808
Bow

Bow

D0881256

s...... & ....
writings

PAUL BOWLES

PAUL BOWLES

COLLECTED STORIES & LATER WRITINGS

The Delicate Prey and Other Stories
A Hundred Camels in the Courtyard
The Time of Friendship
Things Gone and Things Still Here
Midnight Mass
Selected Later Stories
Their Heads Are Green and Their Hands Are Blue
Up Above the World

THE LIBRARY OF AMERICA

DANIEL HALPERN
IS THE EDITOR OF THIS VOLUME

Contents

THE DELICATE PREY
AND OTHER STORIES

CONTENTS

At Paso Rojo

WHEN old Señora Sanchez died, her two daughters Lucha and Chalía decided to visit their brother at his ranch. Out of devotion they had agreed never to marry while their mother lived, and now that she was gone and they were both slightly over forty there seemed just as little likelihood of a wedding in the family as there ever had. They would probably not admit this even to themselves, however. It was with complete understanding of his two sisters that Don Federico suggested they leave the city and go down to Paso Rojo for a few weeks.

Lucha arrived in black crêpe. To her, death was one of the things that happen in life with a certain regularity, and it therefore demanded outward observance. Otherwise her life was in no way changed, save that at the ranch she would have to get used to a whole new staff of servants.

"Indians, poor things, animals with speech," she said to Don Federico the first night as they sat having coffee. A barefooted girl had just carried the dessert dishes out.

Don Federico smiled. "They are good people," he said deliberately. Living at the ranch so long had lowered his standards, it was said, for even though he had always spent a month or so of each year in the capital, he had grown increasingly indifferent to the social life there.

"The ranch is eating his soul little by little," Lucha used to say to Señora Sanchez.

Only once the old lady had replied. "If his soul is to be eaten, then let the ranch do it."

She looked around the primitive dining room with its dry decorations of palm leaves and branches. "He loves it here because everything is his," she thought, "and some of the things could never have been his if he had not purposely changed to fit them." That was not a completely acceptable thought. She knew the ranch had made him happy and tolerant and wise; to her it seemed sad that he could not have been those things without losing his civilized luster. And that he certainly had lost. He had the skin of a peasant—brown

5

and lined everywhere. He had the slowness of speech of men who have lived for long periods of time in the open. And the inflections of his voice suggested the patience that can come from talking to animals rather than to human beings. Lucha was a sensible woman; still, she could not help feeling a certain amount of regret that her little brother, who at an earlier point in his life had been the best dancer among the members of the country club, should have become the thin, sad-faced, quiet man who sat opposite her.

"You've changed a great deal," she suddenly said, shaking her head from side to side slowly.

"Yes. You change here. But it's a good place."

"Good, yes. But so sad," she said.

He laughed. "Not sad at all. You get used to the quiet. And then you find it's not quiet at all. But you never change much, do you? Chalía's the one who's different. Have you noticed?"

"Oh, Chalía's always been crazy. She doesn't change either."

"Yes. She is very much changed." He looked past the smoking oil lamp, out into the dark. "Where is she? Why doesn't she take coffee?"

"She has insomnia. She never takes it."

"Maybe our nights will put her to sleep," said Don Federico.

Chalía sat on the upper veranda in the soft night breeze. The ranch stood in a great clearing that held the jungle at bay all about, but the monkeys were calling from one side to the other, as if neither clearing nor ranch house existed. She had decided to put off going to bed—that way there was less darkness to be borne in case she stayed awake. The lines of a poem she had read on the train two days before were still in her mind: "*Aveces la noche.* . . . Sometimes the night takes you with it, wraps you up and rolls you along, leaving you washed in sleep at the morning's edge." Those lines were comforting. But there was the terrible line yet to come: "And sometimes the night goes on without you." She tried to jump from the image of the fresh sunlit morning to a completely alien idea: the waiter at the beach club in Puntarenas, but she knew the other thought was waiting there for her in the dark.

She had worn riding breeches and a khaki shirt open at the neck, on the trip from the capital, and she had announced to Lucha her intention of going about in those clothes the whole time she was at Paso Rojo. She and Lucha had quarreled at the station.

"Everyone knows Mamá has died," said Lucha, "and the ones who aren't scandalized are making fun of you."

With intense scorn in her voice Chalía had replied, "You have asked them, I suppose."

On the train as it wound through the mountains toward *tierra caliente* she had suddenly said, apropos of nothing: "Black doesn't become me." Really upsetting to Lucha was the fact that in Puntarenas she had gone off and bought some crimson nail polish which she had painstakingly applied herself in the hotel room.

"You can't, Chalía!" cried her sister, wide-eyed. "You've never done it before. Why do you do it now?"

Chalía had laughed immoderately. "Just a whim!" she had said, spreading her decorated hands in front of her.

Loud footsteps came up the stairs and along the veranda, shaking it slightly. Her sister called: "Chalía!"

She hesitated an instant, then said, "Yes."

"You're sitting in the dark! Wait. I'll bring out a lamp from your room. What an idea!"

"We'll be covered with insects," objected Chalía, who, although her mood was not a pleasant one, did not want it disturbed.

"Federico says no!" shouted Lucha from inside. "He says there are no insects! None that bite, anyway!"

Presently she appeared with a small lamp which she set on a table against the wall. She sat down in a nearby hammock and swung herself softly back and forth, humming. Chalía frowned at her, but she seemed not to notice.

"What heat!" exclaimed Lucha finally.

"Don't exert yourself so much," suggested Chalía.

They were quiet. Soon the breeze became a strong wind, coming from the direction of the distant mountains; but it too was hot, like the breath of a great animal. The lamp flickered, threatened to go out. Lucha got up and turned it down.

As Chalía moved her head to watch her, her attention was caught by something else, and she quickly shifted her gaze to the wall. Something enormous, black and swift had been there an instant ago; now there was nothing. She watched the spot intently. The wall was faced with small stones which had been plastered over and whitewashed indifferently, so that the surface was very rough and full of large holes. She rose suddenly and approaching the wall, peered at it closely. All the holes, large and small, were lined with whitish funnels. She could see the long, agile legs of the spiders that lived inside, sticking out beyond some of the funnels.

"Lucha, this wall is full of monsters!" she cried. A beetle flew near to the lamp, changed its mind and lighted on the wall. The nearest spider darted forth, seized it and disappeared into the wall with it.

"Don't look at them," advised Lucha, but she glanced about the floor near her feet apprehensively.

Chalía pulled her bed into the middle of the room and moved a small table over to it. She blew out the lamp and lay back on the hard mattress. The sound of the nocturnal insects was unbearably loud—an endless, savage scream above the noise of the wind. All the vegetation out there was dry. It made a million scraping sounds in the air as the wind swept through it. From time to time the monkeys called to each other from different sides. A night bird scolded occasionally, but its voice was swallowed up in the insistent insect song and the rush of wind across the hot countryside. And it was absolutely dark.

Perhaps an hour later she lit the lamp by her bed, rose, and in her nightgown went to sit on the veranda. She put the lamp where it had been before, by the wall, and turned her chair to face it. She sat watching the wall until very late.

At dawn the air was cool, full of the sound of continuous lowing of cattle, nearby and far. Breakfast was served as soon as the sky was completely light. In the kitchen there was a hubbub of women's voices. The dining room smelled of kerosene and oranges. A great platter heaped with thick slices of pale pineapple was in the center of the table. Don Federico sat at the end, his back to the wall. Behind him was a small niche, bright with candles, and the Virgin stood there in a blue and silver gown.

"Did you sleep well?" said Don Federico to Lucha.

"Ah, wonderfully well!"

"And you?" to Chalía.

"I never sleep well," she said.

A hen ran distractedly into the room from the veranda and was chased out by the serving girl. Outside the door a group of Indian children stood guard around a square of clothesline along which was draped a red assortment of meat: strips of flesh and loops of internal organs. When a vulture swooped low, the children jumped up and down, screaming in chorus, and drove it into the air again. Chalía frowned at their noise. Don Federico smiled.

"This is all in your honor," he said. "We killed a cow yesterday. Tomorrow all that will be gone."

"Not the vultures!" exclaimed Lucha.

"Certainly not. All the cowboys and servants take some home to their families. And they manage to get rid of quite a bit of it themselves."

"You're too generous," said Chalía. "It's bad for them. It makes them dissatisfied and unhappy. But I suppose if you didn't give it to them, they'd steal it anyway."

Don Federico pushed back his chair.

"No one here has ever stolen anything from me." He rose and went out.

After breakfast while it was still early, before the sun got too high in the sky, he regularly made a two-hour tour of the ranch. Since he preferred to pay unexpected visits to the vaqueros in charge of the various districts, he did not always cover the same regions. He was explaining this to Lucha as he untethered his horse outside the high barbed-wire fence that enclosed the house. "Not because I hope to find something wrong. But this is the best way always to find everything right."

Like Chalía, Lucha was skeptical of the Indian's ability to do anything properly. "A very good idea," she said. "I'm sure you are much too lenient with those boys. They need a strong hand and no pity."

Above the high trees that grew behind the house the red and blue macaws screamed, endlessly repeating their elliptical path in the sky. Lucha looked up in their direction and saw Chalía on the upper porch, tucking a khaki shirt into her breeches.

"Rico, wait! I want to go with you," she called, and rushed into her room.

Lucha turned back to her brother. "You won't take her? She couldn't! With Mamá . . ."

Don Federico cut her short, so as not to hear what would have been painful to him. "You both need fresh air and exercise. Come, both of you."

Lucha was silent a moment, looking aghast into his face. Finally she said, "I couldn't," and moved away to open the gate. Several cowboys were riding their horses slowly up from the paddock toward the front of the house. Chalía appeared on the lower porch and hurried to the gate, where Lucha stood looking at her.

"So you're going horseback riding," said Lucha. Her voice had no expression.

"Yes. Are you coming? I suppose not. We should be back soon; no, Rico?"

Don Federico disregarded her, saying to Lucha: "It would be good if you came."

When she did not reply, but went through the gate and shut it, he had one of the cowboys dismount and help Chalía onto his horse. She sat astride the animal beaming down at the youth.

"Now, you can't come. You have no horse!" she cried, pulling the reins taut violently so that the horse stood absolutely still.

"Yes, Señora. I shall go with the señores." His speech was archaic and respectful, the speech of the rustic Indian. Their soft, polite words always annoyed her, because she believed, quite erroneously, that she could detect mockery underneath. "Like parrots who've been taught two lines of Góngora!" she would laugh, when the subject was being discussed. Now she was further nettled by hearing herself addressed as Señora. "The idiot!" she thought. "He should know that I'm not married." But when she looked down at the cowboy again she noticed his white teeth and his very young face. She smiled, saying, "How hot it is already," and undid the top button of her shirt.

The boy ran to the paddock and returned immediately, riding a larger and more nervous horse. This was a joke to the other cowboys, who started ahead, laughing. Don Federico and Chalía rode side by side, and the boy went along behind them, by turns whistling a tune and uttering soothing words to his skittish horse.

The party went across the mile or so of open space that lay between the house and the jungle. Then the high grass swept the riders' legs as the horses went downward to the river, which was dry save for a narrow stream of water in the middle. They followed the bed downstream, the vegetation increasing in height along the banks as they progressed. Chalía had enameled her fingernails afresh before starting out and was in a good humor. She was discussing the administration of the ranch with Don Federico. The expenses and earning capacity interested her particularly, although she had no clear idea of the price of anything. She had worn an enormous soft straw sombrero whose brim dropped to her shoulders as she rode. Every few minutes she turned around and waved to the cowboy who still remained behind, shouting to him: "Muchacho! You're not lost yet?"

Presently the river was divided into two separate beds by a large island which loomed ahead of them, its upper reaches a solid wall of branches and vines. At the foot of the giant trees among some gray boulders was a score or so of cows, looking very small indeed as they lay hunched up in the mud or ambled about seeking the thickest shade. Don Federico galloped ahead suddenly and conferred loudly with the other vaqueros. Almost simultaneously Chalía drew in her reins and brought her horse to a halt. The boy was quickly abreast of her. As he came up she called to him: "It's hot, isn't it?"

The men rode on ahead. He circled around her. "Yes, señora. But that is because we are in the sun. There"—he indicated the island—"it is shady. Now they are almost there."

She said nothing, but took off her hat and fanned herself with the brim. As she moved her hand back and forth she watched her red nails. "What an ugly color," she murmured.

"What, señora?"

"Nothing." She paused. "Ah, what heat!"

"Come, señora. Shall we go on?"

Angrily she crumpled the crown of the sombrero in her fist. "I am not señora," she said distinctly, looking at the men ahead as they rode up to the cows and roused them from their lethargy. The boy smiled. She went on. "I am señorita. That is not the same thing. Or perhaps you think it is?"

The boy was puzzled; he was conscious of her sudden emotion, but he had no idea of its cause. "Yes, señorita," he said politely, without conviction. And he added, with more assurance, "I am Roberto Paz, at your orders."

The sun shone down upon them from above and was reflected by the mica in the stones at their feet. Chalía undid another button of her shirt.

"It's hot. Will they come back soon?"

"No, señorita. They return by the road. Shall we go?" He turned his horse toward the island ahead.

"I don't want to be where the cows are," said Chalía with petulance. "They have *garrapatas*. The *garrapatas* get under your skin."

Roberto laughed indulgently. "The *garrapatas* will not molest you if you stay on your horse, señorita."

"But I want to get down and rest. I'm so tired!" The discomfort of the heat became pure fatigue as she said the words; this made it possible for the annoyance she felt with him to transform itself into a general state of self-pity and depression that came upon her like a sudden pain. Hanging her head she sobbed: "*Ay, madre mía!* My poor mamá!" She stayed that way a moment, and her horse began to walk slowly toward the trees at the side of the river bed.

Roberto glanced perplexedly in the direction the others had taken. They had all passed out of sight beyond the head of the island; the cows were lying down again. "The señorita should not cry."

She did not reply. Since the reins continued slack, her horse proceeded at a faster pace toward the forest. When it had reached the shade at the edge of the stream, the boy rode quickly to her side. "Señorita!" he cried.

She sighed and looked up at him, her hat still in her hand. "I'm very tired," she repeated. "I want to get down and rest."

There was a path leading into the forest. Roberto went ahead to lead the way, hacking at stray vines and bushes with his machete. Chalía followed, sitting listlessly in the saddle, calmed by the sudden entrance into the green world of silence and comparative coolness.

They rode slowly upward through the forest for a quarter of an hour or so without saying anything to each other. When they came to a gate Roberto opened it without dismounting and waited for Chalía to pass through. As she went by him she smiled and said: "How nice it is here."

He replied, rather curtly, she thought: "Yes, Señorita."

Ahead, the vegetation thinned, and beyond lay a vast, open, slightly undulating expanse of land, decorated here and there, as if by intent, with giant white-trunked ceiba trees. The hot wind blew across this upland terrain, and the cry of cicadas was in the air. Chalía halted her horse and jumped down. The tiny thistlelike plants that covered the ground crackled under her boots. She seated herself carefully in the shade at the very edge of the open land.

Roberto tied the two horses to a tree and stood looking at her with the alert, hostile eyes of the Indian who faces what he does not understand.

"Sit down. Here," she said.

Stonily he obeyed, sitting with his legs straight on the earth in front of him, his back very erect. She rested her hand on his shoulder. "*Qué calor*," she murmured.

She did not expect him to answer, but he did, and his voice sounded remote. "It is not my fault, señorita."

She slipped her arm around his neck and felt the muscles grow tense. She rubbed her face over his chest; he did not move or say anything. With her eyes shut and her head pressing hard against him, she felt as if she were hanging to consciousness only by the ceaseless shrill scream of the cicadas. She remained thus, leaning over more heavily upon him as he braced himself with his hands against the earth behind him.

His face had become an impenetrable mask; he seemed not to be thinking of anything, not even to be present.

Breathing heavily, she raised her head to look at him, but found she did not have the courage to reach his eyes with her gaze. Instead she watched his throat and finally whispered, "It doesn't matter what you think of me. It's enough for me to hold you like this."

He turned his head stiffly away from her face, looking across the landscape to the mountains. Gruffly he said, "My brother could come by this place. We must go back to the river."

She tried to bury her face in his chest, to lose herself once more in the delicious sensation. Without warning, he moved quickly and stood up, so that she tumbled forward with her face against the ground.

The surprise of her little fall changed her mood instantly. She sprang up, dashed blindly for the nearer of the two horses, was astride it in an instant, and before he could cry, "It's the bad horse!" had pounded the animal's flanks with her heels. It raised its head wildly; with a violent bound it be-gan to gallop over the countryside. At the first movement she realized dimly that there had been a change, that it was not the same horse, but in her excitement she let her observation stop there. She was delighted to be moving swiftly across the plain against the hot wind. Roberto was left behind.

"*Idiota!*" she screamed into the air. "*Idiota! Idiota!*" with all her might. Ahead of her a tremendous vulture, panic-stricken at the approaching hoof sounds, flapped clumsily away into the sky.

The saddle, having been strapped on for less vigorous ac-tion, began to slip. She gripped the pommel with one hand, and seizing her shirt with the other gave it a convulsive tug that ripped it completely open. A powerful feeling of exulta-tion came to her as she glanced down and saw her own skin white in the sunlight.

In the distance to one side, she dimly saw some palm trees reaching above a small patch of lower vegetation. She shut her eyes: the palms looked like shiny green spiders. She was out of breath from the jolting. The sun was too hot. The sad-dle kept slipping further; she could not right it. The horse showed no sign of being aware of her existence. She pulled on the reins as hard as she could without falling over backward, but it had no effect on the horse, which continued to run at top speed, following no path and missing some of the trees by what seemed no more than inches.

"Where shall I be in an hour?" she asked herself. "Dead, perhaps?" The idea of death did not frighten her the way it did some people. She was afraid of the night because she could not sleep; she was not afraid of life and death because she did not feel implicated to any extent in either one. Only other people lived and died, had their lives and deaths. She, being inside herself, existed merely as herself and not as a part of anything else. People, animals, flowers and stones were objects, and they all belonged to the world outside. It was their juxtapositions that made hostile or friendly patterns. Sometimes she looked at her own hands and feet for several minutes, trying to fight off an indefinite sensation they gave her of belonging also to the world outside. But this never troubled her deeply. The impressions were received and accepted without question; at most she could combat them when they were too strong for her comfort.

Here in the hot morning sun, being pulled forward through the air, she began to feel that almost all of her had slipped out of the inside world, that only a tiny part of her was still she. The part that was left was full of astonishment and disbelief; the only discomfort now lay in having to accept the fact of the great white tree trunks that continued to rush by her.

She tried several times to make herself be elsewhere: in her rose garden at home, in the hotel dining room at Puntarenas, even as a last resort which might prove feasible since it too had been unpleasant, in her bed back at the ranch, with the dark around her.

With a great bound, the horse cleared a ditch. The saddle slipped completely around and hung underneath. Having no pommel to cling to, she kept on as best she could, clutching the horse's flanks with her legs and always pulling on the reins. Suddenly the animal slowed down and stepped briskly into a thicket. There was a path of sorts; she suspected it was the same one they had used coming from the river. She sat listlessly, waiting to see where the horse would go.

Finally it came out into the river bed as she had expected,

and trotted back to the ranch. The sun was directly overhead when they reached the paddock. The horse stood outside, waiting to be let in, but it seemed that no one was around. Making a great effort, she slid down to the ground and found she had difficulty in standing because her legs were trembling so. She was furious and ashamed. As she hobbled toward the house she was strongly hoping Lucha would not see her. A few Indian girls appeared to be the only people about. She dragged herself upstairs and shut herself in her room. The bed had been pushed back against the wall, but she did not have the force to pull it out into the center where she wanted it.

When Don Federico and the others returned, Lucha, who had been reading downstairs, went to the gate. "Where's Chalía?" she cried.

"She was tired. One of the boys brought her back a while ago," he said. "It's just as well. We went halfway to Cañas."

Chalía had her lunch in bed and slept soundly until late in the afternoon. When she emerged from her room onto the veranda, a woman was dusting the rocking chairs and arranging them in a row against the wall.

"Where's my sister?" demanded Chalía.

"Gone to the village in the truck with the señor," the woman replied, going to the head of the stairs and beginning to dust them one by one, as she went down backward.

Chalía seated herself in a chair and put her feet up on the porch railing, reflecting as she did so that if Lucha had been there she would have disapproved of the posture. There was a bend in the river—the only part of it that came within sight of the house—just below her, and a portion of the bank was visible to her through the foliage from where she sat. A large breadfruit tree spread its branches out almost to the opposite side of the stream. There was a pool at the turn, just where the tree's trunk grew out of the muddy bank. An Indian sauntered out of the undergrowth and calmly removed his trousers, then his shirt. He stood there a moment, stark naked, looking at the water, before he walked into it and began to splash and swim. When he had finished bathing he stood again on the bank, smoothing his blue-black hair. Chalía was puzzled, knowing that few Indians would be so

immodest as to bathe naked in full view of the upstairs veranda. With a sudden strange sensation as she watched him,
she realized it was Roberto and that he was wholly conscious
of her presence at that moment.

"He knows Rico is gone and that no one can see him from
downstairs," she thought, resolving to tell her brother when
he came home. The idea of vengeance upon the boy filled her
with a delicious excitement. She watched his deliberate movements as he dressed. He sat down on a rock with only his
shirt on and combed his hair. The late afternoon sun shone
through the leaves and gave his brown skin an orange cast.
When finally he had gone away without once glancing up at
the house, she rose and went into her room. Maneuvering the
bed into the middle of the floor once more, she began to
walk around it; her mood was growing more and more tur-
bulent as she circled about the room.

She heard the truck door slam, and a moment later, voices
downstairs. With her finger to her temple, where she always
put it when her heart was beating very fast, she slipped out
onto the veranda and downstairs. Don Federico was in the
commissary, which he opened for a half hour each morning
and evening. Chalía stepped inside the door, her mouth already open, feeling the words about to burst from her lungs.
Two children were pushing their copper coins along the
counter, pointing at the candy they wanted. By the lamp a
woman was looking at a bolt of goods. Don Federico was on
a ladder, getting down another bolt. Chalía's mouth closed
slowly. She looked down at her brother's desk by the door beside her, where he kept his ledgers and bills. In an open cigar
box almost touching her hand was a pile of dirty bank notes.
She was back in the room before she knew it. She shut the
door and saw that she had four ten-colon notes in her hand.
She stuffed them into her breeches pocket.

At dinner they made fun of her for having slept all the afternoon, telling her that now she would lie awake again all night.

She was busy eating. "If I do, so much the worse," she
said, without looking up.

"I've arranged a little concert after dinner," said Don Federico. Lucha was ecstatic. He went on: "The cowboys have

some friends here, over from Bagaces, and Raul has finished building his marimba."

The men and boys began to assemble soon after dinner. There was laughter, and guitars were strummed in the dark on the terrace. The two sisters went to sit at the end near the dining room, Don Federico was in the middle with the vaqueros, and the servants were ranged at the kitchen end. After several solo songs by various men with guitars, Raul and a friend began to play the marimba. Roberto was seated on the floor among the cowboys who were not performing.

"Suppose we all dance," said Don Federico, jumping up and seizing Lucha. They moved about together at one end of the terrace for a moment, but no one else stirred.

"*A bailar!*" Don Federico shouted, laughing.

Several of the girls started to dance timidly in couples, with loud giggling. None of the men would budge. The marimba players went on pounding out the same piece over and over again. Don Federico danced with Chalía, who was stiff from her morning ride; soon she excused herself and left. Instead of going upstairs to bed she crossed onto the front veranda and sat looking across the vast moonlit clearing. The night was thick with eternity. She could feel it there, just beyond the gate. Only the monotonous, tinkling music kept the house within the confines of time, saved it from being engulfed. As she listened to the merrymaking progress, she had the impression that the men were taking more part in it. "Rico has probably opened them a bottle of rum," she thought with fury.

At last it sounded as though everyone were dancing. Her curiosity having risen to a high pitch, she was about to rise and return to the terrace, when a figure appeared at the other end of the veranda. She needed no one to tell her it was Roberto. He was walking soundlessly toward her; he seemed to hesitate as he came up to her, then he squatted down by her chair and looked up at her. She had been right: he smelled of rum.

"Good evening, señorita."

She felt impelled to remain silent. Nevertheless, she said, "Good evening." She put her hand into her pocket, saying to herself that she must do this correctly and quickly.

As he crouched there with his face shining in the moonlight, she bent forward and passed her hand over his smooth
hair. Keeping her fingers on the back of his neck, she leaned
still further forward and kissed his lips. The rum was very
strong. He did not move. She began to whisper in his ear,
very low: "Roberto, I love you. I have a present for you.
Forty *colones*. Here."

He turned his head swiftly and said out loud, "Where?"

She put the bills into his hand, still holding his head, and
whispered again: "Sh! Not a word to anyone. I must go now.
I'll give you more tomorrow night." She let go of him.

He rose and went out the gate. She went straight upstairs
to bed, and as she went to sleep the music was still going on.

Much later she awoke and lit her lamp. It was half past four.
Day would soon break. Feeling full of an unaccustomed
energy, Chalía dressed, extinguished the lamp and went outdoors, shutting the gate quietly behind her. In the paddock
the horses stirred. She walked by it and started along the road
to the village. It was a very silent hour: the night insects had
ceased their noises and the birds had not yet begun their
early-morning twitter. The moon was low in the sky, so that
it remained behind the trees most of the time. Ahead of her
Venus flared like a minor moon. She walked quickly, with only
a twinge of pain now and then in her hip.

Something dark lying in the road ahead of her made her
stop walking. It did not move. She watched it closely, stepping cautiously toward it, ready to run the other way. As her
eyes grew accustomed to its form, she saw that it was a man
lying absolutely still. And as she drew near, she knew it was
Roberto. She touched his arm with her foot. He did not respond. She leaned over and put her hand on his chest. He was
breathing deeply, and the smell of liquor was almost overpowering. She straightened and kicked him lightly in the
head. There was a tiny groan from far within. This also, she
said to herself, would have to be done quickly. She felt wonderfully light and powerful as she slowly maneuvered his body
with her feet to the right-hand side of the road. There was a
small cliff there, about twenty feet high. When she got him to
the edge, she waited a while, looking at his features in the

moonlight. His mouth was open a little, and the white teeth peeked out from behind the lips. She smoothed his forehead a few times and with a gentle push rolled him over the edge. He fell very heavily, making a strange animal sound as he hit.

She walked back to the ranch at top speed. It was getting light when she arrived. She went into the kitchen and ordered her breakfast, saying: "I'm up early." The entire day she spent around the house, reading and talking to Lucha. She thought Don Federico looked preoccupied when he set out on his morning tour of inspection, after closing the commissary. She thought he still did when he returned; she told him so at lunch.

"It's nothing," he said. "I can't seem to balance my books."

"And you've always been such a good mathematician," said Chalía.

During the afternoon some cowboys brought Roberto in. She heard the commotion in the kitchen and the servants' cries of "*Ay, Dios!*" She went out to watch. He was conscious, lying on the floor with all the other Indians staring at him.

"What's the matter?" she said.

One of the cowboys laughed. "Nothing of importance. He had too much—" the cowboy made a gesture of drinking from a bottle, "and fell off the road. Nothing but bruises, I think."

After dinner Don Federico asked Chalía and Lucha into his little private office. He looked drawn, and he spoke more slowly than usual. As Chalía entered she saw that Roberto was standing inside the door. He did not look at her. Lucha and Chalía sat down; Don Federico and Roberto remained standing.

"This is the first time anyone has done this to me," said Don Federico, looking down at the rug, his hands locked behind him. "Roberto has stolen from me. The money is missing. Some of it is in his pocket still, more than his monthly wages. I know he has stolen it because he had no money yesterday and because," he turned to Chalía, "because he can account for having it only by lying. He says you gave it to him. Did you give Roberto any money yesterday?"

Chalía looked puzzled. "No," she said. "I thought of giving him a *colón* when he brought me back from the ride yesterday morning. But then I thought it would be better to wait until we were leaving to go back to the city. Was it much? He's just a boy."

Don Federico said: "It was forty *colones*. But that's the same as forty *centavos*. Stealing . . ."

Chalía interrupted him. "Rico!" she exclaimed. "Forty *colones*! That's a great deal! Has he spent much of it? You could take it out of his wages little by little." She knew her brother would say what he did say, a moment later.

"Never! He'll leave tonight. And his brother with him."

In the dim light Chalía could see the large purple bruise on Roberto's forehead. He kept his head lowered and did not look up, even when she and Lucha rose and left the room at a sign from their brother. They went upstairs together and sat down on the veranda.

"What barbarous people they are!" said Lucha indignantly. "Poor Rico may learn some day how to treat them. But I'm afraid one of them will kill him first."

Chalía rocked back and forth, fanning herself lazily. "With a few more lessons like this he may change," she said. "What heat!"

They heard Don Federico's voice below by the gate. Firmly it said, "*Adiós*." There were muffled replies and the gate was closed. Don Federico joined his sisters on the veranda. He sat down sadly.

"I didn't like to send them away on foot at night," he said, shaking his head. "But that Roberto is a bad one. It was better to have him go once and for all, quickly. Juan is good, but I had to get rid of him too, of course."

"*Claro, claro*," said Lucha absently. Suddenly she turned to her brother full of concern. "I hope you remembered to take away the money you said he still had in his pocket."

"Yes, yes," he assured her, but from the tone of his voice she knew he had let the boy keep it.

Don Federico and Lucha said good night and went to bed. Chalía sat up a while, looking vaguely at the wall with the spiders in it. Then she yawned and took the lamp into her room.

Again the bed had been pushed back against the wall by the maid. Chalía shrugged her shoulders, got into the bed where it was, blew out the lamp, listened for a few minutes to the night sounds, and went peacefully to sleep, thinking of how surprisingly little time it had taken her to get used to life at Paso Rojo, and even, she had to admit now, to begin to enjoy it.

Pastor Dowe at Tacaté

PASTOR DOWE delivered his first sermon in Tacaté on a bright Sunday morning shortly after the beginning of the rainy season. Almost a hundred Indians attended, and some of them had come all the way from Balaché in the valley. They sat quietly on the ground while he spoke to them for an hour or so in their own tongue. Not even the children became restive; there was the most complete silence as long as he kept speaking. But he could see that their attention was born of respect rather than of interest. Being a conscientious man he was troubled to discover this.

When he had finished the sermon, the notes for which were headed "Meaning of Jesus," they slowly got to their feet and began wandering away, quite obviously thinking of other things. Pastor Dowe was puzzled. He had been assured by Dr. Ramos of the University that his mastery of the dialect was sufficient to enable his prospective parishioners to follow his sermons, and he had had no difficulty conversing with the Indians who had accompanied him up from San Gerónimo. He stood sadly on the small thatch-covered platform in the clearing before his house and watched the men and women walking slowly away in different directions. He had the sensation of having communicated absolutely nothing to them.

All at once he felt he must keep the people here a little longer, and he called out to them to stop. Politely they turned their faces toward the pavilion where he stood, and remained looking at him, without moving. Several of the smaller children were already playing a game, and were darting about silently in the background. The pastor glanced at his wrist watch and spoke to Nicolás, who had been pointed out to him as one of the most intelligent and influential men in the village, asking him to come up and stand beside him.

Once Nicolás was next to him, he decided to test him with a few questions. "Nicolás," he said in his dry, small voice, "what did I tell you today?"

Nicolás coughed and looked over the heads of the assembly to where an enormous sow was rooting in the mud under a mango tree. Then he said: "Don Jesucristo."

"Yes," agreed Pastor Dowe encouragingly. "*Bai,* and Don Jesucristo what?"

"A good man," answered Nicolás with indifference.

"Yes, yes, but what more?" Pastor Dowe was impatient; his voice rose in pitch.

Nicolás was silent. Finally he said, "Now I go," and stepped carefully down from the platform. The others again began to gather up their belongings and move off. For a moment Pastor Dowe was furious. Then he took his notebook and his Bible and went into the house.

At lunch Mateo, who waited on table, and whom he had brought with him from Ocosingo, stood leaning against the wall smiling.

"Señor," he said, "Nicolás says they will not come again to hear you without music."

"Music!" cried Pastor Dowe, setting his fork on the table. "Ridiculous! What music? We have no music."

"He says the father at Yalactín used to sing."

"Ridiculous!" said the pastor again. "In the first place I can't sing, and in any case it's unheard of! *Inaudito!*"

"*Sí, verdad?*" agreed Mateo.

The pastor's tiny bedroom was breathlessly hot, even at night. However, it was the only room in the little house with a window on the outside; he could shut the door onto the noisy patio where by day the servants invariably gathered for their work and their conversations. He lay under the closed canopy of his mosquito net, listening to the barking of the dogs in the village below. He was thinking about Nicolás. Apparently Nicolás had chosen for himself the role of envoy from the village to the mission. The pastor's thin lips moved. "A troublemaker," he whispered to himself. "I'll speak with him tomorrow."

Early the next morning he stood outside Nicolás's hut. Each house in Tacaté had its own small temple: a few tree trunks holding up some thatch to shelter the offerings of fruit and cooked food. The pastor took care not to go near the one that stood near by; he already felt enough like a pariah, and

Dr. Ramos had warned him against meddling of that sort. He called out.

A little girl about seven years old appeared in the doorway of the house. She looked at him wildly a moment with huge round eyes before she squealed and disappeared back into the darkness. The pastor waited and called again. Presently a man came around the hut from the back and told him that Nicolás would return. The pastor sat down on a stump. Soon the little girl stood again in the doorway; this time she smiled coyly. The pastor looked at her severely. It seemed to him she was too old to run about naked. He turned his head away and examined the thick red petals of a banana blossom hanging nearby. When he looked back she had come out and was standing near him, still smiling. He got up and walked toward the road, his head down, as if deep in thought. Nicolás entered through the gate at that moment, and the pastor, colliding with him, apologized.

"Good," grunted Nicolás. "What?"

His visitor was not sure how he ought to begin. He decided to be pleasant.

"I am a good man," he smiled.

"Yes," said Nicolás. "Don Jesucristo is a good man."

"No, no, no!" cried Pastor Dowe.

Nicolás looked politely confused, but said nothing.

Feeling that his command of the dialect was not equal to this sort of situation, the pastor wisely decided to begin again. "Hachakyum made the world. Is that true?"

Nicolás nodded in agreement, and squatted down at the pastor's feet, looking up at him, his eyes narrowed against the sun.

"Hachakyum made the sky," the pastor began to point, "the mountains, the trees, those people there. Is that true?"

Again Nicolás assented.

"Hachakyum is good. Hachakyum made you. True?" Pastor Dowe sat down again on the stump.

Nicolás spoke finally, "All that you say is true."

The pastor permitted himself a pleased smile and went on. "Hachakyum made everything and everyone because He is mighty and good."

Nicolás frowned. "No!" he cried. "That is not true!

Hachakyum did not make everyone. He did not make you. He did not make guns or Don Jesucristo. Many things He did not make!"

The pastor shut his eyes a moment, seeking strength. "Good," he said at last in a patient voice. "Who made the other things? Who made me? Please tell me."

Nicolás did not hesitate. "Metzabok."

"But who is Metzabok?" cried the pastor, letting an outraged note show in his voice. The word for God he had always known only as Hachakyum.

"Metzabok makes all the things that do not belong here," said Nicolás.

The pastor rose, took out his handkerchief and wiped his forehead. "You hate me," he said, looking down at the Indian. The word was too strong, but he did not know how to say it any other way.

Nicolás stood up quickly and touched the pastor's arm with his hand.

"No. That is not true. You are a good man. Everyone likes you."

Pastor Dowe backed away in spite of himself. The touch of the brown hand was vaguely distasteful to him. He looked beseechingly into the Indian's face and said, "But Hachakyum did not make me?"

"No."

There was a long pause.

"Will you come next time to my house and hear me speak?"

Nicolás looked uncomfortable.

"Everyone has work to do," he said.

"Mateo says you want music," began the pastor.

Nicolás shrugged. "To me it is not important. But the others will come if you have music. Yes, that is true. They like music."

"But *what* music?" cried the pastor in desperation.

"They say you have a *bitrola*."

The pastor looked away, thinking: "There is no way to keep anything from these people." Along with all his other household goods and the things left behind by his wife when she died, he had brought a little portable phonograph. It was somewhere in the storeroom piled with the empty valises and cold-weather garments.

"Tell them I will play the *bitrola*," he said, going out the gate.

The little girl ran after him and stood watching him as he walked up the road.

On his way through the village the pastor was troubled by the reflection that he was wholly alone in this distant place, alone in his struggle to bring the truth to its people. He consoled himself by recalling that it is only in each man's own consciousness that the isolation exists; objectively man is always a part of something.

When he arrived home he sent Mateo to the storeroom to look for the portable phonograph. After a time the boy brought it out, dusted it and stood by while the pastor opened the case. The crank was inside. He took it out and wound the spring. There were a few records in the compartment at the top. The first he examined were "Let's Do It," "Crazy Rhythm," and "Strike up the Band," none of which Pastor Dowe considered proper accompaniments to his sermons. He looked further. There was a recording of Al Jolson singing "Sonny Boy" and a cracked copy of "She's Funny That Way." As he looked at the labels he remembered how the music on each disc had sounded. Unfortunately Mrs. Dowe had disliked hymn music; she had called it "mournful."

"So here we are," he sighed, "without music."

Mateo was astonished. "It does not play?"

"I can't play them this music for dancing, Mateo."

"*Cómo nó, señor!* They will like it very much!"

"No, Mateo!" said the pastor forcefully, and he put on "Crazy Rhythm" to illustrate his point. As the thin metallic tones issued from the instrument, Mateo's expression changed to one of admiration bordering on beatitude. "*Qué bonito!*" he said reverently. Pastor Dowe lifted the tone arm and the hopping rhythmical pattern ceased.

"It cannot be done," he said with finality, closing the lid.

Nevertheless on Saturday he remembered that he had promised Nicolás there would be music at the service, and he decided to tell Mateo to carry the phonograph out to the pavilion in order to have it there in case the demand for it should prove to be pressing. This was a wise precaution, because the next morning when the villagers arrived they were talking of nothing but the music they were to hear.

His topic was "The Strength of Faith," and he had got about ten minutes into the sermon when Nicolás, who was squatting directly in front of him, quietly stood up and raised his hand. Pastor Dowe frowned and stopped talking.

Nicolás spoke: "Now music, then talk. Then music, then talk. Then music." He turned around and faced the others. "That is a good way." There were murmurs of assent, and everyone leaned a bit farther forward on his haunches to catch whatever musical sounds might issue from the pavilion.

The pastor sighed and lifted the machine onto the table, knocking off the Bible that lay at the edge. "Of course," he said to himself with a faint bitterness. The first record he came to was "Crazy Rhythm." As it started to play, an infant nearby, who had been singsonging a series of meaningless sounds, ceased making its parrotlike noises, remaining silent and transfixed as it stared at the platform. Everyone sat absolutely quiet until the piece was over. Then there was a hubbub of approbation. "Now more talk," said Nicolás, looking very pleased.

The pastor continued. He spoke a little haltingly now, because the music had broken his train of thought, and even by looking at his notes he could not be sure just how far he had got before the interruption. As he continued, he looked down at the people sitting nearest him. Beside Nicolás he noticed the little girl who had watched him from the doorway, and he was gratified to see that she was wearing a small garment which managed to cover her. She was staring at him with an expression he interpreted as one of fascinated admiration.

Presently, when he felt that his audience was about to grow restive (even though he had to admit that they never would have shown it outwardly) he put on "Sonny Boy." From the reaction it was not difficult to guess that this selection was finding less favor with its listeners. The general expression of tense anticipation at the beginning of the record soon relaxed into one of routine enjoyment of a less intense degree. When the piece was finished, Nicolás got to his feet again and raised his hand solemnly, saying: "Good. But the other music is more beautiful."

The pastor made a short summation, and, after playing "Crazy Rhythm" again, he announced that the service was over.

In this way "Crazy Rhythm" became an integral part of Pastor Dowe's weekly service. After a few months the old record was so badly worn that he determined to play it only once at each gathering. His flock submitted to this show of economy with bad grace. They complained, using Nicolás as emissary.

"But the music is old. There will be no more if I use it all," the pastor explained.

Nicolás smiled unbelievingly. "You say that. But you do not want us to have it."

The following day, as the pastor sat reading in the patio's shade, Mateo again announced Nicolás, who had entered through the kitchen and, it appeared, had been conversing with the servants there. By now the pastor had learned fairly well how to read the expressions on Nicolás's face; the one he saw there now told him that new exactions were at hand.

Nicolás looked respectful. "Señor," he said, "we like you because you have given us music when we asked you for it. Now we are all good friends. We want you to give us salt."

"Salt?" exclaimed Pastor Dowe, incredulous. "What for?"

Nicolás laughed good-naturedly, making it clear that he thought the pastor was joking with him. Then he made a gesture of licking. "To eat," he said.

"Ah, yes," murmured the pastor, recalling that among the Indians rock salt is a scarce luxury.

"But we have no salt," he said quickly.

"Oh, yes, señor. There." Nicolás indicated the kitchen.

The pastor stood up. He was determined to put an end to this haggling, which he considered a demoralizing element in his official relationship with the village. Signaling for Nicolás to follow, he walked into the kitchen, calling as he entered, "Quintina, show me our salt."

Several of the servants, including Mateo, were standing in the room. It was Mateo who opened a low cupboard and disclosed a great stack of grayish cakes piled on the floor. The pastor was astonished. "So many kilos of salt!" he exclaimed. "*Cómo se hace?*"

Mateo calmly told him it had been brought with them all the way from Ocosingo. "For us," he added, looking about at the others.

Pastor Dowe seized upon this, hoping it was meant as a hint and could be recognized as one. "Of course," he said to Nicolás. "This is for my house."

Nicolás looked unimpressed. "You have enough for everyone in the village," he remarked. "In two Sundays you can get more from Ocosingo. Everyone will be very happy all the time that way. Everyone will come each time you speak. You give them salt and make music."

Pastor Dowe felt himself beginning to tremble a little. He knew he was excited and so he was careful to make his voice sound natural.

"I will decide, Nicolás," he said. "Good-bye."

It was clear that Nicolás in no way regarded these words as a dismissal. He answered, "Good-bye," and leaned back against the wall calling, "Marta!" The little girl, of whose presence in the room the pastor now became conscious, moved out from the shadows of a corner. She held what appeared to him to be a large doll, and was being very solicitous of it. As the pastor stepped out into the bright patio, the picture struck him as false, and he turned around and looked back into the kitchen, frowning. He remained in the doorway in an attitude of suspended action for a moment, staring at little Marta. The doll, held lovingly in the child's arms, and swaddled in a much-used rag, was making spasmodic movements.

The pastor's ill-humor was with him; probably he would have shown it no matter what the circumstances. "What is it?" he demanded indignantly. As if in answer the bundle squirmed again, throwing off part of the rag that covered it, and the pastor saw what looked to him like a comic-strip caricature of Red Riding Hood's wolf peering out from under the grandmother's nightcap. Again Pastor Dowe cried, "What is it?"

Nicolás turned from his conversation, amused, and told Marta to hold it up and uncover it so the señor could see it. This she did, pulling away the wrapping and exposing to view a lively young alligator which, since it was being held more or less on its back, was objecting in a routine fashion to the treatment by rhythmically paddling the air with its little black feet. Its rather long face seemed, however, to be smiling.

"Good heavens!" cried the pastor in English. The spectacle struck him as strangely scandalous. There was a hidden obscenity in the sight of the mildly agitated little reptile with its head wrapped in a rag, but Marta was still holding it out toward him for his inspection. He touched the smooth scales of its belly with his fingers, and withdrew his hand, saying, "Its jaws should be bound. It will bite her."

Mateo laughed. "She is too quick," and then said it in dialect to Nicolás, who agreed, and also laughed. The pastor patted Marta on the head as she returned the animal to her bosom and resumed cradling it tenderly.

Nicolás' eyes were on him. "You like Marta?" he asked seriously.

The pastor was thinking about the salt. "Yes, yes," he said with the false enthusiasm of the preoccupied man. He went to his bedroom and shut the door. Lying on the narrow bed in the afternoon was the same as lying on it at night: there was the same sound of dogs barking in the village. Today there was also the sound of wind going past the window. Even the canopy of mosquito netting swayed a little from time to time as the air came into the room. The pastor was trying to decide whether or not to give in to Nicolás. When he got very sleepy, he thought: "After all, what principle am I upholding in keeping it from them? They want music. They want salt. They will learn to want God." This thought proved relaxing to him, and he fell asleep to the sound of the dogs barking and the wind shrilling past the window.

During the night the clouds rolled down off the mountains into the valley, and when dawn came they remained there, impaled on the high trees. The few birds that made themselves heard sounded as though they were singing beneath the ceiling of a great room. The wet air was thick with wood smoke, but there was no noise from the village; a wall of cloud lay between it and the mission house.

From his bed, instead of the wind passing the window, the pastor heard the slow drops of water falling upon the bushes from the eaves. He lay still awhile, lulled by the subdued chatter of the servants' voices in the kitchen. Then he went to the window and looked out into the grayness. Even the nearest trees were invisible; there was a heavy odor of earth. He dressed, shivering as the damp garments touched his skin. On the table lay a newspaper:

BARCELONA BOMBARDEADO POR
DOSCIENTOS AVIONES

As he shaved, trying to work up a lather with the tepid water Quintina had brought him, full of charcoal ashes, it occurred to him that he would like to escape from the people of Tacaté and the smothering feeling they gave him of being lost in antiquity. It would be good to be free from that infinite sadness even for a few hours.

He ate a larger breakfast than usual and went outside to the sheltered platform, where he sat down in the dampness and began to read the seventy-eighth Psalm, which he had thought of using as the basis of a sermon. As he read he looked out at the emptiness in front of him. Where he knew the mango tree stood he could see only the white void, as if the land dropped away at the platform's edge for a thousand feet or more.

"He clave the rocks in the wilderness, and gave them drink as out of the great depths." From the house came the sound of Quintina's giggling. "Mateo is probably chasing her around the patio," thought the pastor; wisely he had long since given up expecting any Indian to behave as he considered an adult should. Every few seconds on the other side of the pavilion a turkey made its hysterical gobbling sound. The pastor spread his Bible out on the table, put his hands to his ears, and continued to read: "He caused an east wind to blow in the heaven: and by His power He brought in the south wind."

"Passages like that would sound utterly pagan in the dialect," he caught himself thinking. He unstopped his ears and reflected: "But to their ears *everything* must have a pagan sound. Everything I say is transformed on the way to them into something else." This was a manner of thinking that Pastor Dowe had always taken pains to avoid. He fixed his eyes on the text with determination, and read on. The giggling in the house was louder; he could hear Mateo too now. "He sent divers sorts of flies among them; . . . and frogs, which destroyed them." The door into the patio was opened and the pastor heard Mateo coughing as he stood looking out. "He certainly has tuberculosis," said the pastor to himself, as the Indian spat repeatedly. He shut his Bible and took off his glasses, feeling about on the table for their case. Not encountering it, he rose, and taking a step forward, crushed it under his heel. Compassionately, he stooped down and picked it up. The hinges were snapped and the metal sides under their artificial leather covering were bent out of shape. Mateo could have hammered it back into a semblance of its form, but Pastor Dowe preferred to think: "All things have their death." He had had the case eleven years. Briefly he summed up its life: the sunny afternoon when he had bought it on the little side street in downtown Havana; the busy years in the hills of southern Brazil; the time in Chile when he had dropped the case, with a pair of dark glasses in it, out the bus window, and everyone in the bus had got out and helped him look for it; the depressing year in Chicago when for some reason he had left it in a bureau drawer most of the time and had carried his glasses loose in his coat pocket. He remembered some of the newspaper clippings he had kept in the case, and many of the little slips of paper with ideas jotted down on them. He looked tenderly down at it, thinking: "And so this is the place and time, and these are the circumstances of its death." For some reason he was happy to have witnessed this death; it was comforting to know exactly how the case had finished its existence. He still looked at it with sadness for a moment. Then he flung it out into the white air as if the precipice were really there. With his Bible under his arm he strode to the door and brushed past Mateo without saying a word. But as he walked into his room it seemed to him that Mateo had looked at him in a strange fashion, as if he knew something and were waiting to see when the pastor would find out, too.

Back in his suffocating little room the pastor felt an even more imperious need to be alone for a time. He changed his shoes, took his cane and went out into the fog. In this weather there was only one path practicable, and that led downward through the village. He stepped ahead over the stones with great caution, for although he could discern the ground at his feet and the spot where he put the tip of his cane each time, beyond that on all sides was mere whiteness. Walking along thus, he reflected, was like trying to read a text with only one letter visible at a time. The wood smoke was sharp in the still air.

For perhaps half an hour Pastor Dowe continued this way, carefully putting one foot before the other. The emptiness around him, the lack of all visual detail, rather than activating his thought, served to dull his perceptions. His progress over the stones was laborious but strangely relaxing. One of the few ideas that came into his head as he moved along was that it would be pleasant to pass through the village without anyone's noticing him, and it seemed to him that it might be managed; even at ten feet he would be invisible. He could walk between the huts and hear the babies crying, and when he came out at the other end no one would know he had been there. He was not sure where he would go then.

The way became suddenly rougher as the path went into a zigzagging descent along the steep side of a ravine. He had reached the bottom before he raised his head once. "Ah," he said, standing still. The fog was now above him, a great gray quilt of cloud. He saw the giant trees that stood around him and heard them dripping slowly in a solemn, uneven chorus onto the wild coca leaves beneath.

"There is no such place as this on the way to the village," thought the pastor. He was mildly annoyed, but more astonished, to find himself standing by these trees that looked like elephants and were larger than any other trees he had seen in the region. Automatically he turned around in the path and started back up the slope. Beside the overpowering sadness of the landscape, now that it was visible to him, the fog up there was a comfort and a protection. He paused for a moment to stare back at the fat, spiny tree trunks and the welter of vegetation beyond. A small sound behind him made him turn his head.

Two Indians were trotting down the path toward him. As they came up they stopped and looked at him with such expectancy on their dark little faces that Pastor Dowe thought they were going to speak. Instead the one ahead made a grunting sound and motioned to the other to follow. There was no way of effecting a detour around the pastor, so they brushed violently against him as they went by. Without once looking back they hurried on downward and disappeared among the green coca leaves.

This unlikely behavior on the part of the two natives vaguely intrigued him; on an impulse he determined to find an explanation for it. He started after them.

Soon he had gone beyond the spot where he had turned back a moment ago. He was in the forest; the plant odor was almost unbearable—a smell of living and dead vegetation in a world where slow growth and slow death are simultaneous and inseparable. He stopped once and listened for footsteps. Apparently the Indians had run on ahead of him; nevertheless he continued on his way. Since the path was fairly wide and well broken in, it was only now and then that he came into contact with a hanging tendril or a projecting branch.

The posturing trees and vines gave the impression of having been arrested in furious motion, and presented a monotonous succession of tortured tableaux vivants. It was as if, for the moment while he watched, the desperate battle for air had been suspended and would be resumed only when he turned away his head. As he looked, he decided that it was precisely this unconfirmable quality of surreptitiousness which made the place so disquieting. Now and then, high above his head, a blood-colored butterfly would float silently through the gloom from one tree trunk to another. They were all alike; it seemed to him that it must be always the same insect. Several times he passed the white grillwork of great spider webs flung across between the plants like gates painted on the dark wall behind. But all the webs looked uninhabited. The large, leisurely drops of water still continued to fall from above; even if it had been raining hard, the earth could not have been wetter.

The pastor was astigmatic, and since he was beginning to be dizzy from watching so many details, he kept his eyes looking straight ahead as he walked, deviating his gaze only when he had to avoid the plant life that had grown across the path. The floor of the forest continued flat. Suddenly he became aware that the air around him was reverberating with faint sounds. He stood still, and recognized the casual gurgle a deep stream makes from time to time as it moves past its banks. Almost immediately ahead of him was the water, black and wide, and considering its proximity, incredibly quiet in its swift flowing. A few paces before him a great dead tree, covered with orange fungus, lay across the path. The pastor's glance followed the trunk to the left; at the small end, facing him, sat the two Indians. They were looking at him with interest, and he knew they had been waiting for him. He walked over to them, greeted them. They replied solemnly, never taking their shining eyes from his face.

As if they had rehearsed it, they both rose at the same instant and walked to the water's edge, where they stood looking down. Then one of them glanced back at the pastor and said simply, "Come." As he made his way around the log he saw that they were standing by a long bamboo raft which was beached on the muddy bank. They lifted it and dropped one end into the stream.

"Where are you going?" asked the pastor. For reply they lifted their short brown arms in unison and waved them slowly in the direction of downstream. Again the one who had spoken before said, "Come." The pastor, his curiosity aroused, looked suspiciously at the delicate raft, and back at the two men. At the same time he felt that it would be pleasanter to be riding with them than to go back through the forest. Impatiently he again demanded, "Where are you going? Tacaté?"

"Tacaté," echoed the one who up to this point had not spoken.

"Is it strong?" queried the pastor, stooping to push lightly on a piece of bamboo. This was merely a formality; he had perfect faith in the Indians' ability to master the materials of the jungle.

"Strong," said the first. "Come."

The pastor glanced back into the wet forest, climbed onto the raft, and sat doubled up on its bottom in the stern. The two quickly jumped aboard and pushed the frail craft from the bank with a pole.

Then began a journey which almost at once Pastor Dowe regretted having undertaken. Even as the three of them shot swiftly ahead, around the first bend in the stream, he wished he had stayed behind and could be at this moment on his way up the side of the ravine. And as they sped on down the silent waterway he continued to reproach himself for having come along without knowing why. At each successive bend in the tunnellike course, he felt farther from the world. He found himself straining in a ridiculous effort to hold the raft back: it glided far too easily along the top of the black water. Further from the world, or did he mean further from God? A region like this seemed outside God's jurisdiction. When he had reached that idea he shut his eyes. It was an absurdity, manifestly impossible—in any case, inadmissible—yet it had occurred to him and was remaining with him in his mind. "God is always with me," he said to himself silently, but the formula had no effect. He opened his eyes quickly and looked at the two men. They were facing him, but he had the impression of being invisible to them; they could see only the quickly dissipated ripples left behind on the surface of the water, and the irregular arched ceiling of vegetation under which they had passed.

The pastor took his cane from where it was lying hidden, and gesticulated with it as he asked, "Where are we going?" Once again they both pointed vaguely into the air, over their shoulders, as if the question were of no interest, and the expression on their faces never changed. Loath to let even another tree go past, the pastor mechanically immersed his cane in the water as though he would stop the constant forward thrusting of the raft; he withdrew it immediately and laid it dripping across the bottom. Even that much contact with the dark stream was unpleasant to him. He tried to tell himself that there was no reason for his sudden spiritual collapse, but at the same time it seemed to him that he could feel the innermost fibers of his consciousness in the process of relaxing. The journey downstream was a monstrous letting go, and he fought against it with all his power. "Forgive me, O God, I am leaving You behind. Forgive me for leaving You behind." His nails pressed into his palms as he prayed.

And so he sat in agonized silence while they slid ahead through the forest and out into a wide lagoon where the gray sky was once more visible. Here the raft went much more slowly, and the Indians propelled it gently with their hands toward the shore where the water was shallow. Then one of them poled it along with the bamboo stick. The pastor did not notice the great beds of water hyacinths they passed through, nor the silken sound made as they rubbed against the raft. Out here under the low-hanging clouds there was occasionally a bird cry or a sudden rustle in the high grass by the water's edge. Still the pastor remained sunk within himself, feeling, rather than thinking: "Now it is done. I have passed over into the other land." And he remained so deeply preoccupied with this emotional certainty that he was not aware of it when they approached a high escarpment rising sheer from the lagoon, nor when they drew up onto the sand of a small cove at one side of the cliff. When he looked up the two Indians were standing on the sand, and one of them was saying, "Come." They did not help him get ashore; he did this with some difficulty, although he was conscious of none.

As soon as he was on land they led him along the foot of the cliff that curved away from the water. Following a tortuous track beaten through the undergrowth they came out all at once at the very foot of the wall of rock.

There were two caves—a small one opening to the left, and a wider, higher one to the right. They halted outside the smaller. "Go in," they said to the pastor. It was not very light inside, and he could see very little. The two remained at the entrance. "Your god lives here," said one. "Speak with him."

The pastor was on his knees. "O Father, hear my voice. Let my voice come through to you. I ask it in Jesus' name. . . ." The Indian was calling to him, "Speak in our tongue." The pastor made an effort, and began a halting supplication in the dialect. There were grunts of satisfaction outside. The concentration demanded in order to translate his thoughts into the still unfamiliar language served to clear his mind somewhat. And the comforting parallel between this prayer and those he offered for his congregation helped to restore his calm. As he continued to speak, always with fewer hesitations, he felt a great rush of strength going through him. Confidently he raised his head and went on praying, his eyes on the wall in front of him. At the same moment he heard the cry: "Metzabok hears you now. Say more to him."

The pastor's lips stopped moving, and his eyes saw for the first time the red hand painted on the rock before him, and the charcoal, the ashes, the flower petals and the wooden spoons strewn about. But he had no sensation of horror; that was over. The important thing now was that he felt strong and happy. His spiritual condition was a physical fact. Having prayed to Metzabok was also a fact, of course, but his deploring of it was in purely mental terms. Without formulating the thought, he decided that forgiveness would be forthcoming when he asked God for it.

To satisfy the watchers outside the cave he added a few formal phrases to his prayer, rose, and stepped out into the daylight. For the first time he noticed a certain animation in the features of the two little men. One said, "Metzabok is very happy." The other said, "Wait." Whereupon they both hurried over to the larger of the two apertures and disappeared inside. The pastor sat on a rock, resting his chin on the hand that held the head of his cane. He was still suffused with the strange triumphant sensation of having returned to himself.

He heard them muttering for a quarter of an hour or so inside the cave. Presently they came out, still looking very serious. Moved by curiosity, the pastor risked a question. He indicated the larger cave with a finger and said, "Hachakyum lives there?" Together they assented. He wanted to go further and ask if Hachakyum approved of his having spoken with Metzabok, but he felt the question would be imprudent; besides, he was certain the answer would be in the affirmative.

They arrived back in the village at nightfall, after having walked all the way. The Indians' gait had been far too swift for Pastor Dowe, and they had stopped only once to eat some sapotes they had found under the trees. He asked to be taken to the house of Nicolás. It was raining lightly when they reached the hut. The pastor sat down in the doorway beneath the overhanging eaves of cane. He felt utterly exhausted; it had been one of the most tiring days of his life, and he was not home yet.

His two companions ran off when Nicolás appeared. Evidently he already knew of the visit to the cave. It seemed to the pastor that he had never seen his face so full of expression or so pleasant. "*Utz, utz*," said Nicolás. "Good, good. You must eat and sleep."

After a meal of fruit and maize cakes, the pastor felt better. The hut was filled with wood smoke from the fire in the corner. He lay back in a low hammock which little Marta, casually pulling on a string from time to time, kept in gentle motion. He was overcome with a desire to sleep, but his host seemed to be in a communicative mood, and he wanted to profit by it. As he was about to speak, Nicolás approached, carrying a rusty tin biscuit box. Squatting beside the hammock he said in a low voice: "I will show you my things." The pastor was delighted; this bespoke a high degree of friendliness. Nicolás opened the box and took out some sample-size squares of printed cloth, an old vial of quinine tablets, a torn strip of newspaper, and four copper coins. He gave the pastor time to examine each carefully. At the bottom of the box were a good many orange and blue feathers which Nicolás did not bother to take out. The pastor realized that he was seeing the treasures of the household, that these items were rare objects of art. He looked at each thing with great seriousness handing it back with a verbal expression of admiration. Finally he said: "Thank you," and fell back into the hammock. Nicolás returned the box to the women sitting in the corner. When he came back over to the pastor he said: "Now we sleep."

"Nicolás," asked the pastor, "is Metzabok bad?"

"*Bai*, señor. Sometimes very bad. Like a small child. When he does not get what he wants right away, he makes fires, fever, wars. He can be very good, too, when he is happy. You should speak with him every day. Then you will know him."

"But you never speak with him."

"*Bai*, we do. Many do, when they are sick or unhappy. They ask him to take away the trouble. I never speak with him," Nicolás looked pleased, "Because Hachakyum is my good friend and I do not need Metzabok. Besides, Metzabok's home is far—three hours' walk. I can speak with Hachakyum here." The pastor knew he meant the little altar outside. He nodded and fell asleep.

The village in the early morning was a chaos of shrill sounds: dogs, parrots and cockatoos, babies, turkeys. The pastor lay still in his hammock awhile listening, before he was officially wakened by Nicolás. "We must go now, señor," he said. "Everyone is waiting for you."

The pastor sat up, a little bit alarmed. "Where?" he cried.

"You speak and make music today."

"Yes, yes." He had quite forgotten it was Sunday.

The pastor was silent, walking beside Nicolás up the road to the mission. The weather had changed, and the early sun was very bright. "I have been fortified by my experience," he was thinking. His head was clear; he felt amazingly healthy. The unaccustomed sensation of vigor gave him a strange nostalgia for the days of his youth. "I must always have felt like this then. I remember it," he thought.

At the mission there was a great crowd—many more people than he had ever seen attend a sermon at Tacaté. They were chatting quietly, but when he and Nicolás appeared there was an immediate hush. Mateo was standing in the pavilion waiting for him, with the phonograph open. With a pang the pastor realized he had not prepared a sermon for his flock. He went into the house for a moment, and returned to seat himself at the table in the pavilion, where he picked up his Bible. He had left his few notes in the book, so that it opened to the seventy-eighth Psalm. "I shall read them that," he decided. He turned to Mateo. "Play the *disco*," he said. Mateo put on "Crazy Rhythm." The pastor quickly made a few pencil alterations in the text of the psalm, substituting the names of minor local deities, like Usukun and Sibanaa for such names as Jacob and Ephraim, and local place names for Israel and Egypt. And he wrote the word Hachakyum each time the word God or the Lord appeared. He had not finished when the record stopped. "Play it again," he commanded. The audience was delighted, even though the sound was abominably scratchy. When the music was over for the second time, he stood and began to paraphrase the psalm in a clear voice. "The children of Sibanaa, carrying bows to shoot, ran into the forest to hide when the enemy came. They did not keep their promises to Hachakyum, and they would not live as He told them to live." The audience was electrified. As he spoke, he looked down and saw the child Marta staring up at him. She had let go of her baby alligator, and it was crawling with a surprising speed toward the table where he sat. Quintina, Mateo, and the two maids were piling up the bars of salt on the ground to one side. They kept returning to the kitchen for more. He realized that what he was saying doubtless made no sense in terms of his listeners' religion, but it was a story of the unleashing of divine displeasure upon an unholy people, and they were enjoying it vastly. The alligator, trailing its rags, had crawled to within a few inches of the pastor's feet, where it remained quiet, content to be out of Marta's arms.

Presently, while he was still speaking, Mateo began to hand out the salt, and soon they all were running their tongues rhythmically over the large rough cakes, but continuing to pay strict attention to his words. When he was about to finish, he motioned to Mateo to be ready to start the record again the minute he finished; on the last word he lowered his arm as a signal, and "Crazy Rhythm" sounded once more. The alligator began to crawl hastily toward the far end of the pavilion. Pastor Dowe bent down and picked it up. As he stepped forward to hand it to Mateo, Nicolás rose from the ground, and taking Marta by the hand, walked over into the pavilion with her.

"Señor," he said, "Marta will live with you. I give her to you."

"What do you mean?" cried the pastor in a voice which cracked a little. The alligator squirmed in his hand.

"She is your wife. She will live here."

Pastor Dowe's eyes grew very wide. He was unable to say anything for a moment. He shook his hands in the air and finally he said: "No" several times.

Nicolás' face grew unpleasant. "You do not like Marta?"

"Very much. She is beautiful." The pastor sat down slowly on his chair. "But she is a little child."

Nicolás frowned with impatience. "She is already large."

"No, Nicolás. No. No."

Nicolás pushed his daughter forward and stepped back several paces, leaving her there by the table. "It is done," he said sternly. "She is your wife. I have given her to you."

Pastor Dowe looked out over the assembly and saw the unspoken approval in all the faces. "Crazy Rhythm" ceased to play. There was silence. Under the mango tree he saw a woman toying with a small, shiny object. Suddenly he recognized his glasses case; the woman was stripping the leatheroid fabric from it. The bare aluminum with its dents flashed in the sun. For some reason even in the middle of this situation he found himself thinking: "So I was wrong. It is not dead. She will keep it, the way Nicolás has kept the quinine tablets."

He looked down at Marta. The child was staring at him quite without expression. Like a cat, he reflected.

Again he began to protest. "Nicolás," he cried, his voice very high, "this is impossible!" He felt a hand grip his arm, and turned to receive a warning glance from Mateo.

Nicolás had already advanced toward the pavilion, his face like a thundercloud. As he seemed about to speak, the pastor interrupted him quickly. He had decided to temporize. "She may stay at the mission today," he said weakly.

"She is your wife," said Nicolás with great feeling. "You cannot send her away. You must keep her."

"*Diga que sí*," Mateo was whispering. "Say yes, señor."

"Yes," the pastor heard himself saying. "Yes. Good." He got up and walked slowly into the house, holding the alligator with one hand and pushing Marta in front of him with the other. Mateo followed and closed the door after them.

"Take her into the kitchen, Mateo," said the pastor dully, handing the little reptile to Marta. As Mateo went across the patio leading the child by the hand, he called after him. "Leave her with Quintina and come to my room."

He sat down on the edge of his bed, staring ahead of him with unseeing eyes. At each moment his predicament seemed to him more terrible. With relief he heard Mateo knock. The people outdoors were slowly leaving. It cost him an effort to call out, "*Adelante.*" When Mateo had come in, the pastor said, "Close the door."

"Mateo, did you know they were going to do this? That they were going to bring that child here?"

"*Sí, señor.*"

"You knew it! But why didn't you say anything? Why didn't you tell me?"

Mateo shrugged his shoulders, looking at the floor. "I didn't know it would matter to you," he said. "Anyway, it would have been useless."

"Useless? Why? You could have stopped Nicolás," said the pastor, although he did not believe it himself.

Mateo laughed shortly. "You think so?"

"Mateo, you must help me. We must oblige Nicolás to take her back."

Mateo shook his head. "It can't be done. These people are very severe. They never change their laws."

"Perhaps a letter to the administrator at Ocosingo . . ."

"No, señor. That would make still more trouble. You are not a Catholic." Mateo shifted on his feet and suddenly smiled thinly. "Why not let her stay? She doesn't eat much. She can work in the kitchen. In two years she will be very pretty."

The pastor jumped, and made such a wide and vehement gesture with his hands that the mosquito netting, looped above his head, fell down about his face. Mateo helped him disentangle himself. The air smelled of dust from the netting.

"You don't understand anything!" shouted Pastor Dowe, beside himself. "I can't talk to you! I don't want to talk to you! Go out and leave me alone." Mateo obediently left the room.

Pounding his left palm with his right fist, over and over again, the pastor stood in his window before the landscape that shone in the strong sun. A few women were still eating under the mango tree; the rest had gone back down the hill.

He lay on his bed throughout the long afternoon. When twilight came he had made his decision. Locking his door, he proceeded to pack what personal effects he could into his smallest suitcase. His Bible and notebooks went on top with his toothbrush and atabrine tablets. When Quintina came to announce supper he asked to have it brought to his bed, taking care to slip the packed valise into the closet before he unlocked the door for her to enter. He waited until the talking had ceased all over the house, until he knew everyone was asleep. With the small bag not too heavy in one hand he tiptoed into the patio, out through the door into the fragrant night, across the open space in front of the pavilion, under the mango tree and down the path leading to Tacaté. Then he began to walk fast, because he wanted to get through the village before the moon rose.

There was a chorus of dogs barking as he entered the village street. He began to run, straight through to the other end. And he kept running even then, until he had reached the point where the path, wider here, dipped beneath the hill and curved into the forest. His heart was beating rapidly from the exertion. To rest, and to try to be fairly certain he was not being followed, he sat down on his little valise in the center of the path. There he remained a long time, thinking of nothing, while the night went on and the moon came up. He heard only the light wind among the leaves and vines. Overhead a few bats reeled soundlessly back and forth. At last he took a deep breath, got up, and went on.

Call at Corazón

B UT WHY would you want a little horror like that to go
along with us? It doesn't make sense. You know what
they're like."

"I know what they're like," said her husband. "It's comforting to watch them. Whatever happens, if I had that to
look at, I'd be reminded of how stupid I was ever to get upset."

He leaned further over the railing and looked intently
down at the dock. There were baskets for sale, crude painted
toys of hard natural rubber, reptile-hide wallets and belts, and
a few whole snakeskins unrolled. And placed apart from these
wares, out of the hot sunlight, in the shadow of a crate, sat a
tiny, furry monkey. The hands were folded, and the forehead
was wrinkled in sad apprehensiveness.

"Isn't he wonderful?"

"I think you're impossible—and a little insulting," she
replied.

He turned to look at her. "Are you serious?" He saw that
she was.

She went on, studying her sandaled feet and the narrow
deck-boards beneath them: "You know I don't really mind all
this nonsense, or your craziness. Just let me finish." He nodded his head in agreement, looking back at the hot dock and
the wretched tin-roofed village beyond. "It goes without saying I don't mind all that, or we wouldn't be here together.
You might be here alone . . ."

"You don't take a honeymoon alone," he interrupted.

"*You* might." She laughed shortly.

He reached along the rail for her hand, but she pulled it
away, saying, "I'm still talking to you. I expect you to be
crazy, and I expect to give in to you all along. I'm crazy too,
I know. But I wish there were some way I could just once feel
that my giving in meant anything to you. I wish you knew
how to be gracious about it."

"You think you humor me so much? I haven't noticed it."
His voice was sullen.

"I don't *humor* you at all. I'm just trying to live with you on an extended trip in a lot of cramped little cabins on an endless series of stinking boats."

"What do you mean?" he cried excitedly. "You've always said you loved the boats. Have you changed your mind, or just lost it completely?"

She turned and walked toward the prow. "Don't talk to me," she said. "Go and buy your monkey."

An expression of solicitousness on his face, he was following her. "You know I won't buy it if it's going to make you miserable."

"I'll be more miserable if you don't, so please go and buy it." She stopped and turned. "I'd love to have it. I really would. I think it's sweet."

"I don't get you at all."

She smiled. "I know. Does it bother you very much?"

After he had bought the monkey and tied it to the metal post of the bunk in the cabin, he took a walk to explore the port. It was a town made of corrugated tin and barbed wire. The sun's heat was painful, even with the sky's low-lying cover of fog. It was the middle of the day and few people were in the streets. He came to the edge of the town almost immediately. Here between him and the forest lay a narrow, slow-moving stream, its water the color of black coffee. A few women were washing clothes; small children splashed. Gigantic gray crabs scuttled between the holes they had made in the mud along the bank. He sat down on some elaborately twisted roots at the foot of a tree and took out the notebook he always carried with him. The day before, in a bar at Pedernales, he had written: "Recipe for dissolving the impression of hideousness made by a thing: Fix the attention upon the given object or situation so that the various elements, all familiar, will regroup themselves. Frightfulness is never more than an unfamiliar pattern."

He lit a cigarette and watched the women's hopeless attempts to launder the ragged garments. Then he threw the burning stub at the nearest crab, and carefully wrote: "More than anything else, woman requires strict ritualistic observance of the traditions of sexual behavior. That is her definition of love." He thought of the derision that would be called forth should he make such a statement to the girl back on the ship. After looking at his watch, he wrote hurriedly: "Modern, that is, intellectual education, having been devised by males for males, inhibits and confuses her. She avenges . . ."

Two naked children, coming up from their play in the river, ran screaming past him, scattering drops of water over the paper. He called out to them, but they continued their chase without noticing him. He put his pencil and notebook into his pocket, smiling, and watched them patter after one another through the dust.

When he arrived back at the ship, the thunder was rolling down from the mountains around the harbor. The storm reached the height of its hysteria just as they got under way.

She was sitting on her bunk, looking through the open porthole. The shrill crashes of thunder echoed from one side of the bay to the other as they steamed toward the open sea. He lay doubled up on his bunk opposite, reading.

"Don't lean your head against that metal wall," he advised. "It's a perfect conductor."

She jumped down to the floor and went to the washstand.

"Where are those two quarts of White Horse we got yesterday?"

He gestured. "In the rack on your side. Are you going to drink?"

"I'm going to *have* a drink, yes."

"In this heat? Why don't you wait until it clears, and have it on deck?"

"I want it now. When it clears I won't need it."

She poured the whisky and added water from the carafe in the wall bracket over the washbowl.

"You realize what you're doing, of course."

She glared at him. "What am I doing?"

He shrugged his shoulders. "Nothing, except just giving in to a passing emotional state. You could read, or lie down and doze."

Holding her glass in one hand, she pulled open the door into the passageway with the other, and went out. The noise of the slamming door startled the monkey, perched on a suitcase. It hesitated a second, and hurried under its master's bunk. He made a few kissing sounds to entice it out, and returned to his book. Soon he began to imagine her alone and unhappy on the deck, and the thought cut into the pleasure of his reading. He forced himself to lie still a few minutes, the open book face down across his chest. The boat was moving at full speed now, and the sound of the motors was louder than the storm in the sky.

Soon he rose and went on deck. The land behind was already hidden by the falling rain, and the air smelled of deep water. She was standing alone by the rail, looking down at the waves, with the empty glass in her hand. Pity seized him as he watched, but he could not walk across to her and put into consoling words the emotion he felt.

Back in the cabin he found the monkey on his bunk, slowly tearing the pages from the book he had been reading.

The next day was spent in leisurely preparation for disembarking and changing of boats: in Villalta they were to take a smaller vessel to the opposite side of the delta.

When she came in to pack after dinner, she stood a moment studying the cabin. "He's messed it up, all right," said her husband, "but I found your necklace behind my big valise, and we'd read all the magazines anyway."

"I suppose this represents Man's innate urge to destroy," she said, kicking a ball of crumpled paper across the floor. "And the next time he tries to bite you, it'll be Man's basic insecurity."

"You don't know what a bore you are when you try to be caustic. If you want me to get rid of him, I will. It's easy enough."

She bent to touch the animal, but it backed uneasily under the bunk. She stood up. "I don't mind him. What I mind is you. *He* can't help being a little horror, but he keeps reminding me that you could if you wanted."

Her husband's face assumed the impassivity that was characteristic of him when he was determined not to lose his temper. She knew he would wait to be angry until she was unprepared for his attack. He said nothing, tapping an insistent rhythm on the lid of a suitcase with his fingernails.

"Naturally I don't really mean you're a horror," she continued.

"Why not mean it?" he said, smiling pleasantly. "What's

wrong with criticism? Probably I am, to you. I like monkeys because I see them as little model men. You think men are something else, something spiritual or God knows what. Whatever it is, I notice you're the one who's always being disillusioned and going around wondering how mankind can be so bestial. I think mankind is fine."

"Please don't go on," she said. "I know your theories. You'll never convince yourself of them."

When they had finished packing, they went to bed. As he snapped off the light behind his pillow, he said, "Tell me honestly. Do you want me to give him to the steward?"

She kicked off her sheet in the dark. Through the porthole, near the horizon, she could see stars, and the calm sea slipped by just below her. Without thinking she said, "Why don't you drop him overboard?"

In the silence that followed she realized she had spoken carelessly, but the tepid breeze moving with languor over her body was making it increasingly difficult for her to think or speak. As she fell asleep it seemed to her she heard her husband saying slowly, "I believe you would. I believe you would."

The next morning she slept late, and when she went up for breakfast her husband had already finished his and was leaning back, smoking.

"How are you?" he asked brightly. "The cabin steward's delighted with the monkey."

She felt a flush of pleasure. "Oh," she said, sitting down, "did you give it to him? You didn't have to do that." She glanced at the menu; it was the same as every other day. "But I suppose really it's better. A monkey doesn't go with a honeymoon."

"I think you're right," he agreed.

Villalta was stifling and dusty. On the other boat they had grown accustomed to having very few passengers around, and it was an unpleasant surprise to find the new one swarming with people. Their new boat was a two-decked ferry painted white, with an enormous paddle wheel at the stern. On the lower deck, which rested not more than two feet above the surface of the river, passengers and freight stood ready to travel, packed together indiscriminately. The upper deck had a salon and a dozen or so narrow staterooms. In the salon the first-class passengers undid their bundles of pillows and opened their paper bags of food. The orange light of the setting sun flooded the room.

They looked into several of the staterooms.

"They all seem to be empty," she said.

"I can see why. Still, the privacy would be a help."

"This one's double. And it has a screen in the window. This is the best one."

"I'll look for a steward or somebody. Go on in and take over." He pushed the bags out of the passageway where the *cargador* had left them, and went off in search of an employee. In every corner of the boat the people seemed to be multiplying. There were twice as many as there had been a few moments before. The salon was completely full, its floor space occupied by groups of travelers with small children and elderly women, who were already stretched out on blankets and newspapers.

"It looks like Salvation Army headquarters the night after a major disaster," he said as he came back into the stateroom. "I can't find anybody. Anyway, we'd better stay in here. The other cubicles are beginning to fill up."

"I'm not so sure I wouldn't rather be on deck," she announced. "There are hundreds of cockroaches."

"And probably worse," he added, looking at the bunks.

"The thing to do is take those filthy sheets off and just lie on the mattresses." She peered out into the corridor. Sweat was trickling down her neck. "Do you think it's safe?"

"What do you mean?"

"All those people. This old tub."

He shrugged his shoulders.

"It's just one night. Tomorrow we'll be at Cienaga. And it's almost night now."

She shut the door and leaned against it, smiling faintly.

"I think it's going to be fun," she said.

"The boat's moving!" he cried. "Let's go on deck. If we can get out there."

Slowly the old boat pushed across the bay toward the dark east shore. People were singing and playing guitars. On the bottom deck a cow lowed continuously. And louder than all the sounds was the rush of water made by the huge paddles.

They sat on the deck in the middle of a vociferous crowd, leaning against the bars of the railing, and watched the moon rise above the mangrove swamps ahead. As they approached the opposite side of the bay, it looked as if the boat might plow straight into the shore, but a narrow waterway presently appeared, and the boat slipped cautiously in. The people immediately moved back from the railing, crowding against the opposite wall. Branches from the trees on the bank began to rub against the boat, scraping along the side walls of the cabins, and then whipping violently across the deck.

They pushed their way through the throng and walked across the salon to the deck on the other side of the boat; the same thing was happening there.

"It's crazy," she declared. "It's like a nightmare. Whoever heard of going through a channel no wider than the boat! It makes me nervous. I'm going in and read."

Her husband let go of her arm. "You can never enter into the spirit of a thing, can you?"

"You tell me what the spirit is, and I'll see about entering into it," she said, turning away.

He followed her. "Don't you want to go down onto the lower deck? They seem to be going strong down there. Listen." He held up his hand. Repeated screams of laughter came up from below.

"I certainly don't!" she called, without looking around.

He went below. Groups of men were seated on bulging burlap sacks and wooden crates, matching coins. The women stood behind them, puffing on black cigarettes and shrieking with excitement. He watched them closely, reflecting that with fewer teeth missing they would be a handsome people. "Mineral deficiency in the soil," he commented to himself.

Standing on the other side of a circle of gamblers, facing him, was a muscular young native whose visored cap and faint air of aloofness suggested official position of some sort aboard the boat. With difficulty the traveler made his way over to him, and spoke to him in Spanish.

"Are you an employee here?"

"Yes, sir."

"I am in cabin number eight. Can I pay the supplementary fare to you?"

"Yes, sir."

"Good."

He reached into his pocket for his wallet, at the same time remembering with annoyance that he had left it upstairs locked in a suitcase. The man looked expectant. His hand was out.

"My money is in my stateroom." Then he added, "My wife has it. But if you come up in half an hour I can pay you the fare."

"Yes, sir." The man lowered his hand and merely looked at him. Even though he gave an impression of purely animal force, his broad, somewhat simian face was handsome, the husband reflected. It was surprising when, a moment later, that face betrayed a boyish shyness as the man said, "I am going to spray the cabin for your señora."

"Thank you. Are there many mosquitoes?"

The man grunted and shook the fingers of one hand as if he had just burned them.

"Soon you will see how many." He moved away.

At that moment the boat jolted violently, and there was great merriment among the passengers. He pushed his way to the prow and saw that the pilot had run into the bank. The tangle of branches and roots was a few feet from his face, its complex forms vaguely lighted by the boat's lanterns. The boat backed laboriously and the channel's agitated water rose to deck level and lapped the outer edge. Slowly they nosed along the bank until the prow once more pointed to midstream, and they continued. Then almost immediately the passage curved so sharply that the same thing happened again, throwing him sideways against a sack of something unpleasantly soft and wet. A bell clanged below deck in the interior of the boat; the passengers' laughter was louder.

Eventually they pushed ahead, but now the movement became painfully slow as the sharpness of the curves in the passage increased. Under the water the stumps groaned as the boat forced its sides against them. Branches cracked and broke, falling onto the forward and upper decks. The lantern at the prow was swept into the water.

"This isn't the regular channel," muttered a gambler, glancing up.

Several travelers exclaimed, "What?" almost in unison.

"There's a pile of passages through here. We're picking up cargo at Corazón."

The players retreated to a square inner arena which others were forming by shifting some of the crates. The husband followed them. Here they were comparatively safe from the intruding boughs. The deck was better lighted here, and this gave him the idea of making an entry in his notebook. Bending over a carton marked *Vermifugo Santa Rosalia*, he wrote: "November 18. We are moving through the blood stream of a giant. A very dark night." Here a fresh collision with the land knocked him over, knocked over everyone who was not propped between solid objects.

A few babies were crying, but most of them still slept. He slid down to the deck. Finding his position fairly comfortable, he fell into a dozing state which was broken irregularly by the shouting of the people and the jolting of the boat.

When he awoke later, the boat was quite stationary, the games had ceased, and the people were asleep, a few of the men continuing their conversation in small groups. He lay still, listening. The talk was all about places; they were comparing the unpleasant things to be found in various parts of the republic: insects, weather, reptiles, diseases, lack of food, high prices.

He looked at his watch. It was half past one. With difficulty he got to his feet, and found his way to the stairs. Above, in the salon, the kerosene lamps illumined a vast disorder of prostrate figures. He went into the corridor and knocked on the door marked with an eight. Without waiting for her to answer, he opened the door. It was dark inside. He heard a muffled cough nearby, and decided that she was awake.

"How are the mosquitoes? Did my monkey man come and fix you up?" he asked.

She did not answer, so he lit a match. She was not in the bunk on the left. The match burned his thumb. With the second one, he looked at the right-hand bunk. A tin insecticide sprayer lay there on the mattress; its leak had made a large circle of oil on the bare ticking. The cough was repeated. It was someone in the next cabin.

"Now what?" he said aloud, uncomfortable at finding himself upset to this degree. A suspicion seized him. Without lighting the hanging lamp, he rushed to open her valises, and in the dark felt hurriedly through the flimsy pieces of clothing and the toilet articles. The whisky bottles were not there.

This was not the first time she had gone on a solitary drinking bout, and it would be easy to find her among the passengers. However, being angry, he decided not to look for her. He took off his shirt and trousers and lay down on the left-hand bunk. His hand touched a bottle standing on the floor by the head of the bunk. He raised himself enough to smell it; it was beer and the bottle was half full. It was hot in the cabin, and he drank the remaining warm, bitter liquid with relish and rolled the bottle across the room.

The boat was not moving, but voices shouted out here and there. An occasional bump could be felt as a sack of something heavy was heaved aboard. He looked through the little square window with the screen in it. In the foreground, dimly illumined by the boat's lanterns, a few dark men, naked save for their ragged underdrawers, stood on a landing made in the mud and stared toward the boat. Through the endless intricacies of roots and trunks behind them he saw a bonfire blazing, but it was far back in the swamp. The air smelled of stagnant water and smoke.

Deciding to take advantage of the relative silence, he lay down and tried to sleep; he was not surprised, however, by the difficulty he found in relaxing. It was always hard to sleep when she was not there in the room. The comfort of her presence was lacking, and there was also the fear of being awakened by her return. When he allowed himself to, he would quickly begin to formulate ideas and translate them into sentences whose recording seemed the more urgent because he was lying comfortably in the dark. Sometimes he thought about her, but only as an unclear figure whose character lent flavor to a succession of backdrops. More often he reviewed the day just completed, seeking to convince himself that it had carried him a bit further away from his childhood. Often for months at a time the strangeness of his dreams persuaded him that at last he had turned the corner, that the dark place had finally been left behind, that he was out of hearing. Then, one evening as he fell asleep, before he had time to refuse, he would be staring closely at a long-forgotten object—a plate, a chair, a pincushion—and the accustomed feeling of infinite futility and sadness would recur.

The motor started up, and the great noise of the water in the paddle wheel recommenced. They pushed off from Corazón. He was pleased. "Now I shan't hear her when she comes in and bangs around," he thought, and fell into a light sleep.

He was scratching his arms and legs. The long-continued, vague malaise eventually became full consciousness, and he sat up angrily. Above the sounds made by the boat he could hear another sound, one which came through the window: an incredibly high and tiny tone, tiny but constant in pitch and intensity. He jumped down from the berth and went to the window. The channel was wider here, and the overhanging vegetation no longer touched the sides of the boat. In the air, nearby, far away, everywhere, was the thin wail of mosquito wings. He was aghast, and completely delighted by the novelty of the phenomenon. For a moment he watched the tangled black wilderness slip past. Then with the itching he remembered the mosquitoes inside the cabin. The screen did not reach quite to the top of the window; there was ample space for them to crawl in. Even there in the dark as he moved his fingers along the frame to find the handle he could feel them; there were that many.

Now that he was fully awake, he lighted a match and went to her bunk. Of course she was not there. He lifted the Flit gun and shook it. It was empty, and as the match went out, he saw that the spot on the mattress had spread even further.

"Son of a bitch!" he whispered, and going back to the window he tugged the screen vigorously upward to close the crack. As he let go of it, it fell out into the water, and almost immediately he was conscious of the soft caress of tiny wings all about his head. In his undershirt and trousers he rushed out into the corridor. Nothing had changed in the salon. Almost everyone was asleep. There were screen doors giving onto the deck. He inspected them: they appeared to be more firmly installed. A few mosquitoes brushed against his face, but it was not the horde. He edged in between two women who were sleeping sitting with their backs against the wall, and stayed there in acute discomfort until again he dozed. It was not long before he opened his eyes to find the dim light of dawn in the air. His neck ached. He arose and went out onto the deck, to which most of the people from the salon had already crowded.

The boat was moving through a wide estuary dotted with clumps of plants and trees that rose out of the shallow water. Along the edges of the small islands stood herons, so white in the early gray light that their brightness seemed to come from inside them.

It was half past five. At this moment the boat was due in Cienaga, where it was met on its weekly trip by the train that went into the interior. Already a thin spit of land ahead was being identified by eager watchers. Day was coming up swiftly; sky and water were the same color. The deck reeked of the greasy smell of mangoes as people began to breakfast.

And now at last he began to feel pangs of anxiety as to where she might be. He determined to make an immediate and thorough search of the boat. She would be instantly recognizable in any group. First, he looked methodically through the salon, then he exhausted the possibilities on the upper decks. Then he went downstairs, where the gambling had already begun again. Toward the stern, roped to two flimsy iron posts, stood the cow, no longer bellowing. Nearby was an improvised lean-to, probably the crew's quarters. As he passed the small door, he peered through the low transom above it, and saw her lying beside a man on the floor. Automatically he walked on; then he turned and went back. The two were asleep, and half-clothed. In the warm air that came through the screened transom there was the smell of whisky that had been drunk and whisky that had been spilled.

He went upstairs, his heart beating violently. In the cabin, he closed her two valises, packed his own, set them all together by the door and laid the raincoats on top of them. He put on his shirt, combed his hair carefully, and went on deck. Cienaga was there ahead, in the mountains' morning shadow: the dock, a line of huts against the jungle behind, and the railway station to the right beyond the village.

As they docked, he signaled the two urchins who were waving for his attention, screaming, "*Equipajes!*" They fought a bit with one another until he made them see his two fingers held aloft. Then to make them certain, he pointed at each of them in turn, and they grinned. Still grinning, they stood beside him with the bags and coats, and he was among the first of the upper-deck passengers to get on land. They went down the street to the station with the parrots screaming at them from each thatched gable along the way.

On the crowded, waiting train, with the luggage finally in the rack, his heart beat harder than ever, and he kept his eyes painfully on the long dusty street that led back to the dock. At the far end, as the whistle blew, he thought he saw a figure in white running among the dogs and children toward the station, but the train started up as he watched, and the street was lost to view. He took out his notebook, and sat with it on his lap, smiling at the shining green landscape that moved with increasing speed past the window.

Under the Sky

Inland from the sea on the dry coastal plain lay the town, open, spread out under the huge high sky. People who lived outside in the country, and even some of the more educated town-dwellers, called the town "the Inferno" because nowhere in the region was the heat so intense. No other place around was quite so shadowless and so dusty; it seemed that the clouds above shrank upwards to their farthest possible positions. Many miles above, and to all sides, they hung there in their massive patterns, remote and motionless. In the spring, during the nights, the lightning constantly jumped from one cloud to another, revealing unexpected distances between them. Then, if anyone ever looked at the sky, he was surprised to see how each flash revealed a seemingly more distant portion of the heavens to which still more clouds had receded. But people in the town seldom turned their heads upward. They knew at what time of the year the rains would come, and it was unnecessary to scan those vast regions in order to say what day that would be. When the wind had blown hard for two weeks so that the dust filled the wide empty streets, and the lightning grew brighter each night until finally there was a little thunder, they could be sure the water would soon fall.

Once a year when the lightning was in the sky Jacinto left his village in the mountains and walked down to the town, carrying with him all the things his family had made since his last trip. There were two days of walking in the sierra where it was cool; the third day the road was through the hot lands, and this was the day he preferred, because the road was flat and he could walk faster and leave the others behind. He was taller and prouder than they, and he refused to bend over in order to be able to trot uphill and downhill as they did. In the mountains he labored to keep up with them, but on the plain he strode powerfully ahead and sometimes arrived at the market before sunset.

Now he stood in the public square with a small paper parcel in his hand. He had arrived the day before. Instead of sitting in the sidestreet near the fountain and discussing the sales with the others from his village, he walked into the municipal garden and sat down on a concrete bench marked "1936." He looked up and down the walk. No one paid him any attention. He was barefoot, so the shoeshine boys passed him by.

Tearing open the paper packet he emptied the dried leaves into his left hand. With his right he picked out all the little round, black berries and tossed them away. Then he crushed the leaves and slowly rolled them into five thin cigarettes. This took all his attention for a half hour.

A voice beside him said: "That's pretty."

He looked up. It was a town-dweller; he had never seen him before, so he did not answer.

"All for you?" said the other in the silken town voice that Jacinto had learned to distrust.

"I bought it. I made them," said Jacinto.

"But I like *grifas* too," smiled the stranger. He was poorly dressed and had black teeth.

Jacinto covered the cigarettes completely with one big hand which he placed on the seat of the bench. The stranger pointed to a soldier sleeping on another bench near the iron bandstand.

"He wants one and I want one. You should be more careful. It's three months now for possessing marijuana. Don't you know?"

"No," said Jacinto. "I don't know." Then he slowly handed over two of the cigarettes. The man took them.

"So long," he said.

Jacinto stood up full of fury, and with the other three cigarettes still in his hand, he walked out into the plaza and down the long street that led to the station. It was nearly time for the daily train from the north. Sometimes crazy people got off, who would give a man enough money for two good meals, just for carrying a bundle into the town for them. There was a cemetery behind the roundhouse where some of the railroad employees went to smoke the weed. He remembered it from the preceding year; he had met an inspector there who had taken him to see a girl. She had proved to be ugly—one side of her face was mottled with blue and purple.

At the station the train had already arrived. The people trying to get on were fighting with those who were trying to get
off. He wondered why with all those open windows everyone
insisted on going through the two little doors at the ends of
the cars. It would have been very simple the other way, but
these people were too stupid to think of it. His defeat at the
hands of the townsman still bothered him; he wanted to have
a gun so he could pull it out and shout: "I am the father of
all of you!" But it was not likely that he ever would have a
gun.

Without approaching the platform where so many people
were moving about, he stood and impassively watched the
confusion. From the crowd three strange-looking people suddenly emerged. They all had very white skin and yellow hair.
He knew, of course, that they were from a faraway place because everyone knows that when people look as strange as
that they are from the capital or even farther. There were two
women and one man, and as they approached him, he noticed
that they were speaking a language which only they could understand. Each one carried a leather bag covered with small
squares of colored paper stuck on at different angles. He
stepped back, keeping his eyes on the face of the younger
woman. He could not be sure whether he found her beautiful or revolting. Still he continued to look at her as she
passed, holding on to the man's arm. The other woman noticed him, and smiled faintly as she went by.

He turned angrily and walked toward the tracks. He was
angry at her stupidity—for thinking he could have enough
money to pay her as much as she would surely want. He
walked on until he came to the cemetery. It was empty save
for the gray lizards that scurried from the path at his feet. In
the farthest corner there was a small square building with a
white stone woman on top. He sat in the shade of the little
building and took out his cigarettes.

The train whistled; it was starting on its trip to the sea
where the people eat nothing but fish and travel on top of the
water. He drew in the first few breaths very slowly and deliberately, holding the smoke in his lungs until he felt it burning
the edges of his soul. After a few minutes the feeling began to
take shape. From the back of his head it moved down to his

shoulders. It was as if he were wearing a tight metal garment. At that instant he looked at the sky and saw far above him the tiny black dots that were vultures, moving ever so slowly in circles as they surveyed the plain in the afternoon sunlight. Beyond them stood the clouds, deep and monumental. "Ay!" he sighed, shutting his eyes, and it occurred to him that this was what the dead people, who were lying on all sides of him, looked at day after day. This was all they could see—the clouds, and the vultures, which they did not need to fear, hidden safely as they were, deep in holy ground.

He continued to smoke, going deeper and deeper into delight. Finally he lay back and murmured: "Now I am dead too." When he opened his eyes it was still the same day, and the sun was very low in the sky. Some men were talking nearby. He listened; they were trainmen come to smoke, discussing wages and prices of meals. He did not believe any of the figures they so casually mentioned. They were lying to impress one another, and they did not even believe each other. He smoked half of the second cigarette, rose, stretched, and jumped over the cemetery wall, going back to the station by a roundabout path in order not to have to speak to the trainmen. Those people, when they smoked, always wanted more and more company; they would never let a fellow smoker go quietly on his way.

He went to the cantina by the station, and standing in the street, watched the railway employees playing billiards inside. As night approached, the lightning became increasingly visible. He walked up the long street toward the center of town. Men were playing marimbas in the doorways and in front of the houses—three or four together, and sometimes only one, indolently. The marimbas and the marijuana were the only good things in the town, reflected Jacinto. The women were ugly and dirty, and the men were all thieves and drunkards. He remembered the three people at the station. They would be in the hotel opposite the plaza. He walked a little faster, and his eyes, bloodshot from lack of sleep and too much of the drug, opened a bit wider.

After he had eaten heartily in the market sitting by the edge of the fountain, he felt very well. By the side wall of the cathedral were all the families from the mountains, some al-

ready asleep, the others preparing for the night. Almost all the
stalls in the market were dark; a few figures still stood in front
of the cold fruit-juice stand. Jacinto felt in his pocket for the
stub and the whole cigarette, and keeping his fingers around
them, walked across to the park. The celestial fireworks were
very bright, but there was no thunder. Throughout the town
sounded the clink and purr of the marimbas, some near and
some far away. A soft breeze stirred the branches of the few
lemon trees in the park. He walked along thoughtfully until
he came to a bench directly opposite the entrance of the hotel, and there he sat down and brazenly began to smoke his
stub. After a few minutes it was easier for him to believe that
one of the two yellow-haired women would come out. He
flicked away the butt, leaned back and stared straight at the
hotel. The manager had put a square loudspeaker over the entrance door, and out of it came a great crackling and hissing
that covered the sound of the marimbas. Occasionally a few
loud notes of band music rose above the chaos, and from
time to time there seemed to be a man's voice speaking behind the noise. Jacinto was annoyed: the women would want
to stay inside where they could hear the sound better.

A long time went by. The radio was silenced. The few
voices in the park disappeared down the streets. By the cathedral everyone was asleep. Even the marimbas seemed to have
stopped, but when the breeze occasionally grew more active,
it brought with it, swelling and dying, long marimba trills
from a distant part of the town.

It grew very late. There was no sound but the lemon leaves
rubbing together and the jet of water splashing into the basin
in the center of the market. Jacinto was used to waiting. And
halfway through the night a woman stepped out of the hotel,
stood for a moment looking at the sky, and walked across the
street to the park. From his bench in the dark he watched her
as she approached. In the lightning he saw that it was not the
younger one. He was disappointed. She looked upward again
before moving into the shade of the lemon trees, and in a
moment she sat down on the next bench and lighted a cigarette. He waited a few minutes. Then he said: "Señorita."

The yellow-haired woman cried: "Oh!" She had not seen
him. She jumped up and stood still, peering toward his bench.

He moved to the end of the seat and calmly repeated the word. "Señorita."

She walked uncertainly toward him, still peering. He knew this was a ruse. She could see him quite clearly each second or so, whenever the sky lighted up. When she was near enough to the bench, he motioned for her to sit down beside him. As he had suspected, she spoke his tongue.

"What is it?" she asked. The talk in the strange language at the station had only been for show, after all.

"Sit down, señorita."

"Why?"

"Because I tell you to."

She laughed and threw away her cigarette.

"That's not a reason," she said, sitting down at the other end of the bench. "What are you doing here so late?" She spoke carefully and correctly, like a priest. He answered this by saying: "And you, what are you looking for?"

"Nothing."

"Yes. You are looking for something," he said solemnly.

"I was not sleeping. It is very hot."

"No. It is not hot," said Jacinto. He was feeling increasingly sure of himself, and he drew out the last cigarette and began to smoke it. "What are you doing here in this town?" he asked her after a moment.

"Passing on my way south to the border," she said, and she told him how she was traveling with two friends, a husband and wife, and how she often took a walk when they had gone to bed.

Jacinto listened as he drew in the smoke and breathed it out. Suddenly he jumped up. Touching her arm, he said: "Come to the market."

She arose, asking: "Why?" and walked with him across the park. When they were in the street, he took her wrist fiercely and pressing it, said between his teeth: "Look at the sky."

She looked up wonderingly, a little fearfully. He went on in a low, intense voice: "As God is my witness, I am going into the hotel and kill the man who came here with you."

Her eyes grew large. She tried to wrest her arm away, but he would not let it go, and he thrust his face into hers. "I have a pistol in my pocket and I am going to kill that man."

"But why?" she whispered weakly, looking up and down the empty street.

"I want his wife."

The woman said: "It is not possible. She would scream."

"I know the proprietor," said Jacinto, rolling his eyes and grinning. The woman seemed to believe him. Now he felt that a great thing was about to happen.

"And you," he said, twisting her arm brutally, "you do not scream."

"No."

Again he pointed to the sky.

"God is my witness. You can save the life of your friend. Come with me."

She was trembling violently, but as they stumbled through the street and he let go of her an instant, she began to run. With one bound he had overtaken her, and he made her stop and look at the sky again as he went through his threats once more. She saw his wide, red-veined eyes in a bright flash of lightning, and his utterly empty face. Mechanically she allowed him to push her along through the streets. He did not let go of her again.

"You are saving your friend's life," he said. "God will reward you."

She was sobbing as she went along. No one passed them as they moved unsteadily on toward the station. When they were nearly there they made a great detour past the edge of town, and finally came to the cemetery.

"This is a holy place," he murmured, swiftly crossing himself. "Here you are going to save your friend's life."

He took off his shirt, laid it on the stony ground, and pushed her down. There was nothing but the insistent, silent flashing in the sky. She kept her eyes shut, but she shuddered at each flash, even with her lids closed. The wind blew harder, and the smell of the dust was in her nostrils.

He took her back as far as the park and there he let go of her. Then he said: "Good night, señorita," and walked away very quickly. He was happy because she had not asked for any money.

*

The next year when he came down to the town he waited at the station four afternoons to see the train come in. The last afternoon he went to the cemetery and sat near the small square building that had the stone woman on top of it. On the ground the dust blew past. The enormous clouds hung in the sky and the vultures were there high above him. As he smoked he recalled the yellow-haired woman. After a time he began to weep, and rolled over onto the earth, clutching the pebbles as he sobbed. An old woman of the town, who came every day to her son's grave, passed near to him. Seeing him, she shook her head and murmured to herself: "He has lost his mother."

Señor Ong and Señor Ha

A T THE END of the town's long street a raw green mountain cut across the sky at a forty-five degree angle, its
straight slope moving violently from the cloudy heights down
into the valley where the river ran. In the valley, although the
land was fertile, there were no farms or orchards, because the
people of the town were lazy and did not want to bother
clearing away the rocks that strewed the ground. And then, it
was always too hot for that sort of work, and everybody had
malaria there, so that long ago the town had fallen into its
little pattern of living off the Indians who came down from
the mountains with food and went back with cheap cloth,
machetes and things like mirrors or empty bottles. Life always
had been easy; although no one in the town was rich, still,
no one ever went hungry. Almost every house had some papayas and a mango tree beside it, and there were plenty of
avocadoes and pineapples to be had in the market for next to
nothing.

Some of this had changed when the government had begun
the building of the great dam up above. No one seemed to
know exactly where the dam was; they were building it somewhere up in the mountains; already the water had covered
several villages, and now after six years the construction was
still going on. This last was the important part, because it
meant that when the Indians came down from above they
now brought with them not only food but money. Thus it
had come about that certain people in the town had suddenly
found themselves rich. They could scarcely believe it themselves, but there was the money, and still the Indians went on
coming down and leaving more and more of it on the counters of their shops. They did not know what to do with all
these unexpected pesos. Most of them bought huge radios
which they kept going from early morning until night, all
tuned in full strength to Tapachula, so that when they walked
the length of the main street they were never out of earshot
of the program and could follow it without a break. But still
they had money. Pepe Jimenez had bought a bright new

67

automobile in the capital, but by the time he had arrived back in town with it, after driving it over the sixty miles of trail from Mapastenango, it was no longer an object to excite admiration, and he felt that he had made an unwise purchase. Even the main street was too bumpy and muddy for him to drive it up and down, and so it stood rusting in front of Mi Esperanza, the bar by the bridge. When they came out of school Nicho and his companions would play in it, pretending it was a fort. But then a group of larger boys from the upper end of the town had come one day and appropriated the car for their own games, so that the boys who lived by the river no longer dared to approach it.

Nicho lived with his aunt in a small house whose garden ended in a wilderness of plants and vines; just below them rushed the river, dashing sideways from boulder to boulder in its shallow mist-filled canyon. The house was clean and simple, and they lived quietly. Nicho's aunt was a woman of too easygoing a nature. Being conscious of this, she felt that one way of giving her dead sister's child the proper care was to attempt to instil discipline in him; the discipline consisted in calling him by his true name, which was Dionisio.

Nor did she have any conception of discipline as far as her own living was concerned, so that the boy was not astonished when the day came that she said to him: "Dionisio, you will have to stop going to school. We have no more money. Don Anastasio will hire you at ten pesos a month to work in his store, and you can get the noonday meal there too. *Lástima*, but there is no money!"

For a week Nicho sat in the shop learning the prices of the articles that Don Anastasio sold, and then one evening when he went home he found a strange-looking man in the house, sitting in the other rocking chair opposite his aunt. The man looked a little like some of the Indians that came down from the furthest and highest mountains, but his skin was lighter, he was plumper and softer-seeming, and his eyes were almost shut. He smiled at the boy, but not in a way that Nicho thought very friendly, and shook hands without getting up from his chair. That night his aunt looked really quite happy, and as they were getting ready for bed she said to him:

"Señor Ong is coming to live with us. You will not have to work any more. God has been good to us."

But it occurred to Nicho that if Señor Ong was to live with them, he would prefer to go on working at Don Anastasio's, in order not to be around the house and so have to see Señor Ong so much. Tactfully he said: "I like Don Anastasio." His aunt looked at him sharply. "Señor Ong does not want you to work. He is a proud man, and rich enough to feed us both. It is nothing for him. He showed me his money."

Nicho was not at all pleased, and he went to sleep slowly, his mind full of misgivings. He was afraid that one day he would fight with Señor Ong. And besides, what would his friends say? Señor Ong was such a strange-looking man. But the very next morning he arrived from the Hotel Paraiso with three boys whom Nicho knew, and each boy carried a large bag on his head. From the garden he watched them accept the generous tips Señor Ong gave them and then run off to school without waiting to see whether Nicho wanted to speak to them or not. "Very bad," he said to himself as he kicked a stone around and around the bare earth floor of the garden. A little while later he went down to the river and sat on top of the highest boulder watching the milky water that churned beneath him. One of his five cockatoos was screaming from the tangle of leaves on the banks. "*Callate!*" he yelled at it; his own ill-humor annoyed him as much as Señor Ong's ar-rival.

And everything turned out much as he had feared—only worse. Two days later, one of the boys from the upper end of the street said to him in passing: "*Hola, Chale!*" He replied to the greeting automatically and walked on, but a second later he said to himself: "*Chale?* But that means Chinaman! Chink!" Of course. Señor Ong must be a Chinaman. He turned to look at the boy, and thought of hitting him in the back with a stone. Then he hung his head and walked on slowly. Nothing would do any good.

Little by little the joke spread, and soon even his own friends called him *Chale* when they met him, and although it was really he who had become less friendly, he imagined that they all were avoiding him, that no one wanted to see him any more, and he spent most of his time playing by the river. The water's sound was deafening, but at the same time it made him feel a little bit better.

Neither Señor Ong nor his aunt paid much attention to him, save for their constant mealtime demands that he eat. "Now that we have more food than we need, you don't want to eat it," said his aunt angrily. "Eat, Dionisio," smiled Señor Ong. "*Bien*," said Nicho, full of resentment, but in a tone of mock-resignation, and pulled off a small piece of tortilla which he chewed very slowly.

There seemed to be no question of his returning to school; at least, the subject was never mentioned, for which he was most grateful, since he had no desire to be back in the midst of his friends just to hear them call him *Chale*. The name by itself would have been bearable if only it had not implied the ridicule of his home life; his powerlessness to change that condition seemed much more shameful than any state of affairs for which he himself might have been at fault. And so he spent his days down by the river, jumping like a goat across the rocks, throwing stones to frighten the vultures away from the carcasses the water left for them, finding deep pools to swim in, and following the river downstream to lie idly naked on the rocks in the hot sun. No matter how pleasant to him Señor Ong might be—and already he had given him candy on several occasions, as well as a metal pencil with red lead in it—he could not bring himself to accept his being a part of the household. And then there were the singular visits of strange, rich townspeople, persons whom his aunt never had known, but who now appeared to find it quite natural to come to the house, stay for five or ten minutes talking to Señor Ong, and then go away again without so much as asking after his aunt, who always made a point of being in the back of the house or in the garden when they came. He could not understand that at all. It was still her house. Or perhaps not! Maybe she had given it to Señor Ong. Women often were crazy. He did not dare ask her. Once he was able to bring himself to inquire about the people, who kept coming in increasing numbers. She had answered: "They are friends of Señor Ong," and had looked at him with an expression which seemed to say: "Is that enough for you, busybody?" He was more than ever convinced that there was something more to know about the visitors. Then he met Luz, and being no longer alone, he ceased for a time to think about them.

When, one windy day, he had first seen her standing on the bridge, her bright head shining against the black mountains behind, he had stopped walking and stood perfectly still in order to look more carefully: he thought there was a mistake in his seeing. Never would he have believed it possible for anyone to look that way. Her hair was a silky white helmet on the top of her head, her whole face was white, almost as if she had covered it with paint, her brows and lashes, and even her eyes, were light to the point of not existing. Only her pale pink lips seemed real. She clutched the railing of the bridge tightly, an expression of intense preoccupation—or perhaps faint pain— on her face as she peered out from beneath her inadequate white brows. And her head moved slowly up and down as if it were trying to find an angle of vision which would be bearable for those feeble eyes that suffered behind their white lashes.

A few weeks back he merely would have stood looking at this apparition; now he watched intently until the girl, who was about his own age, seemed on the point of pitching forward into the road, and then he hurried toward her and firmly took her arm. An instant she drew back, squinting into his face.

"Who?" she said, confused.

"Me. What's the matter?"

She relaxed, let herself be led along. "Nothing," she answered after a moment. Nicho walked with her down the path to the river. When they got to the shade, the heavy lines in her forehead disappeared. "The sun hurts your eyes?" he asked her, and she said that it did. Under a giant breadfruit tree there were clean gray rocks; they sat down and he began a series of questions. She answered placidly; her name was Luz; she had come with her sister only two days ago from San Lucas; she would stay on with her grandfather here because her parents were having quarrels at home. All her replies were given while she gazed out across the landscape, yet Nicho was sure she could not see the feathery trees across the river or the mountains beyond. He asked her: "Why don't you look at me when you talk to me?"

She put her hand in front of her face. "My eyes are ugly."

"It's not true!" he declared with indignation. Then, "They're beautiful," he added, after looking at them carefully for a moment.

She saw that he was not making fun of her, and straightway decided that she liked him more than any boy she had ever known.

That night he told his aunt about Luz, and as he described the colors in her face and hair he saw her look pleased. "*Una hija del sol!*" she exclaimed. "They bring good luck. You must invite her here tomorrow. I shall prepare her a good *refresco de tamarindo.*" Nicho said he would, but he had no intention of subjecting his friend to his aunt's interested scrutiny. And while he was not at all astonished to hear that albinos had special powers, he thought it selfish of his aunt to want to profit immediately by those which Luz might possess.

The next day when he went to the bridge and found Luz standing there, he was careful to lead her through a hidden lane down to the water, so that she might remain unseen as they passed near the house. The bed of the river lay largely in the shadows cast by the great trees that grew along its sides. Slowly the two children wandered downstream, jumping from rock to rock. Now and then they startled a vulture, which rose at their approach like a huge cinder, swaying clumsily in the air while they walked by, to realight in the same spot a moment later. There was a particular place that he wanted to show her, where the river widened and had sandy shores, but it lay a good way downstream, so that it took them a long time to get there. When they arrived, the sun's light was golden and the insects had begun to call. On the hill, invisible behind the thick wall of trees, the soldiers were having machine-gun practice: the blunt little berries of sound came in clusters at irregular intervals. Nicho rolled his trouser legs up high above his knees and waded well out into the shallow stream. "Wait!" he called to her. Bending, he scooped up a handful of sand from the river bed. His attitude as he brought it back for her to see was so triumphant that she caught her breath, craned her neck to see it before he had arrived. "What is it?" she asked.

"Look! Silver!" he said, dropping the wet sand reverently

into her outstretched palm. The tiny grains of mica glistened in the late sunlight.

"*Qué precioso!*" she cried in delight. They sat on some roots by the water. When the sand was drier, she poured it carefully into the pocket of her dress.

"What are you going to do with it?" he asked her.

"Give it to my grandfather."

"No, no!" he exclaimed. "You don't give away silver. You hide it. Don't you have a place where you hide things?"

Luz was silent; she never had thought of hiding anything. "No," she said presently, and she looked at him with admiration.

He took her hand. "I'll give you a special place in my garden where you can hide everything you want. But you must never tell anyone."

"Of course not." She was annoyed that he should think her so stupid. For a while she had been content just to sit there with Nicho beside her; now she was impatient to get back and deposit the treasure. He tried to persuade her to stay a little longer, saying that there would be time enough if they returned later, but she had stood up and would not sit down again. They climbed upstream across the boulders, coming suddenly upon a pool where two young women stood thigh-deep washing clothes, naked save for the skirts wrapped round their waists, long full skirts that floated gently in the current. The women laughed and called out a greeting. Luz was scandalized.

"They should be ashamed!" she cried. "In San Lucas if a woman did that, everyone would throw stones at her until she was buried under them!"

"Why?" said Nicho, thinking that San Lucas must be a very wicked town.

"Because they would," she answered, still savoring the shock and shame she had felt at the sight of the golden breasts in the sunlight.

When they got back to town they turned into the path that led to Nicho's house, and while they were still in the jungle end of the garden, Nicho stopped and indicated a dead tree whose trunk had partially decayed. With the gesture of a conspirator he pulled aside the fringed curtain of vines that hung

down across most of it, revealing several dark holes. Reaching
into one of them, he pulled out a bright tin can, flicked off
the belligerent ants that raced wildly around it, and held it
forth to her.

"Put it in here," he whispered.

It took a while to transfer all the sand from her pocket to
the can; when it was done he replaced it inside the dark trunk
and let the vines fall straight again to cover the place. Then he
conducted Luz quickly up through the garden, around the
house, into the street. His aunt, having caught sight of them,
called: "Dionisio!" But he pretended not to have heard her
and pushed Luz ahead of him nervously. He was suddenly in
terror lest Luz see Señor Ong; that was something which
must be avoided at any cost.

"Dionisio!" She was still calling; she had come out and was
standing in front of the door, looking down the street after
them, but he did not turn around. They reached the bridge.
It was out of sight of the house.

"*Adiós*," he said.

"*Hasta mañana*," she answered, peering up at him with
her strange air of making a great effort. He watched her walk
up the street, moving her head from side to side as if there
were a thousand things to see, when in reality there were only
a few pigs and some chickens roaming about.

At the evening meal his aunt eyed him reproachfully. He
averted her gaze; she did not mention his promise to bring
Luz to the house for *refrescos*. That night he lay on his mat
watching the phosphorescent beetles. His room gave on the
patio; it had only three walls. The fourth side was wide open.
Branches of the lemon tree reached in and rubbed against the
wall above his head; up there, too, was a huge unfolding banana leaf which was pushing its way further into the room
each day. Now the patio was dizzy with the beetles' sharp
lights. Crawling on the plants or flying frantically between
them, they flashed their signals on and off with maddening
insistence. In the neighboring room his aunt and Señor Ong
occupied the bed of the house, enjoying the privacy of quarters that were closed in on all four sides. He listened: the
wind was rising. Nightly it appeared and played on the leaves
of the trees, dying away again before dawn. Tomorrow he

would take Luz down to the river to get more silver. He hoped Señor Ong had not been spying when he had uncovered the holes in the tree trunk. The mere thought of such a possibility set him to worrying, and he twisted on his mat from one side to the other.

Presently he decided to go and see if the silver was still there. Once he had assured himself either that it was safe or that it had been stolen, he would feel better about it. He sat up, slipped into his trousers, and stepped out into the patio. The night was full of life and motion; leaves and branches touched, making tiny sighs. Singing insects droned in the trees overhead; everywhere the bright beetles flashed. As he stood there feeling the small wind wander over him he became aware of other sounds in the direction of the *sala*. The light was on there, and for a moment he thought that perhaps Señor Ong had a late visitor, since that was the room where he received his callers. But he heard no voices. Avoiding the lemon tree's sharp twigs, he made his way soundlessly to the closed doors and peered between them.

There was a square niche in the *sala* wall across which, when he had first arrived, Señor Ong had tacked a large calendar. This bore a colored picture of a smiling Chinese girl. She wore a blue bathing suit and white fur-topped boots, and she sat by a pool of shiny pink tiles. Over her head in a luminous sky a gigantic four-motored plane bore down upon her, and further above, in a still brighter area of the heavens, was the benevolent face of Generalissimo Chiang. Beneath the picture were the words: ABARROTES FINOS. Sun Man Ngai, Huixtla, Chis. The calendar was the one object Señor Ong had brought with him that Nicho could wholeheartedly admire; he knew every detail of the picture by heart. Its presence had transformed the *sala* from a dull room with two old rocking chairs and a table to a place where anything might happen if one waited long enough. And now as he peeked through the crack, he saw with a shock that Señor Ong had removed the calendar from its place on the wall, and laid it on the table. He had a hammer and a chisel and he was pounding and scratching the bottom of the niche. Occasionally he would scoop out the resulting plaster and dust with his fat little hands, and dump it in a neat pile on the table. Nicho waited for a long time without daring to move. Even when the wind blew a little harder and chilled his naked back he did not stir, for fear of seeing Señor Ong turn around and look with his narrow eyes toward the door, the hammer in one hand, the chisel in the other. Besides, it was important to know what he was doing. But Señor Ong seemed to be in no hurry. Almost an hour went by, and still tirelessly he kept up his methodical work, pausing regularly to take out the debris and pile it on the table. At last Nicho began to feel like sneezing; in a frenzy he turned and ran through the patio to his room, scratching his chest against the branches on the way. The emotion engendered by his flight had taken away his desire to sneeze, but he lay down anyway for fear it might return if he went back to the door. In the midst of wondering about Señor Ong he fell asleep.

The next morning when he went into the *sala* the pretty Chinese girl covered the niche as usual. He stood still listening: his aunt and Señor Ong were talking in the next room. Quickly he pulled out the thumbtack in the lower left-hand corner of the calendar and reached in. He could feel nothing there. Disappointed, he fastened it back and went out into the garden. In the tree his treasure was undisturbed, but now that he suspected Señor Ong of having a treasure too, the little can of sand seemed scarcely worth his interest.

He went to the bridge and waited for Luz. When she came they walked to the river below the garden and sat beside the water. Nicho's mind was full of the image of Señor Ong bending over the niche with his tools, and his fancy was occupied with speculation as to what exactly he had been doing. He was uncertain whether or not to share his secret with Luz. He hoped she would not talk about her silver this morning; to forestall inquiries about it he mentioned curtly that he had looked at it only a half hour ago and that it was intact. Luz sat regarding him perplexedly; he seemed scarcely the same person as yesterday. Finally she said, as he continued to fix his gaze on the black pebbles at his feet: "What's the matter with you today?"

"Nothing." He grasped her arm to belie his word; the gesture betrayed him into beginning the confidence. "Listen. In my house there's a lot of gold hidden." He told her everything: Señor Ong's arrival, his own dislike of him, the visits of the town's rich shopkeepers to the house, and finally the suspicious behavior of Señor Ong in the *sala* the night before. She listened, blinking rapidly all the while. And when he had finished she agreed with him that it was probably gold hidden there in the niche, only she was inclined to think that it belonged to his aunt, and that Señor Ong had stolen it from her. This idea had not occurred to Nicho, and he did not really believe it. Nevertheless, it pleased him. "I'll get it and give it back to her," he declared. "Of course," said Luz solemnly, as if there were no alternative. They sat a while without speaking. Up in the garden all the cockatoos were screaming at once. The prospect of stealing back the gold in order to return it to his aunt excited him. But there were dangers. He began to describe the hideousness of Señor Ong's person and character, extemporaneously adding details. Luz shivered and looked apprehensively toward the shadowy path. "*Hay que tener mucho cuidado*," she murmured. Then suddenly she wanted to go home.

Now there was only one thing to wait for: Señor Ong's absence from the house. In Tlaltepec there lived a Chinese man whom he usually visited each week, going on the early bus in the morning and returning in time for the midday meal. Three days went by. People came to the house and went away again, but Señor Ong sat quietly in the *sala* without once going into the street. Each day Nicho and Luz met on the bridge and sat by the river discussing the treasure with an excitement that steadily grew. "*Ay, qué maravilla!*" she would exclaim, holding her hands far apart. "This much gold!" Nicho would nod in agreement; all the same he had a feeling that when he saw the treasure he would be disappointed.

Finally the morning came when Señor Ong kissed Nicho's aunt on the cheek and went out of the house carrying a newspaper under his arm. "Where is he going?" Nicho asked innocently.

"Tlaltepec." His aunt was scrubbing the floor of the *sala*.

He went into the patio and watched a humming-bird buzz from one to another of the *huele-de-noche's* white flowers. When his aunt had finished in the *sala* she shut the door and started on the floor of the bedroom. In agitation he tiptoed

into the room and over to the calendar, whose two lower corners he unfastened from the wall. Again the niche was empty.
Its floor consisted of four large flower-decorated tiles. Without
touching them he could tell which was the loose one. He lifted
it up and felt underneath. It was a paper packet, not very large,
and, which was worse, soft to the touch. He pulled out a fat
manila envelope, replaced the tile and the calendar, and walked
softly out through the patio, into the garden to his tree.

In the large envelope were a lot of little envelopes, and in
some of the little envelopes there was a small quantity of
odorless white powder. The other little envelopes were empty,
held together by a rubber band. That was all there was. Nicho
had expected a disappointment, but scarcely so complete a
one as this. He was furious: Señor Ong had played a joke on
him, had replaced the gold with this worthless dust, just out
of deviltry. But when he thought about it, he decided that
Señor Ong could not have guessed that he knew about the
niche, so that after all this powder must be the real treasure.
Also he felt it unlikely that it belonged to his aunt, in which
case Señor Ong would be even more angry to find it gone.
He took out two of the small empty envelopes, and from each
of the others he poured a tiny bit of powder, until these two
also contained about the same amount. Then he replaced
both empty and full envelopes in the larger folder, and seeing
that his aunt was in the kitchen, went back to the *sala* with it.
Señor Ong would never notice the two missing envelopes or
the powder that Nicho had poured into them. Once back in
the garden he hid the two tiny packets under the tin can full
of sand, and wandered down to the bridge.

It was too early to expect Luz. A thin gray curtain of rain
came drifting up the valley. In another few minutes it would
have arrived. The green mountainside at the end of the street
glared in the half light. Don Anastasio came walking jauntily
down the main street, and turned in at the side street where
Nicho's house was. Obeying a blind impulse, he called to
him: "*Muy buenos, Don Anastasio!*" The old man wheeled
about; he seemed none too pleased to see Nicho. "Good
day," he replied, and then he hurried on. Nicho ran from the
bridge and stood at the entrance of the street watching him.
Sure enough, he was about to go into Nicho's house.

"Don Anastasio!" he shouted, beginning to run toward him.

Don Anastasio stopped walking and stood still, his face screwed up in annoyance. Nicho arrived out of breath. "You wanted to see Señor Ong? He's gone out."

Don Anastasio did not look happy now, either. "Where?" he said heavily.

"I think to Mapastenango, perhaps," said Nicho, trying to sound vague, and wondering if that could be counted as a lie.

"*Qué malo!*" grunted Don Anastasio. "He won't be back today, then."

"I don't know."

There was a silence.

"Can I do anything for you?" faltered Nicho.

"No, no," said Don Anastasio hastily; then he stared down at him. During the week when Nicho had been working at his store, he had had occasion to notice that the boy was unusually quick. "That is," he added slowly, "I don't suppose—did Señor Ong. . . ?"

"Just a minute," said Nicho, feeling that he was about to discover the secret and at the same time become master of the situation. "Wait here," he added firmly. At the moment Don Anastasio showed no inclination to do anything else. He stood watching Nicho disappear around the corner of the house.

In a minute the boy returned panting, and smiled at Don Anastasio.

"Shall we go to the bridge?" he said.

Again Don Anastasio acquiesced, looking furtively up and down the long street as they came out into it. They stood on the bridge leaning over the water below, and Nicho brought one of the little envelopes out of his pocket, glancing up at Don Anastasio's face at the same time. Yes! He had been right! He saw the features fixed in an expression of relief, pleasure and greedy anticipation. But only for an instant. By the time he was handing over the packet to Don Anastasio, the old man's face looked the same as always.

"*Muy bien, muy bien,*" he grumbled. The first small drops of rain alighted softly on their heads, but neither noticed them. "Do I pay you or Señor Ong?" said Don Anastasio, pocketing the envelope.

Nicho's heart beat harder for a few seconds: Señor Ong must not know of this. But he could not ask Don Anastasio not to tell him. He cleared his throat and said: "Me." But his voice sounded feeble.

"Aha!" said Don Anastasio, smiling a little; and he ruffled Nicho's hair in paternal fashion. Finding it wet, he looked up vacantly at the sky. "It's raining," he commented, a note of surprise in his voice.

"*Sí, señor,*" assented Nicho weakly.

"How much?" said Don Anastasio, looking at him very hard. In the valley the thunder groaned faintly.

Nicho felt he must answer immediately, but he had no idea what to say. "Is a peso all right?"

Don Anastasio stared at him even harder; he felt that the old man's eyes would cut through him in another instant. Then Don Anastasio's countenance changed suddenly, and he said: "A peso. Good." And he handed him a silver coin. "Next week you come to my store with another envelope. I'll give you an extra twenty centavos for making the trip. And— sssst!" He put his fingers to his lips, rolling his eyes upward. "Ssst!" He patted Nicho on the shoulder, looking very pleased, and went up the street.

Señor Ong came back earlier than usual, wet through, and in rather a bad humor. Nicho never had paid any attention to the conversations that passed between his aunt and Señor Ong. Now from the kitchen he listened, and heard him say: "I have no confidence in Ha. They tell me he was in town here two days ago. Of course he swears he was in Tlaltepec all the time."

"Three thousand pesos thrown into the street!" declared his aunt savagely. "I told you so then. I told you he would go on selling here as well as in Tlaltepec. *Yo te lo dije, hombre!*"

"I am not sure yet," said Señor Ong, and Nicho could imagine his soft smile as he said the words. Now that he had stolen from him he disliked him more than ever; in a sense he almost wished Señor Ong might discover the theft and accuse him, thereby creating the opportunity for him to say: "Yes, I stole from you, and I hate you." But he knew that he himself would do nothing to hasten such a moment. He went out through the rain to his tree. The earth's dark breath rose all around him, hung in the wet air. He took out the can of sand and dropped the peso into it.

It rained all day and through the night; Nicho did not see Luz until the following day. Then he adopted a mysterious, baffled air and conducted her to the tree.

"Look!" he cried, showing her the tin can. "The silver has made a peso!"

Luz was convinced and delighted, but she did not seem really surprised. "*Qué bueno!*" she murmured.

"Do you want to take it?" He held up the coin. But he was careful to keep his hand over the envelope in the tree's hollow.

"No, no! Leave it! Maybe it will make more. Put it back! Put it back!"

He was a little crestfallen to find that she took his miracle so nearly for granted. They stamped their feet to knock off the ants that were beginning to climb up their legs.

"And the gold?" she whispered. "Did you get it back for your aunt? Was it heavy? What did Señor Ong say?"

"There was nothing there at all," said Nicho, feeling uncomfortable without knowing why.

"Oh." She was disappointed.

They took a long walk down the river, and came upon an enormous iguana sunning himself on a rock above a pool. Nicho threw a stone, and the monster lumbered away into the leaves. Luz clutched his arm tightly as it disappeared from sight; there was the heavy sound of its body dragging through the underbrush. All at once Nicho shook himself free, pulled off his shirt and trousers, and gave a running leap into the pool. He splashed about, beating wildly at the water with his arms and legs, yelling loudly all the while. With an uncertain gait Luz approached the edge, where she sat down and watched him. Presently she said: "Find some more silver." She did not seem at all shocked by his nudity. He sank to the bottom and scrabbled about, touching only rock. Up again, he shouted: "There isn't any!" Her white head followed his movements as he cavorted around the pool. When he came out, he sat on the opposite side, letting the sun dry him. Behind the hill the machine-gun practice was again in progress.

"In San Lucas do you think they'd throw stones at me?" he shouted.

"Why?" she called. "No, no! *Claro que nó!* For boys it's all right."

The next few days were sunny, and they came each afternoon to the pool.

One morning, the other little envelope in his pocket, Nicho went into the center of town to Don Anastasio's shop. The old man seemed very glad to see him. He opened the envelope behind the counter and looked carefully at its contents. Then he handed Nicho a peso and a half.

"I have no change," said Nicho.

"The *tostón* is for you," said Don Anastasio gruffly. "There's a cinema tonight. Come back next week. Don't forget."

Nicho ran down the street, wondering when he would have the chance to fill another envelope for Don Anastasio. It was about time for Señor Ong to make a trip to Tlaltepec.

A moment before he got to the bridge a tall woman stepped out of a shop and confronted him. She had very large eyes and a rather frightening face.

"*Hola, chico!*"

"*Sí, señora.*" He stood still and stared at her.

"Have you got something for me?"

"Something for you?" he repeated blankly.

"A little envelope?" She held out two pesos. Nicho looked at them and said: "*No, señora.*"

Her face became more frightening. "Yes. Yes. You have," she insisted, moving toward him. He glanced up and down the street: there was no one. The shop seemed to be empty. It was the hot hour of the day. He was suddenly terrified by her face. "Tomorrow," he cried, ducking to one side in order to dart past her. But she caught hold of his neck. "Today," she said roughly; her long fingernails were pushing into his skin. "*Sí, señora.*" He did not dare look up at her. "On the bridge," she grated. "This afternoon."

"*Sí, señora.*"

She let go and he walked on, sobbing a little with anger and shame for having been afraid.

In the *sala* Señor Ong and his aunt were talking excitedly. He did not go in, but climbed into a hammock in the patio and listened. Don Anastasio's name was mentioned. Nicho's heart skipped ahead: something had happened!

"Now I am almost sure," Señor Ong said slowly. "It is two weeks since he has been here, and Saenz tells me he is perfectly happy. That means only one thing: He must be supplying him directly."

"Of course," said his aunt bitterly. "You needn't have waited two weeks to know that. Three thousand pesos dropped into the river. What a waste! *Qué idiota, tú!*"

Señor Ong paid no attention to her. "There's also the Fernandez woman," he mused. "She should have been around a few days ago. I know she has no money, but so far she has always managed to scrape together something."

"That old hag!" said his aunt contemptuously. "With her face now, she'll be lucky if she can raise twenty, not to speak of fifty."

"She can raise it," said Señor Ong with confidence in his voice. "The question is, has Ha already found her and is he giving it to her for less?"

"Don't ask *me* all these questions!" cried his aunt with impatience. "Go to Tlaltepec and ask the old man himself!"

"When I go there," said Señor Ong in a quiet, deadly voice, "it will not be to ask him anything."

At that moment a knock came at the front door; his aunt immediately left the room, shutting the door behind her, and went through the patio into the kitchen. For a few minutes Nicho could hear only the confused sound of low voices talking in the *sala*. Presently someone closed the front door. The visitor was gone.

Before the midday meal Nicho went out into the garden and tossed the two silver coins Don Anastasio had given him into the can of sand. It gave him pleasure to think of showing them to Luz; her credulity made him feel clever and superior. He determined never to tell her about the powder. All through lunch he thought about the tall woman he was to meet on the bridge. When the meal was over, Señor Ong did something unusual: he took up his hat and said: "I am going to see Saenz and have a talk with him." And he went out. Nicho watched him disappear into the main street; then he

went into the house and saw his aunt shut herself into the
bedroom for her siesta. Without hesitating he walked straight
to the niche in the *sala* and took out the big yellow envelope.
He knew he was doing a dangerous thing, but he was determined to do it anyway. Quickly he slipped two fat little envelopes into his pocket. He left one in his tree, and with the
other he went out and stood on the bridge to wait for the
woman. She was not long in spotting him from the shop. As
she came toward him, her haggard face seemed to darken the
afternoon. He held the little white envelope out to her even
as she approached, as if to keep her at a certain distance from
him. Frowning mightily, she reached for it, snatched it from
his fingers like a furious bird, and violently pushed it inside
her bodice. With the other hand she put two pesos into his
still outstretched palm; and then she strode away without saying a word. He decided to remain on the bridge, hoping that
Luz would appear presently.

When she came, he suddenly did not want to take her to
the tree, or even to the river. Instead, grasping her hand, he
said: "I have an idea." This was not true: as yet he had no
idea, but he felt the need of doing something new, important.

"What idea?"

"Let's take a trip!"

"A trip! Where to?"

They started up the street hand in hand.

"We can take a bus," he said.

"But where?"

"*No importa adonde.*"

Luz was not convinced the idea was sound; her mind was
encumbered with visions of her older sister's stern face when
she returned. Nevertheless he could see that she would go. As
they came to where the houses and shops began, he let go of
her hand for fear of meeting one of his friends. He had never
walked on the street with her. The sun's light was intense, but
a gigantic white cloud was rising slowly up from behind the
mountains in front of them. He turned to look at her pale
shining head. Her eyes were painful, squinting slits in her
face. Surely no one else in the world had such beautiful hair.
Glancing at the cloud he whispered to her: "The sun will go
in soon."

At the central plaza there was a bus half full of people. From time to time the driver, who stood leaning against its red tin body, shouted: "Tlaltepec! Tlaltepec!" No sooner had they got aboard and taken seats near the back alongside the windows than Luz, in an access of apprehensiveness, asked to get out. But he held her arm and said, hurriedly inventing: "*Oye*, I wanted to go to Tlaltepec because we have something very important to do there. We have to save somebody's life." She listened attentively to his story: the monstrous Señor Ong was going to kill old Señor Ha for not having kept his promise to stay in Tlaltepec. As he recounted the tale, and recalled the wording of Señor Ong's threat, he began to believe the story himself. "When I go there it will not be to ask him anything." The old man would be given no opportunity to explain, no chance to defend himself. As the bus moved out of the plaza, he was as convinced as Luz that they were off to Tlaltepec on an heroic mission.

Tlaltepec was below, in a closed valley with mountains on all sides. The great white cloud, its brilliant edges billowing outward, climbed higher into the sky; as into a cave, the bus entered the precinct of its shadow. Here suddenly everything was green. Scraps of bird-song came in through the open windows, sharp above the rattling of the ancient vehicle.

"*Ay, el pobrecito!*" sighed Luz from time to time.

They came into Tlaltepec, stopped in the plaza. The passengers got out and quickly dispersed in different directions. The village was very quiet. Bright green grass grew in the middle of the streets. A few silent Indians sat around the plaza against the walls. Nicho and Luz walked up the main street, awed by the hush which enveloped the village. The cloud had covered the sky; now it was slowly pulled down like a curtain over the other side of the valley. A sad little churchbell began to ring behind them in the plaza. They turned into a small shop marked *Farmacia Moderna*. The man sitting inside knew Señor Ha: he was the only Chinese in the village. "He lives opposite the convent, in the last house." In Tlaltepec everything was nearby. The bell was still tolling from the plaza. In front of the ruined convent was an open square of sward; basketball posts had been put up at each end, but now they were broken. Before the last house stood a large tree laden with thousands of lavender flowers. In the still air they fell without cease, like silent tears, onto the damp earth beneath.

Nicho knocked on the door. A servant girl came and looked at the two children indifferently, went away. In a moment Señor Ha appeared. He was not quite so old as they had expected; his angular face was expressionless, but he looked closely at both of them. Nicho had hoped he would ask them into the house: he wanted to see if Señor Ha had a calendar like the one at home in the *sala*, but no such hospitality was forthcoming. Luz sat down on the stone step below them and picked up some of the blossoms that had fallen from the tree while Nicho told Señor Ha who he was and why he had come. Señor Ha stood quite still. Even when Nicho said: "And he is going to kill you," his hard little eyes remained in exactly the same position. Nothing in his face moved; he looked at Nicho as though he had not heard a word. For a moment Nicho thought that perhaps he understood nothing but Chinese, but then Señor Ha said, very clearly: "What lies!" And he shut the door.

They walked back to the plaza without saying anything, and sat down on an iron bench to wait for the bus. A warm, mistlike rain moved downward through the air, falling so softly that it was inaudible even in the stillness of the deserted plaza. At one point while they waited Nicho got up and went to the main street in search of some candy. As he came out of the shop, a little man carrying a briefcase walked quickly past and crossed the street. It was Señor Ha.

While they sat eating the candy a battered sedan came out of the main street and bumped across the plaza; on the edge of its back seat, leaning forward talking to the driver, was Señor Ha. They stared. The car turned into the road that led up the mountainside toward the town, and disappeared in the twilight.

"He's going to tell Señor Ong!" cried Nicho suddenly. He let his mouth stay open and fixed the ground.

Luz squeezed his arm. "You don't care," she declared. "They're only Chinamen. You're not afraid of them."

He looked blankly at her. Then with scorn he answered: "No!"

They talked very little on the ride up in the rain. It was night by the time they arrived in the town. Wet and hungry, they went down the street toward the bridge, still without speaking. As they crossed the river Nicho turned to her and said: "Come and have dinner at my house."

"My sister . . ."

But he pulled her roughly along with him. Even as he opened the front door and saw his aunt and Señor Ong sitting inside, he knew that Señor Ha had not been there.

"Why are you so late?" said his aunt. "You're wet." Then she saw Luz. "Shut the door, *niña*," she said, looking pleased.

While they ate in the covered part of the patio, Señor Ong continued with what he apparently had been saying earlier in the evening . . . "She looked directly at me without saying a word."

"Who?" said his aunt, smiling at Luz.

"The Fernandez woman. This afternoon." Señor Ong's voice was edged with impatience. "For me that is proof enough. She's getting it somewhere else."

His aunt snorted. "Still you're looking for proof! *Niña*, take more meat." She piled extra food on Luz's plate.

"Yes, there's no doubt now," Señor Ong continued.

"What beautiful hair! *Ay, Dios!*" She smoothed the top of the girl's head. Nicho was ashamed: he knew that he had invited her to dinner because he had been afraid to come home alone, and he knew that his aunt was touching her hair only in order to bring herself good luck. He sighed miserably and glanced at Luz; she seemed perfectly content as she ate.

Suddenly there were several loud knocks on the front door. Señor Ong rose and went into the *sala*. There was a silence. A man's voice said: "*Usted se llama Narciso Ong?*" All at once there followed a great deal of noise; feet scuffled and furniture scraped on the tile floor. Nicho's aunt jumped up and ran into the kitchen where she began to pray very loudly. In the *sala* there was grunting and wheezing, and then as the racket grew less intense, a man said: "*Bueno.* I have it. A hundred grams, at least, right in his pocket. That's all we needed, my friend. *Vamonos.*"

Nicho slid down from his chair and stood in the doorway. Two men in wet brown ponchos were pushing Señor Ong out the front door. But he did not seem to want to go. He twisted his head and saw Nicho, opened his mouth to speak to him. One of the men hit him in the side of the face with his fist. "Not in front of the boy," said Señor Ong, wriggling his jaw back and forth to see if it was all right. "Not in front of the boy," he said again thickly. The other man slammed the door shut. The *sala* was empty. There was no sound but his aunt's wailing voice in the kitchen, crying aloud to God. He turned to look at Luz, who was sitting perfectly still.

"Do you want to go home?" he said to her.

"Yes." She got up. His aunt came out of the kitchen wringing her hands. Going over to Luz she laid her hand briefly on the white hair, still muttering a prayer.

"*Adiós, niña.* Come back tomorrow," she said.

There was still a light rain falling. A few insects sang from the wet leaves as the two silent children passed along the way to the house where Luz lived. When they rapped on the door it was opened immediately. A tall thin girl stood there. Without speaking she seized Luz with one arm and pulled her violently inside, closing the door with the other.

When Nicho got home and went into the *sala*, his first thought was that Señor Ong had returned, but the next instant he felt that he was in the middle of a bad dream. Señor Ha was sitting there talking with his aunt. She looked up tearfully. "Go to bed," she commanded.

Señor Ha reached out from his chair as Nicho passed and caught his arm—caught it very tightly. "*Ay!*" said Nicho in spite of himself. "One moment," said Señor Ha, still looking at Nicho's aunt, and never for a second relaxing his grip. "Perhaps this one knows." And without turning his face toward Nicho he said: "The police have taken Señor Ong to prison. He will not come back here. He hid something in this house. Where is it?"

It seemed as though the hard fingers would cut through his skin. His aunt looked up at him hopefully. He felt suddenly very important.

"There," he said, pointing to the calendar.

Señor Ha rose and yanked the pretty girl down from the wall. In an instant he had the yellow envelope in his hand. As he examined its contents, he said: "Is there any more?"

"No," said Nicho, thinking of the envelope lying in the safety of his tree out there in the rainy night. Señor Ha began to twist his arm, but the thought of his secret made him feel strong; his pain and his hatred flowed into that feeling of strength. He stood stiffly and let Señor Ha hurt him. A moment later Señor Ha let go of him and gave him a violent push that sent him halfway across the room. "Go to bed," he said.

When Nicho had gone out and closed the door, Señor Ha turned to the aunt. "Tomorrow I shall come back with my clothes," he said. "It is not good to have a boy around the house doing nothing; he gets into trouble. From now on he will deliver it; there will be no one coming to the house."

"But if the police catch him . . ." she objected.

"There will be no trouble with them. It is all arranged. Fortunately I had nearly three thousand pesos on hand." He picked up his briefcase and went to the door. She looked after him with frank admiration and sighed deeply. "You won't stay tonight?" She said the words timidly, and they sounded strangely coquettish.

"No. The car is outside waiting for me. Tomorrow." He opened the door. Rising, she went and took his hand, pressing it warmly between her two hands. "Tomorrow," he repeated.

When the car had driven away and she could no longer hear it, she closed the door, turned off the light, and went out into the patio, where she got into a hammock and lay swinging gently back and forth.

"An intelligent man," she said to herself. "What good luck!" She stopped swinging a moment. "Good luck! Of course! Dionisio must bring her to the house again one day very soon."

The town went on being prosperous, the Indians kept coming down from the heights with money, the thick jungle along the way to Mapastenango was hacked away, the trail widened and improved. Nicho bought a packet of little envelopes. Far down the river he found another hollow tree. Here he kept his slowly increasing store of treasure; during the very first month he picked up enough money on the side to buy Luz a lipstick and a pair of dark glasses with red and green jewels all around the rims.

The Circular Valley

THE abandoned monastery stood on a slight eminence of land in the middle of a vast clearing. On all sides the ground sloped gently downward toward the tangled, hairy jungle that filled the circular valley, ringed about by sheer, black cliffs. There were a few trees in some of the courtyards, and the birds used them as meeting-places when they flew out of the rooms and corridors where they had their nests. Long ago bandits had taken whatever was removable out of the building. Soldiers had used it once as headquarters, had, like the bandits, built fires in the great windy rooms so that afterward they looked like ancient kitchens. And now that everything was gone from within, it seemed that never again would anyone come near the monastery. The vegetation had thrown up a protecting wall; the first story was soon quite hidden from view by small trees which dripped vines to lasso the cornices of the windows. The meadows roundabout grew dank and lush; there was no path through them.

At the higher end of the circular valley a river fell off the cliffs into a great cauldron of vapor and thunder below; after this it slid along the base of the cliffs until it found a gap at the other end of the valley, where it hurried discreetly through with no rapids, no cascades—a great thick black rope of water moving swiftly downhill between the polished flanks of the canyon. Beyond the gap the land opened out and became smiling; a village nestled on the side hill just outside. In the days of the monastery it was there that the friars had got their provisions, since the Indians would not enter the circular valley. Centuries ago when the building had been constructed the Church had imported the workmen from another part of the country. These were traditional enemies of the tribes thereabouts, and had another language; there was no danger that the inhabitants would communicate with them as they worked at setting up the mighty walls. Indeed, the construction had taken so long that before the east wing was completed the workmen had all died, one by one. Thus it was the friars themselves who had closed off the end of the wing with blank walls, leaving it that way, unfinished and blind-looking, facing the black cliffs.

Generation after generation, the friars came, fresh-cheeked boys who grew thin and gray, and finally died, to be buried in the garden beyond the courtyard with the fountain. One day not long ago they had all left the monastery; no one knew where they had gone, and no one thought to ask. It was shortly after this that the bandits, and then the soldiers had come. And now, since the Indians do not change, still no one from the village went up through the gap to visit the monastery. The Atlájala lived there; the friars had not been able to kill it, had given up at last and gone away. No one was surprised, but the Atlájala gained in prestige by their departure. During the centuries the friars had been there in the monastery, the Indians had wondered why it allowed them to stay. Now, at last, it had driven them out. It always had lived there, they said, and would go on living there because the valley was its home, and it could never leave.

In the early morning the restless Atlájala would move through the halls of the monastery. The dark rooms sped past, one after the other. In a small patio, where eager young trees had pushed up the paving stones to reach the sun, it paused. The air was full of small sounds: the movements of butterflies, the falling to the ground of bits of leaves and flowers, the air following its myriad courses around the edges of things, the ants pursuing their endless labors in the hot dust. In the sun it waited, conscious of each gradation in sound and light and smell, living in the awareness of the slow, constant disintegration that attacked the morning and transformed it into afternoon. When evening came, it often slipped above the monastery roof and surveyed the darkening sky: the waterfall would roar distantly. Night after night, along the procession of years, it had hovered here above the valley, darting down to become a bat, a leopard, a moth for a few minutes or hours, returning to rest immobile in the center of the space enclosed by the cliffs. When the monastery had been built, it had taken to frequenting the rooms, where it had observed for the first time the meaningless gestures of human life.

And then one evening it had aimlessly become one of the young friars. This was a new sensation, strangely rich and complex, and at the same time unbearably stifling, as though every other possibility besides that of being enclosed in a tiny, isolated world of cause and effect had been removed forever. As the friar, it had gone and stood in the window, looking out at the sky, seeing for the first time, not the stars, but the space between and beyond them. Even at that moment it had felt the urge to leave, to step outside the little shell of anguish where it lodged for the moment, but a faint curiosity had impelled it to remain a little longer and partake a little further of the unaccustomed sensation. It held on; the friar raised his arms to the sky in an imploring gesture. For the first time the Atlájala sensed opposition, the thrill of a struggle. It was delicious to feel the young man striving to free himself of its presence, and it was immeasurably sweet to remain there. Then with a cry the friar had rushed to the other side of the room and seized a heavy leather whip hanging on the wall. Tearing off his clothing he had begun to carry out a ferocious self-beating. At the first blow of the lash the Atlájala had been on the point of letting go, but then it realized that the immediacy of that intriguing inner pain was only made more manifest by the impact of the blows from without, and so it stayed and felt the young man grow weak under his own lashing. When he had finished and said a prayer, he crawled to his pallet and fell asleep weeping, while the Atlájala slipped out obliquely and entered into a bird which passed the night sitting in a great tree on the edge of the jungle, listening intently to the night sounds, and uttering a scream from time to time.

Thereafter the Atlájala found it impossible to resist sliding inside the bodies of the friars; it visited one after the other, finding an astonishing variety of sensation in the process. Each was a separate world, a separate experience, because each had different reactions when he became conscious of the other being within him. One would sit and read or pray, one would go for a long troubled walk in the meadows, around and around the building, one would find a comrade and engage in an absurd but bitter quarrel, a few wept, some flagellated themselves or sought a friend to wield the lash for them. Always there was a rich profusion of perceptions for the Atlájala to enjoy, so that it no longer occurred to it to frequent the bodies of insects, birds and furred animals, nor even to leave the monastery and move in the air above. Once it almost got into difficulties when an old friar it was occupying suddenly fell back dead. That was a hazard it ran in the frequenting of men: they seemed not to know when they were doomed, or if they did know, they pretended with such strength not to know, that it amounted to the same thing. The other beings knew beforehand, save when it was a question of being seized unawares and devoured. And that the Atlájala was able to prevent: a bird in which it was staying was always avoided by the hawks and eagles.

When the friars left the monastery, and, following the government's orders, doffed their robes, dispersed and became workmen, the Atlájala was at a loss to know how to pass its days and nights. Now everything was as it had been before their arrival: there was no one but the creatures that always had lived in the circular valley. It tried a giant serpent, a deer, a bee: nothing had the savor it had grown to love. Everything was the same as before, but not for the Atlájala; it had known the existence of man, and now there were no men in the valley—only the abandoned building with its empty rooms to make man's absence more poignant.

Then one year bandits came, several hundred of them in one stormy afternoon. In delight it tried many of them as they sprawled about cleaning their guns and cursing, and it discovered still other facets of sensation: the hatred they felt for the world, the fear they had of the soldiers who were pursuing them, the strange gusts of desire that swept through them as they sprawled together drunk by the fire that smoldered in the center of the floor, and the insufferable pain of jealousy which the nightly orgies seemed to awaken in some of them. But the bandits did not stay long. When they had left, the soldiers came in their wake. It felt very much the same way to be a soldier as to be a bandit. Missing were the strong fear and the hatred, but the rest was almost identical. Neither the bandits nor the soldiers appeared to be at all conscious of its presence in them; it could slip from one man to another without causing any change in their behavior. This surprised it, since its effect on the friars had been so definite, and it felt

a certain disappointment at the impossibility of making its existence known to them.

Nevertheless, the Atlájala enjoyed both bandits and soldiers
immensely, and was even more desolate when it was left alone
once again. It would become one of the swallows that made
their nests in the rocks beside the top of the waterfall. In the
burning sunlight it would plunge again and again into the
curtain of mist that rose from far below, sometimes uttering
exultant cries. It would spend a day as a plant louse, crawling
slowly along the under side of the leaves, living quietly in the
huge green world down there which is forever hidden from
the sky. Or at night, in the velvet body of a panther, it would
know the pleasure of the kill. Once for a year it lived in an eel
at the bottom of the pool below the waterfall, feeling the
mud give slowly before it as it pushed ahead with its flat nose;
that was a restful period, but afterward the desire to know
again the mysterious life of man had returned—an obsession
of which it was useless to try to rid itself. And now it moved
restlessly through the ruined rooms, a mute presence, alone,
and thirsting to be incarnate once again, but in man's flesh
only. And with the building of highways through the country
it was inevitable that people should come once again to the
circular valley.

A man and a woman drove their automobile as far as a
village down in a lower valley; hearing about the ruined
monastery and the waterfall that dropped over the cliffs
into the great amphitheatre, they determined to see these
things. They came on burros as far as the village outside
the gap, but there the Indians they had hired to accompany
them refused to go any farther, and so they continued alone,
upward through the canyon and into the precinct of the
Atlájala.

It was noon when they rode into the valley; the black ribs
of the cliffs glistened like glass in the sun's blistering downward rays. They stopped the burros by a cluster of boulders at
the edge of the sloping meadows. The man got down first,
and reached up to help the woman off. She leaned forward,
putting her hands on his face, and for a long moment they
kissed. Then he lifted her to the ground and they climbed
hand in hand up over the rocks. The Atlájala hovered near

them, watching the woman closely: she was the first ever to have come into the valley. The two sat beneath a small tree on the grass, looking at one another, smiling. Out of habit, the Atlájala entered into the man. Immediately, instead of existing in the midst of the sunlit air, the bird calls and the plant odors, it was conscious only of the woman's beauty and her terrible imminence. The waterfall, the earth, and the sky itself receded, rushed into nothingness, and there were only the woman's smile and her arms and her odor. It was a world more suffocating and painful than the Atlájala had thought possible. Still, while the man spoke and the woman answered, it remained within.

"Leave him. He doesn't love you."

"He would kill me."

"But I love you. I need you with me."

"I can't. I'm afraid of him."

The man reached out to pull her to him; she drew back slightly, but her eyes grew large.

"We have today," she murmured, turning her face toward the yellow walls of the monastery.

The man embraced her fiercely, crushing her against him as though the act would save his life. "No, no, no. It can't go on like this," he said. "No."

The pain of his suffering was too intense; gently the Atlájala left the man and slipped into the woman. And now it would have believed itself to be housed in nothing, to be in its own spaceless self, so completely was it aware of the wandering wind, the small flutterings of the leaves, and the bright air that surrounded it. Yet there was a difference: each element was magnified in intensity, the whole sphere of being was immense, limitless. Now it understood what the man sought in the woman, and it knew that he suffered because he never would attain that sense of completion he sought. But the Atlájala, being one with the woman, had attained it, and being aware of possessing it, trembled with delight. The woman shuddered as her lips met those of the man. There on the grass in the shade of the tree their joy reached new heights; the Atlájala, knowing them both, formed a single channel between the secret springs of their desires. Throughout, it remained within the woman, and began vaguely to devise ways of keeping her, if not inside the valley, at least nearby, so that she might return.

In the afternoon, with dreamlike motions, they walked to the burros and mounted them, driving them through the deep meadow grass to the monastery. Inside the great courtyard they halted, looking hesitantly at the ancient arches in the sunlight, and at the darkness inside the doorways.

"Shall we go in?" said the woman.

"We must get back."

"I want to go in," she said. (The Atlájala exulted.) A thin gray snake slid along the ground into the bushes. They did not see it.

The man looked at her perplexedly. "It's late," he said.

But she jumped down from her burro by herself and walked beneath the arches into the long corridor within. (Never had the rooms seemed so real as now when the Atlájala was seeing them through her eyes.)

They explored all the rooms. Then the woman wanted to climb up into the tower, but the man took a determined stand.

"We must go back now," he said firmly, putting his hand on her shoulder.

"This is our only day together, and you think of nothing but getting back."

"But the time . . ."

"There is a moon. We won't lose the way."

He would not change his mind. "No."

"As you like," she said. "I'm going up. You can go back alone if you like."

The man laughed uneasily. "You're mad." He tried to kiss her.

She turned away and did not answer for a moment. Then she said: "You want me to leave my husband for you. You ask everything from me, but what do you do for me in return? You refuse even to climb up into a little tower with me to see the view. Go back alone. Go!"

She sobbed and rushed toward the dark stairwell. Calling after her, he followed, but stumbled somewhere behind her. She was as sure of foot as if she had climbed the many stone steps a thousand times before, hurrying up through the darkness, around and around.

In the end she came out at the top and peered through the small apertures in the cracking walls. The beams which had supported the bell had rotted and fallen; the heavy bell lay on its side in the rubble, like a dead animal. The waterfall's sound was louder up here; the valley was nearly full of shadow. Below, the man called her name repeatedly. She did not answer. As she stood watching the shadow of the cliffs slowly overtake the farthest recesses of the valley and begin to climb the naked rocks to the east, an idea formed in her mind. It was not the kind of idea which she would have expected of herself, but it was there, growing and inescapable. When she felt it complete there inside her, she turned and went lightly back down. The man was sitting in the dark near the bottom of the stairs, groaning a little.

"What is it?" she said.

"I hurt my leg. Now are you ready to go or not?"

"Yes," she said simply. "I'm sorry you fell."

Without saying anything he rose and limped after her out into the courtyard where the burros stood. The cold mountain air was beginning to flow down from the tops of the cliffs. As they rode through the meadow she began to think of how she would broach the subject to him. (It must be done before they reached the gap. The Atlájala trembled.)

"Do you forgive me?" she asked him.

"Of course," he laughed.

"Do you love me?"

"More than anything in the world."

"Is that true?"

He glanced at her in the failing light, sitting erect on the jogging animal.

"You know it is," he said softly.

She hesitated.

"There is only one way, then," she said finally.

"But what?"

"I'm afraid of him. I won't go back to him. You go back. I'll stay in the village here." (Being that near, she would come each day to the monastery.) "When it is done, you will come and get me. Then we can go somewhere else. No one will find us."

The man's voice sounded strange. "I don't understand."

"You do understand. And that is the only way. Do it or not, as you like. It is the only way."

They trotted along for a while in silence. The canyon loomed ahead, black against the evening sky.

Then the man said, very clearly: "Never."

A moment later the trail led out into an open space high above the swift water below. The hollow sound of the river reached them faintly. The light in the sky was almost gone; in the dusk the landscape had taken on false contours. Everything was gray—the rocks, the bushes, the trail—and nothing had distance or scale. They slowed their pace.

His word still echoed in her ears.

"I won't go back to him!" she cried with sudden vehemence. "You can go back and play cards with him as usual. Be his good friend the same as always. I won't go. I can't go on with both of you in the town." (The plan was not working; the Atlájala saw it had lost her, yet it still could help her.)

"You're very tired," he said softly.

He was right. Almost as he said the words, that unaccustomed exhilaration and lightness she had felt ever since noon seemed to leave her; she hung her head wearily, and said: "Yes, I am."

At the same moment the man uttered a sharp, terrible cry; she looked up in time to see his burro plunge from the edge of the trail into the grayness below. There was a silence, and then the faraway sound of many stones sliding downward. She could not move or stop the burro; she sat dumbly, letting it carry her along, an inert weight on its back.

For one final instant, as she reached the pass which was the edge of its realm, the Atlájala alighted tremulously within her. She raised her head and a tiny exultant shiver passed through her; then she let it fall forward once again.

Hanging in the dim air above the trail, the Atlájala watched her indistinct figure grow invisible in the gathering night. (If it had not been able to hold her there, still it had been able to help her.)

A moment later it was in the tower, listening to the spiders mend the webs that she had damaged. It would be a long, long time before it would bestir itself to enter into another being's awareness. A long, long time—perhaps forever.

The Echo

AILEEN pulled out her mirror; the vibration of the plane shook it so rapidly that she was unable to see whether her nose needed powder or not. There were only two other passengers and they were asleep. It was noon; the tropical sun shone violently down upon the wide silver wings and cast sharp reflections on the ceiling. Far below, the uniform green carpet of the jungle moved slowly by. She was sleepy, but she was also excited to be going to a new home. From her handbag she pulled a folded letter which she read again intently, as if to decipher a meaning that did not lie in the sequence of the words. It was in her mother's script:

"Aileen, Sweet—

"I must begin (and finish) this before supper. Prue has gone out for her shower, and that means that by the time she has Luz (the cook) heat the water and can find José (the gardener) to carry it up on the roof to the tank, it will be about an hour. Add to that the time it takes her to do her actual bathing and to dress, and you can see I'll have just about time for a nice chat.

"Perhaps I should begin by saying that Prue and I are sublimely happy here. It is absolute heaven after Washington, as you can pretty well imagine. Prue, of course, never could stand the States, and I felt, after the trouble with your father, that I couldn't face anyone for a while. You know how much importance I have always attached to relaxation. And this is the ideal spot for that.

"Of course I did feel a little guilty about running off down here without seeing you. But I think the trip to Northampton would have sealed my doom. I honestly don't believe I could have stood it. And Prue was nervous about the State Department's passing some new law that would prevent citizens from leaving the U.S. because of the disturbed conditions, and so on. I also felt that the sooner we got down here to Jamonocal the more of a home we could make out of the old place, for you to spend your vacation in. And it *is* going to be beautiful. I won't drag out my reasons for not letting you know beforehand or it will sound apologetic, and I know I never have to apologize to you for anything. So I'll leave that and get on. I'm sure anyway that the eight months passed very quickly up there for you.

"We have had swarms of men working on the house ever since last October. Mr. Forbes happened to be in Barranquilla for a new American project in the interior, and I wanted to be sure of having him supervise the construction of the cantilever in the foundation. That man is really a prince. They don't come much finer. He was up again and again, and gave orders down to the last detail. I felt guilty about making him work so hard, but I honestly think he enjoyed himself with us girls. In any case it seemed silly, when one of the best architects in the U.S. was right here in Colombia and happened to be an old friend, not to use him when I needed him. Anyway, the old house is now the old wing and the new part, which is so exciting I can't wait for you to see it, is built right out over the gorge. I think there's not likely to be another house like it in the world, if I do say it myself. The terrace makes me think of an old cartoon in the *New Yorker* showing two men looking over the edge of the Grand Canyon, and one is saying to the other: 'Did you ever want to spit a mile, Bill? Now's your chance.'

"We are all installed. The weather has been wonderful, and if Luz could only learn a little more about what white people like to eat and how they like it served, the setup would really be perfect. I know you will enjoy being here with Prue. She and you have many things in common, even if you do claim to 'remember not liking her much.' That was in Washington and you were, to put it mildly, at a difficult age. Now, as an adult (because you really are one by now), you'll be more understanding, I'm sure. She loves books, especially on philosophy and psychology and other things your poor mother just doesn't try to follow her in. She has rigged up a kiln and studio in the old guest house which you

probably don't remember. She works at her ceramics
out there all day, and I have all I can do keeping the
house tidy and seeing that the marketing is done. We
have a system by which Luz takes the list to her brother
every afternoon, and he brings the things from town the
following day. It just about keeps him fully busy getting
up and down the mountain on his horse. The horse is a
lazy old nag that has done nothing but plod back and
forth between house and the valley all its life, so it
doesn't know the meaning of the word speed. But after
all, why hurry, down here?

"I think you will find everything to your liking, and
I'm sure you won't require more than five minutes to
see that Prue is a dear, and not at all 'peculiar,' as you
wrote in your letter. Wire me as soon as you receive this,
and let me know just what week you'll be finishing
classes. Prue and I will meet you in Barranquilla. I have
a list of things I want you to get me in New York. Will
wire it to you as soon as I hear. Prue's bath finished.
Must close.

Love,
Mother."

Aileen put the letter away, smiling a little, and watched the
wings diving in and out of the small thick clouds that lay in
the plane's way. There was a slight shock each time they hit
one, and the world outside became a blinding whiteness. She
fancied jumping out and walking on such solid softness, like a
character in an animated cartoon.

Her mother's letter had put her in mind of a much earlier
period in her life: the winter she had been taken to visit Jamonocal. All she could recall in the way of incidents was that
she had been placed on a mule by one of the natives, and had
felt a painful horror that the animal would walk in the wrong
direction, away from the house toward the edge of the gorge.
She had no memory of the gorge. Probably she had never
seen it, although it was only a few paces from the house,
through a short but thick stretch of canebrake. However, she
had a clear memory of its presence, of the sensation of enormous void beyond and below that side of the house. And she

recalled the distant, hollow sound of water falling from a great height, a constant, soft backdrop of sound that slipped into every moment of the day—between the conversations at mealtimes, in the intervals of play in the garden, and at night between dreams. She wondered if really it were possible to remember all that from the time when she had been only five.

In Panama there was a plane change to be made. It was a clear green twilight, and she took a short walk beyond the airport. Parakeets were fighting in the upper branches of the trees; suddenly they became quiet. She turned back and went inside, where she sat reading until it was time to go aboard.

There was no one there to meet her when she arrived at Barranquilla in the early hours of the morning. She decided to go into town and take a room in the hotel. With her two valises she stepped outside and looked about for a cab. They had all gone to the town with passengers, but a man sitting on a packing case informed her that they would soon be coming back. Then suddenly he said, "You want two ladies?"

"What? No. What do you mean?"

"You want two ladies look for you this night?"

"Where are they?" said Aileen, understanding.

"They want a drink," he answered with an intimate grin.

"Where? Barranquilla?"

"No. Here." He pointed down the dark road.

"Where? Can I walk?"

"Sure. I go you."

"No! No thanks. You stay here. Thank you. I can go all right. Where is it? How far?"

"O.K."

"What is it? A bar? What's the name?"

"They got music. La Gloria. You go. You hear music. You look for two ladies. They drinking."

She went inside again and checked the bags with an airline employee who insisted on accompanying her. They strode in silence along the back road. The walls of vegetation on each side sheltered insects that made an occasional violent, dry noise like a wooden ratchet being whirled. Soon there was the sound of drums and trumpets playing Cuban dance music.

"La Gloria," said her escort triumphantly.

La Gloria was a brilliantly lighted mud hut with a thatch-covered veranda giving onto the road. The juke box was outside, where a few drunken Negroes sprawled.

"Are they here?" she said out loud, but to herself.

"La Gloria," he answered, pointing.

As they came opposite the front of the building, she caught a glimpse of a woman in blue jeans, and although instantaneously she knew it was Prue, her mind for some reason failed to accept the fact, and she continued to ask herself, "Are they here or not?"

She turned to go toward the veranda. The record had finished playing. The ditch lay in the dark between the road and the porch. She fell forward into it and heard herself cry out. The man behind her said, "*Cuidado!*" She lay there panting with fury and pain, and said, "Oh! My ankle!" There was an exclamation inside the bar. Her mother's voice cried, "That's Aileen!" Then the juke box began to scratch and roar again. The Negroes remained stationary. Someone helped her up. She was inside the bar in the raw electric glare.

"I'm all right," she said, when she had been eased into a chair.

"But darling, where've you been? We've been waiting for you since eight, and we'd just about given up. Poor Prue's ill."

"Nonsense, I'll recover," said Prue, still seated at the bar. "Been having a touch of the trots, that's all."

"But darling, are you all right? This is absurd, landing here this way."

She looked down at Aileen's ankle.

"Is it all right?"

Prue came over from the bar to shake her hand.

"A dramatic entrance, gal," she said.

Aileen sat there and smiled. She had a curious mental habit. As a child she had convinced herself that her head was transparent, that the thoughts there could be perceived immediately by others. Accordingly, when she found herself in uncomfortable situations, rather than risk the danger of being suspected of harboring uncomplimentary or rebellious thoughts, she had developed a system of refraining from thinking at all. For a while during her childhood this fear of having no mental privacy had been extended to anyone; even persons existing at a distance could have access to her mind. Now she felt open only to those present. And so it was that, finding herself face to face with Prue, she was conscious of no particular emotion save the familiar vague sense of boredom. There was not a thought in her head, and her face made the fact apparent.

Mornings were hard to believe. The primeval freshness, spilled down out of the jungle above the house, was held close to the earth by the mist. Outside and in, it was damp and smelled like a florist's shop, but the dampness was dispelled each day when the stinging sun burned through the thin cape of moisture that clung to the mountain's back. Living there was like living sideways, with the land stretching up on one side and down on the other at the same angle. Only the gorge gave a feeling of perpendicularity; the vertical walls of rock on the opposite side of the great amphitheatre were a reminder that the center of gravity lay below and not obliquely to one side. Constant vapor rose from the invisible pool at the bottom, and the distant, indeterminate calling of water was like the sound of sleep itself.

For a few days Aileen lay in bed listening to the water and the birds, and to the nearby, unfamiliar, domestic sounds. Her mother and Prue both had breakfast in bed, and generally appeared just before the midday meal for a few minutes of conversation until Concha brought the invalid's lunch tray. In the afternoons she thumbed through old magazines and read at murder mysteries. Usually it began to rain about three; the sound at first would be like an augmentation of the waterfall in the distance, and then as its violence increased it came unmistakably nearer—a great roar all around the house that covered every other sound. The black clouds would close in tightly around the mountain, so that it seemed that night would soon arrive. She would ring a small bell for Concha to come and light the oil lamp on the table by the bed. Lying there looking at the wet banana leaves outside the window, with the rain's din everywhere, she felt completely comfortable for the precarious moment. There was no necessity to question the feeling, no need to think—only the subsiding of the rain, the triumphant emergence of the sun into the steaming twilight and an early dinner to look forward to. Each evening after dinner her mother came for a lengthy chat, usually about the servants. The first three nights Prue had come too, carrying a highball, but after that her mother came alone.

Aileen had asked to be put into the old part of the house, rather than into a more comfortable room in the new wing. Her window looked onto the garden, which was a small square of lawn with young banana trees on either side. At the far end was a fountain; behind it was the disordered terrain of the mountainside with its recently cut underbrush and charred stumps, and still further beyond was the high jungle whose frontier had been sliced in a straight line across the slopes many years ago to make the plantation. Here in her room she felt at least that the earth was somewhere beneath her.

When her ankle ceased to pain her, she began going downstairs for lunch, which was served out on the terrace at a table with a beach umbrella stuck in its center. Prue was regularly late in coming from her studio, and she arrived in her blue jeans, which were caked with clay, with smears of dirt across her face. Because Aileen could not bring herself to think what she really felt, which was that Prue was ungracious, ugly and something of an interloper, she remained emotionally unconscious of Prue's presence, which is to say that she was polite but bored, scarcely present in the mealtime conversations. Then, too, Aileen was definitely uncomfortable on the terrace. The emptiness was too near and the balustrade seemed altogether too low for safety. She liked the meals to be as brief as possible, with no unnecessary time spent sipping coffee afterward, but it never would have occurred to her to divulge her reasons. With Prue around she felt constrained to behave with the utmost decorum. Fortunately her ankle provided her with a convenient excuse to get back upstairs to her room.

She soon discovered a tiny patio next to the kitchen where heavy vines with sweet-smelling flowers grew up an arbor that had been placed at one side. The air was full of the humming of hundreds of bees that clung heavily to the petals and moved slowly about in the air. After lunch she would pull a deck chair into the arbor's shade and read until the rain began. It was a stifling, airless spot, but the sound of the bees covered that of the waterfall. One afternoon Prue followed her there and stood with her hands in her hip pockets looking at her.

"How can you take this heat?" she asked Aileen.

"Oh, I love it."

"You do?" She paused. "Tell me, do you really like it here, or do you think it's a bloody bore?"

"Why, I think it's absolutely wonderful."

"Mm. It is."

"Don't you like it?"

Prue yawned. "Oh, I'm all for it. But I keep busy. Wherever I can work, I get on, you know."

"Yes, I suppose so," said Aileen. Then she added, "Are you planning on staying long?"

"What the hell do you mean?" said Prue, leaning backward against the house, her hands still behind her. "I live here."

Aileen laughed shortly. To anyone but Prue it would have sounded like a merry, tinkling laugh, but Prue narrowed her eyes and thrust her jaw forward a bit.

"What's so funny?" she demanded.

"I think you're funny. You're so tied up in knots. You get upset so easily. Perhaps you work too hard out there in your little house."

Prue was looking at her with astonishment.

"God Almighty," she said finally, "your I.Q.'s showing, gal."

"Thank you," said Aileen with great seriousness. "Anyway, I think it's fine that you're happy here, and I hope you go on being happy."

"That's what I came to say to you."

"Then everything's fine."

"I can't make you out," said Prue, frowning.

"I don't know what you're talking about," replied Aileen, fingering the pages of her book impatiently. "It's the most pointless conversation I've ever had."

"That I *don't* think," Prue said, going into the kitchen.

The same evening, when her mother came for her usual after-dinner chat, she looked a little unhappy.

"You don't seem to be getting on very well with Prue," she said reproachfully, as she sat down at the foot of the bed.

"Why, we get on perfectly well. Oh. You're talking about this afternoon, probably."

"Yes, I am, probably. Really, Aileen. You simply can't be rude to a woman her age. She's my guest, and you're my guest, and you've got to be civil to each other. But she's always civil and I have a feeling you're not."

Aileen caught her breath and said, "I'm your guest . . ."

"I invited you here for your vacation and I want things pleasant, and I don't see the slightest reason why they shouldn't be."

Suddenly Aileen cried, "She's a maniac!"

Her mother rose and quickly left the room.

In the quiet days that followed, the incident was not mentioned by any of them. Aileen continued to haunt the little patio after lunch.

There came a morning sweeter than the rest, when the untouched early mist hung inside her bedroom, and the confusion of shrill bird cries came down with perfect clarity from the uncut forest. She dressed quickly and went out. There was a white radiance in the air that she had never seen before. She walked along the path that led by the native huts. There was life stirring within; babies were crying and captive parrots and songbirds laughed and sang. The path swung into a stretch of low trees that had been planted to shield the coffee bushes. It was still almost nocturnal in here; the air was streaked with chill, and the vegetable odors were like invisible festoons drooping from the branches as she walked through. A huge bright spider walked slowly across the path at her feet. She stood still and watched it until it had disappeared in the leaves at one side. She put her hand over her heart to feel how insistently it was beating. And she listened to its sound in her head for a moment, not wanting to break into its rhythm by starting to walk again. Then she began to walk ahead fast, following the path upward toward the lightest part of the sky. When it came out suddenly onto an eminence directly above the plantation, she could barely discern the cluster of roofs through the mist. But here the sound of the waterfall was stronger; she supposed she was near the gorge, although there was no sign of it. The path turned here and went along rough open ground upward. She climbed at a steady gait, breathing slowly and deeply, for perhaps half an hour, and was surprised to find that the jungle had been cut away on all sides in this portion of the mountainside. For a time she thought the sky was growing brighter, and that the sun was about to break through, but as the path leveled out and she was able to see for some distance ahead, she saw that the mist was even thicker up here than down below.

At certain points there was a steep declivity on each side of the path. It was impossible to see how deeply the land fell away. There were a few nearby plants and rocks, the highest fronds of a tree-fern a little beyond, and white emptiness after that. It was like going along the top of a wall high in the air. Then the path would make a wide turn and go sharply upward and she would see a solitary tree above her at one side.

Suddenly she came up against a row of huts. They were less well made than those down at the plantation, and smaller. The mist was full of woodsmoke; there was the smell of pigs. She stood still. A man was singing. Two small naked children came out of the door of one hut, looked at her a moment in terror, and ran quickly back inside. She walked ahead. The singing came from behind the last hut. When she came opposite the hut, she saw that it was enclosed by a tangled but effective fence of barbed wire which left a runway about six feet wide all the way around. A young man appeared from the farther side of the closed-in space. His shirt and pants were tattered; the brown skin showed in many places. He was singing as he walked toward her, and he continued to sing, looking straight into her face with bright, questioning eyes. She smiled and said, "*Buenos dias.*" He made a beckoning gesture, rather too dramatically. She stopped walking and stood still, looking hesitantly back at the other huts. The young man beckoned again and then stepped inside the hut. A moment later he came out, and still staring fascinatedly at her, made more summoning motions. Aileen stood perfectly quiet, not taking her eyes from his face. He walked slowly over to the fence and grasped the wire with both hands, his eyes growing wider as he pressed the barbs into his palms.

Then he leaned across, thrusting his head toward her, his eyes fixing hers with incredible intensity. For several seconds they watched each other; then she stepped a little nearer, peering into his face and frowning. At that point with a cry he emptied his mouth of the water he had been holding in it, aiming with force at Aileen's face. Some of it struck her cheek, and the rest the front of her dress. His fingers unclenched themselves from around the wire, and straightening himself, he backed slowly into the hut, watching her face closely all the while.

She stood still an instant, her hand to her cheek. Then she bent down, and picking up a large stone from the path she flung it with all her strength through the door. A terrible cry came from within; it was like nothing she had ever heard. Or yes, she thought as she began to run back past the other huts, it had the indignation and outraged innocence of a small baby, but it was also a grown man's cry. No one appeared as she passed the huts. Soon she was back in the silence of the empty mountainside, but she kept running, and she was astonished to find that she was sobbing as well. She sat down on a rock and calmed herself by watching some ants demolish a bush as they cut away squares of leaf and carried them away in their mouths. The sky was growing brighter now; the sun would soon be through. She went on. By the time she got back to the high spot above the plantation the mist had turned into long clouds that were rolling away down the mountainside into the ravines. She was horrified to see how near she stood to the ugly black edge of the gorge. And the house looked insane down there, leaning out over as if it were trying to see the bottom. Far below the house the vapor rose up from the pool. She followed the sheer sides of the opposite cliff upward with her eye, all the way to the top, a little above the spot where she stood. It made her feel ill, and she stumbled back down to the house with her hand to her forehead, paying no attention to the natives who greeted her from their doorways.

As she ran past the garden a voice called to her. She turned and saw Prue washing her hands in the fountain's basin. She stood still.

"You're up early. You must feel better," said Prue, drying her hands on her hair. "Your mother's been having a fit. Go in and see her."

Aileen stared at Prue a moment before she said, "I was going in. You don't have to tell me."

"Oh, I thought I did."

"You don't have to tell me anything. I think I can manage all right without your help."

"Help isn't exactly what I'd like to give you," said Prue, putting her hands into her pockets. "A swift kick in the teeth would be more like it. How do you think I like to see your mother worrying about you? First you're sick in bed, then you just disappear into the goddamn jungle. D'you think I like to have to keep talking about you, reassuring her every ten minutes? What the hell d'you think life is, one long - coming-out party?"

Aileen stared harder, now with unmasked hatred. "I think," she said slowly, "that life is pretty awful. Here especially. And I think you should look once in the mirror and then jump off the terrace. And I think Mother should have her mind examined."

"I see," said Prue, with dire inflection. She lit a cigarette and strode off to her studio. Aileen went into the house and up to her room.

Less than an hour later, her mother knocked at her door. As she came into the room, Aileen could see she had been crying only a moment before.

"Aileen darling, I've got something to say to you," she began apologetically, "and it just breaks my heart to say it. But I've got to."

She stopped, as though waiting for encouragement.

"Mother, what is it?"

"I think you probably know."

"About Prue, I suppose. No?"

"It certainly is. I don't know how I can ever make it right with her. She told me what you said to her, and I must say I found it hard to believe. How could you?"

"You mean just now in the garden?"

"I don't know where you said it, but I do know this can't

go on. So I'm just forced to say this. . . . You'll have to go. I can't be stirred up this way, and I can tell just how it'll be if you stay on."

"I'm not surprised at all," said Aileen, making a show of calm. "When do you want me to leave?"

"This is terribly painful . . ."

"Oh, stop! It's all right. I've had a vacation and I can get a lot of work done before the term starts. Today? Tomorrow?"

"I think the first of the week. I'll go to Barranquilla with you."

"Would you think I was silly if I had all my meals up here?"

"I think it's a perfect idea, darling, and we can have nice visits together, you and I, between meals."

Now, when the tension should have been over, somehow it was not. During the four nights before she was to leave, Aileen had endless excruciating dreams. She would wake up in the darkness too agonized even to move her hand. It was not fear; she could not recall the dreams. It was rather as if some newly discovered, innermost part of her being were in acute pain. Breathing quickly, she would lie transfixed for long periods listening to the eternal sound of the waterfall, punctuated at great intervals by some slight, nearby nocturnal noise in the trees. Finally, when she had summoned sufficient energy to move, she would change her position in the bed, sigh profoundly, and relax enough to fall back into the ominous world of sleep.

When the final day came, there was a light tapping on her door just after dawn. She got up and unbolted it. Her mother was there, smiling thinly.

"May I come in?"

"Oh. Good morning. Of course. It's early, isn't it?"

Her mother walked across to the window and stood looking down at the misty garden.

"I'm not so well today," she said. "I'm afraid I can't take you to Barranquilla. I'm not up to getting onto a horse today. It's just too much, that three-hour trip to Jamonocal, and then the train and the boat all night. You'll just have to forgive me. I couldn't stand all three. But it won't matter, will it?" she went on, looking up at last. "We'll say good-bye here."

"But, Mother, how can I go alone?"

"Oh, José'll go all the way to Barranquilla with you and be back by Wednesday night. You don't think I'd let you go off by yourself?"

She began to laugh intensely, then stopped suddenly and looked pensive.

"I rather hate to be here two nights without him, but I don't see any other way to get you down there by tomorrow. You can go shipside to Panama. There's usually a seat somewhere. Now, breakfast, breakfast . . ."

Patting Aileen's cheek, she hurried out and downstairs to the kitchen.

The birds' morning song was coming down from the forest; the mist lay ragged in the tops of the great trees up there. Aileen shifted her gaze to the garden at her feet. Suddenly she felt she could not leave; in a sense it was as if she were leaving love behind. She sat down on the bed. "But what is it?" she asked herself desperately. "Not Mother. Not the house. Not the jungle." Automatically she dressed and packed the remaining toilet articles in her overnight case. But the feeling was there, imperious and enveloping in its completeness.

She went downstairs. There was the sound of voices and the clatter of china in the kitchen. Concha and Luz were preparing her breakfast tray. She went out and watched them until everything was ready.

"*Ya se va la señorita?*" said Concha sadly.

She did not answer, but took the tray from her and carried it through the house, out onto the terrace, where she set it on the table. Everything on the terrace was wet with dew and moisture from the gorge. She turned the chair-cushion over and sat down to eat. The sound of the waterfall took her appetite away, but she thought, "This is the last time." She felt choked with emotions, but they were too disparate and confused for her to be able to identify any one of them as outstanding. As she sat there eating intently, she was suddenly aware that someone was watching her. She started up and saw Prue standing in the doorway. She was wearing pajamas and a bathrobe, and in her hand she held a glass of water. She looked very sleepy.

"How are you?" she said, sipping her water.

Aileen stood up.

"We're all up bright and early this morning," Prue went on cheerily.

"I'm——leaving. I've got to go. Excuse me, it's late," mumbled Aileen, glancing about furtively.

"Oh, take your time, gal. You haven't said good-bye to your mother yet. And José is still saddling the nags. You've got a lot of grips with you."

"Excuse me," said Aileen, trying to slip past her through the doorway.

"Well, shake," Prue said, reaching for Aileen's hand.

"Get away!" cried Aileen, struggling to keep clear of her. "Don't touch me!" But Prue had succeeded in grasping one frantic arm. She held it fast.

"A dramatic entrance is enough. We don't have to have the same sort of exit. Say good-bye to me like a human being." She twisted the arm a bit, in spite of herself. Aileen leaned against the door and turned very white.

"Feel faint?" said Prue. She let go of her arm, and holding up her glass of water, flicked some of it into Aileen's face with her fingers.

The reaction was instantaneous. Aileen jumped at her with vicious suddenness, kicking, ripping and pounding all at once. The glass fell to the stone floor; Prue was caught off her guard. Mechanically, with rapid, birdlike fury, the girl hammered at the woman's face and head, as she slowly impelled her away from the doorway and across the terrace.

From Prue's lips came several times the word "God." At first she did very little to defend herself; she seemed half asleep as she moved toward the outer edge beneath the onslaught. Then suddenly she threw herself to the floor. Aileen continued to kick her where she lay doubled over, trying to protect her face.

"Nobody! Nobody! Nobody! Nobody can do that to me!" she cried rhythmically as she kicked.

Her voice rose in pitch and volume; she stopped for an instant, and then, raising her head, she uttered the greatest scream of her life. It came back immediately from the black wall of rock across the gorge, straight through the noise of water. The sound of her own voice ended the episode for her, and she began to walk back across the terrace.

Concha and Luz stood frightened in the doorway; it was as if they had come to watch a terrible storm pass over the countryside. They stepped aside as Aileen walked through.

Outside the stable, José was whistling as he finished saddling the horses. The valises were already strapped on the burro.

Still in the midst of her deep dream, Aileen turned her head toward the house as they rode past. For a brief second, between the leaves, she saw the two figures of her mother and Prue standing side by side on the terrace, the wall of the gorge looming behind. Then the horses turned and began to descend the trail.

The Scorpion

AN OLD WOMAN lived in a cave which her sons had hollowed out of a clay cliff near a spring before they went away to the town where many people live. She was neither happy nor unhappy to be there, because she knew that the end of life was near and that her sons would not be likely to return no matter what the season. In the town there are always many things to do, and they would be doing them, not caring to remember the time when they had lived in the hills looking after the old woman.

At the entrance to the cave at certain times of the year there was a curtain of water-drops through which the old woman had to pass to get inside. The water rolled down the bank from the plants above and dripped onto the clay below. So the old woman accustomed herself to sitting crouched in the cave for long periods of time in order to keep as dry as possible. Outside through the moving beads of water she saw the bare earth lighted by the gray sky, and sometimes large dry leaves went past, pushed by the wind that came from higher parts of the land. Inside where she was the light was pleasant and of a pink color from the clay all around.

A few people used to pass from time to time along the path not far away, and because there was a spring nearby, those travelers who knew that it existed but not just where it was would sometimes come near to the cave before they discovered that the spring was not there. The old woman would never call to them. She would merely watch them as they came near and suddenly saw her. Then she would go on watching as they turned back and went in other directions looking for the water to drink.

There were many things about this life that the old woman liked. She was no longer obliged to argue and fight with her sons to make them carry wood to the charcoal oven. She was free to move about at night and look for food. She could eat everything she found without having to share it. And she owed no one any debt of thanks for the things she had in her life.

One old man used to come from the village on his way down to the valley, and sit on a rock just distant enough from the cave for her to recognize him. She knew he was aware of her presence in the cave there, and although she probably did not know this, she disliked him for not giving some sign that he knew she was there. It seemed to her that he had an unfair advantage over her and was using it in an unpleasant way. She thought up many ideas for annoying him if he should ever come near enough, but he always passed by in the distance, pausing to sit down on the rock for some time, when he would often gaze straight at the cave. Then he would continue slowly on his way, and it always seemed to the old woman that he went more slowly after his rest than before it.

There were scorpions in the cave all year round, but above all during the days just before the plants began to let water drip through. The old woman had a huge bundle of rags, and with this she would brush the walls and ceiling clear of them, stamping quickly on them with her hard bare heel. Occasionally a small wild bird or animal strayed inside the entrance, but she was never quick enough to kill it, and she had given up trying.

One dark day she looked up to see one of her sons standing in the doorway. She could not remember which one it was, but she thought it was the one who had ridden the horse down the dry river bed and nearly been killed. She looked at his hand to see if it was out of shape. It was not that son.

He began to speak: "Is it you?"

"Yes."

"Are you well?"

"Yes."

"Is everything well?"

"Everything."

"You stayed here?"

"You can see."

"Yes."

There was a silence. The old woman looked around the cave and was displeased to see that the man in the doorway made it practically dark in there. She busied herself with trying to distinguish various objects: her stick, her gourd, her tin can, her length of rope. She was frowning with the effort.

The man was speaking again.

"Shall I come in?"

She did not reply.

He backed away from the entrance, brushing the water drops from his garments. He was on the point of saying something profane, thought the old woman, who, even though she did not know which one this was, remembered what he would do.

She decided to speak.

"What?" she said.

He leaned forward through the curtain of water and repeated his question.

"Shall I come in?"

"No."

"What's the matter with you?"

"Nothing."

Then she added: "There's no room."

He backed out again, wiping his head. The old woman thought he would probably go away, and she was not sure she wanted him to. However, there was nothing else he could do, she thought. She heard him sit down outside the cave, and then she smelled tobacco smoke. There was no sound but the dripping of water upon the clay.

A short while later she heard him get up. He stood outside the entrance again.

"I'm coming in," he said.

She did not reply.

He bent over and pushed inside. The cave was too low for him to stand up in it. He looked about and spat on the floor.

"Come on," he said.

"Where?"

"With me."

"Why?"

"Because you have to come."

She waited a little while, and then said suspiciously: "Where are you going?"

He pointed indifferently toward the valley, and said: "Down that way."

"In the town?"

"Farther."

"I won't go."

"You have to come."

"No."

He picked up her stick and held it out to her.

"Tomorrow," she said.

"Now."

"I must sleep," she said, settling back into her pile of rags.

"Good. I'll wait outside," he answered, and went out.

The old woman went to sleep immediately. She dreamed that the town was very large. It went on forever and its streets were filled with people in new clothes. The church had a high tower with several bells that rang all the time. She was in the streets all one day, surrounded by people. She was not sure whether they were all her sons or not. She asked some of them: "Are you my sons?" They could not answer, but she thought that if they had been able to, they would have said: "Yes." Then when it was night she found a house with its door open. Inside there was a light and some women were seated in a corner. They rose when she went in, and said: "You have a room here." She did not want to see it, but they pushed her along until she was in it, and closed the door. She was a little girl and she was crying. The bells of the church were very loud outside, and she imagined they filled the sky. There was an open space in the wall high above her. She could see the stars through it, and they gave light to her room. From the reeds which formed the ceiling a scorpion came crawling. He came slowly down the wall toward her. She stopped crying and watched him. His tail curved up over his back and moved a little from side to side as he crawled. She looked quickly about for something to brush him down with. Since there was nothing in the room she used her hand. But her motions were slow, and the scorpion seized her finger with his pinchers, clinging there tightly although she waved her hand wildly about. Then she realized that he was not going to sting her. A great feeling of happiness went through her. She raised her finger to her lips to kiss the scorpion. The bells stopped ringing. Slowly in the peace which was beginning, the scorpion moved into her mouth. She felt his hard shell and his little clinging legs going across her lips and her tongue. He crawled slowly down her throat and was hers. She woke up and called out.

Her son answered: "What is it?"

"I'm ready."

"So soon?"

He stood outside as she came through the curtain of water, leaning on her stick. Then he began walking a few paces ahead of her toward the path.

"It will rain," said her son.

"Is it far?"

"Three days," he said, looking at her old legs.

She nodded. Then she noticed the old man sitting on the stone. He had an expression of deep surprise on his face, as if a miracle had just occurred. His mouth was open as he stared at the old woman. When they came opposite the rock he peered more intently than ever into her face. She pretended not to notice him. As they picked their way carefully downhill along the stony path, they heard the old man's thin voice behind them, carried by the wind.

"Good-bye."

"Who is that?" said her son.

"I don't know."

Her son looked back at her darkly.

"You're lying," he said.

The Fourth Day Out from Santa Cruz

R AMÓN signed on at Cádiz. The ship's first call was at Santa
  Cruz de Tenerife, a day and a half out. They put in at
night, soon after dark. Floodlights around the harbor illumined the steep bare mountains and made them grass-green
against the black sky. Ramón stood at the rail, watching. "It
must have been raining here," he said to a member of the
crew standing beside him. The man grunted, looking not at
the green slopes unnaturally bright in the electric glare, but at
the lights of the town ahead. "Very green," went on Ramón,
a little less certainly; the man did not even grunt in reply.

As soon as the ship was anchored, scores of Hindu shopkeepers came aboard with laces and embroidered goods for
the passengers who might not be going ashore. They stayed
on the first-class deck, not bothering to go down below to
third-class where Ramón was scullery boy in the passengers'
cocina. The work so far did not upset him; he had held more
exacting and tiring jobs in Cádiz. There was sufficient food,
and although it was not very good, nevertheless it was better
than what was taken out to the third-class passengers. It had
never occurred to Ramón to want privacy in his living quarters, so that he was unmoved by the necessity of sharing a
cabin with a dozen or so shipmates. Still, he had been acutely
unhappy since leaving Cádiz. Except for the orders they gave
him in the kitchen, the sailors behaved as if he did not exist.
They covered his bunk with their dirty clothes, and lay on it,
smoking, at night when he wanted to sleep. They failed to include him in any conversation, and so far no one had even
made an allusion, however deprecatory, to his existence. For
them it appeared that he simply was not present. To even the
least egocentric man such a state of affairs can become intolerable. In his sixteen years Ramón had not been in a similar
situation; he had been maltreated but not wholly disregarded.

Most of the crew stood at the prow smoking, pointing out
bars to one another, as they scanned the waterfront. Partly
out of perversity born of his grievance, and partly because he
wanted to be by himself for a spell, Ramón walked to the

stern and leaned heavily against the rail, looking down into the darkness below. He could hear an automobile horn being blown continuously as it drove along the waterfront. The hills behind backed up the sound, magnified it as they threw it across the water. To the other side was the dim roar of the sea's waves against the breakwater. He was a little homesick, and as he stood there he became angry as well. It was inadmissible that this state of affairs should continue. A day and a half was too long; he was determined to force a change immediately, and to his undisciplined young mind kept recurring the confused image of a fight—a large-scale struggle with the entire crew, in which he somehow finished as the sole victor.

It is pleasant to walk by the sea-wall of a foreign port at night, with the autumn wind gently pushing at your back. Ramón was in no hurry; he stopped before each café and listened to the guitars and shouting, without, however, allowing himself to be detained by the women who called to him from the darker doorways. Having had to clean up the galley after an extra meal had been served to sixty workmen who had just come aboard here at Santa Cruz, bound for South America, he had been the last to get off the ship, and so he was looking for his shipmates. At the Café del Teide he found several of them seated at a table sharing a bottle of rum. They saw him come in, but they gave no sign of recognition. There was no empty chair. He walked toward the table, slowed down a bit as he approached it, and then continued walking toward the back of the café. The man behind the bar called out to him: "You were looking for something?" Ramón turned around and sat down suddenly at a small table. The waiter came and served him, but he scarcely noticed what he was drinking. He was watching the table with the six men from his ship. Like one fascinated, he let his eyes follow each gesture: the filling of the little glasses, the tossing down the liquor, the back of the hand wiping the mouth. And he listened to their words punctuated by loud laughter. Resentment began to swell in him; he felt that if he sat still any longer he would explode. Pushing back his chair, he jumped up and strode dramatically out into the street. No one noticed his exit.

He began to walk fast through the town, paying no attention to where he was going. His eyes fixed on an imaginary horizon, he went through the *plaza*, along the wide Paseo de Ronda, and into the tiny streets that lie behind the cathedral. The number of people in the streets increased as he walked away from the center of town, until when he had come to what seemed an outlying district, where the shops were mere stalls, he was forced to saunter along with the crowd. As he slowed down his gait, he felt less nervous. Gradually he took notice of the merchandise for sale, and of the people around him. It suddenly occurred to him that he would like to buy a large handkerchief. Outside certain booths there were wires strung up; from these hung, clipped by their corners, a great many of the squares of cloth, their bright colors showing in the flare of the carbide lamps. As Ramón stopped to choose one at the nearest booth he became aware that in the next booth a girl with a laughing face was also buying a bandana. He waited until she had picked out the one she wanted, and then he stepped quickly over to the shopkeeper and pointing down at the package he was making, said: "Have you another handkerchief exactly like that?" The girl paid no attention to him and put her change into her purse. "Yes," said the shopkeeper, reaching out over the counter to examine the bandanas. The girl picked up her little packet wrapped in newspaper, turned away, and walked along the street. "No, you haven't!" cried Ramón, and he hurried after her so as not to lose sight of her in the crowd. For some distance he trailed her along the thoroughfare, until she turned into a side street that led uphill. It smelled here of drains and there was very little light. He quickened his pace for fear she would go into one of the buildings before he had had the opportunity to talk to her. Somewhere in the back of his mind he hoped to persuade her to go with him to the Café del Teide. As he overtook her, he spoke quietly without turning his head: "Señorita." To his surprise she stopped walking and stood still on the pavement. Although she was very near to him, he could not see her face clearly.

"What do you want?"

"I wanted to talk to you."

"Why?"

He could not answer.

"I thought . . ." he stammered.

"What?"

There was a silence, and then as she laughed Ramón remembered her face: open and merry, but not a child's face. In spite of the confidence its recalled image inspired in him, he asked: "Why do you laugh?"

"Because I think you're crazy."

He touched her arm and said boldly: "You'll see if I'm crazy."

"I'll see nothing. You're a sailor. I live here"; she pointed to the opposite side of the street. "If my father sees you, you'll have to run all the way to your ship." Again she laughed. To Ramón her laugh was music, faintly disturbing.

"I don't want to bother you. I only wanted to talk to you," he said, timid again.

"Good. Now you've talked. *Adios.*" She began to walk on. So did Ramón, close beside her. She did not speak. A moment later, he remarked triumphantly: "You said you lived back there!"

"It was a lie," she said in a flat voice. "I always lie."

"Ah. You always lie," echoed Ramón with great seriousness.

They came to a street light at the foot of a high staircase. The sidewalk became a series of stone steps leading steeply upward between the houses. As they slowly ascended, the air changed. It smelled of wine, food cooking, and burning eucalyptus leaves. Up above the city here, life was more casual. People leaned over the balconies, sat in dark doorways chatting, stood in the streets like islands among the moving dogs and children.

The girl stopped and leaned against the side of a house. She was a little out of breath from the climb.

"Tired?" he asked.

Instead of replying she turned swiftly and darted inside the doorway beside her. For a few seconds Ramón was undecided whether or not to follow her. By the time he had tiptoed into the dimly lit passageway she had disappeared. He walked through into the courtyard. Some ragged boys who were running about stopped short and stared at him. A radio was playing guitar music above. He looked up. The building was four stories high; there were lights in almost all the windows.

On his way back to the waterfront a woman appeared from the shadows of the little park by the cathedral and took his arm. He looked at her; she was being brazenly coy, with her head tilted at a crazy angle as she repeated: "I like sailors." He let her walk with him to the Café del Teide. Once inside, he was disappointed to see that his shipmates were gone. He bought the woman a *manzanilla* and walked out on her as she began to drink it. He had not said a word to her. Outside, the night seemed suddenly very warm. He came to the Blanco y Negro; a band was playing inside. Two or three of the men from the ship were on the dark dance floor, trying to instill a bit of life into the tired girls that hung to them. He did not even have a drink here, but hurried back to the ship. His bunk was piled with newspapers and bundles, but the cabin was empty, and he had several hours in the dark in which to brood and doze, before the others arrived. The boat sailed at dawn.

They skirted the island next day—not close enough to see the shore, but within sight of the great conical mountain, which was there all day beside them in the air, clear in distant outline. For two days the ship continued on a southwest course. The sea grew calm, a deep blue, and the sun blazed brighter in the sky. The crew had ceased gathering on the poopdeck, save in the early evening and at night, when they lay sprawled all over it, singing in raucous voices while the stars swayed back and forth over their heads.

For Ramón life continued the same. He could see no difference in the crew's attitude toward him. It still seemed to him that they lived without him. The magazines that had been bought at Santa Cruz were never passed around the cabin. Afternoons when the men sat around the table in the third-class *comedor*, the stories that were recounted could never be interpreted by any gesture in their telling as being directed at a group that included him. And he certainly knew better than to attempt to tell any himself. He still waited for a stroke of luck that might impose him forcibly upon their consciousness.

In the middle of the fourth morning out from Santa Cruz he poked his head from the galley and noticed several of the men from his cabin gathered along the railing at the stern. The sun was blinding and hot, and he knew something must be keeping them there. He saw one man pointing aft. Casually he wandered out across the deck to within a few feet of the group, searching the sea and the horizon for some object—something besides the masses of red seaweed that constantly floated by on top of the dark water.

"It's getting nearer!"

"*Qué fuerza!*"

"It's worn out!"

"*Claro!*"

Ramón looked over their heads, and between them when they changed position from time to time. He saw nothing. He was almost ready to be convinced that the men were baiting him, in the hope of being able to amuse themselves when his curiosity should be aroused to the point of making him ask: "What is it?" And so he was determined to be quiet, to wait and see.

Suddenly he did see. It was a small yellow and brown bird flying crookedly after the boat, faltering as it repeatedly fell back toward the water between spurts of desperate energy.

"A thousand miles from land!"

"It's going to make it! Look! Here it comes!"

"No!"

"Next time."

At each wild attempt to reach the deck, the bird came closer to the men, and then, perhaps from fear of them, it fluttered down toward the boiling sea, missing the wake's maelstrom by an ever closer margin. And when it seemed that this time it surely would be churned under into the white chaos of air and water, it would surge feebly upward, its head turned resolutely toward the bright mass of the ship that moved always in front of it.

Ramón was fascinated. His first thought was to tell the men to step back a little from the rail so that the bird might have the courage to land. As he opened his mouth to suggest this, he thought better of it, and was immediately thankful for having remained quiet. He could imagine the ridicule that would have been directed at him later: in the cabin, at mealtime, evenings on the deck . . . Someone would have invented a shameful little ditty about Ramón and his bird. He stood watching, in a growing agony of suspense.

"Five pesetas it goes under!"

"Ten it makes it!"

Ramón wheeled about and ran lightly across to the galley. Almost immediately he came out again. In his arms he carried the ship's mascot, a heavy tomcat that blinked stupidly in the sudden glare of the sun. This time he walked directly back to the railing where the others stood. He set the animal down at their feet.

"What are you doing?" said one.

"Watch," said Ramón.

They were all quiet a moment. Ramón held the cat's flanks and head steady, waiting for it to catch sight of the fluttering bird. It was difficult to do. No matter how he directed its head it showed no sign of interest. Still they waited. As the bird came up to the level of the deck at a few feet from the boat, the cat's head suddenly twitched, and Ramón knew the contact had been made. He took his hands away. The cat stood perfectly still, the end of its tail moving slightly. It took a step closer to the edge, watching each movement of the bird's frantic efforts.

"Look at that!"

"He sees it."

"But the bird doesn't see him."

"If it touches the boat, the ten pesetas still go."

The bird rose in the air, flew faster for a moment until it was straight above their heads. They looked upward into the flaming sun, trying to shade their eyes. It flew still farther forward, until, if it had dropped, it would have landed a few feet ahead of them on the deck. The cat, staring up into the air, ran quickly across the deck so that it was directly below the bird, which slowly let itself drop until it seemed that they could reach out and take it. The cat made a futile spring into the air. They all cried out, but the bird was too high. Suddenly it rose much higher; then it stopped flying. Swiftly they passed beneath it as it remained poised an instant in the air. When they had turned their heads back it was a tiny yellow thing falling slowly downward, and almost as quickly they lost sight of it.

At the noonday meal they talked about it. After some argument the bets were paid. One of the oilers went to his cabin and brought out a bottle of cognac and a set of little glasses which he put in front of him and filled, one after the other.

"Have some?" he said to Ramón.

Ramón took a glass, and the oiler passed the rest around to the others.

Pages from Cold Point

O UR CIVILIZATION is doomed to a short life: its component parts are too heterogeneous. I personally am content to see everything in the process of decay. The bigger the bombs, the quicker it will be done. Life is visually too hideous for one to make the attempt to preserve it. Let it go. Perhaps some day another form of life will come along. Either way, it is of no consequence. At the same time, I am still a part of life, and I am bound by this to protect myself to whatever extent I am able. And so I am here. Here in the Islands vegetation still has the upper hand, and man has to fight even to make his presence seen at all. It is beautiful here, the trade winds blow all year, and I suspect that bombs are extremely unlikely to be wasted on this unfrequented side of the island, if indeed on any part of it.

I was loath to give up the house after Hope's death. But it was the obvious move to make. My university career always having been an utter farce (since I believe no reason inducing a man to "teach" can possibly be a valid one), I was elated by the idea of resigning, and as soon as her affairs had been settled and the money properly invested, I lost no time in doing so.

I think that week was the first time since childhood that I had managed to recapture the feeling of there being a content in existence. I went from one pleasant house to the next, making my adieux to the English quacks, the Philosophy fakirs, and so on—even to those colleagues with whom I was merely on speaking terms. I watched the envy in their faces when I announced my departure by Pan American on Saturday morning; and the greatest pleasure I felt in all this was in being able to answer, "Nothing," when I was asked, as invariably I was, what I intended to do.

When I was a boy people used to refer to Charles as "Big Brother C.", although he is only a scant year older than I. To me now he is merely "Fat Brother C.", a successful lawyer. His thick, red face and hands, his back-slapping joviality, and his fathomless hypocritical prudery, these are the qualities which make him truly repulsive to me. There is also the fact that he once looked not unlike the way Racky does now. And after all, he still is my big brother, and disapproves openly of everything I do. The loathing I feel for him is so strong that for years I have not been able to swallow a morsel of food or a drop of liquid in his presence without making a prodigious effort. No one knows this but me—certainly not Charles, who would be the last one I should tell about it. He came up on the late train two nights before I left. He got quickly to the point—as soon as he was settled with a highball.

"So you're off for the wilds," he said, sitting forward in his chair like a salesman.

"If you can call it the wilds," I replied. "Certainly it's not wild like Mitichi." (He has a lodge in northern Quebec.) "I consider it really civilized."

He drank and smacked his lips together stiffly, bringing the glass down hard on his knee.

"And Racky. You're taking him along?"

"Of course."

"Out of school. Away. So he'll see nobody but you. You think that's good."

I looked at him. "I do," I said.

"By God, if I could stop you legally, I would!" he cried, jumping up and putting his glass on the mantel. I was trembling inwardly with excitement, but I merely sat and watched him. He went on. "You're not fit to have custody of the kid!" he shouted. He shot a stern glance at me over his spectacles.

"You think not?" I said gently.

Again he looked at me sharply. "D'ye think I've forgotten?"

I was understandably eager to get him out of the house as soon as I could. As I piled and sorted letters and magazines on the desk, I said: "Is that all you came to tell me? I have a good deal to do tomorrow and I must get some sleep. I probably shan't see you at breakfast. Agnes'll see that you eat in time to make the early train."

All he said was: "God! Wake up! Get wise to yourself! You're not fooling anybody, you know."

That kind of talk is typical of Charles. His mind is slow and obtuse; he constantly imagines that everyone he meets is playing some private game of deception with him. He is so utterly incapable of following the functioning of even a moderately

evolved intellect that he finds the will to secretiveness and du-
plicity everywhere.

"I haven't time to listen to that sort of nonsense," I said,
preparing to leave the room.

But he shouted, "You don't want to listen! No! Of course
not! You just want to do what you want to do. You just want
to go on off down there and live as you've a mind to, and to
hell with the consequences!" At this point I heard Racky
coming downstairs. C. obviously heard nothing, and he raved
on. "But just remember, I've got your number all right, and
if there's any trouble with the boy I'll know who's to blame."

I hurried across the room and opened the door so he could
see that Racky was there in the hallway. That stopped his
tirade. It was hard to know whether Racky had heard any of
it or not. Although he is not a quiet young person, he is the
soul of discretion, and it is almost never possible to know any
more about what goes on inside his head than he intends one
to know.

I was annoyed that C. should have been bellowing at me in
my own house. To be sure, he is the only one from whom I
would accept such behavior, but then, no father likes to have
his son see him take criticism meekly. Racky simply stood
there in his bathrobe, his angelic face quite devoid of expression, saying: "Tell Uncle Charley good night for me, will you?
I forgot."

I said I would, and quickly shut the door. When I thought
Racky was back upstairs in his room, I bade Charles good
night. I have never been able to get out of his presence fast
enough. The effect he has on me dates from an early period
of our lives, from days I dislike to recall.

Racky is a wonderful boy. After we arrived, when we found
it impossible to secure a proper house near any town where
he might have the company of English boys and girls his own
age, he showed no sign of chagrin, although he must have
been disappointed. Instead, as we went out of the renting office into the glare of the street, he grinned and said: "Well, I
guess we'll have to get bikes, that's all."

The few available houses near what Charles would have
called "civilization" turned out to be so ugly and so impossibly

confining in atmosphere that we decided immediately on Cold Point, even though it was across the island and quite isolated on its seaside cliff. It was beyond a doubt one of the most desirable properties on the island, and Racky was as enthusiastic about its splendors as I.

"You'll get tired of being alone out there, just with me," I said to him as we walked back to the hotel.

"Aw, I'll get along all right. When do we look for the bikes?"

At his insistence we bought two the next morning. I was sure I should not make much use of mine, but I reflected that an extra bicycle might be convenient to have around the house. It turned out that the servants all had their own bicycles, without which they would not have been able to get to and from the village of Orange Walk, eight miles down the shore. So for a while I was forced to get astride mine each morning before breakfast and pedal madly along beside Racky for a half hour. We would ride through the cool early air, under the towering silk-cotton trees near the house, and out to the great curve in the shoreline where the waving palms bend landward in the stiff breeze that always blows there. Then we would make a wide turn and race back to the house, loudly discussing the degrees of our desires for the various items of breakfast we knew were awaiting us there on the terrace. Back home we would eat in the wind, looking out over the Caribbean, and talk about the news in yesterday's local paper, brought to us by Isiah each morning from Orange Walk. Then Racky would disappear for the whole morning on his bicycle, riding furiously along the road in one direction or the other until he had discovered an unfamiliar strip of sand along the shore that he could consider a new beach. At lunch he would describe it in detail to me, along with a recounting of all the physical hazards involved in hiding the bicycle in among the trees, so that natives passing along the road on foot would not spot it, or in climbing down unscalable cliffs that turned out to be much higher than they had appeared at first sight, or in measuring the depth of the water preparatory to diving from the rocks, or in judging the efficacy of the reef in barring sharks and barracuda. There is never any element of braggadocio in Racky's relating of his exploits—only the joyous excitement he derives from telling how he satisfies his inexhaustible curiosity. And his mind shows its alertness in all directions at once. I do not mean to say that I expect him to be an "intellectual." That is no affair of mine, nor do I have any particular interest in whether he turns out to be a thinking man or not. I know he will always have a certain boldness of manner and a great purity of spirit in judging values. The former will prevent his becoming what I call a "victim": he never will be brutalized by realities. And his unerring sense of balance in ethical considerations will shield him from the paralyzing effects of present-day materialism.

For a boy of sixteen Racky has an extraordinary innocence of vision. I do not say this as a doting father, although God knows I can never even think of the boy without that familiar overwhelming sensation of delight and gratitude for being vouchsafed the privilege of sharing my life with him. What he takes so completely as a matter of course, our daily life here together, is a source of never-ending wonder to me; and I reflect upon it a good part of each day, just sitting here being conscious of my great good fortune in having him all to myself, beyond the reach of prying eyes and malicious tongues. (I suppose I am really thinking of C. when I write that.) And I believe that a part of the charm of sharing Racky's life with him consists precisely in his taking it all so utterly for granted. I have never asked him whether he likes being here—it is so patent that he does, very much. I think if he were to turn to me one day and tell me how happy he is here, that somehow, perhaps, the spell might be broken. Yet if he were to be thoughtless and inconsiderate, or even unkind to me, I feel that I should be able only to love him the more for it.

I have reread that last sentence. What does it mean? And why should I even imagine it could mean anything more than it says?

Still, much as I may try, I can never believe in the gratuitous, isolated fact. What I must mean is that I feel that Racky already has been in some way inconsiderate. But in what way? Surely I cannot resent his bicycle treks; I cannot expect him to want to stay and sit talking with me all day. And I never worry about his being in danger; I know he is more capable than most adults of taking care of himself, and that he is no more likely than any native to come to harm crawling over the cliffs or swimming in the bays. At the same time there is no doubt in my mind that something about our existence annoys me. I must resent some detail in the pattern, whatever that pattern may be. Perhaps it is just his youth, and I am envious of the lithe body, the smooth skin, the animal energy and grace.

For a long time this morning I sat looking out to sea, trying to solve that small puzzle. Two white herons came and perched on a dead stump east of the garden. They stayed a long time there without stirring. I would turn my head away and accustom my eyes to the bright sea-horizon, then I would look suddenly at them to see if they had shifted position, but they would always be in the same attitude. I tried to imagine the black stump without them—a purely vegetable landscape—but it was impossible. All the while I was slowly forcing myself to accept a ridiculous explanation of my annoyance with Racky. It had made itself manifest to me only yesterday, when instead of appearing for lunch, he sent a young colored boy from Orange Walk to say that he would be lunching in the village. I could not help noticing that the boy was riding Racky's bicycle. I had been waiting lunch a good half hour for him, and I had Gloria serve immediately as the boy rode off, back to the village. I was curious to know in what sort of place and with whom Racky could be eating, since Orange Walk, as far as I know, is inhabited exclusively by Negroes, and I was sure Gloria would be able to shed some light on the matter, but I could scarcely ask her. However, as she brought on the dessert, I said: "Who was that boy that brought the message from Mister Racky?"

She shrugged her shoulders. "A young lad of Orange Walk. He's named Wilmot."

When Racky returned at dusk, flushed from his exertion (for he never rides casually), I watched him closely. His behavior struck my already suspicious eye as being one of false heartiness and a rather forced good humor. He went to his room early and read for quite a while before turning off his light. I took a long walk in the almost day-bright moonlight, listening to the songs of the night insects in the trees. And I sat for a while in the dark on the stone railing of the bridge across Black River. (It is really only a brook that rushes down over the rocks from the mountain a few miles inland, to the beach near the house.) In the night it always sounds louder and more important than it does in the daytime. The music of the water over the stones relaxed my nerves, although why I had need of such a thing I find it difficult to understand, unless I was really upset by Racky's not having come home for lunch. But if that were true it would be absurd, and moreover, dangerous—just the sort of the thing the parent of an adolescent has to beware of and fight against, unless he is indifferent to the prospect of losing the trust and affection of his offspring permanently. Racky must stay out whenever he likes, with whom he likes, and for as long as he likes, and I must not think twice about it, much less mention it to him, or in any way give the impression of prying. Lack of confidence on the part of a parent is the one unforgivable sin.

Although we still take our morning dip together on arising, it is three weeks since we have been for the early spin. One morning I found that Racky had jumped onto his bicycle in his wet trunks while I was still swimming, and gone by himself, and since then there has been an unspoken agreement between us that such is to be the procedure; he will go alone. Perhaps I held him back; he likes to ride so fast.

Young Peter, the smiling gardener from Saint Ives Cove, is Racky's special friend. It is amusing to see them together among the bushes, crouched over an ant-hill or rushing about trying to catch a lizard, almost of an age the two, yet so disparate—Racky with his tan skin looking almost white in contrast to the glistening black of the other. Today I know I shall be alone for lunch, since it is Peter's day off. On such days they usually go together on their bicycles into Saint Ives Cove, where Peter keeps a small rowboat. They fish along the coast there, but they have never returned with anything so far.

Meanwhile I am here alone, sitting on the rocks in the sun, from time to time climbing down to cool myself in the water, always conscious of the house behind me under the high palms, like a large glass boat filled with orchids and lilies. The servants are clean and quiet, and the work seems to be accomplished almost automatically. The good, black servants are another blessing of the islands; the British, born here in this paradise, have no conception of how fortunate they are. In fact, they do nothing but complain. One must have lived in the United States to appreciate the wonder of this place. Still, even here ideas are changing each day. Soon the people will decide that they want their land to be a part of today's monstrous world, and once that happens, it will be all over. As soon as you have that desire, you are infected with the deadly virus, and you begin to show the symptoms of the disease. You live in terms of time and money, and you think in terms of society and progress. Then all that is left for you is to kill the other people who think the same way, along with a good many of those who do not, since that is the final manifestation of the malady. Here for the moment at any rate, one has a feeling of staticity—existence ceases to be like those last few seconds in the hour-glass when what is left of the sand suddenly begins to rush through to the bottom all at once. For the moment, it seems suspended. And if it seems, it is. Each wave at my feet, each bird-call in the forest at my back, does *not* carry me one step nearer the final disaster. The disaster is certain, but it will suddenly have happened, that is all. Until then, time stays still.

I am upset by a letter in this morning's mail: the Royal Bank of Canada requests that I call in person at its central office to sign the deposit slips and other papers for a sum that was cabled from the bank in Boston. Since the central office is on the other side of the island, fifty miles away, I shall have to spend the night over there and return the following day. There is no point in taking Racky along. The sight of "civilization" might awaken a longing for it in him; one never knows. I am sure it would have in me when I was his age. And if that should once start, he would merely be unhappy, since there is nothing for him but to stay here with me, at least for the next two years, when I hope to renew the lease, or, if things in New York pick up, buy the place. I am sending word by Isiah when he goes home into Orange Walk this evening, to have the McCoigh car call for me at seven-thirty tomorrow morning. It is an enormous old open Packard, and

Isiah can save the ride out to work here by piling his bicycle into the back and riding with McCoigh.

The trip across the island was beautiful, and would have been highly enjoyable if my imagination had not played me a strange trick at the very outset. We stopped in Orange Walk for gasoline, and while that was being seen to, I got out and went to the corner store for some cigarettes. Since it was not yet eight o'clock, the store was still closed, and I hurried up the side street to the other little shop which I thought might be open. It was, and I bought my cigarettes. On the way back to the corner I noticed a large black woman leaning with her arms on the gate in front of her tiny house, staring into the street. As I passed by her, she looked straight into my face and said something with the strange accent of the island. It was said in what seemed an unfriendly tone, and ostensibly was directed at me, but I had no notion what it was. I got back into the car and the driver started it. The sound of the words had stayed in my head, however, as a bright shape outlined by darkness is likely to stay in the mind's eye, in such a way that when one shuts one's eyes one can see the exact contour of the shape. The car was already roaring up the hill toward the overland road when I suddenly reheard the very words. And they were: "Keep your boy at home, mahn." I sat perfectly rigid for a moment as the open countryside rushed past. Why should I think she had said that? Immediately I decided that I was giving an arbitrary sense to a phrase I could not have understood even if I had been paying strict attention. And then I wondered why my subconscious should have chosen that sense, since now that I whispered the words over to myself they failed to connect with any anxiety to which my mind might have been disposed. Actually I have never given a thought to Racky's wanderings about Orange Walk. I can find no such preoccupation no matter how I put the question to myself. Then, could she really have said those words? All the way through the mountains I pondered the question, even though it was obviously a waste of energy. And soon I could no longer hear the sound of her voice in my memory: I had played the record over too many times, and worn it out.

Here in the hotel a gala dance is in progress. The abominable orchestra, comprising two saxophones and one sour violin, is playing directly under my window in the garden, and the serious-looking couples slide about on the waxed concrete floor of the terrace, in the light of strings of paper lanterns. I suppose it is meant to look Japanese.

At this moment I wonder what Racky is doing there in the house with only Peter and Ernest the watchman to keep him company. I wonder if he is asleep. The house, which I am accustomed to think of as smiling and benevolent in its airiness, could just as well be in the most sinister and remote regions of the globe, now that I am here. Sitting here with the absurd orchestra bleating downstairs, I picture it to myself, and it strikes me as terribly vulnerable in its isolation. In my mind's eye I see the moonlit point with its tall palms waving restlessly in the wind, its dark cliffs licked by the waves below. Suddenly, although I struggle against the sensation, I am inexpressibly glad to be away from the house, helpless there, far on its point of land, in the silence of the night. Then I remember that the night is seldom silent. There is the loud sea at the base of the rocks, the droning of the thousands of insects, the occasional cries of the night birds—all the familiar noises that make sleep so sound. And Racky is there surrounded by them as usual, not even hearing them. But I feel profoundly guilty for having left him, unutterably tender and sad at the thought of him, lying there alone in the house with the two Negroes the only human beings within miles. If I keep thinking of Cold Point I shall be more and more nervous.

I am not going to bed yet. They are all screaming with laughter down there, the idiots; I could never sleep anyway. The bar is still open. Fortunately it is on the street side of the hotel. For once I need a few drinks.

Much later, but I feel no better; I may be a little drunk. The dance is over and it is quiet in the garden, but the room is too hot.

As I was falling asleep last night, all dressed, and with the overhead light shining sordidly in my face, I heard the black woman's voice again, more clearly even than I did in the car yesterday. For some reason this morning there is no doubt in my mind that the words I heard are the words she said. I accept that and go on from there. Suppose she did tell me to keep Racky home. It could only mean that she, or someone else in Orange Walk, has had a childish altercation with him; although I must say it is hard to conceive of Racky's entering into any sort of argument or feud with those people. To set my mind at rest (for I do seem to be taking the whole thing with great seriousness), I am going to stop in the village this afternoon before going home, and try to see the woman. I am extremely curious to know what she could have meant.

I had not been conscious until this evening when I came back to Cold Point how powerful they are, all those physical elements that go to make up its atmosphere: the sea and wind-sounds that isolate the house from the road, the brilliancy of the water, sky and sun, the bright colors and strong odors of the flowers, the feeling of space both outside and within the house. One naturally accepts these things when one is living here. This afternoon when I returned I was conscious of them all over again, of their existence and their strength. All of them together are like a powerful drug; coming back made me feel as though I had been disintoxicated and were returning to the scene of my former indulgences. Now at eleven it is as if I had never been absent an hour. Everything is the same as always, even to the dry palm branch that scrapes against the window screen by my night table. And indeed, it is only thirty-six hours since I was here; but I always expect my absence from a place to bring about irremediable changes.

Strangely enough, now that I think of it, I feel that something *has* changed since I left yesterday morning, and that is the general attitude of the servants—their collective aura, so to speak. I noticed that difference immediately upon arriving back, but was unable to define it. Now I see it clearly. The network of common understanding which slowly spreads itself through a well-run household has been destroyed. Each person is by himself now. No unfriendliness, however, that I can see. They all behave with the utmost courtesy, excepting possibly Peter, who struck me as looking unaccustomedly

glum when I encountered him in the kitchen after dinner. I
meant to ask Racky if he had noticed it, but I forgot and he
went to bed early.

In Orange Walk I made a brief stop on the pretext to Mc-
Coigh that I wanted to see the seamstress in the side street. I
walked up and back in front of the house where I had seen
the woman, but there was no sign of anyone.

As for my absence, Racky seems to have been perfectly content, having spent most of the day swimming off the rocks below the terrace. The insect sounds are at their height now, the
breeze is cooler than usual, and I shall take advantage of these
favorable conditions to get a good long night's rest.

Today has been one of the most difficult days of my life. I
arose early, we had breakfast at the regular time, and Racky
went off in the direction of Saint Ives Cove. I lay in the sun
on the terrace for a while, listening to the noises of the household's regime. Peter was all over the property, collecting dead
leaves and fallen blossoms in a huge basket and carrying them
off to the compost heap. He appeared to be in an even fouler
humor than last night. When he came near to me at one
point on his way to another part of the garden I called to
him. He set the basket down and stood looking at me; then
he walked across the grass toward me slowly—reluctantly, it
seemed to me.

"Peter, is everything all right with you?"

"Yes, sir."

"No trouble at home?"

"Oh, no, sir."

"Good."

"Yes, sir."

He went back to his work. But his face belied his words.
Not only did he seem to be in a decidedly unpleasant temper;
out here in the sunlight he looked positively ill. However, it
was not my concern, if he refused to admit it.

When the heavy heat of the sun reached the unbearable
point for me, I got out of my chair and went down the side
of the cliff along the series of steps cut there into the rock. A
level platform is below, and a diving board, for the water is
deep. At each side, the rocks spread out and the waves break

over them, but by the platform the wall of rock is vertical and the water merely hits against it below the springboard. The place is a tiny amphitheatre, quite cut off in sound and sight from the house. There too I like to lie in the sun; when I climb out of the water I often remove my trunks and lie stark naked on the springboard. I regularly make fun of Racky because he is embarrassed to do the same. Occasionally he will do it, but never without being coaxed. I was spread out there without a stitch on, being lulled by the slapping of the water, when an unfamiliar voice very close to me said: "Mister Norton?"

I jumped with nervousness, nearly fell off the springboard, and sat up, reaching at the same time, but in vain, for my trunks, which were lying on the rock practically at the feet of a middle-aged mulatto gentleman. He was in a white duck suit, and wore a high collar with a black tie, and it seemed to me that he was eyeing me with a certain degree of horror.

My next reaction was one of anger at being trespassed upon in this way. I rose and got the trunks, however, donning them calmly and saying nothing more meaningful than: "I didn't hear you come down the steps."

"Shall we go up?" said my caller. As he led the way, I had a definite premonition that he was here on an unpleasant errand. On the terrace we sat down, and he offered me an American cigarette which I did not accept.

"This is a delightful spot," he said, glancing out to sea and then at the end of his cigarette, which was only partially aglow. He puffed at it.

I said, "Yes," waiting for him to go on; presently he did.

"I am from the constabulary of this parish. The police, you see." And seeing my face, "This is a friendly call. But still it must be taken as a warning, Mister Norton. It is very serious. If anyone else comes to you about this it will mean trouble for you, heavy trouble. That's why I want to see you privately this way and warn you personally. You see."

I could not believe I was hearing his words. At length I said faintly: "But what about?"

"This is not an official call. You must not be upset. I have taken it upon myself to speak to you because I want to save you deep trouble."

"But I *am* upset!" I cried, finding my voice at last. "How can I help being upset, when I don't know what you're talking about?"

He moved his chair close to mine, and spoke in a very low voice.

"I have waited until the young man was away from the house so we could talk in private. You see, it is about him."

Somehow that did not surprise me. I nodded.

"I will tell you very briefly. The people here are simple country folk. They make trouble easily. Right now they are all talking about the young man you have living here with you. He is your son, I hear." His inflection here was sceptical.

"Certainly he's my son."

His expression did not change, but his voice grew indignant. "Whoever he is, that is a bad young man."

"What do you mean?" I cried, but he cut in hotly: "He may be your son; he may not be. I don't care who he is. That is not my affair. But he is bad through and through. We don't have such things going on here, sir. The people in Orange Walk and Saint Ives Cove are very cross now. You don't know what these folk do when they are aroused."

I thought it my turn to interrupt. "Please tell me why you say my son is bad. What has he done?" Perhaps the earnestness in my voice reached him, for his face assumed a gentler aspect. He leaned still closer to me and almost whispered.

"He has no shame. He does what he pleases with all the young boys, and the men too, and gives them a shilling so they won't tell about it. But they talk. Of course they talk. Every man for twenty miles up and down the coast knows about it. And the women too, they know about it." There was a silence.

I had felt myself preparing to get to my feet for the last few seconds because I wanted to go into my room and be alone, to get away from that scandalized stage whisper. I think I mumbled "Good morning" or "Thank you," as I turned away and began walking toward the house. But he was still beside me, still whispering like an eager conspirator into my ear: "Keep him home, Mister Norton. Or send him away to school, if he is your son. But make him stay out of these towns. For his own sake."

I shook hands with him and went to lie on my bed. From there I heard his car door slam, heard him drive off. I was painfully trying to formulate an opening sentence to use in speaking to Racky about this, feeling that the opening sentence would define my stand. The attempt was merely a sort of therapeutic action, to avoid thinking about the thing itself. Every attitude seemed impossible. There was no way to broach the subject. I suddenly realized that I should never be able to speak to him directly about it. With the advent of this news he had become another person—an adult, mysterious and formidable. To be sure, it did occur to me that the mulatto's story might not be true, but automatically I rejected the doubt. It was as if I wanted to believe it, almost as if I had already known it, and he had merely confirmed it.

Racky returned at midday, panting and grinning. The inevitable comb appeared and was used on the sweaty, unruly locks. Sitting down to lunch, he exclaimed: "Gosh! Did I find a swell beach this morning! But what a job to get to it!" I tried to look unconcerned as I met his gaze; it was as if our positions had been reversed, and I were hoping to stem his rebuke. He prattled on about thorns and vines and his machete. Throughout the meal I kept telling myself: "Now is the moment. You must say something." But all I said was: "More salad? Or do you want dessert now?" So the lunch passed and nothing happened. After I had finished my coffee I went into my bedroom and looked at myself in the large mirror. I saw my eyes trying to give their reflected brothers a little courage. As I stood there I heard a commotion in the other wing of the house: voices, bumpings, the sound of a scuffle. Above the noise came Gloria's sharp voice, imperious and excited: "No, mahn! Don't strike him!" And louder: "Peter, mahn, no!"

I went quickly toward the kitchen, where the trouble seemed to be, but on the way I was run into by Racky, who staggered into the hallway with his hands in front of his face.

"What is it, Racky?" I cried.

He pushed past me into the living room without moving his hands away from his face; I turned and followed him. From there he went into his own room, leaving the door open behind him. I heard him in his bathroom running the water. I was undecided what to do. Suddenly Peter appeared in the hall doorway, his hat in his hand. When he raised his head, I was surprised to see that his cheek was bleeding. In his eyes was a strange, confused expression of transient fear and deep hostility. He looked down again.

"May I please talk with you, sir?"

"What was all the racket? What's been happening?"

"May I talk with you outside, sir?" He said it doggedly, still not looking up.

In view of the circumstances, I humored him. We walked slowly up the cinder road to the main highway, across the bridge, and through the forest while he told me his story. I said nothing.

At the end he said: "I never wanted to, sir, even the first time, but after the first time I was afraid, and Mister Racky was after me every day."

I stood still, and finally said: "If you had only told me this the first time it happened, it would have been much better for everyone."

He turned his hat in his hands, studying it intently. "Yes, sir. But I didn't know what everyone was saying about him in Orange Walk until today. You know I always go to the beach at Saint Ives Cove with Mister Racky on my free days. If I had known what they were all saying I wouldn't have been afraid, sir. And I wanted to keep on working here. I needed the money." Then he repeated what he had already said three times. "Mister Racky said you'd see about it that I was put in the jail. I'm a year older than Mister Racky, sir."

"I know, I know," I said impatiently; and deciding that severity was what Peter expected of me at this point I added: "You had better get your things together and go home. You can't work here any longer, you know."

The hostility in his face assumed terrifying proportions as he said: "If you killed me I would not work any more at Cold Point, sir."

I turned and walked briskly back to the house, leaving him standing there in the road. It seems he returned at dusk, a little while ago, and got his belongings.

In his room Racky was reading. He had stuck some adhesive tape on his chin and over his cheekbone.

"I've dismissed Peter," I announced. "He hit you, didn't he?"

He glanced up. His left eye was swollen, but not yet black.

"He sure did. But I landed him one, too. And I guess I deserved it anyway."

I rested against the table. "Why?" I asked nonchalantly.

"Oh, I had something on him from a long time back that he was afraid I'd tell you."

"And just now you threatened to tell me?"

"Oh, no! He said he was going to quit the job here, and I kidded him about being yellow."

"Why did he want to quit? I thought he liked the job."

"Well, he did, I guess, but he didn't like me." Racky's candid gaze betrayed a shade of pique. I still leaned against the table.

I persisted. "But I thought you two got on fine together. You seemed to."

"Nah. He was just scared of losing his job. I had something on him. He was a good guy, though; I liked him all right." He paused. "Has he gone yet?" A strange quaver crept into his voice as he said the last words, and I understood that for the first time Racky's heretofore impeccable histrionics were not quite equal to the occasion. He was very much upset at losing Peter.

"Yes, he's gone," I said shortly. "He's not coming back, either." And as Racky, hearing the unaccustomed inflection in my voice, looked up at me suddenly with faint astonishment in his young eyes, I realized that this was the moment to press on, to say: "What did you have on him?" But as if he had arrived at the same spot in my mind a fraction of a second earlier, he proceeded to snatch away my advantage by jumping up, bursting into loud song, and pulling off all his clothes simultaneously. As he stood before me naked, singing at the top of his lungs, and stepped into his swimming trunks, I was conscious that again I should be incapable of saying to him what I must say.

He was in and out of the house all afternoon: some of the time he read in his room, and most of the time he was down on the diving board. It is strange behavior for him; if I could only know what is in his mind. As evening approached, my problem took on a purely obsessive character. I walked to and fro in my room, always pausing at one end to look out the window over the sea, and at the other end to glance at my face in the mirror. As if that could help me! Then I took a drink. And another. I thought I might be able to do it at dinner, when I felt fortified by the whisky. But no. Soon he will have gone to bed. It is not that I expect to confront him with any accusations. That I know I never can do. But I must find a way to keep him from his wanderings, and I must offer a reason to give him, so that he will never suspect that I know.

We fear for the future of our offspring. It is ludicrous, but only a little more palpably so than anything else in life. A length of time has passed; days which I am content to have known, even if now they are over. I think that this period was what I had always been waiting for life to offer, the recompense I had unconsciously but firmly expected, in return for having been held so closely in the grip of existence all these years.

That evening seems long ago only because I have recalled its details so many times that they have taken on the color of legend. Actually my problem already had been solved for me then, but I did not know it. Because I could not perceive the pattern, I foolishly imagined that I must cudgel my brains to find the right words with which to approach Racky. But it was he who came to me. That same evening, as I was about to go out for a solitary stroll which I thought might help me hit upon a formula, he appeared at my door.

"Going for a walk?" he asked, seeing the stick in my hand.

The prospect of making an exit immediately after speaking with him made things seem simpler. "Yes," I said, "but I'd like to have a word with you first."

"Sure. What?" I did not look at him because I did not want to see the watchful light I was sure was playing in his eyes at this moment. As I spoke I tapped with my stick along the designs made by the tiles in the floor. "Racky, would you like to go back to school?"

"Are you kidding? You know I hate school."

I glanced up at him. "No, I'm not kidding. Don't look so

horrified. You'd probably enjoy being with a bunch of fellows your own age." (That was not one of the arguments I had meant to use.)

"I might like to be with guys my own age, but I don't want to have to be in school to do it. I've had school enough."

I went to the door and said lamely: "I thought I'd get your reactions."

He laughed. "No, thanks."

"That doesn't mean you're not going," I said over my shoulder as I went out.

On my walk I pounded the highway's asphalt with my stick, stood on the bridge having dramatic visions which involved such eventualities as our moving back to the States, Racky's having a bad spill on his bicycle and being paralyzed for some months, and even the possibility of my letting events take their course, which would doubtless mean my having to visit him now and then in the governmental prison with gifts of food, if it meant nothing more tragic and violent. "But none of these things will happen," I said to myself, and I knew I was wasting precious time; he must not return to Orange Walk tomorrow.

I went back toward the point at a snail's pace. There was no moon and very little breeze. As I approached the house, trying to tread lightly on the cinders so as not to awaken the watchful Ernest and have to explain to him that it was only I, I saw that there were no lights in Racky's room. The house was dark save for the dim lamp on my night table. Instead of going in, I skirted the entire building, colliding with bushes and getting my face sticky with spider webs, and went to sit a while on the terrace where there seemed to be a breath of air. The sound of the sea was far out on the reef, where the breakers sighed. Here below, there were only slight watery chugs and gurgles now and then. It was unusually low tide. I smoked three cigarettes mechanically, having ceased even to think, and then, my mouth tasting bitter from the smoke, I went inside.

My room was airless. I flung my clothes onto a chair and looked at the night table to see if the carafe of water was there. Then my mouth opened. The top sheet of my bed had been stripped back to the foot. There on the far side of the bed, dark against the whiteness of the lower sheet, lay Racky asleep on his side, and naked.

I stood looking at him for a long time, probably holding my breath, for I remember feeling a little dizzy at one point. I was whispering to myself, as my eyes followed the curve of his arm, shoulder, back, thigh, leg: "A child. A child." Destiny, when one perceives it clearly from very near, has no qualities at all. The recognition of it and the consciousness of the vision's clarity leave no room on the mind's horizon. Finally I turned off the light and softly lay down. The night was absolutely black.

He lay perfectly quiet until dawn. I shall never know whether or not he was really asleep all that time. Of course he couldn't have been, and yet he lay so still. Warm and firm, but still as death. The darkness and silence were heavy around us. As the birds began to sing, I sank into a soft, enveloping slumber; when I awoke in the sunlight later, he was gone.

I found him down by the water, cavorting alone on the springboard; for the first time he had discarded his trunks without my suggesting it. All day we stayed together around the terrace and on the rocks, talking, swimming, reading, and just lying flat in the hot sun. Nor did he return to his room when night came. Instead after the servants were asleep, we brought three bottles of champagne in and set the pail on the night table.

Thus it came about that I was able to touch on the delicate subject that still preoccupied me, and profiting by the new understanding between us, I made my request in the easiest, most natural fashion.

"Racky, would you do me a tremendous favor if I asked you?"

He lay on his back, his hands beneath his head. It seemed to me his regard was circumspect, wanting in candor.

"I guess so," he said. "What is it?"

"Will you stay around the house for a few days—a week, say? Just to please me? We can take some rides together, as far as you like. Would you do that for me?"

"Sure thing," he said, smiling.

I was temporizing, but I was desperate.

Perhaps a week later—(it is only when one is not fully happy that one is meticulous about time, so that it may have been more or less)—we were having breakfast. Isiah stood by, in the shade, waiting to pour us more coffee.

"I noticed you had a letter from Uncle Charley the other day," said Racky. "Don't you think we ought to invite him down?"

My heart began to beat with great force.

"Here? He'd hate it here," I said casually. "Besides, there's no room. Where would he sleep?" Even as I heard myself saying the words, I knew that they were the wrong ones, that I was not really participating in the conversation. Again I felt the fascination of complete helplessness that comes when one is suddenly a conscious on-looker at the shaping of one's fate.

"In my room," said Racky. "It's empty."

I could see more of the pattern at that moment than I had ever suspected existed. "Nonsense," I said. "This is not the sort of place for Uncle Charley."

Racky appeared to be hitting on an excellent idea. "Maybe if I wrote and invited him," he suggested, motioning to Isiah for more coffee.

"Nonsense," I said again, watching still more of the pattern reveal itself, like a photographic print becoming constantly clearer in a tray of developing solution.

Isiah filled Racky's cup and returned to the shade. Racky drank slowly, pretending to be savoring the coffee.

"Well, it won't do any harm to try. He'd appreciate the invitation," he said speculatively.

For some reason, at this juncture I knew what to say, and as I said it, I knew what I was going to do.

"I thought we might fly over to Havana for a few days next week."

He looked guardedly interested, and then he broke into a wide grin. "Swell!" he cried. "Why wait till next week?"

The next morning the servants called "Good-bye" to us as we drove up the cinder road in the McCoigh car. We took off from the airport at six that evening. Racky was in high spirits; he kept the stewardess engaged in conversation all the way to Camagüey.

He was delighted also with Havana. Sitting in the bar at the Nacional, we continued to discuss the possibility of having C. pay us a visit at the island. It was not without difficulty that I eventually managed to persuade Racky that writing him would be inadvisable.

We decided to look for an apartment right there in Vedado for Racky. He did not seem to want to come back here to Cold Point. We also decided that living in Havana he would need a larger income than I. I am already having the greater part of Hope's estate transferred to his name in the form of a trust fund which I shall administer until he is of age. It was his mother's money, after all.

We bought a new convertible, and he drove me out to Rancho Boyeros in it when I took my plane. A Cuban named Claudio with very white teeth, whom Racky had met in the pool that morning, sat between us.

We were waiting in front of the landing field. An official finally unhooked the chain to let the passengers through. "If you get fed up, come to Havana," said Racky, pinching my arm.

The two of them stood together behind the rope, waving to me, their shirts flapping in the wind as the plane started to move.

The wind blows by my head; between each wave there are thousands of tiny licking and chopping sounds as the water hurries out of the crevices and holes; and a part-floating, part-submerged feeling of being in the water haunts my mind even as the hot sun burns my face. I sit here and I read, and I wait for the pleasant feeling of repletion that follows a good meal, to turn slowly, as the hours pass along, into the even more delightful, slightly stirring sensation deep within, which accompanies the awakening of the appetite.

I am perfectly happy here in reality, because I still believe that nothing very drastic is likely to befall this part of the island in the near future.

You Are Not I

Y OU are not I. No one but me could possibly be. I know
that, and I know where I have been and what I have
done ever since yesterday when I walked out the gate during
the train wreck. Everyone was so excited that no one noticed
me. I became completely unimportant as soon as it was a
question of cut people and smashed cars down there on the
tracks. We girls all went running down the bank when we
heard the noise, and we landed against the cyclone fence like
a lot of monkeys. Mrs. Werth was chewing on her crucifix and
crying her eyes out. I suppose it hurt her lips. Or maybe she
thought one of her daughters was on the train down there. It
was really a bad accident; anyone could see that. The spring
rains had dissolved the earth that kept the ties firm, and so the
rails had spread a little and the train had gone into the ditch.
But how everyone could get so excited I still fail to understand.

I always hated the trains, hated to see them go by down
there, hated to see them disappear way off up the valley toward the next town. It made me angry to think of all those
people moving from one town to another, without any right
to. Whoever said to them: "You may go and buy your ticket
and make the trip this morning to Reading. You will go past
twenty-three stations, over forty bridges, through three tunnels, and still keep going, if you want to, even after you get
to Reading"? No one. I know that. I know there is no chief
who says things like that to people. But it makes it pleasanter
for me when I imagine such a person does exist. Perhaps it
would be only a tremendous voice speaking over a public-
address system set up in all the main streets.

When I saw the train down there helpless on its side like an
old worm knocked off a plant, I began to laugh. But I held
on to the fence very hard when the people started to climb
out the windows bleeding.

I was up in the courtyard, and there was the paper wrapper
off a box of Cheese Tid Bits lying on the bench. Then I was
at the main gate, and it was open. A black car was outside at

the curb, and a man was sitting in front smoking. I thought of speaking to him and asking him if he knew who I was, but I decided not to. It was a sunny morning full of sweet air and birds. I followed the road around the hill, down to the tracks. Then I walked up the tracks feeling excited. The dining car looked strange lying on its side with the window glass all broken and some of the cloth shades drawn down. A robin kept whistling in a tree above. "Of course," I said to myself. "This is just in man's world. If something real should happen, they would stop singing." I walked up and down along the cinder bed beside the track, looking at the people lying in the bushes. Men were beginning to carry them up toward the front end of the train where the road crosses the tracks. There was a woman in a white uniform, and I tried to keep from passing close to her.

I decided to go down a wide path that led through the blackberry bushes, and in a small clearing I found an old stove with a lot of dirty bandages and handkerchiefs in the rubbish around the base of it. Underneath everything was a pile of stones. I found several round ones and some others. The earth here was very soft and moist. When I got back to the train there seemed to be a lot more people running around. I walked close to the ones who were lying side by side on the cinders, and looked at their faces. One was a girl and her mouth was open. I dropped one of the stones in and went on. A fat man also had his mouth open. I put in a sharp stone that looked like a piece of coal. It occurred to me that I might not have enough stones for them all, and the cinders were too small. There was one old woman walking up and down wiping her hands on her skirt very quickly, over and over again. She had on a long black silk dress with a design of blue mouths stamped all over it. Perhaps they were supposed to be leaves but they were formed like mouths. She looked crazy to me and I kept clear of her. Suddenly I noticed a hand with rings on the fingers sticking out from under a lot of bent pieces of metal. I tugged at the metal and saw a face. It was a woman and her mouth was closed. I tried to open it so I could get a stone in. A man grabbed me by the shoulder and pulled at me. He looked angry. "What are you doing?" he yelled. "Are you crazy?" I began to cry and said she was my

sister. She did look a little like her, and I sobbed and kept saying: "She's dead. She's dead." The man stopped looking so
angry and pushed me along toward the head of the train,
holding my arm tightly with one hand. I tried to jerk away
from him. At the same time I decided not to say anything
more except "She's dead" once in a while. "That's all right,"
the man said. When we got to the front end of the train he
made me sit down on the grass embankment alongside a lot
of other people. Some of them were crying, so I stopped and
watched them.

It seemed to me that life outside was like life inside. There
was always somebody to stop people from doing what they
wanted to do. I smiled when I thought that this was just the
opposite of what I had felt when I was still inside. Perhaps
what we want to do is wrong, but why should they always be
the ones to decide? I began to consider this as I sat there
pulling the little new blades of grass out of the ground. And
I thought that for once *I* would decide what was right, and
do it.

It was not very long before several ambulances drove up.
They were for us, the row of people sitting on the bank, as
well as for the ones lying around on stretchers and overcoats.
I don't know why, since the people weren't in pain. Or perhaps they were. When a great many people are in pain together they aren't so likely to make a noise about it, probably
because no one listens. Of course I was in no pain at all. I
could have told anyone that if I had been asked. But no one
asked me. What they did ask me was my address, and I gave
my sister's address because it is only a half hour's drive. Besides, I stayed with her for quite a while before I went away,
but that was years ago, I think. We all drove off together,
some lying down inside the ambulances, and the rest of us sitting on an uncomfortable bench in one that had no bed. The
woman next to me must have been a foreigner; she was
moaning like a baby, and there was not a drop of blood on
her that I could see, anywhere. I looked her all over very carefully on the way, but she seemed to resent it, and turned her
face the other way, still crying. When we got to the hospital
we were all taken in and examined. About me they just said:
"Shock," and asked me again where I lived. I gave them the

same address as before, and soon they took me out again and put me into the front seat of a sort of station wagon, between the driver and another man, an attendant, I suppose. They both spoke to me about the weather, but I knew enough not to let myself be trapped that easily. I know how the simplest subject can suddenly twist around and choke you when you think you're quite safe. "She's dead," I said once, when we were halfway between the two towns. "Maybe not, maybe not," said the driver, as if he were talking to a child. I kept my head down most of the time, but I managed to count the gas stations as we went along.

When we arrived at my sister's house the driver got out and rang the bell. I had forgotten that the street was so ugly. The houses were built one against the other, all alike, with only a narrow cement walk between. And each one was a few feet lower than the other, so that the long row of them looked like an enormous flight of stairs. The children were evidently allowed to run wild over all the front yards, and there was no grass anywhere in sight, only mud.

My sister came to the door. The driver and she spoke a few words, and then I saw her look very worried very suddenly. She came out to the car and leaned in. She had new glasses, thicker than the others. She did not seem to be looking at me. Instead she said to the driver: "Are you *sure* she's all right?"

"Absolutely," he answered. "I wouldn't be telling you if she wasn't. She's just been examined all over up at the hospital. It's just shock. A good rest will fix her up fine." The attendant got out, to help me out and up the steps, although I could have gone perfectly well by myself. I saw my sister looking at me out of the corner of her eye the same as she used to. When I was on the porch I heard her whisper to the attendant: "She don't look well yet to *me*." He patted her arm and said: "She'll be fine. Just don't let her get excited."

"That's what they always said," she complained, "but she just *does*."

The attendant got into the car. "She ain't hurt at *all*, lady." He slammed the door.

"Hurt!" exclaimed my sister, watching the car. It drove off and she stood following it with her eyes until it got to the top of the hill and turned. I was still looking down at the porch floor because I wasn't sure yet what was going to happen. I often feel that something is about to happen, and when I do, I stay perfectly still and let it go ahead. There's no use wondering about it or trying to stop it. At this time I had no particular feeling that a special event was about to come out, but I did feel that I would be more likely to do the right thing if I waited and let my sister act first. She stood where she was, in her apron, breaking off the tips of the pussywillow stems that stuck out of the bush beside her. She still refused to look at me. Finally she grunted: "Might as well go on inside. It's cold out here." I opened the door and walked in.

Right away I saw she had had the whole thing rebuilt, only backward. There was always a hall and a living room, except that the hall used to be on the left-hand side of the living room and now it was on the right. That made me wonder why I had failed to notice that the front door was now at the right end of the porch. She had even switched the stairs and fireplace around into each other's places. The furniture was the same, but each piece had been put into the position exactly opposite to the way it had been before. I decided to say nothing and let her do the explaining if she felt like it. It occurred to me that it must have cost her every cent she had in the bank, and still it looked exactly the same as it had when she began. I kept my mouth shut, but I could not help looking around with a good deal of curiosity to see if she had carried out the reversal in every detail.

I went into the living room. The three big chairs around the center table were still wrapped in old sheets, and the floor lamp by the pianola had the same torn cellophane cover on its shade. I began to laugh, everything looked so comical backward. I saw her grab the fringe of the portiere and look at me hard. I went on laughing.

The radio next door was playing an organ selection. Suddenly my sister said: "Sit down, Ethel. I've got something to do. I'll be right back." She went into the kitchen through the hall and I heard the back door open.

I knew already where she was going. She was afraid of me, and she wanted Mrs. Jelinek to come over. Sure enough, in a minute they both came in, and my sister walked right into the living room this time. She looked angry now, but she had nothing to say. Mrs. Jelinek is sloppy and fat. She shook hands with me and said: "Well, well, old-timer!" I decided not to talk to her either because I distrust her, so I turned around and lifted the lid of the pianola. I tried to push down some keys, but the catch was on and they were all stiff and wouldn't move. I closed the lid and went over to see out the window. A little girl was wheeling a doll carriage along the sidewalk down the hill; she kept looking back at the tracks the wheels made when they left a wet part of the pavement and went onto a dry patch. I was determined not to let Mrs. Jelinek gain any advantage over me, so I kept quiet. I sat down in the rocker by the window and began to hum.

Before long they started to talk to each other in low voices, but of course I heard everything they said. Mrs. Jelinek said: "I thought they was keeping her." My sister said: "I don't know. So did I. But the man kept telling me she was all right. Huh! She's just the same." "Why, sure," said Mrs. Jelinek. They were quiet a minute.

"Well, I'm not going to put up with it!" said my sister suddenly. "I'm going to tell Dr. Dunn what I think of him."

"Call the Home," urged Mrs. Jelinek.

"I certainly am," my sister answered. "You stay here. I'll see if Kate's in." She meant Mrs. Schultz, who lives on the other side and has a telephone. I did not even look up when she went out. I had made a big decision, and that was to stay right in the house and under no condition let myself be taken back there. I knew it would be difficult, but I had a plan I knew would work if I used all my will power. I have great will power.

The first important thing to do was to go on keeping quiet, not to speak a word that might break the spell I was starting to work. I knew I would have to concentrate deeply, but that is easy for me. I knew it was going to be a battle between my sister and me, but I was confident that my force of character and superior education had fitted me for just such a battle, and that I could win it. All I had to do was to keep insisting inside myself, and things would happen the way I willed it. I said this to myself as I rocked. Mrs. Jelinek stood in the hall doorway with her arms folded, mostly looking out the front door. By now life seemed much clearer and more purposeful than it had in a long, long time. This way I would have what I wanted. "No one can stop you," I thought.

It was a quarter of an hour before my sister came back. When she walked in she had both Mrs. Schultz and Mrs. Schultz's brother with her, and all three of them looked a little frightened. I knew exactly what had happened even before she told Mrs. Jelinek. She had called the Home and complained to Dr. Dunn that I had been released, and he had been very much excited and told her to hold on to me by all means because I had not been discharged at all but had somehow *got out.* I was a little shocked to hear it put that way, but now that I thought of it, I had to admit to myself that that was just what I had done.

I got up when Mrs. Schultz's brother came in, and glared at him hard.

"Take it easy, now, Miss Ethel," he said, and his voice sounded nervous. I bowed low to him: at least he was polite.

"'Lo, Steve," said Mrs. Jelinek.

I watched every move they made. I would have died rather than let the spell be broken. I felt I could hold it together only by a great effort. Mrs. Schultz's brother was scratching the side of his nose, and his other hand twitched in his pants pocket. I knew he would give me no trouble. Mrs. Schultz and Mrs. Jelinek would not go any further than my sister told them to. And she herself was terrified of me, for although I had never done her any harm, she had always been convinced that some day I would. It may be that she knew now what I was about to do to her, but I doubt it, or she would have run away from the house.

"When they coming?" asked Mrs. Jelinek.

"Soon's they can get here," said Mrs. Schultz.

They all stood in the doorway.

"I see they rescued the flood victims, you remember last night on the radio?" said Mrs. Schultz's brother.

Nobody answered. I was concentrating on my plan, and it took all my strength, so I sat down again.

"She'll be all right," said Mrs. Schultz's brother. He lit a cigarette and leaned back against the banisters.

The house was very ugly, but I already was getting ideas for making it look better. I have excellent taste in decoration. I tried not to think of those things, and said over and over inside my head: "Make it work."

Mrs. Jelinek finally sat down on the couch by the door, pulled her skirts around her legs and coughed. She still looked red in the face and serious. I could have laughed out loud when I thought of what they were really waiting to see if they had only known it.

I heard a car door slam outside. I looked out. Two of the men from the Home were coming up the walk. Somebody else was sitting at the wheel, waiting. My sister went quickly to the front door and opened it. One of the men said: "Where is she?" They both came in and stood a second looking at me and grinning.

"Well, hel-*lo*!" said one. The other turned and said to my sister: "No trouble?" She shook her head. "It's a wonder you couldn't be more careful," she said angrily. "They get out like that, how do *you* know what they're going to do?"

The man grunted and came over to me. "Wanna come with us? I know somebody who's waiting to see you."

I got up and walked slowly across the room, looking at the rug all the way, with one of the men on each side of me. When I got to the doorway beside my sister I pulled my hand out of the pocket of my coat and looked at it. I had one of my stones in my hand. It was very easy. Before either of them could stop me I reached out and stuffed the stone into her mouth. She screamed just before I touched her, and just afterward her lips were bleeding. But the whole thing took a very long time. Everybody was standing perfectly still. Next, the two men had hold of my arms very tight and I was looking around the room at the walls. I felt that my front teeth were broken. I could taste blood on my lips. I thought I was going to faint. I wanted to put my hand to my mouth, but they held my arms. "This is the turning point," I thought.

I shut my eyes very hard. When I opened them everything was different and I knew I had won. For a moment I could not see very clearly, but even during that moment I saw myself sitting on the divan with my hands in front of my mouth. As my vision cleared, I saw that the men were holding my sister's arms, and that she was putting up a terrific struggle. I buried my face in my hands and did not look up again. While they were getting her out the front door, they managed to knock over the umbrella stand and smash it. It hurt her ankle and she kicked pieces of porcelain back into the hall. I was delighted. They dragged her along the walk to the car, and one man sat on each side of her in the back. She was yelling and showing her teeth, but as they left the city limits she stopped, and began to cry. All the same, she was really counting the service stations along the road on the way back to the Home, and she found there was one more of them than she had thought. When they came to the grade crossing near the spot where the train accident had happened, she looked out, but the car was over the track before she realized she was looking out the wrong side.

Driving in through the gate, she really broke down. They kept promising her ice cream for dinner, but she knew better than to believe them. As she walked through the main door between the two men she stopped on the threshold, took out one of the stones from her coat pocket and put it into her mouth. She tried to swallow it, but it choked her, and they rushed her down the hall into a little waiting room and made her give it up. The strange thing, now that I think about it, was that no one realized she was not I.

They put her to bed, and by morning she no longer felt like crying: she was too tired.

It's the middle of the afternoon and raining torrents. She is sitting on her bed (the very one I used to have) in the Home, writing all this down on paper. She never would have thought of doing that up until yesterday, but now she thinks she has become me, and so she does everything I used to do.

The house is very quiet. I am still in the living room, sitting on the divan. I could walk upstairs and look into her bedroom if I wanted to. But it is such a long time since I have been up there, and I no longer know how the rooms are arranged. So I prefer to stay down here. If I look up I can see the square window of colored glass over the stairs. Purple and orange, an hourglass design, only the light never comes in very much because the house next door is so close. Besides, the rain is coming down hard here, too.

How Many Midnights

H OW MANY midnights, she wondered, had she raised the shade, opened the big window, and leaned out to gaze across the gently stirring city toward the highest towers? Over there behind a certain unmistakable group of them was his building, and at the very top of the building was his apartment, six flights up. In the summer she would look out over the rooftops at some length and sigh, and during the hottest weeks she moved her bed over, directly under the window. Then she would turn off all the lights and sit on the bed combing her hair in the glowing dimness of the city night, or sometimes even by moonlight, which of course was perfect. In the winter however she had to content herself with a moment of looking and a flash of imagining before she bounded across the room into bed.

It was winter now. She was walking crosstown, east, along one of the late Forties. This part of town always had seemed vaguely mysterious to her because of its specially constructed buildings that did not quite touch the pavement. All the buildings just north of the Grand Central were built that way, to absorb the shock, Van had told her; and there were long stretches of grillwork in the sidewalks through which, particularly at night, one could see another world beneath: railway tracks and sometimes a slowly moving train. When it snowed, as it was doing now, the snow filtered down through the grills and covered the ties; then they were even more apparent.

Van worked here in this neighborhood: he was manager of a large bookshop and lending library on Madison Avenue. And he lived in the neighborhood as well, only farther over east, between Third and Second Avenues. His place was not ideal, either as to actual physical comfort or as to locality (since the immediate district was clearly a slum), but with her help he had made it livable, and she used to tell him: "New York and Paris are like that: no clear demarcation of neighborhoods."

In any case, they already had signed a sublease for a place near Gramercy Park which was to be free the first of March. This was of prime importance because they planned to marry on Valentine's Day. They were by no means sentimental souls, either one of them, and for that very reason it seemed to June a little daring to announce to their friends during cocktails: "It's to be Valentine's Day."

Her father, who always was to be counted on to do the thoughtful thing, was staking them to two weeks in Bermuda. "God knows why," Van said. "He hates my guts."

"I don't know how you can say a thing like that about Dad," objected June. "He's never been anything but the essence of politeness with you."

"That's right," said Van, but impenitently.

She crossed Lexington Avenue. The entire sky looked as though it were being illumined from above by gray-violet neons. The tops of the buildings were lost in the cloud made by the falling snow. And the harbor sounds, instead of coming from the river ahead, came from above, as if the tugs were making their careful way around the tips of the towers. "This is the way New York was meant to be," she thought—not the crowded fire-escape, open-hydrant, sumac-leaved summer. Just this quiet, damp, neutral weather when the water seemed all around. She stood still a moment in the middle of the block, listening to the fog horns; there was a whole perspective of them. In the remotest background was a very faint, smothered one that said: "Mmmmm! Mmmmm!" "It must be on the Sound," she thought. She started to walk again.

In her coat pocket she had the keys, because this was to be a special night. Not that there had been any overt reference to that: there was no need for it. It had been implicit in their conversation yesterday afternoon when she had stopped in at the bookshop to see him. They had stood a few minutes talking in the back of the store among the desks, and then he had slipped her the keys. That was surely the most exciting single thing that ever had happened between them—the passage of the keys from his hand to hers. By the gesture he gave up what she knew was most dear to him: his privacy. She did not want him to think that she was in any way unaware of this, and she said in a low voice: "You can trust me with them, I think," laughing immediately afterward so that her remark should not sound ridiculous. He had kissed her and they had gone out for ten minutes to have coffee.

Sitting at the counter he had told how he had caught a man stealing books the night before. (The bookshop was open at night; because of the location it seemed they did almost as much business in the evening as they did during the day.) Van had just finished arranging a display of new books in one of the show windows, and was standing outside in the street looking in. He had noticed a man wearing a long overcoat, standing by the technical books. "I had my eye on him from the beginning. It's a type, you know. You get to spot them. He looked at me right through the window. I suppose he thought I was just another man in the street. I had on *my* overcoat, too." And the man had taken a quick glance around the store to be sure that no one was watching him, had reached up, snatched down a book and dropped it inside his coat. Van had gone quickly to the corner, tapped the traffic policeman on the shoulder and said: "Would you mind coming into my store for a minute? I want you to arrest a man." They had caught him, and when they had opened his coat they found he already had taken three books.

Van always said: "You see some funny things in a bookshop," and often they were really funny. But this story struck June as remotely sinister rather than amusing. Not because it had to do with a theft, certainly. It was not the first case of booklifting he had related to her. Perhaps it was because more than anything else she hated being watched behind her back, and involuntarily she put herself in the place of the thief, with whom she felt that Van had not been quite fair. It seemed to her that he might have gone in and said to him: "I've been watching you. I've seen everything you've been doing. Now, I give you one last chance. Put back whatever you've taken and get the hell out, and don't come back in here." To spring on the man out of the dark after spying on him did seem a little unfair. But she knew she was being absurd. Van could never be unfair with anyone; this was his way of handling the affair, and it was typical of him: he never would argue. She never knew even when he was angry with her until after it was all over, and he told her, smiling: "Gee, I was burned up last Friday."

She crossed Third Avenue. Up to now the snow had been melting as fast as it fell, but the air was getting colder, and the sidewalk began to show silver. The keys jingled in her coat pocket; she pulled off her glove and felt for them. They also were cold. When she had left her house, she had said to her parents: "I'm going out with Van. I'll probably be rather late." They had merely said: "Yes." But she thought she had intercepted a look of mutual understanding between them. It was all right: in ten more days they would be married. She had climbed up the six steep flights of stairs on a good many evenings during the past two years, just to spend an hour or so with him, but never, she reflected with an obscure sort of pride, had anything ever occurred between them which was not what her parents would call "honorable."

She had arrived at the apartment house; it had a gray-stone façade and a good deal of wrought iron around the entrance door. A woman who looked like a West Indian of some sort came out. Noticing that June was carrying a potted plant under her arm, she held the door partially open for her. June thanked her and went in. It was a rubber plant she had bought for Van's apartment. He was inclined to be indifferent about flowers, and, she feared, about decoration in general. She always had hoped to develop aesthetic appreciation in him, and she considered that she had made remarkable progress during the past year. Practically all the adornments in his apartment were objects either of her buying or her choosing.

She knew just how many steps there were to each flight of stairs: nineteen for the first and fifteen for the others. The halls were tiled in black and white, like a bathroom, and tonight, to add to that impression, the stairs and floors were thoroughly wet with the melting snow people had tracked in; the air smelled of wet doormats, wet rubbers, wet clothing. On the third floor a huge perambulator of black leatherette nearly blocked the passageway between the stairs. She frowned at it and thought of the fire regulations.

Because she did not want to be out of breath she mounted the stairs slowly. Not that Van would be there when she arrived—it was still too early—but being out of breath always created in her a false kind of excitement which she particularly wanted to avoid tonight. She turned the key in the lock and stepped inside. It gave her a strange sensation to push open the door all by herself and stand there in the hall alone, smelling the special odor of the place: an amalgam in which she imagined she detected furniture polish, shaving cream and woodsmoke. Woodsmoke there surely was, because he had a fireplace. It was she who had persuaded him to have it installed. And it had not been nearly so expensive to build as he had imagined it was going to be, because since this was the top floor the chimney had only to be built up through the roof. Many times he had said to her: "That was one sensible idea you had," as though the others had not been just as good! They had cut down the legs of all the living-room furniture so that it nestled nearer the floor and made the room seem spacious; they had painted each wall a different shade of gray, adding the occasional wall brackets of ivy; they had bought the big glass coffee table. All these things had made the place pleasanter, and they had all been her ideas.

She shut the door and went into the kitchen. It was a little chilly in the apartment; she lit the gas oven. Then she unwrapped the wet brown paper from around the rubber plant, and set the pot upright on the table. The plant leaned somewhat to one side. She tried to make it stand straight, but it would not. The ice-box motor was purring. She took out two trays of ice and dumped the cubes into a bowl. Reaching up to the top shelf of the cabinet she brought down an almost full bottle of Johnny Walker, and set it, along with two high-ball glasses, onto the big lacquer tray. The room suddenly seemed terribly close; she turned off the oven. Then she scurried about looking for newspapers with which to lay a fire. There were only a few, but she found some old magazines in the kitchen. She rolled the newspapers into thin little logs and set them at various angles across the andirons. Underneath she pushed crumpled pages of the magazines, and on top she put what kindling wood there was. The logs she decided to leave until the kindling already was burning. When the fire was laid, but not lighted, she looked out the window. The snow was coming down thicker than it had been when she came in. She drew the heavy woolen curtains; they covered one entire wall, and they too had been her idea. Van had wanted to have Venetian blinds made. She had tried to make him see how hideous they would be, but although he had agreed that the black-and-white curtains were smart, he never would admit that Venetian blinds were ugly. "Maybe you're right, for this room," he said. "For every room in the world," she had wanted to declare, but she decided against it, since after all, he had given in.

It wasn't that Van had really bad taste. He had an innate sensitivity and a true intelligence which became manifest whenever he talked about the books he had read (and he read a good many during odd moments at the bookshop). But his aesthetic sense had never been fully awakened. Naturally she never mentioned it—she merely made small suggestions which he was free to take or to leave as he saw fit. And usually, if she let her little hints fall at strategic moments, he would take them.

On the mantel were two enormous plaster candelabra covered with angels; she had brought them herself all the way from Matamoros Izúcar in Mexico. Actually she had packed six of them, and all had broken except these two which did not quite match, one of them being somewhat taller than the other. (These were among the few things about which Van was still a bit recalcitrant: he could not be sure he liked them, even yet.) Each one held six candles. She went to a drawer in the desk and got out a dozen long yellow tapers. Often she brought him a dozen at a time. "Where am I supposed to put the damned things?" he would complain. She got a knife from the kitchen and began to scrape the bottoms of the candles to make them fit the holders. "In the middle of this operation he's going to arrive," she said to herself. She wanted the place to be perfect before he got there. Nervously she tossed the paraffine scrapings into the fireplace. She had a feeling that he would not just come up; it would be more like him to ring from the vestibule downstairs. At least, she hoped he would do that. The time it would take him to get up the six flights might make a great difference in the way the room would look. She fitted the last candle into the bright holder and sighed with relief. They were slow-burning ones; she decided to light them now before returning the candelabra to the mantel. Up there they looked beautiful. She stepped back to admire their splendor, and for a moment watched the slowly moving interplay of shadows on the wall. She switched off the electric

lights in the room. With the fireplace aglow the effect would
be breathtaking.

Impetuously she determined to do a very daring thing. It
might possibly annoy Van when he first saw it, but she would
do it anyway. She rushed to the other side of the room and
feverishly began to push the divan across the floor toward the
fireplace. It would be so snug to be right in front of the blaze,
especially with the snow outside. The cushions fell off and a
caster got entangled with the long wool of the goatskin rug
she had given him for his birthday. She got the rug out of the
way and continued to manipulate the divan. It looked absurd
out there in the middle of the room, and she swung one end
around so that it lay at right angles to the fireplace, against
the wall. After she had piled the cushions back she stepped
aside to observe it, and decided to leave it there. Then the
other pieces had to be arranged. The whole room was in disorder at this point.

"I know he's going to open that door this minute," she
thought. She turned the overhead light back on and quickly
began to shift chairs, lamps and tables. The last piece to be
moved was a small commode that she had once helped him
sandpaper. As she carried it across the room its one little
drawer slid out and fell on the floor. All the letters Van had
received in the past months were there, lying in a fairly compact heap at her feet. "Damnation!" she said aloud, and as she
said it, the hideous metallic sound of the buzzer in the
kitchen echoed through the apartment. She let go of the commode and rushed out to press the button that opened the
door downstairs onto the street. Then, without pressing it,
she ran back into the living room and knelt on the floor,
quickly gathering up the letters and dumping them into the
drawer. But they had been piled carefully into that small space
before the accident, and now they were not; as a result the
drawer was overfull and would not close. Again she spoke
aloud. "Oh, my God!" she said. And she said that because for
no reason at all it had occurred to her that Van might think
she had been reading his correspondence. The main thing
now was to get the commode over into the corner; then she
might be able to force the drawer shut. As she lifted it, the
buzzer pealed again, with insistence. She ran into the kitchen,

and this time pressed the answer button with all her might. Swiftly she hurried back and carried the commode into the corner. Then she tried to close the drawer and found it an impossibility. In a burst of inspiration she turned the little piece of furniture around so that the drawer opened toward the wall. She stepped to the fireplace and touched a match to the paper logs. By now he would got only about to the fourth floor; there were three more.

She turned off the light once again, went into the hall and looked at herself briefly in the mirror, put out the light there, and moved toward the entrance door. With her hand on the knob, she held her breath, and found that her heart was beating much too fast. It was just what she had not wanted. She had hoped to have him step into a little world of absolute calm. And now because of that absurd drawer she was upset. Or perhaps it was the dragging around of all that furniture. She opened the door a crack and listened. A second later she stepped out into the hall, and again she listened. She walked to the stairs. "Van?" she called, and immediately she was furious with herself.

A man's voice answered from two floors below. "Riley?" he yelled.

"What?" she cried.

"I'm looking for Riley."

"You've rung the wrong bell," she shouted, enunciating the words very distinctly in spite of her raised voice.

She went in and shut the door, holding onto the knob and leaning her forehead against the panel for a moment. Now her heart was beating even more violently. She returned to the commode in the corner. "I might as well fix it once and for all right now," she thought. Otherwise her mind would be on it every instant. She turned it around, took out all the letters and carefully replaced them in four equal piles. Even then the drawer shut with difficulty, but it did close. When that was done, she went to the window and pulled back the curtain. It seemed to be growing much colder. The wind had risen; it was blowing from the east. The sky was no longer violet. It was black. She could see the snow swirling past the street lamp below. She wondered if it were going to turn into a blizzard. Tomorrow was Sunday; she simply would stay on.

There would be a terrible moment in the morning, of course, when her parents arose and found she had not come in, but she would not be there to see it, and she could make it up with them later. And what an ideal little vacation it would make: a night and day up there in the snow, isolated from everything, shut away from everyone but Van. As she watched the street, she gradually became convinced that the storm would last all night. She looked back into the room. It gave her keen pleasure to contrast its glow with the hostile night outside. She let the curtain fall and went to the fireplace. The kindling was at the height of its blazing and there was no more; she piled two small logs on top of it. Soon they were crackling with such energy that she thought it wise to put the screen across in front of them. She sat on the divan looking at her legs in the blended firelight and candleglow. Smiling, she leaned back against the cushions. Her heart was no longer racing. She felt almost calm. The wind whined outside; to her it was inevitably a melancholy sound. Even tonight.

Suddenly she decided that it would be inexcusable not to let her parents know she was staying the night. She went into the bedroom and lay on the bed, resting the telephone on her stomach. It moved ridiculously while she dialed. Her mother, not her father, answered. "Thank God," she said to herself, and she let her head fall back upon the pillows. Her mother had been asleep; she did not sound too pleased to have been called to the telephone. "You're all right, I hope," she said. They spoke of the storm. "Yes, it's awful out," said June. "Oh, no, I'm at Van's. We have a fire. I'm going to stay. All night." There was a short silence. "Well, I think you're very foolish," she heard her mother say. And she went on. June let her talk a bit. Then she interrupted, letting a note of impatience sound in her voice. "I can't very well discuss it now. You understand." Her mother's voice was shrill. "No, I *don't* understand!" she cried. She was taking it more seriously than June had expected. "I can't talk now," said June. "I'll see you tomorrow." She said good night and hung up, lying perfectly still for a moment. Then she lifted the telephone and set it on the night table, but still she did not move. When she had heard herself say: "We have a fire," a feeling of dread had seized her. It was as if in giving voice to the pretense she thereby became conscious of it. Van had not yet arrived; why then had she taken care to speak as though he had? She could only have been trying to reassure herself. Again her heart had begun to beat heavily. And finally she did what she had been trying not even to think of doing ever since she had arrived: she looked at her watch.

It was a little after midnight. There was absolutely no doubt about it; already he was quite late. He no longer could arrive without going into explanations. Something must have happened, and it only could be something bad. "Ridiculous!" she cried in anger, jumping up and going out into the kitchen. The ice cubes had melted a good deal; she poured the cold water into the sink between her spread fingers, and shook the cubes around in the bowl petulantly, trying to stem the resentment she felt rising up inside her. "It will be interesting to know what his excuse will be," she said to herself. She decided that when he arrived her only possible behavior would be to pretend not to have noticed his lateness.

She dropped some of the ice cubes into one of the glasses, poured in some Scotch, stirred it, and went into the living room with it. The fire was burning triumphantly; the whole room danced in flamelight. She sat on the couch and downed her drink, a little too quickly for a young woman completely at her ease, which was what she was trying to be. When she had finished the last drop, she forced herself to sit without moving for ten minutes by her watch. Then she went out and made herself another drink, a little stronger. This one she drank walking thoughtfully around and around the center of the room. She was fighting against an absurd impulse to put on her coat and go into the street to look for him. "Old woman," she said to herself. Old people always had that reaction—they always expected tragedies. As she came to the end of her second drink she succeeded in convincing herself that the mathematical probabilities of Van's having met with his first serious accident on this particular evening were extremely slight. This moral certitude engendered a feeling of light-heartedness, which expressed itself in the desire for a third drink. She had only just begun this one when an even sharper anguish seized her. If it was not likely that he had had an accident, it was utterly unthinkable that he should have let some unforeseen work detain him until this late; he would have telephoned her anyway. It was even more inconceivable that their rendezvous should have slipped his mind. The final, remaining possibility therefore was that he had deliberately avoided it, which of course was absurd. She tossed another log onto the fire. Again she went to the window and peered between the curtains down into the empty street. The wind had become a gale. She felt each blast against her face through the closed window. Listening for sounds of traffic, she heard none; even the boats seemed to have been silenced. Only the rushing of the wind was left—that and the occasional faint hissing of the fine snow against the glass. She burst into tears; she did not know whether it was out of self-pity, anger and humiliation, loneliness, or just plain nervousness.

As she stood there in the window with the tears covering her sight, it occurred to her how ironic it would be if he should come and find her like this: slightly drunk, sobbing, with her make-up surely in a state of complete ruin. A sound behind her ended her weeping instantly. She let go of the curtain and turned to face the room: through her tears she could see nothing but quivering webs of light. She squeezed her lids tightly together: one of the logs had broken in two. The smaller half lay on the hearth smoking. She went over and kicked it into the fire. Then she tiptoed into the hall to the entrance door and slipped the chain on. As soon as she had done that she was terrified. It was nothing less than a symbol of fear—she realized it as she looked at the brass links stretching across from jamb to door. But once having put it up, she did not have the courage to take it down again.

Still on tiptoe, she returned to the living room and lay on the divan, burying her face in the cushions. She was not crying any longer—she felt too empty and frightened to do anything but lie quite still. But after a while she sat up and looked slowly about the room. The candles had burned down half way; she looked at them, at the ivy trailing down from the little pots on the wall, at the white goatskin by her feet, at the striped curtains. They were all hers. "Van, Van," she said under her breath. Unsteadily she rose and made her way to the bathroom. The glaring light hurt her eyes. Hanging on the inside of the door was Van's old flannel bathrobe. It was too big for her, but she got into it and rolled the sleeves back, turning up the collar and pulling the belt tightly about her waist. In the living room she lay down again on the divan among the cushions. From time to time she rubbed her cheek against the wool of the sleeve under her face. She stared into the fire.

Van was in the room. It was daylight out—a strange gray dawn. She sat up, feeling light-headed. "Van," she said. He was moving slowly across the floor toward the window. And the curtains had been drawn back. There was the rectangle of dim white sky, with Van going toward it. She called to him again. If he heard her he paid no attention. She sat back, watching. Now and then he shook his head slowly from side to side; the gesture made her feel like crying again, but not for herself this time. It was quite natural that he should be there, shuffling slowly across the room in the pale early light, shaking his head from one side to the other. Suddenly she said to herself that he was looking for something, that he might find it, and she began to shiver sitting up there in the cold. "He *has* found it," she thought, "but he's pretending he hasn't because he knows I'm watching him." And even as the idea formed itself in her mind she saw him reach up and swing himself through the window. She screamed, jumped down from the couch and ran across the room. When she got to the window there was nothing to see but the vast gray panorama of a city at dawn, spitefully clear in every tiniest detail. She stood there looking out, seeing for miles up and down the empty streets. It was a foreign city.

The sputtering of a candle as it went out roused her. Several of them had already burned out. The shadows on the ceiling were wavering like bats. The room was cold and the curtains across the closed window moved inward with the force of the wind. She lay perfectly still. In the fireplace she heard the powdery, faintly metallic sound of a cooling ember as it fell. For a long time she remained unmoving. Then she sprang up, turned on all the lights, went into the bedroom and stood for a moment looking at the telephone. The sight of it calmed her a little. She took off the bathrobe and opened the closet door to hang it up. She knew his luggage by heart;

his small overnight valise was missing. Slowly her mouth opened. She did not think to put her hand over it.

She slipped on her coat and unhooked the chain on the entrance door. The hall outside was full of scurrying draughts. Down the six flights she ran, one after the other, until she was at the front door. The snow had drifted high, completely covering the steps. She went out. It was bitter cold in the wind, but only a stray flake fell now and then. She stood there. The street did not tell her what to do. She began to wade through the deep snow, eastward. A taxi, moving cautiously down Second Avenue, its chains clanking rhythmically, met her at the corner. She hailed it, got in.

"Take me to the river," she said, pointing.

"What street?"

"Any street that goes down all the way."

Almost immediately they were there. She got out, paid the driver, walked slowly to the end of the pavement, and stood watching. The dawn was really breaking now, but it was very different from the one she had seen through the window. The wind took her breath away, the water out there was alive. Against the winter sky across the river there were factories. The lights of a small craft moved further down in midstream. She clenched her fists. A terrible anguish had taken possession of her. She was trembling, but she did not feel the cold. Abruptly she turned around. The driver was standing in the street blowing into his cupped hands. And he was looking at her intently.

"You're not waiting for me, are you?" she said. (Was that her voice?)

"Yes, *Ma'am*," he said with force.

"I didn't tell you to." (With her whole life falling to pieces before her, how was it that her voice rang with such asperity, such hard self-assurance?)

"That's right." He put his gloves back on. "Take your time," he said.

She turned her back on him and watched the changing water. Suddenly she felt ridiculous. She went over to the cab, got in, and gave her home address.

The doorman was asleep when she rang, and even after she was inside she had to wait nearly five minutes for the elevator boy to bring the car up from the basement. She tiptoed through the apartment to her room, shutting the door behind her. When she had undressed she opened the big window without looking out, and got into bed. The cold wind blew through the room.

A Thousand Days for Mokhtar

MOKHTAR lived in a room not far from his shop, over-looking the sea. There was a tiny window in the wall above his sleeping-mattress, through which, if he stood on tiptoe, he could see the waves pounding against the rocks of the breakwater far below. The sound came up, too, especially on nights when the Casbah was wrapped in rain and its narrow streets served only for the passage of unexpected gusts of wind. On these nights the sound of the waves was all around, even though he kept the window shut. Throughout the year there were many such nights, and it was precisely at such times that he did not feel like going home to be alone in his little room. He had been by himself ten years now, ever since his wife had died; his solitude never weighed on him when the weather was clear and the stars shone in the sky. But a rainy night put him in mind of the happy hours of his life, when in just such nocturnal wind and storm he and his great-eyed bride would pull the heavy blinds shut and live quietly in each other's company until dawn. These things he could not think about; he would go to the Café Ghazel and play dominoes hour after hour with anyone who came along, rather than return to his room.

Little by little the other men who sat regularly in the café had come to count on Mokhtar's appearance. "It's beginning to rain: Si Mokhtar will be along soon. Save him the mat next to you." And he never disappointed them. He was pleasant and quiet; the latter quality made him a welcome addition to a game, since the café's habitués considered each other far too talkative.

Sitting in the Café Ghazel tonight Mokhtar was unaccountably uneasy. He was disturbed by the bonelike sound of the dominoes as they were shuffled on the tables. The metallic scraping of the old phonograph in the inner room bothered him, and he looked up with an unreasoning annoyance at each new arrival who came in through the door, heralded by blasts of wet wind. Often he glanced out the window beside him at the vast blackness of the sea lying below at the

174

foot of the city. On the other side of the glass, just at the edge of the cliff, a few tall stalks of bamboo caught the light from inside, stood out white against the blackness beyond, bending painfully before the gale.

"They'll break," murmured Mokhtar.

"What?" said Mohammed Slaoui.

Mokhtar laughed, but said nothing. As the evening continued, his discomfort increased. In the inner room they had stopped the phonograph and were singing a strident song. Some of the men around him joined in the noise. He could no longer hear the wind. As that round of dominoes came to an end, he rose precipitately and said: "Good night," not caring how strange his sudden departure might seem to the others.

Outside in the street it was scarcely raining at all, but the wind raged upward from the shore below, bringing with it the bloodlike smell of the sea; the crashing waves seemed very near, almost at his feet. He looked down as he walked along. At each mound of garbage there were cats; they ran across in front of him constantly from one pile to another. As Mokhtar reached his door and pulled out his key, he had the feeling that he was about to perform an irrevocable act, that stepping inside would be a gesture of finality.

"What is happening?" he asked himself. "Am I going to die?" He would not be afraid of that; still, he would like to know it a few moments in advance, if possible. He flexed his arms and legs before opening the door: there was no pain anywhere, everything appeared to be in good condition. "It's my head," he decided. But his head felt clear, his thoughts moved forward in orderly fashion. Nevertheless, these discoveries did not reassure him; he knew something was wrong. He bolted the door behind him and began to mount the stairs in the dark. More clearly than anything else at the moment he sensed that this conviction of having entered into a new region of his life was only in the nature of a warning. "Don't go on," he was being told. "Doing what?" he asked himself as he undressed. He had no secrets, no involvements, no plans for the future, no responsibilities. He merely lived. He could not heed the warning because he could not understand it. And yet there was no doubt that it was there in his room, and it made itself most strongly felt when he lay down.

The wind shook the blinds. The rain had begun to fall again; it showered violently on the panes of glass over the corridor, and rattled down the drainpipe from the roof. And the unappeased roaring of the waves went on, down at the base of the ramparts. He considered the sadness, the coldness of the damp blanket; he touched the straw-covered wall with his finger. In the black night he groaned: "Al-lah!" and fell asleep.

But even in sleep he went on worrying; his dreams were a chaotic, relentless continuation of his waking state. The same accent of implicit warning was present in the sequences of streets and shops which unrolled before his eyes. He was at the entrance to the public market. A great many people were inside, where they had gone to get out of the rain. Although it was mid-morning, the day was so dark that all the stalls were blazing with electric lights. "If only she could have seen this," he said to himself, thinking of how much pleasure it would have given his wife. "Poor girl, in her day it was always dark here." And Mokhtar wondered if really he had the right to go on living and watching the world change, without her. Each month the world had changed a little more, had gone a little further away from what it had been when she had known it.

"Also, since she is not here to eat it, what am I doing buying meat?" He was standing before the stall of his friend Abdallah ben Bouchta, looking at the cuts that were displayed on the slab of white marble in front of him. And all at once he was embroiled in a quarrel with Bouchta. He felt himself seizing the old man by the throat; he felt his fingers pressing with increasing force: he was choking Bouchta and he was glad to be doing it. The violence of the act was a fulfillment and a relief. Bouchta's face grew black, he fell, and his glazed eyes stared like the eyes in a sheep's head served on a platter for the feast of Aïd el Kébir.

Mokhtar awoke, horrified. The wind was still blowing, carrying with it, above the town, wisps of the voice of the muezzin who at that moment was calling from the Jaamâa es Seghira. But the warnings had ceased, and this was comforting enough to make more sleep possible.

The morning was gray and cheerless. Mokhtar rose at the usual hour, made his daily visit to the great mosque for a few moments of prayer and a thorough wash, and proceeded through the rain to his shop. There were few people in the streets. The memory of his dream weighed upon him, saddening him even more than the prospect of a day of infrequent sales. As the morning progressed he thought often of his old friend; he was consumed with the desire to pass by the market, just to assure himself that Bouchta was there as always. There was no reason why he should not be, but once Mokhtar had seen him with his own eyes he would be content.

A little before noon he boarded up the front of his shop and set out for the market. When his eyes became accustomed to the dim inner light of the building, the first person he saw was Bouchta standing behind the counter in his stall, chopping and slicing the meat the same as any other day. Feeling immensely relieved, Mokhtar wandered over to the counter and spoke to him. Perhaps the note of excessive cordiality in his voice surprised Bouchta, for he glanced up with a startled expression in his face, and seeing Mokhtar, said shortly: "*Sbalkheir.*" Then he resumed hacking at a piece of meat for a customer. His rather unfriendly look was lost on Mokhtar, who was so pleased to see him there that he was momentarily unable to perceive anything but that one fact. However, when Bouchta, on completing the sale, turned to him and said abruptly: "I'm busy this morning," Mokhtar stared at him, and again felt his fear stir within him.

"Yes, Sidi?" he said pleasantly.

Bouchta glared. "Twenty-two douro would be a more welcome offering than your foolish smile," he said.

Mokhtar looked confused. "Twenty-two douro, Sidi?"

"Yes. The twenty-two douro you never paid me for the lamb's head at last Aïd el Kébir."

Mokhtar felt the blood leap upward in him like a fire. "I paid you for that the following month."

"*Abaden!* Never!" cried Bouchta excitedly. "I have eyes and a head too! I remember what happens! You can't take advantage of me the way you did of poor old Tahiri. I'm not that old yet!" And he began to call out unpleasant epithets, brandishing his cleaver.

People had stopped in their tracks and were following the conversation with interest. As Mokhtar's anger mounted, he

suddenly heard, among the names that Bouchta was calling
him, one which offended him more than the rest. He reached
across the counter and seized Bouchta's *djellaba* in his two
hands, pulling on the heavy woolen fabric until it seemed that
it would surely be ripped off the old man's back.

"Let go of me!" shouted Bouchta. The people were crowding in to see whatever violence might result. "Let go of me!"
he kept screaming, his face growing steadily redder.

At this point the scene was so much like his dream that
Mokhtar, even while he was enjoying his own anger and the
sight of Bouchta as he became the victim of such a senseless
rage, was suddenly very much frightened. He let go of the
djellaba with one hand, and turning to the onlookers said
loudly: "Last night I dreamed that I came here and killed this
man, who is my friend. I do not want to kill him. I am not
going to kill him. Look carefully. I am not hurting him."

Bouchta's fury was reaching grotesque proportions. With
one hand he was trying to pry Mokhtar's fingers from his garment, and with the other, which held the cleaver, he was making crazy gyrations in the air. All the while he jumped quickly
up and down, crying: "Let go! Let go! *Khlass!*"

"At any moment he is going to hit me with the cleaver,"
thought Mokhtar, and so he seized the wrist that held it,
pulling Bouchta against the counter. For a moment they
struggled and panted, while the slabs of meat slid about under their arms and fell heavily onto the wet floor. Bouchta was
strong, but he was old. Suddenly he relaxed his grasp on
the cleaver and Mokhtar felt his muscles cease to push. The
crowd murmured. Mokhtar let go of both the wrist and the
djellaba, and looked up. Bouchta's face was an impossible
color, like the sides of meat that hung behind him. His mouth
opened and his head slowly tilted upward as if he were looking at the ceiling of the market. Then, as if someone had
pushed him from behind, he fell forward onto the marble
counter and lay still, his nose in a shallow puddle of pinkish
water. Mokhtar knew he was dead, and he was a little triumphant as he shouted to everyone: "I dreamed it! I
dreamed it! I told you! Did I kill him? Did I touch him? You
saw!" The crowd agreed, nodding.

"Get the police!" cried Mokhtar. "I want everyone to be

my witness." A few people moved away quietly, not wishing to be involved. But most of them stayed, quite ready to give the authorities their version of the strange phenomenon.

In court the Qadi proved to be unsympathetic. Mokhtar was bewildered by his lack of friendliness. The witnesses had told the story exactly as it had happened; obviously they all were convinced of Mokhtar's innocence.

"I have heard from the witnesses what happened in the market," said the Qadi impatiently, "and from those same witnesses I know you are an evil man. It is impossible for the mind of an upright man to bring forth an evil dream. Bouchta died as a result of your dream." And as Mokhtar attempted to interrupt: "I know what you are going to say, but you are a fool, Mokhtar. You blame the wind, the night, your long solitude. Good. For a thousand days in our prison here you will not hear the wind, you will not know whether it is night or day, and you will never lack the companionship of your fellow-prisoners."

The Qadi's sentence shocked the inhabitants of the town, who found it of an unprecedented severity. But Mokhtar, once he had been locked up, was persuaded of its wisdom. For one thing, he was not unhappy to be in prison, where each night, when he had begun to dream that he was back in his lonely room, he could awaken to hear on all sides of him the comforting snores of the other prisoners. His mind no longer dwelled upon the earlier happy hours of his life, because the present hours were happy ones as well. And then, the very first day there, he had suddenly remembered with perfect clarity that, although he had intended to do so, he never had paid Bouchta the twenty-two douro for the lamb's head, after all.

Tea on the Mountain

T HE MAIL that morning had brought her a large advance from her publishers. At least, it looked large to her there in the International Zone where life was cheap. She had opened the letter at a table of the sidewalk café opposite the Spanish post office. The emotion she felt at seeing the figures on the check had made her unexpectedly generous to the beggars that constantly filed past. Then the excitement had worn off, and she felt momentarily depressed. The streets and the sky seemed brighter and stronger than she. She had of necessity made very few friends in the town, and although she worked steadily every day at her novel, she had to admit that sometimes she was lonely. Driss came by, wearing a spotless mauve *djellaba* over his shoulders and a new fez on his head.

"*Bon jour, mademoiselle,*" he said, making an exaggerated bow. He had been paying her assiduous attention for several months, but so far she had been successful in putting him off without losing his friendship; he made a good escort in the evenings. This morning she greeted him warmly, let him pay her check, and moved off up the street with him, conscious of the comment her action had caused among the other Arabs sitting in the café.

They turned into the rue du Télégraphe Anglais, and walked slowly down the hill. She decided she was trying to work up an appetite for lunch; in the noonday heat it was often difficult to be hungry. Driss had been Europeanized to the point of insisting on apéritifs before his meals; however, instead of having two Dubonnets, for instance, he would take a Gentiane, a Byrrh, a Pernod and an Amer Picon. Then he usually went to sleep and put off eating until later. They stopped at the café facing the Marshan Road, and sat down next to a table occupied by several students from the Lycée Français, who were drinking *limonades* and glancing over their notebooks. Driss wheeled around suddenly and began a casual conversation. Soon they both moved over to the students' table.

She was presented to each student in turn; they solemnly

acknowledged her *"Enchantée,"* but remained seated while doing so. Only one, named Mjid, rose from his chair and quickly sat down again, looking worried. He was the one she immediately wanted to get to know, perhaps because he was more serious and soft-eyed, yet at the same time seemed more eager and violent than any of the others. He spoke his stilted theatre-French swiftly, with less accent than his schoolmates, and he punctuated his sentences with precise, tender smiles instead of the correct or expected inflections. Beside him sat Ghazi, plump and Negroid.

She saw right away that Mjid and Ghazi were close friends. They replied to her questions and flattery as one man, Ghazi preferring, however, to leave the important phrases to Mjid. He had an impediment in his speech, and he appeared to think more slowly. Within a few minutes she had learned that they had been going to school together for twelve years, and had always been in the same form. This seemed strange to her, inasmuch as Ghazi's lack of precocity became more and more noticeable as she watched him. Mjid noticed the surprise in her face, and he added:

"Ghazi is very intelligent, you know. His father is the high judge of the native court of the International Zone. You will go to his home one day and see for yourself."

"Oh, but of course I believe you," she cried, understanding now why Ghazi had experienced no difficulty in life so far, in spite of his obvious slow-wittedness.

"I have a very beautiful house indeed," added Ghazi. "Would you like to come and live in it? You are always welcome. That's the way we Tanjaoui are."

"Thank you. Perhaps some day I shall. At any rate, I thank you a thousand times. You are too kind."

"And my father," interposed Mjid suavely but firmly, "the poor man, he is dead. Now it's my brother who commands."

"But, alas, Mjid, your brother is tubercular," sighed Ghazi.

Mjid was scandalized. He began a vehement conversation with Ghazi in Arabic, in the course of which he upset his empty *limonade* bottle. It rolled onto the sidewalk and into the gutter, where an urchin tried to make off with it, but was stopped by the waiter. He brought the bottle to the table, carefully wiped it with his apron, and set it down.

"Dirty Jew dog!" screamed the little boy from the middle of the street.

Mjid heard this epithet even in the middle of his tirade. Turning in his chair, he called to the child: "Go home. You'll be beaten this evening."

"Is it your brother?" she asked with interest.

Since Mjid did not answer her, but seemed not even to have heard her, she looked at the urchin again and saw his ragged clothing. She was apologetic.

"Oh, I'm sorry," she began. "I hadn't looked at him. I see now . . ."

Mjid said, without looking at her: "You would not need to look at that child to know he was not of my family. You heard him speak. . . ."

"A neighbor's child. A poor little thing," interrupted Ghazi.

Mjid seemed lost in wonder for a moment. Then he turned and explained slowly to her: "One word we can't hear is tuberculosis. Any other word, syphillis, leprosy, even pneumonia, we can listen to, but not that word. And Ghazi knows that. He wants you to think we have Paris morals here. There I know everyone says that word everywhere, on the boulevards, in the cafés, in Montparnasse, in the Dôme—" he grew excited as he listed these points of interest— "in the Moulin Rouge, in Sacré Coeur, in the Louvre. Some day I shall go myself. My brother has been. That's where he got sick."

During this time Driss, whose feeling of ownership of the American lady was so complete that he was not worried by any conversation she might have with what he considered schoolboys, was talking haughtily to the other students. They were all pimply and bespectacled. He was telling them about the football games he had seen in Malaga. They had never been across to Spain, and they listened, gravely sipped their *limonade*, and spat on the floor like Spaniards.

"Since I can't invite you to my home, because we have sickness there, I want you to make a picnic with me tomorrow," announced Mjid. Ghazi made some inaudible objection which his friend silenced with a glance, whereupon Ghazi decided to beam, and followed the plans with interest.

"We shall hire a carriage, and take some ham to my country

villa," continued Mjid, his eyes shining with excitement. Ghazi started to look about apprehensively at the other men seated on the terrace; then he got up and went inside.

When he returned he objected: "You have no sense, Mjid. You say 'ham' right out loud when you know some friends of my father might be here. It would be very bad for me. Not everyone is free as you are."

Mjid was penitent for an instant. He stretched out his leg, pulling aside his silk *gandoura*. "Do you like my garters?" he asked her suddenly.

She was startled. "They're quite good ones," she began.

"Let me see yours," he demanded.

She glanced down at her slacks. She had espadrilles on her feet, and wore no socks. "I'm sorry," she said. "I haven't any."

Mjid looked uncomfortable, and she guessed that it was more for having discovered, in front of the others, a flaw in her apparel, than for having caused her possible embarrassment. He cast a contrite glance at Ghazi, as if to excuse himself for having encouraged a foreign lady who was obviously not of the right sort. She felt that some gesture on her part was called for. Pulling out several hundred francs, which was all the money in her purse, she laid it on the table, and went on searching in her handbag for her mirror. Mjid's eyes softened. He turned with a certain triumph to Ghazi, and permitting himself a slight display of exaltation, patted his friend's cheek three times.

"So it's set!" he exclaimed. "Tomorrow at noon we meet here at the Café du Télégraphe Anglais. I shall have hired a carriage at eleven-thirty at the market. You, dear mademoiselle," turning to her, "will have gone at ten-thirty to the English grocery and bought the food. Be sure to get Jambon Olida, because it's the best."

"The best ham," murmured Ghazi, looking up and down the street a bit uneasily.

"And buy one bottle of wine."

"Mjid, you know this can get back to my father," Ghazi began.

Mjid had had enough interference. He turned to her. "If you like, mademoiselle, we can go alone."

She glanced at Ghazi; his cowlike eyes had veiled with actual tears.

Mjid continued. "It'll be very beautiful up there on the mountain with just us two. We'll take a walk along the top of the mountain to the rose gardens. There's a breeze from the sea all afternoon. At dusk we'll be back at the farm. We'll have tea and rest." He stopped at this point, which he considered crucial.

Ghazi was pretending to read his social correspondence textbook, with his *chechia* tilted over his eyebrows so as to hide his hopelessly troubled face. Mjid smiled tenderly.

"We'll go all three," he said softly.

Ghazi simply said: "Mjid is bad."

Driss was now roaring drunk. The other students were impressed and awed. Some of the bearded men in the café looked over at the table with open disapproval in their faces. She saw that they regarded her as a symbol of corruption. Consulting her fancy little enamel watch, which everyone at the table had to examine and study closely before she could put it back into its case, she announced that she was hungry.

"Will you eat with us?" Ghazi inquired anxiously. It was clear he had read that an invitation should be extended on such occasions; it was equally clear that he was in terror lest she accept.

She declined and rose. The glare of the street and the commotion of the passers-by had tired her. She took her leave of all the students while Driss was inside the café, and went down to the restaurant on the beach where she generally had lunch.

There while she ate, looking out at the water, she thought: "That was amusing, but it was just enough," and she decided not to go on the picnic.

She did not even wait until the next day to stock up with provisions at the English grocery. She bought three bottles of ordinary red wine, two cans of Jambon Olida, several kinds of Huntley and Palmer's biscuits, a bottle of stuffed olives and five hundred grams of chocolates full of liqueurs. The English lady made a splendid parcel for her.

At noon next day she was drinking an *orgeat* at the Café du Télégraphe Anglais. A carriage drove up, drawn by two horses loaded down with sleighbells. Behind the driver, shielded from the sun by the beige canopy of the victoria, sat Ghazi and Mjid, looking serious and pleasant. They got down to help her in. As they drove off up the hill, Mjid inspected the parcel approvingly and whispered: "The wine?"

"All inside," she said.

The locusts made a great noise from the dusty cliffs beside the road as they came to the edge of town. "Our nightingales," smiled Mjid. "Here is a ring for you. Let me see your hand."

She was startled, held out her left hand.

"No, no! The right!" he cried. The ring was of massive silver; it fitted her index finger. She was immensely pleased.

"But you are too nice. What can I give you?" She tried to look pained and helpless.

"The pleasure of having a true European friend," said Mjid gravely.

"But I'm American," she objected.

"All the better."

Ghazi was looking silently toward the distant Riffian mountains. Prophetically he raised his arm with its silk sleeve blowing in the hot wind, and pointed across the cracked mud fields.

"Down that way," he said softly, "there is a village where all the people are mad. I rode there once with one of my father's assistants. It's the water they drink."

The carriage lurched. They were climbing. Below them the sea began to spread out, a poster blue. The tops of the mountains across the water in Spain rose above the haze. Mjid started to sing. Ghazi covered his ears with his fat dimpled hands.

The summer villa was inhabited by a family with a large number of children. After dismissing the carriage driver and instructing him not to return, since he wanted to walk back down, Mjid took his guests on a tour of inspection of the grounds. There were a good many wells; Ghazi had certainly seen these countless times before, but he stopped as if in amazement at each well as they inspected it, and whispered: "Think of it!"

On a rocky elevation above the farm stood a great olive

tree. There they spread the food, and ate slowly. The Berber woman in charge of the farm had given them several loaves of native bread, and olives and oranges. Ghazi wanted Mjid to decline this food.

"A real European picnic is what we should have."

But she insisted they take the oranges.

The opening of the ham was observed in religious silence. It was no time before both cans were consumed. Then they attacked the wine.

"If my father could see us," said Ghazi, draining a tin cup of it. "Ham and wine!"

Mjid drank a cup, making a grimace of distaste. He lay back, his arms folded behind his head. "Now that I've finished, I can tell you that I don't like wine, and everyone knows that ham is filthy. But I hate our severe conventions."

She suspected that he had rehearsed the little speech.

Ghazi was continuing to drink the wine. He finished a bottle all by himself, and excusing himself to his companions, took off his *gandoura*. Soon he was asleep.

"You see?" whispered Mjid. He took her hand and pulled her to her feet. "Now we can go to the rose garden." He led her along the ledge, and down a path away from the villa. It was very narrow; thorny bushes scraped their arms as they squeezed through.

"In America we call walking like this going Indian fashion," she remarked.

"Ah, yes?" said Mjid. "I'm going to tell you about Ghazi. One of his father's women was a Senegalese slave, poor thing. She made Ghazi and six other brothers for her husband, and they all look like Negroes."

"Don't you consider Negores as good as you?" she asked.

"It's not a question of being as good, but of being as beautiful," he answered firmly.

They had come out into a clearing on the hillside. He stopped and looked closely at her. He pulled his shirt off over his head. His body was white.

"My brother has blond hair," he said with pride. Then confusedly he put the shirt back on and laid his arm about her shoulder. "You are beautiful because you have blue eyes. But even some of us have blue eyes. In any case, you are *magnificent!*" He started ahead again, singing a song in Spanish.

> "*Es pa' mi la màs bonita,*
> *La mujer que yo màs quiero . . .*"

They came to a cactus fence, with a small gate of twisted barbed wire. A yellow puppy rushed up to the gate and barked delightedly.

"Don't be afraid," said Mjid, although she had given no sign of fear. "You are my sister. He never bites the family." Continuing down a dusty path between stunted palms which were quite dried-up and yellow, they came presently to a primitive bower made of bamboo stalks. In the center was a tiny bench beside a wall, and around the edges several dessicated rose plants grew out of the parched earth. From these he picked two bright red roses, placing one in her hair and the other under his *chechia*, so that it fell like a lock of hair over his forehead. The thick growth of thorny vines climbing over the trellises cast a shadow on the bench. They sat awhile in silence in the shade.

Mjid seemed lost in thought. Finally he took her hand. "I'm thinking," he said in a whisper. "When one is far away from the town, in one's own garden, far from everyone, sitting where it is quiet, one always thinks. Or one plays music," he added.

Suddenly she was conscious of the silence of the afternoon. Far in the distance she heard the forlorn crow of a cock. It made her feel that the sun would soon set, that all creation was on the brink of a great and final sunset. She abandoned herself to sadness, which crept over her like a chill.

Mjid jumped up. "If Ghazi wakes!" he cried. He pulled her arm impatiently. "Come, we'll take a walk!" They hurried down the path, through the gate, and across a bare stony plateau toward the edge of the mountain.

"There's a little valley nearby where the brother of the caretaker lives. We can go there and get some water."

"Way down there?" she said, although she was encouraged by the possibility of escaping from Ghazi for the afternoon. Her mood of sadness had not left her. They were running downhill, leaping from one rock to the next. Her rose fell off and she had to hold it in her hand.

The caretaker's brother was cross-eyed. He gave them some foul-smelling water in an earthen jug.

"Is it from the well?" she inquired under her breath to Mjid.

His face darkened with displeasure. "When you're offered something to drink, even if it's poison, you should drink it and thank the man who offers it."

"Ah," she said. "So it is poison. I thought so."

Mjid seized the jug from the ground between them, and taking it to the edge of the cliff, flung it down with elegant anger. The cross-eyed man protested, and then he laughed. Mjid did not look at him, but walked into the house and began a conversation with some of the Berber women inside, leaving her to face the peasant alone and stammer her dozen words of Arabic with him. The afternoon sun was hot, and the idea of some water to drink had completely filled her mind. She sat down perversely with her back to the view and played with pebbles, feeling utterly useless and absurd. The cross-eyed man continued to laugh at intervals, as if it provided an acceptable substitute for conversation.

When Mjid finally came out, all his ill-humor had vanished. He put out his hand to help her up, and said: "Come, we'll climb back up and have tea at the farm. I have my own room there. I decorated it myself. You'll look at it and tell me if you have as pleasant a room in your house in America for drinking tea." They set off, up the mountain.

The woman at the villa was obsequious. She fanned the charcoal fire and fetched water from the well. The children were playing a mysterious, quiet game at a far end of the enclosure. Mjid led her into the house, through several dim rooms, and finally into one that seemed the last in the series. It was cooler, and a bit darker than the others.

"You'll see," said Mjid, clapping his hands twice. Nothing happened. He called peevishly. Presently the woman entered. She smoothed the mattresses on the floor, and opened the blinds of the one small window, which gave onto the sea. Then she lit several candles which she stuck onto the tile floor, and went out.

His guest stepped to the window. "Can you ever hear the sea here?"

"Certainly not. It's about six kilometers away."

"But it looks as though you could drop a stone into it," she objected, hearing the false inflection of her voice; she was not interested in the conversation, she had the feeling that everything had somehow gone wrong.

"What am I doing here? I have no business here. I said I wouldn't come." The idea of such a picnic had so completely coincided with some unconscious desire she had harbored for many years. To be free, out-of-doors, with some young man she did not know—*could* not know—that was probably the important part of the dream. For if she could not know him, he could not know her. She swung the little blind shut and hooked it. A second later she opened it again and looked out at the vast expanse of water growing dim in the twilight.

Mjid was watching her. "You are crazy," he said at last despairingly. "You find yourself here in this beautiful room. You are my guest. You should be happy. Ghazi has already left to go to town. A friend came by with a horse and he got a ride in. You could lie down, sing, drink tea, you could be happy with me . . ." He stopped, and she saw that he was deeply upset.

"What's the matter? What's the matter?" she said very quickly.

He sighed dramatically; perhaps it was a genuine sigh. She thought: "There is nothing wrong. It should have been a man, not a boy, that's all." It did not occur to her to ask herself: "But would I have come if it had been a man?" She looked at him tenderly, and decided that his face was probably the most intense and beautiful she had ever seen. She murmured a word without quite knowing what it was.

"What?" he said.

She repeated it: "Incredible."

He smiled inscrutably.

They were interrupted by the sound of the woman's bare feet slapping the floor. She had a tremendous tray bearing the teapot and its accessories.

While he made the tea, Mjid kept glancing at her as if to

assure himself that she was still there. She sat perfectly still on one of the mattresses, waiting.

"You know," he said slowly, "If I could earn money I'd go away tomorrow to wherever I could earn it. I finish school this year anyway, and my brother hasn't the money to send me to a Medersa at Fez. But even if he had it, I wouldn't go. I always stay away from school. Only my brother gets very angry."

"What do you do instead? Go bathing?"

He laughed scornfully, sampled the tea, poured it back into the pot, and sat up on his haunches. "In another minute it will be ready. Bathing? Ah, my friend, it has to be something important for me to risk my brother's anger. I make love those days, all day long!"

"Really? You mean all day?" She was thoughtful.

"All day and most of the night. Oh, I can tell you it's marvelous, magnificent. I have a little room," he crawled over to her and put his hand on her knee, looking up into her face with an eagerness born of faith. "A room my family knows nothing about, in the Casbah. And my little friend is twelve. She is like the sun, soft, beautiful, lovely. Here, take your tea." He sipped from his glass noisily, smacking his lips.

"All day long," she reflected aloud, settling back against the cushions.

"Oh, yes. But I'll tell you a secret. You have to eat as much as you can. But that's not so hard. You're that much hungrier."

"Yes, of course," she said. A little gust of wind blew along the floor and the candles flickered.

"How good it is to have tea and then lie down to rest!" he exclaimed, pouring her more tea and stretching out beside her on the mattress. She made a move as if to spring up, then lay still.

He went on. "It's curious that I never met you last year."

"I wasn't in town very much. Only evenings. And then I was at the beach. I lived on the mountain."

He sat up. "On this mountain here? And I never saw you! Oh, what bad luck!"

She described the house, and since he insisted, told him the rent she had paid. He was ferociously indignant. "For that miserable house that hasn't even a good well? You had to send your Mohammed down the road for water! I know all about that house. My poor friend, you were robbed! If I ever see that dirty bandit I'll smash his face. I'll demand the money you paid him, and we'll make a trip together." He paused. "I mean, I'll give it to you of course, and you can decide what you want to do with it."

As he finished speaking he held up her handbag, opened it, and took out her fountain pen. "It's a beautiful one," he murmured. "Do you have many?"

"It's the only one."

"Magnificent!" He tossed it back in and laid the bag on the floor.

Settling against the pillows he ruminated. "Perhaps some day I shall go to America, and then you can invite me to your house for tea. Each year we'll come back to Morocco and see our friends and bring back cinema stars and presents from New York."

What he was saying seemed so ridiculous to her that she did not bother to answer. She wanted to ask him about the twelve-year-old girl, but she could find no excuse for introducing the subject again.

"You're not happy?" He squeezed her arm.

She raised herself to listen. With the passing of the day the countryside had attained complete silence. From the distance she could hear a faint but clear voice singing. She looked at Mjid.

"The *muezzin*? You can hear it from here?"

"Of course. It's not so far to the Marshan. What good is a country house where you can't hear the *muezzin*? You might as well live in the Sahara."

"Sh. I want to listen."

"It's a good voice, isn't it? They have the strongest voices in the world."

"It always makes me sad."

"Because you're not of the faith."

She reflected a minute and said: "I think that's true." She was about to add: "But your faith says women have no souls." Instead she rose from the mattress and smoothed her hair.

The *muezzin* had ceased. She felt quite chilled. "This is over," she said to herself. They stumbled down the dark road into town, saying very little on the way.

He took her to her small hotel. The cable she had vaguely expected for weeks was there. They climbed the stairs to her room, the concierge looking suspiciously after them. Once in the room, she opened the envelope. Mjid had thrown himself onto the bed.

"I'm leaving for Paris tomorrow."

His face darkened, and he shut his eyes for an instant. "You must go away? All right. Let me give you my address." He pulled out his wallet, searched for a piece of paper, and finding none, took a calling card someone had given him, and carefully wrote.

"Fuente Nueva," he said slowly as he formed the letters. "It's my little room. I'll look every day to see if there's a letter."

She had a swift vision of him, reading a letter in a window flooded with sunshine, above the city's terraced roofs, and behind him, in the darkness of the room, with a face wise beyond its years, a complacent child waiting.

He gave her the card. Underneath the address he had written the word "Incredible," enclosed in quotation marks and underlined twice. She glanced quickly to see his face, but it betrayed nothing.

Below them the town was blue, the bay almost black.

"The lighthouse," said Mjid.

"It's flashing," she observed.

He turned and walked to the door. "Good-bye," he said. "You will come back." He left the door open and went down the stairs. She stood perfectly still and finally moved her head up and down a few times, as if thoughtfully answering a question. Through the open window in the hallway she heard his rapid footsteps on the gravel in the garden. They grew fainter.

She looked at the bed; at the edge, ready to fall to the floor, was the white card where she had tossed it. She wanted more than anything to lie down and rest. Instead, she went downstairs into the cramped little salon and sat in the corner looking at old copies of *L'Illustration*. It was almost an hour before dinner would be served.

By the Water

THE MELTING SNOW dripped from the balconies. People hurried through the little street that always smelled of frying fish. Now and then a stork swooped low, dragging his sticklike legs below him. The small gramophones scraped day and night behind the walls of the shop where young Amar worked and lived. There were few spots in the city where the snow was ever cleared away, and this was not one of them. So it gathered all through the winter months, piling up in front of the shop doors.

But now it was late winter; the sun was warmer. Spring was on the way, to confuse the heart and melt the snow. Amar, being alone in the world, decided it was time to visit a neighboring city where his father had once told him some cousins lived.

Early in the morning he went to the bus station. It was still dark, and the empty bus came in while he was drinking hot coffee. The road wound through the mountains all the way.

When he arrived in the other city it was already dark. Here the snow was even deeper in the streets, and it was colder. Because he had not wanted to, Amar had not foreseen this, and it annoyed him to be forced to wrap his burnous closely about him as he left the bus station. It was an unfriendly town; he could tell that immediately. Men walked with their heads bent forward, and if they brushed against a passer-by they did not so much as look up. Excepting the principal street, which had an arc-light every few meters, there seemed to be no other illumination, and the alleys that led off on either side lay in utter blackness; the white-clad figures that turned into them disappeared straightway.

"A bad town," said Amar under his breath. He felt proud to be coming from a better and larger city, but his pleasure was mingled with anxiety about the night to be passed in this inimical place. He abandoned the idea of trying to find his cousins before morning, and set about looking for a fondouk or a bath where he might sleep until daybreak.

Only a short distance ahead the street-lighting system terminated. Beyond, the street appeared to descend sharply and lose itself in darkness. The snow was uniformly deep here, and not cleared away in patches as it had been nearer the bus station. He puckered his lips and blew his breath ahead of him in little clouds of steam. As he passed over into the unlighted district he heard a few languid notes being strummed on an oud. The music came from a doorway on his left. He paused and listened. Someone approached the doorway from the other direction and inquired, apparently of the man with the oud, if it was "too late."

"No," the musician answered, and he played several more notes.

Amar went over to the door.

"Is there still time?" he said.

"Yes."

He stepped inside the door. There was no light, but he could feel warm air blowing upon his face from the corridor to the right. He walked ahead, letting his hand run along the damp wall beside him. Soon he came into a large dimly lit room with a tile floor. Here and there, at various angles, figures lay asleep, wrapped in gray blankets. In a far corner a group of men, partially dressed, sat about a burning brazier, drinking tea and talking in low tones. Amar slowly approached them, taking care not to step on the sleepers.

The air was oppressively warm and moist.

"Where is the bath?" said Amar.

"Down there," answered one of the men in the group, without even looking up. He indicated the dark corner to his left. And, indeed, now that Amar considered it, it seemed to him that a warm current of air came up from that part of the room. He went in the direction of the dark corner, undressed, and leaving his clothes in a neat pile on a piece of straw matting, walked toward the warmth. He was thinking of the misfortune he had encountered in arriving in this town at nightfall, and he wondered if his clothes would be molested during his absence. He wore his money in a leather pouch which hung on a string about his neck. Feeling vaguely of the purse under his chin, he turned around to look once again at his clothing. No one seemed to have noticed him as he undressed. He went on. It would not do to seem too distrustful.

He would be embroiled immediately in a quarrel which could only end badly for him.

A little boy rushed out of the darkness toward him, calling: "Follow me, Sidi, I shall lead you to the bath." He was extremely dirty and ragged, and looked rather more like a midget than a child. Leading the way, he chattered as they went down the slippery, warm steps in the dark. "You will call for Brahim when you want your tea? You're a stranger. You have much money. . . ."

Amar cut him short. "You'll get your coins when you come to wake me in the morning. Not tonight."

"But, Sidi! I'm not allowed in the big room. I stay in the doorway and show gentlemen down to the bath. Then I go back to the doorway. I can't wake you."

"I'll sleep near the doorway. It's warmer there, in any case."

"Lazrag will be angry and terrible things will happen. I'll never get home again, or if I do I might be a bird so my parents will not know me. That's what Lazrag does when he gets angry."

"Lazrag?"

"It is his place here. You'll see him. He never goes out. If he did the sun would burn him in one second, like a straw in the fire. He would fall down in the street burned black the minute he stepped out of the door. He was born down here in the grotto."

Amar was not paying strict attention to the boy's babble. They were descending a wet stone ramp, putting one foot before the other slowly in the dark, and feeling the rough wall carefully as they went. There was the sound of splashing water and voices ahead.

"This is a strange *hammam*," said Amar. "Is there a pool full of water?"

"A pool! You've never heard of Lazrag's grotto? It goes on forever, and it's made of deep warm water."

As the boy spoke, they came out onto a stone balcony a few meters above the beginning of a very large pool, lighted beneath where they stood by two bare electric bulbs, and stretching away through the dimness into utter dark beyond. Parts of the roof hung down, "Like gray icicles," thought

Amar, as he looked about in wonder. But it was very warm down here. A slight pall of steam lay above the surface of the water, rising constantly in wisps toward the rocky ceiling. A man dripping with water ran past them and dove in. Several more were swimming about in the brighter region near the lights, never straying beyond into the gloom. The plunging and shouting echoed violently beneath the low ceiling.

Amar was not a good swimmer. He turned to ask the boy: "Is it deep?" but he had already disappeared back up the ramp. He stepped backward and leaned against the rock wall. There was a low chair to his right, and in the murky light it seemed to him that a small figure was close beside it. He watched the bathers for a few minutes. Those standing at the edge of the water soaped themselves assiduously; those in the water swam to and fro in a short radius below the lights. Suddenly a deep voice spoke close beside him. He looked down as he heard it say: "Who are you?"

The creature's head was large; its body was small and it had no legs or arms. The lower part of the trunk ended in two flipper-like pieces of flesh. From the shoulders grew short pincers. It was a man, and it was looking up at him from the floor where it rested.

"Who are you?" it said again, and its tone was unmistakably hostile.

Amar hesitated. "I came to bathe and sleep," he said at last.

"Who gave you permission?"

"The man at the entrance."

"Get out. I don't know you."

Amar was filled with anger. He looked down with scorn at the little being, and stepped away from it to join the men washing themselves by the water's edge. But more swiftly than he moved, it managed to throw itself along the floor until it was in front of him, when it raised itself again and spoke.

"You think you can bathe when I tell you to get out?" It laughed shortly, a thin sound, but deep in pitch. Then it moved closer and pushed its head against Amar's legs. He drew back his foot and kicked the head, not very hard, but with enough firmness to send the body off balance. The thing rolled over in silence, making efforts with its neck to keep from reaching the edge of the platform. The men all looked up. An expression of fear was on their faces. As the little creature went over the edge it yelled. The splash was like that of a large stone. Two men already in the water swam quickly to the spot. The others started up after Amar, shouting: "He hit Lazrag!"

Bewildered and frightened, Amar turned and ran back to the ramp. In the blackness he stumbled upward. Part of the wall scraped his bare thigh. The voices behind him grew louder and more excited.

He reached the room where he had left his clothing. Nothing had changed. The men still sat by the brazier talking. Quickly he snatched the pile of garments, and struggling into his burnous, he ran to the door that led into the street, the rest of his clothes tucked under his arm. The man in the doorway with the oud looked at him with a startled face and called after him. Amar ran up the street barelegged toward the center of the town. He wanted to be where there were some bright lights. The few people walking in the street paid him no attention. When he got to the bus station it was closed. He went into a small park opposite, where the iron bandstand stood deep in snow. There on a cold stone bench he sat and dressed himself as unostentatiously as possible, using his burnous as a screen. He was shivering, reflecting bitterly upon his poor luck, and wishing he had not left his own town, when a small figure approached him in the half-light.

"Sidi," it said, "come with me. Lazrag is hunting for you."

"Where to?" said Amar, recognizing the urchin from the bath.

"My grandfather's."

The boy began to run, motioning to him to follow. They went through alleys and tunnels, into the most congested part of the town. The boy did not bother to look back, but Amar did. They finally paused before a small door at the side of a narrow passageway. The boy knocked vigorously. From within came a cracked voice calling: "*Chkoun?*"

"*Annah!* Brahim!" cried the boy.

With great deliberation the old man swung the door open and stood looking at Amar.

"Come in," he finally said; and shutting the door behind them he led them through the courtyard filled with goats into an inner room where a feeble light was flickering. He peered sternly into Amar's face.

"He wants to stay here tonight," explained the boy.

"Does he think this is a *fondouk*?"

"He has money," said Brahim hopefully.

"Money!" the old man cried with scorn. "That's what you learn in the *hammam*! How to steal money! How to take money from men's purses! Now you bring them here! What do you want me to do? Kill him and get his purse for you? Is he too clever for you? You can't get it by yourself? Is that it?" The old man's voice had risen to a scream and he gestured in his mounting excitement. He sat down on a cushion with difficulty and was silent a moment.

"Money," he said again, finally. "Let him go to a *fondouk* or a bath. Why aren't you at the *hammam*?" He looked suspiciously at his grandson.

The boy clutched at his friend's sleeve. "Come," he said, pulling him out into the courtyard.

"Take him to the *hammam*!" yelled the old man. "Let him spend his money there!"

Together they went back into the dark streets.

"Lazrag is looking for you," said the boy. "Twenty men will be going through the town to catch you and take you back to him. He is very angry and he will change you into a bird."

"Where are we going now?" asked Amar gruffly. He was cold and very tired, and although he did not really believe the boy's story, he wished he were out of the unfriendly town.

"We must walk as far as we can from here. All night. In the morning we'll be far away in the mountains, and they won't find us. We can go to your city."

Amar did not answer. He was pleased that the boy wanted to stay with him, but he did not think it fitting to say so. They followed one crooked street downhill until all the houses had been left behind and they were in the open country. The path led down a narrow valley presently, and joined the highway at one end of a small bridge. Here the snow was packed down by the passage of vehicles, and they found it much easier to walk along.

When they had been going down the road for perhaps an

hour in the increasing cold, a great truck came rolling by. It stopped just ahead and the driver, an Arab, offered them a ride on top. They climbed up and made a nest of some empty sacks. The boy was very happy to be rushing through the air in the dark night. Mountains and stars whirled by above his head and the truck made a powerful roaring noise as it traveled along the empty highway.

"Lazrag has found us and changed us both into birds," he cried when he could no longer keep his delight to himself. "No one will ever know us again."

Amar grunted and went to sleep. But the boy watched the sky and the trees and the cliffs for a long time before he closed his eyes.

Some time before morning the truck stopped by a spring for water.

In the stillness the boy awoke. A cock crowed in the distance, and then he heard the driver pouring water. The cock crowed again, a sad, thin arc of sound away in the cold murk of the plain. It was not yet dawn. He buried himself deeper in the pile of sacks and rags, and felt the warmth of Amar as he slept.

When daylight came they were in another part of the land. There was no snow. Instead, the almond trees were in flower on the hillsides as they sped past. The road went on unwinding as it dropped lower and lower, until suddenly it came out of the hills upon a spot below which lay a great glittering emptiness. Amar and the boy watched it and said to each other that it must be the sea, shining in the morning light.

The spring wind pushed the foam from the waves along the beach; it rippled Amar's and the boy's garments landward as they walked by the edge of the water. Finally they found a sheltered spot between rocks, and undressed, leaving the clothes on the sand. The boy was afraid to go into the water, and found enough excitement in letting the waves break about his legs, but Amar tried to drag him out further.

"No, no!"

"Come," Amar urged him.

Amar looked down. Approaching him sideways was an enormous crab which had crawled out from a dark place in the rocks. He leapt back in terror, lost his balance, and fell heavily, striking his head against one of the great boulders. The boy stood perfectly still watching the animal make its cautious way toward Amar through the tips of the breaking waves. Amar lay without moving, rivulets of water and sand running down his face. As the crab reached his feet, the boy bounded into the air, and in a voice made hoarse by desperation, screamed: "Lazrag!"

The crab scuttled swiftly behind the rock and disappeared. The boy's face became radiant. He rushed to Amar, lifted his head above a newly breaking wave, and slapped his cheeks excitedly.

"Amar! I made him go away!" he shouted. "I saved you!"

If he did not move, the pain was not too great. So Amar lay still, feeling the warm sunlight, the soft water washing over him, and the cool, sweet wind that came in from the sea. He also felt the boy trembling in his effort to hold his head above the waves, and he heard him saying many times over: "I saved you, Amar."

After a long time he answered: "Yes."

The Delicate Prey

THERE WERE three Filala who sold leather in Tabelbala—
two brothers and the young son of their sister. The two
older merchants were serious, bearded men who liked to engage in complicated theological discussions during the slow
passage of the hot hours in their *hanoute* near the marketplace; the youth naturally occupied himself almost exclusively
with the black-skinned girls in the small *quartier réservé*.
There was one who seemed more desirable than the others, so
that he was a little sorry when the older men announced that
soon they would all leave for Tessalit. But nearly every town
has its *quartier*, and Driss was reasonably certain of being
able to have any lovely resident of any *quartier*, whatever her
present emotional entanglements; thus his chagrin at hearing
of the projected departure was short-lived.

The three Filala waited for the cold weather before starting
out for Tessalit. Because they wanted to get there quickly they
chose the westernmost trail, which is also the one leading
through the most remote regions, contiguous to the lands of
the plundering Reguibat tribes. It was a long time since the
uncouth mountain men had swept down from the *hammada*
upon a caravan; most people were of the opinion that since
the war of the Sarrho they had lost the greater part of their
arms and ammunition, and, more important still, their spirit.
And a tiny group of three men and their camels could scarcely
awaken the envy of the Reguibat, traditionally rich with loot
from all Rio de Oro and Mauretania.

Their friends in Tabelbala, most of them other Filali leather
merchants, walked beside them sadly as far as the edge of the
town; then they bade them farewell, and watched them mount
their camels to ride off slowly toward the bright horizon.

"If you meet any Reguibat, keep them ahead of you!" they
called.

The danger lay principally in the territory they would reach
only three or four days' journey from Tabelbala; after a week
the edge of the land haunted by the Reguibat would be left
entirely behind. The weather was cool save at midday. They

took turns sitting guard at night; when Driss stayed awake he brought out a small flute whose piercing notes made the older uncle frown with annoyance, so that he asked him to go and sit at some distance from the sleeping-blankets. All night he sat playing whatever sad songs he could call to mind; the bright ones in his opinion belonged to the *quartier*, where one was never alone.

When the uncles kept watch, they sat quietly, staring ahead of them into the night. There were just the three of them.

And then one day a solitary figure appeared, moving toward them across the lifeless plain from the west. One man on a camel; there was no sign of any others, although they scanned the wasteland in every direction. They stopped for a while; he altered his course slightly. They went ahead; he changed it again. There was no doubt that he wanted to speak with them.

"Let him come," grumbled the older uncle, glaring about the empty horizon once more. "We each have a gun."

Driss laughed. To him it seemed absurd even to admit the possibility of trouble from one lone man.

When finally the figure arrived within calling distance, it hailed them in a voice like a muezzin's: "*S'l'm aleikoum!*" They halted, but did not dismount, and waited for the man to draw nearer. Soon he called again; this time the older uncle replied, but the distance was still too great for his voice to carry, and the man did not hear his greeting. Presently he was close enough for them to see that he did not wear Reguiba attire. They muttered to one another: "He comes from the north, not the west." And they all felt glad. However, even when he came up beside them they remained on the camels, bowing solemnly from where they sat, and always searching in the new face and in the garments below it for some false note which might reveal the possible truth—that the man was a scout for the Reguibat, who would be waiting up on the *hammada* only a few hours distant, or even now moving parallel to the trail, closing in upon them in such a manner that they would not arrive at a point within visibility until after dusk.

Certainly the stranger himself was no Reguiba; he was quick and jolly, with light skin and very little beard. It occurred to Driss that he did not like his small, active eyes which seemed to take in everything and give out nothing, but this passing reaction became only a part of the general initial distrust, all of which was dissipated when they learned that the man was a Moungari. Moungar is a holy place in that part of the world, and its few residents are treated with respect by the pilgrims who go to visit the ruined shrine nearby.

The newcomer took no pains to hide the fear he had felt at being alone in the region, or the pleasure it gave him to be now with three other men. They all dismounted and made tea to seal their friendship, the Moungari furnishing the charcoal.

During the third round of glasses he made the suggestion that since he was going more or less in their direction he accompany them as far as Taoudeni. His bright black eyes darting from one Filali to the other, he explained that he was an excellent shot, that he was certain he could supply them all with some good gazelle meat en route, or at least an *aoudad*. The Filala considered; the oldest finally said: "Agreed." Even if the Moungari turned out to have not quite the hunting prowess he claimed for himself, there would be four of them on the voyage instead of three.

Two mornings later, in the mighty silence of the rising sun, the Moungari pointed at the low hills that lay beside them to the east: "*Timma*. I know this land. Wait here. If you hear me shoot, then come, because that will mean there are gazelles."

The Moungari went off on foot, climbing up between the boulders and disappearing behind the nearest crest. "He trusts us," thought the Filala. "He has left his *mehari*, his blankets, his packs." They said nothing, but each knew that the others were thinking the same as he, and they all felt warmly toward the stranger. They sat waiting in the early morning chill while the camels grumbled.

It seemed unlikely that there would prove to be any gazelles in the region, but if there should be any, and the Moungari were as good a hunter as he claimed to be, then there was a chance they would have a *mechoui* of gazelle that evening, and that would be very fine.

Slowly the sun mounted in the hard blue sky. One camel lumbered up and went off, hoping to find a dead thistle or a bush between the rocks, something left over from a year

when rain might have fallen. When it had disappeared, Driss
went in search of it and drove it back to the others, shouting:
"*Hut!*"

He sat down. Suddenly there came a shot, a long empty in-
terval, and then another shot. The sounds were fairly distant,
but perfectly clear in the absolute silence. The older brother
said: "I shall go. Who knows? There may be many gazelles."

He clambered up the rocks, his gun in his hand, and was
gone.

Again they waited. When the shots sounded this time, they
came from two guns.

"Perhaps they have killed one!" Driss cried.

"*Yemkin.* With Allah's aid," replied his uncle, rising and
taking up his gun. "I want to try my hand at this."

Driss was disappointed: he had hoped to go himself. If only
he had got up a moment ago, it might have been possible,
but even so it was likely that he would have been left behind
to watch the *mehara.* In any case, now it was too late; his uncle had spoken.

"Good."

His uncle went off singing a song from Tafilalet: it was
about date-palms and hidden smiles. For several minutes
Driss heard snatches of the song, as the melody reached the
high notes. Then the sound was lost in the enveloping silence.

He waited. The sun began to be very hot. He covered his
head with his burnous. The camels looked at each other stupidly, craning their necks, baring their brown and yellow
teeth. He thought of playing his flute, but it did not seem the
right moment: he was too restless, too eager to be up there
with his gun, crouching behind the rocks, stalking the delicate prey. He thought of Tessalit and wondered what it would
be like. Full of blacks and Touareg, certainly more lively than
Tabelbala, because of the road that passed through it. There
was a shot. He waited for others, but no more came this time.
Again he imagined himself there among the boulders, taking
aim at a fleeing beast. He pulled the trigger, the animal fell.
Others appeared, and he got them all. In the dark the travelers sat around the fire gorging themselves with the rich
roasted flesh, their faces gleaming with grease. Everyone was

happy, and even the Moungari admitted that the young Filali
was the best hunter of them all.

In the advancing heat he dozed, his mind playing over a
landscape made of soft thighs and small hard breasts rising
like sand dunes; wisps of song floated like clouds in the sky,
and the air was thick with the taste of fat gazelle meat.

He sat up and looked around quickly. The camels lay with
their necks stretched along the ground in front of them.
Nothing had changed. He stood up, uneasily scanned the
stony landscape. While he had slept, a hostile presence had
entered into his consciousness. Translating into thought what
he already sensed, he cried out. Since first he had seen those
small, active eyes he had felt mistrust of their owner, but the
fact that his uncles had accepted him had pushed suspicion
away into the dark of his mind. Now, unleashed in his slumber, it had bounded back. He turned toward the hot hillside
and looked intently between the boulders, into the black
shadows. In memory he heard again the shots up among the
rocks, and he knew what they had meant. Catching his breath
in a sob, he ran to mount his *mehari*, forced it up, and already
had gone several hundred paces before he was aware of what
he was doing. He stopped the animal to sit quietly a moment,
glancing back at the campsite with fear and indecision. If his
uncles were dead, then there was nothing to do but get out
into the open desert as quickly as possible, away from the
rocks that could hide the Moungari while he took aim.

And so, not knowing the way to Tessalit, and without sufficient food or water, he started ahead, lifting one hand from
time to time to wipe away the tears.

For two or three hours he continued that way, scarcely
noticing where the *mehari* walked. All at once he sat erect,
uttered an oath against himself, and in a fury turned the beast
around. At that very moment his uncles might be seated in
the camp with the Moungari, preparing a *mechoui* and a fire,
sadly asking themselves why their nephew had deserted them.
Or perhaps one would already have set out in search of him.
There would be no possible excuse for his conduct, which
had been the result of an absurd terror. As he thought about
it, his anger against himself mounted: he had behaved in an

unforgivable manner. Noon had passed; the sun was in the west. It would be late when he got back. At the prospect of the inevitable reproaches and the mocking laughter that would greet him, he felt his face grow hot with shame, and he kicked the *mehari's* flanks viciously.

A good while before he arrived at the camp he heard singing. This surprised him. He halted and listened: the voice was too far away to be identified, but Driss felt certain it was the Moungari's. He continued around the side of the hill to a spot in full view of the camels. The singing stopped, leaving silence. Some of the packs had been loaded back on to the beasts, preparatory to setting out. The sun had sunk low, and the shadows of the rocks were stretched out along the earth. There was no sign that they had caught any game. He called out, ready to dismount. Almost at the same instant there was a shot from very nearby, and he heard the small rushing sound of a bullet go past his head. He seized his gun. There was another shot, a sharp pain in his arm, and his gun slipped to the ground.

For a moment he sat there holding his arm, dazed. Then swiftly he leapt down and remained crouching among the stones, reaching out with his good arm for the gun. As he touched it, there was a third shot, and the rifle moved along the ground a few inches toward him in a small cloud of dust. He drew back his hand and looked at it: it was dark and blood dripped from it. At that moment the Moungari bounded across the open space between them. Before Driss could rise the man was upon him, had pushed him back down to the ground with the barrel of his rifle. The untroubled sky lay above; the Moungari glanced up at it defiantly. He straddled the supine youth, thrusting the gun into his neck just below the chin, and under his breath he said: "Filali dog!"

Driss stared up at him with a certain curiosity. The Moungari had the upper hand; Driss could only wait. He looked at the face in the sun's light, and discovered a peculiar intensity there. He knew the expression: it comes from hashish. Carried along on its hot fumes, a man can escape very far from the world of meaning. To avoid the malevolent face he rolled his eyes from side to side. There was only the fading sky. The gun was choking him a little. He whispered: "Where are my uncles?"

The Moungari pushed harder against his throat with the gun, leaned partially over and with one hand ripped away his *serouelles*, so that he lay naked from the waist down, squirming a little as he felt the cold stones beneath him.

Then the Moungari drew forth rope and bound his feet. Taking two steps to his head, he abruptly faced in the other direction, and thrust the gun into his navel. Still with one hand he slipped the remaining garments off over the youth's head and lashed his wrists together. With an old barber's razor he cut off the superfluous rope. During this time Driss called his uncles by name, loudly, first one and then the other.

The man moved and surveyed the young body lying on the stones. He ran his finger along the razor's blade; a pleasant excitement took possession of him. He stepped over, looked down, and saw the sex that sprouted from the base of the belly. Not entirely conscious of what he was doing, he took it in one hand and brought his other arm down with the motion of a reaper wielding a sickle. It was swiftly severed. A round, dark hole was left, flush with the skin; he stared a moment, blankly. Driss was screaming. The muscles all over his body stood out, moved.

Slowly the Moungari smiled, showing his teeth. He put his hand on the hard belly and smoothed the skin. Then he made a small vertical incision there, and using both hands, studiously stuffed the loose organ in until it disappeared.

As he was cleaning his hands in the sand, one of the camels uttered a sudden growling gurgle. The Moungari leapt up and wheeled about savagely, holding his razor high in the air. Then, ashamed of his nervousness, feeling that Driss was watching and mocking him, (although the youth's eyes were unseeing with pain) he kicked him over on to his stomach where he lay making small spasmodic movements. And as the Moungari followed these with his eyes, a new idea came to him. It would be pleasant to inflict an ultimate indignity upon the young Filali. He threw himself down; this time he was vociferous and leisurely in his enjoyment. Eventually he slept.

At dawn he awoke and reached for his razor, lying on the ground nearby. Driss moaned faintly. The Moungari turned him over and pushed the blade back and forth with a sawing motion into his neck until he was certain he had severed the windpipe. Then he rose, walked away, and finished the loading of the camels he had started the day before. When this was done he spent a good while dragging the body over to the base of the hill and concealing it there among the rocks.

In order to transport the Filala's merchandise to Tessalit (for in Taoudeni there would be no buyers) it was necessary to take their *mehara* with him. It was nearly fifty days later when he arrived. Tessalit is a small town. When the Moungari began to show the leather around, an old Filali living there, whom the people called Ech Chibani, got wind of his presence. As a prospective buyer he came to examine the hides, and the Moungari was unwise enough to let him see them. Filali leather is unmistakable, and only the Filala buy and sell it in quantity. Ech Chibani knew the Moungari had come by it illicitly, but he said nothing. When a few days later another caravan arrived from Tabelbala with friends of the three Filala who asked after them and showed great distress on hearing that they never had arrived, the old man went to the Tribunal. After some difficulty he found a Frenchman who was willing to listen to him. The next day the Commandant and two subordinates paid the Moungari a visit. They asked him how he happened to have the three extra *mehara*, which still carried some of their Filali trappings; his replies took a devious turn. The Frenchmen listened seriously, thanked him, and left. He did not see the Commandant wink at the others as they went out into the street. And so he remained sitting in his courtyard, not knowing that he had been judged and found guilty.

The three Frenchmen went back to the Tribunal where the newly arrived Filali merchants were sitting with Ech Chibani. The story had an old pattern; there was no doubt at all about the Moungari's guilt. "He is yours," said the Commandant. "Do what you like with him."

The Filala thanked him profusely, held a short conference with the aged Chibani, and strode out in a group. When they arrived at the Moungari's dwelling he was making tea. He looked up, and a chill moved along his spine. He began to scream his innocence at them; they said nothing, but at the point of a rifle bound him and tossed him into a corner, where he continued to babble and sob. Quietly they drank the tea he had been brewing, made some more, and went out at twilight. They tied him to one of the *mehara*, and mounting their own, moved in a silent procession (silent save for the Moungari) out through the town gate into the infinite waste land beyond.

Half the night they continued, until they were in a completely unfrequented region of the desert. While he lay raving, bound to the camel, they dug a well-like pit, and when they had finished they lifted him off, still trussed tightly, and stood him in it. Then they filled all the space around his body with sand and stones, until only his head remained above the earth's surface. In the faint light of the new moon his shaved pate without its turban looked rather like a rock. And still he pleaded with them, calling upon Allah and Sidi Ahmed Ben Moussa to witness his innocence. But he might have been singing a song for all the attention they paid to his words. Presently they set off for Tessalit; in no time they were out of hearing.

When they had gone the Moungari fell silent, to wait through the cold hours for the sun that would bring first warmth, then heat, thirst, fire, visions. The next night he did not know where he was, did not feel the cold. The wind blew dust along the ground into his mouth as he sang.

A Distant Episode

THE September sunsets were at their reddest the week the Professor decided to visit Aïn Tadouirt, which is in the warm country. He came down out of the high, flat region in the evening by bus, with two small overnight bags full of maps, sun lotions and medicines. Ten years ago he had been in the village for three days; long enough, however, to establish a fairly firm friendship with a café-keeper, who had written him several times during the first year after his visit, if never since. "Hassan Ramani," the Professor said over and over, as the bus bumped downward through ever warmer layers of air. Now facing the flaming sky in the west, and now facing the sharp mountains, the car followed the dusty trail down the canyons into air which began to smell of other things besides the endless ozone of the heights: orange blossoms, pepper, sun-baked excrement, burning olive oil, rotten fruit. He closed his eyes happily and lived for an instant in a purely olfactory world. The distant past returned—what part of it, he could not decide.

The chauffeur, whose seat the Professor shared, spoke to him without taking his eyes from the road. "*Vous êtes géologue?*"

"A geologist? Ah, no! I'm a linguist."

"There are no languages here. Only dialects."

"Exactly. I'm making a survey of variations on Moghrebi."

The chauffeur was scornful. "Keep on going south," he said. "You'll find some languages you never heard of before."

As they drove through the town gate, the usual swarm of urchins rose up out of the dust and ran screaming beside the bus. The Professor folded his dark glasses, put them in his pocket; and as soon as the vehicle had come to a standstill he jumped out, pushing his way through the indignant boys who clutched at his luggage in vain, and walked quickly into the Grand Hotel Saharien. Out of its eight rooms there were two available—one facing the market and the other, a smaller and cheaper one, giving onto a tiny yard full of refuse and barrels, where two gazelles wandered about. He took the smaller room, and pouring the entire pitcher of water into the tin basin, began to wash the grit from his face and ears. The afterglow was nearly gone from the sky, and the pinkness in objects was disappearing, almost as he watched. He lit the carbide lamp and winced at its odor.

After dinner the Professor walked slowly through the streets to Hassan Ramani's café, whose back room hung hazardously out above the river. The entrance was very low, and he had to bend down slightly to get in. A man was tending the fire. There was one guest sipping tea. The *qaouaji* tried to make him take a seat at the other table in the front room, but the Professor walked airily ahead into the back room and sat down. The moon was shining through the reed latticework and there was not a sound outside but the occasional distant bark of a dog. He changed tables so he could see the river. It was dry, but there was a pool here and there that reflected the bright night sky. The *qaouaji* came in and wiped off the table.

"Does this café still belong to Hassan Ramani?" he asked him in the Moghrebi he had taken four years to learn.

The man replied in bad French: "He is deceased."

"Deceased?" repeated the Professor, without noticing the absurdity of the word. "Really? When?"

"I don't know," said the *qaouaji*. "One tea?"

"Yes. But I don't understand . . ."

The man was already out of the room, fanning the fire. The Professor sat still, feeling lonely, and arguing with himself that to do so was ridiculous. Soon the *qaouaji* returned with the tea. He paid him and gave him an enormous tip, for which he received a grave bow.

"Tell me," he said, as the other started away. "Can one still get those little boxes made from camel udders?"

The man looked angry. "Sometimes the Reguibat bring in those things. We do not buy them here." Then insolently, in Arabic: "And why a camel-udder box?"

"Because I like them," retorted the Professor. And then because he was feeling a little exalted, he added, "I like them so much I want to make a collection of them, and I will pay you ten francs for every one you can get me."

"*Khamstache*," said the *qaouaji*, opening his left hand rapidly three times in succession.

"Never. Ten."

"Not possible. But wait until later and come with me. You can give me what you like. And you will get camel-udder boxes if there are any."

He went out into the front room, leaving the Professor to drink his tea and listen to the growing chorus of dogs that barked and howled as the moon rose higher into the sky. A group of customers came into the front room and sat talking for an hour or so. When they had left, the *qaouaji* put out the fire and stood in the doorway putting on his burnous. "Come," he said.

Outside in the street there was very little movement. The booths were all closed and the only light came from the moon. An occasional pedestrian passed, and grunted a brief greeting to the *qaouaji*.

"Everyone knows you," said the Professor, to cut the silence between them.

"Yes."

"I wish everyone knew me," said the Professor, before he realized how infantile such a remark must sound.

"*No* one knows you," said his companion gruffly.

They had come to the other side of the town, on the promontory above the desert, and through a great rift in the wall the Professor saw the white endlessness, broken in the foreground by dark spots of oasis. They walked through the opening and followed a winding road between rocks, downward toward the nearest small forest of palms. The Professor thought: "He may cut my throat. But his café—he would surely be found out."

"Is it far?" he asked, casually.

"Are you tired?" countered the *qaouaji*.

"They are expecting me back at the Hotel Saharien," he lied.

"You can't be there and here," said the *qaouaji*.

The Professor laughed. He wondered if it sounded uneasy to the other.

"Have you owned Ramani's café long?"

"I work there for a friend." The reply made the Professor more unhappy than he had imagined it would.

"Oh. Will you work tomorrow?"

"That is impossible to say."

The Professor stumbled on a stone, and fell, scraping his hand. The *qaouaji* said: "Be careful."

The sweet black odor of rotten meat hung in the air suddenly.

"Agh!" said the Professor, choking. "What is it?"

The *qaouaji* had covered his face with his burnous and did not answer. Soon the stench had been left behind. They were on flat ground. Ahead the path was bordered on each side by a high mud wall. There was no breeze and the palms were quite still, but behind the walls was the sound of running water. Also, the odor of human excrement was almost constant as they walked between the walls.

The Professor waited until he thought it seemed logical for him to ask with a certain degree of annoyance: "But where are we going?"

"Soon," said the guide, pausing to gather some stones in the ditch.

"Pick up some stones," he advised. "Here are bad dogs."

"Where?" asked the Professor, but he stooped and got three large ones with pointed edges.

They continued very quietly. The walls came to an end and the bright desert lay ahead. Nearby was a ruined marabout, with its tiny dome only half standing, and the front wall entirely destroyed. Behind it were clumps of stunted, useless palms. A dog came running crazily toward them on three legs. Not until it got quite close did the Professor hear its steady low growl. The *qaouaji* let fly a large stone at it, striking it square in the muzzle. There was a strange snapping of jaws and the dog ran sideways in another direction, falling blindly against rocks and scrambling haphazardly about like an injured insect.

Turning off the road, they walked across the earth strewn with sharp stones, past the little ruin, through the trees, until they came to a place where the ground dropped abruptly away in front of them.

"It looks like a quarry," said the Professor, resorting to French for the word "quarry," whose Arabic equivalent he could not call to mind at the moment. The *qaouaji* did not answer. Instead he stood still and turned his head, as if listening. And indeed, from somewhere down below, but very far below, came the faint sound of a low flute. The *qaouaji* nodded his head slowly several times. Then he said: "The path begins here. You can see it well all the way. The rock is white and the moon is strong. So you can see well. I am going back now and sleep. It is late. You can give me what you like."

Standing there at the edge of the abyss which at each moment looked deeper, with the dark face of the *qaouaji* framed in its moonlit burnous close to his own face, the Professor asked himself exactly what he felt. Indignation, curiosity, fear, perhaps, but most of all relief and the hope that this was not a trick, the hope that the *qaouaji* would really leave him alone and turn back without him.

He stepped back a little from the edge, and fumbled in his pocket for a loose note, because he did not want to show his wallet. Fortunately there was a fifty-franc bill there, which he took out and handed to the man. He knew the *qaouaji* was pleased, and so he paid no attention when he heard him saying: "It is not enough. I have to walk a long way home and there are dogs. . . ."

"Thank you and good night," said the Professor, sitting down with his legs drawn up under him, and lighting a cigarette. He felt almost happy.

"Give me only one cigarette," pleaded the man.

"Of course," he said, a bit curtly, and he held up the pack.

The *qaouaji* squatted close beside him. His face was not pleasant to see. "What is it?" thought the Professor, terrified again, as he held out his lighted cigarette toward him.

The man's eyes were almost closed. It was the most obvious registering of concentrated scheming the Professor had ever seen. When the second cigarette was burning, he ventured to say to the still-squatting Arab: "What are you thinking about?"

The other drew on his cigarette deliberately, and seemed about to speak. Then his expression changed to one of satisfaction, but he did not speak. A cool wind had risen in the air, and the Professor shivered. The sound of the flute came up from the depths below at intervals, sometimes mingled with the scraping of nearby palm fronds one against the other.

"These people are not primitives," the Professor found himself saying in his mind.

"Good," said the *qaouaji*, rising slowly. "Keep your money. Fifty francs is enough. It is an honor." Then he went back into French: "*Ti n'as qu'à discendre, to' droit.*" He spat, chuckled (or was the Professor hysterical?), and strode away quickly.

The Professor was in a state of nerves. He lit another cigarette, and found his lips moving automatically. They were saying: "Is this a situation or a predicament? This is ridiculous." He sat very still for several minutes, waiting for a sense of reality to come to him. He stretched out on the hard, cold ground and looked up at the moon. It was almost like looking straight at the sun. If he shifted his gaze a little at a time, he could make a string of weaker moons across the sky. "Incredible," he whispered. Then he sat up quickly and looked about. There was no guarantee that the *qaouaji* really had gone back to town. He got to his feet and looked over the edge of the precipice. In the moonlight the bottom seemed miles away. And there was nothing to give it scale; not a tree, not a house, not a person. . . . He listened for the flute, and heard only the wind going by his ears. A sudden violent desire to run back to the road seized him, and he turned and looked in the direction the *qaouaji* had taken. At the same time he felt softly of his wallet in his breast pocket. Then he spat over the edge of the cliff. Then he made water over it, and listened intently, like a child. This gave him the impetus to start down the path into the abyss. Curiously enough, he was not dizzy. But prudently he kept from peering to his right, over the edge. It was a steady and steep downward climb. The monotony of it put him into a frame of mind not unlike that which had been induced by the bus ride. He was murmuring "Hassan Ramani" again, repeatedly and in rhythm. He stopped, furious with himself for the sinister overtones the name now suggested to him. He decided he was exhausted from the trip. "And the walk," he added.

He was now well down the gigantic cliff, but the moon, being directly overhead, gave as much light as ever. Only the wind was left behind, above, to wander among the trees, to blow through the dusty streets of Aïn Tadouirt, into the hall of the Grand Hotel Saharien, and under the door of his little room.

It occurred to him that he ought to ask himself why he was doing this irrational thing, but he was intelligent enough to know that since he was doing it, it was not so important to probe for explanations at that moment.

Suddenly the earth was flat beneath his feet. He had reached the bottom sooner than he had expected. He stepped ahead distrustfully still, as if he expected another treacherous drop. It was so hard to know in this uniform, dim brightness. Before he knew what had happened the dog was upon him, a heavy mass of fur trying to push him backwards, a sharp nail rubbing down his chest, a straining of muscles against him to get the teeth into his neck. The Professor thought: "I refuse to die this way." The dog fell back; it looked like an Eskimo dog. As it sprang again, he called out, very loud: "Ay!" It fell against him, there was a confusion of sensations and a pain somewhere. There was also the sound of voices very near to him, and he could not understand what they were saying. Something cold and metallic was pushed brutally against his spine as the dog still hung for a second by his teeth from a mass of clothing and perhaps flesh. The Professor knew it was a gun, and he raised his hands, shouting in Moghrebi: "Take away the dog!" But the gun merely pushed him forward, and since the dog, once it was back on the ground, did not leap again, he took a step ahead. The gun kept pushing; he kept taking steps. Again he heard voices, but the person directly behind him said nothing. People seemed to be running about; it sounded that way, at least. For his eyes, he discovered, were still shut tight against the dog's attack. He opened them. A group of men was advancing toward him. They were dressed in the black clothes of the Reguibat. "The Reguiba is a cloud across the face of the sun." "When the Reguiba appears the righteous man turns away." In how many shops and market-places he had heard these maxims uttered banteringly among friends. Never to a Reguiba, to be sure, for these men do not frequent towns. They send a representative in disguise, to arrange with shady elements there for the disposal of captured goods. "An opportunity," he thought quickly, "of testing the accuracy of such statements." He did not doubt for a moment that the adventure would prove to be a kind of warning against such foolishness on his part—a warning which in retrospect would be half sinister, half farcical.

Two snarling dogs came running from behind the oncoming men and threw themselves at his legs. He was scandalized to note that no one paid any attention to this breach of etiquette. The gun pushed him harder as he tried to sidestep the animals' noisy assault. Again he cried: "The dogs! Take them away!" The gun shoved him forward with great force and he fell, almost at the feet of the crowd of men facing him. The dogs were wrenching at his hands and arms. A boot kicked them aside, yelping, and then with increased vigor it kicked the Professor in the hip. Then came a chorus of kicks from different sides, and he was rolled violently about on the earth for a while. During this time he was conscious of hands reaching into his pockets and removing everything from them. He tried to say: "You have all my money; stop kicking me!" But his bruised facial muscles would not work; he felt himself pouting, and that was all. Someone dealt him a terrific blow on the head, and he thought: "Now at least I shall lose consciousness, thank Heaven." Still he went on being aware of the guttural voices he could not understand, and of being bound tightly about the ankles and chest. Then there was black silence that opened like a wound from time to time, to let in the soft, deep notes of the flute playing the same succession of notes again and again. Suddenly he felt excruciating pain everywhere—pain and cold. "So I have been unconscious, after all," he thought. In spite of that, the present seemed only like a direct continuation of what had gone before.

It was growing faintly light. There were camels near where he was lying; he could hear their gurgling and their heavy breathing. He could not bring himself to attempt opening his eyes, just in case it should turn out to be impossible. However, when he heard someone approaching, he found that he had no difficulty in seeing.

The man looked at him dispassionately in the gray morning light. With one hand he pinched together the Professor's nostrils. When the Professor opened his mouth to breathe, the man swiftly seized his tongue and pulled on it with all his might. The Professor was gagging and catching his breath; he did not see what was happening. He could not distinguish the pain of the brutal yanking from that of the sharp knife. Then there was an endless choking and spitting that went on automatically, as though he were scarcely a part of it. The word "operation" kept going through his mind; it calmed his terror somewhat as he sank back into darkness.

The caravan left sometime toward midmorning. The Professor, not unconscious, but in a state of utter stupor, still gagging and drooling blood, was dumped doubled-up into a sack and tied at one side of a camel. The lower end of the enormous amphitheater contained a natural gate in the rocks. The camels, swift *mehara*, were lightly laden on this trip. They passed through single file, and slowly mounted the gentle slope that led up into the beginning of the desert. That night, at a stop behind some low hills, the men took him out, still in a state which permitted no thought, and over the dusty rags that remained of his clothing they fastened a series of curious belts made of the bottoms of tin cans strung together. One after another of these bright girdles was wired about his torso, his arms and legs, even across his face, until he was entirely within a suit of armor that covered him with its circular metal scales. There was a good deal of merriment during this decking-out of the Professor. One man brought out a flute and a younger one did a not ungraceful caricature of an Ouled Naïl executing a cane dance. The Professor was no longer conscious; to be exact, he existed in the middle of the movements made by these other men. When they had finished dressing him the way they wished him to look, they stuffed some food under the tin bangles hanging over his face. Even though he chewed mechanically, most of it eventually fell out onto the ground. They put him back into the sack and left him there.

Two days later they arrived at one of their own encampments. There were women and children here in the tents, and the men had to drive away the snarling dogs they had left there to guard them. When they emptied the Professor out of his sack, there were screams of fright, and it took several hours to convince the last woman that he was harmless, although there had been no doubt from the start that he was a valuable possession. After a few days they began to move on again, taking everything with them, and traveling only at night as the terrain grew warmer.

Even when all his wounds had healed and he felt no more pain, the Professor did not begin to think again; he ate and defecated, and he danced when he was bidden, a senseless hopping up and down that delighted the children, principally because of the wonderful jangling racket it made. And he generally slept through the heat of the day, in among the camels.

Wending its way southeast, the caravan avoided all stationary civilization. In a few weeks they reached a new plateau, wholly wild and with a sparse vegetation. Here they pitched camp and remained, while the *mehara* were turned loose to graze. Everyone was happy here; the weather was cooler and there was a well only a few hours away on a seldom-frequented trail. It was here they conceived the idea of taking the Professor to Fogara and selling him to the Touareg.

It was a full year before they carried out this project. By this time the Professor was much better trained. He could do a handspring, make a series of fearful growling noises which had, nevertheless, a certain element of humor; and when the Reguibat removed the tin from his face they discovered he could grimace admirably while he danced. They also taught him a few basic obscene gestures which never failed to elicit delighted shrieks from the women. He was now brought forth only after especially abundant meals, when there was music and festivity. He easily fell in with their sense of ritual, and evolved an elementary sort of "program" to present when he was called for: dancing, rolling on the ground, imitating certain animals, and finally rushing toward the group in feigned anger, to see the resultant confusion and hilarity.

When three of the men set out for Fogara with him, they took four *mehara* with them, and he rode astride his quite naturally. No precautions were taken to guard him, save that he was kept among them, one man always staying at the rear of the party. They came within sight of the walls at dawn, and they waited among the rocks all day. At dusk the youngest started out, and in three hours he returned with a friend who carried a stout cane. They tried to put the Professor through his routine then and there, but the man from Fogara was in a hurry to get back to town, so they all set out on the *mehara*.

In the town they went directly to the villager's home, where they had coffee in the courtyard sitting among the camels. Here the Professor went into his act again, and this time there was prolonged merriment and much rubbing together of hands. An agreement was reached, a sum of money paid, and the Reguibat withdrew, leaving the Professor in the house of the man with the cane, who did not delay in locking him into a tiny enclosure off the courtyard.

The next day was an important one in the Professor's life, for it was then that pain began to stir again in his being. A group of men came to the house, among whom was a venerable gentleman, better clothed than those others who spent their time flattering him, setting fervent kisses upon his hands and the edges of his garments. This person made a point of going into classical Arabic from time to time, to impress the others, who had not learned a word of the Koran. Thus his conversation would run more or less as follows: "Perhaps at In Salah. The French there are stupid. Celestial vengeance is approaching. Let us not hasten it. Praise the highest and cast thine anathema against idols. With paint on his face. In case the police wish to look close." The others listened and agreed, nodding their heads slowly and solemnly. And the Professor in his stall beside them listened, too. That is, he was *conscious* of the sound of the old man's Arabic. The words penetrated for the first time in many months. Noises, then: "Celestial vengeance is approaching." Then: "It is an honor. Fifty francs is enough. Keep your money. Good." And the *qaouaji* squatting near him at the edge of the precipice. Then "anathema against idols" and more gibberish. He turned over panting on the sand and forgot about it. But the pain had begun. It operated in a kind of delirium, because he had begun to enter into consciousness again. When the man opened the door and prodded him with his cane, he cried out in a rage, and everyone laughed.

They got him onto his feet, but he would not dance. He stood before them, staring at the ground, stubbornly refusing to move. The owner was furious, and so annoyed by the laughter of the others that he felt obliged to send them away, saying that he would await a more propitious time for exhibiting his property, because he dared not show his anger before the elder. However, when they had left he dealt the Professor a violent blow on the shoulder with his cane, called him various obscene things, and went out into the street, slamming the gate behind him. He walked straight to the street of the Ouled Naïl, because he was sure of finding the Reguibat there among the girls, spending the money. And there in a tent he found one of them still abed, while an Ouled Naïl washed the tea glasses. He walked in and almost decapitated the man before the latter had even attempted to sit up. Then he threw his razor on the bed and ran out.

The Ouled Naïl saw the blood, screamed, ran out of her tent into the next, and soon emerged from that with four girls who rushed together into the coffee house and told the *qaouaji* who had killed the Reguiba. It was only a matter of an hour before the French military police had caught him at a friend's house, and dragged him off to the barracks. That night the Professor had nothing to eat, and the next afternoon, in the slow sharpening of his consciousness caused by increasing hunger, he walked aimlessly about the courtyard and the rooms that gave onto it. There was no one. In one room a calendar hung on the wall. The Professor watched nervously, like a dog watching a fly in front of its nose. On the white paper were black objects that made sounds in his head. He heard them: "*Grande Epicerie du Sahel. Juin. Lundi, Mardi, Mercredi. . . .*"

The tiny inkmarks of which a symphony consists may have been made long ago, but when they are fulfilled in sound they become imminent and mighty. So a kind of music of feeling began to play in the Professor's head, increasing in volume as he looked at the mud wall, and he had the feeling that he was performing what had been written for him long ago. He felt like weeping; he felt like roaring through the little house, upsetting and smashing the few breakable objects. His emotion got no further than this one overwhelming desire. So, bellowing as loud as he could, he attacked the house and its belongings. Then he attacked the door into the street, which resisted for a while and finally broke. He climbed through the

A HUNDRED CAMELS
IN THE COURTYARD

'A pipe of Kif before breakfast gives a man the strength of a hundred camels in the courtyard.'
—Nchaioui Proverb

CONTENTS

A Friend of the World

SALAM rented two rooms and a kitchen on the second floor of a Jewish house at the edge of the town. He had decided to live with the Jews because he had already lived with Christians and found them all right. He trusted them a little more than he did other Moslems, who were like him and said: 'No Moslem can be trusted.' Moslems are the only true people, the only people you can understand. But because you do understand them, you do not trust them. Salam did not trust the Jews completely, either, but he liked living with them because they paid no attention to him. It had no importance if they talked about him among themselves, and they never would talk about him to Moslems. If he had a sister who lived here and there, getting what money she could from whatever man she found, because she had to eat, that was all right, and the Jews did not point at her when she came to visit him. If he did not get married, but lived instead with his brother and spent his time smoking kif and laughing, if he got his money by going to Tangier once a month and sleeping for a week with old English and American ladies who drank too much whiskey, they did not care. He was a Moslem. Had he been rich he would have lived in the Spanish end of the town in a villa with concrete benches in the garden and a big round light in the ceiling of the sala, with many pieces of glass hanging down from it. He was poor and he lived with the Jews. To get to his house he had to go to the end of the Medina, cross an open space where the trees had all been cut down, go along the street where the warehouses had been abandoned by the Spanish when they left, and into a newer, dirtier street that led to the main highway. Halfway down was the entrance to the alley where he and his brother and fourteen Jewish families lived. There were the remains of narrow sidewalks along the edges of the wide gutter, full of mounds of rotten watermelon-rind and piles of broken bricks. The small children played here all day. When he was in a hurry he had to be careful not to step on them as they waded in the little puddles of dishwater and urine that were in front of all the doors. If they had been Moslem children he would have spoken to them, but since they were Jews he did not see them as children at all, but merely as nuisances in his way, like cactuses that had to be stepped over carefully because there was no way of going around them. Although he had lived here for almost two years, he did not know the names of any of the Jews. For him they had no names. When he came home and found his door locked, because his brother had gone out and taken both keys with him, he went into any house where the door was open and dropped his bundles on the floor, saying: 'I'll be back in a little while.' He knew they would not touch his property. The Jews were neither friendly nor unfriendly. They too, if they had had money, would have been living in the Spanish end of the town. It made the alley seem less like a Mellah, where only Jews live, to have the two Moslems staying among them.

Salam had the best house in the alley. It was at the end, and its windows gave onto a wilderness of fig trees and canebrake where squatters had built huts out of thatch and hammered pieces of tin. On the hot nights (for the town was in a plain and the heat stayed in the streets long after the sun had gone) his rooms had a breeze from the south that blew through and out onto the terrace. He was happy with his house and with the life that he and his brother had in it. 'I'm a friend of the world,' he would say. 'A clean heart is better than everything.'

One day he came home and found a small kitten sitting on the terrace. When it saw him it ran to him and purred. He unlocked the door into the kitchen and it went inside. After he had washed his hands and feet in the kitchen he went into his room. The kitten was lying on the mattress, still purring. 'Mimí,' he said to it. He gave it some bread. While it ate the bread it did not stop purring. Bou Ralem came home. He had been drinking beer with some friends in the Café Granada. At first he did not understand why Salam had let the kitten stay. 'It's too young to be worth anything,' he said. 'If it saw a rat it would run and hide.' But when the kitten lay in his lap and played with him he liked it. 'Its name is Mimí,' Salam told him. Nights it slept on the mattress with Salam near his feet. It learned to go down into the alley to relieve itself in the dirt there. The children sometimes tried to catch it, but it ran faster than they did and got to the steps before them, and they did not dare follow it upstairs.

During Ramadan, when they stayed up all night, they moved the mats and cushions and mattresses out on to the terrace and lived out there, talking and laughing until the daylight came. They smoked more kif than usual, and invited their friends home at two in the morning for dinner. Because they were living outside and the kitten could hear them from the alley, it grew bolder and began to visit the canebrake behind the house. It could run very fast, and even if a dog chased it, it could get to the stairs in time. When Salam missed it he would stand up and call to it over the railing, on one side down the alley and on the other over the trees and the roofs of the shacks. Sometimes when he was calling into the alley a Jewish woman would run out of one of the doors and look at him. He noticed that it was always the same woman. She would put one hand above her eyes and stare up at him, and then she would put both hands on her hips and frown. 'A crazy woman,' he thought, and he paid no attention to her. One day while he was calling the kitten, the woman shouted up to him in Spanish. Her voice sounded very angry. '*Oyé!*' she cried, shaking her arm in the air, 'why are you calling the name of my daughter?'

Salam kept calling: 'Mimí! Agi! Agiagi, Mimí!'

The woman moved closer to the steps. She put both hands above her eyes, but the sun was behind Salam, so that she could not see him very well. 'You want to insult people?' she screamed. 'I understand your game. You make fun of me and my daughter.'

Salam laughed. He put the end of his forefinger to the side of his head and made circles with it. 'I'm calling my cat. Who's your daughter?'

'And your cat is called Mimí because you knew my little girl's name was Mimí. Why don't you behave like civilized people?'

Salam laughed again and went inside. He did not think of the woman again. Not many days after that the kitten disappeared, and no matter how much he called, it did not come back. He and Bou Ralem went out that night and searched for it in the canebrake. The moon was bright, and they found it lying dead, and carried it back to the house to look at it. Someone had given it a pellet of bread with a needle inside. Salam sat slowly on the mattress. 'The Yehoudía,' he said.

'You don't know who did it,' Bou Ralem told him.

'It was the Yehoudía. Throw me the mottoui.' And he began to smoke kif, one pipe after another. Bou Ralem understood that Salam was looking for an answer, and he did not talk. After a while he saw that the time had come to turn off the electricity and light the candle. When he had done this, Salam lay back quietly on the mattress and listened to the dogs barking outside. Now and then he sat up and filled his sebsi. Once he passed it to Bou Ralem, and lay back down on the cushions smiling. He had an idea of what he would do. When they went to bed he said to Bou Ralem: 'She's one mother who's going to wet her pants.'

The next day he got up early and went to the market. In a little stall there he bought several things: a crow's wing, a hundred grams of jduq jmel seeds, powdered porcupine quills, some honey, a pressed lizard, and a quarter kilo of fasoukh. When he had finished paying for all this he turned away as if he were going to leave the stall, then he said: 'Khaï, give me another fifty grams of jduq jmel.' When the man had weighed the seeds out and put them into a paper and folded it up, he paid him and carried the paper in his left hand as he went on his way home. In the alley the children were throwing clots of mud at one another. They stopped while he went by. The women sat in the doorways with their shawls over their heads. As he passed before the house of the woman who had killed Mimí he let go of the package of jduq jmel seeds. Then he went upstairs on to his terrace, walked to the door, and pounded on it. No one answered. He stood in the middle of the terrace where everyone could see him, rubbing his hand over his chin. A minute later he climbed to the terrace next to his and knocked on that door. He handed his parcel to the woman who came to open. 'I left my keys in the market,' he told her. 'I'll be right back.' He ran downstairs, through the alley, and up the street.

Behind the Gailan Garage Bou Ralem was standing. When Salam passed him, he nodded his head once and went along without stopping. Bou Ralem began to walk in the other direction, back to the house. As he opened the gate on to the terrace, the woman from next door called to him. 'Haven't you seen your brother? He left his keys in the market.' 'No,' Bou Ralem said, and went in, leaving the door open. He sat down and smoked a cigarette while he waited. In a little while the talking in the alley below sounded louder. He stood up and went to the door to listen. A woman was crying: 'It's jduq jmel! Mimí had it in her hand!' Soon there were many more voices, and the woman from the next terrace ran downstairs in her bathrobe, carrying a parcel. 'That's it,' Bou Ralem said to himself. When she arrived the shouting grew louder. He listened for a time, smiling. He went out and ran downstairs. They were all in the alley outside the woman's door, and the little girl was inside the house, screaming. Without looking toward them he ran by on the far side of the alley.

Salam was inside the café, drinking a glass of tea. 'Sit down,' he told Bou Ralem. 'I'm not going to get Fatma Daifa before eleven.' He ordered his brother a tea. 'Were they making a lot of noise?' he asked him. Bou Ralem nodded his head. Salam smiled. 'I'd like to hear them,' he said. 'You'll hear them," Bou Ralem told him. 'They're not going to stop.'

At eleven o'clock they left the café and went through the back passages of the Medina to Fatma Daifa's house. She was the sister of their mother's mother, and thus not of their family, so that they did not feel it was shameful to use her in the game. She was waiting for them at the door, and together they went back to Salam's house.

The old woman went into the alley ahead of Salam and Bou Ralem, and walked straight to the door where all the women were gathered. She held her haïk tightly around her head so that no part of her face showed, except one eye. She pushed against the Jewish women and held out one hand. 'Give me my things,' she told them. She did not bother to speak Spanish with them because she knew they understood Arabic. 'You have my things.' They did have them and they were still looking at them, but then they turned to look at her. She seized all the packages and put them into her kouffa quickly. 'No shame!' she shouted at the women. 'Go and look after your children.' She pushed the other way and went back into the alley where Salam and Bou Ralem stood waiting. The three went upstairs and into Salam's house, and they shut the door. They had lunch there and stayed all day, talking and laughing. When everyone had gone to bed, Salam took Fatma Daifa home.

The next day the Jews all stared at them when they went out, but no one said anything to them. The woman Salam had wanted to frighten did not come to her door at all, and the little girl was not in the alley playing with the other children. It was clear that the Jews thought Fatma Daifa had put a spell on the child. They would not have believed Salam and Bou Ralem alone could do such a thing, but they knew a Moslem woman had the power. The two brothers were very much pleased with the joke. It is forbidden to practise magic, but the old woman was their witness that they had not done such a thing. She had taken home all the packages just as they had been when she had snatched them away from the Jewish women, and she had promised to keep them that way, so that in case of trouble she could prove that nothing had been used.

The Jewish woman went to the comisaría to complain. She found a young policeman sitting at his desk listening to a small radio he had in his hand, and she began to tell him that the Moslems in her haouma had bought charms to use against her daughter. The policeman did not like her, partly because she was Jewish and spoke Spanish instead of Arabic, and partly because he did not approve of people who believed in magic, but he listened politely until she said: 'That Moslem is a *sinvergüenza.*' She tried to go on to say that there were many very good Moslems, but he did not like her words. He frowned at the woman and said: 'Why do you say all this? What makes you think they put a spell on your little girl?' She told him how the three had shut themselves in all day with the packages of bad things from the market. The policeman looked at her in surprise. 'And for a dead lizard you came all the way here?' he laughed. He sent her away and went on listening to his radio.

The people in the alley still did not speak to Salam and Bou Ralem, and the little girl did not come out to play in the mud with the others. When the woman went to the market she took her with her. 'Hold on to my skirt,' she would tell her. But one day in front of the service station the child let go of the woman's skirt for a minute. When she ran to catch up with her mother, she fell and her knee hit a broken bottle. The woman saw the blood and began to scream. People stopped walking. In a few minutes a Jew came by and helped the woman carry the child to a pharmacy. They bandaged the little girl's knee and the woman took her home. Then she went back to the pharmacy to get her baskets, but on the way she stopped at the police station. She found the same police-man sitting at his desk.

'If you want to see the proof of what I told you, come and look at my little girl now,' she told him. 'Again?' said the po-liceman. He was not friendly with her, but he took her name and address, and later that day on his way home he called at her house. He looked at the little girl's knee and tickled her ribs so that she laughed. 'All children fall down,' he said. 'But who is this Moslem? Where does he live?' The mother showed him the stairs at the end of the alley. He did not in-tend to speak with Salam, but he wanted to finish with the woman once and for all. He went out into the alley, and saw that the woman was watching him from the door, so he walked slowly to the foot of the stairs. When he had decided she was no longer looking, he started to go. At that moment he heard a voice behind him. He turned and saw Salam stand-ing above him on the terrace. He did not much like his face, and he told himself that if he ever saw him in the street he would have a few words with him.

One morning Salam went early to the market to get fresh kif. When he found it he bought three hundred francs' worth. As he went out through the gates into the street the police-man, who was waiting for him, stopped him. 'I want to speak with you,' he told him. Salam stretched his fingers tightly around the kif in his pocket. 'Is everything all right?' said the policeman. 'Everything is fine,' Salam replied. 'No trouble?' the policeman insisted, looking at him as if he knew what Salam had just bought. Salam answered: 'No trouble.' The policeman said: 'See that it stays like that.' Salam was angry at being spoken to in this way for no reason, but with the kif in his pocket he could only be thankful that he was not being searched. 'I'm a friend of the world,' he said, trying to smile. The policeman did not answer, and turned away.

'A very bad thing,' thought Salam as he hurried home with the kif. No policeman had bothered him before this. When he reached his room he wondered if he should hide the package under a tile in the floor, but he decided that if he did that, he himself would be living like a Jew, who each time there is a knock at the door ducks his head and trembles. He spread the kif out on the table defiantly and left it there. During the afternoon he and Bou Ralem cut it. He did not mention the policeman, but he was thinking of him all the time they were working. When the sun had gone down behind the plain and the soft breeze began to come in through the windows he took off his shirt and lay back on the pillows to smoke. Bou Ralem filled his mottoui with the fresh kif and went out to a café. 'I'm staying here,' said Salam.

He smoked for an hour or more. It was a hot night. The dogs had begun to bark in the canebrake. A woman and a man in one of the huts below were cursing one another. Sometimes the woman stopped shouting and merely screamed. The sound bothered Salam. He could not be happy. He got up and dressed, took his sebsi and his mottoui, and went out. Instead of turning toward the town when he left the alley, he walked toward the highway. He wanted to sit in a quiet place in order to find out what to do. If the policeman had not suspected him, he would not have stopped him. Since he had stopped him once, he might do it again, and the next time he might search him. 'That's not freedom,' he said to himself. A few cars went by. Their headlights made the tree-trunks yellow as they passed. After each car had gone, there was only the blue light of the moon and the sky. When he got to the bridge over the river, he climbed down a bank under the girders, and went along a path to a rock that hung out high above the water. There he sat and looked over the edge at the deep muddy river that was moving below in the moonlight. He felt the kif in his head, and he knew he was going to make it work for him.

He put the plan together slowly. It was going to cost a thousand francs, but he had that, and he was willing to spend it. After six pipes, when he had everything arranged in his mind, he stuffed his sebsi into his pocket, jumped up, and climbed the path to the highway. He walked back to the town quickly, going into the Medina by a dirt road where the houses had gardens, and where behind the walls all along the way there were dogs barking at the moon. Not many people walked at night in this part of the town. He went to the house of his cousin Abdallah, who was married to a woman from Sidi Kacem. The house was never empty. Two or three of her brothers were always there with their families. Salam spoke privately with Abdallah in the street outside the door, asking for one of the brothers whose face was not known in the town. Abdallah went in and quickly came out again with someone. The man had a beard, wore a country djellaba, and carried his shoes in his hand. They spoke together for a few minutes. 'Go with him,' said Abdallah, when they had finished talking. Salam and the bearded man said goodnight and went away.

At Salam's house that night the man slept on a mat in the kitchen. When morning came, they washed and had coffee and pastries. While they were eating Salam took out his thousand-franc note and put it into an envelope. On the outside of it Bou Ralem had printed the word GRACIAS in pencil. Soon Salam and the man from the country got up and went out through the town until they came to a side street opposite the back entrance of the police station. There they stood against the wall and talked. 'You don't know his name,' said the man. 'We don't have to,' Salam told him. 'When he comes out and gets into one of the cars and drives away, you run over to the office and give them the envelope, and say you tried to catch him before he left.' He waved the envelope in his hand. 'Ask them to give this to him when he comes back. They'll take it.'

'He may walk,' said the man. 'Then what will I do?'

'The police never walk,' Salam said. 'You'll see. Then you run out again. This street is the best one. Keep going, that's all. I won't be here. I'll see you at Abdallah's.'

They waited a long time. The sun grew hotter and they moved into the shade of a fig tree, always watching the door of the comisaría from where they stood. Several policemen came out, and for each one the man from the country was ready to run, but Salam held on to him and said: 'No, no, no!' When the policeman they were waiting for finally did stand in the doorway, Salam drew in his breath and whispered: 'There he is. Wait till he drives off, then run.' He turned away and walked very fast down the street into the Medina.

When the man from the country had explained clearly who the envelope was for, he handed it to the policeman at the desk, said: 'Thank you,' and ran out quickly. The policeman looked at the envelope, then tried to call him back, but he had gone. Since all messages which came for any of the policemen had to be put on the captain's desk first, he sent the envelope in to his office. The captain held it up to the light. When the policeman came back he called him in and made him open it in front of him. 'Who is it from?' said the captain. The policeman scratched his head. He could not answer. 'I see,' said the captain. The next week he had the man transferred. Word came from the capital that he was to be sent to Rissani. 'See how many friends you can make in the desert,' the captain told him. He would not listen to anything the policeman tried to say.

Salam went to Tangier. When he returned he heard that the policeman had been sent to the Sahara. This made him laugh a great deal. He went to the market and bought a half-grown goat. Then he invited Fatma Daifa and Abdallah and his wife and two of the brothers with their wives and children, and they killed the goat and ate it. It was nearly dawn by the time they all went home. Fatma Daifa did not want to go through the streets alone, and since Salam and Bou Ralem were too drunk to take her, she slept in the kitchen on the floor. When she woke up it was late, but Salam and Bou Ralem were still asleep. She got her things together, put on her haik and went out. As she came to the house of the woman with the little girl, she stood still and looked in. The woman saw her and was frightened. 'What do you want?' she cried. Fatma Daifa knew she was meddling, but she thought this was the right thing to do for Salam. She pretended not to see the woman's frightened face, and she shook her fist back at the terrace, crying into the air: 'Now I see what sort of man you are! You think you can cheat me? Listen to me! None of it's going to work, do you hear?' She walked on down the alley shouting: 'None of it!' The other Jewish women came and stood around the door and sat on the curb in front of it. They agreed that if the old woman had fought with the two men there was no more danger from the magic, because only the old woman had the power to make it work. The mother of the little girl was happy, and the next day the child was playing in the mud with the others.

Salam went in and out of the alley as always, not noticing the children or the people. It was half a month before he said one day to Bou Ralem: 'I think the Jews are feeling better. I saw the wrong Mimí out loose this morning.' He was free again now that the policeman was gone, and he could carry his kif in his pocket without worrying when he went out through the streets to the café. The next time he saw Fatma Daifa she asked him about the Jews in his alley. 'It's finished. They've forgotten,' he said. 'Good,' she replied. Then she went to her house and got out the porcupine quill powder and the crow's wing and the seeds and all the rest of the packages. She put them into her basket, carried them to the market, and sold them there, and with the money she bought bread, oil, and eggs. She went home and cooked her dinner.

He of the Assembly

He salutes all parts of the sky and the earth where it is bright. He thinks the color of the amethysts of Aguelmous will be dark if it has rained in the valley of Zerekten. The eye wants to sleep, he says, but the head is no mattress. When it rained for three days and water covered the flatlands outside the ramparts, he slept by the bamboo fence at the Café of the Two Bridges.

IT SEEMS there was a man named Ben Tajah who went to Fez to visit his cousin. The day he came back he was walking in the Djemaa el Fna, and he saw a letter lying on the pavement. He picked it up and found that his name was written on the envelope. He went to the Café of the Two Bridges with the letter in his hand, sat down on a mat and opened the envelope. Inside was a paper which read: 'The sky trembles and the earth is afraid, and the two eyes are not brothers.' Ben Tajah did not understand, and he was very unhappy because his name was on the envelope. It made him think that Satan was nearby. He of the Assembly was sitting in the same part of the café. He was listening to the wind in the telephone wires. The sky was almost empty of daytime light. 'The eye wants to sleep,' he thought, 'but the head is no mattress. I know what that is, but I have forgotten it.' Three days is a long time for rain to keep falling on flat bare ground. 'If I got up and ran down the street,' he thought, 'a policeman would follow me and call to me to stop. I would run faster, and he would run after me. When he shot at me, I'd duck around the corners of houses.' He felt the rough dried mud of the wall under his fingertips. 'And I'd be running through the streets looking for a place to hide, but no door would be open, until finally I came to one door that was open, and I'd go in through the rooms and courtyards until finally I came to the kitchen. The old woman would be there.' He stopped and wondered for a moment why an old woman should be there alone in the kitchen at that hour. She was stirring a big kettle of soup on the stove. 'And I'd look for a place to hide there in the kitchen, and there'd be no place. And I'd be waiting to hear the policeman's footsteps, because he wouldn't miss the open door. And I'd look in the dark corner of the room where she kept the charcoal, but it wouldn't be dark enough. And the old woman would turn and look at me and say: "If you're trying to get away, my boy, I can help you. Jump into the soup-kettle." The wind sighed in the telephone wires. Men came into the Café of the Two Bridges with their garments flapping. Ben Tajah sat on his mat. He had put the letter away, but first he had stared at it a long time. He of the Assembly leaned back and looked at the sky. 'The old woman,' he said to himself. 'What is she trying to do? The soup is hot. It may be a trap. I may find there's no way out, once I get down there.' He wanted a pipe of kif, but he was afraid the policeman would run into the kitchen before he was able to smoke it. He said to the old woman: 'How can I get in? Tell me.' And it seemed to him that he heard footsteps in the street, or perhaps even in one of the rooms of the house. He leaned over the stove and looked down into the kettle. It was dark and very hot down in there. Steam was coming up in clouds, and there was a thick smell in the air that made it hard to breathe. 'Quick!' said the old woman, and she unrolled a rope ladder and hung it over the edge of the kettle. He began to climb down, and she leaned over and looked after him. 'Until the other world!' he shouted. And he climbed all the way down. There was a rowboat below. When he was in it he tugged on the ladder and the old woman began to pull it up. And at that instant the policeman ran in, and two more were with him, and the old woman had just the time to throw the ladder down into the soup. 'Now they are going to take her to the commissariat,' he thought, 'and the poor woman only did me a favor.' He rowed around in the dark for a few minutes, and it was very hot. Soon he took off his clothes. For a while he could see the round top of the kettle up above, like a porthole in the side of a ship, with the heads of the policeman looking down in, but then it grew smaller as he rowed, until it was only a light. Sometimes he could find it and sometimes he lost it, and finally it was gone. He was worried about the old woman, and he thought he must find a way to help her. No policeman can go into the Café of the Two Bridges because it belongs to the Sultan's sister. This is why there is so much kif smoke inside that a berrada can't fall over even if it is pushed, and why most customers like to sit outside, and even there keep one hand on their money. As long as the thieves stay inside and their friends bring them food and kif, they are all right. One day police headquarters will forget to send a man to watch the café, or one man will leave five minutes before the other gets there to take his place. Outside everyone smokes kif too, but only for an hour or two—not all day and night like the ones inside. He of the Assembly had forgotten to light his sebsi. He was in a café where no policeman could come, and he wanted to go away to a kif world where the police were chasing him. 'This is the way we are now,' he thought. 'We work backwards. If we have something good, we look for something bad instead.' He lighted the sebsi and smoked it. Then he blew the hard ash out of the chqaf. It landed in the brook beside the second bridge. 'The world is too good. We can only work forward if we make it bad again first.' This made him sad, so he stopped thinking, and filled his sebsi. While he was smoking it, Ben Tajah looked in his direction, and although they were facing each other, He of the Assembly did not notice Ben Tajah until he got up and paid for his tea. Then he looked at him because he took such a long time getting up off the floor. He saw his face and he thought: 'That man has no one in the world.' The idea made him feel cold. He filled his sebsi again and lighted it. He saw the man as he was going to go out of the café and walk alone down the long road outside the ramparts. In a little while he himself would have to go out to the souks to try and borrow money for dinner. When he smoked a lot of kif he did not like his aunt to see him, and he did not want to see her. 'Soup and bread. No one can want more than that. Will thirty francs be enough the fourth time? The qahaouaji wasn't satisfied last night. But he took it. And he went away and let me sleep. A Moslem, even in the city, can't refuse his brother shelter.' He was not convinced, because he had been born in the mountains, and so he kept thinking back and forth in this way. He smoked many chqofa, and when he got up to go out into the street he found that the world had changed.

Ben Tajah was not a rich man. He lived alone in a room near Bab Doukkala, and he had a stall in the bazaars where he sold coathangers and chests. Often he did not open the shop because he was in bed with a liver attack. At such times he pounded on the floor from his bed, using a brass pestle, and the postman who lived downstairs brought him up some food. Sometimes he stayed in bed for a week at a time. Each morning and night the postman came in with a tray. The food was not very good because the postman's wife did not understand much about cooking. But he was glad to have it. Twice he had brought the postman a new chest to keep clothes and blankets in. One of the postman's wives a few years before had taken a chest with her when she had left him and gone back to her family in Kasba Tadla. Ben Tajah himself had tried having a wife for a while because he needed someone to get him regular meals and to wash his clothes, but the girl was from the mountains, and was wild. No matter how much he beat her she would not be tamed. Everything in the room got broken, and finally he had to put her out into the street. 'No more women will get into my house,' he told his friends in the bazaars, and they laughed. He took home many women, and one day he found that he had en noua. He knew that was a bad disease, because it stays in the blood and eats the nose from inside. 'A man loses his nose only long after he has already lost his head.' He asked a doctor for medicine. The doctor gave him a paper and told him to take it to the Pharmacie de l'Etoile. There he bought six vials of penicillin in a box. He took them home and tied each little bottle with a silk thread, stringing them so that they made a necklace. He wore this always around his neck, taking care that the glass vials touched his skin. He thought it likely that by now he was cured, but his cousin in Fez had just told him that he must go on wearing the medicine for another three months, or at least until the beginning of the moon of Chouwal. He had thought about this now and then on the way home, sitting in the bus for two days, and he had decided that his cousin was too cautious. He stood in the Djemaa el Fna a minute watching the trained monkeys, but the crowd pushed too much, so he walked on. When he got home he shut the door and put his hand in his pocket to pull out the envelope, because he wanted to look at it again inside his own room, and be sure that the name written on it was beyond a doubt his. But the letter was gone. He remembered the jostling in the Djemaa el Fna. Someone had reached into his pocket and imagined his hand was feeling money, and taken it. Yet Ben Tajah did not truly believe this. He was convinced that he would have known such a theft was happening. There had been a letter in his pocket. He was not even sure of that. He sat down on the cushions. 'Two days in the bus,' he thought. 'Probably I'm tired. I found no letter.' He searched in his pocket again, and it seemed to him he could still remember how the fold of the envelope had felt. 'Why would it have my name on it? I never found any letter at all.' Then he wondered if anyone had seen him in the café with the envelope in one hand and the sheet of paper in the other, looking at them both for such a long time. He stood up. He wanted to go back to the Café of the Two Bridges and ask the qahaouaji: 'Did you see me an hour ago? Was I looking at a letter?' If the qahaouaji said: 'Yes,' then the letter was real. He repeated the words aloud: 'The sky trembles, and the earth is afraid, and the two eyes are not brothers.' In the silence afterwards the memory of the sound of the words frightened him. 'If there was no letter, where are these words from?' And he shivered because the answer to that was: 'From Satan.' He was about to open the door when a new fear stopped him. The qahaouaji might say: 'No,' and this would be still worse, because it would mean that the words had been put directly into his head by Satan, that Satan had chosen him to reveal Himself to. In that case He might appear at any moment. 'Ach haddou laillaha ill'Allah. . . .' he prayed, holding his two forefingers up, one on each side of him. He sat down again and did not move. In the street the children were crying. He did not want to hear the qahaouaji say: 'No. You had no letter.' If he knew that Satan was coming to tempt him, he would have that much less power to keep Him away with his prayers, because he would be more afraid.

He of the Assembly stood. Behind him was a wall. In his hand was the sebsi. Over his head was the sky, which he felt was about to burst into light. He was leaning back looking at it. It was dark on the earth, but there was still light up there behind the stars. Ahead of him was the pissoir of the Carpenters' Souk which the French had put there. People said only

Jews used it. It was made of tin, and there was a puddle in front of it that reflected the sky and the top of the pissoir. It looked like a boat in the water. Or like a pier where boats land. Without moving from where he stood, He of the Assembly saw it approaching slowly. He was going toward it. And he remembered he was naked, and put his hand over his sex. In a minute the rowboat would be bumping against the pier. He steadied himself on his legs and waited. But at that moment a large cat ran out of the shadow of the wall and stopped in the middle of the street to turn and look at him with an evil face. He saw its two eyes and for a while could not take his own eyes away. Then the cat ran across the street and was gone. He was not sure what had happened, and he stood very still looking at the ground. He looked back at the pissoir reflected in the puddle and thought: 'It was a cat on the shore, nothing else.' But the cat's eyes had frightened him. Instead of being like cats-eyes, they had looked like the eyes of a person who was interested in him. He made himself forget he had had this thought. He was still waiting for the rowboat to touch the landing pier, but nothing had happened. It was going to stay where it was, that near the shore but not near enough to touch. He stood still a long time, waiting for something to happen. Then he began to walk very fast down the street toward the bazaars. He had just remembered that the old woman was in the police station. He wanted to help her, but first he had to find out where they had taken her. 'I'll have to go to every police station in the Medina,' he thought, and he was not hungry any more. It was one thing to promise himself he would help her when he was far from land, and another when he was a few doors from a commissariat. He walked by the entrance. Two policemen stood in the doorway. He kept walking. The street curved and he was alone. 'This night is going to be a jewel in my crown,' he said, and he turned quickly to the left and went along a dark passageway. At the end he saw flames, and he knew that Mustapha would be there tending the fire of the bakery. He crawled into the mud hut where the oven was. 'Ah, the jackal has come back from the forest!' said Mustapha. He of the Assembly shook his head. 'This is a bad world,' he told Mustapha. 'I've got no money,' Mustapha said. He of

the Assembly did not understand. 'Everything goes backwards,' he said. 'It's bad now, and we have to make it still
worse if we want to go forwards.' Mustapha saw that He of
the Assembly was mkiyif ma rassou and was not interested in
money. He looked at him in a more friendly way and said:
'Secrets are not between friends. Talk.' He of the Assembly
told him that an old woman had done him a great favor, and
because of that three policemen had arrested her and taken
her to the police station. 'You must go for me to the commissariat and ask them if they have old woman there.' He
pulled out his sebsi and took a very long time filling it. When
he finished it he smoked it himself and did not offer any to
Mustapha, because Mustapha never offered him any of his.
'You see how full of kif my head is,' he said laughing. 'I can't
go.' Mustapha laughed too and said it would not be a good
idea, and that he would go for him.

'I was there, and I heard him going away for a long time,
so long that he had to be gone, and yet he was still there, and
his footsteps were still going away. He went away and there
was nobody. There was the fire and I moved away from it. I
wanted to hear a sound like a muezzin crying Allah akbar! or
a French plane from the Pilot Base flying over the Medina, or
news on the radio. It wasn't there. And when the wind came
in the door it was made of dust high as a man. A night to be
chased by dogs in the Mellah. I looked in the fire and I saw
an eye in there, like the eye that's left when you burn chibb
and you knew there was a djinn in the house. I got up and
stood. The fire was making a noise like a voice. I think it was
talking. I went out and walked along the street. I walked a
long time and I came to Bab el Khemiss. It was dark there
and the wind was cold. I went to the wall where the camels
were lying and stood there. Sometimes the men have fires and
play songs on their aouadas. But they were asleep. All snoring. I walked again and went to the gate and looked out. The
big trucks went by full of vegetables and I thought I would
like to be on a truck and ride all night. Then in another city
I would be a soldier and go to Algeria. Everything would be
good if we had a war. I thought a long time. Then I was so
cold I turned around and walked again. It was as cold as the
belly of the oldest goat of Ijoukak. I thought I heard a

muezzin and I stopped and listened. The only thing I heard was the water running in the seguia that carries the water out to the gardens. It was near the mçid of Moulay Boujemaa. I heard the water running by and I felt cold. Then I knew I was cold because I was afraid. In my head I was thinking: if something should happen that never happened before, what would I do? You want to laugh? Hashish in your heart and wind in your head. You think it's like your grandmother's prayer-mat. This is the truth. This isn't a dream brought back from another world past the customs like a teapot from Mecca. I heard the water and I was afraid. There were some trees by the path ahead of me. You know at night sometimes it's good to pull out the sebsi and smoke. I smoked and I started to walk. And then I heard something. Not a muezzin. Something that sounded like my name. But it came up from below, from the seguia, Allah istir! And I walked with my head down. I heard it again saying my name, a voice like water, like the wind moving the leaves in the trees, a woman. It was a woman calling me. The wind was in the trees and the water was running, but there was a woman too. You think it's kif. No, she was calling my name. Now and then, not very loud. When I was under the trees it was louder, and I heard that the voice was my mother's. I heard that the way I can hear you. Then I knew the cat was not a cat, and I knew that Aïcha Qandicha wanted me. I thought of other nights when perhaps she had been watching me from the eyes of a cat or a donkey. I knew she was not going to catch me. Nothing in the seven skies could make me turn around. But I was cold and afraid and when I licked my lips my tongue had no spit on it. I was under the safsaf trees and I thought: she's going to reach down and try to touch me. But she can't touch me from the front and I won't turn around, not even if I hear a pistol. I remembered how the policeman had fired at me and how I'd found only one door open. I began to yell: "You threw me the ladder and told me to climb down! You brought me here! The filthiest whore in the Mellah, with the pus coming out of her, is a thousand times cleaner than you, daughter of all the padronas and dogs in seven worlds!" I got past the trees and I began to run. I called up to the sky so she could hear my voice behind: "I hope the police put a hose in your mouth and pump you full of salt water until you crack open!" I thought: tomorrow I'm going to buy fasoukh and tib and nidd and hasalouba and mska and all the bakhour in the Djemaa, and put them in the mijmah and burn them, and walk back and forth over the mijmah ten times slowly, so the smoke can clean out all my clothes. Then I'll see if there's an eye in the ashes afterwards. If there is, I'll do it all over again right away. And every Thursday I'll buy the bakhour and every Friday I'll burn it. That will be strong enough to keep her away. If I could find a window and look through and see what they're doing to the old woman! If only they could kill her! I kept running. There were a few people in the streets. I didn't look to see where I was going, but I went to the street near Mustapha's oven where the commissariat was. I stopped running before I got to the door. The one standing there saw me before that. He stepped out and raised his arm. He said to me: "Come here".'

He of the Assembly ran. He felt as though he were on horseback. He did not feel his legs moving. He saw the road coming toward him and the doors going by. The policeman had not shot at him yet, but it was worse than the other time because he was very close behind and he was blowing his whistle. 'The policeman is old. At least thirty-five, I can run faster.' But from any street others could come. It was dangerous and he did not want to think about danger. He of the Assembly let songs come into his head. When it rains in the valley of Zerekten the amethysts are darker in Aguelmous. The eye wants to sleep but the head is no mattress. It was a song. Ah, my brother, the ink on the paper is like smoke in the air. What words are there to tell how long a night can be? Drunk with love, I wander in the dark. He was running through the dye-souk, and he splashed into a puddle. The whistle blew again behind him, like a crazy bird screaming. The sound made him feel like laughing, but that did not mean he was not afraid. He thought: 'If I'm seventeen I can run faster. That has to be true.' It was very dark ahead. He had to slow his running. There was no time for his eyes to get used to the dark. He nearly ran into the wall of the shop at the end of the street. He turned to the right and saw the narrow alley ahead of him. The police had tied the old woman

naked to a table with her thin legs wide apart and were sliding electrodes up inside her. He ran ahead. He could see the
course of the alley now even in the dark. Then he stopped
dead, moved to the wall, and stood still. He heard the footsteps slowing down. 'He's going to turn to the left.' And he
whispered aloud: 'It ends that way.' The footsteps stopped
and there was silence. The policeman was looking into the silence and listening into the dark to the left and to the right.
He of the Assembly could not see him or hear him, but he
knew that was what he was doing. He did not move. When it
rains in the valley of Zerekten. A hand seized his shoulder. He
opened his mouth and swiftly turned, but the man had
moved and was pushing him from the side. He felt the wool
of the man's djellaba against the back of his hand. He had
gone through a door and the man had shut it without making any noise. Now they both stood still in the dark, listening
to the policeman walking quickly by outside the door. Then
the man struck a match. He was facing the other way, and
there was a flight of stairs ahead. The man did not turn
around, but he said: 'Come up,' and they both climbed the
stairs. At the top the man took out a key and opened a door.
He of the Assembly stood in the doorway while the man lit a
candle. He liked the room because it had many mattresses
and cushions and a white sheepskin under the tea-tray in a
corner on the floor. The man turned around and said: 'Sit
down.' His face looked serious and kind and unhappy. He of
the Assembly had never seen it before, but he knew it was not
the face of a policeman. He of the Assembly pulled out his
sebsi.

Ben Tajah looked at the boy and asked him: 'What did you
mean when you said down there: "It ends that way?" I heard
you say it.' The boy was embarrassed. He smiled and looked
at the floor. Ben Tajah felt happy to have him there. He had
been standing outside the door downstairs in the dark for a
long time, trying to make himself go to the Café of the Two
Bridges and talk to the qahaouaji. In his mind it was almost
as though he already had been there and spoken with him.
He had heard the qahaouaji telling him that he had seen no
letter, and he had felt his own dismay. He had not wanted to
believe that, but he would be willing to say yes, I made a mis-

take and there was no letter, if only he could find out where
the words had come from. For the words were certainly in his
head. '. . . and the two eyes are not brothers.' That was like
the footprint found in the garden the morning after a bad
dream, the proof that there had been a reason for the dream,
that something had been there after all. Ben Tajah had not
been able to go or to stay. He had started and stopped so
many times that now, although he did not know it, he was
very tired. When a man is tired he mistakes the hopes of children for the knowledge of men. It seemed to him that He of
the Assembly's words had a meaning all for him. Even though
the boy might not know it, he could have been sent by Allah
to help him at that minute. In a nearby street a police whistle
blew. The boy looked at him. Ben Tajah did not care very
much what the answer would be, but he said: 'Why are they
looking for you?' The boy held out his lighted sebsi and his
mottoui fat with kif. He did not want to talk because he was
listening. Ben Tajah smoked kif only when a friend offered it
to him, but he understood that the police had begun once
more to try to enforce their law against kif. Each year they arrested people for a few weeks, and then stopped arresting
them. He looked at the boy, and decided that probably he
smoked too much. With the sebsi in his hand he was sitting
very still listening to the voices of some passers-by in the
street below. 'I know who he is,' one said. 'I've got his name
from Mustapha.' 'The baker?' 'That's the one.' They walked
on. The boy's expression was so intense that Ben Tajah said
to him: 'It's nobody. Just people.' He was feeling happy because he was certain that Satan would not appear before him
as long as the boy was with him. He said quietly: 'Still you
haven't told me why you said: "It ends that way."' The boy
filled his sebsi slowly and smoked all the kif in it. 'I meant,' he
said, 'thanks to Allah. Praise the sky and the earth where it is
bright. What else can you mean when something ends?' Ben
Tajah nodded his head. Pious thoughts can be of as much use
for keeping Satan at a distance as camphor or bakhour
dropped onto hot coals. Each holy word is worth a high column of smoke, and the eyelids do not smart afterwards. 'He
has a good heart,' thought Ben Tajah, 'even though he is
probably a guide for the Nazarenes.' And he asked himself

why it would not be possible for the boy to have been sent to
protect him from Satan. 'Probably not. But it could be.' The
boy offered him the sebsi. He took it and smoked it. After
that Ben Tajah began to think that he would like to go to the
Café of the Two Bridges and speak to the qahaouaji about the
letter. He felt that if the boy went with him the qahaouaji
might say there had been a letter, and that even if the man
could not remember, he would not mind so much because he
would be less afraid. He waited until he thought the boy was
not nervous about going into the street, and then he said:
'Let's go out and get some tea.' 'Good,' said the boy. He was
not afraid of the police if he was with Ben Tajah. They went
through the empty streets, crossed the Djemaa el Fna and the
garden beyond. When they were near the café, Ben Tajah said
to the boy: 'Do you know the Café of the Two Bridges?' The
boy said he always sat there, and Ben Tajah was not surprised.
It seemed to him that perhaps he had even seen him there.
He seized the boy's arm. 'Were you there today?' he asked
him. The boy said 'Yes,' and turned to look at him. He let go
of the arm. 'Nothing,' he said. 'Did you ever see me there?'
They came to the gate of the café and Ben Tajah stopped
walking. 'No,' the boy said. They went across the first bridge
and then the second bridge, and sat down in a corner. Not
many people were left outside. Those inside were making a
great noise. The qahaouaji brought the tea and went away
again. Ben Tajah did not say anything to him about the letter.
He wanted to drink the tea quietly and leave trouble until
later.

When the muezzin called from the minaret of the
Koutoubia, He of the Assembly thought of being in the Agdal. The great mountains were ahead of him and the olive
trees stood in rows on each side of him. Then he heard the
trickle of water and he remembered the seguia that is there in
the Agdal, and he swiftly came back to the Café of the Two
Bridges. Aïcha Qandicha can be only where there are trees by
running water. 'She comes only for single men by trees and
fresh moving water. Her arms are gold and she calls in the
voice of the most cherished one.' Ben Tajah gave him the
sebsi. He filled it and smoked it. 'When a man sees her face
he will never see another woman's face. He will make love

with her all the night, and every night, and in the sunlight by
the walls, before the eyes of children. Soon he will be an
empty pod and he will leave this world for his home in Je-
hennem.' The last carriage went by, taking the last tourists
down the road beside the ramparts to their rooms in the
Mamounia. He of the Assembly thought: 'The eye wants to
sleep. But this man is alone in the world. He wants to talk all
night. He wants to tell me about his wife and how he beat her
and how she broke everything. Why do I want to know all
those things? He is a good man but he has no head.' Ben Tajah was sad. He said: 'What have I done? Why does Satan
choose me?' Then at last he told the boy about the letter,
about how he wondered if it had had his name on the envelope and how he was not even sure there had been a letter.
When he finished he looked sadly at the boy. 'And you didn't
see me.' He of the Assembly shut his eyes and kept them shut
for a while. When he opened them again he said: 'Are you
alone in the world?' Ben Tajah stared at him and did not
speak. The boy laughed. 'I did see you,' he said, 'but you had
no letter. I saw you when you were getting up and I thought
you were old. Then I saw you were not old. That's all I saw.'
'No, it isn't,' Ben Tajah said. 'You saw I was alone.' He of the
Assembly shrugged. 'Who knows?' He filled the sebsi and
handed it to Ben Tajah. The kif was in Ben Tajah's head. His
eyes were small. He of the Assembly listened to the wind in
the telephone wires, took back the sebsi and filled it again.
Then he said: 'You think Satan is coming to make trouble for
you because you're alone in the world. I see that. Get a wife
or somebody to be with you always, and you won't think
about it any more. That's true. Because Satan doesn't come
to men like you.' He of the Assembly did not believe this
himself. He knew that Father Satan can come for anyone in
the world, but he hoped to live with Ben Tajah, so he would
not have to borrow money in the souks to buy food. Ben Tajah drank some tea. He did not want the boy to see that his
face was happy. He felt that the boy was right, and that there
never had been a letter. 'Two days on a bus is a long time. A
man can get very tired,' he said. Then he called the qahaouaji
and told him to bring two more glasses of tea. He of the Assembly gave him the sebsi. He knew that Ben Tajah wanted

to stay as long as possible in the Café of the Two Bridges. He put his finger into the mottoui. The kif was almost gone. 'We can talk,' he said. 'Not much kif is in the mottoui.' The qahaouaji brought the tea. They talked for an hour or more. The qahaouaji slept and snored. They talked about Satan and the bad thing it is to live alone, to wake up in the dark and know that there is no one else nearby. Many times He of the Assembly told Ben Tajah that he must not worry. The kif was all gone. He held his empty mottoui in his hand. He did not understand how he had got back to the town without climbing up out of the soup kettle. Once he said to Ben Tajah: 'I never climbed back up.' Ben Tajah looked at him and said he did not understand. He of the Assembly told him the story. Ben Tajah laughed. He said: 'You smoke too much kif, brother.' He of the Assembly put his sebsi into his pocket. 'And you don't smoke and you're afraid of Satan,' he told Ben Tajah. 'No!' Ben Tajah shouted. 'By Allah! No more! But one thing is in my head, and I can't put it out. The sky trembles and the earth is afraid, and the two eyes are not brothers. Did you ever hear those words? Where did they come from?' Ben Tajah looked hard at the boy. He of the Assembly understood that these had been the words on the paper, and he felt cold in the middle of his back because he had never heard them before and they sounded evil. He knew, too, that he must not let Ben Tajah know this. He began to laugh. Ben Tajah took hold of his knee and shook it. His face was troubled. 'Did you ever hear them?' He of the Assembly went on laughing. Ben Tajah shook his leg so hard that he stopped and said: 'Yes!' When Ben Tajah waited and he said nothing more, he saw the man's face growing angry, and so he said: 'Yes, I've heard them. But will you tell me what happened to me and how I got out of the soup-kettle if I tell you about those words?' Ben Tajah understood that the kif was going away from the boy's head. But he saw that it had not all gone, or he would not have been asking that question. And he said: 'Wait a while for the answer to that question.' He of the Assembly woke the qahaouaji and Ben Tajah paid him, and they went out of the café. They did not talk while they walked. When they got to the Mouassine mosque, Ben Tajah held out his hand to say goodnight, but He of the As-

sembly said: 'I'm looking in my head for the place I heard
your words. I'll walk to your door with you. Maybe I'll remember.' Ben Tajah said: 'May Allah help you find it.' And he
took his arm and they walked to Ben Tajah's door while He
of the Assembly said nothing. They stood outside the door in
the dark. 'Have you found it?' said Ben Tajah. 'Almost,' said
He of the Assembly. Ben Tajah thought that perhaps when
the kif had gone out of the boy's head he might be able to tell
him about the words. He wanted to know how the boy's
head was, and so he said: 'Do you still want to know how you
got out of the soup-kettle?' He of the Assembly laughed.
'You said you would tell me later,' he told Ben Tajah. 'I will,'
said Ben Tajah. 'Come upstairs. Since we have to wait, we can
sit down.' Ben Tajah opened the door and they went upstairs.
This time He of the Assembly sat down on Ben Tajah's bed.
He yawned and stretched. It was a good bed. He was glad it
was not the mat by the bamboo fence at the Café of the Two
Bridges. 'And so, tell me how I got out of the soup-kettle,'
he said laughing. Ben Tajah said: 'You're still asking me that?
Have you thought of the words?' 'I know the words,' the boy
said. 'The sky trembles. . . .' Ben Tajah did not want him to
say them again. 'Where did you hear them? What are they?
That's what I want to know.' The boy shook his head. Then
he sat up very straight and looked beyond Ben Tajah, beyond
the wall of the room, beyond the streets of the Medina, beyond the gardens, toward the mountains where the people
speak Tachelhait. He remembered being a little boy. 'This
night is a jewel in my crown,' he thought. 'It went this way.'
And he began to sing, making up a melody for the words Ben
Tajah had told him. When he had finished '. . . and the two
eyes are not brothers,' he added a few more words of his own
and stopped singing. 'That's all I remember of the song,' he
said. Ben Tajah clapped his hands together hard. 'A song!' he
cried. 'I must have heard it on the radio.' He of the Assembly shrugged. 'They play it sometimes,' he said. 'I've made
him happy,' he thought. 'But I won't ever tell him another
lie. That's the only one. What I'm going to do now is not the
same as lying.' He got up off the bed and went to the window. The muezzins were calling the fjer. 'It's almost morning,' he said to Ben Tajah. 'I still have kif in my head.' 'Sit

down,' said Ben Tajah. He was sure now there had been no letter. He of the Assembly took off his djellaba and got into the bed. Ben Tajah looked at him in surprise. Then he undressed and got into bed beside him. He left the candle burning on the floor beside the bed. He meant to stay awake, but he went to sleep because he was not used to smoking kif and the kif was in his head. He of the Assembly did not believe he was asleep. He lay for a long time without moving. He listened to the voices of the muezzins, and he thought that the man beside him would speak or move. When he saw that Ben Tajah was surely asleep, he was angry. 'This is how he treats a friend who has made him happy. He forgets his trouble and his friend too.' He thought about it more and he was angrier. The muezzins were still calling the fjer. 'Before they stop, or he will hear.' Very slowly he got out of the bed. He put on his djellaba and opened the door. Then he went back and took all the money out of Ben Tajah's pockets. In with the banknotes was an envelope that was folded. It had Ben Tajah's name written across it. He pulled out the piece of paper inside and held it near the candle, and then he looked at it as he would have looked at a snake. The words were written there. Ben Tajah's face was turned toward the wall and he was snoring. He of the Assembly held the paper above the flame and burned it, and then he burned the envelope. He blew the black paper-ashes across the floor. Without making any noise he ran downstairs and let himself out into the street. He shut the door. The money was in his pocket and he walked fast to his aunt's house. His aunt awoke and was angry for a while. Finally he said: 'It was raining. How could I come home? Let me sleep.' He had a little kif hidden under his pillow. He smoked a pipe. Then he looked across his sleep to the morning and thought: 'A pipe of kif before breakfast gives a man the strength of a hundred camels in the courtyard.'

The Story of Lahcen and Idir

Two friends, Lahcen and Idir, were walking on the beach at Merkala. By the rocks stood a girl, and her djellaba blew in the wind. Lahcen and Idir stopped walking when they saw her. They stood still, looking at her. Lahcen said: 'Do you know that one?' 'No. I never saw her.' 'Let's go over,' said Lahcen. They looked up and down the beach for a man who might be with the girl, but there was no one. 'A whore,' said Lahcen. When they got closer to the girl, they saw that she was very young. Lahcen laughed. 'This is easy.' 'How much have you got?' Idir asked him. 'You think I'm going to pay her?' cried Lahcen.

Idir understood that Lahcen meant to beat her. ('If you don't pay a whore you have to beat her.') And he did not like the idea, because they had done it before together, and it nearly always meant trouble later. Her sister or someone in her family went to the police and complained, and in the end everybody was in jail. Being shut into prison made Idir nervous. He tried to keep out of it, and he was usually able to. The difference between Lahcen and Idir was that Lahcen liked to drink and Idir smoked kif. Kif smokers want to stay quiet in their heads, and drinkers are not like that. They want to break things.

Lahcen rubbed his groin and spat onto the sand. Idir knew he was going over the moves in the game he was going to play with the girl, planning when and where he would knock her down. He was worried. The girl looked the other way. She held down the skirt of her djellaba so the wind would not blow it. Lahcen said: 'Wait here.' He went on to her and Idir saw her lips moving as she spoke to him, for she wore no veil. All her teeth were gold. Idir hated women with gold teeth because at fourteen he had been in love with a gold-toothed whore named Zohra, who never had paid him any attention. He said to himself: 'He can have her.' Besides, he did not want to be with them when the trouble began. He stood still until Lahcen whistled to him. Then he went over to where they stood. 'Ready?' Lahcen asked. He took the girl's arm and started to walk along beside the rocks. 'It's late. I've got to go,' Idir told him. Lahcen looked surprised, but he said nothing. 'Some other day,' Idir told Lahcen, looking at him and trying to warn him. The girl laughed spitefully, as if she thought that might shame him into coming along.

He was glad he had decided to go home. When he went by the Mendoub's fig orchard a dog barked at him. He threw a rock at it and hit it.

The next morning Lahcen came to Idir's room. His eyes were red from the wine he had been drinking. He sat down on the floor and pulled out a handkerchief that had a knot tied in one corner. He untied the knot and let a gold ring fall out into his lap. Picking up the ring, he handed it to Idir. 'For you. I got it cheap.' Idir saw that Lahcen wanted him to take the ring, and he put it on his finger, saying: 'May Allah give you health.' Lahcen rubbed his hand across his chin and yawned. Then he said: 'I saw you look at me, and afterward when we got to the quarry I thought that would be the best place. And then I remembered the night the police took us at Bou Khach Khach, and I remembered you looking at me. I turned around and left her there. Garbage!'

'So you're not in jail and you're drunk,' said Idir, and he laughed.

'That's true,' said Lahcen. 'And that's why I give you the ring.'

Idir knew the ring was worth at least fifty dirhams, and he could sell it if he needed money badly. That would end his friendship with Lahcen, but there would be no help for it.

Sometimes Lahcen came by in the evening with a bottle of wine. He would drink the whole bottle while Idir smoked his kif pipe, and they would listen to the radio until the end of the program at twelve o'clock. Afterward, very late, they would walk through the streets of Dradeb to a garage where a friend of Lahcen's was night watchman. When the moon was full, it was brighter than the street lights. With no moon, there was nobody in the streets, and in the few late cafés the men told one another about what thieves had done, and how there were more of them than ever before. This was because there was almost no work to be had anywhere, and the country people were selling their cows and sheep to be able to pay their taxes, and then coming to the city. Lahcen and Idir worked now and then, whenever they found something to do. They had a little money, they always ate, and Lahcen sometimes was able to afford his bottle of Spanish wine. Idir's kif was more of a problem, because each time the police decided to enforce the law they had made against it, it grew very scarce and the price went up. Then when there was plenty to be had, because the police were busy looking for guns and rebels instead, the price stayed high. He did not smoke any less, but he smoked by himself in his room. If you smoke in a café, there is always someone who has left his kif at home and wants to use yours. He told his friends at the Café Nadjah that he had given up kif, and he never accepted a pipe when it was offered to him.

Back in his room in the early evening, with the window open and the sleepy sounds of the town coming up, for it was summer and the voices of people filled the streets, Idir sat in the chair he had bought and put his feet on the windowsill. That way he could see the sky as he smoked. Lahcen would come in and talk. Now and then they went together to Emsallah to a barraca there near the slaughter house where two sisters lived with their feeble-minded mother. They would get the mother drunk and put her to bed in the inner room. Then they would get the girls drunk and spend the night with them, without paying. The cognac was expensive, but it did not cost as much as whores would have.

In midsummer, at the time of Sidi Kacem, it suddenly grew very hot. People set up tents made of sheets on the roofs of their houses and cooked and slept there. At night in the moonlight Idir could see all the roofs, each one with its box of sheets flapping in the wind, and inside the sheets the red light made by the fire in the pot. Daytimes, the sun shining on the sea of white sheets hurt his eyes, and he remembered not to look out when he passed the window as he moved about his room. He would have liked to live in a more expensive room, one with a blind to keep out the light. There was no way of being protected from the bright summer day that filled the sky outside, and he waited with longing for dusk. His custom was not to smoke kif before the sun went down. He did not like it in the daytime, above all in summer when the air is hot and the light is powerful. When each day came up hotter than the one before it, he decided to buy enough food and kif to last several days, and to shut himself into his room until it got cooler. He had worked two days at the port that week and had some money. He put the food on the table and locked the door. Then he took the key out of the lock and threw it into the drawer of the table. Lying with the packages and cans in his market basket was a large bundle of kif wrapped in a newspaper. He unfolded it, took out a sheaf and sniffed of it. For the next two hours he sat on the floor picking off the leaves and cutting them on a breadboard, sifting, and cutting, again and again. Once, as the sun reached him, he had to move to get out of its heat. By the time the sun went down he had enough ready for three or four days. He got up off the floor and sat in his chair with his pouch and his pipe in his lap, and smoked, while the radio played the Chleuh music that was always broadcast at this hour for the Soussi shopkeepers. In cafés men often got up and turned it off. Idir enjoyed it. Kif smokers usually like it, because of the naqous that always pounds the same design.

The music played a long time, and Idir thought of the market at Tiznit and the mosque with the tree trunks sticking out of its mud walls. He looked down at the floor. The room still had daylight in it. He opened his eyes wide. A small bird was walking slowly along the floor. He jumped up. The kif pipe fell, but its bowl did not break. Before the bird had time to move, he had put his hand over it. Even when he held it between his two hands it did not struggle. He looked at it, and thought it was the smallest bird he had ever seen. Its head was grey and its wings were black and white. It looked at him, and it did not seem afraid. He sat down in the chair with the bird in his lap. When he lifted his hand it stayed still. 'It's a young bird and can't fly,' he thought. He smoked several pipes of kif. The bird did not move. The sun had gone down and the houses were growing blue in the evening light. He stroked the bird's head with his thumb. Then he took the ring from his little finger and slipped it over the smooth feathers of its head. The bird paid no attention. 'A gold collar for the sultan of birds,' he said. He smoked some more kif and looked at the sky. Then he began to be hungry, and he thought the bird might like some breadcrumbs. He put his pipe down on the table and tried to take the ring from the bird's head. It would not come off over the feathers. He pulled at it, and the bird fluttered its wings and struggled. For a second he let go of it, and in that instant it flew straight from his lap into the sky. Idir jumped up and stood watching it. When it was gone, he began to smile. 'The son of a whore!' he whispered.

He prepared his food and ate it. After that he sat in the chair smoking and thinking about the bird. When Lahcen came he told him the story. 'He was waiting all the time for a chance to steal something,' he said. Lahcen was a little drunk, and he was angry. 'So he stole my ring!' he cried. 'Ah,' said Idir. 'Yours? I thought you gave it to me.'

'I'm not crazy yet,' Lahcen told him. He went away still angry, and did not return for more than a week. The morning he came into the room Idir was certain that he was going to begin to talk again about the ring, and he quickly handed him a pair of shoes he had bought from a friend the day before. 'Do these fit you?' he asked him. Lahcen sat down in the chair, put them on, and found they did fit. 'They need new bottoms, but the tops are like new,' Idir told him. 'The tops are good,' said Lahcen. He felt of the leather and squeezed it between his thumb and fingers. 'Take them,' said Idir. Lahcen was pleased, and he said nothing about the ring that day. When he got the shoes to his room he looked carefully at them and decided to spend the money that it would cost to have new soles made.

The next day he went to a Spanish cobbler, who agreed to repair the shoes for fifteen dirhams. 'Ten,' said Lahcen. After a long discussion the cobbler lowered his price to thirteen, and he left the shoes there, saying that he would call for them in a week. The same afternoon he was walking through Sidi Bouknadel, and he saw a girl. They talked together for two hours or more, standing not very near to each other beside the wall, and looking down at the ground so that no one could see they were talking. The girl was from Meknes, and that was why he had never seen her before. She was visiting her aunt, who lived there in the quarter, and soon her sister was coming from Meknes. She looked to him the best thing he had seen that year, but of course he could not be sure of her nose and mouth because her veil hid them. He got her to agree to meet him at the same place the next day. This time they took a walk along the Hafa, and he could see that she would be willing. But she would not tell him where her aunt's house was.

Only two days later he got her to his room. As he had expected, she was beautiful. That night he was very happy, but in the morning when she had gone, he understood that he wanted to be with her all the time. He wanted to know what her aunt's house was like and how she was going to pass her day. In this way a bad time began for Lahcen. He was happy only when she was with him and he could get into bed and see her lying on one side of him and a bottle of cognac on the other, upright on the floor beside his pillow, where he could reach it easily. Each day when she had gone he lay thinking about all the men she might be going to see before she came back to him. When he talked about it to her she laughed and said she spent all her time with her aunt and sister, who now had arrived from Meknes. But he could not stop worrying about it.

Two weeks went by before he remembered to go and get his shoes. On his way to the cobbler's he thought about how he would solve his problem. He had an idea that Idir could help him. If he brought Idir and the girl together and left them alone, Idir would tell him afterward everything that had happened. If she let Idir take her to bed, then she was a whore and could be treated like a whore. He would give her a good beating and then make it up with her, because she was too good to throw away. But he had to know whether she was really his, or whether she would go with others.

When the cobbler handed him his shoes, he saw that they looked almost like new, and he was pleased. He paid the thirteen dirhams and took the shoes home. That night when he was going to put them on to wear to the café, he found that his feet would not go into them. They were much too small. The cobbler had cut down the last in order to stitch on the new soles. He put his old shoes back on, went out, and slammed the door. That night he had a quarrel with the girl. It took him until almost dawn to stop her crying. When the sun came up and she was asleep, he lay with his arms folded behind his head looking at the ceiling, thinking that the shoes had cost him thirteen dirhams and now he was going to have to spend the day trying to sell them. He got rid of the girl early and went in to Bou Aragia with the shoes. No one would give him more than eight dirhams for them. In the afternoon he went to the Joteya and sat in the shade of a grapevine, waiting for the buyers and sellers to arrive. A man from the mountains finally offered him ten dirhams, and he sold the shoes. 'Three dirhams gone for nothing,' he thought when he put the money into his pocket. He was angry, but instead of blaming the cobbler, he felt that the fault was Idir's.

That afternoon he saw Idir, and he told him he would bring a friend with him to Idir's room after the evening meal. Then he went home and drank cognac. When the girl arrived he had finished the bottle, and he was drunk and more unhappy than ever. 'Don't take it off,' he told her when she began to unfasten her veil. 'We're going out.' She said nothing. They took the back streets to Idir's room.

Idir sat in his chair listening to the radio. He had not expected a girl, and when he saw her take off her veil the beating of his heart made his head ache. He told her to sit in the chair, and then he paid no more attention to her and sat on the bed talking only with Lahcen, who did not look at her either. Soon Lahcen got up. 'I'm going out to get some cigarettes,' he said. 'I'll be right back.' He shut the door after him, and Idir quickly went and locked it. He smiled at the girl and sat on the table beside her, looking down at her. Now and then he smoked a pipe of kif. He wondered why Lahcen was taking so long. Finally he said: 'He's not coming back, you know.' The girl laughed and shrugged. He jumped up, took her hand, and led her to the bed.

In the morning when they were getting dressed, she told him she lived at the Hotel Sevilla. It was a small Moslem hotel in the center of the Medina. He took her there and left her. 'Will you come tonight?' she asked him. Idir frowned. He was thinking of Lahcen. 'Don't wait for me after midnight,' he said. On his way home he stopped at the Café Nadjah. Lahcen was there. His eyes were red and he looked as though he had not slept at all. Idir had the feeling that he had been waiting for him to appear, for when he came into the café Lahcen quickly got up and paid the qahouaji. They walked down the main street of Dradeb without saying any-thing, and when they got to the road that leads to the Merkala beach, they turned down it, still without speaking.

It was low tide. They walked on the wet sand while the small waves broke at their feet. Lahcen smoked a cigarette and threw stones into the water. Finally he spoke. 'How was it?'

Idir shrugged, tried to keep his voice flat. 'All right for one night,' he said. Lahcen was ready to say carelessly: 'Or even two.' But then he realized that Idir did not want to talk about the night, which meant that it had been a great event for him. And when he looked at his face he was certain that Idir wanted the girl for himself. He was sure he had already lost her to him, but he did not know why he had not thought of that in the beginning. Now he forgot the true reason why he had wanted to take her to Idir.

'You thought I brought her just to be good to you!' he cried. 'No, sidi! I left her there to see if you were a friend. And I see what kind of friend you are! A scorpion!' He seized the front of Idir's garments and struck him in the face. Idir moved backward a few steps, and got ready to fight. He un-derstood that Lahcen had seen the truth, and that now there was nothing at all to say, and nothing to do but fight. When they were both bloody and panting, he looked for a flash at Lahcen's face, and saw that he was dizzy and could not see very well. He drew back, put his head down, and with all his force ran into Lahcen, who lost his balance and fell onto the sand. Then quickly he kicked him in the head with the heel of his shoe. He left him lying there and went home.

In a little while Lahcen began to hear the waves breaking on the sand near him. 'I must kill him,' he thought. 'He sold my ring. Now I must go and kill him.' Instead, he took off his clothes and bathed in the sea, and when he had finished, he lay in the sun on the sand all day and slept. In the evening he went and got very drunk.

At eleven o'clock Idir went to the Hotel Sevilla. The girl was sitting in a wicker chair by the front door, waiting for him. She looked carefully at the cuts on his face. Under her veil he saw her smile.

The Wind at Beni Midar

A T Beni Midar there is a barracks. It has many rows of small buildings, whitewashed, and everything is in the middle of big rocks, on the side of the mountain behind the town. A quiet place when the wind is not blowing. A few Spanish still live in the houses along the road. They run the shops. But now the people in the street are Moslems, mountain men with goats and sheep, or soldiers from the cuartel looking for wine. The Spanish sell wine to men they know. One Jew sells it to almost anybody. But there never is enough wine in the town for everybody who wants it. Beni Midar has only one street. It comes down out of the mountains, curves back and forth like a snake between the houses for a while, and goes on, back into the mountains. Sunday is a bad day, the one free time the soldiers have, when they can walk back and forth all day between the shops and houses. A few Spaniards in black clothes go into the church at the hour when the Rhmara ride their donkeys out of the souk. Later the Spaniards come out of the church and go home. Nothing else happens because all the shops are shut. There is nothing the soldiers can buy.

Driss had been stationed for eight months in Beni Midar. Because the cabran in charge of his unit had been a neighbor of his in Tetuan, he was not unhappy. The cabran had a friend with a motorcycle. Together they went each month to Tetuan. There the cabran always saw Driss's sister, who made a big bundle of food to send back to the barracks for him. She sent him chickens and cakes, cigarettes and figs, and always many hard-boiled eggs. He shared the eggs with two or three friends, and did not complain about being in Beni Midar.

Not even the brothels were open on Sunday. It was the day when everyone walked from one end of the town to the other, back and forth, many times. Sometimes Driss walked like this with his friends. Usually he took his gun and went down into the valley to hunt for hares. When he came back at twilight he stopped in a small café at the edge of the town and had a glass of tea and a few pipes of kif. If it had not been the only café he would never have gone into it. Shameful things happened there. Several times he had seen men from the mountains get up from the mat and do dances that left blood on the floor. These men were Djilala, and no one thought of stopping them, not even Driss. They did not dance because they wanted to dance, and it was this that made him angry and ashamed. It seemed to him that the world should be made in such a way that a man is free to dance or not as he feels. A Djilali can do only what the music tells him to do. When the musicians, who are Djilala too, play the music that has the power, his eyes shut and he falls on the floor. And until the man has shown the proof and drunk his own blood, the musicians do not begin the music that will bring him back to the world. They should do something about it, Driss said to the other soldiers who went with him to the café, and they agreed.

He had talked about it with his cabran in the public garden. The cabran said that when all the children in the land were going to school every day there would be no more djenoun. Women would no longer be able to put spells on their husbands. And the Djilala and the Hamatcha and all the others would stop cutting their legs and arms and chests. Driss thought about this for a long time. He was glad to hear that the government knew about these bad things. But if they know, he thought, why don't they do something now? The day they get every one of the children in school I'll be lying beside Sidi Ali el Mandri. He was thinking of the cemetery at Bab Sebta in Tetuan. When he saw the cabran again he said: 'If they can do something about it, they ought to do it now.' The cabran did not seem interested. 'Yes,' he said.

When Driss got his permission and went home he told his father what the cabran had said. 'You mean the government thinks it can kill all evil spirits?' his father cried.

'That's right. It can,' said Driss. 'It's going to.'

His father was old and had no confidence in the young men who now ran the government. 'It's impossible,' he said. 'They should let them alone. Leave them under their stones. Children have gone to school before, and how many were hurt by djenoun? But if the government begins to make trouble for them, you'll see what will happen. They'll go after the children first.'

Driss had expected his father to speak this way, but when he heard the words he was ashamed. He did not answer. Some of his friends were without respect for God. They ate during Ramadan and argued with their fathers. He was glad not to be like them. But he felt his father was wrong.

One hot summer Sunday when the sky was very blue Driss lay in bed late. The men who slept in his room at the barracks had gone out. He listened to the radio. It would be good down in the valley on a day like this, he thought. He saw himself swimming in one of the big pools, and he thought of the hot sun on his back afterwards. He got up and unlocked the cupboard to look at his gun. Even before he took it out he said 'Yah latif!' because he remembered that he had only one cartridge left, and it was Sunday. He slammed the cupboard door shut and got back into bed. The radio began to give the news. He sat up, spat as far out as he could from the bed, and turned it off. In the silence he heard many birds singing in the safsaf tree outside the window. He scratched his head. Then he got up and dressed. In the courtyard he saw Mehdi going toward the stairs. Mehdi was on his way to do sentry duty in the box outside the main gate.

'Khai! Does four rials sound good to you?'

Mehdi loooked at him. 'Is this number sixty, three, fifty-one?' he said. This was the name of an Egyptian song that came over the radio nearly every day. The song ended with the word nothing. Nothing, nothing, sung over and over again.

Why not? As they walked along together, Driss moved closer, so that his thighs rubbed against Mehdi's.

'The price is ten, khoya.'

'With all its cartridges?'

'You want me to open it up and show you here?' Mehdi's voice was angry. The words came out of the side of his mouth.

Driss said nothing. They came to the top of the stairs. Mehdi was walking fast. 'You'll have to have it back here by seven,' he said. 'Do you want it?'

In his head Driss saw the long day in the empty town. 'Yes,' he said. 'Stay there.' He hurried back to the room, unlocked his cupboard, and took out his gun. From the shelf he pulled down his pipe, his kif, and a loaf of bread. He put his head outside the door. There was no one in the courtyard but Mehdi sitting on the wall at the other end. Then with the old gun in his hands he ran all the way to Mehdi. Mehdi took it and went down the stairs, leaving his own gun lying on the wall. Driss took up the gun, waited a moment, and followed him. When he went past the sentry box he heard Mehdi's voice say softly: 'I need the ten at seven, khoya.'

Driss grunted. He knew how dark it was in there. No officer ever stuck his head inside the door on Sundays. Ten rials, he thought, and he's running no risk. He looked around at the goats among the rocks. The sun was hot, but the air smelled sweet, and he was happy to be walking down the side of the mountain. He pulled the visor of his cap further down over his eyes and began to whistle. Soon he came out in front of the town, below it on the other side of the valley. He could see the people on the benches in the park at the top of the cliff, small but clear and black. They were Spaniards and they were waiting for the bell of their church to begin to ring.

He got to the highest pool about the time the sun was overhead. When he lay on the rocks afterwards eating his bread, the sun burned him. No animals will move before three, he thought. He put his trousers on and crawled into the shade of the oleander bushes to sleep. When he awoke the air was cooler. He smoked all the kif he had, and went walking through the valley. Sometimes he sang. He found no hares, and so he put small stones on the tops of the rocks and fired at them. Then he climbed back up the other side of the valley and followed the highway into the town.

He came to the café and went in. The musicians were playing an aaita and singing. The tea drinkers clapped their hands with the music. A soldier cried: 'Driss! Sit down!' He sat with his friends and smoked some of their kif. Then he bought four rials' worth from the cutter who sat on the platform with the musicians, and went on smoking. 'Nothing was moving in the valley today,' he told them. 'It was dead down there.'

A man with a yellow turban on his head who sat nearby closed his eyes and fell against the man next to him. The others around him moved to a further part of the mat. The man toppled over and lay on the floor.

'Another one?' cried Driss. 'They should stay in Djebel Habib. I can't look at him.'

The man took a long time to get to his feet. His arms and legs had been captured by the drums, but his body was fighting, and he groaned. Driss tried to pay no attention to him. He smoked his pipe and looked at his friends, pretending that no Djilali was in front of him. When the man pulled out his knife he could not pretend any longer. He watched the blood running into the man's eyes. It made a blank red curtain over each hole. The man opened his eyes wider, as if he wanted to see through the blood. The drums were loud.

Driss got up and paid the qahouaji for his tea. He said good-bye to the others and went out. The sun would soon go below the top of the mountain. Its light made him want to shut his eyes, because he had a lot of kif in his head. He walked through the town to the higher end and turned into a lane that led up into another valley. In this place there was no one. Cactuses grew high on each side of the lane, and the spiders had built a world of webs between their thorns. Because he walked fast, the kif began to boil in his head. Soon he was very hungry, but all the fruit had been picked from the cactuses along the lane. He came to a small farmhouse with a thatched roof. Behind it on the empty mountainside there were more cactuses still pink with hundreds of hindiyats. A dog in a shed beside the house began to bark. There was no sign of people. He stood still for a while and listened to the dog. Then he walked toward the cactus patch. He was sure no one was in the house. Many years ago his sister had shown him how to pick hindiyats without letting the needles get into the flesh of his hands. He laid his gun on the ground behind a low stone wall and began to gather the fruit. As he picked he saw in his head the two blind red holes of the Djilali's eyes, and under his breath he cursed all Djilala. When he had a great pile of fruit on the ground he sat down and began to eat, throwing the peels over his shoulder. As he ate he grew hungrier, and so he picked more. The picture he had in his head of the man's face shiny with blood slowly faded. He thought only of the hindiyats he was eating. It was almost dark there on the mountainside. He looked at his watch and jumped up, because he remembered that Mehdi had to have his gun at seven o'clock. In the dim light he could not see the gun anywhere. He searched behind the wall, where he thought he had laid it, but he saw only stones and bushes.

'It's gone, Allah istir,' he said. His heart pounded. He ran back to the lane and stood there a while. The dog barked without stopping.

It was dark before he reached the gate of the barracks. Another man was in the sentry box. The cabran was waiting for him in the room. The old gun Driss's father had given him lay on his bed.

'Do you know where Mehdi is?' the cabran asked him.

'No,' said Driss.

'He's in the dark house, the son of a whore. And do you know why?'

Driss sat down on the bed. The cabran is my friend, he was thinking. 'It's gone,' he said, and told him how he had laid the gun on the ground, and a dog had been barking, and no one had come by, and still it had disappeared. 'Maybe the dog was a djinn,' he said when he had finished. He did not really believe the dog had anything to do with it, but he could not think of anything else to say then.

The cabran looked at him a long time and said nothing. He shook his head. 'I thought you had some brains,' he said at last. Then his face grew very angry, and he pulled Driss out into the courtyard and told a soldier to lock him up.

At ten o'clock that night he went to see Driss. He found him smoking his sebsi in the dark. The cell was full of kif smoke. 'Garbage!' cried the cabran, and he took the pipe and the kif away from him. 'Tell the truth,' he said to Driss. 'You sold the gun, didn't you?'

'On my mother's head, it's just as I told you! There was only the dog.'

The cabran could not make him say anything different. He slammed the door and went to the café in the town to have a glass of tea. He sat listening to the music, and he began to smoke the kif he had taken from Driss. If Driss was telling the

truth, then it was only the kif in Driss's head that had made
him lose the gun, and in that case there was a chance that it
could be found.

The cabran had not smoked in a long time. As the kif filled
his head he began to be hungry, and he remembered the
times when he had been a boy smoking kif with his friends.
Always they had gone to look for hindiyats afterward, because
they tasted better than anything else and cost nothing. They
always knew where there were some growing. A kouffa full of
good hindiyats, he thought. He shut his eyes and went on
thinking.

The next morning early the cabran went out and stood on
a high rock behind the barracks, looking carefully all around
the valley and the bare mountainside. Not far away he saw a
lane with cactuses along it, and further up there was a whole
forest of cactus. There, he said to himself.

He walked among the rocks until he came to the lane, and
he followed the lane to the farmhouse. The dog began to
bark. A woman came to the doorway and looked at him. He
paid no attention to her, but went straight to the high cactuses on the hillside behind the house. There were many
hindiyats still to be eaten, but the cabran did not eat any of
them. He had no kif in his head and he was thinking only of
the gun. Beside a stone wall there was a big pile of hindiyat
peelings. Someone had eaten a great many. Then he saw the
sun shining on part of the gun's barrel under the peelings.
'Hah!' he shouted, and he seized the gun and wiped it all
over with his handkerchief. On his way back to the barracks
he felt so happy that he decided to play a joke on Driss.

He hid the gun under his bed. With a glass of tea and a
piece of bread in his hand he went to see Driss. He found him
asleep on the floor in the dark.

'Daylight is here!' he shouted. He laughed and kicked
Driss's foot to wake him up. Driss sat on the floor drinking
the tea and the cabran stood in the doorway scratching his
chin. He looked down at the floor, but not at Driss. After a
time he said: 'Last night you told me a dog was barking?'

Driss was certain the cabran was going to make fun of him.
He was sorry he had mentioned the dog. 'Yes,' he said, not
sounding sure.

'If it was the dog,' the cabran went on, 'I know how to get it back. You have to help me.'

Driss looked up at him. He could not believe the cabran was being serious. Finally he said in a low voice: 'I was joking when I said that. I had kif in my head.'

The cabran was angry. 'You think it's a joke to lose a gun that belongs to the Sultan? You did sell it! You haven't got kif in your head now. Maybe you can tell the truth.' He stepped toward Driss, and Driss thought he was going to hit him. He stood up quickly. 'I told you the truth,' he said. 'It was gone.'

The cabran rubbed his chin and looked down at the floor again for a minute. 'The next time a Djilali begins to dance in the café, we'll do it,' he told him. He shut the door and left Driss alone.

Two days later the cabran came again to the dark house. He had another soldier with him. 'Quick!' he told Driss. 'There's one dancing now.'

They went out into the courtyard and Driss blinked his eyes. 'Listen,' said the cabran. 'When the Djilali is drinking his own blood he has power. What you have to do is ask him to make the djinn bring me the gun. I'm going to sit in my room and burn djaoui. That may help.'

'I'll do it,' said Driss. 'But it won't do any good.'

The other soldier took Driss to the café. The Djilali was a tall man from the mountains. He had already taken out his knife, and he was waving it in the air. The soldier made Driss sit down near the musicians, and then he waited until the man began to lick the blood from his arms. Then, because he thought he might be sick if he watched any longer, Driss raised his right arm toward the Djilali and said in a low voice: 'In the name of Allah, khoya, make the djinn that stole Mehdi's gun take it now to Aziz the cabran.' The Djilali seemed to be staring at him, but Driss could not be sure whether he had heard his words or not.

The soldier took him back to the barracks. The cabran was sitting under a plum tree beside the kitchen door. He told the soldier to go away and jumped up. 'Come,' he said, and he led Driss to the room. The air was blue with the smoke of the djaoui he had been burning. He pointed to the middle of the floor. 'Look!' he cried. A gun was lying there. Driss ran and picked it up. After he had looked at it carefully, he said: 'It's the gun.' And his voice was full of fear. The cabran could see that Driss had not been sure the thing was possible, but that now he no longer had any doubt.

The cabran was happy to have fooled him so easily. He laughed. 'You see, it worked,' he said. 'It's lucky for you. Mehdi's going to be in the dark house for another week.'

Driss did not answer. He felt even worse than when he had been watching the Djilali slicing the flesh of his arms.

That night he lay in bed worrying. It was the first time he had had anything to do with a djinn or an affrit. Now he had entered into their world. It was a dangerous world and he did not trust the cabran any longer. What am I going to do? he thought. The men all around him were sleeping, but he could not close his eyes. Soon he got up and stepped outside. The leaves of the safsaf tree were hissing in the wind. On the other side of the courtyard there was light in one of the windows. Some of the officers were talking there. He walked slowly around the garden in the middle and looked up at the sky, thinking of how different his life was going to be now. As he came near the lighted window he heard a great burst of laughter. The cabran was telling a story. Driss stopped walking and listened.

'And he said to the Djilali: "Please, sidi, would you ask the dog that stole my gun——"'

The men laughed again, and the sound covered the cabran's voice.

He went quickly back and got into bed. If they knew he had heard the cabran's story they would laugh even more. He lay in the bed thinking, and he felt poison come into his heart. It was the cabran's fault that the djinn had been called, and now in front of his superior officers he was pretending that he had had nothing to do with it. Later the cabran came in and went to bed, and it was quiet in the courtyard, but Driss lay thinking for a long time before he went to sleep.

In the days that came after that, the cabran was friendly again, but Driss did not want to see him smile. He thought with hatred: In his head I'm afraid of him now because he knows how to call a djinn. He jokes with me now because he has power.

He could not laugh or be happy when the cabran was nearby. Each night he lay awake for a long time after the others had gone to sleep. He listened to the wind moving the hard leaves of the safsaf tree, and he thought only of how he could break the cabran's power.

When Mehdi came out of the dark house he spoke against the cabran. Driss paid him his ten rials. 'A lot of money for ten days in the dark house,' Mehdi grumbled, and he looked at the bill in his hand. Driss pretended not to understand. 'He's a son of a whore,' he said.

Mehdi snorted. 'And you have the head of a needle,' he said. 'It all came from you. The wind blows the kif out your ears!'

'You think I wasn't in the dark house too?' cried Driss. But he could not tell Mehdi about the Djilali and the dog. 'He's a son of a whore,' he said again.

Mehdi's eyes grew narrow and stiff. 'I'll do his work for him. He'll think he's in the dark house himself when I finish.'

Mehdi went on his way. Driss stood watching him go.

The next Sunday Driss got up early and walked into Beni Midar. The souk was full of rows of mountain people in white clothes. He walked in among the donkeys and climbed the steps to the stalls. There he went to see an old man who sold incense and herbs. People called him El Fqih. He sat down in front of El Fqih and said: 'I want something for a son of a whore.'

El Fqih looked at him angrily. 'A sin!' He raised his forefinger and shook it back and forth. 'Sins are not my work.' Driss did not say anything. El Fqih spoke more quietly now. 'To balance that, it is said that each trouble in the world has its remedy. There are cheap remedies and remedies that cost a lot of money.' He stopped.

Driss waited. 'How much is this one?' he asked him. The old man was not pleased because he wanted to talk longer. But he said: 'I'll give you a name for five rials.' He looked sternly at Driss, leaned forward and whispered a name in his ear. 'In the alley behind the sawmill,' he said aloud. 'The blue tin shack with the canebrake in back of it.' Driss paid him and ran down the steps.

He found the house. The old woman stood in the doorway

with a checked tablecloth over her head. Her eyes had turned white like milk. They looked to Driss like the eyes of an old dog. He said: 'You're Anisa?'

'Come into the house,' she told him. It was almost dark inside. He told her he wanted something to break the power of a son of a whore. 'Give me ten rials now,' she said. 'Come back at sunset with another ten. It will be ready.'

After the midday meal he went out into the courtyard. He met Mehdi and asked him to go with him to the café in Beni Midar. They walked through the town in the hot afternoon sun. It was still early when they got to the café, and there was plenty of space on the mats. They sat in a dark corner. Driss took out his kif and his sebsi and they smoked. When the musicians began to play, Mehdi said: 'The circus is back!' But Driss did not want to talk about the Djilala. He talked about the cabran. He gave the pipe many times to Mehdi, and he watched Mehdi growing more angry with the cabran as he smoked. He was not surprised when Mehdi cried: 'I'll finish it tonight!'

'No, khoya,' said Driss. 'You don't know. He's gone way up. He's a friend of all the officers now. They bring him bottles of wine.'

'He'll come down,' Mehdi said. 'Before dinner tonight. In the courtyard. You be there and watch it.'

Driss handed him the pipe and paid for the tea. He left Mehdi there and went into the street to walk up and down because he did not want to sit still any longer. When the sky was red behind the mountain he went to the alley by the sawmill. The old woman was in the doorway.

'Come in,' she said as before. When they were inside the room she handed him a paper packet. 'He has to take all of it,' she said. She took the money and pulled at his sleeve. 'I never saw you,' she said. 'Goodbye.'

Driss went to his room and listened to the radio. When dinner time came he stood inside the doorway looking out into the courtyard. In the shadows at the other end he thought he could see Mehdi, but he was not sure. There were many soldiers walking around in the courtyard, waiting for dinner. Soon there was shouting near the top of the steps. The soldiers began to run toward the other end of the courtyard. Driss looked from the doorway and saw only the running soldiers. He called to the men in the room. 'Something's happening!' They all ran out. Then with the paper of powder in his hand he went back into the room to the cabran's bed and lifted up the bottle of wine one of the officers had given the cabran the day before. It was almost full. He pulled out the cork and let the powder slide into the bottle. He shook the bottle and put the cork back. There was still shouting in the courtyard. He ran out. When he got near the crowd, he saw Mehdi being dragged along the ground by three soldiers. He was kicking. The cabran sat on the wall with his head down, holding his arm. There was blood all over his face and shirt.

It was almost a half hour before the cabran came to eat his dinner. His face was covered with bruises and his arm was bandaged and hung in a sling. Mehdi had cut it with his knife at the last minute when the soldiers had begun to pull them apart. The cabran did not speak much, and the men did not try to talk with him. He sat on his bed and ate. While he was eating he drank all the wine in the bottle.

That night the cabran moaned in his sleep. A dry wind blew between the mountains. It made a great noise in the saf-saf tree outside the window. The air roared and the leaves rattled, but Driss still heard the cabran's voice crying. In the morning the doctor came to look at him. The cabran's eyes were open but he could not see. And his mouth was open but he could not speak. They carried him out of the room where the soldiers lived and put him somewhere else. Maybe the power is broken now, thought Driss.

A few days later a truck came to the barracks, and he saw two men carrying the cabran on a stretcher to the truck. Then he was sure that the cabran's soul had been torn out of his body and that the power was truly broken. In his head he made a prayer of thanks to Allah. He stood with some other soldiers on a rock above the barracks watching the truck grow smaller as it moved down the mountain.

'It's bad for me,' he told a man who stood nearby. 'He always brought me food from home.' The soldier shook his head.

NEW STORIES FROM
THE TIME OF FRIENDSHIP

CONTENTS

The Time of Friendship

THE TROUBLE had been growing bigger each year, ever since the end of the war. From the beginning, although aware of its existence, Fräulein Windling had determined to pay it no attention. At first there were only whispered reports of mass arrests. People said: "Many thousands of Moslems have been sent to prison in France." Soon some of her own friends had begun to disappear, like young Bachir and Omar ben Lakhdar, the postmaster of Timimoun, who suddenly one morning were gone, or so she was told, for when she returned the following winter they were not there, and she never had seen them since. The people simply made their faces blank when she tried to talk about it. After the hostilities had begun in earnest, even though the nationalists had derailed the trains and disrupted the trans-Saharan truck service on several occasions, still it was possible to get beyond the disturbed region to her oasis. There in the south the fighting was far away, and the long hours of empty desert that lay between made it seem much farther, almost as though it had been across the sea. If the men of her oasis should ever be infected by the virus of discontent from the far-off north—and this seemed to her almost inconceivable—then in spite of the fact that she was certain that war could bring them nothing but unhappiness, she would have no recourse but to hope for their victory. It was their own land they would be fighting for, their own lives they would be losing in order to win the fight. In the meantime people did not talk; life was hard but peaceful. Each one was aware of the war that was going on in the north, and each one was glad it was far away.

Summers, Fräulein Windling taught in the Freiluftschule in Bern, where she entertained her pupils with tales of the life led by the people in the great desert in Africa. In the village where she lived, she told them, everything was made by the people themselves out of what the desert had to offer. They lived in a world of objects fashioned out of baked earth, woven grass, palmwood and animal skins. There was no metal. Although she did not admit it to the children, this was no

279

longer wholly true, since recently the women had taken to using empty oil tins for carrying water, instead of the goathide bags of a few years before. She had tried to discourage her friends among the village women from this innovation, telling them that the tins could poison the water; they had agreed, and gone on using them. "They are lazy," she decided. "The oil tins are easier to carry."

When the sun went down and the cool air from the oasis below with its sting of woodsmoke rose to the level of the hotel, she would smell it inside her room and stop whatever she was doing. Then she would put on her burnoose and climb the stairs to the roof. The blanket she lay on while she sunbathed each morning would be there, and she would stretch out on it facing the western sky, and feel the departed sun's heat still strong underneath her body. It was one of the great pleasures of the day, to watch the light changing in the oasis below, when dusk and the smoke from the evening fires slowly blotted out the valley. There always came a moment when all that was left was the faint outline, geometric and precise, of the mass of mud prisms that was the village, and a certain clump of high date palms that stood outside its entrance. The houses themselves were no longer there, and eventually the highest palm disappeared; and unless there was a moon all that remained to be seen was the dying sky, the sharp edges of the rocks on the hammada, and a blank expanse of mist that lay over the valley but did not reach as far up the cliffs as the hotel.

Perhaps twice each winter a group of the village women would invite Fräulein Windling to go with them up into the vast land of the dunes to look for firewood. The glare here was cruel. There was not even the trace of a twig or a stem anywhere on the sand, yet as they wandered along the crests barefoot the women could spot the places where roots lay buried beneath the surface, and then they would stoop, uncover them, and dig them up. "The wind leaves a sign," they told her, but she was never certain of being able to identify the sign, nor could she understand how there might be a connection between the invisible roots in the sand and the wind in the air above. "What we have lost, they still possess," she thought.

Her first sight of the desert and its people had been a trans-figuring experience; indeed, it seemed to her now that before coming here she had never been in touch with life at all. She believed firmly that each day she spent here increased the aggregate of her resistance. She coveted the rugged health of the natives, when her own was equally strong, but because she was white and educated, she was convinced that her body was intrinsically inferior.

All the work in the hotel was done by one quiet, sad-faced man named Boufelja. He had been there when she had first arrived many years ago; for Fräulein Windling he had come to be as much a part of the place as the cliffs across the valley. She often sat on at her table by the fireplace after lunch, playing cards by herself, until the logs no longer gave out heat. There were two very young French soldiers from the fort opposite, who ate in the hotel dining-room. They drank a great amount of wine, and it annoyed her to see their faces slowly turning red as they sat there. At first the soldiers had tipped their caps to her as they went out, and they had stopped their laughing long enough to say, "*Bonjour, madame,*" to her, but now they no longer did. She was happy when they had left, and savored the moment before the fire burned out, while it still glowed under the gusts of wind that wandered down the wide chimney.

Almost always the wind sprang up early in the afternoon, a steady, powerful blowing that roared through the thousands of palms in the oasis below and howled under each door in the hotel, covering the more distant village sounds. This was the hour when she played solitaire, or merely sat, watching the burnt-out logs as they fell to pieces before her eyes. Later she would go along the terrace, a high, bright place like the deck of a great ship sailing through the desert afternoon, hurrying into her room for an instant to get her sweater and cane, and start out on a walk. Sometimes she went southward following the river valley, along the foot of the silent cliffs and through the crooked gorges, to an abandoned village built in a very hot place at a turn in the canyon. The sheer walls of rock behind it sent back the heat, so that the air burned her throat as she breathed it in. Or she went farther, to where the cliff dwellings were, with their animals and symbols incised in the rock.

Returning along the road that led to the village, deep in the green shade of the thickest part of the palm forest, she was regularly aware of the same group of boys sitting at the turn of the road, at a place just before it led up the hill to the shops and the village. They squatted on the sand behind the feathery branches of a giant tamarisk, quietly talking. When she came up to them she greeted them, and they always replied, remained silent a moment until she had passed by, and then resumed their conversation. As far as she could tell, there was never any reference to her by word, and yet this year it sometimes seemed to her that once she had gone by, their inflection had subtly altered, as though there had been a modulation into another key. Did their attitude border on derision? She did not know, but since this was the first time during all her years in the desert that the idea had ever suggested itself to her, she put it resolutely out of her mind. "A new generation requires a new technique if one is to establish contact," she thought. "It is for me to find it." Nevertheless she was sorry that there was no other way of getting into the village save along this main road where they invariably gathered. Even the slight tension caused by having to go past them marred the pleasure of her walks.

One day she realized with a slight shock of shame that she did not even know what the boys looked like. She had seen them only as a group from a distance; when she drew near enough to say good-day to them, she always had her head down, watching the road. The fact that she had been afraid to look at them was unacceptable; now, as she came up to them, she stared into the eyes of one after the other, carefully. Nodding gravely, she went on. Yes, they were insolent faces, she thought—not at all like the faces of their elders. The respectful attitudes into which they had been startled were the crudest sort of shamming. But the important thing to her was that she had won: she was no longer preoccupied with having to pass by them every day. Slowly she even grew to recognize each boy.

There was one, she noted, younger than the others, who always sat a little apart from them, and it was this shy one who stood talking to Boufelja in the hotel kitchen early one morning when she went in. She pretended not to notice him. "I am going to my room to work on the machine for about an hour," she told Boufelja. "You can come then to make up the room," and she turned to go out. As she went through the doorway she glanced at the boy's face. He was looking at her, and he did not turn away when his eyes met hers. "How are you?" she said. Perhaps half an hour later, when she was typing her second letter, she raised her head. The boy was standing on the terrace looking at her through the open door. He squinted, for the wind was strong; behind his head she saw the tops of the palms bending.

"If he wants to watch, let him watch," she said to herself, deciding to pay him no attention. After a while he went away. While Boufelja served her lunch, she questioned him about the boy. "Like an old man," said Boufelja. "Twelve years old but very serious. Like some old, old man." He smiled, then shrugged. "It's the way God wanted him to be."

"Of course," she said, remembering the boy's alert, unhappy face. "A young dog that everyone has kicked," she thought, "but he hasn't given up."

In the days that followed, he came often to the terrace and stood watching her while she typed. Sometimes she waved to him, or said: "Good morning." Without answering he would take a step backward, so that he was out of her range. Then he would continue to stand where he was. His behavior irked her, and one day when he had done this, she quickly got up and went to the door. "What is it?" she asked him, trying to smile as she spoke.

"I didn't do anything," he said, his eyes reproachful.

"I know," she answered. "Why don't you come in?"

The boy looked swiftly around the terrace as if for help; then he bowed his head and stepped inside the door. Here he stood waiting, his head down, looking miserable. From her luggage she brought out a bag of hard candy, and handed him a piece. Then she put a few simple questions to him, and found that his French was much better than she had expected. "Do the other boys know French as well as you?" she asked him.

"*Non, madame,*" he said, shaking his head slowly. "My father used to be a soldier. Soldiers speak good French."

She tried to keep her face from expressing the disapproval

she felt, for she despised everything military. "I see," she said with some asperity, turning back to her table and shuffling the papers. "Now I must work," she told him, immediately adding in a warmer voice, "but you come back tomorrow, if you like." He waited an instant, looking at her with unchanged wistfulness. Then slowly he smiled, and laid the candy wrapper, folded into a tiny square, on the corner of her table. "*Au revoir, madame,*" he said, and went out of the door. In the silence she heard the scarcely audible thud of his bare heels on the earth floor of the terrace. "In this cold," she thought. "Poor child! If I ever buy anything for him it will be a pair of sandals."

Each day thereafter, when the sun was high enough to give substance to the still morning air, the boy would come stealthily along the terrace to her door, stand a few seconds, and then say in a lost voice that was all the smaller and more hushed for the great silence outside: "*Bonjour, madame.*" She would tell him to come in, and they would shake hands gravely, he afterward raising the backs of his fingers to his lips, always with the same slow ceremoniousness. She sometimes tried to fathom his countenance as he went through this ritual, to see if by any chance she could detect a shade of mockery there; instead she saw an expression of devotion so convincing that it startled her, and she looked away quickly. She always kept a bit of bread or some biscuits in a drawer of the wardrobe; when she had brought the food out and he was eating it, she would ask him for news about the families in his quarter of the village. For discipline's sake she offered him a piece of candy only every other day. He sat on the floor by the doorway, on a torn old camel blanket, and he watched her constantly, never turning his head away from her.

She wanted to know what he was called, but she was aware of how secretive the inhabitants of the region were about names, seldom giving their true ones to strangers; this was a peculiarity she respected because she knew it had its roots in their own prehistoric religion. So she forbore asking him, sure that the time would come when he trusted her enough to give it of his own volition. And the moment happened one morning unexpectedly, when he had just recounted several legends involving the great Moslem king of long ago, whose name was Solomon. Suddenly he stopped, and forcing himself to gaze steadily at her without blinking, he said: "And my name too is Slimane, the same as the king."

She tried to teach him to read, but he did not seem able to learn. Often just as she felt he was about to connect two loose ends of ideas and perhaps at last make a contact which would enable him to understand the principle, a look of resignation and passivity would appear in his face, and he would willfully cut off the stream of effort from its source, and remain sitting, merely looking at her, shaking his head from side to side to show that it was useless. It was hard not to lose patience with him at such moments.

The following year she decided not to go on with the lessons, and to use Slimane instead as a guide, bearer and companion, a role which she immediately saw was more suited to his nature than that of pupil. He did not mind how far they went or how much equipment he had to carry; on the contrary, to him a long excursion was that much more of an event, and whatever she loaded onto him he bore with the air of one upon whom an honor is conferred. It was probably her happiest season in the desert, that winter of comradeship when together they made the countless pilgrimages down the valley. As the weeks passed the trips grew in scope, and the hour of departure was brought forward until it came directly after she had finished her breakfast. All day long, trudging in the open sun and in the occasional shade of the broken fringe of palms that skirted the river-bed, she conversed passionately with him. Sometimes she could see that he felt like telling her what was in his head, and she let him speak for as long as his enthusiasm lasted, often reviving it at the end with carefully chosen questions. But usually it was she who did the speaking as she walked behind him. Pounding the stony ground with her steel-tipped stick each time her right foot went down, she told him in great detail the story of the life of Hitler, showing why he was hated by the Christians. This she thought necessary since Slimane had been under a different impression, and indeed had imagined that the Europeans thought as highly of the vanished leader as did he and the rest of the people in the village. She talked a good deal about Switzerland, casually stressing the cleanliness, honesty and good health of her countrymen in short parables of daily life. She told him about Jesus, Martin Luther and Garibaldi, taking care to keep Jesus distinct from the Moslem prophet Sidna Aissa, since even for the sake of argument she could not agree for an instant with the Islamic doctrine according to which the Savior was a Moslem. Slimane's attitude of respect bordering on adoration with regard to her never altered unless she inadvertently tangled with the subject of Islam; then, no matter what she said (for at that point it seemed that automatically he was no longer within hearing) he would shake his head interminably and cry: "No, no, no, no! Nazarenes know nothing about Islam. Don't talk, madame, I beg you, because you don't know what you're saying. No, no, no!"

Long ago she had kept the initial promise to herself that she would buy him sandals; this purchase had been followed by others. At fairly regular intervals she had taken him to Benaissa's store to buy a shirt, a pair of baggy black cotton trousers of the kind worn by the Chaamba camel-drivers, and ultimately a new white burnoose, despite the fact that she knew the entire village would discuss the giving of so valuable an object. She also knew that it was only the frequent bestowing of such gifts that kept Slimane's father from forbidding him to spend his time with her. Even so, according to reports brought by Slimane, he sometimes objected. But Slimane himself, she was sure, wanted nothing, expected nothing.

It was each year when March was drawing to a close that the days began to be painfully hot and even the nights grew breathless; then, although it always required a strenuous effort of the will to make herself take the step which would bring about renewed contact with the outside world, she would devote two or three days to washing her clothing and preparing for the journey. When the week set for her departure had come, she went over to the fort and put in a call to the café at Kerzaz, asking the proprietor to tell the driver of the next northbound truck to take the detour that would enable her to catch him at a point only about three kilometers from the village.

She and Slimane had come back to the hotel on the afternoon of their last excursion down the valley; Fräulein Windling stood on the terrace looking out at the orange mountains of sand behind the fort. Slimane had taken the packs into the room and put them down. She turned and said: "Bring the big tin box." When he had pulled it out from under the bed he carried it to her, dusting it off with the sleeve of his shirt, and she led the way up the stairs to the roof. They sat down on the blanket; the glow of the vanished sun's furnace heated their faces. A few flies still hovered, now and then attacking their necks. Slimane handed her the biscuit tin and she gave him a fistful of chocolate-covered cakes. "So many all at once?"

"Yes," she said. "You know I'm going home in four days."

He looked down at the blanket a moment before replying. "I know," he murmured. He was silent again. Then he cried out aggrievedly: "Boufelja says it's hot here in the summer. It's not hot! In our house it's cool. It's like the oasis where the big pool is. You would never be hot there."

"I have to earn money. You know that. I want to come back next year."

He said sadly: "Next year, madame! Only Moulana knows how next year will be."

Some camels growled as they rolled in the sand at the foot of the fort; the light was receding swiftly. "Eat your biscuits," she told him, and she ate one herself. "Next year we'll go to Abadla with the caid, *incha'Allah*."

He sighed deeply. "Ah, madame!" he said. She noted, at first with a pang of sympathy and then, reconsidering, with disapproval, the anguish that lent his voice its unaccustomed intensity. It was the quality she least liked in him, this faintly theatrical self-pity. "Next year you'll be a man," she told him firmly. Her voice grew less sure, assumed a hopeful tone. "You'll remember all the things we talked about?"

She sent him a postcard from Marseille, and showed her classes photographs they had taken of one another, and of the caid. The children were impressed by the caid's voluminous turban. "Is he a Bedouin?" asked one.

When she left the embassy office she knew that this was the last year she would be returning to the desert. There was not only the official's clearly expressed unfriendliness and suspicion: for the first time he had made her answer a list of questions which she found alarming. He wanted to know what subjects she taught in the Freiluftschule, whether she had ever been a journalist, and exactly where she proposed to be each day after arriving in the Sahara. She had almost retorted: I go where I feel like going. I don't make plans. But she had merely named the oasis. She knew that Frenchmen had no respect for elderly Swiss ladies who wore woolen stockings; this simply made them more contemptible in her eyes. However, it was they who controlled the Sahara.

The day the ship put into the African port it was raining. She knew the gray terraced ramps of the city were there in the gloom ahead, but they were invisible. The ragged European garments of the dock workers were soaked with rain. Later, the whole rain-sodden city struck her as grim, and the people passing along the streets looked unhappy. The change, even from the preceding year, was enormous; it made her sad to sit in the big, cold café where she went for coffee after dinner, and so she returned to her hotel and slept. The next day she got on the train for Perrégaux. The rain fell most of the day. In Perrégaux she took a room in a hotel near the station, and stayed in it, listening to the rain rattle down the gutter by her window. "This place would be a convenient model for Hell," she wrote to a friend in Basel before going to sleep that night. "A full-blown example of the social degeneracy achieved by forced cultural hybridism. Populace debased and made hostile by generations of merciless exploitation. I take the southbound narrow-gauge train tomorrow morning for a happier land, and trust that my friend the sun will appear at some point during the day. *Seien Sie herzlich gegrüsst von Ihrer Maria.*"

As the train crawled southward, up over the high plateau land, the clouds were left behind and the sun took charge of the countryside. Fräulein Windling sat attentively by the smeared window, enveloped in an increasing sadness. As long as it had been raining, she had imagined the rain as the cause of her depression: the gray cloud light gave an unaccustomed meaning to the landscape by altering forms and distances. Now she understood that the more familiar and recognizable the contours of the desert were to become, the more conscious she would be of having no reason to be in it, because it was her last visit.

Two days later, when the truck stopped to let her out, Boufelja stood in the sun beside the boulders waving; one of the men of the village was with him to help carry the luggage. Once the truck had gone and its cloud of yellow dust had fled across the hammada, the silence was there; it seemed that no sound could be louder than the crunch of their shoes on the ground.

"How is Slimane?" she asked. Boufelja was noncommittal. "He's all right," he said. "They say he tried to run away. But he didn't get very far." The report might be true, or it might be false; in any case she determined not to allude to it unless Slimane himself mentioned it first.

She felt an absurd relief when they came to the edge of the cliffs and she saw the village across the valley. Not until she had made the rounds of the houses where her friends lived, discussed their troubles with them and left some pills here and some candy there, was she convinced that no important change had come to the oasis during her absence. She went to the house of Slimane's parents: he was not there. "Tell him to come and see me," she said to his father as she left the house.

On the third morning after her arrival Slimane appeared, and stood there in the doorway smiling. Once she had greeted him and made him sit down and have coffee with her, she plied him with questions about life in the village while she had been in Europe. Some of his friends had gone to become patriots, he said, and they were killing the French like flies. Her heart sank, but she said nothing. As she watched him smiling she was able to exult in the reflection that Slimane had been reachable, after all; she had proved that it was possible to make true friends of the younger people. But even while she was saying, "How happy I am to see you, Slimane," she remembered that their time together was now limited, and an expression of pain passed over her face as she finished the phrase. "I shall not say a word to him about it," she decided. If he, at least, still had the illusion of unbounded time lying ahead, he would somehow retain his aura of purity and innocence, and she would feel less anguish during the time they spent together.

One day they went down the valley to see the caid, and dis-

cussed the long-planned trip to Abadla. Another day they
started out at dawn to visit the tomb of Moulay Ali ben Said,
where there was a spring of hot water. It was a tiny spot of oasis at the edge of a ridge of high dunes; perhaps fifty palms
were there around the decayed shrine. In the shade of the
rocks below the walls there was a ruined cistern into which
the steaming water dribbled. They spread blankets on the
sand nearby, at the foot of a small tamarisk, and took out their
lunch. Before starting to eat, they drank handfuls of the water, which Slimane said was famed for its holiness. The palms
rattled and hissed in the wind overhead.

"Allah has sent us the wind to make us cool while we eat,"
Slimane said when he had finished his bread and dates.

"The wind has always been here," she answered carelessly,
"and it always will be here."

He sat up straight. "No, no!" he cried. "When Sidna Aissa
has returned for forty days there will be no more Moslems
and the world will end. Everything, the sky and the sun and
the moon. And the wind too. Everything." He looked at her
with an expression of such satisfaction that she felt one of her
occasional surges of anger against him.

"I see," she said. "Stand over by the spring a minute. I want
to take your picture." She had never understood why it was
that the Moslems had conceded Jesus even this Pyrrhic victory,
the coda to all creation: its inconsistency embarrassed her.
Across the decayed tank she watched Slimane assume the traditional stiff attitude of a person about to be photographed,
and an idea came into her head. For Christmas Eve, which
would come within two weeks, she would make a crèche. She
would invite Slimane to eat with her by the fireplace, and when
midnight came she would take him in to see it.

She finished photographing Slimane; they gathered up the
equipment and set out against the hot afternoon wind for the
village. The sand sometimes swept by, stinging their faces
with its invisible fringe. Fräulein Windling led the way this
time, and they walked fast. The image of the crèche, illumined by candles, occurred to her several times on the way
back over the rocky erg; it made her feel inexpressibly sad, for
she could not help connecting it with the fact that everything
was ending. They came to the point north of the village

where the empty erg was cut across by the wandering river valley. As they climbed slowly upward over the fine sand, she found herself whispering: "It's the right thing to do." "*Right* is not the word," she thought, without being able to find a better one. She was going to make a crèche because she loved Christmas and wanted to share it with Slimane. They reached the hotel shortly after sunset, and she sent Slimane home in order to sit and plan her project on paper.

It was only when she began actually to put the crèche together that she realized how much work it was going to be. Early the next morning she asked Boufelja to find her an old wooden crate. Before she had been busy even a half-hour, she heard Slimane talking in the kitchen. Quickly she pushed everything under the bed and went out onto the terrace.

"Slimane," she said. "I'm very busy. Come in the afternoon." And that afternoon she told him that since she was going to be working every morning until after the day of the Christ Child, they would not be making any more long trips during that time. He received the information glumly. "I know," he said. "You are getting ready for the holy day. I understand."

"When the holy day comes, we will have a feast," she assured him.

"If Allah wills."

"I'm sorry," she said, smiling.

He shrugged. "Good-by," he told her.

Afternoons they still walked in the oasis or had tea on the roof, but her mornings she spent in her room sewing, hammering and sculpting. Once she had the platform constructed, she had to model the figures. She carried up a great mass of wet clay from the river to her room. It was two days before she managed to make a Virgin whose form pleased her. From an old strip of muslin she fashioned a convincing tent to house the Mother and the Child in its nest of tiny white chicken feathers. Shredded tamarisk needles made a fine carpet for the interior of the tent. Outside she poured sand, and then pushed the clay camels' long legs deep into it; one animal walked behind the other over the dune, and a Wise Man sat straight on top of each, his white *djellaba* falling in long pointed folds to either side of the camel's flanks. The Wise Men would come carrying sacks of almonds and very small liqueur chocolates wrapped in colored tinfoil. When she had the crèche finished, she put it on the floor in the middle of the room and piled tangerines and dates in front of it. With a row of candles burning behind it, and one candle on each side in front, it would look like a Moslem religious chromolithograph. She hoped the scene would be recognizable to Slimane; he might then be more easily persuaded of its poetic truth. She wanted only to suggest to him that the god with whom he was on such intimate terms was the god worshipped by the Nazarenes. It was not an idea she would ever try to express in words.

An additional surprise for the evening would be the new flash-bulb attachment to her camera, which Slimane had not yet seen. She intended to take a good many pictures of the crèche and of Slimane looking at it; these she would enlarge to show her pupils. She went and bought a new turban for Slimane; he had been wearing none for more than a year now. This was a man's turban, and very fine: ten meters of the softest Egyptian cotton.

The day before Christmas she overslept, duped by the heavy sky. Each winter the oasis had a few dark days; they were rare, but this was one of them. While she still lay there in bed, she heard the roar of the wind, and when she got up to look out of the window she found no world outside—only a dim rose-gray fog that hid everything. The swirling sand sprayed ceaselessly against the glass; it had formed in long drifts on the floor of the terrace. When she went for breakfast, she wore her burnoose with the hood up around her face. The blast of the wind as she stepped out onto the terrace struck her with the impact of a solid object, and the sand gritted on the concrete floor under her shoes. In the dining-room Boufelja had bolted the shutters; he greeted her enthusiastically from the gloom inside, glad of her presence.

"A very bad day for your festival, alas, mademoiselle!" he observed as he set her coffee pot on the table.

"Tomorrow's the festival," she said. "It begins tonight."

"I know. I know." He was impatient with Nazarene feasts because the hours of their beginnings and ends were observed in so slipshod a manner. Moslem feasts began precisely, either at sundown or an hour before sunup, or when the new moon was first visible in the western sky at twilight. But the Naza-renes began their feasts whenever they felt like it.

She spent the morning in her room writing letters. By noon the air outside was darker with still more sand; the wind shook the hotel atop its rock as if it would hurl it over the tips of the palms below into the river-bed. Several times she rose and went to the window to stare out at the pink emptiness beyond the terrace. Storms made her happy, although she wished this one could have come after Christmas. She had imagined a pure desert night—cold, alive with stars, and the dogs yapping from the oasis. It might yet be that; there was still time, she thought, as she slipped her burnoose over her head to go in to lunch.

With the wind, the fireplace was an unsure blessing: besides the heat it gave, it provided the only light in the dining-room, but the smoke that belched from it burned her eyes and throat. The shutters at the windows rattled and pounded, covering the noise of the wind itself.

She got out of the dining-room as soon as she had finished eating, and hurried back to her room to sit through the slowly darkening afternoon, as she continued with her letter-writing and waited for the total extinction of daylight. Slimane was coming at eight. There would be enough time to carry everything into the dining-room before that, and to set the crèche up in the dark unused wing into which Boufelja was unlikely to go. But when she came to do it, she found that the wind's force was even greater than she had imagined. Again and again she made the trip between her room and the dining-room, carrying each object carefully wrapped in her burnoose. Each time she passed in front of the kitchen door she expected Boufelja to open it and discover her. She did not want him there when she showed the crèche to Slimane; he could see it tomorrow at breakfast.

Protected by the noise of the gale she succeeded in trans-porting all the parts to the far dark corner of the dining-room without alerting Boufelja. Long before dinner time the crèche was in readiness, awaiting only the lighting of the candles to be brought alive. She left a box of matches on the table be-side it, and hurried back to her room to arrange her hair and change her clothing. The sand had sifted through her garments and was now everywhere; it showered from her under-wear and stuck like sugar to her skin. Her watch showed a few minutes after eight when she went out.

Only one place had been laid at table. She waited, while the blinds chattered and banged, until Boufelja appeared carrying the soup tureen.

"What a bad night," he said.

"You forgot to prepare for Slimane," she told him. But he was not paying attention. "He's stupid!" he exclaimed, be-ginning to ladle out the soup.

"Wait!" she cried. "Slimane's coming. I mustn't eat until he comes."

Still Boufelja misunderstood. "He wanted to come into the dining-room," he said. "And he knows it's forbidden at din-ner time."

"But I invited him!" She looked at the lone soup plate on the table. "Tell him to come in, and set another place."

Boufelja was silent. He put the ladle back into the tureen. "Where is he?" she demanded, and without waiting for him to reply she went on. "Didn't I tell you he was going to have dinner with me tonight?" For suddenly she suspected that in her desire for secrecy she might indeed have neglected to mention the invitation to Boufelja.

"You didn't say anything," he told her. "I didn't know. I sent him home. But he'll be back after dinner."

"Oh, Boufelja!" she cried. "You know Slimane never lies."

He looked down at her with reproach on his face. "I didn't know anything about mademoiselle's plans," he said aggriev-edly. This made her think for a swift instant that he had dis-covered the crèche, but she decided that if he had he would have spoken of it.

"Yes, yes, I know. I should have told you. It's my fault."

"That's true, mademoiselle," he said. And he served the re-maining courses observing a dignified silence which she, still feeling some displeasure with him, did not urge him to break. Only at the end of the meal, when she had pushed back her chair from the table and sat studying the pattern of the flames in the fireplace, did he decide to speak. "Mademoiselle will take coffee?"

"I do want some," she said, trying to bring a note of enthusiasm into her voice. "*Bien*," murmured Boufelja, and he left her alone in the room. When he returned carrying the coffee, Slimane was with him, and they were laughing, she noted, quite as though there had been no misunderstanding about dinner. Slimane stood by the door an instant, stamping his feet and shaking the sand from his burnoose. As he came forward to take her hand, she cried: "Oh, Slimane, it's my fault! I forgot to tell Boufelja. It's terrible!"

"There is no fault, madame," he said gravely. "This is a festival."

"Yes, this is a festival," she echoed. "And the wind's still blowing. Listen!"

Slimane would not take coffee, but Boufelja, ceding to her pressure, let her pour him out a cup, which he drank standing by the fireplace. She suspected him of being secretly pleased that Slimane had not managed to eat with her. When he had finished his coffee, he wished them good-night and went off to bed in his little room next to the kitchen.

They sat a while watching the fire, without talking. The wind rushed past in the emptiness outside, the blinds hammered. Fräulein Windling was content. Even if the first part of the celebration had gone wrong, the rest of the evening could still be pleasant.

She waited until she was sure that Boufelja had really gone to bed, and then she reached into her bag and brought out a small plastic sack full of chocolate creams, which she placed on the table.

"Eat," she said carelessly, and she took a piece of candy herself. With some hesitation Slimane put out his hand to take the sack. When he had a chocolate in his mouth, she began to speak. She intended to tell him the story of the Nativity, a subject she already had touched upon many times during their excursions, but only in passing. This time she felt she should tell him the entire tale. She expected him to interrupt when he discovered that it was a religious story, but he merely kept his noncommittal eyes on her and chewed mechanically, showing that he followed her by occasionally nodding his head. She became engrossed in what she was saying, and began to use her arms in wide gestures. Slimane reached for another chocolate and went on listening.

She talked for an hour or more, aware as from a distance of her own eloquence. When she told him about Bethlehem she was really describing Slimane's own village, and the house of Joseph and Mary was the house down in the *ksar* where Slimane had been born. The night sky arched above the Oued Zousfana and its stars glared down upon the cold hammada. Across the erg on their camels came the Wise Men in their burnooses and turbans, pausing at the crest of the last great dune to look ahead at the valley where the dark village lay. When she had finished, she blew her nose.

Slimane appeared to be in a state bordering on trance. She glanced at him, expected him to speak, but as he did not, she looked more closely at him. His eyes had an obsessed, vacant expression, and although they were still fixed on her face, she would have said that he was seeing something much farther away than she. She sighed, not wanting to make the decision to rouse him. The possibility she would have liked to entertain, had she not been so conscious of its unlikelihood, was that the boy somehow had been captivated by the poetic truth of the story, and was reviewing it in his imagination. "Certainly it could not be the case," she decided; it was more likely that he had ceased some time back to listen to her words, and was merely sitting there, only vaguely aware that she had come to the end of her story.

Then he spoke. "You're right. He was the King of Men."

Fräulein Windling caught her breath and leaned forward, but he went on. "And later Satan sent a snake with two heads. And Jesus killed it. Satan was angry with Him. He said: 'Why did you kill my friend? Did it hurt you, perhaps?' And Jesus said: 'I knew where it came from.' And Satan put on a black burnoose. That's true," he added, as he saw the expression of what he took to be simple disbelief on her face.

She sat up very straight and said: "Slimane, what are you talking about? There are no such stories about Jesus. Nor about Sidna Aissa either." She was not sure of the accuracy of this last statement; it was possible, she supposed, that such legends did exist among these people. "You know those are just stories that have nothing to do with the truth."

He did not hear her because he had already begun to talk. "I'm not speaking of Sidna Aissa," he said firmly. "He was a

Moslem prophet. I'm talking about Jesus, the prophet of the Nazarenes. Everyone knows that Satan sent Him a snake with two heads."

She listened to the wind for an instant. "Ah," she said, and took another chocolate; she did not intend to carry the argument further. Soon she dug into her bag again and pulled out the turban, wrapped in red and white tissue paper.

"A present for you," she said, holding it out to him. He seized it mechanically, placed it on his lap and remained staring down at it. "Aren't you going to open it?" she demanded.

He nodded his head twice and tore open the paper. When he saw the pile of white cotton he smiled. Seeing his face at last come to life, she jumped up. "Let's put it on you!" she exclaimed. He gave her one end, which she pulled taut by walking all the way to the door. Then with his hand holding the other end to his forehead, he turned slowly round and round, going toward her all the time, arranging the form of the turban as it wound itself about his head. "Magnificent!" she cried. He went over to the row of black windows to look at himself.

"Can you see?" she asked.

"Yes, I can see the sides of it," he told her. "It's very beautiful."

She walked back toward the center of the room. "I'd like to take your picture, Slimane," she said, seeing an immediate look of puzzlement appear in his face. "Would you do me a favor? Go to my room and get the camera."

"At night? You can take a picture at night?"

She nodded, smiling mysteriously. "And bring me the yellow box on the bed."

Keeping the turban on his head, he got into his burnoose, took her flashlight and went out, letting the wind slam the door. She hoped the sound had not wakened Boufelja; for an instant she listened while there was no sound but the roar of air rushing through the corridor outside. Then she ran to the dark wing of the room and struck a match. Quickly she lighted all the candles around the crèche, straightened a camel in the sand, and walked back around the corner to the fireplace. She would not have thought the candles could give so much light. The other end of the room was now brighter than the end where she stood. In a moment the door burst open and Slimane came back in, carrying the camera slung over his shoulder. He put it down carefully on the table. "There was no yellow box on the bed," he told her. Then his glance caught the further walls flickering with the unfamiliar light, and he began to walk toward the center of the room. She saw that this was the moment. "Come," she said, taking his arm and pulling him gently around the corner to where the crèche was finally visible, bright with its multiple shuddering points of light. Slimane said nothing; he stopped walking and stood completely still. After a moment of silence, she plucked tentatively at his arm. "Come and see," she urged him. They continued to walk toward the crèche; as they came up to it she had the impression that if she had not been there he would have reached out his hand and touched it, perhaps would have lifted the tiny gold-clad infant Jesus out of His bed of feathers. But he stood quietly, looking at it. Finally he said: "You brought all that from Switzerland?"

"Of course not!" It was a little disappointing that he should not have recognized the presence of the desert in the picture, should not have sensed that the thing was of his place, and not an importation. "I made it all here," she said. She waited an instant. "Do you like it?"

"Ah, yes," he said with feeling. "It's beautiful. I thought it came from Switzerland."

To be certain that he understood the subject-matter, she began to identify the figures one by one, her voice taking on such an unaccustomed inflection of respect that he glanced up at her once in surprise. It was almost as if she too were seeing it for the first time. "And the Wise Men are coming down out of the erg to see the child."

"Why did you put all those almonds there?" asked Slimane, touching some with his forefinger.

"They're gifts for the little Jesus."

"But what are you going to do with them?" he pursued.

"Eat them, probably, later," she said shortly. "Take one if you like. You say there was no yellow box on the bed?" She wanted to take the photographs while the candles were still of equal height.

"There was nothing but a sweater and some papers, madame."

She left him there by the crèche, crossed the room and put on her burnoose. The darkness in the corridor was complete; there was no sign that Boufelja had awakened. She knew her room was in great disorder, and she played the beam of the flashlight around the floor before entering. In the welter of displaced things that strewed the little room there seemed small chance of finding anything. The feeble ray illumined one by one the meaningless forms made by the piling of disparate objects one on the other; the light moved over the floor, along the bed, behind the flimsy curtain of the armoire. Suddenly she stopped and turned the beam under the bed. The box was in front of her face; she had put it with the crèche.

"I mustn't fall," she thought, running along the corridor. She forced herself to slow her pace to a walk, entered the dining room and shut the door after her carefully. Slimane was on his knees in the middle of the room, a small object of some sort in his hand. She noted with relief that he was amusing himself. "I'm sorry it took me so long," she exclaimed. "I'd forgotten where I'd put it." She was pulling her burnoose off over her head; now she hung it on a nail by the fireplace, and taking up the camera and the yellow box, she walked over to join him.

Perhaps a faint glimmer of guilt in his expression as he glanced up made her eyes stray along the floor toward another object lying nearby, similar to the one he held in his hand. It was one of the Wise Men, severed at the hips from his mount. The Wise Man in Slimane's hand was intact, but the camel had lost its head and most of its neck.

"Slimane! What are you doing?" she cried with undisguised anger. "What have you done to the crèche?" She advanced around the corner and looked in its direction. There was not really much more than a row of candles and a pile of sand that had been strewn with tangerine peel and date stones; here and there a carefully folded square of lavender or pink tinfoil had been planted in the sand. All three of the Wise Men had been enlisted in Slimane's battle on the floor, the tent ravaged in the campaign to extricate the almonds piled inside, and the treasure sacks looted of their chocolate liqueurs. There was no sign anywhere of the infant Jesus or of his gold-lamé garment. She felt tears come into her eyes. Then she laughed shortly, and said: "Well, it's finished. Yes?"

"Yes, madame," he said calmly. "Are you going to make the photograph now?" He got to his feet and laid the broken camel on the platform in the sand with the other debris.

Fräulein Windling spoke evenly. "I wanted to take a picture of the crèche."

He waited an instant, as if he were listening to a distant sound. Then he said: "Should I put on my burnoose?"

"No." She began to take out the flash-bulb attachment. When she had it ready, she took the picture before he had time to strike a pose. She saw his astonishment at the sudden bright light prolong itself into surprise that the thing was already done, and then become resentment at having been caught off his guard; but pretending to have seen nothing, she went on snapping covers shut. He watched her as she gathered up her things. "Is it finished?" he said, disappointed. "Yes," she replied. "It will be a very good picture."

"*Incha'Allah.*"

She did not echo his piety. "I hope you've enjoyed the festival," she told him.

Slimane smiled widely. "Ah yes, madame. Very much. Thank you."

She let him out into the camel-square and turned the lock in the door. Quickly she went back into her room, wishing it were a clear night like other nights, when she could stand out on the terrace and look at the dunes and stars, or sit on the roof and hear the dogs, for in spite of the hour she was not sleepy. She cleared her bed of all the things that lay on top of it, and got in, certain that she was going to lie awake for a long time. For it had shaken her, the chaos Slimane had made in those few minutes of her absence. Across the seasons of their friendship she had come to think of him as being very nearly like herself, even though she knew he had not been that way when she first had met him. Now she saw the dangerous vanity at the core of that fantasy: she had assumed that somehow his association with her had automatically been for his ultimate good, that inevitably he had been undergoing a process of improvement as a result of knowing her. In her desire to see him change, she had begun to forget what Slimane was really like. "I shall never understand him," she thought helplessly, sure that just because she felt so close to him she would never be able to observe him dispassionately.

"This is the desert," she told herself. Here food is not an adornment; it is meant to be eaten. She had spread out food and he had eaten it. Any argument which attached blame to that could only be false. And so she lay there accusing herself. "It has been too much head and high ideals," she reflected, "and not enough heart." Finally she traveled on the sound of the wind into sleep.

At dawn when she awoke she saw that the day was going to be another dark one. The wind had dropped. She got up and shut the window. The early morning sky was heavy with cloud. She sank back into bed and fell asleep. It was later than usual when she rose, dressed, and went into the dining-room. Boufelja's face was strangely expressionless as he wished her good-morning. She supposed it was the memory of last night's misunderstanding, still with him—or possibly he was annoyed at having had to clean up the remains of the crèche. Once she had sat down and spread her napkin across her lap, he unbent sufficiently to say to her: "Happy festival."

"Thank you. Tell me, Boufelja," she went on, changing her inflection. "When you brought Slimane back in after dinner last night, do you know where he had been? Did he tell you?"

"He's a stupid boy," said Boufelja. "I told him to go home and eat and come back later. You think he did that? Never. He walked the whole time up and down in the courtyard here, outside the kitchen door, in the dark."

"I understand!" exclaimed Fräulein Windling triumphantly. "So he had no dinner at all."

"I had nothing to give him," he began, on the defensive.

"Of course not," she said sternly. "He should have gone home and eaten."

"Ah, you see?" grinned Boufelja. "That's what I told him to do."

In her mind she watched the whole story being enacted: Slimane aloofly informing his father that he would be eating at the hotel with the Swiss lady, the old man doubtless making some scornful reference to her, and Slimane going out. Unthinkable, once he had been refused admittance to the dining-room, for him to go back and face the family's ridicule. "Poor boy," she murmured.

"The commandant wants to see you," said Boufelja, making one of his abrupt conversational changes. She was surprised, since from one year to the next the captain never gave any sign of being aware of her existence; the hotel and the fort were like two separate countries. "Perhaps for the festival," Boufelja suggested, his face a mask. "Perhaps," she said uneasily.

When she had finished her breakfast, she walked across to the gates of the fort. The sentry seemed to be expecting her. One of the two young French soldiers was in the compound painting a chair. He greeted her, saying that the captain was in his office. She went up the long flight of stairs and paused an instant at the top, looking down at the valley in the unaccustomed gray light, noting how totally different it looked from its usual self, on this dim day.

A voice from inside called out: "*Entrez, s'il vous plaît!*" She opened the door and stepped in. The captain sat behind his desk; she had the unwelcome sensation of having played this same scene on another occasion, in another place. And she was suddenly convinced that she knew what he was going to say. She seized the back of the empty chair facing his desk. "Sit down, Mademoiselle Windling," he said, rising halfway out of his seat, waving his arm, and sitting again quickly.

There were several topographical maps on the wall behind him, marked with lavender and green chalk. The captain looked at his desk and then at her, and said in a clear voice: "It is an unfortunate stroke of chance that I should have to call you here on this holiday." Fräulein Windling sat down in the chair; leaning forward, she seemed about to rest her elbow on his desk, but instead crossed her legs and folded her arms tight. "Yes?" she said, tense, waiting for the message. It came immediately, for which she was conscious, even then, of being grateful to him. He told her simply that the entire area had been closed to civilians; this order applied to French nationals as well as to foreigners, so she must not feel discriminated against. The last was said with a wry attempt at a smile. "This means that you will have to take tomorrow morning's truck," he continued. "The driver has already been advised of your journey. Perhaps another year, when the disturbances are over . . ." ("Why does he say that?" she thought, "when he knows it's the end, and the time of friendship is finished?") He rose and extended his hand.

She could not remember going out of the room and down the long stairway into the compound, but now she was standing outside the sentry gate beside the wall of the fort, with her hand on her forehead. "Already," she thought. "It came so soon." And it occurred to her that she was not going to be given the time to make amends to Slimane, so that it was really true she was never going to understand him. She walked up to the parapet to look down at the edge of the oasis for a moment, and then went back to her room to start packing. All day long she worked in her room, pulling out boxes, forcing herself to be aware only of the decisions she was making as to what was to be taken and what was to be left behind once and for all.

At lunchtime Boufelja hovered near her chair. "Ah, mademoiselle, how many years we have been together, and now it is finished!" "Yes," she thought, but there was nothing to do about it. His lamentations made her nervous and she was short with him. Then she felt guilt-stricken and said slowly, looking directly at him: "I am very sad, Boufelja." He sighed. "Ay, mademoiselle, I know!"

By nightfall the pall of clouds had been blown away across the desert, and the western sky was partly clear. Fräulein Windling had finished all her packing. She went out onto the terrace, saw the dunes pink and glowing, and climbed the steps to the roof to look at the sunset. Great skeins of fiery storm-cloud streaked the sky. Mechanically she let her gaze follow the meanders of the river valley as it lost itself in the darkening hammada to the south. "It is in the past," she reminded herself; this was already the new era. The desert out there looked the same as it always had looked. But the sky, ragged, red and black, was like a handbill that had just been posted above it, announcing the arrival of war.

It was a betrayal, she was thinking, going back down the

steep stairs, running her hand along the familar rough mud wall to steady herself, and the French of course were the culprits. But beyond that she had the irrational and disagreeable conviction that the countryside itself had connived in the betrayal, that it was waiting to be transformed by the struggle. She went into her room and lit the small oil lamp; sitting down, she held her hands over it to warm them. At some point there had been a change: the people no longer wanted to go on living in the world they knew. The pressure of the past had become too great, and its shell had broken.

In the afternoon she had sent Boufelja to tell Slimane the news, and to ask him to be at the hotel at daybreak. During dinner she discussed only the details of departure and travel; when Boufelja tried to pull the talk in emotional directions, she did not reply. His commiseration was intolerable; she was not used to giving voice to her despair. When she got to her room she went directly to bed. The dogs barked half the night.

It was cold in the morning. Her hands ached as she gathered up the wet objects from around the washbowl on the table, and somehow she drove a sliver deep under the nail of her thumb. She picked some of it out with a needle, but the greater part remained. Before breakfast she stepped outside.

Standing in the waste-land between the hotel and the fort, she looked down at the countryside's innocent face. The padlocked gasoline pump, triumphant in fresh red and orange paint, caught the pure early sunlight. For a moment it seemed the only living thing in the landscape. She turned around. Above the dark irregular mass of palm trees rose the terraced village, calm under its morning veil of woodsmoke. She shut her eyes for an instant, and then went into the hotel.

She could feel herself sitting stiffly in her chair while she drank her coffee, and she knew she was being distant and formal with Boufelja, but it was the only way she could be certain of being able to keep going. Once he came to tell her that Slimane had arrived bringing the donkey and its master for her luggage. She thanked him and set down her coffee cup. "More?" said Boufelja. "No," she answered. "Drink another, mademoiselle," he urged her. "It's good on a cold morning." He poured it out and she drank part of it. There was a knocking at the gate. One of the young soldiers had been sent with a jeep to carry her out to the truck-stop on the trail.

"I can't!" she cried, thinking of Slimane and the donkey. The young soldier made it clear that he was not making an offer, but giving an order. Slimane stood beside the donkey outside the gate. While she began to speak with him the soldier shouted: "does he want to come, the *gosse*? He can come too, if he likes." Slimane ran to get the luggage and Fräulein Windling rushed inside to settle her bill. "Don't hurry," the soldier called after her. "There's plenty of time."

Boufelja stood in the kitchen doorway. Now for the first time it occurred to her to wonder what was going to become of him. With the hotel shut he would have no work. When she had settled her account and given him a tip which was much larger than she could afford, she took both his hands in hers and said: "*Mon cher* Boufelja, we shall see one another very soon."

"Ah, yes," he cried, trying to smile. "Very soon, mademoiselle."

She gave the donkey-driver some money, and got into the jeep beside the soldier. Slimane had finished bringing out the luggage and stood behind the jeep, kicking the tires. "Have you got everything?" she called to him. "Everything?" She would have liked to see for herself, but she was loath to go back into the room. Boufelja had disappeared; now he came hurrying out, breathless, carrying a pile of old magazines. "It's all right," she said. "No, no! I don't want them." The jeep was already moving ahead down the hill. In what seemed to her an unreasonably short time they had reached the boulders. When Fräulein Windling tried to lift out her briefcase the pain of the sliver under her nail made the tears start to her eyes, and she let go with a cry. Slimane glanced at her, surprised. "I hurt my hand," she explained. "It's nothing."

The bags had been piled in the shade. Sitting on a rock near the jeep, the soldier faced Fräulein Windling; from time to time he scanned the horizon behind her for a sign of the truck. Slimane examined the jeep from all sides; eventually he came to sit nearby. They did not say very much to one another. She was not sure whether it was because the soldier was with them, or because her thumb ached so constantly, but she sat quietly waiting, not wanting to talk.

It was a long time before the far-off motor made itself heard. When the truck was still no more than a puff of dust between sky and earth, the soldier was on his feet watching; an instant later Slimane jumped up. "It is coming, madame," he said. Then he bent over, putting his face very close to hers. "I want to go with you to Colomb-Bechar," he whispered. When she did not respond, because she was seeing the whole story of their friendship unrolled before her, from its end back to its beginning, he said louder, with great urgency: "Please, madame."

Fräulein Windling hesitated only an instant. She raised her head and looked carefully at the smooth brown face that was so near. "Of course, Slimane," she said. It was clear that he had not expected to hear this; his delight was infectious, and she smiled as she watched him run to the pile of bags and begin carrying them out into the sunlight to align them in the dust beside the edge of the trail.

Later, when they were rattling along the hammada, she in front beside the driver and Slimane squatting in the back with a dozen men and a sheep, she considered her irresponsible action in allowing him to make this absurd trip with her all the way to Colomb-Bechar. Still, she knew she wanted to give this ending to their story. A few times she turned partially around in her seat to glance at him through the dirty glass. He sat there in the smoke and dust, laughing like the others, with the hood of his burnoose hiding most of his face.

It had been raining in Colomb-Bechar; the streets were great puddles to reflect the clouded sky. At the garage they found a surly Negro boy to help them carry the luggage to the railway station. Her thumb hurt a little less.

"It's a cold town," Slimane said to her as they went down the main street. At the station they checked the bags and then went outside to stand and watch a car being unloaded from an open freight train: the roof of the automobile was still white with snow from the high steppes. The day was dark, and the wind rippled the surface of the water in the flooded empty lots. Fräulein Windling's train would not be leaving until late in the afternoon. They went to a restaurant and ate a long lunch.

"You really will go back home tomorrow?" she asked him anxiously at one point, while they were having fruit. "You know we have done a very wicked thing to your father and mother. They will never forgive me." A curtain seemed to draw across Slimane's face. "It doesn't matter," he said shortly.

After lunch they walked in the public garden and looked at the eagles in their cages. A fine rain had begun to be carried on the wind. The mud of the paths grew deeper. They went back to the center of the town and sat down on the terrace of a large, shabby modern café. The table at the end was partly sheltered from the wet wind; they faced an empty lot strewn with refuse. Nearby, spread out like the bones of a camel fallen on the trail, were the rusted remains of an ancient bus. A long, newly-felled date palm lay diagonally across the greater part of the lot. Fräulein Windling turned to look at the wet orange fiber of the stump, and felt an idle pity for the tree. "I'm going to have a Coca Cola," she declared. Slimane said he, too, would like one.

They sat there a long time. The fine rain slanted through the air outside the arcades and hit the ground silently. She had expected to be approached by beggars, but none arrived, and now that the time had come to leave the café and go to the station she was thankful to see that the day had passed so easily. She opened her pocket-book, took out three thousand francs, and handed them to Slimane, saying: "This will be enough for everything. But you must buy your ticket back home today. When you leave the railway station. Be very careful of it."

Slimane put the money inside his garments, rearranged his burnoose, and thanked her. "You understand, Slimane," she said, detaining him with her hand, for he seemed about to rise from the table. "I'm not giving you any money now, because I need what I have for my journey. But when I get to Switzerland I shall send you a little, now and then. Not much. A little."

His face was swept by panic; she was perplexed.

"You haven't got my address," he told her.

"No, but I shall send it to Boufelja's house," she said, thinking that would satisfy him. He leaned toward her, his eyes intense. "No, madame," he said with finality. "No. I have your address, and I shall send you mine. Then you will have it, and you can write to me."

It did not seem worth arguing about. For most of the afternoon her thumb had not hurt too much; now, as the day waned, it had begun to ache again. She wanted to get up, find the waiter, and pay him. The fine rain still blew; the station was fairly far. But she saw that Slimane had something more to say. He leaned forward in his chair and looked down at the floor. "Madame," he began.

"Yes?" she said.

"When you are in your country and you think of me you will not be happy. It's true, no?"

"I shall be very sad," she answered, rising.

Slimane got slowly to his feet and was quiet for an instant before going on. "Sad because I ate the food out of the picture. That was very bad. Forgive me."

The shrill sound of her own voice exclaiming, "No!" startled her. "No!" she cried. "That was good!" She felt the muscles of her cheeks and lips twisting themselves into grimaces of weeping; fiercely she seized his arm and looked down into his face. "*Oh, mon pauvre petit!*" she sobbed, and then covered her face with both hands. She felt him gently touching her sleeve. A truck went by in the main street, shaking the floor.

With an effort she turned away and scratched in her bag for a handkerchief. "Come," she said, clearing her throat. "Call the waiter."

They arrived at the station cold and wet. The train was being assembled; passengers were not allowed to go out onto the platform and were sitting on the floor inside. While Fräulein Windling bought her ticket Slimane went to get the bags from the checkroom. He was gone for a long time. When he arrived he came with his burnoose thrown back over his shoulders, grinning triumphantly, with three valises piled on his head. A man in ragged European jacket and trousers followed behind carrying the rest. As he came nearer she saw that the man held a slip of paper between his teeth.

The ancient compartment smelled of varnish. Through the window she could see, above some remote western reach of waste-land, a few strips of watery white sky. Slimane wanted to cover the seats with the luggage, so that no one would come into the compartment. "No," she said. "Put them in the racks." There were very few passengers in the coach. When everything was in place, the porter stood outside in the corridor and she noticed that he still held the slip of paper between his teeth. He counted the coins she gave him and pocketed them. Then quickly he handed the paper to Slimane, and was gone.

Fräulein Windling bent down a bit, to try and see her face in the narrow mirror that ran along the back of the seat. There was not enough light; the oil lantern above illumined only the ceiling, its base casting a leaden shadow over everything beneath. Suddenly the train jolted and made a series of crashing sounds. She took Slimane's head between her hands and kissed the middle of his forehead. "Please get down from the train," she told him. "We can talk here." She pointed to the window and began to pull on the torn leather strap that lowered it.

Slimane looked small on the dark platform, staring up at her as she leaned out. Then the train started to move. She thought surely it would go only a few feet and then stop, but it continued ahead, slowly. Slimane walked with it, keeping abreast of her window. In his hand was the paper the porter had given him. He held it up to her, crying: "Here is my address! Send it here!"

She took it, and kept waving as the train went faster, kept calling: "Good-by!" He continued to walk quickly along beside the window, increasing his gait until he was running, until all at once there was no more platform. She leaned far out, looking backward, waving; straightway he was lost in the darkness and rain. A bonfire blazed orange by the track, and the smoke stung in her nostrils. She pulled up the window, glanced at the slip of paper she had in her hand, and sat down. The train jolted her this way and that; she went on staring at the paper, although now it was in shadow; and she remembered the first day, long ago, when the child Slimane had stood outside the door watching her, stepping back out of her range of vision each time she turned to look at him. The words hastily printed for him on the scrap of paper by the porter were indeed an address, but the address was in Colomb-Bechar. "They said he tried to run away. But he didn't get very far." Each detail of his behavior as she went back over it clarified the pattern for her. "He's too young to be a soldier," she told herself. "They won't take him." But she knew they would.

Her thumb was hot and swollen; sometimes it seemed almost that its throbbing accompanied the side-to-side jolting of the coach. She looked out at the few remaining patches of colorless light in the sky. Sooner or later, she argued, he would have done it.

"Another year, perhaps," the captain had said. She saw her own crooked, despairing smile in the dark window-glass beside her face. Maybe Slimane would be among the fortunate ones, an early casualty. "If only death were absolutely certain in wartime," she thought wryly, "the waiting would not be so painful." Listing and groaning, the train began its long climb upwards over the plateau.

The Successor

IN THE MIDDLE of the afternoon, lying on his mat, Ali sneezed. A hen that had been drowsing near him screeched and rushed out of the room to a circle of bare dusty ground under the fig tree, where she settled. He listened a while to the distant intermittent thunder in the mountains to the south of the town; then, deciding that he would be able to sleep no more until night, he sat up.

Beyond the partition of upright reeds his brother was talking to El Mehdi, one of the drivers of the carriages that brought people up from the town. From the terrace of the café the eye could wander over the tortured red earth with its old olive trees to the dark caves that lay just below the walls of the town.

The view was something visitors usually considered worth seeing. They would take one of the ancient carriages that waited down in the town and be driven up along the winding road that baked all day in the sunlight; it took less than an hour to reach the café. There they would sit under the trellis in the shade of the vines and drink their tea or their beer. The driver would give the horses water and before twilight they would start back.

On Sundays many carriages and cars came; the café was full all day. His brother, who owned the café and kept the accounts and the money, claimed that he made more on a Sunday than during all the rest of the week. Ali was skeptical of that, not because the statement seemed incredible, but simply because his brother had made it. There was the overwhelming fact that his brother was older than he and therefore had inherited the café from their father. In the face of such crushing injustice there was nothing to be done. Nor was anything his brother had to say of interest to him. His brother was like the weather: one watched it and was a victim to its whims. It was written, but that did not mean it could not change.

He leaned against the wall matting and stretched. His brother and El Mehdi were drinking beer; he was certain of it by the way their voices died down when there was any sound outside the room. They wanted to be able to hide the glasses swiftly if someone should come near the door, so they were listening as they talked. The idea of this childish secrecy disgusted him; he spat on the floor by his feet, and began to rub his bare toe back and forth in the little white mass of saliva.

The thunder rolled in the south mountains, no louder but longer than before. It was a little early in the season for rain, but the rain might come. He reached for the water jug and drank lengthily. Then he sat quite still for a while, his eyes fixed on the framed portrait of the Sultan that hung on the opposite wall.

The thunder came again, still scarcely any louder, but this time unmistakably nearer, the sound more intimate in its movements. It was like a person taking pains to conceal his approach. There was a clapping of hands on the terrace, and a man's voice called: "*Garçon!*" His brother went out, and he heard El Mehdi gulp the rest of his beer and follow him. Presently a woman's voice remarked that it was going to rain. Then El Mehdi shouted, "*Eeeee!*" to his horses, and the carriage began to creak as it started down the road.

After the customers had left, his brother remained outside. Ali went silently to the door, saw him standing by the parapet, his hands behind him, looking out over the town. At the other end of the terrace squatted the boy who washed the glasses and swept the floor. His eyes were closed. There was very little sound from the town below. Occasionally a bird flew out from the hill behind and let itself drop down toward the lower land. The sky was dark. His brother turned and saw him standing in the doorway.

"You slept?"

"Yes."

"It's going to rain."

"*Incha'Allah.*"

"Listen." His brother's hand went up and he turned his face sideways. Very faintly from the town came the sound of the small boys' voices as they ran through the streets chanting the song to Sidi Bou Chta, the song they always sang just before the rain.

"Yes."

Now the thunder was over the nearest mountains. His

brother came toward the door and Ali stepped aside to let him pass.

"We'll close up," said his brother. He called to the boy, who began to carry the chairs and tables into the room where they were kept piled. Ali and his brother sat on the mattress and yawned. When the boy had finished he closed the door, snapped the padlock and came into the front part of the room, where he set to fanning the fire with the bellows. Presently he brought them each a glass of tea.

"Go to the house. We'll eat early," said his brother. The boy went out.

A crash of thunder directly above them made them look at each other. Ali said: "I'll close the house. The boy is an idiot."

The little house was behind the café, built against the low cliff, just beneath the road. When he got to the fig tree he heard his brother talking to someone. Surprised, he stopped and listened. Great drops of rain began to fall here and there on to the dust. It was hard to hear what his brother was saying. He went on to the house.

No one lived there but the two of them and the boy, who slept outside. It was never very clean. If only his brother had been willing to get married, Ali would have had an excuse for going away. Until then, it would be impossible, because his father had told him to stay and help his brother with the café. All he got for staying was a dirty room and the bad food the boy cooked for them.

On the other hand, when his brother walked through the Moulay Abdallah *quartier* he was greeted by the women of every house. The money went on bracelets for them, and on wine and beer for his friends. Besides these women, with whom he spent most of his nights, there was always a young girl of good reputation whom he had hopes of seducing; usually he failed in these endeavors, but his setbacks only increased his interest.

At the moment it was Kinza, the daughter of a shopkeeper from Taza, whose favors he sought. She had granted him short conversations in unfrequented alleys, with a maidservant standing a few feet away; he had met her one twilight outside Bab Segma and put his arm around her (after persuading the servant to stand facing in the other direction), and he even had had a *tête-à-tête* alone with her in a room behind a café, when he had lifted her veil and kissed her. But she had refused any further intimacies, threatening, if he used force, to call the servant who was outside the door. After accepting a good many gifts she had promised him another such rendezvous, so he still had hopes.

Ali knew all about his brother's life and about Kinza, since, in spite of the fact that such subjects cannot be discussed between brothers, it is perfectly proper to talk about them with anyone and everyone else. He knew all about Kinza and he hoped his brother would have no luck with her.

The rain was falling more heavily now. He closed the windows so it would not come in. Then, out of boredom and because he was curious to know who had arrived at the café, he went across the open space between the two establishments, taking long strides, and re-entered the back room. Behind the partition the fire was being fanned again, this time by his brother.

"I'm very fond of your tea here in Morocco," a man's voice was saying; they were speaking French.

His brother said: "Me, I like beer best."

"Have another bottle," said the stranger magnanimously. "Drink to the end of this damned rain. If it keeps up I won't get back to town before dark."

Ali tried to look through the cracks to see what sort of person it was who would walk all the way up to the café, but the man was seated in the doorway looking out at the rain and he could see nothing but his back.

"We are glad to have the rain," said his brother. "Each drop is money. The *fellahin* give thanks."

"*Oui, bien sûr,*" said the stranger without interest.

The thunder had passed over, but the rain was roaring; soon a stream of water burst through the ceiling in a corner of the room and spattered on to the earthen floor. The added noise made it more difficult to hear their talk. He put his ear close to the reeds.

"Isn't Belgium near France?" his brother asked.

"Next door."

"It's a good country?"

"Oh, yes."

His brother handed the stranger a glass of tea.

"Have another bottle of beer," the stranger suggested.

Ali heard the bottle being opened and the cap fall on to the stone door-sill.

"What's that?" said his brother, his voice bright with interest.

"Just a pill. If I'm nervous I take one. It makes me feel better. If I can't sleep I take two."

"And then you sleep?"

"Like a child."

There was a pause. Then his brother asked: "And would they do that to anyone?"

The stranger laughed. "Of course," he said. "Some people might have to take three, some only one."

"And how long does it make you sleep?"

"All night."

"If someone touched you, you'd wake up?"

"Why, yes,"

"But if you took four or five?"

"*Oh, là, là!* You could ride a horse over me then, and I wouldn't know it. That's too many."

This time there was a long silence, and Ali heard only the noise of the rain all around. The water leaking through the roof had made a channel in the mud to the back door. Now and then a distant growl of thunder came from the hills on the north. The air that moved in through the door was cold and smelled of earth.

Presently his brother said: "It's getting dark."

"I suppose you want to close."

"*Oh, ne t'en fais pas!*" said his brother cordially. "Stay until it stops raining."

The stranger laughed. "It's very kind of you, but I'm afraid I'm going to get wet anyway, because it's not going to stop."

"No, no!" his brother cried, an anxious note creeping into his voice. "Wait a few minutes. Soon it will stop. Besides, I enjoy talking with you. You aren't like a Frenchman."

The man laughed again; he sounded pleased and flattered.

Then Ali heard his brother saying timidly: "Those pills. Where could I buy a bottle?"

"My doctor in Belgium gave them to me, but I imagine you could get a doctor here to prescribe some."

"No," said his brother hopelessly.

"Why do you want them? You don't look as though you had trouble sleeping."

His brother squatted down beside the stranger. "It's not that," he said, almost whispering.

Ali peered intently between the reeds, making an effort to follow the movements of his brother's lips. "*C'est une fille*. I give her everything. She always says no. I was thinking, if just once I could——"

The man interrupted him. "You give her enough of these and she won't be able to say anything." He chuckled maliciously. "Here. Hold out your hand."

With a few inarticulate phrases of thanks, his brother rose to his feet, probably to get a box or an envelope for the pills.

Quickly Ali went out of the door through the rain to the house, where he changed his shirt and spread the wet one over the pillows, and lighted the lamp. Then he sat reading, with some difficulty, a newspaper that a customer had left behind the day before. A few minutes later his brother came in, looking pleased and a little mysterious.

It rained most of the night. At dawn, however, when they got up, the sky was clear. His brother drank his coffee hurriedly and went out, saying he would be back about noon.

Two couples came to the café during the morning, but since they took beer the boy did not have to light the fire.

Somewhat later than twelve his brother returned. Ali looked up at his face as he came in the door, and said to himself: "Something has happened." But he pretended to have noticed nothing and turned away unconcernedly after greeting him. Whatever it might be, he knew his brother would never tell him anything.

The afternoon was exceptionally fine. A good many visitors came, as they always did when the weather was clear and the view good. His brother's face did not change. He carried the trays of tea glasses out to the tables like a man walking in his sleep, and he kept his eyes averted from the customers' faces. Each time someone arrived and walked under the arbor onto the terrace, Ali's brother looked as though he were

about to run and jump off the edge of the parapet. Once
when Ali saw him smoking, he noticed his hand trembling
so violently that he had difficulty in getting the cigarette to
his lips, and he looked away quickly so his brother would
not see him watching.

When the evening call to prayer was over and the last carriage had rattled away down the road, the boy brought the tables and chairs in and swept the floor of the terrace. Ali stood
in the doorway. His brother sat on the parapet, looking down
over the olive trees in the dimming light, while the town below sank deeper into the gulf of shadow between the hills. An
automobile came along the road, stopped. Against the sky Ali
saw his brother's head jerk upward. There were the two
sounds of a car's doors being shut. His brother rose, took two
hesitant steps, and sat down again.

Ali moved backward into the room, away from the door. It
was not yet too dark for him to see that the two men walking
across the terrace were policemen. Without slipping into his
babouches he ran barefoot through the inner room of the
café, across the open space to the house. He lay down on his
mattress, breathing rapidly. The boy was in the kitchen preparing the evening meal.

For a long time Ali lay there, thinking of nothing, watching
the cobwebs that dangled from the ceiling move slowly in the
breeze. It seemed so long to him that he thought the two
men must have gone away without his having heard them. He
tiptoed to the door. The boy was still in the kitchen. Ali
stepped outside. The crickets were singing all around and the
moonlight looked blue. He heard voices on the terrace. Without making a sound he crept into the café's back room and
lay down on the mat.

The policemen were making fun of his brother, but not
pleasantly. Their voices were harsh and they laughed too loud.

"A Belgian, no less!" cried one with mock surprise. "He fell
out of the sky like an angel, *bien sûr*, with the veronal in one
hand. But nobody saw him. Only you."

Ali caught his breath, sprang up. Then very slowly he lay
down again, scarcely breathing now, still listening. "Nobody,"
said his brother, his voice very low. It sounded as though he
had his hands over his face. "He said she'd just go to sleep."

They thought this very funny. "She did that, all right," said one at length. Then their speech became abrupt, the tone brutal: "*Allez, assez! On se débine!*" They rose, yanking him up with them.

As they pushed him into the car, his brother was still saying: "I didn't know. He didn't tell me."

The motor started up; they turned the car around and drove down the road. Soon the distant sound of its motor was covered by the song of the crickets.

For a while Ali lay very still. Then, being hungry, he went to the house and had his dinner.

The Hours After Noon

> "If one could awaken all the echoes of one's memory
> simulanteously, they would make a music, delightful or sad as
> the case might be, but logical and without dissonances. No
> matter how incoherent the existence, the human unity is not
> affected."
>
> —Baudelaire

O H, YOU'RE a *man*! What does a man know about such
things? I can tell you how much: absolutely nothing!"
When she argued with her husband at mealtimes, Mrs. Callender often sought the support of the other diners in the
room. In this instance, however, her appeal was purely formal,
since at the moment she was the only woman present, and
thus assumed she had their attention anyway. Her bright eyes
flashed indignantly from one male diner to the next, and she
even turned around in her chair to include old Mr. Richmond, the teller in the Bank of British West Africa. He looked
up from his food and said: "Eh? Oh, yes. I dare say."

The Pension Callender was surprisingly empty these
days—empty even for the hot season. Besides old Mr. Richmond, who had been with them since they had started
eleven years ago, there was Mr. Burton down from London
to write a book; he had come last autumn and as yet had
given no indication of being ready to leave. Mr. Richmond
and Mr. Burton were the only true residents of the pension.
The others either came and went irregularly, like Mr. Van
Siclen the archeologist and Clyde Brown who was in business in Casablanca, or were merely there for a few days waiting for money or visas before they continued southward or
northward, like the two young Belgians who had left that
morning.

"A young girl—any young girl—is unbelievably sensitive.
Like a thermometer, or a barometer. She catches hold of
whatever's in the air. It's true, I tell you." Mrs. Callender
looked around at each one defiantly; her black eyes flashed.

Mr. Callender was in a good humor. "That may be," he
said indulgently. "But I wouldn't worry about Charlotte. And

anyway, we don't even know for sure whether Monsieur Royer's coming or not. You know how he is, always changing his mind. He's probably on his way to Marrakesh right now."

"Oh, he *will* come. You know he will! You simply don't want to face facts." (Sometimes this was true of Mr. Callender. When it was obvious that one of the Moslem servants was systematically stealing foodstuffs from his pantry, he would make no effort to discover who the culprit was, preferring to wait until he might possibly catch him red-handed.) "You hope that somehow he won't get here. But he will, and he's a filthy, horrible man, and he's going to be sitting opposite your own daughter at every meal. I should think that might mean something to you."

Her husband looked around at the other diners, an expression of amusement on his face. "I don't think sitting opposite to him at mealtimes'll bring about her downfall, do you?"

"Abdallah! *Otra taza de café!*" The boy who had been standing by the fireplace trying to follow the conversation stepped forward and filled her cup. "Silly boy!" she cried, sipping the coffee. "It's quite cold." He understood, and lifted the cup to carry it out. "No, no," she said sighing, reaching out for it. "*Déjalo, déjalo.*" And without pausing: "He has a sinister personality. It has an effect on one. Women *feel* those things. I've felt it myself."

Her husband raised his eyebrows. "Aha! So now we come to the meat of the conversation. Gentlemen! Wouldn't you say that my wife is the one to watch? Don't you think *she* should be kept from Monsieur Royer?"

Mrs. Callender simpered. "Bob! You're positively appalling!" At the same time Mr. Richmond raised his head in a startled fashion and said: "Monsieur Royer? Oh?"

Clyde Brown was the only one of the four guests who had been following the conversation from the beginning. His watery blue eyes stared with interest. "Who is this Monsieur Royer? A Latin Quarter Don Juan?"

There was a slight silence. The wind was blowing a blind outside the dining-room window back and forth; the distant sound of heavy waves pounding against the cliffs came up from below. "Don Juan?" echoed Mrs. Callender, laughing thinly. "My dear, I wish you could see him! He looks like a furious lobster, one that's just been cooked. Absolutely hideous! And he's at least fifty."

"You're treading on delicate ground," said Mr. Callender into his plate.

"I know, darling, but you don't go about annoying young girls and getting into messes. He gets into the most frightful messes. You haven't forgotten Señora Coelho's niece last year, when he . . ."

Mr. Callender pushed back his chair; the scraping sound it made on the tile floor was very loud in the room. "Probably does, and probably richly deserves whatever trouble he gets into," he announced. Then impatiently, quickly, to his wife: "I know all about him. What do you want me to do—wire him we're full up?" He knew she would say no, and she did. There was always something in one of the stores in town which she coveted at the time: a silk scarf, a pair of shoes or gloves, and the only money which came in was that paid by the guests who stayed at the pension. "But I should think you'd show more interest where your own daughter is concerned," she added.

Mr. Burton, who had just become aware that a discussion was in progress, raised his head from the book he had been reading and smiled affably at Mrs. Callender. Old Mr. Richmond folded his napkin, stuffed it into its aluminum ring, and said: "I expect it's time to be getting back into town." Mr. Callender announced that he was going to his cottage to take his afternoon siesta. Soon only Mr. Van Siclen remained at his table by the window, sipping his coffee and looking distractedly out at the windblown landscape. He was a young man who had let his beard grow during the war when he had been stationed on some distant island in the Pacific; now finding that he looked more impressive with it (he was very young to be an archeologist, people told him), he still wore it. Mrs. Callender found herself watching him, wondering whether or not he would be better-looking without its black decoration: he would be less romantic, she decided, perhaps even a little frail of face. As he turned to look at her she felt a tiny thrill of excitement, but his expression swiftly effaced it. He always seemed pleasantly preoccupied; the cynical smile that flickered about his lips made him more remote than if there had been no smile at all. His way of being friendly was to look up from his book and say: "Good morning. How are you today?" in a very firm voice; then by the time you had replied he would be buried again in the book. She considered his behavior insufferably rude, but then, she never had met an American who did not impress her as wanting in courtesy. It was more their attitude than it was anything they did or failed to do. She herself had been born in Gibraltar of an English father and a Spanish mother, her school days had been passed in Kent, and, although Mr. Callender was an American, she considered herself English through and through. And Charlotte was going to be a typical English girl, a wholesome, simple lass without the ridiculous attitudes and featherbrained preoccupations of most American girls. Nor would she be granted the freedom so many American mothers allowed their daughters. Mrs. Callender had enough of the Mediterranean in her to believe that while a boy should have complete liberty, a girl should have none at all. The wind continued to bang the shutter.

"I see. Trying to get rid of old Royer," said Mr. Van Siclen lazily, shaking his head with mock disapproval. "Poor old Royer who never did any harm except ruin a girl's life here and there."

"Oh, I'm so glad!" she cried; the force of her emotion startled him. He glanced at her suspiciously.

"Glad about what?"

"Glad that you agree with me about Monsieur Royer."

"That he's a useless old rake who'll be up to no good until the day he dies? Sure I agree."

"Of course you do," she assured him; she did not see that he was baiting her.

"But I don't agree with you about keeping him away from anybody. Why? *Sauve qui peut,* I always say. And the devil take the hindmost."

She was genuinely indignant. "How can you talk that way? I'm being perfectly serious, even if you're not."

"I'm perfectly serious, too. After all, a girl's education has to start somewhere, some time."

"I think you're quite revolting. Education, indeed!" Her eyes looked beyond his face, through the window, to the

stunted cypresses below, at the top of the cliff. She could remember some experiences she would have liked to avoid, or
at least have put off until later, when she might have been
ready for them. Her aunt in Málaga had been far too lenient,
otherwise it never would have been possible for her to meet
the sailor from the *Jaime II*, much less to have made an appointment with him in the Alameda for the following day.
And the two students she had gone on the picnic with to An-
tequera, who had thought they could take advantage of her
because she was not Spanish. "I must still have had a slight
accent," she thought. She was sure it was because of such
memories as these that she now had "sad days," when she felt
that life would never be right again. There were many things
a girl should not know until she was married, and they were
the very things it seemed every man was determined to im-
part to her. Once she was married and it all mattered so much
less, precisely then the opportunities for learning were cut
down to a minimum. But of course it was better that way.

Slowly her expression was changing from indignation to
wistfulness. Voluptuous memories burned in the mind like fire
in a tree stump: they were impossible to put out, and they
consumed from within, until suddenly nothing was left. If she
had a great many memories instead of only a few, she reflected, she would surely be lost.

"You wouldn't talk that way, so playfully, if you knew the
hazards of bringing up a girl in this place," she said wearily.
"With these Moors all about, and strange new people coming
to the pension every day. Of course, we try to get the good
Moors, but you know how they are—utterly undependable
and mad as hatters, every one of them. One never knows
what any of them will take it into his head to do next. Thank
God we can afford to send Charlotte to school in England."

"I'm chilly," said Mr. Van Siclen. He rose from the table
rubbing his hands together.

"Yes, it's cool. It's the wind. Mind, I have absolutely nothing personal against Monsieur Royer. He's always been a
model of fine behavior with me. It isn't that at all. If he were
a young man" (she almost added: "like you"), "I'd think it
was amusing. I don't object to a young man who's sowing his
wild oats. That's to be expected. But Monsieur Royer is at

least fifty. And he goes after such mere children. A young man is more likely to be interested in older women, don't you think? That isn't nearly so dangerous." She followed him with her gaze, turning her head as he went toward the door. "Not nearly."

He paused in the doorway, the same inexpressive smile on his lips. "Send him out to El Menar." He had a little native house at El Menar, where he was digging through the Roman and Carthaginian layers of rubble, trying to get at the earlier material. "If he chases the girls around out there they'll find him in a couple of days behind a rock with a coil of wire around his neck."

"Such brutes!" she cried. "How can you stay out there all alone with those wild men?"

"They're fine people," he said, going out.

She looked around the empty room, shivered, and went out on to the terrace, feeling unpleasantly nervous. The wind was near to being a gale, but the clouds, which until now had covered the sky, were breaking up, letting the hard blue backdrop of the sky show through in places. In the cypresses the wind whistled and hissed, and when it hit her face it took her breath away. The air was sharp with the odor of eucalyptus, and damp from the fine spray of the breaking waves below. Then, when the landscape was least prepared for such a change, the sun came out. In all these years of living in Morocco she never had ceased wondering at the astonishing difference made by the sun. Immediately she felt the heat seeping in through her pores, the wind was warm, no longer hostile; the countryside became greener, smiled, and slowly the water down there turned to a brilliant blue. She breathed deeply and said tentatively to herself that she was happy. She was not sure it was true, for it seldom happened, but sometimes she could bring it about in this way. It seemed to her that long ago she had known happiness, and that the brief moments of it she found now were only faint memories of the original state. Now, she always felt surrounded by the ugliness of humanity; the scheming little human mind was always present. A certain awareness of what went on around her was essential if she were to find even normal contentment.

She saw a Moroccan coming towards her from the driveway. Vaguely she knew that his arrival would entail something unpleasant, but for the moment she refused to think about it. She ran her hand through her hair which the wind had blown awry, and tried to bring her mind back to the pension. There was Mr. Richmond's mirror which was broken, Brahim needed a new electric bulb in the pantry, she had to look in the laundry for an undershirt of Bob's that was missing, she must catch Pedro before he drove the station wagon into town, to remind him to stop at the Consulate and pick up Miss Peters whom she had invited for tea.

The Moroccan, his ragged *djellaba* whipping in the wind, emerged from the shadows of the nearest eucalyptus. She exclaimed with annoyance and turned to face him. He was old and he carried a basket. Suddenly she remembered him from last year: she had bought mushrooms from him. And as she remembered, she glanced involuntarily at the withered hand holding the basket and saw the six dark fingers that she knew would be there. "Go away!" she cried passionately. "*Cir f'ha-lak!*" She wheeled about and began to run down the path to her cottage in the garden below. Without looking behind she went in and slammed the door behind her. The room smelled of damp plaster and insecticide. She stood a moment at the window looking apprehensively up the path through the bushes. Then, feeling slightly absurd, she drew the curtains across and began to remove her make-up. As a rule the mornings took care of themselves; it was the hours after noon that she had to beware of, when the day had begun to go toward the night, and she no longer trusted herself to be absolutely certain of what she would do next, or of what unlikely idea would come into her head. Once again she peered between the curtains up the sunlit path, but there was nobody.

2

The months in Spain had been not at all relaxing; he was fed up with the coy promises of eyes seen above fans, furious with mantillas, crucifixes and titters. Here in Morocco, if love lacked finesse, at least it was frank. The veils over the faces did not disturb him; he had learned long ago to decipher the features beneath. Only the teeth remained a hazard. And the eyes he could read as easily as words. When they showed any interest at all, they expressed it clearly, with no hint of the prudishness he so hated.

Above a bank of thick clouds the twilight sky burned with a fierce blueness. He turned into the crowded native quarter. He had sent his luggage to the Pension Callender by taxi and had arranged to take Mr. Callender's station wagon when it started up from the market just before dinner. That left him free to wander a half-hour or so in the Casbah, nothing on his mind, nothing in his hands. He turned into the Rue Abdessadek. The hooded figures in the street moved from stall to stall, their hands making the decorative oriental gestures, their voices strident with disagreement over prices. It was all familiar to Monsieur Royer, and very comforting. He felt he could again breathe easily. Slowly he ascended the hill, trying to recall a passage of something he once had read and loved: "*Le temps qui coule ici n'a plus d'heures, mais—*" He could not get beyond this point into the other thought. Turning into a smaller street, he was suddenly met by an overpowering odor of jasmine; it came from behind the wall beside him. He stood still a moment beneath the overhanging branch of a fig tree on the other side of the wall, and inhaled slowly, deliberately, still hoping to get beyond that part of the thought which had to do with time. The jasmine would help. It was coming to him: "*mais, tant le loisir—*" No.

A child brushed against him, and he had the impression that it had done so purposely. He glanced down: sure enough, it was begging. In a cajoling, unnatural little voice that set his nerves on edge it was asking alms, raising a tiny cupped hand toward him. He began to walk quickly, still sniffing the jasmine, feeling the elusive phrase he sought moving a little further away from him. The child hurried along beside him, continuing its odious chant. "No!" he cried explosively, without looking down at it again, and forcing his legs to take enormous strides in the hope of escaping its singsong voice.

"*Le temps qui coule ici n'a plus d'heures, mais tant—*" he murmured aloud, to cover the sound beside him. It was impossible. Now his mood was irrevocably shattered. The child, growing bolder, touched his leg with a tentative finger. "*Dame una gorda,*" it whined. With a suddenness and ferocity which astonished him even as he acted, he dealt it a savage blow in the face, and a fraction of a second later heard it moan. Then he watched it duck and run to the side of the street where it stood against the wall holding its hand to its face and staring at him with an expression of reproach and shocked disbelief.

Already he was feeling a sharp pang of regret for his behavior. He stepped toward the cowering child, not aware of what he was about to say or do. The child looked up; its pinched face was pale in the light of the arc-lamp that swung above. He heard himself say in a tremulous voice: "*Porqué me molestas así?*" It did not answer, and he felt its silence making an unbridgeable abyss between them. He took hold of its thin arm. Again, without stirring, it made its absurd, animal moan. In a new access of rage he struck it again, much harder. This time it made no sound; it merely stood. Completely unnerved and miserable, Monsieur Royer turned and walked off in the direction from which he had just come, colliding with a shrouded woman who was emptying garbage from a pan into the middle of the street. She called after him angrily, but he paid no attention. The idea that the Moroccan urchin must consider him with the same dread and contempt it felt for any other Christian interloper was intolerable to him, for he considered himself a particularly understanding friend of the Moslems. He hurried back through the town to the market, found the station wagon, and got into it. By the light of the many flares in the vegetable stands opposite, he recognized old Mr. Richmond of the Bank of British West Africa sitting on the seat facing him.

"Good evening," said Monsieur Royer, feeling that any kind of conversation at all would help him to recover from the ill-humor induced by his walk.

Mr. Richmond grunted a reply, and after a pause said: "You're Royer, I believe?"

"Aha, you remember me," smiled Monsieur Royer. But Mr. Richmond said no more.

Presently Pedro arrived, his arms full of bundles which he piled on the floor between them. He greeted Monsieur Royer ceremoniously, and explained that they would not be going directly to the pension because they had to stop by the airport to call for Miss Charlotte, who was coming down from London. As they drove slowly through the crowded market, several times Monsieur Royer saw Mr. Richmond glance across at him with a surreptitiousness which bordered on the theatrical. "*Pauvre vieux*," he thought. "He's losing his grip."

3

It had been a nerve-racking flight down, through clouds most of the way, with sudden terrifying exits into regions of pitiless burning sunlight against which the softness of the clouds seemed a protection. She was not afraid of flying; the uneasiness had begun long before she had left school. Each morning on waking she had smelled the freshly-cut grass, heard the birds' familiar chirping in the bushes, and said to herself that she did not want to leave.

Of course there was no question of her not going home to visit her family; although her mother had come to England the year before to spend the vacation months with her, she had not seen her father for two years, and she really cared more for him than she did for her mother. He was quiet, he looked at her in a strange, appraising manner that enormously flattered her and, above all, he let her alone, refrained from making suggestions for the betterment of her appearance or character, which ostensibly meant that he considered her a fully formed individual. And while she had to admit that her mother was sweet, at the same time she could not help thinking her silly and something of a nuisance: she was so laden with advice and so eternally ready to bestow it. And the more one took, the more of it she attempted to unload upon one. There was no end to the chain of suggestions and admonitions. She told herself that this constant watching was a very common misapplication of maternal love, but that did not make it any easier to bear.

Her last two days at school she had spent packing slowly, automatically; they had been filled with a particular anguish which she finally brought herself to diagnose. It was sheer apprehensiveness at the prospect of being again with her mother. Other years she had prepared to go home without feeling this tremulous dread. It was as they left London Airport and she was bracing herself against the plane's banking that the reason came to her; without realizing it she already had determined to resist. The discovery was a shock. For a moment she felt like a monster. "I can't go home feeling like this," she thought. But as the plane righted itself, and, soaring higher, broke through the pall of fog into the clarity above, she sighed and sat back to read, reflecting that after all the decision was purely private and could scarcely be read in her face. However, throughout the flight, as the plane moved onward from sunlight into shadow and out again, she continued from time to time to be plagued by the feeling that she had become disloyal; and with this suspicion went the fear that in some way she might hurt her mother.

It was a small airport. Before the plane had landed Charlotte had sighted the station wagon, standing in the glare of the floodlights near the shack which served as waiting-room and customs office. She was not surprised to find that her father had not come to meet her; he left the pension only when he was forced to. Pedro piled her luggage on top and helped her into the back of the car.

"Pleasant journey?" Mr. Richmond asked when they had greeted each other and she was seated beside him.

"Yes, thank you," she said, waiting to be presented to the other gentleman sitting opposite them. He was obviously from the Continent and of a rather distinguished appearance, she thought. But Mr. Richmond looked unconcernedly out at the lights of the airport, and so she spoke with the gentleman anyway.

They chatted about the weather and the natives. The car climbed the steep road; at each turn its headlights swept the white walls along the sides, crowned with masses of trailing flowers and vines. High in the dark trees a few cicadas continued to rasp their daytime song. She and the gentleman were still talking when the station wagon pulled into the garage. Mr. Richmond, however, had not said another word.

4

At the pension nothing had changed since her last visit. Her mother looked younger and prettier than ever, and seemed, if

possible, still more scatteredbrained and distraught—so much
so that she too forgot to introduce her to the French gentleman. However, since he was seated in the farthest corner of
the dining-room by the window, and was already finishing
when the family sat down to eat, it did not matter much.

Her father looked at her across the table and smiled.

"So there you are," he said with satisfaction. He paused
and turned to his wife: "Better get Señorita Marchena busy
on a dress." And to Charlotte: "There's a big shindig Saturday night at the Country Club."

"Oh, but I have plenty of things to wear!" she objected.

"Yes, but this is very special. And calls for something very
special. Señorita Marchena'll be equal to the occasion." He
looked at her carefully. "And all I can say is, the Ramirez girls
had better look to their laurels."

She felt herself blushing. The Ramirez girls were three sisters who held the reputation of having a local monopoly on
beauty.

"The Ramirez girls!" cried Mrs. Callender, a note of scorn
in her voice.

"What's the matter with them?" demanded her husband.
"They're nice girls."

"Oh, they're pretty, yes, Bob, but they're scarcely what one
would call nice girls." (For Mrs. Callender all Spaniards by
definition were inclined to dubious morality.)

"Mother! How can you say that!" Charlotte exclaimed.

Mrs. Callender looked about uneasily; it seemed to her that
Monsieur Royer was listening to their conversation. She had
purposely delayed sitting down to dinner until she thought
he would be finished eating, but he was still toying with his
fruit. "I'll tell you about them later," she said *sotto voce* to
Charlotte, and changed the subject, fervently hoping that in a
moment he would leave and go down to his cottage.

In the middle of the meal the door from the terrace
opened and Mr. Van Siclen burst in, fresh from El Menar,
dressed in earth-stained overalls. He had a way of appearing
unannounced at any hour of the day or night. Sometimes it
was inconvenient for the servants, but since he paid full pension and ate few meals there, the Callenders never remarked
upon his impromptu arrivals. He shut the door carefully so

the wind sweeping through the room from the kitchen would not slam it.

"Hello, everybody!" he said, running his hand through his hair. Mrs. Callender glanced toward the window where Monsieur Royer was slicing an apple into paper-thin sections. "Oh, how terrible! Monsieur Royer has your table! Do sit here with us. Abdallah! *Trae otra silla!*" She moved her own chair up a bit and indicated the space beside her. "Before you sit down, this is my daughter Charlotte." He acknowledged the introduction dryly, with a minimum of civility, and seated himself, sighing mightily.

"What a night!" he exclaimed as his soup was placed before him. "An ocean breeze, a full moon, and big clouds. I just came in from El Menar in my jeep," he told Charlotte. (She had decided he was pretentious, with that beard.)

"How enchanting!" cried Mrs. Callender. "Now, do tell us. Have you stumbled on something fantastic out there? Gold coins? Lapis lazuli cups?"

As he spoke, Charlotte watched his face, complacent and slightly mocking. It summed up all the things she disliked most in men: conceit, brashness, insensitivity. Still, he could not be as bad as he looked, she thought; some of it must be the beard. No one his age had a right to such a decoration.

From time to time she stole a glance at her mother, who was following his dull discourse as if it were of the greatest interest, punctuating it with little cooing sounds and exclamations of rapture. Somehow she had expected to find her less silly this time (perhaps because of her determination to resist) and instead, here she was, worse than ever. "It must be her age," she decided. At some point she would probably change suddenly, overnight. And now, becoming aware that it was precisely this quality of superficiality to which she most objected, she no longer felt even a twinge of guilt at her own rebelliousness. Trying to manage other people's lives was a definite thing. It had its limits. But the kind of irresponsibility she saw in her mother amounted to a denial of all values. There was no beginning and no end; anything was equal to anything else.

Two nurses on leave from the hospital in Gibraltar pushed back their chairs and walked across the room to the door.

"Good nayt," they said. Both wore glasses; both were dressed in execrable taste. Charlotte watched them and thought: "To have reached thirty and to look like that—!"

Someone laid a hand lightly on her shoulder. She twisted her head around. The French gentleman was standing behind her chair, smiling at her mother.

"I wish to compliment you, madam. A lovely girl like this could only be the daughter of so charming a mother as you."

He bowed low, from behind her, so that for a second his head was level with hers; his hand remained on her shoulder. A short silence fell upon the table. To Mr. Van Siclen Monsieur Royer said: "Good evening, my dear fellow! How are you? Have you made any remarkable discoveries recently?"

"Hello, Royer. I was just telling the Callenders a little about the new wall I came to yesterday."

"But it's splendid! Only yesterday! I want to hear about it."

"Sit down," said Mr. Van Siclen. Mrs. Callender flashed him a furious glance.

"I'm afraid it'll be rather crowded," she said, scraping her chair back and forth on the tiles as noisily as possible, and failing to move it an inch.

"Oh, no. There's room," objected Charlotte. "Here beside me."

But Monsieur Royer laughed.

"No, no! You are very kind and I want very much to hear about the latest developments of this prodigious excavating. Perhaps tomorrow, Mr. Van Siclen?" Ceremoniously he kissed the hands of Mrs. Callender and Charlotte, and went out.

Mrs. Callender rolled her eyes at her husband. "One needs the patience of Job," she said. "What an insufferable fool!"

Charlotte hesitated an instant before saying: "Why? I think he's rather sweet."

Her mother gave a little shriek, part giggle, and looked at Mr. Callender as if seeking support. Then she said very seriously: "I'm sorry to hear it, darling, because it only shows what faulty judgment you have. The man's an utter cad, a complete bounder. They don't come lower."

Charlotte in turn looked at her father. "Is that really true?" she asked.

"He's a bad egg, all right," he said.

They sat a while over coffee exchanging news. The dining-room was empty now save for their table. Abdallah leaned by the fireplace more asleep than awake. Mr. Van Siclen had ceased taking part in the talk, and tilted his chair back, puffing on a pipe. From time to time the wind shook the house. Slowly the conversation had centered itself upon Charlotte. She was telling her parents about school, about her classes and friends; she had almost forgotten Mr. Van Siclen was present. Suddenly she stopped short.

"This must all be the most frightful bore for Mr. Van Siclen," she said apologetically.

"Nonsense; go on," said her father. "If he doesn't like it he can leave."

Mr. Van Siclen smiled sleepily through the smoke. "I'm not bored at all," he assured her. "It's very instructive."

She was convinced he was making fun of her, and she grew hot with anger.

"I'm dreadfully tired. I think I should go to sleep." It was the only way to avoid going on with it; now that she was conscious of his amused eyes she could not possibly continue talking.

Her mother jumped up. "Of course she's tired, poor baby. Come along. You must get to bed immediately." She tried to take her arm, to pull her toward the door, but Charlotte could not allow that. Gently she disengaged herself and went over to kiss her father good night; she took leave of Mr. Van Siclen with more civility than she felt; then, back at the door, she seized her mother's arm and led her down the steps through the garden to the cottages below. Mrs. Callender went in and sat on the bed while she unpacked, gossiping about the servants. Hassan's eleven-year-old brother had been put in prison for reaching in through the open window into Mr. Burton's room and taking a hundred-peseta note which lay on the table.

"But, mother! that's terribly young to be in prison."

"Darling, I've said for years that the child was a thief. I've told Hassan to watch him, or we should have trouble. Isn't that the bathrobe Mrs. Grey gave you? It's rather pretty, but it seems a bit long." Eventually she went out, leaving Charlotte wide awake in the dark, listening to the rhythmical roar of

the waves. They were not very loud tonight; she could remember many nights when they had seemed right in the
room. But tonight the wind was from the west.

5

It was not long before she realized how foolish of her it had
been to drink coffee after dinner; she would not be sleepy for
hours. And since her mother generally read for an hour or so
before going to sleep, and could see across to her cottage, she
could not very well get up. Directly she turned on her light,
her mother would be over to see what was wrong. She
wanted to take a walk—perhaps down on the beach. But it
would mean getting dressed in the dark and stealing out
quietly at the risk of meeting her father. She had not yet heard
him go into his own cottage. If she waited, it would be safer,
but she did not feel like waiting. As she groped about cautiously for her skirt she heard him shut his door. She sighed
with relief. Now that everyone was in, it would be much
easier.

It all went very smoothly; she did not make a sound. Under the grape-arbor, through the vegetable garden, down
across the open field towards the promontory where the cypresses and rocks overlooked the water beneath. The low
clouds scudding overhead made waves of shadow that moved
slowly across the moonlit country. She hummed happily as
she walked along. To the right, under the big bent cypress,
through the little ravine, up again; she knew the way perfectly.
What she had not counted on was meeting Mr. Van Siclen sitting on a rock directly in the path, as she reached the edge of
the cliff. He sat there looking out to sea; at her involuntary
"Oh!" he turned and smiled at her in the moonlight.

The sight of him there had so thoroughly disrupted her
state of mind that she merely stood still and looked at him.

"I *thought* you'd be out," he said with satisfaction.

She could only say, stupidly: "Why?"

"I didn't think you were sleepy."

She said nothing. Her impulse was to be unfriendly, but she
decided it would be childish. "I thought I'd go for a walk
down on the beach for a bit."

He laughed. "I saw you come sneaking out." (Why did he have to be so objectionable?) "Care to go for a little ride?"

"Oh, I don't think so, thank you," she said politely, conscious at the same time that her voice lacked forcefulness.

"Sure you would. Come on!"

He sprang up, seized her hand, and began to pull her along, back up the path. "No, really! No! Listen to me!" She wanted to resist physically, but she was afraid of seeming a whining creature—a poor sport. Presently she was obliged to stop for a moment. "Please!" she gasped. "Not so fast!" This he appeared to construe as a tacit acceptance of his suggestion; he laughed, loosened his grip, and said: "The jeep's in the upper driveway."

And once she was in the car, going up the mountain with the night wind in her face, she thought that perhaps she had meant to accept from the moment he had invited her. There was a sharp, spicy odor in the air: they were in the eucalyptus forest. It was like going through a high dark tunnel. The sound of the motor reverberated overhead. A minute later the walls of Sultan Moulay Hafid's palace loomed, growing higher as they approached the entrance. In another moment there were no walls at all; the car was on the high, flat section of road leading through the olive-grove to Bou Amar. The rolling hills stretched away to the south in a vast misty panorama whitened by the moonlight. Here and there the uncertain shadow of a cloud moved up a slope, assuming a new form as it reached the summit and spread over the valley beyond. The clouds were low and moved swiftly. She wanted to say: "It's lovely." But he had turned the windshield horizontal, and her breath was cut by the onrushing blast of air. The little white native houses of Bou Amar flitted past, and again they were in the country, among the pines now. The road did not deviate from its straight line, but it rose and dipped like a roller-coaster over the hills. He closed the windshield.

"Shall I open her up?" he called.

"Don't go any faster, if that's what you mean."

"That's what I mean."

"No!"

"This thing can't go, anyway!" he yelled.

But it seemed to her he had increased the speed.

Now there were no more trees; it was a high, open, rocky region dotted with clumps of holly and heather that glistened under the moon. Far ahead the lighthouse on the cape sent out its recurrent message. All at once he brought the jeep to a stop. It was absolutely silent up here save for the wind: there were no insects and the sea was too far away to be heard. He lit a cigarette without offering her one, and looked at her sideways.

"Are you what's laughingly called a virtuous young lady?" Her heart sank.

"What?" (And it was so idiotic, in any case.) She waited, then said: "I expect so. Why?"

"*Very* virtuous?"

"Did you bring me out here to inquire after my morals?"

"They don't mean a damn thing to me, if you want to know. I'm just asking to be polite. You know—how's your lumbago? How's your abscessed tooth?"

In spite of herself she said: "You know, I think you're quite disgusting."

He blew some smoke in her face. "All disgust, my dear young lady, is nothing but lack of appetite—desire not to touch with the mouth."

"What?"

"Eating an object. Kissing somebody. Same thing."

"I don't know what you are talking about." She began to be alarmed: it was like conversing with a madman.

"I'm just trying to tell you that I don't really disgust you."

The lighthouse was flashing. "How can I get him to go back?" she thought.

"I should think I'd be the best judge of that," she said a bit shakily.

"And yet you want me to kiss you."

"What?" she cried shrilly. After a moment she said in a low voice: "Why should I want you to kiss me?"

"I'm damned if I know. But you do."

"It's not true. I don't."

He tossed his cigarette away. "I think we've argued enough about this little thing," he said, turning toward her.

She had never been treated this way before. When he seized her, she could do nothing. When with all her might she tried to pull her head away, he caught hold of her lip with his teeth, so that she cried out with pain. After a prolonged struggle he let go and sat grinning at her. She tried to speak, but sobbed and choked.

"Have a handkerchief," he said. Automatically she accepted it and blew her nose. Then she dabbed at her lip and saw the dark blood on the white linen. For some reason this gave her the courage to raise her head and look at him.

"I——"

"Don't try to talk," he said shortly.

She stared at him, overcome by her hatred of him, opened her mouth to speak, and choked afresh. When she had calmed herself sufficiently to be able to think: "That was beastly," rather than "This is beastly," she handed him his handkerchief and said quietly: "My mother was wrong. She said they don't come lower than Monsieur Royer."

He laughed delightedly. "Oh, he's much worse! *Mu-u-uch* worse!"

"If you don't mind, I'd prefer not to talk about it any more."

"Ah, it wasn't as bad as all that," he said.

She did not answer.

"As a matter of fact," he pursued, "this ride was good for you."

"I don't think my father would agree," she said somewhat primly.

"Probably not. But he'll never be asked his opinion, will he?"

Remembering her sigh of relief when she had heard her father shut the door of his cottage, she was silent. He started up the engine, turned the jeep around, and they went back over the road as quickly as they had come. When they arrived at the garage, she jumped out without speaking again, and hurried to her cottage. All the lights in the other cottages were out. She undressed in the dark, turning on the light over the wash-basin just long enough to put a drop of iodine on her lip. As she got into bed she noticed that she was trembling. Even so, it was not long before the sound of the waves had lulled her to sleep.

6

In the morning she awoke in rather a bad humor. Perhaps the trip was just having its effect, or perhaps the unpleasantness of last night had upset her nerves. Halima, the younger of Mustapha the cook's two wives, brought her breakfast. When she had finished eating, she got out of bed and looked in the mirror. Her lower lip was still swollen. "Maybe by lunchtime it will be gone," she thought hopefully, and she put on her bathing suit and rushed down to the beach where she spent the whole morning swimming and sunbathing. About noon she caught sight of Monsieur Royer coming around the point at the base of the cliffs. He was in while flannels and flourished a cane. She watched him approach, glad he was not Mr. Van Siclen.

"Aha! A mermaid today!" he cried. "Is the sea comfortable?"

"Oh, yes. It's lovely."

He stood above her, making designs in the sand with the tip of his cane, and they talked. Finally he said: "May I be seated?"

"Oh, please! Of course!" She felt rude for not having suggested it.

When he was beside her he continued to chat and plough up the sand with his cane. After a few minutes he turned and looked into her face, smiling in such a way that his eyes seemed to shine more brightly, and said: "It is not too many times in his life that a man has the privilege of sitting with a real mermaid, you know. So you must forgive me if I enjoy this privilege."

She did not know what she ought to say, but his manner amused her, and so she laughed and said: "Thank you."

He did not seem entirely satisfied. "I don't want to embarrass you, my dear. You must realize that what I say is said quite sincerely. It is not meant to be flattery. If it seems comic, that is merely my English vocabulary."

"But it's not comic at all," she protested. "It's very charming, really. And you speak English beautifully."

His conversation consisted of very little else besides these elaborate compliments, but she found them inoffensive, a little touching, and on the whole enjoyable. As they talked, her sympathy for him increased, and she found herself wishing she could confide in him—not about anything in particular or anything serious, she thought—just about whatever came into her head at the moment. He was friendly, detached, sincere, and, she was sure, very wise. As a little fishing-boat rounded the point, bobbing up and down in the rough water, she suddenly said: "Monsieur Royer, tell me your honest opinion. Do you think it's despicable for a man to kiss a girl against her will?" She was shocked to hear the words coming out; she had not known they would be exactly those words, but apparently she needed to say them, and there was no one else to say them to.

A cloud seemed to spread across Monsieur Royer's sunburned face. Slowly he said: "Ah. I see that people have been talking to you about me."

"No! No!" she cried, startled and then horrified.

"Naturally they have," he said calmly. "We have never even been presented one to the other. Do you realize that? Yes. Of course they have. Why not? They are quite right." He paused. "Luncheon will be ready soon, and I must first prepare. But I want to answer your question. Yes. I think such a thing is despicable. You used the words: 'against her will.' But there are a great many girls who have no will, like the natives here, or even the Spanish girls of the lower class. It is all the same to them, as long as they receive a gift. They have no wish one way or the other. And if they have no will, one can scarcely go against it, can one?"

She was silent. "I wasn't talking about you," she finally said.

He looked at her very seriously; he seemed not to have heard her. "Do you see what I mean to say?"

"I'm not sure," she said, letting the sand run between her fingers. "But I really didn't mean——"

He had risen.

"Good morning, madame."

She looked around: her mother stood there. She greeted Monsieur Royer crisply. Then she looked down.

"Charlotte, it's lunchtime. Come up and dress." There was

an edge of fury in her voice that recalled long-forgotten days of childhood misbehavior and recrimination.

The upward climb was steep. Charlotte went first, with her mother panting behind her. "Charlotte, I'm extremely angry with you. You're not a child any more, you know—" Between each sentence she ceased speaking and took a breath. "Your father and I as much as told you to have nothing to do with Monsieur Royer. How explicit must one be? I was going to tell you all about him this morning. But of course you disappeared. I don't know why— I couldn't be more annoyed with you. You're thoroughly throughtless and egotistical—"

Charlotte listened with apathy to the diatribe, walking quickly so that her mother, in attempting to keep up with her, would have the maximum of difficulty in delivering it. At one point she had been about to protest that Monsieur Royer had only happened by a short while ago, and that she had been sitting with him only a few minutes, but she felt that this would seem to put her in the wrong; it would sound like an excuse, and she was determined to admit to no fault. Since she did not answer at all, her mother's voice softened tentatively as she continued: "Don't you think it's time you changed, and thought of others?"

"I expect so," she said vaguely, adding in a louder voice, "But I can't see what you have against poor Monsieur Royer to say such horrid things about him."

Mrs. Callender snorted impatiently.

"Oh, good heavens, Charlotte! I know all about the man. Please believe me, he has a most unsavory reputation. If only for that, he's no one for you to see. But I happen to know as well that his reputation is completely justified. He's a confirmed roué and a scoundrel. In any case, I don't intend to argue the point with you. It's an established fact. But what I do intend to have is your promise—your promise that you won't speak to him again unless either your father or I, one of us is present."

They were at the top of the cliff. Mrs. Callender would have liked to stop a moment and catch her breath, but Charlotte hurried on. The path was less steep here, and her mother quickly caught up with her, breathing heavily. She sounded angrier now.

"I refuse to stand by and watch an old libertine like that try to ruin your life—I won't *have* you seeing him. Do you understand me?"

Charlotte spoke without looking around. "Yes, of course I understand. But I don't agree."

"It's of no interest to me whether you agree or not!" cried Mrs. Callender shrilly. "I expect you think it's brilliant and becoming to show spirit—"

They had reached the vegetable garden. One of the nurses from Gibraltar was sitting on the porch of her cottage sunning herself. Mrs. Callender lowered her voice and became cajoling. "Darling, please don't ruin my pleasure in your stay by being stubborn and belligerent about this."

"Do you want me to be rude to him?"

"It's not necessary. But if you disobey me I shall be the one to be rude. I shall simply ask him to leave. And I've never done that to anyone."

"Then the only thing for me to do is to tell him in front of you that you've forbidden me to speak to him."

They stood in the garden between their respective cottages.

"If that's the pleasantest way you can devise, do so by all means," said her mother acidly. "I'm sure I don't mind." She went into her room and shut the door. Charlotte stood a moment looking after her.

In her mirror she examined her lip; the salt water had brought the swelling down. She dressed quickly and went up to the dining-room, noting to her immense relief that Mr. Van Siclen was not there. During lunch she glanced out of the window and saw Monsieur Royer being served on the terrace in the sun; she wondered if he were eating outside because he liked it, or out of consideration for her. While her parents were still finishing their dessert she excused herself and went out. She paused an instant on the steps, and then walked casually toward the table where Monsieur Royer sat sipping his coffee. He rose and seized a chair from the next table for her. Knowing she was being watched through the window, she sat down with him. Hassan brought her a cup of coffee and they talked brightly for a quarter of an hour or so. She fully expected her mother to appear and precipitate a scene, but nothing happened. When she got up and went down to her cottage she thought, "Now she'll come," but she lay awake a long time listening for her mother's footsteps, and they did not arrive. At last she sank into a heavy slumber.

7

In the rose garden behind the bar Mr. and Mrs. Callender walked back and forth, conversing in low tones.

"You saw it!" exclaimed Mrs. Callender in an intense whisper. "Pure infatuation, nothing else. It's not like Charlotte to behave this way. She'd never defy me like this. I admit it was only a provocation, the whole little act, yes. But she's never been this way before. The man has bewitched her, it's perfectly clear. We must do something. Immediately."

Back and forth along the short, bordered path they walked. "We've got to send him away," she said.

"Impossible," said Mr. Callender.

"Then I shall take Charlotte and go to a hotel until he leaves," she declared.

Mr. Callender grunted.

"All she needs," he said at length, "is to meet some boys her own age. The ones she used to know here are mostly gone. Too bad the dance at the Club isn't tonight or tomorrow night. She'd forget about Royer in short order."

Mrs. Callender sighed. "If he could only be put on ice until the dance," she mused. Then she straightened and tried once more. "Oh, Bob, we *must* get rid of him."

Her husband stood still. "The time to get rid of Monsieur Royer was before he came. You had your chance. I asked you if you wanted me to wire him there was no room, and you said no. It's one thing to tell someone the place is full up. And another to send a man away for no reason at all. You can't do it."

"No reason at all, indeed!" she snorted.

Now she sat in her room on the edge of the bed and fidgeted. The long windswept afternoon depressed her. There was too intimate and mysterious a connection between what she felt, and the aspect of the countryside, now brilliant under the ardent sun, now somber in shadow as the endless procession of separate clouds raced past. It was easy to say, "This is a sad day," and attribute it to the unfortunate coincidence which had brought Charlotte and Monsieur Royer here at the same time. But that did not really explain anything. The aching nostalgia for her own youth remained—the bright Andalusian days when each hour was filled to bursting with the promise of magic, when her life lay ahead of her, inexhaustible, as yet untouched. It was true that she had not always been happy then, but there had been the imminent possibility of it, at every moment. And the people around her had not had the strange faculty they now had of becoming suddenly sinister. Even her husband, when she looked at him quickly, sometimes seemed to be coming hurriedly back from somewhere not in the light. It disconcerted her, and if she ever had dwelt on it for very long at a time, it would have terrified her.

A *rhaïta* was being played fairly far away on the mountain, announcing a wedding. It would probably go on for several days and nights. She put her hands over her ears. As if that could help! Whenever she took them away, the slippery little sound would be there, twisting thinly around itself like a treesnake. She pressed her palms more tightly against her head, until the vacuum hurt her eardrums. But the images had been awakened: the donkeys laden with blankets and painted wooden chests, the procession of lanterns, the native women in white with their drums. . . . She jumped up, looked at her watch, stepped to the mirror and powdered her face. Then she went down to Mr. Van Siclen's cottage. He had had lunch in town with the American Vice-Consul, saying that he would be back early as he was returning to El Menar before dark. She knocked; there was no answer. She went up to the bar where he often sat thumping out old tunes with one finger on the piano. He was talking with the barman.

"Mr. Van Siclen, I must speak with you."

"Sure." He followed her outside.

"I know all this won't interest you in the least, but it's the only favor I shall ever ask of you. Monsieur Royer has his eye on Charlotte. No, don't laugh. It's most serious. I'm counting on you. You *must* help me."

"Well, well!" he said. And after a bit: "O.K. What do you want me to do?"

"I thought if you could invite him out to El Menar . . . Just for a few days . . ." she hastily added as he frowned. ". . . Just for two or three days. At least until I've had the opportunity of talking with her. You see, for some mad reason *she* seems quite taken with *him* as well. There's no explaining these things. But one must act. I shall be eternally grateful to you."

"Well," he said slowly, smoothing his hair, "I'm willing to extend the invitation, but how do I know he'll accept?"

"I think you can make it attractive to him if you really try," she said, smiling significantly. "Playing up the native life a bit . . . You know him, after all. You know what amuses him."

"Damn it!" he cried, suddenly annoyed. "I don't want him out there trailing me around all day while I work."

And seeing her face, he added resignedly: "But I'll ask him, I'll ask him."

"You *are* a darling," she said.

It was done. For some reason she felt no doubt that Monsieur Royer would accept. Fittingly, the sun was shining as she went through the garden to her cottage. It was almost an anticlimax when at tea-time Monsieur Royer came to announce his departure.

"We shall miss you," she smiled. "I expect you'll want to keep your cottage." And when he said that he did, she generously suggested: "We'll put you on demi-pension for those days. That way you'll only be paying a little more than the price of the room."

"No, no," he protested politely, but she saw that he was pleased.

A little while later she watched her two guests drive off in the open jeep into the twilight.

At dinner Mr. Callender looked around the room. "Where's everybody?" he said.

"Oh, Mr. Van Siclen's gone back to El Menar and taken Monsieur Royer along with him."

"*What?*" He was incredulous.

Charlotte said nothing. Several times during the meal Mrs. Callender glanced across at her, but if she was feeling any emotion she did not betray it.

"She's rather a little sneak," said Mrs. Callender to herself, disappointed; she had expected a little more reaction than this.

Charlotte was thinking: "He's gone, thank Heavens." But she meant Mr. Van Siclen. She went to bed immediately after dinner, slept soundly, and awoke early with a desire to see Gloria Gallegos, a friend from her *lycée* days. She breakfasted, dressed, and in the fresh of the morning set out on foot for town. It was not a great walk; she could make it in an hour. The moving air was a tonic. The sun had not yet begun to weight it down with its heat, nor the flowers with their noonday scent, nor the insects with their droning. When she arrived in the market she was startled to see Mr. Van Siclen's jeep parked by the Ciné Régis. She kept her face averted as she passed, lest he should be in it. But she came face to face with him at the corner.

"Hi there!" he said, grasping her arm, quite, she thought, as if nothing had ever occurred between them.

She was not effusive in her greeting. The crowd of Berbers passing pushed them this way and that.

"Where are you off to so early?" he demanded.

"Just up to the Boulevard," she said coldly.

"It's quite a walk. Let me take you up."

"I enjoy walking."

"Come on, be a good sport. Don't go on having hard feelings. You'll get old before your time."

He did not let go of her arm; the easiest way out was to accept. She let him lead her back to the jeep and help her in. As they went around the north end of the market they met the pension's station wagon which had just deposited Mr. Richmond at the bank. She waved to Pedro, who waved back.

"Am I forgiven?" asked Mr. Van Siclen.

"Only if you don't go on talking about it," she replied.

"That's the spirit," he said approvingly. "I had to come in for kerosene. There wasn't even enough for the lamps last night. Poor old Royer had to go to bed by moonlight, I guess. I didn't hear him come in."

He let her out at the Boulevard. At lunchtime she tried to telephone her mother to tell her that she was eating at the Gallegoses', but the line was having one of its frequent bad days, and she was unable to reach the pension.

"Bob, I *am* worried about Charlotte." Mrs. Callender was saying at lunch. (If the telephone had not been out of order it would have rung at that instant.) "She was already gone at eight when I went in to see her. It's not like her to go out so early. Where can she be?"

"Don't get so wrought up," said Mr. Callender gently. "Quit thinking she's a kid. She's in town somewhere and she can't get through on the phone, that's all."

Mrs. Callender pouted. "She's been intolerable since the moment she arrived. Inconsiderate and perverse. I've done nothing all morning but worry about her."

"I know."

"And I've a fearful migraine as a result. It's that *beastly* Monsieur Royer," she added with vehemence.

At the next table Mr. Burton laid aside his book and feebly inquired: "I expect your daughter is pleased to be back home?"

Mrs. Callender turned to face him. "Oh, yes! She adores it here. Of course it's ideal for young people."

"Oh, quite! Yes, indeed."

After lunch she took more aspirin. Now she felt a slight nausea as well. She lay on her bed, the curtains drawn, reflecting with a dim satisfaction that at least Charlotte would know she had made her mother ill. The wind still blew, the trees still swayed and roared, and through their sound from time to time crept the shrill, tiny notes of the distant *rhaïta*. She dozed, woke, dozed. At tea-time Halima knocked to ask if she wanted tea in her room. She inquired if Señorita Charlotte had returned. Halima had not seen her.

Although she wanted Charlotte to find her ill in bed when she returned, she disliked having tea in her cottage alone and, deciding to run the risk of rising, went up to the salon in the main house for her tea. Only the nurses were there, but she sat down anyway. Soon she heard Pedro's voice in the hall and excused herself.

"*Oiga*, Pedro," she called, running out. "You haven't seen Señorita Charlotte this afternoon, have you?"

"*Esta tarde? Nó, señora*. Not since this morning in the market, riding with Señor Van Siclen in his car."

"*Cómo!*" she cried; the word was like an explosion. Her

eyes had become very large. Pedro looked at her and thought that perhaps Señora Callender was about to faint.

"Get the *camioneta*," she said weakly. "*Vamos a El Menar.*"

"Now?" he asked, surprised.

"Immediately."

8

She sat in front with Pedro, her head pounding so hard that it was merely an enormous and imprecise pain she carried with her. The familiar landmarks as they passed made no sense. She could not have identified one. Nor did she know which of the three enraged her most: Charlotte, for her effrontery and disobedience, Mr. Van Siclen for his perfidy, or Monseiur Royer, for existing at all.

As long as she was sitting in the moving car her anger remained at fever pitch. But when Pedro stopped in the wilderness, pointing to a road strewn with large stones, and remarking that they would have to walk up to get to the village, her annoyance at this unexpected obstacle somewhat calmed her. It was quite dark by this time, and the faint light from Pedro's torch wavered uncertainly. Out here the wind came directly off the Atlantic; it was violent and damp.

The road led upward, zigzagging among huge boulders. Each minute the sound of the sea became more audible. She had never been here before; the idea of this absurd village perched on the crags above the ocean filled her with terror. They met a Berber on his way down, and by the flashlight's feeble glimmer she saw him, stocky and dark-skinned, and carrying a shepherd's crook. "*Msalkheir*," he said as he passed. He was in the darkness back of them before they could ask him how far the village was. Suddenly they came to a hut. There was a flickering light inside, and the sound of many goats and sheep. A little farther on Pedro spied the jeep. She caught herself thinking, "How does he ever drive up that trail?" and quickly remembered the seriousness of her errand.

"*Pregúnteles*," she whispered to Pedro, indicating a group of dark figures at the right. The barnyard odors were overwhelming. As Pedro left her side to approach the men, she glanced up and saw the sky, uniformly black. Not a star showed through the huge curtain of cloud. Yet, far out over the invisible sea she thought she saw one shining, but it could have been a boat. She had neglected to bring a wrap, and she was shivering.

The house was up ahead, at the top of the village. She could see the lamp through the open door, the brightest light in the landscape. Several dogs went slinking away into the dark as they approached the house. Pedro called out, "*Señor!*" and Mr. Van Siclen appeared.

"Good God!" he cried when he saw them standing in the doorway. "What are you doing here?"

She pushed past him into the tiny room. There was a chair, a table littered with papers, and a mattress on the floor in the corner. And there were large native baskets everywhere, full of pieces of stone. The light hurt her eyes.

"Where's my daughter?" she said, going to the door of the adjoining room and peering in.

"What?"

She looked at him; for the first time since she had known him he seemed really perturbed—even frightened.

"Charlotte. Where is she?"

The expression on his face did not change. Her question seemed not to have reached it. "I have no idea. I let her off early this morning on the Boulevard by the French Consulate."

Mrs. Callender hesitated, not completely sure he was telling the truth. He took the initiative. "It'd be more to the point to ask where Monsieur Royer is. You haven't seen *him* by any chance? I don't mind telling you I'm worried."

"Monsieur Royer? Certainly not! Isn't he here with you?"

He shrugged his shoulders helplessly. "I'm afraid not. I don't know what's up. But it doesn't look good to me."

She sat down sideways on the straight-backed chair. For a second she heard the sea much closer that it should have been.

"He went out last night right after supper. There were some drums beating."

She had her hand to her head. And as so often happens in moments of great fatigue, she felt that the scene was one whose outcome she knew by heart, that although she was in it, it would go on and play itself through to the end without her participation. Mr. Van Siclen would reach into his hip-pocket, pull out a packet of cigarettes, extract one, light it, and hold the match a moment before blowing it out, just as he did do each of these things a fraction of a second after she had known he would. And he would go on speaking.

"—but I don't quite know what the hell to do. The worst thing about it is that the natives all claim not to have seen him, ever. They don't know there is such a person. I know damned well they're lying. It's too unanimous. I don't think he ever came back at all. The blankets on his mattress in there"—he indicated the next room—"haven't been touched. I didn't notice that until I got back from town this morning. I thought he was asleep."

She said nothing because she felt she was getting much too far ahead of him now. At the moment this bare room with the wind outside was the less strong of two realities. The other was a spoken sentence, a dreadful image, but she could recall neither the sentence nor the image it had evoked—only the brief horror she had felt at the time.

She was standing up, walking toward the door.

"I feel a bit ill." To say the words demanded a monstrous effort.

Outside, the sea-wind battered her face. She breathed deeply several times. Mr. Van Siclen's voice came from the door, so-licitous. "Are you all right?"

"Yes," she said.

"Be careful out there. There's barbed wire strung along the edge where you are."

Now it was complete. Everything had been said. All she had to do was go on breathing deeply, facing the sea. Of course. A coil of wire around his neck. Behind a rock. A minute or two later she went back in.

"Better?"

"If I could have a drink," she said wanly. (She could not say to him: "It's not my fault. You yourself put the idea into my head," because to admit that much would establish her guilt firmly, for all time.)

"Whisky, you mean? Or water?"

"I think whisky."

As she drank it he said: "We'll have a searching party out looking for him the first thing in the morning. That is, if he doesn't turn up tonight. I'll drive you back now so you won't have to walk down the hill. And I think it might be a good idea to call the *comisaría* tonight, anyway."

She smiled ruefully. "The police won't be of much use, will they?"

"Never know," he said, slipping into his jacket. "He may be lying only a half mile from here with a broken leg."

Again she smiled: she was so sure it was not that. And so was he, she thought, but now that she was upset too he could afford to pretend.

"Well, shall we get going?" he asked her.

The wind blew, the great black cloud from the sea had covered everything. He put his arm about her waist as they stumbled downward. She thought of nothing, let herself bump against him as they avoided rocks.

They were in the jeep. At the foot of the hill Pedro got out. "Do you want to go in your own car?" said Mr. Van Siclen. "It'd be more comfortable, I guess."

"No. This air is just what I need."

Swiftly they left El Menar behind in the darkness.

From the spot where he lay, he could have heard the two motors grow fainter and be drowned by the vaster sound of the sea; he could have seen the two little red tail-lights moving away across the empty countryside. Could have, if all that had not been decided for him twenty-one hours earlier. In the bright moonlight he had sat with the child on his knee (for she was really no more than a child) letting her examine his watch. For some reason—probably the sight of this innocent animal holding the thin gold toy in her tattooed hands—he was put in mind of the phrase he had not been able to recall the evening of his arrival. He began to murmur it to himself, even at the moment her expression changed to one of terror as, looking up over his shoulder, she saw what was about to happen.

"*Le temps qui coule ici n'a plus d'heures, mais, tant l'inoccupation de chacun est parfaite——*"

This time he might have completed it.

The Hyena

A STORK was passing over desert country on his way north.
He was thirsty, and he began to look for water. When he
came to the mountains of Khang el Ghar, he saw a pool at the
bottom of a ravine. He flew down between the rocks and
lighted at the edge of the water. Then he walked in and drank.

At that moment a hyena limped up and, seeing the stork
standing in the water, said: "Have you come a long way?"
The stork had never seen a hyena before. "So this is what a
hyena is like," he thought. And he stood looking at the hyena
because he had been told that if the hyena can put a little of
his urine on someone, that one will have to walk after the
hyena to whatever place the hyena wants him to go.

"It will be summer soon," said the stork. "I am on my way
north." At the same time, he walked further out into the
pool, so as not to be so near the hyena. The water here was
deeper, and he almost lost his balance and had to flap his
wings to keep upright. The hyena walked to the other side of
the pool and looked at him from there.

"I know what is in your head," said the hyena. "You believe
the story about me. You think I have that power? Perhaps
long ago hyenas were like that. But now they are the same as
everyone else. I could wet you from here with my urine if I
wanted to. But what for? If you want to be unfriendly, go to
the middle of the pool and stay there."

The stork looked around at the pool and saw that there was
no spot in it where he could stand and be out of reach of the
hyena.

"I have finished drinking," said the stork. He spread his
wings and flapped out of the pool. At the edge he ran quickly
ahead and rose into the air. He circled above the pool, looking down at the hyena.

"So you are the one they call the ogre," he said. "The
world is full of strange things."

The hyena looked up. His eyes were narrow and crooked.
"Allah brought us all here," he said. "You know that. You are
the one who knows about Allah."

The stork flew a little lower. "That is true," he said. "But I am surprised to hear you say it. You have a very bad name, as you yourself just said. Magic is against the will of Allah."

The hyena tilted his head. "So you still believe the lies!" he cried.

"I have not seen the inside of your bladder," said the stork. "But why does everyone say you can make magic with it?"

"Why did Allah give you a head, I wonder? You have not learned how to use it." But the hyena spoke in so low a voice that the stork could not hear him.

"Your words got lost," said the stork, and he let himself drop lower.

The hyena looked up again. "I said: 'Don't come too near me. I might lift my leg and cover you with magic!'" He laughed, and the stork was near enough to see that his teeth were brown.

"Still, there must be some reason," the stork began. Then he looked for a rock high above the hyena, and settled himself on it. The hyena sat and stared up at him. "Why does everyone hate you?" the stork went on. "Why do they call you an ogre? What have you done?"

The hyena squinted. "You are very lucky," he told the stork. "Men never try to kill you, because they think you are holy. They call you a saint and a sage. And yet you seem like neither a saint nor a sage."

"What do you mean?" said the stork quickly.

"If you really understood, you would know that magic is a grain of dust in the wind, and that Allah has power over everything. You would not be afraid."

The stork stood for a long time, thinking. He lifted one leg and held it bent in front of him. The ravine grew red as the sun went lower. And the hyena sat quietly looking up at the stork, waiting for him to speak.

Finally the stork put his leg down, opened his bill, and said: "You mean that if there is no magic, the one who sins is the one who believes there is."

The hyena laughed. "I said nothing about sin. But you did, and you are the sage. I am not in the world to tell anyone what is right or wrong. Living from night to night is enough. Everyone hopes to see me dead."

The stork lifted his leg again and stood thinking. The last daylight rose into the sky and was gone. The cliffs at the sides of the ravine were lost in the darkness.

At length the stork said: "You have given me something to think about. That is good. But now night has come. I must go on my way." He raised his wings and started to fly straight out from the boulder where he had stood. The hyena listened. He heard the stork's wings beating the air slowly, and then he heard the sound of the stork's body as it hit the cliff on the other side of the ravine. He climbed up over the rocks and found the stork. "Your wing is broken," he said. "It would have been better for you to go while there was still daylight."

"Yes," said the stork. He was unhappy and afraid.

"Come home with me," the hyena told him. "Can you walk?"

"Yes," said the stork. Together they made their way down the valley. Soon they came to a cave in the side of the mountain. The hyena went in first and called out: "Bend your head." When they were well inside, he said: "Now you can put your head up. The cave is high here."

There was only darkness inside. The stork stood still. "Where are you?" he said.

"I am here," the hyena answered, and he laughed.

"Why are you laughing?" asked the stork.

"I was thinking that the world is strange," the hyena told him. "The saint has come into my cave because he believed in magic."

"I don't understand," said the stork.

"You are confused. But at least now you can believe that I have no magic. I am like anyone else in the world."

The stork did not answer right away. He smelled the stench of the hyena very near him. Then he said, with a sigh: "You are right, of course. There is no power beyond the power of Allah."

"I am happy," said the hyena, breathing into his face. "At last you understand." Quickly he seized the stork's neck and tore it open. The stork flapped and fell on his side.

"Allah gave me something better than magic," the hyena said under his breath. "He gave me a brain."

The stork lay still. He tried to say once more: "There is no power beyond the power of Allah." But his bill merely opened very wide in the dark.

The hyena turned away. "You will be dead in a minute," he said over his shoulder. "In ten days I shall come back. By then you will be ready."

Ten days later the hyena went to the cave and found the stork where he had left him. The ants had not been there. "Good," he said. He devoured what he wanted and went outside to a large flat rock above the entrance to the cave. There in the moonlight he stood a while, vomiting.

He ate some of his vomit and rolled for a long time in the rest of it, rubbing it deep into his coat. Then he thanked Allah for eyes that could see the valley in the moonlight, and for a nose that could smell the carrion on the wind. He rolled some more and licked the rock under him. For a while he lay there panting. Soon he got up and limped on his way.

The Garden

A MAN who lived in a distant town of the southern country was working in his garden. Because he was poor his land was at the edge of the oasis. All the afternoon he dug channels, and when the day was finished he went to the upper end of the garden and opened the gate that held back the water. And now the water ran in the channels to the beds of barley and the young pomegranate trees. The sky was red, and when the man saw the floor of his garden shining like jewels, he sat down on a stone to look at it. As he watched, it grew brighter, and he thought: "There is no finer garden in the oasis."

A great happiness filled him, and he sat there a long time, and did not get home until very late. When he went into the house, his wife looked at him and saw the joy still in his eyes.

"He has found a treasure," she thought; but she said nothing.

When they sat face to face at the evening meal, the man was still remembering his garden, and it seemed to him that now that he had known this happiness, never again would he be without it. He was silent as he ate.

His wife too was silent. "He is thinking of the treasure," she said to herself. And she was angry, believing that he did not want to share his secret with her. The next morning she went to the house of an old woman and bought many herbs and powders from her. She took them home and passed several days mixing and cooking them, until she had made the medicine she wanted. Then at each meal she began to put a little of the *tseuheur* into her husband's food.

It was not long before the man fell ill. For a time he went each day to his garden to work, but often when he got there he was so weak that he could merely sit leaning against a palm tree. He had a sharp sound in his ears, and he could not follow his thoughts as they came to him. In spite of this, each day when the sun went down and he saw his garden shining red in its light, he was happy. And when he got home at night his wife could see that there was joy in his eyes.

"He has been counting the treasure," she thought, and

she began to go secretly to the garden to watch him from behind the trees. When she saw that he merely sat looking at the ground, she went back to the old woman and told her about it.

"You must hurry and make him talk, before he forgets where he has hidden the treasure," said the old woman.

That night the wife put a great amount of *tseuheur* into his food, and when they were drinking tea afterward she began to say many sweet words to him. The man only smiled. She tried for a long time to make him speak, but he merely shrugged his shoulders and made motions with his hands.

The next morning while he was still asleep, she went back to the old woman and told her that the man could no longer speak.

"You have given him too much," the old woman said. "He will never tell you his secret now. The only thing for you to do is go away quickly, before he dies."

The woman ran home. Her husband lay on the mat with his mouth open. She packed her clothing and left the town that morning.

For three days the man lay in a deep sleep. The fourth day when he awoke, it was as if he had made a voyage to the other side of the world. He was very hungry, but all he could find in the house was a piece of dry bread. When he had eaten that, he walked to his garden at the edge of the oasis and picked many figs. Then he sat down and ate them. In his mind there was no thought of his wife, because he had forgotten her. When a neighbor came by and called to him, he answered politely, as if speaking to a stranger, and the neighbor went away perplexed.

Little by little the man grew healthy once more. He worked each day in the garden. When dusk came, after watching the sunset and the red water, he would go home and cook his dinner and sleep. He had no friends, because although men spoke to him, he did not know who they were, and he only smiled and nodded to them. Then the people in the town began to notice that he no longer went to the mosque to pray. They spoke about this among themselves, and one evening the imam went to the man's house to talk with him.

As they sat there, the imam listened for sounds of the man's wife in the house. Out of courtesy he could not mention her, but he was thinking about her and asking himself where she might be. He went away from the house full of doubts.

The man went on living his life. But the people of the town now talked of little else. They whispered that he had killed his wife, and many of them wanted to go together and search the house for her remains. The imam spoke against this idea, saying that he would go and talk again with the man. And this time he went all the way to the garden at the edge of the oasis, and found him there working happily with the plants and the trees. He watched him for a while, and then he walked closer and spoke a few words with him.

It was late in the afternoon. The sun was sinking in the west, and the water on the ground began to be red. Presently the man said to the imam: "The garden is beautiful."

"Beautiful or not beautiful," said the imam, "you should be giving thanks to Allah for allowing you to have it."

"Allah?" said the man. "Who is that? I never heard of him. I made this garden myself. I dug every channel and planted every tree, and no one helped me. I have no debts to anyone."

The imam had turned pale. He flung out his arm and struck the man very hard in the face. Then he went quickly out of the garden.

The man stood with his hand to his cheek. "He has gone mad," he thought, as the imam walked away.

That night the people spoke together in the mosque. They decided that the man could no longer live in their town. Early the next morning a great crowd of men, with the imam going at the head of it, went out into the oasis, on its way to the man's garden.

The small boys ran ahead of the men, and got there long before them. They hid in the bushes, and as the man worked they began to throw stones and shout insults at him. He paid no attention to them. Then a stone hit the back of his head. He jumped up quickly. As they ran away, one of them fell, and the man caught him. He tried to hold him still so he could ask him: "Why were you throwing stones at me?" But the boy only screamed and struggled.

And the townspeople, who were on their way, heard the

screaming, and they came running to the garden. They pulled the boy away from him and began to strike at the man with hoes and sickles. When they had destroyed him, they left him there with his head lying in one of the channels, and went back to the town, giving thanks to Allah that the boy was safe.

Little by little the sand covered everything. The trees died, and very soon the garden was gone. Only the desert was there.

Doña Faustina

No one could understand why Doña Faustina had bought the inn. It stood on one of the hairpin curves in the old highway leading up from the river valley to the town, but the route had been made useless by the building of the new paved road. Now it was impossible to reach the inn except by climbing up a stony path over the embankment and walking several hundred feet down the old road which, no longer kept in repair, already was being washed away by the rains and strangled by the shiny vegetation of that lowland region.

On Sundays the people used to walk out from the town, the women carrying parasols and the men guitars (for this was before the days of the radio, when almost everyone knew how to make a little music); they would get as far as the great breadfruit tree and look up the road at the faded façade of the building, more than half hidden by young bamboo and banana plants, stare a few seconds, and turn around to go back. "Why does she leave the sign up?" they would say. "Does she think anyone would ever spend the night there now?" And they were quite right: no one went near the inn any more. Only the people of the town knew that it existed, and they had no need of it.

There remained the mystery of why she had bought it. As usual when there is something townspeople cannot understand, they invented a whole series of unpleasant explanations for Doña Faustina's behavior. The earliest and most common one, which was that she had decided to transform the place into a house of ill-repute, soon fell to pieces, for there was absolutely nothing to substantiate such a theory. No one had been seen to go near the inn for weeks, except Doña Faustina's younger sister Carlota who arrived from Jalapa, and the old servants José and Elena, who went to market each morning and minded their business strictly enough to satisfy even the most vicious gossips. As for Carlota, she appeared occasionally at Mass, dressed in black. It was said that she had taken their father's death very much to heart, and would probably not remove the mourning, ever.

The other suppositions evolved by the people of the town in their effort to bring light to the mystery proved as unlikely as the first. It was rumored that Doña Faustina was giving asylum to Chato Morales, a bandit whom the police of the region had been trying for months to capture, but he was caught soon afterward in a distant part of the province. Then it was said that the inn was a depository for a drug ring; this also proved to be false. The leaders of the ring, having been arrested, divulged their secrets, and the cache proved to be in a room above the Farmácia Ideal. There were darker hints to the effect that Carlota might be luring lone voyagers to the inn, where they met the fate that traditionally befalls such solitary visitors to lonely inns. But people did not take such suggestions seriously. The opinion grew that Doña Faustina had merely gone a little mad, and that her madness, having taken an antisocial turn, had induced her to retire to the out-skirts of town where she could live without ever seeing any-one. To be sure, this theory was contested by certain younger members of the community who claimed that she was no more crazy than they, that on the contrary she was extremely crafty. They said that having a great deal of money she had bought the inn because of the ample lands which surrounded it, and that there in the privacy of the plant-smothered gar-dens and orchards she had devised all kinds of clever ways of hiding her riches. The older citizens of the town took no stock in this, however, since they clearly remembered both her husband and her father, neither of whom had evinced any unusual prowess in collecting money. And she had bought the inn for practically nothing. "Where would she have got the pesos?" they said sceptically. "Out of the trees, perhaps?"

2

Once when a child disappeared from the town (small children were often stolen in those days and taken off to distant places where they were made to work), the parents insisted that the police search the inn. Doña Faustina, who was a large woman in the prime of life, met the little policeman at the door and refused to let him in. Indeed, she was so brusque with him and glared at him with such malignity that he felt obliged to go back to the *comisaría* and get reinforcements. When he and the three extra men returned to the inn, they made a complete but unrewarding search of the place, followed at every step by Doña Faustina, who did not cease to shower them with insults until they had left the premises. But they returned to town with a story. The rooms were a shambles, they said, the furniture was broken, there was rubbish and garbage everywhere in the corridors, the railing of the second-story balcony had given way and been replaced by a single strand of barbed wire, and the place looked generally as though innumerable picnic parties had been held there over a period of years. This report helped to fortify people in their belief that Doña Faustina had more or less lost her mind, and for a time the town ceased thinking about her.

Some time afterward it was noted that she and her sister had taken to making trips to neighboring towns; they had been seen in such widely separated places as Tlacotalpam and Zempoala. But even these peregrinations failed to elicit true interest. Heads were shaken, sympathetically or otherwise, and it was remarked that Doña Faustina was growing less and less sane, but that was all.

When the mistresses of the house were absent they did not return for three or four days, and José and Elena remained alone to guard the property, not even venturing forth to the town for marketing until the two reappeared. On their return the sisters would take an old covered carriage that went each day to the station to await the train. They would pile their numerous bundles and baskets in and drive as far as the curve, where they would get down, the driver helping them up the embankment with their effects and then leaving them to get to the house in whatever way they could. Carlota would go and bring up José to help carry the things, but Doña Faustina always insisted on carrying the heaviest baskets herself. A few trips would be made back and forth through the undergrowth, and then the abandoned road would be quiet again until the old servants went to market the next morning.

In another fortnight or so they would set out once more, always to a new place; necessarily this led them farther and farther afield. Someone even claimed to have seen them once in Vera Cruz, although, given the number of false stories which were circulated about the two women, there was no particular reason to believe this.

Before the house had been made into an inn it had been a prosperous *finca*, with terraced lands planted with fruit trees, leading downward rather steeply for a mile or so to a high bluff above the river. For fifty years or more the land had been totally neglected, so that now it was hard to find the avocado and mango trees in the tangle of new, eager parasites which had sprung up on every side and often reached above even the tallest of the older trees. Lianas looped down from the branches, climbing plants stretched up to clutch at them, and a person could not stray more than fifty feet down one of the orchard paths from the house without coming face to face with an impenetrable curtain of leaves. And now no one really knew how far it was from the house to the river, because the borders of the property gave on even thicker jungle.

3

Not even José would have known the tank existed, if he had not strayed a bit farther down than usual one afternoon, to see if he could find some *zapotes*. In the deep silence of the undergrowth there, far beneath the regions where the sun could reach, he had heard a heavy splash not far distant, as though a boulder had been flung into deep water. He had listened intently, but there had been no other sound. The next afternoon during siesta time he went back to the same spot carrying a machete, and laboriously hacked his way through the stubborn vegetation. It was nearly twilight when he caught sight of the water ahead. Finally he stood near the edge of the tank. The stagnant water gave off a heavy odor, and insects hovered in swarms in the still air above it. And as he watched, it seemed to him that there was a faint movement down in the brown depths; for some reason the water was not completely motionless. For a while he stood there staring downward, lost in contemplation; then, as the light was fading, he turned and started back, resolving without knowing why he did so, to say nothing about the tank to Elena when he returned to the house.

Several times in the course of the following months José returned there, always with the hope of discovering what had
made the splash. Even a man diving into the tank could
scarcely have caused such a noise. There was a stone-paved
ramp at the far end (the tank doubtless had been built to
bathe cattle) and on two occasions he found the ramp partially wet, which merely added to his perplexity. The second
time he noticed this, he began to cut his way through the
vines along the edge, in order to examine the ramp closely.
And half-way along he found the path. Someone had cleared
a narrow but practicable passage to the tank from some point
back near the house. Abandoning his project, he followed the
path and came out in a corner of what had once been a rose
garden, on a lower terrace between the door to the laundry
and the ruined stables. As he stood blinking in the sunlight,
Doña Faustina appeared coming down the short flight of
steps outside the laundry door. By its handle she carried a basket with a newspaper tucked over the top. Automatically old
José walked toward her to take the basket from her. Evidently
she had not been expecting to see him, for when she looked
up and realized he was near her, her face took on an extraordinary expression. But all she said was: "What are you doing
down here? Go to the kitchen." Then she stepped to a stone
bench under an arbor near her and sat down, putting the basket on the bench beside her.

As he went on up towards the house José thought he had
never seen his *patrona* look quite so fierce. She was always severe, and often forbidding, but not to the point of being able
to frighten him as she had today. It was as if a demon had
peered out at him for a moment from beneath her heavy lids.

"It must be true," he thought. "Doña Faustina is going
mad. What will become of Elena and me?"

This time when he got to the kitchen he took Elena into a
corner and whispered to her, telling her his fears, and of how
strange the señora had looked in the garden. Elena crossed
herself. "Oh, God," she murmured. But he did not mention
the tank to her, either now or later. He did not even want to
think about it, because he suspected that in some way it was
connected with Doña Faustina's madness, and being the only

one who knew about it gave him a certain feeling of security which he would have lost had he shared the knowledge with Elena.

One cold evening of *llovizna*, as the mealy fog slowly turned to water and drenched the countryside, there was a knock at the entrance door. Doña Faustina, who spent much of her time pottering about in the basement where the baths and laundry were, heard it from there, and straightway mounted the stairs, her face dark with fury. Carlota stood in the *comedor*, undecided as to whether she should answer. The knocking was repeated as Doña Faustina reached her.

"Again the police?" said Carlota a bit fearfully.

"*Ya veremos*," muttered Doña Faustina. And she went out and stood behind the door, calling out in a loud voice: "Who?"

There was no answer.

"Don't open it," whispered Carlota, who stood behind her.

Doña Faustina made an impatient gesture to silence her sister. They waited several minutes, but the knock did not come again. There was only the irregular dripping of the water from the balcony above on to the ground.

"Stay here," said Doña Faustina, and she went through the *comedor*, down the stairs and into the laundry again. Here she gathered up all the refuse that strewed the floor and the wash-tubs, and packing it into two large baskets, continued out the side door which gave on the grape arbor. From here, descending the steps slowly, she disappeared into the darkness of the rose garden.

Within a half-hour she was back in the entrance hall where Carlota still stood listening by the door.

"Nothing," said Carlota in answer to Doña Faustina's questioning gesture. Doña Faustina's beckoned to her. They went into the *comedor* and whispered together. One candle flame cowered behind a pitcher on the newspaper-covered sideboard.

"It's not the police," said Doña Faustina. "Your room has a key. Go immediately. Lock the door and go to bed."

"But you . . . ?"

"I'm not afraid."

Left alone in the *comedor*, Doña Faustina poured herself a glass of water and drank it. Then she took the candle and

went up the long staircase to her room. She closed the door
and set the candle down. By her sagging bed, around which
Elena had draped the patched mosquito-net, stood a man.
Swiftly he stepped over to her, and putting one arm around
her neck tightly, stuffed a crumpled cloth into her mouth. She
swung her arms about wildly, and managed to hit him once in
the face, but almost immediately he had tied her wrists together. There was no further struggle. He propelled her
roughly to the bed, yanked aside the netting and pushed her
down. She looked at him: he was a tall young man, a *mestizo*
probably, and badly dressed. As he moved about the room
looking into the crates and boxes that lay in wild disorder
about the floor, he snorted with distaste. Finally he overturned a chair in anger and with a scornful gesture swept all
the empty bottles and piles of newspapers off the bureau onto
the floor. He approached the bed again and looked at Doña
Faustina in the wavering light. Then, to her surprise (although it cannot be said to her annoyance) he lay down and
had his way with her quietly, impersonally. A few minutes later
he sat up and pulled the cloth out of her mouth. She lay perfectly still and looked up at him. Finally she said: "What do
you want here? I have no money."

"Who knows if you have or not?"

"I tell you there is none."

"We'll see."

He got up. Again he spent a quarter of an hour or so
searching the room, scuffing piles of refuse under the tables,
kicking the furniture over to examine the under part, emptying drawers of their dust and litter. He lit a small cigar and returned to the bed. His oblique eyes looked almost closed in
the light of the candle.

"Where is it?" he said.

"There is none. But I have something more precious."

"What?" He looked at her with scornful disbelief. What
could be more precious than money?

"Untie my hands."

He gave her the use of one hand, holding the other arm
firmly while she fumbled in her clothing. In a moment she
drew forth a small parcel done up in newspaper, and handed
it to him. He placed it on the bed and bound her hands to-

gether. Then in a gingerly fashion he lifted the parcel and smelled of it. It was soft, and slightly wet.

"What is it?"

"Open it, *hombre*. Eat it. You know what it is."

Suspiciously he removed the outer layer of paper and held the contents close to the candle.

"What is this?" he cried.

"*Ya sabes, hombre,*" she said calmly. "*Cómelo.*"

"What is it?" he said again, trying to sound stern; but there was fear in his voice.

"Eat it, son. You don't have the chance every day."

"Where did you get it?"

"Ah!" Doña Faustina looked mysterious and wise, and gave no further answer.

"What do I want of it?" said the young man presently, looking down at the little object in his hand.

"Eat it! Eat it and have the power of two," she said cajolingly.

"*Brujerías!*" he exclaimed, still without putting the thing down.

A moment later he added, speaking slowly: "I don't like witchcraft. I don't like it."

"Bah!" Doña Faustina snorted. "Don't be stupid, son. Don't ask questions. Eat it, and go on your way with the force of two. Who will ever know? Tell me that! Who?"

This argument appeared to weigh with the young man. Suddenly he lifted the thing to his mouth and bit into it as if it had been a plum. While he ate he looked once at Doña Faustina darkly. When he had finished, he walked around the room tentatively for a moment, his head slightly on one side. Doña Faustina watched him closely.

"How do you feel?" she inquired.

"*Bien,*" he said.

"Two," she reminded him. "Now you have the power of two."

As if inspired by the fortifying suggestion, he walked to the bed, threw himself down on it and lay with her again briefly. This time she kissed his forehead. When it was over he rose, and without undoing the rope that bound her hands, without saying a word, he went out of the door and down the stairs.

A minute or so later she heard the front door close. At the same time the candle, which had burned down to its base, began to flicker wildly, and soon the room was in darkness.

5

All night Doña Faustina lay perfectly still on her bed, sleeping now and then, and during the periods of wakefulness listening to the slow dripping of the mist outside her windows. In the morning Carlota, still fearful, opened her door a crack, and apparently finding everything in the corridors in a normal state went to Doña Faustina's room.

"*Ay, Dios!*" she cried when she saw Doña Faustina lying with her clothing partially ripped away and her hands lashed together. "Oh, God! Oh, God!"

But Doña Faustina was calm. As Carlota undid the rope, she said: "He did no harm. But I had to give him the heart."

Carlota looked at her sister with horror.

"You're mad!" she cried. "The police will be here any minute."

"No, no," Doña Faustina reassured her, and she was right: no police arrived to search the house again. Nothing happened. At the end of two weeks they made another trip, and a little while later still another. Two days after they had returned from this one, Doña Faustina called Carlota into her room and said to her: "There will be a child."

Carlota sat down slowly on the bed.

"How terrible!"

Doña Faustina smiled. "No, no. It's perfect. Think. It will have the power of thirty-seven."

But Carlota did not seem convinced. "We don't know about those things," she said. "It may be a vengeance."

"No, no, no," said Doña Faustina, shaking her head. "But now we must be more careful than ever."

"No more trips?" said Carlota hopefully.

"I shall think about it."

A few days later they were both in the rose garden sitting on a bench.

"I have thought," said Doña Faustina. "And there will be no more trips."

"Good," replied Carlota.

Toward the end of the year Doña Faustina was confined to bed, awaiting the birth of the child. She lay back comfortably in the crooked old bed, and had Elena come and sweep out the room for the first time in many months. Even when the floor was clean, the room still reeked of the garbage that had lain there for so long. Carlota had bought a tiny crib in the town; the purchase had awakened interest in their activities on the part of the townspeople.

When the time arrived, Elena and Carlota were both in the room to assist at the birth. Doña Faustina did not scream once. The baby was washed and laid beside her in the bed.

"A boy," said Elena, smiling down at her.

"Of course," said Doña Faustina, beginning to nurse him.

Elena went down to the kitchen to tell José the good news. He shook his head gloomily.

"Something bad in all this," he muttered.

"In all what?" said Elena sharply.

"Who is the father?" said José, looking up.

"That is Doña Faustina's secret," Elena replied smugly, rather as if it had been her own.

"Yes. I think so too," said José meaningfully. "I think there is no father, if you want to know. I think she got the child from the Devil."

Elena was scandalized. "Shameless!" she cried. "How can you say such a thing?"

"I have reasons," said José darkly. And he would say no more.

Things went smoothly at the inn. Several months passed. The baby had been named Jesus Maria and was in perfect health—"*un torito,*" said Elena, "a real little bull."

"Of course," Doña Faustina had replied on that occasion. "He has the power of thirty-seven . . ." Exactly then Carlota had been taken with a violent fit of coughing which managed to cover the rest of the sentence. But Elena had noticed nothing.

The rainy season had finished again, and the bright days of sunlight and green leaves had come. José went in search of fruit once more, wandering down through the garden, crouching over most of the time to creep beneath the hanging walls of vines and tendrils. Again one day he cut his way to the tank, and stood on the edge of it looking toward the ramp. And this time he saw the monster just as it slid forward and disappeared beneath the surface of the water. His mouth dropped open. Only one word came out: "*Caimán!*"

He stood still for several minutes looking down at the dark water. Then he edged along the side of the tank to the place where the path had been the year before. It had completely disappeared. No one had been to the tank in many months; there was no indication that such a corridor had ever existed there in the mass of vegetation. He returned the way he had come.

It was a scandal, thought José, that such a beast should be living on Doña Faustina's property, and he determined to speak to her about it immediately. He found her in the kitchen talking with Elena. From his face she saw that something was wrong, and fearful perhaps that he was going to say just what he did say a moment later, she tried to get him out of the room.

"Come upstairs. I want you to do something for me," she said, walking over to him and pulling him by the arm.

But José's excitement was too great. He did not even notice that she was touching him. "Señora!" he cried. "There is a crocodile in the garden!"

Doña Faustina looked at him with black hatred. "What are you saying?" she said softly and with a certain concern in her voice, as if the old man needed to be treated with gentleness.

"An enormous *caimán*! I saw it!"

Elena looked at him apprehensively. "He's ill," she whispered to Doña Faustina. José heard her. "Ill!" he laughed scornfully. "Come with me and wait a little. I'll show you who's ill! Just come!"

"You say in the garden?" repeated Doña Faustina incredulously. "But where?"

"In the great tank, señora."

"Tank? What tank?"

"The señora doesn't know about the tank? There's a tank down below in the orchard. *Sí, sí, sí,*" he insisted, seeing Elena's face. "I've been there many times. It's not far. Come."

Inasmuch as Elena seemed to be on the point of removing her apron and accepting his invitation, Doña Faustina changed her tactics. "Stop this nonsense!" she shouted. "If you're ill, José, go to bed. Or are you drunk?" She stepped close to him and sniffed suspiciously. "No? *Bueno.* Elena, give him some hot coffee and let me know in an hour how he is."

But in her room Doña Faustina began to worry.

6

They got out just in time. Carlota was not sure they ought to leave. "Where shall we go?" she said plaintively.

"Don't think about that," said Doña Faustina. "Think about the police. We must go. I know. What good does it do me to have the power of thirty-seven if I pay no attention to what they tell me? They say we must leave. Today."

As they sat in the train, ready to pull out of the station, surrounded by baskets, Doña Faustina held Jesus Maria up to the window and made his tiny arm wave good-by to the town. "The capital is a better place for him in any case," she whispered.

They went to a small *fonda* in the capital, where the second day Doña Faustina conceived the idea of applying at the nearest *comisaría* for employment as police matron. Her physical build, plus the fact that, as she told the lieutenant, she was afraid of no human being, impressed those who interviewed her, and after various examinations, she was accepted into the force.

"You'll see," she said to Carlota when she returned that evening in high spirits. "From now on we have nothing to worry about. Nothing can harm us. We have new names. We are new people. Nothing matters but Jesus Maria."

At that very moment the inn was swarming with police. The news of the *caimán*, which José in his obstinacy insisted was really there, first to Elena and then to others in the market, had reached them and awakened their curiosity once again. When it was found that there was not one, but a pair of the beasts, in the hidden tank, the police began to look more closely. No one really believed even now that it was Doña Faustina and her sister who were responsible for the disappearance of the dozens of infants who had vanished during the past two or three years, but it was felt that it would do no harm to investigate.

In a dark corner of the laundry, under one of the washtubs, they found a bundle of bloodstained rags which on closer inspection proved beyond a doubt to be the garments of an infant. Then they discovered other such rags stuffed in the windows to fill the spaces left by broken panes. "They must be Jesus Maria's," said the loyal Elena. "The señora will be back in a day or so, and she will tell you." The police leered.

The *jefe* came and looked around the laundry. "She was not stupid," he said admiringly. "She did the work here, and *they*"—he pointed out toward the orchard—"took care of the rest."

Little by little all the stories from roundabout concurred to make one unified mass of evidence; there was no longer much doubt as to Doña Faustina's guilt, but finding her was another matter. For a while the papers were full of the affair. Indignant articles were spread across the pages, and always there was the demand that the readers be on the lookout for the two monstrous women. But it turned out that no picture was available of either of them.

Doña Faustina saw the newspapers, read the articles, and shrugged her shoulders. "All that happened long ago," she said. "It has no importance now. And even if it had, they could not catch me. I have too much power for them." Soon the papers spoke of other things.

Fifteen years passed quietly. Jesus Maria, who was unusually bright and strong for his age, was offered a position as servant in the home of the Chief of Police. He had seen the boy about with his mother for several years, and liked him. This was a great triumph for Doña Faustina.

"I know you will be a great man," she told Jesus Maria, "and will never bring dishonor upon us."

But eventually he did, and Doña Faustina was inconsolable.

After three years he grew bored with his menial work, and went into the army, carrying with him a recommendation from his employer to a close friend, a certain colonel who saw to it that Jesus Maria was pleasantly treated in the barracks. Everything went well for him; he was constantly promoted, so that by the time he was twenty-five he had become a colonel himself. It may be observed that to be a colonel in the Mexican army is not so great an attainment, nor is it necessarily a sign of exceptional merit. However, there is little doubt that Jesus Maria's military career would have continued its upward course, had he not happened to be in Zacatecas at the time of the raids on the villages thereabout by Fermín Figueroa and his band. As one more privilege in the endless chain of favors granted him by his superiors he was put in charge of the punitive expedition that was sent out in pursuit of Figueroa. Jesus Maria could not have been completely without ability, nonetheless, since on the third day out he succeeded in taking the leader prisoner along with thirty-six of his men.

No one ever really knew what happened in the small mountain village where the capture took place, save that Figueroa and the bandits had all been tied up in a sheep corral, ready to be shot, and when a few hours later a corporal had arrived with six soldiers to carry out the execution, the corral was empty. And it was even said, after Jesus Maria had been stripped of his rank, that a sheepherder had seen him enter the corral in the bright afternoon sunlight when everyone else was asleep, loosen the ropes that bound Figueroa, and then hand him his knife, whereupon he turned his back and walked away. Few believed the sheepherder's story: colonels do not do such things. Still, it was agreed that he had been inexcusably careless, and that it was entirely his fault that the thirty-seven bandits had escaped and thus lived to continue their depredations.

The evening Jesus Maria arrived back at his barracks in the capital, he stood alone in the latrine looking at himself in the fly-specked mirror. Slowly he began to smile, watching the movements of his facial muscles. "No," he said, and tried again. He opened his eyes wider and smiled with all his might. The man's face had looked something like that; he would never be able to get it exactly, but he would go on trying because it made him happy to recall that moment—the only time he had ever known how it feels to have power.

Tapiama

JUST behind the hotel was the river. If it had come from very far inland it would have been wide and silent, but because it was really only a creek swollen by the rains, and its bed was full of boulders, it made a roaring noise which the photographer briefly mistook for more rain. The heat and the trip had tired him out; he had eaten the cold fried fish and the leathery omelet that oozed grease, the brown bean paste with rice and burned bananas, and had been overtaken suddenly by a sleepiness powerful as the effect of a drug. Staggering to his bed, he had ripped off his shirt and trousers, lifted the stiff mosquito-net that reeked of dust, and dropped like a stone onto the mattress, only distantly noticing its hardness before he lost himself in sleep.

But in the night when he awoke he realized he had been in the false sleep of indigestion; staring into the blackness over his head he told himself that it was going to be hard to find the way back into oblivion. It was then that he had become aware of the night's changeless backdrop of sound, and had taken it for rain. Now and then, far above his head (how could the ceiling be that high?) a firefly's nervous little light flashed its indecipherable code for an instant or two. He was lying on his back; something small was crawling down his chest. He put his hand there: it was a slowly moving drop of sweat. The rough sheet under him was wet. He wanted to move, but if he did there would be no end to the shifting, and each new position would be more uncomfortable than the last. In the anonymous darkness of a nearby room someone coughed from time to time; he could not tell whether it was a man or a woman. The meal he had eaten lay like ten meals in his stomach. Slowly the memory of it was being suffused with a nebulous horror—particularly the heavy cold omelet shining with grease.

Lying there smelling the dust from the netting was like being tied up inside a burlap bag. To get out into the street and walk—that was what he wanted, but there were difficulties. The electricity went off at midnight; the old man who ran the hotel had told him that. Instead of putting the matches under his pillow he had left them in his trouser-pocket, and the idea of stepping out on to the floor barefoot without a light did not appeal to him. Besides, he reminded himself, listening again to the wide, strangely distant clamor out there, it was raining. But to move along the dead streets even under the invisible rain would be a pleasure. . . . If he lay quite still, sleep might return. Finally, in desperation he yanked the net aside and sprang out of bed, across the room in the direction of the chair over which he had thrown his clothes.

He managed to get into his shirt and trousers in the space of three matches; his shoes he pounded on the concrete floor in the dark, to tumble out a possible centipede or scorpion. Then he struck a fourth match and opened the door into the *patio*. Here it was no longer pitch-black. The huge potted plants were visible in the night's lead-colored light, but the sky, stifled by a cloud that no starlight could pierce, seemed not to be there at all. It was not raining. "The river must be very close," he thought.

He walked along the covered *corredor*, grazing the tentacles of orchids that hung in baskets and jars from the eaves, bumping into the pieces of wicker furniture, and found the entrance door, closed and doubly bolted. Carefully he slid back the metal bars and opened the door, pulling it shut after him. The gloom of the street was as profound as that of the *patio*, and the air as still as it had been under the mosquito-net. But it had an indefinite vegetable scent—a sweet odor of both fulfilment and exhaustion.

He turned to the left: the long empty main street, lined with one-story buildings, led straight down to the *paseo* along the sea. As he walked, the unmoving hot-house air became veined with the fresher smell of seaweed on the beach. At each intersecting street he had to go down six steps to the road level, cross, and climb up again to the sidewalk. In the rainy season, the *propietario* of the hotel had told him, there was a rowboat at each corner to ferry the pedestrians across. Like the intermingling of the land and sea odors that he breathed, two opposing but entwined sensations took possession of him: a relief amounting almost to delight, and a faint feeling of nausea which he decided to combat because he felt

that not to have been able to leave all suggestion of illness behind showed a lack of strength. He tried to put more springi-
ness into his walk, but discovered almost immediately that it
was too hot to make any more than a minimum of effort. He
was sweating even more now than he had been in his bed.
He lighted an Ovalado. The taste of the sweet tobacco was a
part of the night.

The *paseo* bordering the sea-front was about half a mile
long. He had imagined there would be some slight stirring of
the air here, but he could detect no difference. Still, now and
then there was the soft intimate sound of a small wave breaking gently on the sand just below. He sat down on the
balustrade and rested, in the hope of cooling off a little. The
sea was invisible. He could have been sitting on the peak of a
cloud-covered mountain—the gloom in front of him would
have been that formless and all-embracing. Yet the sea's casual
noises had no element of distance in them, as sea sounds
have. It was as though they were taking place in a vast, closed
courtyard. The concrete slabs on which he sat were damp,
and a little cooler than his flesh. He smoked two cigarettes
and strained his ears to hear some sound, made even indirectly, by human agency. But there was nothing more than
the desultory slipping and sucking of the lazy water on the
beach below. He glanced up and down the empty *paseo*. Far
out along the shore to the west there was a light. It was
orange, it flickered: a bonfire? He resumed walking, more
slowly than before, ahead of him the distant blaze, the one
point of light in the landscape.

A wide flight of steps led down on to the beach. Just beyond, he could see the flimsy structure of a pier that had been
built out over the water. He stood still and listened. The fitful licking of small waves around the piles sounded as though
it were happening in an echo-chamber.

He ran lightly down the steps and passed underneath the
pier. It was definitely cooler walking along on the sand than it
had been up on the *paseo*. He felt wide-awake now, and decided to see how much nearer to the light down the shore fifteen minutes would put him. Night-colored crabs hurried
along the sand just ahead of his moving feet, completely
soundless and almost invisible. A little beyond the end of the

paseo the sand gave place to a hard coral surface which was easier to walk on. Out of prudence he kept as near to the water's edge as possible.

There was a difference between this walk and innumerable other midnight jaunts he had made, and he was inclined to wonder what made it so pleasant. Perhaps he was enjoying it simply because the fabric here was of pure freedom. He was not looking for anything; all the cameras were back in the hotel room.

Occasionally he lifted his eyes from the dim brainlike configurations of coral beneath his feet and looked inland, to see whether he could make out any signs of habitation. It seemed to him that there might be sand dunes a few hundred feet back, but in the absence of light it was impossible to be certain of even that much. The sweat trickled down his spine and over his coccyx, sliding in between his buttocks. Maybe the best idea would be to undress completely. But then there would be the bother of carrying his clothing, and he wanted his hands free, even at the risk of chafing.

The question of freedom was governed by the law of diminishing returns, he said to himself, walking faster. If you went beyond a certain point of intensity in your consciousness of desiring it, you furnished yourself with a guarantee of not achieving it. In any case, he thought, what is freedom in the last analysis, other than the state of being totally, instead of only partially, subject to the tyranny of chance?

There was no doubt that this walk was dispelling the miasma of indigestion that had lain within him. Three minutes to go, said the bright minute-hand of his watch; the orange light ahead seemed smaller than it had from the town. Why an arbitrary fifteen minutes? He smiled at the precise urban pattern in which his mind had automatically moved. If he lifted his arm he could touch the sky, and it would be moist, tepid and voluptuously soft.

And now in the distance ahead, on the landward side, he heard sounds which he quickly identified as the voices of hundreds of young frogs. The light, now that he studied it, was moving in a strange fashion: slightly up and down, and sideways as well, but without appearing to alter its position. All at once it became a huge flame belching upward, an instant later scattering cascades of red sparks, and he understood that he had arrived. The bonfire burned on the floor of a gently swaying craft not a hundred feet ahead of him. A naked man stood above it, tossing it palm branches. The photographer stopped walking and listened for the sound of human voices, but the happy chorus of frogs filled the air.

He stepped ahead several paces and decided to call out. "*Hola!*" The man wheeled about, jumped over the nearer side of the boat (the water was extremely shallow) and came running up to him.

Without greeting him, taking him perhaps for someone else, the man said: "*Tapiama? Vas a Tapiama?*" The photographer, never having heard of Tapiama, stuttered a bit and finally said, "*Sí,*" whereupon the other seized his arm and pulled him along to the edge of the water. "The tide's all the way out. We'll start in a minute."

He could see two other people in the craft, lying flat on the floor, one on each side of the fire, as far from its heat as possible. The photographer squatted down and removed his shoes and socks, then waded to the boat. When he stood in the center of it (the fire was still crackling brightly) he turned and watched the naked man loosening the rope that held the craft in place.

"The whole thing is absurd." He could only distrust the very naturalness with which all this was coming about—the indifference to his unexpected arrival on the part of the two passengers, and perhaps even more, the highly suspect readiness of the boatmen to take off the moment he had appeared. He told himself, "Things don't happen this way," but since beyond a doubt they were doing so, any questioning of the process could lead only in the direction of paranoia. He dropped to the floor of the boat and pulled out his packet of Ovalados. The naked boatman, the coil of dripping rope around his black forearm like a bracelet, sprang aboard, and with his big toe nudged one of the supine passengers who stirred, rose to his knees, and glanced about with annoyance. "Where is it?" he demanded. Without replying, the boatman handed him the shorter of two poles that had lain along the gunwale. Together they began to propel the punt along the invisible surface of the water. The frogs' canticle and the fire's flare filled the night.

Having answered "*Sí*" to the Tapiama question, the photographer felt he could scarcely take the retrogressive step of asking "What is Tapiama?" or "Where is Tapiama?" And so, much as he would have liked to know, he decided to wait. This shallow body of water beneath them—estuary, lagoon? River more likely, since the boatman had said the tide was out. But not the stream whose troubled passage among the boulders he had heard from his bed.

They pushed on, now and then passing beneath clumps of high vegetation where the frogs' song was briefly covered by another sound, inexplicable and brutal, like the sudden tearing of a vast sheet of strong linen. From time to time something solid and heavy splashed nearby, as if a man had fallen into the water. And occasionally the other passenger raised himself on one elbow and without too much effort managed to revive the dying fire with another dry palm-leaf.

Probably it was less than an hour before they came to a landing in the mud. The two passengers leapt out and hurried away into the darkness. The boatman, after carefully donning a pair of short underpants, tapped the photographer on the arm and asked him for sixty centavos. He gave him seventy-five and clambered out into the soft mud, his shoes in his hand.

"Wait a minute," said the man. "I'll go with you." The photographer was pleased. When the boatman, looking blacker now in his white shorts, had secured the punt to an upright log driven into the mud, he led the way upward through a tangle of undergrowth, saying casually at one point: "Are you going across tomorrow?"

"Across? No."

"Aren't you here for the company?" The voice implied that to be here otherwise than for the company laid one open to unnameable suspicion.

The time had come to be truthful, he feared, although he did not relish the position he knew it would put him in. "I never heard of the company," he said. "I just arrived in Rio Martillo tonight. What sort of company?"

"Sugar," said the other. Then he stood still in the dark and spoke slowly: "*Entonces*—why have you come to Tapiama? They don't like *millonarios* here, you know." Understanding that this was the contemptuous coastal term for Americans, the photographer quickly lied. "I'm Danish," he said, but feeling that his voice lacked conviction he immediately added: "Do we go through any more mud, or can I put my shoes on?"

The man had started up again. "Wash your feet at the *cantina*, if you like," he told him over his shoulder. In another minute they were there: all in the dimness an open space, a dozen or so palm-leaf huts at one end of it, at the other a platform which must be a loading dock, the empty night and openness of water behind it; and half-way between the dock and the cluster of dwellings, the *cantina*, itself only a very large hut without a front wall.

A faint light came from within; there was no sound but the frogs on all sides, and the occasional tearing rasp in the branches high overhead. "Why is the place open at this hour?" demanded the photographer. The boatman stopped in the middle of the clearing and adjusted his shorts briefly. "Don Octavio runs it from six in the morning until six at night. His brother runs it from six at night until six in the morning. The company lets the men off from work at different hours. They come here with their *pago* and spend it. They like it better here than at home. Not so many mosquitoes." It could have been the photographer's imagination that made the man's voice sound bitter as he spoke the last words. They continued across the clearing and stepped into the *cantina*.

There was no floor; the ground was covered with white sand. A counter of boards had been built diagonally across a far corner. Here an oil lamp smoldered and two men stood drinking. Wooden packing-cases were scattered here and there, some standing on end with empty beer bottles on them, and others on their sides, to be used as seats. "*Muy triste*," commented the boatman, glancing around. Then he went behind the bar and disappeared through a small door in the wall there. Apart from the two at the bar, who had ceased their conversation and now stood staring at the photographer, there was no one else in the place. "When in doubt, speak," he told himself, advancing toward them, although it occurred to him that he might just as well have made it, "When in doubt, keep quiet," even as he opened his mouth to say, "*Buenas noches,*" for their expressions did not alter in any manner that he could detect. For a full three seconds they continued to gaze at him before they replied, which they then did more or less simultaneously. These two had nothing in common, he noted: one was a soldier in uniform, an Indian boy of perhaps eighteen, the other a tired-looking mulatto civilian of indeterminate age. Or perhaps—the idea came to him as he put his elbow on the bar with a show of casualness—they did have at least a common antagonism, now that he had entered the *cantina*. "Oh, well, I'm barefoot and my shoes are covered with mud," he thought.

"*Hay alguien?*" he said aloud to the palm-leaf wall behind the bar. The two neither resumed their conversation nor spoke further with him, and he did not turn his head again toward them. Presently the small door opened and a fat man pushed through. He stood with his hands outspread on the bar, his eyebrows raised in anticipation. "I'll have a *cumbiamba*," said the photographer, remembering the name of the coastal region's favorite drink, a herbal concoction famous for its treacherous effects.

It was foul-tasting but strong. The second one seemed less objectionable. He walked across to the open side of the *cantina* and sat down on a packing-case, looking out at the formless night. The two at the bar were talking again now in low tones. It was not long before five men appeared from the platform end of the clearing; they straggled in and stood at the bar, laughing as they waited for their drinks. All of them were black, and wore only underpants, like the boatman. Now a mulatto girl with gold teeth came through the little door behind the bar and joined them. Almost immediately, however, she became aware of the photographer sitting by himself, and with her hands on her hips, half dancing, she made her way across the open space toward him. When she arrived, she squatted down beside him grinning and with one thin yellow hand reached out to unfasten his fly. His reaction was instantaneous and automatic: he drew back his leg and kicked her full in the breast, so that she toppled over back-

ward in silence on to the sand. The noise of the resulting
laughter at the bar was not sufficient to cover her thin voice,
made sharp by rage: "*Qué bruto, tú! Pendejo!*" Hands on hips
again, she retreated to the bar and was given a beer by one of
the workmen. Although the photographer had not meant to
kick her, he felt no regret at the turn the incident had taken.
The *cumbiambas* seemed to be having their effect; he was beginning to feel very well. He sat still a while, tapping rhythms
on the side of his empty glass. Soon more Negro workmen
came in and joined the others at the bar. One carried a guitar
on which he set to work strumming a syncopated chordal accompaniment for a melody which failed to appear. However,
it was music of a sort, and everyone was pleased with it. Perhaps awakened by the sound, the dogs of the village had now
started an angry chorus of barking; this was particularly audible to the photographer who sat at the entrance, and it
bothered him. He rose and moved over to an empty crate
alongside the opposite wall, resting his head against a rough-
hewn pole that was one of the supports of the roof. A foot or
so above his head there was a strange object dangling from a
nail. Now and then he rolled his eyes upward and studied it.

All at once he jumped up and began violently to brush the
back of his neck and head. The pole behind him was swarming with tiny ants, thousands upon thousands of them: someone had hung a small crushed coral snake over the nail, and
they had come to eat the flesh. It took him a good while not
to feel any more of the insects running over his back; during
that time two other individuals had come into the *cantina*
(whether from the outside or through the door behind the
counter, he had not noticed), and now sat between him and
the bar in such a fashion that both of them faced him. The
old man looked Nordic, the innocent-looking one-legged boy
with him could be Spanish; the old man was telling the boy a
humorous story, leaning toward him with great interest, occasionally poking his arm with a forefinger to drive home a
point, but the boy was distraughtly making designs in the
sand with the tip of his crutch.

The photographer stood up; he had never before had such
an effect from two drinks. "A very peculiar sensation," he said
to himself. "Very peculiar," he repeated aloud under his

breath as he started toward the bar to order another. It was not that he felt drunk so much as that he had become someone who was not he, someone for whom the act of living was a thing so different from what he had imagined it could be, that he was left stranded in a region of sensation far from any he had heretofore known. It was not unpleasant: it was merely indefinable. "*Dispénseme,*" he said to a tall Negro in pink and white striped BVD's, and he handed his empty glass to the fat man. He wanted to see what went into a *cumbiamba*, but the barman did everything quickly beneath the counter and handed him back the glass, brimming with the slightly frothy mixture. He took a good swallow of it and set it down, turning a little to his right as he did so. Standing beside him was the Indian soldier, his cap at an angle atop a pre-Colombian face. "Why does the army put such big visors on them?" he wondered.

He saw that the soldier was about to speak. "Whatever he says is going to turn out to be an insult," he warned himself, in the hope that this would help him to avoid possible anger later.

"Do you like this place?" the soldier said; his voice was silken.

"*Es simpático.* Yes, I like it."

"Why?" The dogs outside had come nearer; he could hear their yapping now above the laughter.

"Can you tell me why they hung that dead snake on the wall there?" he found himself asking, and supposed it was to change the subject. But the soldier was going to be even more boring than he had feared. "I asked you why you like this *cantina,*" he insisted.

"And I told you it was *simpático.* Isn't that enough?"

The soldier tilted his head back and looked down his nose.

"Far from being enough," he replied, his manner pedantic, his expression infuriating.

The photographer returned to his drink, picked it up, slowly finished it off. Then he pulled out his cigarettes and offered one to the other. With exaggerated deliberateness the soldier reached for the cigarette, took it, and began to tap it on the counter. The man playing the guitar at last had started to sing in a small falsetto voice along with it, but most of the words were in a dialect the photographer could not understand. When the cigarettes were lighted, he found himself wondering who had lighted them—he or the soldier.

"Just where did you come from?" asked the soldier.

He was not bothering to answer, but the soldier misunderstood even this. "I can see you're inventing something," he said, "and I don't want to hear it."

The photographer, disgusted, exclaimed, "Aaah!" and ordered another *cumbiamba*. This most recent one had done something extraordinary to him: he felt that he had become very precise, thin and hard, an object made of enamel or some similar material, something other than a living being, but intensely conscious all the same. "Four ought to do the trick," he thought.

The empty glass was in his hand, the fat barman was staring at him, and at that point he had not the slightest idea whether he had already drunk the fourth one or whether it was still the moment just after he had ordered it. He felt himself laughing, but he could not hear whether any sound was coming out or not. The mangled snake, seething with ants, had upset him a little; recognizing it, he had then been made aware of its smell, which he was not sure he had escaped even now. Here at the bar the kerosene lamp smoked heavily; its strong fumes choked him. "*Gracias a Dios,*" he confided to the barman, handing him the glass.

The old man who had been sitting on the crate behind them rose and came vaguely toward the bar. "Where did this come from?" said the photographer, laughing apologetically, looking at the full glass in his hand. The frenzied dogs out in the clearing yapped and howled, an exasperating sound. "*Qué tienen esos perros?*" he demanded of the soldier.

The old man had stopped beside them. "Say, Jack, I don't mean to butt in or anything," he began. He was bald, sunburned; he wore a fishnet shirt. The furrows between his ribs showed as parallel shadows, and irregular tufts of gray hair waved out from his chest between the meshes of the shirt. He stretched his lips in a smile, showing naked white gums. The soldier's stance became over-nonchalant; he stared at the newcomer, open hatred suddenly in his eyes, and gently blew the smoke from his cigarette into the old man's face.

"You from Milwaukee? Siddown."

"In a little while, thanks," said the photographer.

"A little while?" the old man echoed incredulously, running his hand over the top of his head. Then he called out in Spanish to the one-legged boy. The photographer was thinking: "This is not going to work out right, at all. It's just not going to work out." He wished the Negro would stop singing and the dogs would stop barking. He looked at the glass in his hand, full of what looked like soapsuds. Someone tapped him on the shoulder. "Say, bud, lemme give you a little advice." The old man again. "There's money in this country if you know where to look. But the guy that finds it is the guy that sticks to his own kind, if you know what I mean." He put his face nearer and lowered his voice. Three skeletal fingers touched the photographer's arm. "You take it from me, from one white man to another. I'm tellin' you!" The three fingers, dark with tobacco stain, lifted themselves, trembled, and dropped back. "These guys all mean trouble from the word go."

The boy having both gathered up his crutch and managed to rise from where he had been sitting, had now arrived at the bar. "Take a look at this, Jack," the old man said. "Show him," he told the boy in Spanish, and the boy, leaning on his crutch, bent over and rolled up the right leg of his ragged khaki shorts until he had exposed the stump of his amputated leg. It was not far below the groin; the scar tissue had puckered and wrinkled curiously in countless tiny convolutions. "See?" cried the old man. "Two hundred and sixty tons of bananas went over that. Feel it."

"You feel it," said the photographer, wondering how it was possible for him to go on standing and talking exactly as if he were a person like the rest of them. (Could it be that what had happened to him did not show?) He turned his head and looked towards the entrance. The mulatto girl was vomiting just outside. With a cry the barman rushed across and furiously pushed her farther away, out into the clearing. When he came back in he was theatrically holding his nose. "That prostitute ape!" he yelled. "In another minute we'd have had the dogs inside here."

The boy was still looking expectantly at the old man, to see if it was time to lower his trouser leg. "You think he got a centavo from them?" said the old man sadly. "Hah!"

The photographer had begun to suspect that something had gone very wrong inside him. He felt sick, but since he was no longer a living creature he could not conceive it in those terms. He had shut his eyes and put his hand over his face. "It's going around backward," he said. The undrunk *cumbiamba* was in his other hand.

Saying the sentence had made it more true. It was definitely going around backward. The important thing was to remember that he was alone here and that this was a real place with real people in it. He could feel how dangerously easy it would be to go along with the messages given him by his senses, and dismiss the whole thing as a nightmare in the secret belief that when the breaking-point came he could somehow manage to escape by waking himself up. A little unsteadily he set his drink down on the counter. An argument which had arisen a while ago between the Indian soldier and his sad companion had now reached its noisy stage, with the companion attempting to drag the soldier away from the bar against his will, and the soldier, his two booted legs firmly apart, breathing rapidly, noisily in his resistance. Suddenly there was a small, shining knife in his right hand, and his face assumed the look of a little boy about to burst into tears. The old man quickly moved around to the photographer's other side. "That guy's bad news in any language," he muttered, gesturing nervously to the boy with the crutch as he bade him move out of the way.

The photographer was saying to himself: "If I can hold out. If I can only hold out." The whole place was slipping away from him, downward and outward; the guitar strummed and the dogs barked, the soldier flashed his knife and pouted, the old American talked about caves with buried emeralds only six days up the Tupurú, the lamp grew redder and more smoke came out of it. He understood nothing except that he must stay there and suffer; to try to escape would be fatal. The soldier's face was very near his own now, breathing black tobacco smoke at him. Languorously, with an insane natural coquetry, he made his long lashes tremble as he asked: "Why have you not offered me a *copita*? All night I have been waiting for you to invite me." The hand holding the knife hung listlessly at his side; the photographer thought of a sleeping baby still clutching its rattle.

"*Sí quieres. . . . Qué tomas?*" he murmured, reflecting that his shoes should be in his hand and were not; then where were they? Someone had brought a large spider monkey into the *cantina* and was forcing it to dance to the guitar's syncopations, making it stand upright by holding its two front paws. With an air of distraught gravity it stepped about, peering this way and that, grimacing nervously at the loud peals of laughter that came from those at the bar watching its antics. The dogs, having noticed its arrival, had rushed to the very entrance of the *cantina*, where they braced themselves to shriek and snap with determined fury.

The soldier's drink had been bought and paid for, but he was not drinking it. He was leaning far back against the bar, reclining on his elbow almost as though he were in bed, his eyes simple black slits, whispering: "You don't like it here. You want to go, *verdad*? But you are afraid to go."

In spite of the constant sliding away, everything had remained just as it was. It would have been better if he could have sat down. "Oh, God," he asked himself. "Am I going to be able to stand this?"

"Why are you afraid to go?" pursued the other tenderly, smiling so that the photographer could admire his small, perfect teeth. The photographer laughed silently, did not reply.

The face of the soldier, ovoid, honey-colored, so near to his, moved now with consummate smoothness into another face, that of a general. ("*Sí, mi general*," with stiff *bigotes* sprouting from beneath the nostrils, almond eyes, black, deadly with a delicate lust, the uniform svelte, plaited steel riding crop in hand, sharpened spurs shining by the anklebone. "*Bien, mi general.*" Lying on the hot barrack mattress, *tarde tras tarde*, the soldier had dreamed of being the general. Which mountain village had he said he was from? How long had he been talking?)

". . . and that day alone they killed forty-one pigs before my eyes. There in the corral. *Me hizo algo; no sé. . . .*" His smile was apologetic, intimate; he lowered his eyes imperceptibly, made the effort and raised them again to look at the photographer in such a way that, since they were wider than before, they glistened. "I never forgot it; I don't know why."

Between them the gold-toothed girl came sliding, her hands wriggling over her head, her hips circling, her thin voice shouting: "*Ahii! Ahii! El fandango de la Guajira!*" The soldier must have pushed her, for all at once she slapped him. But it was happening very slowly. How could it take the soldier so long to bring up his knife, and as he raised his hand, how could the stupid girl wait that way before screaming and ducking aside? Even so, the blade caught her only on the arm; she was in the middle of the floor, kneeling on the sand, moaning: "He cut me! Oh, God! He cut me!" And because the man who had been dancing with the spider monkey let go of it to get as quickly as all the others to the bar, the beast toddled over to the girl and distractedly wrapped one long hairy arm around her neck. But then the photographer was being roughly jostled, his bare feet were being stepped on as everyone tried to get at the soldier and disarm him. (A demon mask shiny with venom, a voice of barbed wire that rasped: "*Os mato a todos! A todos!*")

It was exactly nineteen steps from the place where he had stood to the trunk of a small papaya tree in front of the entrance. The tree was not very strong; it swayed slightly as he leaned against it. The dogs were yelping now from inside the *cantina*. Here the air was sweet and almost cool; the faintest glimmer of morning was in the sky and water behind the landing. "I must start to walk," he told himself; it seemed important to believe it. The shouts and screams inside the *cantina* were growing in volume, and people were beginning to call to one another from the doors of their huts. The landing platform was empty—just boards and no railing. Shuffling along with great care because he was not used to going barefoot, he followed what he thought was the path he had taken earlier, through the undergrowth back down to the river's edge, and there was the punt, mud-beached in the mangroves.

It was easy to get in, easy to untie the rope, and easy (for the level of the water had risen considerably since the craft had been left) to pry it loose from the shelf of mud where it rested. But once he was floating among the now nearly visible trunks and branches, bumping against them and being spun to face first the dark chaotic riverbank and then the wide whitening emptiness of open sky and water, he understood dimly that it was not going to be possible to pole his way back to the beach whence he had come, since the tide was still coming in. It was a comforting thought, he decided, because it meant that everything was going ahead instead of backward. A minute later he was floating quietly by the base of the landing: people were running around the clearing. Quickly he lay down flat on the bottom of the punt, and there he stayed, looking straight up at the gray sky, hoping in this way to remain invisible until he had been carried out of sight, beyond Tapiama.

It was going to be one of those stillborn tropical days, when there would be no sun, no wind, no clouds—because the entire sky was enfolded in one vast suffocating blanket of cloud—when nothing at all would happen save that hourly it would grow hotter until an approximate dusk came along. Already the eastern side of the sky was the hot side, arching above the flatness of the swampland. The punt scarcely moved now, the channel having broadened into this wide marshy lake. The photographer lay still and groaned. Little by little the fear that someone might see him gave way to the hope that what current there was would propel the craft in the direction of the shore rather than out toward the wilderness of water and tiny islands; sometimes, even though suffering be implicit in it, contact with others is preferable to the terror of solitude and the unknown. He laid an arm over his eyes to shield them from the corrosive gray light that beat down upon him from the spaces above. The other hand lay in the ashes of last night's fire. And he floated in utter silence on the calm bosom of the lagoon, not stirring as the morning hours moved along, but growing increasingly conscious of the infernal seething of the *cumbiambas* in his brain, a seething which expressed itself as a senseless nightmare imposed from without, in the face of which he could only be totally passive. It was an invisible spectacle whose painful logic he followed with the entire fiber of his being, without, however, once being given a clear vision of what agonizing destinies were at stake.

Some time towards mid-morning the punt grazed a sub-
merged root and was swung into an eddyless pool in the shelter of the vegetation near the shore. Here fierce flies stung
him, and from among the leaves high above, a talking bird remarked casually, over and over again: "*Idigaraga. Idigaraga.
Idigaraga.*"

It was no particular consolation to him, so intent was he on
the obscure drama being enacted within him, to hear human
voices presently, or to feel the craft seized by the hands of
someone splashing in the water alongside. Only when several
people had climbed in and crouched chattering around him
did he move his arm and squint up at them. Five young men,
all of whom looked remarkably alike, surrounded him. Water
dripped down upon him from their naked bodies. He shut his
eyes again: it was too unlikely a scene. During this time one
of them dived overboard, was gone a short while, and returned with a green coconut whose top he had sliced off. He
began to let the water dribble into the photographer's face,
whereupon the photographer partially sat up and drank the
rest of it. In a minute he looked around at them again, and
said: "Are you brothers?"

"*Sí, sí*," they chorused. This was for some reason a consolation. "*Hermanos*," he sighed, sliding down into the ashes
again. Then he added desperately, hoping they could still hear
him: "Please take me to Rio Martillo."

It had been a brief interlude of clarity. Now they poled the
punt back out under the hot sky, letting him lie there and
moan as he liked. At one point he felt he must try to explain
that he would give them each seventy-five centavos for their
trouble, but they giggled and pushed him back down.

"My shoes!" he cried. "There are no shoes," they told him.
"Lie still."

"And when we get to the beach," he panted, seizing a
brown ankle beside his face, "how will you get me to Rio
Martillo?" "We are not going to any beach," they replied.
"We go through the swamp and the canal."

He lay still a while, trying to disassociate himself from the
irrational ideas boiling up in his head. "Is this the way to Rio
Martillo?" he demanded, thrusting himself up a little and
gasping, trying to see beyond the enclosing thicket of brown

legs and arms, and feeling a deep unreasoned shame at having once again accepted defeat. They laughed, pushed him gently down to the floor, and went on rhythmically poling the craft eastward. "The factory chimney," they said to one another, pointing into the distance. His mind took him back to the quiet region by the riverbank where the small bird had spoken, high up in the trees, and he heard again the ridiculous conversational tone. "*Idigaraga*," he said aloud, imitating perfectly its voice and intonation. There was an explosion of mirth around him. One of the youths took his arm, shook it lightly. "You know that bird?" he said. "It is a very comic bird. It goes to the nests of other birds and wants to sit there, and when the other birds fight with it and drive it away, it sits down in the same tree there and says: '*Idigaraga*.' That means: '*Iri garagua, nadie me quiere*, nobody likes me.' And it says it over and over, until they make it go farther away so they can't hear it any more. You said it just right. Say it again." "*Sí, sí*," the others agreed, "*otra vez!*"

The photographer had no intention of saying it again. His shame at having accepted defeat already troubled him less. It was hard in his present condition to fit the bird correctly into the pattern, but he knew it had to be done.

When the Compañía Azucarera Riomartillense blew a long blast on its whistle to announce the advent of noon, the sound hovered for an instant over the empty swampland like an invisible trail of smoke. "*Las doce*," said one of the brothers. A great black and gold dragonfly came skimming across the water and lighted on the photographer's bare foot. After raising and lowering its wings twice, it was away again on its crooked course, curving and swooping over the lagoon toward Tapiama. "Say it again," the brothers begged him.

If I Should Open My Mouth

A T LAST succeeded in finding the correct mixture of gum-arabic, sugar and essence of peppermint. Had the most complicated time getting Mrs. Crawford out of the house and keeping her out for a sufficiently long time so that I could clean up the kitchen properly before she returned. I find this plan most exhilarating, however, and I intend to carry it through to its conclusion in the face of all obstacles. The subway station details are clear in my mind, and I have worked out the entire plan of action. In fact, the project is so extremely simple that it seems at times almost suspect. It is as if I were constantly being reassured by an invisible person whose face, if only I could see it, might easily prove to be wearing a falsely benign expression. However, it is only in the evenings that I begin to think of such things. A seconal or two ought to arrange matters, at least for tonight, so that I can knit up some of that raveled sleeve of care. Curious how disturbing the sound of a motorcycle can be out here in the still night air. There has been one idling somewhere up the road for the past ten minutes, popping and sputtering in a way calculated to drive a listener crazy. When it finally purred off into the distance it was like a relief from a constant pain. Why were machines ever invented? And what is this strange calm confidence that mankind has placed in these senseless toys it has managed to put together? That question I don't expect ever to be able to answer. I can only say that I know it is wrong.

Wednesday 28th——

More complications, getting rid of Mrs. C. while I dipped the tablets. The rest, gluing the ends of the boxes and so on, can be done up here in my room. A ridiculous facet of my feeling about all this is that while I am quite aware of the reprehensible aspects of my silly little project, for some unfathomable reason I feel hugely righteous about it all—more satisfyingly virtuous than I have in years. A quirk of human nature, I suppose.

Saturday 1st——

I don't know why it is that ideas never occur to me except when I lack the time to put them down or when it is literally impossible to do so, as for instance when I am seated in a dentist's chair or surrounded by talking people at a dinner party, or even sound asleep, when often the best things come to light and are recognized as such by a critical part of my mind which is there watching, quite capable of judging but utterly unable to command an awakening and a recording. Sick-bed and fever often bring up astonishing things, but again, to what avail? A less ingenuous man than I might ask just why it should be of any importance to me that what goes on inside my mind should be put down. I am not a literary person and I never expect to be one, nor have I any intention of showing my notebooks to my friends. But that is a point not even to be discussed; long ago I determined to extract from my mind whatever by-products it could furnish. I have done it, I am still doing it, and I expect to continue to do it. The only difficulty is that whatever I am able to catch hold of is captured only after engaging in the most elaborate intrigues with my mind, playing hide-and-seek with various parts of it, exhausting myself in inventing disguises with which to surprise it, and in general having a most unpleasant time. Such as this very moment, this very page. A typical example of an occasion when there is not a single idea in view on the vast inner horizon. I am using up pages of my notebook, minutes when I might be strolling on the beach smelling the sea, in scribbling these absurd excuses, inventing alibis for not living, trying to find one more reason why I should feel justified in keeping these nonsensical journals year after year. Year after year, and life does not last for ever, not even an unsatisfactory one like mine. Perhaps this is the very thing which is keeping my life so unsatisfactory. If I could argue myself into stopping it all, even into destroying the notebooks, would it be better? Yes. Each minute would be complete in itself, like a room with four walls in which one can stand, sit, move about. Each day would be like a complete city shining in the sun, with its streets, parks and crowds. And the years would be whole countries to roam in. That much is certain. But the whole? That is to say, the interstices in time, the tiny chinks in consciousness when the total is there, enveloping one, and one knows that life is not made of time any more than the world is made of space. They would still occur, and they would be illicit because there would have been no arrangements made for them. What a man can distil and excrete will necessarily have some value for him (if only for him, as in my case) because its essence is of the interstices in time. One more justification, as idiotic as all the others, of the need for living an unsatisfactory life.

It seems to me that if one could accept existence as it is, partake of it fully, the world could be magical. The cricket on my balcony at the moment piercing the night repeatedly with its hurried needle of sound, would be welcome merely because it is there, rather than an annoyance because it distracts me from what I am trying to do. Here I am, a man of fifty-five, who enjoys a certain respect on the part of his friends, cursing a small black insect outside the window. But I dare say all this is merely procrastination. I am probably trying to put off writing down what is really on my mind. It must go down, of course, because everything must go down, and truthfully. (I thought the cricket had stopped just then, but it has started again, quite the same as before.) I delivered the first twenty boxes today.

Sunday 2nd——

The cricket got to be too much for me last night. It seemed to keep increasing its tempo, although I don't know how it could have managed to chirp any faster than it had been doing at the beginning. In any case, when I put down the great fact, I waited a while trying to decide how to go about describing the distribution. Nothing untoward happened, it is quite true, while I was making the deliveries, but still, it seemed to me last night in my overwrought condition that a special effort was required for me to be able to go into the details. And while I waited, the cricket went on and on and on; faster and faster, or so it seemed to me, until it would have been impossible to set down another word. This morning, however, I am in fine shape.

It was raining a little when I started out, a warm, fine summer drizzle. One of the things I have noticed about myself since Anna and I split up is the fact that I have a sneaking fondness for walking in the rain without rubbers or a hat. Doubtless this is a predilection I have always had without realizing it, since first it was Mother and then Anna who always seemed somehow to prevent me from indulging in it. Quite rightly, too; I should probably have caught pneumonia and died long before this if it had not been for them. But since Anna left me and I have been here in Manor Heights alone, I occasionally slip out bareheaded and without rubbers, if the rain is not too heavy. Mrs. Crawford, like a good housekeeper, has sometimes caught me at it, and brought it to my attention, hurrying to supply the needed accessories and thus obliging me to wear them. Yesterday morning, however, I managed to get out of the front door while she was in the kitchen talking to the delivery man from Macy's. I knew he would be coming, and I had everything ready, the twenty little boxes in the left-hand pocket of my jacket, the pennies in the right-hand trouser-pocket. The only way to do anything is to have it so well rehearsed in one's imagination that when the moment comes one does it automatically, as though for the hundredth time. Then it is all natural, and there is little likelihood of a slip-up. And there was no slip-up anywhere along the way. It was a heavy day, but not too hot because of the rain, which fell quietly as I walked down the road to the station. On the train I was not in the slightest degree perturbed: I knew there was no chance of any trouble. I kept marveling at the peculiar pleasure afforded by the knowledge that one has planned a thing so perfectly there can be no room for the possibility of failure, all the while being conscious that both the pleasure and the idea itself were completely childish, and that my conviction of success was, at the very least, ill-founded. But certain situations call forth certain emotions, and the mind is a thing entirely apart. I have cakes of soap that I bought twenty-five years ago, still in their wrappers, and I am saving them in the perfect confidence that the right day will come to unwrap each one and use it. And there are probably a hundred books downstairs in the library that I am eager to read, have been eager to read for years, yet refuse to read until the days comes, the day that says to me: This is the morning to start Villiers de l'Ile Adam, or George Borrow, or Psichari, or someone else. Now, in my logical mind, I know quite well that these promised days are not likely ever to arrive: I shall never use those old cakes of soap that are stored in the linen closet, and I am reasonably sure of never reading *Romany Rye*, because it doesn't interest *me*. But there is that other person, the ideal one that I ought to be, and whom it does interest, and it comforts me to think that those things are there waiting for him. Certainly, the mind is a thing absolutely apart.

From Grand Central I took the shuttle across to Times Square, then walked underground to the Eighth Avenue Subway. I chose the Independent as my territory, because of the great length of the stations. The air in that tunnel was almost steamy, and smelled of wet cement, hot metal and sewage. I took an express all the way up to Fort Tryon, worked slowly down through Harlem and then all the way to Canal Street. There was no hitch, no real difficulty, anywhere. The only place where there was even a meeting of any sort was at Twenty-third Street, where a colored woman who was standing near the machine came up behind me as I was reaching in to take out the real package, which of course made it impossible for me to put in the one I held in my left hand. I did not hesitate for a fraction of a second. It was my determination that everything be carried off perfectly. I turned aside, put my left hand back into my coat pocket, and proceeded to open the little box, shake out its two white candy-coated pellets into my hand and pop them into my mouth. If I were to suggest to anyone that this was an excellent piece of strategy, it would sound laughable, and yet it required quick thinking and a certain courage. In the first place, I have never chewed gum, and the idea of it disgusts me. (It occurs to me now that this distaste may easily have had some bearing on my choice of method for carrying out my project.) But much more than that secondary consideration was the fact that my co-ordination is not always of the best. On occasion it takes terrific concentration for me to distinguish right from left. And a second before, I had held in my left hand the *other* box, one of *my* boxes. What if, I said to myself, through some dark perversity of the subconscious, I should somehow have opened the wrong box? And as I crunched through the enamal walls of mint-sugar I found myself wondering if what I was tasting was the normal flavor, or whether it might be my flavor, my special mixture. I did not wait to get at that machine again, but continued downtown, skipping the West Fourth Street station because of the central platforms and the undesirable placing of the machines.

At Canal Street I had the pleasure of actually seeing the bait snapped up. I had no sooner put the penny in, retrieved the untouched box, and placed one of mine at the back of the shelf, when a young girl (Italian, I think) pushed past me and worked the machine. There was an expression of amusement on her face as she rejoined her friends at the edge of the platform. "Gee, I'm gettin' good," she said. "I got two."

I delivered the three final boxes in Brooklyn, returned to Manhattan, had a light meal at a Longchamps on Madison Avenue, and came home, feeling that the day had certainly not been wasted. I venture to say that I am embarked on the biggest comedy to be played in the subways of New York until the day Russia's super-bombs lay them all bare to the sun. This is an infantile pastime I have devised, but at the same time it carries its own weight, and thus must have a meaning. However, I paid for my jaunt with a feeling of considerable fatigue, mostly of nervous origin, I suppose. Naturally, it was something of a strain. On an ordinary evening a cricket would not have been able to disturb me. Mrs. Crawford was indignant about the rubbers and the hat and the fact that my clothes were quite damp, of course. She is a good old soul. Today I have done nothing but sit in the garden reading the Sunday *Times*. The sun was out and in, all day, but it was not too hot.

This morning the Stewarts very kindly invited me on a picnic to Rye Beach. I could not entertain the thought of going, certainly. It's bad enough to have them living next door, to have to hear their abominable radio at all hours of the day and night, and put up with the depredations wrought in the garden by that untrained brat of theirs, without going out of my way to accompany them on an outing. It was a kind thought, however, and I have decided to go downtown the first thing tomorrow morning and buy a toy of some sort for little Dorothy. Maybe a tricycle, or something that will keep her on the sidewalk. Anywhere, anywhere, out of my garden!

Monday 3rd——

I scarcely dared open the paper this morning, for fear of what I should find. Still, reading of the consequences is most assuredly a part of the procedure, and so I went ahead. But for some reason the police are keeping it quiet. There was nothing, anywhere. This silence managed to make me feel uncomfortable; in a way I feel as though I were being watched.

The Stewarts were most pleased with the velocipede, or whatever the chromium-plated contraption is called. Little Dorothy seemed quite overwhelmed by its splendor. As yet I have not seen her use it. I dare say she is too small to pull it by herself, up and down the two flights of steps between the front door and the sidewalk. I imagine for a while her parents will have to take it up and down for her.

Thursday 6th——

The newspapers continue to maintain a stubborn silence, being filled instead with asinine stories about the electoral campaign. As if it could possibly change the course of history which of the two scarecrows gets into the seat of power. It was already too late to do that a hundred and seventy-five years ago. Too late to avert the sheer, obscene horror that has been on its way ever since, and is nearly here now. Voltaire, Marx, Roosevelt, Stalin, what were they but buds along the branch, like sores that have a way of bursting through the skin where it is thinnest? Who planted the tree of poison, who infected the blood? I am not qualified to say; the complexities of the question are endless. But I believe that one of the culprits was our friend Rousseau. That unpardonable mechanism, the intellect, has several detestable aspects. Perhaps the worst is the interpenetration of minds; the influence, unconscious, even, that one mind can have over millions, is unforeseeable, immeasurable. You never know what form it will take, when it will make itself manifest.

Saturday 8th——

The police assuredly are playing some sort of game. There must have been at least fifteen deaths, and not a word about one of them has appeared. That of course is their business, but I am amused and a little mystified to see how they are conducting it. Mrs. C. has a heavy summer cold. I tried hard to make her stay in bed, but she is the soul of conscientiousness, and insists on continuing with her regular work.

Sunday 9th——

It is an odd thing, that part of the mind which invents dreams and retains them, sometimes making of a certain dream a colored lens, as it were, which comes between one's consciousness and one's vision of what passes for reality. That is, the feeling of the dream can remain when every detail has been lost. For several days now a particular atmosphere, taste, sensation, or whatever it may be called, has been haunting me. It can only be a dream-vestige, yet in spite of the fact that I have forgotten the dream it is very strong. And since it is gone it is unlocatable in time. It may have been this week or many years ago that the dream itself took place. The feeling, if it can be put into words at all, is one connected with languor, forgetfulness, lostness, emptiness, endlessness—one thing which would be all those things. Living my life and thinking my thoughts through that lens makes for a certain melancholy. I have tried desperately to find a door into the dream; perhaps if I could recall it, get back there, I could destroy its power. It is often a way. But it is almost as if it were an entity in itself, aware of my efforts to find it, and determined to remain hidden. As I feel I am approaching it I seem to sense a springing away, a definite recoil into some airless, unreachable region within. I don't like it; it worries me.

Monday 10th——

When things become wholly unbelievable, all one can do is laugh. There is nothing to fall back upon but the bare fact of one's existence; one must forsake logic for magic. Because it was raining this morning (a morning rather like the day of my excursion to the city) and I wanted to take a short stroll, I went to the clothes closet and took out my gray flannel suit.

I was entirely dressed when I suddenly recalled that there was a large hole in the right trouser-pocket. A strange feeling of confusion came over me, even before I started to think. But then the mental process commenced. How had the pennies stayed in my pocket that day? It was quite simple. I had changed my suit; now I remembered clearly taking off the gray flannel and putting on the herring-bone tweed. Perhaps if I had been able to live completely in the mind at that moment, I should have given it no further thought, and the unacceptable discovery would not have been made—at least, not then. But evidently I could not be satisfied with anything so simple. Another reflex sent my left hand to the pocket of the jacket, and that was the instant of my undoing. Later I took them all out and counted them sitting on the bed, but then I merely stood still, my hand inside the pocket feeling the jumble of small cardboard boxes, my mouth hanging open like an idiot's. It was inescapable—they were there. A second later I said aloud: "Oh." And I rushed over to the bureau drawer and opened it, because I wanted to be sure that these were not the untouched boxes I had collected. But they too were there, scattered among the piles of clean handkerchiefs. Then the others——? There is nothing to think. I *know* I delivered them.

At least, I believe I know. If I am to doubt my own eyes and ears, then it is time I gave up entirely. But in connection with that idea a ghastly little thought occurs to me: am I doubting my eyes and ears? Obviously not; only my memory. Memory is a cleverer trickster by far. In that case, however, I am stark, raving mad, because I remember every detail of those hours spent in the subway. But here are the boxes piled in front of me on the desk, all twenty. I know them intimately. I glued down each little flap with the maximum of care. There is no mistaking them. It is a shattering experience, and I feel ill, ill in every part of my being. A voice in me says: "Accept the impossible. Leave off trying to make this fit in with your preconceived ideas of logic and probability. Life would be a sad affair if it reserved no surprises at all." "But not this sort!" I reply. "Nothing quite so basically destructive of my understanding of the world!" I am going to bed. Everything is all wrong.

3:15 A.M. ——

The dream has emerged from its wrappings of fog. Not all of it, but that does not matter. I recognized it immediately when only a piece of it appeared, as I was lying here in the dark, half asleep. I relaxed and let more of it come. A senseless dream, it would seem, and yet powerful enough to have colored all these past few days with its sadness. It is almost impossible to put down, since nothing *happens* in it: I am left only with vague impressions of being solitary in the park of some vast city. Solitary in the sense that although life is going on all around me, the cords that could connect me in any way with that life have been severed, so that I am as alone as if I were a spirit returned from the dead. Traffic moves past at some distance from where I am reclining on the ground under the trees. The time—timeless. I know there are streets full of people behind the trees, but I will never be able to touch them. If I should open my mouth to cry out, no sound would come forth. Or if I should stretch my arms toward one of the figures that occasionally wanders along the path nearby, that would have no effect, because I am invisible. It is the terrible contradiction that is unbearable: being there and yet knowing that I am not there, for in order to *be*, one must not only be to one's self: it is absolutely imperative that one be for others. One must have a way of basing one's being on the certainty that others know one is there. I am telling myself that somewhere in this city Mrs. Crawford is thinking of me. If I could find her, she would be able to see me, and could give me a sign that would mean everything was all right. But she will never come by this place. I am hidden. I cannot move, I was born here, have always been here under these trees on this wet grass. And if I was born, perhaps I can die, and the city making its roar out beyond this park will stop being. That is my only hope. But it will take almost for ever. That is about all there is to the dream. Just that static picture of sadness and lostness.

The boxes are still there on my desk. They at least are no dream!

That little Dorothy is a horror. This evening at dusk I was returning from a short walk. It was nearly dark, and for some reason the street lights had not yet been put on. I turned into the front walk, climbed up the steps, and had almost reached the house, when I banged full-force into her damned tricycle. I am afraid my anger ran away with me, for I deliberately gave it such a push that it bumped all the way down both flights of steps and ran out into the middle of the street. A truck coming down the hill finished it off in a somewhat spectacular fashion. When I got inside I found the child in the kitchen talking with Mrs. C. I did not mention the incident, but came directly upstairs.

It is a lovely evening. After dinner I am going to take all forty boxes to the woods behind the school and throw them on to the rubbish heap there. It's too childish a game to go on playing at my age. Let the kids have them.

The Frozen Fields

THE TRAIN was late because the hot-box under one of the coaches had caught fire in the middle of a great flat field covered with snow. They had stayed there about an hour. After the noise and rushing of the train, the sudden silence and the embarrassed stirring of people in their seats induced a general restlessness. At one point another train had shot by on the next track with a roar worse than thunder; in the wake of that, the nervousness of the passengers increased, and they began to talk fretfully in low voices.

Donald had started to scratch pictures with his fingernail in the ice that covered the lower part of the windowpane by his seat. His father had said: "Stop that." He knew better than to ask "Why?" but he thought it; he could not see what harm it would do, and he felt a little resentful toward his mother for not intervening. He could have arranged for her to object to the senseless prohibition, but experience had taught him that she could be counted on to come to his defense only a limited number of times during any given day, and it was imprudent to squander her reserve of good will.

The snow had been cleared from the station platform when they got out. It was bitter cold; a fat plume of steam trailed downward from the locomotive, partially enveloping the first coach. Donald's feet ached with the cold.

"There's Uncle Greg and Uncle Willis!" he cried, and he jumped up and down several times.

"You don't have to shout," said his father. "We see them. And stand still. Pick up your bag."

Uncle Willis wore a black bearskin coat that almost touched the ground. He put his hands under Donald's arms and lifted him up so that his head was at a level with his own, and kissed him hard on the mouth. Then he swung him over into Uncle Greg's arms, and Uncle Greg did the same thing. "How's the man, hey?" cried Uncle Greg, as he set him down.

"Fine," said Donald, conscious of a feeling of triumph, because his father did not like to see boys being kissed. "Men shake hands," he had told him. "They don't kiss each other."

The sky was crystal clear, and although it was already turning lavender with the passing of afternoon, it still shone with an intense light, like the sky in one scene at the Russian Ballet. His mother had taken him a few weeks earlier because she wanted to see Pavlova; it was not the dancing that had excited him, but the sudden direct contact with the world of magic. This was a magic sky above him now, nothing like the one he was used to seeing above the streets of New York. Everything connected with the farm was imbued with magic. The house was the nucleus of an enchanted world more real than the world that other people knew about. During the long green summers he had spent there with his mother and the members of her family he had discovered that world and explored it, and none of them had ever noticed that he was living in it. But his father's presence here would constitute a grave danger, because it was next to impossible to conceal anything from him, and once aware of the existence of the other world he would spare no pains to destroy it. Donald was not yet sure whether all the entrances were safely guarded or effectively camouflaged.

They sat in the back of the sleigh with a brown buffalo robe tucked around them. The two big gray horses were breathing out steam through their wide nostrils. Silently the white countryside moved past, its frozen trees pink in the late light. Uncle Greg held the reins, and Uncle Willis, sitting beside him, was turned sideways in his seat, talking to Donald's mother.

"My feet hurt," said Donald.

"Well, God Almighty, boy!" cried Uncle Willis. "Haven't you got 'em on the bricks? There are five hot bricks down there. That's what they're there for." He bent over and lifted up part of the heavy lap-robe. The bricks were wrapped in newspaper.

"My feet are like blocks of ice, too," said Donald's mother. "Here, take your shoes off and put your feet on these." She pushed two of the bricks toward Donald.

"He just wants attention," said Donald's father. But he did not forbid him to have the bricks.

"Is that better?" Uncle Willis asked a moment later.

"It feels good. How many miles is it to the farm?"

"Seven miles to The Corner, and a mile and a half from there."

"Oh, I know it's a mile and a half from The Corner," said Donald. He had walked it many times in the summer, and he knew the names of the farms along the road. "First you come to the Elders, then the Landons, then the Madisons——"

His father pushed him hard in the ribs with his elbow. "Just keep quiet for a while."

Uncle Willis pretended not to have heard this. "Well, well. You certainly have a good memory. How old are you now?"

Donald's throat had constricted; it was a familiar occurrence which did not at all mean that he was going to cry—merely that he felt like crying. He coughed and said in a stifled voice: "Six." Then he coughed again; ashamed, and fearful that Uncle Willis might have noticed something amiss, he added: "But I'll be seven the day after New Year's."

They were all silent after that; there were only the muffled rhythm of the horses' trot and the soft, sliding sound of the runners on the packed snow. The sky was now a little darker than the white meadows, and the woods on the hill-side beyond, with their millions of bare branches, began to look frightening. Donald was glad to be sitting in the middle. He knew there were no wolves out there, and yet, could anybody be really certain? There had been wolves at one time—and bears as well—and simply because nobody had seen one in many years, they now said there weren't any. But that was no proof.

They came to The Corner, where the road to the farm turned off from the main road. Seven rusty mail-boxes stood there in a crooked row, one for each house on the road.

"R. F. D. Number One," said Uncle Willis facetiously. This had always been a kind of joke among them, ever since they had bought the farm, because they were townspeople and thought the real farmers were very funny.

Now Donald felt he was on home ground, and it gave him the confidence to say: "Rural Free Delivery." He said the words carefully, since the first one sometimes gave him difficulty. But he pronounced it all right, and Uncle Greg, without turning round, shouted: "That's right! You go to school now?"

"Yes." He did not feel like saying more, because he was following the curves in the road, which he knew by heart. But everything looked so different from the way he remembered it that he found it hard to believe it was the same place. The land had lost its intimacy, become bare and unprotected. Even in the oncoming night he could see right through the leafless bushes that should have hidden the empty fields beyond. His feet were all right now, but his hands in their woolen mittens under the buffalo skin were numb with cold.

The farm came into view; in each downstairs window there was a lighted candle and a holly wreath. He bent over and put his shoes on. It was hard because his fingers ached. When he sat up again the sleigh had stopped. The kitchen door had opened; someone was coming out. Everyone was shouting "Hello!" and "Merry Christmas!" Between the sleigh and the kitchen he was aware only of being kissed and patted, lifted up and set down, and told that he had grown. His grandfather helped him take off his shoes again and removed a lid from the top of the stove so he could warm his hands over the flames. The kitchen smelled, as in summer, of woodsmoke, sour milk and kerosene.

It was always very exciting to be in the midst of many people. Each one was an added protection against the constant watchfulness of his mother and father. At home there were only he and they, so that mealtimes were periods of torture. Tonight there were eight at the supper table. They put an enormous old leather-bound dictionary in a chair so he would be high enough, and he sat between his grandmother and Aunt Emilie. She had dark brown eyes and was very pretty. Uncle Greg had married her a year ago, and Donald knew from many overheard conversations that none of the others really liked her.

Gramma was saying: "Louisa and Ivor couldn't get down till tomorrow. Mr. Gordon's driving them down as far as Portersville in his car. They'll all stay in the hotel tonight, and we've got to go in first thing in the morning and bring them out."

"Mr. Gordon, too, I suppose," said his mother.

"Oh, probably," Uncle Greg said. "He won't want to stay alone Christmas Day."

His mother looked annoyed. "It seems sort of unnecessary," she said. "Christmas is a *family* day, after all."

"Well, he's part of the family now," said Uncle Willis with a crooked smile.

His mother replied with great feeling: "I think it's terrible."

"He's pretty bad these days," put in Grampa, shaking his head.

"Still on the old fire-water?" asked his father.

Uncle Greg raised his eyebrows. "That and worse. You know. . . . And Ivor too."

Donald knew they were being mysterious because of him. He pretended not to be listening, and busied himself making marks on the tablecloth with his napkin ring.

His father's mouth had fallen open with astonishment. "Where do they get it?" he demanded.

"Prescription," said Uncle Willis lightly. "Some crooked Polack doctor up there."

"Oh, honestly," cried his mother. "I don't see how Louisa *stands* it."

Aunt Emilie, who had been quiet until now, suddenly spoke. "Oh, I don't know," she said speculatively. "They're both very good to her. I think Mr. Gordon's very generous. *He* pays the rent on her apartment, you know, and gives her the use of the car and chauffeur most afternoons."

"You don't know anything about it," said Uncle Greg in a gruff, unpleasant voice which was meant to stop her from talking. But she went on, a bit shrilly, and even Donald could hear that they were in the habit of arguing.

"I *do* happen to know that Ivor's perfectly willing to give her a divorce any time she wants it, because she told me so herself."

There was silence at the table; Donald was certain that if he had not been there they would all have begun to talk at that point. Aunt Emilie had said something he was not supposed to hear.

"Well," said Uncle Willis heartily, "how about another piece of cake, Donald, old man?"

"How about bed, you mean," said his father. "It's time he went to bed."

His mother said nothing, helped him from his chair and took him upstairs.

The little panes of his bedroom window were completely covered with ice. Opening his mouth, he breathed on one pane until a round hole had been melted through and he could see blackness outside. "Don't do that, dear," said his mother. "Gramma'll have to clean the window. Now come on; into bed with you. There's a nice hot brick under the covers so your feet won't get cold." She tucked the blankets around him, kissed him, and took the lamp from the table. His father's voice, annoyed, came up from the foot of the stairs. "Hey, Laura! What's going on up there? Come on."

"Won't there be any light in my room at all?" Donald asked her.

"I'm coming," she called. She looked down at Donald. "You never have a light at home."

"I know, but home I can turn it on if I need it."

"Well, you're not going to need it tonight. Your father would have a fit if I left the lamp. You know that. Now just go to sleep."

"But I won't be able to sleep," he said miserably.

"Laura!" shouted his father.

"Just a *minute*!" she cried, vexed.

"Please, Mother. . . ?"

Her voice was adamant. "This cold air will put you to sleep in two shakes of a lamb's tail. Now go to sleep." She went to the doorway, the lamp in her hand, and disappeared through it, closing the door behind her.

There was a little china clock on the table that ticked very loud and fast. At infrequent intervals from below came a muffled burst of laughter which immediately subsided. His mother had said: "I'll open this window about an inch; that'll be enough." The room was growing colder by the minute. He pushed the sole of one foot against the heated brick in the middle of the bed, and heard the crackle of the newspaper that enfolded it. There was nothing left to do but go to sleep. On his way through the borderlands of consciousness he had a fantasy. From the mountain behind the farm, running silently over the icy crust of the snow, leaping over the rocks

and bushes, came a wolf. He was running toward the farm.
When he got there he would look through the windows
until he found the dining-room where the grownups were sitting around the big table. Donald shuddered when he saw his
eyes in the dark through the glass. And now, calculating every
movement perfectly, the wolf sprang, smashing the panes, and
seized Donald's father by the throat. In an instant, before
anyone could move or cry out, he was gone again with his
prey still between his jaws, his head turned sideways as he
dragged the limp form swiftly over the surface of the snow.

The white light of dawn was in the room when he opened
his eyes. Already there were bumpings in the bowels of the
house: people were stirring. He heard a window slammed
shut, and then the regular sound of someone splitting wood
with a hatchet. Presently there were nearer noises, and he
knew that his parents in the next room had gotten up. Then
his door was flung open and his mother came in, wearing a
thick brown flannel bathrobe, and with her hair falling loose
down her back. "Merry Christmas!" she cried, holding up a
gigantic red mesh stocking crammed with fruit and small
packages. "Look what I found hanging by the fireplace!" He
was disappointed because he had hoped to go and get his
stocking himself. "I brought it up to you because the house
is as cold as a barn," she told him. "You stay put right here in
bed till it's warmed up a little."

"When'll we have the tree?" The important ritual was the
tree: the most interesting presents were piled under it.

"You just hold your horses," she told him. "You've got
your stocking. We can't have the tree till Aunt Louisa gets
here. You wouldn't want her to miss it, would you?"

"Where's my present for Aunt Louisa and Uncle Ivor?
Uncle Ivor's coming, too, isn't he?"

"Of course he's coming," she replied, with that faintly different way of speaking she used when she mentioned Uncle
Ivor. "I've already put it under the tree with the other things.
Now you just stay where you are, all covered up, and look at
your stocking. I'm going to get dressed." She shivered and
hurried back into her room.

The only person he had to thank at breakfast was his grandfather, for a box of colored pencils which had been jammed

into the foot of the stocking. The other gifts had been tagged: "For Donald from Santa." Uncle Willis and Uncle Greg had eaten an early breakfast and gone in the sleigh to the hotel in Portersville to fetch Aunt Louisa and Uncle Ivor. When they got back, Donald ran to the window and saw that Mr. Gordon had come. Everyone had talked so mysteriously about Mr. Gordon that he was very eager to see him. But at that moment his mother called him upstairs to help her make the beds. "We all have to do as much as we can for Gramma," she told him. "Lord knows she's got all she can manage with the kitchen work."

But eventually he heard Aunt Louisa calling up the staircase. They went down: he was smothered in kisses, and Aunt Louisa asked him: "How's my boy? You're *my* boy, aren't you?" Then Uncle Ivor kissed him, and he shook hands with Mr. Gordon, who was already sitting in Grampa's armchair, where nobody else ever sat. He was plump and pale, and he wore two big diamond rings on one hand and an even bigger sapphire on the other. As he breathed he wheezed slightly; now and then he pulled an enormous yellow silk handkerchief out of his breast pocket and wiped his forehead with it. Donald sat down on the other side of the room and turned the pages of a magazine, from time to time looking up to observe him. He had called Donald "my lad," which sounded very strange, like someone talking in a book. At one point he noticed Donald's attention, and beckoned to him. Donald went and stood beside the armchair while Mr. Gordon reached into his pocket and pulled out a fat watch with a little button near the stem. "Push it," he said. Donald pushed the button, and tiny chimes struck inside the watch. A few minutes later he signaled to him afresh; Donald bounded over to him and pressed the button again. The next time, his mother told him to stop bothering Mr. Gordon.

"But he *asked* me to," objected Donald.

"Sit down right there. We're all going in and have our tree in a little while. Uncle Ivor's going to be Santa Claus."

Presently Uncle Willis came into the room. "Well, everybody," he said, rubbing his hands together, "I think the parlor's warm enough now. How about our tree?"

"It's about time," said Aunt Emilie. She was wearing a red

taffeta dress which Donald had heard his mother discussing with his father earlier. "*Most* inappropriate," she had said. "The girl doesn't seem to realize she's living on a farm." Aunt Emilie reached down and took Donald's hand. "Would you care to accompany me, sir?" she said. They walked into the parlor holding hands. The fire in the fireplace roared and crackled.

"Where's Ivor?" said Uncle Greg. "Has everybody got a seat?"

"Here he is," said Uncle Ivor, coming in from the hallway. He had put on an old red knitted skull-cap and a red dressing gown, and he had a wreath of green fluted paper around his neck. "This is all Santa Claus could find," he announced.

Aunt Louisa began to laugh. "Look at your Uncle Ivor," she told Donald. "I am," said Donald. But he was really looking at the tree. It was a tall hemlock that reached to the ceiling, and underneath it was piled the most enormous assortment of packages he had ever seen. "Look at that!" they all cried.

"What *do* you suppose is in them all?" said Aunt Louisa.

"I don't know," he replied.

Uncle Ivor sat down on the floor as near the tree as he could get, and lifting up a large crate he passed it to Uncle Greg, who stood in the middle of the room. "Let's get this out of the way first," he said. Then Uncle Greg intoned: "To Donald from the Folks at Rutland."

While Uncle Ivor went on passing out packages, Donald struggled with his box. He was vaguely aware of the little cries that were being uttered around him: "How lovely! But it's too much!" "Oh, you shouldn't have!" "Why did you do it?" as the others opened their gifts, but he was too preoccupied to notice that most of the exclamations were being addressed to Mr. Gordon, who sat in the window looking very pleased.

It was too good to believe: a fire engine three feet long, with rubber tires and a bell and a siren and three ladders that shot upward automatically when it stopped. Donald looked at it, and for a moment was almost frightened by the power he knew it had to change his world.

"Oh . . . isn't . . . that . . . lovely!" said his mother, her annoyance giving a sharp edge to each word. "Louisa, why did you do it?" Donald glanced up quickly and saw Aunt Louisa indicate Mr. Gordon with a jerk of her head, as if she were saying: "Everything is his fault."

His mother moved along the floor towards the crate and fished out the greeting card. "I want you to keep each card in with the present it came with," she told Donald, "because you'll have a lot of thank-you notes to write tomorrow, and you don't want to get them mixed up. But you can thank Aunt Louisa and Uncle Ivor right now."

He hated to be told to thank a person in that person's presence, as though he were a baby. But he said the words bravely, facing Mr. Gordon: "Thank you so much for the beautiful fire engine."

"There's more there, my lad," beamed Mr. Gordon; the diamonds flashed in the sunlight.

Aunt Emilie was holding out her arm in front of her, looking at her new wrist-watch. Grampa had put on a black silk dressing gown and was smoking a cigar. He looked perfectly content as he turned to Mr. Gordon and said: "Well, you've spoiled us all." But Donald's mother interpreted his phrase as a reproach, and added in explanation: "We're not used to getting such *elaborate* gifts, Mr. Gordon."

Mr. Gordon laughed, and turning to Donald, told him: "You've barely started, my lad. Tell your Uncle Ivor to get on with it."

Now it seemed as though nearly every package was for Donald. He opened them as fast as he could, and was freshly bewildered by the apparition of each new marvel. There were, of course, the handkerchiefs and books and mufflers from the family, but there was also a Swiss music box with little metal records that could be changed; there were roller skates, a large set of lead soldiers, a real accordion, and a toy village with a streetcar system that ran on a battery. As Donald opened each package, the little cries of admiration made by his parents came closer to sounding like groans. Finally his father said, in a voice loud enough for Mr. Gordon to hear him above the general conversation: "It's bad business for one kid to get so much."

Mr. Gordon had heard him. "You were young once yourself," he said airily.

Aunt Emilie was trying on a fur jacket that Uncle Greg had given her. Her face was flushed with excitement; she had just planted a big kiss on Uncle Greg's cheek.

"The little Astor baby got five thousand dollars' worth of toys on its last birthday," she said to Donald's father, running her hand back and forth along the fur.

Donald's father looked at her with narrowed eyes. "That," he said, enunciating very clearly, "is what might be called an *asinine* remark."

Save for the crackling of the fire there was silence for a moment in the room. Those who had not heard knew that something had happened. Uncle Greg looked quickly at Donald's father, and then at Aunt Emilie. Maybe there would be a quarrel, thought Donald, with everyone against his father. The idea delighted him; at the same time he felt guilty, as though it were his doing.

Uncle Ivor was handing him a package. Automatically he untied the ribbon, and pulled out a tan cashmere sweater. "That's Mother's and Daddy's present to you," his mother said quietly. "It's a little big for you now, but I got it big purposely so you could grow into it." The small crisis had passed; they all began to talk again. Donald was relieved and disappointed. "How about christening that bottle of brandy?" cried Uncle Willis.

"You menfolk sit here," Gramma told them. "We've got to to get out into the kitchen."

"I'll bring yours out to you," said Uncle Ivor to Aunt Louisa as she got up.

On her way out of the room Donald's mother bent over and touched his shoulder. "I want you to put every present back into its box just the way it was. After that you carry them all up into our room and stack them carefully in the corner under the window. You hear me?"

She went out. Donald sat a moment; then he jumped up and ran after her to ask if he might save out just one thing—the fire engine, perhaps. She was saying to Gramma: ". . . quite uncalled for. Besides, I don't know how we're *ever* going to get it all back to New York. Owen can take the big things at least with him tomorrow, I suppose."

He stopped running, and felt peace descend upon him. His

father was leaving the farm. Then let him take everything with him, fire engine and all; it would not matter. He turned and went back into the parlor, where he meticulously packed the toys into their boxes, put the covers on, and tied them up with lengths of ribbon and string.

"What's all this?" exclaimed Mr. Gordon suddenly, noticing him. "What are you doing?"

"I have to take everything upstairs," said Donald.

His father joined the conversation. "I don't want to find those boxes lying all over the place up there, either. See that you pile 'em neatly. Understand?"

Donald continued to work without looking up.

After a moment Mr. Gordon said under his breath: "Well, I'll be damned." Then to Donald's father: "I've seen some well-behaved kids in my time, but I don't mind telling you I never saw one like *that*. Never."

"Discipline begins in the cradle," said his father shortly.

"It's sinister," murmured Mr. Gordon to himself.

Donald glanced up and saw his father looking at Mr. Gordon with hatred.

In the kitchen his grandmother, his aunts and his mother were busy preparing dinner. Donald sat by the window mashing potatoes. The blue of the sky had disappeared behind one curtain of cloud, uniformly white. "We'll have more snow before night," said Gramma, looking out of the window above the sink.

"Want to smell something good?" Donald's mother asked him. He ran across to the stove and she opened the oven door: the aroma of onions mingled with that of the roasting turkey. "He's coming along beautifully," she announced. She shut the oven door with a bang and hung the pot-holders on their hooks. Then she went into the pantry. Donald followed her. It was very cold in here, and it smelled of pickles and spices. His mother was searching for something along the shelves, among the jars and tin boxes.

"Mother," he said.

"Hmm?" she replied distraughtly, without looking down at him.

"Why does Mr. Gordon live at Uncle Ivor's?"

Now she did look at him, and with an intensity that startled

him. "What was that?" she demanded sharply. Then, before
he could repeat his question, she went on in a suddenly matter-of-fact voice: "Dear, don't you know that Uncle Ivor's
what they call a male nurse? Like Miss Oliver, you remember,
who took care of you when you had influenza? Only a man.
A man nurse."

"Is Mr. Gordon sick?"

"Yes, he is," she said, lowering her voice to little more than
a whisper. "He's a very sick man, but we don't talk about it."

"What's he got?" He was conscious of being purposely
childish at the moment, in the hope of learning more. But
his mother was already saying: "I don't know, dear. You go
back into the kitchen now. It's too cold for you in here.
Scoot! Out with you!" He giggled, ran back into the kitchen,
satisfied for having definitely established the existence of a
mystery.

During dinner his father looked across at him and, with the
particular kind of sternness he reserved for remarks which he
knew were unwelcome, said: "You haven't been outside yet
today, young man. We'll take a walk down the road later."

Aunt Louisa had brought a large glass of brandy to the
table with her, and was sipping it along with her food. "It's
too cold, Owen," she objected. "He'll catch his death o'
cold." Donald knew she was trying to help him, but he
wished she had kept quiet. If it became an issue, his father
would certainly not forget about the walk.

"Too cold!" scoffed his father. "We have a few basic rules
in *our* little family, and one of them is that he has to get some
fresh air every day."

"Couldn't you make an exception for Christmas? Just for
one day?" demanded Aunt Louisa.

Donald did not dare look up, for fear of seeing the expression on his father's face.

"Listen, Louisa," he said acidly. "I suggest you just stay on
your side of the fence, and I'll stay on mine. We'll get along
a lot better." Then as an afterthought he snapped: "That all
right with you?"

Aunt Louisa leaned across Grampa's plate toward Donald's
father and spoke very loud, so that everyone stopped eating.
"No, it's not all right with me!" she cried. "All you do is pick

on the child from morning till night. It's shameful! I won't sit by and watch my own flesh and blood plagued that way!"

Both Gramma and Donald's father began to speak at once. Gramma was saying, "Louisa," trying to soothe her. Donald's father shouted: "You've never *had* a kid. You don't know the first thing *about* raising kids."

"I know when a man's selfish and plain cussed," Aunt Louisa declared.

"Louisa!" cried Gramma in a tone of surprise and mild reproof. Donald continued to look at his plate.

"Have I ever come up to Rutland and stuck my nose in your affairs and criticized? Have I?" demanded Donald's father.

"Now come on," said Uncle Willis quickly. "Let's not spoil a beautiful Christmas."

"That's right," Grampa said. "We're all happy. Let's not say anything we'll be sorry for later."

But Aunt Louisa would not retreat. She took a fast gulp of brandy and almost choked on it. Then, still leaning toward Donald's father, she went on: "What do you mean, come to Rutland and criticize? What've you got to criticize in Rutland? Something wrong there?"

For an instant Donald's father did not reply. During that instant it was as though everyone felt the need to say something without being able to say it. The one who broke the short silence was Donald's father, using a peculiar, soft voice which Donald recognized immediately as a vicious imitation of Uncle Ivor. "Oh, *no!* There's nothing wrong in *Rut*land!"

Suddenly, with two simultaneous motions, Donald's mother slapped her napkin into her plate and pushed her chair back violently. She rose and ran out of the room, slamming the door. No one said anything. Donald sat frozen, unable to look up, unable even to breathe. Then he realized that his father had got up, too, and was on his way out.

"Leave her alone, Owen," said Gramma.

"You keep out of this," his father said. His footsteps made the stairs creak as he went up. No one said anything until Gramma made as if to rise. "I'm going up," she declared.

"For God's sake, Abbie, sit still," Grampa told her. Gramma cleared her throat, but did not get up.

Aunt Louisa looked very red, and the muscles of her face

were twitching. "Hateful," she said in a choked voice. "Just hateful."

"I felt like slapping his face," confided Aunt Emilie. "Did you hear what he said to me when we were having our presents?"

At a glance from Uncle Greg, Aunt Emilie stopped. "Why, Donald!" she exclaimed brightly, "you've scarcely touched your dinner! Aren't you hungry?"

In his mind's eye he was seeing the bedroom upstairs, where his father was twisting his mother's arm and shaking her to make her look at him. When she wouldn't, he punched her, knocking her down, and kicked her as hard as he could, all over her body. Donald looked up. "Not very," he said.

Without warning Mr. Gordon began to talk, holding his glass in front of him and examining it as he turned it this way and that. "Family quarrels," he sighed. "Same old thing. Reminds me of my boyhood. When I look back on it, it seems to me we never got through a meal without a fight, but I suppose we must have once in a while." He set the glass down. "Well, they're all dead now, thank God."

Donald looked quickly across at Mr. Gordon as if he were seeing him for the first time.

"It's snowing!" cried Gramma triumphantly. "Look, it's snowing again. I knew we'd have more snow before dark." She did not want Mr. Gordon to go on talking.

Aunt Louisa sobbed once, got up, and went out into the kitchen. Uncle Ivor followed her.

"Why, Donald! You've got the wishbone!" cried Aunt Emilie. "Eat the meat off it and we'll hang it up over the stove to dry, and tomorrow we'll wish on it. Wouldn't that be fun?"

He picked it up in his fingers and began to chew on the strips of white meat that clung to it. When he had carefully cleaned it, he got down and went out into the kitchen with it.

The room was very quiet; the tea-kettle simmered on the stove. Outside the window the falling snowflakes looked dark against the whiteness beyond. Aunt Louisa was sitting on the high stool, doubled over, with a crumpled handkerchief in her hand, and Uncle Ivor was bending over her talking in a very low voice. Donald laid the wishbone on the sink shelf and started to tiptoe out, but Uncle Ivor saw him. "How'd you like to go up to the henhouse with me, Donald?" he said. "I've got to find us a dozen eggs to take back to Rutland."

"I'll get my coat," Donald told him, eager to go out before his father came back downstairs.

The path up the hill to the henhouse had been made not by clearing the snow away, but by tramping it down. The new snow was drifting over the track; in some places it already had covered it. When Uncle Ivor went into the henhouse Donald stood still, bending his head back to catch some snowflakes in his mouth. "Come on in and shut the door. You'll let all the heat out," Uncle Ivor told him.

"I'm coming," said Donald. He stepped through the doorway and closed the door. The smell inside was very strong. As Uncle Ivor approached the hens, they set up a low, distrustful murmur.

"Tell me, Donald," said Uncle Ivor as he explored the straw with his hands. "What?" said Donald.

"Does your mother often run to her room and shut the door, the way she did just now?"

"Sometimes."

"Why? Is your father mean to her?"

"Oh," said Donald vaguely, "they have fights." He felt uncomfortable.

"Yes. Well, it's a great pity your father ever got married. It would have been better for everybody if he'd stayed single."

"But then I wouldn't have been born at all," cried Donald, uncertain whether Uncle Ivor was serious or not.

"At least, we *hope* not!" said Uncle Ivor, rolling his eyes and looking silly. Now Donald knew it was a kind of joke, and he laughed. The door was flung open. "Donald!" roared his father.

"What is it?" he said, his voice very feeble.

"Come out here!"

He stumbled toward the door; his father was peering inside uncertainly. "What are you doing in there?" he demanded.

"Helping Uncle Ivor look for eggs."

"Hmmph!" Donald stepped out and his father shut the door.

They started to walk along the road in the direction of the Smithson farm. Presently his father fell in behind him and prodded him in the back, saying: "Keep your head up. Chest out! D'you want to get round-shouldered? Before you know it you'll have curvature of the spine."

When they had got out of sight of the house, in a place where the tangle of small trees came to the edge of the road on both sides, his father stopped walking. He looked around, reached down, picked up a handful of the new snow, and rolled it into a hard ball. Then he threw it at a fairly large tree, some distance from the road. It broke, leaving a white mark on the dark trunk. "Let's see you hit it," he told Donald.

A wolf could be waiting here, somewhere back in the still gloom of the woods. It was very important not to make him angry. If his father wanted to take a chance and throw snowballs into the woods, he could, but Donald would not. Then perhaps the wolf would understand that he, at least, was his friend.

"Go on," said his father.

"No. I don't want to."

With mock astonishment his father said: "Oh, you don't?" Then his face became dangerous and his voice cracked like a whip. "Are you going to do what I told you?"

"No." It was the first time he had openly defied him. His father turned very red.

"Listen here, you young whippersnapper!" he cried, his voice tight with anger. "You think you're going to get away with this?" Before Donald knew what was happening, his father had seized him with one hand while he bent over and with the other scooped up as much snow as he could. "We'll settle this little matter right now," he said through his teeth. Suddenly he was rubbing the snow violently over Donald's face, and at the same time that Donald gasped and squirmed, he pushed what was left of it down his neck. As he felt the wet, icy mass sliding down his back, he doubled over. His eyes were squeezed shut; he was certain his father was trying to kill him. With a desperate lunge he bounded free and fell face-downward into the snow.

"Get up," his father said disgustedly. He did not move. If he held his breath long enough he might die.

His father yanked him to his feet. "I've had just about enough of your monkeyshines," he said. Clutching him tightly with both hands, he forced him to hobble ahead of him, back through the twilight to the house.

Donald moved forward, looking at the white road in front of him, his mind empty of thoughts. An unfamiliar feeling had come to him: he was not sorry for himself for being wet and cold, or even resentful at having been mistreated. He felt detached; it was an agreeable, almost voluptuous sensation which he accepted without understanding or questioning it.

As they advanced down the long alley of maple trees in the dusk his father said: "Now you can go and cry in your mother's lap."

"I'm not crying," said Donald loudly, without expression. His father did not answer.

Fortunately the kitchen was empty. He could tell from the sound of the voices in the parlor that Aunt Louisa, Uncle Ivor and Mr. Gordon were getting ready to leave. He ran upstairs to his room and changed his clothes completely. The hole he had breathed in the ice on the windowpane had frozen over thickly again, but the round mark was still visible. As he finished dressing his mother called him. It was completely dark outside. He went downstairs. She was standing in the hallway.

"Oh, you've changed your clothes," she said. "Come out and say good-by to Aunt Louisa and Uncle Ivor. They're in the kitchen." He looked quickly at her face to see if there were signs of her recent tears: her eyes were slightly bloodshot.

Together they went into the kitchen. "Donald wants to say good-by to you," she told Mr. Gordon, steering Donald to Aunt Louisa. "You've given him a wonderful Christmas"— her voice became reproachful—"but it was *much* too much."

The thick beaver collar of Mr. Gordon's overcoat was turned up over his ears, and he had on enormous fur gloves. He smiled and clapped his hands together expectantly; it made a cushioned sound. "Oh, it was a lot of fun," he said. "He reminds me a little of myself, you know, when I was his age. I was a sort of shy and quiet lad, too." Donald felt his mother's hand tighten on his shoulder as she pushed him toward Aunt Louisa. "Mm," she said. "Well, Auntie Louisa, here's somebody who wants to say good-by to you."

Even in the excitement of watching Uncle Willis and Uncle

Greg drive the others off in the sleigh, Donald did not miss the fact that his father had not appeared in the kitchen at all. When the sleigh had moved out of sight down the dark road, everyone went into the parlor and Grampa put another log on the fire.

"Where's Owen?" Gramma said in a low voice to Donald's mother.

"He must be upstairs. To tell the truth, I don't care very much where he is."

"Poor child," said Gramma. "Headache a little better?"

"A little." She sighed. "He certainly managed to take all the pleasure out of *my* Christmas."

"A mean shame," said Gramma.

"It was all I could do to look Ivor in the face just now. I mean it."

"I'm sure they all understood," said Gramma soothingly. "Just don't you fret about it. Anyway, Owen'll be gone to-morrow, and you can rest up."

Shortly after Uncle Willis and Uncle Greg got back, Donald's father came downstairs. Supper was eaten in almost complete silence; at no time did his father speak to him or pay him any attention. As soon as the meal was over his mother took him upstairs to bed.

When she had left him, he lay in the dark listening to the sound of the fine snow as the wind drove it against the panes. The wolf was out there in the night, running along paths that no one had ever seen, down the hill and across the meadow, stopping to drink at a deep place in the brook where the ice had not formed. The stiff hairs of his coat had caught the snow; he shook himself and climbed up the bank to where Donald sat waiting for him. Then he lay down beside him, putting his heavy head in Donald's lap. Donald leaned over and buried his face in the shaggy fur of his scruff. After a while they both got up and began to run together, faster and faster, across the fields.

THINGS GONE AND
THINGS STILL HERE

TABLE OF CONTENTS

Allal

H E WAS born in the hotel where his mother worked. The
hotel had only three dark rooms which gave on a courtyard behind the bar. Beyond was another smaller patio with
many doors. This was where the servants lived, and where
Allal spent his childhood.

The Greek who owned the hotel had sent Allal's mother
away. He was indignant because she, a girl of fourteen, had
dared to give birth while she was working for him. She would
not say who the father was, and it angered him to reflect that
he himself had not taken advantage of the situation while he
had had the chance. He gave the girl three months' wages
and told her to go home to Marrakech. Since the cook and
his wife liked the girl and offered to let her live with them for
a while, he agreed that she might stay on until the baby was
big enough to travel. She remained in the back patio for a few
months with the cook and his wife, and then one day she disappeared, leaving the baby behind. No one heard of her
again.

As soon as Allal was old enough to carry things, they set
him to work. It was not long before he could fetch a pail of
water from the well behind the hotel. The cook and his wife
were childless, so that he played alone.

When he was somewhat older he began to wander over the
empty table-land outside. There was nothing else up here but
the barracks, and they were enclosed by a high blind wall of
red adobe. Everything else was below in the valley: the town,
the gardens, and the river winding southward among the
thousands of palm trees. He could sit on a point of rock far
above and look down at the people walking in the alleys of
the town. It was only later that he visited the place and saw
what the inhabitants were like. Because he had been left behind by his mother they called him a son of sin, and laughed
when they looked at him. It seemed to him that in this way
they hoped to make him into a shadow, in order not to have
to think of him as real and alive. He awaited with dread the
time when he would have to go each morning to the town

and work. For the moment he helped in the kitchen and served the officers from the barracks, along with the few motorists who passed through the region. He got small tips in the restaurant, and free food and lodging in a cell of the servants' quarters, but the Greek gave him no wages. Eventually he reached an age when this situation seemed shameful, and he went of his own accord to the town below and began to work, along with other boys of his age, helping to make the mud bricks people used for building their houses.

Living in the town was much as he had imagined it would be. For two years he stayed in a room behind a blacksmith's shop, leading a life without quarrels, and saving whatever money he did not have to spend to keep himself alive. Far from making any friends during this time, he formed a thorough hatred for the people of the town, who never allowed him to forget that he was a son of sin, and therefore not like others, but *meskhot*—damned. Then he found a small house, not much more than a hut, in the palm groves outside the town. The rent was low and no one lived nearby. He went to live there, where the only sound was the wind in the trees, and avoided the people of the town when he could.

One hot summer evening shortly after sunset he was walking under the arcades that faced the town's main square. A few paces ahead of him an old man in a white turban was trying to shift a heavy sack from one shoulder to the other. Suddenly it fell to the ground, and Allal stared as two long dark forms flowed out of it and disappeared into the shadows. The old man pounced upon the sack and fastened the top of it, at the same time beginning to shout: Look out for the snakes! Help me find my snakes!

Many people turned quickly around and walked back the way they had come. Others stood at some distance, watching. A few called to the old man: Find your snakes fast and get them out of here! Why are they here? We don't want snakes in this town!

Hopping up and down in his anxiety, the old man turned to Allal. Watch this for me a minute, my son. He pointed at the sack lying on the earth at his feet, and snatching up a basket he had been carrying, went swiftly around the corner into an alley. Allal stood where he was. No one passed by.

It was not long before the old man returned, panting with triumph. When the onlookers in the square saw him again, they began to call out, this time to Allal: Show that berrani the way out of the town! He has no right to carry those things in here. Out! Out!

Allal picked up the big sack and said to the old man: Come on.

They left the square and went through the alleys until they were at the edge of town. The old man looked up then, saw the palm trees black against the fading sky ahead, and turned to the boy beside him.

Come on, said Allal again, and he went to the left along the rough path that led to his house. The old man stood perplexed.

You can stay with me tonight, Allal told him.

And these? he said, pointing first at the sack and then at the basket. They have to be with me.

Allal grinned. They can come.

When they were sitting in the house Allal looked at the sack and the basket. I'm not like the rest of them here, he said.

It made him feel good to hear the words being spoken. He made a contemptuous gesture. Afraid to walk through the square because of a snake. You saw them.

The old man scratched his chin. Snakes are like people, he said. You have to get to know them. Then you can be their friends.

Allal hesitated before he asked: Do you ever let them out?

Always, the old man said with energy. It's bad for them to be inside like this. They've got to be healthy when they get to Taroudant, or the man there won't buy them.

He began a long story about his life as a hunter of snakes, explaining that each year he made a voyage to Taroudant to see a man who bought them for the Aissaoua snake-charmers in Marrakech. Allal made tea while he listened, and brought out a bowl of kif paste to eat with the tea. Later, when they were sitting comfortably in the midst of the pipe-smoke, the old man chuckled. Allal turned to look at him.

Shall I let them out?

Fine!

But you must sit still and keep quiet. Move the lamp nearer.

He untied the sack, shook it a bit, and returned to where he had been sitting. Then in silence Allal watched the long bodies move cautiously out into the light. Among the cobras were others with markings so delicate and perfect that they seemed to have been designed and painted by an artist. One reddish-gold serpent, which coiled itself lazily in the middle of the floor, he found particularly beautiful. As he stared at it, he felt a great desire to own it and have it always with him.

The old man was talking. I've spent my whole life with snakes, he said. I could tell you some things about them. Did you know that if you give them majoun you can make them do what you want, and without saying a word? I swear by Allah!

Allal's face assumed a doubtful air. He did not question the truth of the other's statement, but rather the likelihood of his being able to put the knowledge to use. For it was at that moment that the idea of actually taking the snake first came into his head. He was thinking that whatever he was to do must be done quickly, for the old man would be leaving in the morning. Suddenly he felt a great impatience.

Put them away so I can cook dinner, he whispered. Then he sat admiring the ease with which the old man picked up each one by its head and slipped it into the sack. Once again he dropped two of the snakes into the basket, and one of these, Allal noted, was the red one. He imagined he could see the shining of its scales through the lid of the basket.

As he set to work preparing the meal Allal tried to think of other things. Then, since the snake remained in his mind in spite of everything, he began to devise a way of getting it. While he squatted over the fire in a corner, he mixed some kif paste in a bowl of milk and set it aside.

The old man continued to talk. That was good luck, getting the two snakes back like that, in the middle of the town. You can never be sure what people are going to do when they find out you're carrying snakes. Once in El Kelaa they took all of them and killed them, one after the other, in front of me. A year's work. I had to go back home and start all over again.

Even as they ate, Allal saw that his guest was growing sleepy. How will things happen? he wondered. There was no way of knowing beforehand precisely what he was going to do, and the prospect of having to handle the snake worried him. It could kill me, he thought.

Once they had eaten, drunk tea and smoked a few pipes of kif, the old man lay back on the floor and said he was going to sleep. Allal sprang up. In here! he told him, and led him to his own mat in an alcove. The old man lay down and swiftly fell asleep.

Several times during the next half hour Allal went to the alcove and peered in, but neither the body in its burnous nor the head in its turban had stirred.

First he got out his blanket, and after tying three of its corners together, spread it on the floor with the fourth corner facing the basket. Then he set the bowl of milk and kif paste on the blanket. As he loosened the strap from the cover of the basket the old man coughed. Allal stood immobile, waiting to hear the cracked voice speak. A small breeze had sprung up, making the palm branches rasp one against the other, but there was no further sound from the alcove. He crept to the far side of the room and squatted by the wall, his gaze fixed on the basket.

Several times he thought he saw the cover move slightly, but each time he decided he had been mistaken. Then he caught his breath. The shadow along the base of the basket was moving. One of the creatures had crept out from the far side. It waited for a while before continuing into the light, but when it did, Allal breathed a prayer of thanks. It was the red and gold one.

When finally it decided to go to the bowl, it made a complete tour around the edge, looking in from all sides, before lowering its head toward the milk. Allal watched, fearful that the foreign flavor of the kif paste might repel it. The snake remained there without moving.

He waited a half hour or more. The snake stayed where it was, its head in the bowl. From time to time Allal glanced at the basket, to be certain that the second snake was still in it. The breeze went on, rubbing the palm branches together. When he decided it was time, he rose slowly, and keeping an eye on the basket where apparently the other snake still slept, he reached over and gathered together the three tied corners of the blanket. Then he lifted the fourth corner, so that both the snake and the bowl slid to the bottom of the improvised sack. The snake moved slightly, but he did not think it was angry. He knew exactly where he would hide it: between some rocks in the dry river bed.

Holding the blanket in front of him he opened the door and stepped out under the stars. It was not far up the road, to a group of high palms, and then to the left down into the oued. There was a space between the boulders where the bundle would be invisible. He pushed it in with care, and hurried back to the house. The old man was asleep.

There was no way of being sure that the other snake was still in the basket, so Allal picked up his burnous and went outside. He shut the door and lay down on the ground to sleep.

Before the sun was in the sky the old man was awake, lying in the alcove coughing. Allal jumped up, went inside, and began to make a fire in the mijmah. A minute later he heard the other exclaim: They're loose again! Out of the basket! Stay where you are and I'll find them.

It was not long before the old man grunted with satisfaction. I have the black one! he cried. Allal did not look up from the corner where he crouched, and the old man came over, waving a cobra. Now I've got to find the other one.

He put the snake away and continued to search. When the fire was blazing, Allal turned and said: Do you want me to help you look for it?

No, no! Stay where you are.

Allal boiled the water and made the tea, and still the old man was crawling on his knees, lifting boxes and pushing sacks. His turban had slipped off and his face ran with sweat.

Come and have tea, Allal told him.

The old man did not seem to have heard him at first. Then he rose and went into the alcove, where he rewound his turban. When he came out he sat down with Allal, and they had breakfast.

Snakes are very clever, the old man said. They can get into places that don't exist. I've moved everything in this house.

After they had finished eating, they went outside and looked for the snake between the close-growing trunks of the palms near the house. When the old man was convinced that it was gone, he went sadly back in.

That was a good snake, he said at last. And now I'm going to Taroudant.

They said good-bye, and the old man took his sack and basket and started up the road toward the highway.

All day long as he worked, Allal thought of the snake, but it was not until sunset that he was able to go to the rocks in the oued and pull out the blanket. He carried it back to the house in a high state of excitement.

Before he untied the blanket, he filled a wide dish with milk and kif paste, and set it on the floor. He ate three spoonfuls of the paste himself and sat back to watch, drumming on the low wooden tea-table with his fingers. Everything happened just as he had hoped. The snake came slowly out of the blanket, and very soon had found the dish and was drinking the milk. As long as it drank he kept drumming; when it had finished and raised its head to look at him, he stopped, and it crawled back inside the blanket.

Later that evening he put down more milk, and drummed again on the table. After a time the snake's head appeared, and finally all of it, and the entire pattern of action was repeated.

That night and every night thereafter, Allal sat with the snake, while with infinite patience he sought to make it his friend. He never attempted to touch it, but soon he was able to summon it, keep it in front of him for as long as he pleased, merely by tapping on the table, and dismiss it at will. For the first week or so he used the kif paste; then he tried the routine without it. In the end the results were the same. After that he fed it only milk and eggs.

Then one evening as his friend lay gracefully coiled in front of him, he began to think of the old man, and formed an idea that put all other things out of his mind. There had not been any kif paste in the house for several weeks, and he decided to make some. He bought the ingredients the following day, and after work he prepared the paste. When it was done, he mixed a large amount of it in a bowl with milk and set it down for the snake. Then he himself ate four spoonfuls, washing them down with tea.

He quickly undressed, and moving the table so that he could reach it, stretched out naked on a mat near the door.

This time he continued to tap on the table, even after the snake had finished drinking the milk. It lay still, observing him, as if it were in doubt that the familiar drumming came from the brown body in front of it.

Seeing that even after a long time it remained where it was, staring at him with its stony yellow eyes, Allal began to say to it over and over: Come here. He knew it could not hear his voice, but he believed it could feel his mind as he urged it. You can make them do what you want, without saying a word, the old man had told him.

Although the snake did not move, he went on repeating his command, for by now he knew it was going to come. And after another long wait, all at once it lowered its head and began to move toward him. It reached his hip and slid along his leg. Then it climbed up his leg and lay for a time across his chest. Its body was heavy and tepid, its scales wonderfully smooth. After a time it came to rest, coiled in the space between his head and his shoulder.

By this time the kif paste had completely taken over Allal's mind. He lay in a state of pure delight, feeling the snake's head against his own, without a thought save that he and the snake were together. The patterns forming and melting behind his eyelids seemed to be the same ones that covered the snake's back. Now and then in a huge frenzied movement they all swirled up and shattered into fragments which swiftly became one great yellow eye, split through the middle by the narrow vertical pupil that pulsed with his own heartbeat. Then the eye would recede, through shifting shadow and sunlight, until only the designs of the scales were left, swarming with renewed insistence as they merged and separated. At last the eye returned, so huge this time that it had no edge around it, its pupil dilated to form an aperture almost wide enough for him to enter. As he stared at the blackness within, he understood that he was being slowly propelled toward the opening. He put out his hands to touch the polished surface of the eye on each side, and as he did this he felt the pull from within. He slid through the crack and was swallowed by darkness.

On awakening Allal felt that he had returned from somewhere far away. He opened his eyes and saw, very close to him, what looked like the flank of an enormous beast, covered with coarse stiff hair. There was a repeated vibration in the air, like distant thunder curling around the edges of the sky. He sighed, or imagined that he did, for his breath made no sound. Then he shifted his head a bit, to try and see beyond the mass of hairs beside him. Next he saw the ear, and he knew he was looking at his own head from the outside. He had not expected this; he had hoped only that his friend would come in and share his mind with him. But it did not strike him as being at all strange; he merely said to himself that now he was seeing through the eyes of the snake, rather than through his own.

Now he understood why the serpent had been so wary of him: from here the boy was a monstrous creature, with all the bristles on his head and his breathing that vibrated inside him like a far-off storm.

He uncoiled himself and glided across the floor to the alcove. There was a break in the mud wall wide enough to let him out. When he had pushed himself through, he lay full length on the ground in the crystalline moonlight, staring at the strangeness of the landscape, where shadows were not shadows.

He crawled around the side of the house and started up the road toward the town, rejoicing in a sense of freedom different from any he had ever imagined. There was no feeling of having a body, for he was perfectly contained in the skin that covered him. It was beautiful to caress the earth with the length of his belly as he moved along the silent road, smelling the sharp veins of wormwood in the wind. When the voice of the muezzin floated out over the countryside from the mosque, he could not hear it, or know that within the hour the night would end.

On catching sight of a man ahead, he left the road and hid behind a rock until the danger had passed. But then as he approached the town there began to be more people, so that he let himself down into the seguia, the deep ditch that went along beside the road. Here the stones and clumps of dead plants impeded his progress. He was still struggling along the floor of the seguia, pushing himself around the rocks and through the dry tangles of matted stalks left by the water, when dawn began to break.

The coming of daylight made him anxious and unhappy. He clambered up the bank of the seguia and raised his head to examine the road. A man walking past saw him, stood quite still, and then turned and ran back. Allal did not wait; he wanted now to get home as fast as possible.

Once he felt the thud of a stone as it struck the ground somewhere behind him. Quickly he threw himself over the edge of the seguia and rolled squirming down the bank. He knew the terrain here: where the road crossed the oued, there were two culverts not far apart. A man stood at some distance ahead of him with a shovel, peering down into the seguia. Allal kept moving, aware that he would reach the first culvert before the man could get to him.

The floor of the tunnel under the road was ribbed with hard little waves of sand. The smell of the mountains was in the air that moved through. There were places in here where he could have hidden, but he kept moving, and soon reached the other end. Then he continued to the second culvert and went under the road in the other direction, emerging once again into the seguia. Behind him several men had gathered at the entrance to the first culvert. One of them was on his knees, his head and shoulders inside the opening.

He now set out for the house in a straight line across the open ground, keeping his eye on the clump of palms beside it. The sun had just come up, and the stones began to cast long bluish shadows. All at once a small boy appeared from behind some nearby palms, saw him, and opened his eyes and mouth wide with fear. He was so close that Allal went straight to him and bit him in the leg. The boy ran wildly toward the group of men in the seguia.

Allal hurried on to the house, looking back only as he reached the hole between the mud bricks. Several men were running among the trees toward him. Swiftly he glided through into the alcove. The brown body still lay near the door. But there was no time, and Allal needed time to get back to it, to lie close to its head and say: Come here.

As he stared out into the room at the body, there was a great pounding on the door. The boy was on his feet at the first blow, as if a spring had been released, and Allal saw with despair the expression of total terror in his face, and the eyes with no mind behind them. The boy stood panting, his fists clenched. The door opened and some of the men peered inside. Then with a roar the boy lowered his head and rushed through the doorway. One of the men reached out to seize him, but lost his balance and fell. An instant later all of them turned and began to run through the palm grove after the naked figure.

Even when, from time to time, they lost sight of him, they could hear the screams, and then they would see him, between the palm trunks, still running. Finally he stumbled and fell face downward. It was then that they caught him, bound him, covered his nakedness, and took him away, to be sent one day soon to the hospital at Berrechid.

That afternoon the same group of men came to the house to carry out the search they had meant to make earlier. Allal lay in the alcove, dozing. When he awoke, they were already inside. He turned and crept to the hole. He saw the man waiting out there, a club in his hand.

The rage always had been in his heart; now it burst forth. As if his body were a whip, he sprang out into the room. The men nearest him were on their hands and knees, and Allal had the joy of pushing his fangs into two of them before a third severed his head with an axe.

Mejdoub

A MAN who spent his nights sleeping in cafés or under the trees or wherever he happened to be at the time when he felt sleepy, wandered one morning through the streets of the town. He came to the market place, where an old mejdoub dressed in rags cavorted before the populace, screaming prophecies into the air. He stood watching until the old man had finished and gathered up the money the people offered him. It astonished him to see how much the madman had collected, and having nothing else to do, he decided to follow him.

Almost before he got out of the market he was aware that small boys were hurrying from under the arcades to run alongside the mejdoub, who merely strode forward, chanting and waving his sceptre, and from time to time threatening the children who came too close. Walking at some distance behind, he saw the old man go into several shops. He came out each time with a banknote in his hand, which he promptly gave to one of the small boys.

It occurred to him then that there was much he could learn from this mejdoub. He had only to study the old man's behavior and listen carefully to the words he uttered. Then with practice he himself could make the same gestures and shout the same words. He began to look each day for the mejdoub and to follow him wherever he went in the town. At the end of a month he decided that he was ready to put his knowledge to use.

He travelled south to another city where he had never gone before. Here he took a very cheap room by the slaughterhouse, far from the centre of town. In the flea-market he bought an old and tattered djellaba. Then he went to the ironmongers and stood watching while they made him a long sceptre like the one the mejdoub had carried.

The next day, after practicing for a while, he went into the town and sat down in the street at the foot of the largest mosque. For a while he merely looked at the people going past. Slowly he began to raise his arms to the sky, and then to gesture with them. No one paid him any attention. This reassured him, as it meant that his disguise was successful. When he began to shout words the passers-by looked toward him, but it was as if they could not see him, and were only waiting to hear what he had to say. For a time he shouted short quotations from the Koran. He moved his eyes in a circular motion and let his turban fall over his face. After crying the words *fire* and *blood* several times he lowered his arms and bent his head, and said no more. The people moved on, but not before many of them had tossed coins on the ground in front of him.

On succeeding days he tried other parts of the city. It did not seem to matter where he sat. The people were generous to him in one place the same as in another. He did not want to risk going into the shops and cafés until he was certain that the town had grown used to his presence. One day he stormed through the streets, shaking his sceptre to the sky and screaming: Sidi Rahal is here! Sidi Rahal tells you to prepare for the fire! This was in order to give himself a name for the townspeople to remember.

He began to stand in the doorways of shops. If he heard anyone refer to him as Sidi Rahal, he would step inside, glare at the proprietor, and without saying a word, hold out his hand. The man would give him money, and he would turn and walk out.

For some reason no children followed him. He would have been happier to have a group of them with him, like the old mejdoub, but as soon as he spoke to them, they were frightened and ran away. It's quieter like this, he told himself, but secretly it bothered him. Still, he was earning more money than he ever had thought possible. By the time the first rains arrived, he had saved up a large sum. Leaving his sceptre and ragged djellaba in his room by the slaughterhouse, he paid the landlord several months' rent in advance. He waited until night. Then he locked the door behind him and took a bus back to his own city.

First he bought a great variety of clothing. When he was richly dressed he went out and looked for a house. Soon he found one that suited him. It was small and he had enough money left to pay for it. He furnished two rooms and prepared to spend the winter eating and smoking kif with all his old friends.

When they asked him where he had been all summer, he spoke of the hospitality and generosity of his wealthy brother in Taza. Already he was impatient for the rains to stop. For there was no doubt that he truly enjoyed his new work.

The winter finally came to an end. He packed his bag and told his friends that he was going on a business trip. In the other town he walked to the room. His djellaba and sceptre were there.

This year many more people recognized him. He grew bolder and entered the shops without waiting in the doorways. The shopkeepers, eager to show their piety to the customers, always gave a good deal more than the passers-by.

One day he decided to make a test. He hailed a taxi. As he got in he bellowed: I must go to Sidi Larbi's tomb! Fast! The driver, who knew he was not going to be paid, nevertheless agreed, and they rode out to a grove of olive trees on a hill far from the town.

He told the driver to wait, and jumped out of the taxi. Then he began the long climb up the hill to the tomb. The driver lost patience and drove off. On the way back to the town he missed a curve and hit a tree. When he was let out of the hospital he spread the word that Sidi Rahal had caused the car to go off the road. Men talked at length about it, recalling other holy maniacs who had put spells on motors and brakes. The name of Sidi Rahal was on everyone's lips, and people listened respectfully to his rantings.

That summer he amassed more money than the year before. He returned home and bought a larger house to live in, while he rented out the first one. Each year he bought more houses and lands, until finally it was clear that he had become a very prosperous man.

Always when the first rains fell he would announce to his friends that he was about to travel abroad. Then he would leave secretly, never allowing anyone to see him off. He was delighted with the pattern of his life, and with the good luck he had been granted in being able to continue it. He assumed that Allah did not mind if he pretended to be one of His holy maniacs. The money was merely his reward for providing men with an opportunity to exercise their charity.

One winter a new government came to power and announced that all beggars were to be taken off the streets. He talked about this with his friends, all of whom thought it an excellent thing. He agreed with them, but the news kept him from sleeping at night. To risk everything by going back, merely because that was what he wanted to do, was out of the question. Sadly he resigned himself to spending the summer at home.

It was not until the first few weeks of spring had gone by that he realized how close it had been to his heart, the starting out on a fine starry night to go in the bus to the other city, and what a relief it had been each time to be able to forget everything and live as Sidi Rahal. Now he began to understand that his life here at home had been a pleasure only because he had known that at a certain moment he was going to leave it for the other life.

As the hot weather came on he grew increasingly restless. He was bored and lost his appetite. His friends, noticing the change in him, advised him to travel, as he always had done. They said that men had been known to die as a result of breaking a habit. Again he lay awake at night worrying, and then secretly he determined to go back. As soon as he had made the decision he felt much better. It was as though until then he had been asleep, and suddenly had awakened. He announced to his friends that he was going abroad.

That very night he locked up his house and got onto a bus. The next day he strode joyously through the streets to sit in his favorite spot by the mosque. Passers-by looked at him and remarked to one another: He's back again, after all. You see?

He sat there quietly all day, collecting money. At the end of the afternoon, since the weather was very hot, he walked down to the river outside the gates of the town, in order to bathe. As he was undressing behind some oleander bushes, he glanced up and saw three policemen coming down the bank toward him. Without waiting he seized his slippers, threw his djellaba over his shoulder, and began to run.

Sometimes he splashed into the water, and sometimes he slipped in the mud and fell. He could hear the men shouting after him. They did not chase him very far, for they were laughing. Not knowing this, he kept on running, following the river, until he was breathless and had to stop. He put on the djellaba and the slippers, thinking: I can't go back to the town, or to any other town, in these clothes.

He continued at a slower gait. When evening came he was hungry, but there were no people or houses in sight. He slept under a tree, with only the ragged djellaba to cover him.

The next morning his hunger had grown. He got up, bathed in the river, and set out again. All that day he walked under the hot sun. In the late afternoon he sat down to rest. He drank a little water from the river and looked around him at the countryside. On the hill behind him stood a partially ruined shrine.

When he was rested, he climbed up to the building. There was a tomb inside, in the center of the big domed room. He sat down and listened. Cocks crowed, and he heard the occasional barking of dogs. He imagined himself running to the village, crying to the first man he met: Give me a piece of bread, for the love of Moulay Abdelqader! He shut his eyes.

It was nearly twilight when he awoke. Outside the door stood a group of small boys, watching him. Seeing him awaken, they laughed and nudged one another. Then one boy tossed in a piece of dry bread, so that it fell beside him. Soon they were all chanting: He's eating bread! He's eating bread!

They played the game for a while, throwing in clods of earth and even uprooted plants along with the scraps of bread. In their faces he could read wonder, malice and contempt, and shining through these shifting emotions the steady gleam of ownership. He thought of the old mejdoub, and a shiver ran through him. Suddenly they had gone. He heard a few shrill cries in the distance as they raced back to the village.

The bread had given him a little nourishment. He slept where he was, and before it grew light he set out again along the river, giving thanks to Allah for having allowed him to get beyond the village without being seen. He understood that heretofore the children had run from him only because they knew that he was not ready for them, that they could not make him theirs. The more he thought about this, the more fervently he hoped never to know what it was like to be a true mejdoub.

That afternoon as he turned a bend in the river, he came suddenly upon a town. His desperate need for food led him straight to the market, paying no heed to the people's stares. He went into a stall and ordered a bowl of soup. When he had finished it and paid, he entered another stall for a dish of stew. In a third place he ate skewered meat. Then he walked to the bread market for two loaves of bread to carry with him. While he was paying for these, a policeman tapped him on the shoulder and asked for his papers. He had none. There was nothing to say. At the police station they locked him into a small foul-smelling room in the cellar. Here in this closet he passed four days and nights of anguish. When at the end of that time they took him out and questioned him, he could not bring himself to tell them the truth. Instead he frowned, saying: I am Sidi Rahal.

They tied his hands and pushed him into the back of a truck. Later in the hospital they led him to a damp cell where the men stared and shivered and shrieked. He bore it for a week, and then he decided to give the officials his true name. But when he asked to be taken before them, the guards merely laughed. Sometimes they said: Next week, but usually they did not answer at all.

The months moved by. Through nights and days and nights he lived with the other madmen, and the time came when it scarcely mattered to him any more, getting to the officials to tell them who he was. Finally he ceased thinking about it.

You Have Left Your Lotus Pods on the Bus

I SOON learned not to go near the windows or to draw aside the double curtains in order to look at the river below. The view was wide and lively, with factories and warehouses on the far side of the Chao Phraya, and strings of barges being towed up and down through the dirty water. The new wing of the hotel had been built in the shape of an upright slab, so that the room was high and had no trees to shade it from the poisonous onslaught of the afternoon sun. The end of the day, rather than bringing respite, intensified the heat, for then the entire river was made of sunlight. With the redness of dusk everything out there became melodramatic and forbidding, and still the oven heat from outside leaked through the windows.

Brooks, teaching at Chulalongkorn University, was required as a Fulbright Fellow to attend regular classes in Thai; as an adjunct to this he arranged to spend much of his leisure time with Thais. One day he brought along with him three young men wearing the bright orange-yellow robes of Buddhist monks. They filed into the hotel room in silence and stood in a row as they were presented to me, each one responding by joining his palms together, thumbs touching his chest.

As we talked, Yamyong, the eldest, in his late twenties, explained that he was an ordained monk, while the other two were novices. Brooks then asked Prasert and Vichai if they would be ordained soon, but the monk answered for them.

"I do not think they are expecting to be ordained," he said quietly, looking at the floor, as if it were a sore subject all too often discussed among them. He glanced up at me and went on talking. "Your room is beautiful. We are not accustomed to such luxury." His voice was flat; he was trying to conceal his disapproval. The three conferred briefly in undertones. "My friends say they have never seen such a luxurious room," he reported, watching me closely through his steel-rimmed spectacles to see my reaction. I failed to hear.

They put down their brown paper parasols and their reticules that bulged with books and fruit. Then they got themselves into position in a row along the couch among the cushions. For a while they were busy adjusting the folds of their robes around their shoulders and legs.

"They make their own clothes," volunteered Brooks. "All the monks do."

I spoke of Ceylon; there the monks bought the robes all cut and ready to sew together. Yamyong smiled appreciatively and said: "We use the same system here."

The air-conditioning roared at one end of the room and the noise of boat motors on the river seeped through the windows at the other. I looked at the three sitting in front of me. They were very calm and self-possessed, but they seemed lacking in physical health. I was aware of the facial bones beneath their skin. Was the impression of sallowness partly due to the shaved eyebrows and hair?

Yamyong was speaking. "We appreciate the opportunity to use English. For this reason we are liking to have foreign friends. English, American; it doesn't matter. We can understand." Prasert and Vichai nodded.

Time went on, and we sat there, extending but not altering the subject of conversation. Occasionally I looked around the room. Before they had come in, it had been only a hotel room whose curtains must be kept drawn. Their presence and their comments on it had managed to invest it with a vaguely disturbing quality; I felt that they considered it a great mistake on my part to have chosen such a place in which to stay.

"Look at his tattoo," said Brooks. "Show him."

Yamyong pulled back his robe a bit from the shoulder, and I saw the two indigo lines of finely written Thai characters. "That is for good health," he said, glancing up at me. His smile seemed odd, but then, his facial expression did not complement his words at any point.

"Don't the Buddhists disapprove of tattooing?" I said.

"Some people say it is backwardness." Again he smiled. "Words for good health are said to be superstition. This was done by my abbot when I was a boy studying in the *wat*. Perhaps he did not know it was a superstition."

We were about to go with them to visit the *wat* where they lived. I pulled a tie from the closet and stood before the mirror arranging it.

"Sir," Yamyong began. "Will you please explain something? What is the significance of the necktie?"

"The significance of the necktie?" I turned to face him. "You mean, why do men wear neckties?"

"No. I know that. The purpose is to look like a gentleman."

I laughed. Yamyong was not put off. "I have noticed that some men wear the two ends equal, and some wear the wide end longer than the narrow, or the narrow longer than the wide. And the neckties themselves, they are not all the same length, are they? Some even with both ends equal reach below the waist. What are the different meanings?"

"There is no meaning," I said. "Absolutely none."

He looked to Brooks for confirmation, but Brooks was trying out his Thai on Prasert and Vichai, and so he was silent and thoughtful for a moment. "I believe you, of course," he said graciously. "But we all thought each way had a different significance attached."

As we went out of the hotel, the doorman bowed respectfully. Until now he had never given a sign that he was aware of my existence. The wearers of the yellow robe carry weight in Thailand.

A few Sundays later I agreed to go with Brooks and our friends to Ayudhaya. The idea of a Sunday outing is so repellent to me that deciding to take part in this one was to a certain extent a compulsive act. Ayudhaya lies less than fifty miles up the Chao Phraya from Bangkok. For historians and art-collectors it is more than just a provincial town; it is a period and a style—having been the Thai capital for more than four centuries. Very likely it still would be, had the Burmese not laid it waste in the eighteenth century.

Brooks came early to fetch me. Downstairs in the street stood the three bhikkus with their book bags and parasols. They hailed a cab, and without any previous price arrangement (the ordinary citizen tries to fix a sum beforehand) we got in and drove for twenty minutes or a half hour, until we got to a bus terminal on the northern outskirts of the city.

It was a nice, old-fashioned, open bus. Every part of it rattled, and the air from the rice fields blew across us as we pieced together our bits of synthetic conversation. Brooks, in high spirits, kept calling across to me: "Look! Water buffaloes!" As we went further away from Bangkok there were more of the beasts, and his cries became more frequent. Yamyong, sitting next to me, whispered: "Professor Brooks is fond of buffaloes?" I laughed and said I didn't think so.

"Then?"

I said that in America there were no buffaloes in the fields, and that was why Brooks was interested in seeing them. There were no temples in the landscape, either, I told him, and added, perhaps unwisely: "He looks at buffaloes. I look at temples." This struck Yamyong as hilarious, and he made allusions to it now and then all during the day.

The road stretched ahead, straight as a line in geometry, across the verdant, level land. Paralleling it on its eastern side was a fairly wide canal, here and there choked with patches of enormous pink lotuses. In places the flowers were gone and only the pods remained, thick green disks with the circular seeds embedded in their flesh. At the first stop the bhikkus got out. They came aboard again with mangosteens and lotus pods and insisted on giving us large numbers of each. The huge seeds popped out of the fibrous lotus cakes as though from a punchboard; they tasted almost like green almonds. "Something new for you today, I think," Yamyong said with a satisfied air.

Ayudhaya was hot, dusty, spread-out, its surrounding terrain strewn with ruins that scarcely showed through the vegetation. At some distance from the town there began a wide boulevard sparingly lined with important-looking buildings. It continued for a way and then came to an end as abrupt as its beginning. Growing up out of the scrub, and built of small russet-colored bricks, the ruined temples looked still unfinished rather than damaged by time. Repairs, done in smeared cement, veined their facades.

The bus's last stop was still two or three miles from the center of Ayudhaya. We got down into the dust, and Brooks declared: "The first thing we must do is find some food. They can't eat anything solid, you know, after midday."

"Not noon exactly," Yamyong said. "Maybe one o'clock or a little later."

"Even so, that doesn't leave much time," I told him. "It's quarter to twelve now."

But the bhikkus were not hungry. None of them had visited Ayudhaya before, and so they had compiled a list of things they most wanted to see. They spoke with a man who had a station wagon parked nearby, and we set off for a ruined *stupa* that lay some miles to the southwest. It had been built atop a high mound, which we climbed with some difficulty, so that Brooks could take pictures of us standing within a fissure in the decayed outer wall. The air stank of the bats that lived inside.

When we got back to the bus stop, the subject of food arose once again, but the excursion had put the bhikkus into such a state of excitement that they could not bear to allot time for anything but looking. We went to the museum. It was quiet; there were Khmer heads and documents inscribed in Pali. The day had begun to be painful. I told myself I had known beforehand that it would.

Then we went to a temple. I was impressed, not so much by the gigantic Buddha which all but filled the interior, as by the fact that not far from the entrance a man sat on the floor playing a *ranad* (pronounced *lanat*). Although I was familiar with the sound of it from listening to recordings of Siamese music, I had never before seen the instrument. There was a graduated series of wooden blocks strung together, the whole slung like a hammock over a boat-shaped resonating stand. The tones hurried after one another like drops of water falling very fast. After the painful heat outside, everything in the temple suddenly seemed a symbol of the concept of coolness—the stone floor under my bare feet, the breeze that moved through the shadowy interior, the bamboo fortune sticks being rattled in their long box by those praying at the altar, and the succession of insubstantial, glassy sounds that came from the *ranad*. I thought: If only I could get something to eat, I wouldn't mind the heat so much.

We got into the center of Ayudhaya a little after three o'clock. It was hot and noisy; the bhikkus had no idea of where to look for a restaurant, and the idea of asking did not appeal to them. The five of us walked aimlessly. I had come to the conclusion that neither Prasert nor Vichai understood spoken English, and I addressed myself earnestly to Yamyong. "*We've got to eat.*" He stared at me with severity. "We are searching," he told me.

Eventually we found a Chinese restaurant on a corner of the principal street. There was a table full of boisterous Thais drinking *mekong* (categorized as whiskey, but with the taste of cheap rum) and another table occupied by an entire Chinese family. These people were doing some serious eating, their faces buried in their rice bowls. It cheered me to see them: I was faint, and had half expected to be told that there was no hot food available.

The large menu in English which was brought us must have been typed several decades ago and wiped with a damp rag once a week ever since. Under the heading SPECIALITIES were some dishes that caught my eye, and as I went through the list I began to laugh. Then I read it aloud to Brooks.

> *"Fried Sharks Fins and Bean Sprout*
> *Chicken Chins Stuffed with Shrimp*
> *Fried Rice Birds*
> *Shrimps Balls and Green Marrow*
> *Pigs Lights with Pickles*
> *Braked Rice Bird in Port Wine*
> *Fish Head and Bean Curd"*

Although it was natural for our friends not to join in the laughter, I felt that their silence was not merely failure to respond; it was heavy, positive.

A moment later three Pepsi-Cola bottles were brought and placed on the table. "What are you going to have?" Brooks asked Yamyong.

"Nothing, thank you," he said lightly. "This will be enough for us today."

"But this is terrible! You mean no one is going to eat *anything*?"

"You and your friend will eat your food," said Yamyong. (He might as well have said "fodder.") Then he, Prasert, and Vichai stood up, and carrying their Pepsi-Cola bottles with them, went to sit at a table on the other side of the room. Now and then Yamyong smiled sternly across at us.

"I wish they'd stop watching us," Brooks said under his breath.

"They were the ones who kept putting it off," I reminded him. But I felt guilty, and I was annoyed at finding myself placed in the position of the self-indulgent unbeliever. It was almost as bad as eating in front of Moslems during Ramadan.

We finished our meal and set out immediately, following Yamyong's decision to visit a certain temple he wanted to see. The taxi drive led us through a region of thorny scrub. Here and there, in the shade of spreading flat-topped trees, were great round pits, full of dark water and crowded with buffaloes; only their wet snouts and horns were visible. Brooks was already crying: "Buffaloes! Hundreds of them!" He asked the taxi driver to stop so that he could photograph the animals.

"You will have buffaloes at the temple," said Yamyong. He was right; there was a muddy pit filled with them only a few hundred feet from the building. Brooks went and took his pictures while the bhikkus paid their routine visit to the shrine. I wandered into a courtyard where there was a long row of stone Buddhas. It is the custom of temple-goers to plaster little squares of gold leaf onto the religious statues in the *wats*. When thousands of them have been stuck onto the same surface, tiny scraps of the gold come unstuck. Then they tremble in the breeze, and the figure shimmers with a small, vibrant life of its own. I stood in the courtyard watching this quivering along the arms and torsos of the Buddhas, and I was reminded of the motion of the bô-tree's leaves. When I mentioned it to Yamyong in the taxi, I think he failed to understand, for he replied: "The bô-tree is a very great tree for Buddhists."

Brooks sat beside me on the bus going back to Bangkok. We spoke only now and then. After so many hours of resisting the heat, it was relaxing to sit and feel the relatively cool air that blew in from the rice fields. The driver of the bus was not a believer in cause and effect. He passed trucks with oncoming traffic in full view. I felt better with my eyes shut, and I might even have dozed off, had there not been in the back of the bus a man, obviously not in control, who was intent on making as much noise as possible. He began to shout, scream, and howl almost as soon as we had left Ayudhaya, and he did this consistently throughout the journey. Brooks and I laughed about it, conjecturing whether he was crazy or only drunk. The aisle was too crowded for me to be able to see him from where I sat. Occasionally I glanced at the other passengers. It was as though they were entirely unaware of the commotion behind them. As we drew closer to the city, the screams became louder and almost constant.

"God, why don't they throw him off?" Brooks was beginning to be annoyed.

"They don't even hear him," I said bitterly. People who can tolerate noise inspire me with envy and rage. Finally I leaned over and said to Yamyong: "That poor man back there! It's incredible!"

"Yes," he said over his shoulder. "He's very busy." This set me thinking what a civilized and tolerant people they were, and I marvelled at the sophistication of the word "busy" to describe what was going on in the back of the bus.

Finally we were in a taxi driving across Bangkok. I would be dropped at my hotel and Brooks would take the three bhikkus on to their *wat*. In my head I was still hearing the heartrending cries. What had the repeated word patterns meant?

I had not been able to give an acceptable answer to Yamyong in his bewilderment about the significance of the necktie, but perhaps he could satisfy my curiosity here.

"That man in the back of the bus, you know?"

Yamyong nodded. "He was working very hard, poor fellow. Sunday is a bad day."

I disregarded the nonsense. "What was he saying?"

"Oh, he was saying: 'Go into second gear,' or 'We are coming to a bridge,' or 'Be careful, people in the road.' Whatever he saw."

Since neither Brooks nor I appeared to have understood, he went on. "All the buses must have a driver's assistant. He watches the road and tells the driver how to drive. It is hard work because he must shout loud enough for the driver to hear him."

"But why doesn't he sit up in the front with the driver?"

"No, no. There must be one in the front and one in the back. That way two men are responsible for the bus."

It was an unconvincing explanation for the grueling sounds we had heard, but to show him that I believed him I said: "Aha! I see."

The Fqih

ONE MIDSUMMER afternoon a dog went running through
a village, stopping just long enough to bite a young man
who stood on the main street. It was not a deep wound, and
the young man washed it at a fountain nearby and thought no
more about it. However, several people who had seen the animal bite him mentioned it to his younger brother. You must
take your brother to a doctor in the city, they said.

When the boy went home and suggested this, his brother
merely laughed. The next day in the village the boy decided
to consult the fqih. He found the old man sitting in the shade
under the figtree in the courtyard of the mosque. He kissed
his hand, and told him that a dog no one had ever seen before had bitten his brother and run away.

That's very bad, said the fqih. Have you got a stable you
can lock him into? Put him there, but tie his hands behind
him. No one must go near him, you understand?

The boy thanked the fqih and set out for home. On the way
he determined to cover a hammer with yarn and hit his brother
on the back of the head. Knowing that his mother would never
consent to seeing her son treated in this way, he decided that
it would have to be done when she was away from the house.

That evening while the woman stood outside by the well,
he crept up behind his brother and beat him with the hammer until he fell to the floor. Then he fastened his hands behind him and dragged him into a shed next to the house.
There he left him lying on the ground, and went out, pad-
locking the door behind him.

When the brother came to his senses, he began a great outcry. The mother called to the boy: Quick! Run and see what's
the matter with Mohammed. But the boy only said: I know
what's the matter with him. A dog bit him, and the fqih said
he has to stay in the shed.

The woman began to pull at her hair and scratch her face
with her fingernails and beat her breasts. The boy tried to calm
her, but she pushed him away and ran out to the shed. She
put her ear to the door. All she could hear was her son's loud

panting as he tried to free his hands from the cords that bound them. She pounded on the wood and screamed his name, but he was struggling, his face in the dirt, and did not reply. Finally the boy led her back to the house. It was written, he told her.

The next morning the woman got astride her donkey and rode to the village to see the fqih. He, however, had left that morning to visit his sister in Rhafsai, and no one knew when he would be back. And so she bought bread and started out on the road for Rhafsai, along with a group of villagers who were on their way to a souq in the region. That night she slept at the souq and the following morning at daybreak she started out again with a different group of people.

Each day the boy threw food in to his brother through a small barred window high above one of the stalls in the shed. The third day he also threw him a knife, so he could cut the ropes and use his hands to eat with. After a while it occurred to him that he had done a foolish thing in giving him the knife, since if he worked long enough with it he might succeed in cutting his way through the door. Thus he threatened to bring no more food until his brother had tossed the knife back through the window.

The mother had no sooner arrived at Rhafsai than she fell ill with a fever. The family with whom she had been travelling took her into their house and cared for her, but it was nearly a month before she was able to rise from the pallet on the floor where she had been lying. By that time the fqih had returned to his village.

Finally she was well enough to start out again. After two days of sitting on the back of the donkey she arrived home exhausted, and was greeted by the boy.

And your brother? she said, certain that by now he was dead.

The boy pointed to the shed, and she rushed to the door and began to call out to him.

Get the key and let me out! he cried.

I must see the fqih first, aoulidi. Tomorrow.

The next morning she and the boy went to the village. When the fqih saw the woman and her son come into the courtyard he raised his eyes to heaven. It was Allah's will that your son should die as he did, he told her.

But he's not dead! she cried. And he shouldn't stay in there any longer.

The fqih was astounded. Then he said: But let him out! Let him out! Allah has been merciful.

The boy however begged the fqih to come himself and open the door. So they set out, the fqih riding the donkey and the woman and boy following on foot. When they got to the shed, the boy handed the key to the old man, and he opened the door. The young man bounded out, followed by a stench so strong that the fqih shut the door again.

They went to the house, and the woman made tea for them. While they sat drinking, the fqih told the young man: Allah has spared you. You must never mistreat your brother for having shut you away. He did it on my orders.

The young man swore that never would he raise his hand against the boy. But the boy was still afraid, and could not bring himself to look at his brother. When the fqih left to return to the village, the boy went with him, in order to bring back the donkey. As they went along the road, he said to the old man: I'm afraid of Mohammed.

The fqih was displeased. Your brother is older than you, he said. You heard him swear not to touch you.

That night while they were eating, the woman went to the brazier to make the tea. For the first time the boy stole a glance at his brother, and grew cold with fear. Mohammed had swiftly bared his teeth and made a strange sound in his throat. He had done this as a kind of joke, but to the boy it meant something very different.

The fqih should never have let him out, he said to himself. Now he'll bite me, and I'll get sick like him. And the fqih will tell him to throw me into the shed.

He could not bring himself to look again at Mohammed. At night in the dark he lay thinking about it, and he could not sleep. Early in the morning he set out for the village, to catch the fqih before he began to teach the pupils at the msid.

What is it now? asked the fqih.

When the boy told him what he feared, the old man laughed. But he has no disease! He never had any disease, thanks to Allah.

But you yourself told me to lock him up, sidi.

Yes, yes. But Allah has been merciful. Now go home and forget about it. Your brother's not going to bite you.

The boy thanked the fqih and left. He walked through the village and out along the road that led finally to the highway. The next morning he got a ride in a truck that took him all the way to Casablanca. No one in the village ever heard of him again.

Istikhara, Anaya, Medagan
and the Medaganat

I N THE SAHARA, where the air, the light, even the sky suggest some as yet unvisited planet, it is not surprising to
find certain patterns of human comportment equally unfamiliar. Behavior is strictly formulated, with little margin allowed
for individual variations. If circumstances offer the opportunity for attack and pillage, the action is expected; indeed, custom demands it.

This is common knowledge. What may be less well-known
are the two institutions of *istikhara* and *anaya*. The first is an
invocation, offered up just before going to sleep, in which the
supplicant implores Allah to send a dream which will make it
possible for him to solve his difficulties. The prayer must be
uttered in full four times over before the request is made for
the specific revelatory details that will determine the sleeper's
course of action when he awakens. The orison may or may
not be answered. It is up to the supplicant to decide whether
his dream is a result of *istikhara* or not, and, if it seems to him
that it is, to interpret its material correctly. The practice seems
a sound one: not only does it assume that dreams can be therapeutic, but it offers Moslems a practical technique for pro-
ducing them.

Anaya, on the other hand, is a custom devoid of meaning
save in a feudal society. It is the last feeble hope left to a soldier defeated in battle. If he can manage to crawl to one of
the enemy and get his head totally under the folds of the
other's burnous, he is automatically saved from death. His
pardon, however, involves him with the wearer of the
burnous for the rest of his life, or until the wearer dies. He
becomes his enemy's permanent possession and responsibility.
At the time when the events cited here took place, which is to
say roughly a hundred years ago, *anaya* still functioned as an
integral part of Saharan military etiquette.

A man named Medagan appeared one day in Ouargla, accompanied by seven of his sons. They sat with the Chaamba

and told them of how for some misdemeanor or other their own tribe of Kelkhela Tuareg had driven them out of their homeland in the Hoggar, and how they had wandered and suffered ever since. The Chaamba listened and took them in to live with them. First they lent them some of their camels, and later let them have large quantities of dates and wheat on credit. This gave the Tuareg the mobility they seemed to require. For several months they lived in the vicinity of Ouargla, hunting and getting themselves into good health. Then they went back to Ouargla and robbed the Chaamba of twenty of their best camels, which they proceeded to drive off into an uninhabited region. There, hidden in the deep ravines of the desolate Tademait country, they lived for two years or more, moving out of their lair only to attack caravans that passed nearby. At length, apparently considering themselves invulnerable, they had the audacity to ride up to the very gates of El Golea and capture thirty camels from under the eyes of the Chaamba who owned them.

A Chaambi from Ouargla happened to be with the other Chaamba when the raid took place. He was one of those who had been willing to give Medagan wheat on credit. When he had finished telling the others that part of the story, the men determined to go in pursuit of the Tuareg. A few days later sixty men set out on fast *mehara*.

When Medagan and his sons arrived back at their hiding place they suspected that they might be followed, but they were fairly confident that the Chaamba would not venture into the maze of gorges and narrow passageways which characterize the terrain. Nevertheless, before lying down to sleep that night, Medagan prayed for a dream that could guide his behavior in the event the Chaamba did manage to catch up with them. In the morning when he awoke and realized with dismay that he had had no dream whatever, or none that he could recall, he conferred with his sons. They read this as an unfavorable omen, and agreed that if they were forced into battle they would seek *anaya*, throwing themselves upon the mercy of the Chaamba once again, this time definitively. Then Medagan sent off his youngest son, who was no more than a child, with some camels they had captured earlier, to sell them in El Golea. Since the group had just returned from there, this act would seem to indicate that Medagan foresaw the possibility of serious trouble, and hoped to save this son at least. In this he was successful, for the boy reached El Golea with the camels, unharmed.

The Chaamba meanwhile found the group with ease, and heard Medagan call out to them that Allah had advised him to seek *anaya*. Seeing that the Tuareg in truth were not even attempting to defend themselves, the Chaamba settled the matter by sending their black slaves against them. This ruled out the possibility of *anaya*, since a slave is powerless to grant it. The blacks cut the throat of each man, thus ending the saga of Medagan and his sons.

This took place in 1863, just as the French were making strenuous efforts to extend their hegemony southward into the desert. It marked the beginning of a twenty-year period of excessive lawlessness throughout the Sahara. Bandit groups sprang up on all sides to sweep down on oases, plunder passing caravans, and massacre voyagers. Some of this activity was legitimate retaliation for French incursions, but the greater part was simple outlawry, due no doubt to the breakdown in moral conventions attendant upon the prolonged infidel presence.

A small group of the Mekhadema tribe having been attacked and murdered in the same region of the Tademait where Medagan had met his death, the popular imagination around Ouargla was quick to attribute the raid to Medagan and his sons, who were declared to be wreaking vengeance from beyond the grave in return for having been denied the possibility of *anaya* by the Chaamba. Thereafter, as the raids proliferated, each new *razzia* was attributed to the ghosts of the Medaganat, and the word fast came to be a Saharan synonym for outlaw. Every petty thief, agitator, pillager, renegade or highwayman was labeled a Medagani. Only the empty shell of the word remained, its original and secondary meanings both having been lost in the general confusion that existed in the region. The assaults became organized and took on a more openly political character. Now it was the Chaamba themselves en masse who decided to be outlaws, and who in 1871 adopted the name of Medaganat as their official designation.

In 1876 they boasted of killing the three French priests, Fathers Paulmier, Menoret, and Boujard. The French press reacted with hysteria: the situation in the Sahara was utterly intolerable. Meanwhile the attacks increased in number and violence. The Medaganat conducted raids along the Tunisian border, in Libya, in Morocco, and throughout the Algerian desert. It was only several years later, in 1883, when they were careless enough to attack a group of Reguibat, that they finally met with an enemy able to destroy them.

At the very beginning of the battle a good many of the Medaganat, sensing likely defeat, defected outright to the Reguibat. The others, once it became clear that they could not win, then tried like their original namesakes to obtain *anaya*. But the women of the Reguibat, who were with them in the camp, repeatedly warned their menfolk not to grant it. Thus the Reguibat were obliged to chop the Medaganat into pieces with their swords to prevent them from touching the folds of their capes. The women furthermore insisted that even those who had surrendered at the outset be slaughtered. This was a grave infraction of desert law, but to oblige them the men cut a few dozen throats, and finally the women were quiet.

In this instance it is clear that neither *anaya* nor *istikhara* produced what was desired of it, and yet the results were by no means the same as they would have been had neither been practiced. To a Moslem, the failure of Medagan's attempt at *istikhara* is implicit in the facts. One may pray, but if one is not in a state of grace the prayer fails to get through. Once Medagan had betrayed his protectors, he was not in a condition which permitted contact with the Deity. And having construed his dreamless night as an instruction to seek *anaya*, by going out and requesting it immediately, without making even a gesture of self-defense, he doubtless helped to bring about his own defeat. To the Chaamba this behavior could only have seemed a proof of cowardice; the sending of slaves to despatch the bandits thus gave a flavor of contempt to their refusal. Apparently, Medagan and his sons were beyond the radius of normal functioning with regard to both *istikhara* and *anaya*. Many of the Chaamba Medaganat, however, would have been saved by *anaya* if the Reguibat had not happened to have their women along.

Thus there was no *istikhara*, no *anaya*, Medagan was not a Medagani, and the Medaganat had never heard of Medagan.

The Waters of Izli

No one would have guessed, from seeing the two villages spread out there, one higher up than the other on the sunny slope of the mountain, that enmity existed between them. And yet, if you looked closely, you would see certain marked differences in the respective designs they made on the landscape. Tamlat was higher, the houses were farther apart, and there were trees between them. In Izli everything was crowded together, for there was not enough space. The entire village seemed to have been built on top of boulders and at the edges of cliffs. Green fields and meadows surrounded Tamlat. It lay above, where the valley was wide, so that there was ample room for farming, and thus the people lived well. But the orchards down in Izli were little more than steep stairways of terraces. No matter how hard they worked trying to raise vegetables and fruit, the villagers never had enough.

What ought to have helped compensate for Izli's unlucky site was the large spring just outside the village, whose water was the sweetest in the region. The people of Izli claimed great curative powers for it, an idea that was dismissed by the inhabitants of Tamlat, although they themselves often went down and filled their skins and jars with it to take home with them. There was no way of fencing off the land around the spring, or the natives of Izli long ago would have seen to it that no one else had access to the water. If only the people of Tamlat had been willing to admit that the water was superior to their own, eventually they might have been persuaded to trade a few vegetables for it. However, they were careful never to mention it, and except for going casually to fetch it, behaved as if it did not exist.

The man whose land lay nearest to the spring was Ramadi, said to be the most prosperous one in Izli. By the standards of Tamlat he would not have been considered well-off. But his black mare was the only horse in Izli, and his orchard had twenty-three almond trees growing on eight different levels, and on each level he had built a channel that ran with clear water. The mare was a beautiful animal, and he kept her in perfect condition. When he dressed in his white selham and rode the mare through the street out of the village, the people of Izli remarked to each other that he looked almost like Sidi Bouhajja. This was a great compliment, since Sidi Bouhajja was the most important saint in the region. He too wore white garments and rode a black horse, although his was a stallion.

For a long time Ramadi had been on the lookout for a fitting mate for his mare. However, not one stallion among all those he had looked at in the neighboring villages could be called her equal. In fact, the only horse he would have accepted for her was the shining black stallion ridden by Sidi Bouhajja, and this was out of the question, since there was no way of asking a saint for such a favor.

It was assumed by many people that Sidi Bouhajja and his horse were able to converse together. And it was common knowledge, for he had proclaimed it in public on several occasions, that at the moment of his death it was to be the horse that would decide on his burial place. He asked that his body be fastened astride the animal, which was then to be allowed to go where it pleased. Where it stopped, at that spot Sidi Bouhajja was to be interred. This doubtless lent weight to the belief that the old man and his horse had a secret language between them.

It was a subject for much speculation around the countryside as to which region might prove fortunate enough to witness this event, but everything was cut short by Sidi Bouhajja's sudden collapse one afternoon as he sat outside the mosque at Tamlat.

The saint had ridden up through Izli earlier in the day, passing by Ramadi's house as the mare stood in front of it, shaded by an old olive tree. The stallion wanted to stop, and Sidi Bouhajja had some difficulty in getting him to continue. Ramadi watched, fingering his beard, thinking what a great thing it would be if the stallion should suddenly rise up, saint and all, and mount the mare. Then, feeling ashamed, he looked away.

Later in the day Ramadi got onto the mare and rode up to Tamlat. There in a corner of the market he caught sight of an Aissaoui snake charmer from Izli whom he knew, and he sat down to talk with him. It was then that he heard the news of Sidi Bouhajja's death.

He sat up very straight. The Aissaoui added that soon they would be tying the saint to his horse.

Where do you think it'll go? Ramadi asked him.

It'll probably come here and go into the grain market, the Aissaoui said.

Have you got your snakes with you?

The Aissaoui looked surprised. Yes, I have them, he said.

Get them out there to the turn-off and let him see them, Ramadi told him. He's got to go down the hill instead.

He rose, jumped onto his mare, and rode off.

The Aissaoui ran to the fondouq where he had left his basket of vipers and cobras. Then he hurried up to the corner where the road turned off from the main street and led down the side of the mountain.

Since everyone in Tamlat was watching the elders strap Sidi Bouhajja's body onto the back of the stallion, Ramadi on his mare passed unnoticed as he galloped down the road to Izli. When he got to his house, he left the mare standing under the olive tree and waited.

Up in Tamlat the Assaoui sat by the edge of the road with his basket. At length he saw the horse come into view, its sacred burden strapped to its back. It cantered down the street toward him, followed at some distance by the elders. He opened his basket and took out two of the larger serpents, holding one in each hand. As the horse approached him, he stood up and made the reptiles writhe in the air. Immediately the horse opened its eyes very wide and turned to the right, down the road leading out of the village.

The Aissaoui put the snakes back into the basket and sauntered out of the bushes which until then had hidden him from the approaching elders. They paid him no attention, and he set out along the road to Izli. Far ahead of him he could see the black form of the stallion racing down the mountainside, the white bundle it carried flopping in the sunlight. After he had walked along for a while, he turned to look back. The elders stood up there at the corner, shading their eyes as they peered down into the valley.

And as Ramadi sat in his doorway waiting, the stallion stormed into the village, stood quiet for an instant, and then trotted directly to Ramadi's house. The mare still stood under the olive tree, switching her tail against the flies. Before anyone arrived to watch, the stallion reared himself up to a great height, bursting the straps that had bound Sidi Bouhajja to his back. The body in the white selham dropped to the ground at the same moment the stallion seized the mare. Ramadi ran forward and pulled it out of the way. Then he returned to the doorway to look on.

A little later some neighbors arrived, and they carried Sidi Bouhajja into Ramadi's courtyard, all the while praising Allah. By the time the men of Tamlat had got down to Izli, the stallion and the mare were standing quietly under the olive tree, and the tolba of Izli chanted inside Ramadi's house.

The men from Tamlat hid their chagrin and accepted the will of Allah. The horse had come to Izli and stopped here, therefore this was where Sidi Bouhajja had to be buried. They helped the men of Izli dig the grave, and the news went out to all the villages around, so that tolba came from many places to chant at the tomb.

It was no time before crowds of pilgrims began to arrive in Izli, seeking baraka at Sidi Bouhajja's tomb. Soon it was necessary to demolish Ramadi's house and in its place to build a sanctuary where the pilgrims could sleep. At the same time they constructed a domed qoubba over the saint's resting place by the olive tree, and then built a high wall around it. Ramadi was given another house nearby.

Since the pilgrims all carried away with them water from the spring, the water's fame soon spread, and it took on great importance. Even those who did not venerate Sidi Bouhajja came to drink it and take it home with them. In exchange they left offerings of food and money in the sanctuary. Before a year was up, Izli had become more prosperous than Tamlat.

Only Ramadi and the Aissaoui knew of the part they had played in bringing about the stroke of good luck that had changed their village, and they considered it of slight importance, since everything is decided by Allah. What mattered to Ramadi was the beauty of the black colt that now followed the mare wherever he rode her, even if it was down to the plain or up to the market in Tamlat.

Afternoon with Antaeus

YOU wanted to see me? They told you right. That's my name. Ntiuz. The African Giant's what they've called me ever since I started fighting. What can I do for you? Have you seen the town? It isn't such a bad place. You're lucky the wind's not blowing these days. We have a bad wind that comes through here. But without it the sun's too hot. Argos? Never heard of it. I've never been over to the other side.

A man named Erakli? Yes, yes, he was here. It was a long time ago. I remember him. We even put on a fight together.

Killed me! Is that what he told them back there? I see. And when you got here you heard I was still around, and so you wanted to meet me? I understand.

Why don't we sit here? There's a spring in the courtyard that has the coldest water in town. You asked about Erakli. No, he had no trouble here, except losing his fight. Why would anyone bother him? A man alone. You never saw him before. You let him go on his way. You don't bother him. Only savages attack a stranger walking alone. They kill him and fight over his loincloth. We let people go through without a word. They come in on one side and go out on the other. That's the way we like it. Peaceful and friendly with everyone. We have a saying: Never hit a man unless you know you can kill him, and then kill him fast. Up where I come from we're rougher than they are down here on the coast. We have a harder life, but we're healthier. Look at me, and I could almost be your father. If I'd lived down here on the coast all my life I wouldn't be like this now. And still I'm nothing to what I was twenty years ago. In those days I went to every festival and put on shows for the people. I'd lift a bull with one hand and hit him between the horns with the other, so he'd fall dead. People like to see that. Sometimes I broke beams with my head. That was popular, too, but the bull was religious, of course, so it was the one people wanted to see most. There was nobody who didn't know about me.

Have some nuts? I eat them all day. I get them up in the forest. There are trees up there bigger than any you ever saw.

It was at least twenty years ago he came through here, but I remember him, all right. Not because he was any good as a fighter, but because he was so crazy. You can't help remembering a man as crazy as Erakli.

Have some more. I've got a whole sack full. That's true, the flavor's not quite like anything else. I don't suppose you have them over on the other side.

I'll be only too glad to take you up to the forest, if you'd like to see it. It's not far. You don't mind climbing a little?

Of course he didn't make any friends here, but a man like that can't have friends. He was so full of great ideas about himself that he didn't even see us. He thought we were all savages, ready to swallow his stories. Even before the fight everybody was laughing at him. Strong, yes, but not a good fighter. An awful boaster and a terrible liar. And ignorant.

We'll turn here and go up this path. He talked all the time. If you believed him, there was nothing he couldn't do, and do it better than anybody else.

You'll get a fine view on the way. The edge of the world. How does it feel, when you're used to being in the middle, to be out here at the end? It must be a different feeling.

Erakli came into town without anyone noticing him. He must have had a little money with him, because he began to meet two or three men I knew every day and pay for their drinks. They told me about him, and I went along one day just to see what he looked like, not to meet him. Right away I knew he was no good. No good as a fighter, no good as a man. I didn't even take him seriously enough to challenge him. How can you take a man seriously when he has a beard that looks like the wool on a sheep?

He stayed around town a while and saw me kill a few bulls. I fought a match or two, too, while he was here, and it seems he came each time to watch me. The next thing I knew, he'd challenged me. It was he who wanted the match. It was hard to believe. And what's more, they told me he held it against me that I hadn't been the one who challenged him. It just never entered my mind.

All this land you see up here is mine. This and the forest up ahead. I keep everybody out. I like to walk, and I don't want to meet people while I'm walking. It makes me nervous. I used to fight every man I met. At least, in the beginning.

When I was a small boy in my village I liked to go late in the afternoon to a big rock. I'd sit on it and look down the valley and pretend enemies were coming. I'd let them get to a certain point, and then I'd start a boulder rolling down the mountain to hit them. I killed them every time. My father caught me and I got punished. I might have hit sheep or goats, or even men down there.

But I'm not dead, as you can see, no matter what Erakli may be saying. I want you to look at my trees. Look at the size of the trunk of that one. Follow it up, up, up, to where the first branches begin. Have you ever seen trees this big anywhere?

When I got a little older I learned how to throw a calf, and later a bull. By that time I was fighting. Never lost yet. They forgot my name was Ntiuz and began to call me The Giant. Not because of my size, of course. I'm not so big. But because nobody could beat me in a match. They came from all around, and afterwards from far away. You know how they do when they hear of a fighter who's never lost. They can't believe that somehow or other they won't manage to get him down. That was the way with your Erakli. I didn't meet him until the fight, but I'd heard all about him from my friends. He told them he'd studied me, and he knew how to beat me. He didn't say how he was going to do it. And I never even found out what he thought he was going to do until after the fight.

No, I'm not dead. I'm still the champion. Anybody here can tell you. It's too bad you never met Erakli yourself. You wouldn't be so surprised. You'd understand that whatever he said when he got back home was what he wanted to tell and nothing more. He couldn't tell the truth if he wanted to.

Are you tired? It's a steep climb if you're not used to it. The fight itself? It didn't last long. He was so busy trying to use the system he'd worked out. He'd back away, and then come up to me and just stand there with his hands on me. I couldn't understand what he was trying to do. The crowd was jeering. For a minute I thought: He's the kind that gets his pleasure this way, running his hands over a man's chest and squeezing his waist. He didn't like it because I laughed and shouted to the crowd. He was very serious the whole time. And I was wrong anyway. Are we going too fast? And you're carrying that heavy pouch at your waist. We can go as slowly as you want to. There's no hurry.

That's a good idea. Why don't we sit a minute and rest? Do you feel all right? No. Nothing. I thought you looked a little pale. It may be the light. The sun never gets down in here.

It was only after the fight that one of my friends told me what Erakli wanted to do. Instead of trying to throw me, the crazy fool was trying to lift me off the ground and hold me in the air! Not so he could throw me down better, but just to hold me up there. It's hard to believe, isn't it? But that's what he had in his mind. That was his great system. Why? Don't ask me. I'm an African. I don't know what goes on in the heads of the men of your country.

Have some more nuts. No, no, they couldn't have hurt you. It's the air. Our climate doesn't suit people from the other side. While he was trying to make up his mind how to lift me I finished him. They had to drag him out.

Shall we go on? Or would you rather wait a while? Are you still out of breath? There's no air here in the forest.

Don't you think we ought to wait a while? Of course, if you want to go. We can walk slowly. Let me help you up. It's too bad we couldn't have gone further. The biggest trees are up that way.

Yes, they dragged him out, and he stayed three days lying on a mat before he left here. Finally he limped out of town like a dog, with everybody laughing at him along the way. Hang on to me. I won't let you fall. You're walking all right. Just keep going. He didn't look left or right on his way out of town. Must have been glad to get into the mountains.

Relax. First one foot, then the other foot. I don't know where he went. I'm afraid there's no water here. We'll get some as soon as we get to town. You'll be all right. I suppose he went back where he came from. We never saw him again here, in any case.

Does it seem like such a long time that we've been walking? It's only a few minutes. You recognize the path but you don't know where you are? Why should you know where you are? It's not your forest. Relax. Step. Step. Step.

You're right. It's the rock where we were sitting a few minutes ago. I wondered if you'd notice. Of course I know my way! I thought you'd better rest again before we started into town. That's right, you just lie back there. You'll be fine as soon as you've had a little sleep. It's very quiet here.

No, you haven't been asleep so long. How do you feel now? Good. I knew a little sleep would do it. You're not used to the air here. A pouch? I don't think you were carrying anything.

There's no need to make a face like that. You don't think I took it, do you?

I thought we were friends. I treated you like a friend. And now you pay me back.

I'm not going to take you anywhere. Get down to the town by yourself. I'm going the other way.

Go on back to your country and tell them about me. You can walk all right.

Just keep going.

And get out of the forest fast!

Reminders of Bouselham

WHEN I was a boy, Mother's favorite spot for reading, the place where she sat when she was going to read for a long time, was an old chaise longue, kept always in the same position in a corner of the east room, far enough from the walls so that the light came in over her shoulders on both sides. The back of the chaise longue was piled with dozens of small down-stuffed cushions. It was a comfortable seat to recline in. Sometimes I would use it for a few minutes in the morning before she was up. Once she caught me there and ridiculed me.

Getting decrepit in your old age! she scoffed. You're a growing boy. That's a chair for an adult.

The garden was the place to lie on a summer afternoon. Overhead the wind hissed in the high eucalyptus and cypress trees. There were flying skeins of fog that swept by very fast, just above, sometimes catching the tops of the trees and swooping down through the branches. One summer when I was back from school in England I did all my studying out there on the ground behind bushes or hedges, or anywhere that was hidden from the sight of the house.

And I would lie face-down in the hot garden, and look beneath the cut tips of the grass spears, into the miniature forest where the ants lived. Most of them were very small, and were not troubled by the mat I spread out over their domain. If the large red ones discovered it, as now and then they did, they attacked at once, and there was nothing to do but carry the mat somewhere else.

It went without saying that the Medina was forbidden territory. Mother would have reacted very badly had she known I had ever been in it alone. But from time to time I went on an errand and had the opportunity to slip into the old town and find my way along the alleys for a few minutes. I loved the way they suddenly changed direction and burrowed under the houses. In fact, you went under a house to get into the alley where Mama Tiemponada's brothel stood. Hers was not the only one there, but it was the biggest. All the houses in

468

the alley were brothels. The women leaned in the doorways and made remarks to the men walking by. I found the place mysterious and sinister. It seemed natural enough that Mother should not want me to come to the Medina.

One evening as I stood outside Mama Tiemponada's in the alley watching the door, it opened and a single Moroccan boy came out. He stood still for an instant, and looking up at the full moon directly above, whistled once at it, then walked away. This struck me as very strange, and I remembered it. The whistle was casual and intimate, suggesting that the moon and he had been good friends for a long time. A year or two later, when Bouselham came to work for us, I thought I recognized him as the same boy.

Probably it would have been better for me if I'd got to know Father, but I never did. It did not occur to me to wonder what sort of man he was. His fiftieth birthday was well behind him when I was born, and by then he was interested primarily in golf. He paid no attention to me, and very little to Mother. At daybreak he would get up, eat a big breakfast, and ride his favorite horse to the country club at Boubana. We would not see him again until evening. The ladies said to Mother: Colonel Driscoll is so impressive up there on his horse! Their own husbands drove in their cars to the country club. I was convinced that they were secretly laughing at us because Father was so odd.

As a boy I sometimes played with Amy, because she lived on the property next to ours, down the road. She was five years older than I, a tomboy, and full of sadistic impulses which she often vented on me. When she was twenty her mother died, and Amy was left alone in a house far too big for her. Then she began to spend almost all her time with Mother.

I was not surprised when Mother announced casually one day: Amy has a buyer for Villa Vireval. She's coming to stay with us for a while.

Soon Amy was with us. She had changed with the years, and was now an introverted, nervous young woman with a passion for precision. She had an annoying tic: the constantly repeated clearing of her throat. In the beginning Father made an effort to converse with her, even though he was very much against having her with us. She was neurotic, he said; she was morbid and self-centered, and she sapped Mother's energy.

What's wrong with that girl? Can't she leave you alone for a minute?

Mother, who like anyone else enjoyed being admired, was grateful even for Amy's devotion.

She's a well-balanced girl. I can't think what you have against her.

As usual the gossip got the basic facts fairly straight, but the motivations wrong. Everyone was certain that Father had left home because of Bouselham, when actually it was because he could no longer bear to be in the same house with Amy. He put up with her for six months. Then, seeing that she had no intention of leaving, and that Mother was adamant in her refusal to suggest to her that she find another place to live, he suddenly went off to Italy. Mother was unperturbed. Your father needs a holiday, she said to me after he had gone. Of course she assumed he would return.

It was precisely at that point that Bouselham emerged from his obscurity. Father had engaged him a year or so earlier, when he was sixteen, as an assistant gardener. He weeded, raked, and carried water in the lower garden, and one seldom saw him anywhere near the house. But when Father left, he began to come into the kitchen, where the maids would give him tea. Before long he was eating regularly there with them, rather than sitting under a tree with whatever he had brought with him from home.

How did the relationship start between him and Mother? What was the beginning of it? There is no way of bringing up the subject with Bouselham, since it has never been mentioned and thus does not exist between us. But I know that whatever the beginning may have been, it was Mother who set it in motion.

Often Bouselham had nothing to do but sit in a café smoking kif, and it was not always certain that there would be someone who could play cards with him. Most men worked during the day and came into the café after they had finished. Bouselham did not have to work. Ever since the colonel had gone away he had been with the colonel's wife. She did not want him to work, because then he would have to get up very early every morning, whereas she liked to sleep late and have him with her. All the men in the café knew that Bouselham had a rich Nazarene woman who gave him whatever he wanted.

And this was what Amy eventually began to say to Mother in one way or another, over and over. In her view it was wrong of Mother to have Bouselham with her, not only because his culture, religion and social class were not hers, but also because he was too young for a woman of her age. Usually Mother replied blandly that she didn't agree, but now and then she said a bit more. I heard her say one day: You're trying to encroach on my private life, Amy, and you have no right to.

Not too long after that, Amy decided to go to Paris where a friend had invited her. She packed up very quickly and was suddenly gone. Mother limited her comment to saying: Amy's a very sweet girl who has everything to learn, I'm afraid. And whether she will or not, I wonder.

The day Amy left I wandered into her room and looked around. It needed a thorough cleaning. I pulled the bureau out from the wall and peered down behind it. Underneath, wedged behind a back leg, was a crumpled postcard-size glossy print of Bouselham in bathing trunks on the beach at Sidi Qanqouch. For me this put Amy's quarrel with Mother in a new light. For a moment I was even sorry she was gone; it would have been fun to see what a few leading questions might have brought out from behind those thin precise lips of hers. Had she coveted Bouselham for herself? Or did Mother interrupt something that was already going on between them when she brought Bouselham into the house to sleep in her room?

The tale had been going around Tangier for many months. I heard it first from an English woman; she had just arrived here, and so had no way of knowing that the subject of her story was my mother. The colonel's wife used to disappear every night into the dark corners of the garden to meet the gardener, who was no more than a boy, an ordinary Moroccan workman. And when the colonel had had enough of her nonsense he had left, whereupon she had calmly taken the servant into the house and lived with him. I'm told she's even given him a racing car! she added, pretending to burst into laughter.

Probably, I said.

There is no doubt that Mother changed in certain respects during the time Bouselham was living in the house. She did buy a second-hand Porsche convertible for him, and this was certainly most unlike her. Her manner became distant; she seemed uninvolved in all the things that heretofore had been her life. When I suggested that I move out of the house and take a flat in town, she merely raised her eyebrows. You'll come to dinner twice a week, was all she said.

What finally decided her against Bouselham was a long and complicated saga involving his sister. Once she had carefully checked on the details of the story, her resolve to get rid of him was instantaneous. However, the only way she could devise for accomplishing this was so drastic as to be laughable. Mother has lived in this country for many years, and should not have been so deeply disturbed by Bouselham's behavior, particularly since it had nothing whatever to do with her. To me what he did seems natural enough, but then, I was born here. I first heard about it from Bouselham himself, not long after I moved out of the house and took the apartment in town.

I had been out to dinner and had walked home afterward. A thunderstorm was approaching from the direction of the strait. Soon hail showered against the windows. There was a very bright bolt of lightning, and the electricity was gone. I got out a flashlight, started some candles burning, and stood in front of the fireplace for a while. The thunderstorm circled around and came back, and it rained harder. In the midst of this there was a banging on the door, and when I opened it I found Bouselham standing there, completely wet.

He looked as wild and as pleased with himself as ever, in spite of the rivulets of rain running down his face. Immediately he took off his shoes and socks and crouched in front of the fireplace, almost inside it, while he talked. Every day, he said, he was seeing a lawyer friend of his who was helping him.

To do what? I asked.

Avoiding a direct answer, he pivoted on his heels to face me, and asked if I could let him have ten thousand francs. The lawyer had to have the money for photocopies and notarizations. His fee would be contingent upon the success of his case, later. As soon as I had agreed to let him have the money, the story began to come out.

A certain rich merchant of the Medina, intent on the pleasures of the twilight hour, used to go each day and sit in a café at the end of the city. Here he could see in three directions, and hundreds of people were visible nearby and in the distance, walking along the roads. Each day, sooner or later, a girl passed by with an older woman who carried a basket. He sat at a table on the sidewalk, facing in the direction from which they always came, so that he could see them from far away, and watch the girl as she approached. Every afternoon he saw her eyes pick him out from among the others at the café, but from that moment on she would give no sign of knowing he was there.

How many years since I've seen such a beauty? he sighed. He would notice them coming far down the road under the eucalyptus trees, long before she could see him, for they were walking into the sunset light. The instant came when she saw him, and then her head bent forward. The rich merchant would watch her as she came nearer, his eyes never leaving her. It seemed to him that she was dancing rather than walking, and as she went past, often so near that he could have touched her djellaba by stretching out his arm, he was exasperated by the impossibility of speaking with her.

Maybe one day they'll let her out by herself, he thought, and so he waited.

The day finally came when he saw her walking along carrying the basket herself, and no one was with her. Ah, he said softly, rubbing the ends of his fingers together. He called the waiter and paid him. Then he sat quietly until she had gone by. As the girl turned the corner he got up and began to walk after her.

He caught up with her only after she had gone into another street. May I drive you somewhere? he asked her.

You may drive me home if you like, she said.

This was not what the rich merchant had hoped to hear. However, he led her to his car, which was parked not far away.

I brought Bouselham a cup of coffee. He sipped it, still crouching by the fire, and said nothing for several minutes. Then abandoning his story-telling manner, he went on casually, as though recapitulating a tale I already knew.

And I was just coming out of a bacal there, and I saw this Mercedes parked up ahead. And not with Belgian license-plates, either. Moroccan ones, and that means money. And then, while I was still looking, I stopped believing what I was seeing, because the door of the car opened and my sister got out and ran up toward the corner. I knew she'd seen me and didn't think I'd seen her. The first thing I thought of was going after her and killing her. While I stood there the car drove away. I didn't see the man or get the number.

What good would that have done, if you'd killed her? I said, although I knew that for him it was one of those meaningless European remarks. Surprisingly, he laughed and said: I'm not that stupid. I felt sorry for her, though, that night when I got her alone at home and saw how frightened she was.

I saw you get out of the car, I told her. But then I said: You say he's always at the Café Dakhla. Tomorrow you're going to show me which one he is. As you walk past him you're going to cough.

And she did, and when he left the café I followed him and saw him get into his Mercedes. I watched him drive away and I thought: Maybe. Maybe. Incha' Allah!

Once he had identified the man through his license-plate, he began to ask questions, first going to the qahouaji there in the café, and then having narrowed his search, to several merchants and bazaar-keepers in the city.

I found out more about him than his mother knows, said Bouselham. He owns half the textile factory at the Plaza Mozart, and an apartment house in the Boulevard de Paris. And three bazaars. So one night when I got home I took my sister up on the roof where we could talk, and I said to her: You like this Qasri?

She began to stammer and protest. I don't even know him. How can I say if I like him?

That made me angry and I grabbed her. You don't know whether you like him. But you got into his car and sat beside him. What does that mean?

She thought I was going to hit her, and she hid her face in her hands and backed away. I had the right to beat her, of course. But I let her know I was on her side, and would never mention it to the rest of the family. I even bought her new clothes the next day, so El Qasri could get some idea of how she could look if she wanted to. And I decided to wait and see if things happened by themselves.

He kept after her and she went on putting him off. Then once my father and mother and the whole family had to go to Meknes overnight, and she and I were the only ones who stayed home. I thought: I'm going to spend the night in Tetuan and see what happens. So I told her I wasn't going to be there that night, and that she would have to sleep at our aunt's house. And I asked her please not to mention my trip to Tetuan to our parents, because of course I was supposed to be in the house taking care of her. I thought: If anything's going to happen by itself, tonight's the night when it'll happen. And I was right. I went to Tetuan and she went with him to his house, and it wasn't a long time later when she came to me and said she thought there was a child in her belly.

Right away I took her over to Gibraltar, to the biggest hospital. We stayed there four days, and I got the papers on each test, and there was no doubt about it, they said: there was a child inside.

Having nothing more urgent to do with his time, Bouselham continued to go each day to the café at the end of the city. Here he fell into conversation and eventual companionship with the rich merchant. Even after he had brought his sister back from Gibraltar, and the lawyer was busy preparing his strategy, even after the lawyer had called on the rich merchant to advise him that the only way of avoiding a scandal was to ask for the girl in marriage, before her family discovered her pregnancy, Bouselham sat daily with him in the café listening to the story of his troubled romance.

She's got a brother, the rich merchant told him. He's the one who wants my blood. The son of a whore found out about it.

Then Bouselham said to him: But why son of a whore? He's letting you marry her. If he wanted to, he could put you in jail today. Are you crazy? She was a virgin.

The rich merchant agreed that this was so. Less than a week later he made the offer of marriage to Bouselham's father.

After he stopped talking, I looked down at him, trying to see the expression on his face, but his head was outlined against the flames, and there was only the light of two candles in the room.

He's not going to like it much when he finds out you're her brother, I said.

He only laughed. Some day, he said. Some day.

I brought a fresh log, and he finally stood up.

Bouselham did not keep silent about the dubious part he'd played in the arranging of his sister's wedding; on the contrary, he discussed it at length with his Moroccan friends. To him it was a business matter in whose success he took a healthy pride. Thus several garbled versions of the story began to travel around Tangier. Mother heard them, but discounted them as fables invented purely out of spite. It was not until months after Bouselham's visit to me at the flat that she brought herself to accepting them as fact. At that instant she became irrational.

The whole thing is vile! she said. I've got rid of him. His dismissal had been summary, with no explanation offered. She had handed him a sum of money and told him to leave the premises instantly. Two days later she had set out for Italy. It was clear to me that she half expected to be blackmailed, but was ashamed to put it into words. If only she had mentioned her fear, I could have tried to reassure her. I believe I know Bouselham better than she did.

Until the day when he called to me from inside the Café Raqassa, I had not seen him for several weeks. We sat in a back corner where it was dark and the air smelled of damp cement and charcoal smoke. Bouselham spoke briefly of Mother, shaking his head ruefully. There was no mention of anything more than that he had lost his job as gardener when Madame went away. He was aware of somehow having offended her, but her arbitrary behavior had bewildered and aggrieved him. The way he saw it, he had been turned out of the house for no reason at all. Still, as we parted, he said: When you write to Madame, tell her Bouselham sends his greetings.

I did not pass on the message, or any subsequent ones, from him to Mother. She sold the house without returning to Tangier, and it seemed to me that living over there in Italy with Father she must be miserable enough without getting reminders of Bouselham from me.

Things Gone and Things Still Here

TANGIER—if I were to move into the house at Ain Chqaf I should go to great expense to have the workmen install a fountain in the center of the courtyard. The water would fall into a marble basin and run out along marble troughs into a ditch. Running water, they say, rests the soul before the hour of prayer. On occasion, perhaps too much. An example: the familiar story of Hadj Allal, who came to grief through no fault of his own.

"As if he had stepped on a mine," explained one divinity student. "Only the mine was invisible and made no sound when it exploded. No one knew anything about it. He was there looking into the stream. Then he came into the mosque. For all of us he had been out there perhaps five minutes. But in the place where he had fallen two years had gone by. He tried to explain it to us. We took him home and told his wife to put him to bed and cover him up."

There is the tale of the fqih who taught in a local mosque some two centuries ago. No trace of his passage through life would remain now had it not been for an inexplicable psychic misadventure: the man must have stumbled upon one of those rare fissures in time—an open fault, as it were, in the surface of time—and fallen in.

Another fqih, this one in Hajra den Nahal, is said to have slipped between two instants and fallen into a deep well of time. The accident occurred while he was washing in the stream outside the mosque. As he squatted by the running water two tolba passed by on their way into the mosque to pray. They were having a conversation. Later the fqih stated that he had heard only one phrase: "in the twinkling of an eye." That seems to have been the signal. Everything around him stopped existing and he was in darkness.

In all versions the entry into this bubble in time is decisive for the protagonist. The two false years, according to the Nahali's story, were spent by him in India in a state of invisibility. During that time he did nothing but observe a famous goldsmith at work. When he was cast out of the time trap and returned to the stream by the mosque, he had brought with him all the Indian master's secrets, knowledge which he immediately put to use by becoming a goldsmith himself. His fame as a master artisan spread throughout Islam, so that the Indian goldsmith, on hearing of it, could not rest until he had visited Morocco and seen the designs himself. Unwisely, he traveled with his wife. The dénouement and meaning of the story for those who tell it is the Nahali's double victory. Not only did the Indian see all his own designs improved upon by the Moroccan, but he also lost his wife to him.

Another unfortunate fqih passed his sojourn in the time bubble as a woman, but returned to the world with greater wisdom.

A brilliant account could be written of the saga of the Haddaoua and their destruction. The patron saint sat smoking kif in a nargilah all day every day, it is said; even seven or eight years ago adepts could still be found smoking beside the ruined tomb. The brotherhood has been painstakingly eradicated by the authorities. Sometimes you see a lone man walking along the road wearing the dusty rags and wild hairdo of a Haddaoui, but since the cult no longer exists (and, perhaps more importantly, has no headquarters) such a man no longer deserves the respect which being a member of a brotherhood would give him, and so for most citizens he slips into the category of ordinary madman.

In the eyes of the government, the Haddaoua were not a religious sect at all, but an organized group of brigands to be finished off with bullets. Apart from their uncanny powers over goats, which made it possible for them to arrange the wholesale theft of these animals all over northern Morocco, and their use of magic spells as a threat in order to extort money from the rural populace, there would seem to be no valid reason for their persecution and extermination. Perhaps it was the fact that they built a fortress and kept a good many women shut into the cellars. They claimed that the women had come of their own volition and asked to be taken in as adepts. Whether or not that was the case, once the women had been present at the rituals they were not permitted to leave the premises, but were locked into the basement where they performed domestic duties.

The Haddaoua placed great stress on food. Each meal was a banquet. This emphasis on eating may have been a result of the vast quantities of cannabis the men ingested each day, but the meals themselves were made possible by the easy availability of edible livestock. A Haddaoui could go out alone into the countryside and return in a few days with hundreds of goats following him in single-file formation. This alone was enough to strike fear to the hearts of the peasants. No one appears to know exactly how they imposed their will on the animals, but all agree that it was a special art which took time and patience to learn. When you consider that the men learned the technique by lying down among the animals and conversing with them at night during their sleep, it does not seem so improbable. The Haddaoui lying in the Marrakech dust forty years ago "became" a goat while I watched, and there in front of me was a man's body with a goat inside it, as if the goat had been able to assume the visible form of a man, while at the same time it remained unmistakably a goat. Whatever it was that they stumbled upon in the way of esoteric knowledge, their misuse of it was their undoing.

For people living in the country today the djinn is an accepted, if dreaded, concomitant of daily life. The world of djenoun is too close for comfort. Among the Moroccans it is not a question of summoning them to aid you, but simply of avoiding them. Their habitat is only a few feet below ours, and is an exact duplication of the landscape aboveground. Each tree, rock and house has its identical counterpart beneath the earth's surface. The only difference is that there the sky is made of earth instead of air, and so it is totally dark. But since the lower world is a faithful reproduction of the upper world, it follows that the djenoun are perfectly equipped for life down there, and actually prefer it to our world. The trouble occurs when they emerge and take on human or animal form, for they are our traditional enemies, an alien tribe always on the lookout for an opportunity to infiltrate our ranks, and they do this merely by establishing contact with us.

Once a djinn has revealed himself to you your life changes.

You can suspect his influence or presence whenever things have not gone as they should have, whenever there is a suspect or inexplicable element in a situation, whenever, in short, you are confronted with anything you don't understand. This is your warning; you begin to look for the djinn, and sooner or later you come across it and recognize it, no matter in what form you find it. What counts is your behavior and method of dealing with it at that point. Losing out in your struggle with a djinn can involve you in years of harassment or illness; it can also be fatal.

Above all you must guard against becoming emotionally involved with a djinn or a djinniya. There are many instances of miscegenation, but these are usually not discovered until after one partner has killed the other. "I watched her for months and I noticed that she never ate anything with salt in it. That was how I knew she was not a woman."

The open points along the frontier between the two worlds can conceivably occur anywhere, but exist generally in caves and under water, particularly under running water. If your itinerary involves crossing a stream, best have something made of steel (or at least iron) handy. City people often say there are no djenoun, not any more, or in any case not in the city. In the country, where life is the same as before and where there are not many automobiles and other things containing iron, they admit that djenoun probably still exist. But they add that the automobiles will eventually drive them all away, for they can't stand the proximity of iron and steel. Then it will be only in the distant mountains and the desert where you will need to worry about them.

Notwithstanding the rationalizations, djenoun continue to raise havoc now and then in the very center of the city by coming suddenly out of sink drains and attacking housewives. With this in mind, many women will not allow any hot water to fall into the sink, which means they must wash the dishes in cold water for fear of burning the possible inhabitant of the pipe. Djenoun have been known to be extremely vindictive in such cases, and commonly retaliate by causing paralysis in the offender.

*

If you go to the outskirts of any town, to where the fields begin and sheep are grazing, and dig in the earth under certain trees, you will come upon a knife. If you dig somewhere a few yards away from there, you may find another. There are many of them, all of the folding sort, and each one is clasped shut on a scrap of paper. Even though you open every knife you find, each time releasing a man from the spell of some accursed woman, still you are not going to spend all your time doing good turns for a whole group of men you have never known and never will meet. There would be no reason in the first place to go and dig for knives unless you suspect that a woman has shut a knife on you. Then, depending on who you think it might have been and where she would be most likely to go in order to bury it, you get busy and start to dig.

Sometimes you come upon other men digging, and when they see you they look ashamed and pretend to be looking for some change they have dropped. Often they stand up, shrug, and walk away. But if you go some distance and wait, they come back and start again to dig. Where is the justice in a world in which a woman with a simple folding knife can make so much trouble for a man?

"Twice I've found folded knives deep in the water at the bottom of the cliffs along the strait. The women who do this are even worse than the ones who bury them in the ground. They are willing to walk all the way to the cliffs so they can ruin the lives of the men they hate. There is not much chance of these knives being found and opened. And even if the paper where the curse was written has dissolved in the water, the man can have no sort of life again until the blade is opened. It's the shutting of the blade on the curse that keeps a man from being able to get hard. If I ever come across a woman burying a knife, she'll never get back home."

MIDNIGHT MASS

TABLE OF CONTENTS

Midnight Mass

H<small>E ARRIVED</small> in Tangier at noon and went straight to the house. In the rain the outer courtyard was uninviting. Several dead banana plants had fallen over and been left to rot on the tile floor. Even as old Amina, seeing him from the kitchen doorway, waddled out into the rain to greet him, he was aware of the piles of empty crates, and of the frame of an ancient garden swing looming behind her.

At lunch he tasted his childhood in Amina's soup. The recipe had not changed; pumpkin and cumin still predominated. All at once he was aware of a cold wind blowing through the room. He called to Amina: the big window in the kitchen was broken. He reminded her that money had been sent to have it repaired. But the wind had come and blown it in again, she said, and this time they had simply left it that way. He told her to shut the door to the kitchen. When she had done it he could not see that it made any difference.

He went through the rooms. The place was only a shell of the house he remembered. Most of the furniture was gone, and there were no rugs or curtains. When he discovered that all six of the fireplaces belched smoke, he had his first doubts about the usefulness of the house as a place to spend the Christmas holidays—at least, that year. It was the only bequest his mother had made him, and she had been reluctant even about that. "You don't want the house in Tangier. You'll never use it." "But I love it," he had objected. "I grew up in it, after all." Once she had agreed to leave it to him, she had proceeded to strip it of everything of value. A rug went to one friend, a highboy to another, a chest to someone else, so that by the time she died, the house must have been in more or less its present state. Several times during the eight years since her death his wife had urged him to go and "take stock" of the house, but since her interest was based on the possibility of selling it, a thing he intended never to do, he had taken no action.

The house was in even worse condition than he had expected it to be. Ingenuously, he had assumed that because he paid their wages promptly each month, the servants would make an attempt to keep it in order. He hoped for some hot water to get the chimney soot off his hands, but Mohammed told him that the water heater had not functioned since the year before Madame had died. The man she called in to repair it had said it would have to be replaced by a new system, so she had used cold water after that. As he dried his hands on a flimsy linen guest-towel (she had given away all the bath-towels) he thought grimly: She could let old Madame Schreiber go off with a rug worth several thousand pounds, but she couldn't afford to bathe in hot water.

He went out into the garden. The rain had stopped, but the wind moved the trees, so that large scattered drops still fell as they swayed. He looked up at the huge white façade, marvelling that he ever could have thought it majestic. Now it looked like a pavilion left over from a long-forgotten exposition.

By the end of the afternoon he was thoroughly chilled. The house was too close to the sea. The wind came up over the cliff laden with the salt mist of the waves, and sprayed it against the windows. If he looked out at the garden he saw it only confusedly through the curtain of salt that had coated the panes. In the library closet he found an electric heater. It was ancient, but it gave off a modest glow. With the shutters bolted and the door closed, he seized a book at random from the bookshelves and threw himself into a chair. He read for a moment, then turned to the back of the book and on a blank page began to compose a telegram to his wife. CANCEL FLIGHT HOUSE DISASTROUS REPAIRS IMPERATIVE RETURNING FIRST WEEK JANUARY ALAS NO CHRISTMAS TOGETHER PLAN FOR EASTER HERE BETTER SEASON ALL LOVE. Early spring could be very cold, too, he suddenly remembered, but at least the fire-places would be working.

He had instructed his Tangier bank to have the telephone connected; it was an agreeable surprise to hear the operator's voice. The difficulties began as he tried to spell out the name and address. "*M comme en Marseille? R comme en Robert?*" There was an explosion of clicks, and the connection faded.

He hung up and dialled the taxi service. The cab waited for him outside the post-office.

The first few nights he slept badly. The sheets were damp and there were not enough blankets. Even with the windows shut the sea wind raced through the big bedroom. Each morning well before dawn a pair of owls settled in the cypress trees beside the house and began to call back and forth. In his childhood he had heard the sound many times, but it never had kept him awake.

When the wind had turned and the days grew sunny, the workmen were able to start rebuilding the chimneys. The house was full of Moroccans in overalls and rubber boots. It was Ramadan; they worked without speaking, feeling their hunger and thirst in silence.

On the Sunday before Christmas the sky was bright blue and cloudless. The north wind had brought the mountains in Spain unusually near. Since no workmen would be coming, he decided to go out for a walk. The puddles in the road had dried. Plant odors and the scent of woodsmoke laced the wind. In a better mood, he conceived the idea of asking a few people to come by on Christmas Eve for drinks; it would be pleasanter than having to go out, and he could not envisage remaining alone in the house on that night.

A small white car came into view and drew up outside an iron-grilled gate a hundred feet or so ahead of him. As he approached, he recognized Madame Dervaux. As soon as they had greeted one another, he mentioned Christmas Eve, suggesting that she bring along anyone she wished. She accepted immediately; she would try, she said, to be with interesting people. He was about to make a facetious reply, but seeing that she was perfectly serious, he held his tongue.

During the next few days he invited a few more people. Although he did not much care who came, since he wanted only to see someone in the house on Christmas Eve, he reflected with satisfaction that not one of the prospective guests would have been asked to the house by his mother.

Christmas Eve was clear and almost windless. The moon, directly overhead, filled the courtyard with its hard light. Amina had just carried the last tray of glasses into the hall when the doctor arrived. Once he was seated, a gin and tonic in his hand, he looked around the room and frowned.

"Your mother had a great deal to put up with here in this house," he said. "It was far too damp for her to live in, and far too big for her to manage."

He heard the sharpness in his voice as he replied. "It was her own choice to go on living here. She loved it. She wouldn't have agreed to live anywhere else."

The rector came in, out of breath and smiling. This was his first winter in Morocco, so the doctor described the climate to him.

Leaving the two talking, he went into the library and lighted the fire Mohammed had laid in the fireplace there. Then he had Amina bring more candles and set them around the room, knowing that the library was where the guests eventually would gather. The other rooms had very little furniture in them.

The sound of laughter came from the courtyard. Madame Dervaux entered, with several younger people in her wake. Going straight up to her host, she presented him with a huge bunch of narcissus. "Smell," she told him. "I picked them this afternoon at Sidi Yamani. The fields are covered."

He hurried to the kitchen to have Amina put the flowers into water. Madame Dervaux followed, talking rapidly. She had come, she said, with a poet, a painter and a philosopher, all of them Moroccans. As an afterthought she added: "And a very charming Indian girl from Paris. So you see?"

Understanding this as a reference to her promise to bring "interesting" people, he set his jaw. Finally he murmured: "Aha."

When they returned to the salon, Vandeventer stood in the middle of the room, slightly the worse for having just come from another party. The rector had gone with the younger people into the library. Madame Dervaux, hearing their laughter, walked quickly in their direction.

He settled Vandeventer near the doctor, poured himself a neat Scotch, and wandered in the direction of the library. As he got to the doorway, the rector was saying playfully to one of the young Moroccans: "You'd better be careful. One of these mornings you may wake up and find yourself in Hell."

"No, no," the young man said easily. "Hell is only for people who haven't suffered enough here." The rector seemed taken aback.

Fearful that the conversation might be about to degenerate into a quasi-religious discussion among his guests, he went quickly toward the group. "And you," he said, singling out the Moroccan, "you've suffered enough?"

"Too much," he said simply.

Madame Dervaux rose to her feet and asked to be taken on a tour of inspection of the house. He protested that there was nothing to see but empty rooms.

"But we can see the rooms! And go up into the tower, and out onto the roof. The view is superb."

"In the dark?"

"In the moonlight, in the moonlight," she said rapturously. The Moroccans murmured with approval.

"Come," he told them, and they all followed him out. A young Frenchman and his wife, both of whom taught at the Lycée Regnault, had arrived, bringing with them another couple from Casablanca. He had to leave his little party of sightseers at the foot of the stairs while he saw to it that the new arrivals were supplied with drinks. He poured himself another glass of whisky to take with him on the tour.

Some of the electric bulbs along the way failed to come on, so that there was more darkness than light on the stairways. Even before they got to the tower door they could hear the roar of the sea below.

He went ahead and opened one of the windows, so they could lean out and see the black cliffs of the coastline. The only lights in the landscape were a few twinkling points across the strait in Spain. "The end of the world," the rector remarked as he drew in his head.

A moment later when they were back in the hallway, the young Moroccan with whom he had spoken in the library came up from behind and walked along beside him. "Letting me look at all these empty rooms is very bad," he said. "Like showing food to a starving man."

"How is that?" he asked absently.

"It's only that I have to live with my family, and there's no space anywhere, so what I want most is a room. Nearly every night I dream that I have a room of my own where I can paint. So of course when I see so many rooms with no one in them, the saliva runs in my mouth. It's natural."

"I suppose it is." He found the young man's confidences embarrassing; they emphasized the disparities between them, and gave him a vague sense of guilt.

Now Madame Dervaux was clamoring to be taken out onto the roof. He refused. "There's no railing."

"We'll just stand in the moonlight," she insisted. "No one will go near the edge."

He stopped walking and stared at her. "That's exact, since no one is going onto the roof."

She pouted for an instant, and then resumed her chatter.

On the way downstairs he turned to the painter, who was still beside him. "I ought to spend more time here," he said, a note of apology in his voice. "But the truth is, the house isn't very livable."

"How can you say that? It's a magnificent house."

"The wind blows straight through it," he went on, as though the other had not spoken. "There are rats in the walls, there's no hot water, half the time the telephone doesn't function."

"But all houses here are like that. The difference is that this one has ten times as much space."

So far he had pretended not to see where the painter was attempting to direct the conversation, but now he said: "I'd like nothing better than to be able to slice off a room for you and wrap it up, so you could take it home."

The Moroccan smiled. "Why does it have to be taken home? It could be consumed on the premises just as well."

He laughed, liking the Moroccan's appropriation of his metaphor. "Ah yes. There's that too," he agreed as they arrived back at the library door. "Just pass by the bar," he said to those behind him. "Mohammed will give you what you want."

Beyond the library was a farther room, forming a separate wing of the house. In bygone days it had been referred to as the conservatory. Now there was nothing in it, and the door into it was kept shut because the many windows let in the sea-wind. When he returned from the bar presently, he caught sight of Madame Dervaux striking a theatrical pose as she flung open the door.

"*Mon dieu!*" she cried. "So *this* is where the corpses are buried!"

Now the library was crowded, so that he was unable to get to the door before she had led both the painter and poet into the dark room. He leaned in and called to them. "There's no light in there, and we can't have the door open. Please come back." When they failed to answer, he shut the door.

He heard Madame Dervaux's squeal, waited, then opened the door a crack and held it, so they could find their way back.

Madame Dervaux came out laughing, although she shot a resentful glance at him. The poet continued imperturbably to criticize Baudelaire, but the painter was not listening. "What a studio!" he murmured.

"It was terrifying, that horrible place, without a ray of light!" Madame Dervaux confided to the Indian girl.

She was insufferable. "But Madame," he said. "Corpses are generally enjoyed in the dark."

"A fantastic studio," the painter went on. "North light, nothing but trees and the sea. A paradise!"

He faced the young man. "The ceiling is in shreds. The rain has come in everywhere. I doubt one could use it for anything."

The doctor and the rector were leaving, and the two French couples were conferring on the shortest route to the site of the next party. Vandeventer, leaning against the wall for support, was arguing with the Indian girl. There was a general consulting of timepieces. "If we're going to Midnight Mass we must leave now," Madame Dervaux declared.

Vandeventer had begun to walk slowly toward the group. "Have you ever heard such nonsense?" he demanded of his host, indicating the others with his glass. "Three Moslems, one Hindu and one atheist, all running off to Midnight Mass? Ridiculous, no?"

He shrugged. "Ah, well, *de gustibus*. You know." To himself he said fervently: "Thank God for Midnight Mass." Without it they would have stayed indefinitely. The workmen were coming in the morning, the same as on other days, the holiday not being one of theirs.

Vandeventer seized his arm. "I must leave you. Delightful evening. Already I'm drunk, and now I must take my wife to the reveillon at the Minzah.

He walked with him to the gate, to prevent him from stumbling in the courtyard. Once Vandeventer had managed to get into the car, he had no difficulty in driving it.

And now the remainder of his guests came filing out. The two French couples said good-night, and Mohammed shut the gate after them. As she slowly led her little group across the open space, Madame Dervaux suddenly announced that they must all take a quick glance at the kitchen, which she qualified as "superb." The others followed her, all but the painter, who lagged behind and walked over to his host.

"I hope you enjoy the service," his host told him.

"Oh, I'm not going with them. I live near here."

The wind had risen somewhat. He heard Madame Dervaux's shrill expletives and Amina's easy laughter. He stared at the painter. "Good. Stay a minute after they've gone. I'd like to talk to you." His mind was made up. "What difference does it make?" he thought. "Let him use the room. No one else is ever going to use it."

The young man nodded, his face taking on an air of secrecy. When the others went out through the gate he said nothing. Instead of getting into the car with Madame Dervaux, he slammed the door shut and waved.

Immediately her head emerged. "*Oh, le méchant!*" she scolded. "*Il va avoir une gueule de bois affreuse!*"

The painter smiled and waved again.

He watched the scene standing in the open gateway. When the tail lights had disappeared up the dark road, he turned to the young man and said: "I simply wanted to say that I see no objection to letting you use the conservatory."

The young man's eyes glowed; he expressed his gratitude at some length. When they had shaken hands and he had gone out through the gate, he looked back and said: "Tonight I won't have to dream of having a room to paint in."

His host smiled fleetingly and bolted the door. The wind whipped around the banana plants, slapping their leaves one against the other. He was pleased with his decision. The house seemed more real now that he knew someone would be using even that small part of it. He went from room to room, blowing out the candles and switching off the lights. Then he went upstairs to bed. Amina had set a bowl of Madame Dervaux's narcissus on the night table. Their scent reached him, borne on the sea air, as he fell into sleep.

He did not go to Tangier at Easter time, nor yet during the summer. In September he got word that the painter's very rich and influential family had taken possession of the entire house. His lawyer was unable to evict them. Just before Christmas he received notice that the property, having been certified as agricultural land, no longer belonged to him. He reacted quietly to the loss, but his calm was shattered when, a few months later, he learned that the top floor and the tower had been rented by Madame Dervaux.

The Little House

THE LITTLE HOUSE had been built sixty or seventy years ago on the main street of what had been a village several miles outside the town; now the town had crept up on all sides. Originally there had been only the ground floor, but at some point an extra room had been added above the kitchen. In clear weather from one window of the upstairs room it was still possible to see the line of distant mountains to the southwest. It was here that Lalla Aïcha liked to sit, running her fingers over the beads of her chaplet while she considered how greatly her life had changed since her son had brought her to the town to stay with him. Somewhere behind the mountains was the valley where she had passed her life. She did not expect to see it again.

At first she had felt that moving to the town was a great triumph for her, but now she was not certain. It was true that the food was better, and there was plenty of it, but the house was very small, and she felt cramped living in it. Privately she was sorry that Sadek had not found a better wife than Fatoma, even though Fatoma's parents owned a large house not far away. It seemed to her that in return for having married their useless daughter, Sadek might have been offered a part of their house to live in. They all could have lived there easily, without getting in each other's way. But when she mentioned it to Sadek, he merely laughed.

The young people had been married for more than a year, and there was no sign of a child, a circumstance which Lalla Aïcha blamed on the girl, unaware that the couple had agreed to start a family only when they had some money set aside for the purpose.

As for Fatoma, she had been nervous and unhappy since the day Lalla Aïcha had moved in with them. The old woman was particular about her food, and found constant fault with Fatoma's method of keeping house. Whatever the girl happened to be doing, Lalla Aïcha would stand watching her closely, then shake her head and say: That's not the way we did it in my day, when Moulay Youssef was alive. She felt that

496

Fatoma was too casual about serving Sadek's dinner to him when he came in from work.

Why should he have to wait half an hour before he can eat? she demanded. Why don't you have everything ready so you can bring in the taifor as soon as you hear him come in? He's too good to you, that's the trouble, and you take advantage of his easy nature.

Then Lalla Aïcha would get Sadek aside and tell him how much Fatoma disliked her and how insultingly she treated her. She won't take me out for a walk, and she won't let me go to market with her. I like to get out once in a while, but I can't go by myself. And the other day when she took me to the doctor's, she went so fast I couldn't catch my breath. I know, she wishes I were dead, that's all.

Sadek laughed and said: You're crazy.

Ever since the older woman had moved in with them, Fatoma had been trying to persuade her to discard her haik and wear a djellaba like other women of the town, but Lalla Aïcha disapproved strongly of djellabas on women, saying that Moulay Youssef would surely have forbidden such a shameless custom. For Fatoma the haik was an emblem of rusticity; above all she did not want to be taken for a girl from the country. It filled her with shame to walk in the street beside a tottering old woman in a haik.

Each time she could slip it into the conversation, Fatoma reminded Lalla Aïcha that she had been given the best room in the house. They both knew this was not the case. True, it had more windows and better light than the room where the married couple slept. But it was upstairs, and with each heavy rain the roof sprang new leaks, while Sadek and Fatoma were snug in a room near the kitchen.

Neither of them was sure enough of her position in the household to risk a show of open hostility; each had the fear that Sadek might unaccountably side with the other. Thus they were quiet in his presence, and life in the house continued with relative tranquility.

For a long time Lalla Aïcha had been aware that a fleshy growth was developing in the middle of her spine, although she had mentioned it to no one. One day as he helped her rise from the floor where she had been sitting, Sadek felt the bulbous object beneath her clothing, and cried out in surprise. It was not an easy matter to persuade her to see a doctor, but Sadek was determined, and eventually had his way. The doctor advised prompt removal of the tumor, and set a date for the operation.

During the days immediately prior to her hospitalization the old woman fretted. She had heard that the anaesthetic was something to be dreaded, she was afraid she might bleed to death, and she made it very clear that she had no faith in Nazarene medicines.

It's all right, Sadek told her. You're going to be fine.

The night before she was to leave, Sadek and Fatoma sat in their room discussing the probable cost of the operation. Lalla Aïcha had gone upstairs and was getting her things together to be packed.

All the money I've saved trying to make cheap meals, Fatoma said with bitterness.

If it were your own mother you wouldn't feel that way, he told her.

She did not answer. There was a knock at the door. Lalla Halima, an elderly woman who lived across the street, had come to call on Lalla Aïcha and bid her good-bye.

She's upstairs, said Fatoma listlessly. Sighing and groaning, the woman mounted the staircase, and Sadek and Fatoma continued their unhappy discussion.

In the morning after Lalla Aïcha had gone to the hospital, and Sadek and Fatoma were having breakfast, Sadek looked around the room. It seems different, having her gone, doesn't it?

It's quiet, said Fatoma.

He turned quickly to her. I know you don't like having her here. I know she makes you nervous. But she's my mother.

Fatoma assumed an injured air. I only said it was quiet, and it is.

That afternoon when Sadek came home from work, Fatoma handed him a large basket. He lifted it. It's heavy, he said.

Take it to your mother in the hospital. It's a tajine with lemon, still hot.

It was his mother's favorite dish. By Allah, she's going to be very happy! he said, and he kissed Fatoma, happy that she should have gone to such trouble.

When he got to the hospital the doors were locked. He tapped on the glass. A guard came who told him that visiting hours were over, and that in any case no food from outside could be taken in. Sadek cajoled, pleaded, threatened, but it had no result. The guard shut the door, leaving him on the steps with the basket.

Both he and Fatoma heartily disliked tajine with lemon, so that he saw no purpose in carrying it back home. It would be a sin to waste it; someone must eat it while it was hot. Then he thought of Fatoma's parents, who lived just down the street from the hospital. They liked the old-fashioned dishes, and would surely appreciate being brought a fresh tajine.

He found Fatoma's mother in the kitchen, greeted her, and took the pot out of the basket. Here's a tajine Fatoma just made, he told her.

She burst into smiles. Si Mohammed's going to be very happy when he sees what we're going to eat tonight, she said.

Early the following morning, before Sadek had eaten his breakfast, there was a great banging on the door. The two police officers who stood outside seized him and without allowing him to say good-bye to Fatoma, forced him into a jeep.

His mystification did not last long. At the comisaría they confronted him with the basket and the pot, which still had a good amount of the tajine in it. He was made to understand that the food was full of poison, and that his mother-in-law was dead. Si Mohammed, who lay in the hospital, had accused him of her murder.

At that point only one thought occupied Sadek's mind: Fatoma had tried to kill his mother. Confused by the lengthy questioning, he muttered aloud some of his inward preoccupations; these scraps caught the attention of the police.

Allah has punished her! She meant to kill mine, and she killed her own.

They soon learned that he was talking about his wife, but placed no credence in his account until the hospital guard had been called in and had verified it. The man remembered

Sadek very distinctly, he said, because he had been so annoy-
ingly insistent upon getting the food delivered to his mother.

They sent for Fatoma. She was overcome by the news of
her mother's death, and stunned by Sadek's sudden arrest.
Her replies were inarticulate beyond her admission that she
had given Sadek the basket with the pot of tajine in it, and
told him to take it to the hospital. She was locked into a cell.

Several weeks passed before the trial was held. Lalla Aïcha
had been discharged from the hospital and gone home to find
the empty house. She received the bad news about Sadek and
Fatoma with no show of emotion, save that she shook her
head and murmured: It was written.

She doesn't understand what has happened, they whispered
behind her back. It's too much for her, poor thing.

They brought her food each day so she would not have to
go to the market. Instead of climbing up to her room to sleep,
Lalla Aïcha installed herself downstairs in the matrimonial
bedroom, explaining to the neighbors that by the time Sadek
and Fatoma came home she would be entirely recovered from
her operation, and could then climb the stairs with more ease.

She still doesn't realize, they told one another.

At the trial Fatoma testified that she had given Sadek the
basket with the food in it, but that she knew nothing about
any poison.

Yet you admit that the tajine came from your kitchen.

Of course, said Fatoma. I was there while the old woman
was making it. The afternoon before she went to the hospital
she put everything together the way she likes her tajine. She
told me to cook it the next day and have Sadek take it to her
in the hospital.

This struck the court as an unlikely tale. It was decided to
adjourn and call in Lalla Aïcha at the next session.

The old woman arrived on the witness stand entirely covered in her haïk. She was asked to remove it from around her
head so they could hear what she was saying. Then they were
startled to hear her declare with a note of pride in her voice
that indeed she had made the tajine with her own hands. Yes,
yes, she said. I like to use lots of marinated lemons.

And what else did you put into it? the qadi asked in a deceptively gentle voice.

Lalla Aïcha began the recital of a list of ingredients. Then she stopped and said: Do you want the whole recipe?

Everyone laughed. The qadi called for silence, and fixing her with a baleful stare, said: I see. We have a humorist with us. Sit down. We'll come back to you later.

Lalla Aïcha sat and looked into her lap, murmuring as she told the beads on her chaplet. The qadi glared at her from time to time, incensed by her unconcern. He was waiting for a report from some special police who had been left behind in Sadek's house when Lalla Aïcha had been brought in. It came soon enough. Upstairs in her closet among her clothes they had come across a half-empty container of the same rat-killer that had been found in the tajine.

The qadi's expression was triumphant when he next called Lalla Aïcha to the stand. In his left hand he held a tin box which he shook in front of her face. Have you ever seen this box? he demanded.

Lalla Aïcha did not hesitate. Of course I've seen it. It belongs to me. That's what I used in the tajine.

The sound of whispering moved through the chamber: the spectators had decided that the old woman was feeble-minded. For an instant the qadi's eyes and mouth opened wide. Then he frowned.

Ah, you admit that it was you who put the poison into the tajine?

Lalla Aïcha sighed. I asked you if you wanted the recipe, and you didn't. I put half a kilo of lemons in. It covers up the taste of the powder.

Go on, said the qadi, looking fixedly at her.

That was special food for me, she continued, a note of indignation in her voice. Not for anybody else. It was medicine. You don't think I was going to eat it, do you? I wanted to let the poison in the tajine draw out the poison in my body.

I don't know what you're talking about, the qadi told her.

You put it into your mouth and spit it out. Then you put more in and spit it out, and keep doing it, and you wash your mouth out with water in between. That's an old medicine from my tchar. It gets rid of all the poison.

Don't you know you killed a woman with your nonsense?

Lalla Aïcha shook her head. No, no. It was written, that's all.

From another part of the chamber came Fatoma's shrill voice: Lies! It's not true! She knew they weren't going to let the food in! She knew before she went to the hospital!

Fatoma was silenced. The qadi, nevertheless, made a note, and the following day when she was called to the witness stand, he asked her to elaborate. As a result of Fatoma's tale, they next called in Lalla Halima, the neighbor from across the street. She too had to be asked to loosen her haïk, which she did with visible distaste.

Two, maybe three days before Lalla Aïcha was going to leave for the hospital, I went to see her. I wanted to be good to her, so I said: I'm going to have my daughter make some cabrozels and maybe some mrozeiya, and take them around to you in the hospital. She said: That's very kind of you, but it's no use. They have a new law, so the doctor told me, and they don't let anything in from the outside. So I had my daughter make some cabrozels anyway, and I took them to her myself the night before she went. I thought maybe she could wrap her clothes around them and put them into her bag, and they wouldn't see them.

That's all, said the qadi, making a gesture of dismissal. His eyes glittered as he said to Lalla Aïcha: And now what are you going to tell me?

I've told you everything, she said calmly. I was very busy trying to get my medicine made, and I forgot they wouldn't let it in. I'm an old woman. It went out of my head.

There was a commotion in one corner of the hall as Fatoma screamed: She didn't forget! She knew Sadek would leave it at my mother's!

Fatoma was hustled out of the court, still shouting and struggling. Lalla Aïcha stood quietly, waiting to be addressed. The qadi merely looked at her, an expression of doubt on his face.

Finally he said with exasperation: You're a stupid, ignorant woman. Who ever heard of poison in the mouth absorbing poison in the blood? Do you think anyone believes that nonsense?

Lalla Aïcha was unmoved. Yes, she said patiently. Everybody knows that Nazarene medicine works better if you take

Moslem medicine at the same time. The power of Allah is very great.

In despair the qadi dismissed the case and sent the three defendants home, after warning Sadek that he would be held responsible for any further trouble caused by his mother, since she was clearly not responsible for her actions.

That night, when Lalla Aïcha was asleep in her room upstairs, Fatoma presented Sadek with an ultimatum. Either he sent his mother away, or she would leave him and go to live with her father.

She killed my mother. I won't stay in the house with her.

Sadek was wise enough to accept this; he offered no objection. In the light of what she had done, he himself had come to the conclusion that it would be better to take his mother back to the country to live with the rest of her family.

She received the news quietly; indeed, she seemed to have been expecting it. In the hope of persuading her that he was not being arbitrary, was not merely getting rid of her, he added: You see what your foolishness has done.

Then she faced him and looked into his eyes. You have no right to blame me for anything, she told him. It's not my fault if you're still living in this little house.

At the time the remark meant nothing to him; it was merely a senile non-sequitur. Later, when he had returned from the tchar in the valley and was living quietly with Fatoma, he recalled it. After that, he often thought about it.

The Dismissal

IT WAS not his fault that he had lost his job, Abdelkrim explained to his friends. For more than a year and a half he had worked at Patricia's, and they always had got on smoothly. This is not to say that she did not find fault with him; but Nazarenes always criticize the work Moslems do for them, and he was used to that. Although at such moments she looked at him as though he were a small child, her objections came out in a gentler voice than most Nazarenes use. His tasks were simple enough, but they had demanded his constant presence on the property. Unless he were given specific permission to go to the cinema or sit in a café for an hour or two, he was obliged to be on hand. Patricia relied solely upon taxis; she had no car, so that Abdelkrim was able to live comfortably in the garage, where he cooked his own meals and listened to his radio.

Patricia had come from California a few years ago and bought the house. She was not exactly a girl, because she told him she had already been married to three different men, but she looked like a girl, and behaved, he said, like a nervous virgin who suspected she was never going to find a husband. I swear, he said, you wouldn't think she'd ever had a man.

She wore peculiar clothes, and pounds of jangling jewelry (it was all silver and copper, he said, not gold). Even her long earrings made a constant clicking sound. Abdelkrim's feeling about her was that she was a nice girl, but crazier than most Nazarenes. Even when the weather was not cold she wanted a fire roaring in the fireplace. There were plenty of electric lights, but she would only burn candles; she said electricity gave a dead light. The house was crammed with zebra hides and leopard pelts, and there was a collection of monstrous wooden heads which she claimed were African gods. Abdelkrim could see for himself that they represented devils. He always looked past them rather than at them.

For the six months prior to his dismissal Patricia's mother had been staying with her. She was a small excitable woman with bulging black eyes. In her frequent arguments with

Patricia she shrieked and sometimes wept, and he decided that it was her mother who had made Patricia crazy.

Abdelkrim's job consisted of three distinct kinds of work. In the morning he had to walk two miles to the market in the city, buy the food for the day and carry it back to the house. Afternoons he worked in the garden, and at night he acted as watchman. Patricia had presented her terms at the beginning, and he had accepted them. Since then he had never been absent for an hour without permission.

It was not a good garden to be in on a hot afternoon. Since the house was new, there was not one bush or tree big enough to provide any shade. Abdelkrim did not mind working in the sun, but he liked to rest fairly often and smoke a pipe of kif, and in order for that to give him the greatest relaxation and pleasure, he must be sitting somewhere deep in the shade. As a boy fifteen years ago, he had known shady places nearby where he and his friends played. He had vivid memories of the pine woods at Moujahiddine, the grove of high eucalyptus trees that covered the hillside at Ain Chqaf, and the long shaded tunnels the boys cut through the jungle of matted vines and blackberry bushes outside his house. All this was gone now; new villas covered the countryside.

There did remain one place where he could find the sort of shade he had loved to seek out in his boyhood. Half an hour's walk from Patricia's house, around the long cemetery wall, over the fields, and down into the valley of Boubana, took him to the country club, nestling in an oasis of greenery. Behind the clubhouse lay a strip of the original forestland, with a slow-moving stream that meandered noiselessly through it. The golf course was more often than not deserted; he could run across the fairways without fear of being seen, and then follow the stream until he came to the forest. Where the big trees began, it was like entering a huge silent building. The screaming of the cicadas was left outside with the sunlight. Once inside, all he could hear was the stirring of leaves in the upper branches, a distant watery sound that seemed to him the perfect music for a hot summer afternoon.

One Friday Abdelkrim asked if he might be absent in the afternoon of the following day, since it was a national holiday. Without replying Patricia went into another room and began to confer with her mother. When she came out she said that they had been planning to go on a picnic with some American friends, but that they could arrange to go on Sunday just as well.

Saturday came up hot and still. Since there was to be a parade, his friends had gone off to the town to see it. When Abdelkrim had carried the food back from the market and left it in the kitchen, he went quietly to his room in the garage. There he put his bread, tunafish and olives into a small bag, along with everything else that would help him to pass a pleasant afternoon, and went out through the gate bound for Boubana. Probably he would not have undertaken the long walk in the heat of the day (for it was unusually hot) if only there had been a dark corner of the garden where he could have sat and smoked and drunk his tea in shadowed privacy. This sun is poison, he said to himself as he went along.

When he entered the forest he was already hungry. Not far from one of the paths that snaked through the underbrush, he found a large flat rock where he spread out his things and ate a leisurely lunch. This is the place to be, he thought, not standing in the sun on the Boulevard along with fifty thousand others, waiting to see a few floats go past. He smoked a few pipes of kif, and laying his sebsi beside him on the rock, he yawned, leaned back, and stretched. At that moment he became aware of a commotion in the bushes on the other side of the stream. There were grunts and wheezes, and then a heavy thud as something hit the ground. He remained immobile for an instant, then swiftly threw himself face downward, flat on the earth.

The sounds came closer. He raised his head a bit and saw, not far away, five men carrying a big black cube as they stumbled along the path among the trees. In another instant he knew that the object, which seemed to be almost too heavy for them to manage, was a safe. There was a crackling sound as they dropped it into a mass of bushes. Rapidly they uprooted plants and gathered armfuls of leaves, tossing them in piles, to cover all signs of the object.

With great caution Abdelkrim crawled in the opposite direction, still flat on his belly. A dry branch cracked under him as he slid across it. The sounds of activity behind him ceased. A voice said: Someone's there.

Then he got to his feet wildly and ran. At one point he made the mistake of looking back. The five men stood there, staring after him. But he had recognized one of them, and in turn had been recognized.

He ran panting out of the woods, across a field, and into a lane bordered by thorn bushes. Three farmers were stretched out under a tree, eyeing him with surprise. He slowed his pace. When he was out of their sight he pulled off his sweat-soaked shirt. The police might easily question the farmers.

He was now certain that no one was following him. He got to the paved road, where an occasional car went by, and breathed more easily.

What he had seen in that brief instant of looking back was the brutal face of Aziz, the waiter in the bar at the Country Club. Everyone feared and disliked him, but the director kept him working there because one blow of his huge fist on the top of the head landed a troublesome client on the floor. They said of Aziz, and only half in jest, that the only times he prayed were just after he had killed someone.

If the farmers should mention that they had seen a young man hurrying along the lane, the police could find him and ask him questions, and no matter what he told them, if Aziz were caught, he would never believe it had not been Abdelkrim who had betrayed him.

It was even hotter once he had crossed the bridge and started to climb the hill. He had heard enough about Aziz to know that the most prudent thing for him to do at the moment was to get out of Tangier. His brother Mustapha would be happy to see him. Agadir was a long way off, but once he was there he would have no expenses.

He walked to the house with the afternoon sun beating down on his back. In the garage he threw himself onto the mattress and thought about his bad luck. His kif, his pipe, everything he had taken with him to the woods, had remained behind, there on the rock.

He would catch the night bus for Casablanca, the one that left the beach at half past eleven. Patricia and her mother must suspect nothing; indeed, his main consideration was how to get out of the garage and through the big gate without their hearing him, for at night the only sounds near the house came from the crickets. If one of them were to hear the gate click behind him when he crept out, he knew they would rush out and go screaming along the road after him in their bathrobes.

Soon Patricia knocked on the door, interrupting his meditations. I thought I heard you come in, she said with satisfaction. Afraid that his disturbed state might somehow show in his face, he forced himself to smile, but she did not notice because she had more to say. They had been invited by Monsieur and Madame Lemoine to attend a Jilala party at half past seven, and he could come too for a half hour if he wanted. It was to be at Hadj Larbi's house, which was not far away, so that it would be easy for him to walk back before dark.

Abdelkrim nodded vigorously in agreement, an expression of unfeigned satisfaction on his face. He saw his problem being solved for him.

Now that he no longer dreaded the night, he was eager for it to arrive. The suitcase he would take with him was ready; he hid it in a dark corner of the garage. At precisely half past seven Monsieur Lemoine was outside in the road, sounding his car horn; Madame Lemoine sat stiffly beside him. Patricia, loaded down with chains and medallions, ran to the car and leaned in to speak with Madame Lemoine. Now and then she raised her head and shouted the word Mother! toward the house.

Abdelkrim could hear the older woman complaining in her bedroom as she got her things together. Finally she came out, looking more irritable than usual. He sat between them on the back seat.

Hadj Larbi's garden was bounded at one end by a row of tall cypresses, black against the twilit sky. As they went in, one of Hadj Larbi's sons, whom Abdelkrim knew, came up to him and led him to the musicians' side of the courtyard. We have the Jilala in for my uncle every year during the smayyim, he told him.

Abdelkrim sat down on a mat beside the moqqaddem. An old man in a white djellaba came out of the house and stood facing the musicians. The drums began a leisurely rhythm, and he bent forward and slowly shuffled back and forth over the paving stones.

As the drummers increased their speed, the old man's feet ceased to scrape and drag; his legs now seemed to be springing upward of their own accord. He strained at the end of the sash that was wound about his waist and held by the man behind him. His eyes were on the fire, and he wanted to hurl himself into it. The music swelled in volume, the drummers began to hit the ground with the rims of their benadir, and the old man's frenzy increased. His face constantly changed its expression, distorted as if by waves of water washing over it. He was coming into the presence of the saint who would lead him far beyond the visible world to a place where his soul would be cleansed.

When he finally toppled to the ground there was a concerted rush of men to pull him away from the fire. They clustered around, touching his head, covering him with a blanket, lifting him carefully and carrying him away, out of sight.

Above the riad's wall Abdelkrim saw the dark obelisks of the cypresses. If he himself were to invoke Sidi Maimoun or Sidi Rahal, he was certain they would pay him no attention; it was too late for young men to expect to get in touch with the saints. He slipped out into the garden, said good-night to a servant standing in the doorway, and was on his way.

At the garage he picked up his valise, locked the gate behind him, and set out for the bus terminal on the beach, trying not to imagine the scene that would ensue the next morning when they found him gone. He waited nearly three hours for the bus to open its doors and let the passengers in.

Two months later he had reliable word that Aziz and his accomplices had been caught the very day after the robbery, there in the same part of the woods while they hammered at the safe, trying to get it open. He returned to Tangier and went directly to Patricia's house. But a maid whom he did not know brought him word that she would not see him.

The maid's expression was apologetic; out of friendliness she added: The old one and the young one, they both say they'll never forgive you. The idea of this struck her as strangely comic, and she laughed.

Abdelkrim turned to look with scorn at the garden. More to himself than to her he said: One real tree, and it would have been different.

But in any case she had not heard him, or had not understood, for she continued to smile. No, they don't want to see you, she said again.

Here To Learn

MALIKA needed no one to tell her she was pretty. From the beginning of her memory people had murmured about her beauty, for even when she was a baby girl the symmetry of her head, neck and shoulders was remarkable. Before she was old enough to go to the spring to fetch water she knew she had eyes like a gazelle and that her head was like a lily on its stalk. At least, these were the things older people said about her.

On a hill above the town stood a large building with palm-shaded walks leading up to it. This belonged to the Hermanas Adoratrices. Certain of these nuns, upon catching sight of Malika, had gone to her father, offering to take her in charge and teach her to speak Spanish and to embroider. Enthusiastically he had agreed. Allah has sent us here to learn, he would say. Malika's mother, who disapproved of her daughter's spending her time with Nazarenes, did her utmost to make him change his mind. Nevertheless Malika stayed with the sisters for five years, until her father died.

Malika's grandmother was fond of saying that when she had been Malika's age she had looked exactly like her, and that if it were possible for her to become a little girl again and stand beside Malika, no one would be able to tell them apart. At first Malika found this impossible to believe; she studied the old woman's ravaged face and straightway rejected the idea. After her grandmother had died, she began to understand what the old woman had meant when she said: Only Allah remains the same. One day she would no longer be pretty, but now she was. Thus, when she was able to go by herself to the spring and carry back two full pails of water, it meant nothing to her if the older boys and the young men called to her and tried to speak with her. They would do better, she thought, to say all those flattering things to girls who needed such reassurance.

A barracks full of soldiers stood just outside the town. The men were rough and brutal. When she caught sight of one of them, even in the distance, Malika would hide until he had disappeared. Fortunately the soldiers seldom strayed into the arroyo that lay between her house and the spring; they preferred to saunter in groups up and down the main road leading through the town.

There came a day when her mother insisted that she go to sell a hen at the market on the main highway. Her older sister always had done this, but she was at a neighbor's house helping prepare for a wedding. Malika begged her mother to lend her her haïk so she could cover her face.

Your sister's been a thousand times. She never wears a haïk.

Malika knew this was because no one paid any attention to her sister, but she could not say it to her mother. I'm afraid, she said, and burst into tears. Her mother had no patience with the silly behavior of girls, and refused to let her take the haïk. As Malika ran out of the house, holding the hen by its legs, she snatched up a soiled bathtowel. As soon as she was out of sight, she wrapped it loosely around her head, so that when she got to the highway she could pull it down and cover at least a part of her face.

Several dozen women lined one side of the road, each sitting on the ground with her wares spread out around her. Malika went to the end of the row, which was opposite a small park where the soldiers sat on benches. People wandered past and picked up the hen to squeeze it and shake it, so that it constantly squawked and fluttered. She had pulled the towel down so far over her eyes that she could see only the earth at her feet.

After an hour or so had gone by, a woman came along who began to discuss the price of the hen with her. Eventually she bought it, and Malika, once she had tied the coins up in a piece of cloth, jumped to her feet. The towel slipped over her face and fell to the ground. She picked it up and started to hurry along the highway.

II

The town was derelict; it smelled of the poverty in which its people were accustomed to live. Nor was there any indication that in some past era something more had existed. The wind from the sea raised the dust of the streets high into the air and showered it angrily over the countryside. Even the leaves of

the fig trees were coated white. The hot sand flying stung the
skin on the backs of her legs as she turned the corner of the
side street that led to the lower end of the gully. She draped
the towel over her head and held onto it with one hand. It
had never occurred to her to hate the town, for she assumed
that anywhere else would be more or less the same.

The street was scarcely more than an alley, with walls on either side. All at once she heard the sound of heavy boots
pounding the earth behind her. She did not turn around.
Then a hard hand seized her arm and pushed her roughly
against the wall. It was a soldier, and he was smiling. He
braced his arms against the wall on each side of her so she
could not escape.

Malika said nothing. The man stood gazing at her. He was
breathing deeply, as though he had been running. Finally he
said: How old are you?

She looked directly into his eyes. Fifteen.

He smelt of wine, tobacco and sweat.

Let me go, she said, and she tried desperately to duck under the barricade. The pain she felt as he twisted her arm made
her open her eyes very wide, but she did not cry out. Two
men in djellabas were approaching from the direction of the
gully, and she fixed her eyes on them. The soldier turned, saw
them, and began to walk quickly back toward the highway.

When she got home, she tossed the bit of cloth with the
money in it onto the taifor, and indignantly showed her
mother the marks on her arm.

What's that?

A soldier grabbed me.

Her mother dealt her a stinging blow across the face. Malika had never seen her in such a rage.

You young bitch! she screamed. That's all you're good for!

Malika ran out of the house and down into the gully, where
she sat on a rock in the shade, wondering if her mother might
be going mad. The unexpectedness and injustice of the sudden blow had removed all thought of the soldier from her
mind. She felt that she must find an explanation of her
mother's behavior; otherwise she would hate her.

That night at dinner things were not much better; her
mother would not look at her, and directed all her remarks to

her other daughter. This proved to be the pattern for the days that followed. It was as if she had decided that Malika no longer existed.

Good, thought Malika. If I'm not here, then she's not here. She's not my mother and I do hate her.

This silent war between them did not mean that Malika was exempt from having to continue to go to the market. Nearly every week she would be sent off to sell a hen or a basket of vegetables and eggs. She had no further trouble with the soldiers, perhaps because she now stopped on her way down the gully each time and smeared a little mud over her face. It was always dry by the time she reached the highway, and although the women there sometimes stared at her with surprise, the men paid her no attention. On her way home, going up the gully, she would wash her face.

There was always suspicion in her mother's glance now when she returned to the house. If you get into trouble, she said, I swear I'll kill you with my own hands. Malika sniffed and left the room. She knew what her mother meant, but it astonished her to see how little she knew about her own daughter.

III

One day as Malika sat in the front row of women and girls in the market on the highway, a long yellow car without a top drove up silently and stopped. There was only one man in it, and he was a Nazarene. The women began to murmur and cry out, for the man held a camera in his hands and was pointing it at them. A girl sitting next to Malika turned to her and said: You speak Spanish. Tell him to go away.

Malika ran over to the car. The man lowered his camera and stared at her.

Señor, you mustn't take pictures here, she said, looking at him gravely. She pointed back at the row of indignant women.

The Nazarene was big, with light-colored hair. He understood and smiled. *Muy bien, muy bien*, he said good-naturedly, still looking fixedly at her. She was suddenly conscious of the dirt on her face. Without thinking she rubbed her cheek with the back of her hand. The man's smile became broader.

Will you let me take your picture?

Malika's heart began to beat painfully. No! No! she cried, aghast. Then by way of explanation she added: I have to go and sell my eggs.

The Nazarene looked more pleased than ever. You have eggs for sale? Bring them over.

Malika went and fetched the little packet of eggs, tied in a cloth. A group of boys had caught sight of the dazzling yellow car, and now they surrounded it, demanding money. The Nazarene, trying to wave them away, opened the door for Malika and pointed to the empty seat. She laid the bundle on the leather cushion and bent to undo the knot, but the arms of the boys kept pushing in front of her and jostling her. The Nazarene shouted angrily at the urchins in a foreign language, but this deterred them only for an instant. Finally, in a rage, he said to Malika: Get in. She lifted the eggs and obeyed, seating herself with the bundle on her lap. The man reached in front of her and slammed the door shut. Then he raised the window. But two beggars now had joined the boys, and they were able to reach over the top of the window.

Without warning the Nazarene started up the motor with a great roar. The car shot forward. Startled, Malika turned to see some of the boys sprawling in the road. When she looked again, they were almost out of the town. The Nazarene still seemed to be very angry. She decided not to ask him how far he was going before he stopped and bought the eggs. Her emotions hovered between delight at being in the fine car and anxiety about walking back to the town.

The trees were going by very fast. It seemed to her that she had always known something strange like this would happen to her one day. It was a comforting thought, and it kept her from feeling actual fear.

IV

Soon they turned onto a dirt road that burrowed deep into a eucalyptus grove. Here in the dubious shade the Nazarene shut off the motor and turned to Malika with a smile. He took the bundle of eggs from her lap and put it into the back of the car. From a basket behind her seat he brought out a bottle of mineral water and a napkin. He poured a little water onto the napkin and with one hand on her shoulder set to work wiping the streaks of mud from her cheeks. She let him rub, and she let him remove the towel wrapped around her head, so that her hair fell to her shoulders. Why shouldn't he see me? she thought. He's a good man. She had already noticed that he did not smell at all, and his gentleness with her gave her a pleasant sensation.

Now shall I take your picture?

She nodded. There was no one to witness the shameful act. He made her sit lower in the seat, and held the camera above her. It clicked so many times, and he looked so peculiar with the big black apparatus in front of his face, that she began to laugh. She thought he might stop then, but he seemed even more pleased, and went on clicking the camera until it would click no more. Then he spread a blanket on the ground and set a basket of food in the center of it. They sat with the basket between them and ate chicken, cheese and olives. Malika was hungry, and she thought this great fun.

When they had finished, he asked her if she wanted him to take her back to the market. It was as if darkness had fallen over the world. She thought of the women there, and of what they would say when they saw her. She shook her head vigorously. The present moment was real; she would not help it to end. No, not yet, she said lightly.

He looked at his watch. Shall we go to Tetuan?

Her eyes brightened. It was less than an hour's ride from her town, but she had only heard about it. The trees sped by again. Here a stiff breeze blew in from the Mediterranean, and Malika was chilly. The man took out a soft camel's hair cape and put it around her shoulders.

Tetuan was very exciting with all its traffic. The guards in scarlet and white stood at attention in front of the Khalifa's palace. But she would not get out of the car and walk with him in the street. They were parked there in the Feddane, where the hot afternoon sun beat down on them. Finally the man shrugged and said: Well, if I'm going to get to Tangier tonight, I'd better take you back home.

Malika made a strange sound. She seemed to have become very small inside the cape.

What's the matter?

I can't!

The man stared at her. But you've got to go back home.

Malika began to wail. No, no! she cried. The man glanced nervously at the passersby, and tried to comfort her with words. But a possibility had just revealed itself to her, and at that moment the idea was powerful enough to occupy her totally. Seeing her too immersed in inner turmoil even to hear him, he started the car and slowly made his way through the throng of people to the other side of the plaza. Then he drove along the principal street to the outskirts of the city, stopped the car by the side of the road, and lighted a cigarette.

He turned to her. One would almost have said that on the seat beside him there was nothing but the cape. He tugged at it, and heard a sob. Gently slipping his hand inside, he smoothed her hair for a moment. Finally she began to push herself upward into a sitting position, and her head appeared.

I'm going to take you with me to Tangier, he said. She made no reply to this, nor did she look at him.

They sped westward, the late afternoon sun in front of them. Malika was conscious of having made an irrevocable choice. The results, already determined by destiny, would be disclosed to her one by one, in the course of events. It was only slowly that she became aware of the landscape around her and of the summer air rushing past.

They came to a tiny café, alone on the mountainside, and stopped. Come in and we'll have some tea, he said. Malika shook her head, pulling the cape more tightly around her.

The man went inside and ordered two glasses of tea. A quarter of an hour later a boy carried them to the car on a tray. The tea was very hot, and it took them a while to drink it. Even when the boy had come and taken away the tray, they went on sitting there. Eventually the man switched on the headlights, and they started down the mountainside.

V

Malika was frightened by the elevator, but she relaxed somewhat when the man had shown her into the apartment and shut the door behind them. There were thick rugs and soft couches piled with pillows, and lights that could be turned on and off by pushing a button. Most important of all, the Nazarene lived there by himself.

That night he showed her to a room, telling her it was to be hers. Before he said goodnight he took her head in his hands and kissed her on the forehead. When he had gone she wandered into the bathroom and amused herself for a long time turning the hot and cold taps on and off, to see if sooner or later one of them would make a mistake. Finally she undressed, put on the muslin gandoura the man had left for her, and got into the bed.

A pile of magazines lay on the table beside her, and she began to look at the pictures. There was one photograph which caught her attention and held it. The picture showed a luxurious room, with a beautiful woman lying back in a chaise longue. A wide collar of diamonds flashed from her neck, and in her hand she held a book. The book was open but she was not looking at it. Her head was raised, as though someone had just come into the room and found her reading. Malika studied the photograph, glanced at others, and returned to it. To her it illustrated the perfect pose to adopt when receiving guests, and she resolved to practice it by herself, so that when the time came she could put it to use. It would be a good idea to be able to read, too, she thought. One day she would ask the man to show her how.

They had breakfast on the terrace in the morning sun. The building overlooked a spacious Moslem cemetery. Beyond it was the water. Malika told him it was not good to live so near to a graveyard. Later, she looked over the railing, saw the elaborate domed mausoleum of Sidi Bou Araqia, and nodded her head in approval. As they sat over their coffee, he answered more of her questions. His name was Tim, he was twenty-eight years old, but he had no wife and no children. He did not live in Tangier all the time. Sometimes he was in Cairo and sometimes in London. In each of these places he had a small flat, but he kept his car in Tangier because that was where he came when he was not working.

As they sat there Malika heard sounds inside the apartment. Presently a fat black woman in a yellow zigdoun came onto the terrace. *Bonjour*, she said, and she began to carry out the dishes. Each time she appeared Malika sat very straight, looking fixedly out across the water at the mountains in Spain.

Someone would be coming in a little while, Tim said, an Italian woman who was going to take her measurements and make some clothes for her.

Malika frowned. What kind of clothes?

When he said: Whatever you want, she jumped up and went to her room, returning with a copy of *The New Yorker*, which she opened at a page showing a girl in a knit sports suit standing by a set of matched luggage. Like this one, she said. An hour or so later the Italian woman came in, very businesslike, tickled Malika with her tape measure for a while, and left, notebook in hand.

VI

Late that afternoon when the black woman had gone, Tim took Malika into her bedroom, pulled the curtains across the windows, and very gently gave her her first lesson in love. Malika did not really want this to happen then, but she had always known it would sooner or later. The slight pain was negligible, but the shame of being naked in front of the man was almost more than she could bear. It never had occurred to her that a body could be considered beautiful, and she did not believe him when he told her she was perfect in every part. She knew only that men used women in order to make children, and this preoccupied her, as she had no desire for a child. The man assured her that he was not hoping for children either, and that if she did as he told her there was no danger of having any. She accepted this as she accepted everything else he said. She was there in order to learn, and she intended to learn as much as possible.

When, during the next few weeks, she finally consented to go with him to the houses of his friends, he did not guess that she agreed to appear in public only because she had studied herself in the new clothes, and had found them sufficiently convincing to act as a disguise. The European garments made it possible for her to go into the streets with a Nazarene and not be reviled by other Moroccans.

After taking Malika to a photographer's studio and making several lengthy visits to the authorities, Tim returned triumphant one day, waving a passport at her. This is yours, he said. Don't lose it.

Nearly every day there were parties on the Mountain or picnics on the beach. Malika particularly loved the night picnics around a fire, with the sound of the waves breaking on the sand. Sometimes there were musicians, and everyone danced barefoot. One evening eight or ten of the guests jumped up and ran shouting toward the breakers to swim naked in the moonlight. Since the moon was very bright, and there were men and women together, Malika gasped and hid her face. Tim thought this amusing, but the incident caused her to question the fitness of the people in Tangier to be her models for the elegance she hoped to attain.

One morning Tim greeted her with a sad face. In a few days, he told her, he had to go to London. Seeing her expression of chagrin, he quickly added that in two weeks he would be back, and that she would go on living in the flat just as though he were there.

But how can I? she cried. You won't be here! I'll be all alone.

No, no. You'll have friends. You'll like them.

That evening he brought two young men to the apartment. They were handsome and well-dressed, and very talkative. When Malika heard Tim address one of them as Bobby, she burst into laughter.

Only dogs are called Bobby, she explained. It's not a man's name.

She's priceless, said Bobby. A teen-age Nefertiti.

Absolute heaven, agreed his friend Peter.

After they had gone, Tim explained that they were going to keep Malika company while he was in England. They would live in the apartment with her. On hearing this, she was silent for a moment.

I want to go with you, she said, as if anything else were inconceivable.

He shook his head. *Ni hablar.*

But I don't want love with them.

He kissed her. They don't make love with girls. That's why I asked them. They'll take good care of you.

Ah, she said, partially reassured, and at the same time thinking how clever Tim was to have been able to find two such presentable eunuchs with so little apparent effort.

As Tim had promised, Bobby and Peter kept her amused. Instead of taking her out to parties they invited their friends in to meet her. Soon she realized that there were a good many more eunuchs in Tangier than she had suspected. Since, according to Bobby and Peter, these tea-parties and cocktail hours were given expressly for Malika, she insisted on knowing exactly when the guests would be coming, so she could receive them in the correct position, lying back on the cushions of the divan with a book in her hand. When the new arrivals were shown in, she would raise her head slowly until its noble proportions were fully evident, fix her gaze on a point far behind anything in the room, and let the beginning of a smile tremble briefly on her lips before it vanished.

She could see that this impressed them. They told her they loved her. They played games and danced with each other and with her. They tickled her, nuzzled her, took her on their laps and fussed with her hair. She found them more fun to be with than Tim's friends, even though she was aware that the things they said had no meaning. To them everything was a game; there was nothing to learn from them.

VII

Tim had been gone for more than a week when they first brought Tony to the flat. He was a tall, noisy Irishman for whom the others of the group seemed to have a certain respect. At first Malika assumed that this was because he was not a eunuch like them, but quickly she discovered that it was only because he had far more money to spend than they did. Tony's clothing always smelled delicious, and his car, a green Maserati, attracted even more attention than Tim's. One day he came by at noon, while Bobby and Peter were still at the market. The black woman had received orders from Bobby to let no one in under any circumstances, but Tony was an expert in getting around such things. Malika had been playing a record of Abdelwahab's; now she quickly silenced it and gave all her attention to Tony. In the course of their dialogue, he remarked casually that her clothes were pretty. Malika smoothed her skirt.

But I'd like to see you in some other clothes, he went on. Where are they?

Not here. In Madrid.

They heard the door slam, and knew that Bobby and Peter had returned. The two had quarreled and were communicating only in acid monosyllables. Malika saw that the game of dominoes they had promised to play with her when they got back would not take place. She sat and sulked for a while, turning the pages of one of Tim's financial magazines. Eunuchs were extremely childish, she reflected.

Bobby came into the room and stood at the other end, arranging books on the bookshelves in silence. Soon the black woman appeared in the doorway and announced to him in French that Monsieur Tim had telephoned from London and would not be in Tangier until the eighteenth.

When Tony had translated the information into Spanish, Malika merely sat staring at him, an expression of despair on her face.

Bobby hurried out of the room. Ill at ease, Tony stood up and followed him. A moment later Bobby's sharp voice cried: No, she can't go out to eat with you. She can't go out at all, anywhere, unless we go along. One of Tim's rules. If you want to eat here, you can.

Very little was said at lunch. In the middle of the meal Peter flung down his napkin and left the room. Afterward the black woman served coffee on the terrace. Bobby and Peter were arguing farther back in the flat, but their shrill voices were strangely audible.

For a while Malika sipped her coffee and said nothing. When she spoke to Tony, it was as if there had been no interruption to their earlier conversation. Can we go to Madrid? she said.

You'd like that? He grinned. But you see how they are. And he pointed behind him.

A mí me da igual cómo son. I only promised to stay with them for two weeks.

The next morning, while Bobby and Peter were at the market buying food, Tony and Malika put some valises into the Maserati and drove to the port to catch the ferry to Spain. Tony had left a short note for Bobby, saying that he had borrowed Malika for a few days, and would see to it that she telephoned.

VIII

They slept in Córdoba the first night. Before setting out for Madrid in the morning, Tony stopped at the cathedral to show it to her. When they walked up to the door, Malika hesitated. She peered inside and saw an endless corridor of arches extending into the gloom.

Go on in, said Tony.

She shook her head. You go. I'll wait here.

Driving out of the city, he scolded her a bit. You should look at things when you have the chance, he told her. That was a famous mosque.

I saw it, she said firmly.

The first day in Madrid they spent at Balenciaga's, morning and afternoon. You were right, Malika said to Tony when they were back in the hotel. The clothes here are much better.

They had to wait several days for the first items to be ready. The Prado was almost next door to the hotel, but Tony decided against making the attempt to entice Malika into it. He suggested a bullfight.

Only Moslems know how to kill animals, she declared.

They had been in Madrid for more than a week. One evening as they sat in the bar downstairs at the Ritz, Tony turned to her and said: Have you called Tangier? No, you haven't. Come.

Malika did not want to think of Tangier. Sighing, she rose and went with Tony up to his room, where he put in the call.

When finally he heard Bobby at the other end of the wire, he gestured and handed the telephone to Malika.

At the sound of her voice, Bobby immediately began to reproach her. She interrupted him to ask for Tim.

Tim can't get back to Tangier quite yet, he said, and the pitch of his voice rose as he added: But he wants *you* to come back right now!

Malika was silent.

Did you hear what I said? yelled Bobby. *Oíste?*

Yes, I heard. I'll let you know. She hung up quickly so as not to hear the sounds of outraged protest at the other end.

They went several more times to Balenciaga for fittings. Malika was impressed by Madrid, but she missed the comforting presence of Tim, particularly at night when she lay alone in her bed. While it was pleasant to be with Tony because he paid so much attention to her and constantly bought her gifts, she knew he did this only because he enjoyed dressing her the way he wanted her to look when they went out together, and not because he cared about her.

Although the deliveries continued to be made, and the gowns and ensembles were perfect, Malika's pleasure was somewhat lessened by her discovery that the only places where people really looked at what she was wearing were two restaurants and the bar downstairs. When she remarked about this to Tony, he laughed.

Ah! What you want is Paris. I can see that.

Malika brightened. Can we go there?

When the last garment had arrived, Tony and Malika ate a final dinner at Horcher, and started early the next morning for Paris. They spent the night in Biarritz, where the streets were rainswept and empty.

IX

Paris was far too big. She was frightened of it even before they arrived at the hotel, and she determined not to let Tony out of her sight unless she was safe in her room. At the Hôtel de la Trémoaille she watched him lying back on his bed, making one telephone call after the other while he joked, shouted, waved his legs, and screamed with laughter. When he was through telephoning he turned to her.

Tomorrow night I'm going to take you to a party, he said. And I know just what you'll wear. The oyster-colored satin number.

Malika was excited by the sumptuous house and the guests in evening clothes. Here at last, she was certain, she had reached a place where the people were of the ultimate degree of refinement. When she found that they looked at her with approval, she was filled with a sense of triumph.

Soon Tony led her up to a tall, pretty girl with flashing black eyes. This is my sister Dinah, he announced. She speaks better Spanish than I do.

Indicating Malika, he added: And this is the new Antinea. He left the two together and disappeared into another room.

Dinah's manner with her made her feel that they had been friends for a long time. When they had chatted for a few minutes, she led her over to a group of South Americans. The women were covered with jewels and some of them carried the pelts of animals over their shoulders. Even the men wore huge diamonds on their fingers. Malika suspected that Tim would disapprove of these people, but then it occurred to her that perhaps he could not be relied upon as an arbiter of taste in a city like this.

Paris es muy grande, she said to a man who smiled at her invitingly. I never saw it until yesterday. I'm afraid to go out. Why did they make it so big?

The man, smiling more broadly, said he was at her service, and would be delighted to go with her wherever she wished, whenever it suited her.

Oh, she said, looking pensive. That would be nice. *Mañana?*

Somehow Dinah had caught the end of their dialogue. Not tomorrow, I'm afraid, she said briskly, taking Malika's arm. As she led her away she whispered furiously: His wife was standing there watching you.

Malika stole a frightened glance over her shoulder. The man was still smiling after her.

During the next few days Dinah, who lived nearby in the Avenue Montaigne, came regularly to the hotel. She and Tony had long discussions while Malika listened to Radio Cairo. One afternoon when Tony had gone out and Malika was bored, she asked Dinah to put in a call to Bobby in Tangier. A half hour later the telephone rang, and she heard Bobby's voice.

Hola, Bobby!

Malika! His voice was already shrill. You can't do this to me! Why are you in Paris? You've got to come back to Tangier.

Malika was silent.

We're waiting for you. What will Tim say if you're not here?

Tim! she said with scorn. Where is Tim?

He's coming back next week. I want to speak to Tony.

Tony's gone out.

Listen to me! Bobby shouted. What hotel are you in?

I don't know its name, she said. It's in Paris. It's a nice hotel. *Adiós.*

One morning not long afterward Tony announced abruptly that he was leaving for London in an hour. Dinah came in shortly before he set out. They seemed to be involved in a dispute, which ended only when he kissed each of them good-bye. After he had gone, Malika nodded her head sagely. London, she mused. He won't come back.

X

The day after Malika moved into Dinah's flat the weather turned rainy and cold. Dinah often went out, leaving her alone with the housemaid and cook. She was just as glad to stay indoors where it was warm. Her wardrobe, impressive as it was, failed to include any kind of covering for cold weather. Dinah had told her that the cold was just beginning, and that it would not be warm again for many months. It seemed to Malika that somewhere in Paris there must be a *joteya*, where she could take two or three evening gowns and exchange them for a coat, but Dinah shook her head when she asked her about it.

The apartment was spacious, and there were plenty of magazines to study. Malika spent her time curled up on a divan, examining the details in the fashion photographs.

Tony called from London, postponing his return for a few days. When Dinah gave her the news, Malika smiled and said: *Claro.*

I'm having lunch today with a friend. She has mountains of clothes, said Dinah. I'll see if I can't get a coat for you.

What she brought back that afternoon was a mink coat badly in need of repairs. Malika gazed at the rips with visible distaste.

You haven't any idea of how lucky you are, Dinah told her. She shrugged.

When the garment had been fitted at the furrier's and the skins resewn, it looked completely new, as if it had just been made for Malika. She ran her fingers over its glistening surface and examined herself in the mirror, and quickly decided that it was a very fine coat after all.

Dinah's friend came to lunch. Her name was Daphne. She was not very pretty and she tried to speak Italian with Malika. During the course of the meal she invited them both to a house-party at Cortina d'Ampezzo.

Dinah was enthusiastic. She brought out an album of photographs after Daphne had left, and spread it in Malika's lap. Malika saw that the ground was white and the people, whose clothing was not at all elegant, wore long boards on their feet. She was doubtful, but the strange white landscape and the groups of festive people intrigued her. It might be more interesting than Paris, which in the end had turned out to be rather dull.

They went to the office to book plane passage. Have you any money at all? Dinah asked her as they waited.

Malika was suddenly very much ashamed. Tony never gave me any.

It's all right, Dinah told her.

Before they left there was a lively argument between them as to whether Malika should take all her valises with her on the plane to Milano.

But you won't need all those clothes there, Dinah objected. And besides, it would cost so much.

I have to take everything, Malika said.

All of her belongings went with them on the plane. They had bad weather on the way to Milano, where Daphne's car met them. She was already in Cortina.

Malika had not enjoyed the plane ride. She did not understand why people with cars took planes. There was nothing to see but clouds, and the rocking of the plane made some of the passengers sick, so that by the end of the flight everyone seemed to be nervous and unhappy. For a while as they sped along the autostrada Malika thought she was back in Spain.

According to the driver, there were already so many friends staying at Daphne's chalet that no place was left for them. Daphne was putting them up in a hotel. Dinah received this news in silence; presumably she was displeased. Malika, when she understood the situation, secretly rejoiced. There would be many more people in the hotel than in the house.

XI

It was cold in Cortina. At first Malika would not go out of the hotel. The air is like poison, she complained. Then she began to experiment a bit, finally discovering that it was an agreeable kind of cold.

She would sit with the others on the terrace of the hotel in the brilliant sunshine, wearing her warm coat, sipping hot chocolate while they had their cocktails. The red-cheeked jollity of the people around her was a new experience, and the snow never ceased to fascinate her. Each morning when Daphne and her guests came to fetch Dinah, Malika would watch the noisy group rush out toward the ski fields. Then she would wander through the public rooms. The employees were polite, and often smiled at her. There was a shop in the hotel that sold skis and the clothes that had to be worn when using them. The window displays were changed daily, so that Malika was often to be seen standing outside the door, inspecting the merchandise through the glass.

Twice a tall young man had sauntered up to the shop windows as she stood there, giving the impression that he was about to speak to her. Both times she had turned away and resumed her aimless meandering. Tony and Dinah had warned her repeatedly against entering into conversation with strangers, and she thought it better to observe the etiquette they considered so important. She had discovered that Otto the barman spoke Spanish, and in the morning when the bar was often empty she would go in and talk with him. One morning he asked her why she never went out to ski with her friends.

I can't, she said in a muffled voice.

At that moment, in the mirror behind the bar, she saw the tall young man come into the room and remain standing by the door, as if he were listening to their conversation. She hoped Otto would not continue it, but he did.

That's no reason, he said. Take lessons. There are plenty of good skiing professors in Cortina.

Malika shook her head slowly several times.

The young man stepped to the bar, saying, in Spanish: He's right, our friend Otto. That's what Cortina's for. Everybody skis here.

Now he leaned on the bar and faced Malika. I spend a lot of time south of the border myself, he said as though in confidence. I have a little hacienda down in Durango.

Malika stared at him. He was speaking in Spanish, but she had no idea of what he was talking about. He misunderstood her expression and frowned. What's the matter. Don't you like Durango?

She looked at Otto and back at the tall young man. Then she burst into laughter, and the sound filled the bar agreeably. The tall young man's face seemed to melt as he heard it.

She slid down from the barstool, smiled at him, and said: I don't understand. *Hasta luego*, Otto. While the young man was still making a visible effort to collect his thoughts, she turned and walked out of the bar.

This marked the beginning of a new friendship, one which grew to substantial proportions later that same day. At the end of the afternoon Malika and the young man, who said his name was Tex, went for a walk along the road outside the hotel, where the snow had been packed down. The peaks of the mountains around them were turning pink. She sniffed the air with enthusiasm.

I like it here, she said, as though the subject had been under discussion.

You'd like it more if you learned to ski, he told her.

No, no!

She hesitated, then went on quickly: I can't pay for lessons. I haven't any money. They don't give me any.

Who's they?

She walked on beside him without answering, and he took her arm. By the time they got back to the hotel she had agreed to let Tex pay for lessons, skis and clothes, on condition that the clothes be bought at a shop in the town and not at the hotel.

Once she had been fitted out, the lessons were begun, Tex being always present. Dinah did not like the idea at all. She said it was unheard-of, and she asked Malika to point Tex out to her.

Malika, who had felt no resentment at being left each day to her own devices, could not understand Dinah's objections. She was delighted with her new friend, and arranged for Dinah to meet him in the bar, where she sat for a half hour listening to them speak in English. Later that night Dinah told her Tex was uncivilized. Malika did not understand.

He's an idiot! Dinah cried.

Malika laughed, for she took this to mean that Dinah also liked him. He has a good heart, she replied calmly.

Yes, yes. You'll see that good heart soon enough, Dinah told her with a crooked smile.

Having observed that Tex's interest in her was due in part to the mystery with which she seemed to be surrounded, Malika offered him as little information about herself as possible. He was still under the impression that she was Mexican and a member of Dinah's family, and that for one reason or another Dinah was in charge of her. His misconception amused Malika, and she did nothing to correct it. She knew Dinah and Daphne were persuaded that she and Tex were having an affair, and this pleased her, too, since it was not true.

Sometimes, in spite of Malika's efforts to restrain him, Tex drank too much whiskey. This generally happened in the bar after dinner. At such moments his face often took on an expression that made her think of a fish dragged up onto the beach. His eyes bulging, his jaw slack, he would take one of her hands in both of his, and groan: Oh, Honey! To Malika this was an expression of momentary despair. She would sigh and shake her head, and try to comfort him by saying that he would feel better in a little while.

The lessons were going very well; Malika spent most of the daylight hours on the snow with Tex. She would have eaten at his table, too, if Dinah had not indignantly forbidden it.

One day at lunch Dinah lit a cigarette and said: You're going to have your last skiing lesson tomorrow. We're leaving for Paris on Thursday.

Malika saw that she was watching her closely to observe the effect of her announcement. She decided to look slightly crestfallen, but not enough to give Dinah any satisfaction.

It's been a marvelous holiday, Dinah went on, and we've all had a fine time, but now it's over.

Así es la vida, murmured Malika with lowered head.

XII

That afternoon when the lesson was over, Malika and Tex sat side by side in the snow, looking out across the valley in the fading light. All at once she found that she was sobbing. Tex stared at her in consternation, then drew her to him, trying to comfort her. Through her sobs, she repeated what Dinah had told her at lunch.

When she felt his arms around her, she knew that the only reason for her unhappiness was that she did not want to leave him. She leaned her head on his chest and sobbed: *Me quiero quedar contigo, Tex, contigo.*

These words transformed him. He began to glow. While he soothed her with gestures, he told her he would do anything in the world for her. If she wanted him to, he would take her away that very night. She stopped weeping and listened.

Before they rose from the snowbank, they had agreed upon the following morning for their departure, while Dinah would be out skiing. Tex was determined to have no further meeting with Dinah, but Malika made him leave a note behind for her, which she dictated.

Dinah, I don't want to go to Paris now. Thank you and thank Daphne. I loved Cortina. Now I'm going to learn to ski. I'll be in Switzerland for a while. Good luck, Malika.

Tex had made arrangements to have a chauffeur-driven car large enough to hold Malika's many valises pick them up at the hotel at half past nine in the morning. Everything went off smoothly. Malika handed the note for Dinah to the receptionist. He did not mention the subject of her bill, which she had feared he might do, but merely nodded gravely.

As they left Cortina behind them, Malika said: Dinah's going to be very angry.

I'm thinking of that, said Tex. Will she make trouble?

She can't do anything. She never saw my passport. She doesn't even know my name.

Tex appeared to be stunned by this information, and began to put a whole series of questions to her, but she, being happy to see the beautiful white landscape outside, replied without answering them, seized his hand now and then to draw his attention to a detail in the landscape, and, by taking gentle command, succeeded in putting him off without his being aware of it.

They had lunch at a small restaurant in Mezzolombardo. The waiter brought a bottle of wine and poured out two glasses. No, said Malika, pushing it away.

Your friend Dinah's not here now, Tex reminded her. You can do whatever you like.

Dinah! she scoffed. What's Dinah beside the words of God?

He stared at her, mystified, without pursuing the matter further, and drank the bottle of wine by himself, so that he was in a happy and relaxed state when they got back into the car. As they rolled southward on the autostrada he devoted himself to crushing her hand in his, nuzzling her neck with his lips, and finally kissing her feverishly on the lips. Malika could not have hoped for more.

XIII

At dinner that night in Milano she watched him drink two bottles of wine. Later in the bar he had several whiskeys. At Cortina she would have begged him to stop, but this night she affected not to notice that he was resolutely sliding into a drunken state. Instead, she began to tell him a complicated story she had known since her childhood, about a female ghoul that lived in a cave and unearthed newly buried corpses to extract their livers. Seeing his expression of total bewilderment, she stopped halfway through the tale.

He shook his head. What an imagination! he said.

I want to learn how to speak English, Malika went on, leaving the ghoul behind. That's what I'm going to do in Switzerland.

Tex was drunk by the time they went upstairs. She regretted this, for she liked him much better when he was sober. But she suspected that he was going to want to sleep with her and she thought it wiser for their first time together that he be in a state of befuddlement. It was imperative that he believe himself to be the first to have had her.

In the morning when he awoke staring, trying to remember, she confided that it had not been as painful as she had expected. Tex was contrite; he nearly wept as he begged her forgiveness. She smiled and covered him with kisses.

Having won this much, she pressed on, not with any specific purpose in mind, but simply to gain a stronger foothold. While he was still in the slough of early-morning remorse, she made him promise to abjure whiskey.

At the Grand Saint Bernard, as the police handed back their passports, Malika saw Tex stare at hers briefly with astonishment. When they were in the car, he asked to see the passport again. The Arabic characters seemed to cause him great excitement. He began to ask her questions about Morocco which she could not have answered even if she had been in the mood for such conversation. She assured him it was like any other country. Now I'm looking at Switzerland, she said.

They arrived in Lausanne at sunset and took rooms in a large hotel by the lake, at Ouchy. It was far grander than the hospice at Cortina, and the people living there, not being dressed for skiing, seemed to Malika much more elegant.

I like it here, she said to Tex that night at dinner. How long can we stay?

The next morning, at Malika's insistence, they went together to the Berlitz School for intensive language courses: she in English and he in French. She saw that Tex imagined she would soon tire of the strict schedule, but she was determined not to leave Lausanne before she could converse in English. They spent each morning in their respective classes, had lunch together, and returned to the school at three for further tutoring.

Every Friday afternoon Tex would rent a car, and they would drive to Gstaad, stopping to have dinner on the way. Saturdays and Sundays if no snow fell, they skied at Wasserngrat or Eggli. Sometimes he would insist on staying over until Monday, even though it meant missing their morning classes. Malika could see that if she had let him have his way he always would have done this, and very likely would have extended the weekends further and further. He approved of Malika's learning English, but he could not fathom her obsessive preoccupation with it. Nor, had he asked her, could she have explained it to him. She knew only that unless she kept on learning she was lost.

XIV

During the winter there in Lausanne they made no friends, being entirely satisfied with each other's company. One day as they were coming out of the Schweizerische Kreditanstalt, where Tex had opened an account for Malika, he turned to her and apropos of nothing asked her if she had ever thought of being married.

She looked at him wonderingly. I think of it all the time, she said. You know it makes me happy to be married to you.

He stared at her as if he had understood nothing she had said. After a moment he seized her arm and pulled her to him. It makes me happy, too, he told her. She could see, however, that something was on his mind. Later when they were alone, he said that of course it was true that they were married, but that what he had been speaking of was marriage with papers.

With papers or not with papers! It's the same thing, isn't it? If two people love each other, what have papers got to do with it?

It's the governments, he explained. They like married people to have papers.

Of course, she agreed. In Morocco, too. Many people are married with papers.

She was about to add that papers were important if you expected to produce children, but she checked herself in time, sensing that the observation bordered on dangerous ground. Already, from certain questions he had put to her, she suspected that he had begun to wonder if she were pregnant. His questions amused her, based as they were on the supposition that there had been no Tim before Tex, to show her how always to be safe.

One morning in early spring when she complained of feeling tired, he asked her outright.

You think Moroccan women don't know anything? she cried. If they want to make children they make them. If they don't, they don't make them.

He nodded dubiously. Those home remedies don't always work.

She saw that she was safe. He knew nothing about Morocco. Mine does, she said.

If she never mentioned America to him or asked about his family, it was because she could not envisage his life there with enough clarity to be curious about it. For his part, he spoke of America with increasing frequency. Never before had he stayed away for so long, he said. Malika interpreted these remarks as warnings that he had had enough of his present life and was contemplating a change. The thought struck terror to her heart, but she would not let him perceive this.

From time to time she would catch him in the act of staring at her, an expression of utter incomprehension on his face. By now, at Malika's insistence, they often spoke together in English. She thought it suited him much better than Spanish; he seemed to have an altogether different voice.

Would you like to be married? With papers, I mean.

Yes, if you want to.

And you? he insisted.

Of course I want to, if you want to.

They were married in the rectory office of a Protestant minister, who remarked in an aside to Tex that personally he was not in favor of marriage where the bride was as young as Malika. In my experience, he said, very few such unions prove to be permanent.

To Malika the episode was a bit of nonsense of the sort that Nazarenes appear so much to enjoy. Nevertheless she saw clearly that it was a matter of great importance to Tex. Indeed, his character seemed to have undergone a subtle metamorphosis since the ceremony, in that he was now more self-assertive. She liked him rather better this way, and concluded that secretly he was a very devout man. The papers were obviously a requirement of the Nazarene religion; now that he had them he felt more secure.

It was only a fortnight later that Tex, after drinking a little more wine than was his habit, announced to her that they were going home. Malika received the news with a sinking sensation. She could see that he was glad to be leaving the world of hotels and restaurants, and she suspected that life in a house would be very different and not nearly so much fun.

Once again she saw nothing from the plane, but this time the journey went on for such a long time that she grew worried. Tex was sleepy, nevertheless she disturbed him several times to ask: Where are we?

Twice he answered jovially: In the air. The next time he said: Somewhere over the ocean, I suppose. And he stole a glance at her.

We're not moving, she told him. We're standing still. The plane is stuck.

He only laughed, but in such a way that she realized she had made a mistake of some sort. I don't like this plane, she said.

Go to sleep, Tex advised her.

She shut her eyes and sat quietly, feeling that she had gone much too far away—so far that now she was nowhere. Outside the world, she whispered to herself in Arabic, and shivered.

XV

Being in Los Angeles persuaded Malika that she was right, that she had left behind everything that was comprehensible, and was now in a totally different place whose laws she could not know. They went from the airport to the top of the mountain, where a house was hidden in the woods. Tex had told her about it, but she had imagined something very different, like the Mountain in Tangier, where the villas had big gardens around them. This house was buried among the trees; she could not see the rest of it even when they went up to the door.

In the middle of the forest, she said wonderingly.

An ugly little Filipino in a white jacket opened the door for them. He bowed low and made a short formal speech of welcome to Malika. She knew he was speaking English, but it was not the English she had been taught in Lausanne. At the end she thanked him gravely.

Later she asked Tex what the little man had been saying.

He was hoping you'd be happy here in your new house, that's all.

My house? But it's your house, not mine!

Of course it's yours! You're my wife, aren't you?

Malika nodded. She knew, no matter what anyone pretended, that when men grew tired of their wives they put them out, and took new ones. She loved Tex and trusted him, but she did not expect him to be different from other men. When the time came, she knew he would find a pretext to rid himself of her. The important point was to know how to fight off the fatal moment, to make it come as late as possible. She nodded again and said with a smile: I like this house, Tex.

The rooms had irregular shapes, with unexpected alcoves and niches where there were soft couches with piles of cushions. As she inspected the house she noted with satisfaction that the windows were barred with iron grillwork. She had already seen the massive front door with its heavy bolts.

That night as they sat in front of the fireplace they heard the yapping of coyotes.

Jackals, murmured Malika, turning her head to listen. Very bad.

She found it incomprehensible that anyone should waste money building such a pretty house in a place so far from everything. Above all she could not understand why the trees had been left growing so close to the house. Silently she determined never to go outside unless Tex accompanied her, and never under any circumstances to remain in the house without him.

The next morning, when Tex was about to drive down into the city, Malika began to run from room to room, crying: Wait! I'm going with you.

You'd be bored, he told her. I've got to go to a lawyer's office. You stay here with Salvador.

She could not let Tex know that she was afraid to stay in the house; it would be an unforgivable affront. No, no, no. I want to see the town, she said.

He kissed her and they set out for the city. It was a bigger car than the one he had rented at the airport the day before.

I always want to go with you no matter where you go, she confided, hoping that this declaration would aid in establishing a precedent.

During these weeks, when she watched the life in the streets, she could find no pattern to it. The people were always on their way somewhere else, and they were in a hurry. She knew better than to imagine that they were all alike; still, she had no way of knowing who was who. In Morocco, in Europe, there had been people who were busy doing things, and there had been others watching. Always, no matter where one was or what one was doing, there were watchers. She had the impression that in America everyone was going somewhere and no one sat watching. This disturbed her. She felt herself to be far, far away from everything she had ever known. The freeways inspired her with dread, for she could not rid herself of the idea that some unnameable catastrophe had occurred, and that the cars were full of refugees fleeing from the scene. She had ample opportunity to observe the miles of small houses set side by side, and compare these simple dwellings with the house on the mountain. As a result it occurred to her that perhaps she was fortunate to live where she did. One day as they drove into the city she turned to Tex and said: Do you have more money than these people?

What people?

She moved her hand. The ones who live in these houses.

I don't know about other people's money, he said. I know I never have enough of my own.

She looked out at the rows of frail wooden houses with their dusty shrubbery, and could not believe him. You *do* have more money, she declared. Why don't you want to say it?

This made him laugh. Whatever I have, I made myself. The day I was twenty-one my father handed me a check and said: Here. Let's see what you can do with this. In three years I changed it into four and a half times as much. Is that what you meant, Dad? I asked him. That's what I meant, son, he said.

Malika thought a moment, saying finally: And now when he needs money you give it to him.

Tex looked sideways at her and said gravely: Of course.

She wanted to ask him if he had no friends in Los Angeles. Since their arrival she had not met anyone, and she thought this strange. It could be a custom here for recently married couples to keep strictly to themselves during a specified period. Or perhaps Tex's friends here were all girls, which would automatically preclude her knowing them. When she asked him, he said he seldom came to Los Angeles. I'm generally with my family in Texas, he said, or down at the hacienda.

There was a studio upstairs with a wide sun-deck that was not hidden by trees in the middle of the day. Malika did not feel entirely at ease sitting out there, with nothing between her and the dark forest. She suspected that the trees harbored dangerous birds. Sometimes she and Tex sat up here between dips in the pool, which, being below inside the closed patio, she considered safe. Tex would observe her as she lay stretched on a mattress, and assure her she was more beautiful than ever. She had noticed this herself, but she was pleased to know that he too had seen it.

XVI

One day Tex told her that a man named F. T. was coming to dinner. F. T. was an old friend of his father's, who managed his financial affairs for him. Malika was interested to hear what such work entailed, so Tex made an effort to explain the mechanics of investment. She was quiet for a while. But then you can't make money unless you already have it, she said.

That's about it, Tex agreed.

F. T. was middle-aged and well-dressed, with a small gray moustache. He was delighted with Malika, and called her Little Lady. This struck her as vaguely insulting, but since she could see that he was a pleasant and well-behaved man otherwise, she made no objections. Besides, Tex had told her: Remember. If you should ever need anything, anything at all, just call F. T.'s number. He's like my father.

During dinner she decided that she really liked F. T., even though he seemed not to take her very seriously. Afterward

he and Tex talked together for a long time. The words went
on for so long that Malika fell asleep on a divan and awoke
only after F. T. had gone. She was apologetic for having been
rude, but she blamed Tex for allowing it to happen.

He threw himself down beside her. F. T. thought you were
great. He says you're beyond a doubt the most beautiful girl
he's ever seen.

He's a nice man, she murmured.

Ever since her arrival in California, her life had seemed static. When she thought back about it, she decided that it had
stopped moving when she had left the Berlitz School. Innocently, she asked Tex if she might continue the lessons here.
To her astonishment he ridiculed the suggestion, claiming
that all she needed was practice in conversation. Because he
was not in the habit of refusing her anything, she did not take
him at his word, and continued to dwell on her desire for further instruction. All at once she saw that he was going to be
firm; he seemed to consider her dissatisfaction a criticism of
him. Finally she realized that he was angry.

You don't understand! she cried. I have to study English
more before I can study anything else.

Study!

Of course, she said calmly. I'm always going to study. You
think I want to stay like this?

I hope you do, Honey, for my sake. You're perfect.

He took hold of her, but she wriggled free.

That evening Tex said to her: I'm going to get an extra
woman in the kitchen and let Salvador give you lessons in
cooking. That's something you should learn, don't you think?

Malika was silent. Do you want me to learn? You know I
want to make you happy.

She began to spend several hours each day in the kitchen
with Salvador and Concha, a Mexican girl of whose work the
little Filipino was scornful. It was a pleasant enough room,
but the number of strange machines and the little bells that
kept sounding as Salvador rushed from one spot to another
awed and confused her. She was even a bit afraid of Salvador,
because his face never changed its fixed expression—that of a
meaningless grin. It seemed to her that when he was annoyed
the grin became even wider. She took care to pay strict atten-

tion to everything he told her. Soon he had her making simple dishes which they ate at lunch. If the recipe called for a
béchamel or a chasseur, he made it himself and incorporated
it, since the timing was more than Malika could manage. It
gratified her to see that Tex thought her food good enough
to be served at table. She continued to spend two hours in
the kitchen each morning, and another hour or so before
dinner in the evening. Sometimes she helped Salvador and
Concha prepare a picnic hamper, and they went to the beach.
She would have liked to tell Tex about the picnics on the
beach at Tangier, but there was no way of doing that.

XVII

Occasionally, despite Malika's entreaties, Tex would take advantage of her morning session in the kitchen to drive the
small car into the city on an errand. She would be uneasy until he returned, but he was always back in time for lunch. One
morning he failed to appear at the usual hour. The telephone
rang. Salvador wiped his hands and stepped into the butler's
pantry to answer it, while Malika and Concha went on chatting together in Spanish. In a moment Salvador reappeared in
the doorway, and with a radiant smile told Malika the police
had called to say that Mister Tex had met with an accident
and was in a hospital in Westwood.

Malika rushed at the little man and seized him by the
shoulders. Telephone to F. T.!

She hopped up and down while he searched for the number and dialed it. As soon as she saw that he was speaking to
F. T., she snatched the telephone from his hand.

F. T.! Come and get me! I want to see Tex.

She heard F. T.'s voice, calm and reassuring. Yes. Now you
just wait quietly for me. I'll be there as soon as I can. Don't
you worry. Let me speak to Salvador again.

She left Salvador talking into the telephone and rushed upstairs to the studio, where she began to walk back and forth.
If Tex was in the hospital, he probably would not be home to
sleep that night, and she would not stay in the house without
him. She went out onto the sun-deck and stared at the trees.
Tex is dead, she thought.

It was mid-afternoon before F. T.'s car drew up at the door. He found her in the studio lying face down on a couch. When she heard his voice she sprang up, wide-eyed, and ran to him.

That night Malika slept at F. T.'s house. He had insisted upon taking her home with him and leaving her in the care of his wife. For it was true that Tex was dead; he had succumbed not long after reaching the hospital.

F. T. and his wife did not commiserate with Malika. Mrs. F. T. said a show of sympathy could induce hysteria. Malika merely talked on and on, weeping intermittently. Sometimes she forgot that her listeners did not know Arabic or Spanish, until at their prompting she would go back into English. She had sworn to accompany Tex whenever he went out, and she had not done so, therefore he had been killed, he was the only being in the world she loved, and she was far from home, and what was going to become of her here alone?

That night as she lay in the dark listening to the occasional passing wail of a police siren, she was assailed afresh by the sensation she had felt on the plane—that of having gone too far for the possibility of return. Being with Tex had made it possible to accept the strangeness of the place; now she saw herself as someone shipwrecked on an unknown shore peopled by creatures whose intentions were unfathomable. And no one could come to rescue her, for no one knew she was there.

She slept at F. T.'s house for several nights. During the days she visited supermarkets and other points of interest with Mrs. F. T. You've got to keep busy, her hostess told her. We can't have you brooding.

There was no way, however, of preventing Malika from worrying about what was to become of her, stranded in this unlikely land without a peseta to buy herself bread, and only the caprice of F. T. and his wife between her and starvation.

XVIII

One morning F. T. himself drove Malika to his office. Out of respect for him she had dressed with great care in a severe gray silk suit from Balenciaga. Her entrance into the office with F. T. caused a stir of interest. When she sat facing him across his desk in a small inner room, he pulled a sheaf of papers from a drawer. As he leafed through them he began to talk.

Betty tells me you're worried about money.

Seeing Malika nod, he went on. I take it you haven't any at all. Is that right?

She felt in her handbag and pulled out a crumpled twenty dollar bill that Tex had given her one day when they were shopping.

Only this, she said, showing him.

F. T. cleared his throat.

Well, I want you to stop worrying. As soon as we get everything cleared up you'll have a regular income. In the meantime I've opened a checking account for you at the bank downstairs in this building.

He saw anxiety flitting across her face, and added hastily: It's your money. You're his sole beneficiary. After taxes and all the rest, you'll still have a substantial capital. And if you're wise, you'll leave it all just where it is, in certificates of deposit and treasury notes. So stop worrying.

Yes, she said, understanding nothing.

I never let Tex play with stocks, F. T. went on. He had no head for business.

She was shocked to hear F. T. denigrate poor Tex in this way, but she said: I see.

When we get everything straight and running smoothly, you ought to have around fifty thousand a month. Possibly a little more.

Malika stared at F. T. Is that enough? she asked cautiously.

He shot a quick glance at her over his spectacles. I think you'll find it's enough.

I hope so, she said with fervor. You see, I don't understand money. I never bought anything myself. How much does a thing cost? I don't know. Only in my own country.

Of course. F. T. pushed a checkbook along the top of the desk toward her. You understand, this is a temporary account for you to draw on now, until all the legal work is finished. I hope you won't overdraw. But I'm sure you won't.

He smiled encouragingly at her. Remember, he went on. There are only twenty-five thousand dollars there. So be a good girl and keep track of your checks.

But I can't do what you tell me! she exclaimed. Please do it for me.

F. T. sighed. Can you write your name? he asked very quietly.

Tex showed me in Lausanne, but I've forgotten.

In spite of himself, F. T. raised his arms. But my dear lady, how do you expect to live? You can't go on this way.

No, she said miserably.

F. T. pushed back his chair and stood up. Well, he said jovially, what you don't know you can always learn. Why don't you come up here every morning and study with Miss Galper? She's as smart as a whip. She'll teach you everything you need to know. That's my suggestion for you.

He was not prepared for her vehement response. She jumped up and hugged him. Oh, F. T.! That's what I want! That's what I want!

XIX

The following day Malika moved her luggage into a hotel in Beverly Hills. Under F. T.'s advice she kept Salvador on, living in the house, but now functioning solely as chauffeur. Each morning he called at the hotel for her and drove her to F. T.'s office. She found this routine stimulating. Miss Galper, a pleasant young woman with glasses, would spend the forenoon working with her, after which they generally went to lunch together. There had not been much glamor in Miss Galper's life, and she was fascinated by Malika's accounts of Europe and Morocco. There remained a basic mystery in her story, nevertheless, since she never explained how she came to be living at Tim's flat in Tangier. In her version, she might have come into being during a picnic on the beach at Sidi Qacem.

When after two months F. T. saw that Malika was, if anything, even more serious and determined about pursuing her practical education, he suggested that the lessons continue at the hotel. Now it was Miss Galper whom Salvador drove to and from Beverly Hills. Occasionally they went shopping— small expeditions to Westwood that delighted Malika because for the first time she was aware of prices, and could gauge the

buying power of her money. F. T. had told her that with what
Tex had left for her she would be able to live better than most
people. At the time she had supposed this was a part of his attempt to comfort her, but now that she understood the prices
she realized that he had been stating a fact. She said nothing
to Miss Galper of her surprise at finding the cost of goods so
low. Instead, she overwhelmed her with a constant flow of
small gifts.

You've got to stop this, Malika, Miss Galper told her.

The first month they had done nothing but arithmetic. After that there was the telling of time, the names of the days
and the months. With some difficulty Miss Galper taught her
to sign the two forms of her name: *Malika Hapgood* and *Mrs.
Charles G. Hapgood*. By the time the lessons were moved to
the hotel, Malika had begun to practice writing out in words
complicated sums given her in figures. They went back to
dates, and she had to learn to write them correctly.

You can leave everything else to a secretary, Miss Galper
told her. But you've got to take care of your money yourself.

To this end she gave Malika a course in reading bank statements, and another in spacing the purchase of securities to assure regular turnover.

As the months went by and Malika's insight into the functioning of the world around her grew, she began to understand the true extent of her ignorance, and she conceived a
passionate desire to be able to read the texts of newspapers
and magazines.

I'm not an English teacher, Miss Galper told her. F. T.
doesn't pay me for that. We can get you a good professor
whenever you want.

Malika, being persuaded that she could learn only from
Miss Galper, consulted F. T. about it. After a certain amount
of deliberation, he devised a plan which delighted Malika and
pleased Miss Galper as well. He would give Miss Galper a
year's holiday with salary if Malika wanted to take her on as a
paid companion during that time. In this way, he implied to
Malika, she would be able to get the reading lessons she
wanted. He added that he did not think Miss Galper was the
person to give them, but since Malika had her heart set on
being taught by her, this seemed to him a viable strategy.

It was Miss Galper's idea to make a tour of Europe. F. T. suggested they buy a big car, put it on a freighter, and take Salvador along with them to pick it up over there and drive it. When Malika heard this, she asked why they could not all go on the ship with the car. It might be possible, F. T. told her.

Eventually F. T. had arranged to get Malika a new passport, had even helped Miss Galper and Salvador expedite theirs, and, accompanied by Mrs. F. T., had bidden them a lengthy farewell at the dock in San Pedro. It was a comfortable Norwegian freighter bound for Panama and eventually for Europe.

The ship was already in tropical waters. Malika said she had imagined it could be this hot only in the Sahara, and certainly not on the sea. She had nothing to do all day. Salvador spent most of his time sleeping. Miss Galper sat in a deck chair reading. She had refused to give Malika any kind of lessons while they were on the ship. It would make me seasick, she assured her. But she noticed Malika's boredom, and talked with her for long periods of time.

XX

Malika could not sit, as Miss Galper could, looking at the sea. The flat horizon on all sides gave her much the same sensation of unreality she had experienced on the plane with Tex. Panama came as a relief, making it clear that the ship had not been static during all those days, and that they had reached a very different part of the world.

It took all day to go through the canal. Malika stood on deck in the sun, waving back to the men working along the locks. But from Panama on, her restlessness increased daily. She was reduced to playing endless games of checkers with a yawning Salvador each afternoon in the narrow passengers' lounge. They never spoke during these sessions. From the beginning of the voyage the captain had urged Malika to visit the bridge. At some point Miss Galper had mentioned that he had the power to seize anyone on the ship and have him locked into a dark cell somewhere below. When Malika finally accepted his invitation she took Miss Galper along.

Standing at the prow, Malika stared ahead at the white buildings of Cadiz. As the ship moved into the port, the combination of the light in the air, the color of the walls and the odors on the wind told her that she was back in her part of the world and close to home. For a long time she had refused to think about the little house above the gully. Now that it no longer frightened her, she was able to imagine it almost with affection.

It was her duty to go and visit her mother, however hostile a reception she might get from her. She would try to give her money, which she was certain she would refuse to take. But Malika was ready with a ruse. If her mother spurned the money, she would tell her she was leaving it next door with Mina Glagga. Once Malika was out of the way, her mother would lose no time in going to claim it.

Miss Galper had hoped to spend the night in Cadiz, but Malika insisted on driving straight to Algeciras. Now that she was so near home, she wanted to get there as soon as she could. I must see my mother, she said. I must see her first.

Of course, said Miss Galper. But you haven't seen her in two years or more and she isn't expecting you. One day sooner or later?

We can come back. Now I have to go and see my mother.

In Algeciras at the hotel that night they saw Salvador eating at the other end of the long dining room. He had changed from his uniform into a gray flannel suit. Malika observed him carefully, and said: He's drinking wine.

He'll be all right tomorrow, Miss Galper told her. They always drink, Filipinos.

He was at the door grinning when they came out of the hotel in the morning to be driven to the dock. Most of the passengers going to Tangier were Moroccans. Malika had forgotten the shameless intensity with which her countrymen stare at women. Now she was back among her own kind. The realization startled her; she felt both excitement and apprehension.

XXI

After they had settled into their quarters at the hotel, Malika went down to the desk. She hoped to visit her mother in the evening, when she was sure to be in the house, and when there would be a valid excuse for not staying too long. She intended to reserve two rooms in Tetuan for the night, one for Salvador and one for herself, and return to Tangier in the morning. In the lobby they told her of a new hotel on the beach only a mile or so from her town. She asked them to telephone for reservations.

Miss Galper's room was down the corridor from hers. Malika knocked on her door and told her she would be leaving about five o'clock, in order to get to the hotel before dark.

Miss Galper looked at her searchingly. I'm glad you're doing it now and getting it over with, she said.

You can have a good time, Malika told her. There are bars where you can go.

No, thank you. The men here give me the creeps. They all try to talk to you.

Malika shrugged. What difference does it make? You can't understand what they're saying.

This was fortunate, she thought. The brutally obscene remarks made by the men to women passing in the street disgusted and infuriated her. Miss Galper was lucky not to know any Arabic.

She said a lame good-bye and hurried to her room. The prospect of seeing her mother had unsettled her. Mechanically she put a few articles of clothing into an overnight bag. On the way out she cashed some traveler's checks at the office, and soon she and Salvador were on the road to Tetuan.

The mountains had scarves of white cloud trailing outward from their summits. Salvador criticized the narrow highway. Malika scarcely heard his complaints. Her heart was beating unusually fast. It was true that she was going back to help her mother; she was going because it was included in the pattern. Since the day she had run away, the vision of the triumphant return had been with her, when she would be the living proof that her mother had been mistaken, that she was not like the other girls of the town. Now that the moment was drawing near, she suspected that the visit was foredoomed to failure. Her mother would feel no pleasure at seeing her—only rancor and bitterness at the thought that she had been with Nazarenes.

Salvador said: In Pilipinas we got better roads than this
one.

Don't go fast, she told him.

They skirted Tetuan and turned to the left along the road
that led to her town. The sea wind rushed through the car.
Bismil'lah, she murmured under her breath, for now she was
entering the crucial part of the journey.

She did not even know they had reached the town until
they were in the main street. It looked completely different.
There were big new buildings and bright lights. The idea that
the town might change during her absence had not occurred
to her; she herself would change, but the town would remain
an unmoving backdrop which would help her define and
measure her transformation.

A moment later they had arrived at the new hotel, spread
out along the beach in a glare of green floodlights.

XXII

Malika soon discovered that it was not a real hotel. There was
no room service, and in the dining room they served only
snack-bar food. Before eating, she changed into blue jeans,
bought in Los Angeles at Miss Galper's suggestion. She wore
a sweater and wrapped a silk kerchief tightly around her head.
In this costume she felt wholly anonymous.

Salvador was already eating at the counter in the comedor.
She sat on a stool near him and ordered pinchitos. Her stomach rebelled at the thought of eating, but she chewed and
swallowed the meat because she had learned that to feel well
she must eat regularly. Through the rasping of a transistor
radio at the end of the counter she heard the dull, repeated
sound of the waves breaking over the sand below. If her
mother flew into a rage and began to beat her, she would go
directly to Mina Glagga and give her the money, and that
would finish it. She signed the chit and went out into the
wind to the car.

The town's new aspect confused her. They had moved the
market; she could not see it anywhere, and she felt a wave of
indignation at this betrayal. Salvador parked the car at the service station and they set out on foot up the narrow street that

led to the house. There were street lights only part of the way; beyond, it would have been dark had it not been for the moon. Salvador glanced ahead and said it would be better to turn around and come again in the morning.

You wait here, she said firmly. I'll come back as soon as I can. I know the way. And she quickly went on, before he could argue about it.

She made her way up along the empty moonlit street until she came to a small open square from which, in the daytime at least, her mother's house was visible ahead, at the edge of the barranca. Now as she looked, the moon's light did not seem to strike it at all; she could see no sign of it. She hurried on, already assailed by a nightmarish premonition, and then she stopped, her mouth open in disbelief. The house was not there. Even the land where it had stood was gone. Mina Glagga's and all the houses bordering on the gully had disappeared. Bulldozers had made a new landscape of emptiness, a great embankment of earth, ashes and refuse that stretched downward to the bottom of the ravine. The little house with its garden had been just below where she now stood. She felt her throat tighten painfully as she told herself that it no longer existed.

Ceasing finally to stare at the meaningless terrain, she turned and went back to the square, where she knocked at the door of one of the houses. The woman who opened the door was a friend of her mother's whose name she had forgotten. She eyed Malika's blue jeans with distaste and did not ask her inside. They talked standing in the doorway. In an expressionless voice the woman told her that her mother had died more than a year earlier, during Ramadan. It was fortunate, she added, that she had not lived to see them destroy her house in order to build the new road. She thought Malika's sister had gone to Casablanca, but she was not certain.

By now the woman had pushed the door so that it was nearly shut. Malika thanked her and said good night.

She went over and stood at the edge of the landfill, staring down at the uniform surface of the hillside, unreal even in the careful light dropped over it by the moon. She had to force her eyes shut to clear them of the tears that kept forming, and she found it strange, for she had not felt tenderness for her mother. Then she saw more clearly. It was not for her mother that she felt like weeping; it was for herself. There was no longer any reason to do anything.

She let her gaze wander over the dim expanse toward the mountains beyond. It would be good to perish here in the place where she had lived, to be buried along with the house under the hateful mass. She pounded the edge of it with her heel, lost her footing, and slid downward some distance through mounds of ashes and decayed food. In that instant she was certain it was happening, as a punishment for having wished to be dead a moment ago; her weight had started a landslide that would roll her to the bottom, leaving her under tons of refuse. Terrified, she lay still, listening. There were faint stirrings and clinks around her, but they quickly died away into silence. She scrambled up to the roadbed.

A cloud had begun to move across the moon. She hurried down the hill toward the street light where Salvador waited.

Madame and Ahmed

UNLESS it was raining very hard, Mrs. Pritchard spent roughly half of each day working outdoors in the garden. It was a garden to be admired, but not a place where one could sit. Her house was at the top of a cliff overlooking the sea; the winds sweeping through the Strait of Gibraltar struck the spot first, and blew harder there. If Ahmed thought of Madame in the garden, he saw her with her skirt fluttering in the wind and her hand over her hair, trying vainly to keep it in place.

The land sloped off at a moderate angle for a few hundred feet before the sheer drop, and the terraced garden followed it down to the end. On some levels there were long tiled pools full of goldfish; others were bounded by arbors sheltering small fountains whose water dribbled from the mouths of marble fish into basins.

She had planted the land in such a way that the flowers were superb throughout the year, thus transforming the bleak and forbidding strip of land, and she took pride in the result. Recently, however, certain large shrubs she had imported from England seemed to be doing very poorly, and since they were within sight of the house, she was upset by their sickly aspect. If guests peered out of a window she would beg them not to look, saying sadly: I'm ashamed of my garden this year.

Her friends commiserated with her, most of them advising her to find a new gardener. This worried her, for she shrank from the idea of getting rid of Ahmed. He had kept her garden in order for the past eleven years. In that time, she wondered how many hundreds of hours she had spent squatting beside him as, working together with trowels and clippers, they discussed the ways of plants. She felt that they knew and understood one another in a basic and important fashion, even though Ahmed never had learned even to pronounce her name. For him she was Madame.

One day she came to him in excitement and said she had just bought a large number of beautiful plants from a man in the city who would bring them in a truck tomorrow and, she added, help her plant them. Seeing Ahmed's expression of hurt surprise, she explained to him that this service was included in the price of the plants. The cost, she confessed, had been extremely high, and she saw no reason not to take advantage of the man's offer to assist in the work. Ahmed was unable to follow her logic; he understood only that she was allowing an outsider to come in and work in the garden. Yes, Madame, he said; no more.

The following morning a stout man in a grey business suit appeared with Madame at the top of the garden. They talked and occasionally pointed. Ahmed, squatting on a terrace some distance below, stared up at the man and recognized him as the chief gardener for the municipality. A little later, returning from a trip to the tool shed, he was able to pass near enough to the new plants to recognize them as having come from the Jardin Municipal. For a moment he was impelled to go and tell Madame that she had bought stolen goods, but then he thought better of it. During the years of working for her he had observed that if one Moroccan spoke ill of another Moroccan to her, she automatically took the side of the accused rather than that of the complainer. When the time came, he might make use of what he knew about the plants.

A second man was carrying in more pots from the truck outside, setting them down in rows on the top terrace. Madame was saying to the stout man: Now these will go here along the wall, and those there in that circular bed, and I think the tuberoses should go all the way down at the end of this path by themselves.

I know the best place for each plant, Madame, the fat man told her. You'll see.

Wait! she cried nervously, glancing around as if for help. I'll send my gardener up.

The man rejected this suggestion. No, no! My assistant and I will do everything. Each plant will be in the right place. You leave it to me.

Mrs. Pritchard seemed to wilt. She turned and went inside the house.

The thief had taken command of the garden, not even allowing Madame to have her plants where she wanted them. From the lower terrace where he knelt, Ahmed watched the two men. They were putting the plants in hurriedly, paying little heed to what they were doing. When they had finished, they began to walk back and forth along the two topmost terraces, examining the flowers. He tried to hear what they were saying, but they spoke too low. On seeing their prolonged stop beside the giant hibiscus Madame had brought from Hawaii, he suspected that the fat man would find a pretext for returning to see Madame.

After the truck had driven away, Madame came out of the house and called to Ahmed. Together they surveyed the hasty workmanship. Madame laughed. It doesn't matter. We can replant them later. Give them plenty of water.

He glanced at the row of agapanthus without interest. When she mentioned the price she had paid for them, he was indignant. You could have bought bulbs, he said reproachfully.

But I wouldn't have had the flowers until next year.

He nodded gloomily.

That evening Johara, the black cook, stopped him as he passed the kitchen door. Do you know what he was telling Madame, that man? He told her you weren't a real gardener, and she should get rid of you and let him work here.

He's a criminal! Ahmed shouted.

In the shack where he lived behind the greenhouse, Ahmed sat and thought. He must save his job, and he must save the garden. Again he recalled the visitors' scrutiny of the hibiscus bushes. If they came there to work they would methodically strip the garden of its most valuable plants.

Once he had convinced himself that he was acting partially in Madame's interest, he felt less guilt about what he was planning to do. It was simple enough. He waited until long after all the lights in the main house had been put out. Then, taking up a sack into which he dropped a sharp knife, he stole out into the garden, to the end of the topmost terrace, and knelt down among the newly interred plants. One after the other he yanked them up, severed their roots or tubers with a swift stroke of the blade, and carefully replanted them exactly where they had been. The sack was full of roots and bulbs when he took it back to his room. He built a fire in his mijmah and charred them beyond recognition before carrying them

out and scattering them over the compost heap. Then he
went to bed.

In the morning Madame was out looking at the new plants.
They're very pretty, she said to Ahmed. Each one needs to be
watered with a sprinkling can, and before the sun hits them.
Just sprinkle a little around each stalk so it can soak in.

She watched for a while as Ahmed, in resentful silence, carried out her instructions. Then, apparently satisfied, she went
inside. It was many years since she had stood over him like
that, waiting to see if he did as he was told, and he understood that the fat man's poison was working in her, that in
spite of his open indifference to her wishes she had not rejected the idea of hiring him to run her garden.

By mid-afternoon some of the flowers were not looking as
crisp as they had looked in the morning. Ahmed noted their
state as he passed by them, and decided to put off reporting
it until evening, when the sun would have carried its destructive work still further.

It was Madame herself who first remarked on the poor
complexion of the transplants. She called to Ahmed, who
came up from the bottom of the garden.

I don't know, she said, shaking her head. As she pulled at a
leaf of one of the plants, it fell over, a dry stick exposing its
rootless base. She seized the next plant and lifted it up.

Ahmed! she cried. These things are just stems stuck into
the ground. They're not growing plants at all!

He examined the two plants, and gazed at her, feeling sorry
for her. The wind was blowing her hair all across her face, and
she seemed ready to burst into tears.

They looked so healthy, she said.

Together they went to examine the agapanthus, the tuberoses. The filthy swine! cried Madame. No wonder he didn't
want me around while he planted them!

Suddenly she stared at Ahmed. He's coming back. He said
he was going to bring me some rose bushes.

He won't dare come back after what he's done, Ahmed declared.

Madame looked even more distraught. And to think—she
began, checking herself as she realized that up to a few minutes ago she still had been considering the possibility of dis-

missing Ahmed and hiring the man. She could not admit to such disloyalty. Ahmed knew what she had stopped herself from saying, and he smiled grimly.

If he comes back, don't let him in. Don't even talk to him. Call me and I'll take care of him.

I'd much prefer that, she said. I don't want to see that disgusting face again.

The wind blew, the dead plants were dumped onto the compost heap, and the brief scandal was no longer mentioned. Ahmed was certain, however, that the man would return.

One day he did. Johara came to the toolshed to say that the bad man was at the door, and Madame was very nervous.

Ahmed put on his djellaba and walked out to the entrance door. He opened it, and looking sternly at the fat man, intoned, as though repeating an order he had learned by rote: Madame said to tell you she knows where you got the flowers, and not to come back here unless you want to explain it to the police.

Then he shut the door and listened while the truck drove away. Madame was waiting in the doorway of the entrance hall.

He's gone, he said.

Ahmed, what would I do without you? She stared at him for a moment, shaking her head. What did you say to him?

I told him no true Moslem would play tricks on a woman with no husband.

Mrs. Pritchard reflected. I'm sure that was exactly the right thing to say. I'm afraid I should have insulted him and gone to bed with a headache afterward. I'm very grateful to you.

Still uneasy because of the deception he had practised upon Madame, and more than a little guilty for having destroyed so many healthy, expensive plants, he found that it made him feel better to say: Everybody plays tricks nowadays, Madame. Everybody.

For him it served as a comforting admission of his wrongdoing, but she took it as a hint. Oh, I shan't do it again, I promise you, she said. He glanced at her approvingly and turned to go.

You're right, Madame, he told her. Don't believe anybody.

Kitty

KITTY lived in a medium-sized house with a big garden around it. She loved some things, like picnics and going to the circus, and she hated other things, like school and going to the dentist's.

One day she asked her mother: "Why is my name Kitty?"

"Your name is really Catherine," her mother said. "We just call you Kitty."

This reply did not satisfy Kitty, and she decided that her mother did not want to tell her the truth. This made her think even more about her name. Finally she thought she had the answer. Her name was Kitty because some day she was going to grow up into a cat. She felt proud of herself for having found this out, and she began to look into the mirror to see if perhaps she was beginning to look like a cat, or at least like a kitten.

For a long time she could see nothing at all but her own pink face. But one day when she went up to the glass she could hardly believe what she saw, for around her mouth tiny gray whiskers were beginning to sprout. She jumped up and down with delight, and waited for her mother to say something about them. Her mother, however, had no time for such things, and so she noticed nothing.

Each day when Kitty looked at her reflection she saw more wonderful changes. Slowly the whiskers grew longer and stood out farther from her face, and a soft gray fur started to cover her skin. Her ears grew pointed and she had soft pads on the palms of her hands and the soles of her feet. All this seemed too good to be true, and Kitty was sad to find that nobody had said a word about the marvelous change in her. One day as she was playing she turned to her mother and said: "Meow. I'm Kitty. Do you like the color of my fur?"

"I don't know," her mother said. "What color is it?"

"It's gray!"

"Oh, gray. Very pretty," said her mother, and Kitty saw with a sinking heart that she did not care what color the fur was.

After that she tried to make several neighbors remark on her fine whiskers, her velvety ears and her short fluffy tail, and they all agreed that these things were very nice, and then paid no more attention to them. Kitty did not care too much. If *they* could not see how different she had become, at least she herself could.

One summer morning when Kitty awoke, she discovered that her fingernails and toenails had been replaced by splendid new pearly gray claws that she could stick out or pull in as she chose. She jumped out of bed and ran into the garden. It was still very early. Her mother and father were asleep, but there were some birds walking around on the lawn.

She slipped behind some bushes and watched. After a long time she began to crawl forward. The branches caught her nightgown, so she tore it off. When one of the birds came very close to her, she sprang forward and caught it. And at that moment she knew that she was no longer a girl at all, and that she would never have to be one again.

The bird tasted good, but she decided not to eat it. Instead, she rolled on her back in the sun and licked her paws. Then she sat up and washed her face. After a while she thought she would go over to Mrs. Tinsley's house and see if she could get some breakfast. She climbed up to the top of the wall and ran quickly along it to the roof of the garage. From there she scrambled down the trellis into Mrs. Tinsley's backyard. She heard sounds in the kitchen, so she went up to the screen door and looked in. Then she said: "Meow." She had to keep saying it for quite a while before Mrs. Tinsley came and saw her.

"Well, if that isn't the cutest kitten!" Mrs. Tinsley said, and she called to her husband and her sister. They came and saw the small grey kitten with one paw raised, scratching at the screen. Of course they let her in, and soon Kitty was lapping up a saucer full of milk. She spent the day sleeping, curled up on a cushion, and in the evening she was given a bowl of delicious raw liver.

After dinner she decided to go back home. Mr. Tinsley saw her at the kitchen door, but instead of opening the door for her, he picked her up and locked her into the cellar. This was not at all what Kitty wanted, and she cried all night.

In the morning they let her go upstairs, and gave her a big bowl of milk. When she had drunk it she waited in the kitchen until Mrs. Tinsley opened the door to go out into the yard. Then she ran as fast as she could between Mrs. Tinsley's feet, and climbed up onto the roof of the garage. She looked down at Mrs. Tinsley, who was calling: "Kitty, Kitty, Kitty." Then she turned and ran the other way. Soon she was in her own garden. She went up to all the doors and looked in. There were policemen inside the house with her mother and father. They were holding Kitty's torn nightgown in their hands, and her mother was crying and sobbing. No one paid the slightest attention to Kitty.

She went sadly back to Mrs. Tinsley's house, and there she stayed for many weeks. Sometimes she would go over to her own house and peek again through the doors, and often she saw her mother or her father. But they looked very different from the way they had looked before, and even if they noticed her, they never came to the door to let her in.

It was nice not having to go to school, and Mr. and Mrs. Tinsley were very good to her, but Kitty loved her mother and father more than she could love anyone else, and she wanted to be with them.

Mr. and Mrs. Tinsley let her go out whenever she pleased now, because she always came back. She would go to her house at night and look in through the window to see her father sitting alone reading the paper. This was how she knew that her mother had gone away. Even if she cried and pushed her claws against the window, her father paid no attention to her, and she knew that he would never let her in. Only her mother would do that. She would come and open the door and take her in her arms and rub the fur on her forehead and kiss her.

One day several months later when Kitty climbed over the wall into her own garden, she saw her mother sitting in a chair outside. She looked much better, almost the way she had used to look. Kitty walked slowly toward her mother over the grass, holding her tail in the air. Her mother sat up straighter, watching as she came nearer. Then she put out her hand and wriggled her fingers at Kitty. "Well, the pretty pussycat," she said. "Where did *you* come from?"

Kitty went near enough so that her mother could rub her head and scratch her cheeks. She waved her tail and purred with delight as she felt her mother's fingers stroking her fur. Then she jumped up into her mother's lap and lay curled up there, working her claws joyously in and out. After a long time her mother lifted her up and held her against her face, and then she carried her into the house.

That evening Kitty lay happily in her mother's lap. She did not want to try her father's lap because she was afraid he might push her off. Besides, she could see that it would not be very comfortable.

Kitty knew that her mother already loved her, and that her father would learn to love her. At last she was living exactly the life she always had wished for. Sometimes she thought it would be nice if she could make them understand that she was really Kitty, but she knew there was no way of doing that. She never heard them say the word *Kitty* again. Instead, because her fur was so long and fine that when she moved she seemed to be floating, they named her Feather. She had no lessons to worry about, she never had to go to the dentist's, and she no longer had to wonder whether her mother was telling her the truth or not, because she knew the truth. She was Kitty, and she was happy.

The Husband

ABDALLAH lived with his wife in a two-room house on a hillside several miles from the center of town. They had two children. The girl was in school and the boy lived at the house of an Englishman for whom he did gardening.

Long ago the woman had set the pattern of their life by going out to work as a maid in Nazarene houses. She was strong and jolly, and the Nazarenes liked her. They recommended her to their friends, so that she was never without employment, and was able to work at several houses each day. Since she turned over all her wages to Abdallah, there was no need for him to work. Sometimes he suspected that the Nazarenes were paying her more than she claimed, but he said nothing.

The woman was also expert at carrying things out of the houses of the Nazarenes without their being aware of it. In earlier days she had handed over these bits of plunder to him along with the money; what they brought at the joteya was a welcome bonus. Working so long for the Nazarenes, however, had given her a taste for the way the Nazarenes lived. She began to complain when Abdallah tried to carry off a bath towel or a sheet or a fancy serving dish, for she wanted these things in the house with her. When he took away a small traveling alarm clock which she particularly prized, she stopped speaking to him and would have nothing to do with him. He was angry and mortified, and he began to sleep in the other room, sending the girl to sleep with her mother.

The silent war between them had not gone on for very long before Abdallah took a great interest in Zohra, a young woman living up the road, whose husband only recently had left her. Because she needed money, she encouraged Abdallah's attentions, and soon he was eating and sleeping in her house with her, not caring that his behavior was causing unfavorable comment throughout the neighborhood.

Zohra was not long in discovering that Abdallah could not pay for anything. Having moved out of his house, he could scarcely go back at the end of the month and ask his wife for money. Once she saw how matters stood, Zohra thought only of getting rid of him, and she did her utmost to make his life unbearable.

Early one afternoon he paid a visit to his house, knowing that his wife would be away at work. It was a Friday, so that his daughter was not at school. She was in the patio, washing out some clothes. He greeted her, but she scarcely looked up. Her mother has filled her head with lies about me, he thought. Then he went inside and called his wife's name. At the same time his eye alighted on a transparent plastic bag, stuffed into a niche in the wall. He stepped nearer and saw something shining inside the bag. Without looking further, he hid it inside his djellaba, called his wife's name once more, and returned to the patio.

Tell your mother I was here, he said to the girl. She did not reply, and he added: Don't listen to the neighbors.

She fixed him for a second with a resentful stare before she bent again to scrub the clothes.

He climbed up the hillside and sat down in the woods so he could examine the contents of the bag in private. There were twelve big spoons there, all of them exactly alike. After admiring them for a while, he wrapped them up and set out for the town to show them to a friend in Emsallah who knew about such things.

The man assured him that the soup spoons were of the purest silver, and offered to give him seventy thousand francs for them. Abdallah said he needed time to consider it, and that he would return. From Emsallah he went directly to the joteya and put the silver in the hands of a dillal, who began to make the rounds of the market with it. The bids finally reached a hundred thousand francs, and the spoons were sold.

That night at Zohra's he lay awake, fully dressed, with the banknotes clutched in his hand. Early in the morning he went out and bought ten goats, all of them black. Then he rented a shack with a shed beside it where he could keep them at night. He was careful to choose a quarter that lay at some distance from his own, one that was reached by a different road, reasoning that this would reduce the likelihood of an unexpected encounter with Zohra or his wife.

He found his new life agreeably restful. Each morning at daybreak he went out with the goats, driving them along the back road to Boubana and then through the valley toward Rehreh. Here he would sit in the shade of a ruined farmhouse and look down at the goats as they wandered over the hillside.

Sometimes he fell asleep for a while as he sat watching them. This was dangerous: they could get into a patch of cultivated ground and he would have trouble with the farmer. Even more important was a recently passed law stipulating that henceforth no motorist would be held responsible for any livestock he happened to hit on the highway. Worse than that, it was the owner of the animals who had to pay a stiff fine for each one killed. The country people were unable to fathom the reasons for an order that seemed so perverse, but they understood that it was wiser to keep their animals far from the roads.

Often when the weather was hot Abdallah did not take the trouble to drive the goats up the valley, but sat under a pine tree in a field not far from the road to Rmilat. Here he was obliged to force himself to stay awake and keep his eye on them, for they could easily stray onto the road. One breathless afternoon, however, he felt a powerful need for sleep overtaking him, and even though he fought against it, he was unable to keep from dropping into a deep slumber.

He awoke to a squealing of brakes, looked down at the road, and saw what had happened. Two of his goats had wandered in front of a truck, and lay dead on the asphalt.

He jumped up, drove the others away from the road, and then hurried back to drag the two dead animals over to the ditch. If the police were to pass by now, they would immediately identify them as part of his flock, and take him with them.

A youth whom he recognized as the son of the man who lived next door to his shack came along, pushing an empty wheelbarrow. He called to him, and pointed to the bodies in the ditch.

Get rid of these for me, will you? I don't care where you hide them, but don't go along the road with them. When you come back here with the empty wheelbarrow you get the money.

He did not explain to the boy why he was so eager to remove the carcasses instead of simply leaving them there in the ditch for the dogs. If the boy realized the importance of his task, he would be dissatisfied with the small amount Abdallah intended to give him.

The lad heaved the two goats into the wheelbarrow and set off along a path that led through the scrub down toward the river. It was a Sunday, and scores of women were doing their washing along the banks of the stream; the bushes were tents of drying sheets. He pushed the wheelbarrow along until he came to the bridge over the sluice. On the upper side the water was deep and black; on the other side a rivulet trickled at the bottom of a twisting gulley. He decided to dump the goats into the deep water, and rolled up his sleeves.

At that moment a woman standing on the bank at the foot of the bridge began to shout at him. It was her land he was standing on, she cried, and he could take his carrion somewhere else. He let her shout and watched her wave her arms for a long time, saying nothing. Then, seeing that a crowd was gathering, he spat contemptuously, tipped the wheelbarrow and let the animals splash into the water. The woman's voice rose to a scream as she announced that she was going to the police.

I know you! she shrieked. I know where your father lives! You'll sleep in jail!

The boy did not even look at her as he pushed his wheelbarrow ahead of him. To get to where Abdallah was waiting for him, he went along the highway.

When Abdallah saw him coming, he walked to meet him, noted the empty wheelbarrow, and paid him, assuming that the goats were hidden somewhere among the bushes and brambles near the bend in the river.

Less than an hour later the woman was at the comisaría waving her arms as she denounced the boy. The police listened attentively, feeling certain that they were on their way to collecting some fines.

When they had fished the goats out of the water and dumped them in a back room at the police station, the woman led them to the house of the boy's father.

The boy was indignant. Deep water's the best place to throw them, he protested. The man paid me to take them away. Ask him.

On the adjoining plot of land they found Abdallah sitting dejectedly with his eight remaining goats. Come on, they said. We've got something to show you. And they made him go with them to the comisaría, where they confronted him with the two wet carcasses, and demanded an immediate payment of forty thousand francs.

Abdallah was shocked. I haven't even got ten, he said.

That's all right, they told him. We'll take four of your goats.

At this Abdallah set up an outcry. How can two goats be worth four? he kept shouting. They laughed and pushed him out, but the scene had been so noisy that people had gathered outside the entrance, trying to see in through the front door. Zohra, who was waiting for a bus on the other side of the road, quickly got the story from others who stood nearby.

Ah, so he has goats, she said to herself, and as she rode up the hill in the bus all her rancor against Abdallah returned. He could never even pay for a loaf of bread, but he has goats.

She set about spreading the news around the neighborhood that Abdallah, contrary to what everyone thought, had not left Tangier at all, but lived below Vasco da Gama with a flock of goats. She was certain that this would get to Abdallah's wife, which it very soon did.

Abdallah's wife had never bothered to file a complaint against him for having abandoned her and the children, since she knew she would get nothing out of it. Now however she determined to go and claim support. If Abdallah had goats, he had them only because of her spoons; of that she was certain. He must not be allowed to keep them.

The following day, instead of reporting to work at the Nazarenes', she went to declare that her husband had left her. After a long wait, she was allowed into an office. As he filled out a paper, the official asked her where Abdallah worked.

He doesn't work. He has no money.

The man raised his arms. Then what do you expect us to do? If he has no money, why did you come here?

He has goats, she said.

A few weeks later a message from the government arrived for her, telling her to go to the comisaría of her quarter. There a policeman was assigned to her, and together they started to walk to the shack where Abdallah lived.

Ever since the police had gone away with half his flock, Abdallah had not taken the trouble to drive the four remaining goats out to the fields where they could graze. He merely sat in the doorway of his shack, watching the starving animals wander around the small enclosure. Once in a while he brought in an armful of weeds for them.

The policeman told the woman to wait in the road while he went in and got the goats. She peered through the gate and saw the four bony, dried-up creatures. The policeman was talking, and then he came out through the gate, driving the goats ahead of him.

As he shut the gate she stole another glance inside and saw Abdallah sitting by the door of the shack, his face buried in his hands. At that moment, if only he had looked up, she would have called out something to him, to make him understand that it was all right, that he could return to her. But he did not move. The gate cut across her view of him, and she was in the road, walking with the policeman and the goats.

For an instant she regretted not having spoken to him: he looked so solitary and hopeless. Then she remembered the shawl. Three days earlier, after months of planning, she had managed to avail herself of a huge soft cashmere shawl which she intended to keep. She thought she had done well to hold her tongue.

In this world it's not possible to have everything, she told herself.

At the Krungthep Plaza

IT WAS the day when the President of the United States was due to arrive with his wife on a visit to the King and Queen. Throughout the preceding afternoon squads of men had been running up and down the boulevard, dragging with them heavy iron stands to be used as barricades along the curbs. Mang Huat rose from his bed sweaty and itching, having slept very little during the night. Ever since he had been advised that the procession would be passing in front of the hotel he had been awaiting the day with mounting dread. The smallest incident could jeopardize his career. It needed only one lunatic with a hand grenade.

With distaste he pulled aside the curtains near his bed and peered out into the light of the inauspicious day. Later, when he had showered, he returned to the window and stood for a long time. Above the city the grey sky was ahum with helicopters; so far none had hit the tops of the highest chedis towering above the temples, but people in the street watched with interest each time an object clattered overhead in the direction of a nearby spire. At times, when a police car was on its way through the quarter, all traffic was suspended, and there would follow an unusual, disturbing hush in which he could hear only the whir of the insects in the trees. Then there would come other sounds of life, farther away: the cries of children and the barking of dogs, and they too were disturbing, these naked noises in place of the unceasing roar of motors.

No one seemed to know when the royal cortege would go by. The radio had announced the time as ten o'clock, but gossip in the lobby downstairs, reportedly straight from police headquarters, fixed the starting hour as noon. Mang Huat decided not to have breakfast, nor indeed to eat at all until the danger had passed and he was free from tension.

He sat behind his desk tapping the point of an eyetooth with his fingernail, and looking thoughtfully across at Miss Pakun as she typed. The magenta silk curtains at his office windows stirred slightly with the breath of an oscillating fan. They gave the room a boudoir glow in which a motion or a posture sometimes could seem strangely ambivalent. Today the phenomenon, rather than stimulating him, merely increased the distrust he had been feeling with regard to his secretary. She was unusually attractive and efficient, but he had to tell himself that this was not the point. He had engaged her in what he considered good faith, assuming that the information she had written on her application form was true. He had chosen her from among several other equally presentable applicants because she bore the stamp of a good bourgeois upbringing.

His equivocal feelings about Miss Pakun dated from the previous week, when his cashier, Udom by name, had reported seeing her walking along the street in an unsanitary and disreputable quarter of Thonburi on the other side of the river. Udom knew the area well; it was a neighborhood of shacks, mounds of garbage, opium houses and brothels. If she lived over there, why had she given the Sukhumvit address? And if not, what legitimate excuse could she have for visiting this unsavory part of the city? He had even wondered if Pakun were her true name.

Mang Huat was proud of his three-room suite at the Krungthep Plaza. At thirty-two he was manager of the hotel, and that pleased him. Through a small window in the wall of his salon he could, if he felt so inclined, look down into the lobby and see what was happening in almost every corner of it. He never used the peephole. It was enough that the staff knew of its existence.

From where he sat he could hear the trickle of the fountain in the next room. A friend, recently moved to Hong Kong, had left it with him, and he had spent a good deal of money getting it installed. Miss Pakun coughed, probably to remind him that he was smoking. She always coughed when he smoked. On a few occasions when she had first come to work for him he had put out his cigarette. Today he was not much concerned with the state of her throat. Nor, he thought, did he care whether she lived at the elegant address in Sukhumvit or in a slum alley of Thonburi. He no longer had any intention of forging an intimate friendship with her.

Late in the morning Udom knocked on his door. Udom was a friend from university days, down on his luck, who had begged for work at the hotel. Mang Huat, persuaded that it was unrealistic to expect any man to possess more than one good quality, had given the job of cashier to Udom, who was unreliable but honest.

Ever since his uncle's partner had placed him in his present exalted position, Mang Huat had experienced the bliss of feeling sheltered from the outside world. Today for the first time that delicious peace of mind was being threatened. It was absurd, he knew; there was little likelihood of an accident, but any situation beyond his control caused him undue anxiety.

Udom came over to the desk and murmured gloomily that the American Security men were downstairs asking for a passkey to the rooms. I told them I'd have to speak to you, he went on. It's not obligatory, you know. Only the keys of certain specific rooms, if they ask for them.

I know that, said Mang Huat. Give them a passkey.

The guests are going to object.

Mang Huat bridled. What difference does that make? Give them whatever keys they ask for. Just be sure you get them all back.

It scandalized him that anyone should hesitate to accept this added protection, but then Udom could be counted on to create complications and find objections. Mang Huat suspected that he had not entirely outgrown his youthful Marxist sympathies, and sometimes he wondered if it had been wise to take him on to the staff.

Pangs of hunger were making his nervousness more acute. It was twenty-five minutes past one. Miss Pakun had not yet returned from lunch. All at once he realized that a new sound which filled the air outside had been going on for some time. He stepped to the window. The big official cars were rolling past, and at a surprising speed. His eye suddenly caught the two white Bentleys from the palace, enclosed by their escort of motorcycles. He held his breath until they were gone. Even then he listened for a minute before he telephoned to order his lunch.

Late in the afternoon the receptionist rang his office to say that a guest was demanding to see him. Suddenly the threat was there again. I can't see anyone, he said, and hung up.

Five minutes later Udom was on the wire. I was afraid this would happen, he said. An Englishman is complaining that the police searched his room.

Tell him I'm not in my office, said Mang Huat. And to Miss Pakun: No incoming calls. You hear?

Twilight had come down all at once, brought on by a great black cloud that swelled above the city. The thought occurred to him that he could let Miss Pakun go now, before the rain came. He stood at the window staring out. The city sparkled with millions of extra lights; they were looped in fanciful designs through the branches of the trees across the canal. A triumphal arch had been built over the entrance to the bridge, spectacularly floodlighted in red and blue to show a thirty-foot-high face of the visiting president, with appropriate words of welcome beneath, in English and Thai.

The buzzer in the antechamber sounded. Miss Pakun answered it, and a bellboy in scarlet uniform came in with a note on a tray. He's had smallpox, Mang Huat said to himself. Who can have hired him? On his pad he scribbled a reminder to have the boy discharged in the morning, and took the note from him. Udom had written: *The man is in the bar getting the guests to sign a petition. I think you should see him.*

Mang Huat read the note twice in disbelief. Then he pounded the desk once with his fist, and Miss Pakun glanced up. Because he was angry, he reminded himself that above all he must keep his composure. With such malcontents it was imperative to be adamant, and not to allow oneself to be drawn into discussion, much less argument.

The buzzer sounded. Tell him I'll be free in five minutes, he said to Miss Pakun.

There was no longer any question of letting her go before the storm broke. She would simply have to take her shoes off, like other people in that squalid quarter where she surely lived, and wade barefoot through the puddles and ponds, to the end of the alley where a taxi could not take her. In a moment she came back in and sat down, patting her hair and smoothing her skirt. At that moment a police car must have been in the neighborhood, for there was one of the sudden ominous silences outside. While Miss Pakun carefully applied a whole series of cosmetics to her features, he sat in the stillness and heard a gecko chatter just beyond the air-conditioning box behind him; the tentative chirruping pierced the slight whir of the motor. And the insects in the trees still droned. He was sorry he had made a time limit. The five minutes of silence seemed like twenty. When the time was up Miss Pakun, resplendent, rose once more and turned to go out. Mang Huat stopped her.

No typing, please, while the man is here, he said crisply. Only shorthand. You can do it. (Her face had begun to change its expression.) This is an agitator, he stressed. We must have a record of everything he says.

Miss Pakun always grew timid and claimed insufficient knowledge of English if he asked her to transcribe a conversation in that language. The results of her work, however, were generally successful. Mang Huat glowered. You must get every word. He may threaten me.

The visitor came in, followed by Miss Pakun. He was young, and looked like a university student. With a brief smile he sat down in a chair facing Mang Huat, and said: Thank you for letting me in.

Mang Huat took this as sarcasm. You came to complain?

You see, the young man began, I'm trying to get an extension of my tourist visa without leaving the country.

Mang Huat slapped the desk hard with the flat of his hand. Someone has made a mistake. You are looking for the Immigration Department. My secretary will give you the address.

The young man raised his voice. I was trying to lead up to my complaint. But I'll make it now. It's an affront to your guests to allow the Americans into the rooms.

Ah! Perhaps you should complain to the Thai police, Mang Huat suggested, standing up to show that the meeting was at an end. My secretary can also give you that address.

The young Englishman stared at him for an instant with patent disgust. You're the perfect manager for this abject institution, he muttered. Then, seeing that Miss Pakun had risen and was holding the door open for him, he got up and stalked out, doing his best to slam the outer door of the antechamber behind him. Equipped against such rough treatment, the door merely gave its usual cushioned hiss. Coming at that moment, the sound, which to Mang Huat represented the very soul of luxury, caused him to heave a sigh of pure sensuous pleasure.

That will be all, he told Miss Pakun. She took up her handbag, showed him her most luscious smile for the fraction of a second, and shut the door behind her.

It was now night, and the rain was falling heavily. Miss Pakun would get very wet, he thought, a twinge of pity spicing his satisfaction. He went into the next room and lay back on the divan to watch television for a few minutes. Then he got up. It was the moment to make his evening excursion to the kitchen and, having examined the food, order his dinner. He lighted a cigarette and took the elevator down to the lobby.

In front of the reception desk he frowned with disapproval at the spots left on the carpet by the wet luggage being brought in. At that moment he happened to glance across the crowded lobby, and saw Miss Pakun emerge from the bar, accompanied by the young Englishman. They went directly out into the street. By the time Mang Huat was able to get over to the door, walking at a normal pace, they were climbing into a taxi. He stepped outside, and, sheltered by the marquee, stood watching the cab disappear into the downpour.

On his way to the kitchen he stopped at the cashier's desk, where he recounted to Udom what he had just seen. He also told him to give Miss Pakun her final paycheck in the morning and to see that under no circumstances was she to get upstairs to his office.

A prostitute, he said with bitter indignation. A common prostitute, masquerading as an intelligent, educated girl.

The Empty Amulet

HABIBA'S father, who was the concierge at the principal hotel of the city, provided a comfortable life for his family, but he was unusually strict. Some of Habiba's friends among girls of her age had been to school and even passed their examinations, so that they could become secretaries and bookkeepers and dentists' assistants. Habiba's father, however, considered all this highly immoral, and would not hear of allowing her to attend school. Instead, she learned embroidery and knitting, which she accomplished using modern German machines he bought for her.

When Moumen, a young man of the neighborhood, came to ask for Habiba's hand in marriage, her father accepted because he knew that the young man worked at a nearby hospital as interne, and thus had permanent employment. Habiba was not consulted. She was delighted to escape from the parental home and the everlasting embroidery.

Since Moumen was a young man with modern ideas, he did not lock his bride into the house when he went out to work. On the contrary, he urged her to get to know the young married women of the quarter. Soon she was part of a group whose members met each day, first at one house and then another.

Habiba was not long in discovering that the principal topic of conversation among these ladies was the state of their health. Every one of them claimed to suffer from some affliction or indisposition. This discountenanced Habiba, for, always having been in the best of health, she could only sit and listen when the subject of ailments arose.

One day she awoke with a headache. When her friends arrived that morning to see her, she complained of the pain. Immediately she was the center of attention. The following day when they inquired about her health, she told them she still had the pain in her head. And indeed, as she thought about it, it seemed to her that she could feel an occasional throb. Each woman was ready with a different remedy, but they all agreed that a visit to the tomb of Sidi Larbi would provide the surest relief.

There were three other women in the group who were eager to make the pilgrimage. Accordingly, a few days later Habiba went off with them in a large taxi to Sidi Larbi. They took along a picnic lunch, which Habiba, following their advice, washed down with a glass of water containing a large pinch of black earth from outside the mausoleum. Each of them gathered a pile of this dirt to take home for future use. At the end of the day in the open air, Habiba was unable to feel even a trace of headache. Drink the dirt five nights in a row, they told her.

When she got home she hid the packet of earth, knowing that Moumen disapproved of Moroccan medicine. His objections to it were so vehement that she suspected him of being afraid of it, in the same way that she was frightened of entering the hospital where he worked. The nauseating medicinal odors, the bins of bloody bandages, the shining syringes, all filled her with dread.

Scarcely a week passed that some one of the young women among her friends did not make a pilgrimage to the tomb of Sidi Hussein or Sidi Larbi or some other not too distant shrine. It seemed to Moumen that Habiba was always on the verge of visiting one saint or another; either she had pains in her back, or cramps, or a stiff neck. Whatever trouble she named, there was always a saint who could cure it.

One evening Moumen went unexpectedly into the kitchen and found Habiba stirring some earth into a glass of water.

Habiba! You can't do that! he cried. It's what they did a hundred years ago.

And two hundred and five hundred, she retorted, her eyes on the glass.

You're a savage! It makes me sick to look at you!

Habiba was unperturbed. She knew he considered the pills and injections used by the Nazarenes superior to the baraka of the saints. This had nothing to do with her, she decided; she was not going to be influenced by him.

I have pains in my side, she said. Rahma had the same pains, and the mud from Sidi Yamani got rid of them in twenty-four hours.

If you'll come to the hospital tomorrow morning, I'll give you some pills, he told her, intending, if she agreed, to hand her some sugar-coated pills containing nothing at all, since he knew her to be in perfect health.

This is my medicine, she said, moving the glass in a circular fashion, to dissolve all the mud.

It cost him an effort not to wrest the glass away from her and dash it to the floor. He shook his head. A beautiful girl like you swallowing dirt!

Habiba leaned back against the sink and calmly drank the contents of the glass.

The day Moumen learned that Habiba was carrying a child, he sat for a long time in a café, trying to think of a way to keep her from going on any more of her absurd pilgrimages. At one point he looked up and noticed a book of cigarette papers that someone had left on the table next to him. He reached over for it. Idly he pulled out two of the little sheets of rice-paper and crumpled them between his fingers. As he glanced down at the tiny ball of paper, the idea came to him.

He paid the qahouaji, and taking the book of cigarette papers with him, he made his way down into the Medina to see a friend who worked as a goldsmith. He wanted him to make a tiny gold cage just big enough to hold a baraka. While they were discussing the size and price of the piece of jewelry, Moumen surreptitiously reached into his pocket and pulled out two cigarette papers, which he rolled into a ball. When they had come to an agreement, he asked the goldsmith for a bit of silk thread, and wound a short length of it around the ball of paper.

Here's the baraka, he told the man, who dropped it into an envelope on which Moumen wrote his name, and promised to have the chain and pendant ready the following afternoon.

The small gold cage on its slender chain made a pretty necklace. When he took it home and fastened it around Habiba's neck, he told her: This baraka is from a very great fqih. It's to protect the baby.

He was a bit ashamed, but greatly relieved, to see how much the gift meant to her. During the months that followed, when she might have been expected to suffer discomfort, she was uncomplaining and happy. She told her friends that her husband did not want her to ride in taxis on country roads because it might be bad for the baby, and they nodded their heads sagely. Besides, said Habiba, I don't need to go any more.

Hamdoul'lah, they said.

The baby was born: a robust little creature who passed through his infancy unscathed by illness. Habiba herself was radiantly healthy; since the day she had begun to wear the cage over her heart she had not once complained of a symptom. It was the possession she valued above all others. The days of making pilgrimages and swallowing mud were far behind; Moumen was pleased with himself for having found such a simple solution to a difficult problem.

One summer afternoon when Habiba rose from her siesta, she took the necklace from the table to fasten it around her neck, for she did not like to be without it. For some reason the chain snapped, and the cage slid to the floor, where it rolled out of sight. As she moved around the room looking for it, she felt a light crunch beneath her foot, and realized that she had stepped on it. The lid had broken off and the ball of paper had tumbled out. She gathered up the broken cage and the baraka that had been inside. The silk thread slipped off and the cigarette papers sprang open.

Habiba uncreased them both. Nothing was written on either paper. She held them up to the light and saw the watermarks; then she understood what they were. She sat perfectly still for a long time, while her sense of injury was slowly replaced by fury with Moumen for having deceived her, and for so long a period of time. When Moumen got home that evening and saw her face, he knew that the hour of reckoning had come. Habiba shouted at him, she wept, she sulked, she said she would never believe him again as long as she lived.

For several days she would not speak to Moumen; when finally one morning she did, it was to announce that she felt dizzy and had pains in her stomach. To his dismay he saw that for the first time she did look ill.

Thanks to your lies I went all that time without any baraka, she said bitterly.

Yes, but you were well all that time, he reminded her.

And that's why I'm sick now! she screamed. It's your fault!

Moumen did not attempt to answer her; he had learned the futility of expecting her to follow a logical train of thought.

Before the week was out, Habiba was on her way to Sidi Larbi with two of her friends. From that time onward Moumen heard nothing from her but an unvarying stream of complaints, cut short only on the day they were divorced.

Bouayad and the Money

THE AID EL KEBIR would be arriving in a month or so.
Each year sheep cost more, Bouayad told Chaouni.
This year they're going to be higher than ever. Why don't we
buy twenty and split the cost? When the holiday comes we'll
split the proceeds.

Chaouni always had some ready cash. He agreed. They
went out to Sidi Yamani and bought the animals cheap from
a friend of Bouayad's. They hired a truck to carry them to
Tangier. There they put them into a shed at Bouayad's and
went together every day, driving them to graze in the country. The sheep had to be fat and beautiful before the Aid.

One day some soldiers came across the meadow where
Bouayad and Chaouni sat watching the sheep. The colonel
stopped and looked. Then he went over to Bouayad and
asked him if he wanted to sell the sheep.

Maybe, Bouayad said.

The price the colonel offered was exactly what they had
been planning to ask in the market. They both thought it
would be a good idea to sell them all at once and save themselves the bother of taking them out to pasture every day. The
colonel told them to go to his office at the qachla the next
morning and he would give them the money. Because he was
well-known they did not question his word. The soldiers
drove the sheep ahead of them, and Bouayad and Chaouni
were left alone in the meadow.

The next day when Bouayad went to the qachla he discovered that the colonel had been called to Rabat. This news
made Chaouni decide to go himself the next day. The colonel
was still in Rabat. They took turns going to the qachla.

This continued for several weeks. Finally they learned that
the colonel was back in Tangier. Now when they went he was
not in his office. They were convinced that the colonel had no
intention of paying them.

Bouayad was the kind of man who would not admit to
having lost. He went to Chaouni and said: Are you with me?

Whatever happens? We get that money or we put him out of commission. Are you with me?

No, Chaouni said. I've got a wife and children to think of.

You say good-bye to all that money?

It's gone. I'm sorry I ever listened to you.

That means whatever I get is mine, said Bouayad.

Yes. And the trouble is yours too. You'll be lucky if you stay alive.

It's in the hands of Allah. I'll get the money or you won't see me again.

He went to the Amalat and tried to see the secretary of the governor. The guards refused to let him in. At this point luck began to shine on Bouayad. As he ranted to the guards in front of the office door a man walked past and stopped to listen. Then he spoke to Bouayad. They went outside and Bouayad recounted his tale. The man said: I can help you. Go tomorrow morning to the king's palace at Sidi Amar.

Bouayad did not understand what connection the man could have with the palace, but he trusted him because he had a serious face. The next morning he went up to Sidi Amar and stepped through the open gate. Immediately he was surrounded by soldiers. They asked him again and again why he had walked through the gate. He tried to tell them about the sheep and the appointment he had made the day before outside the Amalat, but they would not stop yanking him this way and that.

Here is where Bouayad's luck became greater than seems possible. The king does not spend even one day a year in Tangier, but he had come from Rabat the day before. Not only was he in residence; he was in the garden not far from the gate, and he saw the commotion. He beckoned to the soldiers to let go of Bouayad so he could approach and present his case.

The king listened until he had finished. Then he told Bouayad to wait, and went down to the palace. As he stood in the garden a man in the uniform of the royal guard walked past Bouayad and smiled at him. He recognized him then as the one who had told him to come to the palace. Later a servant brought out a letter signed by the king, with the instructions that he go to Tetuan and present the letter to the official whose name was on the envelope.

Bouayad did not even stop off at home for lunch. He went straight to the Avenida de España and, sharing a taxi with three others, set out for Tetuan.

Again he was not allowed in. Nor did he trust anyone sufficiently to show him the letter. For several hours he stayed there, insisting that he had a highly secret message that must be delivered to the official by him personally. Finally they allowed him to go inside.

The official took the letter and read it. Then he went into the adjoining room for a moment and returned with the cash for the full amount. Bouayad thanked him.

He went back to Tangier in a state of elation. After his family, the first person he told was Chaouni.

I'm back, he said, and that means I've got the money.

All of it? Chaouni could not believe it.

That's right.

Chaouni said nothing. The next day he went to see Bouayad. I've been thinking. You've got my money too.

Your money? You said good-bye to it. Remember?

Chaouni went home. It was not long before he started a lawsuit against Bouayad, demanding not only his share but Bouayad's as well. When the case was heard, Bouayad was allowed to keep his share. Out of the other half Chaouni was forced to pay a heavy lawyer's fee and Bouayad's fare both to and back from Tetuan.

Rumor and a Ladder

ALONE in Paris, Monsieur Ducros sat in his spacious hotel room, preparing to write a letter to his daughter in Kuala Lumpur. He frowned at the hotel stationery, which now was merely printed, instead of being embossed as it had been on his last visit. A symbol of the times, he thought automatically. The slow encroachment of poverty on all sides. Then he glanced down at the cast encasing his leg, smiled briefly at it, and started to write.

My dear Clotilde:

I hope my unwonted silence hasn't disturbed you. Ordinarily I'm a good correspondent; admit it. I can't believe Kuala Lumpur has altered much since 1965. As you know, it was my last post. I was pleased to hear that Abd er Rahman and his wife are still there; one never knows. I passed my eighty-fifth birthday quietly in Tangier. In a moment you will see what I mean by "quietly."

The incredible irony of certain situations in which life insists upon involving us! What was I doing, standing at the top of a stepladder in the library on a Sunday morning? You may well ask. I also asked myself that, but a good deal too late.

When I felt the ladder tilting (for this is the way it all began) and knew I was going to fall, I was aware of several things simultaneously: that everything was unfinished; that I had been an idiot to climb up there; that people would believe I had been drunk or the victim of an assault (suppositions equally damaging to one's posthumous reputation in that vicious city where, as you're aware, no one thinks well of anyone); and above all the conviction that everything would go wrong, with the result that you and Pierrot somehow would not be able to inherit El Hafa. Because, my girl, I was certain that it was the end. Then the leg got involved with the ladder as we went down, there was a crash, and I lay there, my head pounding, and quite aware that my leg was broken above the knee. Fortunately the big Chichaoua rug was underneath, or I should have hit marble. I called endlessly for Annamaria. When she finally appeared, she claimed the wind was rattling the shutters so hard that she hadn't heard me at first. It's true that her room faces northeast, and there was a gale blowing outside. Still—

I had her send Abdeslam on foot to Dr. Rinaldi's clinic. (The telephone had been out of order for more than three weeks.) Rinaldi arrived. The femur was fractured. He saw the stepladder by the bookshelves, and looked at me reprovingly. Off I went to the clinic; in traction for what seemed an eternity. Actually it was something less than a month and a half. . . .

II

It's essential that I go to Paris, said Monsieur Ducros, surveying his leg, still in its cast. As you can see, I manage perfectly well now with the cane.

Dr. Rinaldi shrugged. Luck has been with you so far, he said. Why shouldn't we expect it to continue?

They sat sipping whiskey in the library where the accident had taken place. After a certain hesitation Dr. Rinaldi inquired if the rumor were true that his host planned to sell El Hafa.

Monsieur Ducros bristled. But what an idea! Certainly not! I haven't the slightest intention of selling. I know, that Saudi is interested, and the offer would be generous. I intend my daughter and her husband to have the property after my death. I've spent all my retired years in this house, and everything I own in the world is in it.

Dr. Rinaldi looked around the room approvingly. There are many treasures, yes. Astonishing how Japanese, Tibetan, Khmer and Persian can blend in a room.

Not really, if you think about it, said Monsieur Ducros, without elaborating. The point is, I don't want to give up anything. You understand. With my things around me, it's as though I were still out there in the Far East. I enjoy my little life, and I can assure you I have no intention of interrupting it by selling El Hafa.

There's one thing I'm curious about, Dr. Rinaldi said after a moment. Those paintings at the far end of the hall. I couldn't help noticing them.

Monsieur Ducros chuckled. Yes, it's a jarring note, I know. But they're not really much in evidence. I keep it fairly dark at that end, purposely. Madame Ducros bought those things shortly after the First World War. They say less than nothing to me, I confess. I've been told they have a certain value, but I don't take that too seriously. I've kept them because my wife was so fond of them.

A Moroccan in a white jacket announced that dinner was served. Dr. Rinaldi handed Monsieur Ducros his cane, and they rose from their chairs.

At the table Monsieur Ducros pointed to the carafes in the center, saying: The white is simply Valpierre. The red is a fairly good Bordeaux. You've taken Mademoiselle Herzler's tray up, Abdeslam?

When they were alone in the dining-room, he spoke confidentially: My secretary insists upon eating by herself in her room. I think she's not entirely happy here. She objects very much to the wind. Swiss, he added, as if by way of explanation.

Dr. Rinaldi, busying himself with his sole meunière, did not reply. Presently he looked up and said with great seriousness: I suspect you of grossly underestimating the worth of those canvases. May I ask what you imagine they'd fetch on the market today?

Monsieur Ducros stopped eating, and thought for a moment. I have no idea, he said.

For the five Soutines alone I can get you two million French francs tomorrow. As he made the statement he stared fixedly at his host, as if to measure his reaction. He saw a flash of interest, followed immediately by disbelief.

Ridiculous. They're not Titians, after all.

I'm entirely serious.

Monsieur Ducros was quiet. Then he sighed. Even if your estimate is not dramatically exaggerated, and even if I wanted to dispose of them, what would be the point? The money would be of no use here, and it couldn't be taken out of Morocco.

Oh, come, said Dr. Rinaldi. There are ways.

No, thank you, Monsieur Ducros said firmly. The law is generally illogical and often unjust, but I'm not one to flout it.

My friend, you function according to the ethos of a bygone era. But I approve, I approve.

In my experience the rational man is the one who obeys the law.

But alas! sighed Dr. Rinaldi. How human it is to be irrational!

Monsieur Ducros glanced furtively at his guest: he suspected these last words to be a veiled reference to his accident. The doctor already had upbraided him severely for allowing the absurd thing to happen. What were servants for, if not to climb stepladders? He had not mentioned Monsieur Ducros' age, but this show of discretion counted for little because of the stern manner in which he had voiced his opinion. Monsieur Ducros recognized the minatory tone; since he had passed his eightieth birthday all his doctors had used it with him.

They spoke of other things. But later, over coffee and Armagnac in the den, Monsieur Ducros turned with a puzzled expression to his guest.

To return for a moment to the subject of those paintings. How would your buyer have arranged to get them out of the country? I'm curious.

The question wouldn't have arisen, the doctor told him. An American collector is building a house in Marrakech. Why? Are you tempted?

Monsieur Ducros shook his head. No, no! Not in the least.

III

Their next encounter, less than a week later, was unexpected and tempestuous. In the middle of a weekday afternoon Monsieur Ducros was brought by a taxi-driver to Dr. Rinaldi's clinic in a state bordering on apoplexy. The cast on his leg had been split open, and tatters of gauze trailed out from inside it.

Seeing that Monsieur Ducros was not in a state to speak coherently, Dr. Rinaldi questioned the taxi-driver. He was struck by a car?

The driver did not know. He had been summoned by an official at the airport and instructed to take the passenger home, but on the way the old man had demanded to be brought to the clinic.

Monsieur Ducros was put to bed and given an injection. Later that evening, after an enforced sleep of several hours, he was sufficiently rested to tell his tale to Dr. Rinaldi.

Abdeslam had driven him to the airport, given his luggage to a porter, and left. The plane for Paris arrived. As his passport was being examined, a man had appeared from nowhere, and asked him to go with him into an inner office, where he and two others had made him undress. Not content with that, they had refused to believe that his leg was broken, and had held him by force while they smashed open the cast and pulled the inside to pieces in their search for money.

It's that rumor! They had the effrontery to tell me they were acting on secret information that I'd sold El Hafa.

Dr. Rinaldi was deeply shocked. Unheard-of! Herbier must be informed immediately at the consulate.

I shall sue for damages! Monsieur Ducros cried feebly.

My poor friend, that would produce an enormous zero. You've lived here long enough to realize that. All you can do is accept what has happened, be sure the leg is all right, put on a new cast, and start out again.

Monsieur Ducros shut his eyes for a moment, and opened them again. You can help me, he said.

Naturally. As your doctor I can attest to the authenticity of the fracture. Perhaps they'd like to see the X-ray, too, he added acidly.

Monsieur Ducros did not seem to be listening. He was looking at the ceiling. Yes, you can help me, he repeated.

Dr. Rinaldi decided that the time had come for his patient to rest. You can count on me, he told him.

The next day he went into the sickroom and announced that he was ready to make a new cast. Monsieur Ducros waved him away. No, no. I don't want it.

But you must have a cast. You can't walk without one.

I shan't walk. I'll stay in my bed at home until you come to do it.

As you like, Dr. Rinaldi said shortly, feeling that he was being foolish to humor the caprice of an unreasonable old man.

Abdeslam can take me home this afternoon. Will you come by at five o'clock?

Fleetingly the idea occurred to the doctor that the experience at the airport might have caused a small cerebral lesion. In some subtle way Monsieur Ducros' personality seemed very slightly altered.

You must not use the leg, he said frowning. Not even to take a few steps in your room. Are we agreed?

IV

At El Hafa Dr. Rinaldi found his patient propped up in an enormous antique bed; the damask curtains that hung from the baldaquin overhead nearly hid him from view.

I've obeyed you to the letter, he called out, even before the doctor and his assistant had got inside the room.

Dr. Rinaldi laughed. When do you plan your next escape attempt?

I haven't thought about it, said Monsieur Ducros. May I have a five-minute conversation with you in private?

Dr. Rinaldi spoke with the Moroccan, and he left the room. When they were alone, Monsieur Ducros leaned forward and beckoned to the other to approach.

I'll explain, he whispered. You see, I don't want you to put the cast on today. I merely wanted you to come by. And I've decided to sell those paintings, if you can get in touch with the American.

This inconsequential coupling of ideas confirmed Dr. Rinaldi's previous suspicions; he saw in it a clear instance of mental dysfunction. Come, he said, sitting down on the edge of the bed. One thing at a time. May I ask why you prefer to remain without the cast?

Because I must know whether or not the paintings can be sold. I should think that would be obvious.

I hadn't connected the two things, the doctor said drily. But since what interests you most is evidently the sale of the paintings, I can say: yes, they definitely can be sold, and in short order, if you like. I myself will buy them and resell them.

At a reasonable profit, I hope, added Monsieur Ducros, smiling.

Very likely.

You said two million, as I recall.

Dr. Rinaldi laughed. If you want to throw in the Vlaminck, the Rouault and the Kokoschka, two and a quarter.

Monsieur Ducros threw up his hands. Kokoschka, indeed! I don't know one from the other. They're all equally inept. That would make all eight of them, wouldn't it? I have some old Thai things I'll hang at that end of the hall. They'll be far more in keeping.

Dr. Rinaldi looked searchingly at his patient. This is serious? You really want my check now?

But not at all! The currency. In French francs.

Dr. Rinaldi opened his mouth. But, he began.

You don't agree?

It will take time. Perhaps by tomorrow evening.

Monsieur Ducros was waving his hands again. Just bring the francs here to me.

Shaking his head with disapproval, Dr. Rinaldi said: Far too much money to leave lying around the house.

This seemed to mystify Monsieur Ducros. Surely you've understood by now what I expect you to do with the banknotes? You'll build them into the cast. And what they imagined was happening the first time will actually happen this time.

After a long silence Dr. Rinaldi said slowly: You can scarcely expect me to be eager to risk my professional status simply to help you perpetrate a fraud.

Monsieur Ducros cried excitedly: Fraud! I've already been punished. Now I want to *deserve* that punishment!

The doctor stood up. I find it quite extraordinary, the total change in your views on morality.

Nothing has changed. What was a question of ethics has become a question of honor.

As Dr. Rinaldi moved around the room, following the patterns of the rug, he said: You realize how much more work it would mean for me, having to do it all without my assistant?

Monsieur Ducros, knowing he had won, pressed on. Herbier has been in touch with Rabat, no? He has a formal apology for the incident. There's absolutely no question of a repetition. The element of risk has been removed.

The doctor returned to the bed and placed his hands on the footboard. I retract what I said about you at dinner not too long ago. You are indeed a product of our times.

I don't see it that way at all, Monsieur Ducros said quickly. This little ploy of revenge in no way affects my point of view. We're playing a game of extra-legal tit-for-tat, nothing more.

It's quite all right, said Dr. Rinaldi. You won't need any medical attestations if Herbier himself is accompanying you to the airport.

. . . And that is the bare outline of how your father took the first step along the pathway to crime. But criminals can be fiercely fond of their families, you know. So, go to the Hongkong and Shanghai Bank in Kuala and ask for Mister Nigel Dawson. He will explain to you that you now have an account with them, and that it has seventy-five thousand British pounds in it at the moment. I'm sure there are many things for which it will be useful, including, I hope, a visit by you and Pierrot to Tangier before too long.

I had the paintings thanks to your mother. And I think she would appreciate the ridiculous turn of events which made it possible for me to sell them for a small fortune. But luck is always absurd.

I imagine you sitting in the dubious freshness of that air-conditioned apartment, looking down at the wet trees and traffic of "*Kuala l'impur*", as Cocteau called it. But there are places far more impure!

Know that I think of you, and, I beg you, let me have news soon.

ton père qui t'aime

The Eye

TEN or twelve years ago there came to live in Tangier a man who would have done better to stay away. What happened to him was in no way his fault, notwithstanding the whispered innuendos of the English-speaking residents. These people often have reactions similar to those of certain primitive groups: when misfortune overtakes one of their number, the others by mutual consent refrain from offering him aid, and merely sit back to watch, certain that he has called his suffering down upon himself. He has become taboo, and is incapable of receiving help. In the case of this particular man, I suppose no one could have been of much comfort; still, the tacit disapproval called forth by his bad luck must have made the last months of his life harder to bear.

His name was Duncan Marsh, and he was said to have come from Vancouver. I never saw him, nor do I know anyone who claims to have seen him. By the time his story reached the cocktail-party circuit he was dead, and the more irresponsible residents felt at liberty to indulge their taste for myth-making.

He came alone to Tangier, rented a furnished house on the slopes of Djamaa el Mokra—they were easy enough to find in those days, and correspondingly inexpensive—and presently installed a teen-age Moroccan on the premises to act as night-watchman. The house provided a resident cook and gardener, but both of these were discharged from their duties, the cook being replaced by a woman brought in at the suggestion of the watchman. It was not long after this that Marsh felt the first symptoms of a digestive illness which over the months grew steadily worse. The doctors in Tangier advised him to go to London. Two months in hospital there helped him somewhat. No clear diagnosis was made, however, and he returned here only to become bedridden. Eventually he was flown back to Canada on a stretcher, and succumbed there shortly after his arrival.

In all this there was nothing extraordinary; it was assumed that Marsh had been one more victim of slow poisoning by native employees. There have been several such cases during my five decades in Tangier. On each occasion it has been said that the European victim had only himself (or herself) to blame, having encouraged familiarity on the part of a servant. What strikes the outsider as strange is that no one ever takes the matter in hand and inaugurates a search for the culprit, but in the total absence of proof there is no point in attempting an investigation.

Two details complete the story. At some point during his illness Marsh told an acquaintance of the arrangements he had made to provide financial aid for his night-watchman in the event that he himself should be obliged to leave Morocco; he had given him a notarized letter to that effect, but apparently the boy never tried to press his claim. The other report came from Dr. Halsey, the physician who arranged for Marsh's removal from the house to the airport. It was this last bit of information which, for me, at least, made the story take on life. According to the doctor, the soles of Marsh's feet had been systematically marked with deep incisions in the form of crude patterns; the cuts were recent, but there was some infection. Dr. Halsey called in the cook and the watchman: they showed astonishment and dismay at the sight of their employer's feet, but were unable to account for the mutilations. Within a few days after Marsh's departure, the original cook and gardener returned to take up residence, the other two having already left the house.

The slow poisoning was classical enough, particularly in the light of Marsh's remark about his provision for the boy's wellbeing, but the knife-drawn designs on the feet somehow got in the way of whatever combinations of motive one could invent. I thought about it. There could be little doubt that the boy was guilty. He had persuaded Marsh to get rid of the cook that came with the house, even though her wages had to continue to be paid, and to hire another woman (very likely from his own family) to do the cooking. The poisoning process lasts many months if it is to be undetectable, and no one is in a better position to take charge of it than the cook herself. Clearly she knew about the financial arrangement that had been made for the boy, and expected to share in it. At the same time the crosses and circles slashed in the feet were inexplicable. The slow poisoner is patient, careful, methodical; his principal concerns are to keep the dosage effective and to avoid leaving any visible marks. Bravado is unknown to him.

The time came when people no longer told the story of Duncan Marsh. I myself thought of it less often, having no more feasible hypotheses to supply. One evening perhaps five years ago, an American resident here came to me with the news that he had discovered a Moroccan who claimed to have been Marsh's night-watchman. The man's name was Larbi; he was a waiter at Le Fin Bec, a small back-street restaurant. Apparently he spoke poor English, but understood it without difficulty. This information was handed me for what it was worth, said the American, in the event that I felt inclined to make use of it.

I turned it over in my mind, and one night a few weeks later I went down to the restaurant to see Larbi for myself. The place was dimly lit and full of Europeans. I studied the three waiters. They were interchangeable, with wide black moustaches, blue jeans and sport shirts. A menu was handed me; I could scarcely read it, even directly under the glow of the little table lamp. When the man who had brought it returned, I asked for Larbi.

He pulled the menu from my hand and left the table. A moment later another of the triumvirate came up beside me and handed me the menu he carried under his arm. I ordered in Spanish. When he brought the soup I murmured that I was surprised to find him working there. This brought him up short; I could see him trying to remember me.

"Why wouldn't I be working here?" His voice was level, without inflection.

"Of course! Why not? It was just that I thought by now you'd have a bazaar or some sort of shop."

His laugh was a snort. "Bazaar!"

When he arrived with the next course, I begged his pardon for meddling in his affairs. But I was interested, I said, because for several years I had been under the impression that he had received a legacy from an English gentleman.

"You mean Señor Marsh?" His eyes were at last wide open.

"Yes, that was his name. Didn't he give you a letter? He told his friends he had."

He looked over my head as he said: "He gave me a letter."

"Have you ever showed it to anyone?" This was tactless, but sometimes it is better to drive straight at the target.

"Why? What good is it? Señor Marsh is dead." He shook his head with an air of finality, and moved off to another table. By the time I had finished my crème caramel, most of the diners had left, and the place seemed even darker. He came over to the table to see if I wanted coffee. I asked for the check. When he brought it I told him I should like very much to see the letter if he still had it.

"You can come tomorrow night or any night, and I'll show it to you. I have it at home."

I thanked him and promised to return in two or three days. I was confused as I left the restaurant. It seemed clear that the waiter did not consider himself to be incriminated in Duncan Marsh's troubles. When, a few nights later, I saw the document, I no longer understood anything.

It was not a letter; it was a *papier timbré* of the kind on sale at tobacconists. It read, simply: *To Whom It May Concern: I, Duncan Whitelow Marsh, do hereby agree to deposit the sum of One Hundred Pounds to the account of Larbi Lairini, on the first of each month, for as long as I live.* It was signed and notarized in the presence of two Moroccan witnesses, and bore the date June 11, 1966. As I handed it back to him I said: "And it never did you any good."

He shrugged and slipped the paper into his wallet. "How was it going to? The man died."

"It's too bad."

"*Suerte.*" In the Moroccan usage of the word, it means *fate*, rather than simple luck.

At that moment I could have pressed on, and asked him if he had any idea as to the cause of Marsh's illness, but I wanted time for considering what I had just learned. As I rose to leave I said: "I'm sorry it turned out that way. I'll be back in a few days." He held out his hand and I shook it. I had no intentions then. I might return soon or I might never go back.

For as long as I live. The phrase echoed in my mind for several weeks. Possibly Marsh had worded it that way so it would be readily understandable to the *adoul* of Tangier who had affixed their florid signatures to the sheet; yet I could not help interpreting the words in a more melodramatic fashion. To me the document represented the officializing of a covenant already in existence between master and servant: Marsh wanted the watchman's help, and the watchman had agreed to give it. There was nothing upon which to base such an assumption, nevertheless I thought I was on the right track. Slowly I came to believe that if only I could talk to the watchman, in Arabic, and inside the house itself, I might be in a position to see things more clearly.

One evening I walked to Le Fin Bec and without taking a seat motioned to Larbi to step outside for a moment. There I asked him if he could find out whether the house Señor Marsh had lived in was occupied at the moment or not.

"There's nobody living there now." He paused and added: "It's empty. I know the guardian."

I had decided, in spite of my deficient Arabic, to speak to him in his own language, so I said: "Look. I'd like to go with you to the house and see where everything happened. I'll give you fifteen thousand francs for your trouble."

He was startled to hear the Arabic; then his expression shifted to one of satisfaction. "He's not supposed to let anyone in," he said.

I handed him three thousand francs. "You arrange that with him. And fifteen for you when we leave the house. Could we do it Thursday?"

The house had been built, I should say, in the fifties, when good construction was still possible. It was solidly embedded in the hillside, with the forest towering behind it. We had to climb three flights of stairs through the garden to get to the entrance. The guardian, a squinting Djibli in a brown djellaba, followed close on our footsteps, eyeing me with mistrust.

There was a wide terrace above, with a view to the southeast over the town and the mountains. Behind the terrace a shadowed lawn ended where the forest began. The living room was large and bright, with French doors giving onto the lawn. Odors of damp walls and mildew weighted the air. The absurd conviction that I was about to understand everything had taken possession of me; I noticed that I was breathing more quickly. We wandered into the dining-room. There was a corridor beyond, and the room where Marsh had slept, shuttered and dark. A wide curving stairway led down to a level where there were two more bedrooms, and continued its spiral to the kitchen and servants' rooms below. The kitchen door opened onto a small flagstoned patio where high phylodendron covered the walls.

Larbi looked out and shook his head. "That's the place where all the trouble began," he said glumly.

I pushed through the doorway and sat down on a wrought-iron bench in the sun. "It's damp inside. Why don't we stay out here?"

The guardian left us and locked up the house. Larbi squatted comfortably on his heels near the bench.

There would have been no trouble at all, he said, if only Marsh had been satisfied with Yasmina, the cook whose wages were included in the rent. But she was a careless worker and the food was bad. He asked Larbi to find him another cook.

"I told him ahead of time that this woman Meriam had a little girl, and some days she could leave her with friends and some days she would have to bring her with her when she came to work. He said it didn't matter, but he wanted her to be quiet."

The woman was hired. Two or three days a week she came accompanied by the child, who would play in the patio where she could watch her. From the beginning Marsh complained that she was noisy. Repeatedly he sent messages down to Meriam, asking her to make the child be still. And one day he went quietly around the outside of the house and down to the patio. He got on all fours, put his face close to the little girl's face, and frowned at her so fiercely that she began to scream. When Meriam rushed out of the kitchen he stood up smiling and walked off. The little girl continued to scream and wail in a corner of kitchen, until Meriam took her home. That night, still sobbing, she came down with a high fever. For several weeks she hovered between life and death, and when she was finally out of danger she could no longer walk.

Meriam, who was earning relatively high wages, consulted one fqih after another. They agreed that "the eye" had been put on the child; it was equally clear that the Nazarene for whom she worked had done it. What they told her she must do, Larbi explained, was to administer certain substances to Marsh which eventually would make it possible to counteract the spell. This was absolutely necessary, he said, staring at me gravely. Even if the señor had agreed to remove it (and of course she never would have mentioned it to him) he would not have been able to. What she gave him could not harm him; it was merely medicine to relax him so that when the time came to undo the spell he would not make any objections.

At some point Marsh confided to Larbi that he suspected Meriam of slipping soporifics into his food, and begged him to be vigilant. The provision for Larbi's well-being was signed as an inducement to enlisting his active support. Since to Larbi the mixtures Meriam was feeding her master were relatively harmless, he reassured him and let her continue to dose him with her concoctions.

Tired of squatting, Larbi suddenly stood up and began to walk back and forth, stepping carefully in the center of each flagstone. "When he had to go to the hospital in London, I told her: 'Now you've made him sick. Suppose he doesn't come back? You'll never break it.' She was worried about it. 'I've done what I could,' she said. 'It's in the hands of Allah.'"

When Marsh did return to Tangier, Larbi urged her to be quick about bringing things to a head, now that she had been fortunate enough to get him back. He was thinking, he said, that it might be better for the señor's health if her treatment were not continued for too long a time.

I asked no questions while he talked; I made a point of keeping my face entirely expressionless, thinking that if he noticed the least flicker of disapproval he might stop. The sun had gone behind the trees and the patio was chilly. I had a strong desire to get up and walk back and forth as he was doing, but I thought even that might interrupt him. Once stopped, the flow might not resume.

Soon Marsh was worse than ever, with racking pains in his abdomen and kidneys. He remained in bed then, and Larbi brought him his food. When Meriam saw that he was no longer able to leave the bed, even to go into the bathroom, she decided that the time had come to get rid of the spell. On the same night that a fqih held a ceremony at her house in the presence of the crippled child, four men from Meriam's family came up to Djamaa el Mokra.

"When I saw them coming, I got onto my motorcycle and went into the city. I didn't want to be here when they did it. It had nothing to do with me."

He stood still and rubbed his hands together. I heard the southwest wind beginning to sound in the trees; it was that time of afternoon. "Come. I'll show you something," he said.

We climbed steps around the back of the house and came out onto a terrace with a pergola over it. Beyond this lay the lawn and the wall of trees.

"He was very sick for the next two days. He kept asking me to telephone the English doctor."

"Didn't you do it?"

Larbi stopped walking and looked at me. "I had to clean everything up first. Meriam wouldn't touch him. It was during the rains. He had mud and blood all over him when I got back here and found him. The next day I gave him a bath and changed the sheets and blankets. And I cleaned the house, because they got mud everywhere when they brought him back in. Come on. You'll see where they had to take him."

We had crossed the lawn and were walking in the long grass that skirted the edge of the woods. A path led off to the right through the tangle of undergrowth, and we followed it, climbing across boulders and fallen treetrunks until we came to an old stone well. I leaned over the wall of rocks around it and saw the small circle of sky far below.

"They had to drag him all the way here, you see, and hold him steady right over the well while they made the signs on his feet, so the blood would fall into the water. It's no good if it falls on the side of the well. And they had to make the same signs the fqih drew on paper for the little girl. That's hard to do in the dark and in the rain. But they did it. I saw the cuts when I bathed him."

Cautiously I asked him if he saw any connection between all this and Marsh's death. He ceased staring into the well and turned around. We started to walk back toward the house.

"He died because his hour had come."

And had the spell been broken? I asked him. Could the child walk afterward? But he had never heard, for Meriam had gone to Kenitra not much later to live with her sister.

When we were in the car, driving back down to the city, I handed him the money. He stared at it for several seconds before slipping it into his pocket.

I let him off in town with a vague sense of disappointment, and I saw that I had not only expected, but actually hoped, to find someone on whom the guilt might be fixed. What constitutes a crime? There was no criminal intent—only a mother moving in the darkness of ancient ignorance. I thought about it on my way home in the taxi.

In the Red Room

WHEN I had a house in Sri Lanka, my parents came out one winter to see me. Originally I had felt some qualms about encouraging their visit. Any one of several things—the constant heat, the unaccustomed food and drinking water, even the presence of a leprosy clinic a quarter of a mile from the house—might easily have an adverse effect on them in one way or another. But I had underestimated their resilience; they made a greater show of adaptability than I had thought possible, and seemed entirely content with everything. They claimed not to mind the lack of running water in the bathrooms, and regularly praised the curries prepared by Appuhamy, the resident cook. Both of them being in their seventies, they were not tempted by the more distant or inaccessible points of interest. It was enough for them to stay around the house reading, sleeping, taking twilight dips in the ocean, and going on short trips along the coast by hired car. If the driver stopped unexpectedly at a shrine to sacrifice a coconut, they were delighted, and if they came upon a group of elephants lumbering along the road, the car had to be parked some distance up ahead, so that they could watch them approach and file past. They had no interest in taking photographs, and this spared me what is perhaps the most taxing duty of a cicerone: the repeated waits while the ritual between man and machine is observed. They were ideal guests.

Colombo, where all the people I knew lived, was less than a hundred miles away. Several times we went up for week-ends, which I arranged with friends by telephone beforehand. There we had tea on the wide verandahs of certain houses in Cinnamon Gardens, and sat at dinners with professors from the University, Protestant ministers, and assorted members of the government. (Many of the Sinhalese found it strange that I should call my parents by their first names, Dodd and Hannah; several of them inquired if I were actually their son or had been adopted.) These week-ends in the city were hot and exhausting, and they were always happy to get back to the house, where they could change into comfortable clothing.

One Sunday not long before they were due to return to America, we decided to take in the horse races at Gintota, where there are also some botanical gardens that Hannah wanted to see. I engaged rooms at the New Oriental in Galle and we had lunch there before setting out.

As usual, the events were late in starting. It was the spectators, in any case, who were the focus of interest. The phalanx of women in their shot-silk saris moved Hannah to cries of delight. The races themselves were something of a disappointment. As we left the grounds, Dodd said with satisfaction: It'll be good to get back to the hotel and relax.

But we were going to the Botanical Gardens, Hannah reminded him. I'd like to have just a peek at them.

Dodd was not eager. Those places cover a lot of territory, you know, he said.

We'll just look inside and come out again, she promised.

The hired car took us to the entrance. Dodd was tired, and as a result was having a certain amount of difficulty in walking. The last year or so I find my legs aren't always doing exactly what I want 'em to do, he explained.

You two amble along, Hannah told us. I'll run up ahead and find out if there's anything to see.

We stopped to look up at a clove tree; its powerful odor filled the air like a gas. When we turned to continue our walk, Hannah was no longer in sight. We went on under the high vegetation, around a curve in the path, looked ahead, and still there was no sign of her.

What does your mother think she's doing? The first thing we know she'll be lost.

She's up ahead somewhere.

Soon, at the end of a short lane overhung by twisted lianas, we saw her, partially hidden by the gesticulating figure of a Sinhalese standing next to her.

What's going on? Dodd hastened his steps. Run over there, he told me, and I started ahead, walking fast. Then I saw Hannah's animated smile, and slowed my pace. She and the young man stood in front of a huge bank of brown spider orchids.

Ah! I thought we'd lost you, I said.

Look at these orchids. Aren't they incredible?

Dodd came up, nodded at the young man, and examined the display of flowers. They look to me like skunk cabbage, he declared.

The young man broke into wild laughter. Dodd stared at him.

This young man has been telling me the history of the garden, Hannah began hurriedly. About the opposition to it, and how it finally came to be planted. It's interesting.

The Sinhalese beamed triumphantly. He wore white flannels and a crimson blazer, and his sleek black hair gave off a metallic blue glint in the sunlight.

Ordinarily I steer a determined course away from the anonymous person who tries to engage me in conversation. This time it was too late; encouraged by Hannah, the stranger strolled beside her, back to the main path. Dodd and I exchanged a glance, shrugged, and began to follow along behind.

Somewhere up at the end of the gardens a pavilion had been built under the high rain-trees. It had a verandah where a few sarong-draped men reclined in long chairs. The young man stopped walking. Now I invite you to a cold ginger beer.

Oh, Hannah said, at a loss. Well, yes. That would be nice. I'd welcome a chance to sit down.

Dodd peered at his wrist-watch. I'll pass up the beer, but I'll sit and watch you.

We sat and looked out at the lush greenness. The young man's conversation leapt from one subject to another; he seemed unable to follow any train of thought farther than its inception. I put this down as a bad sign, and tried to tell from the inflections of Hannah's voice whether she found him as disconcerting as I did.

Dodd was not listening. He found the heat of low-country Ceylon oppressive, and it was easy to see that he was tired. Thinking I might cover up the young man's chatter, I turned to Dodd and began to talk about whatever came into my head: the resurgence of mask-making in Ambalangoda, devil-dancing, the high incidence of crime among the fishermen converted to Catholicism. Dodd listened, but did no more than move his head now and then in response.

Suddenly I heard the young man saying to Hannah: I have just the house for you. A godsend to fill your requirements. Very quiet and protected.

She laughed. Mercy, no! We're not looking for a house. We're only going to be here a few weeks more.

I looked hard at her, hoping she would take my glance as a warning against going on and mentioning the place where she was staying. The young man was not paying attention, in any case. Quite all right. You are not buying houses. But you should see this house and tell your friends. A superior investment, no doubt about that. Shall I introduced myself, please? Justus Gonzag, called Sonny by friends.

His smile, which was not a smile at all, gave me an unpleasant physical sensation.

Come anyway. A five-minute walk, guaranteed. He looked searchingly at Hannah. I intend to give you a book of poems. My own. Autographed for you with your name. That will make me very happy.

Oh, Hannah said, a note of dismay in her voice. Then she braced herself and smiled. That would be lovely. But you understand, we can't stay more than a minute.

There was a silence. Dodd inquired plaintively: Can't we go in the car, at least?

Impossible, sir. We are having a very narrow road. Car can't get through. I am arranging in a jiffy. He called out. A waiter came up, and he addressed him in Sinhalese at some length. The man nodded and went inside. Your driver is now bringing your car to this gate. Very close by.

This was going a little too far. I asked him how he thought anyone was going to know which car was ours.

No problem. I was present when you were leaving the Pontiac. Your driver is called Wickramasinghe. Up-country resident, most reliable. Down here people are hopeless.

I disliked him more each time he spoke. You're not from around here? I asked him.

No, no! I'm a Colombo chap. These people are impossible scoundrels. Every one of the blighters has a knife in his belt, guaranteed.

When the waiter brought the check, he signed it with a rapid flourish and stood up. Shall we be going on to the house, then?

No one answered, but all three of us rose and reluctantly moved off with him in the direction of the exit gate. The hired car was there; Mr. Wickramasinghe saluted us from behind the wheel.

The afternoon heat had gone, leaving only a pocket here and there beneath the trees where the air was still. Originally the lane where we were walking had been wide enough to admit a bullock-cart, but the vegetation encroaching on each side had narrowed it to little more than a footpath.

At the end of the lane were two concrete gate-posts with no gate between them. We passed through, and went into a large compound bordered on two sides by ruined stables. With the exception of one small ell, the house was entirely hidden by high bushes and flowering trees. As we came to a doorway the young man stopped and turned to us, holding up one finger. No noises here, isn't it? Only birds.

It was the hour when the birds begin to awaken from their daytime lethargy. An indeterminate twittering came from the trees. He lowered his finger and turned back to the door. Mornings they are singing. Now not.

Oh, it's lovely, Hannah told him.

He led us through a series of dark empty rooms. Here the dhobi was washing the soiled clothing! This is the kitchen, you see? Ceylon style. Only the charcoal. My father was refusing paraffin and gas both. Even in Colombo.

We huddled in a short corridor while he opened a door, reached in, and flooded the space inside with blinding light. It was a small room, made to seem still smaller by having been given glistening crimson walls and ceiling. Almost all the space was filled by a big bed with a satin coverlet of a slightly darker red. A row of straight-backed chairs stood along one wall. Sit down and be comfy, our host advised us.

We sat, staring at the bed and at the three framed pictures on the wall above its brass-spoked headboard: on the left a girl, in the middle our host, and on the right another young man. The portraits had the imprecision of passport photographs that have been enlarged many times their original size.

Hannah coughed. She had nothing to say. The room gave off a cloying scent of ancient incense, as in a disused chapel.

The feeling of absurdity I got from seeing us sitting there side by side, wedged in between the bed and the wall, was so powerful that it briefly paralyzed my mental processes. For once the young man was being silent; he sat stiffly, looking straight ahead, like someone at the theatre.

Finally I had to say something. I turned to our host and asked him if he slept in this room. The question seemed to shock him. Here? he cried, as if the thing were inconceivable. No, no! This house is unoccupied. No one sleeping on the premises. Only a stout chap to watch out at night. Excuse me one moment.

He jumped up and hurried out of the room. We heard his footsteps echo in the corridor and then grow silent. From somewhere in the house there came the sonorous chiming of a grandfather's clock; its comfortable sound made the shiny blood-colored cubicle even more remote and unlikely.

Dodd stirred uncomfortably in his chair; the bed was too close for him to cross his legs. As soon as he comes back, we go, he muttered.

He's looking for the book, I imagine, said Hannah.

We waited a while. Then I said: Look. If he's not back in two minutes, I move we just get up and leave. We can find our way out all right.

Hannah objected, saying it would be unpardonable.

Again we sat in silence, Dodd now shielding his eyes from the glare. When Sonny Gonzag returned, he was carrying a glass of water which he drank standing in the doorway. His expression had altered: he now looked preoccupied, and he was breathing heavily.

We slowly got to our feet. Hannah still looking expectant.

We are going, then? Come. With the empty glass still in his hand he turned off the lights, shut the door behind us, opened another, and led us quickly through a sumptuous room furnished with large divans, Coromandel screens and bronze Buddhas. We had no time to do more than glance from side to side as we followed him. As we went out through the front door, he called one peremptory word back into the house, presumably to the caretaker.

There was a wide unkempt lawn on this side, where a few clumps of high areca palms were being slowly strangled by the sheaths of philodendron roots and leaves that encased their trunks. Creepers had spread themselves unpleasantly over the tops of shrubs like the meshes of gigantic cobwebs. I knew that Hannah was thinking of snakes. She kept her eyes on the ground, stepping carefully from flagstone to flagstone as we followed the exterior of the house around to the stables, and thence out into the lane.

The swift twilight had come down. No one seemed disposed to speak. When we reached the car Mr. Wickramasinghe stood beside it.

Cheery-bye, then, and tell your friends to look for Sonny Gonzag when they are coming to Gintota. He offered his hand to Dodd first, then me, finally to Hannah, and turned away.

They were both very quiet on the way back to Galle. The road was narrow and the blinding lights of oncoming cars made them nervous. During dinner we made no mention of the afternoon.

At breakfast, on the verandah swept by the morning breeze, we felt sufficiently removed from the experience to discuss it. Hannah said: I kept waking up in the night and seeing that awful bed.

Dodd groaned.

I said it was like watching television without the sound. You saw everything, but you didn't get what was going on.

The kid was completely non compos mentis. You could see that a mile away, Dodd declared.

Hannah was not listening. It must have been a maid's room. But why would he take us there? I don't know; there's something terribly depressing about the whole thing. It makes me feel a little sick just to think about it. And that bed!

Well, stop thinking about it, then! Dodd told her. I for one am going to put it right out of my mind. He waited. I feel better already. Isn't that the way the Buddhists do it?

The sunny holiday continued for a few weeks more, with longer trips now to the east, to Tissamaharana and the wild elephants in the Yala Preserve. We did not go to Colombo again until it was time for me to put them onto the plane.

The black weather of the monsoons was blowing in from the southwest as we drove up the coast. There was a violent downpour when we arrived in mid-afternoon at Mount Lavinia and checked into our rooms. The crashing of the waves outside my room was so loud that Dodd had to shut the windows in order to hear what we were saying.

I had taken advantage of the trip to Colombo to arrange a talk with my lawyer, a Telugu-speaking Indian. We were to meet in the bar at the Galleface, some miles up the coast. I'll be back at six, I told Hannah. The rain had abated somewhat when I started out.

Damp winds moved through the lobby of the Galleface, but the smoky air in the bar was stirred only by fans. As I entered, the first person I noticed was Weston of the Chartered Bank. The lawyer had not yet come in, so I stood at the bar with Weston and ordered a whiskey.

Didn't I see you in Gintota at the races last month? With an elderly couple?

I was there with my parents. I didn't notice you.

I couldn't tell. It was too far away. But I saw the same three people later with a local character. What did you think of Sonny Gonzag?

I laughed. He dragged us off to his house.

You know the story, I take it.

I shook my head.

The story, which he recounted with relish, began on the day after Gonzag's wedding, when he stepped into a servant's room and found his bride in bed with the friend who had been best man. How he happened to have a pistol with him was not explained, but he shot them both in the face, and later chopped their bodies into pieces. As Weston remarked: That sort of thing isn't too uncommon, of course. But it was the trial that caused the scandal. Gonzag spent a few weeks in a mental hospital, and was discharged.

You can imagine, said Weston. Political excitement. The poor go to jail for a handful of rice, but the rich can kill with impunity, and that sort of thing. You still see references to the case in the press now and then.

I was thinking of the crimson blazer and the Botanical Gardens. No. I never heard about it, I said.

He's mad as a hatter, but there he is, free to do whatever he feels like. And all he wants now is to get people into that house and show them the room where the great event took place. The more the merrier as far as he's concerned.

I saw the Indian come into the bar. It's unbelievable, but I believe it, I told Weston.

Then I turned to greet the lawyer, who immediately complained of the stale air in the bar. We sat and talked in the lounge.

I managed to get back to Mount Lavinia in time to bathe before dinner. As I lay in the tepid water, I tried to imagine the reactions of Hannah and Dodd when I told them what I had heard. I myself felt a solid satisfaction at knowing the rest of the story. But being old, they might well brood over it, working it up into an episode so unpleasant in retrospect that it stained the memory of their holiday. I still had not decided whether to tell them or not, when I went to their room to take them down to dinner.

We sat as far away from the music as we could get. Hannah had dressed a little more elaborately than usual, and they both were speaking with more than their accustomed animation. I realized that they were happy to be returning to New York. Halfway through the meal they began to review what they considered the highlights of their visit. They mentioned the Temple of the Tooth, the pair of Bengal tiger cubs in Dehiwala which they had petted but regretfully declined to purchase, the Indonesian dinner on Mr. Bultjens's lawn, where the mynah bird had hopped over to Hannah and said: "Eat it up," the cobra under the couch at Mrs. de Sylva's tea-party.

And that peculiar young man in the *strange* house, Hannah added meditatively.

Which one was that? asked Dodd, frowning as he tried to remember. Then it came to him. Oh, God, he muttered. Your special friend. He turned to me. Your mother certainly can pick 'em.

Outside, the ocean roared. Hannah seemed lost in thought. *I* know what it was like! she exclaimed suddenly. It was like being shown around one of the temples by a bhikku. Isn't that what they call them?

Dodd sniffed. Some temple! he chuckled.

No, I'm serious. That room had a particular meaning for him. It was like a sort of shrine.

I looked at her. She had got to the core without needing the details.

I felt that, too, I said. Of course, there's no way of knowing.

She smiled. Well, what you don't know won't hurt you.

I had heard her use the expression a hundred times without ever being able to understand what she meant by it, because it seemed so patently untrue. But for once it was apt. I nodded my head and said: That's right.

SELECTED LATER STORIES

Monologue, Tangier 1975

I FIRST met her just after she'd bought the big villa over-looking the valley Saudis have it now they've got most of the good properties I remember she asked Anton and me to tea we hadn't been married very long then she seemed very much interested in him she'd seen him dance years ago in Paris before his accident and they talked about those days it was all very correct she had delicious petits fours strange how that impressed itself on my mind of course at that time you must remember we were frightfully poor living on the cheap-est sort of food fortunately Anton was a fantastic cook or we should have starved he knew how to make a meal out of nothing at all I assure you well it wasn't a fortnight later that she invited us to lunch terribly formal a large staff everything perfect and afterward I remember we were having coffee and liqueurs beside the fireplace and she suddenly offered us this little house she had on the property there were several extra cottages hidden around you know guest-houses but most of them were up above nearer the big house this one was way down in the woods far from everything except a duck pond I was absolutely stunned it was the last thing I should have ex-pected of her then she took us down to see it very simple but charming tastefully furnished and a rather primitive kitchen and bath but there were heaps of flowers growing outside and lovely views from the windows we were enchanted of course you understand there was nothing to pay we were simply given the use of the house for as long as we wished I admit it was a very kind gesture for her to make although at the time I suspected that she had her eye on Anton I was quite wrong as it happened in any case having the house made an enor-mous difference to us it was a gift from the gods there was as a matter of fact one drawback for me Anton didn't seem to mind them but there were at least twenty peacocks in an enormous aviary in the woods not far away and some nights they'd scream you know how hair-raising the sound is espe-cially in the middle of the night it took me weeks to get used to it lying there in the dark listening to those insane screams eventually I was able to sleep through it well once we'd moved in our hostess never came near us which was her privilege naturally but it did seem a bit peculiar at least she wasn't after Anton the months went by and we never caught sight of her you see we had a key to the gate at the bottom of the estate so we always used the lower road to come and go it was much easier than climbing up past the big house so of course in order for us to see her she'd have had to come down to our part of the property but she never ventured near us time went on then all at once we began to hear from various directions a strange rumour that whenever she spoke of us she referred to us as her squatters I was all for going up and having it out with her on the spot is that why you invited us here so you could ridicule us wherever you go but Anton said I'd got no proof it could simply be the typical sort of malicious gossip that seems to be everywhere in this place he said to wait until I heard it with my own ears well clearly she wasn't likely to say it in front of me then one morning I went to take a little walk in the woods and what should I see but several freshly painted signs that had been put up along the paths all saying DEFENSE DE TOUCHER AUX FLEURS obviously they'd been put there for us there was no one else isn't it extraordinary the way people's minds work we didn't want her beastly flowers we'd never touched them I don't like cut flowers I much prefer to see them growing Anton said best pay no attention if we have words she'll put us out and he was right of course but it was very hard to take at all events you know she had lovers always natives of course what can one expect that's all right I'm not so narrow-minded I'd begrudge her that dubious pleasure but there are ways and ways of doing things you'd expect a woman of her age and breeding to have a certain amount of discretion that is she'd make everything as unnoticeable as possible but no not at all in the first place she allowed them to live with her quite as if they were man and wife and that gave them command over the servants which is unthinkable but worse she positively flourished those wretched lovers of hers in the face of the entire town never went out without the current incumbent if people didn't include him she didn't accept the invitation she was the sort of woman one couldn't imagine ever having felt embarrassment but she could have managed to live here without alienating half the Europeans you know in those days people felt strongly about such things natives couldn't even enter the restaurants it wasn't that she had lovers or even that her lovers were natives but that she appeared with them in public that was a slap in the face for the European colony and they didn't forgive it but she couldn't be bothered to care what anybody felt what I'm leading up to is the party we never caught a glimpse of her from one month to the next you understand and suddenly one day she came to call on us friendly as you please she said she had a favour to ask of us she was giving this enormous party she'd sent out two hundred invitations that had to be surrendered at the gate she said there were always too many gate-crashers at her parties the tourists would pay the guides to get them in and this time nobody was to get in excepting the ones she'd invited what she wanted us to do was to stand in a booth she'd built just outside the gate it had a little window and a counter Anton was to examine the invitations and give a sign to one of the policemen stationed outside to admit the holder I had a big ledger with all the names alphabetically listed and as Anton passed me the invitation I was to make a red check opposite the name she wanted to be sure later who had come and who hadn't I've got ten servants she said and not one of them can read or write it's discouraging then I thought of you and decided to ask this great favour of you is everything all right in your little house do you enjoy living here so of course we said oh yes everything is lovely we'd be glad to help you what fools we were it won't take long she said two hours at most it's a costume party drinks dinner and dancing by moonlight in the lower garden the musicians begin to play at half-past seven after she'd gone I said to Anton two hundred invitations indeed she hasn't got twenty friends in this entire city well the night of the party came and we were up there in our little sentry-box working like coolies the sweat was pouring down my back sometimes a dozen people came all together half of them already drunk and they didn't at all like having to wait and be admitted one at a time they kept arriving on and on I thought they'd never stop coming at midnight we were still there finally I told Anton this is too much I don't care who comes I'm not going to stand here another minute and Anton said you're right and he spoke to the guard and said that's it no more people are coming don't let anybody else in and good night and so on and we went down to where the party was the costumes were very elaborate we stood for a few minutes at the end of the garden watching them dancing suddenly a tall man in robes with a false beard and a big turban came up to us I had no idea who he was but Anton claimed he recognized him at once anyway it was her lover if you please she'd sent him to tell us that if we were going to come to the party would we please go and put on our costumes as if we had any costumes to put on I was staggered after getting us to stand for almost five hours in a suffocating little box she has the infernal gall to ask us to leave yes and not even the common courtesy to come and speak to us herself no she sends her native lover to do it I was starved there was plenty of food on the buffet but it was a hundred feet away from us at the other end of the garden when we got back down to our house I told Anton I hate that woman I know it's wrong but I really hate her to make things worse the next day she came down to see us again not as you might think to thank us far from that on the contrary she'd come to complain that we'd let in people who had no invitations what do you mean I cried look at the cards and look at the book they tally what are you talking about and she said the Duchesse de Saint Somethingorother was missing her evening bag where she'd put her emerald earrings and I said just what has that got to do with us will you please tell me well she said we'd left our post our post she called it as though we were in the army and after we'd gone some other people had arrived and the police let them in Anton asked if they'd presented their invitations well she said she hadn't been able to get hold of that particular policeman so she didn't know but if we'd been there it wouldn't have happened my dear lady I said do you realize we were in that booth for five hours you told us it wouldn't take more than two I hope you're aware of that well it's most unfortunate she said I've had to call in the police that made me laugh eh bien madame I said since according to you it was the police who let the thief in it ought to be very simple I don't see that we have anything to do with it then she raised her voice all I can say is I'm sorry I was foolish enough to count on you I shall know better another time and she went out it was then that I said to Anton look we can't go on living in this woman's house we've got to find somewhere else he was earning a little at that time working in an export-import office practically nothing but enough to pay rent on a small cottage he thought we should hang on there and hope that things would return to normal but I began to go out by myself nearly every day to look for somewhere we could move to this turned out later to have been very useful at least I'd seen a good many houses and knew which ones were possible you see the party was only the prelude to the ghastly thing that happened less than a month afterward one night some teenage hoodlums got into the big house the lover had gone to Marrakesh for the weekend so she was alone yes she made the servants sleep in cabins in the upper garden she was alone in the house and you know these people they're always convinced that Europeans must have vast sums of money hidden about the premises so they tortured her all night long trying to make her tell where it was she was beaten and burned and choked and cut and both her arms were broken she must have screamed I should think but maybe they covered her face with pillows at all events no one heard a thing the maids found her in the morning she was alive but she died in hospital that afternoon we knew nothing about it until the police suddenly arrived two days later and said the property was being padlocked and everybody had to leave immediately meaning the servants and gardeners and us so out we went with all our things it was terrible but as Anton said at least we lived for more than a year without paying rent he always insisted on seeing the positive side of things in a way that was helpful later when I heard the details I was frightfully upset because you see the police traced the hooligans through a gold cigarette case and some other things they'd taken the night they tortured her and then it was discovered that they also had the Duchess's evening-bag one of the criminals had arrived late the night of the party and slipped in along with a group of Spaniards after Anton and I had left the gate and of course that gave him the opportunity of examining the house and grounds for the break-in later so I felt terribly guilty of course

I knew it wasn't my fault but I couldn't keep myself from thinking that if we'd only stayed on a little longer she'd still have been alive I was certain at first that the lover had had some part in it you see he never left her side she wouldn't hear of it and all at once he goes off to Marrakesh for a weekend no it seemed too pat it fitted too well but apparently he had nothing to do with it besides he'd had every chance to make off with whatever he wanted and never had touched a thing so he must have been fairly intelligent at least he knew better than to bite the hand that was feeding him except that in the end he got nothing for his good behaviour poor wretch I've tried to think back to that night and sometimes it seems to me that in my sleep maybe I did hear screams but I'd heard those blasted peacocks so many times that I paid no attention and now it makes my blood run cold to think that perhaps I actually did hear her calling for help and thought it was the birds except that the big house was so far away she'd have had to be screaming from a window that looked over the valley so I keep telling myself I couldn't possibly have heard her they wouldn't have let her get near a window but it's upsetting all the same

Monologue, Massachusetts 1932

just applejack little mint little lemon nothing better on a hot
afternoon you want more ice it's here I don't like ice in my
drink nor ice-cream either funny when I was a little tyke they
gave me some and I spit it out said it burned my mouth yep
that's thunder all right I figured we were about due for a
shower we get some bad ones here they come rolling up the
valley God you'd think it was bombs sit here wondering
where it's going to hit next got the barn out there twice once
two years ago didn't do any harm other time oh fifteen years
ago more than half of it burned down got the horses out all
right though had horses then that was one time when the
family was lucky we get some corkers here generally come in
August the worst ones my wife my first wife that is as soon as
she'd hear thunder she'd go to pieces all white and start trembling couldn't do anything with her lightning rods didn't
mean a thing to her I'd tell her Susan even if it hits the house
it's not going to hurt you when women get nervous no use
trying to make 'em listen to reason go right on with the same
thing over and over yep this is the house I was born in always
lived here didn't use to look like this it was my second wife
brought all this furniture here it doesn't belong in an old
place like this yes the house is pretty old seventeen ninety-six
you can see the numbers chiselled on the doorstep out front
all these old houses have little rooms there's no space for big
chairs and tables I told her the only room in this house big
enough to hold that grand piano is the kitchen but there it is
takes up half the room that was a loud one it's coming this
way all right look at the sky out there over the top of the hill
black as sin yep live here alone since my last wife died haven't
even got a dog to keep me company I don't mind it too
much never could stand a lot of commotion around anyway
can't abide noise that radio there never turn it on except I
want to hear the news how's that drink coming here I'll fix
you another yes hits the spot but you know you can't use
peppermint got to use spearmint funny the peppermint won't
give it the flavour so you saw my ad came all the way here to

see the place not much to see just the old house got a hundred and forty-five acres of woods down back there's a pretty good brook runs through got some fruit trees out on that side that's about all I keep busy got fifty-odd cord of wood stacked in the shed for cold weather too bad you didn't get here an hour sooner we could have gone down to the woods I presume you'd like to see the whole property well we can look around outside a little we'll have to stick close to the house though you can smell the rain in the air bring your drink along that's all right those four old maples were just as big when I was a boy I recall my grandfather told me he couldn't remember a time when they weren't there the two little windows upstairs well there's two bedrooms and a garret up there here it comes it's going to come down hard too bad well we didn't get wet this room on the right is the parlour I keep it shut off never come in here got plenty of room without it it's stuffy you can smell the dust come on in the other room and get a fresh drink the applejack glad you like it that's right make it myself down cellar I've got a little still down there my father had it before me it's real good stuff if you make it right Christ that was near must have been over by the Henderson farm hit something I've got to shut the windows the rain's coming in I make it every year God no I don't sell it that would be asking for trouble it's just for household consumption except I've got no household no no more marriage for me I've tried it twice and both times it turned out bad tragic awful they were both of them very refined and sensitive the first one had a little money the second was as broke as I am a few shares of Tel and Tel but she did have all this furniture well it's nigh on ten years since I married my first wife my old man died and the place was up to here in mortgages she wanted to get them cleared up first thing so I got that off my mind yes I did say tragic terrible I'm coming to that after about a year I begin to notice that Susan isn't in such good shape she's sort of going to pieces I don't know nervous as a witch and can't sleep and I have to put up with her nagging nag nag day and night night most of all wouldn't let me sleep so finally I slept on a sofa we used to have in here I don't know if you noticed this shot-gun in the corner in the parlour I always keep it there ready for action so I can get at it fast maybe a woodchuck in the garden or a red squirrel can't leave them around tear your house to pieces anyway Susan knew it was there only she never even touched it when she dusted she was afraid of it well she'd been going from bad to worse finally she just clammed up on me wouldn't say a word that was all right with me I had this new Ford truck I used to drive into town every few days stock up on food it's only eighteen miles if you go straight through by the back road some of it's pretty rough didn't bother me any in the truck though I generally went in the morning so I'd be back by noon but this day I didn't start out till after lunch about two it took me longer than usual in town got home a little after sundown went into the house looked around for Susan no sign of her when I went into the room across the hall there the parlour I found her dead yes she'd shot herself she sat down in a chair rested the stock on the floor leaned way over put the barrel into her mouth and pulled the trigger a terrible thing you don't want to hear all this how did I start on it don't see so many people these days somebody comes I open up I guess can I make you another no not even a small one you're right it packs a wallop well you don't mind if I help myself I don't have to drive anywhere well this awful thing damn near broke me up after the funeral I went down to New York took in a few shows Christ I'd have gone crazy if I'd stayed here it was down there I first met Laura didn't see much of her that year the next year I went to New York again and we saw a lot more of each other wasn't till the year after that we got married she was wild about the house always wanted to live in one just like this we got rid of the old tables and chairs weren't any great shakes anyhow and she shipped all her stuff here Laura she was very delicate high-strung used to having her own way she loved the country she'd walk for hours in the woods at least she did the first year or so she was artistic too set up her easel out in the orchard and paint the trees she didn't do anything with the pictures she just liked to paint 'em there's a whole stack up in the garret she was a good sport we used to go berrying up on Hawk Mountain fix sandwiches stay there all day don't know how many quarts we'd bring back could hardly carry it all between us it's letting up a little going on down the valley still coming down all

right though the trouble was my fault ought to have told her
about Susan I mean how she died I ought to have told her
right off might have known she'd hear about it somehow you
know women's gossip so she wants to know all about it and
why I didn't tell her in the first place instead of letting her
find out she kept asking questions how Susan could have
reached the trigger with such a long barrel figure it out for
yourself I told her she thought there was something I was trying to hide she got so she wanted to talk about it all the time
she'd say oh sometimes I get to thinking about Susan and it
makes me feel so blue I wonder what she was feeling and how
she could have done that to herself I'd tell her for Christ's
sake you never even met Susan how can you think about her
that's why I didn't want to tell you because I knew you'd take
it this way it wasn't long before I see we were never going to
get on together she didn't exactly nag but she was sarcastic
and she had her own ideas anyway too late now I thought just
have to make the best of it well one way of making the best
of it was to get out of the house whenever she started playing
the piano it's stopped going to open the windows no air in
here sure you don't want another I'm helping myself again
hope you don't mind don't drink much when I'm alone don't
enjoy it no fun to drink if you've got nobody to talk to right
and worse to drink with somebody who won't drink and
doesn't want you to drink either Laura couldn't drink claimed
it gave her a headache so she took exception to it when I
drank even wanted me to get rid of the still said it made her
nervous knowing it was down there did my drinking out in
the tool shed you know it's a bad thing when a man can't do
as he's a mind to in his own house we were getting on each
other's nerves something terrible and she was spending more
and more time at the piano what kind of music God I don't
know but it was always loud I didn't stay to listen I got out
she'd be pounding there all afternoon long I put up with it
till one day I told her look we've got to have an understanding about that piano right now it seems to me an hour in the
morning and an hour in the afternoon's enough for anybody
and by God that's all you're going to play I'm going to time
you and if you go on after your time's up I'm going to come
in and drag you out of here by force you hear well that didn't

go down with her after that she wouldn't play at all said I'd
ruined it for her you see this was just part of her nervous
breakdown cutting off her nose to spite her face but she held
it against me right up to the end I even tried once in a while
to get her to play but she wouldn't wouldn't even come into
this room any more sat in the kitchen by the big window
mooning I didn't know then but she must have had Susan on
her mind the whole time I think even if I'd told her myself instead of her finding out from the neighbours the way she did
I think it would have been the same anyway one morning I
was out in the field hoeing and I heard a funny noise in the
house by God I said she's playing with that shot-gun and I
started to run well I found her in the parlour she'd done it
the same way as Susan both of them I couldn't believe it
couldn't believe it things like that don't happen I mean twice
exactly the same way no well it was terrible I asked Doc Syn-
der about it later if he thought it was my interfering with her
piano but he said no she was melancholic and would have
done the same thing anyway so I mustn't feel to blame but I
still did he told me Caleb when a woman like your wife gets
an idea into her head you might as well give up you're not
going to get it out he didn't help Laura any he'd joke with
her but she just nodded her head Doc said he wasn't much
surprised at what she'd done he'd sort of been expecting
something bad well it was a pleasure talking to you come back
if you still want to see the place in good weather be glad to
see you any time a pleasure take it easy on the road you won't
get back before dark anyway

Monologue, New York 1965

a dazzling accomplishment Kathleen Andrews has succeeded in forging a language capable of bearing her to the
highest reaches of lyrical expressivity the poems soar above
the stratosphere what idiotic reviews they write you know her
mother has a certain amount of influence she's also very rich
so I wouldn't be surprised if there'd been a bit of quid pro
quo under the table publishers and critics are human too no
I'm afraid I'm unconvinced I've read her poetry you see we
were classmates at Sarah Lawrence I knew her well she's not
someone you'd forget easily either she was always impossible
writing poetry even back then and publishing it right and left
a lot of people were impressed she probably did have some
talent but what a waste it was she could be held up as the classical example of the person who systematically ruins her own
life purely self-destructive in college she would always go out
of her way to say things nobody could possibly have agreed
with she'd explain I'm for giving the world shock treatment
that's what it needs people enjoy being scandalized more than
anything else yes that may be Kathleen I'd tell her but don't
you see that every time you shock them they put a little more
distance between you and them can't you see that in the end
they're not going to take anything you say seriously you're
going to be some sort of freak as far as they're concerned
have you thought about it I used to argue with her almost
plead with her you know the way you do when you see a
friend doing everything wrong I took her seriously I thought
I could help her but her reaction was oh if they want to think
I'm a freak what difference does it make well this childish attitude was all right then I suppose but later on it wasn't so
amusing anyway as far as I could see she had no interest in
men she was far too busy thinking about herself she did say
she wanted the experience of having a child but wouldn't
dream of marrying I told her she'd better think twice before
doing anything so scatter-brained actually she was pregnant
the first year after graduation but she didn't tell me I was
about the only one of her old friends who kept on seeing her

she simply shut herself off anyway as soon as she knew she
was pregnant it seems she began holding long conversations
with the baby she had this strange idea that she could influence it by talking to it all the time Kathleen I'd tell her come
back to reality you can't go on this way you've got to be serious a baby's not an idea or a poem it's real and you're
going to have to take care of it oh that's all right she said I've
got my trust fund it ought to be enough that's not what I'm
talking about I told her you're going to be a mother a flesh-
and-blood mother do you know what that means what it involves oh of course I'll find out what it means all right when
the time comes and I thought but will you and that poor
child but she was stubborn she had an idea she liked and she
was going to hold on to it come hell or high water she
wouldn't listen she'd just smile her superior smile and say my
life is my own to do with as I please yes I said but not the life
of your child that isn't to do as you please with think about it
and for God's sake try to make sense it's not a game Kathleen
you know she was ashamed of being pregnant she didn't want
anyone to see her she wouldn't go out at all she simply hid
herself away in that little apartment in the Village month
after month every two weeks or so I'd drop in to see her
because we were really close friends practically everybody else
was fed up with her nonsense but I guess I imagined I might
be able to appeal to her common sense we always think we
can help even when we ought to know better it would be sad
if it hadn't been so funny I remember that winter there was a
blizzard and I walked all the way from Gramercy Park to
Bank Street one day so that by the time I got to her place I
was half frozen and my feet were soaked Little Missy had all
the lights out she was lying in bed with one candle burning
on the table beside her and a book in her hand but she
jumped up and turned on the lights she had only about a
month to go I sat by the fireplace warming my feet while she
brewed tea well she seemed to be making perfectly good
sense but then she suddenly got back into bed and said excuse
me I want to finish it'll only take a minute I'm reading the
Analects of Confucius to Alaric isn't the name perfect isn't it
precisely what you'd expect her to choose no one's been
named Alaric for the past fifteen hundred years oh I love it

and then my dear she began to read out loud looking down
at herself the Master said this and the Master said that well it
was grotesque it made my flesh crawl but I couldn't very well
interrupt her her voice was so sepulchral so I sat twiddling my
toes by the fire after a while she shut the book and spoke up
in a normal voice you see while he's still with me I want to be
as close to him as I can because once he's born there's no
more I can do she said all this in such a reasonable tone of
voice that I was suddenly furious Kathleen I said you ought to
know by now you can't shock me I'm shockproof as far as
you're concerned tell me what are you trying to prove but she
simply opened her eyes wide and said I don't know what you
mean well I said in the first place what makes you so sure it's
going to be a boy oh of course it's a boy I decided that at the
beginning the thing is I want to give him a good pre-natal education so when he's born he won't be so much at the mercy
of outside negative influences it's the most important part of
a child's upbringing but most mothers don't feel close to
their babies until they can actually see them human stupidity
as always and she began to tell me what was wrong with
everybody look I said I don't suppose it's occurred to you
that you might as well be reading to that table you know
damned well it can't even hear much less understand what
you're saying why do you insist on playing games with yourself can't you just relax and be natural for a while oh she said
of course he understands how can he help it we're the same
person I know once he's born he won't understand anything
after all I'm not living in Fantasy Land so you see that's why
I have to spend all my time with him until then because once
he's left me he's on his own and I can't do anything more for
him I must have had a strange expression on my face because
she suddenly straightened up and said I'm sorry you feel so
strongly about it I know most people think it's their duty to
press their own ideas on others but I'd always imagined you
were more tolerant and she looked at me as if I'd been a great
disappointment to her well Kathleen all I can say is I hope the
baby's healthy I have the feeling that when you've taken care
of it for a while you'll see things differently and we talked a
little and I told her Jack and I were off to Rio and I'd see her
when I got back and not to worry worry she said what would

I worry about I'm happy so I went out into the blizzard again
and got a cab home thinking it would have been a lot better
if I hadn't gone my God not living in Fantasy Land indeed
and I thought then I'm not going to go on seeing her when
I get back it's a lost cause and I really meant it but you know
me curiosity killed a cat oh yes I looked her up again the next
summer the baby must have been about five months old perfectly healthy as far as I could see although I noticed it didn't
smile once what got me was her offhand attitude toward it
when she first showed it to me she said there he is the little
horror and I thought here comes more of the same but for
once I'm not going to react he's lovely I said do you breast-
feed him yes she said but once he's weaned I'm going to take
him to my mother's in Lake Forest she'll find a good nanny
for him she said she didn't ever want to have to correct or discipline him because it would destroy their relationship and it
was so important for him to have confidence in her and she
went on the whole thing getting more outrageous by the
minute I should have realized long before that she was never
going to change but somehow I'd thought having the baby
might have done something of course I couldn't have been
more wrong as the twig is bent baby or no baby that's it I
thought well better for him to have a good nanny at least
than to be left to the tender mercies of Kathleen seeing all
this made me rather thankful that Jack and I had never had
any children so she went off to her mother's but the most incredible episode of all came several years later by then I'd
more or less stopped thinking about her once in a while I did
wonder what had become of her well one fine day I got a letter covered with Moroccan stamps from Kathleen she'd left
her mother's and gone to Europe with Alaric her mother paid
for the trip probably to get rid of her she'd been living here
and there and had ended up in Tangier being Kathleen she
was in the native quarter of course and Alaric was learning
about life with his peers playing with the Moroccan boys in
the neighbourhood and she thought it was wonderful and
wanted to stay for ever and hoped sometime I'd pass through
Tangier it all sounded suspiciously like a continuation of the
pattern anyway a year or so later when Jack and I were in
Europe I decided to fly down to Tangier for a weekend and

look in on Kathleen I was intrigued American girl living alone
in the native quarter well Jack didn't want to go so he stayed
in London and I went flying off down to Morocco I can't tell
you it was incredible the whole thing it took me hours to find
her house I finally had to go back to the hotel and get a guide
and we went through all the dark alleys eventually we came to
the door it was wide open to the street I told the guide to
wait ouside I'd never have found my way back to the hotel
well she was there dressed in some sort of flashy native costume the place had no furniture in it just mats and cushions
and a big table in the middle of the room and here's the pay-
off on the table was an enormous pile a mountain of marijuana I saw it from the street before I went in without
knowing what it was Kathleen I said that stuff is forbidden
you know that how can you leave it out in plain sight like that
anyone going past can see it my guide must have seen it I was
feeling damned nervous sitting there can't you shut the door
please she shrugged and went to shut it I asked her where
Alaric was I was curious to see how he'd turned out she
looked vague oh outside he has lots of friends this made me
think of the awful kids I'd just seen playing in the street each
time we saw a crowd of them the guide would say hold on to
your handbag madame it's nice he has friends I said and you
how are you I was thinking how can she possibly live like this
it smelt exactly like a stable she began to walk back and forth
looking preoccupied and once she stood and stared down at
the table this stuff's not mine she said it's Todd's Todd's staying with me he's gone to the store, he'll be back in a minute
oh I see I said and pretty soon Todd came in about six foot
three and jet black this was interesting I thought it showed a
new side of Kathleen not a very original one I admit but still
something different from before anyway I was sitting there
trying to make conversation with the two of them and suddenly there was this terrible gurgling animal sound in the next
room it echoed my God what's that I asked her she was perfectly matter-of-fact about it it's just our sheep we've had it
now a month fattening it up for the festival next week Alaric
is all excited about it he lives for that sheep it's hard to get
him away from it but in the house I said how can you stand
it well the boy finally came in and he had a whole crew of

other kids with him all jabbering in Arabic it must have been but at least he looked healthy through the dirt he was as filthy as the rest of them and hadn't had his hair cut in a year incredible they trooped in and all rushed to the room where the sheep was tied up and it began to make its awful bleat I decided this was a good moment to disappear I said I had to go because my guide was waiting but I'd come back the next day Kathleen looked at me as if it were the end of the world but you just got here she kept saying then the kids all went out all except Alaric and he climbed on to Todd's lap and began to hug him that kid was starved for affection I said to him Alaric it's nice you have the sheep he can be your friend and follow you around wherever you go and that kid looked straight at me and said oh no we're going to cut his throat next Tuesday I thought he was making it up but Kathleen said yes Tuesday's the day of the sacrifice as I went out she said she'd been writing lots of poetry and I thought I'll bet you have and what a blessing I don't have to read it I said goodbye see you tomorrow and I really meant to go back and try to talk with her just the two of us but it was all so abject and sordid and she was so childish it was really depressing I couldn't face looking for that alley again the next morning I got a plane out to London I've never heard from her since what a waste I don't think she has any idea of what she's done to herself I suppose I'm getting less tolerant but I have no patience with people who refuse to abide by the rules of the game and that boy of hers I'd be willing to bet he ends up behind bars it's inevitable but she has no one to blame she's brought it all on herself the sad part is that she'll never realize how much harm she's caused it'll never cross her mind that her life has been one great mistake from the beginning pretty ridiculous isn't it

Unwelcome Words

I'M GLAD you replied to my letter from the blue, although sorry to see that you imagine I think of you as a captive audience merely because you're confined to your room. Or was that said simply to make me feel guilty for having remained mobile?

Of course prices began to rise here long before the international oil blackmail of the seventies. We watched them go up, always thinking: They can't go any higher. Everything's five times as expensive as it was ten years ago. Since 1965 importation has been forbidden. So instead of imported goods we had smuggled goods, which fetched whatever people were willing to pay for them. (I suppose one should remember that prices here were incredibly low in the thirties and forties, so that they could keep on rising more or less indefinitely before they were equal to those of Europe or America. Then came the oil inflation, so that they're still going up, and still lower than other countries.)

Five years or so after independence, Christopher was talking with an old Berber somewhere in the south. In the midst of a general conversation the old man leaned toward him and said confidentially: "Tell me. How long is this Independence going to go on?"

I remember in 1947 I sent to New York for a thousand dollars. (If you care to remember, that was enough to live on for three or four months in those days, at least here.) The bank where it was supposed to have been sent didn't have it, but they advised me to try all the other banks in town. There were more than forty of them here then. I'd try two or three a day; nobody knew anything. A month later I still didn't have my money. The American Legation suggested I go to the first bank and demand it, at the same time hinting that the American Minister would take steps if they failed to produce it. Magic result: the clerk went straight to a filing cabinet and pulled out the check. But I've always wondered what they hoped to gain by holding it up for such a long time. (It seemed very long to me then, and I was indignant about it.)

Now things are much worse. All foreign money coming into the country is thrown into a pool in Casablanca and kept there while interest is collected from those who borrow it, generally over a period of three months. Eventually the sum shows up on your bank statement, charged at whatever was the lowest rate during that period. It's perfectly understandable considering that the war goes on and is expensive, but that doesn't lessen the inconvenience. We're probably lucky not to have to pay a special war tax, and God knows, that may yet come. Sufficient unto the day.

You ask for news about me: my daily life, what I think about, my opinions on exterior events. All in good time, if I can do it. But what happens here in the city carries much more weight than what we hear from outside. There are plenty of crimes, but each year we seem to have one murder which interests everyone. The special interest lies in the victims having been non-Moslems. This fascinates Moslems as well as infidels, although doubtless for different reasons.

For instance, two years ago, while the workmen were still building the new mosque between here and the Place de France, an elderly woman used to appear from a building across the street, carrying pots of tea and coffee to the men. She'd come early in the morning, before sunrise, when the air was still cold, and the workmen looked forward to her arrival. One day she failed to appear, and later the same day they heard that she'd been murdered in her bed. Someone had managed to climb up to her window and get into her apartment, and before leaving he had prudently cut her throat. He'd expected to find hidden money (which, the woman being Jewish, he naturally assumed he'd unearth somewhere). But she lived in poverty; he found nothing but a blue plastic transistor radio, and he took it. After that, although the workmen got no more tea or coffee, they had music from the blue transistor, but only for a few days. A neighbor of the murdered woman noticed the radio there among the mounds of tiles, and was so certain she had recognized it that she mentioned it to a policeman in the street. So of course they caught the workman, who said he wouldn't have cut the old Jewess's throat if he'd known how poor she was!

Then there was the case, last year, of the two old Americans (I don't think you ever knew them) who lived in a small house high up on the Old Mountain, at the very end of the navigable road, where it turns into what's left of the Roman road. They were truly isolated there, without a telephone or another house in sight. So after several decades of living up there in peace, they were suddenly attacked. The husband was in the garden at the edge of the woods, filling a ditch with water. The attackers felled him and pushed his head into the ditch. The wife saw everything through the window before they went into the house and beat her up, trying to make her tell where "the money" was hidden. (These people were penniless, living on their Social Security checks.) There was no money, so after landing a few more kicks in the woman's face, the marauders went on their way. The husband died; the wife survived. The incident alarmed the Europeans living on the Old Mountain Road, all of whom have large properties and are already guarded by night watchmen; the muggers chose the old couple precisely because they were unprotected, and of course got nothing at all out of it. The grapevine claims that the criminals were caught about two months later. They were part of a gang that lived in a cave on the coast to the west. But who knows? These things are taken more seriously by the European residents than food riots and battles with the so-called Polisario in the Sahara. The bridge-table mentality, if you'll pardon the slur.

So anyway, that's that for now.

II

Good that we're back in touch.

You're wrong; I do remember the last time we saw each other. You were living in that crazy apartment on the roof of the castle, and there was a terrible wind coming from the harbor. You had a few people there for dinner, and I remember the door onto the roof being opened and the wind blowing through the entire flat, so that everyone was calling out: Shut the door! What the precise year was, I don't know, because the episode seems to have no context. The only other detail I recall is your remark that you couldn't read anything written after the eighteenth century. I accepted it as a personal idio-syncrasy; since then I've thought about it, wondering how healthy such a self-imposed stricture is for a twentieth-century author. Is it that you don't read contemporary writing any longer in order to escape from its possibly pernicious influence, or that any contact with present-day fiction is repugnant to you because it suggests the idea of competition? Of course your reasons for excluding the nineteenth century remain un-explained in any case. Although in music I could easily make a similar sweeping statement, relegating to oblivion all the music of the nineteenth century. But that kind of generaliza-tion is never fruitful, it seems to me, and I wonder how closely you adhere to your dictum.

Half the time I haven't even been sure where you were dur-ing these past fifteen years or so. Through others I heard you'd been living in Hong Kong, Tokyo and even Malaysia. (There was a town there which you were said to be fond of, but I can't remember its name. On the east coast, and fairly far north.) Once you'd got out of the habit of writing to me, you no longer knew where to write, which is understandable. The excuse applies even more strongly to me, since you had no fixed residence, whereas I always had a home base.

I needn't ask you if you remember Betty and Alec Howe, since they were your bridge and canasta partners, along with all the other residents I avoided knowing for years. Both of them died ten days or so ago; who knows of what? He first, and she a few days later. Smina is convinced that Betty did herself in so as not to have to go through Alec's funeral. She could be right; I never knew the Howes except at parties and in the market. I suspect you won't bemoan their passing.

And of course there's the incredible Valeska. She's been back here several times since you have, although not in the past five years or so. Abdelouahaïd conceived a strong dislike for her, mainly because she steadfastly refused to sit in the front seat of the Mustang, even though it was the only com-fortable passenger's seat in the car. Her insistence upon riding in back rubbed him the wrong way, since he assumed, and probably quite correctly, that she wanted to make it clear to the public that he was the chauffeur. This basic antipathy made it easy for him to criticize other facets of her behavior.

This he constantly did to me, but of course not to her. Then one day he found his chance and sprang. The result was so insane that I couldn't upbraid him afterwards as I should have.

On the days when I went to fetch Valeska at the hotel she always sat by a table in the courtyard, reading, doing crossword puzzles or whatever, but very busy. Abdelouahaïd would drive right up to the head of the stairs so she couldn't help seeing us, and she always glanced up once, so that it was certain she'd noticed. For some reason I couldn't fathom, she never budged until I got out of the car and went down into the courtyard and crossed it and stood within a foot of her table. This was a sacred rite. One day I stayed at home and sent Abdelouahaïd for her. When she saw him going down into the courtyard she jumped up and followed him up to the car, he said, asking again and again: "Where's Paul? Where's Paul?"

At this point Satan must have arrived and prompted Abdelouahaïd to look at the ground and say sadly: "Paul's dead." You'll be able to imagine the screeches and squawks that followed on this announcement. He helped her into the car and they set off for Itesa. As you know, he doesn't speak English, but he knew enough words to convey to her that I was lying on the floor, and that people were standing around looking at me.

He said that as they got to the Plaza del Kuweit, Valeska suddenly cried out: "Oh Christ! My camera's at the hotel. Never mind. Go on."

She was literally hysterical when she saw me, safe and sound, and I thought: This is too much, and saw myself taking her to Beni Makada to the psychiatrist. Then she wheeled and shrieked at Abdelouahaïd: "You son of a bitch!"

I don't think she's ever forgiven him for his joke, but he's still delighted by the memory of it. As I say, I couldn't bring myself to criticize him, since in a way he did it for me, thinking that she might change her behavior as a result. But naturally it changed nothing, she considering it merely an arbitrary action by a crazy Arab who was curious to see how she'd react.

They're building fancy villas all around me. They're well-built but hideous, and look like old-fashioned juke boxes, their façades plastered with wrought iron and tile work. Each one is required by law to have a chimney, but in no case is the chimney connected with anything inside the house, being purely decorative. The builders are waiting for buyers who don't arrive. Will they ever? The prices seem very high: between $125,000 and $200,000, and there's no heat, of course—no furnace, no fireplaces—and often no space outside for a garden. Yet it's that space which determines whether they're to be considered officially villas, or merely houses (which don't have to have chimneys).

I hope all's well with you, and that you'll reply.

III

I've made it an objective to write you regularly if not frequently, to keep you in touch with this section of the outside world; it may help to aerate your morale. Clearly the only way to give you an idea of my life is for me to write whatever comes into my head. In the conscious selection of material to include, there is the possibility of imposing a point of view, a parti pris. I think my procedure will give you a more accurate picture of my daily life—at least, that part of it which goes on inside my head, by far the most important part.

I've often imagined being in your unenviable situation in the event of a fire or a earthquake. Not to be able to get out of your bed and try to run to safety. Or if you're in your wheelchair, not to be able to go anywhere in it save up and down the corridors. I think that would be my main preoccupation, but again, maybe it wouldn't, since one doesn't live in constant expectation of fires and earthquakes. But I can see myself lying awake at night imagining in detail what it would be like to be asphyxiated by smoke or suddenly flung to the floor with a girder on top of my legs and the dust of plaster choking me. I hope you don't do that, and I somehow doubt that you do. By now you must have become enough of a fatalist to be able to consider all objective phenomena as concomitants of your condition. If that's the case, it may be partially due to your having had to put up for eight years with an impossible wife—a kind of training for the ultimate attainment of a state of total acceptance. At the same time it has occurred to me that the constant presence of a woman like Pamela may easily have augmented the tension which led eventually to the stroke. You suffered unnecessarily for those eight years. Pamela was a racist. She felt she operated on a higher level than yours because she was aware that three hundred years ago her ancestors were living in Massachusetts, whereas yours were living in some benighted region of the Ukraine. "We were here first, so of course it's ours, but we love to have you here, because it makes life more interesting." Am I wrong, or was Pamela like that? Weren't you always aware of a profound contradiction between what she said and the way she acted? At this great remove, I don't remember her very well. That is to say, her face escapes me; I can't project an image of it. I do remember her voice however. It was beautifully modulated and a pleasure to listen to, except when she was angry. This was to be expected: one purposely changes one's voice and delivery as a means of communicating one's emotion. Yet now I have to ask: was Pamela *ever* angry? When I replay the mental tape I have of the breakfast in Quito (in that crazy ice-cream parlor with the balcony where they served food) I hear those trenchant staccato phrases of hers not as expressions of annoyance but as orders being given to an inferior. They had the desired effect: you shrank into your shell and said no more. Everything was delightful as long as there was no resistance; then commands had to be issued.

The truth is that for two or three decades I haven't thought of her at all. I thought of her this morning only because I was trying, from what I knew of your life, to imagine possible causes of a cerebral lesion. I admit that after the fact it's of purely academic interest. The autopsy doesn't cure the patient.

After I woke up this morning I recalled a silly song I heard as a child, when it was sung to me by a woman named Ethel Robb. (I don't know who she was, but I seem to remember that she was a schoolteacher.) The words struck me as so strange that I learned them by heart.

> In der vintertime ven der valley's green
> And der vind blows along der vindowsill
> Den der vomen in der vaudeville
> Ride der velocipedes around der vestibule.

(The melody was a variant of "Ach, du lieber Augustin.") Surely you never heard the song. I wonder if anyone ever did, outside Miss Robb's circle of acquaintances.

The early twenties was the time for absurd lyrics: witness "Oh by Jingo," "The Ogo Pogo," "Lena Was the Queen of Palestina," "Yes, We Have No Bananas," "Barney Google" and God knows what else. There was also a Fanny Brice song called "Second-Hand Rose," which got me into trouble with the mother of my hostess when I sang it at a party here in the sixties. She paid no attention to: "Even the piano in the parlor Papa bought for ten cents on the dollar." But when I got to "Even Abie Cohen, that's the boy I adore, had the nerve to tell me he'd been married before," the lady jumped up and ran across to the divan where I was sitting. She seized my face between her thumb and fingers and squeezed, crying: "Even you, Paul Bowles, even you?" It was all so sudden and dramatic that I felt I'd committed a major solecism. Fortunately there were other guests who knew the song, and they were able to convince her that I hadn't been extemporizing for the occasion, although she didn't seem completely mollified.

I think the most important characteristic you and I have in common (although you'd be within your rights in claiming that we have no points at all in common) is a conviction that the human world has entered into a terminal period of disintegration and destruction, and that this will end in a state of affairs so violent and chaotic as to make any attempts at maintaining government or order wholly ineffective. I've always found you excoriating the decay of civilization even more vehemently than I. This of course was when the worst we could imagine was destruction by nuclear warfare. But now we can imagine conditions under which sudden death by fire might be a welcome release from the inferno of life; we might long for a universal euthanasia. Can we *hope* for nuclear war—I mean ethically—or are we bound out of loyalty to wish for the continuation of the human species at no matter what costs in suffering? I used the word ethical because it seems to me that unethical desires are bound to engender false conclusions.

I suppose what is at the bottom of my mind in all this is that I'm curious to know whether being totally incapacitated has altered your point of view in any way. Has it left you angrier, more resigned, or entirely indifferent? (Although that you never were, under any circumstances, so that I doubt the likelihood of such a major alteration in personality.) I have a feeling that you may consider these things a purely private matter, and as a result may resent my prurient probing.

IV

I can see that you don't really remember the weekend you referred to earlier. There's nothing shameful about not having total recall: still, it seems doubly unfortunate that you should have been deprived of both external *and* internal mobility: I mean the freedom to wander in the past, to explore the closets of memory. I know, it was forty years ago and you say you don't remember, that all three of us were so drunk none of us could possibly recall the details of that absurb excursion. But neither you nor I was drunk when we arrived in the village (and had to get off the train because that was as far as they'd built the railroad). It was still daylight, and we crossed the river on that unfinished bridge to get to the so-called hotel. Surely you remember that there was nothing to drink but mescal; you kept saying that it smelled like furniture polish, which as I recall it did. Have you ever drunk any since? And what a night, with Bartolomé sitting there getting drunker and drunker and giggling his head off. And at one point (search well—you *must* remember this) the mosquito net over my bed collapsed onto my head so that I was swathed in folds of netting, and the dust made me sneeze, and Bartolomé in his chair pointed at me while I struggled, and cried: *Pareces al Niño Dios!* And you and he laughed interminably while I sneezed and flailed my arms, trying to find an opening in the net. By then there was nothing to do but send Bartolomé down for another bottle of Tehuacan and go on drinking our mescal. I think it was he who finally extricated me from the netting. I admit that you were more or less intoxicated, but certainly not enough so to have drawn a blank. All that was fun, and belongs on the credit side of the ledger. As usual, however, I was more conscious of the unpleasant details than of all the amusement. The next day was eternal. It was agony to be on that plunging rattletrap little train, and I looked with loathing at the miles of cactus on the parched hillsides. Each jolt of the train increased the pounding in my head. Bartolomé slept. You seemed to have no hangover, for which I felt some bitterness; but then, you were used to alcohol and I was not. But since you say you don't remember, I'm left alone with the memory; I might as well have dreamed it all.

Sometimes I suspect you of exaggerating your present deficiencies, not, certainly, to evoke pity, since that would be unlike you, and besides, the desire to exaggerate is probably unconscious in its origin. Nevertheless, you do emphasize your unfortunate situation, so that one can't help feeling sorry for you. The question is: Why do you italicize your misfortune? My feeling is that it's simply out of bitterness. I feel you thinking: Now I'm in a wheelchair. That's that, and that's what the world wanted. In other words, *they* have done it to you. If only you were religious you could blame it on God, or wouldn't that be any more satisfactory?

As I remember, you're not particularly fond of animals. I've always been an ailurophile myself as opposed to a dog-lover. It seemed to me there'd be time enough later to make friends with the canines. Here there's not much likelihood of that. At night they're out in packs, and sometimes attack passersby in the street. A sextet of them chased an American friend for a quarter of a mile one evening along the new road that goes from the foot of the Old Mountain to the new section of Dradeb. When one particular dog gets to be a continuous sleep-disturber I've twice resorted to drastic measures. It would be better to describe the drastic measures, I realize, than let you think that I poisoned the beasts. Naturally that was the first thing that occurred to me, but I decided against it because of the suffering it causes. Also, the symptoms of death from rat poison (the only lethal product I'd have been able to find here) are so classical that the owner of the animal would immediately suspect that his watchdog had been poisoned. My system with the first brute, which used to bark all night from the garden next door, was time-consuming but effective. It involved my staying up half the night for a week in my wait for a completely deserted street. About half past one

I would go to the kitchen and prepare the half pound of raw hamburger. One night I would mix Melleril and Largactyl with the meat, the following night I would grind up several tablets of Anafranil. I continued the alternation until the dog's owner decided it was rabid, and had it shot. There was no more barking after the first night of treatment. This seemed the most humane way of getting rid of the animal.

Another year a bitch whelped in the garage, which is always open. The night watchman gave her a carton to lie in with her pups. When these had been given away, she remained in the garage, encouraged by an eccentric Ethiopian woman who sent her maid at all hours with food for her. As soon as she felt thoroughly at home in the garage, she began to engage in long-distance conversations with friends in Ain Hayani and Dradeb. I complained about this to Abdelouahaïd; I thought he might have a solution. He had a very simple one. He picked up the bitch and put her into the boot of the car. We drove to the Forêt Diplomatique, to the edge of the beach, where there's a restaurant run by a Moroccan with a crew of dogs. Before letting her out of the boot, Abdelouahaïd turned the Mustang around, to be able to start up quickly. She stood on the beach for a second, bewildered; the other dogs saw her and came to investigate. While they surrounded her Abdelouahaïd started up, and we escaped, even though I saw her running behind the car for a good distance as we drove through the woods. She wasn't stupid: as soon as she heard the motor she pushed the other dogs aside and rushed toward the car.

Something has happened to the Moroccans. Fifty years ago dogs were execrated. Only people living in the country owned them. Too dirty to live in the city. Somehow they noticed that practically all French women went into the street accompanied by dogs on leashes, and gradually began to imitate them. At first it was boys leading curs by ropes which they tied tightly around the animals' necks. French ladies passing by would be indignant. *Mais ce pauvre chien! Tu vas l'étrangler!* Now every Moroccan child in neighborhoods such as mine has a canine pet. Most are German shepherds: fathers think they provide better protection.

The French are unpredictable. Last month a young photographer from Paris was here taking pictures for *Libération*.

The only thing which moved him to exclamations of surprise was the size of a peanut-butter jar full of birdseed. Is that authentic? he wanted to know. Do they really sell such large jars of peanut butter? When I said yes, I'm not sure he didn't suspect me of pulling his leg, as he went across the room and examined it carefully. Merry Christmas.

V

Someone sent me a box of American chocolate creams last week. On the cover are the words *Home Fashioned*. On another facet of the same cover is a list of ingredients included in the home-fashioning. Among these are: invert sugar, partially hydrogenated vegetable oils, sorbitol, lecithin, butylated hydroxytoluene, butylated hydroxyanisole, propyl gallate, potassium sorbate, sulphur dioxide and benzoate of soda. Even the most modern home isn't likely to have all these delicacies in its kitchen. Although I haven't been in an American kitchen in many years, I know that they're inclined to look more and more like laboratories. Perhaps by now they have chemical cabinets stocked with everything from triethylene glycol to metoclopramide.

The kitchens in farmhouses at the time of the First World War were not too pleasant to be in either, as I remember, in spite of all the propaganda romanticizing them. There were mingled odors of sour milk, dill and iron from the well water. Spirals of flypaper hung from every convenient hook, and the flies still buzzed on all sides. If there were dogs, they smelled. If there were children, they smelled. It was unbelievable that serious people should want to live that way. What's the matter with them? Nothing. They just don't know any better, that's all. This answer never satisfied me. It implied a double standard that made it possible for my parents to overlook these people's shortcomings. But they never forgave *me* for not knowing something I ought to know, and the severity was applied precisely because I was not a farm boy. Seventy years ago there existed that class difference between those brought up in the city and those brought up on the farm. Now there seems to be very little distinction made. The concept of class has been carefully destroyed. Either you have money or you don't. The result of democracy, I suppose, when it's misunderstood to mean similarity rather than equality.

You couldn't have known the typical small, medium-priced hotel of Paris in the twenties. (By the time you got to Paris, after the Second World War, things had changed somewhat.) There were only three or four rooms per floor, the staircases and corridors were heavily carpeted and the windows were hidden by two sets of curtains. Normally there were two lights in the room, one hanging from the center of the ceiling and the other above the bed's headboard. Both were affixed to a system of pulleys, so that they could be propelled upward or downward according to the needs of the moment. The wallpaper was always dark with wide stripes in colors which might at one time have been garish, although there was no way of knowing, since the patina of age had long since darkened them. It was easy to feel encased and protected in those rooms, and I often dream about them even now. Such dreams however aren't pleasant, since I seem always to be on the point of having to leave in order to let someone else move in. No dream without at least subliminal anxiety.

Incidentally, you have no reason to upbraid me for not giving my specific reactions to your most recent tale of woe. Such reactions can only be emotional in content, and there's never any point in expressing emotions in words, it seems to me. I assure you, nevertheless, that I experienced a feeling of profound chagrin when I read your letter and realized that you were undergoing further torments, and I thought I'd conveyed that impression earlier.

You may remember (although probably not, since you never crack a book written in our century) a phrase used by the Castor in *La Nausée*: "*Je me survis.*" (Ineptly translated in the American edition as "I outlive myself.") I understand the Castor's feeling of being her own survivor; it's not unlike my feeling, save that I'd express mine as: "*Ma vie est posthume.*" Do you make sense of that?

I've often wished that someone would rewrite the end of *Huckleberry Finn*, delivering it from the farcical closing scenes which Twain, probably embarrassed by the lyrical sweep of the nearly completed book, decided were necessary if the work were to be appreciated by American readers. It's the great American novel, damaged beyond repair by its author's senseless sabotage. I'd be interested to have your opinion, or do you feel that the book isn't worth having an opinion about, since a botched masterpiece isn't a masterpiece at all? Yet to counterfeit the style successfully, so that the break would be seamless and the prose following it a convincing continuation of what came before—that seems an impossible task. So I shan't try it, myself.

I think a warning sign of creeping senility is the shortening of the attention span, which strikes me as a form of regression to childhood. We'll see.

VI

I haven't mentioned the mounting hostility I've noted in your letters because I've assumed that it was directed at the world in general, and not at me. Now I see how mistaken I was. First you tell me that my letters are self-indulgent. I let that pass: it was merely a criticism of my method. But I can't overlook the word "gloating." On seeing that, I realize that I'd have done better to limit my correspondence to one necessarily cruel *Get Well* card, and let it go at that.

It seems to me that for this final period of your life it might be profitable to stop encouraging your masochistic tendencies. I can see that you don't feel that way at all, and that on the contrary you intend to go on giving free rein to them. Too bad. There's obviously nothing I can do from here to help you, so I may as well let it rest. But as you sink into your self-imposed non-being, I hope you'll remember (you won't) that I made this small and futile attempt to help you remain human.

Hasta el otro mundo, as Rosa Lopez used to say.

In Absentia

(*sent to Pamela Loeffler*)

I'LL TRY to keep this short so it won't take you too much time to read it. I know how women worry when they have to settle into a new house, with new servants to take charge of, and when they're faced with all those terrible decisions about how to place the furniture and where to store things.

This is a beautiful sunny day for a change. It's been raining on and off this past week, so that the sudden appearance of bright sunlight is a tonic. And the sun made me think of you, who have always loved it as much as I. Do you still sunbathe, out there where you are, or is it too hot? I gave up the practice years ago. Too many of my friends developed skin cancer from it.

So this morning I woke up thinking: I shall write to Pamela today. I know it's been a long time since we saw each other or communicated, but I've followed your activities from afar via what are admittedly unreliable sources: *Time* and the *International Herald Tribune*. And I can now congratulate you. (Nothing is sacred; everyone knows how much you got. But even that amount won't ruin old Loeffler, so don't ever feel guilt.) I can only remark that occasionally the scale tips in favour of justice, and I'm happy that you've been able to experience the phenomenon concretely.

I now have a vague concept of where you are: on the north shore of Maui. I've even found Kahului and Paukokalo. As I studied the map I couldn't help noticing that the entire west coast of the island of Hawaii is decorated with lava flows, as you no doubt know. What amuses me is that each one is named after the year the stuff slid down the mountainside, so that you get *Lava Flow of 1801*, *Lava Flow of 1859*, *Lava Flow of 1950*. It puts me in mind of the streets in Latin American countries, named after important dates. 'He lives on the corner of the Fourth of April and the Nineteenth of October.'

I remember, when people used to ask me what Pamela was doing, I'd reply: Oh, she's busy being beautiful. I remember, also, being taken to task for my flippant answer. But what's wrong with it? Isn't it true? You *are* beautiful (as we know) and you've remained beautiful thanks to your determination to do so. That requires concentration and effort. How otherwise would there have been a Loeffler?

Now I'm trying to imagine you in the un-American decor of our fiftieth state. Do you wear jodhpurs, like Karen Blixen in Kenya? When you have a moment, send a snapshot. I'll be waiting for it.

(sent to Pamela Loeffler)

No, a three-month silence is quite forgivable. I wonder you were able to find the time even when you did. Most of the matters I felt like asking you about in my last, but refrained from mentioning out of tact, seem to have been arranged more or less happily: plumbing, staff, provisions, neighbours. The last named would be rather important, I should think. Great that you should have discovered the Hollywood people only six miles up the road. I don't remember ever having seen his name. But then, he could have been the most famous director in the US and I still wouldn't have heard of him. As you know, I was never a film enthusiast. Anyway, it's nice that they're there, and companionable to boot. They sound *echt* Beverly Hills, but that may be only because I'm relying on your description.

Above all I was happy to hear that a few old friends will be visiting you soon. If Florence actually arrives (does she ever know what she's doing?) give her my love. I can see her getting to San Francisco and deciding to go to Carmel instead of Honolulu, and then two months later suddenly arriving at your place without a word of warning, just when the house is *archicomplet.* I remember one winter when she kept the house in Turtle Bay open, with the housekeeper in residence, to take care of her cat while she was away (but for six months or more) because she believed that cats grow fond of places rather than people, and the cat would have been too unhappy if it had been taken away from the house. Then as soon as she got back home she gave the cat to somebody who lived in Connecticut.

Tell me—you ought to know this by now, being surrounded by exotic flora—is frangipani the same tree which is known in the Philippines as ylang-ylang, and in India as champak? I'm not trying to test you; I don't know myself, and there's no reason why I should expect you to. And yet it's just the sort of thing you might know. If you don't, perhaps one of your friends from Boston will. Bostonians often know the most unlikely things. At least, they used to. Or are there no true Bostonians left?

I see you understand the pleasure that can be got from writing letters. In other centuries this was taken for granted. Not any longer. Only a few people carry on true correspondences. No time, the rest tell you. Quicker to telephone. Like saying a photograph is more satisfying than a painting. There wasn't all that much time for writing letters in the past, either, but time was found, as it generally can be for whatever gives pleasure.

And when *you* find the time, send me a few recent snapshots of yourself and the place. I imagine they'll have to be Polaroids, since from what you write you haven't easy access to what we like to call the amenities of civilization. It sounds to me as though most of your supplies had to be flown over from Honolulu. That's all too reminiscent of the situation here. 'We're waiting for a new shipment. Maybe in three or four months.' Those are the honest baqals; the others say: 'Next week, incha'Allah', knowing it's untrue. You may, or you may never, get your saucepan or your powdered milk or your trowel or your broom or your Gruyère or your spatula. More likely you never will, for such things are not allowed entry into the country these days. *Tant pis et à bientôt.*

(sent to Pamela Loeffler)

Thank you for the year-old photo of the house-in-progress. Even without its finishing touches I can see how handsome it must be now. It's really very sumptuous, very grand. You must have room for a dozen visitors, in case you ever should feel afraid of succumbing to melancholia. But I see no sign of *you*, nor of anyone else. Incredibly fine vegetation.

What makes you think I should be able to interpret your dream? In the first place, I don't believe X can explain to Y what Y dreamed. How do I know what the act of running along a pier represents to you, or what your usual reaction to seaweed is? I don't understand my own dreams, much less those of others. I do notice that people have a tendency to re-count dreams in which there is action, to such an extent that I often wonder if they don't unconsciously supply the action in the telling. Because I can't ever recall any narrative content in my own dreams. They're more like a succession of unre-lated still photographs, rather than a film. But dream tellers go right on saying: 'And then. And then.' I'd like to know if it's really that way with them, or if they only feel that it should be that way.

And besides, why interpret a dream? If it's a warning from your unconcious mind, you'll get the message eventually in any case. Tell me, can you force a dream to recur? I can't. Anyway, good dreaming.

(sent to Pamela Loeffler)

Still at me about dreams? Why do you say that I 'of all peo-ple' should know about them? I don't think about them in the way you do. For me they're a psychic barometer, useful only to the person who does the dreaming, in the way a clin-ical thermometer is useful to the one running a fever. It seems a mistake to attach particular importance to one image rather than another (no matter how significant it may seem at the time of dreaming) since the images themselves are only dele-gates for other, unformulated images. How can you expect anyone to give you the 'meaning' of masses of red seaweed floating in the water? Seaweed means seaweed. You also claim that there was total lack of affect connected with the sight of it. Then why in God's name are you interested in discovering its 'meaning'? If it meant nothing to you in the dream, how can it mean anything in retrospect?

You ask if the Muslims here have a system for explaining dreams. They have, of course, as they have (theoretically) a system for everything, but it's divination using approved reli-gious symbology. I can't see that it's in any sort of agreement with Freudian theory. (How could it be?) It all might have come out of a little book called *Ali Baba's Dream Almanac.* But they believe it, just as the Hindus believe in that idiotic zodiac with its twelve signs. (And not only the Hindus, alas.)

Dear Pamela, the value of a letter can't be measured quantitatively. If you haven't time to write what you call a 'real' letter, then write a few lines. I don't expect anyone to compose long-winded epistles, as I sometimes do. I write letters because I enjoy doing it. It doesn't even matter too much whether the recipient takes pleasure in reading what I write: I've had my pleasure.

So don't decide not to write merely because you know it can be only a few lines. You could send me a note that read: 'A muggy day and I'm depressed. I had baked ham and fruit salad for lunch.' And I'd be delighted. But if you send nothing at all, you leave the field to the imagination, which is always ready with its angst. I want to hear how you feel about the house, as well as about the guests who are staying with you. You wouldn't need much time to tell me that, would you?

(sent to Pamela Loeffler)

I think Tangier is getting less and less liveable. One of the principal reasons why I've continued to stay here has been the good air that we breathe. But the traffic has increased tenfold in the past five years, and with practically all the recent cars equipped with diesel engines, the streets are full of smoke. The buses and trucks constantly whoof out fat black columns of it. At home it doesn't bother me, because I live high up. It's walking in the street that's troublesome. Apart from the pollution, the sidewalks are crowded with obstacles: cars parked in the middle, groups of students sitting along the curb, and beggars installed against the walls. If you mention the beggars to a Moroccan, he'll tell you: Not one of them is from Tangier. They're all down from the mountains. Don't give them anything.

You underestimate the intelligence of the Moroccans at your peril. They know when you're lying and when you're only exaggerating, they know when you mean what you say and when you're only talking, and these things they know directly and not as a result of deduction. It's true that they sometimes scent deceit where there is none. I've argued with Moroccans who refuse to believe that anyone has been to the moon. 'Just America advertising.' Others, admitting the moonwalk, think the money should have been spent feeding hungry people. 'What good did it do?' They're not fascinated or excited by the idea of exploring space, because they have no concept of historic movement or growth; for them time is an eternal stasis. Everything is as it always has been, and will remain thus for ever. A comforting philosophy, if you can subscribe.

(sent to Pamela Loeffler)
Your letter about the Palmers very amusing, I thought. Surely you're not encouraging Dick to look for property in your vicinity? That would be catastrophic, wouldn't it? I agree that it's nice to have acquaintances living only fifteen or twenty miles away, if your first reaction each time you see them doesn't express itself as a sudden sinking sensation. It takes such a lot of energy to fight that. I've got to the point of pre-ferring solitude to being under that sort of stress.

Of course Ruth was always a negative quantity, even before she married Dick. Collecting potsherds, pieces of quartz and crinoids, when I knew her. So the butterfly business is quite in line. It must be marvellous to see her bounding around as she wields the net! Hyperthyroid and graceless. Dick is merely obstinate and dictatorial; that's how I remember him. (I haven't seen him in fifteen years, more or less, but I feel pretty certain that he hasn't changed much. Perhaps extra years have decreased his energy, but it doesn't take much energy to be egotistical if that's one's nature.) When he had a flat here he was completely wrapped up in the Rolling Stones, who were friends he'd known in London. The name meant nothing to me, but Dick insisted they were the greatest rock group in existence. He got me out of bed one night at one o'clock, came pounding on my door, very excited. I must go with him to his flat because he had the Stones there. I, sleepy: 'What stones?' He explained, and I went. A man named Jag-ger, dressed for a costume party, reclined on the bed, gnaw-ing on a leg of lamb. A girl lay face down at his feet, and there were other people spread out asleep on the floor. It wasn't bright enough in the room for me to see their costumes in detail. Mr Jagger said nothing. His muzzle was shiny with lamb fat. Dick saw my surprise at the sight of the inert bodies on the floor, and confided that everyone had taken a new drug which apparently induced a comatose state. It's strange: Dick has this air of breathless enthusiasm. It's a physical attribute which ought to be contagious, but isn't. Instead, it comes across as sales talk, and creates next to no empathy.

After about an hour I thanked him and said I was off to bed. This didn't go down at all well. He took it as an offence, assuming, quite correctly, that I hadn't appreciated my great opportunity of meeting the Stones. I considered that I had been patient, but as I went out and turned to thank Dick again, he drew himself up and, pretending to be a very proper English governess, said: 'Oh, urfty turfty wiffy bibben bibben, oh yes!' and slammed the door.

If the moment seems right, you may mention this episode to Dick, and see if he remembers it. What he's sure to remember is that they all went to Marrakesh the next morning at seven o'clock, Dick included. That was in the pre-Ruth days.

I'm not surprised that Florence postponed her visit; in fact, I predicted it. What does strike me as strange is that you should have Dick and Ruth Palmer there, because I know they're not the ones you'd most like to have staying with you. But of course, that's what happens when one has a large house in a remote place. Still, it's certainly better for you to have guests than to be alone. This next guest of yours, Fronda Farquhar, who is she and what is she? And that name, at the far end of credibility! You speak of her as if I should know who she is, but I don't. What does she do? Or is she another Ruth, searching for arrowheads and shells?

Well, it all sounds like fun.

                                                    (*sent to Susan Choate*)
Now what? Hippocrates strikes again. I wondered at your long silence and now I understand. Hepatitis B is not so amusing. What astonishes me is that you got rid of it in a hospital, which I thought was a place where one contracted it rather than cured it. Do you think it's really gone? I must say I hope so. That hospital bill you enclosed is staggering. How can you be sure that I'll be able to pay it? Clearly I can't keep

sending larger and larger amounts. All your expenses grow like weeds. I realize that you can't help it; money has less and less value, but that simply means that people like me can buy less and less. I'm not lecturing; I'm just bewailing this hospital bill. It's surprising they let you out of the institution without some sort of guarantee that it would be paid. Naturally you took it for granted that I could pay it, without considering the possibility that I might be short of funds. And I can pay it, yes, but not with pleasure. How did you ever get hepatitis? Did they have any theories as to the origin? I hope they gave you some pointers as to how to avoid it in the future.

Did you get the caftan? It should be ideal for dressy occasions in New York or Boston, if indeed there are any more such things. (Although I'm told that girls are becoming interested once more in clothes, and can conceive of wearing something besides those proletarian blue jeans they've been affecting for the past few decades.) Anyway, the caftan is a museum piece. That very heavy silk brocade is no longer woven—not even by Fortuny. I bought it from a Moroccan friend in whose family it had been since the turn of the century. I know you'll look superb in it, and I only hope you'll wear it. (Not in a hospital, however!) I hope to hear from you.

(sent to Susan Choate)

Glad to hear you've had no further trouble with your liver. But good God, Suky, no wonder you came down with hepatitis. Haiti, of all insane places to go, even for a short holiday. I'm not surprised you didn't mention it to me. You must have known I'd do my best to discourage you. You seem to think it was all right because you were invited, so that it cost you nothing. But it did cost you six weeks of classes, not to mention that it cost me a fortune to pay for it.

You say Haiti was picturesque, and I'm sure it is. But it's precisely in this sort of poverty-induced picturesqueness that diseases are rampant. I myself have spent plenty of time enjoying the poverty of others in exotic places, and have paid for it with ailments and aches, as you know. But the point is that hepatitis is a serious disease, and you must take it seriously, something I suspect you don't do, to judge by your flippant references to the experience. Remember that your great-grandmother Gray caught it on a trip to Mexico and died of it, and very quickly. So for God's sake stay put, there at Mount Holyoke, and don't add to my insomnia by going to places you know may be dangerous.

It's a help to know you don't drink. A heavy diet of cannabis can be almost as harmful to the liver, you know. (Likewise tobacco and coffee!) Your doctor must have told you all this, but that doesn't mean that you listened. Having withstood an attack doesn't make you immune; on the contrary, you're more vulnerable to another attack.

Forgive me if I lapse into pedantry, but you spoke of 'convincing' the manager of the bookshop to extend credit. It's not possible to convince 'to'. If you're going to use *convince*, you need either 'of' or 'that'. Otherwise use *persuade*. End of lecture, and until soon.

(*sent to Pamela Loeffler*)

There's no point in asking for news from here. News isn't generally made in this part of the world, or if something occurs here which becomes news in the rest of the world, we hear about it in foreign broadcasts. And the broadcasts of course are full of talk about terrorism. For most Europeans and Americans the word *terrorist* is unqualifiedly pejorative; while to the people here it suggests a patriot. Thus actions some consider criminal and contemptible are to others heroic. How can the two ever see eye to eye?

A theatrical agency in Sydney! I didn't know they had them. I understand her being called Fronda Farquhar if that's where she's from. You make the picnics sound like something out of Waugh or early Angus Wilson. How did you weather three of them, all with F. Farquhar as well as Ruth P.? My suspicion is that the reason Dick refused to go with you is that he was loath to get too far away from the source of supply: your refrigerator. He's always been a glutton. I shan't ask your opinion on that: you're too far away to put irrelevant questions to. But it must be something of a relief to have all of them gone, in spite of feeling alone and missing them. I can't believe you actually miss those three particular people, though. Isn't what you miss the presence of someone, anyone, to talk to now and then? That's not an irrelevant question, by the way, and I do put it to you. Because it's occurred to me that Sue Choate, my father's sister's great-granddaughter, will be visiting a college friend in Honolulu, and might enjoy a visit with you. (I think I told you I was financing her education, so it's of great interest to me where she spends her vacations.) The last time she was out of the States she went to Haiti and caught hepatitis. One can't ask a seventeen-year-old to be circumspect in matters like that, of course. Haiti was there, she was invited, it sounded exciting, so she went.

Let me know about that. I think it might be pleasant for you both. She's charming, lively, and very attractive. Talkative, but intelligently so, and can be turned off with ease. (I'm describing her as she was at the age of fifteen; I haven't seen her since.)

If you have crowds of people scheduled to arrive, and Suky would be in the way, that's of course another story. But let me know when you can, so I can plan her summer.

What happened to those people from California who lived only six miles from you? Don't they like picnics?

See enclosed sheet with Sue's address and phone number at Mount Holyoke, in case.

(sent to Susan Choate)

It was good of you to write so soon, even if I wasn't exactly pleased to hear you'd sold the caftan. And without ever wearing it! I admit that you got an unbelievable price for it. Your friend Myra must be wallowing in dollars. But that wasn't why I sent it to you, so that you could sell it to have spending money. I was hoping it would be a very special item of your wardrobe. You say that one has to get used to doing without things when one becomes poor, and that you couldn't face asking me for money when I was paying for the hospital. All that I appreciate completely. Still, I'm sorry you didn't bring the subject up before getting rid of the garment. I'd have tried to dissuade you, even though I couldn't have sent you the twelve hundred you got for it——at least, not all at once, which is obviously the way you wanted it.

Have you thought of how you'll spend the summer? Much as I'd like to see you, I wouldn't advise your coming here. There's nothing much here to interest you, I'm afraid. Hotels are relatively inexpensive, yes, but not cheap enough for my purse. And the friends with guest-houses where you might have stayed gratis have died or moved away.

It has occurred to me that you might like to visit Hawaii. I know the suggestion sounds absurd, coming directly after the song of poverty. But there I do know someone who might put you up, and probably would be delighted to do so. You've never met her, but you may have heard me speak of her when you were a child. More likely not. Your summer would cost me only the round-trip fare and what's more, I shouldn't be worrying that you might have sneaked off to Mexico or Jamaica, or, God forbid, Haiti. You, of course, know what you want and how you feel like spending your vacation. This is just one suggestion; others may appear in the course of time.

I should add that I do appreciate your concern about money, and understand that you sold the caftan to help me, so I'm not too chagrined that you never wore it, and that I haven't a photo of you modelling it. The postal system, incidentally, is worse than ever.

(*sent to Susan Choate*)

I can't help wondering why you're so eager to know how much I paid for that caftan. It's clear that you hope it was very little, as if that would somehow justify your having sold it. But your logic is ailing. It's not a question of how much *I* paid for it; it's a question rather of how much *you* paid for it, and the answer is nothing. Therefore you cleared your twelve hundred and ought not to bother your head with what it cost me. I can see how your mind is working, and I suppose it shows family solidarity: that is, what's mine is ours. Since you write about practically nothing else in your short letter, I have to assume that it's important to you to know how much more your selling price was than my purchase price. You want to know how much 'we' made on the deal. So in spite of your not seeming to be aware that it's unheard-of to inquire the price of a gift, I think you deserve an answer, since you made 'us' a profit of an even thousand, minus the mailing charges. Does that please you?

You don't seem to take my suggestion about Hawaii very seriously. I can see why, with all our talk about scarce money. Nevertheless I meant it in all seriousness, as a way of solving the vacation problem. I can see that you may not be eager to be the guest of a woman you don't know , or of anyone else, for that matter. But Pamela is what's called easy-going—tolerant and gregarious. She gives the impression of being twenty years younger than she really is. (She's in her late fifties, and may have had cosmetic surgery, but I somehow doubt it. That sort of thing she'd be secretive about.) Do I make her sound like someone to be avoided? I hope not, as I'd be delighted to see you established there for the summer. Besides solving the vacation problem, your sojourn there could prove advantageous in other ways.

Or perhaps I'm crazy, in which case nothing I've said makes sense.

Anyway, let me hear.

(*sent to Susan Choate*)

Your friend McCall sounds like a real slob. Why would he drive you to Hartford knowing you were going to have to take the bus back, and not mention it to you beforehand? You didn't seem to find that unusual; I suppose this sort of irresponsible rudeness is part of today's etiquette. I don't find it appealing, but then, young people go out of their way to be as unattractive as possible, both in their persons and their behaviour. So your date from Amherst is probably no worse than the rest.

I can see you're beginning to give the Hawaiian idea a little thought. You're wrong, however, to use the word *directive*, and to suggest that I've been 'pressuring' you, as you put it. To issue a directive is one thing, and to request a favour is something else. Perhaps I didn't make myself clear in the last letter. Staying with Pamela out there you would be in a position, if you were clever enough, to receive financial assistance for the coming year. That wouldn't have occurred to you in your youthful innocence. But it occurred to me, and I see it as a distinct possibility. Pamela has more money than she can spend, and she's generous. She and I are old friends as you know, and if she took a fancy to you and offered to help you, she'd know she was also helping me. Obviously, once you were there it would be up to you to decide how to play it. A question of choosing the right moment in which to be perfectly truthful. Clearly it's in my interest that you go (and even more in your own, I suspect).

Meditate some more, and when you come up with an answer, let me know. But don't wait too long.

(sent to Susan Choate)

Pamela has risen to the occasion. She's asked me to tell you that she'd be delighted to have you stay with her for as long as it suits you—the entire summer if you like. As soon as she knows what you've decided she'll be in touch directly with you. But if you make up your mind to go, wire or phone her immediately, even before you let me know. Because if you accept her invitation through me, it will take the rest of the spring. Massachusetts–Morocco, Morocco–Hawaii.

If I had access to a telephone I'd call you. And if sending a telegram didn't involve standing in line for an hour first, I'd wire you, and save that much more time. But I'm not up to that.

In any case, the machinery has been set in motion. Let me hear.

(sent to Susan Choate)

Your letter was the best sort of news. Thank God for Lucy Piper! Knowing that you had a friend who lived in Hawaii, I went out on a limb and lied a bit to Pamela, telling her that you'd been asked by this girl's family for a visit. I needed a pretext on which to hang my suggestion that Pamela invite you to Maui. (Since you were going to be in Hawaii, etc.) Now it turns out not to be a lie, after all. The two weeks in Honolulu ought to be fun, particularly if her parents aren't going to be there. The Pipers may be paragons of charm for all I know, but things are generally better when families are not around.

I'll have the New York bank send you fifteen hundred. With what you have, that should be enough for fare both ways. Send me a wire when you get to San Francisco before the Hawaii flight. I shan't write more now. I only wanted to let you know how delighted I am that you decided to go.

(sent to Susan Choate)

The wire Pamela sent you is essentially the same as the one she sent me. She'll pick you up at the Pipers' June 20th and fly you on to Maui. It's an ideal solution. Providential. She wanted to be in Honolulu anyway that week, so she's not putting herself out for you. It just happened to fall right.

In spite of your trepidation, I'd say the possibility that Pamela will be bored by your presence is nil. You by her, who knows? But very unlikely.

What do you mean, 'procedure' to follow with Pamela? Of course there is none. You simply play everything by ear. How can I advise you from here, or dictate a course of behaviour? Or foresee the complex choreography of subterfuges and dissimulations which will make up your conversation? Women know how to handle each other, and need no man's advice.

Don't think about these things now. It will just interfere with your studying. Time enough for that later. Finish up your work and go with Lucy Piper. I hope she's fun to travel with.

Postscriptum: Destroy my letters once you've read them. There won't be all that many, in any case. The summer's too short.

(sent to Pamela Loeffler)

So everything meshed, *grace à Dieu.* And now Suky's with you. Could you gauge her immediate reaction to the new environment? I ask you because I don't expect her to tell me accurately in her letters, if she ever decides to write me. I'm a little surprised that she hasn't sent me even a few words. I suppose she thought a letter from you would be enough.

While we're still talking about Suky, I'm so glad you find her companionable. One never knows with the very young; their moods are mercurial. She's been alone far too much. Her parents both died when she was twelve, and I've seen her only once, and briefly, since then. She will have changed.

There never was such a thing as hashish in Morocco; it was the Americans who first manufactured it here. Kif is volatile, and they were looking for a more compact and durable form of it, so they used a vice. This made an ersatz sort of hashish. The Moroccans, not knowing hashish, good or bad, followed suit, and found the product saleable abroad. They've been pressing this inferior merchandise ever since, and are still making great fortunes exporting it. There's a direct relationship between the commerce in hashish and the prevalence of corruption. A huge sum can silence anyone. I take it the situation is very different where you are; do you know anything about it? That is, more than you can read in the press?

Suggest to Sue that she write me a note at least, if she can find the time between dates. Two boy-friends? Who are they? I imagined you as fairly isolated. Apparently you're not.

What makes you say I'm 'obsessed' by the girl? If you've even suggested such an idea to her, inevitably she'll see it in a Freudian light. This would give her a perfect pretext for not writing. In what other way could she take it? And in what way did *you* mean it, for that matter? 'Obsessed' is a word used too often.

(*sent to Pamela Loeffler*)

I can't help feeling some anxiety over not having had some word from Sue. I know you say she's fine, but I'm not convinced. If she were her usual self, she'd write. It's clear that something is troubling her that she shrinks from telling me, something more than this nonsense she's been feeding you about being 'terrified' of me. She knows that's laughable. How can she speak of me as 'authoritarian'? We haven't seen each other in several years, and no one can terrify by mail.

What's got into her? The difficulty is that you don't know her, so you can't notice any little changes that might have come over her recently. Have you tried to persuade her to sit down and scribble a few words?

It goes without saying that I don't expect you to choose her friends for her. I have no objection to her seeing a Japanese mechanic three nights a week, or every night, so you needn't feel uneasy on my account. Please understand that I don't consider you in any way responsible for her behaviour. She's old enough to account for it herself. As she undoubtedly has told you, she's a partisan of feminine 'liberation'.

(sent to Susan Choate)

I saw something this morning that amused me. Two little boys about five years old were playing at bullfighting. The bull was a perambulator containing a strapped-in baby under blankets, and the one pushing the pram was making frantic attempts to gore the torero, who dodged and sidestepped the attacks. At one point the bull made an all-out desperate attempt and charged with such force that it banged into a telephone pole. Torero delighted. Baby jolted but impervious.

Do write a few lines about the place, about the general set-up. Remember, I've never been there, and am curious. A few sentences in a personal report mean more than pages of a travel article. I'm not asking for an essay; you can tell it all in two paragraphs. One on the place and the other on Pamela. *Finis.*

(sent to Susan Choate)

And now you write me, when you're just about ready to leave, so that I can't even be sure this will reach you in time. At least you gave what is probably an honest reason for your silence: you were having too good a time. That is of course the best reason, and I'm glad it turned out that way. It would have been awful if you'd hated the place and been bored by Pamela. But what a peculiar creature you are, to keep me waiting all summer for a sheet of paper it would have taken five minutes to cover.

The last message I had from you was the wire you sent from San Francisco, so I have no idea of your present finances, or even whether you bought a round-trip passage. One can only worry so much, however; then one becomes philosophical. I suppose philosophy is merely sublimated worry. If this were a telephone conversation I could say: Let me speak to Pamela. So I shall speak to her, in a letter I'll write as soon as I get this one into its envelope. I'm very happy you've loved your vacation.

(sent to Pamela Loeffler)

I just finished a note to the culprit. As you probably know, she finally decided to write me before she returned to college. She describes everything and all in glowing terms—particularly you, about whom she made some highly astute observations, all favourable. I think she has seen the entire spectrum of your personality, complex though it is, and for that I give her good marks. I can see from your last letter that you loved having her there with you.

Does she seem at all preoccupied by the thought of money? If she's been sensible, she should have more than enough to get her back to Massachusetts. Nevertheless, if you get this in time, and think she should have a bit more, please let her have it. I'll repay you immediately.

I'll try to write an actual letter soon, which this is not. What I'd call a true letter ought to be an amalgam of personal conversation, diary (what happened) and journal (what one thinks about what happened). But anyway.

(sent to Pamela Loeffler)

Your letter was indeed bad news. Are you really satisfied with the doctor? I ask because I'm surprised that he didn't seem to be sure whether it was a return of the hepatitis she caught in Haiti, or simple dysentery (non-amoebic, I mean).

Poor Suki! Tell her to relax, and not to worry about being late in getting back to classes. She can make up the work easily.

I wonder if it occurred to your doctor that she might have sunstroke. You spoke of her long hours at the beach. Her symptoms sound a little like my own when I was struck by the sun in Cuba. It's at times like this that I wish I had a telephone. Wire me if there's any sudden change for the worse in her condition.

I saw something incredible in a French magazine last week. A friend of de Gaulle was being interviewed. One question: 'Then de Gaulle was not anti-Semitic?' The reply: 'Well, in 1940, I remember that André Maurois came and asked to speak to de Gaulle privately. The general turned to someone beside him and said: "What's that kike doing here?" But that was just his way of speaking. De Gaulle was never anti-Semitic.' Little things like that make life worth living.

The dog may be man's best friend, but only if he has a master who feeds him. Here the dogs with no human ties are a menace. They hunt in packs of fifteen or twenty and have formed the habit of attacking tethered donkeys when night comes. They crowd around the donkey's head, trying to reach its neck. It backs up, and slowly winds its chain tightly around the tree. When it can no longer move, it belongs to the dogs, which devour it. In Tangier there used to be a dog-catcher, who piled ownerless dogs into his little truck and took them to the pound. Now there's neither catcher nor pound. The dogs are considered a natural hazard, like wild boars and snakes.

I hope it doesn't make too much extra bother for you to have Suki laid up in bed. I'm sorry I was instrumental in bringing this on you. You're an angel, as always. Write me soon.

(*sent to Pamela Loeffler*)
You don't sound very sanguine about Sue's improvement. Of course she hasn't written me, but I can scarcely expect her to if she feels miserable. She knows you keep in touch.

So now Florence pays her visit, and unannounced. And naturally she defends herself with the story of the letter she sent from Santa Barbara, even though she saw that it hadn't arrived until three days after her own arrival. And of course she appears just when you've got Suky in bed sick. I know you say guests never bother you, but it always takes a lot of one's time to care for a sick person. I hope by now that sick person is on

her feet. It's almost a month since she came down with whatever she has.

Still the doctor doesn't want to commit himself on what's
wrong with her? After all the laboratory tests? I find that unheard-of, but apparently you don't, since you calmly quote
him as though he were Pasteur. This sort of thing strikes me
as one of the disadvantages of living in Kahului. You can see
that I'm not at home with illness. I'd much rather be ill myself than have to cope with a sufferer.

And you, are you all right? I'm sorry that Sue's holiday had
to end this way. I hope she's already on her way back to
Mount Holyoke.

In any case, I'll be waiting to hear from you. And tell me
more about Florence; she's always amused me. (At a distance.)

                                        (*sent to Pamela Loeffler*)
You're as bad as Suky herself, if not worse, for as far as I know
you're in good health, whereas I have to assume she's still in
bed, having heard nothing to the contrary. How can you let
an entire month go by without sending me some sort of
word? I'm not berating you, but I'm curious and *blessé* at the
same time. I get an indistinct impression that in spite of my
being what you call 'obsessed' by Suky, you think I don't care
deeply about her.

It's true that I don't really know her; I've never had the opportunity. But that's beside the point. I've taken on the responsibility for her education and I want it to go well. Surely
you can understand that.

As I was waking up this morning (a moment when things
of the distant past can suddenly reappear in detail) I recalled
the opening lines of two songs my mother used to sing when
I was very young. They were both songs of rejection, I now
realize. One went: 'Take back your gold, for gold will never
buy me', and the other, even more absurd: 'I don't want to
play in your yard; I don't love you any more.' According to
her, they were both very popular ditties. Have you ever heard
of either?

I'm in a hurry to get this off, because I have a forlorn hope
that in the event you haven't written, my pleas will make you

decide to do so. Consider this note to be one long supplication. Let me hear about Sue!

(sent to Pamela Loeffler)

Your postcard from Fiji was a slap in the face. You think I'll be 'amused' to see where you are, but I'm not. I'm astounded and exasperated that you should be dragging Sue off on a South Pacific trip when she should be in college. And I don't subscribe to your theory that such a voyage is a part of her convalescence. In fact, I think you don't believe it yourself. Obviously you imagine that old age makes people ingenuous. Or was that remark merely the first pretext that came to your mind? Do you find it incredible that having invested nervous energy, time and money in her education, I should want to see her complete it?

It goes without saying that this year is lost. It strikes me as an irresponsible act to gather the girl under your wing and fly off with her to God knows where and for God knows how long.

I suppose you won't receive this for many weeks. Tell S. that I'm disappointed to see how basically indifferent she is to her own well-being. Tell her I'm glad she's well (if indeed she ever was as ill as you gave me to believe) and tell her that when she gives a sign of life I'll reply. But she probably feels guilty and doesn't want to be in touch with me.

I'll get over my shock and indignation, but it won't be right away.

(sent to Pamela Loeffler)

In the past ten weeks I've had three postcards from you: from Fiji, Apia and Papeete, plus Sue's silly attempt at humour: 'Having wonderful time. Glad you're not here.' Tell her that message doesn't count. (Although it does show me it was only thanks to the security she felt in your presence that she was able to express her hostility toward me.) She'll have to write me a letter if she wants to hear from me.

If you've followed the schedule you outlined on your card from Papeete, you're back at home now. I'll expect to hear from you.

I'm still at a loss to understand why you went on that senseless trip. Perhaps when you're settled again you'll feel like explaining. Or perhaps you won't. It really doesn't matter. I think I perceive the general pattern.

(sent to Pamela Loeffler)

We seem to have arrived at an impasse: mutual misunderstandings due to IPI (insufficient preliminary information). You take exception to whatever I say. You're unreasonable. I get the impression that you two are arrayed against me. I can also see that S. confided in you completely, and at my expense. I did tell her you were generous, which you always have been.

My mistake with her, I think, was in advising her to destroy my letters. It was foolish because there was nothing incriminating in them, as I'm sure you're aware, having read them. But it must have set her to thinking, so that she now imagines I used her as a 'pawn' in my own 'financial planning'. It must be clear to you that this line of reasoning is unjustified. If it's not clear, there's nothing I can do about it, and it doesn't matter.

I had a brief note from Florence—the first in at least fifteen years. She wanted me to know what a fine time she'd had with you, and how much she liked Sue. Loved the climate, the landscape, the picnics and the bathing, and incidentally had not a word to say about anyone being sick in bed. According to her you all went everywhere together, and it was perfect. This deviates considerably from the official version.

(sent to Pamela Loeffler)

A few postmortem thoughts. You can tell S. that I've written her Aunt Emily West (who became her guardian when her parents died) informing her that her niece has left college and has an address in Hawaii where she can reach her. I've also been in touch with my lawyer in New York, explaining that my financial obligations to Susan Choate terminated with the end of her academic career, and asking him to cancel whatever future arrangements he had expected to make.

As to my writing S. herself, there doesn't seem to be any reason for it. She's made it very clear that she prefers not to hear from me. And what could I say at this point? 'I hope you won't regret your decision'? As you tell me, she already suspects that I disapprove of that decision, so that anything I might say would change suspicion to conviction. It would be hard to get her to believe that I have no objection to what she's doing. She probably prefers to imagine me as being scandalized by her behaviour; it would be more fun for her that way. She expects me to mind that things didn't work out in the way I thought they would. But that's only because she doesn't know me. What she must consider to be my archaic epistolary style has helped her to think of me as an opinionated and uncompromising old bastard.

Nevertheless, please believe me when I tell you that she can fall in love with a Japanese garage mechanic, sleep with you, and marry an orang-utan, and it will all be the same to me. There's not enough time in life for recriminations.

Too Far From Home

B Y DAY her empty room had four walls, and the walls enclosed a definite space. At night the room continued forever into the darkness.

"If there are no mosquitos why do we have mosquito nets?"

"The beds are low and we have to tuck ourselves in with the nets, so that our hands can't fall out and touch the floor," Tom said. "You don't know what might be crawling there."

The day she arrived, the first thing he did after showing her the room where she would sleep, was to take her on a tour of the house. It was dim and clean. Most of the rooms were empty. It seemed to her that the help occupied the greater part of the building. In one room five women sat in a row along the wall. She was presented to all of them. Tom explained that only two of them were employed in the house; the others were visitors. There was the sound of men's voices in another room, a sound which turned swiftly to silence at Tom's knock on the door. A tall, very black man in a white turban appeared. She had the instant impression that he resented her presence, but he bowed gravely. "This is Sekou," Tom told her. "He runs things around here. You might not guess it, but he's extremely bright." She glanced at her brother nervously; he seemed to know why. "Don't worry," he added. "Nobody knows a word of English here."

She could not go on talking about this man while she stood facing him. But when they were on the roof later, under the improvised awning, she continued the conversation. "What made you assume that I thought your man was stupid? I know you didn't say that; but you as much as said it. I'm not a racist, you know. Do *you* think he looks slow-witted?"

"I was just trying to help you see the difference between him and the others, that's all."

"Oh," she said. "There's an obvious difference, of course. He's taller, blacker, and with finer features than the others."

sanatorium. And who knows? Even that might not have done
the trick. And financially it would have been ausgeschlossen,
in any case. With Tom coming on his Guggenheim this
seemed perfect. The idea was to get away from everything
that could remind me in any way of what I'd been going
through. This is certainly the antithesis of New York and of
any place you can think of in the U.S.A. I was worried about
food, but so far neither of us has been sick. Probably the important thing is that the cook is civilized enough to believe
in the existence of bacteria, and is very careful to sterilize
whatever needs sterilizing. The Niger River Valley is no place
to come down with any disease. Fortunately we can get
French mineral water for drinking. If its delivery should be
cut off, or if it should not arrive in time, we'd have to drink
what there is here, boiled and with Halazone. All this may
sound silly, but living here makes one into a hypochondriac.
You may wonder why I don't describe the place, tell you
what it looks like. I can't. I don't believe I could be objective about it, which would mean that when I finished you'd
have less of an idea what it's like than before I started. You'll
have to wait until you see what Tom does with it, although
he hasn't yet painted any landscapes at all—only what he sees
in the kitchen: vegetables, fruit, fish, and a few sketches of
natives bathing in the river. You'll see it all when we get
back.

Elaine Duncan is such a nut. Imagine her asking me if I
don't miss Peter. How does a mind like that work? At first I
thought she was pulling my leg, but then I realized she was
perfectly serious. I suppose it's just her kind of sentimentality.
She knows what I was going through and what it cost me to
make the final decision. She also knows me well enough to realize that once I'd decided to get out of it, it was because I
understood I couldn't stay any longer with Peter, and most
assuredly wasn't of two minds about it. It's clear she's hoping
I regret having got out of the marriage. I'm afraid she's in for
a big disappointment. At last I feel free. I can have my own
thoughts, without anybody offering me a penny for them.
Tom works all day in silence, and doesn't notice whether I
talk or not. It's so refreshing to be with somebody who pays
no attention to you, doesn't notice whether you're there or

not. All feelings of guilt evaporate. This is all very personal, of course. But in a place like this you become autoanalytical.

I do hope you're completely recovered from the effects of the accident, and that you'll keep warm. Here it's generally just a little over a hundred degrees Fahrenheit. You can imagine how much energy I have!

Devotedly,
Anita

III

Nights were slow in passing. Sometimes as she lay in the silent blackness it seemed to her that the night had come down and seized the earth so tightly that daylight would be unable to show through. It could already be noon of the next day and no one would know it. People would go on sleeping as long as it remained dark, Tom in the next room, and Johara and the watchman whose name she never could remember, in one of the empty rooms across the courtyard. They were very quiet, those two. They retired early and they rose early, and the only sound she ever heard from their side of the house was an occasional dry cough from Johara. It bothered her that there was no door to her room. They had hung a dark curtain over the doorway between Tom's room and hers, so that the light of his roaring Coleman lamp would not bother her. He liked to sit up reading until ten o'clock, but immediately after the evening meal she was always somnolent, and had to go to bed, where she would sleep heavily for two or three hours before she awoke to lie in the dark, hoping that it was nearly morning. The crowing of cocks near and far was meaningless. They crowed at any time during the night.

In the beginning it had seemed quite natural that Johara and her husband should be black. In New York there had always been two or three black servants around the house. There she thought of them as shadows of people, not really at home in a country of whites, not sharing the same history or culture and thus, in spite of themselves, outsiders. Slowly, however, she had begun to see that these people here were masters of their surroundings, completely at home with the culture of the place. It was to be expected, of course, but it was something of a shock to realize that the blacks were the real people and that she was the shadow, and that even if she went on living here for the rest of her life she would never understand how their minds worked.

IV

Dear Elaine:

I should have written you ages ago when I first got here, but I've been under the weather for the past few weeks—not physically, really, except that the spirit and the flesh aren't separated. When I'm depressed, everything in my body seems to go to pieces. I suppose that's normal, perhaps it isn't. God knows.

It's true, when I first looked out at the flat land that went on and on to the horizon, I felt my depression dissolving in all that brightness. It didn't seem possible that there could be so much light. And the stillness that surrounded each little sound! You feel that the town is built on a cushion of silence. That was something new—an amazing sensation, and I was very conscious of it. I felt that all this was exactly what I needed, to get my mind off the divorce and the rest of the trouble. There was nothing that had to be done, no one I had to see. I was my own master, and didn't even have to bother with the servants if I didn't want to. It was like camping out in a big empty house. Of course in the end I did have to bother with the servants, because they did everything wrong. Tom would tell me: Leave them alone. They know what they're doing. I suppose they do know what they mean to do, but they don't seem to be able to do it. If I find fault with the food, the cook looks bewildered and aggrieved. This is because she knows she's famous in the Gao region as the woman whose cuisine pleases the Europeans. She listens and agrees, but in the manner of one soothing a deranged invalid. I suspect she thinks of me in just such terms.

By being completely aware of, and focusing his attention on the smallest details of the life going on around him, Tom manages to objectify the details, and so he remains outside, and far from them. He paints whatever is in front of his eyes at any moment, in the kitchen, or the market, or the edge of the river: vegetables and fruit being sliced, often with the knife still embedded in the flesh, bathers and fish from the Niger. My trouble is that this life sweeps me along with it in spite of me. I mean that I am being forced to participate in some sort of communal consciousness that I really hate. I don't know anything about these people. They're all black, but nothing like "our" blacks in the States. They're simpler, more friendly and straightforward, and at the same time very remote.

Something is wrong with night here. Logic would have it that night is only the time when the sky's door is open and one can look out on infinity, and thus that the spot from which one looks out is of no importance. Night is night, no matter from where perceived. Night here is no different from night somewhere else. It's only logic that says this. Day is huge and bright and it's impossible to see farther than the sun. I realize that by "here" I don't mean "here in the middle of the Sahara on the banks of the River Niger" but "here in this house where I'm living." Here in this house with the floors of smooth earth where the servants go barefoot and you never hear anyone coming until he's already in the room.

I've been trying to get used to this crazy life here, but it takes some getting used to, I can tell you. There are many rooms in the house. In fact, it's enormous, and the rooms are big. And they look even larger, without furniture, of course. There is no furniture at all except for the mats on the floors of the rooms where we sleep and our suitcases and the wardrobes where we hang the few clothes we have with us. It was because of these wardrobes that the house was available, because they made it count as a "furnished house," and that made the rent so high that no one wanted to take it. By our standards, of course, it's very cheap, and God knows it should be, with no electricity and no water, without even a chair to sit in or a table to eat at, or, for that matter, a bed to sleep in.

Naturally I knew it was going to be hot, but I hadn't imagined this sort of heat—solid, no change from day to day, no breeze. And remember, no water, so to take even a sponge bath is an entire production number. Tom is angelic about the water. He lets me have about all we can get hold of. He says females need more than men do. I don't know whether that's an insult or not, and I don't care as long as I can get the water. He also says it's not hot. But it is. I don't know how to convert Centigrade into Fahrenheit, but if you do, change 46° C into F., and you'll see that I'm right. 46° was what my thermometer registered this morning.

I don't know which is worse, day or night. In the daytime, of course, it's a little hotter, although not much. They don't believe in windows here, so the house is dark inside, and that gives you a shut-in feeling. Tom does a lot of his work on the roof in the sun. He claims he doesn't mind it, but I can't believe it's not bad for him. I know it would be the end of me if I sat up there the way he does, hours at a time and with no break.

I had to laugh when I read your question about how I felt after the divorce, whether I "still cared" a little for Peter. What a crazy question! How could I still care for him? The way I feel now, if I never see another man it will be too soon. I'm really fed up with their hypocrisy, and I'd willingly send them all to Hell. Not Tom, of course, because he's my brother, even though trying to live with him under these conditions isn't easy. But trying to live at all in this place is hard. You can't imagine how remote from everything it makes you feel.

The mail service here is not perfect. How could it be? But it's not impossible. I do get letters, so be sure and write me. After all, the post office is this end of the umbilical cord that keeps me attached to the world. (I almost added: *and to sanity.*)

I hope all is well with you, and that New York hasn't grown any worse than it was last year; although I'm sure it has.

Much love, and write.
Anita

v

At first there would be memories—small, precise images complete with the sounds and odors of a certain incident in a certain summer. They had not meant anything to her at the time of experiencing them, but now she strove desperately to stay with them, to relive them and not let them fade into the enveloping darkness where a memory lost its contours and was replaced by something else. The formless entities which followed on the memories were menacing because indecipherable, and her heartbeat and breathing accelerated at this point. "As though I'd had coffee," she thought, although she never drank it. Whereas a few moments earlier she had been living in the past, she was now fully surrounded by the present instant, face to face with a senseless fear. Her eyes would fly open, to fix on what was not there in the blackness.

She was not fond of the food, claiming that it was much too hot with red pepper and at the same time without flavor.

"And you realize," he said, "that we've got the most famous cook in these parts."

She remarked that it was hard to believe.

They were eating lunch on the roof, not in the sun, but in the vicious glare of a white sheet stretched above them. There was an expression of distaste on her face.

"I feel sorry for the girl who marries you," she said presently.

"It's an abstraction," he told her. "Don't even think about it. Let her pity herself once she's married to me."

"Oh, she will, all right. I can promise you that."

After a fairly long silence he looked at her.

"What's making you so belligerent all of a sudden?"

"Belligerent? I was just thinking how hard it is for you to show sympathy. You know I haven't been feeling too well lately. But have I ever noticed a shred of sympathy?" (She wondered, too late, if she ought to have made this admission.)

"You're perfectly well," he said, adopting his gruff manner.

VI

Dear Peg:

It's evident that Tom is doing everything in his power to keep any day from being exactly like the preceding one. He arranges a walk down to the river or a jaunt into "town," as he calls the nondescript collection of shacks around the market. No matter where we go, I'm expected to snap pictures. Some of it can be fun. The rest is tiring. It's quite clear that he does all this to keep me from boredom, which means it's a kind of therapy, which in turn means that he believes I might become a mental case and is afraid. This I find very troubling. It means that there is something between us that can't be mentioned. It's embarrassing and makes for tension. I'd like to be able to turn to him and say: "Relax. I'm not about to crack up." But I can pretty well imagine the disastrous effect such a straightforward statement would have. For him it would only be proof that I was not certain of my mental stability, and of course, all he needs to ruin his year is a jittery sister. Why should there be any question of my being in anything but the best of health? I suppose it's simply because I'm terrified that he'll suspect I'm not. I can't bear the idea of being a spoilsport, or of his thinking that I am.

We were walking, Tom and I, along the edge of the river yesterday. A wide beach of hard dirt. He tries to get me to walk nearer the water where the ground is softer, saying it's easier on the bare feet. God knows what parasites live in this water. It seems dangerous enough to me to go barefoot anywhere around here, without going into the water. Tom has very little patience with me when I take care of myself. He claims it's just part of my generally negative approach to life. Being used to his critical remarks, I let them slide off my duck's back. He did say one thing which stuck in my mind, which was that extreme self-centeredness invariably caused dissatisfaction and poor health. It's clear he considers me a paragon of egocentricity. So today when I went up onto the roof I faced him with it. The dialogue went something like this:

"You seem to be under the impression that I'm incapable of being interested in anything besides myself."

"Yes. That's the impression I'm under."

"Well, you don't have to be so cavalier about it."

"As long as we've started this conversation we might as well push ahead with it. Tell me then; what are you interested in?"

"When you're asked point-blank like that, it's hard to pluck something out of the air, you know."

"But don't you see that that means you can't think of anything? And that's because you have no interests. Apparently you don't realize feigning interest, kindles interest. Like the old French saying about love being born through making the gestures of love."

"So you think salvation lies in pretending?"

"Yes, and I'm serious. You've never yet looked at my work, much less thought about it."

"I've looked at everything you've done here."

"Looked at. But seen?"

"How do you expect me to appreciate your paintings? I have a poor visual sense. You know that."

"I don't care whether you appreciate them, or even like them. We're not talking about my paintings. We're talking about you. That's just a small example. You could take an interest in the servants and their families. Or how the architecture in the town fits the exigencies of the climate. I realize that's a pretty ridiculous suggestion, but there are a thousand things to care about."

"Yes, if you care in the first place. Hard to do if you don't."

I knew (or felt pretty certain) when I agreed to come here that I was letting myself in for something unpleasant. I realize that I'm writing now as though there had been some dreadful occurrence, when as a matter of fact nothing whatever has happened. And let's hope it doesn't.

Lots of love.

Anita

VII

Hi, Ross! The enclosed shows the view looking south from the roof. It certainly is a lot of nothing. Yet it's strange how one lone man in such a vast landscape takes on importance. It's not a place I'd recommend to anybody. I didn't recommend it even to Anita; she just came. I think she's happy here—that is, as much as she's ever happy. Some days she's crankier than usual, but I disregard that. I don't think she enjoys celibate life. Too bad she didn't think of that before she came. Myself, I do very little besides work. I can feel it's going well. It would take a major act of God to stop me at this point.

Tom

VIII

One morning when she had finished her breakfast and set her tray on the floor beside her bed, she ran up onto the roof for a little sunlight and fresh air. Normally she was careful not to climb up because Tom sat there most of the day, generally not working, merely sitting. When she once had been thoughtless enough to inquire what he was doing, instead of answering "Communing with nature" or "meditating" as more pretentious painters might have replied, he said: "Getting ideas." This directness was tantamount to expressing a desire for privacy; so she respected that privacy and seldom went up onto the roof. This morning he gave no sign of minding. "I heard the call to prayer this morning for the first time," she told him. "It was still dark."

"Yes, you can sometimes hear that one," he said, "when there's no other sound to cover it."

"It was sort of comforting. Made me feel that things were under control."

He did not seem to be paying attention. "Listen, Nita, you could do me a great favor, if you will. Yes?"

"Well, sure," she said, with no idea of what was coming next. It was something she was not expecting, given his unusual manner of prefacing it.

"Could you go into town and get some films? I want to take a lot more pictures. You know Mother's been asking for shots of you and me together. I've got plenty of photos, but not of us. I'd go myself, but I can't spare the time. It's not nine yet. The shop that sells films is on the other side of the market. They don't shut until ten."

"But Tom, you seem to forget that I don't know my way anywhere."

"Well, Sekou'll go with you. You won't get lost. Tell them you want black and white."

"I know Mother'd rather have them in color."

"You're right. Old people and kids like color better. Get two rolls of color and two black and white. Sekou's waiting for you by the front door."

She was sorry she needed a guide to show her the shop, and even more sorry that the guide had to be the black man she had already decided was hostile toward her. But it was still early and the air in the street would feel relatively fresh.

"Don't wear those sandals," Tom told her, continuing to work, not looking up. "Wear thick socks and regular shoes. God knows what germs are in the dust."

So she stood at the door in the prescribed footgear, and Sekou came across the courtyard and greeted her in French. His wide smile made her think that perhaps she had been mistaken, that he did not resent her presence in the house after all. And suppose he does? she thought defiantly. There was a limit to the depth at which one could decently bury one's ego. Beyond that depth the whole game of selflessness became abject. She knew it was in her nature to refuse to admit being a "person." It was so much simpler to hide in the shadow of neutrality, even when there was no possibility of a confrontation. One could scarcely care about the reactions of an African servant. For in spite of what Tom had told her, she still thought of Sekou as a kind of servant—a factotum, perhaps with the stature of a jester.

It was an insane thing to be doing, walking along the main street of the town, side by side with this tall black man. An unlikely couple, God knows. The idea of being photographed at the moment made her smile. If she were to send a copy of such a picture to her mother she knew more or less what the reply would be. "The ultimate in exoticism." She certainly did not feel that this street was exotic or picturesque: it was dirty and squalid.

"He may try to make conversation," she thought, and determined to pretend not to understand. Then she would have only to smile and shake her head. Presently he did say something which, since she had already decided that there were to be no words between them, she failed to understand. An instant later she heard his phrase with its interrogatory inflection, and realized that he had said: "*Tu n'as pas chaud?*" He had slowed his gait; he was waiting for her reply.

"The hell with it," she thought, and so she answered his question, but indirectly. Rather than saying: "Yes, I am hot," she said: "It's hot."

Now he stopped walking altogether, and indicated, on their left, an improvised nook between piles of crates, where a table and two chairs had been placed. A large sign was laid across the entire space, creating an inviting area of shade, which quickly grew to be irresistible once one had even entertained the possibility of stepping in and sitting down.

Obsessively, her thoughts turned to her mother. What would be her reaction if she could see her only daughter sitting beside a black man in this dark little refuge? "If he takes advantage of you, remember that you asked for it. It's just tempting Providence. You can't treat people like that as equals. They don't understand it."

The drink was Pepsi Cola, surprisingly cold, but unusually sweet. "Ah," she said, appreciative.

Sekou's fluent French put her to shame. "How can this be?" she thought, with a certain indignation. Being conscious of her own halting French made it more difficult to engage in conversation. These empty moments when neither of them had anything to say made the silence more apparent, and for her more embarrassing. The sounds of the street—footsteps on the sand, children running and now and then a dog's bark, were curiously muted by the piles of crates and the covering overhead. It was an astonishingly quiet town, she reflected. Since they had left the house she had not heard the sound of one automobile, even in the distance. But now, as she became aware of listening, she could discern the far-off alternative whining and braying of a motorcycle, sounds she particularly disliked.

Sekou rose and went to pay the owner. She had meant to do that, but now it seemed quite impossible. She thanked him. Then they were back in the street, and the air was hotter than ever. This was the moment to ask herself why she had allowed Tom to send her off on this absurd errand. It would have been better, she thought, if she had gone to the kitchen and asked the cook not to serve fried potatoes. The woman seemed to consider potatoes, no matter how prepared, a succulent dish, but those available here did not lend themselves to any mode of cooking save perhaps mashing. She had mentioned this to Tom on various occasions, but his opinion was that mashing would be more work for Johara, and that most likely she would not know how to perform the operation properly, so that the result would be less tasty than what she served now.

The insane noise of the motorcycle in imitation of a siren came from a good deal nearer at present. "It's coming this way," she thought. If only we could get to the market before it arrives. She had been once with Tom to buy food, and she remembered the colonnades and pillars. No motorcycle could roar through there. "Where *is* the market?" she demanded suddenly. Sekou gestured. "Ahead."

Now the dragonlike machine was visible, far up the long street, bouncing and raising a cloud of dust which seemed partly to precede it. Even that far away she could see pedestrians bolting and scurrying to keep out of its way.

The noise was growing unbelievably loud. She had an impulse to cover her ears, like a child. The thing was coming. It was coming straight at them. She jumped to the side of the road just as the motorcyclist braked to avoid hitting Sekou straight on. He had refused to duck and escape its impact. The flamboyant vehicle lay in the dust, partially covering the bare legs and arms of the riders. Two nearly naked youths pulled themselves up, holding their red and yellow helmets in their hands. They glared and shouted at Sekou. She was not surprised to hear American speech.

"You blind?"

"You're one lucky son of a bitch. We could have killed you."

As Sekou paid no attention to them, but continued to walk, they became abusive.

"A real downhome uppity nigger."

Sekou ignored the two with supreme aplomb.

From her side of the road Anita stepped forth to face them. "If we're going to talk about who might be killed by your impossible apparatus, I'm first on the list. You came straight at me. Isn't that what's known as sowing panic? Does it make you feel better to frighten people?"

"Sorry we scared you, ma'am. That wasn't what we had in mind."

"I'll bet it wasn't." Now being startled had turned to being indignant. "I'll bet what you had in mind was one big zero." She had not heard the apology. "You've gone too far from home, my friends, and you're going to have trouble."

A leer. "Oh yeah?"

She could feel her anger pushing up inside her. "Yeah!" she cried. "Trouble! And I hope I'll have a chance to see it." A moment later she spat: "Monsters."

Sekou, who had not even glanced at them once, now stopped and turned to see if she were coming. As she caught up with him, he remarked without looking at her that tourists were always ignorant.

When they got to the shop that sold films, she was surprised to find it being run by a middle-aged French woman. If Anita had not been breathless with rage and excitement, she would have liked to engage the woman in conversation: to ask how long she had been living here and what her life was like. The moment was not propitious for such a move.

As they walked back toward the house in the increasing heat, there was no sign or sound of the hellish machine. She noticed that Sekou was limping a bit, and looked carefully at him. There was blood on the lower part of his white robe, and she realized that the motorcycle had collided with his leg. Her appraisal seemed to annoy him; she could not bring herself to ask to see the injury, or even to speak of it.

IX

At lunch she avoided all mention of the motorcycle accident.

"It wasn't too far, was it?"

"It was hot," she replied.

"I've been thinking," Tom said at length. "This house would be so cheap to buy. It would be worthwhile. I wouldn't mind coming here regularly."

"I think you'd be out of your mind!" she cried. "You could never really live here. It's an uncomfortable temporary campsite, nothing more. Anyway, whatever property you buy in a third-world country is lost before you even pay for it. You know that. Renting makes sense. Then when things go crazy, you're free."

Johara stood beside her, offering her more creamed onions. She served herself.

"Things don't always go crazy," Tom said.

"Oh, yes they do!" she cried. "In these countries? It's inescapable."

After a bit, she went on. "Well, of course. You'll do as you please. I don't suppose you'd lose much."

While they were having fruit, Anita volunteered: "I dreamed of Mother last night."

"You did?" said Tom without interest. "What was she doing?"

"Oh, I can't even remember. But when I woke up I began thinking about her. You know she had absolutely no sense of humor, and yet she could be very funny. I remember she was giving a rather fancy dinner one night, and suddenly she turned to you and said: 'How old are you, Tom?' And you said: 'Twenty-six.' She waited a little, and then said: 'When William the Silent was your age he had conquered half of Europe.' And she sounded so disgusted that everyone at the table burst out laughing. Do you remember? I still think that's funny, although I'm sure she didn't mean it to be."

"I wouldn't be too sure. I think she was playing to the gallery. She couldn't laugh herself, naturally. Too dignified. But she wasn't above making others laugh."

X

Another day they sat on the floor having breakfast in Tom's room. The cook had just brought them more toast.

"I'd like to drive a few miles down the river and have a look at the next village," said Tom, signalling to the cook to wait. "How about it? I can rent Bessier's old truck. How does that strike you?"

"I'm game," she said. "The road's straight and flat, isn't it?"

"We won't get lost. Or stuck in the sand."

"Is there something special you want to see?"

"I just need to see something else. The smallest change gives me all sorts of new ideas."

They agreed to go the following day. When he asked Johara to prepare them a *casse-croûte*, she became excited upon hearing that they planned to go to Gargouna. Her sister lived there, she said, and she gave Tom instructions as to how to find her house, along with messages she hoped he would deliver.

The little truck had no cabin. They were cooled by the breeze they created. It was stimulating to be driving along the edge of the river in the early morning air. The road was completely flat, with no potholes or obstacles.

"It's fine now," said Tom, "but it won't be so good coming back, with nothing between us and the sun."

"We've got our topis," she reminded him, glancing at the two helmets on the seat between them. She had with her a pair of powerful field glasses, bought in Kobe the previous year, and in spite of the movement she kept them trained on the river where men fished and women bathed.

"It's nice, isn't it?" said Tom.

"It's certainly a lot prettier with the black bodies than it would be if they were all whites."

This was only moderate enthusiasm, but it seemed to please him. He was very eager for her to appreciate the Niger Valley. But at the moment he was intent on not passing the road on the left that led to Gargouna. "Fifty kilometres, more or less," he murmured. Soon he said: "Here it is, but I'm not going to risk that sand." He stopped the truck and shut off the motor. The silence was overpowering. They sat without moving. Occasionally there was a cry from the river, but the open and wide landscape made the voices sound like birdcries.

"One of us has to stay with the car, and that's you."

Tom jumped down. "I'm going to do it on foot, find the village and Johara's sister. It ought to take ten minutes, not much more. You'll be all right here, won't you?" They had not seen another vehicle since setting out. "We're right in the middle of the road," she told him.

"I know, but if I move off to the right, I'll be in the sand. That's the one thing I don't want. If it makes you nervous, get out and walk around. It's not hot yet."

She was not afraid to have been left alone, but she was nervous. This was one occasion when Tom could have brought along one of the several men who spent their days sitting in the kitchen. It suddenly occurred to her that she had not seen Sekou since the day of the motorcycle incident, and this made her wonder how badly his leg or foot had been hurt. Thinking of him, she got down and began to walk along the same path Tom had taken. She could not see him ahead, because the region was one of low dunes with occasional thorn bushes. She wondered why it was impossible for the sky here to be really blue, why instead it always had a grey tinge.

Thinking that she might get a glimpse of Gargouna, she climbed one of the small hills of sand, but had a view only of rather larger thorn bushes ahead. She was particularly eager to see the village; she could imagine it: a group of circular huts lying fairly far apart, each with a cleared space around it, where poultry pecked in the sand. She turned to the right, where the dunes appeared to be somewhat higher, and followed a kind of path which led over and around them. There were little valleys between the dunes, some of them quite deep. The crests of the dunes all seemed to run parallel to each other, so that it was difficult to get from one dune to the next without going down and then climbing immediately. There was one dune not far ahead which dominated the others, and from which she felt certain she could see the truck waiting in the road. She reached it and stood atop it, a bit breathless. With the aid of the field glasses she saw that the truck was there, and to the left in the distance there were a few leafless trees. The village was in that direction, she supposed. Then, looking across into the depression between two dunes, she saw something that accelerated the beating of her heart, a senseless sculpture in vermillion enamel and chromium. There were large boulders down there; the cycle had skidded, hurling the suntanned torsos against the rocks. The machine was twisted grotesquely and the two bodies were jumbled together and uniformly spattered with blood. They were not in a condition to call for help; they lay motionless there in the declivity, invisible to all save to one who might stand exactly where she was standing. She turned and ran quickly down the side of the dune. "Monsters," she muttered, but without indignation.

She was sitting in the truck when Tom returned. "Did you find her, Johara's sister?"

"Oh, yes. It's a tiny village. Everybody knows everybody, of course. Let's eat. Here or down the shore?"

Her heart was still beating rapidly and with force. She said: "Let's go down to the river. There might be a little breeze down there." She was surprised now to recall that her first feeling upon seeing the wreck of the motorcycle had been one of elation. She could still induce the little chill of pleasure that had run through her at that instant. As they walked along the shore, she was thankful once again that she had never mentioned to Tom the confrontation with the two Americans.

XI

"Are you sleeping better now?" Tom asked her.

She hesitated. "Not really."

"What do you mean, not really?"

"I have a problem," she sighed.

"A problem?"

"Oh, I might as well tell you."

"Of course."

"Tom, I think Sekou comes to my room at night."

"What?" he cried. "You're crazy. What do you mean, he comes to your room?"

"Just that."

"What does he do? Does he say anything?"

"No, no. He just stands beside my bed in the dark."

"That's insane."

"I know."

"You've never seen him?"

"How could I? It's pitch dark."

"You've got a flashlight."

"Oh, that terrifies me more than anything. To turn it on and actually see him. Who knows what he'd do then, once he knew I'd seen him."

"He's not a criminal. God, why are you so damned nervous? You're safer here than you would be anywhere back in New York."

"I believe you," she said. "But that's not the point."

"What *is* the point? You think he comes and stands by your bed. Why do you think he does that?"

"That's the worst part of all. I can't tell you. It's too frightening."

"Why? Do you think he's planning to rape you?"

"Oh, no! It's nothing like that. What I feel is that he's *willing* me to dream. He's willing me to dream a dream I can't bear."

"A dream about him?"

"No. He's not even in the dream."

Tom was exasperated. "But what is this? What are we talking about, finally? You say Sekou wants you to have a certain dream, and you have it. So then he comes the next night, and you're afraid you'll have it again. According to you, why does he do this? I mean, what interest would he have in doing it?"

"I don't know. That makes it more horrible. I know you think it's ridiculous. Or you think I'm imagining it all."

"No, I don't say that. But since you've never seen anything, how can you be sure it's Sekou and not somebody else?"

Later in the day he said to her, "Anita, are you taking vitamins?"

She laughed. "Lord, yes. Dr. Kirk gave me all kinds. Vitamins and minerals. He said the soil here probably was deficient in mineral salts. Oh, I'm sure you think I have some sort of chemical imbalance that causes the dreaming. That could be. But it isn't the dream itself that scares me. Although God knows it's too repulsive to talk about."

He interrupted. "Is it sexual?"

"If it were," she said, "it would be a lot easier to describe. The thing is, I *can't* describe it." She shuddered. "It's too confusing. And it makes me feel sick to think of it."

"Maybe you should let me be your analyst. What happens during the dream?"

"Nothing happens. I only know something terrible is on its way. But as I say, it's not the dream that bothers me. It's knowing I'm being obliged to have it, knowing that black man is standing there inventing it and forcing me into it. That's too much."

XII

A wooden sign, nailed above a wooden door, with the words *Yindall & Fambers, Apothecaries* painted on it. Inside, a counter, an athletic young man standing behind it. At first glance he looks naked, but he is wearing red and blue shorts. Instead of saying: "Hi, I'm Bud," he says: "I'm Mr. Yindall. May I help you?" The voice is dry and grey.

"I want a small bottle of Sweet Spirits of Nitre and a box of Slippery Elm lozenges."

"Right away." But something is wrong with his face. He turns to go into the back room, hesitates. "You haven't come to see Mr. Yindall, have you?"

"But you said you were Mr. Yindall."

"He gets mixed up sometimes. As a rule he doesn't admit people."

"I didn't say I wanted to see him."

"But you do." He reaches across the counter, and a hand of steel takes hold. "He's waiting in the basement. Fambers speaking."

"I don't want to see Mr. Yindall, thank you."

"It's too late to say that."

A portion of the counter is on hinges. He lifts it up to allow passage, still pressing with a hand of steel.

Protestations all the way to the cellar. A chromium throne against one wall shining in the glare of spotlights trained upon it. Two muscular thighs growing from a man's shoulders, the legs bent at the knees. Between the thighs a thick neck from which the head has been severed. The arms, attached to the hips, hang loosely, the fingers twitching.

"This is Mr. Fambers. He can't see you, of course. His head had to be removed. It got in the way. But his neck is filled with highly sensitive protoplasm. If you bite it or even nibble it, you establish instant communication. Just lean over and push your mouth into his neck."

The hand of steel guides. The substance inside the neck feels like water-soaked bread, its slightly sulfurous odor is like that of turnips.

"Push with your tongue. Don't gag."

At the first pressure of the tongue, the substance in the neck pulses, bubbles, splashes warm liquid upward.

"It's only blood. I think you'd better stay here a while."

"No, no, no, no!" Rolling in her vomit on the floor.

"No, no, no!" Trying to rub the blood from her lips and face.

Down, down, blood and all, vomit and all, into the feather-bedded floor. Only the turnip stench to breathe in an airless pocket. Then, choking, having been smothered, she rose from below and breathed deeply of the open black air around her, sickened by the nature of the dream, certain that it would be repeated, terrified above all by the thought that the orders governing this phenomenon should be coming from without, from another mind. This was unacceptable.

XIII

Tom found her reasoning faulty. "You had a nightmare, and of course that's not something to worry about. But to be obsessed by the idea that Sekou or anyone else is in charge of your dreams is pure paranoia. It's based on nothing at all. Can't you see that?"

"I can see how *you* think that, yes."

"I'm convinced that once you told it, all of it, it would stop worrying you."

"It makes me feel like throwing up just to think of it."

The steady burning of the pressure lamp between them on the floor inspired Anita to exclaim: "It's too bright, too noisy, and too hot."

"Don't pay it any attention. Forget about it."

"It's rather hard to do that."

"You know if I turn it down we won't be able to see anything."

After a moment she said: "These vegetables here are really abject. I don't understand you. You paint practically nothing but food, yet you don't care what you eat."

"What d'you mean, I don't care? I care very much. I don't complain, if that's what you're expecting. The vegetables here are what there is, unless you want French canned food, which, knowing you, I don't believe you do. I think it's a miracle they can get even this much out of the sand."

Suddenly Johara was in the room; she announced the next course.

"I didn't hear her come upstairs, did you?"

She snorted. "With this lamp going you wouldn't hear an elephant."

"No, but even without the lamp, have you noticed that you never hear any footsteps in this house?"

She laughed. "I'm only too aware of it. That's part of what bothers me at night. I've never heard a sound in my room when it's night. Any number of people could be there and I wouldn't know it."

Tom said nothing; his mind obviously was on something else. For a few minutes they sat in silence. When she began to speak again, her voice made it clear that she had been ruminating.

"Tom, did you ever hear of slippery elm?"

He sat up straight. "Of course. Granny used to swear by it for sore throat. They put it out in tablets, like cough-drops. I remember how upset she was when they stopped manufacturing them. I doubt that slippery elm exists today in any form."

He stole a glance at her, suspecting that this was her devious way of dealing with the material of the dream. He waited.

Her next question struck him as comic. "Isn't saltpeter what they put into prisoners' food?"

"They used to, I don't know whether they do nowadays. What are you doing, preparing a compendium of useless knowledge?"

"No, I just wondered."

He arranged the cushions behind him and stretched out.

"You want to know who I think Sekou is?" he asked her.

"How do you mean, who he is?"

"Who he is for you, I mean. I think he's Mother."

"What?" she cried, very loud.

"I'm serious. I remember how Mother used to come and stand beside my bed in the dark, and just stand there. And I was always terrified she'd know I was awake. So I had to breathe calmly and not move a muscle. And she used to do the same thing by your bed. I'd hear her go into your room. Didn't you ever find her there, right beside your bed, standing perfectly still?"

"I don't remember. It's a pretty crazy idea, to have a black African play the role of your mother."

"You're just looking at it from the outside. But I'm willing to bet it's a guilt dream, and who's the one who always makes you feel guilty? Mother, every time."

"I'm not a Freudian," she told him. "But even if you admit—which I don't for a minute—that the dream comes from feeling guilt, and that I'm remembering Mother from when I was little, it gets nowhere in explaining why I'm so sure Mother's being played by Sekou. Haven't you got a theory for that?"

"A very good one. There's just no connection between what's in the dream and why you think you dream it. Try putting Sekou into the dream when you go over it in your mind, and see how he reacts."

"I never go over it in my mind. It's bad enough to have to experience it without playing around with it when I'm awake."

"Well, all I can say, Nita, is that it'll go on bothering you until you pull it to pieces and examine it carefully."

"The day I decide what I'm guilty of, I'll tell you."

XIV

Everyone in the town knew of Mme. Massot. She and her husband had lived there when the French ruled the region. Then, just after Independence, when Mme. Massot was not yet twenty years old, her husband had died, leaving her with a photographer's studio and very little else. She had a darkroom and she had learned how to develop and print photographs. Having a monopoly on this service was not as remunerative as it might have been elsewhere, for there was very little call for it. Of late the number of young people with cameras had increased, so that she not only developed and printed, but sold film as well. A few young natives who had lived in Europe repeatedly tried to persuade her to stock video tapes, but she explained that she did not have the capital to invest.

After the death of Monsieur Massot she had briefly entertained the idea of returning to France, but she soon decided that she did not really want to do that. Life in Montpellier would be a good deal more expensive, and there was no guarantee that she would find a suitable place to live, with an extra room to be used as a darkroom.

Only a handful of white people found it strange that she was willing to stay on alone in a city of blacks. As for her, from the day of her arrival directly after her marriage, she had found the black people sympathetic, kind, generous and well-disposed. She could find no fault in them save a tendency to be careless about time. Often they seemed not to know either the hour or the day. The younger citizens were aware that Europeans considered this a defect in their countrymen, and did their utmost to be punctual when they were dealing with foreigners. Although Mme. Massot was cordial with the other French inhabitants, she had established her particular friendships with the families of the native bourgeoisie. She had never learned to speak any of the local tongues, but these people spoke a passable French, and their sons were surprisingly proficient in the language. Seldom did she find herself wishing to be in France, and then only fleetingly. The climate here was pleasant if one did not mind the heat, which she did not, and with her asthmatic condition it was ideal. People in Europe continually surprised her by assuming that the city must be dirty and unhealthy, and very likely she surprised them by maintaining that the streets were cleaner and more free of objectionable odors than those of any European city. She knew how to live in the desert, and she managed to remain in excellent health all during the year. The difficult months were May and June, when the heat became trying and the wind covered one with sand if one went outside, and July and August, when rain fell and the air was damp, and reminded her that she had suffered from asthma in her early days.

Before Anita's arrival Mme. Massot and Tom had become friends, principally, he supposed, because she had worked for a year at a small art gallery in the rue Vignon, and being unusually aware had absorbed a good deal of painter lore during that time, all of which had remained with her since then. She was still able to discuss the private lives of several painters of the era and the prices fetched by their canvases, and Tom found this appealing. Her year in Paris had made a kind of gossip between them possible. He thought now of inviting her once again for a meal. This was always a risky undertaking because she was an expert cook, particularly of local dishes using native ingredients. Unlike many autodidacts she was not averse to sharing her discoveries with anyone who had the same interest in cooking as she. With her encouragement Tom had learned to prepare two or three dishes successfully.

"I'll have her for lunch on Monday," he told Anita. "And you can do me a great favor once again if you go to her shop and invite her. You can get some films at the same time. You know the way now, so you won't need anybody to go with you. Do you mind? I'd lose a morning's work if I went."

"I don't mind. But I should think a little exercise would be good for you."

"I get my exercise running on the shore before breakfast. You know that. I don't need more. So you tell Mme. Massot we'll expect her for lunch Monday, will you? She speaks English."

"You forget I majored in French."

She had no desire to walk through the town, but she rose, saying, "Well, I'm off while the air is only at blood temperature."

When she came to the stand where she and Sekou had sat and had cold drinks, she found it shut. She had not been eager to come on this errand for Tom because she had a superstitious conviction that the encounter with the two American barbarians might repeat itself. She even found herself listening for the detestable sound of their motorcycle in the distance. Before she got to the market she decided that the two had left the town and gone to another place where they could terrify a new lot of natives, the people here undoubtedly having grown used to their presence.

Mme. Massot seemed to be delighted with the invitation. "How's Tom?" she said. "You came to the shop not long ago, but I haven't seen Tom in a very long time."

Back in the house she climbed to the roof where Tom was working, and told him: "She'll come Monday. Is she a dyke, d'you think?"

Tom cried: "Good Lord! How would I know? I never asked her. Where'd you get such an idea?"

"I don't know. It just occurred to me as we were talking. She's so serious."

"I'd be very surprised if she were."

Recently the air had been charged with dust, and each day there seemed to be more of it. Apparently it was politer to call it sand, or so Tom said, but he agreed that if it was sand, it was pulverized sand, which is another term for dust. There was no avoiding it. Certain downstairs rooms let less of it in, but the doors could not really be shut, and the powder was being propelled by a constant wind which carried it into the narrowest spaces.

XV

When Monday came, the dust had reached such a state of opacity that from the roof it was impossible to distinguish forms in the street below. Tom decided that they would have to eat in one of the downstairs rooms with the door shut. "It'll be claustrophobic," he said, "but what else can we do?"

"I know one thing we can do," Anita told him. "Not to-day, but fast, just the same. And that's to get out of this town. Think of our lungs. We might as well be living in a coal mine. And it's going to start raining soon. Then what do we have? Mud City. You've always said the place was uninhabitable half the year."

Mme. Massot was shown upstairs by a kitchen maid, light-ing the way in the gloom with a guttering candle. She held in front of her what looked like a shoe box, which she immedi-ately presented to Tom.

"The herbs I promised you," she said. "Only it's a little late to be giving them to you now."

He opened the box. Inside, it was divided into three small compartments, all filled with black earth, out of which grew small fringes and feathers of green. "Oregano, marjoram and tarragon," she said, pointing. "But you have to keep the box covered at this season. The sand will choke the plants."

"I love it," Anita volunteered, examining the box. "It's like a little portable garden."

"I keep all my herbs inside the house and covered up."

"We should have made this appointment two weeks ago," Tom said. "I hate to think of you walking all the way through this hellish weather. And how do you manage to arrive here looking so unruffled, so svelte and chic?"

Anita had been thinking exactly that. Mme. Massot was impeccably clothed in a khaki ensemble, clearly something de-signed for use in the desert, but which would have been equally elegant on the rue de Faubourg St. Honoré. "Ah," she said, unwinding the turban from her head and shaking it. "The secret is that Monsieur Bessier passed me in the market and drove me straight here in his truck. So it was a question of two minutes rather than forty."

"What a fantastic garment!" Anita cried with enthusiasm, stretching forth her hand to touch the lower part. "Do you mind?"

Mme. Massot raised her arms behind her head to facilitate the examination. "It's really an adaptation of Saharan serrouelles combined with the local boubou," she explained. "It's my own invention."

"It's absolutely perfect," Anita told her. "But you didn't get the material here."

"No, no. I got it in Paris, and had it made up there. I'm not very good with a needle and thread. But the design is so simple that I'm convinced a local tailor could make a copy easily. The trick is in the cutting on the bias, so that the top seems to be a part of the trousers, and the whole thing, from the shoulders to the ankles, is one line, seamless."

"It's certainly the right color for today," Tom told her.

"I don't mind the weather," she said. "This is the price we have to pay for what we get the rest of the year. It's a nuisance, but I find it a challenge. That doesn't mean that I don't often rush off to France at this time of the year, because I do. My brother has a farm not far from Narbonne. Summer in Provence is lovely. But you know, I'm here today primarily to see your pictures."

"Yes." Tom looked unhappy. "Too bad you can't see them by daylight, but it'll have to be downstairs, and by pressure lamp. I can't unpack them up here with this dust and sand."

Lunch was announced by Johara, and the same kitchen maid guided them down the dark stairway, holding her candle aloft. "It's really a shame," Anita remarked, "having to eat down here. It's so much pleasanter on the terrace under the awning. But there's certainly no help for it."

As she ate, Mme. Massot demanded suddenly: "Who is responsible for this delicious food, monsieur? You?"

"I'm afraid not. It was Johara."

"How lucky you are to have that woman. As soon as you're gone, I'm going to try to get her."

"But you don't need her. You can prepare any dish you want by yourself."

"Yes, if I don't mind spending the entire day in the kitchen. Besides, it's less of a pleasure to eat the food one has cooked oneself."

"I imagine she'll be delighted to go from one job directly to another," said Tom.

"Oh, you never know with these people. They're not greedy. They're not ambitious. What seems to be most important for them is their relationship with their employer. He may be impossibly severe or completely casual. If they like him, they like him. This dish is superb," she went on. "I know how it's made, but I haven't had much luck with it so far."

"How *is* it made?" asked Tom.

"The base is tiny millet cakes. The caramel sauce is no problem, but the cream over it is a bit difficult. It's the white meat of the coconut, macerated in a little of the coconut milk. It's hard to get the right consistency. But your cook has done it to perfection."

Tom was busy removing his paintings from the metal case in which he kept them. "I'll just bring out the most recent things. I think they're the best, anyway."

"Oh, no!" objected Mme. Massot. "I want to see everything. Whatever you've done here, in any case."

"That would take all night. You don't realize how prolific I am."

"Just show me what you want to show me, and I'll be happy." He passed her a sheaf of gouaches done on paper.

She studied each piece intently and at length. Suddenly she cried out in delight. "But these paintings are phenomenal! Of a subtlety! And of a beauty! Let me see more! They're like nothing I've ever seen, I assure you."

As she continued to look, from time to time she murmured: "*Invraisemblable.*"

Anita, until now a spectator, spoke. "Show her *La Boucle du Niger*," she urged Tom. "Can you get at it? I think it's one of the most successful of all."

He seemed annoyed by her declaration. "In what way successful?"

"I love the landscape on the far side of the river," she explained.

"I'll come to it," he said gruffly. "I've got them arranged the way I want them."

Mme. Massot continued to study the pictures. "I begin to understand your method," she murmured. "It's very clever. Often a question of letting pure chance in one detail decide the treatment of the entire painting. You remain flexible up to the final moment. Isn't that true?"

"Sometimes," he agreed, noncommittally. A moment later he said: "I think that's enough to give you an idea of what I've been doing here."

Mme. Massot's eyes shone. "You're a genius! You'll surely have an enormous success with these. They're irresistible."

When Johara had cleared away the coffee cups, Mme. Massot rose. "I still intend to try to get that woman when you've gone," she told them. "You're going this week?"

"As soon as we can get out," Anita said.

"Let's go upstairs and see how the weather is behaving," Tom suggested. "You haven't got Monsieur Bessier to drive you home."

"He and Mme. Massot walked to the door. "You coming?" he asked Anita. She shook her head, and he shut the door from the outside.

They were gone longer than was necessary for determining whether or not the wind had diminished. She sat in the shut-in room, feeling that the lunch had been a waste of time. When they came down, Mme. Massot was insisting that it was unnecessary for Tom to accompany her home. Anita saw, however, that he was determined to go with her. "But everyone knows me here," she was objecting, "and it's not yet dark. No one would think of bothering me. Anyway, the wind has died down and there's practically no dust in the air. Do stay here."

"I wouldn't dream of it."

XVI

When Mme. Massot had made a somewhat formal adieu to Anita, they went out, and Anita hurried upstairs onto the roof, to breathe some fresh air. The wind was no longer raging, and the town's soft landscape of mud was once more visible. It was very quiet; only an occasional dog barked to pierce the silence.

The knowledge that very soon she would be leaving buoyed up her spirits, so that she was able to feel a certain sense of responsibility vis-à-vis the house. It seemed to her that it would be a good idea to go down and thank Johara for having taken such pains to prepare an excellent dinner for their guest. Johara, standing in the kitchen lighted by two candles, received the praise with her usual imperturbable dignity. Communication with her was difficult, so Anita smiled and went out into the courtyard, turning her flashlight in all directions. Then she went back to the room where they had eaten, and where the pressure lamp was roaring. She had left the door open when she had gone up onto the roof, and the room was now aired. She sat down on the cushions and began to read.

Sooner than she expected, he was back, his T-shirt completely wet.

"Why all the sweat?" she said. "It's not that hot."

"I practically jogged all the way back."

"You didn't have to do that. There's no hurry."

She read a few more lines, and put the book on the couch beside her. "Anyway, now we know she's not a dyke," she said.

"Are you out of your mind?" he cried. "Still thinking about that? Besides, why do we know now and didn't before? Because she didn't make a pass at you?"

She glanced at him an instant. "Ah, shut your beak! It was pretty clear to me that she's interested in you."

"What made it so clear?"

"Oh, the way she purred over your pictures, for one thing."

"Just French manners."

"Yes. I know. But no etiquette demands such fulsome praise as she was dishing out."

"Fulsome? It was perfectly sincere. As a matter of fact, a lot of what she said was very much to the point."

"I can see you respond to flattery."

"You can't believe that anyone could get excited about my painting, I know."

"Oh, Tom, you're impossible. I didn't say that, but my personal opinion is that it wasn't your pictures that excited her today."

"You mean she has a sexual interest?"

"What do you think I mean?"

"Well, suppose she did, and suppose I reciprocated it, would that be important?"

"Obviously not. But I think it's interesting."

"You were just trying to keep me on the straight and narrow as far as my work is involved. You're right, of course, and I ought to appreciate it. But I don't. It's too much fun to be told how good you are. You want to stay up there for a while, savoring all the nice things you've just been told."

"I'm sorry," she said. "I certainly didn't mean to belittle your work, or depress you."

"Probably you didn't, but talking about it now depresses me."

"Sorry," she said, not sounding sorry. "On the way to her house did Mme. Massot go on about your painting?"

He was angry. "She did not." A moment later he continued. "She had a long complicated story to tell, about two students from Yale who were found dead last week out near Gargouna. We never hear anything here. Old Monsieur Bessier was called in. The police had heard that his truck had been seen out there a couple of days before they found them. Of course it had, because we were in it. The kids had a motorcycle, and they were trying to run it in the sand."

"They had an accident?" She managed to keep her voice normal. "There's no need," she thought. "No one knows anything."

"They went into some big rocks, and were pretty much cut up. But apparently it wasn't their injuries that killed them."

"What was it?" Her voice was much too feeble, but he did not notice. "I've got to continue this dialogue as though it meant absolutely nothing," she told herself.

"It was insolation. The damn fools were wearing no clothes. Only shorts. Nobody's sure when the accident happened, but they must have lain there naked for two or three days, getting more burned and scorched by the hour. It's a mystery why nobody from the village saw them before that. But people don't wander around in the dunes much, of course. And by the time somebody did see them, the sun had finished them off."

"What a shame." She saw the two again, the bright red and blue shorts, the blood on the bronzed bodies and the bent chromium cage above them. "The poor boys. How awful."

Tom went on talking, but she did not hear him. A little later she murmured: "How terrible."

XVII

Now, when they were within a few days of leaving to go to Paris, Anita began to feel an acute need to clear her mind of the fog of doubts and fears that had been plaguing her since the day at Gargouna. The dream was of course at the core; she had not experienced it for several nights. There was also the question of Sekou. If she left here without a satisfactory explanation of his connection with the dream, she would consider it a major failure on her part. The monsters were dead. Sekou was alive; he might be of help.

"Is Sekou around?" she inquired of Tom. He looked surprised. "Why? You want to see him?"

"I'd like to take a walk along the river, and I thought he might go with me."

Tom hesitated. "I don't know whether he's up to it. He's been having trouble with an infected leg. I'll see if he's in the house somewhere and let you know."

He found him sitting in a room near the kitchen, and suggested that he let him sterilize the wound again. Sekou became hesitant when he saw Anita standing outside the door.

"You can come in and watch, if you want," Tom told her. He had no patience with the excessive prudery of the local males. "It's a mean gash, all the way from the ankle up to the knee. I don't wonder it got infected. But it's a lot better." He tore away the strips that held the bandage in place. "It's all dry," he announced. There's no use asking him if it hurts, because he'll say no, even if the pain is killing him. "*Tout va bien maintenant?*" Sekou smiled and said: "*Merci beaucoup. La plaie s'est fermee.*"

"He'll be able to walk with you," Tom said.

Sekou seemed relieved when Tom pulled his gandoura down and covered the leg.

As they went along the edge of the river, Anita inquired what had happened to cause such a deep cut. "You saw," he said, surprised at the question. "You were there. You saw how the tourists ran their machine into me."

"I thought so," she said. "Oh, those two monsters." It helped to speak of them thus, even knowing that she was partially responsible for their deaths.

The wind was beginning again to blow, and the air was being filled with dust. There were not many fishermen in the river today. It was twilight at mid-morning.

"You say they were devils," proceeded Sekou. "But they weren't devils. They were ignorant young men. I know you were very angry with them, and you put a curse on them."

Anita was astonished. "What?" she cried.

"You said they were going to be in trouble and you would be happy to see them suffering. I think they have gone away."

Her impulse was to say: "They're dead," but she held her tongue, thinking it strange that he had not heard the news.

"I had already forgiven them, but I know you had not. When my leg hurt very much, Monsieur Tom gave me an injection. I told myself maybe the pain would stop if you forgave them, too. One night I dreamed I went and spoke to you. I wanted to hear you say it. But you said: 'No. They are devils. They nearly killed me. Why should I forgive them?' Then I knew that you would never forgive them."

"Monsters," Anita murmured, "not devils." He seemed not to have heard her.

"Then thanks to God, Monsieur Tom made my leg well again."

"Shall we go back? The air is full of dust." They turned and began to walk in the other direction. For some minutes they were silent. Eventually Anita said: "In your dream, did you want me to go and see them, tell them I forgave them?"

"It would have made me very happy, yes. But I did not dare ask you to do that. I thought it would be enough to hear you say 'I forgive them.'"

"It doesn't do any good for me to say now 'I forgive them,' does it? But I do forgive them." Her voice was a bit tearful. He noticed it, and stood still.

"Of course it does! It does good for you. If you have anger inside yourself it's poison for you. Everyone should always forgive everyone."

During the rest of the walk she was silent, thinking of her own dream in which forgiveness played no part, for Yindall and Fambers could only be what she had decided they were beforehand. They were monsters, thus her unconscious had to supply a world for them where everything was monstrous.

She thought of Sekou's interpretation of her furious words to the cyclists. In a sense it was quite accurate. Her behavior was exactly what constituted putting a curse on someone, although she would not have described the thing in those terms. Without understanding the words, he had seized their import. Basic emotions have their own language.

She had been right. Sekou's intense desire had, through his dream, put him in contact with the dark side of her mind and forced her to seek out Yindall and Fambers. (She had no other names to give them.)

XVIII

The following morning Tom, who had gone out early not to run beside the river, but to walk to the market, returned in a state of excitement. "A real stroke of luck!" he cried. "I ran into Bessier. His nephew's here and he's leaving tomorrow, and he says there's room for us in his Land Rover. That way we're sure of getting to Mopti before the rain starts."

Anita, delighted by the prospect of going, nevertheless asked: "Why Mopti before the rain?"

"Because the road between here and there is impassable once the rain begins. From Mopti on it's relatively smooth sailing. The ride'll save us a lot of worry. And I won't have to pay out a fortune to rent a vehicle that would get us through. So, can you get packed?"

She laughed. "I've got practically nothing with me, you know. I can get it all together in a half hour."

The idea of leaving, of seeing a landscape different from the endless lightstruck emptiness here stimulated her. She felt, however, a certain ambivalence. She had begun to care for the flat sand-colored town, knowing that she would never see another place quite like it. Nor, it occurred to her, would she ever find another person with the same uncomplicated purity of Sekou. (She knew that she would continue to think of him in the days to come.)

The morning of departure Tom was busy handing out money to those who had performed services of one sort or another in the house. Anita went with him to the kitchen and shook Johara's hand. She was hoping to see Sekou and bid him good-bye, but it was too early for him to have come around.

"I'm really disappointed," she said, as they stood outside the house waiting for Bessier's nephew.

"You finally decided to like Sekou," Tom remarked. "You see, he didn't want to rape you."

She could not help saying: "But he dreamed of me."

"He did?" Tom seemed amused. "How do you know that?"

"He told me. He dreamed he came and stood by my bed." She decided to stop there and say no more. Tom's expression was despairing. He shook his head. "Well, it's all too much for me."

She was glad to see the Land Rover approaching.

When they were far out in the desert she was still reviewing the no longer painful story. Sekou knew much of it, but she knew it all, and she promised herself that never would anyone else hear of it.

THEIR HEADS ARE GREEN AND
THEIR HANDS ARE BLUE

Far and few, far and few,
  Are the lands where the Jumblies live;
Their heads are green, and their hands are blue,
  And they went to sea in a Sieve.

—from *The Jumblies*
by EDWARD LEAR

FOREWORD

Each time I go to a place I have not seen before, I hope it will be as different as possible from the places I already know. I assume it is natural for a traveler to seek diversity, and that it is the human element which makes him most aware of difference. If people and their manner of living were alike everywhere, there would not be much point in moving from one place to another. With few exceptions, landscape alone is of insufficient interest to warrant the effort it takes to see it. Even the works of man, unless they are being used in his daily living, have a way of losing their meaning, and take on the qualities of decoration. What makes Istanbul worth while to the outsider is not the presence of the mosques and the covered *souks*, but the fact that they still function as such. If the people of India did not have their remarkable awareness of the importance of spiritual discipline, it would be an overwhelmingly depressing country to visit, notwithstanding its architectural wonders. And North Africa without its tribes, inhabited by, let us say, the Swiss, would be merely a rather more barren California.

The concept of the status quo is a purely theoretical one; modifications occur hourly. It would be an absurdity to expect any group of people to maintain its present characteristics or manner of living. But the visitor to a place whose charm is a result of its backwardness is inclined to hope it will remain that way, regardless of how its inhabitants may feel. The seeker of the picturesque sees the spread of technology as an unalloyed abomination. Still, there are much worse things.

M. Claude Lévi-Strauss, the anthropologist, claims that in order for the Western world to continue to function properly it must constantly get rid of vast quantities of waste matter, which it dumps on less fortunate peoples. "What travel discloses to us first of all is our own garbage, flung in the face of humanity."

At the other end of the ideological spectrum are those who regard any objective description of things as they are today in an underdeveloped country as imperialist propaganda. Having been subjected to attack from both camps, I am aware that such countries are a delicate subject to write about. With reference to one of the pieces in this volume, "Fish Traps and Private Business," a British resident of Ceylon declared, "Other authors have found peace and beauty here in the simple life of our coolies." Whereas, when I wrote "Mustapha and His Friends," a strong-minded French lady translated it into her language, had two hundred copies mimeographed, and distributed them among Moslem politicians to illustrate the typical reactionary attitude of Americans toward oppressed peoples.

My own belief is that the people of the alien cultures are being ravaged not so much by the by-products of our civilization, as by the irrational longing on the part of members of their own educated minorities to cease being themselves and become Westerners. The various gadget-forms of our "garbage" make convenient fetishes to assist in achieving the magic transformation. But there is a difference between allowing an organism to evolve naturally and trying to force the change. Many post-colonial regimes attempt to hasten the process of Europeanization by means of campaigns and decrees. Coercion can destroy the traditional patterns of thought, it is true; but what is needed is that they be transformed into viable substitute patterns, and this can be done only empirically and by the people themselves. A cultural vacuum is not even productive of nationalism, which at least involves a certain consciousness of identity.

Since human behavior is becoming everywhere less differentiated, the Jumblie hunters are having to increase the radius of their searches and lower their standards. For a man to qualify as a Jumblie today he need not practice anthropophagy or infibulation; it is enough for him to sacrifice a coconut or bury a packet of curses in his neighbor's garden. It may be, says W. H. Auden, "that in a not remote future, it will be impossible to distinguish human beings living on one area of the earth's surface from those living on any other." It is comforting to imagine that when that day arrives we may be in a position to have the inhabitants of a nearby planet as our Jumblies. There is always the possibility, too, that they may have us as theirs.

CONTENTS

Fish Traps and Private Business

Welideniya Estate, Ceylon
May, 1950

THE LANDSCAPE is restless—a sea of disorderly hills rising steeply. In all directions it looks the same. The hills are sharp bumps with a thin, hairy vegetation that scarcely covers them. Most of this is rubber, and the rubber is wintering. Mr. Murrow, the planter, says that in another week or two the present brownish-yellow leaves will be replaced by new ones. Where the rubber stops the tea begins. There the earth looks raw. The rocks show between the low bushes; here and there a mulberry tree with lopped branches, planted for shade.

On top of one of these steep humps is the bungalow, spread out all along the crest. Directly below to the southwest, almost straight down, is the river with its sandy banks. But in between, the steep declivity is terraced with tea, and by day the voices of the Tamil pickers are constantly audible. At night there are fires outside the huts on the opposite bank of the river.

The air is hot and breathless, the only respite coming in the middle of the afternoon, when it rains. And afterward, when it has stopped, one has very little energy until night falls. However, by then it is too late to do anything but talk or read. The lights work on the tea-factory circuit. When everyone is in bed, Mr. Murrow calls from under his mosquito net through the open door of his bedroom to a Tamil waiting outside on the lawn. Five minutes later all the lights slowly die, and the house is in complete darkness save for the small oil lamps on the shelves in the bathrooms. Nothing is locked. The bedrooms have swinging shutters, like old-fashioned barroom doors, that reach to within two feet of the floor. The windows have no glass—only curtains of very thin silk. All night long a barefoot watchman shouldering a military rifle pads round and round the bungalow. Sometimes, when it is too hot to sleep, I get up and sit out on the verandah. Once there was no air even there, and I moved a chair to the lawn. On his first trip around, the watchman saw me, and made a grunting sound which I interpreted as one of disapproval. It may not have been; I don't know.

The nights seem endless, perhaps because I lie awake listening to the unfamiliar sounds made by the insects, birds and reptiles. By now I can tell more or less how late it is by the section of the nocturnal symphony that has been reached. In the early evening there are things that sound like cicadas. Later the geckos begin. (There is a whole science of divination based on the smallest details of the behavior of these little lizards; while the household is still up they scurry silently along the walls and ceiling catching insects, and it is only well on into the night that they begin to call out, from one side of the room to the other.) Still later there is a noise like a rather rasping katydid. By three in the morning everything has stopped but a small bird whose cry is one note of pure tone and unvarying pitch. There seem always to be two of these in the rain tree outside my room; they take great care to sing antiphonally, and the one's voice is exactly a whole tone above the other's. Sometimes in the morning Mrs. Murrow asks me if I heard the cobra sing during the night. I have never been able to answer in the affirmative, because in spite of her description ("like a silver coin falling against a rock"), I have no clear idea of what to listen for.

We drink strong, dark tea six or seven times a day. No pretext is needed for Mr. Murrow to ring the bell and order it. Often when it seems perfectly good to me, he will send it back with the complaint that it has been poorly brewed. All the tea consumed in the bungalow is top-leaf tea, hand-picked by Mr. Murrow himself. He maintains that there is none better in the world, and I am forced to agree that it tastes like a completely different beverage from any tea I have had before.

The servants enter the rooms bowing so low that their backs form an arch, and their hands are held above their heads in an attitude of prayer. Last night I happened to go into the dining room a few minutes before dinner, and old Mrs. Van Dort, Mrs. Murrow's mother, was already seated at her place. The oldest servant, Siringam, suddenly appeared in the doorway of the verandah leading to the kitchen, bent over double with his hands above his head, announcing the entrance of a kitchen maid bearing the dog's meal. The woman carried the dish to the old lady, who sternly inspected it and then commanded her in Singhalese to put it down in a corner for the animal. "I must always look at the dog's food," she told me, "otherwise the servants eat part of it and the poor dog grows thinner and thinner."

"But are the servants that hungry?"

"Certainly not!" she cried. "But they like the dog's food better than their own."

Mrs. Murrow's son by a former marriage came to spend last night, bringing his Singhalese wife with him; she had already told me at some length of how she resisted the marriage for three years because of the girl's blood. Mrs. Murrow is of the class which calls itself Burgher, claiming an unbroken line of descendency from the Dutch settlers of two centuries ago. I have yet to see a Burgher who looks Caucasian, the admixture of Singhalese being always perfectly discernible. It is significant that the Burghers feel compelled to announce their status to newcomers; the apparent reason is to avoid being taken for "natives." The tradition is that they are Europeans, and one must accept it without question. The son is a tall, gentle man who wears a gray cassock and keeps his hands folded tightly all the time, a habit which makes him look as though he were prey to a constant inner anguish. He is a minister of the Anglican church, but this does not keep him from being of the extreme left politically. His joy is to stir up dissension among his parishioners by delivering sermons in which Communists are depicted as holding high posts in heaven. He has told me some amusing anecdotes of his life as a teacher in the outlying provinces before he was ordained. Of these the ones I remember have to do with the strange faculty the children have for speaking passable English without knowing the meaning of the words they use. One boy, upon being asked to answer which he would prefer to be, a tailor or a lawyer, was unable to reply. "You know what a tailor is, don't you?" said Mr. Clasen. The boy said he did, and he also knew the functions of a lawyer, but he could not answer the question. "But why?" insisted Mr. Clasen, thinking that perhaps some recondite bit of Buddhist philosophy was about to be forthcoming. But the boy finally said, "I know tailor and I know lawyer, but please, sir, what is be?" Another boy wrote, "The horse is a noble animal, but when irritated will not do so."

When you ask a question of a Singhalese who does not know English, he is likely to react in a most curious fashion. First he looks swiftly at you, then he looks away, his features retreating into an expression of pleasant contemplation, as if your voice were an agreeable but distant memory that he had just recalled and thought it worth while to savor briefly. After a few seconds of giving himself up to this inward satisfaction he goes on about his business without ever looking your way again—not even if you insist, or wait a bit and make your inquiry afresh. You have become invisible. At the resthouses in the country, where the members of the personnel feel they must put up some sort of front, they say, "Oh, oh, oh," in a commiserating tone, ("oh" is "yes") as if they understood only too well, and were forbearing to say more for the sake of decorum. Then they wag their heads back and forth, from side to side, a gesture which reminds you of a metronome going rather too quickly, keeping their bright eyes on you, listening politely until you have finished speaking, whereupon they smile beautifully and walk away. The servants who do speak English insist upon calling you "master," which is disconcerting because it seems to imply responsibility of some sort on your part. They also use the third person instead of the second: "Master wishing eat now?" The youngest generation, however, has almost unanimously adopted the more neutral "sir," (pronounced "sar") as a substitute for the too colonial-sounding "master."

There is a long, thin, green adder that likes to lie in the sun on top of the tea bushes; one of these bit a woman recently while she was picking. Mr. Murrow hurried to the scene and, taking up a pruning knife, cut off the tip of her finger, applying crystals of potassium permanganate to the flesh. She was saved in this way, but as soon as she regained consciousness, she went to the police and filed a complaint, accusing Mr. Murrow of causing irreparable damage to her finger. When the investigator came to the estate, he heard the details of the case and told the woman that thanks to Mr. Murrow's quick action she was still alive; without it she would have been dead.

The woman's husband, who was present at the hearing, jumped up and drew a knife on the investigator, but was prevented from hurting him. When they had subdued the man, he wailed across at the investigator: "You have no sense! I could have collected plenty of rupees for that finger, and I would have given you half."

The public toilets in the villages, instead of being marked *Ladies* or *Women*, bear signs that read: *Urinals for Females.*

A sign on the side of a building in Akmimana: *Wedding Cakes and other thing Supplied for Weddings in Convenient Times.*

Another, in Colombo: *Dr. Rao's Tonic—a Divine Drug.*

A Burgher who works in the travel agency of the Grand Oriental Hotel and who had seen me when I first arrived, said to me a few weeks later when I stopped in, "You're losing your color." "What?" I cried incredulously. "After all this time in the sun? I'm five shades darker than I was." He looked confused, but continued patiently, "That's what I say. You're losing your color."

Kaduwela

The Lunawa resthouse was a disagreeable place to stay, being directly opposite the railway station in the middle of a baking and unshaded patch of dried-up lawn. In the concrete cell I was given it was impossible to shut out the sounds made by the other guests, who happened to be extremely noisy. The room next to mine was occupied by a party of eight men, who spent the entire afternoon and evening giggling and guffawing. When I would walk past their door I could see them lying in their sarongs across the two beds which they had pushed together. In the dining room the radio never ceased blaring at maximum volume. The food was ghastly, and there was no mosquito net available for my bed and, therefore, no protection against the tiny insects that constantly brushed against my face in the dark, seeking to get under the sheet with me. When I finally got into the state of nerves they had been trying to induce, I jumped up, dressed and rushed out, to the horror of the boy lying on his mat across the front doorway. He too sprang up, went to an inner room to fetch

the keeper, and together they cried out after me across the
dark lawn: "Master going?"

"Coming back, coming back!" I called, and began to walk
quickly up the road toward the lagoon. When I got to the
bridge I stood awhile. The water was absolutely still, and
there were dozens of pinkish flames guttering in lamps placed
just at the surface, each with its unmoving reflection. And
each lamp illumined a complex scaffolding of bamboo poles;
these pale constructions scattered across the black expanse of
water looked like precarious altars, and the fact that I knew
they were fish traps made them no less extraordinary, no less
beautiful. To break the silence a drum began to beat on the
far shore. Presently a man came riding by on a bicycle; as he
passed me he turned his flashlight into my face. The sight of
me standing in that spot startled him, and he pedaled madly
away across the bridge.

I walked on to Lunawa Junction, where I stood in the road
listening to a radio in a corner "hotel" play Tamil music.
(What the Singhalese call hotels are merely teahouses with
three or four tables and a tiny space back of a screen or partition where there are mats on the floor for those who wish
to rest.) People wandered past now and then and stared at
me; I was clearly an object of great interest. Europeans never
appear at night in such places. When I sat down on a culvert
I was soon the center of a semicircle of men, some clad only
in G-strings and with hair that reached halfway down their
backs. It was no use talking to me in Singhalese, but they
went right on trying. One who spoke English finally arrived
and asked me if I would like to race him down the road. I declined, saying I was tired. This was true; it was after midnight,
and I was beginning to wish there were some comfortable
place in the neighborhood where I could lay my head. The
English-speaking man then told me that they had all been
asleep but had got up because someone had arrived with the
news that a stranger was standing in the road. While I sat
there doing my best to make some sort of polite conversation, three older men in white robes came by and, seeing the
crowd, stopped. These were obviously of a higher social station, and they were most disapproving of what they saw. One
of them, who had rapidly been delegated as spokesman,

stepped forward, indicated the band of wild-eyed, long-haired individuals, and said: "Hopeless people." I pretended not to understand, whereupon all three set to work repeating the same two words over and over, accenting equally each syllable. I was so fascinated with their performance that nearly all the nudists had disappeared into the dark before I realized they were leaving, and all at once I was sitting there facing only these three serious, chanting men. "Come," said the leader, and he took me by the arm and helped me up and started me walking—I won't say *forcing* me to walk, because his firmness was expressed with too much gentleness for that—but seeing to it that I did walk, with him and his friends, back to the road intersection where bats dipped in the air under the one street light. "Now you go to resthouse," he said, showing that he knew more English than the two-word refrain which had sufficed him until then. But then a second later, "Hopeless people," he sang, and the others, looking still more grave beneath the light, agreed with him once more. Lamely I protested that I should go back presently, when I felt like it, but they were adamant; it was clear that my personal desires were quite beside the point. They called to a boy who stood under a tree near the "hotel" and charged him to walk the mile with me back to the resthouse. For perhaps a minute I argued, half laughingly, half seriously, and then I turned and started up the road. They called good night and went on their way. The boy kept close beside me, partly out of fear, I imagine; and when I got to the bridge and stood still for a moment to look at the water and the lights, he pressed me to go on quickly, pretending there were crocodiles in the lagoon and that they came out of the water at night. I don't think he believed it at all, but he wanted to accomplish his mission and get to the safety of the resthouse as fast as he could. Trees harbor spirits here; the older and larger ones have niches carved into their trunks where the people put long-burning altar candles. The flickering lights attract the spirits, like moths, and keep them from leaving the tree and doing harm beyond its immediate vicinity. At the resthouse the man and the boy were waiting up for me. My road companion had no intention of augmenting his ordeal by going back across the lagoon unaccompanied; he curled up on the

floor of the verandah and spent the night there. The gigglers
had gone to sleep and there was quiet at last, but the insects
were more numerous and active than they had been earlier. I
did not have a very successful night.

I had already made arrangements to spend the next night at
Homagama, where the resthouse is, or at least appears to be,
somewhat superior. When the elderly resthouse keeper
showed me his rooms there, he tried to get me to take an extension of the dining room, on the pretext that it would be
quieter. The only other available room was next to his quarters, and that, he said apologetically, he was sure Master
would not like at all. Since the room he was trying to give me
had only three complete walls, the fourth being merely a
wooden screen about five feet high over which I could see
two gentlemen drinking ginger beer at a table, I unwisely decided upon the room adjoining his quarters. Once I was settled, with my luggage partially unpacked, and the servants
had hung the mosquito net and brought in a very feeble oil
lamp, I discovered my error. This room also was only a section of another room; in the part not inhabited by me a baby
began to wail, and presently the voice of an extremely old
woman rose in incantation. Whether it was a lullaby, a prayer,
or merely a senile lamentation, I am still too unfamiliar with
the culture of the land to tell. But it went on intermittently
until dawn, when the sounds of the poultry, the crows in the
mango trees, and the locomotives which passed by the doorway, blotted it out. Whenever the old lady would stop, the infant would wake her up; as soon as the baby ceased crying,
she would start afresh and awaken the baby.

In the morning I discovered that there was a third room
but that it was due to be occupied any moment by what is euphemistically called a "honeymoon couple." At six-thirty in
the morning they arrived, and when they had left in the late
afternoon, I was allowed to take it. It was vastly better, and I
kept it for the next two nights, much to the keeper's disgust,
since he had to put all the couples that arrived during that
time into the other rooms. Given the fact that by far the
larger part of his personal revenue comes in the form of gra-
tuities from such parties, it is understandable that he should
like to provide them with the best accommodations. Another

expression used by resthouse keepers to refer to their honeymoon couples is "private business." Those concerned do not sign their names in the register, and for that privilege leave relatively large tips. The keeper at Kesbewa informed me that his rooms were all reserved for private business for the next six weeks.

During the late afternoon of the third day I had to leave. Unless one has special permission from the government to remain longer, one's stay in a resthouse is strictly limited to three nights, which is presumably ample time for whatever private business one may wish to conduct.

I engaged a bullock-cart with the body of an old-fashioned buggy, drawn by a small beige-colored *zebu*, and with the driver, who had never heard the English words "yes" and "no," started along the back roads through the forest for Kaduwela. There were a good many small villages on the way, and we had to stop at one so that the luggage, which was constantly slipping and falling out into the dust, could be rearranged and tied more securely. The driver brought a great length of thick but feeble rope for the purpose, and we went ahead. The incredible jolting became unbearable after a while; I had pains everywhere from my knees to my neck. The rope, of course, kept breaking, and the valises continued to slip and fall out. The charm of the landscape however had induced in me such a complete euphoria that nothing mattered. I only wanted it to stay light as long as possible so I could go on being aware of my surroundings. The forest was not constant; it opened again and again onto wide stretches of green paddy fields where herons waded. Each time we plunged again into the woods it was darker, until finally I could no longer distinguish areca palms from bamboo. People walking along the road were carrying torches, made of palm leaves bound tightly together that burned with a fierce red flame, they held them high above their heads, and the sparks dropped behind them all along the way. In one village, cinnamon bark had been piled against the houses. The odor enveloped the whole countryside. Now every ten minutes or so the driver stopped, got down, and put a new wax taper into one or the other of the two little lamps at the sides of the buggy. It was very late when we got to Kaduwela.

Here the resthouse is on the river, the Kelani Ganga, which flows by at the base of the rocks, just a few feet below the verandah. At night in the quiet I can sometimes hear a slight gurgle out there, but I am never sure whether it is a fish or merely the current. Occasionally a whole string of bamboo barges floats swiftly by without a sound; if one did not see the moving red spots, the braziers where the members of the crew are cooking their food, one would not know it was there.

Hikkaduwa

In Ceylon the Christmas-tree light is a favorite decoration. They use thousands of them at once, string them across the fronts of the houses and shops, through the trees, and up and down the *dagobas* of the temples. If there is a religious procession, whatever is carried through the streets is covered with colored electric bulbs. During Perahera in Kandy as many as eighty elephants parade at night, wearing strings of lights which take the place of the emeralds, rubies and diamonds that cover the beasts in the daytime processions. Last week while I was in Kandy the Moslems had a festival, and they carried a pagoda-like tower, every square inch of whose area was ablaze with tiny colored lights. It looked rather like a colossal, glittering wedding cake. I followed it up and down Trincomalee Street and Ward Street, and then I went to bed. Until then I had not realized that there was a mosque across the garden from my room (they seem to have dispensed with muezzins here—at least, one never hears them), but that evening there was magnificent music coming from a courtyard behind the mosque. It went on all night, like a soft wind in the trees. I listened until nearly three, and then it carried me off into sleep.

Last night there was a *pirith* ceremony at a house across the road. The family that lived next door to the one holding the ceremony had offered their verandah for the installation of a generator, for there had to be electric light and a great deal of it. So, the clanking of the motor all but covered the chanting of the men. In one corner of the main room they had built a small cubicle. Its walls were of translucent paper, cut into designs along the edges of the partitions, so that each section looked like the frame of a fancy valentine. There were lights everywhere, but the greatest amount of light came from inside the cubicle. Earlier in the evening I had noticed two men winding or unwinding a white silk thread between them; now there was a decanter full of an unidentified liquid on the table, and the thread connected its neck with a part of the ceiling that was invisible from where I stood. The table was surrounded by men sitting pressed close to one another, chanting. One of the onlookers who stood with me in the road said that the chanting was being done in Pali, not in Singhalese. As if it were necessary to excuse the use of such an ancient language, he added that Catholic services were conducted in Latin, not in English, and I said I understood.

I asked what the white silk thread meant and was told that it was a decoration; but since everything in the ceremony had been arranged with show-window precision, and since the thread, shooting upward at its crazy angle toward the ceiling, was clearly not an adornment to anything, I was not inclined to accept that version of its function. The men shouted in a desperate fashion, so that they were obliged to lean against the table for support. All night long they kept it up. When I awoke at quarter to five they were still at it, but the sound now had a different contour; one could say that in a way it had subsided, being now a succession of short wails with a *tessitura* never exceeding a major third, a sequence that repeated itself exactly, again and again, with no variation. I was told today that the pirith chant is allowed four distinct tones and no more, since the addition of a fifth would put it into the category of music, which is strictly forbidden. Perhaps the celebrants are too much preoccupied with observing the letter of the law. In any case, within the allowed gamut they hit every quarter-tone they could find. The dogs of the resthouse objected now and then with howls and yapping, until the guard silenced them with a shout.

A young Buddhist who had been standing outside the house while I was there offered to explain a few details about the ceremony to me. "You see the women?" he said. They were sitting in the outer part of the room, conversing quietly. "They are not allowed inside." The chanting begins, he said (in this case it was at nine in the evening), with all the men shouting together. Then as they tire, only the two strongest continue, while the others gather their forces. At daybreak once again everyone joins in, after six hours or so of alternating shifts. Purpose of ceremony: to keep evil in abeyance. The young man did not hold the custom in very high esteem and suggested that I visit a monastery four miles away on an island where the *bhikkus* behaved in a really correct manner. Even Buddhism is riddled with primitive practices. Practically speaking, the pirith is merely a quiet variation of devil-dancing.

Colombo

The Pettah is the only part of the city where the visitor can get even a faint idea of what life in Colombo might have been like before the twentieth century's gangrene set in. It is at the end of a long and unrewarding walk across the railroad tracks and down endless unshaded streets, and no one in Ceylon seems to be able to understand how I can like it. It is customary to assume an expression of slight disgust when one pronounces the word Pettah.

The narrow streets are jammed with zebu-drawn drays which naked coolies (no one ever says "laborers") are loading and unloading. Scavenging crows scream and chuckle in the gutters. The shops specialize in unexpected merchandise: some sell nothing but fireworks, or religious chromolitho-graphs depicting incidents in the lives of Hindu gods, or sarongs, or incense. With no arcades and no trees the heat is more intense; by noon you feel that at some point you have inadvertently died and are merely reliving the scene in your head. A rickshaw or taxi never passes through, and you must go on and on until you come out somewhere. Layers of dried betel spit coat the walls and sidewalks; it looks somewhat like dried blood, but it is a little too red. The pervading odor is that of any Chinese grocery store: above all, dried fish, but with strong suggestions of spices and incense. And there are, indeed, a few Chinese here in Pettah, although most of them appear to be dentists. I remember that one is named Thin Sin Fa and that he advertises himself as a Genuine Chinese dentist.

The mark of their profession is painted over the doorway: a huge red oval enclosing two rows of gleaming white squares. If there is a breeze, pillars of dust sweep majestically through the streets, adding an extra patina of grit to the sweat that covers your skin. In one alley is a poor Hindu temple with a small *gopuram* above the entrance. The hundreds of sculpted figures are not of stone, but of brilliantly painted plaster; banners and pennants hang haphazardly from crisscrossed strings. In another street there is a hideous red brick mosque. The faithful must wear trousers to enter.

There are Hindus and Moslems in every corner of Ceylon, but neither of these orthodoxies seems fitting for the place. Hinduism is too fanciful and chaotic, Islam too puritanical and austere. Buddhism, with its gentle agnosticism and luxuriant sadness, is so right in Ceylon that you feel it could have been born here, could have grown up out of the soil like the forests. Soon, doubtless, it will no longer be a way of life, having become, along with the rest of the world's religions, a socio-political badge. But for the moment it is still here, still powerful. And in any case, *après nous le déluge!*

Africa Minor

I T HAD taken the truck fourteen hours to get from Kerzaz to Adrar and, except for the lunch stop in the oasis of El Aougherout, the old man had sat the whole time on the floor without moving, his legs tucked up beneath him, the hood of his burnoose pulled up over his turban to protect his face from the fine dust that sifted up through the floor. First-class passage on vehicles of the Compagnie Générale Transsaharienne entitled the voyager to travel in the glassed-in compartment with the driver, and that was where I sat, occasionally turning to look through the smeared panes at the solitary figure sitting sedately in the midst of the tornado of dust behind. At lunch, when I had seen his face with its burning brown eyes and magnificent white beard, it had occurred to me that he looked like a handsome and very serious Santa Claus.

The dust grew worse during the afternoon, so that by sunset, when we finally pulled into Adrar, even the driver and I were covered. I got out and shook myself, and the little old man clambered out of the back, cascades of dust spilling from his garments. Then he came around to the front of the truck to speak to the driver, who, being a good Moslem, wanted to get a shower and wash himself. Unfortunately he was a city Moslem as well as being a good one, so that he was impatient with the measured cadence of his countryman's speech and suddenly slammed the door, unaware that the old man's hand was in the way.

Calmly the old man opened the door with his other hand. The tip of his middle finger dangled by a bit of skin. He looked at it an instant, then quietly scooped up a handful of that ubiquitous dust, put the two parts of the finger together and poured the dust over it, saying softly, "Thanks be to Allah." With that, the expression on his face never having changed, he picked up his bundle and staff and walked away. I stood looking after him, full of wonder, and reflecting upon the difference between his behavior and what mine would have been under the same circumstances. To show no outward sign of pain is unusual enough, but to express no resentment against the person who has hurt you seems very strange, and to give thanks to God at such a moment is the strangest touch of all.

Clearly, examples of such stoical behavior are not met every day, or I should not have remembered this one; my experience since then, however, has shown me that it is not untypical, and it has remained with me and become a symbol of that which is admirable in the people of North Africa. "This world we see is unimportant and ephemeral as a dream," they say. "To take it seriously would be an absurdity. Let us think rather of the heavens that surround us." And the landscape is conducive to reflections upon the nature of the infinite. In other parts of Africa you are aware of the earth beneath your feet, of the vegetation and the animals; all power seems concentrated in the earth. In North Africa the earth becomes the less important part of the landscape because you find yourself constantly raising your eyes to look at the sky. In the arid landscape the sky is the final arbiter. When you have understood that, not intellectually but emotionally, you have also understood why it is that the great trinity of monotheistic religions—Judaism, Christianity and Islam—which removed the source of power from the earth itself to the spaces outside the earth—were evolved in desert regions. And of the three, Islam, perhaps because it is the most recently evolved, operates the most directly and with the greatest strength upon the daily actions of those who embrace it.

For a person born into a culture where religion has long ago become a thing quite separate from daily life, it is a startling experience to find himself suddenly in the midst of a culture where there is a minimum of discrepancy between dogma and natural behavior, and this is one of the great fascinations of being in North Africa. I am not speaking of Egypt, where the old harmony is gone, decayed from within. My own impressions of Egypt before Nasser are those of a great panorama of sun-dried disintegration. In any case, she has had a different history from the rest of Mediterranean Africa; she is ethnically and linguistically distinct and is more a part of the Levant than of the region we ordinarily mean when we speak of North Africa. But in Tunisia, Algeria and Morocco there are still people whose lives proceed according to the ancient pattern of concord between God and man, agreement between theory and practice, identity of word and flesh (or however one prefers to conceive and define that pristine state of existence we intuitively feel we once enjoyed and now have lost).

I don't claim that the Moslems of North Africa are a group of mystics, heedless of bodily comfort, interested only in the welfare of the spirit. If you have ever bought so much as an egg from one of them, you have learned that they are quite able to fend for themselves when it comes to money matters. The spoiled strawberries are at the bottom of the basket, the pebbles inextricably mixed with the lentils and the water with the milk, the same as in many other parts of the world, with the difference that if you ask the price of an object in a rural market, they will reply, all in one breath, "Fifty, how much will you give?" I should say that in the realm of *beah o chra* (selling and buying; note that in their minds selling comes first), they are surpassed only by the Hindus, who are less emotional about it and therefore more successful, and by the Chinese, acknowledged masters of the Oriental branch of the science of commerce.

In Morocco you go into a bazaar to buy a wallet and somehow find yourself being propelled toward the back room to look at antique brass and rugs. In an instant you are seated with a glass of mint tea in your hand and a platter of pastries in your lap, while smiling gentlemen modeling ancient caftans and marriage robes parade in front of you, the salesman who greeted you at the door having completely vanished. Later on you may once again ask timidly to see the wallets, which you noticed on display near the entrance. Likely as not, you will be told that the man in charge of wallets is at the moment saying his prayers, but that he will soon be back, and in the meantime would you not be pleased to see some magnificent jewelry from the court of Moulay Ismail? Business is business and prayers are prayers, and both are a part of the day's work.

When I meet fellow Americans traveling about here in North Africa, I ask them, "What did you expect to find here?" Almost without exception, regardless of the way they express it, the answer, reduced to its simplest terms, is: a sense of mystery. They expect mystery, and they find it, since fortunately it is a quality difficult to extinguish all in a moment. They find it in the patterns of sunlight filtering through the latticework that covers the souks, in the unexpected turnings and tunnels of the narrow streets, in the women whose features still go hidden beneath the *litham*, in the secretiveness of the architecture, which is such that even if the front door of a house is open it is impossible to see inside. If they listen as well as look, they find it too in the song the lone camel driver sings by his fire before dawn, in the calling of the muezzins at night, when their voices are like bright beams of sound piercing the silence, and, most often, in the dry beat of the *darbouka*, the hand drum played by the women everywhere, in the great city houses and in the humblest country hut.

It is a strange sensation, when you are walking alone in a still, dark street late at night, to come upon a pile of cardboard boxes soaked with rain, and, as you pass by it, to find yourself staring into the eyes of a man sitting upright behind it. A thief? A beggar? The night watchman of the quarter? A spy for the secret police?

You just keep walking, looking at the ground, hearing your footsteps echo between the walls of the deserted street. Into your head comes the idea that you may suddenly hear the sound of a conspiratorial whistle and that something unpleasant may be about to happen. A little farther along you see, deep in the recess of an arcade of shops, another man reclining in a deck chair, asleep. Then you realize that all along the street there are men both sleeping and sitting quietly awake, and that even in the hours of its most intense silence the place is never empty of people.

It is only since the end of 1955 that Morocco has had its independence, but already there is a nucleus of younger Moslems who fraternize freely with the writers and painters (most of whom are American girls and youths) who have wandered into this part of the world and found it to their liking. Together they give very staid, quiet parties which show a curious blend of Eastern and Western etiquette. Usually no Moslem girls are present. Everyone is either stretched out on mattresses or seated on the floor, and *kif* and hashish are on hand, but half the foreigners content themselves with highballs. A good many paintings are looked at, and there is a lot

of uninformed conversation about art and expression and religion. When food is passed around, the Moslems, for all their
passionate devotion to European manners, not only adhere to
their own custom of using chunks of bread to sop up the oily
mruq at the bottom of their plates, but manage to impose the
system on the others as well, so that everybody is busy rubbing pieces of bread over his plate. Why not? The food is
cooked to be eaten in that fashion, and is less tasty if eaten in
any other way.

Many of the Moslems paint, too; after so many centuries of
religious taboo with regard to the making of representational
images, abstraction is their natural mode of expression. You
can see in their canvases the elaboration of design worked out
by the Berbers in their crafts: patterns that show constant
avoidance of representation but manage all the same to suggest recognizable things. Naturally, their paintings are a great
success with the visiting artists, who carry their admiration to
the point of imitation. The beat-generation North Africans
are music-mad, but they get their music via radio, phonograph and tape-recorder. They are enthusiastic about the music of their own country, but unlike their fathers, they don't
sing or play it. They are also fond of such exotic items as
Congo drumming, the music of India, and particularly the
more recent American jazz (Art Blakey, Horace Silver, Can-
nonball Adderley).

At the moment, writing about any part of Africa is a little
like trying to draw a picture of a roller coaster in motion. You
can say: It *was* thus and so, or, it *is becoming* this or that, but
you risk making a misstatement if you say categorically that
anything *is*, because likely as not you will open tomorrow's
newspaper to discover that it has changed. On the whole the
new governments of Tunisia and Morocco wish to further
tourism in their respective countries; they are learning that
the average tourist is more interested in native dancing than
in the new bus terminal, that he is more willing to spend
money in the Casbah than to inspect new housing projects.
For a while, after the demise of the violently unpopular Pasha
of Marrakech, Thami el Glaoui, the great public square of
Marrakech, the Djemaa el Fna, was used solely as a parking
lot. Anyone will tell you that the biggest single attraction for

tourists in all North Africa was the Djemaa el Fna in Marrakech. It was hard to find a moment of the day or night when tourists could not be found prowling around among its acrobats, singers, storytellers, snake charmers, dancers and medicine men. Without it Marrakech became just another Moroccan city. And so the Djemaa el Fna was reinstated, and now goes on more or less as before.

North Africa is inhabited, like Malaya and Pakistan, by Moslems who are not Arabs. The *Encyclopaedia Britannica's* estimate of the percentage of Arab stock in the population of Morocco dates from two decades ago, but there has been no influx of Arabs since, so we can accept its figure of ten percent as being still valid. The remaining ninety percent of the people are Berbers, who anthropologically have nothing to do with the Arabs. They are not of Semitic origin, and were right where they are now long before the Arab conquerors ever suspected their existence.

Even after thirteen hundred years, the Berbers' conception of how to observe the Moslem religion is by no means identical with that of the descendants of the men who brought it to them. And the city Moslems complain that they do not observe the fast of Ramadan properly, they neither veil nor segregate their women and, most objectionable of all, they have a passion for forming cults dedicated to the worship of local saints. In this their religious practices show a serious deviation from orthodoxy, inasmuch as during the *moussems*, the gigantic pilgrimages which are held periodically at the many shrines where these holy men are buried, men and women can be seen dancing *together*, working themselves into a prolonged frenzy. This is the height of immorality, the young puritans tell you. But it is not the extent, they add, of the Berbers' reprehensible behavior at these manifestations. Self-torture, the inducing of trances, ordeal by fire and the sword, and the eating of broken glass and scorpions are also not unusual on such occasions.

The traveler who has been present at one of these indescribable gatherings will never forget it, although if he dislikes the sight of blood and physical suffering he may try hard to put it out of his mind. To me these spectacles are filled with great beauty, because their obvious purpose is to prove the power of the spirit over the flesh. The sight of ten or twenty thousand people actively declaring their faith, demonstrating *en masse* the power of that faith, can scarcely be anything but inspiring. You lie in the fire, I gash my legs and arms with a knife, he pounds a sharpened bone into his thigh with a rock—then, together, covered with ashes and blood, we sing and dance in joyous praise of the saint and the god who make it possible for us to triumph over pain, and by extension, over death itself. For the participants exhaustion and ecstasy are inseparable.

This saint-worship, based on vestiges of an earlier religion, has long been frowned upon by the devout urban Moslems; as early as the mid-thirties restrictions were placed on its practice. For a time, public manifestations of it were effectively suppressed. There were several reasons why the educated Moslems objected to the brotherhoods. During the periods of the protectorates in Tunisia and Morocco, the colonial administrations did not hesitate to use them for their own political ends, to ensure more complete domination. Also, it has always been felt that visitors who happened to witness the members of a cult in action were given an unfortunate impression of cultural backwardness. Most important was the fact that the rituals were unorthodox and thus unacceptable to true Moslems. If you mentioned such cults as the Derqaoua, the Aissaoua, the Haddaoua, the Hamatcha, the Jilala or the Guennaoua to a city man, he cried, "They're all criminals! They should be put in jail!" without stopping to reflect that it would be difficult to incarcerate more than half the population of any country. I think one reason why the city folk are so violent in their denunciation of the cults is that most of them are only one generation removed from them themselves; knowing the official attitude toward such things, they feel a certain guilt at being even that much involved with them. Having been born into a family of adepts is not a circumstance which anyone can quickly forget. Each brotherhood has its own songs and drum rhythms, immediately recognizable as such by persons both within and outside the group. In early childhood rhythmical patterns and sequences of tones become a part of an adept's subconscious, and in later life it is not difficult to attain the trance state when one hears them again.

A variation on this phenomenon is the story of Farid. Not

long ago he called by to see me. I made tea, and since there was a fire in the fireplace, I took some embers out and put them into a brazier. Over them I sprinkled some *mska*, a translucent yellow resin which makes a sweet, clean-smelling smoke. Moroccans appreciate pleasant odors; Farid is no exception. A little later, before the embers had cooled off, I added some *djaoui*, a compound resinous substance of uncertain ingredients.

Farid jumped up. "What have you put into the *mijmah*?" he cried.

As soon as I had pronounced the word djaoui, he ran into the next room and slammed the door. "Let air into the room!" he shouted. "I can't smell djaoui! It's very bad for me!"

When all trace of the scent released by the djaoui was gone from the room, I opened the door and Farid came back in, still looking fearful.

"What's the matter with you?" I asked him. "What makes you think a little djaoui could hurt you? I've smelled it a hundred times and it's never done me any harm."

He snorted. "You! Of course it couldn't hurt *you*. You're not a Jilali, but I am. I don't want to be, but I still am. Last year I hurt myself and had to go to the clinic, all because of djaoui."

He had been walking in a street of Emsallah and had stopped in front of a café to talk to a friend. Without warning he had collapsed on the sidewalk; when he came to, he was at home and a drum was being beaten over him. Then he recalled the smoke that had been issuing from the café, and knew what had happened.

Farid had passed his childhood in a mountain village where all the members of his family were practicing Jilala. His earliest memories were of being strapped to his mother's back while she, dancing with the others, attained a state of trance. The two indispensable exterior agents they always used to assure the desired alteration of consciousness were drums and djaoui. By the time the boy was four or five years old, he already had a built-in mechanism, an infallible guarantee of being able to reach the trance state very swiftly in the presence of the proper stimulus. When he moved to the city he ceased to be an adept and, in fact, abandoned all religious practice.

The conditioned reflex remained, as might be expected, with the result that now as a man in his mid-twenties, although he is at liberty to accept or refuse the effect of the specific drum rhythms, he is entirely at the mercy of a pinch of burning djaoui.

His exposition of the therapeutic process by which he is "brought back" each time there is an accident involves a good many other details, such as the necessity for the presence of a member of the paternal side of his family who will agree to eat a piece of the offending djaoui, the pronouncing of certain key phrases, and the playing on the *bendir* the proper rhythms necessary to break the spell. But the indisputable fact remains that when Farid breathes in djaoui smoke, whether or not he is aware of doing so, straightway he loses consciousness.

One of my acquaintances, who has always been vociferous in his condemnation of the brotherhoods, eventually admitted to me that all the older members of his family were adherents to the Jilala cult, citing immediately afterward, as an example of their perniciousness, an experience of his grandmother some three years before. Like the rest of the family, she was brought up as a Jilalia but had grown too old to take part in the observances, which nowadays are held secretly. (Prohibition, as usual, does not mean abolition, but merely being driven underground.) One evening the old lady was alone in the house, her children and grandchildren having all gone to the cinema, and since she had nothing else to do she went to bed. Somewhere nearby, on the outskirts of town, there was a meeting of Jilala going on. In her sleep she rose and, dressed just as she was, began to make her way toward the sounds. She was found next morning unconscious in a vegetable garden near the house where the meeting had taken place, having fallen into an ant colony and been badly bitten. The reason she fell, the family assured me, was that at a certain moment the drumming had stopped; if it had gone on she would have arrived. The drummers always continue until everyone present has been brought out of his trance.

"But they did not know she was coming," they said, "and so the next morning, after we had carried her home, we had to send for the drummers to bring her to her senses." The younger generation of French-educated Moslems is infuriated

when this sort of story is told to foreigners. And that the latter are interested in such things upsets them even more. "Are
all the people in your country Holy Rollers?" they demand.
"Why don't you write about the civilized people here instead
of the most backward?"

I suppose it is natural for them to want to see themselves
presented to the outside world in the most "advanced" light
possible. They find it perverse of a Westerner to be interested
only in the dissimilarities between their culture and his. However, that's the way some of us Westerners are.

Not long ago I wrote on the character of the North Africa
Moslem. An illiterate Moroccan friend wanted to know what
was in it, and so, in a running translation into Moghrebi, I
read him certain passages. His comment was terse: "That's
shameful."

"Why?" I demanded.

"Because you've written about people just as they are."

"For us that's not shameful."

"For us it is. You've made us like animals. You've said that
only a few of us can read or write."

"Isn't that true?"

"Of course not! We can all read and write, just like you.
And we would, if only we'd had lessons."

I thought this interesting and told it to a Moslem lawyer,
assuming it would amuse him. It did not. "He's quite right,"
he announced. "Truth is not what you perceive with your
senses, but what you feel in your heart."

"But there is such a thing as objective truth!" I cried. "Or
don't you attach importance to that?"

He smiled tolerantly. "Not in the way you do, for its own
sake. That is statistical truth. We are interested in that, yes,
but only as a means of getting to the real truth underneath.
For us there is very little visible truth in the world these
days." However specious this kind of talk may seem, it is still
clear to me that the lawyer was voicing a feeling common to
the great mass of city dwellers here, educated or not.

With an estimated adult illiteracy rate of eighty to ninety
percent, perhaps the greatest need of all for North Africa is
universal education. So far there has been a very small
amount, and as we ourselves say, a little learning is a dan-

gerous thing. The Europeans always have been guilty of massive neglect with regard to schools for Moslems in their North African possessions. In time, their shortsighted policy is likely to prove the heaviest handicap of all in the desperate attempt of the present rulers to keep the region within the Western sphere of influence. The task of educating these people is not made easier by the fact that Moghrebi, the language of the majority, is purely a spoken tongue, and that for reading and writing they must resort to standard Arabic, which is as far from their idiom as Latin is from Italian. But slowly the transition is taking place. If you sit in a Moroccan café at the hour of a news broadcast, the boy fanning the fire will pause with the bellows in his hand, the card players lay down their cards, the talkers cease to argue as the announcer begins to speak, and an expression of ferocious intensity appears on every countenance. Certainly they are vitally interested in what is being said (even the women have taken up discussing politics lately), for they are aware of their own increasing importance in the world pattern, but the almost painful expressions are due to each man's effort to understand the words of standard Arabic as they come over the air. Afterward, there is often an argument as to exactly what the news contained.

"The British are at war with Yemen for being friendly to Gamal Abd el Nasser."

"You're crazy. He said Gamal Abd el Nasser is making war against Yemen because the British are there."

"No. He said Gamal Abd el Nasser *will* make war against Yemen if they let the British in."

"No, no! Against the *British* if they send guns to Yemen."

This state of affairs, if it does not keep all members of the populace accurately informed, at least has the advantage of increasing their familiarity with the language their children are learning at school.

There is a word which non-Moslems invariably use to describe Moslems in general: fanatical. As though the word could not be applied equally well to any group of people who care deeply about anything! Just now, the North African Moslems are passionately involved in proving to themselves that they are of the same stature as Europeans. The attainment of political independence is only one facet of their problem. The North African knows that when it comes to appreciating his culture, the average tourist cannot go much closer toward understanding it than a certain condescending curiosity. He realizes that, at best, to the European he is merely picturesque. Therefore, he reasons, to be taken seriously he must cease being picturesque. Traditional customs, clothing and behavior must be replaced by something unequivocally European. In this he is fanatical. It does not occur to him that what he is rejecting is authentic and valid, and that what he is taking on is meaningless imitation. And if it did occur to him, it would not matter in the least. This total indifference to cultural heritage appears to be a necessary adjunct to the early stages of nationalism.

Hospitality in North Africa knows no limits. You are taken in and treated as a member of the family. If you don't enjoy yourself, it is not your host's fault, but rather the result of your own inadaptability, for every attempt is made to see that you are happy and comfortable. Some time ago I was the guest of two brothers who had an enormous house in the *medina* of Fez. So that I should feel truly at home, I was given an entire wing of the establishment, a tiled patio with a room on either side and a fountain in the center. There were great numbers of servants to bring me food and drink, and also to inquire, before my hosts came to call, whether I was disposed to receive them. When they came they often brought singers and musicians to entertain me. The only hitch was that they went to such lengths to treat me as one of them that they also assumed I was not interested in going out into the city. During the entire fortnight I spent with them I never once found my way out of the house, or even out of my own section of it, since all doors were kept locked and bolted, and only the guard, an old Sudanese slave, had the keys. For long hours I sat in the patio listening to the sounds of the city outside, sometimes hearing faint strains of music that I would have given anything really to hear, watching the square of deep-blue sky above my head slowly become a softer and lighter blue as twilight approached, waiting for the swallows that wheeled above the patio when the day was finally over and the muezzins began their calls to evening prayer, and merely existing in the hope that someone would come, something would happen before too many more hours had gone past. But as I say, if I was bored, that was my own fault and not theirs. They were doing everything they could to please me.

Just as in that twelfth-century fortress in Fez I had been provided with a small hand-wound phonograph and one record (Josephine Baker singing "*J'ai deux amours*," a song hit of that year), so all over North Africa you are confronted with a mélange of the very old and the most recent, with no hint of anything from the intervening centuries. It is one of the great charms of the place, the fact that your today carries with it no memories of yesterday or the day before; everything that is not medieval is completely new. The younger generation of French and Jews, born and raised in the cities of North Africa, for the most part have no contact with that which is ancient in their countries. A Moroccan girl whose family moved from Rabat to New York, upon being asked what she thought of her new home, replied: "Well, of course, coming from a new country as I do, it's very hard to get used to all these old houses here in New York. I had no idea New York was so *old*." One is inclined to forget that the French began to settle in Morocco only at the time of World War I, and that the mushroom cities of Casablanca, Agadir and Tangier grew up in the 'thirties. Xauen, whose mountains are visible from the terrace of my apartment in Tangier, was entered by European troops for the first time in 1920. Even in southern Algeria, where one is likely to think of the French as having been stationed for a much longer time, there are war monuments bearing battle dates as recent as 1912. Throughout the whole first quarter of the century the North African frontier was continuously being pushed southward by means of warfare, and south of the Grand Atlas it was 1936 before "pacification" came to an end and European civilians were allowed, albeit on the strict terms laid down by the military, to look for the first time into the magic valleys of the Draa, the Dadès and the Todra.

Appearing unexpectedly in out-of-the-way regions of North Africa has never been without its difficulties. I remember making an impossible journey before the last world war in a produce truck over the Grand Atlas to Ouarzazat, full of excitement at the prospect of seeing the Casbah there with its strange painted towers, only to be forced to remain three days inside the shack that passed for a hotel, and then sent on another truck straight back to Marrakech, having seen nothing but Foreign Legionnaires, and having heard no music other than the bugle calls that issued every so often from the nearby camp. Another time I entered Tunisia on camelback from across the Great Eastern Erg. I had two camels and one hardworking camel driver, whose job it was to run all day long from one beast to the other and try, by whacking their hind legs, to keep them walking in something resembling a straight line. This was a much more difficult task than it sounds; although our course was generally due east, one of the animals had an inexplicable desire to walk southward, while the other was possessed by an equally mysterious urge to go north. The poor man passed his time screaming: "Hut! Aïda!" and trying to run both ways at once. His turban was continually coming unwound, and he had no time to attend to the scarf he was knitting, in spite of the fact that he kept the yarn and needles dangling around his neck, ready to work on at any moment.

We did finally cross the border and amble into Tunisia, where we were immediately apprehended by the police. The camel driver and his beasts were sent back to Algeria where they belonged, and I started on my painful way up through Tunisia, where the French authorities evidently had made a concerted decision to make my stay in the country as wretched as possible. In the oasis at Nefta, in the hotel at Tozeur, even in the mosque of Sidi Oqba at Kairouan, I was arrested and lugged off to the commissariat, carefully questioned and told that I need not imagine I could make a move of which they would not be fully aware.

The explanation was that in spite of my American passport they were convinced I was a German; in those days anybody wandering around *l'Afrique Mineure* (as one of the more erudite officers called this corner of the continent), if he did not satisfy the French idea of what a tourist should look like, was immediately suspect. Even the Moslems would look at me closely and say: "*Toi pas Français. Toi Allemand*," to which I never replied, for fear of having to pay the prices that would have been demanded if my true status had been revealed to them.

Algeria is a country where it is better to keep moving around than to stay long in one place. Its towns are not very interesting, but its landscapes are impressive. In the winter, traveling by train across the western steppes, you can go all day and see nothing but flat stretches of snow on all sides, unrelieved by trees in the foreground or by mountains in the distance. In the summer these same desolate lands are cruelly hot, and the wind swirls the dust into tall yellow pillars that move deliberately from one side of the empty horizon to the other. When you come upon a town in such regions, lying like the remains of a picnic lunch in the middle of an endless parking lot, you know it was the French who put it there. The Algerians prefer to live along the wild and beautiful seacoast, in the palm gardens of the south, atop the cliffs bordering the dry rivers, or on the crests of the high mountains in the center of the country. Up there above the slopes dotted with almond trees, the Berber villages sit astride the long spines of the lesser ranges. The men and women file down the zigzagging paths to cultivate the rich valleys below, here and there in full view of the snowfields where the French formerly had their skiing resorts. Far to the south lie the parallel chains of red sawtooth mountains which run northeast to southwest across the entire country and divide the plains from the desert.

No part of North Africa will again be the same sort of paradise for Europeans that it has been for them these last fifty years. The place has been thrown open to the twentieth century. With Europeanization and nationalism have come a consciousness of identity and the awareness of that identity's commercial possibilities. From now on the North Africans, like the Mexicans, will control and exploit their own charms, rather than being placed on exhibit for us by their managers, and the result will be a very different thing from what it has been in the past. Tourist land it still is, and doubtless will continue to be for a while; and it is on that basis only that we as residents or intending visitors are now obliged to consider it. We now come here as paying guests of the inhabitants themselves rather than of their exploiters. Travel here is certain not to be so easy or so comfortable as before, and prices are many times higher than they were, but at least we meet the people on terms of equality, which is a healthier situation.

If you live long enough in a place where the question of colonialism versus self-government is constantly being discussed, you are bound to find yourself having a very definite opinion on the subject. The difficulty is that some of your co-residents feel one way and some the other, but all feel strongly. Those in favor of colonialism argue that you can't "give" (quotes mine) an almost totally illiterate people political power and expect them to create a democracy, and that is doubtless true; but the point is that since they are inevitably going to take the power sooner or later, it is only reasonable to help them take it while they still have at least some measure of good will toward their erstwhile masters. The die-hard French attitude is summed up in a remark made to me by a friendly immigration officer at the Algiers airport. "Our great mistake," he said sadly, "was ever to allow these savages to learn to read and write." I said I supposed that was a logical thing to say if one expected to rule forever, which I knew, given the intelligence of the French, that they did not intend to try, since it was impossible. The official ceased looking sad and became much less friendly.

At a dinner in Marrakech during the French occupation, the Frenchman sitting beside me became engaged in an amicable discussion with a Moroccan across the table. "But look at the facts, *mon cher ami*. Before our arrival, there was constant warfare between the tribes. Since we came the population has doubled. Is that true or not?"

The Moroccan leaned forward. "We can take care of our own births and deaths," he said, smiling. "If we must be killed, just let other Moroccans attend to it. We really prefer that."

Notes Mailed at Nagercoil

Cape Comorin, South India
March, 1952

I HAVE been here in this hotel now for a week. At no time during the night or day has the temperature been low enough for comfort; it fluctuates between ninety-five and one hundred and five degrees, and most of the time there is absolutely no breeze, which is astonishing for the seaside. Each bedroom and public room has the regulation large electric fan in its ceiling, but there is no electricity; we are obliged to use oil lamps for lighting. Today at lunch time a large Cadillac of the latest model drove up to the front door. In the back were three fat little men wearing nothing but the flimsy *dhotis* they had draped around their loins. One of them handed a bunch of keys to the chauffeur, who then got out and came into the hotel. Near the front door is the switch box. He opened it, turned on the current with one of the keys, and throughout the hotel the fans began to whir. Then the three little men got out and went into the dining-room where they had their lunch. I ate quickly, so as to get upstairs and lie naked on my bed under the fan. It was an unforgettable fifteen minutes. Then the fan stopped, and I heard the visitors driving away. The hotel manager told me later that they were government employees of the State of Travancore, and that only they had a key to the switch box.*

Last night I awoke and opened my eyes. There was no moon; it was still dark, but the light of a star was shining into my face through the open window, from a point high above the Arabian Sea. I sat up, and gazed at it. The light it cast seemed as bright as that of the moon in northern countries; coming through the window, it made its rectangle on the opposite wall, broken by the shadow of my silhouetted head. I held up my hand and moved the fingers, and their shadow too was definite. There were no other stars visible in that part of the sky; this

---

*Subsequently Travancore and Cochin have merged to make the province of Kerala.

one blinded them all. It was about an hour before daybreak, which comes shortly after six, and there was not a breath of air. On such still nights the waves breaking on the nearby shore sound like great, deep explosions going on at some distant place. There is the boom, which can be felt as well as heard and which ends with a sharp rattle and hiss, then a long period of complete silence, and finally, when it seems that there will be no more sound, another sudden boom. The crows begin to scream and chatter while the darkness is still complete.

The town, like the others here in the extreme south, gives the impression of being made of dust. Dust and cow dung lie in the streets, and the huge crows hop ahead of you as you walk along. When a gust of hot wind wanders in from the sandy wastes beyond the town, the brown fans of the palmyra trees swish and bang against each other; they sound like giant sheets of heavy wrapping paper. The small black men walk quickly, the diamonds in their earlobes flashing. Because of their jewels and the gold thread woven into their dhotis, they all look not merely prosperous, but fantastically wealthy. When the women have diamonds, they are likely to wear them in a hole pierced through the wall of one nostril.

The first time I ever saw India I entered it through Dhanushkodi. An analogous procedure in America would be for a foreigner to get his first glimpse of the United States by crossing the Mexican border illegally and coming out into a remote Arizona village. It was God-forsaken, uncomfortable and a little frightening. Since then I have landed as a bonafide visitor should, in the impressively large and unbeautiful metropolis of Bombay. But I'm glad that my first trip did not bring me in contact with any cities. It is better to go to the villages of a strange land before trying to understand its towns, above all in a complex place like India. Now, after traveling some eight thousand miles around the country, I know approximately as little as I did on my first arrival. However, I've seen a lot of people and places, and at least I have a somewhat more detailed and precise idea of my ignorance than I did in the beginning.

If you have not taken the precaution of reserving a room in advance, you risk having considerable difficulty in finding one when you land in Bombay. There are very few hotels, and the two or three comfortable ones are always full. I hate being committed to a reservation because the element of adventure is thereby destroyed. The only place I was able to get into when I first arrived, therefore, was something less than a first-class establishment. It was all right during the day and the early hours of the evening. At night, however, every square foot of floor space in the dark corridors was occupied by sleepers who had arrived late and brought their own mats with them; the hotel was able in this way to shelter several hundred extra guests each night. Having their hands and feet kicked and trodden on was apparently a familiar enough experience to them for them never to make any audible objection when the inevitable happened. Here in Cape Comorin, on the other hand, there are many rooms and they are vast, and at the moment I am the only one staying in the hotel.

It was raining. I was on a bus going from Alleppey to Trivandrum, on my way down here. There are two little Indian nuns on the seat in front of mine. I wondered how they stood the heat in their heavy robes. Sitting near the driver was a man with a thick, fierce mustache who distinguished himself from the other passengers by the fact that in addition to his dhoti he also wore a European shirt; its scalloped tail hung down nearly to his knees. With him he had a voluminous collection of magazines and newspapers in both Tamil and English, and even from where I sat I could not help noticing that all this reading matter had been printed in the Soviet Union. (After years of practice one gets to recognize it without difficulty.)

At a certain moment, near one of the myriad villages that lie smothered in the depths of the palm forests, the motor suddenly ceased to function and the bus came to a stop. The driver, not exchanging a single glance with his passengers, let his head fall forward and remain resting on the steering wheel in a posture of despair. Expectantly the people waited a little while, and then they began to get up. One of the first out of the bus was the man with the mustache. He said a hearty good-bye to the occupants in general, although he had not been conversing with any of them, and started up the road carrying his umbrella, but not his armful of printed matter.

Then I realized that at some point during the past hour, not foreseeing the failure of the motor and the mass departure which it entailed, he had left a paper or magazine on each empty seat—exactly as our American comrades used to do on subway trains three decades ago.

Almost at the moment I made this discovery, the two nuns had risen and were hurriedly collecting the "literature." They climbed down and ran along the road after the man, calling out in English, "Sir, your papers!" He turned, and they handed them to him. Without saying a word, but with an expression of fury on his face, he took the bundle and continued. But it was impossible to tell from the faces of the two nuns when they returned to gather up their belongings whether or not they were conscious of what they had done.

A few minutes later everyone had left the bus and walked to the village—everyone, that is, but the driver and me. I had too much luggage. Then I spoke to him.

"What's the matter with the bus?"

He shrugged his shoulders.

"How am I going to get to Trivandrum?"

He did not know that, either.

"Couldn't you look into the motor?" I pursued. "It sounded like the fan belt. Maybe you could repair it."

This roused him sufficiently from his apathy to make him turn and look at me.

"We have People's Government here in Travancore," he said. "Not allowed touching motor."

"But who *is* going to repair it, then?"

"Tonight making telephone call to Trivandrum. Making report. Tomorrow or other day they sending inspector to examine."

"And then what?"

"Then inspector making report. Then sending repair crew."

"I see."

"People's Government," he said again, by way of helping me to understand. "Not like other government."

"No," I said.

As if to make his meaning clearer, he indicated the seat where the man with the large mustache had sat. "That gentleman Communist."

"Oh, really?" (At least it was all in the open and the driver was under no misapprehension as to what the term "People's Government" meant.)

"Very powerful man. Member of Parliament from Travancore."

"Is he a good man, though? Do the people like him?"

"Oh, yes, sir. Powerful man."

"But is he *good*?" I insisted.

He laughed, doubtless at my ingenuousness. "Powerful man all rascals," he said.

Just before nightfall a local bus came along, and with the help of several villagers I transferred my luggage to it and continued on my way.

Most of the impressively heavy Communist vote is cast by the Hindus. The Moslems are generally in less dire economic straits, it is true, but in any case, by virtue of their strict religious views, they do not take kindly to any sort of ideological change. (A convert from Islam is unthinkable; apostasy is virtually nonexistent.) If even Christianity has retained too much of its pagan décor to be acceptable to the puritanical Moslem mind, one can imagine the loathing inspired in them by the endless proliferations of Hindu religious art with its gods, demons, metamorphoses and avatars. The two religious systems are antipodal. Fortunately the constant association with the mild and tolerant Hindus has made the Moslems of India far more understanding and tractable than their brothers in Islamic countries further west; there is much less actual friction than one might be led to expect.

During breakfast one morning at the Connemara Hotel in Madras the Moslem head waiter told me a story. He was traveling in the Province of Orissa where, in a certain town, there was a Hindu temple which was famous for having five hundred cobras on its premises. He decided he would like to see these legendary reptiles. When he had got to the town he hired a carriage and went to the temple. At the door he was met by a priest who offered to show him around. And since the Moslem looked prosperous, the priest suggested a donation of five rupees, to be paid in advance.

"Why so much?" asked the visitor.

"To buy eggs for the cobras. You know, we have five hundred of them."

The Moslem gave him the money on condition that the priest let him see the snakes. For an hour his guide dallied in the many courtyards and galleries, pointing out bas-reliefs, idols, pillars and bells. Finally the Moslem reminded him of their understanding.

"Cobras? Ah, yes. But they are dangerous. Perhaps you would rather see them another day?"

This behavior on the priest's part had delighted him, he recalled, for it had reinforced his suspicions.

"Not at all," he said. "I want to see them now."

Reluctantly the priest led him into a small alcove behind a large stone Krishna, and pointed into a very dark corner.

"Is this the place?" the visitor asked.

"This is the place."

"But where are the snakes?"

In a tiny enclosure were two sad old cobras, "almost dead from hunger," he assured me. But when his eyes had grown used to the dimness he saw that there were hundreds of eggshells scattered around the floor outside the pen.

"You eat a lot of eggs," he told the priest.

The priest merely said, "Here. Take back your five rupees. But if you are asked about our cobras, please be so kind as to say that you saw five hundred of them here in our temple. Is that all right?"

The episode was meant to illustrate the head waiter's thesis, which was that the Hindus are abject in the practice of their religion; this is the opinion held by the Moslems. On the other hand, it must be remembered that the Hindu considers Islam an incomplete doctrine, far from satisfying. He finds its austerity singularly comfortless and deplores its lack of mystico-philosophical content, an element in which his own creed is so rich.

I was invited to lunch at one of the cinema studios in the suburbs north of Bombay. We ate our curry outdoors; our hostess was the star of the film then in production. She spoke only Marathi; her husband, who was directing the picture, spoke excellent English. During the meal he told how, as a

Hindu, he had been forced to leave his job, his home, his car and his bank account in Karachi at the time of partition—when Pakistan came into existence—and emigrate empty-handed to India, where he had managed to remake his life. Another visitor to the studio, an Egyptian, was intensely interested in his story. Presently he interrupted to say, "It is unjust, of course."

"Yes," smiled our host.

"What retaliatory measures does your government plan to take against the Moslems left here in India?"

"None whatever, as far as I know."

The Egyptian was genuinely indignant. "But why not?" he demanded. "It is only right that you apply the same principle. You have plenty of Moslems here still to take action against. And I say that even though I am a Moslem."

The film director looked at him closely. "You say that *because* you are a Moslem," he told him. "But we cannot put ourselves on that level."

The conversation ended on this not entirely friendly note. A moment later packets of betel were passed around. I promptly broke a tooth, withdrew from the company and went some distance away into the garden. While I, in the interests of science, was examining the mouthful of partially chewed betel leaves and areca nut, trying to find the pieces of biscuspid, the Egyptian came up to me, his face a study in scorn.

"They are afraid of the Moslems. That's the real reason," he whispered. Whether he was right or wrong I was neither qualified nor momentarily disposed to say, but it was a classical exposition of the two opposing moral viewpoints—two concepts of behavior which cannot quickly be reconciled.

Obviously it is a gigantic task to make a nation out of a place like India, what with Hindus, Moslems, Parsees, Jainists, Jews, Catholics and Protestants, some of whom may speak the arbitrarily imposed national idiom of Hindi, but most of whom are more likely to know Gujarati, Marathi, Bengali, Urdu, Telugu, Tamil, Malayalam or some other tongue. One wonders whether any sort of unifying project can ever be undertaken, or, indeed, whether it is even desirable.

When you come to the border between two provinces you often find bars across the road, and you are obliged to undergo a thorough inspection of your luggage. As in the

United States, there is a strict control of the passage of liquor between wet and dry districts, but that is not the extent of the examination.

Sample of conversation at the border on the Mercara-Cannanore highway:

Customs officer: "What is in there?"

Bowles: "Clothing."

"And in that?"

"Clothing."

"And in all those?"

"Clothing."

"Open all, please."

After eighteen suitcases have been gone through carefully: "My God, man! Close them all. I could charge duty for all of these goods, but you will never be able to do business with these things here anyway. The Moslem men are too clever."

"But I'm not intending to sell my clothes."

"Shut the luggage. It is duty-free, I tell you."

A professor from Raniket in North India arrived at the hotel here the other day, and we spent a good part of the night sitting on the window seat in my room that overlooks the sea, talking about what one always talks about here: India. Among the many questions I put to him was one concerning the reason why so many of the Hindu temples in South India prohibit entry to non-Hindus, and why they have military guards at the entrances. I imagined I knew the answer in advance: fear of Moslem disturbances. Not at all, he said. The principal purpose was to keep out certain Christian missionaries. I expressed disbelief.

"Of course," he insisted. "They come and jeer during our rituals, ridicule our sacred images."

"But even if they were stupid enough to want to do such things," I objected, "their sense of decorum would keep them from behaving like that."

He merely laughed. "Obviously you don't know them."

The post office here is a small stifling room over a shop, and it is full of boys seated on straw mats. The postmaster, a tiny old man who wears large diamond earrings and gold-rimmed spectacles, and is always naked to the waist, is also a professor; he interrupts his academic work to sell an occasional stamp.

At first contact his English sounds fluent enough, but soon one discovers that it is not adapted to conversation, and that one can scarcely talk to him. Since the boys are listening, he must pretend to be omniscient, therefore he answers promptly with more or less whatever phrase comes into his head.

Yesterday I went to post a letter by airmail to Tangier. "Tanjore," he said, adjusting his spectacles. "That will be four annas." (Tanjore is in South India, near Trichinopoly.) I explained that I hoped my letter would be going to Tangier, Morocco.

"Yes, yes," he said impatiently. "There are many Tanjores." He opened the book of postal regulations and read aloud from it, quite at random, for (although it may be difficult to believe) exactly six minutes. I stood still, fascinated, and let him go on. Finally he looked up and said, "There is no mention of Tangier. No airplanes go to that place."

"Well, how much would it be to send it by sea mail?" (I thought we could then calculate the surcharge for air mail, but I had misjudged my man.)

"Yes," he replied evenly. "That is a good method, too."

I decided to keep the letter and post it in the nearby town of Nagercoil another day. In a little while I would have several to add to it, and I counted on being able to send them all together when I went. Before I left the post office I hazarded the remark that the weather was extremely hot. In that airless attic at noon it was a wild understatement. But it did not please the postmaster at all. Deliberately he removed his glasses and pointed the stems at me.

"Here we have the perfect climate," he told me. "Neither too cold nor too cool."

"That is true," I said. "Thank you."

In the past few years there have been visible quantitative changes in Indian life, all in the one direction of Europeanization. This is in the smaller towns; the cities of course have long since been westernized. The temples which before were lighted by bare electric bulbs and coconut-oil lamps now have fluorescent tubes glimmering in their ceilings. Crimson, green and amber floodlights are used to illumine bathing tanks, deities, the gateways of temples. The public-address system is the bane of the ear these days, even in the temples. And it is impossible to attend a concert or a dance recital without discovering several loudspeakers whose noise completely destroys the quality of the music. A mile before you arrive at the cinema of a small town you can hear the raucous blaring of the amplifier they have set up at its entrance.

This year in South India there are fewer men with bare torsos, dhotis and sandals; more shirts, trousers and shoes. There is at the same time a slow shutting-down of services which to the Western tourist make all the difference between pleasure and discomfort in traveling, such as the restaurants in the stations (there being no dining cars on the trains) and the showers in the first-class compartments. A few years ago they worked; now they have been sealed off. You can choke on the dust and soot of your compartment, or drown in your own sweat now, for all the railway cares.

At one point I was held for forty-eight hours in a concentration camp run by the Ceylon government on Indian soil. (The euphemism for this one was "screening camp.") I was told that I was under suspicion of being an international spy. My astonishment and indignation were regarded as almost convincing in their sincerity, thus proof of my guilt.

"But who am I supposed to be spying *for*?" I asked piteously.

The director shrugged. "Spying for international," he said.

More than the insects or the howling of pariah dogs outside the rolls of barbed wire, what bothered me was the fact that in the center of the camp, which at that time housed some twenty thousand people, there was a loudspeaker in a high tower which during every moment of the day roared forth Indian film music. Fortunately it was silenced at ten o'clock each evening. I got out of the hell-hole only by making such violent trouble that I was dragged before the camp doctor, who decided that I was dangerously unbalanced. The idea in letting me go was that I would be detained further along, and the responsibility would fall on other shoulders. "They will hold him at Talaimannar," I heard the doctor say. "The poor fellow is quite mad."

Here and there, in places like the bar of the Hotel Metropole at Mysore, or at the North Coorg Club of Mercara, one may still come across vestiges of the old colonial life: ghosts in the form of incredibly sunburned Englishmen in jodhpurs and boots discussing their hunting luck and prowess. But these visions are exceedingly rare in a land that wants to forget their existence.

The younger generation in India is intent on forgetting a good many things, including some that it might do better to remember. There would seem to be no good reason for getting rid of their country's most ancient heritage, the religion of Hinduism, or of its most recent acquisition, the tradition of independence. This latter, at least insofar as the illiterate masses are concerned, is inseparable not only from the religious state of mind which made political victory possible, but also from the legend which, growing up around the figure of Gandhi, has elevated him in their minds to the status of a god.

The young, politically-minded intellectuals find this not at all to their liking; in their articles and addresses they have returned again and again to the attack against Gandhi as a "betrayer" of the Indian people. That they are motivated by hatred is obvious. But what do they hate?

For one thing, subconsciously they cannot accept their own inability to go on having religious beliefs. Then, belonging to the group without faith, they are thereby forced to hate the past, particularly the atavisms which are made apparent by the workings of the human mind with its irrationality, its subjective involvement in exterior phenomena. The floods of poisonous words they pour forth are directed primarily at the adolescents; this is an age group which is often likely to find demagoguery more attractive than common sense.

There are at least a few of these enlightened adolescents in every town; the ones here in Cape Comorin were horrified when by a stratagem I led them to the home of a man of their own village who claims that his brother is under a spell. (They had not imagined, they told me later, that an American would believe such nonsense.) According to the man Subramaniam, his brother was a painter who had been made art director of a major film studio in Madras. To substantiate his story he brought out a sheaf of very professional sketches for film sets.

"Then my brother had angry words with a jealous man in the studio," said Subramaniam, "and the man put a charm on him. His mind is gone. But at the end of the year it will return." The brother presently appeared in the courtyard; he was a vacant-eyed man with a beard, and he had a voluminous turkish towel draped over his head and shoulders. He walked past us and disappeared through a doorway.

"A spirit doctor is treating him . . ." The modern young men shifted their feet miserably; it was unbearable that an American should be witnessing such shameful revelations, and that they should be coming from one in their midst.

But these youths who found it so necessary to ridicule poor Subramaniam failed to understand why I laughed when, the conversation changing to the subject of cows, I watched their collective expression swiftly change to one of respect bordering on beatitude. For cow worship is one facet of popular Hinduism which has not yet been totally superseded by twentieth-century faithlessness. True, it has taken on new forms of ritual. Mass cow worship is often practiced now in vast modern concrete stadiums, with prizes being distributed to the owners of the finest bovine specimens, but the religious aspect of the celebration is still evident. The cows are decorated with garlands of jewelry, fed bananas and sugar cane by people who have waited in line for hours to be granted that rare privilege; and when the satiated animals can eat no more they simply lie down or wander about, while hundreds of young girls perform sacred dances in their honor.

In India, where the cow wishes to go she goes. She may be lying in the temple, where she may decide to get up to go and lie instead in the middle of the street. If she is annoyed by the proximity of the traffic streaming past her, she may lumber to her feet again and continue down the street to the railway station, where, should she feel like reclining in front of the ticket window, no one will disturb her. On the highways she seems to know that the drivers of trucks and buses will spot her a mile away and slow down almost to a stop before they get to her, and that therefore she need not move out from under the shade of the particular banyan tree she has chosen for her rest. Her superior position in the world is agreed upon by common consent.

The most satisfying exposition I have seen of the average Hindu's feeling about this exalted beast is a little essay composed by a candidate for a post in one of the public services, entitled simply "The Cow." The fact that it was submitted in order to show the aspirant's mastery of the English language, while touching, is of secondary importance.

THE COW

The cow is one wonderful animal, also he is quadruped and because he is female he gives milk—but he will do so only when he has got child. He is same like God, sacred to Hindu and useful to man. But he has got four legs together. Two are foreward and two are afterwards.

His whole body can be utilized for use. More so the milk. What it cannot do? Various ghee, butter, cream, curds, whey, kova and the condensed milk and so forth. Also, he is useful to cobbler, watermans and mankind generally.

His motion is slow only. That is because he is of amplitudinous species, and also his other motion is much useful to trees, plants as well as making fires. This is done by making flat cakes in hand and drying in the sun.

He is the only animal that extricates his feedings after eating. Then afterwards he eats by his teeth which are situated in the inside of his mouth. He is incessantly grazing in the meadows.

His only attacking and defending weapons are his horns, especially when he has got child. This is done by bowing his head whereby he causes the weapons to be parallel to ground of earth and instantly proceeds with great velocity forwards.

He has got tail also, but not like other similar animals. It has hairs on the end of the other side. This is done to frighten away the flies which alight on his whole body and chastises him unceasingly, whereupon he gives hit with it.

The palms of his feet are so soft unto the touch so that the grasses he eats would not get crushed. At night he reposes by going down on the ground and then he shuts his eyes like his relative the horse which does not do so. This is the cow.

The moths and night insects flutter about my single oil lamp. Occasionally, at the top of its chimney, one of them goes up in a swift, bright flame. On the concrete floor in a fairly well-defined ring around the bottom of my chair are the drops of sweat that have rolled off my body during the past two hours. The doors into both the bedroom and the bathroom are shut; I work each night in the dressing room between them, because fewer insects are attracted here. But the air is nearly unbreathable with the stale smoke of cigarettes and *bathi* sticks burned to discourage the entry of winged creatures. Today's paper announced an outbreak of bubonic plague in Bellary. I keep thinking about it, and I wonder if the almost certain eventual victory over such diseases will prove to have been worth its price: the extinction of the beliefs and rituals which gave a satisfactory meaning to the period of consciousness that goes between birth and death. I doubt it. Security is a false god; begin making sacrifices to it and you are lost.

Mustapha and His Friends

To qualify as Mustapha a man must be an illiterate city-dweller. All visitors to North Africa have known him, and most of them recall instances of his personal charm. In the not-too-distant future he will not exist; there is no room for his kind of innocence and spontaneous behavior in the world now being planned for him.

Mustapha may observe his religion to the letter, or partially, or not at all, but he will always call himself a Moslem. His first loyalty is to fellow Moslems from whatever country. The differences between the concepts of nationality, religion and race are indistinct. "I don't care whether that man is Portuguese or Christian or Negro or Greek. I'm a Moslem. He can't talk that way to me."

The difference between Mustapha and us is possibly even greater than it would be were he a Buddhist or a Hindu, for there is no religion on earth which demands stricter conformity to the tenets of its dogma than that supra-national brotherhood called Islam. Even the most visionary and idealistic among us of the Western world is more than likely to explain the purpose of life in terms of accomplishment. Our definition of that purpose will be a dynamic one in which it will be assumed desirable for each individual to contribute his share, however infinitesimal, to the total tangible or intangible enrichment of life. Mustapha does not see things that way at all. To him it is slightly absurd—the stress we lay upon work, our craving to "leave the world better than we found it," our unceasing efforts to produce ideas and objects. "We are not put on earth to work," he will tell you. "We are put here to pray; that is the purpose of life." This does not mean that Mustapha himself ever prays, for he doesn't. "There is no use in praying now and then," he insists. Either one prays properly or not at all, and it is too late for him to join the ranks of the devout. Any allusions, however, to his religious laxity must be made by himself and not by anyone else.

With a divergency of such proportions in so basic a matter, it is not surprising that the moral and social accompaniments should show at least the same degree of deviation from ours. Mustapha does not believe in the same good or evil as we do. Such personal concepts as continence and honesty, such social virtues as a taste for the "democratic way of life" and a sense of civic responsibility, mean very little to him. He thinks of peace as that boring and meaningless interlude between wars, of democracy as a weak and corrupt substitute for autocracy. The best ruler is a benevolent tyrant; there never was so good a sultan as Haroun el Rashid. The people of Fez are fond of singing the praises of one El Baghdadi, who was Pasha of Fez in the early part of the present century. He was, according to their accounts, a completely unscrupulous politician, a bandit, a racketeer. But he possessed a quality which for them far outweighed his greed and dishonesty: he was adamant in his equitable administering of justice. In their opinion no greater tribute can be given a ruler. I myself suspect that the Pasha el Baghdadi's justice had much in common with that of a certain *caid* in the Middle Atlas about whom the people were enthusiastic because, as they explained, he invariably ruled in favor of the man who paid him most (instead of accepting gifts from all sides and then clapping everyone into prison). This is, I presume, simple straightforward honesty; in any case, the caid in question earned the respect of his subjects for exercising it.

Mustapha knows that virtue is rewarded and evil is punished; his religion tells him that, but he is a past-master at juggling the two concepts in order to befuddle himself and ease his not-too-active conscience. In the home, save to professional thieves, property is theoretically sacred. But an object inadvertently left on a windowsill or outside a door for a moment no longer falls into the category of private property. Even if you leave something on your terrace whose removal requires the use of hooks, rope and a twenty-foot length of bamboo pole, you will eventually find that your neighbors have appropriated it. After all, it was not *in* your house, and so how can they be blamed for imagining that perhaps it was theirs and had fallen from their terrace down to yours? And anyway, it had been out there so long that you couldn't possibly have wanted it. And besides, they will remind you, if you are so ingenuous as to allow yourself to fall into an altercation with them about it, everything you have really belongs to them in any case, since you are in their country uninvited by them. There is no viable reply to this argument; it is best to avoid situations in which they can proffer it. What Mustapha is primarily interested in is the spoils, and he must be the victor. Force and ruse go hand in hand; he is adroit in combining them. Even in friendship, love, marriage and family relationships, at one time or another he will try in some way to get the better of the others. Only that can give him the glow of satisfaction which he seems to need so urgently.

Mustapha knows his fellow countrymen. He is aware that often all he needs to do is to mention a price in order to involve an intended victim in the game of bargaining—even if the object to be sold is of little or no interest to the possible buyer. It will assume importance as a result of playing with the price, and he is correct in counting on the other's inability to let what he thinks is an advantageous purchase go by the boards. In each town there is an extensive *joteya*, or flea market, where practically anything Mustapha could want can be bought at second-hand. What he finds particularly fascinating is clothing for himself, usually cast-off European clothing. He can look at shoes all day, trying them on and taking them off, inspecting their soles and lasts and stitches. A good fit is not uppermost in his mind; shoes are objects of art first, and wearing apparel only incidentally. If he buys a pair, he will limp about in them for a few days and then very likely go and sell them again, perhaps making a little something on the sale if he is clever, perhaps losing; it is not important. To appear among his friends in different garments as often as possible is a way of raising his prestige. He will go off to the joteya with a new shirt, sell it, and pay the same sum of money for a second-hand one in order to sit down in his usual café that evening in a shirt which is not the same one he wore the night before.

It is not the complete truth to say that he has lost all semblance of taste and wants to Europeanize himself at whatever cost. Certainly once he has abandoned his own esthetic traditions he no longer knows which way to turn, and thus will take whatever is available in the way of clothing. His preference is not necessarily for Nazarene trousers and shoes; however, preference plays a small part in his life. Native garments are prohibitively expensive these days. They are hand sewn and decorated, and the material for the *djellaba* is hand woven. The shoes are also fashioned entirely by hand. Only the relatively well-to-do city-dwellers can afford such luxuries in this age of transition. And so Mustapha wears what he can get, and gives thanks to Allah for it, though it be an old G.I. shirt and a pair of Levis.

If he is in a playful mood, Mustapha will wait, after making purchases in a shop, for the opportunity of making away with a postcard, a packet of needles, or some equally worthless and uncoveted object, simply in order to experience the pleasurable sensation of having bested the shopkeeper. There is, in addition, a certain superstitious element in the insistence upon getting something for nothing: success in such little exploits, like receiving an unexpected gift, is a proof of being in a state of grace.

In games, knowing the rules and being a competent player are merely a basic *sine qua non*, such as being able to move one's fingers in order to play the flute. The expert proves his mastery of the fine points through his ability both to engage in undetected cheating and to carry out the successful unmasking of the cheating done by his adversary. Very seldom is a player reconciled to losing. The vanquished generally complains vehemently of the victor's underhanded comportment. This would seem illogical, considering that not only has he been unable to detect it during his close scrutiny of his opponent's game, but has employed the same methods himself; but logic is the last thing to look for in Mustapha's behavior.

And yet this ever-present distrust (including the locking away of one's clothing at home, for fear the other members of the family may steal it and sell it), this constant suspicion and openly expressed hostility to everyone, qualities which at first sight may appear unworthy of a civilized people, provide a healthy outlet to the emotions, if one can judge from the scarcity of serious crime in the community. Petty offenses abound; that is inevitable when Moslems have been subjected to the rule of a foreign nation whose laws, not being based on Koranic precepts, they neither understand nor respect. But premeditated murder is extremely rare, and so-called sex maniacs are unknown. Perhaps this is because Mustapha, not being well-versed in the art of self-control, nor even, doubtless, able to see any particular virtue in it, is inclined to do what he feels like doing at any given moment, and thus remains relatively unrepressed. His enthusiasms and rages are likely to be short-lived. Sometimes one has the fleeting impression, living in his world, that one is living among children playing at being grownups. But the act is played with such artistry, and so amusingly, that one is willing to accept the impersonations at their face value.

Although Mustapha may do what he feels like doing, simply because no other course has suggested itself to him, he will almost never say what is in his mind. For, according to his devious reasoning, if he were to utter his true thoughts, he would be giving himself away, playing recklessly into your hands. Thus it is extremely important for him to make conversation which will lead you away from, rather than toward, whatever is in his mind or what he believes to be the truth. His words make, as it were, a two-dimensional decoration to cover the wall of time, with little concern for representation and none at all for giving the illusion of depth. They may be amusing or dull, orderly or chaotic, rational or utterly self-contradictory, but only by some miracle brought about by the laws of chance will they be a sincere attempt to convey a true picture of the pattern of his mind, or a straightforward recounting of what he knows to be a fact. He is a genius at forging the most involved, and sometimes even briefly plausible, chains of improbabilities. His excuses are masterpieces of fictional inventiveness, his resources inexhaustible. Assuredly he does not expect you to give credence to his tales; if for reasons of courtesy you let it appear that you do so, you fall into the category of persons to be treated with contempt. On the other hand, he does expect you to refrain from being such a boor as to suggest to him that he is not telling you the truth. The middle course consists in listening and being entertained, and perhaps handing him back a fairly obvious lie in exchange; this strikes him as properly civilized behavior. It never occurs to him that he may risk losing your respect with his lies, because he assumes that you would naturally like to be as accomplished a liar as he but simply haven't the virtuosity. He and his friends have often remarked upon my disinclination to go in for this form of amusement, but their comment has ordinarily taken the form of commiseration for my hopeless ineptitude at deception. "Only a fool tries to say the truth," they tell me. The more speculative ones will go off into a fancy and specious kind of argument according to which, since only Allah knows the nature of truth, man can scarcely take it upon himself to pass judgment as to what is true and what is false.

Since Mustapha's behavior at any given moment is considerably more affected by the emotional factors involved than would be thought entirely normal among us, there is a good deal of latitude in the list of his possible reactions to a set of circumstances. The same kind of incident may make him quarrelsome on one occasion, fearful on another, or depressed or merely philosophical; it depends upon how he felt beforehand.

He is the adventurer par excellence. He expects life to have something of the variety and flavor of *The Thousand and One Nights*, and if that pungency is lacking he does his best to supply it. A whole-hearted believer in dangerous living, he often takes outrageous chances. This is not bravery (although he can be remarkably courageous and even stoical if he feels it to be necessary) nor sheer bravado, nor is it simple ignorance of the nature or presence of peril. Say, rather, it is a refusal to believe that action entails result. To him each is separate, everything having been determined at the beginning of time, when the inexorable design of destiny was laid out. All of life is a desperate gamble, and everyone has the odds against him. It is the most monstrous absurdity to fear death, the future, or the consequence of one's acts, since that would be tantamount to fearing life itself. Thus to be prudent is laughable, to be frugal is despicable, and to be provident borders on the sinful. How can a man be so presumptuous as to assume that tomorrow, let alone next year, will actually arrive? And so how dare he tempt fate to the point of preparing for any part of the future, either immediate or distant? The wise man is complete in himself at every moment, with no strings of hopefulness stretching out toward the future, entangling his soul and possibly making it loath to leave this life. Mustapha will tell you that the true Moslem is always ready for death at an instant's notice.

Should Mustapha ever get hold of any more money than he needs for his immediate living, he will not put it into the bank, because he says that, along with investments and usury, it is a sinful thing to use a bank. While dogma supports his contention, a more immediate and cogent reason is that he places absolutely no trust in banks. He wants his money where he can take it out and count it when he feels that need.

He has a passion for personal independence. He does not look for assistance from others; indeed, he is incapable of receiving it; nor does he believe in the possibility of one person helping another, since all aid comes from Allah. Even the gift of money a beggar has managed to elicit from a stranger in the street will be shown triumphantly to a friend with the remark, "See what God gave me." Provided with sufficient aid and impetus from the outside, he will accomplish exactly nothing with it, since it has never occurred to him that a man might be able to influence the course of his own existence. His general idea about life is that it is a visit: you come, stay awhile and go away again. The circumstances and length of the stay are beyond anyone's control and, therefore, only of slight interest. He does not know the meaning of ambition, which is a long-term drive and must be fairly constant. One might say that the difference between ambition and the fitful pangs of longing for wealth and property felt by Mustapha is one of tense: ambition is properly expressed in the future tense, whereas the latter is best defined by using the conditional.

Probably the facet of Mustapha's life which interests the West more than any other is his attitude toward the women of his society, the fact that he and his co-religionists insist upon keeping them sequestered and out of touch with the world. This is perhaps the very heart of his civilization, conditioning almost every aspect of it; even the architecture has evolved with an eye to providing the females of the family group with a maximum of seclusion. It is all very well for outsiders to complain that the system is barbarous and to clamor for "progress," but even assuming that a relaxation of the strictures is desirable, the far-reaching results of such a change will affect the entire social and moral fabric of the civilization; and if imposed from the outside by law it can produce only

disintegration and anarchy. The campaign for feminine liberation will inevitably come, but it must come from within, from
the women themselves, at the time and in the way they feel
the need for it. The men are fond of saying, "A woman
should go out only three times." These are: once when she
emerges from her mother's womb, once when she marries
(that is, when she leaves her father's house and goes to her
husband's), and once when she leaves the world. This is still
the opinion in many orthodox homes, but in others a much
wider latitude is being allowed the girls and women than
would have seemed possible in the mid-'fifties.

Mustapha has very little of what we would call "respect" for
women, and this is not surprising, since during his childhood
and adolescence he has been kept away from them by the traditional division of the sexes which operates throughout his
society, and thus has been denied the opportunity of learning
much about them. Whatever contacts he has had before marriage will have been with prostitutes, and he is likely to consider their manner of thinking the norm; he believes they are
more or less what every girl would like to become if she were
not kept from it by sheer force. He will of course except his
mothers and sisters from the general wickedness he attributes
to women, but they are about the only ones who escape his
censure. He shares the widespread conviction among his kind
that females are wild beasts and must be kept caged.

Listen to the conversation in a café. If it is not about
money or politics, the chances are that it will be a vociferous
attack on women—their perfidy, their cunning, their greed
and their general malevolence. The men never waste time describing their charms. Instead they exhibit scars, mutilations,
and the various marks left by slow poison (recognized in time
for them to escape before its effects proved lethal). These are
the battle scars of which they are neither proud nor ashamed;
it's a part of life, and a man has to expect it. But they do get
a certain pleasure out of using their exhibits as object lessons
to accompany their excoriations of woman. At a dramatic
point in the lecture, the turban will be raised to show the
place where the ear used to be, or the arm bared to expose
the purple and black mottles on the flesh, left by the poison.
The direct attack with knife or razor while the man sleeps is

understandable; it corresponds to the classical rolling pin or the stray plate hurtling through the kitchen doorway, immortalized for our culture by the comic strip, but it is also far less usual than poison.

Living in an atmosphere in which this sort of thing is taken for granted as a normal attribute of daily life, the men can scarcely be blamed for claiming that women should be kept in cages, and for considering them a dangerous if highly necessary evil. To point out to them that the man-versus-woman feud is a vicious circle, and that the women behave the way they do as a result of centuries of subjection and incarceration, produces no reaction at all. But if Mustapha's attitude toward the female of the species may seem at times to border on the pathological, the women, on the other hand, live in a world of their own where there is no particular deep-seated terror of the lord and master. They have always known they were cleverer than men and that to get around them it was necessary only to put them in the right humor. If a man *feels* like believing his wife, for instance, that's all she asks; it would be too much to expect him really to believe her, since she knows it is axiomatic in the man's world that a woman *never* tells the truth under any conditions.

The behavior of a group of women together resembles that of the children of a classroom where the teacher has stepped outside for a moment. If a man's voice is heard, conversation and giggling stop, and the ladies adopt a serious mien. When they think they are alone again, they go back to their joking and ribaldry; this deportment is conditioned more by traditional respect, however, than by fear.

Let us assume that Aicha's husband has gone to work. She thinks it would be fun to go down the street to Yamina's house and see her new baby, so, since it would be improper to set out alone, she climbs up onto the roof and suggests the idea to Haddouj, the servant girl who works next door and at the moment is hanging some clothes up to dry. Haddouj cautions her not to speak too loud, as her mistress may hear; that would not do, because she would be sure to forbid the excursion, and in any case, the fun consists in sneaking out behind the lady's back. Somewhat later Aicha has tied on her litham, which covers all of her face but her eyes, and got into her *haik*, which gives her the shape of an enormous, full laundry bag. Haddouj has done likewise. They open their respective doors a crack, communicate in stage whispers their readiness to depart, and slip out into the street, where they hurry along among the donkeys and passers-by to the door of the house of Kinza. Here they pick up not only Kinza, but her two cousins who are visiting from out of town, her sister, and two more neighbors. This makes the mission far more respectable. Then they go unabashedly in a body to Zodeiya's house and bang on the door. Unfortunately her husband is at home. "Who is it?" he growls. (No one ever opens a door without first asking who is there. The answer must be "I." Then the one inside says, "Who are you?" Only then may the knocker give his name, which normally is insufficient to warrant having the door opened for him until further information has been gathered as to the purpose of the call.) The sound of the husband's voice disconcerts the little group of ladies, and they hurry away, tittering. Poor Zodeiya will have to miss the fun, and she will be sad when she hears how they all went to see Yamina's baby, because, although she could go more or less any time by getting a neighbor to accompany her, it is not every day that she could find eight other ladies with whom to pay the call. The larger the group, the greater the prestige which accrues to each member of it.

Yamina's husband, thanks to Allah, is out, but her brother happens to have stopped by to see her. After they have knocked, and their separate identities have been properly checked on, there is a long wait, and presently the brother slams out of the house, bumping into the ladies clustered around the door as if they were invisible to him. He slouches sullenly down the street to a café, where he will sit during their visit, for the house is a small one and there is no corner in which he could decently remain while they are present. The daughter of the maid who works for the people who live next door to Yamina's mother has agreed to come and help out during the first few weeks after the baby's arrival. She is nine years old, but she does all the heavy work in the house as well as caring for the two babies while Yamina is busy preparing the meals. The ladies troop in and amid much laughter remove their haiks and veils. Yamina sends the girl out to buy a pack of cigarettes; it is very daring and elegant to smoke. The girl goes to the front door with the money and hands it to a six-year-old boy playing in the street, and gives him the instructions as to what he must do with it. She would really like to go herself, but the presence of so many ladies has made her feel very grown-up, and it is not really proper that she be seen in the street. The boy returns with the cigarettes, she delivers them to Yamina, and the ladies light up. When the party is at its height and everyone is screaming with laughter at the bawdy gyrations of Kinza, who is performing a belly dance in the center of the room, a hammering comes at the door. In a split second there is silence, and the ladies look at one another in alarm. "Who is it?" cries Yamina. The answering voice proves to be that of her husband. There are squeals of consternation as lithams and haiks are reached for and hastily donned. During this time the master of the house continues to pound on the door, although Yamina has already explained through the din that he will have to wait until her guests have left. By the time they are all dressed and ready to leave, the banging has ceased and he has gone away. Yamina climbs up onto two packing cases piled one upon the other, and peers out the tiny window near the ceiling to be certain that he has disappeared, whereupon they all sit down again and go on talking until he returns an hour or so later and shouts that if her guests don't get out he will break down the door. This is merely a figure of speech. Yamina unbolts the door and the ladies file out with dignity, pretending not to see Yamina's husband as he stands their glaring at them. And thus ends a pleasant episode in the day's activities.

The simple life that Mustapha leads fosters simple virtues. His famous hospitality is a point of honor with him, and goes hand in hand with his generosity. Like most people unencumbered with the latter-day passion for general information, his memory is fantastically clear; he can often recall in detail what he had to eat on a certain day five years ago (although he may think it was two years ago, since he has practically no sense of time). His powers of observation are extraordinarily acute, and his sense-impressions, while perhaps not highly differentiated, are intense; he is very conscious of smell, color, sound and texture, and he takes it for granted that the senses with which he perceives them were given him to be gratified on every possible occasion. He can spend hours merely sitting on the ground, looking out over a landscape, in a kind of contemplation that you and I will never know. He is not engaging in metaphysical reflections; you might say, rather, that he is enjoying the act of existing. He has not yet abrogated the pact between nature and man, according to whose terms she commands and he obeys. And so he has unlimited patience and faith—not in Allah's mercy, but in His might. That which is all-powerful goes far beyond the realm of moral considerations. The supreme law of the universe is that what is inexorable is thereby right, and he wants to feel that there is something of this quality in the character of his earthly ruler. As long as he remains the way he is, he will align himself with the faction which has the greatest number of visible attributes of ruthless power. This is something which the statesmen, both Moslem and otherwise, seem inclined to overlook when they speak of imposing upon him the onus of universal suffrage and make their perilous plans for initiating him into the mysteries of the democratic way of life.

A Man Must Not Be Very Moslem

Aboard m/s Tarsus,
Turkish Maritime Lines
September 25, 1953

WHEN I announced my intention of bringing Abdeslam along to Istanbul, the general opinion of my friends was that there were a good many more intelligent things to do in the world than to carry a Moroccan Moslem along with one to Turkey. I don't know. He may end up as a dead weight, but my hope is that he will turn out instead to be a kind of passkey to the place. He knows how to deal with Moslems, and he has the Moslem sense of seemliness and protocol. He has also an intuitive gift for the immediate understanding of a situation and at the same time is completely lacking in reticence or inhibitions. He can lie so well that he convinces himself straightway, and he is a master at bargaining; it is a black day for him when he has to pay the asking price for anything. He never knows what is printed on a sign because he is totally illiterate; besides, even if he did know he would pay no attention, for he is wholly deficient in respect for law. If you mention that this or that thing is forbidden, he is contemptuous: "Agh! a decree for the wind!" Obviously he is far better equipped than I to squeeze the last drop of adventure out of any occasion, I, unfortunately, *can* read signs but can't lie or bargain effectively, and will forgo any joy rather than risk unpleasantness or reprimand from whatever quarter. At all events, the die is cast: Abdeslam is here on the ship.

My first intimation of Turkey came during tea this afternoon, as the ship was leaving the Bay of Naples. The orchestra was playing a tango which finally established its identity, after several reprises, as the "Indian Love Call," and the cliffs of Capri were getting in the way of the sunset. I glanced at a biscuit that I was about to put into my mouth, then stopped the operation to examine it more closely. It was an ordinary little arrowroot tea-biscuit, and on it were embossed the words HAYD PARK. Contemplating this edible tidbit, I recalled what friends had told me of the amusing havoc that results

when the Turks phoneticize words borrowed from other languages. These metamorphosed words have a way of looking
like gibberish until you say them aloud, and then more likely
than not they resolve themselves into perfectly comprehensible English or French or, even occasionally, Arabic. SKOÇ
TUID looks like nothing; suddenly it becomes Scotch Tweed.
TUALET, TRENÇKOT, OTOTEKNIK and SEKSOLOJI likewise reveal their messages as one stares at them. Synthetic orthogra-
phy is a constantly visible reminder of Turkey's determination
to be "modern." The country has turned its back on the East
and Eastern concepts, not with the simple yearning of other
Islamic countries to be European or to acquire American
techniques, but with a conscious will to transform itself from
the core outward—even to destroy itself culturally, if need be.

Tarabya, Bosporus
     This afternoon it was blustery and very cold. The water in
the tiny Sea of Marmara was choppy and dark, laced with
froth; the ship rolled more heavily than it had at any time
during its three days out on the open Mediterranean. If the
first sight of Istanbul was impressive, it was because the perfect hoop of a rainbow painted across the lead-colored sky
ahead kept one from looking at the depressing array of factory smokestacks along the western shore. After an hour's
moving backward and forward in the harbor, we were close
enough to see the needles of the minarets (and how many of
them!) in black against the final flare-up of the sunset. It was
a poetic introduction, and like the introductions to most
books, it had very little to do with what followed. "Poetic" is
not among the adjectives you would use to describe the dis-
embarkation. The pier was festive; it looked like an elegant
waterside restaurant or one of the larger Latin-American air-
ports—brilliantly illumined, awnings flapping, its decks
mobbed with screaming people.
     The customs house was the epitome of confusion for a half-
hour or so; when eventually an inspector was assigned us, we
were fortunate enough to be let through without having to
open anything. The taxis were parked in the dark on the far
side of a vast puddle of water, for it had been raining. I had

determined on a hotel in Istanbul proper, rather than one of those in Beyoğlu, across the Golden Horn, but the taxi driver and his front-seat companion were loath to take me there. "All hotels in Beyoğlu," they insisted. I knew better and did some insisting of my own. We shot into the stream of traffic, across the Galata Bridge, to the hotel of my choosing. Unhappily I had neglected, on the advice of various friends back in Italy, to reserve a room. There was none to be had. And so on, from hotel to hotel there in Istanbul, back across the bridge and up the hill to every establishment in Beyoğlu. Nothing, nothing. There are three international conventions in progress here, and besides, it is vacation time in Turkey; everything is full. Even the m/s *Tarsus*, from which we just emerged, as well as another ship in the harbor, has been called into service tonight to be used as a hotel. By half past ten I accepted the suggestion of being driven twenty-five kilometers up the Bosporus to a place, where they had assured me by telephone that they had space.

"Do you want a room with bath?" they asked.

I said I did.

"We haven't any," they told me.

"Then I want a room without bath."

"We have one." That was that.

Once we had left the city behind and were driving along the dark road, there was nothing for Abdeslam to do but catechize the two Turks in front. Obviously they did not impress him as being up-to-the-mark Moslems, and he started by testing their knowledge of the Koran. I thought they were replying fairly well, but he was contemptuous. "They don't know anything," he declared in Moghrebi. Going into English, he asked them: "How many times one day you pray?"

They laughed.

"People can sleep in mosque?" he pursued. The driver was busy navigating the curves in the narrow road, but his companion, who spoke a special brand of English all his own, spoke for him. "Not slep in mosque many people every got hoss," he explained.

"You make sins?" continued Abdeslam, intent on unearthing the hidden flaws in the behavior of these foreigners. "Pork, wine?"

The other shrugged his shoulders. "Muslim people every not eat pork not drink wine but maybe one hundred year ago like that. Now different."

"*Never* different!" shouted Abdeslam sternly. "You not good Moslems here. People not happy. You have bad government. Not like Egypt. Egypt have good government. Egypt one-hundred-percent Moslem."

The other was indignant. "Everybody happy," he protested. "Happy with Egypt too for religion. But the Egypts sometimes fight with Egypts. Arab fight Arabs. Why? I no like Egypt. I in Egypt. I ask my way. They put me say bakhshish. If you ask in Istanbul, you say I must go my way, he can bring you, but he no say give *bakhshish*. Before, few people up, plenty people down. Now, you make your business, I make my business. You take your money, I take my money. Before, *you* take *my* money. You rich with *my* money. Before, Turkey like Egypt with Farouk." He stopped to let all this sink in, but Abdeslam was not interested.

"Egypt very good country," he retorted, and there was no more conversation until we arrived. At the hotel the driver's comrade was describing a fascinating new ideology known as democracy. From the beginning of the colloquy I had my notebook out, scribbling his words in the dark as fast as he spoke them. They express the average uneducated Turk's reaction to the new concept. It was only in 1950 that the first completely democratic elections were held. (Have there been any since?) To Abdeslam, who is a traditionally-minded Moslem, the very idea of democracy is meaningless. It is impossible to explain it to him; he will not listen. If an idea is not explicitly formulated in the Koran, it is wrong; it came either directly from Satan or via the Jews, and there is no need to discuss it further.

This hotel, built at the edge of the lapping Bosporus, is like a huge wooden box. At the base of the balustrade of the grand staircase leading up from the lobby, one on each side, are two life-sized ladies made of lead and painted with white enamel in the hope of making them look like marble. The dining room's decorations are of a more recent period—the early 'twenties. There are high murals that look as though the artist had made a study of Boutet de Monvel's fashion drawings of the era; long-necked, low-waisted females in cloches and thigh-length skirts, presumably picnicking on the shores of the Bosporus.

At dinner we were the only people eating, since it was nearly midnight. Abdeslam took advantage of this excellent opportunity by delivering an impassioned harangue (partly in a mixture of Moghrebi and Standard Arabic and partly in English), with the result that by the end of the meal we had fourteen waiters and bus boys crowded around the table listening. Then someone thought of fetching the chef. He arrived glistening with sweat and beaming; he had been brought because he spoke more Arabic than the others, which was still not very much. "Old-fashioned Moslem," explained the head-waiter. Abdeslam immediately put him through the *chehade*, and he came off with flying colors, reciting it word for word along with Abdeslam: "*Achhaddouanlaillahainallah. . . .*" The faces of the younger men expressed unmistakable admiration, as well as pleasure at the approval of the esteemed foreigner, but none of them could perform the chef's feat. Presently the manager of the hotel came in, presumably to see what was going on in the dining room at this late hour. Abdeslam asked for the check, and objected when he saw that it was written with Roman characters. "Arabic!" he demanded. "You Moslem? Then bring check in Arabic." Apologetically the manager explained that writing in Arabic was "dangerous," and had been known on occasion to put the man who did it into jail. To this he added, just to make things quite clear, that any man who veiled his wife also went to jail. "A man must not be *very* Moslem," he said. But Abdeslam had had enough. "I *very very* Moslem," he announced. We left the room.

The big beds stand high off the floor and haven't enough covers on them. I have spread my topcoat over me; it is cold and I should like to leave the windows shut, but the mingled stenches coming from the combined shower-lavatory behind a low partition in the corner are so powerful that such a course is out of the question. The winds moving down from the Black Sea will blow over me all night. Sometime after we had gone to bed, following a long silence during which I thought he had fallen asleep, Abdeslam called over to me:

"That Mustapha Kemal was carrion! He ruined his country. The son of a dog!" Because I was writing, and also because I am not sure exactly where I stand in this philosophical dispute, I said: "You're right. *Allah imsik bekhir.*"

Sirkeci, September 29

We are installed at Sirkeci on the Istanbul side, in the hotel I had first wanted. Outside the window is a taxi stand. From early morning onward there is the continuous racket of men shouting and horns being blown in a struggle to keep recently arrived taxis from edging in ahead of those that have been waiting in line. The general prohibition of horn-blowing, which is in effect everywhere in the city, doesn't seem to apply here. The altercations are bitter, and everyone gets involved in them. Taxi drivers in Istanbul are something of a race apart. They are the only social group who systematically try to take advantage of the foreign visitor. In the ships, restaurants, cafés, the prices asked of the newcomer are the same as those paid by the inhabitants. (In the bazaars buying is automatically a matter of wrangling; that is understood.) The cab drivers, however, are more actively acquisitive. For form's sake, their vehicles are equipped with meters, but their method of using them is such that they might better do without them. You get into a cab whose meter registers seventeen liras thirty kuruş, ask the man to turn it back to zero and start again, and he laughs and does nothing. When you get out it registers eighteen liras eighty kuruş. You give him the difference—one lira and a half. Never! He may want two and a half or three and a half or a good deal more, but he will not settle for what seems equitable according to the meter. Since most tourists pay what they are asked and go on their way, he is not prepared for an argument, and he is likely to let his temper run away with him if you are recalcitrant. There is also the pre-arranged-price system of taking a cab. Here the driver goes as slowly and by as circuitous a route as possible, calling out the general neighborhood of his destination for all in the streets to hear, so that he can pick up extra fares en route. He will, unless you assert yourself, allow several people to pile in on top of you until there is literally no room left for you to breathe.

The streets are narrow, crooked and often precipitous; traffic is very heavy, and there are many tramcars and buses. The result is that the taxis go like the wind whenever there is a space of a few yards ahead, rushing to the extreme left to get around obstacles before oncoming traffic reaches them. I am used to Paris and Mexico, both cities of evil repute where taxis are concerned, but I think Istanbul might possibly win first prize for thrill-giving.

One day our driver had picked up two extra men and mercifully put them in front with him, when he spied a girl standing on the curb and slowed down to take her in, too. A policeman saw his maneuver and did not approve: one girl with five men seemed too likely to cause a disturbance. He blew his whistle menacingly. The driver, rattled, swerved sharply to the left, to pretend he had never thought of such a thing as stopping to pick up a young lady. There was a crash and we were thrown forward off the seat. We got out; the last we saw of the driver, he was standing in the middle of the street by his battered car, screaming at the man he had hit, and holding up all traffic. Abdeslam took down his license number in the hope of persuading me to instigate a lawsuit.

Since the use of the horn is proscribed, taxi drivers can make their presence known only by reaching out the window and pounding violently on the outside of the door. The scraping of the tramcars and the din of the enormous horse-drawn carts thundering over the cobbled pavements make it difficult to judge just how much the horn interdiction reduces noise. The drivers also have a pretty custom of offering cigarettes at the beginning of the journey; this is to soften up the victim for the subsequent kill. On occasion they sing for you. One morning I was entertained all the way from Sulemaniye to Taksim with "Jezebel" and "Come On-a My House." In such cases the traffic warnings on the side of the car are done in strict rhythm.

Istanbul is a jolly place; it's hard to find any sinister element in it, notwithstanding all the spy novels for which it provides such a handsome setting. A few of the older buildings are of stone; but many more of them are built of wood which looks as though it had never been painted. The cupolas and minarets rise above the disorder of the city like huge gray fungi growing out of a vast pile of ashes. For disorder is the visual keynote of Istanbul. It is not slovenly—only untidy; not dirty—merely dingy and drab. And just as you cannot claim it to be a beautiful city, neither can you accuse it of being uninteresting. Its steep hills and harbor views remind you a little of San Francisco; its overcrowded streets recall Bombay; its transportation facilities evoke Venice, for you can go many places by boats which are continually making stops. (It costs threepence to get across to Üsküdar in Asia.) Yet the streets are strangely reminiscent of an America that has almost disappeared. Again and again I have been reminded of some New England mill town in the time of my childhood. Or a row of little houses will suggest a back street in Stapleton, on Staten Island. It is a city whose esthetic is that of the unlikely and incongruous, a photographer's paradise. There is no native quarter, or, if you like, it is all native quarter. Beyoğlu, the site of the so-called better establishments, concerns itself as little with appearances as do the humbler regions on the other side of the bridges.

You wander down the hill toward Karaköy. Above the harbor with its thousands of caïques, rowboats, tugs, freighters and ferries, lies a pall of smoke and haze through which you can see the vague outline of the domes and towers of Aya Sofia, Sultan Ahmet, Süleyimaniye; but to the left and far above all that there is a pure region next to the sky where the mountains in Asia glisten with snow. As you descend the alleys of steps that lead to the water's level, there are more and more people around you. In Karaköy itself just to make progress along the sidewalk requires the best part of your attention. You would think that all of the city's million and a quarter inhabitants were in the streets on their way to or from Galata Bridge. By Western European standards it is not a well-dressed crowd. The chaotic sartorial effect achieved by the populace in Istanbul is not necessarily due to poverty, but rather to a divergent conception of the uses to which European garments should be put. The mass is not an ethnically homogeneous one. The types of faces range from Levantine through Slavic to Mongoloid, the last belonging principally to the soldiers from eastern Anatolia. Apart from language there seems to be no one common element, not even shabbiness, since there are usually a few men and women who do understand how to wear their clothing.

Galata Bridge has two levels, the lower of which is a great dock whence the boats leave to go up the Golden Horn and the Bosporus, across to the Asiatic suburbs, and down to the islands in the Sea of Marmara. The ferries are there, of all sizes and shapes, clinging to the edge like water beetles to the side of a floating stick. When you get across to the other side of the bridge there are just as many people and just as much traffic, but the buildings are older and the streets narrower, and you begin to realize that you are, after all, in an oriental city. And if you expect to see anything more than the "points of interest," you are going to have to wander for miles on foot. The character of Istanbul derives from a thousand disparate, nonevident details; only by observing the variations and repetitions of such details can you begin to get an idea of the patterns they form. Thus the importance of wandering. The dust is bad. After a few hours of it I usually have a sore throat. I try to get off the main arteries, where the horses and drays clatter by, and stay in the alleyways, which are too narrow for anything but foot traffic. These lanes occasionally open up into little squares with rugs hanging on the walls and chairs placed in the shade of the grapevines overhead. A few Turks will be sitting about drinking coffee; the *narghilehs* bubble. Invariably, if I stop and gaze a moment, someone asks me to have some coffee, eat a few green walnuts and share his pipe. An irrational disinclination to become involved keeps me from accepting, but today Abdeslam did accept, only to find to his chagrin that the narghileh contained tobacco, and not kif or hashish as he had expected.

Cannabis sativa and its derivatives are strictly prohibited in Turkey, and the natural correlative of this proscription is that alcohol, far from being frowned upon as it is in other Moslem lands, is freely drunk; being a government monopoly it can be bought at any cigarette counter. This fact is no mere detail; it is of primary social importance, since the psychological effects of the two substances are diametrically opposed to each other. Alcohol blurs the personality by loosening inhibitions. The drinker feels, temporarily at least, a sense of participation. Kif abolishes no inhibitions; on the contrary it reinforces them, pushes the individual further back into the recesses of his own isolated personality, pledging him to contemplation and inaction. It is to be expected that there should be a close relationship between the culture of a given society and the means used by its members to achieve release and euphoria. For Judaism and Christianity the means has always been alcohol; for Islam it has been hashish. The first is dynamic in its effects, the other static. If a nation wishes, however mistakenly, to Westernize itself, first let it give up hashish. The rest will follow, more or less as a matter of course. Conversely, in a Western country, if a whole segment of the population desires, for reasons of protest (as has happened in the United States), to isolate itself in a radical fashion from the society around it, the quickest and surest way is for it to replace alcohol by cannabis.

October 2

Today in our wanderings we came upon the old fire tower at the top of the hill behind Süleymaniye, and since there was no sign at the door forbidding entry, we stepped in and began to climb the one hundred and eighty rickety wooden steps of the spiral staircase leading to the top. (Abdeslam counted them.) When we were almost at the top, we heard strains of Indian music; a radio up there was tuned in to New Delhi. At the same moment a good deal of water came pouring down upon us through the cracks above. We decided to beat a retreat, but then the boy washing the stairs saw us and insisted that we continue to the top and sit awhile. The view up there was magnificent; there is no better place from which to see the city. A charcoal fire was burning in a brazier, and we had tea and listened to some Anatolian songs which presently came over the air. Outside the many windows the wind blew, and the city below, made quiet by distance, spread itself across the rolling landscape on every side, its roof tiles pink in the autumn sun.

Later we sought out Pandeli's, a restaurant I had heard about but not yet found. This time we managed to discover it, a dilapidated little building squeezed in among harness shops and wholesale fruit stores, unprepossessing but cozy, and with the best food we have found in Istanbul. We had *pirinç çorba*, *beyendeli kebap*, *barbunya fasulya* and other good things. In the middle of the meal, probably while chewing on the *taze makarna*, I bit my lip. My annoyance with the pain was not mitigated by hearing Abdeslam remark unsympathetically, "If you'd keep your mouth open when you chew, like everybody else, you wouldn't have accidents like this." Pandeli's is the only native restaurant I have seen which doesn't sport a huge refrigerated showcase packed with food. You are usually led to this and told to choose what you want to eat. In the glare of the fluorescent lighting the food looks pallid and untempting, particularly the meat, which has been hacked into unfamiliar-looking cuts. During your meal there is usually a radio playing ancient jazz; occasionally a Turkish or Syrian number comes up. Although the tea is good, it is not good enough to warrant its being served as though it were nectar, in infinitesimal glasses that can be drained at one gulp. I often order several at once, and this makes for confusion. When you ask for water, you are brought a tiny bottle capped with tinfoil. Since it is free of charge, I suspect it of being simple tap water; perhaps I am unjust.

In the evening we went to the very drab red-light district in Beyoğlu, just behind the British Consulate General. The street was mobbed with men and boys. In the entrance door of each house was a small square opening, rather like those through which one used to be denied access to American speak-easies, and framed in each opening, against the dull yellow light within, was a girl's head.

The Turks are the only Moslems I have seen who seem to have got rid of that curious sentiment (apparently held by all followers of the True Faith), that there is an inevitable and hopeless difference between themselves and non-Moslems. Subjectively, at least, they have managed to bridge the gulf created by their religion, that abyss which isolates Islam from the rest of the world. As a result the visitor feels a specific connection with them which is not the mere one-sided sympathy the well-disposed traveler has for the more basic members of other cultures, but is something desired and felt by them as well. They are touchingly eager to understand and please—so eager, indeed, that they often neglect to listen carefully and consequently get things all wrong. Their good will, however, seldom flags, and in the long run this more than compensates for being given the breakfast you did not order, or being sent in the opposite direction from the one in which you wanted to go. Of course, there is the linguistic barrier. One really needs to know Turkish to live in Istanbul and because my ignorance of all Altaic languages is total, I suffer. The chances are nineteen in twenty that when I give an order things will go wrong, even when I get hold of the housekeeper who speaks French and who assures me calmly that all the other employees are idiots. The hotel is considered by my guidebook to be a "de luxe" establishment—the highest category. Directly after the "de luxe" listings come the "first class" places, which it describes in its own mysterious rhetoric: "These hotels have somewhat luxury, but are still comfortable with every convenience." Having seen the lobbies of several of the hostelries thus pigeonholed, complete with disemboweled divans and abandoned perambulators, I am very thankful to be here in my de-luxe suite, where the telephone is white so that I can see the cockroaches on the instrument before I lift it to my lips. At least the insects are discreet and die obligingly under a mild blast of DDT. It is fortunate I came here: my two insecticide bombs would never have lasted out a sojourn in a first-class hotel.

October 6

Santa Sophia? Aya Sofya now, not a living mosque but a dead one, like those of Kairouan which can no longer be used because they have been profaned by the feet of infidels. Greek newspapers have carried on propaganda campaigns designed to turn the clock back, reinstate Aya Sofya as a tabernacle of the Orthodox Church. The move was obviously foredoomed to failure; after having used it as a mosque for five centuries the Moslems would scarcely relish seeing it put back into the hands of the Christians. And so now it is a museum which contains nothing but its own architecture. Sultan Ahmet, the mosque just across the park, is more to my own taste; but then, a corpse does not bear comparison to a living organism. Sultan Ahmet is still a place of worship, the *imam* is allowed

to wear the classical headgear, the heavy final syllable of Allah's name reverberates in the air under the high dome, boys
dahven in distant corners as they memorize surat from the
Koran. When the tourists stumble over the prostrate forms of
men in prayer, or blatantly make use of their light meters and
Rolleiflexes, no one pays any attention. To Abdeslam this incredible invasion of privacy was tantamount to lack of respect
for Islam; it fanned the coals of his resentment into flame. (In
his country no unbeliever can put even one foot into a
mosque.) As he wandered about, his exclamations of indignation became increasingly audible. He started out with the
boys by suggesting to them that it was their great misfortune
to be living in a country of widespread sin. They looked at
him blankly and went on with their litanies. Then in a louder
voice he began to criticize the raiment of the worshipers, because they wore socks and slippers on their feet and on their
heads berets or caps with the visors at the back. He knows
that the wearing of the *tarboosh* is forbidden by law, but his
hatred of Kemal Ataturk, which has been growing hourly ever
since his arrival, had become too intense, I suppose, for him
to be able to repress it any longer. His big moment came
when the imam entered. He approached the venerable gentleman with elaborate salaams which were enthusiastically reciprocated. Then the two retired into a private room, where
they remained for ten minutes or so. When Abdeslam came
out there were tears in his eyes and he wore an expression of
triumph. "Ah, you see?" he cried, as we emerged into the
street. "That poor man is very, *very* unhappy. They have only
one day of Ramadan in the year." Even I was a little shocked
to hear that the traditional month had been whittled down to
a day. "This is an accursed land," he went on. "When we get
power we'll soak it in petrol and set it afire and burn everyone in it. May it forever be damned! And all these dogs living in it, I pray Allah they may be thrown into the fires of
Gehennem. Ah, if we only had our power back for one day,
we Moslems! May Allah speed that day when we shall ride
into Turkey and smash their government and all their works
of Satan!" The imam, it seems, had been delighted beyond
measure to see a young man who still had the proper respect

for religion; he had complained bitterly that the youth of Turkey was spiritually lost.

Today I had lunch with a woman who has lived here a good many years. As a Westerner, she felt that the important thing to notice about Turkey is the fact that from having been in the grip of a ruthless dictatorship it has slowly evolved into a modern democracy, rather than having followed the more usual reverse process. Even Ataturk was restrained by his associates from going all the way in his iconoclasm, for what he wanted was a Turkish adaptation of what he had seen happen in Russia. Religion was to him just as much of an opiate in one country as in another. He managed to deal it a critical blow here, one which may yet prove to have been fatal. Last year an American, a member of Jehovah's Witnesses, arrived, and as is the custom with members of that sect, stood on the street handing out brochures. But not for long. The police came, arrested him, put him in jail, and eventually effected his expulsion from the country. This action, insisted my lunch partner, was not taken because the American was distributing Christian propaganda; had he been distributing leaflets advocating the reading of the Koran, it's likely that his punishment would have been more severe.

October 10

At the beginning of the sixteenth century, Selim the Grim captured from the Shah of Persia one of the most fantastic pieces of furniture I have ever seen. The trophy was the poor Shah's throne, a simple but massive thing made of chiseled gold, decorated with hundreds of enormous emeralds. I went to see it today at the Topkapi Palace. There was a bed to match, also of emerald-studded gold. After a moment of looking, Abdeslam ran out of the room where these incredible objects stood into the courtyard, and could not be coaxed back in. "Too many riches are bad for the eyes," he explained. I could not agree; I thought them beautiful. I tried to make him tell me the exact reason for his sudden flight, but he found it difficult to give me a rational explanation of his behavior. "You know that gold and jewels are sinful," he began.

To get him to go on, I said I knew. "And if you look at sinful things for very long you can go crazy; you know that. And I don't want to go crazy." I was willing to take the chance, I replied, and I went back in to see more.

October 16

These last few days I have spent entirely at the covered souks. I discovered the place purely by accident, since I follow no plan in my wanderings about the city. You climb an endless hill; whichever street you take swarms with buyers and sellers who take up all the room between the shops on either side. It isn't good form to step on the merchandise, but now and then one can't avoid it.

The souks are all in one vast ant hill of a building, a city within a city whose avenues and streets, some wide, some narrow, are like the twisting hallways of a dream. There are more than five thousand shops under its roof, so they assure me; I have not wondered whether it seems a likely number or not, nor have I passed through all its forty-two entrance portals or explored more than a small number of its tunneled galleries. Visually the individual shops lack the color and life of the *kissarias* of Fez and Marrakech, and there are no painted Carthaginian columns like those which decorate the souks in Tunis. The charm of the edifice lies in its vastness and, in part, precisely from its dimness and clutter. In the middle of one open space where two large corridors meet, there is an outlandish construction, in shape and size not unlike one of the old traffic towers on New York's Fifth Avenue in the 'twenties. On the ground floor is a minute kitchen. If you climb the crooked outside staircase, you find yourself in a tiny restaurant with four miniature tables. Here you sit and eat, looking out along the tunnels over the heads of the passers-by. It is a place out of Kafka's *Amerika*.

The antique shops here in the souks are famous. As one might expect, tourists are considered to be a feeble-minded and nearly defenseless species of prey, and there are never enough of them to go around. Along the sides of the galleries stand whole tribes of merchants waiting for them to appear. These men have brothers, fathers, uncles and cousins, each of whom operates his own shop, and the tourist is passed along from one member of the family to the next with no visible regret on anyone's part. In one shop I heard the bearded proprietor solemnly assuring a credulous American woman that the amber perfume she had just bought was obtained by pressing beads of amber like those in the necklace she was examining. Not that it would have been much more truthful of him had he told her that it was made of ambergris; the amber I have smelled here never saw a whale, and consists almost entirely of benzoin.

If you stop to look into an antiquary's window you are lost. Suddenly you are aware that hands are clutching your clothing, pulling you gently toward the door, and honeyed voices are experimenting with greetings in all the more common European languages, one after the other. Unless you offer physical resistance you find yourself being propelled forcibly within. Then as you face your captors over arrays of old silver and silk, they begin to work on you in earnest, using all the classic clichés of Eastern sales-patter. "You have such a fine face that I want my merchandise to go with you." "We need money today; you are the first customer to come in all day long." A fat hand taps the ashes from a cigarette. "Unless I do business with you, I won't sleep tonight. I am an old man. Will you ruin my health?" "Just buy one thing, no matter what. Buy the cheapest thing in the store, if you like, but buy something. . . ." If you get out of the place without making a purchase, you are entitled to add ten to your score. A knowledge of Turkish is not necessary here in the bazaars. If you prefer not to speak English or French or German, you find that the Moslems love to be spoken to in Arabic, while the Jews speak a corrupt Andalucían version of Spanish.

Today I went out of the covered souks by a back street that I had not found before. It led downward toward the Rustempaşa Mosque. The shops gave the street a strange air: they all looked alike from the outside. On closer inspection I saw that they were all selling the same wildly varied assortment of unlikely objects. I wanted to examine the merchandise, and since Abdeslam had been talking about buying some rubber-soled shoes, we chose a place at random and went into it. While he tried on sneakers and sandals I made a partial inventory of the objects in the big, gloomy room. The shelves and counters exhibited footballs, Moslem rosaries, military belts, reed mouthpieces for native oboes, doorhooks, dice of many sizes and colors, narghilehs, watch-straps of false cobraskin, garden shears, slippers of untanned leather—hard as stone, brass taps for kitchen sinks, imitation ivory cigarette holders—ten inches long, suitcases made of pressed paper, tambourines, saddles, assorted medals for the military and plastic game counters. Hanging from the ceiling were revolver holsters, lutes, and zipper fasteners that looked like strips of flypaper. Ladders were stacked upright against the wall, and on the floor were striped canvas deck chairs, huge tin trunks with scenes of Mecca stamped on their sides, and a great pile of wood shavings among whose comfortable hills nestled six very bourgeois cats. Abdeslam bought no shoes, and the proprietor began to stare at me and my note-book with unconcealed suspicion, having decided, perhaps, that I was a member of the secret police looking for stolen goods.

October 19

Material benefits may be accrued in this worldwide game of refusing to be oneself. Are these benefits worth the inevitable void produced by such destruction? The question is apposite in every case where the traditional beliefs of a people have been systematically modified by its government. Rationalizing words like "progress," "modernization," or "democracy" mean nothing because, even if they are used sincerely, the imposition of such concepts by force from above cancels whatever value they might otherwise have. There is little doubt that by having been made indifferent Moslems the younger generation in Turkey has become more like our idea of what people living in the twentieth century should be. The old helplessness in the face of *mektoub* (it is written) is gone, and in its place is a passionate belief in man's ability to alter his destiny. That is the greatest step of all; once it has been made, anything, unfortunately, can happen.

Abdeslam is not a happy person. He sees his world, which he knows is a good world, being assailed from all sides, slowly crumbling before his eyes. He has no means of understanding me should I try to explain to him that in this age what he considers to be religion is called superstition, and that religion today has come to be a desperate attempt to integrate metaphysics with science. Something will have to be found to replace the basic wisdom which has been destroyed, but the discovery will not be soon; neither Abdeslam nor I will ever know of it.

The Rif, to Music

THE most important single element in Morocco's folk culture is its music. In a land like this, where almost total illiteracy has been the rule, the production of written literature is of course negligible. On the other hand, like the Negroes of West Africa the Moroccans have a magnificent and highly evolved sense of rhythm which manifests itself in the twin arts of music and the dance. Islam, however, does not look with favor upon any sort of dancing, and thus the art of the dance, while being the natural mode of religious expression of the native population, has not been encouraged here since the arrival of the Moslem conquerors. At the same time, the very illiteracy which through the centuries has precluded the possibility of literature has abetted the development of music; the entire history and mythology of the people is clothed in song. Instrumentalists and singers have come into being in lieu of chroniclers and poets, and even during the most recent chapter in the country's evolution—the war for independence and the setting up of the present pre-democratic regime—each phase of the struggle has been celebrated in countless songs.

The neolithic Berbers have always had their own music, and they still have it. It is a highly percussive art with complicated juxtapositions of rhythms, limited scalar range (often of no more than three adjacent tones) and a unique manner of vocalizing. Like most Africans, the Berbers developed a music of mass participation, one whose psychological effects were aimed more often than not at causing hypnosis. When the Arabs invaded the land they brought with them music of a very different sort, addressed to the individual, seeking by sensory means to induce a state of philosophical speculativeness. In the middle of Morocco's hostile landscape they built their great walled cities, where they entrenched themselves and from which they sent out soldiers to continue the conquest, southward into the Sudan, northward into Europe. With the importation of large numbers of Negro slaves the urban culture ceased being a purely Arabic one. (The child of a union between a female slave and her master was considered

778

legitimate.) On the central plains and in the foothills of the mountains of the north the Berber music took on many elements of Arabic music; while in the pre-Sahara it borrowed from the Negroes, remaining a hybrid product in both cases. Only in the regions which remained generally inaccessible to non-Berbers—roughly speaking, the mountains themselves and the high plateaux—was Berber music left intact, a purely autochthonous art.

My stint, in attempting to record the music of Morocco, was to capture in the space of the six months which the Rockefeller Foundation allotted to me for the project, examples of every major musical genre to be found within the boundaries of the country. This required the close coöperation of the Moroccan government, everyone agreed. But with which branch of it? No one knew. Because the material was to belong to the archives of the Library of Congress in Washington, the American Embassy in Rabat agreed to help me in my efforts to locate an official who might be empowered to grant the necessary permission, for I needed a guarantee that I would be allowed to move freely about the untraveled parts of the country, and once in those parts, I needed the power to persuade the local authorities to find the musicians in each tribe and round them up for me.

We approached several ministries, some of which claimed to be in a position to grant such permission, but none of which was willing to give formal approval to the project. Probably there was no precedent for such an undertaking, and no one wanted to assume the responsibility of creating such a precedent. In desperation, working through personal channels, I managed eventually to evolve a document to which was stapled my photograph, with official stamps and signatures; this paper made it possible to start work. By this time it was early July. In October, when I had been at work for more than three months, I received a communication from the ministry of foreign affairs which informed me that since my project was ill-timed I would not be allowed to undertake it. The American Embassy advised me to continue my work. By December the Moroccan government had become aware of what was going on; they informed me summarily that no recordings could be made in Morocco save by special permission from the Ministry of the Interior. By then I had practically completed the project, and the snow was beginning to block the mountain passes, so this blow was not too bitter. However, from then on it was no longer possible to make any recordings which required the coöperation of the government; this deprived the collection of certain tribal musics of southeastern Morocco. But I already had more than two hundred and fifty selections from the rest of the country, as diversified a body of music as one could find in any land west of India.

Christopher is a level-headed Canadian with a Volkswagen and all the time in the world. Mohammed Larbi, a good contact man and assistant, as a youth had spent a year accompanying an expedition across the Sahara to Nigeria. The three of us set out together from Tangier following four roughly circular itineraries of five weeks' duration each: southwestern Morocco, northern Morocco, the Atlas, and the pre-Sahara. Between trips we recuperated in Tangier. The pages which follow were written from day to day during the course of the second journey, most of whose days were spent in the mountains of the Rif, in what used to be the Spanish protectorate.

Alhucemas
August 29, 1959

The road to Ketama goes along the backbone of the western Rif. You can see for miles, both to the Mediterranean side and to the southern side, big mountains and more big mountains—mountains covered with olive trees, with oak trees, with bushes, and finally with giant cedars. For two or three hours before getting up to Ketama we had been passing large gangs of workmen repairing the road; it needed it badly. We had been going to cook lunch in a little pine grove just above a village between Bab Taza and Bab Berret, but when we got in among the trees, wherever we looked there were workmen lying on the dry pine needles in the shade, sleeping or smoking kif, so we set up our equipment in the sun and wind, a little below the crest where the pine grove was. The wind kept blowing out the butagaz flame, but in the end we managed to eat. Christopher drank his usual Chaudsoleil *rosé*, and Mohammed Larbi and I drank piping hot Pepsi-Cola, since there was no water left in the thermos we had filled in Xauen. That one thermosful proved to be the last good water we were to have for three weeks.

During lunch Mohammed Larbi insisted on amusing himself with the radio; he was trying to get Damascus on the nineteen-meter band in order to hear the news. When eventually he did get it he could not understand it, of course, because it was in Syrian Arabic, but that made no difference to him. It was news, and they were talking about Kassem and excoriating the French, which was easy enough for even me to understand. Mohammed Larbi had been smoking kif constantly all morning and was a bit exalted. We packed up and started on our way again.

It was about half past four when we came in sight of the wide plain of Ketama they call Llano Amarillo. It is aptly named, at least in summer, for then it is dry and yellow. Here and there, scattered over a distance which went toward infinity, was a herd of cattle or a flock of sheep. They looked as though they had been put there purposely to give the place scale. At first you saw nothing but the yellow flatness with the great cedar trees along the sides. Then you saw the dots that were the nearest sheep, then to the right the pinpoints that were cows, but smaller than the sheep, then far over to the left almost invisible specks that were another herd.

The *parador* of Bab Berret, which has about twenty rooms, looked completely abandoned, but there was a chair on the wide front terrace, and the door was open. I went in to inquire about sleeping quarters. The inside seemed deserted too. The dining room had furniture in it; the other rooms had been stripped. In the town of Bab Berret, the Spanish, when they relinquished their protectorate, took the generator with them; the vicinity has been without electricity ever since. There was no sign of life at the reception desk, no piece of paper or ledger in sight—nothing but the keys hung in three rows on the wall. I called out, "*Hay alguien?*" and got no answer. Finally, behind the big door of what had been the bar, I saw a pair of legs lying on a decayed divan and peered around the door. A young man lay there with his eyes open, but he wasn't looking at me; he was staring at the ceiling. When he did see me, he slowly sat up and stretched a little, never answering my "excuse me's" and "good afternoons." I decided he must be a guest and went out again into the main hall, but in a minute he was there behind me, and then he did not ask me what he could do for me, but what was the matter.

When he heard I wanted rooms he turned away with disgust. "There are no rooms," he said.

"None at all?"

"None at all."

"Is the hotel open?"

"The hotel's open and there are no rooms. Tomorrow you can have some if you want."

"And tonight where am I going to sleep?"

He turned around again and looked at me blankly. Too much kif, I could see that. He was scratching his crotch voluptuously all this time. He yawned and began to walk around toward the bar. "You couldn't put up a cot somewhere?" I called after him. But he continued to move away. I went out to the car to report. Christopher and Mohammed Larbi came back in with me; they didn't believe any of it.

The scratcher was already back on his broken-down couch, getting himself into a comfortable position. This time he looked really hostile. I decided to go back out onto the terrace. I didn't want to see him any more. Mohammed Larbi was examining the main entrance hall and the staircase. When Christopher came out he said there were plenty of rooms, that the young man was finally awake, and that we could stay after all. The foremen of the various road construction gangs had requisitioned several rooms (for which they were not paying), but there were a dozen or more vacant ones.

The scratcher was manager, bellboy, waiter, dishwasher and accountant. Besides him there was a crazy-looking cook and an old Riffian woman who made the beds and scrubbed the floors, but that was the entire personnel. The cook also ran a small generator in the garage; he took us out to admire it later on.

Someone had removed the doorknobs from the bedroom doors, so that if the door of your room happened to blow shut, you had to pound on it until the manager heard you and came upstairs with a piece of metal of his own fashioning which he stuck through the hole where the knob had been and turned the lock to let you either in or out, depending on where you happened to be. This was true of the hotel's one toilet, too, but that was of no importance because the place was so filthy that you didn't go into it anyway. The toilet bowl had been filled up and so people had begun using the floor. In 1950 I had spent a night in that one bathroom. They put a cot beside the tub and hung a scribbled sign on the door saying the bathroom was out of order, but that didn't prevent a steady stream of French tourists from pounding indignantly on the door throughout the long night. Some of them tried to break the door in, but the bolt was strong. Now that I stuck my head into the stinking room, I remembered that endless night and the noise of the unloading bus beneath my window at five in the morning, the bugle calls from the barracks back in the cedar forest and the gobbling of the turkeys in crates out on the terrace.

We wanted to get down to Laazib Ketama as quickly as possible, in order to see the caid or the *khalifa* before the government offices closed, so after leaving our luggage in our rooms we started out, bumping down the crazy, wide Tirak d'l Ouahada. Hundreds of Riffians on horseback, muleback and donkeyback, the women walking, were on their way up. We covered them all with layers of white dust; there was no help for it. They were in a fine humor, however, laughing and waving.

At one point you could look directly down from the road into a deep ravine whose sides were planted wholly with kif. Ketama is the kif center of all North Africa, and very likely of the world now. It is the only region where it is legal to grow it, and that is because the Sultan has agreed to allow the cultivation of it to continue until the land has been made feasible for other crops. At present the only crop that will grow is kif, and although any Moroccan can plant a few stalks in his garden, the only really good kif is the Ketami. So you have miles and miles of it growing out of the stony soil on the edges of the steep slopes, and under the present ruling this will go on until some other means of livelihood has been found for the inhabitants.

At present the kif situation is ridiculous. Tons of the drug are grown each year and shipped out of Ketama in all directions.

That is legal. But if anyone is caught selling it he is immediately given a heavy fine and/or a prison sentence. No penalties are attached to the possession of it, but the official attitude toward the smoking of it in public places differs according to the way the local authorities of each town feel about it. I was in Marrakech in August and found it wide open. In Fez I saw only one old man holding a *sebsi*. In Tangier and Tetuan clouds of kif smoke pour out of the cafés. In Rabat, Essaouira, Oujda, nothing. In some towns it's easy to get and cheap and good; in others, you almost might as well not even try. These conditions are of course far from static. The city in which two months ago you could run around the corner for a paper of kif is suddenly closed tight, whereas in another town where previously there was strict vigilance, men are observed puffing on their pipes in the street, in full view of police headquarters. Generally speaking, when you get to the southern side of the Grand Atlas, kif is a luxury and greatly prized, whereas in the extreme north, among the Djebala, for instance, the average village male over fourteen has his little mottoui full of it and his sebsi in his pocket.

We stopped the car and climbed down a way to examine the phenomenon. None of us had ever before seen so much kif. We could have filled the back of the car with it and no one would have known. Mohammed Larbi stroked a stalk lovingly and murmured, "Like green diamonds everywhere. *Fijate.*" An old man ambled by and sat down beside the road to look at us with curiosity. Mohammed Larbi shouted to him in Moghrebi: "Is this kif yours?" It was clear that next he was going to ask to be given some. But the old man did not understand. He merely stared at us. "Like donkeys!" snorted Mohammed Larbi. He never fails to be annoyed with the Riffians when they speak only Tarifcht; if a Moroccan does not understand at least some Moghrebi he takes it as a personal affront. When we got back to the car he pulled out his enormous sheep's bladder, packed with three pounds of the powerful greasy green kif he prepares himself, and filled a cigarette paper with it. "I've got to smoke!" he cried in great excitement. "I can't see all that kif and not feel some of it in me." He continued to smoke until we got down to Laazib Ketama.

The main body of the tribesmen had already left (it was market day), but there were still several hundred men lying around on rugs and sacks under the cedars in the three big courtyards where the souk had been taking place. The merchants were winding bolts of cloth and packing sugar and toys and cutlery away into big bundles. The dust that hung in the air, where it came in contact with the last rays of the sun, made blinding golden streamers across the scene. We sneezed repeatedly as we picked our way through the emptying market. There were the customary blank faces when we inquired after the khalifa's office, but we found it, and eventually managed to get into it. I had forgotten about the short war of 1958 between the Riffians and the forces of the Rabat government, but the memory of it came back soon enough. They told me that since we were in a military zone we would have to consult the *comandante* if we expected to be allowed to record. Yes, the comandante had been down here in Laazib Ketama all day, but now he had left, and who knew where he was now? However, they were building a bridge just below the village, and perhaps he was down there watching. We went further down the trail. It looked a hopeless task to find anyone in the midst of such chaos. In any case, it was already twilight and we had about fifteen miles of rough trail to climb in order to get back to the parador. So we backed up, nearly went over a small cliff, and headed toward Llano Amarillo.

Because the khalifa had also suggested that we stop off at the barracks on the way back to the parador, we turned in toward a three-story log cabin that looked like an expensive hotel in a skiing resort, and were met by a dozen wide-eyed Moroccan youths in uniform who immediately trained their submachine guns on us, just in case it turned out that we needed to be captured. A sergeant made them back up and told us that the comandante would be coming in about eight o'clock.

The khalifa in Laazib Ketama had mentioned a village some thirty kilometers further on where there were some *rhaita* players. His news did not stimulate me particularly, because I already had taped a good many sequences of rhaita music, including some excellent ones from Beni Aros, the capital of Djebala musicians. The rhaita among the Djebala is not noticeably different from the rhaita in the Rif, save perhaps that the Rif-fians' playing shows a more accurate rhythmical sense. What I was looking for was the *zamar*, a double-reed instrument fitted with a pair of bull's horns. The khalifa had assured me that the Beni Uriaghel in the Central Rif would supply that; for lack of anything better I had shown polite interest in his offer of rhaitas, and I was ready to devote a day to recording them. It would depend upon whether the comandante proved willing to collect the musicians for me; I did not want to waste any energy or time having to persuade him, even if it meant no recording in the Ketama region. I was eager to get on eastward to where the true Riffian music is.

We drove back to the hotel. The mountain night had settled over the valley. The wind was whistling through the rooms; doors were squeaking and banging all by themselves. Each minute I was becoming less interested in finding the comandante. We went to my room and turned on the shivering little electric light bulb over the bed. Christopher and Mohammed Larbi make a habit of meeting in my room because I have the equipment with me: the two tape recorders, the radio, the food and drink, and the fire. There is seldom a reason for either of them ever to go to his own room save to sleep. On our twilight visit to the generator in the garage we had learned that it supplied two-hundred-and-twenty-volt direct current to the parador, and so I already knew that it was not going to be possible to work the tape recorders, either for studying tapes already recorded or for our amusement. This was bad news. The night would be cold and uncomfortable, once we were in those forbidding beds. We needed a reason to stay up late.

Ketama is fairly high for the Rif: about six thousand feet up. With the setting of the sun a mountain chill had crept down through the forest from the heights. The road menders were eating sardines in their rooms. It was cold in the empty *comedor* at dinner time. As soon as we had eaten we went upstairs and made coffee. Mohammed Larbi brought out the bottle of Budapest kümmel, and Christopher handed us the half-kilo bag of *majoun* someone had sold him in Xauen. We all drank kümmel, but only Mohammed Larbi ate any majoun. If someone is entirely comfortable and contented, majoun can enhance his pleasure, but there is no point in italicizing an unsatisfactory experience.

It suddenly occurred to me that the lights might be turned off and that we had no candles. I went down to look for the manager. He was drying dishes in the kitchen with the cook, who was smoking kif in a very long sebsi. I was right, he said; the lights would be going off within twenty minutes, at ten o'clock, and there were no candles in the parador. That I did not believe. I objected that there must be at least one, somewhere.

"No candles," he said, firmly.

"Haven't you got a piece of one?"

"No pieces of candles," he replied, drying dishes, not looking up. "Nothing."

It was clearly a provocation. I had seen what had happened when I had tried to get the rooms. Christopher had been able to get them out of him, I had not, and he was aware of this. He was playing his inexplicable little game again. I stood there. Finally I said: "I don't understand this hotel."

Now he set down his dish and turned to face me. "Señor," he said deliberately, "don't you know this is the worst hotel in the world?"

"What?"

He repeated the words slowly, "It's the worst hotel in the world."

"No, I didn't know," I said. "Who owns it?"

"A poor slob who lives around here." He and the cook exchanged mysterious, amused glances. I could think of nothing to retort save that I had been under the impression that it was run by the government. Formerly it was the family or religion that one criticized, if in the course of one's personal relations one found it expedient to infuriate a Moroccan; nowadays one gets the same reaction by ridiculing the government, since at last it is Moroccans who are responsible for it. But neither one of them understood my remark as the insult I had intended. "No, no, no!" they laughed. "Just a *pobre desgraciado*."

I went back upstairs and reported all this; it was greeted with loud laughter. Christopher got up and left the room. A minute or two later he was back with three new candles and two half-burned ones. The lights stayed on until half past ten.

We went to bed. In the morning there was a blinding fog and it was still cold. I had a hacking cough and decided that I must be about to come down with something. Christopher and Mohammed Larbi came in and made coffee. I told them I wanted no music from Ketama; we were leaving immediately for Alhucemas. When I went down to pay the bill, for the first time the manager looked nearly awake. I got back my change, and out of curiosity I handed him two hundred francs as a tip, determined, if he threw the coins on the floor, merely to pick them up and leave. But his face suddenly came alive.

"I'm going crazy here," he confided. "How can I do anything? There's nothing here, nothing works, everything's broken, there's no money, nobody comes but road workers. Anybody would go crazy."

I nodded in sympathy.

"I'll be leaving soon, of course," he continued. "I'm not used to places like this. I'm from Tetuan."

"Is that so?"

"I've been here two months almost, but next week I'm getting out."

"I'd say that's lucky for you." I did not believe he would really be leaving, although at the moment he looked passionate enough to walk out the door and down the highway and never return. Some Moroccans can work themselves into a state of emotional imbalance with astonishing speed.

"I'm going, all right. You've got to be crazy to live up here. *Ma hadou.*"

I said good-bye and he wished me good luck.

The road east of Ketama was extremely bad: a rough surface sprinkled with small sharp stones, and unbanked curves every few yards. At times the fog was so thick that nothing at all was visible but the dirt bed of the road three feet ahead of the car. We crawled along. The fog dissolved. There were villages down in the valleys at our feet. The earth was whitish gray, and so were the enormous, square earthen houses. Traditional Riffian architecture, untouched. The landscape was timeless.

We bought gasoline in Targuist. The place was the last refuge of poor old Abd el Krim; the French captured him here in 1926. There are many Jews, speaking Spanish; and the modern town is a monstrous excrescence with long dirty streets, the wind blowing along them, whipping clouds of dust and filth against the face, stinging the skin. The Moslem village across the highway was of a more attractive aspect, but proved to be unreachable in the car. Beyond Targuist were a dark sky and a high wind and a countryside which grew more arid and forlorn by the mile. Finally it was raining, but the storm passed in time for us to have our lunch beside a culvert where the dirt in the wind cut less (for in this valley it had not rained), and where we could keep the flame of the butagaz alive.

We drove into Alhucemas at about half past four. The sea looked like lead. The town itself has a certain paranoid quality: the classic Spanish fishing village seen as in a bad dream. There is a vague atmosphere of impending disaster, of being cut off from the world, as in a penal colony. A penal colony, yes. It is in the faces of the few Spaniards sitting in the shabby cafés. Most of the Spanioline have gone away. The ones who remain are not likely to admit that the only reason they are still here is that it is impossible for them to go anywhere else.

The Moroccans have taken over Alhucemas—all of it except the Hotel España. I am in a luxurious room with a tile shower; there is hot water in the pipes, which is unbelievable; it is the first since Tangier. The weather remains lowering, and suddenly it is dark. At dinner the fat Spanish waiter is the principal source of amusement: he is definitely drunk and even staggers classically as he brings in the food. Mohammed Larbi makes fairly brutal fun of him all through the meal.

This morning we went to see the governor. He is friendly, speaks in Tarifcht to his assistants; in the government offices of the south they are likely to use French. He says that to-morrow evening we are to report to the fort at Ajdir. There the Caid of Einzoren will meet us and take over. We have agreed. The sky is still dark and the air heavy.

August 31—4 A.M.

The Caid of Einzoren proved to be a jolly young man from Rabat, not much more than twenty years old. He is enjoying himself enormously up here in the Rif, he confided, because he has a girl in Einzoren, a "hundred percent Española," named Josefina. In the middle of our recording session he invited us to have dinner with him and Josefina. We accepted, but were given a table where we sat alone eating the food he had ordered for us, while he sat with Josefina and her family.

We had set up the recording equipment in an empty municipal building which stood in the middle of the main plaza. It gave the impression of being a school which was no longer in use. When we arrived, we found one of the rooms already filled with women and girls, three dozen or so of them, singing and tapping lightly on their drums. They sat in straight-backed chairs, their heads and shoulders entirely hidden under the bath towels they wore. A great hushed crowd of men and boys stood outside in the plaza, pressing against the building, trying to peer over the high window sills. Now and then someone whispered; I was grateful for their silence.

The tribe was the Beni Uriaghel, but in spite of that there was no zamar. It was a great disappointment. I questioned the caid about the possibilities of finding one. He knew even less than I about it; he had never suspected the existence of such an instrument. The musicians themselves shook their heads; the Beni Uriaghel did not use it, they said. Not even in the country, I pursued, outside Einzoren? They laughed, because they were all rustics from the mountains roundabout and had been summoned to the village to take part in the "festival."

No one had told me that the girls were going to sing in competitive teams, or that each village would be represented by two rival sets of duo-vocalists, so that I was not prepared for the strange aspect of the room. They sat in pairs, their heads close enough together so that each couple could be wholly covered by the one large turkish towel. The voices were directed floorward through the folds of cloth, and since no gesture, no movement of the head, accompanied the singing, it was literally impossible to know who was performing and who was merely sitting. The song was surprisingly repetitious even for Berber music; nevertheless I was annoyed to have it marred by the constant sound of murmurs and whispers and sotto-voce remarks during the performance, an interference the microphone would inevitably register. But there was no way of catching anyone's eye, since no eyes were visible. Even the matrons, who were supplying the drumming, were covered. The first selection went on and on, strophe after strophe, the older women tapping the membranes of their disc-shaped bendirs almost inaudibly on arbitrary offbeats. I took advantage of the piece's length to leave the controls and go over to whisper a question to the caid, who sat beaming in an honorific armchair, flanked by his subordinates who were crouching on the floor around him. "Why are they all talking so much?" I asked him.

He smiled. "They're making up the words they're going to sing next," he told me. I was pleased to hear that the texts were improvised and went back to my Ampex and earphones to wait for the song to end. When the girls had gone on for thirty-five minutes more, and the tape had run out, I tiptoed across the room once again to the caid. "Are all the pieces going to be this long?" I inquired.

"Oh, they'll go on until I stop them," he said. "All night, if you like."

"The same song?"

"Oh, yes. It's about me. Do you want them to sing a different one?"

I explained that it was no longer being recorded, and he called a halt. After that I was able to control the length of the selections.

Presently word arrived that the rhaita group was sitting in a café somewhere at the edge of town, waiting for transportation; and so, accompanied by a *cicerone*, Christopher drove out to fetch them. The café proved to be in a village about twenty kilometers distant. The men were playing when he arrived; when he told them to get into the car they did so without ceasing to play. They played all the way to Einzoren and walked into the building where I was without ever having interrupted the piece. I let them finish it, and then had them taken back outside into the public square. Mohammed Larbi carried the microphone out and set it up in the middle of the great circle formed by the male onlookers. The rhaita, a superoboe whose jagged, strident sound has been developed precisely for long-distance listening, is not an indoor instrument.

While we were away in the restaurant, the men and the women in the public square somehow got together and put on a *fraja*. This would not have happened in the regions of

Morocco where Arab culture has been imposed on the population, but in the Rif it is not considered improper for the two sexes to take part in the same entertainment. Even here the men did not dance; they played, sang and shouted while the women danced. I heard the racket from the restaurant and hurried back to try and tape it, but as soon as they saw what I was doing they became quiet. There was a group of excellent musicians from a village called Tazourakht; their music was both more primitive and more precise rhythmically than that of the others, and I showed open favoritism in asking for more of it. This proved to be not too good an idea, for they were the only men to belong to another tribe, the Beni Bouayache. The recording session, which had been in progress since dusk, gave signs of being about to degenerate into a wild party somewhere around two o'clock in the morning. I suggested to the caid that we stop, but he saw no reason for that. At twenty to three we disconnected the machines and packed them up. "We're going on with this until tomorrow," said the caid, declining our offer of a ride to Alhucemas. The sounds of revelry were definitely growing louder as we drove away.

August 31

Last night was really enough; we ought to go on eastward. But the governor has gone out of his way to be helpful and has arranged another session in Ismoren, a village in the hills to the west, for tomorrow evening. Today I succeeded in enticing the two Riffian maids at the hotel here into my room to help me identify sixteen pieces on a tape I recorded in 1956. I knew it was all music from the Rif, but I wanted to find out which pieces were from which tribes, in order to have a clearer idea of what each genre was worth in terms of the effort required to capture it. The girls refused to come into the room without a chaperone; they found a thirteen-year-old boy and brought him with them. This was fortunate, because the boy spoke some Moghrebi, while they knew only Tarifcht and a few words of Spanish. I would play a piece and they would listen for a moment before identifying its source. Only two pieces caused them any hesitation, and they soon agreed on those. I still need examples of the Beni Bouifrour, the Beni Touzine, the Ait Ulixxek, the Gzennaia and the Temsaman. The girls were delighted with the small sum I gave them; upon leaving the room they insisted on taking some soiled laundry with them to wash for me.

Nador, September 6

We went up to Ismoren as scheduled, at twilight on the following day. The landscape reminded me of central Mexico. The trail from the highway up to the village was a constant slow climb along a wide, tilting plain. The caid was not at home; there had been a misunderstanding and he was in Alhucemas. The villagers invited us into his home, saying that the musicians were ready to play when we wanted to begin. It was a Spanish house with large rooms, dimly lit and sparsely furnished. There were great piles of almonds lying about in the corners; they reached almost up to the ceiling. The dank odor they gave off made the place smell like an abandoned farmhouse. The feeble electricity trembled and wavered. I had Mohammed Larbi test the current because I suspected it of being direct. Unhappily, that was what it proved to be, and I had to announce that in spite of all the preparations it was not going to be possible to record in Ismoren. There was incredulity and then disappointment on all faces. "Stay the night," they told us, "and tomorrow perhaps the electric force will be better." I thanked them and said we could not do that, but Mohammed Larbi, exasperated by their ignorance, launched into an expository monologue on electricity. Nobody listened. Men were beginning to bang drums outside on the terrace, and someone who looked like the local schoolteacher was delegated to serve tea. He invited me to preside at the caid's big desk. When they saw me sitting there, they laughed. An elderly man remarked, "He makes a good caid," and they all agreed. I opened three packs of cigarettes and passed them around. Everyone was looking longingly at the equipment, wanting very much to see it set up. We had tea, more tea, and still more tea, and finally got off for Alhucemas to a noisy accompaniment of benadir, with two men running ahead of us along the cactus-bordered lanes to show us the way out of the village.

And so each morning I continued to go down to the government offices to study their detailed wall maps and try to locate the tribes with which I hoped to make contact. The first day I had spotted an official surreptitiously looking up our police records; apparently they were satisfactory. The governor and his aides had begun with a maximum of cordiality; but as the novelty of seeing us wore off, their attitude underwent a metamorphosis. It seemed to them that we were being arbitrary and difficult in our insistence upon certain tribes instead of others, and they had had enough of telephoning and making abortive arrangements. It involved about two hours' work for them each day. It was the electricity which frustrated us every time; we had been supplied with a transformer but not with a generator, and Einzoren appeared to be the only village in the region with alternating current.

One night when we went in to have dinner in the comedor of the Hotel España there was a murderous-looking soldier sitting at the table with Mohammed Larbi. We sat down; he was drunk and wanted to deliver a political lecture. He and Mohammed Larbi went out together. At three in the morning there was a great racket in the corridors. Mohammed Larbi was finding the way to his room with the help of various recruits from the street and with the voluble hindrance of the hotel's night watchman. The next day, which had been set as the day of departure, he was moaning sick. He managed to pack the car for us, and then fell into the back with the luggage, to say no more. The weather had gone on being dramatic and threatening. South of Temsaman the mountains, even in normal weather, look like imaginary sketches of another planet. Under the black sky and with the outrageous lighting effects that poured through unexpected valleys, they were a disquieting sight. Mohammed Larbi moaned occasionally.

The trail was execrable, but fortunately we did not meet another car all day—at least, not until late afternoon when we had got down into the plain to Laazib Midar, where a real road is suddenly born. My idea was to find some sort of place thereabouts where we could stay when we returned after seeing the Governor at Nador (since we were now in the Province of Nador and had to go all the way to the capital to get permission to work). But, Laazib Midar being only a frontier-like agglomeration of small adobe houses strung along the road, we went on through.

From the back seat Mohammed Larbi began once more to wail. "Ay, *yimma habiba*! Ay, what bad luck!" I told him that nobody had forced him to drink whatever he had drunk. "But they did!" he lamented. "That's just what happened. I was forced." I laughed unsympathetically. No one can smoke as much kif as Mohammed Larbi does and be able to drink, too. I thought it was time he knew it, inasmuch as he has been smoking regularly since he was eleven and he is now twenty-five.

"But it was at the barracks, and there were eight soldiers, and they said if I didn't drink I must be a woman. Is that *b'd drah* or not?"

"It's very sad," I said, and he was quiet.

It was black night and raining quietly when we got into Nador. After driving up and down the muddy streets we stopped at a grocery store to ask about a hotel. A Spaniard in the doorway said there was no hotel and that we should go on to Melilla. That was completely out of the question, since Melilla, although in Morocco, has been Spanish for the past four hundred and fifty years, and still is; even if Christopher and Mohammed Larbi had been in possession of Spanish visas, which they were not, we could never have got the equipment across the border. I said we had to stay in Nador no matter what. The Spaniard said: "Try Paco Gonzalez at the gasoline pump. He might put you up. He's a European, at least."

A small Moroccan boy who was listening shouted: "Hotel Mokhtar is good!" The word "hotel" interested me, and we set out in search of it. Less than an hour later we came across it; it was over a Moslem café. Above the door someone had printed in crooked letters: H. MOKHTAR. The place reminds me somewhat of the Turkish baths that used to exist in the Casbah of Algiers thirty years ago. It is run by a bevy of inquisitive Riffian women; I know there are a great many of them, but I haven't yet been able to distinguish one from the others. After assigning us three uniformly melancholy rooms, they all came, one at a time, to examine our luggage and equipment; then apparently they held a conference, after which they put a "kitchen" at our disposal. This room was strewn with garbage, but it had two grids where charcoal fires could be built if you had charcoal. It also had a sink which was stopped up and full, I should guess, of last year's dishwater. We threw the garbage out the window onto the flowers in the patio, (there was nowhere else to put it) and installed ourselves. By now we are used to inhaling the stench of the latrines at each breath, but that first night it bothered us considerably. I flung my window open and discovered that the air outside was worse. The interior odor was of ancient urine, but the breeze that entered through the window brought a heavy scent of fresh human excrement. Just how that could be was unascertainable for the moment. However, I shut the window and lighted several bathi sticks, and then we settled down to prepare some food.

The next morning when I looked out into the sunlight I understood. The Hotel Mokhtar is built at the edge of town; for about five hundred yards beyond it the earth is crisscrossed by trenches three feet deep. These are the town's lavatories; at any moment during the day you can always see a dozen or more men, women and children squatting in the trenches. Until 1955 Nador was just another poor Moroccan village with a few Spaniards in it; suddenly it was made the capital of a newly designated province. The Spanish still have several thousand troops stationed here to "protect" Melilla—which Rabat more or less openly claims and will undoubtedly sooner or later recover. And so, naturally enough, the Moroccans have that many thousand soldiers, plus several thousand more, quartered here in order to protect Nador. There are many more people here than there should be. Water has to be got in pails and oil tins from pumps in the street; food is at a premium and all commodities are scarce. Dust hangs over the town and refuse surrounds it, except on the east, where the shallow waters of the Mar Chica lap against the mud, disturbing the dead fish that unaccountably float there in large numbers. The Mar Chica is a useless inland sea with an average depth of about six feet—just enough to drown a man. At the horizon, glistening and white, is the sandbar where the Mediterranean begins, and toward which one gazes wistfully, imagining the clean-smelling breeze that must sometimes blow out there. Nador is a prison. The presence of a wide, palm-and-flower-planted boulevard leading down the half-mile from the administration building to the dead shore of the Mar Chica only makes the place more revolting. At the lower end of the thoroughfare is a monstrous edifice built to look like a huge juke box, and supported by piles that raise it above the water. This is the town's principal restaurant, where we eat each noon. The *paseo* is lined with sidewalk cafés and concrete benches. When the benches are full of the hundreds of desperate-looking Spanish and Moroccan soldiers who roam the streets, the only place for new arrivals to sit is in the chairs put out under the palms by the café-keepers. They sit there, but they stare down the boulevard and order nothing. At night it's a little less depressing because the thoroughfare is not at all well lighted and the intense shabbiness doesn't show. Besides, after dark the two military populations are shut into their respective barracks.

Late this morning we went to the governor's office; he was in Meknès with the Sultan, but his voluble *katib* had stayed behind, and it was he who took charge of us. "Let's see. You want the Beni Bouifrour tribe. You will have them tomorrow without fail. Go now to Segangan."

That sounded too easy. He saw my hesitation. "You can still catch the khalifa before he goes out for his aperitif. Wait. I shall telephone him. He will wait." And when I looked dubious, "By my order he will wait. Go."

To get us out of the way, I thought. When we come back, this one will be gone, and I'll lose the whole day. Maybe two days. My doubt must have made itself even more noticeable, for he became dramatic. "I am telephoning. Now. Look. My hand is on the telephone. As soon as you go out that door I shall speak with the khalifa. You can go with the certainty that I shall keep my word." I understood that the longer I listened to him go on in this vein, the less I was going to believe anything that he said. There seemed to be nothing to do but start out for Segangan immediately.

But the katib had telephoned, after all, and the khalifa of Segangan, once we found the military headquarters where he had his office, proved to be pleasant and unreserved. He closed his office and walked with us into the street. As we strolled under the acacias he said, "We have many charming gardens here in Segangan." (He pronounced it Az-rheung-ng'n, in the Riffian fashion.) "It only remains for you to choose the garden of your preference for the recording."

"Haven't you a room somewhere?" I suggested. "It would be quieter, and besides, I need to plug my equipment into the electric current."

"Gardens are better than rooms," he said. "And we have our own electrician who will do whatever you ask him."

We examined bowers and arbors and fountains and nooks. I explained that I did not care where we did it, if outside noises were kept at a minimum, and that bearing this in mind, it seemed that indoors would perhaps be preferable.

"Not at all!" cried the khalifa. "I shall have all traffic deflected during the recording."

"But then the people of the town will know something is going on, and they'll come to find out what it is, and there will be more noise than ever!"

"No, no," he said reassuringly. "Foot traffic will not be allowed to circulate."

It was clear that any such measures would call attention to us straightway, because they never would be fully enforced. But his excessive proposals were a part of his desire to appear friendly, and so I ceased objecting, and resolved to speak to the katib about it when I got back here to Nador. We found a place in which to record, a remote corner of one of the parks, as shady as a thicket and quiet save for the crowing of roosters in the distance. The session was arranged for tomorrow morning. Back here in Nador I went to find the katib, but he had left his office for the day; we shall be at the mercy of the well-meaning khalifa.

September 7

My anxiety was unnecessary. When we got to Segangan this morning, we were taken to a completely different garden, quite outside the town. The khalifa's electrician had already installed the cable, and everything went with beautiful smoothness.

Among the Berbers, not only in the Rif, but much further south in the Grand Atlas, the professional troubadour still exists; the social category allotted him is not exactly that of an accepted member of the community, but neither is he a pariah. As an entertainer he is respected; as an itinerant worker he is naturally open to some suspicion. The Riffians are fond of drawing an analogy between the *imdyazen* (as the minstrels are called both here and in the Atlas) and the *gitanos* of Spain—only, as they point out, the imdyazen live in houses like other people, and not in camps outside the towns like the gypsies. If you ask them why that is, they will usually reply: "Because they are of the same blood as we." In Segangan I had my first encounter with the imdyazen. Their *chikh* looked like a well-chosen extra in a pirate film—an enormous, rough, good-natured man with a bandanna around his head instead of a turban. He, at last, had a zamar with him. Even Mohammed Larbi had never seen one before. We examined it at some length and photographed it from various angles. It consists of two separate reed pipes wired together, each with its own mouthpiece and perforations; fitted to the end of each reed is a large bull's horn. The instrument can be played with or without the horns, which are easily detached. Yesterday the effusive khalifa promised me two zamars, and even this morn-ing he let me go on believing, for the first half-hour or so, that a second player would be forthcoming. But when I began to seem anxious about his arrival and made inquiries among some of the officials, meaningful glances were exchanged, and the language abruptly shifted from Moghrebi into Tarifcht. I realized then that I was being boorish; one does not bring a lie out into the open. For some personal reason the chikh did not want another zamar, and that was that. He was an expert on his instrument, and he played it in every conceivable man-ner: standing, seated, while dancing, with horns, without, in company with drums and vocal chorus, and as a solo. He in-sisted on playing it even when I asked him not to. Within two hours my principal problem was to make him stop playing it, because its sound covered that of the other instruments to such an extent that there was a danger of monotony in sonorous effect. I finally seated him ten or twelve yards away from the other musicians. He went on playing, his cheeks puffed out like balloons, sitting all alone under an orange tree, happily unaware that his music was not being recorded.

One very good reason why I wanted to cut out the zamar was the presence among the players of an admirable musician named Boujemaa ben Mimoun, one of the few North African instrumentalists I have seen who had an understanding of the concept of personal expression in interpretation. His instrument was the *qsbah*, the long reed flute with the low register, common in the Sahara of southern Algeria but not generally used in most parts of Morocco. I had been trying to get a qsbah solo ever since I had found a group of Rhmara musicians in Tetuan. The Rhmara had agreed to do it, but their technique was indifferent and their sound was not at all what I had hoped for. Again I tried at Einzoren, and got good results musically, but once more not in the deep octave, which because of the demands it makes on breath control is the most difficult register to manage.

When I drew ben Mimoun aside and asked him if he would be willing to play a solo, he was perplexed. He wanted to please me, but as he said, "How is anybody going to know what the qsbah is saying all by itself, unless there is somebody to sing the words?" The chikh saw us conferring together and came over to investigate. When he heard my request, he immediately proclaimed that the thing was impossible. Ben Mimoun hastily agreed with him. I continued to record, but clandestinely carried my problem to the caid of the village from which the imdyazen had been recruited. He was sitting, smoking kif with some other notables in a small *pergola* nearby. He seemed to think that a qsbah could play alone if it were really necessary. I assured him that it was, that the American government wished it. After a certain length of time spent in discussion, during which Mohammed Larbi passed out large quantities of kif to everyone, the experiment was made. The chikh saved face by insisting that two versions of each number be made—one for qsbah solo and one with sung text. I was delighted with the results. The solos are among the very best things in the collection. One called "Reh dial Beni Bouhiya" is particularly beautiful. In a landscape of immensity and desolation it is a moving thing to come upon a lone camel driver, sitting beside his fire at night while the camels sleep, and listen for a long time to the querulous, hesitant cadences of the qsbah. The music, more than any other I know, most completely expresses the essence of solitude. "Reh dial Beni Bouhiya" is a perfect example of the genre. Ben Mimoun looked unhappy while he played, because there was a tension in the air caused by general disapproval of my procedure. Everyone sat quietly, however, until he had finished.

After that they went back to ensemble playing and dancing. The kif had sharpened not only their sense of rhythm but their appetites as well, and I could see that we had come to the end of the session. As the drummers frantically leapt about, nearly tripping over the microphone cable, a tall man in a fat turban approached the microphone and began to shout directly into it. "It's a dedication," explained the caid. First there was praise of the Sultan, Mohammed Khamiss, as well as of his two sons, Prince Moulay Hassan and Prince Moulay Abdallah. After that came our friend the Governor of Alhucemas Province (because in the 1958 Riffian war of dissidence he found a solution which pleased nearly everybody), and finally, with the highest enthusiasm, came a glorification of the Algerian fighters who are being slaughtered by the French next door, may Allah help them. (Drums and shouting, and the bulls' horns pointing toward the sky, spouting wild sound). We drank far too much tea and got back here to Nador too late to eat in the juke box restaurant on stilts, so we opened some baked beans and ate them in the filth and squalor of my room.

September 10

Mohammed Larbi is still fairly ill as a result of his experience in Alhucemas; his liver is not functioning properly, and he is trying to remedy it by doubling the amount of kif he smokes. The device is not working. It does, however, have one advantage: the stink of urine in the corridor is somewhat tempered by the overpowering but cleaner smell of burning kif, particularly if he leaves his door open, a habit I am trying to encourage. He lies in his room all day on the bed in an intense stupor, somewhere above the stratosphere, with the radio tuned constantly into either Cairo or Damascus. We cook breakfast and supper in my room, which gradually has come to look like a stall in any Moroccan joteya, with the most diverse objects covering every square foot of floor space. The only way I can get out of bed is to climb over the footboard and land in front of the lavabo. Each day several of the bright-eyed Riffian proprietresses come and look in happily, saying: "We don't have to make up the room today, either?" The bed has never yet been made, and the floor never swept; I don't want anyone in the room.

This morning Mohammed Larbi's sickness put him in mind of the time his stepmother tried to poison him. This is a favorite story of his which he recounts often and graphically. It seems to have been a traumatic experience for him, and this is scarcely surprising. As a result of it he walked out the door of his home and remained in hiding from his family for more than five years. It is merely incidental that during that time he married two former prostitutes; they were the only girls he knew personally. All others were potential poisoners. To him they still are; his fulminations against human females are hair-raising.

It appears that his mother left his father when the latter took a fourth wife, because although she had put up with the other two, she did not want to live in the house with the latest addition. So she packed up and went back to Tcharhanem where she had a little mud hut with nothing in it but a straw pallet and some earthenware pots. Mohammed Larbi stayed on with his father and the other wives. The new one, being the youngest, tried to get him into bed with her while his father was away from the house, and being a normally moral young man he indignantly refused. The girl was then overcome by fear that he might talk, and so she decided to get rid of him. Soon after, she pretended that something had gone wrong with the lunch, and that she would have to cook it again. It was half past four in the afternoon before she appeared with Mohammed Larbi's food. She was counting, and correctly, on his being more than ordinarily hungry. However, while he was wolfing his meal he caught sight of a bit of thread sticking out of the meat in the middle of the tajine. He pulled on it to no avail, and finally bit into the meat. It was only then that it occurred to him what the string might mean, and he ripped open the meat with his fingers, to find that a small inner pocket of meat enclosing various powders and other things had been sewn into the larger piece. He also discovered that he had eaten a certain amount of that pocket and its contents. He said nothing, scrambled up off the floor and ran out of the house, and to this day he has never been back there, although subsequently he did manage to persuade his father to get rid of that particular wife. The "other things" in the food, in addition to the assorted drugs, were, by his reluctant admission, powdered fingernails and finely cut hair—pubic hair, he maintains—along with bits of excrement from various small creatures. "Like what?" I wanted to know. "Like bats, mice, lizards, owls . . . how should I know what women find to feed to men?" he cried aggrievedly. At the end of a month his skin began to slough off, and one arm turned bluish purple. That is usual; I have seen it on occasion. It is also considered a good sign; it means that the poison is "coming out." The concensus of opinion is that if it stays in, there is not much that anyone can do in the way of finding an antidote. The poisons are provided by professionals; Larache is said to be a good place to go if you are interested in working magic on somebody. You are certain to come back with something efficacious.

Every Moroccan male has a horror of *tseuheur*. Many of them, like Mohammed Larbi, will not eat any food to which a Moslem woman has had access beforehand, unless it be his mother or sister, or, if he really trusts her, his wife. But too often it is the wife of whom he must be the most careful. She uses tseuheur to make him malleable and suggestible. It may take many months, or even several years, but the drugs are reliable. Often it is the central nervous system which is attacked. Blindness, paralysis, imbecility or dementia may occur, although by that time the wife probably has gone off to another part of the country. If the husband dies, there is no investigation. His hour has come, nothing more. Even though the practice of magic is a punishable offense, in the unlikely event that it can be proven, hundreds of thousands of men live in daily dread of it. Fortunately Mohammed Larbi is sure of his present wife; he beats her up regularly and she is terrified of him. "She'll never try to give me tseuheur," he boasts.

"I'd kill her before she had it half made." This story is always essentially the same, but at each telling I gather a few more descriptive details.

"That's why I can't drink any more," he laments. "It's the tseuheur still in there somewhere, and it turns the drink to poison."

"It's the kif," I tell him.

September 13

The cough that began at Ketama is still with me. The dry air at Alhucemas helped to keep it somewhat in abeyance; the conditions here in the Hotel Mokhtar seem to aggravate it. But now it's too late. We've stayed too long and I feel feverish.

September 15

Two days later. Still in bed but much better. Christopher is disgusted with the situation and Mohammed Larbi is in a state of advanced disintegration. The idea of going back to Midar does not bother me so much as knowing that after that we shall have to return here to Nador once again. The pail of dark water provided for us by the women, out of which I have been filling empty wine bottles and adding Halazone tablets to them so we could have some kind of water to drink, proved to have a large, indescribably filthy cleaning rag buried in the silt at the bottom. I discovered it only this morning when all the water had been drunk. At that moment I wanted more than anything merely to escape from here. During lunch I said tentatively, "What do you think of going east, soon?" Christopher thought well of the idea, and so did Mohammed Larbi. I have renounced Temsaman, the Beni Touzine and the Ait Ulixxek.

Oujda, September 17

Even the weather seemed brighter when we had left Nador behind and were hurrying toward the Algerian border. We crossed the chastened, dry-weather Oued Moulouya and the flat rich farmlands north of the Zegzel country where the Beni Snassen live. It was getting dark as we went through Berkane, new and resplendent. The town was full of people, palms and fluorescent lights. After Nador it looked like Hong Kong; but we decided not to stop, because we wanted to get to Oujda in time to have dinner at the hotel—that is, if the hotel was still functioning.

About seven o'clock we saw the lights of Martimprey spread out ahead, perhaps twenty miles away, slightly below us. While we were still looking out across the plain, three flares exploded overhead and sailed slowly earthward. Very strong searchlight beams began to revolve, projected from behind the mountains in Algeria. There was a turn-off before Martimprey; we got onto the Saidia road just south of the town. That avoided possible difficulties with the authorities, for Martimprey is literally on the frontier, and is little more than a military headquarters these days. On this road there was a certain small amount of traffic. About every ten minutes we met a car coming toward us. Ahead there was a nervous driver who steadfastly refused to let us pass him. But when Christopher slowed down, in order to let him get well ahead of us, he slowed down too; there was no way of not being directly behind him. In exasperation Christopher finally drew up beside the road and stopped, saying, "I want to see a little of this war, anyway. Let's watch awhile." The red flares illumined the mountainsides to the east, and the sharp beams of blue light intersected each other at varying angles. It was completely silent; there were not even any crickets. But the other car had stopped too, perhaps five hundred feet ahead of us, and soon we saw a figure approaching. Mohammed Larbi whispered: "If he asks questions, just answer them. He has a pistol." "How do you know?" I countered, but he did not reply. Christopher had turned off the headlights and the road was very dark, so we were not able to see the man's face until he had come right up to us.

"*Vous êtes en panne?*" he inquired, looking in through the front window like a customs inspector. In the reflection from the dashboard light I could see that he was young and well-dressed. He made a swift examination of the interior by turning his head slowly from one side to the other. The searchlights continued to move across the sky. We said we were only watching, as though we were in a shop where we didn't want to buy anything. "I see," he said presently. "I thought maybe you were in trouble." We thanked him. "Not at all," he said lightly, and he went back into the darkness. A minute or two later we heard the door of his car shut, but the motor did not start up. We waited another ten minutes or so; then Christopher turned on the headlights and the motor. The other car did likewise, started up and kept ahead of us all the way to Oujda. Before we got to the center it turned down a side street and disappeared.

I had been afraid that with the Algerian border closed, the *raison d'être* of the Hotel Terminus would be gone, and it might no longer exist. It is open as usual, but its prices are much higher and the food has deteriorated. What the food now lacks in quality the service compensates for in pretentiousness. Dinner was served outdoors under the palms, around a large circular basin of water. The popping of corks punctuated the sequences of French conversation. Suddenly there was a very loud explosion; the ground under my feet shuddered a little with the force of it. No one seemed to have noticed; the relaxed monotone of words and laughter continued as before. Within the minute there was another boom, somewhat less strong but still powerful. When the waiter came up I questioned him.

"It's the bombardments in the Tlemcen sector," he said. "*Un engagement.* It's been going on for the past two nights. Sometimes it's quiet for a week or so, sometimes it's very active." During dessert there was a long string of machine-gun fire not more than half a mile distant—in Oujda itself. "What's that?" I demanded. The waiter's face did not change. "I didn't hear anything," he said. All kinds of things happen in Oujda nowadays, and no one asks any questions.

This was the night De Gaulle was to make his long-awaited "peace" offer to the F.L.N. via the radio. Out of idle curiosity, we went immediately upstairs after eating to listen to it. While the General intoned his pious-sounding syllables the deep-toned explosions continued outside, sometimes like nearby thunder and sometimes quite recognizably bombs. Mohammed Larbi sat quietly, filling empty cigarette papers with kif and tamping them down before closing the ends. Now and then he demanded: "What's he saying?" (for he has never learned French), and each time he made the query I quickly said: "*Reh.*" (Wind.) Christopher was annoyed with both of us. He has never been violently partisan in the Algerian dispute, because he is willing to credit the French with a modicum of good will. In order not to disturb his listening, I went to stand on the balcony, where I could hear the bombs instead of the words. There was no hypocrisy in their sound, no difference between what they meant and what they said, which was: death to Algerians. I wondered how many millions of Moslems in North Africa were hearing the radio words at that instant, and imagined the epithets of contempt and hatred coming from their lips as they listened. "*Zbil!*" "*Jiffa!*" "*Kharra!*" "*Ouild d'l qhaba!*" "*Inaal dinou!*" "*El khannez!*" When the General had finished his monologue, Christopher said sadly: "I only hope they believe him." I didn't think there was much danger of that, so I said nothing. The noise from the front kept going until a little after midnight. I felt feverish again, and I had to hunt for my clinical thermometer. It registered a little over 39 degrees. "Multiply by one point eight and add thirty-two. A hundred and two point two. My God! I'm sick."

"I've got to go to bed," I announced.

September 18

I stayed in bed yesterday morning. About three in the afternoon I got up long enough to drive to the governor's office. He too was in Meknès with the Sultan, and his katib was politely uncoöperative. His jurisdiction extended to the Beni Snassen, he agreed, but the truth was that the Beni Snassen had absolutely no music; in fact, he declared, they hire their musicians from the Beni Uriaghel when they need music. Nothing. And Figuig? I suggested. "There is no music in Figuig," he said flatly. "You can go. But you will get no music. I guarantee you that." I understood that he meant he would see to it that we got none. The anger was beginning to boil up inside me, and I thought it more prudent to get out of his office quickly. I thanked him and went back to bed. He is not an unusual type, the partially educated young Moroccan for whom material progress has become such an important symbol that he would be willing to sacrifice the religion, culture, happiness, and even the lives of his compatriots in order to achieve even a modicum of it. Few of them are as frank about their convictions as the official in Fez who told me, "I detest all folk music, and particularly ours here in Morocco. It sounds like the noises made by savages. Why should I help you to export a thing which we are trying to destroy? You are looking for tribal music. There are no more tribes. We have dissolved them. So the word means nothing. And there never was any tribal music anyway—only noise. *Non, monsieur,* I am not in accord with your project." In reality, the present government's policy is far less extreme than this man's opinion. The music itself has not been much tampered with—only the lyrics, which are now indoctrinated with patriotic sentiments. Practically all large official celebrations are attended by groups of folk musicians from all over the country; their travel and living expenses are paid by the government, and they perform before large audiences. As a result the performing style is becoming slick, and the extended forms are disappearing in favor of truncated versions which are devoid of musical sense.

Oujda, September 20

I have lain in bed for the past three days, feverish and depressed, having lost the Beni Snassen as well as the others. Now all that remains open to me in the way of Riffian music is that of the Gzennaia. They live in the Province of Taza, and it will probably be difficult to get to them because of the roads.

During the day there seems to be no sound from the front, but at night the bombardments begin, shortly after dark, and continue for three or four hours. Mohammed Larbi refuses to go out of the hotel; he claims Oujda is a dangerous place these days. According to him, there are ambushes and executions daily. I suspect that most of the explosions we hear during the day are fireworks celebrating the beginning of Mouloud, but I agree that some of the sounds are hard to ex-

plain away in that manner. In any case, the city is too close to
the border to be restful. All I want is to be well enough to
leave for Taza.

Taza, September 22

Yesterday morning I had no fever at all, so in spite of feeling a little shaky, I got up and packed, and we set out on the
road once more. It was a cool, sunny morning when we left.
As we got into the desert beyond El Ayoun, however, the
heat waves began to dance on the horizon. We ate in a wheat-
field outside Taourirt. Passers-by stopped under the tamarisk
trees and sat down to watch us. When we got back into the
car there was a struggle going on among several of them for
possession of the empty tins and bottles we had left.

By the time we arrived in Taza it was nearly sunset, and I
was ready again for bed. But since the government buildings
had not yet shut for the night I decided to try and see the
governor while I was still up and walking around. I had a feeling that the fever had returned. I went straight to the hotel
from there to get into bed, and I have not yet got out of it,
so it is just as well that I stayed up an extra hour and saw the
katib. The governor, not surprisingly, was in Meknès with the
Sultan.

This katib was a young intellectual with thick-lensed
glasses. He made it clear that he thought my project an absurdity, but he did not openly express disapproval. He even
went through the motions of telephoning all the way to
Aknoul to a subordinate up there in the mountains.

"I see, I see," he said presently. "He died last year. Ah, yes.
Too bad. And Tizi Ouzli?" he added, as I gestured and stage-
whispered to him. "Nothing there, either. I see." He listened
awhile, commenting in monosyllables from time to time, then
finally thanked his informant and hung up.

"The last chikh in Aknoul died last summer. He was an old
man. There is no music in the region. In Tizi Ouzli the
people won't come out. When the Sultan went through, the
women refused to leave their houses to sing for him. So you
see"—he smiled, spreading his hands out, palms up—"it will
not be possible with the Gzennaia."

I sat looking at him while he spoke, already aware of what he was going to report, letting fragments of thoughts flit through my tired head. How they mistrust and fear the Riffians! But how naïve this one is to admit openly that the alienation is so great! Were the women punished? And I remembered a remark a Riffian had once made to me, "You have your Negroes in America, and Morocco has us."

"End of the Rif," I said sadly to Christopher.

The young katib pointed to the wall map behind his desk. "In the Middle Atlas, on the other hand, I can arrange something for you. Within a very few days, if you like. The Ait Ouaraine."

"Yes, I should like it very much," I told him.

"Come, please, tomorrow morning at ten o'clock."

"Thank you," we said.

I came back here to the Hôtel Guillaume Tell and got into bed. The room is not made up here, either, but there is plenty of space in it and my meals are brought up on a tray, so it is not important. Yesterday Christopher and Mohammed Larbi made contact in the street with a group of professional musicians who agreed to record today. Their ensemble consisted of three rhaitas, four *tbola* (beaten with sticks) and eight rifles. The first price asked was high; then it was explained that if the rifles were not to be fired during the playing the cost would be cut in half. The agreement reached provided that only the rhaitas and tbola would perform.

Mohammed Larbi's excessive consumption of kif has given him a serious chronic liver disorder; he feels ill most of the time. Last night he went out for a walk after dinner. At the end of an hour he came in, his expression more determined than usual, and announced to us: "I'm finished with kif." Christopher laughed derisively. To implement his words, Mohammed Larbi tossed both his *naboula*, bulging with kif, and his cherished pipe, on my bed, saying, "Keep all this. You can have it. I don't want to see any of it again." But this morning before breakfast he went out and bought a fifth of Scotch, which he sampled before his morning coffee. When he came into my room later to pack up the recording equipment, he had the bottle with him, and Christopher made loud fun of him.

"*O chnou brhitsi?*" he cried indignantly. "I'm not smoking kif any more. Do you expect me to leave my poor head *empty?*" This amused Christopher and depressed me. I foresee difficulties with a belligerent Mohammed Larbi. Kif keeps men quiet and vegetative; alcohol sends them out to break shop windows. In Mohammed Larbi's case it often means a fight with a policeman. I watched with misgivings as he prepared to go out.

This was the first time any recording had been done in my absence. But it all went smoothly, said Christopher on their return. There was a slight altercation at the moment of payment, because in spite of the agreement by which the men were not to discharge their rifles, they had not been able to resist participating, so that at three separate points in the music they fired them off, all eight of them, and simultaneously. At the end they presented a bill for twenty-four cartridges, which Mohammed Larbi, by then well fortified with White Label, steadfastly refused to pay. "All right. Good-bye," they said, and they went happily off to play at a wedding in a nearby village.

September 22

The whiskey has done its work, but in a fashion I had not expected. This evening, when the bottle was nearly empty, Mohammed Larbi spent two hours trying to telephone his wife in Tangier. Finally he got the proprietor of a grocery near his house to go and fetch her, and had a stormy conversation with her for five minutes. I could hear him bellowing from where I lay, at the other end of the hotel. When he came into my room he looked maniacal.

"I've heard my wife's voice!" he shouted. "Now I've got to see her. She may have somebody else. I'm going tonight. I'll get there by tomorrow night."

"You're walking out on your job?"

"I'm going to see my *wife!*" he cried, even louder, as though I had not understood. "I *have* to do that, don't I?"

"You're going to leave me here, sick in bed?"

He hesitated only an instant. "Christopher knows how to take care of you. Besides, you're not sick. You just have a fever. I'll give you the grocer's number, and you telephone me when you get to Fez. I'll see you in a week or ten days. In Fez."

"All right," I said, without any intention of calling him. If he is going to be on whiskey, it would be better not to have him along, in any case.

And so now I have at least a pound of very strong kif among my possessions. In another two or three days I should be well enough to go up to Tahala and capture the Ait Ouaraine. The Rif is finished, and I managed to record only in two places.

Baptism of Solitude

IMMEDIATELY when you arrive in the Sahara, for the first or the tenth time, you notice the stillness. An incredible, absolute silence prevails outside the towns; and within, even in busy places like the markets, there is a hushed quality in the air, as if the quiet were a conscious force which, resenting the intrusion of sound, minimizes and disperses sound straightway. Then there is the sky, compared to which all other skies seem faint-hearted efforts. Solid and luminous, it is always the focal point of the landscape. At sunset, the precise, curved shadow of the earth rises into it swiftly from the horizon, cutting it into light section and dark section. When all daylight is gone, and the space is thick with stars, it is still of an intense and burning blue, darkest directly overhead and paling toward the earth, so that the night never really grows dark.

You leave the gate of the fort or the town behind, pass the camels lying outside, go up into the dunes, or out onto the hard, stony plain and stand awhile, alone. Presently, you will either shiver and hurry back inside the walls, or you will go on standing there and let something very peculiar happen to you, something that everyone who lives there has undergone and which the French call *le baptême de la solitude*. It is a unique sensation, and it has nothing to do with loneliness, for loneliness presupposes memory. Here, in this wholly mineral landscape lighted by stars like flares, even memory disappears; nothing is left but your own breathing and the sound of your heart beating. A strange, and by no means pleasant, process of reintegration begins inside you, and you have the choice of fighting against it, and insisting on remaining the person you have always been, or letting it take its course. For no one who has stayed in the Sahara for a while is quite the same as when he came.

Before the war for independence in Algeria, under the rule of the French military, there was a remarkable feeling of friendly sympathy among Europeans in the Sahara. It is unnecessary to stress the fact that the corollary of this pleasant state of affairs was the exercise of the strictest sort of colonial control over the Algerians themselves, a regime which amounted to a reign of terror. But from the European viewpoint the place was ideal. The whole vast region was like a small unspoiled rural community where everyone respected the rights of everyone else. Each time you lived there for a while, and left it, you were struck with the indifference and the impersonality of the world outside. If during your travels in the Sahara you forgot something, you could be sure of finding it later on your way back; the idea of appropriating it would not have occurred to anyone. You could wander where you liked, out in the wilderness or in the darkest alleys of the towns; no one would molest you.

At that time no members of the indigent, wandering, unwanted proletariat from northern Algeria had come down here, because there was nothing to attract them. Almost everyone owned a parcel of land in an oasis and lived by working it. In the shade of the date palms, wheat, barley and corn were grown, and those plants provided the staple items of diet. There were usually two or three Arab or Negro shopkeepers who sold things such as sugar, tea, candles, matches, carbide for fuel, and cheap European cotton goods. In the larger towns there was sometimes a shop kept by a European, but the merchandise was the same, because the customers were virtually all natives. Almost without exception, the only Europeans who lived in the Sahara were the military and the ecclesiastic.

As a rule, the military and their aides were friendly men, agreeable to be with, interested in showing visitors everything worth seeing in their districts. This was fortunate, as the traveler was often completely at their mercy. He might have to depend on them for his food and lodging, since in the smaller places there were no hotels. Generally he had to depend on them for contact with the outside world, because anything he wanted, like cigarettes or wine, had to be brought by truck from the military post, and his mail was sent in care of the post, too. Furthermore, the decision as to whether he was to have permission to move about freely in the region rested with the military. The power to grant those privileges was vested in, let us say, one lonely lieutenant who lived two hundred miles from his nearest countryman, ate badly (a condition anathema to any Frenchman), and wished that neither camels, date palms, nor inquisitive foreigners had ever been created. Still, it was rare to find an indifferent or unhelpful comandante. He was likely to invite you for drinks and dinner, show you the curiosities he had collected during his years in the *bled*, ask you to accompany him on his tours of inspection, or even to spend a fortnight with him and his *peloton* of several dozen native meharistes when they went out into the desert to make topographical surveys. Then you would be given your own camel—not an ambling pack camel that had to be driven with a stick by someone walking beside it, but a swift, trained animal that obeyed the slightest tug of the reins.

More extraordinary were the Pères Blancs, intelligent and well-educated. There was no element of resignation in their eagerness to spend the remainder of their lives in distant outposts, dressed as Moslems, speaking Arabic, living in the rigorous, comfortless manner of the desert inhabitants. They made no converts and expected to make none. "We are here only to show the Moslem that the Christian can be worthy of respect," they explained. One used to hear the Moslems say that although the Christians might be masters of the earth, the Moslems were the masters of heaven; for the military it was quite enough that the *indigène* recognize European supremacy here. Obviously the White Fathers could not be satisfied with that. They insisted upon proving to the inhabitants that the Nazarene was capable of leading as exemplary a life as the most ardent follower of Mohammed. It is true that the austerity of the Fathers' mode of life inspired many Moslems with respect for them if not for the civilization they represented. And as a result of the years spent in the desert among the inhabitants, the Fathers acquired a certain healthy and unorthodox fatalism, an excellent adjunct to their spiritual equipment, and a highly necessary one in dealing with the men among whom they had chosen to live.

With an area considerably larger than that of the United States, the Sahara is a continent within a continent—a skeleton, if you like, but still a separate entity from the rest of Africa which surrounds it. It has its own mountain ranges, rivers, lakes and forests, but they are largely vestigial. The mountain ranges have been reduced to gigantic bouldery bumps that rise above the neighboring countryside like the mountains on the moon. Some of the rivers appear as such for perhaps one day a year—others much less often. The lakes are of solid salt, and the forests have long since petrified. But the physical contours of the landscape vary as much as they do anywhere else. There are plains, hills, valleys, gorges, rolling lands, rocky peaks and volcanic craters, all without vegetation or even soil. Yet, probably the only parts that are monotonous to the eye are regions like the Tanezrouft, south of Reggane, a stretch of about five hundred miles of absolutely flat, gravel-strewn terrain, without the slightest sign of life, or the smallest undulation in the land, nothing to vary the implacable line of the horizon on all sides. After being here for a while, the sight of even a rock awakens an emotion in the traveler; he feels like crying, "Land!"

There is no known historical period when the Sahara has not been inhabited by man. Most of the other larger forms of animal life, whose abode it formerly was, have become extinct. If we believe the evidence of cave drawings, we can be sure that the giraffe, the hippopotamus and the rhinoceros were once dwellers in the region. The lion has disappeared from North Africa in our own time, likewise the ostrich. Now and then a crocodile is still discovered in some distant, hidden oasis pool, but the occurrence is so rare that when it happens it is a great event. The camel, of course, is not a native of Africa at all, but an importation from Asia, having arrived approximately at the time of the end of the Roman Empire—about when the last elephants were killed off. Large numbers of the herds of wild elephants that roamed the northern reaches of the desert were captured and trained for use in the Carthaginian army, but it was the Romans who finally annihilated the species to supply ivory for the European market.

Fortunately for man, who seems to insist on continuing to live in surroundings which become increasingly inhospitable to him, gazelles are still plentiful, and there are, paradoxically enough, various kinds of edible fish in the water holes—often more than a hundred feet deep—throughout the Sahara. Certain species which abound in artesian wells are blind, having always lived deep in the subterranean lakes.

An often-repeated statement, no matter how incorrect, takes a long time to disappear from circulation. Thus, there is a popular misconception of the Sahara as a vast region of sand across which Arabs travel in orderly caravans from one white-domed city to another. A generalization much nearer to the truth would be to say that it is an area of rugged mountains, bare valleys and flat, stony wasteland, sparsely dotted with Negro villages of mud. The sand in the Sahara, according to data supplied by the Geographical Service of the French Army, covers only about a tenth of its surface; and the Arabs, most of whom are nomads, form a small part of the population. The vast majority of the inhabitants are of Berber (native North African) and/or Negro (native West African) stock. But the Negroes of today are not those who originally peopled the desert. The latter never took kindly to the colonial designs of the Arabs and the Islamized Berbers who collaborated with them; over the centuries they beat a constant retreat toward the southeast until only a vestige of their society remains, in the region now known as the Tibesti. They were replaced by the more docile Sudanese, imported from the south as slaves to work the constantly expanding series of oases.

In the Sahara the oasis—which is to say, the forest of date palms—is primarily a man-made affair and can continue its existence only if the work of irrigating its terrain is kept up unrelentingly. When the Arabs arrived in Africa twelve centuries ago, they began a project of land reclamation which, if the Europeans continue it with the aid of modern machinery, will transform much of the Sahara into a great, fertile garden. Wherever there was a sign of vegetation, the water was there not far below; it merely needed to be brought to the surface. The Arabs set to work digging wells, constructing reservoirs, building networks of canals along the surface of the ground and systems of subterranean water-galleries deep in the earth.

For all these important projects, the recently arrived colonizers needed great numbers of workers who could bear the climate and the malaria that is still endemic in the oases. Sudanese slaves seemed to be the ideal solution of the problem, and these came to constitute the larger part of the permanent population of the desert. Each Arab tribe traveled about among the oases it controlled, collecting the produce. It was never the practice or the intention of the sons of Allah to live there. They have a saying which goes, "No one lives in the Sahara if he is able to live anywhere else." Slavery has, of course, been abolished officially by the French, but only recently, within our time. Probably the principal factor in the process by which Timbuktu was reduced from its status of capital of the Sahara to its present abject condition was the closing of the slave market there. But the Sahara, which started out as a Negro country, is still a Negro country, and will undoubtedly remain so for a long time.

The oases, those magnificent palm groves, are the blood and bone of the desert; life in the Sahara would be unthinkable without them. Wherever human beings are found, an oasis is sure to be nearby. Sometimes the town is surrounded by the trees, but usually it is built just outside, so that none of the fertile ground will be wasted on mere living quarters. The size of an oasis is reckoned by the number of trees it contains, not by the numbers of square miles it covers, just as the taxes are based on the number of date-bearing trees and not on the amount of land. The prosperity of a region is in direct proportion to the number and size of its oases. The one at Figuig, for instance, has more than two hundred thousand bearing palms, and the one at Timimoun is forty miles long, with irrigation systems that are of an astonishing complexity.

To stroll in a Saharan oasis is rather like taking a walk through a well-kept Eden. The alleys are clean, bordered on each side by hand-patted mud walls, not too high to prevent you from seeing the riot of verdure within. Under the high waving palms are the smaller trees—pomegranate, orange, fig, almond. Below these, in neat squares surrounded by narrow ditches of running water, are the vegetables and wheat. No matter how far from the town you stray, you have the same impression of order, cleanliness, and insistence on utilizing every square inch of ground. When you come to the edge of the oasis, you always find that it is in the process of being enlarged. Plots of young palms extend out into the glaring wasteland. Thus far they are useless, but in a few years they will begin to bear, and eventually this sun-blistered land will be a part of the green belt of gardens.

There are a good many birds living in the oases, but their songs and plumage are not appreciated by the inhabitants. The birds eat the young shoots and dig up the seeds as fast as they are planted, and practically every man and boy carries a slingshot. A few years ago I traveled through the Sahara with a parrot; everywhere the poor bird was glowered at by the natives, and in Timimoun a delegation of three elderly men came to the hotel one afternoon and suggested that I stop leaving its cage in the window; otherwise there was no telling what its fate might be. "Nobody likes birds here," they said meaningfully.

It is the custom to build little summerhouses out in the oases. There is often an element of play and fantasy in the architecture of these edifices which makes them captivating. They are small toy palaces of mud. Here, men have tea with their families at the close of day, or spend the night when it is unusually hot in the town, or invite their friends for a few hands of *ronda*, the favorite North African card game, and a little music. If a man asks you to visit him in his summerhouse, you find that the experience is invariably worth the long walk required to get there. You will have to drink at least the three traditional glasses of tea, and you may have to eat a good many almonds and smoke more kif than you really want, but it will be cool, there will be the gurgle of running water and the smell of mint in the air, and your host may bring out a flute. One winter I priced one of these houses that had particularly struck my fancy. With its garden and pool, the cost was the equivalent of twenty-five pounds. The catch was that the owner wanted to retain the right to work the land, because it was unthinkable to him that it should cease to be productive.

In the Sahara as elsewhere in North Africa, popular religious observances often include elements of pre-Islamic faiths in their ritual; the most salient example is the institution of religious dancing, which persists despite long-continued discouragement of the custom by educated Moslems. Even in the highly religious settlement of the M'Zab, where puritanism is carried to excessive lengths, the holding of dances is not unknown. At the time I lived there children were not allowed to laugh in public, yet I spent an entire night watching a dozen men dance themselves into unconsciousness beside a bonfire of palm branches. Two burly guards were necessary to prevent them from throwing themselves into the flames. After each man had been heaved back from the fire several times, he finally ceased making his fantastic skyward leaps, staggered, and sank to the ground. He was immediately carried outside the circle and covered with blankets, his place being taken by a fresh adept. There was no music or singing, but there were eight drummers, each one playing an instrument of a different size.

In other places, the dance is similar to the Berber *ahouache* of the Moroccan Atlas. The participants form a great circle holding hands, women alternating with men; their movements are measured, never frantic, and although the trance is constantly suggested, it seems never to be arrived at collectively. In the performances I have seen, there has been a woman in the center with her head and neck hidden by a cloth. She sings and dances, and the chorus around her responds antiphonally. It is all very sedate and low-pitched, but the irrational seems never very far away, perhaps because of the hypnotic effect produced by the slowly beaten, deep-toned drums.

The Touareg, an ancient offshoot of the Kabyle Berbers of Algeria, were unappreciative of the "civilizing mission" of the Roman legions and decided to put a thousand miles or more of desert between themselves and their would-be educators. They went straight south until they came to a land that seemed likely to provide them the privacy they desired, and there they have remained throughout the centuries, their own masters almost until today. Through all the ages during which the Arabs dominated the surrounding regions, the Touareg retained their rule of the Hoggar, that immense plateau in the very center of the Sahara. Their traditional hatred of the Arabs, however, does not appear to have been powerful enough to keep them from becoming partially Islamized, although they are by no means a completely Moslem people. Far from being a piece of property only somewhat more valuable than a sheep, the woman has an extremely important place in Targui society. The line of succession is purely maternal. Here, it is the men who must be veiled day and night.

The veil is of fine black gauze and is worn, so they explain, to protect the soul. But since soul and breath to them are identical, it is not difficult to find a physical reason, if one is desired. The excessive dryness of the atmosphere often causes disturbances in the nasal passages. The veil conserves the breath's moisture, is a sort of little air-conditioning plant, and this helps keep out the evil spirits which otherwise would manifest their presence by making the nostrils bleed, a common occurrence in this part of the world.

It is scarcely fair to refer to these proud people as Touareg. The word is a term of opprobrium meaning "lost souls," given them by their traditional enemies the Arabs, but one which, in the outside world, has stuck. They call themselves *imochagh*, the free ones. Among all the Berber-speaking peoples, they are the only ones to have devised a system of writing their language. No one knows how long their alphabet has been in use, but it is a true phonetical alphabet, quite as well planned and logical as the Roman, with twenty-three simple and thirteen compound letters.

Unfortunately for them, the Touareg have never been able to get on among themselves; internecine warfare has gone on unceasingly among them for centuries. Until the French military put a stop to it, it had been a common practice for one tribe to set out on plundering expeditions against a neighboring tribe. During these voyages, the wives of the absent men remained faithful to their husbands, the strict Targui moral code recommending death as a punishment for infidelity. However, a married woman whose husband was away was free to go at night to the graveyard dressed in her finest apparel, lie on the tombstone of one of her ancestors, and invoke a certain spirit called Idebni, who always appeared in the guise of one of the young men of the community. If she could win Idebni's favor, he gave her news of her husband; if not, he strangled her. The Touareg women, being very clever, always managed to bring back news of their husbands from the cemetery.

The first motor crossing of the Sahara was accomplished in 1923. At that time it was still a matter of months to get from, let us say, Touggourt to Zinder, or from the Tafilelt to Gao. In 1934, I was in Erfoud asking about caravans to Timbuktu.

Yes, they said, one was leaving in a few weeks, and it would take from sixteen to twenty weeks to make the voyage. How would I get back? The caravan would probably set out on its return trip at this time next year. They were surprised to see that this information lessened my interest. How could you expect to do it more quickly?

Of course, the proper way to travel in the Sahara is by camel, particularly if you're a good walker, since after about two hours of the camel's motion you are glad to get down and walk for four. Each succeeding day is likely to bring with it a greater percentage of time spent off the camel. Nowadays, if you like, you can leave Algiers in the morning by plane and be fairly well into the desert by evening, but the traveler who gives in to this temptation, like the reader of a mystery story who skips through the book to arrive at the solution quickly, deprives himself of most of the pleasure of the journey. For the person who wants to see something the practical means of locomotion is the trans-Saharan truck, a compromise between camel and airplane.

There are only two trails across the desert at present (the Piste Impériale through Mauretania not being open to the public) and I should not recommend either to drivers of private automobiles. The trucks, however, are especially built for the region. If there is any sort of misadventure, the wait is not likely to be more than twenty-four hours, since the truck is always expected at the next town, and there is always an ample supply of water aboard. But the lone car that gets stuck in the Sahara is in trouble.

Usually, you can go to the fort of any town and telephone ahead to the next post, asking them to notify the hotelkeeper there of your intended arrival. Should the lines be down—a not unusual circumstance—there is no way of assuring yourself a room in advance, save by mail, which is extremely slow. Unless you travel with your own blankets this can be a serious drawback, arriving unannounced, for the hotels are small, often having only five or six rooms, and the winter nights are cold. The temperature goes to several degrees below freezing, reaching its lowest point just before dawn. The same courtyard that may show 125° when it is flooded with sun at two in the afternoon will register only 28° the following morning. So it is good to know you are going to have a room and a bed in your next stopping place. Not that there is heating of any sort in the establishments, but by keeping the window shut you can help the thick mud walls conserve some of the daytime heat. Even so, I have awakened to find a sheet of ice over the water in the glass beside my bed.

These violent extremes of temperature are due, of course, to the dryness of the atmosphere, whose relative humidity is often less than five percent. When you reflect that the soil attains a temperature of one hundred and seventy-five degrees during the summer, you understand that the principal consideration in planning streets and houses should be that of keeping out as much light as possible. The streets are kept dark by being built underneath and inside the houses, and the houses have no windows in their massive walls. The French have introduced the window into much of their architecture, but the windows open onto wide, vaulted arcades, and thus, while they do give air, they let in little light. The result is that once you are out of the sun you live in a Stygian gloom.

Even in the Sahara there is no spot where rain has not been known to fall, and its arrival is an event that calls for celebration—drumming, dancing, firing of guns. The storms are violent and unpredictable. Considering their disastrous effects, one wonders that the people can welcome them with such unmixed emotions. Enormous walls of water rush down the dry river beds, pushing everything before them, often isolating the towns. The roofs of the houses cave in, and often the walls themselves. A prolonged rain would destroy every town in the Sahara, since the *tob*, of which everything is built, is softer than our adobe. And, in fact, it is not unusual to see a whole section of a village forsaken by its occupants, who have rebuilt their houses nearby, leaving the walls and foundations of their former dwellings to dissolve and drop back into the earth of which they were made.

In 1932 I decided to spend the winter in the M'Zab of southern Algeria. The rattletrap bus started out from Laghouat at night in a heavy rain. Not far to the south, the trail crossed a flat stretch about a mile wide, slightly lower than the surrounding country. Even as we were in it, the water began to rise around us, and in a moment the motor died.

The passengers jumped out and waded about in water that soon was up to their waists; in all directions there were dim white figures in burnouses moving slowly through the flood, like storks. They were looking for a shallow route back to dry land, but they did not find it. In the end they carried me, the only European in the party, all the way to Laghouat on their backs, leaving the bus and its luggage to drown out there in the rain. When I got to Ghardaia two days later, the rain (which was the first in seven years) had made a deep pond beside an embankment the French had built for the trail. Such an enormous quantity of water all in one place was a source of great excitement to the inhabitants. For days there was a constant procession of women coming to carry it away in jugs. The children tried to walk on its surface, and two small ones were drowned. Ten days later the water had almost disappeared. A thick, brilliant green froth covered what was left, but the women continued to come with their jugs, pushing aside the scum and taking whatever fell in. For once they were able to collect as much water as they could store in their houses. Ordinarily, it was an expensive commodity that they had to buy each morning from the town water-sellers, who brought it in from the oasis.

There are probably few accessible places on the face of the globe where one can get less comfort for his money than the Sahara. It is still possible to find something flat to lie down on, several turnips and sand, noodles and jam, and a few tendons of something euphemistically called chicken to eat, and the stub of a candle to undress by at night. Inasmuch as it is necessary to carry one's own food and stove, it sometimes seems scarcely worth while to bother with the "meals" provided by the hotels. But if one depends entirely on tinned goods, they give out too quickly. Everything disappears eventually—coffee, tea, sugar, cigarettes—and the traveler settles down to a life devoid of these superfluities, using a pile of soiled clothing as a pillow for his head at night and a burnous as blanket.

Perhaps the logical question to ask at this point is: Why go? The answer is that when a man has been there and undergone the baptism of solitude he can't help himself. Once he has been under the spell of the vast, luminous, silent country, no

other place is quite strong enough for him, no other surroundings can provide the supremely satisfying sensation of
existing in the midst of something that is absolute. He will go
back, whatever the cost in comfort and money, for the absolute has no price.

(*Since this piece was written, the Algerian war has changed
the Saharan picture. Now the hypothetical voyager would probably not go back, because without special documents it is very
unlikely that he would be allowed in. The Sahara is not on
display at the present time.*)

All Parrots Speak

P ARROTS are amusing, decorative, long-lived, and faithful
in their affections, but the quality which distinguishes
them from most of God's other inventions is their ability to
imitate the sounds of human speech. A parrot that cannot talk
or sing is, we feel, an incomplete parrot. For some reason it
fascinates us to see a small, feather-covered creature with a ludicrous, senile face speaking a human language—so much,
indeed, that the more simple-minded of us tend to take seriously the idea suggested by our subconscious: that a parrot
really is a person (in disguise, of course), but capable of
human thought and feeling.

In Central America and Mexico I have listened for hours
while the Indian servants in the kitchen held communion
with the parrot—monologues which the occasional interjec-
tions from the perch miraculously transformed into conversations. And when I questioned the Indians I found a recurrent
theme in their replies: the parrot can be a temporary abode
for a human spirit. Our own rational system of thought unhappily forbids such extravagances; nevertheless the atavism is
there, felt rather than believed.

The uneducated, unsophisticated Indian, on the other
hand, makes an ideal companion and mentor for the parrot.
The long colloquies about what to put into the soup, or
which rebozo to wear to the fiesta, are in themselves education of a sort that few of us have the time or patience to provide. It is not surprising that most of the parrots that have
found their way to the United States have been trained by
rural Latin-Americans. As important as the spoken word in
these relationships is a continuous association with one or two
individuals. A parrot is not a sociable bird; it usually develops
an almost obsessive liking for a very few people, and either indifference or hatred toward everyone else. Its human relationships are simple extensions of its monogamous nature.
There is not much difference between being a one-man bird
and a one-bird bird.

I remember the day when I first became parrot-conscious.

It was in Costa Rica; my wife and I had been riding all morning with the vaqueros and were very thirsty. At a gatehouse between ranch properties we asked a woman for water. When we had drunk our fill, rested and chatted, she motioned us into a dim corner and said "*Miren, qué graciosos!*" There, perched on a stick, were seven little creatures. She carried the stick out into the light, and I saw that each of the seven tiny bags of pinkish-gray skin had a perfectly shaped, hooked yellow beak, wide open. And when I looked closely, I could see miniature brilliant green feathers growing out of the wrinkles of skin. We discussed the diet and care of young parrots, and our hostess generously offered us one. Jane claimed she couldn't bear to think of breaking up the family, and so we went on our way parrotless.

But a week later, while waiting for a river boat, we had to spend the night in the "hotel" of a hamlet called Bebedero. Our room was built on stilts above a vast mud welter where enormous hogs were wallowing, and it shook perilously when they scratched their backs against the supporting piles. The boat came in fifteen hours late, and there was nothing we could do but sit in the breathlessly hot room and wait. Nothing, that is, until the proprietor appeared in the doorway with a full-grown parrot perched on his finger and asked us if we wanted to converse with it.

"Does it speak?" I asked.

"*Claro que sí.* All parrots speak." My ignorance astonished him. Then he added, "Of course it doesn't speak English. Just its own language."

He left the bird with us. It did indeed speak its own language, something that no philologist would have been able to relate to any dialect. Its favorite word, which it pronounced with the utmost tenderness, was "Budupple." When it had said that several times with increasing feeling, it would turn its head downward at an eighty-degree angle, add wistfully: "Budupple mah?" and then be quiet for a while.

Of course we bought it; the proprietor put it into a burlap sugar sack, and we set out downstream with it. The bend of the river just below Bebedero was still visible when it cut its way out of the bag and clambered triumphantly onto my lap. During the rest of the two-day trip to San José the bird was

amenable enough if allowed to have its own way uncondi-
tionally. In the hotel at San José it ate a lens out of a lorgnette,
a tube of toothpaste, and a good part of a Russian novel. Most
parrots merely make mincemeat out of things and let the debris fall where it will, but this one actually ate whatever he
destroyed. We were certain that the glass he had swallowed
would bring about a catastrophe, but day after day passed, and
Budupple seemed as well as ever. In Puerto Limón we had a
cage made for him; unfortunately the only material available
was tin, so that by the time we got off the ship at Puerto
Barrios and were inside its customshouse the convict had
sawed his way through the bars and got out on top of his
cage. With his claws firmly grasping the cage roof, the bird
could lean far out and fasten his beak into whatever presented
itself. As we waited in line for the various official tortures to
begin, what presented itself was a very stout French lady under whose skirt he poked his head, and up whose fleshy calf he
then endeavored to climb, using beak and claw. The incident
provided an engrossing intermission for the other voyagers.

The next morning, with six porters in tow, we were running
through the streets to catch the train for the capital; at one
point, when I set the cage down to shift burdens, Budupple
slid to the ground and waddled off toward a mango tree. I
threw the cage after him and we hurried on to where the train
was waiting. We got in; it had just begun to move when there
was a commotion on the platform and Budupple was thrust
through the open window onto the seat. The Indian who had
perpetrated this enormity had just time to say, "Here's your
parrot," and wave the battered cage victoriously up and down
as a gesture of farewell. Tin is evidently worth more than parrot flesh in Puerto Barrios.

A few days later we arrived in Antigua, where we let
Budupple get up into an avocado tree in the back patio of the
pension and stay. I have often wondered if he managed to survive the resident iguana that regularly took its toll of ducks
and chickens.

It might seem that after so inauspicious an introduction to
parrot-keeping, I should have been content to live quietly
with my memories. But I kept wondering what Budupple
would have been like under happier circumstances. After all, a

parrot is not supposed to travel continually. And the more I reflected, the more firmly I determined to try another bird. Two years later I found myself in Acapulco with a house whose wooded patio seemed to have ample room for whatever birds or beasts I might wish.

I started out with a Mexican *cotorro*. To a casual observer a cotorro looks like a rather small parrot. Its feathers are the same green—perhaps a shade darker—and it has the general characteristics of a parrot, save that the beak is smaller, and the head feathers, which would be yellow on a *loro real* (the Latin American's name for what we call parrot), are orange instead. Neither this cotorro, nor any other I ever had, learned to say anything intelligible. If you can imagine a tape-recording of an old-fashioned rubber-bulbed Parisian taxi horn run off at double speed, you have a fair idea of what their conversation sounds like. The only sign of intelligence this cotorro displayed was to greet me by blowing his little taxi horn immediately, over and over. After I had set him free I went out and got a true parrot.

This one came to be the darling of the servants, because, although he had no linguistic repertory to speak of, he could do a sort of Black Bottom on his perch and perform correctly, imitating the sound of a bugle, a certain military march almost to the end. The kitchen was his headquarters, where, when things got dull for Rosa, Amparo and Antonio, they could bribe him into performing with pieces of banana and tortilla. Occasionally he wandered into the patio or along the *corredor* to visit the rest of the house, but he liked best the dimness and smoke of the kitchen, where five minutes seldom passed without his being scratched or fed, or at least addressed.

The next psittacine annexation to the household (in the interim there came an armadillo, an ocelot and a tejón—a tropical version of the raccoon) was a parakeet named Hitler. He was about four inches high and no one could touch him. All day he strutted about the house scolding, in an eternal rage, sometimes pecking at the servants' bare toes. His voice was a sputter and a squeak, and his Spanish never got any further than the two words *periquito burro* (stupid parakeet), which always came at the end of one of his diatribes; trembling with emotion, he would pronounce them in a way that recalled the classical orator's "I have spoken." He was not a very interesting individual because his personality was monochromatic, but I became attached to him; his energy was incredible. When I moved away he was the only member of the menagerie that I took with me.

For some time I had had my eye on a spectacular macaw that lived up the street. She was magnificently red, with blue and yellow trimmings, and she had a voice that could have shouted orders in a foundry. I used to go in the afternoon to study her vocal abilities; after a while I decided I wanted her, although I remained convinced that the few recognizable words she was capable of screaming owed their intelligibility solely to chance. It was unlikely that anyone had ever spoken to her of the Oriental dessert known as baklava, or of the Battle of Balaklava, and even less probable that she had overheard discussions concerning Max Ernst's surrealist picture book, *La femme cent têtes*, in which the principal character is a monster called Loplop. These words, however, figured prominently in her monologues. Sometimes she threw in the Spanish word *agua*, giving equal and dire stress to each syllable, but I think even that was luck. At all events, soon she was in my patio, driving the entire household, including the other birds, into a frenzy of irritability. At five o'clock every morning she climbed to the top of the lemon tree, the highest point in the neighborhood, flapped her clipped wings with a sound like bedsheets in the wind, and let loose that unbelievable voice. Nothing could have brought her down, save perhaps the revolver of the policeman who lived three doors away and who came early one morning to the house, weapon in hand, ready do the deed if he could get into the patio. "I can't stand it any longer, *señor*," he explained. (He went away with two pesos to buy tequila.)

There is a certain lizardlike quality still discernible in the psittacine birds; this is particularly striking in the macaw, the most unlikely and outlandish-looking of the family. Whenever I watched Loplop closely I thought of the giant parrots whose fossils were found not so long ago in Brazil. All macaws have something antediluvian about them. In the open, when they fly in groups, making their peculiar elliptical spirals, they look like any other large bright birds; but when they are reduced by the loss of their wing tips and tail feathers to waddling, crawling, climbing and flopping, they look strangely natural, as if they might have an atavistic memory of a time when they were without those appendages and moved about as they do now in captivity.

The word "captivity" it not really apt, since in Latin America no one keeps macaws in cages; they are always loose, sometimes on perches or in nearby trees, and it seems never to occur to them to want to escape. The only macaws I have seen chained or caged belonged to Americans; they were vicious and ill-tempered, and the owners announced that fact with a certain pride. The parrot, too, although less fierce in its love of freedom and movement, loathes being incarcerated. It has a fondness for its cage (provided the floor is kept clean), but it wants the door left open so it can go in and out as it pleases. There is not much point in having a parrot if you are going to keep it caged.

Loplop was headstrong and incurably greedy. She had her own bowl of very sweet *café con leche* in a corner on the floor, and whatever we gave her she dipped into the bowl before devouring it. The edible contributions we made during mealtimes were more like blood money than disinterested gifts, for we would have handed her practically anything on the table to keep her from climbing onto it. Once she did that, all was lost: silverware was scattered, cups were overturned, food flew. She went *through* things like a snowplow. It was not that we spoiled her, but anyone will reflect a moment before crossing a creature with a beak like a pair of hedge clippers.

The afternoon Jane left for a weekend in Taxco, Loplop decided that I was lonely. She came to tell me so while I was lying in a hammock. Reaching up from the floor and using my posterior for leverage, she climbed into the hammock. I moved quickly to another, taking care first to raise it well into the air. She gurgled. If I wanted to make things difficult, it was quite all right with her; she had plenty of time to achieve her aim. She clambered down, pushed across the floor, shinnied up one of the posts that held the hammock, and slid down the rope into my lap. By the time I realized what had happened, it was too late. I was in my bathing trunks, and she made it quite clear that if I attempted to lift her off she would show no mercy. All she wanted was to have her belly scratched, but she wanted it badly and for an indefinite period of time. For two hours I half-heartedly tickled and scratched her underside, while she lay on her back opening and closing her idiotic eyes, a prey to some mysterious, uncatalogued avian ecstasy. From that day onwards she followed me through the house, ogling me, screaming "Baklava! Loplop!" trying to use my legs as a tree trunk to climb up to my face. Absolute devotion, while admirable, tends to become tedious. I sold Loplop back to the ladies from whom I had bought her.

The following year I found the best of all my Amazons, a perfect *loro real* with a great gift for mimicry. I looked into a little garden and there it was, perched in its cage, demurely conscious of being stared at. I approached it, asked it its name, and it slowly turned itself upside down before it put its head to the bars nearest me and replied in a coquettish falsetto that was almost a whisper: "*Co-to-rri-to.*" This, although it was in truth its name, was obviously a misnomer, for the bird was not a cotorro but a parrot, and a large-sized one. We had a short conversation about the weather, after which I bought my new friend, cage and all, for six dollars and carried it home, to the delight of the Indian maids, who felt that the kitchen was not complete without a *loro* to talk to during the long hours they spent combing their hair. They wanted beauty advice. "Do you like it this way?" they would ask, and then, changing the position of the tresses, comb in mouth, "Or like this?"

Cotorrito was an intelligent bird—well-balanced emotionally, and with a passion for regularity. He wanted his cage uncovered at half past six in the morning, and bananas at seven. At about nine he had to be let out so he could perch on top of his cage, where he would stay until noon. Then he made his tour of inspection of the house, toddling from room to room, just to be sure the place was in order. After that he climbed on to an old bicycle tire, hung in a shady part of the patio, and remained perched there while we ate lunch nearby, joining in the conversation with short comments such as "*Verdad?*" "*Cómo?*" or "*Ay!*" and bursting into hysterical giggles if the talk became more animated than usual. During the afternoon he took his siesta along with the rest of the household. When the shadows lengthened he grew lyrical, as parrots have a way of doing toward the end of the day; and when the maids gathered in the kitchen to prepare dinner he went back there, climbed atop his cage and superintended their work for two hours or so. When he got sleepy, he stepped into the cage and softly demanded to have the door shut and the cover put over him.

His performing repertory seemed to be a matter of degree of excitement rather than of choice. Tranquillity expressed itself in a whispered monologue, quite unintelligible, punctuated with short remarks in Spanish. One step above that took him completely into Spanish. From there he went into his giggles, from that into strident song. (At some point he must have lived within hearing of a very bad soprano, because the flatted notes of a song which began "*No sé qué frio extraño se ha metido en mi corazón,*" were always identical.) Beyond that there came a strange rural domestic scene which began with a baby that cried, sobbed, and choked for lack of breath, went on to a comforting mother, an effete-sounding father who shouted "*Cállate!*" a very nervous dog that yapped, and several varieties of poultry including a turkey. Lastly, if his emotion exceeded even this stage, which happened very seldom, he let loose a series of jungle calls. Whoever was within hearing quickly departed, in sheer self-protection. Under normal circumstances these different emotional planes were fairly widely separated, but a good loud jazz record could induce a rough synopsis of the entire gamut. The sound of the clarinet, above all, stimulated him: giggling went into wailing and wailing into barking, barking turned swiftly into jungle calls— and at that point one had to take the record off or leave the house.

Cotorrito was a good parrot: he bit me only once, and that was not his fault. It was in Mexico City. I had bought a pair of new shoes which turned out to be squeaky, and I was wearing them when I came into the apartment after dark. I neglected to turn on the light, and without speaking walked straight to where Cotorrito was perched on top of his cage. He heard the unfamiliar shoes, leaned out and attacked the stranger. When he discovered his shameful error he pretended it had been due to extreme sleepiness, but I had previously roused him from sleep innumerable times with no such deplorable result.

Two parrots live with me now. I put it thus, rather than, "I own two parrots," because there is something about them that makes them very difficult to claim as one's property. A creature that spends its entire day observing the minutiae of your habits and vocal inflections is more like a rather critical friend who comes for an indefinite stay. Both of my present birds have gone away at various times; one way or another they have been found, ransomed from their more recent friends and brought back home. Seth, the African Grey, is the greatest virtuoso performer I have ever had. But then, African Greys are all geniuses beside Amazons; it is unfair to compare them. He was born in a suburb of Leopoldville in August, 1955, and thus by parrot standards is still an infant-in-arms. If he continues to study under his present teacher, a devout Moslem lady who works in my kitchen, he ought, like any good Moslem, to know quite a bit of the Koran by the time he reaches adolescence. The other guest, who has been with me for the past fourteen years, is a yellow-headed Amazon. I bought him from a Moroccan who was hawking him around the streets of Tangier, and who insisted his name was Babarhio, which is Moghrebi for parrot. I took him to a blacksmith's to break the chains which fettered his legs. The screams which accompanied this operation drew an enormous crowd; there was great hilarity when he drew blood from the blacksmith's hand. Much more difficult was the task of finding him a cage—there was not one for sale in Tangier strong enough to hold him. I finally got wind of an English lady living far out on the Old Mountain whose parrot had died some years ago; possibly she would still have its cage. During the week it took her to find it, Babarhio made a series of interesting wire sculptures of the two cages I had bought him in the market, and wreaked general havoc in my hotel room. However much freedom one may give a parrot once it has become accustomed to its surroundings, it certainly is not feasible at the outset; only chaos can ensue.

Almost immediately I got Babarhio used to traveling. I kept him warm by wrapping around the cage two of the long woolen sashes that are worn by the men here, and putting a child's djellaba of white wool over everything. The little sleeves stuck out, and the cage looked vaguely like a baby with a large brass ring for a head. It was not a reassuring object, particularly when the invisible parrot coughed and chuckled as he often did when bored with the darkness of his cage.

There is no denying that in tropical and subtropical countries a parrot makes a most amusing and satisfactory companion about the house, a friend you miss very much when it is no longer with you. Doña Violeta, a middle-aged widow who sold bread in the market of Ocosingo, had hers for some thirty years, and when a dog killed it, she was so deeply affected that she closed her stall for three days. Afterward, when she resumed business, with the embalmed body of her pet lying in state in a small glass-covered coffin on her counter, she was shattered, disconsolate, and burst into tears whenever one showed signs of commiserating with her. "He was my only friend in the world," she would sob. This, of course, was quite untrue; one can forgive its exaggeration only by considering her bereavement. But when she added, "He was the only one who understood me," she was coming nearer the truth—a purely subjective one, perhaps, but still a truth. In my mind I have a picture of Doña Violeta in her little room, pouring her heart out to the bird that sat before her attentively and now and then made a senseless remark which she could interpret as she chose. The spoken word, even if devoid of reason, means a great deal to a lonely human being.

I think my susceptibility to parrots may have been partly determined by a story I heard when I was a child. One of the collection of parrots from the New World presented to King Ferdinand by Columbus escaped from the palace into the forest. A peasant saw it, and never having encountered such a bird before, picked up a stone to hit it, so he could have its brilliant feathers as a trophy. As he was taking aim, the parrot cocked its head and cried "*Ay, Dios!*" Horrified, the man dropped the stone, prostrated himself, and said, "A thousand pardons, señora! I thought you were a green bird."

The Route to Tassemsit

WHENEVER I leave Tangier to go south, my home takes on the look of a place where serious disaster has just struck. The night before I set out on this particular trip the usual disorder prevailed. There were crates of canned food-stuffs and bundles of blankets and pillows in the living room. The recording equipment was scattered over an unnecessarily large area, so that coils of extra cable hid the portable butane-gas stove and boxes of tape covered the road maps. The ser-vants had induced me to write down the specifications of the things they hoped I would remember to buy for them while I was away. Fatima wanted a white woolen blanket at least eight meters long, and Mina a silver-plated circular tray with three detachable legs. Following tradition, they had scrupulously insisted that these things were to be paid for out of their wages after I returned, and I had agreed, although each of us was aware that such deductions would never be made. Moroccan etiquette demands that when the master of the house goes on a journey he bring back souvenirs for every-one. The farther he goes and the longer he stays, the more substantial these gifts are expected to be.

In this country, departure is often a pre-dawn activity. After the half-hour of early morning prayer-calling is finished and the muezzins have extinguished the lights at the tops of the minarets, there is still about an hour of dark left. The choir of roosters trails on in the air above the rooftops of the city un-til daybreak. It is a good moment to leave, just as the sky is growing white in the east and objects are black and sharp against it. By the time the sun was up Christopher and I were far out in the country, rolling along at a speed determined only by the curves and the occasional livestock in the road. The empty highway, visible far ahead, measured off the miles of grandiose countryside, and along the way no billboards came between us and the land.

During the last six months of 1959 I traveled some twenty-five thousand miles around Morocco, recording music for the Library of Congress on a grant from the Rockefeller Foundation. The quality of the material was uniformly splendid; nevertheless, one always has preferences. After a great deal of listening, the tapes which interested me most were the ones I had recorded in Tafraout, a region in the western Anti-Atlas. Since I had managed to get only six selections there, I wanted now to go back and try to find some more, although this time it would have to be without the assistance of the Moroccan government. By my inland itinerary there was a distance of 1,370 kilometers (855 miles) to be covered between Tangier and Tafraout, and the roads would be fairly good all the way. The direct route to Marrakech via Rabat runs over flat terrain and has a certain amount of traffic along it. The unfrequented interior route we used, which leads through the western foothills of the Rif Mountains and over the Middle Atlas, takes an extra day, but is beautiful at every point.

Beyond Xauen we followed the River Loukos for a while, here a clear, swift stream at the bottom of a narrow valley. Christopher, who was driving, suggested that it was time for lunch. We stopped, spread a rug under an old olive tree and ate, listening to the sound of the water skipping over the stones beside us. The hills rose steeply on both sides of the river; there was not a person or a dwelling in sight. We started out again. A half-hour further on, we rounded a corner and came upon a man lying face down on the paved surface of the road, his djellaba covering his head. Immediately I thought: he's dead. We stopped, got out, prodded him a bit, and he sat up, rubbing his eyes, mumbling, annoyed at being awakened. He explained that the clean, smooth road was a better place to sleep than the stony ground beside it. When we objected that he might easily be killed, he replied with fine peasant logic that no one had killed him yet. Nevertheless, he got up and walked a few yards off the highway, where he slumped down again all in one motion, wrapped the hood of his djellaba around his head, and went back into the comfortable world of sleep.

The next day was hotter. We climbed up along the slowly rising ramp of the Middle Atlas, a gray, glistening landscape. The shiny leaves of the scrub live oaks, and even the exposed bedrock beneath, reflected the hot light of the overhead sun. Further along, on the southern slope of the mountains, we passed the mangled body of a large ape that had not got out of the road fast enough—an unusual sight here, since the monkeys generally stay far from the highways.

All afternoon we had been speeding along the gradually descending valley between the Middle Atlas and the Grand Atlas. The sun went down ahead of us and the moon rose behind us. We drank coffee from the thermos and hoped we would get into Marrakech in time to find some food. The new Moroccan regime has brought early closing hours to a land where heretofore night was merely a continuation of day.

After the lunar brightness of the empty waste land, the oasis seemed dark. The highway went for miles between high mud walls and canebrakes; the black tracery of date palms rose above them, against the brilliant night sky. Suddenly the walls and the oasis came to an end, and ahead, standing in the rubble of the desert, was a big new cinema trimmed with tubes of colored neon, the tin and straw shacks of a *bidonville* clustering around it like the cottages of a village around the church. In Morocco the very poor live neither in the country nor in the city; they come as far as the outer walls of the town, build these desperate-looking squatters' colonies out of whatever materials they can find, and there they stay.

Marrakech is a city of great distances, flat as a table. When the wind blows, the pink dust of the plain sweeps into the sky, obscuring the sun, and the whole city, painted with a wash made of the pink earth on which it rests, glows red in the cataclysmic light. At night, from a car window, it looks not unlike one of our own Western cities: long miles of street lights stretching in straight lines across the plain. Only by day does one see that most of these lights illumine nothing more than empty reaches of palm garden and desert. Over the years, the outer fringes of the medina have been made navigable to automobiles and horse-drawn carriages, of which there are still a great many, but it takes a brave man to drive his car into the maze of serpentine alleys full of porters, bicycles, carts, donkeys and ordinary pedestrians. Besides, the only way to see anything in the medina is to walk. In order to be really present, you must have your feet in the dust, and be aware of the hot, dusty smell of the mud walls beside your face.

The night we arrived in Marrakech, Christopher and I
went to a café in the heart of the medina. On the roof, under the stars, they spread matting, blankets and cushions for
us, and we sat there drinking mint tea, savoring the cool air
that begins to stir above the city after midnight, when the
stored heat of the sun is finally dissipated. At a certain moment, out of the silence of the street below, there came a
succession of strange, explosive cries. I leaned over the edge
and peered down into the dim passageway three floors beneath. Among the few late strollers an impossible, phantom-
like figure was dancing. It galloped, it stopped, it made great
gravitation-defying leaps into the air as if the earth under its
feet were helping. At each leap it yelled. No one paid any attention. As the figure came along below the café, I was able
to identify it as a powerfully built young man; he was almost
naked. I watched him disappear into the dark. Almost immediately he returned, doing the same inspired dance, occasionally rushing savagely toward other pedestrians, but always
stopping himself in time to avoid touching them. He passed
back and forth through the alley in this way for a quarter of
an hour or so before the *qahouaji* climbed the ladder again
to the roof where we sat. When he came I said casually,
"What's going on down there?" Although in most places it
would have been clear enough that a madman was loose in
the streets, in Morocco there are subtle distinctions to be
made. Sometimes the person turns out to be merely holy, or
indisposed.

"Ah, poor man," said the qahaouaji. "He's a friend of
mine. We were in school together. He got high marks and
played good soccer."

"What happened?"

"What do you think? A woman, of course."

This had not occurred to me. "You mean she worked
magic on him?"

"What else? At first he was like this—" He let his jaw drop
and his mouth hang open; his eyes became fixed and vacant.
"Then after a few weeks he tore off his clothes and began to
run. And ever since, he runs like that, in the summer and in
the winter. The woman was rich. Her husband had died and
she wanted Allal. But he's of a good family and they didn't

like her. So she said in her head: 'No other woman is going to have him either.' And she gave him what she gave him."

"And his family?"

"He doesn't know his family. He lives in the street."

"And the woman? What happened to her?"

He shrugged. "She's not here any more. She moved somewhere else." At that moment the cries came up again.

"But why do they let him run in the street like that? Can't they do anything for him?"

"Oh, he never hurts anybody. He's just playful. He likes to scare people, that's all."

I decided to ask my question. "Is he crazy?"

"No, just playful."

"Ah, yes. I see."

At twilight one day we were the tea guests of Moulay Brahim, one of the Moroccans who previously had helped me make contacts with musicians. He lived in a rooming house near the dyers' souk. The establishment, on the second floor, consisted of a dozen or more cubicles situated around an open central court with a dead fountain in the middle. No women were allowed in the building; it was a place for men who have left home and family behind. Not an object was visible that could even remind one of the existence of traditional Moroccan life.

Moulay Brahim is militantly of his epoch; his life is almost wholly abstract. He spends his hours in an attitude of prostration on his mattress, his head touching a large short-wave radio. He knows what time it is in Jakarta, just where the Nigerian representative to the United Nations is at this moment, and what Sékou Touré said to Nkrumah about Nasser. The radio is never silent save for a useless five minutes now and then while he waits impatiently for a program in Cairo or Damascus or Baghdad to begin. He follows the moves of the cold war like an onlooker at a chess match, making searing comments on what he considers the blunders of both sides. Only the neutralist powers have his sympathy. We sat in the dusk around the dimly illumined radio and listened to it hiss and crackle. Moulay Brahim dispensed kif silently, intent on the panel of the instrument, weighing each gradation of static with the expression of a connoisseur certain of his ground.

Fifteen minutes might go by without a trace of any sort of program coming out—only the unvarying noise of interference. His face did not change; he knows how to wait. At any moment he may hear something more, something identifiable. Then he can relax for a bit, while the tea-concession man from across the courtyard brings in the big tray, sets up the glasses and rolls the mint between his hands before stuffing it into the pot. But soon it is not enough for Moulay Brahim to know that he is in touch with the BBC service to the Middle East, and he begins once again the painful search for the unfindable.

Inhabitants of the other rooms came in and squatted, but it was difficult to engage them in anything more than desultory conversation. They had learned from experience that in Moulay Brahim's room it was better to be quiet. At one point, when a particularly confused noise had for some time been issuing from the loudspeaker, I rashly suggested that he adjust the dial. "No, no!" he cried. "This is what I want. I've got five stations here now. Sometimes others come in. It's a place where they all like to get together and talk at once. Like in a café." For a young and deracinated Moroccan like Moulay Brahim, radio is primarily neither a form of entertainment nor a medium of information. It is a sort of metaphysical umbilical cord—a whole manner of existence, an essential adjunct to feeling that he is in contact with life.

When we had finally persuaded him that it was time for us to leave, he reluctantly rose from the radio and took us out into the streets to the apothecary market, where I had expressed a desire to go. It is the place you visit if you want the ingredients for making black magic. There were six stalls in a row, all bristling with the dried parts of birds, reptiles and mammals. We wandered slowly by, examining the horns, quills, hair, eggs, bones, feathers, feet and bills that were strung on wires in the doorways. I was put in mind of the unfortunate Allal and the rich widow, and I described Allal to Moulay Brahim. He knew him; everybody in Marrakech knew him, he declared, adding as he pointed to the rows of glass containers in front of us, "You can get everything for that sort of business here. But you've got to know how to blend them. That takes an expert." He raised his eyebrows significantly,

and approached the nearest merchant to mutter a few words
to him. A packet containing tiny seeds was brought out.
Moulay Brahim examined them at some length, and bought
fifty grams. "What is it?" I asked him. But he was enjoying his
brief role as mystery man, and merely rattled the seeds in their
paper, saying, "Something very special, very special."

Taroudant
October 6, 1961

*Brilliant day. Sky like a blue enamel bowl overhead. Left
Marrakech at noon, driving straight up to Ouirgane, in a valley only about three thousand feet above the plain. Lunch outside
in the sun at Le Sanglier Qui Fume. Our table midway between
a chained eagle and a chained monkey, both of which watched
us distrustfully while we ate. Below, hidden, somewhere nearby,
the little river roared over its rocks. The Grand Atlas sun fiery.
Monsieur gave us drooping old straw sombreros to wear while we
ate. A tame stork, very proprietary, strutted around, poking its
beak into everything. It was wary, however, of the monkey, which
had a long bamboo pole in its hand and patiently tried to trip
it up each time it came past. Everything excellent: hors d'oeuvre,
frogs' legs and chicken paprika. Madame is Hungarian, said
she lives in the hope that people coming through Ouirgane will
prove to speak her language, "Or at least know Budapest," she
added. Obviously disappointed in us. On up to the pass at Tizi
n'Test and over the top. The valley of the Souss thick with a mist
that looked like smoke. Only the long sloping rim of the Anti-
Atlas showed in the sky to the south, fifty miles across. Below, a
gulf of vapor. Got into Taroudant at seven. The heat was still
everywhere inside the walls. While I was unpacking, a procession
of Guennaoua shuffled by in the street. Tried to get out through
a door into the patio, but it was padlocked. I peeked through a
crack and saw them going past slowly, carrying candle lanterns.
The pounding of the drums shook the air.*

After Taroudant—Tiznit, Tanout, Tirmi, Tiffermit. Great
hot dust-colored valleys among the naked mountains, dotted
with leafless argan trees as gray as puffs of smoke. Sometimes
a dry stream twists among the boulders at the bottom of the

valley, and there is a peppering of locust-ravaged date palms whose branches look like the ribs of a broken umbrella. Or hanging to the flank of a mountain a thousand feet below the road is a terraced village, visible only as an abstract design of flat roofs, some the color of the earth of which they are built, and some bright yellow with the corn that is spread out to dry in the sun.

The argan trees are everywhere, thousands of them, squat and thorny, anchored to the rocks that lie beneath in their dubious shade. They flourish where nothing else can live, not even weeds or cacti. Their scaly bark looks like crocodile hide and feels like iron. Where the argan grows the goats have a good life. The trunk is short and the branches begin to proliferate only a few feet from the ground. This suits the goats perfectly; they climb from branch to branch eating both the leaves and the greasy, bitter, olive-like fruit. Subsequently their excrement is collected, and the argan-pits in it are pressed to make a thick cooking oil.

Tafraout is rough country—the Bad Lands of South Dakota on a grand scale, with Death Valley in the background. The mountains are vast humps of solid granite, their sides strewn with gigantic boulders; at sunset the black line of their crests is deckle-edged in silhouette against the flaming sky. Seen from a height, the troughs between the humps are like long gray lakes, the only places in the landscape where there is at least a covering of what might pass for loose earth. Above the level surface of this detritus in the valleys rise the smooth expanses of solid rock.

The locusts have fed well here, too. Tafraout could never subsist on its dates. But the bourgeois Berbers who live here learned long ago that organized commerce could provide greater security than either the pastoral or the agricultural life. They inaugurated a successful campaign to create a virtual monopoly on grocery and hardware stores all over Morocco. Taking his male children with him, a man goes to a city in the north where he has a shop, or several shops, and remains there for two or three years at a stretch, living usually in conditions of extreme discomfort on the floor behind the counter. Being industrious, thrifty and invariably successful, he is naturally open to a good deal of adverse criticism from those of his compatriots who are less so, and who despise his frugal manner of living and deride his custom of leaving small boys of eight in charge of his shops. But the children run the establishments quite as well as their elders; they know the price of every object and are equally difficult to deal with in the national pastime of persuading the seller to lower his asking price. The boys merely refuse to talk; often they do not even look at the customer. They quote the price, and if it is accepted, hand over the article and return the change. It is a very serious matter to be in charge of a store, and the boys behave accordingly.

As you come up from Tiznit over the pass, the first Tafraout settlements on the trail occur at the neck of a narrow valley; built in among, underneath, and on top of the great fallen lumps of granite, the fortress-houses dominate the countryside. It is hard to reconcile the architectural sophistication of these pink and white castles with the unassuming aspect of their owners back in the north, just as it is difficult to believe that the splendid women, shrouded in black and carrying copper amphoras or calfskin-covered baskets on their shoulders, can be these inconspicuous little men's wives and sisters. But then, no one would expect a tribe of shopkeepers to have originated in the fortresses of this savage landscape.

Tafraout
October 9

Arrived yesterday about five, after having a puncture ten miles up the trail. Hotel completely empty, save for a handful of ragged children and one old gentleman in a djellaba who has been left in charge of the premises while the regular guardian is down in Tiznit. He helped with luggage, hung up our clothes, prepared the beds, brought pails of washing water and bottles of drinking water, and filled the lamps with kerosene. Slept heavily and late for the first time since Meknès. Woke once in the night to hear a great chorus of howling and barking below in the village. Lunch better than dinner last night, but everything was drowned in an inch of hot oil. Tajine of beef, almonds, grapes, olives and onions. Came back up to the hotel to make Nescafé on the terrace afterward. The old man who received us last night was sitting in a corner, buried under his djellaba. He saw we were looking at magazines, got up and came over. Soon he said timidly, "Is that an American book you are reading?" I said it was. He pointed to a color photograph and asked, "And are the mountains in America really all green like that?" I told him many of them were. He stood a while studying the picture. Then he said bitterly, "It's not pretty here. The locusts eat the trees and all the rest of the plants. Here we're poor."

During the next few days I discovered how unrealistic my recording project had been. We visited at least two dozen villages in the region, and made no progress toward uncovering an occasion where there might prove to be music. The previous year even the government had needed thirty-six hours' notice for sending its directives via a network of caids and messengers up into the heights before the musicians had put in their appearance in Tafraout. When Friday morning arrived, Christopher said to me at breakfast, "What do you think? Do we leave tomorrow for Essaouira?" I said I supposed there was nothing else to do. Then I suggested we go down to the hospital to see if they had any Rovamycine.

A bearded Moroccan intern stood under a pepper tree in the hospital's patio, a syringe in his hand; he said the doctor had gone to Agadir for the weekend, but that if I wished I could speak with the French pharmacist, who in the absence of his chief was in charge of the institution.

The pharmacist arrived rubbing his eyes. He had been working all night, he told us. There was no Rovamycine. "It's an expensive drug. They don't supply us with that sort of thing here."

Christopher invited him to come up to the hotel for a whiskey. "*Avec plaisir*," he said. Alcoholic drinks are not on sale in Tafraout, since Moslems cannot drink legally. The only two Europeans in the region were the doctor and the pharmacist, and they got by with the occasional bottle of wine or cognac they brought up from Tiznit.

The pharmacist had with him a young Moroccan medical student who had just arrived from Rabat the day before; he thought Tafraout the strangest place he had ever seen. We sat on the terrace in the scalding sun and watched the crows flying in a slowly revolving circle high above the valley. I was disappointed in my sojourn this time, I told Monsieur Rousselot, because I hadn't got into the life of the people and because there was no edible food. The second reason touched the Frenchman. "I shall do my best to fill these unfortunate lacunae," he said. "First let us go to my house for lunch. I have a good chef."

The house behind the hospital was comfortable. There were several servants. Walls were lined with books, particularly art books, for like many French men of medicine, Monsieur Rousselot loved painting, and had a hankering to try his hand at it himself one day.

During lunch he announced, "I have a little excursion in mind for this afternoon. Have you ever drunk *mahia*?" I said I had, many years ago, with Jewish friends in Fez. "Ah!" he exclaimed happily. "Then you are acquainted with its virtues. You will have an opportunity to drink mahia again later this afternoon." I smiled politely, having already determined that when the moment arrived I should decline the offer. I am not fond of *eau de vie*, even when it is made of figs, as it is in Fez. In the Anti-Atlas they use dates, said Monsieur Rousselot; this didn't seem an improvement.

After coffee and cognac, we started out down the Tiznit trail. Some thirty miles to the south, in a parched lower valley, we came to a poor-looking village called Tahala, which, besides its Moslem population, contains a Jewish colony of considerable size. The air was breathless as we got out of the car in front of the primitive little mosque. Five or six Moslem elders sat on the dusty rocks in the shade, talking quietly. "The Israelites add to their modest revenue by selling us the ambrosia they distill," explained Monsieur Rousselot. Seddiq, the medical student, now expressed himself on the subject for the first time. "It's terrible!" he said with feeling. "*Bien sûr,*" agreed Monsieur Rousselot, "but you'll drink it."

Several children who had seen us arrive and park the car had run ahead into the village to announce our advent; now as we went along the oven-hot alleys, on all sides doors were being unceremoniously slammed shut and bolted. There was no one visible. But Monsieur Rousselot knew where he was going. He sent us ahead around a corner to wait out of sight while he pounded on one of the doors. It was a quarter of an hour before he reappeared and called to us. In the doorway where he had been standing talking stood an exceptionally pretty girl. The baby she held had an infected arm. Its forehead and nose were decorated in simple designs applied with kohl; one would have said that its face had been inexpertly tattooed. The room we went into was as dark and cool as a farmhouse cellar; the dirt floor slanted in various directions. A short flight of mud steps led up into an open patio with a well in its center. Seven or eight very white-skinned women sat there on a bench around the well; they wore medieval head-dresses like those Tenniel gave the duchess in his illustrations for *Alice in Wonderland*. But they were all exceptionally handsome—even the old ones. No pictures could be taken, Monsieur Rousselot warned. The excuse they gave was that it was Friday afternoon. We were beckoned on into a further patio, this one full of men and boys, all wearing *yamalkes* on their heads. From there we went into a small room with a brass bed at one end and a straw mat on the floor at the other. Asleep in the bed was a baby, naked and beseiged by flies. We sat down on the mat in the sunlight, disturbing several hundred groggy flies; the men and boys came in from the patio one by one and solemnly shook hands with us. The big tray they put on the mat in front of us was piled high with almonds, dates, and flies—both alive and dead. Then the patriarch of the house was helped into the room by a younger man and eased into a sprawling position on the floor. His face was drawn and sad, and his replies to Monsieur Rousselot's questions were apathetic. "You must come to the hospital and let us examine you," urged Monsieur Rousselot. The old man frowned and shook his head slowly. "They're all afraid," Monsieur Rousselot explained to me in French. "They consider the hospital a place where one goes to die, nothing more."

"Do you know what's wrong with him?" I asked.

"I'm almost certain it's the scourge."

"The scourge?"

"Cancer," snapped Monsieur Rousselot, as if the word itself were evil. "It carries them off, *whsht, whsht*." He clicked his fingers twice.

Someone came and carried the baby away, still asleep. The flies remained behind. A small bottle of mahia was produced, and miniature glasses of it were passed around. Surreptitiously I poured mine into Monsieur Rousselot's glass. Only the old man and I went without.

"He can't eat anything," explained one of the sons to Monsieur Rousselot. "Haven't you any pills for him?"

"Yes, yes, yes," said Monsieur Rousselot jovially, opening his doctor's bag. He took out two large jars, one filled with aspirin tablets, the other with Vitamin-C pills, and poured a pile of them onto the mat. A murmur went around the patio, started by those who were crowding the doorway watching. "This is the only medicament I ever carry with me. It's all I have to give them. *Mais vous allez voir.* The pills will all stay behind here in Tahala." The flies crawled on our faces, trying to drink from the corners of our eyes. Monsieur Rousselot conferred quietly with one of the younger members of the family; presently two liter-bottles of mahia appeared and were packed into the medical bag. When we got up to leave, Monsieur Rousselot said to the old man, "Then it's agreed. You'll bring your grandson on Tuesday." To me he muttered, "Perhaps for the baby he'll come, and I can get him to stay for an examination. But it's doubtful."

Outside the front door a crowd of people had gathered. Word had got around that the *toubib* was there with his medicine. Monsieur Rousselot's prediction was accurate; there were not enough pills to go around.

On the way back up to Tafraout I said to him; "This has been an unforgettable day. Without it our trip to Tafraout would have been a failure." And I thanked him and said we would be leaving in the morning.

"Oh, no! You can't go!" he cried. "I have something much better for you tomorrow."

I said we had to start moving northward.

"But this is something special. Something I discovered. I've never shown it to anyone before."

"It's not possible. No, no."

He pleaded. "Tomorrow is Saturday. Leave on Monday morning. We can spend tomorrow night in the palace and have Sunday morning for exploring the oases."

"Two days!" I cried. But the curiosity he had counted on awakening must have shown through my protestations. Before we left his house, I had agreed to go to Tassemsit. I could scarcely have resisted after his description of the place. According to him, Tassemsit was a feudal town at the bottom of a narrow canyon, which by virtue of being the seat of an influential religious brotherhood had so far escaped coming under governmental jurisdiction and was still functioning in a wholly traditional fashion. Absolute power was nominally in the hands of a nineteen-year-old girl, the present hereditary saint whose palace was inside the walls. In reality, however, said Monsieur Rousselot, lowering his voice to a whisper, it was the family chauffeur who held the power of life and death over the citizens of Tassemsit. The old Cherif, father of the girl-saint, for many years had run the *zaouia* where religious pilgrims came to pray and leave offerings. Not long ago he had bought a car to get up to Tafraout now and then, and had hired a young Marrakchi to drive it. The old Cherif's somewhat younger wife had found the chauffeur interesting, as wives sometimes do, and *l'inévitable* had happened: the old Cherif had suddenly died and the wife had married the young Marrakchi, who had taken charge of everything: the woman, the holy daughter, the car, the palace and the administration of the shrine and the town around it. "It's an equivocal situation," said Monsieur Rousselot with relish. "You'll see."

Tassemsit, October 16
Early morning. Others still asleep. Big grilled window right beside my head. A world of dappled sunlight and shadow on the other side of the wrought-iron filigree, an orchard of fig trees where small birds dart and chirp. Then the mud wall, and beyond, the stony floor of the canyon. A few pools of water in the river bed. The women are out there, getting water, bringing it back in jugs. Background to all views: the orange sidewall of the canyon, perpendicular and high enough to block out the sky from where I sit on the mattress.

More lurid details about the place from Rousselot yesterday during lunch. When the chauffeur took over, he instituted a novelty in Tassemsit: it seems he conceived the idea of providing

*girls to keep the pilgrims occupied at night, when the zaouia is
closed. A great boost to the local economy. "A holy city of sin,"
said Rousselot with enthusiasm. Merely speak to the chauffeur,
and you get any woman in town, even if she happens to be married. He had hardly finished telling us all this when a little fat
man came in. Rousselot's face was a study in chagrin, dropped
jaw and all. He rallied then, introduced the little man around
as Monsieur Omar, and made him sit down with us for coffee.
Some sort of government employee. When he heard that we were
about to leave for Tassemsit, Monsieur Omar said very simply
that he would go with us. It was clear enough that he wasn't
wanted, but since nobody said anything to the contrary, he came
along, sitting in back with Monsieur Rousselot and Seddiq.*

*Trail rough in spots on the way up over the peaks just south of
Tafraout. Going down the other side it was narrower, but the
surface was no worse. Had we met another car, one of us would
have had to back up for a half-hour. The landscape became constantly more dramatic. For two hours the trail followed a valley
that cut itself deeper and deeper into the rock walls as it went
downward. Sometimes we drove along the bed of the stream for
a half-mile or so. At the date-palm level we came across small
oases, cool and green, that filled the canyon floor from cliff to
cliff. The lower we went, the higher the mountain walls rose
above, and the sunlight seemed to be coming from further away.
When I was a child I used to imagine Persephone going along a
similar road each year on her way down to Hades. A little like
having found a back way out of the world. No house, no car, no
human being all afternoon. Later, after we had been driving in
shadow a good while, the canyon widened, and there on a
promontory above a bend in the dry river bed, was Tassemsit,
compact, orange-gold like the naked rock of the countryside
around it, still in the sunlight. A small, rich oasis just below it
to the south. The zaouia with its mosque and other buildings
seemed to occupy a large part of the town's space. A big, tall
minaret in northern style, well-preserved. We stopped and got
out. Complete silence throughout the valley.*

Monsieur Rousselot had seemed pensive and nervous all
during the afternoon, and now I understood why. He got me
aside on some pretext, and we walked together down the trail

a way, he talking urgently the whole time. It worried him
very much that Monsieur Omar should be with us; he felt
that his presence represented a very real danger to the status
quo of the place. "One false move, and the story of Tassemsit can be finished forever," he said. "*C'est très délicat.* Above
all, not a word about what I told you. Any of it." I said he
could count on me, and promised to warn Christopher. It
came to me as we walked back up toward the car that there
was probably another reason, besides the fact that he wanted
to keep the place as his private playground, why Monsieur
Rousselot was worried. A Frenchman's job in Morocco, if he
works for the government, is never too secure in any case; it
is easy to find a pretext which will dispose of him and replace
him with a Moroccan. When we got to the car I spoke to
Christopher, but he had already guessed the situation. At
Monsieur Rousselot's insistence we waited another half-hour;
then we drove down a side trail to the right, to within two
hundred feet of the town gate. A mist of sweet-smelling
wood smoke hung over the canyon. Several tall black men in
white cotton robes appeared at the top of the rocks above us,
came down to the car, and recognized Monsieur Rousselot.
Smiling, they led us through a short alley into the palace itself, which was small, primitive and elegant. The big room
where they left us was a conscious synthesis of luxury and
wild fantasy; with its irresponsible color juxtapositions it was
like something Matisse would have produced had he been
asked to design a Moorish salon. "This is our room," said
Monsieur Rousselot. "Here we are going to eat and sleep, the
five of us." While we were unpacking, our host, the late
Cherif's chauffeur, came in and sat down in our midst for a
while. He was pleasant-mannered, quick-witted, and he spoke
a little French. A man in his late twenties, born in the country, one would guess, but used to living in the city. At one
point I became aware of the conversation he was having with
Monsieur Rousselot, who had sat down beside him on the
mattress. It concerned the possibility of an ahouache, performed by the citizens of Tassemsit later on in the evening.
Afterward, when the host had left, Monsieur Rousselot announced that not only would we have the entertainment, but
that there would be a certain number of women taking part

in it. "Very unusual," he commented, looking owlishly at Monsieur Omar. Monsieur Omar grinned. "We are fortunate," he said; he was from Casablanca and might as well have been visiting Bali for all he knew about local customs. "You understand, of course," Monsieur Rousselot went on to say to me with some embarrassment, "this ahouache will have to be paid for."

"Of course," I said.

"If you and Monsieur Christopher can give three thousand, I should be glad to contribute two."

I protested that we should be delighted to pay the whole five thousand francs, if that was the price, but he wouldn't consider it.

Through the windows, from the silence in the canyon outside, came the thin sound of the muezzin's voice calling from the mosque, and as we listened, two light bulbs near the ceiling began to glow feebly. "It's not possible!" cried Christopher. "Electricity *here*?" "*Tiens*," murmured Monsieur Rousselot. "He's got his generator going at last." I looked wistfully up at the trembling filaments above my head, wondering whether the current and voltage might conceivably be right for recording. A tall servant came in and announced that the Cherif was expecting us on the floor above. We filed out under the arcade and up a long flight of stairs. There at the top, on an open terrace, surrounded by roaring pressure-lamps, sat our host with two women. We were presented to the mother first. She would have been considered elegant anywhere in the world, with her handsome head, her regal white garments and her massive gold jewelry. The daughter, present titular ruler of Tassemsit, was something else; it was difficult to believe that the two had anything in common, or even that they inhabited the same town. The girl wore a pleated woolen skirt and a yellow sweater. She had had her front teeth capped with gold, and noisily snapped her chewing gum from time to time as she chatted with us. Presently our host rose and conducted us back down the stairs into our room, where servants had begun to arrive with trays and small tables.

It was an old-fashioned Moroccan dinner, beginning with soap, towels, and a big ewer of hot water. When everyone had washed and dried himself, an earthenware dish at least a foot and a half across was brought in and set in our midst; it held a mountain of *couscous* surrounded by a sea of sauce. We ate in the traditional manner, using our fingers, a process which demands a certain minimum of technique. The sauce was bubbling hot, and the tiny grains of semolina (since the cook knew his business) did not adhere to each other. Some of the food we extracted from the mound in front of us got to our mouths, but a good deal of it did not. I decided to wait a bit until someone had uncovered some of the meat buried in the center of the mass, and when my opportunity came I seized a small piece of lamb which was still too hot to touch with comfort, but which I managed nevertheless to eat.

"I see that even the rudiments of local etiquette remain unknown to you," remarked Monsieur Rousselot to me in a voice which carried overtones of triumph rather than the friendly concern it might have expressed. I said I didn't know what he meant.

"Have I committed an infraction?" I asked him.

"Of the gravest," he said solemnly. "You ate a piece of meat. One is constrained to try some of every other element in the dish first, and even then one may not try the meat until one's host has offered one a piece of it with his own fingers."

I said this was the first time I had eaten in a home of the region. Seddiq, the medical student, observed that in Rabat such behavior as Monsieur described would be considered absurd. But Monsieur Rousselot was determined to be an old Moroccan hand. "*Quelle décadence!*" he snorted. "The younger generation knows nothing." A few minutes later he upset a full glass of tea on the rug.

"In Rabat we don't do that, either," murmured Seddiq.

Shortly after tea had been served for the third time, the electricity began to fail, and eventually it died. There was a pause in the talking. From where he sat, the head of the house shouted an order. Five white-dustered black men brought in candle lanterns; they were still placing them in strategic positions around the room when the lights came on again, brighter than before. The lanterns were quickly blown out. Candles are shameful. Twenty minutes later, in the midst of a lion story (stories about lions are inevitable whenever city people gather in the country in South Morocco, although according to reliable sources the beasts have been extinct in the region for several generations), the current failed again, abruptly. In the silence of sudden darkness we heard a jackal yapping; the high sharp sound came from the direction of the river bed.

"Very near," I remarked, partly in order to seem unaware of the host's probable embarrassment at having us witness the failure of his power system.

"Yes, isn't it?" He seemed to want to talk. "I have recorded them many times. Not one jackal—whole packs of them."

"You've recorded them? You have a tape-recorder here?"

"From Marrakech. It doesn't work very well. At least, not always."

Monsieur Rousselot had been busy scrabbling around his portion of the rug; now he suddenly lit a match and put it to the candle of the lantern near him. Then he stood up and went the length of the big room, lighting the others. As the patterns painted on the high ceiling became visible again, there was the sound of hand drums approaching from the town.

"The entertainers are coming," said our host.

Monsieur Rousselot stepped out into the courtyard. There was the increasing sound of voices; servants had appeared and were moving about beyond the doorway in the gloom. By the time we all went to look out, the courtyard had some fifty or sixty men in it, with more arriving. Someone was building a fire over in a corner under the far arcade. A drum banged now and then as its owner tested the membrane. Again the electricity came on. The master of the palace smiled at Monsieur Rousselot, disappeared, and returned almost immediately with a servant who carried a tape-recorder. It was a small model made by Philips of Holland. He set it up on a chair outside the doorway and had great difficulty connecting it because none of the wall plugs appeared to work. Eventually he found a live one. By that time there were more than a hundred men massed under the arches around the open center of the courtyard, and in the middle were thirty or more musicians standing in an irregular circle. The host had propped the microphone against the machine itself, thus dooming his recording from the outset. "Why not hang it up there on the wall?" I suggested.

"I want to talk into it once in a while," he said. When he turned the volume up the machine howled, of course, and there was laughter from the spectators, who until then had been very quiet, just standing and watching. The host had another chair brought, and he sat down in it, holding the microphone in his hand—a position not likely to produce much better results than the first one. Christopher caught my eye and shook his head sadly. More chairs were provided from out of the darkness, and someone arrived bringing a pressure-lantern, which was set inside the musicians' circle. That was where the fire ought to have been, but there was not enough space in the courtyard to put it there.

The performers, all Negroes, wore loose white tunics, and each carried a *poignard* in a silver scabbard at his waist. Their drums were the regulation bendir—a skin stretched over a wooden hoop about a foot and a half in diameter. This sim-ple instrument is capable of great sonorous variety, depending on the kind of blow and the exact spot on the membrane struck by the fingertips or palm. The men of South Morocco do not stand still when they play the drums; they dance, but the purpose of their choreography is to facilitate the produc-tion of rhythm. No matter how involved or frenzied the body movements of the players (who also sing in chorus and as soloists), the dancing is subordinate to the sound. It is very difficult to hear the music if one is watching the performance; I often keep my eyes shut during an entire number. The par-ticular interest of the Anti-Atlas ahouache is that drummers divide themselves into complementary groups, each of which provides only certain regularly recurring notes in the complex total of the rhythmical pattern.

The men began to play; the tempo was exaggeratedly slow. As they increased it imperceptibly, the subtle syncopations be-came more apparent. A man brandishing a *gannega*, a smaller drum with a higher pitch and an almost metallic sonority, moved into the center of the circle and started an electrifying counter-rhythmic solo. His virtuoso drumbeats showered out over the continuing basic design like machine-gun fire. There was no singing in this prelude. The drummers, shuffling their feet, began to lope forward as they played, and the circle's counterclockwise movement gathered momentum. The laughter and comments from our side of the courtyard ceased, and even the master of the palace, sitting there with his microphone in his hand, surrendered to the general hypnosis the drummers were striving to create.

When the opening number was over, there was a noisy rearranging of chairs. These were straight-backed and completely uncomfortable, no matter how one sat in them, and it seemed clear that no one ever used them save when Europeans were present. Few chairs are as comfortable as the Moroccan *m'tarrba* with its piles of cushions.

"Art Blakey'd enjoy this," said Christopher. "There's a lot of material here for him."

Our host leaned sideways, holding the microphone in front of his mouth, and said, "*Comment?*" Then he held it closer to Christopher for his reply.

"I was talking about a great Negro drummer in America."

He shifted it again. "Ah, yes. The Negroes are always the strongest."

Out in the open part of the courtyard, groups of three or four men were going across into the far corner to tune their drums over the fire. Almost at once they began again to perform; a long, querulous vocal solo was the prelude. One might have thought it was coming from the silence of the town, from somewhere outside the palace, it was so thin and distant in sound. This was the leader, creating his effect by standing in the darkness under the arches, with his face turned to the wall, as far away as he could get from the other performers. Between each strophe of his chant there was a long, profound silence. I became more aware of the night outside, and of the superb remoteness of the town between the invisible canyon walls, whose only connection with the world was the unlikely trail we had rattled down a few hours earlier. There was nothing to listen for in the spaces between the plaintive cries, but everyone listened just the same. Finally, the chorus answered the far-away soloist, and a new rhythm got under way. This time the circle remained stationary, and the men danced into and out of the center in pairs and groups, facing one another.

About halfway through the piece there was whispering and commotion in the darkness by the entrance door. It was the women arriving *en masse*. By the time the number was finished, sixty or seventy of them had crowded into the courtyard. During the intermission they squeezed through the ranks of standing men and seated themselves on the floor, around the center—bundles without form or face, wrapped in great dark lengths of cloth. Still, one could hear their jewelry clinking. One of them on my left suddenly rearranged her outer covering, revealing a magnificent turquoise robe embroidered in gold; then swiftly she became a sack of laundry once more. Several set pieces by the men followed, during which the women kept up a constant whispering among themselves; they watched politely, but it was evident that their minds were on the performance they themselves were about to give. When the men had finished and had retired from the center, half the women present stood up and set about removing their outer garments. As they moved into the light they created a fine theatrical effect; the beauty of the scene, however, came solely from the variety of color in the splendid robes and the flash of heavy gold adornments. There were no girls at all among them—which is another way of saying that they were all very fat. A curious phenomenon among female musicians in Morocco is that at the beginning of their performance they seldom give much evidence of rhythmic sense. This has to be worked up by the men playing the drums. At the outset they seem distraught, they talk and fidget, smooth their clothing, and seem interested in everything but the business at hand. It took a good deal of insistent drumming to capture the women on this occasion, but after two numbers the men had them completely. From then on the music grew consistently more inspired. "*N'est-ce pas qu'elles sont magnifiques?*" whispered Monsieur Rousselot. I agreed that they were wonderful; at the same time I found it difficult to reconcile what I was seeing with his earlier description of Tassemsit as a holy city of sin. Still, doubtless he knew best.

As the shrill voices and the drumming grew in force and excitement, I became convinced that what was going on was indeed extraordinarily good, something I would have given a good deal to be able to record and listen to later at my leisure. Watching my host in the act of idly ruining what might have been a valuable tape was scarcely a pleasure. Throughout their performance, the women never stirred from where they stood, limiting their movements to a slight swaying of the body and occasional fantastic outbursts of antiphonal hand-clapping that would have silenced the Gypsies of Granada. With all that excess flesh, it was just as well they had no dance steps to execute. When the final cadence had died away, and while we applauded, they filed back to the shadows of the arcade and modestly wrapped their great cloths around them, to sit and listen to the ahouache's purely percussive coda. This was vigorous and brief; then a great crash of drums announced the end of the entertainment. We all stood up quickly, in considerable discomfort for having sat so long in the impossible chairs, and went back into the big room.

Five inviting beds had been made up along the mattresses at intervals of perhaps twenty feet. I chose one in a corner by a window and sat down, feeling that I should probably sleep very well. The courtyard emptied in no time, and the servants carried away the chairs, the lantern and the tape-recorder. Monsieur Rousselot stood in the middle of the room, yawning as he took off his shirt. The host was shaking hands with each one of us in turn and wishing us elaborate good-nights. When he came to me, he held out the flat box containing the tape he had just recorded. "A souvenir of Tassemsit," he said, and he bowed as he handed it to me.

The final irony, I thought. Of course, the spoiled tape has to be given to me, so that I can know in detail just what I failed to get. But my words to him were even more florid than his to me; I told him that it had been an unforgettable occasion, and that I was eternally indebted to him for this undeserved favor, and I wished him a pleasant night. Monsieur Omar was lying in his bed smoking, clad only in his shorts, a delighted and indestructible Humpty Dumpty. He was blowing smoke rings toward the ceiling. I did not feel that the future of Tassemsit was in immediate danger. Our host went out, and the door into the courtyard was shut behind him.

After everyone had gone to sleep, I lay there in the dark, listening to the jackals and considering my bad luck. Yet the original objective of the trip had been attained, a fact I discovered only when I got to the next place that had electricity. When I tried the tape in the hotel at Essaouira, fourteen out of its eighteen pieces proved to be flawless. There was no point in wondering why, since logically the thing was impossible; it had to be accepted as a joyful mystery. It is always satisfying to succeed in a quest, even when success is due entirely to outside factors. We bought blankets, trays, rugs and teapots, and set out again for the north.

GLOSSARY

ahouache In the Grand Atlas and in territories to the south of it, a formal festival involving groups of dancers, singers and percussionists.

bakhshish A gratuity.

bendir A large disc-shaped drum with one membrane.

bhikku A Buddhist monk.

bidonvilles The shanty towns that have grown up during the past three decades around the urban centers of North Africa. Not a geographically restrictive term.

bled The countryside.

butagaz Butane gas, used for cooking.

caid The chieftan of a tribe (or fraction of a tribe).

caique A rowboat or sailing boat.

chehade The spoken sentence affirming the Islamic faith.

chikh The leader, in this case, of a group of folk musicians.

cicerone A tourist guide.

comedor The dining room in a small hotel.

couscous (properly couscsou) A form of pasta, made by sprinkling drops of water over flour.

dagoba Buddhist burial mound.

dahven The repeated backward and forward motion of the torso of a seated person.

darbouka Large ceramic hand drum.

dhoti A loincloth worn by men in India.

djaoui Resin for burning, especially with benzoin in it.

djellaba A hooded overgarment with sleeves. Formerly a man's garment, but now worn by both sexes.

fraja Mass dancing.

gannega A small disc-shaped drum with a single fine membrane.

gitanos Gypsies.

gopuram Ornamented tower at the gateway to a Hindu temple.

Guennaoua (singular Guennaoui) A religious brotherhood, most of whose members are of Sudanese extraction, descendents of slaves. Their choreographed ritual is useful in the curing of madness, seizures and scorpion stings. They also rid houses of undesirable spirits.

haik Woman's traditional outer covering, generally of fine white wool.

imam Leader of prayer in the mosque.

imdyazen In certain Berber-speaking regions of Morocco, professional itinerant musicians.

Imochagh Tamachek term for Touareg.

joteya Second-hand market.

katib Secretary.

khalifa A deputy official.

kif The fine leaves at the base of the flowers of the common hemp plant, chopped and mixed (ideally in a ratio of seven to four) with tobacco grown in the same earth.

kissaria In a Moslem town, the quarter of the souqs devoted to the sale of textiles, clothing and luxury articles.

litham The cloth worn over the lower half of a woman's face.

mahia Alcohol distilled from fruit.

majoun In North Africa *majoun* is the word for jam. Used in its special sense it is the word for any sweet preparation eaten with the purpose of inducing hallucinations; its active ingredient is the hemp plant.

medina The Arabic word for city. In North Africa it indicates in particular that part of any city which was built by the Moslems and was already in existence at the time of the arrival of the Europeans.

meharistes Saharan military cavalrymen mounted on trained camels.

mektoub Destiny.

mijmah A brazier.

mottoui Leather pouch for carrying kif on one's person.

Mouloud The holiday commemorating the birthday of the Prophet Mohammed; also the month in which it occurs.

moussem Seasonal festival held at the tomb of a saint.

mruq Sauce.

m'tarrba The high narrow mattresses that line the walls of the rooms in a Moslem house.

mska A clear yellow gum resin.

naboula Bladder. Specifically a lamb's bladder, dried and softened, in which to store kif hermetically.

nargileh A water-pipe consisting of a jar and a hose with a mouthpiece.

parador An inn. In Spain and Morocco a specific term for government-run tourist hostelries.

paseo An avenue, generally with a strip of garden in the center.

peloton In French military usage, a detachment of soldiers.

pirith Buddhist purification ceremony.

qahaouaji Tea-maker.

qsbah Large reed transverse flute with a low register.

rhaita Reed instrument, equivalent to oboe.

ronda Card game, suggestive of gin rummy.

sebsi Long thin pipe for smoking kif.

semolina Grains made from grinding any cereal. In North Africa the process is slow: drops of water are sprinkled over the surface of flour, and the resulting accretions are shaken until they are globular and of the desired size.

souk (properly *souq*) The word is used throughout North Africa to mean a market. In the larger cities it has a second, more specific use in designating a street or quarter devoted to the buying and selling (and often the manufacture) of one given commodity.

Spanioline Plural of Spanioli, a Spaniard.

tarboosh High-crowned skullcap, a fez.

tbola Plural of *tbel*, North African side-drum, played with sticks.

tob Mixture of straw and earth (and often manure) for masonry.

toubib Doctor.

tseuheur The theory and practice of black magic.

yamaka The small black skullcap worn by male Jews.

zamar Riffian double-reed musical instrument.

zaouia The seat of a religious brotherhood, generally comprising a mosque, a school and the tomb of the sect's founder.

zebu The East Indian humped ox.

UP ABOVE THE WORLD

One

THE SLADES sat down to their breakfast more asleep than awake. The ship was in; they had heard its mournful whistle when it had arrived out in the harbor at some dark hour during the night. Now it was only a question of getting aboard with the luggage. Last night, when they returned from their pre-bedtime walk around the deserted town, the proprietor had told them to set their minds at rest: the night watchman would wake them at half past five, and breakfast would be served in the dining room at six. It was now twenty to seven. In the center of the room a black woman on her knees scrubbed the already spotless board floor. There was no one else in evidence, although faint sounds came from the region of the kitchen. Someone, they assumed, was making the coffee that would finally persuade them they were alive. The table had not been cleared away after last night's meal; at each place lay a half-eaten custard.

"I'll kill myself if we miss it," she declared.

"Oh, God." Then as if correcting himself, he said, "We won't miss it."

Outside the window the morning mist dripped from banana leaf to banana leaf. The clock over the sideboard ticked fast and loud. Time bomb, Dr. Slade thought as he looked out over the wet greenness of the hotel gardens.

"Just don't get nervous," he said, yawning. "We've got plenty of time." There was a difference between an ordinary relaxed yawn and this tight trembling one that came up convulsively from the bottom of his stomach. He counted to ten and jumped up.

"Where the *hell* is that coffee?" he cried in a sudden fury, wheeling in search of a door to the kitchen. A heavy red-faced woman was coming into the dining room; as he approached her he was aware of her bright cheeks, and he wondered fleetingly if she would be the wife of the proprietor. His *Buenos días* was a mutter, but she was already greeting him in English, and with a broad smile. He went on in the direction of the kitchen sounds and found the place, a dark cavern where a sleepy Negro fanned a smoking wood fire in a stove. "*Café! Café!*" cried Dr. Slade.

The man pointed to the garden, and Dr. Slade stepped out through the doorway onto the coarse sand. Poinsettia bushes grew under the young papaya trees; the flowers looked like wet red tissue paper. He went back into the dining room through a side door, cursing, and saw the steam rising from the two cups of coffee on the table. Mrs. Slade was no longer in the room.

The prospect of drinking the coffee while it was still hot, even with its usual complement of condensed milk, was too tempting to be disregarded. He sat down. "I trust that was a useful trip," he would say when she came back. Or, "Your digestion's important too, you know." A dog was barking furiously in the street just outside the window, and excited voices called. "When you're really pressed for time, there's an art in making each second count. You merely fit each thing you've got to do into the right bit of time." A girl appeared with a plate of bread.

"*Hay mantequilla?*" he asked her. She stared at him, shrugged her shoulders, and said she would go and see. He called after her to bring another cup of coffee, and glanced at the clock: twelve minutes to seven.

There was the sound of heel-taps behind him, approaching quickly from the hall. Mrs. Slade was at the table before he could put down his cup and turn. There was an expression of amused preoccupation on her face as she seated herself.

"Terribly funny," she said, more to herself than to him, and then she sipped her coffee while he waited for an explanation. The girl returned without the butter, but with two plates of ham and eggs. Before he began to eat, he said, "What?"

Mrs. Slade seemed not to have heard him, and plunged into her food with gusto.

2

The dock was at the end of the street; from there they could see the ship, huge and unmoving in the center of the circular bay. A motor launch with a green canopy crossed and re-crossed the bright water between the dock and the vessel while they stood waiting to get into the customs shed.

"It's going to be a nice day, after all," Dr. Slade announced with satisfaction. "That fog was just decoration." He set his briefcase down so that it leaned against his leg.

"It'd be just like them to pull up the anchor and start off while we stand here waiting," Mrs. Slade said grimly.

Dr. Slade laughed. Had such a thing really happened, he would have minded it even more than she, but in his experience the world was a rational place. "I only hope they can make frozen daiquiris," he said; it was a remark which might momentarily set her mind at rest.

The little motor launch chugged up to the dock, and out of it climbed the big woman with the pink cheeks, her wide forehead glistening with sweat. In her hand she held some papers which she waved at the two uniformed men standing nearby; they pointed to the customs shed.

"Look at Mrs. Crazy," said Dr. Slade with interest. "Isn't she something? She's already been out to the ship and back."

"She forgot her letter of credit," said Mrs. Slade.

Dr. Slade looked at his wife. "How do you know that?"

"She told me. She's a passenger. They won't honor the letter of credit on the ship, and she thinks if she can find a bank she may be able to get hold of some money. It's a whole saga. I lent her ten dollars."

"You lent *her money?*" cried Dr. Slade, scandalized. Then hearing his voice, he tried to alter its tone, and with discernibly false gentleness continued, "What for?"

"She'll give it back, dear." Mrs. Slade's voice was one calculated to calm a small child.

The woman was approaching them, panting. Dr. Slade had the time only to whisper, "That's not the point."

"Don't you let the ship go off without me!" she cried, shaking her black leather handbag at them playfully.

Mrs. Slade smiled. "Oh, I think you have time."

"I hope so," said Dr. Slade, not quite *sotto voce*. His inflection made it sound as if he had said "I hope not."

"Tell them they've *got* to wait," she called over her shoulder.

"Ridiculous," said Dr. Slade.

"I think she's rather touching," Mrs. Slade murmured pensively, looking after the retreating figure.

Dr. Slade did not reply. He stared out across the still harbor, and there came to him the idea that it was sometimes possible for two people who were close to one another to be very separate indeed. His eye followed the fuzzy line of forested mountains above the landlocked harbor, and the word *touching* took on an unaccustomed, disturbing dimension for him as he pursued the course of his thought.

3

The coastwise journey from La Resaca to Puerto Farol took only a day and a half, but Mrs. Slade, being uncertain which articles were in which valises, had found it necessary to unpack everything. Aware that he was not going to be able to prevent the operation, Dr. Slade had retired to the library to avoid having to witness it. Later in the afternoon he went in search of her and found her, shining with sun oil, prostrate on a deck mattress by the pool. He knelt proudly beside her, conscious of the other sunbathers' interest.

"How're you weathering lap two?" he asked her.

"What?" She squinted up at him.

"The second lap of the Slade Anniversary Expedition."

"Oh." She stretched with pleasure and waited a while before saying, "I meant to tell you. We're having drinks with Mrs. Rainmantle at six. Down in the bar."

He was mystified. "What for?" he asked, but his wife merely looked at him.

"You don't have to come," she told him.

He stood up. "Don't I?"

He walked slowly back to the stern of the ship and stood looking over the rail down into the soapy wake below. Along the horizon distant cumulus clouds leaned in a row like crooked pillars. Suddenly he felt very much alone. He stared for a long time at the far-off slanting cloud-towers. Before coming on the trip, during his medical checkup, he had forced himself to refer to the subject. "She could be my daughter. Or even my granddaughter, for that matter." The other physician had laughed. "Won't hurt to keep it in mind," he said.

He began to walk again, finally, and took the first stairway he found up to the boat deck, where he went eight times around.

Mrs. Rainmantle was already in the bar when they got there, seated on a high stool, wearing the same loosely fitting gray silk suit. Her hair was matted and stiff. Pretty bad, thought Dr. Slade; he would have liked to take out his handkerchief and wipe the grease and sweat from her forehead. It was something that required attention, like a child whose nose needs blowing.

When they had their planter's punches safely set on a table in the corner, he rubbed a drop of water from his lapel and said to Mrs. Rainmantle, "Was the bank obliging?" He saw the furious glance his wife darted in his direction.

"Oh, no! It was a completely useless trip," she replied airily.

"You mean it was shut?" said Dr. Slade, narrowing his eyes as he looked at her. He was aware of a whole series of tiny agitated movements being gone through by his wife in her attempt to catch his eye, but he would not look at her.

Smiling vaguely, Mrs. Rainmantle took a large gulp of her drink.

"It was open, all right. But they wouldn't help me."

"What?" he exclaimed. "I should think if you'd contacted your consul he might have done something." (Although would he? he thought. Perhaps not, if he took a good look at you.)

"I saw him," she explained. "He was perfectly pleasant. But he didn't feel he could take the responsibility. I didn't have the identification card with me. I showed him my passport and letters . . ." Her voice died as she recalled the details in the scene of her failure.

To his relief Mrs. Slade laughed. Good girl! he thought, daring to hope that her annoyance with him would now be mitigated. But even as she was laughing, she glanced at him, and he recognized his error.

They had another round of drinks. While they were talking, Mrs. Rainmantle drew the steward aside and had signed the chit before either of them was aware of what was happening. "Of course I invited you," she announced regally, and succeeded in silencing them both.

She rose. "I'm going to have one of those wonderful hot salt baths. See you anon."

"Ah," said Dr. Slade. When she was gone, he sat down. "It still wasn't ten dollars."

After dinner they wandered along the promenade deck; there was a warm wind and a bright moon. "How can you say I was rude?" he cried. "Is there any reason why I should go out of my way to treat that woman with kid gloves?"

She had her hands on the railing and was looking out across the shimmering expanse of moonlit water. "Yes! Yes!" she said, in a low but passionate voice. "There is! I always make an effort with your friends."

"Friends! Yes, but is she a friend?"

"You saw I was on friendly terms with her."

He was silent a moment while he thought, I'm making too much of it. "How did we get into all this?" he said. Then he laughed, caught hold of her hand, and pulled her away from the railing. They started to walk.

"It won't happen again," he told her. Still holding her hand, he pressed it as he spoke. Later, while they were dancing, he remained on the lookout for Mrs. Rainmantle, to be more certain of being able to avoid her, but she was not among the guests in the Bahia Bar.

A very fine rain was falling as the ship pushed into the harbor of Puerto Farol. It dimmed the steep outlines of the mountains that climbed upward to disappear in the enormous heavy sky. Even before the anchor had been cast, Dr. Slade heard the calling of countless frogs from the land. A shore excursion had been arranged for the passengers who were interested in visiting the stelae of San Ignacio.

"Is there anything as physically depressing as the sight of a lot of people together in one place?" said Mrs. Slade. "Thank God, we're leaving this ark." They stood by the rail, looking toward the land; a slight backward toss of her head indicated the passengers behind them.

"Are there sharks in the water, Daddy?" A small girl with pigtails standing beside Dr. Slade pointed downward. "Daddy, are there?" No one paid her any attention, and so Dr. Slade said to her in a matter-of-fact voice, "Of course there are, dear."

"Don't you believe him, honey," Mrs. Slade told her. "He's just teasing."

Dr. Slade laughed. "You fall in and see what happens," he said. The child looked from one of them to the other and backed away from the railing.

"Why are you so mean?" demanded Mrs. Slade. "Why do you want to frighten the poor little thing?"

Dr. Slade was impatient. "She asked for information and she got it," he said with finality. Through his binoculars he was scanning the seaside forest of coconut palms ahead. He had just caught sight of Mrs. Rainmantle coming along the deck, and he hoped to avoid having to greet her. Above all, he wanted not to go ashore in the same launch with her. Out of the corner of his eye, while he pretended to be looking through the glasses, he saw her work her way through the crowd to the rail farther astern, and was relieved.

4

They stood at the desk in the front hall of the hotel, listening to the wide sound of the rain that fell; it came down heavily now. The man behind the desk was eating a mango. Short strings of the fruit's pulp had got caught in his bushy mustache and hung from the hairs like tiny yellow worms above his lip. "*Pues sí, señores*," he resumed, without wiping his face. "The train for the capital leaves every morning at half past six. But there are many things to see here in Puerto Farol."

Dr. Slade looked out of the doorway across the veranda with its broken wicker furniture, past the waterfall of rain that splattered down from the door, to the empty garden beyond. A large buzzard suddenly appeared and settled clumsily on the bare plank that was the veranda's railing. For a moment he thought it was going to topple over. Like a mass of charred newspaper it wavered there for an instant, then steadied itself, folded its wings and let its raw red head fall to one side on its breast.

The man picked his nose with his forefinger now as he spoke. "There is a place called Paraíso only thirty-two kilometers from here. There are the ruins of San Ignacio. Very interesting. Big stones in the jungle, with faces in them. They'll give you nightmares!" His laugh broke into a cough, and he spat straight down from where he stood, watching the mass of sputum fall to the floor. Then he seemed to be doing a little dance by himself behind the desk as he scuffed it with the sole of his shoe. "*Sabe lo que son, las pesadillas?*"

"Yes, yes, of course," said Dr. Slade. "We'll be taking the train tomorrow morning, and we'll need at least three men to help with our luggage. I just wanted to let you know now."

"It's fantastic!" Mrs. Slade exclaimed, looking up at her husband. "A town as big as this without a single taxi!"

"A town as big as this with only this one hotel," he retorted. "The walk's nothing. Fifteen minutes. But God, we've got to sleep here. And we've got to eat here. The taxi's the least of my worries."

The man behind the desk was tearing the skin from another mango; the tart varnish-like odor filled the hall. Mrs. Slade spoke very little Spanish. "*Mango bueno?*" she said to the man.

"*Regular,*" he answered without looking up.

They wandered out onto the veranda; the buzzard did not move. The air smelled of flowers, and there was a constant tapestry of insect sounds audible behind the roar of the rain. They sat down in two worn wicker rocking chairs and stared out at the blinding watery gray noon. From time to time there was the very loud sound of a rooster crowing from somewhere nearby.

"I think I'll change before lunch. I feel wet and dirty," said Mrs. Slade.

"At least we got the good room," Dr. Slade replied with satisfaction.

Mrs. Slade laughed derisively; he supposed it was the idea of using the word *good*. "It's going to be rice and beans, I can tell you," he said. "But you like that, of course." He looked at her with indulgence.

"I'm so lucky!" She smiled and rocked a bit; the chair creaked dangerously.

Around the edge of the empty plaza, avoiding the deeper puddles, moved a small car; it came to a stop in front of them, at the foot of the veranda steps. The buzzard on the railing flopped down out of sight, the car door opened, and Dr. Slade saw what he immediately told himself he had expected to see: the red face and high gray coiffure of Mrs. Rainmantle emerging from the little sedan. She nodded her head to the driver, slammed the door, and hurried up the steps, panting and wet. When she recognized the Slades sitting there in front of her, her preoccupied expression altered to one of astonishment and pleasure. Dr. Slade rose slowly and extended his hand.

"Don't tell me you missed all *three* of the buses to San Ignacio!" she cried. "May I?" She dropped into his chair. He looked down at her apathetically, half hoping to see the chair collapse under her weight, but it was deceptively resistant. "Oh, of course. I forgot. You're disembarking here, too, aren't you?" She squeezed her hair with both hands, and rivulets of rain ran down her face.

"You're wet through to the skin," observed Mrs. Slade.

She laughed. "To the bone, I think."

Mrs. Slade watched the car making its way through the mud on the opposite side of the public garden. "Was that a taxi you had?" she asked suddenly.

"That was the British consul. More trouble. Now they won't let me take my luggage off the ship. I have a bar bill. But don't let me get started on it."

"Hah!" said Dr. Slade, who was walking slowly back and forth in front of the two women.

"It sounds very strange to me," Mrs. Slade said cautiously. Then she added, "You're getting off the ship here at Puerto Farol, then?"

Mrs. Rainmantle laughed. "Of course I'll get off all right. The consul is going to take care of it the first thing this afternoon. If only my son had been able to meet me. . . . So unnecessary." She sneezed violently.

Mrs. Slade stood up. "You're wet and you have nothing to change into. That can't *be*."

"I know. It's an impossible situation."

"I was wondering . . ." Mrs. Slade looked doubtful.

"Mercy!" laughed Mrs. Rainmantle. "A little thing like you, with your waist? Never in the world! You couldn't possibly have anything."

Mrs. Slade hesitated another instant. "No," she said suddenly. "Come up with me. I've got something. Really."

At the end of a series of facetious protests, Mrs. Rainmantle let herself be led upstairs, and Dr. Slade sat down again in the rocking chair he had given her. The rain was lessening, and the mechanical sound of the insects in the trees came louder. He sat looking straight ahead. A skeletal and nearly furless cat crawled around the corner of the veranda and stretched out near his feet. Now and then he drummed with his fingers on the chair arm, and once he said aloud incredulously, in a voice heavy with disgust, "I'll be damned."

5

Dr. Slade went in to lunch in a state of desperate boredom tempered with resentment; it had shaken him a little to see how bad luck could be prolonged to such unlikely lengths. Only three other passengers from the ship had finished their voyage at Puerto Farol. They were all in the dining room at the moment—three men sitting at three separate tables along the wall, watching the center, where the *turistas* sat. Here Mrs. Rainmantle, heavily made up now, and wearing Mrs. Slade's most baroque Japanese kimono, was dispensing bloody marys. She had ordered a large can of tomato juice from the refrigerator in the corner, and pulled a bottle of vodka from her handbag.

"I oughtn't to do this before lunch," she was saying. "But there are times when the call must be obeyed. And I feel the call."

"Well, I'm with you," Mrs. Slade told her. "Here's to you." She held up her glass. "May you arrive tomorrow night in the capital! Complete with luggage!"

Mrs. Rainmantle made a sad face. "I can't go tomorrow. I've got to see the consul again in the morning. I won't be able to leave until the *next* morning."

"What a shame!" said Dr. Slade. He could see from the expression on his wife's face that she was beginning to consider the possibility of delaying their own departure, and so he said firmly, "We're going tomorrow." Then, less certainly, "But we're bound to see you up there."

"I should think so!" agreed Mrs. Slade with warmth. "You'll call us at the hotel as soon as you have a minute."

Dr. Slade drank deeply from his glass and let their conversation flow over his head. Without listening, he perceived the outline of the story. A cockatoo in a back patio screamed twice; it was the voice of a demon. "Good God! We're back in the violent ward," said Mrs. Rainmantle.

By now he knew that she was a Canadian who lived in London and who was in the habit of coming here to visit her son. Still it was not necessary to listen: the high points of the story were so often reiterated that the graph was clear. He yawned and tapped his fingers on the table, looking out of the window at the wet leaves and tin roofs.

The three solitary diners had left the room and gone for their siestas. Now and then Dr. Slade glanced at his wife apprehensively to see if she resented his long silence, but she seemed not to mind. Occasionally she even sent him a sweet little smile, as though it were understood that he appreciated the extended monologue as much as she; with his answering smile he tried to project an expression of forbearance. Now the rain had ceased, the sun was blazing, and steam rose from the earth outside the window.

"I always try to see something worthwhile when I come out to visit Grover." One year she had been to the lake district, one year to see the volcanoes near the southern border of the republic. Again she had come via Trinidad and Georgetown in order to go up the Mazaruni to Roraima.

The waiter came in to clear off the table. "Ask him if he hung the señora's clothes near the stove, darling," said Mrs. Slade.

He spoke with the waiter. "They're dry," he announced.

"Hurray!" cried Mrs. Rainmantle. "Now we can go out. I had visions of myself sitting inside all afternoon, waiting, while you two went out on the town."

"We wouldn't have gone off without you," said Mrs. Slade.

"Gone where?" Dr. Slade asked. His wife looked at him once, rose from the table, and followed Mrs. Rainmantle and the waiter into the kitchen. He remained sitting alone in the room, looking out at the shining day, and wondering what a single man's sex life would be like in Puerto Farol. A few sad sick whores near the railway station, most likely. No moonlit idyls under the palms while the surf rolled over the warm sand nearby. These people read no books. A town of corrugated iron, raw concrete and barbed wire. He had seen enough of it on his way from the dock to the hotel.

Mrs. Slade called to him from the kitchen door. "We're going upstairs. We'll be right down."

6

The single window, next to the door, gave directly onto the veranda that encircled the whole second story. This balcony was the one pleasant spot to be found on the premises of the Gran Hotel de la Independencia. Over the years a great collection of potted tropical plants had been set on the floor along its railings; these had flourished, pushed forth fronds and spikes, extended creepers and branches, with the result that in places they constituted a veritable forest to be got through as one made one's way along the gallery. In some of the open spots there was a lone rocking chair of the same variety as those downstairs at the entrance. "The older sisters," Mrs. Slade had said as they passed by them a few minutes ago.

They lay on their beds now, partially undressed, with the netting prudently tucked under the mattresses, relaxing, absently exchanging half-thoughts across the no-man's-land between the beds. The hot dusk had closed down upon the town and swiftly sealed it off. Darkness here was tangible and intimate; it palpitated on all sides. There were the waves of flower and plant odors that drifted through the open window, the steady chorus of insects and tree frogs from the high vegetation beyond the veranda, the flashing on and off of the fireflies that moved high above their heads, just under the palmwood beams of the ceiling.

"If we want air we've got to leave the window open," said Dr. Slade.

"We certainly can't sleep with it shut. Under these nets?"

"It's safe enough. There must be a man on duty downstairs."

Presently she murmured, "It's like being in a tent."

"What's that?" he asked. Another minute and he might have dozed.

"This room." Her voice became more animated. "It's like being outdoors. Listen!"

After a moment he said, "Wonderful music for sleeping. I wish we didn't have to get up for dinner."

"Mmm," she answered uncertainly.

They were silent for a long time, as he fell into a series of light naps. Every few minutes he opened his eyes and then allowed himself to slip comfortably off again. She thought of what she would wear down to dinner, of the unbelievable dimness of the light in the room. Lack of light made everything more difficult. This was the sort of room where there could be spiders and one would not see them. She decided to unpack nothing and to put the same things back on, damp with sweat though they were. It was Puerto Farol that was at fault; anywhere else it would have struck her as an unsavory idea to dress in damp clothes.

All at once it was later, and people were approaching along the veranda outside the window.

"Taylor! What time is it?" she cried.

Dr. Slade moaned. She waited. Presently he said, "Ten after eight."

"You've been asleep a long time," she told him, as though it required forgiving.

He stretched voluptuously and yawned. There were several people on the balcony outside the door, and they were making a surprising amount of noise. Valises were dropped carelessly onto the bare board floor; then came the sound of their being slid along it. Several men were speaking in Spanish, and then unmistakably there was Mrs. Rainmantle's high voice mixed in with the others. "*Pero . . . pero . . .*" she seemed to be saying.

"Sounds as if she got her bags, all right," said Dr. Slade, sitting up. He opened the curtains of the net, got out of the bed quickly, and pulled the gap shut after him. Taking care to get into his slippers, he shuffled over to the window and stood there, watching. After a moment he came back to his wife's bed and said in a low voice, "They've put her in next door."

Mrs. Slade made a sharp "Shhhh!"

The porters' footsteps were still banging and shaking the veranda as they went on their way downstairs. He saw her sit up indignantly and try to catch his eye through the curtain of netting. She struggled into her kimono and pulled the net open, staring out at him, looking rumpled and angry, and, he thought, very desirable. He gave a pleased chuckle and said, "She can't hear, she can't hear. Believe me. Listen." He held up his hand for a second. "All those insects. It's a kind of soundproofing. Unless you're going to shout."

"I was afraid she might be outside the door."

Her clothes were not appreciably drier than when she had taken them off. It seemed to her they had an odor of rum about them. "I wonder if perspiration can smell of what you've drunk," she said.

"Absolutely."

She did not question the information. Using an atomizer filled with Tabac Blond, she set to work trying to neutralize the scent.

Dr. Slade waited, watching her. "The room's full of it," he observed aloud.

"I'm ready," she said.

They went out. He had a small flashlight in his hand to help them through the bottlenecks of vegetation. "You're so clever to have brought that along," she told him.

Dinner was identical to lunch; they were alone in the nearly dark dining room. They got through the meal as quickly as possible, refusing coffee afterward. It was surprising that Mrs. Rainmantle had not come down.

"I'd like to take a little turn around the square before I go back into my box," said Dr. Slade.

"All right." Her voice lacked enthusiasm. "I'll probably have insomnia anyway."

"No, you won't." He stroked her arm.

"God, it's hot," she said, jumping up. "Let's go."

7

They had chosen a narrow, well-lighted alley to walk in rather than a street; suddenly they found themselves not among houses and trees, but on a boardwalk above a swamp. The street lights began again much farther ahead; here it was dark, and their footsteps banged loud on the boards. As they advanced, the frogs directly under them stopped calling, but on all sides the sound continued.

"Strange place," said Dr. Slade. Had he been alone, he would surely have turned back, but with his wife along that was harder to do. She would store away the memory of his action for use as ammunition some day in an unrelated context. "You were afraid, for instance, to cross that swamp at Puerto Farol. Of course you were quite right. I was just waiting to see how far you'd go. But you have to admit you *were* afraid, darling."

"Bats!" she exclaimed. "I saw some bats back there just before we came onto the bridge."

"We're almost to the end of it."

"Do they have vampire bats here?"

"I don't know. Probably." An instant later he added, "It seems they've discovered that just being in the same room with *any* bat can give you rabies."

They had come to high vegetation now. It was the end of the boardwalk. "I don't think I've ever seen so many fireflies," he mused.

"Rabies? That was in *Time*," she said accusingly. "I saw it."

"Therefore it's false. Is that it?"

Their heels no longer rapped in the silence; they were walking again on sand. Some of the houses here had thatched roofs. The banana leaves looked very green under the street lights. Not a person was visible.

"I'm being eaten by mosquitoes," she announced.

"Why don't we go back?"

"They're not going to stop just because we're walking the other way."

"The street lights end up ahead here," he said, pointing.

"All right." She swung sharply around and they began to walk in the other direction.

On the boardwalk, amid the clamor of the frogs, she told him, "I've got the horrors now. I'm going to hold my breath when I go under those bat trees."

"The mosquitoes are getting my ankles," he said. "I don't know why we came out this way."

She laughed her little-girl laugh. "I didn't choose it," she said gaily.

Once back on the ground, they got quickly to the plaza. There was one electric bulb burning on the hotel veranda. They went into the dark front hall, were met by the odor of garbage and cooking. Something moved at his side; Dr. Slade jumped and clicked on the flashlight. It was Mrs. Rainmantle sitting in a rocking chair in the dark.

"Oh, I've been waiting for you!" she cried, her voice calamitous. "I can't find anyone. They've *got* to give me a different room."

"Is it awful?" asked Mrs. Slade.

"There's no key in the door, no bolt, no possible way of locking it. I refuse to sleep in it, that's all." Her voice had risen; it was as if she were already making her official complaint.

Dr. Slade turned the flashlight's beam into distant corners. "Isn't there anybody around down here? Must be a watchman or somebody."

"Nobody! And there's the front door wide open. Anyway, the bed sags like a hammock. How are your beds?" There was the odor of fresh whiskey on her breath.

"They're all right," said Mrs. Slade.

"She's used to roughing it," explained her husband quickly.

"It's the door that makes the room impossible," Mrs. Rainmantle said in a dead voice. They were silent.

"Well, we might as well go up," Mrs. Slade said at last. "There's at least a light upstairs."

When they stood outside the Slades' bedroom Mrs. Rainmantle pushed on, crying, "Come in here. I want to show you." She led the way into the dark further chamber and turned on the light. The place was clearly nothing more than a storeroom for old pieces of furniture, with a crooked bed pushed into one corner. A ten-year-old calendar dangled by one corner on the wall beside the bureau. The air was hot and still.

"This is awful!" exclaimed Mrs. Slade. "I don't understand how they dare put anyone in a room like this."

A narrow passageway between the stacked chairs and Mrs. Rainmantle's unpacked valises made it just possible to get through to the bed.

"But look at the door!" cried Mrs. Rainmantle; her voice again sounded hysterical. "I'll sit downstairs out on the porch. Anywhere. It doesn't matter. I won't sleep here."

"Come into our room," Mrs. Slade urged her. "We can sit down."

At the far end of the veranda the light spilled out onto the boards through an open door. There was the faint sound of men's voices. Perhaps only two men, Dr. Slade thought, pausing to listen as he followed the two women from one room to the other; he got the impression that they were sitting over a bottle. He saw his wife lay her hand on the older woman's arm as they went through the door, and he had an immediate premonition of the way in which the situation was going to be resolved. Indeed, the ladies had scarcely sat down facing one another in the two chairs under the light before Mrs. Slade was saying, "You simply stay in here with me, Mrs. Rainmantle, and everything will be all right. Just forget about it."

"Oh, I couldn't!"

"Dr. Slade doesn't mind whether his door is locked or not. Do you, Taylor?"

"No, I don't mind," he said slowly.

"It doesn't matter to him, really," pleaded Mrs. Slade. "And it matters so much to you."

"Well," Mrs. Rainmantle sighed, looking at him timidly. "It *would* be a godsend."

"It's quite all right," he assured her. "Only I suggest we do it now." He wanted to be by himself quickly, so that his ill-humor should not become visible. But instead of leaving the room, he strode over to the wash basin and began to brush his teeth. "Excuse me if I do this," he said thickly, spitting into the basin. "I don't want to carry anything into the other room. Do you need anything of yours from there, Mrs. Rainmantle?"

She emerged from a brief reverie. "No, no. I have everything I want in my handbag."

"I'll pound on the door at half past five," he said to his wife. She was looking at him sadly, as if she suspected that there would be no swift forgiving of her treason. He stared at her with what he hoped was no expression at all and said, "Good night." "Good night," he said also to Mrs. Rainmantle, and then he was out of the room, having failed to take along any pajamas.

He'll sleep naked, she thought. She heard the door of the next room shut. The men down at the end of the balcony were still talking; the louder words made their sounds heard even above the insects.

Mrs. Rainmantle fished in her handbag and pulled out a pint of whiskey she had bought that afternoon at a Chinese shop on the waterfront. It was about half empty. "I'm going to have myself a little drink before I undress," she said with satisfaction, walking over to the washbasin. "One for you?"

"A nightcap."

She poured far too much Scotch into Mrs. Slade's glass, but being able to relax for a moment seemed to be giving her so much pleasure that Mrs. Slade did not protest.

"This may look like rank self-indulgence to you," began Mrs. Rainmantle, settling back in her chair, "but today was a day I'll always remember. And not for its pleasantness, either. *Nothing* happened the way it was supposed to."

Mrs. Slade thought: Does it ever?

"You must be very tired," she said, certain that the other expected a more lively demonstration of sympathy than she was giving her. She hoped that when she had drunk the whiskey she might feel more like going out of her way to say kind words. She looked at the wall and imagined her husband on the other side of it, unable to sleep in the leaning bed, trying to get into a bearable position, cursing the stagnant air and the smell of dust.

Mrs. Rainmantle was talking; it was a monologue and there seemed no need to listen carefully. She tried nevertheless to follow, fearing that otherwise her eyes would shut of their own accord.

"I want my house to have space in it," Mrs. Rainmantle declared. "I want my rooms to be enormous."

Although Mrs. Slade had drunk all the whiskey in her glass,

the awaited feeling of benevolence toward her guest still had not manifested itself; she only wanted very much to go to bed.

She heard herself asking blankly, "Where is this house?"

"Oh, it's going to be in Hawaii. I've bought the property." Mrs. Rainmantle poured herself another small drink.

"How wonderful!" said Mrs. Slade.

"I really think I'm going to be happy there. In the end, living in hotel rooms is dehumanizing."

Some minutes later Mrs. Slade sprang up. "I've got to go to bed. I'm sorry."

"Yes, we must."

Through the confused folds of her mosquito netting she saw Mrs. Rainmantle go to the wall by the door and turn off the light. "Can you see to undress?" she asked.

"I never have any trouble undressing," Mrs. Rainmantle replied cheerfully from inside her garments.

She heard the other bed creak as it was charged with the weight of the heavy body. Mrs. Rainmantle sighed deeply. "It feels good," she said with contentment.

The insects sang, a door closed somewhere. Mrs. Slade wished she had refused the whiskey; it was the wrong thing to have put into her stomach. She tried hard not to think of Dr. Slade, lying in the awful room, but the image was there in front of her.

8

Dr. Slade shut his door, undressed, and laid his clothes out along the top of the dusty bureau. When he was naked, he stood under the light and adjusted the alarm of his watch. Then, looking once apprehensively at the deformed bed, he switched off the light. With his flashlight he found his way through the chaos to the foot of the mosquito net and climbed up onto the bed. After a certain number of experiments he discovered that if he lay diagonally across its sloping surface he could be reasonably comfortable. Coming in here without pajamas had been purposeful on his part. It was a mute protest, a way of refusing the room existence. When morning came, he would dress and walk out of it empty-handed, as if he had never been aware of it. Underneath the encompassing sound of the insects he sometimes could hear the two women's voices, but not their words.

The smell of the dust was in the air inside here; his hot breath came back at him from the netting near his face. Mrs. Rainmantle, he thought wryly, had merely shown normal animal intelligence in refusing to use the room, lock or no lock on the door.

It had been his hope to sleep in the same bed with his wife, at least for a part of the night. The past two nights they had been on the ship, where the size and disposition of the berths had discouraged any project of love-making. The fantasy occurred to him that he might be doing a reckless thing in leaving Day alone with Mrs. Rainmantle; there was no certainty that she was not psychopathic. He tried to listen to the voices, to guess at the kind of conversation they were having, but he was getting sleepy, and the steady song of the night creatures filled the air. Surprised that it had been so easy, he recognized the fact that he was sliding down the incline into sleep.

His first thought when he heard the frantic buzzing of the alarm on his watch was that he had set it wrong; he had been ready to sleep, and he still had not achieved it. But when he pulled the flashlight out from under the pillow and turned it on, he saw that the time was five twenty-five. The sounds outside were entirely different now; the background consisted largely of isolated honks and chirps. Nearby a night bird of some sort made a series of clear low-pitched calls. Then he heard a second bird farther away, echoing the sound. He ·waited an instant and then, the flashlight still in his hand, he sprang out of bed and snapped the light switch. The room remained dark.

Soon he had his clothes on and was out on the veranda, rapping on the other door. He heard Day's muffled response and said quietly, "Five thirty."

"Yes," she answered. "Right."

There was no sign of dawn in the sky. The air was tepid and still. He went back into the dark room and, leaving the flashlight on, washed his face over the basin and combed his hair. He intended to shave the last thing before they left for the station.

He turned the flashlight off and sat down on the bed in the dark. Now the roosters were crowing in the distance, and dogs were barking, and below in the garden a cockatoo began to scream—probably the same bird they had heard at lunch the day before. The wandering fingers of a fresh predawn breeze reached him from time to time, and he thought, This is the good hour, when the stars are still shining and it's finally cool, and you can't see anything of the town.

He heard the key turn and the door of the next room open. Then there was the tapping of Mrs. Slade's mules along the veranda as she went in the direction of the bathrooms. The feeblest suggestion of daylight had begun to show in the sky; each minute it would be stronger. After a long time he heard the mules coming back, and then the door was shut again.

Mrs. Slade's night had been long and bristling with nightmares. She had lain on the sheet sweating inside the mosquito net, hating the room, hating even the idea of poor Mrs. Rainmantle lying in all her flesh on the other bed. With the whiskey's acid flame still flickering in her stomach, she had forced herself to breathe slowly, regularly, but the possibility of being seized and paralyzed by her own nightmare had never been far off. How many times had she forced herself to turn over in the bed to dispel the forming tornado of dreams? At first, during her waking spells, she had listened intently in order to pick out, this side of the screaming metallic backdrop, the nearer, softer sound of Mrs. Rainmantle's snoring. Sometimes, aware of the open window, she was certain that a third presence had come into the room. She would fix a point in the dark, her eyes very wide, and lie absolutely still, trying to breathe like someone asleep. Once she had felt a heavy insect or a lizard land on the canopy above her head, and remain clinging there, moving the netting lightly from time to time. Then there had been only the monstrous hairy darkness that clicked and pulsed out there from its black insect throat.

She had not dared, even with her flashlight, to get out of bed to look for a Seconal, for fear of stepping on a scorpion or a centipede, and so she had lain there in a suspended state between sleeping and waking. When the knock came at the door, she said, "Uh," and, seizing the flashlight as if it had been a weapon, tore open the netting and stood upright on

the floor to play the beam around the room. In the dimness
she could distinguish Mrs. Rainmantle's body like a great pillow entangled with the sheets on the far side of the bed. She
moved the beam along the wall. There by the door was the
light switch. She walked over and pushed it. The light did not
come on. It was still night—the same night; her stomach
burned and her head ached. Dr. Slade was knocking on the
door. Suddenly she was fearful that Mrs. Rainmantle would
waken. She put her face near the panel of the door and said
calmly, "Yes. Right." It stopped the knocking, and she heard
him go back into his room.

A moment later she hurried out toward the bathroom,
cursing the plants as they rubbed against her face in the dark.
Even before she got to the end of the balcony she realized
that she was not going to take a shower. There would be
nowhere to put the flashlight; it would get wet or fall off onto
the floor, and she would be there in the dark with the water
running over her. She went into one of the rooms and locked
the door behind her. It was hot, dark, airless. A small table
stood between the washbasin and the shower. She set the
flashlight down. The walls were impregnated with the ancient
stench of the latrine. Later, when the sun was up, she would
be all right, she knew, but at the moment she felt ill. If I can
throw it up, she thought. But it was as impossible as trying to
retch up the night; the night was still there, and the fiery
sourness still inside her.

When she came out, the air seemed a little cooler, and she
could almost see her way through the ferns and palms without the flashlight. She pressed it intermittently as she walked
along; when she got to her room she turned it all the way on,
went in, and shut the door. In order to minimize the chances
of waking Mrs. Rainmantle (for she did not relish the idea of
having to talk with her at this point) she got into her clothing quickly and silently. Then she packed her two cases and
gathered up her handbag, all the while reflecting that it was
going to seem a little unfriendly of her to run off this way
without saying goodbye. No. We've got to go, she told herself; she wanted to get out of the room once and for all. The
surest way for her to accomplish this was for her to pack

Taylor's things herself and set all the luggage outside the door.
That way the room would remain quiet. He would not have
to come in at all, and Mrs. Rainmantle would go on sleeping.

She had his bags shut in a minute; he had taken practically
nothing out of them. She opened the door onto the veranda.
Slowly, one by one, she carried the suitcases out and set them
down, making as little sound as possible. Then, when everything was out, she stood in the doorway and played the flashlight rapidly once around the room, saying a silent goodbye
to Mrs. Rainmantle as it reached her corner. The beam went
on along the wall past the mirror and coat hooks.

She shut the door and stood perfectly still, listening for a
sound from within, and trying to be certain of what she had
just seen. Mrs. Rainmantle still lay in her uncomfortable position on the wall side of the bed, and one great leg hung over
the edge. In that instant of faint light, and with the draperies
of the mosquito netting in the way, she could not be certain,
but it seemed to her that Mrs. Rainmantle's eyes had been
open. Her reaction had been to pull the door shut even more
quickly. And now she listened. If Mrs. Rainmantle were
awake, it was likely that even at this moment she was getting
up and coming to the door.

There was no sound from inside the room. She tried to recapture the picture once more as she had seen it. The eyes
seemed to be shut this time. But then it became like a chromolithograph of Jesus where the closed lids suddenly flew
open and the eyes were there, looking straight ahead. She
turned and knocked on Dr. Slade's door.

9

Following the course of a roaring stream, the small train
wound slowly uphill. Tree smells and birdsong blew in
through the open windows. At the hotel they had managed
to get only coffee; breakfast had been some bananas bought
through the car window before the train had pulled out of
Puerto Farol. One sickly boy had been available to carry the
luggage to the station, instead of the three men Dr. Slade had
asked for. They had made the train only by dividing the valises

among them, with Mrs. Slade carrying a basket and her own
overnight bag.

Her headache, largely dissipated by the coffee, had revived
during the rush to the station. Now, as the train swerved violently from one side to the other, an occasional throb made
her wince. She took a pair of dark glasses from her handbag
and put them on. A moment later she slipped her hand into
the bag again and began to touch the objects there, until she
had found a tube of Optalidon, which she surreptitiously removed. While Dr. Slade was occupied in looking at the landscape she popped one of the pills into her mouth, but
apparently he had noticed the motion of her hand, out of the
corner of his eye. He turned to look at her.

"You sleep all right?"

"Did *you*?" she countered. The night was too recent for her
to want to discuss it. "You had a horrible bed."

"I slept fine," he said, still looking at her. "I could have
done with a little more, yes."

She wanted to change the subject, but she could not think
of anything to talk about. It was as though her mind were
working there in her head all by itself, hoping to find an answer to an unformulated question.

Perhaps an hour and a half later they were atop the first
ridge of sierra, overlooking the misty green coastal plain. The
wind that came in through the windows was suddenly cold.
Dr. Slade slipped on his jacket.

"Are you chilly?" he said.

"No."

She would have been happy to sit back and tell Taylor how
strange Mrs. Rainmantle had looked, and how it had made her
feel at the time, after she had shut the door. It would have
been a relief to describe how she had kept thinking of it since.
But if she began to talk about it, she would see again the circle of dim yellow light moving along the discolored wall, and
Mrs. Rainmantle's head lying at an unlikely angle to the
mountainous body, with the sheet pulled tight around her
neck. If she got that far, she knew she would find the eyes
open, staring senselessly out through the netting. She put her
hand quickly to her face to keep the picture from forming.
Seeing that Dr. Slade was watching her, she pretended to have

a cinder in her eye. If he suspected any preoccupation in her, he would end by prying it all out; it was his belief that what he called negative emotions immediately ceased to exist once they had been exposed to the blazing light of reason. He would force her to put it into words, and words in this case were not what she wanted: they might only make it all the more real.

There was a forty-minute stop at a place called Tolosa, a pockmarked, dusty town with a short main street that ran along beside the railroad track. In company with a few passengers from the train they walked to a shabby restaurant opposite the station. The two elderly Chinese men who ran the place clearly had no interest in food.

"Nothing Chinese at all?" said Dr. Slade wistfully to the one who stood before them. The man said something in unintelligible Spanish and brought them the same dishes they had eaten back in Puerto Farol: brown beans, rice, plantain and fried eggs.

"This would have been a shock to Ruth," murmured Dr. Slade. "You know, the Chinese were the only good cooks in the world. But this is unbelievable. These two don't eat this food. They have their own in the kitchen."

Ruth had been Dr. Slade's first wife. By tacit mutual consent they never spoke of her. He supposed the understanding between them was a product of atavism: by itself it had come into being. Mention of the first Mrs. Slade was thus uncommon enough to make Day now look up from her plate. Then she understood that he had been expecting exactly that reaction, had provoked it purposely in order to be able to catch her eye and smile encouragingly at her. He's doing his best, she thought, resentful of having failed to conceal her nervousness. As if there had been no maneuver on his part, she smiled blandly. "The rice grains are fairly separate, at least," she said, looking back down at her plate. "I don't really mind this sort of bad food. There's so little difference here between good and bad, it doesn't matter much one way or the other."

She stopped talking and stared for a moment out into the bright sunlight. The train was there in front of her, stretching to left and right of the station. Everyone was leaning out of the car windows, buying food and soft drinks. Beyond was the open countryside of distant barren mountains and nearby wasteland. A factory siren wailed. She went on eating; Dr. Slade said nothing.

Back in their compartment, however, they both felt better. It was a relief to be on the train rather than looking across at it, expecting to see it start up without them. They relaxed and slept a while.

When Mrs. Slade awoke her headache was gone; she remained lying stretched out on the seat. Just after sunset, when they were scarcely an hour from the capital, the ticket collector came in, and she sat upright. The man went back out into the corridor and shut the door. Still they did not speak, their heads nodding with the movement of the train as they looked out at the red landscape and the coming of dusk across it. Some time after the rhythms of the train had taken over her consciousness although her eyes were still open, he said unexpectedly, "I wonder if she got in touch with her son today."

Mrs. Slade heard her own voice saying unsurely, "No . . ."

"You don't think she did?"

She shook her head with impatience. "I don't know any more than you do about it. I was thinking of something else."

10

After midnight the capital was deserted; the long straight avenues, sparsely illumined, stretched for great distances into the stony plain beyond. For an hour or two the cold mountain wind swept over the highland, and after that the air was still. There were long periods during the night when the silence was like a fine needle in her ears. But a locomotive sometimes whistled from far out in the country as the train labored up a barranca from a lower valley. Or a caged bird in someone's patio nearby called a few clear notes. A cricket chirped, a plane flew overhead, far above even the invisible mountain peaks, and the *guardia* blew his soft pipe in the street below; in the lower part of the city the cathedral clock chimed the hour. With the silences in between, the night passed.

At the desk she had asked for a separate room. "What I really need is sleep," she told Dr. Slade. "I didn't sleep last night." Knowing she had already told him this, she was about to elaborate.

Dr. Slade spoke first. "Of course. Naturally."

When the bellboys let them into the room meant for her, she walked ahead of them to the window, opened it, and looked down at the tops of the trees in the dark street below. She listened.

"It's sublimely quiet."

She lay on the bed, comfortable in the cold dry air that came in through the window. Even now she did not feel sleepy; she supposed it was due to the altitude. It was a joy merely to lie still and be comfortable. The quiet room and the soft bed relaxed her; there were the added luxuries of feeling secure and being alone. A little before dawn she slept.

Dr. Slade woke and telephoned downstairs for breakfast. In the bathroom he dashed cold water into his eyes, seized a bath towel, and, after vigorously drying himself, stepped onto the small balcony outside his window. The city shone in the strong early sunlight, and the tops of the mountains looked absurdly near. His eye moved down the slopes to the forested regions, the lesser summits, and the vast detailed countryside of hills and valleys still lower down.

On his breakfast tray was a newspaper bearing a gummed label: BUENOS DÍAS. LA DIRECCIÓN. GOOD MORNING. THE MANAGEMENT. The coffee was good and there was a big pitcher of it. He glanced at the headlines and poured himself another cup. Presently he got up, shaved, dressed, and went downstairs to look for a barbershop. There was none in the hotel; the desk clerk suggested he take a cab to the center of the city.

He decided to walk. It would be downhill nearly all the way. The shabby provincial capital was saved from ugliness only by its trees and parks. When he was seated in the swivel chair and covered by the sheet, the barber handed him a newspaper, which, even as he accepted it, he recognized as the same one that had been sent upstairs with his breakfast. He ran his eye over *El Globo*'s already familiar front page; a short item at the bottom caught his attention. The dateline

contained the words *Puerto Farol*. He read on, his mouth
dropping open. It was the account of a fire, which shortly after daybreak the preceding morning had destroyed a part of
the Gran Hotel de la Independencia. It had claimed the life
of one guest, Mrs. Agnes Rainmantle, a tourist of Canadian
nationality who had arrived on the M.S. *Cordillera*. There
was a description of the property damage caused to the building, and that was all, save that the piece ended with the
words "*a lamentar*," which somehow removed it from the
realm of the serious or possible. No further disgraces to
lament!

Poor woman, he thought, his natural chagrin weighted by
a small sense of guilt because he had been rude to her at the
end of her last evening.

Day mustn't see this, he said to himself suddenly. I've got
to keep it away from her.

II

Mrs. Slade opened her eyes and looked at her watch: five
minutes past eleven. Six hours, more or less, she thought; it
was not really enough sleep, but she felt wide-awake and full
of energy. She called down for breakfast and took a quick
shower. When the maid arrived she had her set the tray on
the balcony, and there in the hot sunlight she drank her coffee and ate her toast. There was a local newspaper on the
tray; without looking at it she laid it on the table. Only
when she had finished breakfast did she call Dr. Slade's
room. There was no answer. He's rushed out to see the
town, she thought, feeling a faint resentment that he should
have gone without her, yet aware that had he come to her
room and wakened her she would have been furious. She
dressed and decided to take a short walk herself, while the
morning smell was still in the air. Yesterday's nervousness
was gone.

It was cool enough at last to wear the new pink linen suit
she had been longing to put on. Its color complemented her
suntan in a manner she had only partially foreseen. From the
closet mirror she walked out onto the terrace and lit a cigarette while she stood looking down across the red tile roofs of

the city. The towering distant mountains behind it looked nearer than the town itself, half lost down there in its pool of haze. She tapped her ashes into the street, put on her sunglasses, and went back into the bedroom.

In the lobby, next to the reception desk, there was a small brightly lighted newsstand, and in front of it an assortment of comfortable chairs, each with its reading lamp. At the moment the reception hall was empty of guests save for one young man, who was sprawled in one of the chairs, his legs over the side, reading a magazine.

At the counter she examined the display of newspapers from two and three days earlier, choosing a San Francisco *Chronicle* and a New York *Times*. A man appeared from an inner room and stood facing her; she asked him for *Newsweek* and handed him a banknote. "Oh," he said, looking at it. "Excuse me one minute." He went back into the room where he had been.

Wheeling slowly around, she leaned against the counter, her hands behind her, and gazed across the lobby. It surprised her to see it so empty at this hour of the morning. Although she told herself that she did not particularly want to, she glanced again at the young man and found herself forming an opinion. If a man was wholly and dramatically handsome, she looked for a character defect. To her way of thinking, no man could look as this one did and not have ended by taking unfair advantage of it.

The young man flicked his cigarette ashes into a tall jar by his hand, and went on reading. She turned back to the stand; the man counted out her change for her. "Did you take out for *Newsweek*?" she asked him, running her eye over the display of publications. "Where is it?"

"*Newsweek*? You come back in one-half hour."

There was a small garden off the lobby, crowded with philodendron and cages of parakeets. She chose a comfortable chair in the sun, put on her dark glasses, and sat there reading the newspapers for exactly thirty minutes, expecting Dr. Slade to appear at any moment. Then, convinced that the clerk behind the desk would not yet have managed to get hold of her magazine, and not much caring, she went back to ask him.

The young man, still in his armchair, took no notice of her as she went past. Even as she approached the counter and saw the face of the clerk behind it, she knew she had been right. "No more *Newsweek!*" he cried in an unnecessarily loud voice. "All sold out."

There was a movement behind her; she turned and saw the young man advancing. He held several magazines out in front of him and smiled tentatively. "I'm sorry," he told her. "I couldn't help hearing. Here's a *Newsweek*. I've got one here. Will you take it?"

The tone of her voice as she said, "No. No, thank you," made her feel that she was being unfriendly, and so she smiled back and added, "I wouldn't have read it anyway. You keep it."

He still held it out. "I've looked at it. You won't find another anywhere else in town. They all go the first few hours."

She had no intention of accepting the magazine. "It's not important," she said. "It doesn't matter at all. They don't sell books anywhere here in the hotel, do they?"

The man behind the counter had disappeared into the inner room, and the young man was holding a pack of cigarettes in front of her. She took one. As he lighted it for her he was saying, "There's only one store in town where you can get books in English. I've got my car outside."

She was tempted, but she hesitated. "Oh," she said. "You see, I'm sort of expecting to see my husband here in the lobby any minute." It seemed an ungracious way of refusing, and it was not what she had meant to say.

The young man stepped over to the reception desk and spoke briefly with the clerk. She stood there with the cigarette in her hand, thankful now that there was no one else to witness the equivocal scene. He came back, smiling more broadly. "Your husband's gone to the barbershop," he told her. "So it's up to you."

The long open convertible had a crumpled fender.

"You *are* American?" she said. The motor roared and they moved ahead through the shadows of the high trees.

He laughed. "No! I'm just another irresponsible citizen. I've lived here so long I'm one of them."

That's no answer, she thought, nettled.

The streets in the lower city were narrow and crowded with traffic. "I'm enjoying this," she told him. Again he made an ambiguous reply. "Why not?" he said brightly.

She chose three paperbacks in swift succession while he watched. "Something to look at in bed," she said over her shoulder while she paid the woman.

"Good to have," he answered, and she turned further and glanced at him. His smile was there, but it said nothing.

"I'm glad to know about this place," she went on. "I'll come down again when I can look around."

"Take as long as you like."

She laughed and stepped ahead of him through the doorway. "I've got plenty for now," she told him. "I'm really delighted."

The car moved up a long steep ramp lined with palms and azaleas. At the top there was a park with a railing that ran along the edge of a cliff, where crowds of people leaned, looking down at the city in the haze below.

"You understand I've got to go to the hotel," she began, trying to make the words sound like a command and immediately aware of her failure.

"Look up there!" the young man said. He pointed to the summit of a steep green slope where a few dozen high pines grew; a large white building towered above them.

"I'm going to be a bore now," she warned him. "Is this the way to the hotel?"

"It's one way," he replied, turning toward her and shaking his head sadly. "You imagining what it would be like to be kidnaped? Snatched by somebody who hasn't got money on his mind at all, never gets in touch with anybody, just keeps you there, on and on? Now, *that* would be something to worry about."

"I'll worry about it when I come to it," she said crisply. "You mean you're taking a long way around; isn't that it?"

He looked at her again, this time with amazement. "You're a nervous one, aren't you? We've been gone about twenty minutes so far. We'll be back at the hotel in another twenty. How's that?"

"It's not tragic, I suppose. You did say ten originally, if you remember."

He finally spoke, after he had navigated the last hairpin curve. "Twenty minutes. Eighteen now. I give you my word."

They came out on top of the hill. The tall white building was an apartment house, and he stopped the car in front of it. Then he got out and came around to her door. "Come up for a minute. I want to get a jacket."

"What about the seventeen minutes?"

"That's only if you don't argue." He opened the door. She picked up her handbag and the parcel and got out. As they went into the building she had an impression of glass and metal, rocks and plants. In the elevator mirror she saw that her hair had been blown into an unrecognizable shape. "The wind has ruined me," she complained, fussing with it.

"You can fix it upstairs," he told her.

They went to the top. The door opened onto a patio where a jet of water splashed into a pool. There was a colonnade on the right, a short flight of steps to go down, and they walked into a vast room.

"It's breathtaking," she said; at the same time, her opinion of him dropped still further. She went slowly down the steps. "I'd hate to be responsible for keeping this place clean." She wanted him to know that she thought it impractical, absurd, for a young man to have such an excessively luxurious apartment.

She sat down. "It's all leather, fur and glass!" she exclaimed.

"There's no problem," he told her, looking mildly surprised. "The air's free of dust up here. What can I give you? Want to fix your hair? In there, through that door, and I'll make you a drink. A quick vodka martini?"

She gave a deliberately mirthless laugh. "Go on. I can't stop you."

The wall in front of her was entirely hidden by a barrage of trees and vines that reached to the ceiling; illumined dimly from within, it gave her the feeling of being at the edge of a forest. Sweet-smelling mountain air moved slowly through the room, stirring the upper tendrils and fronds. Somewhere out in the bright daylight a military band was playing; the distant sounds floated up on the breeze, now louder, now softer.

She ran her hand tentatively over the vicuña skin that covered the couch where she sat. Then she rose and went to arrange her hair in the little room he had indicated.

From some part of the apartment she heard the clear voice of a small child call out, "Where, Mommy?" Standing before the mirror, drawing her upper lip taut over her teeth as she applied her lipstick, she realized with faint astonishment that she had not foreseen a wife. Why not? she wondered.

There were sounds in the big room. "Your drink's here," he called.

"Well, that was quick!" She came out of the dressing room to join him.

He had his glass in his hand, was in fact already drinking from it. She lifted hers from the tray; it was very cold. "Come on outside," he told her.

On the terrace there was a grotto with a pool inside it, and a stream that ran in a crooked course, winding among the groups of chairs and tables. Below was the city with its far-off murmur, and on all sides the sky was cut across by the mountains' gray crests. "This is magnificent!" she exclaimed when they got to the edge and looked out.

He drained his glass. "When you've got the scenery in front of you, you take advantage of it, no?"

"You have a child here," she said; it was not a question, but its inflection demanded a reply. "I heard it talking."

"In this country you never know whether it's a child or a parrot," he told her, looking very serious.

"What *I* heard sounded very much like a child." She was not used to being put off in this manner.

"It probably was a child, then. There's one here. It's time to go. Seven minutes."

Before they got to the door, she took a last look around the terrace. "It gives me such a wonderful feeling of *freedom*," she said, and stepped inside.

They drove through a short stretch of forest, and down the side of the mountain to a boulevard that led to the hotel. This time she kept her hands over her hair. He drew up at the entrance and stopped the car.

"Have I been exact?" He looked at his wristwatch.

"Yes, indeed, you've been exact," she said, delighted with the episode, now that she was back and it was over. "And you've been very kind."

They got out and stood on the sidewalk in the sun. "How about tomorrow?" he said suddenly. "You and your husband. You and Dr. Slade. I'd like to have you meet Luchita."

"Oh," she said. "Yes. Well, when I've met *you*, maybe you can arrange it."

"The name's Soto." She had the impression that it was an unpleasant experience for him to have to pronounce it; at the same time he drew himself up and looked at her defiantly. "S—O—T—O. Easy. If we make it around six-thirty you'll get the sunset. Try and persuade the doctor. I'll pick you up right here. Why don't I phone you around ten tomorrow morning?"

"I think ten would be fine," she said.

He got into the car, backed, smiling at her, eased ahead, waved slowly once, and drove off. She heard him opening the motor up as the car sped down the boulevard.

On her way across the lobby the clerk at the newsstand called out to her, "That's a very fine young man, Mr. Soto!"

She glanced with apprehension around the lobby: it was as empty as it had been before. At least, she thought, if she went nearer to the counter he would lower his voice. "Yes?" she said, walking over to within a few paces of him.

"Ah, yes! A very important family. His father is Don José García Soto. But he don't like *him*." He smiled and shrugged; apparently that was the end of the story, even though the emphasis on the final "him" made its meaning ambiguous.

"His father doesn't like him, you mean?"

"No. He don't like *him*."

Since the words had been said in precisely the same way as before, she did not know whether to understand it as a correction or a reiteration. "Why not?" she asked him, thinking she might get at it that way.

He wagged his head from side to side. "Young man, he likes a good time. The old man, he don't go with that, he don't see it the same way. So what they going to do?"

Dr. Slade had taken a cab back to the hotel. In a quiet corner of the lounge, behind a screen of climbing plants, he caught sight of Mrs. Slade standing by a counter, engaged in conversation with the clerk. Always he made a point of leaving her the maximum of privacy and freedom of movement. And now, although he thought of joining her, he decided not to, and continued through the lobby to the elevators. As he stood waiting, a *botónes* in a brilliant green uniform came running up to him, crying, "*Señor!*"

He followed the boy back to the newsstand. While he bent to kiss her, she said with an admonitory smile, "I saw you sneak by."

They walked slowly through the lobby.

"Better today?"

"Yes. I'm fine. I had a ride."

"Who with? Where to?"

She sighed. It seemed suddenly tedious to have to tell the story. "Somebody. I don't know. His name is Soto."

"Well, well!" He smiled at her, and as always she was aware of the beam of ownership in his eyes. "Why don't we eat? Do you want to go up to your room first?"

"No."

"I'm going up for a minute," he told her. "I'll be right down."

His bedroom had been made up; there was a bowl of wine-colored dahlias on the coffee table. He noted with approval that the window had been left open and the curtains drawn. *El Globo* lay on the desk. He folded and refolded it, until he had made it as small as possible. Then he took it out onto the balcony and dropped it over the railing. He watched it hit the paving stones below. The leaves of the trees down there glistened in the midday sunlight.

At lunchtime the hotel's dining room was crowded with the sleek upper-class local population. "Here where they don't need it they've got air conditioning," Dr. Slade remarked. Because he felt well, he was still delighted with the climate. "It's like a spring day out."

"Ideal," she agreed. "He had an open car, and I'm already dead. I got to sleep sometime this morning."

"Not again!" he said, frowning.

"No," she corrected him. "I *slept*, at least. Night before last I didn't sleep."

"You may have dropped off even then," he said in a matter-of-fact tone. "It often happens during those bad nights. Only you don't remember it."

Not listening, she went back to eating her melon.

"Who's this who took you in his car?"

She ran through the principal points in the encounter. "He's invited us out for drinks with them tomorrow night."

Dr. Slade frowned again. She knew him well enough to be certain he was thinking that people ought to be thoroughly scrutinized before one accepted invitations from them. "Well," he said, "if you've just been there, I should think it would be better to have them here, wouldn't it?"

Up until then she had felt indifferent to the invitation. Now that he seemed on the point of refusing it, she found that on the contrary she was rather eager to go. "They have a spectacular apartment. I just got a glimpse of it for a minute. We stopped on the way up from the bookstore. I didn't even see *her*."

When lunch was over, they went upstairs. She slept immediately. At four o'clock she was up, tapping on his door.

"Let's go out for a walk this minute while the sun's still shining," she said, peering into his room from the corridor.

The hotel was not far from the edge of town. From a pavilion in a park higher up they watched the sun set behind the mountains and the valley come alive with the lights of the capital.

"The city looks so small, doesn't it, in the middle of all these mountains," she said with wonder.

"There's supposed to be a pretty good nightclub, called the Costa de Oro," he told her. They never went out at night without having a lengthy discussion afterwards whose point was to prove that the excursion had been an indefensible waste of time and money.

"It might be fun some night," she said uncertainly. Then she added in a hearty voice, "Tonight I'm going to sleep or know the reason why."

"Of course, you've got to sleep," he said gravely.

The early night wind, spiced with the smell of pine, had begun to stir through the valley. They shivered and started to walk briskly down the hill; on the way out of the park they found a taxi.

Two

12

W HAT had happened was that Luchita, unusually ingenuous for her seventeen years, had made a serious miscalculation. To her it had seemed reasonable, and therefore likely, that if Vero were willing to supply fifty dollars a week and allow Pepito and her to live with him, Señor Guzman, who was middle-aged and much more difficult in his demands, would at least furnish her fare back to Paris. Thus, observing what she imagined was the greatest secrecy, she had "escaped" from Vero and gone to live with Señor Guzman. (Even now, when she had been back at Vero's for three weeks, she did not know that Vero and Señor Guzman had discussed the switch in detail before the idea of making it had occurred to her.) All she had to show for her trouble was three pairs of shoes, a wristwatch, and a transistor tape recorder covered in lizard skin; and although Señor Guzman had pointed out to her that the aggregate value of these items was a good deal more than the seventy-five dollars a week he had vaguely mentioned at the outset, she had decided after a fortnight to return to Vero.

He took her back into the household with good grace, but in the meantime he had made some new laws. Pepito was to sleep in one of the servants' rooms and at no time was to be allowed beyond the kitchen, while she, instead of occupying the big blue room with her favorite bathroom, was to share Vero's room with him. She had objected strongly to this last provision; not that she minded the loss of privacy, but the arrangement clearly lowered her bargaining power. However, the situation at Señor Guzman's had been growing steadily more unbearable; twice he had found her *yerba* and thrown it out, so that she had had to spend a lot of time and money getting more, and when Pepito had tossed his iron locomotive and broken the big mirror in the dining room, Señor Guzman had hit him in the face with the back of his hand, so hard that the big diamond ring had cut his cheek. While she was crying in her room afterwards, she had decided that there was something wrong with Señor Guzman and that it would be better for her to get out of his house.

The day she had gone back to see Vero she had done without smoking for hours beforehand, trying to plan the course of the conversation they would have, at the same time certain that however it went, it would be completely different from the way she was imagining it. This proved to be the case. He merely nodded his head now and then while she was talking, and suddenly expounded the new laws which would apply if she returned. Then he held his cigarette case in front of her, snapped it open, and said, "The filter tips." And she pulled out a fat grifa and lit it. Afterwards she thought it had been this gesture which had made her decide to accept the new laws and the change in her status they implied. It was impossible to live with a man who never smoked anything but tobacco, who hated even the smell of marijuana and could detect it in the air an hour afterward, and who thought he had the right to go through her bags in his search for hidden stores of it.

Before the "escape," the rule with Vero had been three times a week. She never knew which nights, because sometimes he liked them one after the other, and sometimes he spaced them. Now that she was going to sleep in his room, she suspected that she would have no more free nights at all.

The evening of her return they were talking across the space between the two beds. "I want you to be civilized," he was telling her. "That means you should do exactly as you feel like doing. But you have to *know* you want to do it, and know *why* you want to, too."

"I know what I want," she said, blinking her eyes. "I want to go to Paris. But I'm not civilized, am I? Because I haven't got the money for the ticket. *La plata, hombre, la plata!*"

"I'm trying to explain something and you're wailing about Paris. Why don't we finish one thing first?"

"You want to finish something?" she demanded fiercely. "I want to finish something, too. I want to say goodbye to this lousy country. The people! The way they act! *Petits bourgeois!* Pah!" She raised herself and remained leaning on one elbow. "If it's true you want to see me be civilized, you know how to do it. Let me go to Paris. I don't care if it's on a ship, tourist class. If you want to see me lying dead, leave me here longer, that's all."

Luchita had learned English in her native Havana; Spanish she spoke here only with the servants, and occasionally when she had smoked heavily and was feeling exceptionally *cotorra*. This was not the case tonight; the effects of her morning grifas were dissipated, and with an eye to being as astute as possible in the argument she expected, she had not smoked since lunch.

"You won't listen! You won't let me talk!" he was complaining. Then he lowered his voice. "You know what I was really talking about? You *want* to know?"

"Yes," she said in a small voice, but guardedly.

"I was trying to say that whenever you want to go to the Embajadores or the Tahiti or any of those places, go ahead. If you really want to go and you know why, then go on. When you'd rather stay here and be with me, here I am!" He held out his arms as if in expectation of an embrace.

She smiled. "That's very sweet," she said, lying down, talking into the pillow. "You do trust me, Vero."

"Of course I do. I practically always have."

She sat up again. "Well, thank God!" she cried with feeling, and slowly let her head fall back onto the pillow.

"I don't trust all of *them*, I can tell you that," he went on. "Not when they buy a hundred dollars' worth of pictures all at once. Come on!" he said, angry suddenly that she should be making sounds of protest. "I saw him. I saw where his hand was. I don't have to listen to anything."

"Because you think the pictures stink," she said bitterly.

He was dramatically silent for a moment. "Have I ever said they stank?"

"But you can't believe somebody could like them."

"Not that much, no! There's a limit to everything."

"Well, thank God Mr. Mason's limit's not your limit. At least I'm a hundred dollars nearer to Paris."

"What is it? Can't you wait till June? Or don't you believe me, or what?"

"How do I know what to believe?" she demanded fiercely. "You say you'll have it. But you said that before and you didn't have it."

"I'll have it," he said quietly.

She lay on her stomach and kicked her feet up and down in the air. "Oh, if I could really be sure!" she cried. "You know I'd stay every night with you, and the hell with the pictures." She sat up once more and looked across at him. "But I can't be sure! I've got to keep going until I see the ticket in my hand."

"You're free, tan, and seventeen," he said. "You do just what you feel you ought to do."

"Wait." She slid down off the bed, put on a peignoir and went out to the kitchen. Pepito's room gave onto a narrow corridor beyond.

She opened the door; Pepito was sleeping. From the bookcase she took a small metal box and carried it back with her into the bedroom. The jazz was playing very softly behind the plants on the terrace. She got into his bed beside him and took a cigarette from the box. It was one of the last batch she had rolled, two days before, at Señor Guzman's.

"I'm sleepy," she told him. "I'm going to turn on a little. I can go to the Embajadores tomorrow."

Later, a little before daybreak, she murmured, "I do love you, Vero, and Pepito loves you too. Why won't you be sweet to us? Why?"

She had long been aware that these attempts at persuasion, ill-timed or not, were useless, but the image kept suggesting itself to her: she was letting herself into the apartment with her own keys because she was the *señora*, and Pepito was running in to meet her from the big terrace, where even at the beginning he had never been allowed to go.

"You know the whole goddamned story," he said yawning. "You wouldn't even have your fifty a week."

"Don José García Soto," she intoned scornfully. "The lousy *bourgeois*! Do I talk about my grandfather's uncle? He was the Cardinal Gonsalvez y Alcántara, and so what?"

"So he knows you're from a good family. Jesus!" He was silent an instant before going on. "Can't you understand he doesn't give a shit *who* you are? He doesn't like you. It's simple."

"You don't have to use that talk with me."

She knew she was not going to be able to extend the argument into new territory, into regions that had not already been covered on other occasions, but the subject was always there, and it was irresistible. "Because I don't hang furs on me like the *putas* at his house."

"Yes! You've said it!" he cried. "A lot of it's the way you look. You had time to change the other night. You didn't have to come in to dinner with dirt on your face, and wearing those stinking Levis. You're just a lazy little slut."

She hit him with her fist on the shoulder as hard as she could, sprang out of bed, and stood there naked, looking down at him. "You take his side now," she whispered, as if the thought were more than she could bear. "I knew you were just like him."

"Agh!" he said with disgust, and rolled over to sleep.

Luchita got into her bed. Listening to the sounds of the waking city, she thought once again about Paris.

13

Other nights since then had been much the same; she did go a few times to the nightclubs and even managed to sell several more pictures, although she told Vero it had been only two. It seemed logical to her that the less she appeared to be earning, the more generous he would be when the moment came to supply her with passage money to Paris. As the days went by, she found herself almost believing him when he assured her that the money was going to be available. There was no single reason for the change in the way she felt; it could have been a combination of several things. Vero had never talked with her very much in any case, but now he spoke practically not at all unless they were in bed. He would lie naked on the terrace all day, reading; then he would dress and go out with friends to dinner, and she would not see him until he came home to bed. Twice he had taken her out to a Chinese roadhouse at kilometer 12 on the highway. She had enjoyed the dancing after dinner, but the clientele was pitifully provincial; she told him so, and it put him into a bad humor.

During the most recent days, Vero had been seeing a good deal more of Thorny, whom she disliked increasingly. "I hate the way he smiles," she told Vero. "Thank God Pepito lives

with the servants. At least he can't see Thorny." Then she
added suspiciously, "What does he want?"

"Want? He doesn't want anything as far as I know. I'm taking him down to the ranch this weekend."

She looked at him unbelievingly. "Vero, you're crazy," she
declared. "Why do you want to take him down there?"

"Because he's working for me. Is that important to you?"

Luchita was contemptuous. "Work? What sort of work
could Thorny do? He's never worked in his life."

"Yes, yes, yes. I know," Vero said patiently. "For the record,
he did have a job once at Radio Nacional. But anyway, he's
got one now for a few weeks. He's going to put in the sound
system for me."

"Thorny?"

"He's going to supervise, for God's sake! Make them follow my instructions. If they're left alone there, they'll do it all
ass backwards. What difference does it make to you whether
Thorny's down at the ranch or not?"

"I don't like him," she said simply.

He laughed. "You're not going to be there."

"Me at San Felipe? I'd rather be in jail!"

He looked at her darkly. "You seemed to enjoy yourself all
right."

She was evasive. "Snakes and centipedes, and the vines always slap you in the face. And so hot, my God!" She opened
her mouth and gasped, remembering it.

"You never saw a snake the whole time you were there."

"I saw a centipede."

"It's an old house. They're in the foundation."

"In this country," she told him, "there's only one thing
worse than the mountains, and that's your lousy *tierra
caliente.*"

Thorny came at eight on Friday morning. They took the
station wagon because they were going to pick up farm imple-
ments and parts for a new generator on the way out of the city.
As soon as Vero had left, Luchita went hunting through his
bedroom and bathroom, collecting her things. She had decided to sleep on the couch in Pepito's room for the two
nights, and she wanted to move her effects quickly, before
Paloma, the housemaid, saw her and got her into conversation

about her reasons. When she was alone she smoked more, out of nervousness. But the result of the smoking was to make her apprehensive; she knew she would sleep better locked into the little room with Pepito than by herself in the big bedroom where the masses of plants and the high screens frightened her.

When she had carried everything through the apartment to Pepito's room, she lay back on the couch against the cushions and lit a grifa. Pepito was kneeling on a chair opposite, playing with something on the table.

"Mommy, what's this?"

She looked up through the smoke and saw that he had found her handbag and was holding up some partially folded banknotes.

"What do you mean, what is it? It's money. Put it back."

"I know," he said, suddenly looking worldly-wise. "If we had money we'd go to Paris, wouldn't we?"

She stared at him in admiration; for a boy of five he was quick.

"You remember Paris: *Abuelita* and the bird in the cage?" she said hopefully.

"No."

"The green bird that used to say, '*Apaga la luz, hombre!*' And everybody used to laugh? You remember him."

"I do not!" Pepito said, looking intently at her.

"It was only a year ago." She fell silent, to think about Paris. In a moment she rose, picked up her handbag, and walked across the room.

"Where are you going?" His voice was sharp with resentment.

"Out on the terrace."

"Why can't I go? Why?"

"You stop that. Let go of me!" His fingernails scratched against the rough material of her blue jeans as he clung to her leg. The force of her push threw him off balance; he fell over backward onto the floor. Slowly he sat up, rubbing the back of his head, his face preparing for tears.

It was hot on the terrace; she lay on a couch with a wide canopy over it, writing a letter to her mother in Paris. Everything was fine at the nightclub where she worked, she said, and by summer she would surely have enough saved up to come home. In a little while she got up and went to the kitchen to get a glass of water. Vero, of course, would have rung for it, but she did not like to give orders to the servants; she merely let them know when she was ready to eat. With the cold water inside her, she returned to the terrace and finished her letter. Then she lay back and daydreamed a while, enjoying the first passage of the breeze that announced the possible advent of rain. When she went in for lunch, the cumulus clouds had advanced and expanded upward from all sides into what remained of the clear sky above.

She and Pepito had their sandwiches and salad at the table in the little bedroom. She had trained him to go directly from lunch to bed for his nap, principally because she herself could not do without a siesta at that hour. She sat on the couch reading for a few minutes after he was quiet, and then she stretched out and fell asleep.

The awakening from a heavy afternoon slumber is slow. She had seen Pepito go out of the room, she had heard the rain splattering on the balcony, and then she had been asleep again, perhaps for a long time. Next, Pepito was pushing his fingers into her neck. "Mommy! Mommy! Telephone!"

She stood up and staggered out into the kitchen. Paloma sat at the big table in the center, pointing to the corner of the room. She went over and picked up the receiver. It was Vero.

"What's the matter?" she said.

She could hear him laughing. "I just wanted to say Hi! See how you were. We're in Mi Cielo, you remember? The little cantina on the plaza. Got in here about fifteen minutes ago." They talked a little. Behind his voice, in the background, a church bell had begun to ring. She heard it booming through the air, above the noises of the bar. "See you around eight tomorrow night," he told her, and hung up.

She walked past Paloma, smiling self-consciously, and on into the library, where she stood gazing out at the terrace awash with rain under the dark sky. The air beyond the windows had become a gray expanse of falling water. "The rain is raining all around," she recalled. She had liked the verses as a child when she was learning English; they had made the rain into a friendly phenomenon. Here they meant nothing; it was a different kind of rain, violent and menacing.

In her head she could still hear the deep, full-throated sound of the church bell. But San Felipe was a village with one small church, and she knew the sound of its bell. It had a high, cracked ring like a metal pipe clanging, more like an alarm than a church bell. Vero was not in San Felipe at all. Where he might be she had no idea, but she knew it was not San Felipe Tonatan. She was thinking only that he had lied to her and she did not know why. I'm glad he won't marry me, she told herself.

14

He got back a little after seven on Sunday evening. Luchita was sitting in Pepito's room reading when she heard him come in. As he entered the kitchen a moment later, he shouted to someone, "Go on outside! I'll be right out." Pepito had already rushed into the kitchen to meet him. She put the book down and stepped into the bathroom, where she stood before the mirror combing her hair. How am I going to look at him? she thought. It was as if she had been the one who had lied, rather than he. Then she heard him come into the bedroom, and she opened the door and walked toward him, still running the comb through her hair.

"Hi, Chita!" he cried, seizing her arm and spinning her around to kiss her. She submitted miserably, not looking into his eyes.

"How's everything?" he said.

She looked toward him but not at him. "Fine. Who's that with you?"

"Just Thorny."

"But I thought he was staying down at the ranch."

"He's going back down in a day or two." He let go of her, and she started back toward the bathroom.

"Where the hell's everybody?" he shouted from the kitchen. "Where's Manuel?"

"You said you'd come at eight, and I told them," she called. She could not hear the words of his reply, but their tone seemed to express dissatisfaction. A moment later she heard him putting bottles and glasses on a tray. Pepito was helping; he cried, "This one, Vero?"

"Pepito!" she called. When he appeared in the doorway she said, "Now you take your bath. I'll be back in fifteen minutes."

"I want to help Vero," he complained.

She seized him and pulled his shirt off over his head. Then she began to draw the water in the tub. "Where are you going?" he demanded. Thinking once again about the church bell, she did not answer. Because he was slow in undressing, she lent a hand; when he was naked, she patted him on the buttocks and pointed at the clock on the shelf. "Fifteen minutes," she repeated, and went out.

Vero was carrying the tray through the kitchen. "Bring some crackers and stuff," he told her.

It was warm on the terrace. Thorny stood at the edge, looking over the railing. The night sky was blue, crowded with stars, the mountains were black, and the long strands of street lamps were draped like cobwebs of light all across the valley below. Luchita walked over to the edge and leaned against the railing. "Hello," she said, looking toward Thorny. He was wearing a sweatshirt with a blazer over it, and his hair was rumpled.

"Oh," he said. "Hi, Luchita." He sighed deeply.

"You sick, or you just feel gloomy?" she inquired turning around and facing the terrace. He did not move.

"It isn't that, baby!" His voice was deep, and so husky as to be almost a whisper. "No, not gloomy! I just feel bad all over inside." He ran his hand vaguely down his torso.

"What'd you eat?" she demanded.

Vero came over with a drink for Thorny. "This'll help. Thorny's upset, that's all. We hit a dog and we heard it yelling while it died."

"Who was driving?" Vero glanced toward her, but there was not enough light for her to see the expression on his face.

"*He* was driving! That's why he's upset," Vero said sharply; she could see that he did not want to talk about it, so she said no more. But she thought: He lets that maniac drive the station wagon.

Thorny turned to Luchita. "Baby, it was a terrible thing. A dog, yes; I know. But it's *life*, baby. It's life! Each time he screamed, a little of his life came out. And then it was gone. It made me feel bad, I don't know, to think that's all life is."

"Well, yes," said Luchita vaguely. "You can't tell. Maybe it isn't always that bad. Some people never even know they're dying."

"Or maybe it's worse," said Vero. "The dog was dead in five seconds. Who could ask for better than that?"

"You can't measure it!" Thorny cried in a stage whisper. "Five seconds, five years, forever! I swear to you, I'll *never* forget it!" He hesitated. Luchita took advantage of the break to observe, "Forever! Don't worry. *Your* life's not going to be so long."

Thorny had started to go on, but at the same instant Vero interrupted: "How's your drink? Can I fill it up?" He was squinting at Thorny's glass, trying to see the level in it. "What's the matter with you?" he cried. "Why aren't you drinking? Until you drink you're going to go on talking about it. Nobody wants to hear you talk about it." He said the last words a little more slowly. "You know?"

Thorny coughed, stood up straight, and drank.

"I think you got too much sun," Vero told him. "Why don't you sit down?"

Thorny finished his drink and held out his glass for more.

They listened while a plane flew over; when its roar had become only a reverberation passing farther down the valley, Thorny said, "Put on the new Cecil Taylor."

"Give me the glass." Vero filled it again, set the shaker down, and went inside. Luchita hummed for an instant. Then she said, "What's the matter with you?"

"I'm tired. The heat was rough." Faint strains of music began to come from behind the plants.

As Vero came back onto the terrace he called, "Thorny! Come and sit down. Or lie here and put your feet up."

Luchita went to the kitchen. Manuel and Paloma sat in a flood of fluorescent light at the table, talking. "*Buenas noches,*" they said.

Pepito was still in the tub, squeezing soapsuds from a washcloth. As she pulled out the plug and the water began to suck into the drainpipe, she heard the telephone ringing.

"Mommy, did Vero see any rattlesnakes?"

"I'll ask him," she said.

"Did he see any iguanas?"

"How do I know what he saw?" She was trying to get him dry with the damp towel. "Ask him tomorrow. They hit a dog on the way home. That's all he said."

"Oh!" Pepito was shocked.

"Thorny was driving," she went on quickly. "Vero couldn't do anything about it."

"Ah." He was relieved. "Vero wouldn't run over a dog, would he?"

She was sorry she had mentioned it. "It was an accident, Pepito. Get into your pajamas."

When Pepito was finally in bed and silenced, she went back out onto the terrace. Thorny lay in a swing couch, lightly swaying, listening to the jazz. He got up as she approached and put his forefinger conspiratorially to his lips. Taking her arm, he walked with her over to the parapet.

"Listen! Don't go inside. He's just had bad news. His mother's dead."

"His mother?" She was silent for a moment. Then, trying to unfasten his fingers from around her arm, she turned to face him, and cried, "Why shouldn't I go in?" She pulled away and ran a few steps, then walked the rest of the way to the library door. It was dark inside.

Vero lay on a couch staring upward, his hands behind his head. When she first went into the room she could scarcely see him. He turned toward her. "Did Thorny tell you?"

"Yes. I'm sorry, Vero. I'm very sorry."

"I just came in here for a few minutes. I wanted to be by myself."

"I know!" she cried, and, in spite of herself she reached down suddenly and seized his head in her two hands to kiss his forehead and cheeks. Then she stood up without saying any more and started to walk away.

"You and Thorny go ahead with dinner. I'll have something later."

At this she stood still and turned around. "You said he wasn't staying to dinner," she said in a stage whisper. "Why can't he go out?"

Vero looked at her in the way she did not like. "He's sick. Can't you see that? He should eat and go to bed. He's sleeping in the little bedroom tonight."

"Why can't he go home? It's not so far."

"Because I want him here in the morning, early."

She stepped nearer to the couch. "I'm not going to eat with him," she declared, still in her stage whisper.

He sprang up and seized her wrist, forcing her to be motionless for a moment. "Yes, you are." He looked at her steadily. "You're going to see that he gets to bed afterward, too. Jesus Christ! Is that so much to do for a man when his mother dies?"

Luchita shut her eyes and opened them. "I didn't mean to argue. I'm sorry. Lie down. I'll take care of him."

"Come back in when he's gone to bed. I'll be home by then."

"You're going out?"

"To the police station for a minute."

"Poor Vero," she said, shaking her head.

Manuel had set a formal table in the dining room. Apart from the candles, the only light came from behind the thicket of bamboo which filled one end of the room. While they were having soup they heard Vero go out. Luchita's spirits sank. Poor, poor Vero, she thought; the idea of having any sort of contact with the police filled her with dread. It did not occur to her to wonder why they wanted to see him.

Thorny, in spite of being a little drunk, still seemed depressed. In a way, that was fortunate, because he was less likely to talk. In any case, it was her duty to get through the meal somehow. When it was over, she reflected that he had not once spoken about the dog. And she hoped it was partly her doing. She wanted to help Vero however she could; to feel that she had done even that much made her happy.

They stood beside the table. "Well, good night," she said. "I know you want to go to bed. I've got to go and look at Pepito."

She did not hear any reply, but she turned and went through the pantry into the kitchen. When she came back with her cigarette-rolling machine, he had gone into his room.

Out on the terrace the jazz was still playing. She let herself drop onto a mattress beside the swimming pool and began to make grifas to pass the time. The young frogs Vero had put into the smaller pool on the west terrace tried to croak, gave up, tried again. When she had five grifas prepared, she heard the library door shut.

"Vero?"

He came out and stood looking down at her, his hands in his pockets. "Well, that's that, at least," he said.

She moved over and touched the mattress beside her, and he sat down. "Wait," she said. She held a match to one of the cigarettes and handed it to him; then she lit another for herself and waited for him to speak. The minutes went past; the music played and the frogs chirped. When she had finished her cigarette she said, "What did the police want?"

He sighed. "They called about my mother. They wanted me to go down and look at something. I had to sign a paper."

"What for?"

"She died here. That's the point."

"Here!" Luchita's eyes opened very wide. She had seen many photographs of Vero's formidable mother; the thought of her being nearby, even in death, filled her with awe. (When she was really surprised, he thought fleetingly, she was cuter than at any other time. He wished he had waited until bedtime to tell her.)

"Well, not up here. Puerto Farol. I went down there to meet her." He flicked his butt into the air; it made a bright arc and disappeared over the edge of the building. Some day he would hit somebody and there would be trouble, she had repeatedly told him. Neither one spoke for a while. Then Luchita began excitedly, "But why'd you say you were going to the ranch? I knew you weren't in San Felipe. Why'd you lie to me?"

He hesitated. "I was going to surprise you," he said. "Meet her and bring her up."

Another lie, she thought. He would never even have let his mother know she existed, much less have brought her to the apartment while she was in it.

"You didn't meet her?"

"No," he said hopelessly.

She waited before she said, "But what happened?"

With a convulsive movement he stretched out beside her, looking toward her, his face twisted into what resembled an expression of agony.

"God! There was a fire! In the hotel! They brought up her gold mirror and some jewelry. I had to identify them." He was silent a while; then he turned slowly over onto his back. "It was a favor."

"What was a favor?"

"They let me do it here. Otherwise I'd have had to go all the way down to Puerto Farol."

"I see," she said with a sour smile. "Because you're you."

"It's a favor I appreciate," he said defensively.

"Yes. It wouldn't be the same down there a second time."

He looked at her.

"I mean, you had it the first time."

"Oh, God! *Had* it!" He put his arm over his eyes and left it there. "I got conscious around twilight, I remember, and we drove back into town. I know we went swimming. It was too late then even to go and see her at the Independencia. If I'd only met her at the boat she would never have been in the hotel at all."

"But what *happened*?" she said impatiently.

"Well, we were at one of those rat-hole cantinas on the waterfront. Some hacendero walks in. I've seen him here in town. He's telling us: *Hombre*, my finca's only six minutes from town, and so on. All right, we'll go to the finca. It's in the jungle. Not six minutes, of course. It's about twenty-five, a track full of mud and bushes, terrible! So we see the finca and his friends come in from other fincas and it's a big party. A long party. The boat anchored at seven the next morning, and I was asleep all day. I'd missed the boat anyway, and she was already in the hotel. I couldn't go and have her see me the way I was. I thought I'd wait and see her here."

"Oh, Vero! You didn't meet her, and then you just turned around and came back! That's terrible!"

"Ah," he said, almost with satisfaction. "You understand what I'm talking about, why I feel the way I do."

"Yes, but you shouldn't think it's your fault. That's not true, baby."

She lit another grifa and was silent while she smoked it. "It's lucky you didn't really care much about her," she said after reflection. "Think how much more you'd mind."

"My God! Your mother's your mother! Can't you see the shock would be just as great, no matter how you *felt* about her?"

Luchita shook her head in a matter-of-fact manner. "No. It would be worse. You don't know. You never loved your mother. You told me yourself."

"What's that got to do with it?" he cried. "It's much more than that. She's inside you! And when she dies something happens. It's the way life is made, that's all."

Luchita was thinking of her own mother in Paris. "Of course. But if you love her too, it's worse when she dies."

"You've got no mind," Vero said with finality.

The pile of records had given out; only the sound of the frogs remained.

"Thorny went to bed right after dinner," she told him.

"Did he go on with the dog business?"

"No," she said proudly. "He just ate his dinner."

He stood up and stretched. "He's tired out. It's a long drive up. You want to make me a sandwich?"

"You stay here," she said, happy to be put to use. "I'll bring everything."

"Bring it to bed. I'm going in."

15

With Luchita there were no scenes of flirtation, no voluptuous undressings; she kept him at arm's length until they were there, side by side, in the bed. Tenderness between them she could accept only as a by-product of love-making. Sometimes he tried merely looking at her steadily across the table, or from the other side of the room; she pretended not to notice, but always she ended by showing an emotional reaction of some kind, so that he felt he had at least partially imposed his will. However, she made it clear that she considered these tactics unfair, an invasion of her privacy. And yet, when the moment came, no one could be so carefree and passionate. It was an unalloyed blessing to be with her. Thus he was continually weighing the hindrances against the advantages. Making it possible for her to get back to Paris seemed safe enough: she was going back to face a degree of poverty she had not yet known. Soon she would be clamoring for a short vacation with him. At that time he would decide whether he really wanted her with him again or not, whether or not the intimacy he had to do without in his daily life was compensated for by the unusually high quality of her performance in bed.

Normally there were neither big days nor small ones in Grove's calendar. What he had had in mind when he had fitted together the various possibilities that would form and maintain his present life was an eternally empty schedule in which he would enjoy the maximum liberty to make sudden decisions. He wanted the basic pattern of each day to be as much as possible like that of the one before it. Friends and servants presented no problem; his father and Luchita, on the other hand, in all innocence did interfere occasionally with the smooth functioning of his personal pattern. This was to be expected: the one supplied him with money and the other with pleasure. But as a permanent situation it was unacceptable. To have moral support he had encouraged Thorny to forsake Canada and come to live in the capital. Thorny was a ruin, but so had he been during their student days together, and since he was quick, intuitive, and appreciative of every facet of Grove's personality (without, however, being easy to manipulate), it was natural for Grove to have decided to make him available. He wanted to have him around—in the background, but nearby. Each time old Señor Soto threatened to precipitate a crisis, or the struggle with Luchita grew too acute to go on bearing without a hiatus, he would get hold of Thorny, and they would go off somewhere together. Because Thorny's monthly income was barely sufficient to pay for a cheap apartment and the simple food he ate in it, he was always ready to accept an invitation; the more involved the expedition and the longer it took, the more money he had left when he returned to wait for his next check to arrive from home. Although Señor Soto and Luchita seldom were of the same opinion on anything, both objected strongly to Thorny, and for the same reasons. "Can't you see when a man is taking advantage of you?" demanded old Señor Soto. It seemed to him that Thorny's influence was not a civilizing one in Grove's life. And Luchita: "That bum! He thinks this is a hotel. You encourage him."

The present project had presented itself rather suddenly and was not a direct outgrowth of domestic pressures. It was only about three weeks earlier that the idea had occurred to him. There was work being done on the ranch at San Felipe. He would tell Luchita he was going there, and instead slip down to Puerto Farol with Thorny for a day or two.

The trip could be successful only if he made it in a state of absolute calm. This tranquility was something he had studied to attain. It was fairly easy: using an empirical system of auto-hypnosis he obliged himself to believe that the present was already past, that what he felt himself to be doing he had already done before, so that present action became merely a kind of playback of the experience. By ridding himself of all sense of immediacy with his surroundings, he was able to remain impervious to them.

However, when he had set the calming apparatus in motion he became untalkative. Thorny knew all about it; he had noticed that the functioning of the device made Grove silent and morose. It was an unimportant concomitant of the process whereby Grove assumed certain attributes of superhumanity; there was no question of his infallibility at such times. Knowing that the master was going to be operating under pressure, Thorny was prepared for an unpleasant journey.

They drove down the highway under the hanging orchids, a *mejorana* wailing into their faces from the radio panel. The day was clear, the air light. When they got into the lowlands the giant sky turned gray. There were stretches where the road was narrow and curving, and the vegetation, reaching out from both sides, hit the car and scraped along its body. The back of Grove's shirt was wet and cold; he turned and saw the sweat running down the plastic fabric of the cushion. The hot filthy villages went past, the forest between them black and rotting.

Now that the trip was all over, he lay on the fur under the frozen menace of the plants, his hands behind his head, triumphant at having managed so far not to have reviewed even once any of its details. When the telephone call came from the police he thought only of how he was going to behave in front of Luchita. "Tell her, but keep her away from me for a while if you can," he said to Thorny; but he was not surprised when she had sought him out immediately, as soon as she had heard. He had not had time; he had had to play it by ear. Still he did not think he had done too badly, and when he returned from his visit to police headquarters he resolved to go ahead in the same improvised vein of behavior. It seemed to him that tonight could prove to be one of their really good nights; her tender outburst upon hearing about his mother suggested that.

In the dimness of the room, while Luchita looked for food in the kitchen, he lay on the bed and considered his reflection. He had installed electrically adjustable mirrors in place of the headboard and footboard—ridiculous gadgets that he sometimes set up to amuse Luchita during their bed games. Since her return from Señor Guzman's he had been prudent enough to refrain from using them. Tonight?

There was no mystery; it was perfectly clear to him, as he followed the line of his cheeks and chin down to his neck and shoulders, why any girl would be happy to be in bed with him. He grinned lasciviously into the mirror of the footboard. Faintly he heard the kitchen sounds. It was his habit to stay away from that part of the house. In spite of all the white enamel and conspicuous hygiene, there was always a hint of the sour smell of garbage out there, as though rotten papaya rinds might be lying behind the doors. And then there was the boy.

After he had eaten, many grifas were smoked, the Baluba drummers played behind the bamboo plants, the mirrors tilted and flashed, the night was transformed. Eden on all sides, with him at the heart of it.

Although he was aware that all was well because he was in the big bed and had Luchita with him, pressed against him all the way down to his faraway feet, nevertheless he dreamed he was lying face down on a narrow cot. The two glass walls on either side of his mattress met in a point, not far from the pillow where his head lay. It was like having a bed that was fitted into the prow of a ship, save that he was poised high above an illimitable city whose streets were so far below that the traffic which filled them was soundless.

Attached to the cot by a complicated chromium fixture was an outsize Easter egg made of sparkling pink and white sugar crystals, and lighted from within. He peered into the lens at the end of the egg: a television program was being flashed across a surface which, thanks to the extraordinary amplifying power of the tiny lens, proved to be an enormous screen in a darkened hall full of spectators.

He had got in at the beginning of a program. As the music blared, he raised himself slightly off the cot and glanced behind him. Through the glass walls at the footboard he saw the actual hall below; the glass cage was one of several hundred such cells, a honeycomb of niches built into the walls of the auditorium. Now that he was sitting up, he felt dizzy. He lay down again and tried to make himself comfortable. Before adjusting the angle of the egg to his eye, he examined a group of three small press-buttons arranged in a vertical row at the side of the lens. Keeping his finger on the top button, he arranged the angle of the egg and peered through the lens once more. Credits were still unfolding on the screen. As the first image came on, he pressed the button.

Immediately he knew that the little sugar egg was a priceless gadget. There was a slight whirring, as of a generator being set in motion, and the already extremely dim lights in the auditorium were further lowered momentarily. Then they slowly returned to their former intensity. The important point was that the machine gave him the illusion of actually standing in the auditorium. It occurred to him that it would be a triumph if he could arrange to unscrew the egg from the fixture and take it with him when he left.

It was then that he felt terror, sat up, and lifted his hand above his head. His fingers touched the glass before he had stretched his arm very far. It was a box, this chamber where he lay. He was enclosed; there was no air-conditioning panel. And he was convinced that the air was already growing heavy and foul; he imagined he could detect the stink of his own breath. He lay down again, vastly depressed but in the particular state of paralyzed acceptance which the dreamer does not combat. There was a faint but distinct smell of ozone coming, as in a fine spray, from the direction of the egg. The first button was still down. Suddenly he understood that the buttons constituted an escape; they provided an exit to be used in emergencies. He looked again into the egg and straightway had the illusion of being in the auditorium, standing back in the dark at the head of an interminable aisle. Beyond was the screen. Staring up at the great bright rectangle now for the first time, he saw the face of a well-known, faded, middle-aged actress; he could not remember her name. The thirty-foot-high figure stood there sadly, her hair disheveled, in the pathetic role of a distraught matron. There was a strong flavor of remonstrance in her voice. He noticed that she had made even the single word *yes* sound recriminatory.

Repelled by the character she was playing but fascinated by the quality of the acting, he began to walk down the aisle. An end seat was empty. As he sat down he was aware of a certain agitation in the audience. The woman on the screen was pointing with her forefinger; suddenly he saw her in the flesh, tiny and down at one side of the screen, with brilliant spotlights focused on her head. He watched the small bright figure raise its arms as if welcoming the audience, and he had an unreasonable conviction that things were going to go badly from this moment on. Stealthily he stretched out his hand and felt along the armrest of his seat. The top button was still depressed; he waited an instant, trying to understand what the actress was saying. It was a complaint; she sobbed, her words were unintelligible and the inflections of her voice were growing hysterical. And constantly the music was rising in volume and dramatic intensity. If it went on, he would be paralyzed, unable even to push a button. Carefully he moved his finger a half-inch along the surface of the armrest until it touched the second button. He hesitated an instant, and then he pushed it down with a click.

The actress screamed and twitched, as though a powerful electric current had been sent through her. Immediately he knew that something terrible was going to happen: he had set the wrong forces in motion. He raised his head to stare at the screen. There was no element of surprise in his emotions as he watched the transformation take place—only a dull horror at the inevitability of it. The woman's features faded, slid away, melted swiftly, and the face took on its true identity, the one he now knew he had been expecting from the start—that of his mother.

Even here, he thought miserably. What does she want here? Now he watched both the screen and the doll-like figure in the flesh-colored pool of light at the foot of it, feeling his heart beat faster. With her "jolly" look, which never once had fooled him even as a small child, she began to talk as though she were addressing one of her clubs, as though the audience were made up only of women. Underneath the jovial flesh was the supremely calculating consciousness, the dark destroying presence. No matter what part she was playing (for her role depended upon her audience), to him her basic expression was always the same, cunning and omniscient, with an undertone of implicit menace, as though it had been universally conceded that woman's state, entailing persecution and suffering, included her right to seek vengeance.

"I came here," she was saying (he grew tense) . . . "to see my son. I thought they might be working on him tonight." Her smile was an apology for the boundlessness of human frailty; he looked straight into its amplified folds on the screen as he rose to his feet and felt himself dissolving in horror. If he went up the aisle they would stop him. He crossed over and entered a row of seats, squeezing himself along in front of the seated spectators toward an exit door near the end. There was a certain amount of whispered protest as he pushed his way through, but he felt certain he had not been identified. When he got to the side aisle he flung the door open and in spite of himself turned for a last glimpse of the screen. She was looking straight at him. That means she's looking at the camera, he reminded himself.

"Grover!" Her voice was cool and imperious; it became contemptuous as she asked, "Have you finished?"

With all his might he screamed back, "No!" and felt the hall tremble with the force of his cry. As he began to run along the dark corridors he thought, She knows about the glass room upstairs. She's the one who had me committed.

The backstage world was a labyrinth of narrow stairways and dingy storerooms. The place was empty of people, but he had no idea where he was going, and it seemed to him that he could hear a murmur of disturbance back in the auditorium. And he kept running, through the corridors, up circular staircases, down interior fire escapes and along galleries that overhung unlighted depths, increasingly convinced that this was a flight to save his life; by rising from his seat in the audience he had in some way interfered with institutional processes. He would be caught and punished. At that point Luchita coughed and moved her hand roughly along his thigh.

The sweetness of the night came pouring in from all sides. The fountain gurgled on the terrace, there was a slight sound of wind in the leaves, and somewhere a motorcycle labored upward from the valley below. Luchita moved into a new position and went on breathing regularly. He lay completely still, feeling shame because his heart still pounded so wildly.

Still without moving, in a half-sleep, he tried to reconstruct the world of the little nightmare: he had to understand whatever he was afraid of. Was it possible that even knowing she was dead, he was not going to be able to diminish the dread of her that was still there inside him? He listened to the fountain, to the wind below in the pines. His heart went on beating oppressively; in an effort to calm it, he tried taking deep and regular breaths.

He had backed out of the garage and was sitting at the wheel of the Cadillac, ready to be off, but his mother had appeared in the driveway and now leaned against the car door, her head inside, and she was talking. "Just remember, when you're out on that highway, the difference between the brake and the accelerator is the difference between life and death. Will you try to remember that, just for me?"

The words made him squirm. "For God's sake, Mother!"

"If only you weren't always on the defensive," she said wistfully, adding, as if to herself, "Of course, with no father—"

In simulated anger he had started up, so that she nearly lost her balance. This had taken days to smooth over, but he knew it had been the correct move. The inevitable pattern of his life had been one of exploiting the enmity between her and his father; yet in the presence of each he had preserved what appeared to be a basic loyalty toward the other. If he came back to the capital after a visit to Montreal and described his mother's civic campaigns and her women's club banquets, he was careful to include details which he knew would infuriate Señor Soto, who had his own Latin ideas on female behavior;

and before he went back to Montreal he made lists of seemingly anodyne details which had to be innocently incorporated into his conversations with his mother. It was necessary to hint that Señor Soto's house might be one of the last places on earth where a mother would want her son to be. If there were any overt criticism from her, however, he assumed a disturbed air and begged her gently, "Please . . . Please!"

The winter when he was sixteen, Señor Soto had tried to persuade him to go with him to mass on Sunday; in an offhand, dogmatic fashion he told him that the only way to be free in life was to adhere so strictly to an orthodoxy that everything save the spirit became a matter of reflex. Grove had given a good deal of thought to this; it seemed a viable technique, providing you found a valid orthodoxy. Later in the year he expounded the theory to his mother.

"You're not turning out to be a fanatic, I hope!" she cried, going on ruefully, "I don't understand it. You don't get this taste for excess from my side of the family. That goes with the Church. You can smell it a mile away. I thought you had more balance."

"It's a question of discipline," he told her.

She shook her head slowly back and forth. "Don't let him rope you into the Church, Grove. I warn you. It's fatal."

"You know he's an agnostic," he said quietly.

"Is that what he claims to be?" She looked up, startled. That had done it; later in the day she suggested buying a motorboat and spending the autumn at Percé. "I don't have to have a boat," he told her. "Don't spend the money." She had bought the boat and they had gone together up to the Gaspé. The college propaganda began again during this long holiday. She wanted to enter him at McGill the following year. Grove, knowing that he was in the position of the head of a neutralist state, instead spent the winter with his father in the beach house at Puerto Pacífico, persuaded that the following summer would bring forth something more substantial than a motorboat. Señor Soto's opinion of the value of a college education was very low; he wanted to give him practical experience in administering one of the haciendas. "But if you want to try it, you've got one of the oldest universities in the world right here in the capital."

"I don't want to try it!" Grove told him. "I just want to keep the peace."

"Don't let yourself be pressured," his father advised him.

His moves had all been correct. Summer brought the Cadillac, a bonus for agreeing to live with his mother and attend the University; he would have been happier if a truck had not backed into it one night after he had parked it in front of a roadhouse. It was more than he could do to face her with the news. He had bought a plane ticket to Panama and gone directly up to Puerto Pacífico. The end of his academic career had not shaken his mother so deeply as the fact that he had left without letting her know, without giving her a chance to say goodbye. In spite of all the times he had seen her since, even now he found himself frowning there in the dark as he recalled it; but the feeling of guilt could no longer be reshaped into anger, because there was nothing left to fear. It was long past, he told himself, and it was something she should have expected, in any case. When the daylight began to show from the terrace he fell back into sleep.

16

In the morning the first sound Luchita heard was the splashing of water in the swimming pool. She reached down and pulled the sheet up over her, for she was naked. Then she felt tentatively along the mattress beside her for Vero. His place was empty. She went back to sleep. Later she woke to see him dressing; he seemed to be in a great hurry. Presently he stepped over to the bed and spoke to her, and she came really awake. He had put on a business suit.

"What time is it?" she asked.

"Ten to eight."

"What's wrong? What are you doing up so early?"

"I've got to go out. I'll be back for lunch."

"You look high." She squinted at him.

"You never heard of feeling good in the morning?" He pulled down the sheet and set to tickling her savagely. She struggled, buried her face in the pillows to stifle her screams, tried unsuccessfully to kick him. At the moment when she felt she could stand it no longer, he stopped and stood up.

"You be here for lunch, though," he said, adjusting his tie. "You can help me."

She had yanked the sheet up around her neck. "My God, what'd they lay on you, anyway?" she cried.

"Go back to sleep," he told her.

Just before lunch was ready he returned, still in a state of excitement, and began to rush noisily around the kitchen. Luchita came out of Pepito's room. He was putting ice cubes into a bowl. Leaning against the refrigerator, smoking, she listened to him describe the visit to the bookshop. At length she said impassively, "You like her?"

"I'm not planning to screw her, if that's what you mean."

She shrugged and went back into the bedroom. Over lunch they discussed the morning visitor. "You were right not to come out if you were going to look like that," he told her. "You'll meet her tomorrow night. If you can arrange to wear something else instead of those Levis, I'd appreciate it."

"Whatever you like," she said meekly; she had determined to make an attempt to please him during this period. She waited, then said, "Where's Thorny?"

"He went out to Los Hermanos. He won't be back till late tonight."

"That's a good place for him," she declared. "I wish he'd stay there. I'm going down to the movies with Pepito."

After lunch, instead of taking his accustomed siesta, he shut himself into the library with a notebook and a sheaf of papers. When Luchita had been gone for a half hour or so, he switched on a tape recorder and listened. Here he had been preparing one of his discussions with Luchita. Often he improvised these one-sided conversations, recorded them, and then wrote out notes on the more convincing passages. Using these, he plotted the course of a verbal procedure from which he allowed himself almost no deviation when the moment came for actual speaking.

"All right. You don't know me. You always say you have no idea what I'm like. But at least you know what I'm *not* like. I'm not like most people. I want the same thing, always. I don't like changes. You ought to know. You've checked up. You know I never brought anybody back nights, before you came. I want you here next to me when I wake up. That's not so hard to understand, is it?"

He reversed the tape to its beginning, set the microphone on the coffee table, and began to record over the month-old monologue. For an instant he stood staring down at the slowly turning reels. "Day," he said tentatively, as if the uttering of the word might effect some palpable change in the room. "Wait while I get a cigarette."

When he came in from the terrace he lay down on the divan facing the table. He spoke for a while; his voice was gentle, his inflections those of one seeking agreement at the most basic level of rationality. The pauses for her hypothetical replies were brief. He lit another cigarette and balanced it on the edge of the ashtray. The smoke rose in a long line, straight into the air. It was too soon for the late-afternoon wind to have arrived. He watched the little cylinder of white paper with its thin blue column of smoke, and thought, If it were now. This was a recurrent fantasy, an obsessive pastime in which he often indulged during periods of stress. If he should vanish at this moment and *they* should come, wanting to learn about him, what would they find? One British cigarette, burning, balancing on the edge of the ashtray, the tape recorder turning, carrying only silence to the tape. They could talk with the servants and with one retarded Cuban girl (Luchita knew nothing about him and would be hostile anyway), and they would get nowhere. Making himself into one of them for the instant and generously granting that one an intelligence akin to his own, he ran his eye approvingly over the nearest row of books. *Ferien am Waldsee, Erinnerungen eines Überlebenden. L'Enfer Organisé. Netchaiev. Cybernation and the Corporate State. L'Univers Concentrationnaire. Auschwitz, Zeugnisse und Berichte.* Even though the man were an enemy, for they were all enemies, those who would come after his disappearance to verify his essence, the inspector would be profoundly impressed by the sum of the evidence. The report could read: "This kind of genius for achieving total perfection has no application in an era of collective consciousness." Imagining his own nonexistence never failed to stimulate him; he continued to speak, now in an even calmer voice.

"But if we're going to be friends, you've got to know me completely. Isn't that always the case if there's going to be understanding? You've got to know what I'm all about and why I'm the way I am. If we're going to talk to each other we've got to be in the same psychic room, as it were. You say I'm difficult. I'm like anyone else. But I care a great deal about the truth. It's hard to come by and it makes trouble, but it's worth it. Or don't you admit that?" He looked quizzically at the microphone standing on its chromium tripod; often it reminded him of a machine gun. *Ametralladora, modelo bolsillo*, he thought, and smiled at it. Then he got up and walked to the bar by the window, threw a proprietary glance at the city shining below in the sudden gold light of sunset beneath the storm clouds, and poured out a glass of cherry brandy. He began to talk on his way back to the table, walking slowly, holding the glass at eye level, staring into it. "We're machines for realizing the inconceivable, and we go on living like animals, being subjective, with personal tastes and preferences. In India, you know, there are people who claim that love is obscene unless both parties are so conscious of what they are doing—I mean so absolutely aware of themselves and each other during sex—that they can concentrate on God all the way through to the end, both of them. What it really means is that you've got to be both intelligent and shameless. But the Hindus always turn out to be practical." He sipped from his glass. "I believe they've hit it. Sex will never be any good until we're free. At least free enough to be able to focus on God while we're doing it." He laughed self-consciously. "You can see that it could be a great discipline, just in order to improve the quality of the experience. The whole point of sex is that it should be as good as possible."

At this point he imagined her saying, "Were we talking about sex?" She had a dry authoritative way of cutting a conversation short; she allowed the traffic to circulate only along the main highway. This was a hindrance, but stupid women are more difficult to manage than bright ones. And it occurred to him that the school-principal element in her character might be a sign that she was already ruined for unashamed love-making.

It would be impossible, without being explicit, to convey to her a sense of the necessity of an immediate decision; he could not hope for that. If when he finished talking to her he could not be certain that he had won, he would give up the sex project entirely. He knew just where in the garden at Los Hermanos the talk would take place. By a circular pool there was a wide balustrade from which you looked down across the terraced land to the tangled forest beyond. A relaxing landscape, made voluptuous by moonlight.

A violent rainstorm broke while Luchita and Pepito were in the theater. When they came out, it had passed, but the streets had become rushing brooks. Before she could find a taxi, Pepito had managed to step into the water and get wet as far up as his waist.

"Oh, Pepito! You're so stupid!"

"I like to be wet," he said. "It feels good."

When she had got him into dry clothes it was nearly dinnertime. She walked out onto the terrace and looked through the door into the library. Vero was there, sitting at the desk under the light, writing. She stepped inside. "You still busy?" she asked him.

He looked up. "That's right." He yawned and stretched. "I'll finish later, before I go to bed."

After dinner he went into the library, shut the doors, and was back with his papers. Luchita wandered from the terrace into the bedroom and back a few times. It was one of those nights, frequent at the end of the dry season, when there seemed to be no air anywhere. From the library she heard the distant clicking of the typewriter. She went into the bedroom and stood in front of the mirror. Whatever he was doing, she reflected, it was better than thinking about his mother; also she had an irrational conviction that his work had some hidden connection with the eventual purchase of her ticket to Paris. She lit a grifa and pulled on it a few times. Suddenly she went to the library door. She hesitated an instant and threw it open.

"I've got to have some music!" she cried. "I can't just sit in here alone with nothing."

He did not look up. "Play it on the terrace and keep it low."

She stood there with her eyes fixed on the bright desk as if it might help her to divine what was written on the papers in front of him. Very slowly she swung the door, and still watched through the crack before she shut it entirely, taking care not to let the knob click when she lifted her hand from it.

17

The motor roared as they went up the mountain. The valley below was almost sunk in shadow. Dr. Slade sniffed the air noisily. "Now, if you could make a perfume that smelled like *that*!" he exclaimed. He sat up straight at each hairpin curve and peered over the drop. The day of visits to parks and palaces had been tiring; his nerves were a little on edge. It was pleasant when they got to the top and parked on level ground in front of the apartment house.

They came out of the elevator, were in a patio where a fountain played above a pool. There was a girl standing in an arched doorway, very young and extraordinarily beautiful. In her white gown she looked to Mrs. Slade just about old enough to write her first love letter.

"Here's Luchita!" cried Señor Soto. "This is Luchita. Mrs. Slade. Dr. Slade."

"Come in," said Luchita. "Please come in."

"This room! It's a work of art!" Mrs. Slade raised her arms upon entering it again, and turned to her husband.

"Yes, yes. It certainly is," he agreed, standing still an instant to look around, and then following Señor Soto across the room and out onto the terrace. The air in there had seemed stuffy; there had been a faint animal smell in it, or, if not exactly animal, something he connected with "native" life. He could not identify it, but he knew it was surprising to find the smell here in this apartment.

"Yes, this is quite an amazing place you've got here, Señor Soto. Quite amazing." He felt a bit insincere as he said the words; it looked to him more like an overpoweringly elegant hotel than a home. A hotel or a department store. "Yes. It's very fine indeed." He turned to the sunset over the valley. "What a sight!"

Señor Soto smiled. "Yes. Sunset up here is something big. Wait. I'll get you a drink. What is it?"

"Scotch and soda."

Dr. Slade watched the young man as he walked away across the terrace. He frowned. The all-enveloping charm of his young host made him uneasy; without hesitation he rejected it. There was no chance of its being real. And he thought with annoyance that it was typical of Day to be taken in by such a couple. She could disregard all the pretense and vulgarity, if only she found them "fun." He walked back toward the doorway. She and the girl were sitting among mountains of fur-covered cushions; each had a cocktail glass in her hand. Señor Soto appeared, carrying drinks. He joined Dr. Slade in the doorway, and they remained there talking.

Mrs. Slade was being a guest. "I think this apartment is the most beautiful thing I've ever seen!"

"I'm just invited here," Luchita said, looking downward. "I live in Paris."

Mrs. Slade shut her lips together and rearranged her skirt over her knees. "Paris. I don't think I could live there. The traffic."

"I hate it here," said Luchita.

"Really?" She laughed uneasily, and with a glance took in the entire room. "Oh, come on. You don't like living in this incredible place?"

"I'm going to Paris soon. The people in these small towns are lousy."

"Yes, I see how they could be," she began uncertainly, thinking of the overdressed crowd in the hotel dining room. "But really it's a very pleasant little city. We've been sightseeing today, so I have a fresh eye."

"Yes. I suppose it looks pretty to tourists," Luchita said thoughtfully.

"I don't think you could call us exactly tourists," Mrs. Slade said. "We just move around where we please, when we please. It's the only way to do it. Group travel's a degradation. The whole point is to be free. Not to have to make reservations ahead of time."

Luchita was not listening; she did, however, hear the last sentence, and it struck no sympathetic chord in her. "I like my reservations a long time before, I can tell you."

Mrs. Slade was thrown off balance. "Oh, well, of course . . ." She laughed, not knowing what she had intended to say, and then smiled in order to camouflage her scrutiny of reappraisal. She looked carefully into Luchita's eyes, and had the peculiar feeling that she was studying an alien species. Señor Soto and Taylor stood talking in the doorway, with the sunset behind them.

"It's getting brighter every minute!" she cried.

Señor Soto came over and squatted, facing her.

"I was reading some Javanese poems today," he told her. "And I came across a line that won't go away."

"Javanese poetry?"

"That's right. 'The moon is more splendid than a young girl who looks the other way.' You like it?"

"I'm not quite sure I understand it," she said evenly, as if she thought that might stop him.

He laughed, took her arm, and pulled her up. "Come outside and look at the sunset while I explain it." They passed in front of Dr. Slade as they went through the doorway.

"Do you want to see the sunset again?" said Luchita, smiling at Dr. Slade.

"No, I don't think I do."

"Why don't you come and sit down?"

She told him about her father's orchestra, and how they all had left Havana and gone to Paris and become very successful, so that she had had many fine clothes. But then her father had died and the orchestra had broken up, and her mother had had to lend many of the musicians money to get back to Havana, until they had become extremely poor, which was why she must get to Paris soon. "How do I even know if my mother is alive?" she cried.

"I should think you'd want to go back," he said in tones of concern. "I shouldn't think it would be much pleasure being on vacation if you're going to worry like this. It'll wear you down."

"I know."

"You'd better go soon," he said, meaning to sound fatherly; he suspected that she thought him senile.

Earlier in the evening Luchita had smoked a great deal, and was now so bewitched by the sound of her own story that she was aware of him only in his capacity as listener. Overstimulated, he thought, but not drunk; she had not touched her drink since Day had gone out onto the terrace. Suddenly she stopped talking and stood up. "I have to go and feed my son," she told him, and went out of the room.

Mrs. Slade had been standing with her host, looking out over the darkening valley, while he explained the several possible meanings of the line of poetry; she had no idea what he was talking about, because she was not listening. When she thought he had finished, she said. "That girl. Your guest. She's a real crazy kid, isn't she?"

He frowned. "It's very hard to know what she's like," he said reflectively.

"Oh, come! You must be in a position to manage *that* much!"

"It's not exactly what you think," he protested.

"God forbid!" she exclaimed, laughing.

He looked at her but said nothing, and she felt rebuffed. After a moment he went on. "For one thing, she lives on grass. You know, marijuana." He gave it the Spanish pronunciation.

"Can't you stop her? Haven't you any influence at all over her? She's so young to be ruining her life."

"It keeps her quiet," he said, laughing. "I'm not one for trying to change people."

Mrs. Slade frowned at him. "I'm afraid I could never sit by and watch someone I cared about, or *didn't* care about, even, destroy himself, and not at least make an effort to do something about it."

"You see," he said with great seriousness, "I haven't noticed any signs of self-destructiveness in Luchita, so it's hard to know what to say."

Mrs. Slade was suddenly prim. "Of course, it's none of my business."

"Let me bring you another," he said, reaching for her glass. She held on to it and shook her head. "I think I'd like to go in. It's getting cool out here."

Inside she found Dr. Slade sitting alone, absently running his fingers back and forth over the chinchilla spread on which he sat. "Oh! I thought you were talking to—" she hesitated— "the young lady."

"She's gone to feed her child," he said very distinctly, and she glanced at him to see his face. At the same instant he looked up at her, and she recognized the glint of accusation in his eyes. It was the expression he always wore when he wanted to remind her that he was suffering for her sake. He was bored with the girl and bored with Señor Soto, and it was her fault. She walked over and sat down beside him.

"It's lovely, isn't it?" she said, watching his hand smooth the fur.

"Lovely?" he said blankly.

The telephone rang. They heard Señor Soto say, "*Diga. Quién habla?*" and then go into English. Shortly after that he laughed. "I thought he'd want to. Well, all I can do is ask. Put Dirk on." He called across the room. "Dr. Slade! Will you talk to this friend of mine who's sick? He's coming to the phone now. I told him you were here."

Dr. Slade stood up, and was already walking toward the end of the room where Señor Soto stood with the receiver in his hand. "Why, of course. Gladly."

And so it was that less than five minutes later he found himself, with considerable relief, back in the car with Señor Soto, breathing the resinous evening air as they sped around the mountain in the direction of an upland valley.

"It's only as far as Los Hermanos, if that means anything to you. A little place about twenty minutes out. He's going to appreciate this more than you realize."

"I can't do anything for him, you understand. I haven't been a practicing physician in a good many years."

"No, but it'll boost his morale. He's an American, after all, so he only really trusts American doctors."

"Naturally," said Dr. Slade.

They went over a mountain pass. Without warning, the air was bitterly cold. The stars that shone in the still twilit sky seemed abnormally large and bright. Then the road pirouetted downward through matted forest into a warm, windless valley choked with lush vegetation. "This is Los Hermanos," Señor Soto said, turning to see his guest's reaction to the inglorious line of thatched huts and adobe boxes going past on each side of the road. Ever since they had come into the valley there had been the constant croaking of frogs; even in the middle of the town it was still audible.

Dr. Slade did not give any visible sign that he had heard the

words. He was looking up the grass-filled streets as they
passed them. Each one had two or three arc lights where the
children clustered. Beyond, in the background, was the darkness of the forest. He had the impression that each street, as
they approached it and he saw the swiftly changing vignette
of light and shadow, was concerned intimately with some part
of him, that he had even lived here for great periods of time.
And the thought occurred to him that this shabby little town
was very likely a model village in the eyes of the Creator; this
was probably the kind of place in which all men were meant
to live. The sound of the frogs could have been going on
since the beginning of life. Another thing: he had begun to
be aware of a general discomfort; there was a heaviness in
him. He shut his eyes. I've caught a chill, he thought. At that
moment the car swung off the highway onto a dirt road.
Soon jungle arched above them. Señor Soto drove slowly,
now and then turning to look at the doctor. The noise made
by the frogs and insects was tremendous.

Slumping in his seat, Dr. Slade looked up at the vines and
branches above his head. Then he shut his eyes again. What
he had perceived was too unpleasant. Only a moment before,
he had made the discovery that the frogs were aware of being
a chorus; they sang together in rhythm. Then, for the fraction
of a second, looking up at the chaos of vegetation overhead,
he had very clearly seen each bough and leaf pulsating with
the frogs, in exactly the same rhythmic patterns. He folded his
hands over his chest and sighed.

"You need a jeep for this," said Señor Soto.

"Yes," he answered absently. Recovering for a second, he
thought, "Alcohol is dangerous at this altitude," and resolved
to drink more slowly.

The car stopped. An Indian in overalls, with a rifle in one
hand, swung the big gate inward. "*Sí señor*," he said, and they
drove on through a garden. Squat palms lined the driveway.
Ahead, a car was parked beside a great dark mass of bushes.
Señor Soto eased in beside it and shut off the motor. The
frogs were singing here too, and the noise was as loud as it
had been back in the jungle. The headlights went off; the garden glowed with impossible colors in the dim starlight.

"This has got to be done," Dr. Slade said to himself. He

reached out his hand and pressed the door handle, took two or three steps on the spongy grass, and raised his head. In front of him, not three feet away, there was a face—a muzzle, rather, for it surely belonged to an animal—looking at him with terrible intensity. It was unmoving, fashioned from a nameless, constantly dripping substance. Unmoving, yet it must have moved, for now the mouth was much farther open; long twisted tendons had appeared in each cheek. He watched, frozen and unbelieving, while the whole jaw swiftly melted and fell away, leaving the top part of the muzzle intact. The eyes glared more savagely than before; they were telling him that sooner or later he would have to pay for having witnessed that moment of its suffering. He took a step backward and looked again. There were only leaves and shadows of leaves—no muzzle, no eyes, nothing. But the leaves were pulsating with energy. At any moment they could swell and become something other than what they were.

"The door's around this way," a man's voice was saying. He looked, and could see no one. Slowly he squatted and sat down on the grass with his knees up, his arms folded around them and his head bent over facing the earth.

"Is anything wrong?" the voice asked.

"I don't—" He could not say it. The frogs' song slurred upward, over and over again. If there was a person nearby, it could only be a stranger.

The stranger was pulling him to his feet. It was not really any harder to walk than it had been to sit doubled over listening to the frogs. A part of him had been shut out and was trying in anguish to join the other part that was shut in, but there was not even a way of thinking about it. A gill-like orifice gaped on each side of his neck; he could feel the pair of them opening and shutting regularly.

"You were out in the sun today. No?"

This was a red jungle. There were floor lamps and rugs in the clearings, and rows of books back in the shadows. The wilderness was peopled, but the men were all strangers. They held a cup of something hot to his lips. "Can you drink this?"

"I'm all right." This was what one was supposed to say, and he said it; yet he was aware of the outside world rushing away, retreating before the onslaught of a vast sickness that welled up inside him, and he knew that soon there would be only the obscene reality of himself, trapped in the solitary chambers of existence.

18

After Vero and the old American had left, Luchita went around turning on all the lights in the apartment. "Sometimes I like lots of light," she explained. "You know, it makes me feel something's happening." She returned to the couch and lay back on the cushions with her hands behind her head.

"Yes, I suppose."

"Do you ever feel nothing is happening?"

Mrs. Slade looked at her disapprovingly. "I don't think I do. No."

Luchita sat partially up. "You mean you've *never* bumped into it?"

But Mrs. Slade did not seem to want to talk about that. "How old is your child?" she asked her.

"You want to see him?"

Now she looked happier. "Oh, yes!"

Luchita led her to the little bedroom where Pepito was spooning up his food.

"Pepito, this is Mrs. Slade."

He smiled and continued to eat.

They went back into the library. There was no light left in the sky. "How long do you think they'll be gone?" Mrs. Slade asked her; she did not find it reassuring to have been left alone with this strange girl.

"They'll be back soon. It's not far," said Luchita. Part of helping Vero was to keep this not very friendly young woman occupied while he was gone. She spoke once again of Paris.

Suddenly Mrs. Slade cut her short. "Your husband," she said, and shook her head back and forth anxiously. "Where is he?"

"I've never been married," Luchita said earnestly, as if astonished that anyone should have supposed such a thing. "And *he's* not going to marry me!" She laughed to make it clear that she was free of illusions.

Mrs. Slade was silent. After a while she said, "Who's the boy's father?"

"Some English guy," Luchita said indifferently.

"Won't he help?"

"It was somebody in England. I don't know who," she explained. "Pepito looks English, too, a little. Don't you think?"

This could only be purposeful, thought Mrs. Slade. The girl was trying to provoke a reaction; she would not oblige her by supplying one. "There are so many different English types," she said evenly. "You can't really say that anyone looks English or anything else. Anybody can look anything."

"That's crazy," Luchita objected, thinking of Havana. Hastily she went on, "I lived in England for a while when I was young."

Mrs. Slade laughed merrily as she recalled her first impression of the girl standing in the patio.

"I went to art school there. That was when I decided to be an artist."

"Oh, you paint?" She sounded, but did not look, interested.

"I make drawings on paper. With pastels."

"Pastels are pretty," Mrs. Slade said in a colorless voice.

"If you want to see them I'll show them to you." At this point Luchita unconsciously applied a professional touch: a long look designed to convey an impression of sexy, childish innocence. Mrs. Slade gave no sign of having noticed it. She said, "Do bring them out. I'd love to see some."

Luchita sprang up, a little girl in her mother's new party dress, rustled across the room to a cabinet and drew out a portfolio.

The drawings were of uniform size. Carefully she laid them out in the middle of the floor in four rows, like playing cards. They were the work of a bright child that has absorbed certain formulas from looking at comic books. There were sunsets over the sea, heavily made-up film stars, and a few unidentifiable animals. Luchita stood up and remained looking down at them in an attitude of fond appreciation, her hands behind her back.

"What's that one?" Mrs. Slade asked in a toneless voice, pointing to an orange creature with many teeth, sprawled under a giant plant that looked like a cactus.

"Oh, that's a lion. I almost sold him one night at the Embassy Club. Then the man met a friend of his and they went away. He got too drunk, I guess."

"You sell them?" She tried to keep from sounding incredulous.

"Of course! That's why I make them. I'm trying to get the money to go back to Paris."

"But I don't understand," she began. "Aren't you living here? I mean, in this apartment?"

"Sometimes I stay," Luchita said vaguely. "Sometimes I go home."

"I see." Mrs. Slade was silent. "And you sell these in bars and places."

"A few weeks ago a man bought twenty. But it's not always like that."

"Twenty!"

"Vero thinks I should charge different prices. But I sell them for five dollars apiece."

"That seems reasonable," said Mrs. Slade guardedly. "They're awfully good. I hope you sell them all."

"Which ones do you like best?"

Here it comes, thought Mrs. Slade. "Oh, I like all of them," she said airily. "But I've never bought a picture in my life. I'd have no place to put it."

"Paris was fine. I used to make around eight thousand francs a day."

"You mean with your pictures?"

"I did them with chalk on the sidewalk. I always had a crowd."

"On the sidewalk!" she cried. "Have you done that here?"

"Vero says they don't allow it. But I could do it all right."

"You'd better not try."

Luchita knelt down and studied the drawings silently for a moment before gathering them up.

The girl's a mental case, she thought as she watched.

While Luchita was trying to get the portfolio back into the cabinet, the door opened and Señor Soto came in. "Sorry to be so long," he said smiling.

Mrs. Slade looked at him. "Where's Taylor?" And when he did not answer she said, "Where's Dr. Slade?"

He walked toward her with the same casual smile, as if he had not heard, and stood in front of her, regarding her quizzically from above. "He's all right. He wasn't feeling very well, so I had him lie down."

Mrs. Slade's eyes had opened wide. "Wasn't feeling well? What's the matter with him?"

Luchita had sunk down upon a hassock. She was convinced that once again Vero was lying, and it alarmed her because she could see no motive for it. He was patting Mrs. Slade on the shoulder. "If you want, I'll drive you out there right now, and we can all come back together. Or if not, I'll go out in a little while and get him. Either way."

"What's she going to do out at Los Hermanos?" demanded Luchita suddenly.

He did not take his eyes from Mrs. Slade's face. "Whichever you like."

Mrs. Slade sat for a moment, not moving; then she stood up. "May I have a vodka on the rocks?"

He moved one step backwards, his face showing dismay. "How about a sandwich and some salad? It's after nine."

She was protesting, "No, no, no," but he seemed not to hear her, and sent Luchita hurrying toward the kitchen.

"All I want is a drink," insisted Mrs. Slade, but he was already talking again. "You haven't seen this balcony out here. It's got a pool full of frogs."

She said nothing, and went with resentment; he was using the same tactics he had tried on her the previous day. As they passed through the doorway he seized her arm. Outside, they stood for an instant, looking up at the stars. He did not let go of the arm.

"This is more private," he was saying. "You don't get the wind. There's no view either, of course, except the trees."

Now he guided her toward the railing, and they leaned over, looking down at the street below, and out at the high pines not far away, black against the night-blue sky.

He sighed. "I thought we'd be going out on the town tonight. I wanted to show you and the Doctor a few spots, two or three little places where the tourists never get." He paused. "Maybe we can make it for tomorrow. A good night's sleep tonight and he'll be back to normal. How old a man is he?"

"I believe he's sixty-seven," she said, resenting the question, and feeling somehow that she ought to have lied.

"Really. I'd have thought less than that by several years." He waited a moment. "Are you coming out there with me? The hacienda's worth seeing. Seventeenth century."

"I want a drink." Even in the dimness she knew he could see her looking straight at him.

"It's a magnificent old place," he went on, returning her stare, but decreasing the pressure of his fingers on her arm.

"A drink," she said again, slowly and clearly, her voice flickering with fury. She felt him let go of her.

"Yes. Of course." He turned and started inside.

You must calm down, she told herself. She moved nearer to the pool and parted the great smooth leaves of a liana that hung from the trellis above. A frog dived into the basin; the water made the sound of the word *blip*. She heard Señor Soto sliding open panels and clicking shut cabinet doors. She stood still.

When he came back out he was subdued, almost melancholy. "Well, here it is," he said, slowly handing her the glass. She imagined that his expression was wistful as he watched her drink. Soon Manuel arrived with a tray of sandwiches and brought her a plate.

"I'm glad to see you eating at last," he told her. "It'll be cold in the mountains."

She turned. "I'm not going. I'd rather stay here, if you don't mind."

"Of course, it's as you like." He did not try to conceal the displeasure in his voice.

"Look," she said. "I just don't feel like having to make an effort to control my nerves. Driving at night makes me nervous. You say he's not in danger and I take your word for it."

"Of course he's not in danger."

Luchita was standing in the doorway. "You need anything?" she asked.

"If you're not coming, I think I'll start out there now. I ought to be back here in about an hour."

"I'm sorry," she said, and then she began to flutter a bit. "We've made you so much trouble."

He turned at the doorway and looked back at her a second as if in surprise. Inside, he began to speak with Luchita. She heard their voices fading as they walked away into another room. It was about ten minutes before he went out.

19

Even on the small sheltered terrace it was too cool; she stepped inside. Luchita was sprawled on a pile of cushions, busy with cigarette papers. There was a feline-scented herbal smoke in the air.

"It's chilly outside," she announced.

Luchita looked up. "What's your name?" she said, as one small child to another.

Mrs. Slade stood still. "Why—"

"I mean, I heard the doctor call you Day. I wondered what it really was."

She was uncomfortable. "Well, it was—I mean it still is—" She laughed. "—Désirée. Dr. Slade never liked it, so he began calling me Day. You know. Anyway, I hate Désirée."

She felt that she had been clumsy in her explanation, for the girl did not appear to have understood. "You ought to make him call you Désirée," she said, looking straight ahead.

"He never would," Mrs. Slade said listlessly. He had told her that Day suited her; it was he who had to use the name. Suddenly she felt a physical dread, something pulling downward on each side of her body, and it seemed to her that the floor moved slightly. She stood very still, her heart beating fast.

"Do you have earthquakes here?" she asked presently, thinking of the emptiness beyond the balcony outside.

Luchita was more direct. "I didn't feel anything," she said, huddling with her knees up, wrapping her arms around her legs. "Did you?"

"I don't know." She stood in the middle of the room, irresolute, aware of an approaching wave of anguish. Luchita eyed her carefully. "You must be tired," she said. "Why don't you relax?"

Obediently she stretched out on the chinchilla spread. It might be possible to drive off the feeling of nausea. "I'm rather tense," she explained from where she lay.

"Relax," Luchita advised. Then she got up and turned down the lighting.

A while later Mrs. Slade spoke again. "I really don't feel very well. I don't think I'm going to be sick, though."

A gaseous blue light was beginning to glow somewhere behind her vision, and she had the impression that there was a never-ending music, a music that was silent, yet present; it was like the wheezing, low notes of a harmonium. If she cleared her throat, she merely heard the sound of that over the music.

"You did too much today. You went too many places. You're not used to being up so high. It's awful. I hate it," Luchita was saying. She poured the chopped leaves into the machine and rolled out a new cigarette.

Presently Mrs. Slade sat up and stared across the room. "Malaria. Do you think I could have malaria? I really feel miserable. Terrible." The dread had seized her again, was twisting through her bowels.

"Malaria's nothing," Luchita said impassively. "You take a couple of pills."

Mrs. Slade lay down again. "It's so strong," she heard herself say as she shut her eyes. Then she fell back almost voluptuously into a world of undifferentiated flapping things where words were silent and colors became textures. There were blossomings and explosions. From where she had floated far down the coastline of her consciousness, she called out.

"I'm cold!" she cried.

Luchita came over to her quickly. She pressed her palm against Mrs. Slade's forehead.

"You haven't got malaria," she told her. Then she tossed another light fur spread over her. In her mind was the idea that if she got too close to Mrs. Slade she might carry the disease to Pepito.

"You ought to have a doctor," she said uncertainly. "Only you'll have to wait until Vero comes back. He knows the name of a doctor." Then she began to laugh. "I'm crazy! Your husband. He's your doctor!"

Mrs. Slade heard her words, but she heard each one separately; each was a point of departure for a new idea, something completely different. A vast novel was unfolding; she recognized the backdrop as a sinister distortion of the actual landscape outside the apartment. The countryside was peopled, but she could not see the faces. Now and then, with the regularity of a nerve aching, the conviction swept over her that the faces belonged to an unknown monstrous race. She was being propelled toward a time when they would no longer be hidden.

She moaned a little. Luchita looked up, apprehensive. "I'll put on some music," she said. Vero had told her, "Please don't monkey with the tape recorder or the phonograph. I've got them both set up the way I want." She flicked the tape recorder on anyway: African drumming, incisive, perfect in rhythm, endlessly repetitive. Then she went back to her work. The precise patterns played on, minute after minute. He had said another thing that struck her as peculiar: "If I'm not back by midnight, have Mrs. Slade stay here. Put her in your old room." She hoped he would come early. It was bad enough that she herself should not be allowed to have the room, without being obliged to offer it to a stranger.

The landscape was flaking off, crumbling. Day sat erect again, staring around the room. Luchita saw the movement and looked up.

"Can I get you something? Some hot tea? Some cold Coke?"

Mrs. Slade saw the room becoming gelatinous; she watched the opposite wall quiver and shimmer like the top of an aspic. "Cold Coke," she repeated thickly, without inflection. "Cold Coke."

A moment later, when Luchita returned from the kitchen, she was lying out flat. She spoke to her, but there was no reply. Luchita set the glass down. "It's there on the table when you want it," she told her. Then it occurred to her that if Mrs. Slade were really ill, it would be wiser to put her to bed now, before she fell asleep or became delirious.

She finally got her to her feet, but she would not walk. "I can't be pushed any further!" she cried desperately, and looked at Luchita, her eyes starting out of her head, as if she were seeing her for the first time. "Where's my husband?"

She's acting, thought Luchita, seeing the distraught, haunted expression on her face. She took her arm, said, "We have to go out through the patio," and led her on a crooked course in that direction. When they got to the bedroom the long silk curtains were blowing inward with the breeze. "The bathroom's here." Luchita reached her arm through a dark doorway and switched on a light. Out of the corner of her eye she saw Mrs. Slade about to sink down onto the bed. "No, no!" she cried, running back to stop her. "Sit here." She eased her into a chair and pressed a wall button fiercely. While she waited for the maid she took the fur spread off the bed, turned the sheets back and patted the pillows. There was a knock at the door; she opened it and spoke in a low voice with Paloma for a moment. Then she turned back to Mrs. Slade, who sat slumped in the chair wringing her hands. "Paloma's going to help you. Just relax and go to sleep."

Since Mrs. Slade did not appear to have heard her, Luchita went out and shut the door.

Paloma eyed the foreign lady mistrustfully; she had seen enough gringas to decide straightway that this one was drunk. She forced her up out of the chair and pulled off her dress and slip. Then she got a challis dressing gown from the closet. The wind was still blowing in through the doors that gave on to the balcony, and the curtains rippled fitfully into the room. The lady was shivering; she continued to tremble and shake uncontrollably as she got into the bed with the bathrobe belt finally tied around her waist. Paloma watched her for a moment, and came to a different conclusion: the lady took drugs. She had seen films in which addicts were shown behaving very much as she was behaving now. And she continued to stare downward, an expression of disgust spreading over her face as she watched. Mrs. Slade's palsied hands clawed frantically at the sheet; she was trying to cover herself. Paloma only looked. She did not lean over to help her. The gringa was not a person. That's what they come to, she told herself.

The smooth linen sheets were painfully cold; wherever they touched her, they hurt—on the high peaks where the snow glistened and in the valleys where the glaciers creaked. It was all painful, the pain of cold like the aching of an inmost nerve.

Even while she was balancing at the edge of the abyss, she found herself wondering that it was possible to be in so decentralized a state and yet be aware, not only of everything inside and outside herself, but also of the fact that the disintegration was still in process.

There was, of course, no bottom to the abyss, once she had
been drawn into it. It was merely a further stage of decom-
position, the inability to respond to the law of gravity. The fall
was slow, almost luxurious. When it gathered speed and she
grew dizzy, she opened her eyes. A strange woman stood
over her; she had a face of luminous white wax. Her eyes were
staring down at the bed with an expression of hatred. She
screamed once and sat up, stretched out her arm to drive
away the demon. It turned swiftly and clicked off all the
lights. Then it went out of the room and shut the door.

The distant sound of the wind blowing through the pines
was a little like the roar of the sea; it rose up from below now
and then and came through the doors into the room.

Inside, in the dark vault of her consciousness, there was an
endless entry into Hell, where cities toppled and crashed
upon her, and she died each time slowly, imprisoned at the
bottom of the wreckage. And on the fiery horizon still more
cities towered, postponing their imminent collapse until she
should be within reach.

20

There is a cold wind blowing along the floor; it is that way in
all the rooms so far. It comes from the patio. The doors are
shut but it blows under them. He can feel it on his ankles. He
is walking without shoes, wearing a bathrobe, but he is not
thinking about that. Thus far he has found a door from each
room into the next, so that he has not had to go out into the
patio. There are dim lights out there among the bushes. The
rooms are in darkness. That is good, because it is safer in
the dark, even though he bumps into things sometimes as he
feels his way along.

He listens and hears frogs singing, but they sound far away.
The rooms smell old; they have that inner stillness found only
in ancient houses. As he passes an open door into the patio,
he looks out for an instant and sees stone pillars and arches.
He moves ahead, but with such caution that even when he
comes suddenly upon a piece of furniture, he makes no sound
as he touches it.

He does not know where he is trying to go; he only wants to get as far as possible from the bed. The dream he has left there was so terrible he cannot remember it. But this could still be part of the dream, he thinks, bristling with fear, this unchanging silent house with the men somewhere in it waiting to catch him. In a dream, what does it matter? Strike out, smash the furniture, yell. Let them come rushing through the rooms.

He holds his breath, listens again. Frogs. A dog yaps in the distance. Now he knows that he wants to get out of the house. When he starts to move again he is less cautious, and comes up short against a chair. To keep as far as he can from the patio, he makes his way toward the opposite wall. On the far side of one of the rooms he may find a door, and the door could open onto the garden. When his outstretched hand touches a curtain, his fingers follow the cloth to its end; he pulls the curtain back a bit and steps behind its folds. The window is high and has iron grillwork over it. But the sight of the stars excites him. They're still there, he thinks. At the same instant a twinge of fear makes him peer around, back into the room. He had forgotten fear for a while; he had merely been on his way. He remembers: it began as a nightmare. Now it is beginning to turn back into one. He waits for the signs of transformation, and because there is no change in the silence and darkness of the room, he suddenly becomes aware that neither the silence nor the darkness is complete. There is the sound of leaves being moved by a faint breeze in the patio; the basic glow of the stars coming in through a door, a window, can sometimes help to determine the size and even the shape of a desk or chair. At this moment he is convinced that he is awake, that the soles of his bare feet actually are touching the soft rugs and icy tiles; they are surfaces that supply varying sensations. But what is the world? he thinks. How many more rooms are there in it?

The stucco wall along which he has been feeling his way ends in a smooth wooden pillar. A little more light comes from the patio into the next room, and he hears a cricket outside. A variation in the quality of the acoustics, and he glances upward. This room is much higher than the others; he imagines he sees a balcony up there in the dark at the far end.

The big room proves to have no door leading into a further room. His eyes follow the curve of an archway that gives onto the patio. As he approaches it, the sweet nocturnal smell of plant life comes in, on an eddy of breeze, and the odor disturbs him. To escape its impact he makes himself take a step forward through the archway and peer outside. A small lantern hangs some distance back in the bushes beyond the arcade, masked by moving leaves. To the left is a wide staircase leading upward. There is still no sound but the frogs calling in chorus from a distance and the drier chirp of a few crickets in the patio. Quickly he walks across that corner of the cloistered passage and starts to climb. The steps are made of smooth stone, and they slant slightly toward the center, where the tread of feet has worn them down.

Now he hears a voice. It seems to be calling from one room to another, far at the other end of the house. "Yes," it says. Then he can hear nothing. He continues silently. Up here the patio looks the same; the arched balcony stretches out to the left and straight ahead. The stars are more in evidence: no branches hide them.

He goes swiftly to the nearest open door and enters. In the patio he would be visible. He believes that he is likely to find a way out of the house in one of these rooms up here. This floor is much more difficult. The rooms are only partially furnished, and there are crates and piles of boxes along the walls. The first two rooms are filled with the heavy odor of ancient dust. The third makes him stop short: it smells lived in. He moves ahead uncertainly. All at once there is an object in front of him, very near to his right eye. He draws back and looks up. It is a piece of sculpture, towering dimly above him. He feels he is going to lose his balance and takes a step sideways, bending exaggeratedly to avoid the statue. His arm stretches out ahead of him and his hand strikes something cold and very smooth, and during that instant there is a loud sound in the room.

In the following silence he listens first and hears nothing. He has not even asked himself what has happened, what has caused the sound. He listens, still hears nothing. While he is listening, he is growing used to his surroundings: he is standing in front of a grand piano, his head bent, looking downward. But now he hears something. It is at first as much felt under his feet as heard, like a bump. Then in the patio a slight stirring of sound is added to the call of the crickets and the air moving the leaves.

They are coming up the stairs, indifferent to the noise their shoes are making on the steps. He stands there and waits. Without warning, the room is bursting with light, as from a great altitude he gazes down upon the precise black-and-white landscape of the keyboard.

They are being very polite, joking carefully with him as they gently guide him through the door and across the covered passage to the stairway. One of them keeps telling him that he has a fever and ought to be in bed. He replies that it is not true, but that he was expecting them to come in any case. They seem a little in awe of him, and he feels that this respect is predicated upon his complete obedience; at the first sign of a divergency of opinion or behavior on his part their attitude will change. He has always known the world is like this. There is no way of escaping. They come and get you and quietly lead you away. As they go down the stone steps they are telling him that he is risking pneumonia, that he must understand he is ill, that he must stay in bed.

Now they are back down in the other half of the world. He feels that he knows it intimately: the lantern behind the leaves as they go along under the arches, the crickets' song, the open doors into the dark rooms, and the doors that are shut, where the wind blows underneath.

When they are in his room and he sees the bed, he looks up at them, waiting to be told to get in. One of them announces he is going to make him some hot tea, that he may have caught a chill. He says that if it were not for the fever he would give him brandy instead.

"Fever?" he repeats thickly, climbing into the bed. "Fever?" He turns his head to one side, shuts his eyes, and lies still. In one respect they are right, the two young strangers: he feels very ill.

Much later, as someone comes in, he opens his eyes. The only light is behind a high screen; the bed is in shadow. One of the young men is walking toward him carrying a cup and saucer. He stares up from the pillows; it does not surprise him to see that his captor's face is painted in stripes of blue and black. Around the snout the stripes run together in a more delicate design; this part of the face is faintly incandescent. He thinks he has motioned to him to put the cup on the table. He tells himself that he expected it, but the striped mask disturbs him and he does not want any contact with its owner.

He has made no signal at all; he has not moved. The creature forces him to sit up and drink the tea, so hot that it burns his lips. It seems a long time before he has drunk it and is allowed to lie down. He has not glanced at the face again. The young man walks away. As he is leaving the room he stands in the doorway an instant and tells him that Mr. Soto will soon be there. He says it with an air of promising something pleasant, as if he too is looking forward to the arrival.

When he lies alone in the darkened room once more, the absurd idea comes into his head that these people are invaders from outer space. No one ever had such a face, he is certain; he looked directly at it and saw the miniature designs around the muzzle.

The visitor, when he comes, proves to be another like the first two, only larger and more officious; he is clearly their commander. This one has no stripes on his face. On the contrary, it would seem that no effort had been spared to make him as realistic as possible. He is a facsimile made with the most meticulous regard for detail; he is a perfect imitation of a man. And now that the lights have been turned on, he sees that the other one no longer bears the stripes on his snout. They burned away, he thinks.

The chief comes toward the bed, his hands in his pockets. "How you feeling now, Doctor? A little better?" He cocks his head to one side.

"I'm all right."

"The pills helped." The chief says this as a question, with a note of faint astonishment.

He only grunts, and moves a little in the bed, aware that the chief has come closer and is standing over him, moving objects on the table by his pillow.

"May have brought it down," he hears him say, and he feels the end of a thermometer being pushed against his lip.

Yes, he is sick, he thinks, but the synthetic man has no idea of what is the matter with him; he is playing the doctor tonight. He rolls the thermometer under his tongue and looks up at him distrustfully. Later the chief pulls it out of his mouth and holds it under the lamp on the table to read it; he turns his head toward the wall and keeps his eyes shut while this is going on.

"Very good," the chief says after a moment. "Down to a hundred and three point two."

He makes a momentous decision—that of forcing himself to go to the trouble of sitting up. The chief looks at him in surprise as he sees him begin to struggle upward.

"May I see it?" he hears himself say. The chief quickly hands him the thermometer, saying, "You ought not to be making any effort."

"I can read a thermometer," he replies tonelessly. It takes him a long time; he is trying to focus on the painted notches and catch the magnified gleam of the mercury behind the curve of the glass. He holds it very close to his eyes. The silver band inside is there, but then he loses it, and the effort to regain it is more than he can make. He grunts and hands it back, certain, as he pushes his head into the pillows, that there is no fever. He cries out, "Why don't you just try leaving me alone?"

The chief laughs indulgently. "You've got to eat. It's essential to keep something inside you."

When he has drunk the consommé and eaten the sandwich he lies down with his head facing away from the lamp. A moment later someone comes quietly in and switches off all the lights.

There is a mistake about the time. He is in a house, caught in the body of a man who is being kept in bed. People come and bother him, go away. Doors are opened and shut. It is daytime; it is night. Sometimes he is impaled on the wind as he rushes through space. There are long periods when he is imprisoned in a muddy submarine world, aware of the room beyond the bed, knowing that time is creeping past, but able only to lie there without motion, clinging mollusk-like to the underside of consciousness until someone comes and touches him, and once again changes everything.

21

There came a moment when she found herself knowing it was daytime rather than night, and when she was aware of one hour following upon another. She was in the open air, lying in bed on a balcony. Birds chirped from the railing; the wind smelled of gardenias and pine trees. But this is real, she thought with a shock, and in the desperate hope of finding it possible to remain with the reality she decided to make no effort, merely to watch and see what would happen.

Several times that morning the nurse brought her food and cold drinks. It was logical to suppose there must be someone else nearby, but she had no memory of anyone but the nurse. Often she suspected her of not being a nurse at all; the woman's ill-humor was more like that of a sullen menial. She felt that for her to have been left in the hands of such a person was a serious oversight on someone's part, and she intended to complain about it when the right time came. She tried not to let herself dislike the nurse too much: she suspected the other would sense it and retaliate in some indirect manner. Always the woman came in a hurry, tapping along the tiles on her little high heels, did what had to be done on the balcony with visible distaste and a great deal of noise, and then went away again without even looking at her. When she was gone and the balcony was quiet once more, she would lie in a state of sheer happiness, grateful for having been returned to the world outside. Convalescence, she told herself comfortably, without troubling to wonder from what.

At sunset she heard hushed voices in the room off the balcony. She opened her eyes and stared ahead of her, listening, thinking she recognized one of the voices. "Doctor," she cried feebly. The murmur stopped; there was silence. For a while she waited, expecting the conversation to start up once more, and when it did not, trying to hear at least the sound of retreating footsteps. After a while she called out again, "Nurse!" The word seemed to have come up out of a distant valley; it was hard to believe that it was she who had uttered it. Still there was no sound from the room. She waited a long time; no one came, and there were no more voices. The birds had gone and it was almost dark. Feeling hurt and resentful, she drifted off into sleep.

A floor lamp had been put beside the bed. The light was shining into her face, and a man stood there looking down at her. She assumed he was the doctor. Behind him stood another man, much younger; this one she recognized, without connecting him with any specific place or particular period of her life.

She tried to smile at the doctor, but she was not sure whether the muscles of her face had moved or not. "I'm better," she said.

The doctor, without ceasing to look at her, said something to the other in Spanish. Then he bent over and lifted her hand to his lips, letting it drop gently back onto the coverlet. He straightened, turned, and walked inside, followed by the younger man. She wanted to call after them; instead, she lay still under the blinding light, listening to their voices recede as they went through the rooms, finally hearing them die out entirely.

Some time later there were approaching footsteps. The young man came out onto the balcony, smiling, his hands in his pockets. "Sorry to leave that light in your eyes," he said, and turned it off. The balcony was half in light, half in shadow.

"You're a lot better, aren't you?" It was a statement which he expected her to confirm, but she said nothing. "Are you really out of the tunnel now?"

Still she did not answer; she imagined herself walking in a tunnel and seeing the opening ahead. At first the mouth of the tunnel was fairly near, but then it grew smaller and smaller. She opened her eyes quickly. He was looking at her with undisguised interest.

"This is the first day," she said, and wondered if he understood what she meant. There she lay at the bottom of her soft world while he talked of symptoms, treatment and reactions, idly asking herself now and then what his function was in the hospital. It was all one unchanging scene; he ended it rather abruptly, she thought, by saying "Good night" and walking away. At some point the nurse must have come, for when she awoke later the balcony was in darkness, and she could see the stars in the sky beyond the railing.

The next day she was more at home inside herself. When the young man came she said to him, "I'm out of the tunnel."

"I can see that." He was wearing a red and gray striped shirt and a pair of shorts. She stared with mild astonishment at his bare legs.

"You're not the doctor, are you?"

He smiled condescendingly. "You saw the doctor yesterday. You've finished with him. He's seeing Dr. Slade today. Also for the last time. You're both out of your respective tunnels."

He went on talking, but for a moment she did not hear what he was saying. She had been lying here all this time, and not once had the thought of Taylor crossed her mind. If he'd asked me was I married, I'd have said no, she marveled. After a while the meaning of his words came to her, and she interrupted him, crying, "Is Dr. Slade ill?"

"He's fine. He's fine." The young man patted her hand. "You've both been sick, and you're both well." He looked carefully at her.

She did not reply. If she had known who the young man was, in what capacity he served on the staff, she reflected, it would have been easier for her to talk with him. There were the complaints she wanted to make about the service and the nurse they had assigned to her. But she had a feeling that the young man had the answers to all possible questions written out and hidden away for safekeeping, and that under no circumstances would she ever get from him more than a small part of the truth. With this in mind, it seemed scarcely worth while to ask; nevertheless she did. "Where is he? Where is Taylor?"

"Right there at Los Hermanos where he's been the whole time." If he had said, "Still undergoing gravitational therapy on Venus," she would have understood just as much. But she answered, "I see," as though she now had a clear picture of a life being led in a place called The Brothers, and as though it were to be expected that her husband should be leading that life. Even as he said the words, however, her mind was brushed by the shadow of another question she could not even formulate. An intensity in the young man's eyes had belied the simulated casualness of his reply.

Since she said no more, he ceased staring at her and lit a cigarette. "I think you can plan on seeing him tomorrow night," he told her presently. "Would you like some music?"

"I don't think so. Not particularly."

It was as though the world no longer contained anything certain. There were only unstable elements; everything had been cut free, was floating. Her head was clear; she was aware of being able to follow and assess her thoughts. Yet without finding it possible to name it specifically, she was convinced that something in the situation was amiss, something outside and beyond her own lassitude. As she grew stronger, she reflected, it was likely that she would be less conscious of it, and precisely for that reason she made a mental note to remind herself of it the next day.

He talked for a while. She pretended to be drifting off now and then into sleep. At length he left her.

She swung her legs over the side of the bed and took a few tentative steps, barefoot, on the cold tiles. Feeling surprisingly full of energy, she began to walk up and down alongside the railing, looking out at the patterns made by the occasional street lights of some remote suburb across the valley.

At the far end of the balcony there was a small lavatory; a mirror hung above the washbasin. In its reflection she searched for signs of illness or fatigue and was mildly astonished to find none. But then a whole series of unanswerable questions flooded her mind simultaneously. Where was her handbag? Where had they put her clothes? What hospital was it? In the mirror she saw her eyes open a little wider as she was seized by the realization that she could remember nothing of arriving, whether she thought of the hospital or of the city whose lights she had seen a moment ago.

She looked down into the washbasin, bent over, and began to splash cold water into her face. She understood that she had not yet fully recovered; probably it had been unwise of her to get up and walk even this much. At all events, and she said this to herself with great firmness, it was important not to be afraid. She dried her face pleasurably with a large bath towel; the best thing would be to get back into bed and sleep.

When she awoke at dawn the problem was there with her, an invisible, total curtain between her and everything outside. The frail strand of cockcrow that came over the still air was filtered through the curtain, and thus reached her devoid of meaning. She knew that somewhere roosters were crowing, but because she could not remember how she had got to this high balcony in a town she did not know, the roosters' very existence was unacceptable. She felt her heart begin to beat very hard, like something wholly apart from her. Coughing nervously, she thought of adrenalin, the product of fear. It was imperative to hold out until Taylor came. She sat up and looked out at the large moon still casually giving light, like a street lamp left on after day has come. The pointed black tips of some pine trees not far away showed above the railing. There was only the unnecessary moon to look at, and as she looked, life began to move again, because all at once she had remembered. The fact that an hour or so later she discovered a few empty spots in the landscape of the past did not bother her greatly; she felt that she had found the important material.

The nurse brought her a fine breakfast. She ate it all and lay quietly watching the sparrows arrive and shower drops of water from the birdbath. It was on the ship where the story began to blur, where details became uncertain. She could not recapture the image of their cabin; had it been port or starboard? And in the dining room. She thought she recalled a meal when she had been eating rice, sitting across from Taylor, but had it been on the ship?

When she saw the young man arriving at half-past ten, the unwelcome idea came to her that he might be a supervising psychiatrist: he was so cocksure, so clearly in command.

"Paloma says you're back into yourself, as she put it," he told her, beaming with pleasure. "Yes. You look about ready to set forth."

"Set forth?"

"Yes." He smiled harder and, leaning over, rested his hands on the knobs of the footboard. "For the country."

"I don't know what you're talking about!" she cried excitedly. "The country? What for? Didn't you tell me Dr. Slade would be here tonight?"

He shook his head, still smiling. "You misunderstood. Not here. At San Felipe."

She sat very stiff and severe, certain that an edge of anger must show in her voice. "Look!" she said. "I'm not the kind that takes orders. My mechanism doesn't work. There's just no reaction." She waited a moment, and then, since he did not answer, she went on. "Why can't my husband come here and see me? Is it forbidden, or what?"

The young man straightened and viewed her with surprise.

"Come on," she urged him. "I'm very dense, I know, but is there any reason why Dr. Slade can't visit me here at the hospital?"

"Hospital! You don't recognize the apartment?"

Without ceasing to look at her, he lowered himself slowly into a chair. After a moment he went on calmly, "It can come after the fever. It's nothing. It goes away." He leaned forward. "You had an extremely high fever for a while, in case you don't know."

"I don't want to hear about it." Apartment, she was thinking.

He laughed. "Better not to."

The nurse came clacking onto the balcony, saw the young man, and stood still. Then she bowed respectfully toward the bed and said, "*Muy buenos días, señora.*"

"I'm going to leave you with Paloma." He started away, then paused in the doorway to say, "Your things are in here, in this room. I think you'll find everything. When you're dressed, why don't you call Luchita on the phone? Push number four. I'll be back here for lunch." He chuckled. "And you really thought this was a hospital!"

The room was large and pleasantly cool. All the valises, hers and Taylor's, stood in a corner. She went into the bathroom and turned on the hot water. The tub was a good place for lying back and thinking. Her outburst had been regrettable, but he had taken it very well. She smiled at her toes, seeing them sticking out above the water level. It was still an embarrassing situation, to be the house guest of people whose name she did not even know.

When she went back into the bedroom Paloma was waiting for her to unlock her bags. Finally she was dressed, and although she had no desire to meet her hostess, she took up the telephone and pressed the number four button. Fortunately it was the young man who answered; a minute later he was at the door, and together they walked through a patio and several rooms, out onto a spacious terrace. I've probably seen all this before, she told herself; it even seemed to her that she recalled certain things, but it was more as though she had read about them or seen them in a film.

They stood talking in the shade by a pool where some lianas hung; still he had given her no clue. Suddenly she saw the city gleaming in the haze far below, and as she became aware of the great height, she took a few steps back toward the wall of the building.

"You remember this terrace?" he inquired.

"I can't even tell you. That means I don't, I suppose."

"We came out here. And we talked about a building. The building at the end of the dock. How it seemed to collapse, you remember, when you fell?"

As he spoke, she lowered her head a little and passed her hand over her eyes. She had a static image, in which she and Taylor were in a huge dusty windowless tin-covered shed—an inferno of heat and noise. They were both sick, and being sick they were afraid. Remembering it now was like skirting the black flames of a noonday nightmare. Taylor had just remarked that if only he could get to the door and breathe some fresh air he would be all right. And then he had fallen, and she must have run ahead to the door to look for help. Now she saw what was like a color photo in an advertisement: a pair of handsome young people attractively dressed in beach clothes standing by a sports car under a coconut palm. The world had suddenly turned sideways like a plane banking, and as she fell she had seen a frame building at the end of the next pier cave in as if a giant foot had kicked it.

"The sun's hot," she said. "Could we go in?"

"You did tell me about how the building seemed to buckle and collapse?"

"Yes," she said in a faint voice, walking on toward the door. "In Puerto Farol. We can never thank you for all you've done."

"You were a sick couple, that I'll say."

When they were inside she sat on a pile of cushions and

shielded her eyes. "The sun makes me dizzy," she confided. She remembered the fur and the glass and the tall plants, the strange child with her pictures spread out on the floor, the moment when she had begun to be cold, and then the slow journey down into the cloaca of horror that had been the disease. She was silent.

"I'm going to fix you a drink," he said.

When the girl came in and he cried, "Ah, Luchita!" it was the same child who had shown the drawings, the same child who had stood glistening in the picture postcard of the car under the palms.

"Hello," she said. "Are you all right now?"

"Yes. I'm fine."

He spoke from the other side of the room. "Everybody ought to be at San Felipe by seven at the latest. Luchita can drive you down in the station wagon."

"I want a bottle of Seven-Up," Luchita announced.

"You'll have to get it from the kitchen," he told her.

Mrs. Slade and her host were alone for a moment. "What does she call you?" she asked him. "Vero?"

"Evolved from Grover through Grovero. Sort of a joke, like *pocho* talk in reverse." He eyed her sharply. "I thought it would be good if you and Dr. Slade saw something of the country before you left. Some of the mountains, some of the jungle. It's a beautiful drive down to San Felipe." He described a series of hairpin turns with his forefinger. "If you like scenery."

"I do. I never get tired of it."

Luchita had come back into the room carrying a tall glass; ice cubes clinked daintily against its sides. "It's *tierra caliente*," she said, looking meaningfully at Mrs. Slade, and he glanced her way with annoyance.

"Is it very hot there?" Mrs. Slade wanted to know.

Luchita had caught his warning. "Not too bad," she said.

"I somehow don't think it would be good to stay too long in a place where it was very hot, do you?"

"It isn't hot," he told her. "That wasn't what Luchita meant. *Tierra caliente* isn't necessarily hot. She just doesn't like *tierra caliente*. The ranch isn't in the selva. It's in the open, just above where the selva begins."

The drink was helping. After a moment she said, "All I can

tell you is that I'm overcome by so much attention. You have to come all the way here to find out what real hospitality is."

It would be better not to show any hesitation in accepting; then when she and Taylor got together they could make their plans. Lunch was an elaborate curry; the big table was entirely covered with side dishes. When they had finished coffee, she felt a good deal livelier.

"About the luggage, you want to take everything, I imagine," he told her. "You may want to go on to wherever you're going from there."

He helped the doorman pack the car, and waved as Luchita swung the station wagon around and started down the mountainside. In the city, after they had left the business district, Luchita got a traffic ticket for being on the left of the white line in the center of the street. "Vero's going to be mean when I tell him," Luchita sighed.

"You have to pick the right moment."

Steering her way slowly between oxcarts and crowds of barefoot pedestrians, Luchita laughed derisively. Soon they were in the country.

22

There was the sky, and then trees went past, first nearby, overhead, with huge shining green leaves. The sky came again, and more trees far away on the side of a stony hill, gray, leafless, spiked, hundreds of them, while more of the hill came into view. The train jerked as it went along, making his head rock from side to side. The air that blew in through the window above his head was foul with coal gas. Now and then a tiny cinder pellet hit his face. He was about to move his hand up to cover his forehead, but at the same instant his mind began to move. His eyes shut and he lay still. He would wait until he knew more before venturing out of his hiding place. The idea came to him that perhaps it would be better to go all the way back in; if he were surprised out there he would be helpless. Let him begin to think too much, and they would sense it. He wanted to spy on them from the safety of the dark.

The next time he came back, his eyes were open again, and

he saw the sky and trees the same as before. Then he glanced once down along his body and shut his eyes. He was intact, and he wore his gray slacks and had sandals on his feet. His heart was beating too fast and hard, but inside his mind there was calm.

He slept a little, aware betweentimes of the train running on and on, roaring over trestles, the sound of its wheels echoing against hillsides.

He opened his eyes and looked across the compartment. Only one man was sitting there, young, carefully dressed, heavily tanned by the sun. Yes, he thought. I know him. It was surprising that there should be only this one; he had been sure there were several. Then it occurred to him that the young man was speaking to him, and that he in turn was expected to say something. He pushed himself up a bit and shook his head dubiously. The sensation of helplessness was real now; it was like early morning in a strange hotel room when for a moment the waker has no idea of where he is. But that nowhereness is always dispelled after a few instants of effort, and this was still going on.

He peered more closely at the young man. He looked like a film star, and he spoke in the almost convincing manner of a character in a film, his face constantly changing a little in its expression as it accompanied his sentences. It was important to know what he was talking about.

"I don't know," he said dubiously; now he too was a character in the same film. He studied the gray eyes behind the handsome mobile face.

The young man smiled reassuringly. There was a large pigskin valise in the rack over his head; a raincoat lay folded on top of it.

They were together on a train. He was making a trip with this young man whose name escaped him, and he was getting old. Old. That was the only explanation. But it seemed likely that if the other talked enough, he would remember. Some word would come out which would make the connection and bring him entirely awake.

The young man looked at his watch. "The girls ought to be at Escobar around about now. There's a sort of inn there where they'll probably stop for something."

What he was saying conveyed no message. "You'll have to excuse me," he said, endeavoring to sit up a bit straighter. "I'm a little muzzy. How long have I been asleep?"

"I don't know. A while."

They rushed into the dark of a tunnel and were out again into the open, the train straining around a long curve. "What were you saying a few minutes ago?" he said.

The young man laughed shortly. "Whatever it was, it was just an opening gambit. I didn't want to startle you."

"Startle me?"

"You see, I was sure you'd make sense one of these times when you came around, and finally you did."

For some reason he felt a surge of anger. "Why don't you say whatever it is you're trying to say? Haven't I been making sense?"

The other leaned forward on the seat and looked at him intently. "You're fine now. But you weren't so hot a few days ago. You know, it's tricky where the brain's involved. You might easily have waked up just now without any idea of who the hell you were."

The word "brain" carried dark echoes with it. "I know who I am," he said grimly, shutting his eyes. But it was true: he was still muzzy. He occupied a small center of unknown territory, and on all sides there was wilderness. And that was exactly what the young man had meant: amnesia.

"What was it? What did I manage to pick up?"

The young man sat back. "There's a lot of it around," he said. "They don't really know much about how it works. A man named Newbold isolated the virus a few years ago. It's called after him. Hits like lightning and goes away just as fast, without doing any visible harm. Except, as I say, sometimes there's this temporary memory loss."

"Hmmm." He let his eyes follow the pattern in the lace on the armrest. It was like a first-class compartment on a European train. This disturbed him: he did not want to be in Europe.

"How temporary is it?" he finally said. "I ask because I've got it. I'm *lost*!" He shook his head slowly.

"No, you're not. Look. You remember landing in Puerto Farol with Day?"

The names were enough; the contact was made. Once more he shut his eyes. As the darkness inside was banished, he recalled the sea-smell of the town, green and steaming after rain. The train swerved, whistled, clattered along the edge of a cliff. "Where is she?" he said.

"On the highway down there somewhere, behind those nearest mountains, in a white station wagon." The young man thrust his arm out the window and pointed.

He lay back for a bit, having decided against asking all the other questions. If he waited until he was clearer-headed, perhaps he would not have to ask them at all.

"We came in this contraption because I wanted you to be able to lie out flat. Anyway, Los Hermanos is on the line to San Felipe. It's the easiest way."

He grunted a reply and realized that he was half asleep once again. Then the young man said no more; the sounds and movements of the train took over.

He felt his shoulder being prodded; the rasping sound of brakes filled the coach. He sat up and put his feet on the floor. The train was winding through a narrow gorge with sheer rock walls on either side. "Is this it?" he asked, and the other nodded. The gorge widened, the train kept braking, and he saw a small dust-colored town ahead.

"I take it the bags are all in the car," he said to the young man.

"That's right. Everything."

The train stopped and they stood up. Taking his suitcase and raincoat, the young man pushed him ahead into the corridor. "You go ahead and I'll be right behind."

"This is really something," he muttered, shuffling along with difficulty. "Come on a vacation and wind up like this. . . ."

"You're doing fine. Just keep going."

They rode in a truck, down into warmer land, the three of them: the mestizo driver, the young man and he. The countryside was covered with flat-topped, leafless thorn trees. Ahead the orange sky flared, then faded, and the spiny landscape went ghost-gray.

"Day's been down with it too, you know," the young man said suddenly, adding, "You'd never believe it, though. I swear, she looks better now than she did before. I didn't know whether to tell you or let her tell you."

"Hell, don't keep any secrets from me. She's all right?"

"Blossoming. I took care of a case of Newbold's right here at the ranch last year. This friend of mine was really sick. But it was incredible! He was up and running around five days later, exactly as if nothing had happened. When I say sick, I mean I thought he wasn't going to pull through. Photism and convulsions and all the trimmings."

"Good God!"

The truck stopped and they got out. In the near-dark he could see only a long windowless wall. The air, warm and dry, was sweet with the smell of woodsmoke. Half a dozen servants ran up, each carrying a flashlight. There were greetings and handshakings; these continued as they went into the house and more servants appeared.

"If you'll just come through here," the young man said. "I'm putting you two in this wing by yourselves. You'll have absolute privacy. It's a pretty big house. Used to be a monastery, you know." He pointed to the beamed ceiling. A barefoot Indian girl carrying a thermos bottle appeared through a doorway ahead of them; she smiled shyly as they passed her.

"You'd probably like to eat something light, right in your room, and go to bed."

"You're right," he said with feeling.

The young man knocked on the door through which the maid had just come, and Day opened it.

Three

23

D R. SLADE had finished his breakfast. The table was set under a khaki-colored parasol in the small patio off the bedroom. He turned his chair around so he could look across the garden. "They've done everything they could for us," he said.

"They've been marvelous, of course. I often wonder what we must have looked like, staggering out of that customs office." Being with Taylor had brought her all the way back into the world; she sat and enjoyed the powerful early morning sunlight and the country smells. "No! I only meant—you don't want to stay here *very* long, do you? They couldn't be sweeter and more generous." She hesitated and took a sip of coffee. "But what have we got in common?"

This of course was the position he had originally taken with regard to his hosts, but at the moment he was in an expansive mood. He stretched back in his chair and yawned. "You're talking too soon, Day. You can't tell. You may love it here."

"You keep inferring there's something here I don't like. I'm divinely happy. I wouldn't want to be anywhere else. But from something you said, I got the impression you felt like staying for quite a while, and I'm just trying to find out how long."

"Since we're here, why don't we just enjoy ourselves? Whenever you want, we can leave."

She sighed. He was not in the habit of being relaxed and casual when it was a question of travel plans. It could be a sign of fatigue. At his age, she reflected, and considering the virulence of the disease, he was fortunate to have rallied this quickly.

"I suppose you're right," she said, feeling a sudden surge of protectiveness toward him. It seemed likely that he needed a thorough rest, and this was the opportunity. She stretched out her feet in front of her and looked at her sandals. "We'll save money, too," she added archly.

He grunted. "It's usually about the same as a hotel by the time you get out, as far as that goes." Her abrupt gesture of agreement had not escaped him; however, he was wary of its motive, and waited.

Late in the afternoon, when the shadows were oblique, they set forth on a walking tour of inspection under the guidance of Señor Soto. Luchita was sullen and silent, and made a point of looking at the sky or the ground beneath her feet each time they stopped to admire a view or examine a plant. She wore a torn shirt, a pair of exaggeratedly dirty Levis, and from what Day could see, nothing else. At one point they came out onto a point of tableland overlooking the river valley and the forest below. "It's dry jungle," said their host. "You can see it's really only a strip that follows the river. We've got about ten thousand acres of good grazing land on the other side over there. Down below here there's a little coffee. Not much, yet. It costs more than it brings in at this point."

Day glanced around for Luchita, and saw her some distance away, seated on a rock, smoking a cigarette. She inhaled with great deliberateness, each time holding the smoke carefully in her lungs for a moment before expelling it. She can't even smoke like other people, she thought. Then she saw that Grove had noticed her, too, and watched his expression cloud over with annoyance. "Come on!" he called. "The *fábrica*, before it gets dark." He led them downward, along a narrow path between boulders and large ceiba trees with fat gray roots.

The *fábrica* was a vast wooden construction, built into the side hill on several levels, partly covered and partly roofless, a chaos of chutes and bins. In Indian file, with Grove leading, they picked their way among the mounds of coffee beans and got to a small office on the dim far side of the shed. A wizened, swarthy young man sat at a desk. "This is my foreman, Enrique Quiroga," said Grove, and they shook hands. Several workmen had taken up unmoving positions from which they could watch through the open door into the office. Grove seized one of several large sombreros that hung from a row of nails on the wall and threw it on his head at an angle. "I feel as though we were on our way to the captain's dinner," Day said to him.

"Not quite. Watch."

A few thin beams of late sunlight pierced the makeshift wall and slanted across the dark interior far above their heads. "Piranese," said Grove, walking ahead.

No one answered. "Come over here and look at this," he said.

Luchita was talking with the foreman. "*Hombre!*" she shouted.

In the corner, up and down, were dozens of webs, like hammocks carelessly slung between the two walls. An enormous black-and-yellow spider lay in each one.

"My God, their bodies are as big as plums!" cried Dr. Slade.

Crushing the crown of the sombrero in one hand, Grove made a long downward scooping gesture with it; the sticky membranes snapped. Then he held the hat up so they could see inside. Dr. Slade adjusted his glasses and stared.

"How many'd I get?"

"Seven or eight."

As Luchita came over to them, Grove bunched the crown together again. "Hold the shadow-maker a minute, will you?"

Dutifully she took it and carried it a few paces. One of the insects, climbing up to escape, touched her hand. She glanced down, screamed, and flung the hat away.

"Oh, I'll kill you, you lousy son of a bitch!" she cried, rushing at Grove to pound him with her fists.

"She hates them," he explained over her shoulder to Day, keeping her hands away from his face.

Behind the *fábrica* were several rows of thatched-roof huts where women chattered and children shrieked. They stood outside of one and looked in at the mud walls and dirt floor; an old woman lay on a pile of burlap sacks in one corner.

"Pretty primitive," said Dr. Slade. Day caught the inflection of criticism in his voice. Perhaps Grove noticed it also. "They're primitive people," he said. "Give them a bed and they put it out for the chickens to roost on. Give them money and they're drunk for two days."

"Still, they must have money sometimes," objected Dr. Slade.

"They don't see it from one year to the next. They get paid in scrip and buy their food at the company store on credit."

"I've read about the system," said Dr. Slade drily.

"They seem happy enough," Day began in an uncertain tone. She was ready to say anything which might forestall discussion of the subject: she knew Taylor.

At one side of the *fábrica*, under a large tree, there was a truck. "Enrique's giving us a lift back to the house," said Grove.

The bumpy trail led through scrub most of the way; it was almost dark when they arrived back at the house. Luchita had made a point of involving herself in a conversation with the foreman as soon as they had got into the truck. When it stopped she jumped down and disappeared.

The main courtyard of the monastery, terraced and open at one end, had not been changed. By daylight there was a view down through the cloistered garden and across the headlands to the curving river with its band of forest. In a corner on the highest terrace, glass walls had been built, and behind these they had dinner. The candles flickered in the breeze. Luchita was sleek and glowing in a close-fitting black gown. As she ate, she stared moodily out toward the invisible river, and when she spoke, her voice was sharp with emotion, alternately indignant and insolent.

"The poor child's still shaken," said Day to Grove. "Those spiders! Why did you do it?"

"Do what?" he cried disgustedly. "It's that very childishness she should be fighting against."

In principle Day agreed with him, but she raised her eyebrows to show disapproval. Looking at him, ruddy and beaming in the candlelight, she thought with faint repulsion: Men are all brutal with young girls. And even Taylor. He too had been sadistic to a small girl, but where had it been? And had he, really, or was it a false memory left over from her sickness?

All day long, here and there, at odd moments, something had been bothering her, and she had put off taking the time to see what it was. And now, as she suddenly came face to face with it, even as Luchita was refusing salad from the bowl the servant held in front of her, she knew in a flash that there was still an empty spot in the past.

She watched the man coming toward her with the salad bowl. Nothing of what was happening was understandable; it could as easily have been something completely different. Until she knew what had gone on before she could not fully accept what was going on now.

For one thing, it struck her as extremely strange that she should feel she knew Grove so well. His voice particularly—it was like a sound she had known all her life. There was something abnormal in the terrible familiarity she felt with its cadence and inflections. And then, What has he got against me? she wondered. Why is he practically vibrating with hostility? Several times during the day she had been nettled by his air of insolent triumph as he looked at her.

All at once she realized that Grove and Taylor were engaged in the argument she had been afraid they would have when they had stood among the workers' huts outside the *fábrica*.

"Yes, but what does the term 'human rights' mean? The American idea is based completely on the fact that Americans have always had more than their share." Grove fixed Dr. Slade with his forefinger. "Put them in the same position as the rest of the people in the world, and they'll understand soon enough that what they've had so far have been only privileges, not rights."

"But for your own protection, in a country like this," pursued Dr. Slade blandly, "it seems you'd do better to cut down the area of possible discontent, don't you think?"

Grove laughed. "Shall we go inside for coffee?" They rose from the table, leaving the candles to gutter in the rising breeze.

In the *sala* Grove stood facing Dr. Slade. "I know, I know," he said with impatience. "A liberal can't say no because he's got nothing to say yes to. But, Doctor, in political theory you keep up with research too."

Dr. Slade bridled. "I'm afraid I don't see the parallel."

They walked over and sat down by the coffee table. Luchita, seeing Grove come into the room, had stopped talking and had assumed a chastened attitude.

"Taylor! Listen to what Pepito said. Tell him, Luchita. It's marvelous!"

Luchita glanced apprehensively at Grove, who seemed amused by her sudden shyness.

"I don't know what's come over her. Ordinarily she doesn't mention the product of her childhood indiscretions," he said.

"Who's Pepito?" demanded Dr. Slade, still ruffled by what he considered Grove's unwarranted attack. But Luchita had risen silently, her face transformed by rage, and was already on her way out of the room. The sound of her heels tapping on the flagstones in the patio died away, and there was silence for an instant.

Finally Day said, "Well!" Grove went on to tell about Indian customs; there was no further reference to the angry exit. A half hour later he too got up, saying he had some work to do, and bade them good night.

They sat on in the *sala* for another few minutes, leafing through magazines in silence. Then, more with mutterings than with words, they agreed to get up and go to their room. Day took with her a copy of *Country Life* and one of *Réalités*. There was a barefoot Indian girl in their bedroom turning down the coverlets and laying out their bathrobes and slippers. She smiled at them and went out.

Dr. Slade stood by the window staring into the faintly lighted patio. Day had gone into the bathroom and was drawing water in the washbasin. He tried without success to remember the last occasion when he and Day had been together in bed. It was unimportant, and yet not knowing when or where it had been disturbed him.

At last she came into the room, radiant in a white peignoir. She walked over to him and put her arm through his. "Darling," he said, turning toward her to embrace her. The smell of her hair always reminded him of sunlight and wind. She did not raise her face to his.

He put his hand under her chin. "What's the matter?"

"Nothing very much," she said smiling; she pulled gently away from him and went to sit at the dressing table.

When he came out of the bathroom in his pajamas, she was sitting up with her sheet over her, looking at *Réalités*. She had tossed the copy of *Country Life* onto his bed. He lay down and stared for a minute at photographs of yew trees and English sitting rooms; then he turned off the lamp on his night table and let the magazine slide to the floor. A moment later Day clicked off her light; the room was in darkness. He heard her yawn faintly. After that there was silence, and then she spoke, tentatively: "Taylor."

"Yes," he murmured, forcing himself back into wakefulness. "What?"

"I wanted to ask you. Have you had any trouble trying to remember things? Since you were sick? Have you noticed anything?"

"A little." He was already wide-awake.

"I've got a big blank in my head. The whole trip is completely gone. It's awful."

"He mentioned the possibility of it. He said it would all come back."

"It's as though a whole section had been simply rubbed out."

"I know. I went through it yesterday," he said hesitantly. "This is one time when you've just got to be patient."

"You have no blank spots?" she insisted.

"I think they've all gone now." He fabricated a yawn; he hoped she would take the hint, and go to sleep. About his own situation he was not so happy as he had tried to appear. Very definitely there was a blind spot in his memory; he could recall nothing that had happened beyond the first two or three days on the ship out of San Francisco. But he had no intention of admitting it to Day; it would deprive her of the very support she most needed at the moment. Besides, he was convinced that between them they would be able to put together the jumbled pieces. Each day one or the other would supply more details, until the picture was complete for both of them.

He listened. She was still; he assumed she was asleep.

Words were deceptive, the very short ones most of all; she thought of the crucial importance of the two small words Taylor had just used: *he said*. He said the forgetfulness would quickly be dissipated. He said it was a result of something called Newbold's Disease. He said the best doctor in the capital had attended them. But would the faculty return intact? Taylor had never heard of Newbold's Disease. It was conceivable that a different doctor could have prescribed a treatment which would have obviated the aftereffects she was suffering. It was demoralizing to know that everything depended on the word of this particular young man. More than ever she distrusted him, and was annoyed only because she could find no more specific material to help her account for her feeling. It seemed to her that the mere fact of his having taken them in and having bothered to bring them all the way here to the ranch could be viewed in a suspicious light. There was a fundamental contradiction in his behavior: he had gone far out of his way to be hospitable and helpful, yet when she was with him she could not perceive even a glimmer of friendliness. He served his charm and courtesy mechanically; it was as if she and Taylor were paying guests and he a professional host. She was convinced that when he had left them an hour ago he had heaved a sigh of relief finally to be rid of them, free to get back to his own life. What his private world was like she could only surmise, but she was certain there was no corner in it for either her or Taylor; in that realm they counted as objects, not as people.

At some point in the night she had a dream. Or it was possible that she was partially awake, and was only remembering a dream? She was alone among the rocks on a dark coast beside the sea. The water surged upward and fell back languidly, and in the distance she heard surf breaking slowly on a sandy shore. It was comforting to be this close to the surface of the ocean and gaze at the intimate nocturnal details of its swelling and ebbing. And as she listened to the faraway breakers rolling up onto the beach, she became aware of another sound entwined with the intermittent crash of waves: a vast horizontal whisper across the bosom of the sea, carrying an ever-repeated phrase, regular as a lighthouse flashing: *Dawn will be breaking soon.* She listened a long time: again and again the scarcely audible words were whispered across the moving water. A great weight was being lifted slowly from her; little by little her happiness became more complete, and she awoke. Then she lay for a few minutes marveling at the dream, and once again fell asleep.

24

The next morning, some time after they had finished breakfast, Grove knocked on their door. Day, who had been sunbathing, pulled her bathrobe around her.

"I hate to invade your privacy like this," he said, striding into the patio where they sat. "Everything all right? Anything you need?" As they protested that all the details combined to make perfection, he settled back on a chaise lounge and lit a cigarette. In a few minutes the purpose of his visit became clear: he had come to ask Dr. Slade to go with him to visit a nearby silver mine.

"A silver mine! Is that right?" said Dr. Slade with inflections of interest. "Why, I think I might enjoy it."

"Are you going *into* the mine?" Day inquired, looking intently at Grove.

He smiled. "It would be hard to see it from the outside."

"I hate places inside the earth!" she said with feeling, not removing her eyes from his.

"It's a common enough complaint," he told her, his smile even more bland. Suddenly she felt that he was encouraging her to make herself absurd beyond a point of dignified retreat, and so for a while she let the talk go on to other things. Then without warning she asked him, "Is this a modern mine?"

"It's safe, if that's what you mean. It's at least two centuries old. Very solid."

When Dr. Slade got up to leave and was about to follow Grove through the doorway, she said to him in a low voice, but loud enough so that he heard, "I wish you wouldn't go, Taylor."

He stopped and turned. "This is a fine time to tell me! I'll take it easy on the climbs and see you about twelve."

"Yes," she said tonelessly, waving her hand in his direction. He took it as a gesture of dismissal and went on.

When they were in the cloister of the main courtyard, Grove looked at him. "Day's full of anxieties, isn't she?"

"Not at all. She's unusually well balanced," said Dr. Slade. "Her nerves have been a little raw since she was sick, that's all."

Grove smiled tolerantly, shook his head. "Well, Doctor, she's *your* wife. You ought to know. On the other hand, that very intimacy you have might make it impossible for you to see what somebody else meeting her for the first time would see right off. You can't tell."

"I doubt that very much," Dr. Slade said with some force. Grove understood that he was not going to be receptive.

"Why should she be nervous?" he demanded. "She's completely recovered. You can see that."

Dr. Slade stopped walking. "But is she? She's got the same business I have." He tapped his forehead. "There are a whole lot of things she can't remember."

Grove snorted. "More likely it's imaginary. She knows she was out cold for a few days, so she feels the thread's been broken. I think you'll find she can remember, if you ask her the right questions."

They resumed walking, slowly. "I don't know," said Dr. Slade dubiously. "Certainly in my case it's real enough. There's a whole period that's just gone."

"Still missing!" Grove exclaimed.

Since he felt himself being encouraged to talk about it, during the drive he went into describing for Grove the extent of the lapse, using certain landmark dates and counting the days before and after them on his fingers. Between them they calculated that the lost time embraced a period of between thirteen and fifteen days.

"It's my main interest in life at the moment, getting back those days," said Dr. Slade, trying to smile. The hot wind cut violently across his face, making it hard to breathe.

"They'll come home, dragging their tails behind them." Grove was driving much too fast along the rough trail; he never moved his eyes from the track ahead.

Day, continuing her sunbath alone in the increasingly hot patio, went on striving to reconstruct key scenes whose details might call into being a fragment of the missing material. But it was like looking on the shore for yesterday's footprints. She held it against Taylor that he had gone out in spite of her having asked him not to: his absence left her alone with her preoccupation. She was certain that together they had a better chance of solving their difficulties than they ever could have separately.

When the maids came to make up the room she slipped on a shirt and some slacks, and wandered through the house to the front entrance. Outside in the road it seemed a little cooler. There were several dusty trails leading in various directions; the one she chose went along for a way beside the walls of the house and gardens. Soon it dipped and turned to the left. In spite of the heat she continued slowly, scuffing the dust with her sandals as she went along. Then she turned and went back toward the ranch more quickly than she had come. Once in the courtyard, she heard voices coming from the *sala*, and looked in.

"You should have seen it," Taylor told her. "There were brooks of cyanide everywhere."

She laughed shortly and took the cocktail Grove was holding out to her. "That's what I need, some good cyanide."

The dining room was a small museum of pre-Columbian art; its walls were peppered with niches that held masks and sculptures. Grove had wanted to eat here, insisting that it was too hot to be outside. There was a discussion then with Luchita, who protested that the air conditioning made it too cold to be in the dining room. As they sat down to lunch she brought it up again.

"And besides that, you give us vichyssoise with ice in it," she complained.

"Ah, the old teahead freeze. It's hot in here." Grove looked to Day for support.

"It feels just right to me," she said lightly, at the same time twining her legs together, for it seemed uncomfortably chilly.

"Delightful," said Dr. Slade.

"You've got a jacket on," Day told him, and stopped. "What god is that?" she inquired presently, pointing to the huge stone figure that towered at the far end of the room.

Grove glanced at the statue with respect. "That's Xiuloc, god of the life force. They called him the Father of Boils. He weighs fourteen tons."

"I'd have thought a good deal more," said Dr. Slade morosely; he considered it an absurdity to surround a dining table with grimacing faces and snarling muzzles.

"That's the point," Grove told him. "The stone is porous. They broke their boils on it and the stone sucked out the pus."

"Oh," said Day, looking down at her vichyssoise.

"God of the life force," repeated Dr. Slade, as if considering the idea.

"How'd you ever corral all these things?" she asked Grove.

"Everything was dug up on our own land somewhere. The government got the big ones. But there's one mammoth in the studio you've got to see."

"You won't sleep for two weeks if you look at that. I'm telling you the truth," Luchita warned her, speaking with great seriousness.

"I can't wait," she said to Grove. "What is it?"

"Just a divinity. But it's got snakes and spiders in it, and that bothers her."

What am I doing here? she asked herself. It was absurd to be sitting in this glacial room with these two disconnected young people; to prolong the visit would be senseless. She suspected that it was going to be hard to spur Taylor to action. Perhaps a scene would not be necessary, but she was prepared to produce one if he demurred. At least there was satisfaction in knowing that she was no longer of two minds about it.

Immediately after lunch, while Luchita and Dr. Slade were having coffee in the cloister, Grove took her into the room where the big statue was. The light behind it came down from windows high above; she had a strong impression that the object was alive and conscious. A gigantic piece of stone, waiting. Whether it was decorated with snakes and spiders, or hearts and skulls, was beside the point. It was the stone itself that was alive.

From somewhere above their heads came the desperate buzzing of a solitary fly as it banged against a pane of glass. The air in the room was hot and still. The longer they sat without speaking, the more importance the statue would assume.

"I think Luchita and I see it the same way," she finally said. "These Indian things down here give me the shudders."

"Don't you think it's a beauty?" Grove demanded.

"It's magnificent. But I wouldn't want to live anywhere near it. I don't even like to touch these things." Her tone had become one of apology; then it resumed its natural sound. "I think these were pretty terrible civilizations, don't you?"

"Terrible compared to what? Sit down here on the couch where you can look up at it. It has a sense of balance all its own."

She laughed and obligingly seated herself. "It's much worse from here, of course. But you said, Compared to what? Well, to our own Christian civilization, for instance."

Abruptly he sat down beside her. "The one thing Christianity has given the world is a lesson in empathy. Jesus's words are a manual on the technique of putting yourself in the other's place."

"Is that what they are?" If he was hoping to make her angry, she would disappoint him.

"Your husband worries too much about you," he went on, as though continuing the conversation.

"Worries about me?" she exclaimed, astonished.

"I suppose he's concerned about your aftereffects, your hangover of amnesia."

"That's ridiculous," she said, annoyed to hear that they had discussed her. "It's not permanent, is it?"

"No, no." He said only that, and then there was the sound of the fly's agonized attempt to escape. They sat there.

Finally he spoke. "You have to work at it, you know. For instance, when we were out on the terrace, up in the capital, you spoke about coming out of the customhouse at Puerto Farol, and from the way you described it, it seemed like a very sharp and detailed memory."

"Yes," she said uncertainly. The picture as she saw it now was not sharp and detailed at all; it was like remembering a photograph she had once looked at rather than an experience she had lived through.

"You know the part I mean." His voice had overtones of impatience. "When the side of the building and the signboard seemed to buckle as you were falling, and the water in the harbor was flowing like a river? And the uprooted palm trees lying along the waterfront?"

She shut her eyes for a few seconds. When she opened them again her heart was beating violently. Without saying anything she shook her head slowly back and forth.

"Anyway," he went on, "it's not what you saw or thought you saw at that moment, but the fact that those clear memories came right in the middle of your blocked-out period."

She was silent for a moment. Her heart still pounding, she got up quietly and said, "Couldn't we go back?" Without looking again at the statue, she walked toward the door leading out to the cloister.

In the *sala* there was no sign of Luchita or Dr. Slade, and the coffee tray had been cleared away. "Taylor must have gone for his siesta," she said. "I'm going in too, if you don't mind."

"It's hot today," he told her. "The end of the dry season it gets like this."

Taylor had told her about the end of the dry season in that part of the world, how all of nature seemed to be straining to pull a little moisture out of the sky, until one could feel the tension in everything, and the scorpions came out and the lightning flashed more each night, and human nerves grew taut. As she lay back on her pillow, with Taylor snoring gently on the other bed, she tried to find the reason why it had been such an unpleasant experience to have Grove remind her of the arrival in Puerto Farol. It had been like hearing her own dream being told by someone who could tell it far better than she ever could. A few days ago the mention of it on the terrace in the city had been bad, but today's reminder had been infinitely worse, because his unexpected inclusion of the forgotten details of the water in the harbor pouring out to sea and the broken palm trees had given her a terrifying sensation of being dependent upon him, as if she would remember whatever he chose to have her remember. This was manifestly nonsense. She determined not to speak of it to Taylor, who already was treating her with a little of the condescension one shows to invalids.

She listened: the dry wind bore the sound of singing insects as it blew through the patio, and the long, hard leaves of the pandanus bumped one against the next. It would have made her happy to lean across the space between the two beds and take Taylor by the arm. When he was awake she would say, I want to go tomorrow morning.

She sat up. There was no question of relaxing enough to be able to doze off, and if she could not sleep she did not want to be lying there. A walk, even in the burning mid-afternoon sun, would be preferable. She could try a different road—one that might take her to a vantage point where she could see the entire ranch from above.

A few minutes later she stepped out into the wind. There was not a person in sight on any of the roads. The monastery was prolonged by walls for a great distance at each end; she turned to the right and followed the wall. Soon she came to an open door. She peered through and saw some avocado trees. There was a primitive hut back in the deep shade. Turkeys pecked at the dust. One of the maids came out of the hut, caught sight of her, and waved.

She walked on. In the air was the simple odor of the dusty plains, tinged occasionally with a whiff of plant life from the jungle below. The road led upward, over the crest of a small hill. On each side was a living fence of high cactus, and each plant was entirely wrapped in a thick coating of spiderwebs that quivered in the wind. The dust in the road was thick and satiny; no tracks were visible on its recently deposited surface. And in the maze of webs there was nothing but an occasional dry twig or scrap of insect. Yet she repeatedly found herself staring carefully into the tattered gossamer world, as if somewhere inside might be lurking something which would translate itself into the answer to an as yet unformulated question.

The bare hillside had a few rocks and prickly shrubs scattered over it. There was nothing to look at. But the mere act of walking made it easier to accept the fact that she was only waiting for Taylor to finish his nap.

Up here the whole landscape looked scraggy and desolate; its leafless trees and slag-colored expanses made her want to shut her eyes. Whichever way she looked, it was the same: gray and burned out—a landscape imitating death. But when she got to the crest of the hill she found that on the other side it overlooked a bend in the river valley. The tufted tops of the big trees lay steeply below, and in the middle distance she could see stretches of the river as it wandered through the jungle, back and forth across the valley. From where she stood there was no sign of human presence—only the wasteland around her, the valley below, and beyond that more wasteland, rising on and on, to shadows of high mountains on the farthest horizon. After she had stood a while she went back, feeling frustrated.

In the bedroom he was still asleep. She continued into the bathroom and, leaving the door partly open, took a noisy shower. When she came out, he was stirring.

"You're so lucky to be able to sleep that way. Do you want me to ring for tea?"

"I suppose. I've been sweating. It's hot in here."

Ten minutes later, while he was eating an éclair, she began. "You know what I'd like?" she said. "I'd like to pack my things tonight and leave tomorrow morning."

He stared at her. "That seems like rather short notice, doesn't it? They'll think something's wrong."

It annoyed her to hear him include Luchita along with Grove, as if she carried some weight in his household. "Plenty's wrong, and it's all with him. I could fly out of my skin."

"Day, you can't just walk out on people. How do you know what they've got planned for us?"

"Planned!" she cried piteously.

"We can't do it. We've got to give them a little notice."

"I really hate it here," she said in a small, pathetic voice. "I'd like to be in a hotel."

"I got to know him a little this morning," Dr. Slade said meditatively. "You can't help liking the boy. He's had a pretty tough time."

She was contemptuous. "Oh, stop it! He was brought up in the lap of luxury."

"What's that got to do with it? There are other things besides comfort and financial security."

"You'd never guess it."

He shrugged. "You want to be harsh on him, that's all." Then he turned and saw the anxiety in her face. "Why don't we compromise and tell them at dinner we've got to leave day after tomorrow?"

"But definitely? No matter what?"

"Well, of course definitely."

She was silent a moment. "That makes another forty or more hours to get through. God!"

"I wish you'd just relax," he told her.

By dinnertime it had cooled off enough so that they were able to eat in the courtyard under the stars. About halfway through the meal Dr. Slade cleared his throat, and she knew he was going to begin. "Grove, Day and I have been talking it over, and we feel we've got to be getting on." There was a long period of protestation and mutual flattery; she was aware of what Taylor was going through, and she felt sorry for him.

Luchita, looking very pale and sophisticated, had finished her steak and lighted one of her aromatic cigarettes. Her humor was better tonight; from time to time she looked derisively at Grove as he attempted to persuade Dr. Slade to put off his departure. What a rude little bitch she is, Day thought. She might as well have been saying aloud, This isn't what he tells *me*.

It was understood that Grove would drive them to the station at San Felipe and put them on the train for the capital. As they went across the cloister into the *sala*, Grove added, "Luchita's going up anyway on Friday."

Quick as a lizard Luchita turned in the doorway. "Oh, I am?" she cried hoarsely. "You think I am? On the train?"

Day sat down in the place indicated for her, while Grove piled cushions behind her back. She watched the girl closely. Grove turned to her and said in an offhand manner, "Luchita, do you remember a restaurant near the Place de l'Alma called A la Grenouille de Cantal?" Looking earnestly at her, he waited for the reply. And Day was first astonished and then incensed, with the result that she felt impelled to side with the girl. It was a shamefully unequal struggle; Luchita wilted, melted, as if an invisible blow had been struck her. After a moment she said in an almost inaudible voice, "Yes, Vero."

A little while later, when she had the opportunity, Day said in an aside to Grove, "You seem to have *all* the answers."

"Not all," he said, looking carefully at her.

She had hoped to keep the hard edge of her voice covered, but she knew it had cut through; his look at her had been swift and keen. And his astuteness in discerning the hostility she had meant to keep hidden surprised her; it ran counter to certain key prejudices she had regarding him.

When they got to the bedroom and the door was shut behind them, Day stood motionless. "You see what I mean about him?" she demanded.

"He and the girl were on the outs, that's all."

It seemed useless to discuss it. From her bed, propped up against the pillows, she watched Dr. Slade as he shuffled about the room in his bathrobe. Soon he got into the other bed, took off his wristwatch, and reached out to lay it on the night table.

"Has it ever occurred to you," she said, looking at him steadily, "to ask yourself *why* he brought us here?"

He looked incredulous. "*Why?* My God, girl, he's just being hospitable! How can you ask *why?*"

"I can ask anything," she said.

25

It was twenty-five minutes past eight. From her bed Day heard the rustling of small birds in the patio's shrubs. Because the air was so still she could hear even the distant sounds from the kitchen: a pail being set down, the chatter of women, a door slamming. Taylor lay on his side, asleep. Tomorrow at this time I'll be on the train, she thought, wondering how she would get through the enormous day of waiting that lay ahead of her.

In the dim bathroom as she washed, she was telling herself that each hour equaled about four per cent of the time left, which meant that every fifteen minutes one per cent would tick by. At first her reckoning made the time seem finite and bearable, but after several carefully spaced glances at her watch, she understood that fifteen minutes was a long period of time.

During the course of the morning she gave several small things to the chambermaid to wash out for her, explaining that she must have them all back by evening. Between bouts of packing she sunbathed in the patio with Taylor. Just before they went in to lunch, the girl brought all the clothing back, washed, dried and ironed. "Of course. Everything dries in two minutes in this climate," said Taylor.

At one o'clock they assembled in the *sala* for cocktails. Now there was no sign of friction between Grove and Luchita. "One last round before we go into that icebox," Grove advised, pouring out the drinks for everyone but Luchita, who was still sipping her first.

"Wise girl," commented Dr. Slade. "You don't ever drink much, do you?"

"It makes me feel sick," she told him.

Sitting at the table directly across from Luchita, Day had the opportunity of examining her at close range. What she saw struck her as extraordinarily unpleasant: for the first time in her life she felt she was looking at a zombie. The girl's eyes were almost closed, and a gigantic, meaningless smile lay over her face. When she was spoken to, she appeared to have difficulty finding her voice in order to reply. At least, thought Day, this beatific state augured a quiet meal.

"Well, so this is our last lunch together," said Dr. Slade, spooning up his gazpacho. "It's been so pleasant I hate to get out of the rut. This is certainly one part of the trip I'll never forget."

Day tittered and turned red. Dr. Slade did not seem to have heard. Luchita stared at her, suddenly wide-eyed; then she put her head back and looked down from her own remote heights upon the antics of the alcohol drinker.

"You've missed a great chance, you know, Day." Grove pointed a cigarette at her. "I'd have taken you into San Felipe. A local fiesta."

Day had brought her cocktail in with her; now she sipped it. "Don't tell me," she pleaded. "I don't want to know what I'm missing."

While the others talked, she was busy calculating that already about twenty-two per cent of her time had gone past.

"How about it, Day? You put off your trip and take in the fiesta?"

"You're not serious?"

"Yes."

"Of course we're not going to put off anything. We're leaving tomorrow morning." She laughed in order to seem less ungracious and looked toward Taylor, fearful that he might yet allow the departure to be placed in question. She would not have been astonished at that moment if Grove had spoken out suddenly, declaring that it would be impossible for them to leave. Then she understood that the danger was past and that he would say no more about it.

As they got up from the table, Dr. Slade put his hand on Grove's arm. "Now if you'll forgive me this once, I'll cut the coffee and make straight for my bed."

"Yes," Day said. "I'm sleepy too."

Trying to keep out of the stinging sunlight, they walked slowly along the cloister toward their room. Grove called after them, "Tea in your room at five?"

"Lovely!" said Day. Then she muttered, "Breakfast and tea are the best meals in *this* house. I thought the lunch would never end."

"He makes his drinks too damned strong," Dr. Slade declared.

The curtains were drawn against the glare of the patio. "Will it bother you if I go on packing?" she asked him. He was wrapping his beach bathrobe around him. "Go right ahead," he said. Then, "Whew!" he exclaimed fervently as he fell onto the bed.

For a while she moved aimlessly around the darkened room, carrying objects from one place to another. Finally it became clear to her that everything was packed except the things that had to be left out until the last moment. Common sense told her to stay in the room, where there was no risk of running into Grove and having to engage in conversation with him, but the prospect of lying quietly in the gloom for two or three hours was more than she could face. She was too nervous to read. There was nothing to do but go outside.

It was unlikely that Grove would be wandering around the servants' garden at this hour. There was always life in the neighborhood of the kitchen, and it was soothing to watch people in the act of performing simple tasks. She went out through the big door and followed the road that went along beside the wall. When she came to the garden door, she pushed it open and stepped inside.

At once she had the impression that the place was deserted. The turkeys were there, furrowing the dust with their stiff tailfeathers, and somewhere behind one of the huts farther back in the shade a dog yapped; but she did not hear a human sound.

Leading back to the kitchen door was a long pergola with a trelliswork top where flowering vines drooped. She walked along slowly, marveling at the silence of the afternoon. As she came out into sunlight, she saw on a flagstone at her feet the remains of a small bonfire. Several sheets of typewritten paper had been partially burned; the black-edged, irregular yellow scraps lay beside her foot. She craned her neck a bit and, with her head on one side, looked at what was written there. The word "scaffolding" caught her eye. Then she straightened and walked on to the kitchen door.

There was no sound inside but the steady cheerful dripping of a tap into a sink full of water. The room was very bright; there were glass bricks in the ceiling. She walked in front of the enormous fireplace. It was, of course, the hour of the siesta, when everyone managed to crawl away and lose consciousness for an hour or two, but she would expect to find at least one maid somewhere about. As she continued into the pantry, her movements became stealthy; she felt she had had no right to go through the kitchen. Surely Grove would consider it a kind of trespassing. In the dining room's cold vault the silence was at its most strident. She went quickly through without glancing at the grinning faces. There was no one in the courtyard. A hammock had been slung across between two pillars, and a book lay open in it, face down. The wind hissed among the thousands of twigs in the lemon tree and pushed the tendrils of overhanging vines out to touch her.

When she came to the turning that led to their room, she hesitated an instant, and then continued straight ahead to the front door. This time she took the road that led downward toward the river. On the promontory that was visible from where they had sat at lunch there were a few low shaggy trees where buzzards perched, and a small partially ruined chapel. This was where the workmen were installing the swimming pool; half of it would be shaded by the apse and the rest would be in the sunlight. She could see the mounds of earth and the wheelbarrows in front of the baroque façade, but no workmen.

It gave her pleasure to scuff her feet through the thick dust, raising a long cloud that moved off behind her across the empty land. The dust was everywhere on her; she thought voluptuously of the shower she would take on returning. It would be more fun to have something visible to wash off.

When the road began to descend too steeply she climbed up over the rocks at the side to get a view across the highest branches of the trees that loomed ahead, and if possible to get a glimpse of the river. Then she stood there staring out at the savage landscape. Directly below her, half covered by trees, was the red roof of the coffee *fábrica*. The ribbon of jungle wound deliberately through the barren country, covering great distances back and forth across the valley; of the river itself there was no sign. Only one more meal to sit through, she reflected with satisfaction.

It was not quite ten to five when she got back to the room, but Taylor had already drunk his tea and gone back to sleep. The tray was there, the teapot empty. He would always drink it while it was hot, without waiting for her, no matter when they brought it. But she was annoyed with Grove. He had said five; here she was, just in time, and there was no tea for her.

Taylor was asleep on his back. It looked like an uncomfortable position, but there was no question of waking him to make him change it. After she had taken her shower she lay out flat on her bed, hoping to relax for a few minutes. Occasionally she rose and walked slowly around the room. When it was twilight she went through the curtained door and into the rosy gray light of the patio. She stood, feeling the slight wind go past.

When the stars are really out I'll wake him up, she thought. With the trip in view it was good that he was sleeping so long. If she changed for dinner now, he could have the bathroom to himself when he got up.

A half hour later, when she was dressed to go in for cocktails, she wandered once more out into the patio and stared up at the sky. The wind had dropped; there were a few stars, but most of them were hidden by great masses of distant cumulus, still white with daylight from behind the horizon. As she watched, tongues of lightning moved between the clouds, and they glowed and flickered with yellow light from deep inside.

She went back in and, opening one of Taylor's valises, took out a pack of playing cards. She sat sideways on her bed and unthinkingly began to play a kind of solitaire she had not thought of since her childhood. Suddenly she made her decision. "Taylor!" she said. She looked over at him and thought she saw him breathe more deeply. "Come on. It's seven-thirty."

His eyes were still shut, and his hands were folded comfortably on his chest.

"Taylor!" she cried. She leaned across and seized his arm, shook it roughly. Already she was certain that nothing was going to rouse him. She jumped up. Standing directly over him, looking down upon his head, feeling his forehead, she thought: He's going to die. This time he's going to die.

It was not much later when she pushed the wall button to call the maid. Then she felt his pulse, and sat intent on the insistent throbs beneath the ball of her finger. There was no knock at the door; she rang again. In the bathroom she dampened a towel and brought it to put around his head. As she pushed the folds of wet linen against his hair she saw that she should have wrung out the towel much more firmly. The water trickled onto the pillow. If by now no one had come in answer to her call, no one was going to come, because the house was empty.

She went in the direction of the corridor. The lights were burning there. When she got to the far side of the courtyard she saw Grove standing inside the doorway of the *sala*.

26

Together they stood in the room looking at Taylor, Grove nodding his head slowly as he studied the inert form that lay there.

"Can't we call a doctor?" she said finally.

"I'm afraid he wouldn't thank us for calling in Dr. Solera." He smiled wryly at her. "It's nothing, nothing," he added almost impatiently. "If he doesn't come around by midnight I'll give him a shot."

He led her into the *sala*, where he handed her a double vodka martini.

"I'm really master of the house tonight," he said with relish. "I let the whole staff go to the fiesta. Everybody."

"I noticed the quiet. You mean there are really just the four of us in the house tonight?"

"Three," he said, rising to take his cigarette case from the mantel. "Luchita went up this afternoon." He smiled ingenuously. "You were wrong. You see what happened. She took the station wagon."

She felt her eyes growing wide with dismay. To offset the impression that might make, she slowly let her face expand into a delighted grin.

"No trains for Luchita!" she said, trying to laugh, shaking her head. Suddenly she knew he was at her again, studying each muscle of her face as it moved from one expression to another. I can't let him see I'm afraid, she kept thinking. It was as though he were waiting for her to betray herself.

"Who's getting dinner?" she said.

"I am. We are. If you don't mind helping me."

"No," she said, trying to sound pleasant.

"I'll show you the kitchen."

In her mind's eye she saw the whitewashed walls, the black beams overhead, and the huge fireplace. "Have you installed gadgets?" she asked him. "Or do you use the old kitchen, the way it was?"

"It's not old. It's just smoky." He was eying her in a curious manner, perhaps a little in the way a painter would look at a model he was about to begin sketching. "It looks old, I admit. It's an addition from the turn of the century."

Feeling the wind sweep all at once into the room and inundate her with its sweet forest smell, she looked around toward the door. "What's happening out there?"

"It's capricious this time of year," he said. "Off and on, up and down."

The wind had brought the wilderness into the room; her ear now focused on the sounds it was making in the vegetation outside.

"You never talk about yourself," she told him, as he handed her a second double martini.

"I'm always talking about myself."

"I mean your life. When you were a boy, for instance."

He laughed scornfully, but although she waited, he still said nothing.

She rose. "I've got to get something to put around my shoulders. The wind's blowing right on me."

He did not offer to go with her. As she hurried along toward the bedroom, she found herself marveling that she should be able to go on talking while Taylor lay unconscious. It seemed to help prove the truth of a suspicion she had long

entertained: people could not really get very close to one another; they merely imagined they were close. (It was not a re-
lapse, merely a part of the tapering off, Grove had said. There
was no danger.)

She hunted out the stole she wanted and put it around
her shoulders. "Don't disturb him. The thing is to leave him
alone." She went over to Taylor's bed and took away the
wet towel from around his head. With a fresh towel she
dried the strands of damp hair as well as she could. His
breathing was regular, slow and profound, and his face
looked neither flushed nor pale. It seemed cruel to leave him
alone in order to go and sit in the *sala* making meaningless
conversation.

As she turned the corner of the cloister, she glanced down
the long corridor that lost itself in a dim confusion of plants
and furniture. A man in a white shirt had stood for a second
at the far end before stepping ahead into the darkness of the
courtyard; he did not reappear.

Grove had turned on some jazz and was stretched out full-
length on the floor. She went in, and since he did not get up,
she stood a moment and then sat down in a chair by the door,
where the sound of the music was not so deafening. When
the final cymbal crash had announced the end of the piece, he
rose and turned off the machine.

"Sometimes I like it so loud it hurts," he told her.

"You said there was no one in the house," she began. "But
there's somebody out there. I just saw him."

"Where?" he demanded, staring at her. The idea hovered in
her mind that he might be afraid.

"Way down at the end of the colonnade. He went out into
the bushes."

"There's a night guard on, down at the generator. He must
have come up for something."

"I was surprised," she said, laying her hand over her heart.
"I'm on edge, naturally."

"Yes." It was clear that he was thinking about something
different. "Of course." Then he turned to her abruptly. "If
you're worrying about the doctor, don't."

She looked at him almost tearfully for an instant. "Of
course I'm worried!" she cried.

"But you're a fool—" he raised his hand—"if you let him take that trip tomorrow, no matter how he feels."

"I'm for calling your doctor right now." She felt certain of being able to manage the doctor; he would give his permission, and Taylor could go. "Is he so bad?"

"He's not so good; I can tell you that."

"At least he's a doctor," she said reproachfully.

"You don't want another drink, do you? Let's go out and get dinner. We can talk while we work."

As he piloted her through the dim dining room she was telling herself that from the instant they went through the doorway into the pantry she must behave as though she were seeing everything for the first time. Halfway through the pantry she said, "This is an older wing, isn't it?"

He was not listening. "There are some mangoes and papayas in the icebox that have got to be cut up." They were in the kitchen; she looked up at the vaulted beams.

Grove filled a large pot, and another small one, with water, set them on the stove, and lighted the gas burners. "Now we've got direct contact," he said under his breath. While the water heated, she helped him cut up the fruit on the big center table. Then she stood back against the sink and watched while he opened tins and packets and began silently to stir up a sauce over the flame.

"Do you think Luchita's gone for good?" she asked him.

He looked up in surprise. "Why would I think that? She didn't run away."

"Why don't you marry her, Grove?" she said softly.

"You're serious?" He stopped stirring for an instant and saw that she was. "You've seen her," he said, emptying a box of spaghetti into the cauldron of boiling water.

"Oh, marry her, for God's sake! What's the matter with you?"

Turning to the smaller vessel he held up his arm and let some of the sauce drip from the spoon back into the pot, watching it carefully as it fell. "In this country," he told her, speaking slowly, "they say you might as well make a political speech as give unwanted advice. Nobody's going to listen in either case."

She dropped her cigarette into the sink behind her. "Well, I can tell you, you'll never be happy until you do what you know's the right thing. That's what life's about, after all."

"What life's about!" he cried incredulously. "What *is* life about? Yes. What's the subject matter?" He stirred the sauce. "It's about who's going to clean up the shit."

"I don't know what you mean," she said, her voice hostile.

"The work's got to be done. If *you* don't want to do it, you've got to be able to make somebody else do it. That's what life's about. Or isn't that the way you like to hear it?"

She hesitated. "I don't understand. You seem like a mature man. Why you haven't outgrown all this, I mean. If you were ten years younger it wouldn't be so surprising." She would have enjoyed being able to say "so repulsive," because that was the way she felt, but to risk a break would be a kind of abdication; she must stay with him and prove, at least to herself, that she was not afraid of him. Turning her head so he would not see the expression of distaste she knew was on her face, she finally said, "But, isn't it boring eventually? All this animosity, year after year, hating, hating? How do you keep up interest?"

"Life makes it easy. You don't have to worry about that."

She shrugged. "It's not my problem."

"Only a drooling idiot would tell his troubles to a woman," he said suddenly, with some bitterness.

"Troubles?" She eyed him as she lighted another cigarette. "You have troubles?"

His face darkened; he studied the sauce more closely. "Yes. I have troubles." He had said the word without choosing it, but now he seemed to be considering its meaning.

She looked at him and believed him. "I'm sorry," she said. "But whatever they are, I have a feeling you'll get them behind you. It's a question of making up your mind."

He seemed to stiffen. "In what way?"

"I mean setting your mind to putting them behind you."

He wheeled to face her, and she saw with a cold dread that he had had his eyes shut for the past few seconds; they were still shut as he turned. When he opened them, he opened his mouth as well, and laughed once. It sounded like a young dog trying to bark.

"*Abajo* San Felipe!" he cried. "I'm no cook." She had the impression now that he had clambered back inside himself and shut the door.

"I didn't have to let them all go," he went on. "It seemed like a cheap way of reinforcing goodwill between master and servant. You have to keep shoring it up, you know. It wears away like a sea wall. Why don't we sit down right here? Or would you rather put everything on trays and take it into the dining room?"

She went on looking at him, aware suddenly that there was a shadowy bond between them. It was at that instant she first felt the cold impact of physical fear. And for some hidden reason she hoped never to discover, he was afraid of her.

They sat down at a long marble-topped table near the fireplace. The smell of garlic and spices was in the steam that rose from the sauce, but she had no appetite for it when he passed it to her. It had been a fraction of a second that she had looked into his eyes as they opened after having been focused on an inner world of torment, but she had been caught up and drawn into orbit along with him. By the time she had thought: I am I, it was finished, yet for that flash the difference between them had been next to nothing. It was a fact as much as the water dripping from the tap (now into a shallow dish) or the electric clock whirring on top of the refrigerator, or the smoky façade of the chimney above the fireplace.

After the first few mouthfuls she found it easier to eat. He told her several unlikely stories about the abbot of the monastery; she listened and watched him, remembering that at least time was going past. The trouble with Grove was, she thought, trying to be objective about him for a minute, that it was impossible to be relaxed in his presence: he was too desperate and final in his manner.

"There's always a pan of ice cream in the fridge for me," he said when they had finished. "I hope to hell it's there tonight. They get excited by fiestas. Anything can happen."

He got up and peered into the freezing compartment. "It's here," he announced. "Would you like some?"

She let him heap it into a bowl for her. "We'll eat it by the fire," he told her.

Reclining on piles of cushions in the familiar *sala*, she felt a little better, although she longed to get to her own room. He turned on the tape recorder; this time the jazz was a scarcely audible background.

They talked sporadically. Betweentimes the music went on playing. Finally the soft curtain of jazz had become empty silence; the machine continued to run. She could hear the long trills of the night insects in the higher branches of the lemon tree outside. Now and then a languorous stirring of the wind reached her where she sat.

Grove was up, had stopped the tape recorder, was spinning the tape ahead. "I have a wonderful jungle sequence somewhere on here. Just sounds at night." He started the tape, turned up the volume, and the dry, metallic song of the forest night filled the room.

"Beautiful," she said. After a suitable period of listening, she stood up.

"He's all right. Believe me," he told her, rising. "The thing is to let him wake up by himself. If he's hungry, or you want anything, my room's the last one on the right going down, at the end."

"Thank you." She was too tired to think of anything else to say.

27

Everything was the same in the room: the lighted floor lamp, the curtains across the doorway into the little garden, the nightgown draped over the cowhide back of the chair. Dr. Slade, however, was not in the bed. She saw the depression in the mattress, and the flattened part of the pillow where his head had been lying. It was too much what she had hoped for; it could not be true. "Taylor," she called softly, standing beside the bathroom door.

No sound. She opened the door a crack; it was dark inside. She pushed open the door and stared into the empty bathroom. She pulled aside the curtains and went out into the patio. It was fairly dark out there, but she could see the whitewashed walls all around, and the sharp black forms of the plants against them. There was no one there.

Back in the room standing near the foot of her bed, she turned slowly, looking at each wall in succession. There was no point in going to the door and shouting his name up and down the cloister; nevertheless she stepped outside for an instant and cried "Taylor!" once, into the darkened courtyard. A moment later she began to walk swiftly along under the arches toward the far open end of the cloister. The last door had a sliver of light under it. She knocked four times, quickly.

It seemed a long time before Grove, wearing a white bathrobe, stepped outside and shut the door behind him.

They stood in the dark. He waited, and so she spoke. "He's gotten up and gone out of the room. I don't know where to look for him."

He knotted the belt of the bathrobe tighter about his waist. "He's somewhere around. He won't have gone far."

"Somewhere around," she repeated without conviction. "In the dark?" She gestured with an arm, indicating the vast unlighted expanse of the courtyard. "He shouldn't be wandering around. Suppose he's delirious or walking in his sleep?"

He patted her on the shoulder. "Why don't you just go to bed? He'll be back. He probably wanted a little air."

This was more than she could take. "Are you out of your mind?" she cried. "I've got to find him."

"Feel free to go anywhere. There's generally a light switch on the right inside each door. I don't think you'll find him. As you say, he's not likely to be standing around in a dark house." He stepped toward the doorway.

There was a long silence. "I see," she said. "I thought you might be willing to help."

He did not reply, merely stood there with his hand on the doorknob.

At last he's showing his true colors, she thought. She listened to the wind in the vines. A rooster crowed nearby.

"If he's not in the house, he's gone out," he said. "If he's gone out he'll be back. He's not a child."

"The fact that he's been sick, the fact that only an hour ago he was still unconscious, none of that means anything to you?"

He opened his door a crack and started in. "It doesn't because it's irrelevant. I'd advise you to go back and get into bed."

"You're incredible!" she told him, but her voice was so tight with rage that she doubted he heard her. In her anger she spun around and began to walk very fast. The sound of her heeltaps on the stones struck her as ridiculous even as she heard his door shut. Her fancy was beset with images of pummeling him, clawing his face, kicking him; the black hatred he had aroused spread to the house itself and the countryside around it, and she found herself at the main entrance door, which she opened. She stood there, looking out at the road and the trees swimming in the moonlight. Suddenly she felt certain that Taylor was out here—not in the house.

First she went to the gate that led into the garden. It was unlocked. Inside, the huts were all dark, and the thatch of their roofs was mottled with tiny patches of moonlight that sifted down through the high trees. She stepped uncertainly ahead into the gloom, and then she stopped moving and listened. What she heard in the distance sounded like a drum beating a fast, irregular rhythm. The generator, she thought, and there was a man on duty there. She walked on into the tunnel of shadow. When the avenue of trees and huts had finished, she came out into an open space, and there was a flight of steps leading down. The sound was very loud here; she could see a little building in the bushes below, but no light. The moonlight was bright on the steps. Until she got around to the other side of the cabin and walked under the banana plants that grew in front of it she did not hear the radio. Then she saw a man squatting just outside the open door, his transistor on the ground in front of him. He grunted, jumped up and snapped on a light in the doorway; a tawny Indian youth in a visored cap stared at her with suspicion. She smiled, but could think of no explanation to give for her sudden intrusion. The boy did not return the smile. Instead, he called out, "Señor Torny!"

There was the sound of heavy boots coming nearer on the other side of the plants. A tall young man in cowboy uniform moved into view, and remained looking impassively in her direction for what seemed a long time. Like the nasty one in a

Western, she thought. The Indian boy did not move again. Suddenly the cowboy spoke in a low thin voice, and she jerked her head up in surprise. His English was perfect.

"Looking for something in particular or just taking a walk?"

"Oh, I heard the sound and I came down," she said, knowing that what she was saying was absurd, unconvincing. He still waited, and an idea came to her. "I think you were right in the beginning. I did want something."

She waited again. "Yes," he finally said.

"What I really needed but didn't dare hope for was a ride into San Felipe."

"You mean tonight, now?"

"That's what I meant."

He stepped toward her. "I'd do it, baby, but the truck isn't mine."

She hesitated. "I just wanted to get to a doctor."

Again he merely looked at her.

She was not certain how he was going to react, but she went ahead anyway. "It would be worth a hundred dollars to me to get there."

"I see." Now he stared at the ground.

Eventually he looked up at her. "The problem's still the same, but I'll risk it. When do you want to go?"

"Right now."

"I'll have to get the keys. Wait there." He turned away. The sound of his boots on the gravel became fainter. She moved aimlessly around in the open space in front of the banana plants while the Indian boy stared at her. Now and then she felt a compulsion to go back to the bedroom: Taylor could be there waiting. But she did not believe it, and she would not go into the house again until she had Dr. Solera with her. She heard the cowboy's feet pounding the earth as he approached.

"Ready," he said from behind the wall of banana leaves. They walked, partly through garden and partly through wasteland, to the garage where a truck stood in the moonlight. He got in, leaned across and opened the door for her. The hard seat was very high off the floor, and the motor made a fantastic amount of noise when he started it. Then they swung around and began to move along the driveway. As a precaution he had opened the gate when he went to get the keys. They slid through and the ranch was behind them.

He turned to her. "Have you got enough clothes on, baby? It's a lot cooler up there, you know."

Even had she known that the streets of San Felipe were going to be deep with snow, she would not have considered going back to get a coat. She looked through the windshield at the sky full of stars. "Why do you say baby?" she asked him.

He was startled. "Why do I say baby? It's the way I talk, that's all. Why, don't you like it?"

"I don't mind it," she said thoughtfully.

He did not reply. The truck roared along the highway, in and out of arroyos, through desert and brushland. At a gap between two hills he stopped and jumped out, slamming the door. After she had managed to get her door open, she too got down. He was standing in the cold at the back of the truck, looking down into the valley they had just left behind. Seeing her, he turned and began to kick the tires. "I'm paranoid about flats," he said. Far down the valley she saw the lights of a car moving along toward them.

"O.K.?" They got in, slammed the doors, and moved off. As they approached the first cantinas on the outskirts of the town, he looked briefly over at her. "You want a doctor? That means Solera."

"Yes," she said impatiently.

"But with this fiesta, I don't know. We'll have to walk." He had slowed down. Through the window, above the sound of the truck's motor, came the ceaseless rattle of firecrackers, and she could hear two or three bands playing at once.

He stopped under some tamarind trees near the empty marketplace. Men were lying at the base of the trees and in front of the dark stalls. They got out, and he locked the doors. "Come on," he said.

"Do you know where he lives?"

"Sure I know. That doesn't mean much tonight, though."

The din of marimbas, cornets, fireworks and screams came closer as they walked through the market; the crowd was at the end of the street, ahead of them. Now and then a sky-rocket rushed almost horizontally to explode just above their heads.

Day was not used to seeing several thousand masked men and women shouting into one another's faces. It was clear that the fireworks were dangerous: several rockets had gone directly into the mass of people. She tried to slow their pace a bit, but he kept going until they were in the crowded plaza, under the lights and streamers, engulfed by the mob. They began to fight their way through in order to cross the square.

"Do we have to get into the middle of it?" she shouted. He seemed not to hear her, and only shoved her ahead. She felt the bodies pushing and twisting against her on all sides, saw the shiny painted masks: skulls, monkeys, demons—and the purpose of the fiesta came to her. It was not meant to celebrate the glory of God, or the saint in whose honor it was named. Instead, it was a night of collective fear, when everyone agreed to be frightened. Each person was out to scare the next; their voices were sharp with apprehensiveness. And no one knew where the skyrockets and Roman candles were going to belch their fire.

The crush had started out by being overwhelming; then it had become painful and a little unpleasant. She was sure that beneath the masks the faces were unfriendly.

In the center of the plaza was a kiosk plastered over with posters. REVINDICACIÓN, REDENCIÓN, REVOLUCIÓN, they proclaimed. She let herself be forced back into the pocket against the wall of the kiosk, where there was partial shelter from the moving throng.

"I sort of hoped we might find him here," he told her. "The important citizens are usually up there sitting with the band."

"Is he really a very bad doctor?"

"Couldn't tell you."

They stood a while watching; the uproar did not encourage conversation. But once she looked and he was not there, and her heart missed a beat. Then she began desperately to examine all the taller men nearby, thinking, He can't just have walked off without his hundred dollars. When she was satisfied that he was not there, she lowered her head. Suddenly she understood that he had betrayed her to Grove. She started ahead fiercely into the crowd. I'll get to Dr. Solera by myself. She clamped her jaws together and put all her force into pushing her body forward.

Eventually she was ejected from the central core of pressure, spinning and staggering, to land against a concrete bench. A group of youths stood on top of it, peering over the heads of the multitude. As she bumped against their legs, they stared at her in surprise. One of them jumped down and stood on the ground beside her. Quickly she began in careful Spanish, "*Buenas noches*. I should like a hotel."

They started to walk. She was being buffeted so often by people rushing past that he took her arm to steady her. A sky-rocket emptied its fire into a group just ahead of them, and a girl was led away sobbing, her hands over her face.

They finally left the plaza behind and walked in the small dark streets. From time to time, when the breeze shifted and blew up from across the swampland below, an evil odor filled the air—a wide, greasy stench that expanded slowly through the streets until a new wind dispersed it. The Indians sat quietly in the dust, burning candles and carbide lamps, arranging their herbs and copal in small designs on the ground in front of them, their empty eyes fixed upon a point beyond the town.

There was another plaza, smaller and deserted save for a few drunken mestizos lying on the benches and against the tree trunks. On the far side at the end of a row of humble houses was a door with a small plaque above it: PENSIÓN FÉNIX. CAMAS.

She stood quietly, listening to the distant excitement while he knocked. There might be no one to open the door. But then an old woman stood there, her black rebozo pulled tightly about her head, blinking and frowning at them. When the youth had spoken with her for a moment, she opened the door wider. "*A sus órdenes*," he murmured, turning and running down the street. Day stepped inside.

There was a small patio full of furniture and plants. From there the old woman led her into a room that had nothing in it but a brass bed and a round table that held a bowl of dusty wax flowers. "Dr. Solera," she began. "Where is his house? I want to see him."

The old woman spoke for a while; Day interpreted her words as meaning that the thing would not be possible before morning. Still she insisted. She could be shown his house at least. But the old woman pulled the rebozo more firmly around her wrinkled forehead and began to mutter and sigh to herself. "*No se puede*," she said, going out into the patio. Day followed her.

In the center was a tall cage covered with chicken wire where birds fluttered and hopped among the branches of a dead tree. The old woman stood by the cage watching the birds move in the dark, and her face assumed an expression which could have denoted satisfaction.

Day hovered in the background, waiting for a propitious moment, when the old woman might become receptive again. On a small wicker table covered with lace doilies was a frayed photograph album. She held it under the light bulb and fingered the pages. The pictures were old postcards, all of them views of a local volcano. She put the album back and took up a magazine. There were photographs of huge groups of nuns standing in rows, and a full-page portrait of the Pope. When she heard the four quick knocks on the entrance door she was absolutely certain it was Grove; it was almost as if his voice had spoken. She dropped the magazine to her side and, standing very still, looked up at the stars.

Four

28

I N THE GLARE of the truck's headlights the trail looked even rougher than it was; each oncoming hummock stood out sharply against the darkness behind it. Thorny drove as fast as possible, trying to keep the roar of the motor and the rattle of the chassis at a constant level. Variations in pitch and volume weakened the hypnotic power of the sound upon which, at the present moment, his thoughts depended for their sequence. Not that he believed there was any point in thinking, much less in worrying, about the mess that Grove had made. His own part in it was finished; he had done exactly as he had been told, and now once again it was merely a question of waiting, this time in doubt rather than with faith. Grove had always had the power to pull the world out from under his feet, but until now he had not done it. Trying to imagine how he would have gone about the whole thing, had he been Grove, brought him to the conclusion that everything Grove had done, from the first night on, had been done wrong.

He had telephoned Thorny at his apartment, saying he would meet him outside in the street, and there Thorny had found him, walking quickly up and down in front of the shabby entrance door, ignoring the stares of the passers-by. First he slipped Thorny a handful of grifas. They each lighted one, and started walking fast in the direction of the even poorer outskirts, past the slaughterhouse where the streets were not paved. Here there was a small park, overgrown with vegetation; at this late hour the place was completely deserted.

They sat on a bench and talked. Thorny always counted his grifas, and it was during his fourth that Grove, in his own roundabout fashion, offered Thorny a hundred thousand dollars. Grove had been smoking earlier in the evening, before coming to see him, and so Thorny assumed he was spinning one of his fantasies. He played the game for a while, and then, the talk about money having inevitably reminded him of his own precarious position, he grew morose and stared at the shadows of the leaves on the ground beside the bench.

And the little buses went past on their way through the valley to outlying villages, rattling along with their dim blue lights inside, and Thorny was thinking that there was something about being rich that made people sadistic. Grove, who was certainly very high, had gone on at such length and in such detail that he had finally cut him short. "Listen," he said. "The day I see a hundred mil I'll be down with either polio or cancer."

And Grove had cried out, "Jesus Christ! You don't know yet when I'm serious? Haven't you listened?"

They were up again, walking, with the wind swooping down out of the trees into their faces, the street lights swinging behind the leaves. Once more Grove went through the exposition of his project. At the end Thorny, although tremendously excited, shook his head. "It can't be that easy, baby. It never is."

The doubt, which he now understood had been there from the beginning, had been overshadowed by the habit of unquestioning acceptance. One day a month or so later, Grove handed him a great sheaf of typed pages. "I'm coming along on it," he told him modestly. "These are just random notes, if you want to look through them." They made the desired impression on Thorny; when he had read them he announced his willingness to collaborate on the venture. Grove did not show the surprise or pleasure he had expected. It was clear that he had counted on him from the outset.

Thorny had found it strange enough that Grove should not have observed strict secrecy in the matter; if you were going to do something like that, you went ahead and did it yourself, and said nothing to anyone. But the great question, which, had he not known Grove so well, would have put him off completely, was the size of the sum he had offered. True, it was no more than a promise, but Grove's word was good.

"I'll do it, baby. You know that," he had told Grove. "But I can't help asking myself why you don't want to save the cash and take care of it yourself."

Grove had stared at him, appalled by his lack of understanding. "What?" he cried. "Tie myself to that kind of guilt for the rest of my life? God!"

"Oh, I see," said Thorny. "You going to keep Luchita on?"

"As soon as this is fixed up I'll be able to let her go to Paris."

"I wouldn't mind a trip myself," Thorny mused. "Maybe on a freighter, the kind that takes ninety days to get to Palembang."

Grove's look had chilled all fantasy. "You'll wait a long time for that. Because you're going to live on the interest. A windfall, in a town like this?"

Thorny nodded unhappily. "You're right. God, yes!"

Now and then, at a sharp curve in the trail, the dust he was raising blew ahead and enveloped the truck, blotting out the white rocks and bushes at the sides, but he did not shift gears or slow down. At the time he had accepted Grove's explanation. It was a childish desire to feel unimplicated; very likely the handing over of money would be the gesture of charity that would help him to believe in his innocence. Even accepting all this, Thorny had worried.

One time he had thought about it all night. When morning came he had telephoned Grove. In a café opposite the Correo Central he began by babbling, "I've been thinking. I don't believe I can manage it."

Grove cut him short. "Look. No matter how you picture it, it's going to turn out different. So don't picture it."

After that he was silent about his anxieties. The day they set out for Puerto Farol, Grove handed him a small box. "One now, and another every two hours." By noon he was in a state of happy indifference. As they were speeding down the eastern flank of the sierra, he said, "Nice little pills. I've got cushions all the way around."

"Good," said Grove, and was silent again. Thorny relaxed completely, happy merely to be sitting beside Grove, the one constant in a totality of flux and chaos. (Grove had remembered every detail—even, he reflected with admiration, to the playing cards.)

The bungalow was under coconut palms near the beach. Rain had discolored the dark walls, and there was the hopeless smell of mildew. "And this is the best Romero could do!" Grove snorted. "Try once to get him up off his big ass."

"But he cooperates, baby. And you've got a couch there," Thorny told him. Then he went off in the car with everything to the hotel. As he drove into the plaza he saw Romero on the steps, standing in the late-afternoon sunlight.

"*Hombre, cómo estás?*" The fraternal back-slaps, the close-up of the rotten teeth. Upstairs, in the fetid little cubicle near the bathrooms, Romero sat on the edge of the bed and spat out the pieces of toothpick he had been chewing. More imminent and insidious than the stink from the latrines was the expanding odor of Romero's sneakered feet. Following instructions, Thorny had brought up only one bottle of whiskey from the car. He took it out and poured Romero the first drink.

He ate in his room. After supper there were the cards, with Romero winning and sweating and drinking more, until his gestures were without much control, and Thorny made a show of putting the bottle on the bureau. They went on playing. One by one the guests clattered by the door to use the lavatories, returned to their rooms, and shut their doors. Then Thorny got up and went out to the latrine himself; this would give Romero the chance to take another drink. While he was out he walked softly along the balcony to the other room. The light was out. Now his heart was going too fast, and the pill was not due until twelve. On his return trip along the balcony he ran into the plants several times. Romero was in the chair with his elbows on the table when Thorny walked through the doorway, but he had taken a stiff drink; he sat with the tears coming out of his eyes, trying to keep from coughing.

Thorny took a pocket radio out of his valise, sat down, and began to move the dial. Thundershowers in the mountains made a constant crashing of static. Knowing that Romero was not going to continue the game, he sat still, waiting for him to get up and clump downstairs to bed; instead he laid his head on the table and stayed that way. Thorny sat on for a while, playing with the radio.

29

The noise of the palms swishing in the dark came through the screens into the bungalow. Grove had been allowing himself to chain-smoke his grifas since eleven o'clock; he was aware of being excessively nervous, and he realized that the grifas had been a mistake. He stepped outside and stood in the sand for a moment, sniffing the still air. Then he began to walk toward the open beach ahead. The air under the trees was close and hot, but by the water there was a slight breeze stirring. It could be happening at this very moment; without being conscious of what he was doing he shut his eyes tightly and continued to walk ahead. Then he opened them. There was no one on the beach. He walked along for a way, and then turned and went back, still feeling taut and irritable. When he got to the bungalow, Thorny stood in the doorway looking out. He pushed inside past him and turned to stare at him.

"They switched rooms on us."

Grove did not answer; his mouth fell open. Then he shut it. "Where's Romero?"

"He's fine. Practically out." He gestured. "I went myself and looked. There was an old guy in there. She must have antennae. She's locked in the next room with the guy's wife."

It hit Grove like a hammer blow. She had thought of it; she was afraid. She knew him. And she was still there.

"What are you doing here?" he demanded, his voice harsh.

"I had to let you know, didn't I?"

Thorny's defensive tone infuriated him. "No! You didn't! What the bloody Christ are you down here for?"

"You want me to go in through the window?" Thorny cried. "With the other one there?"

Grove reached out and seized his shoulder roughly. "Look, Thornwald," he said, squeezing his flesh still harder. "This is your problem. You're doing it. You understand?"

He had never seen Grove's face so excessively distorted. When he felt the grip on his shoulder slowly lessen, he swung abruptly around, ran outside and got into the car.

Back at the hotel he climbed up the rickety stairs; Romero had got up from the chair and fallen onto the bed. He was snoring heavily. Thorny pushed him over against the wall and sat down on the edge of the mattress. Time began to go by, while he sat looking at the door, at the window. At one o'clock the electricity went off; he lighted a candle and watched the shadows, getting himself ready. Finally he took off his shoes and went out.

The night noises covered whatever tiny sounds he might have made climbing through the window. With the syringe in his hand he walked to the bed on the left. As he shot the curare into the fleshy neck he found his lips forming the words, "Goodbye, you old bag." (From the beginning she had disapproved of him as a friend for Grove.) There was no more motion in the bed than as if she had turned over in her sleep. He pulled the sheet up tight around her chin and went back to the window.

30

Later, when it was daylight and the old American and his wife had left, and the servants were clattering in the kitchen, he went in again and finished his work. Driving back to the bungalow he felt a glow of pleasure as he recalled the speed and precision with which he had accomplished this last part of the venture. Grove was waiting for him outside the bungalow, sitting on a palm stump. They drove inland through the green world of a banana plantation to the top of a hill behind the town, where they stopped and watched until the fire was brought under control. The plaza was black with people. Then they cut through the jungle along a narrow back trail and came out onto the coast-capital highway.

It was all done, and done in the only way possible, as Thorny saw it, yet Grove was not content; he was fretting about the American girl. Over and over he said he would never be sure what she had seen. She had gone on her way quietly, yes, but how could he know she hadn't happened onto the truth (it must have been fairly evident, if for any reason she had really looked), and rather than see herself getting involved, had merely shut the door and gone away, free to tell everything later?

"That's got to be changed," Grove said with finality.

"It's a little late in the day to change anything," Thorny told him, stung to realize that Grove did not consider his work a brilliant success.

Grove said nothing. As they rounded a curve, Thorny stole a glance at him, and decided that he had been shut out. Grove was going to do something crazy, and without taking him into his confidence.

Even so, he could scarcely believe Grove was serious when, two days later after getting him down to Los Hermanos, he expounded the outrageous new project to him.

"You *want* trouble, don't you?" he said slowly. "Have you got to walk another tightrope now, when everything's all right?"

"The answer is yes," Grove snapped. "You'll be stuck here for a few days, that's all. They're coming down tonight."

He did not ask Grove why the girl never appeared. Three mornings later, after they had managed to calm the old man somewhat, Grove remarked, "It's a good thing she's responsive to treatment. If she were anything like him, Paloma'd never be able to manage her."

Forbearing to criticize, since criticism was useless, Thorny merely said, "The old guy's a handful." He would not have thought Grove capable of such protracted nonsense. Instead of living a normal life, waiting quietly for word from London and Montreal, he was hysterically involved in a round-the-clock game with two American tourists: feeding them LSD, shooting them full of scopolamine and morphine, putting them under and bringing them out again, and providing special sound effects for each phase of the program. (This preoccupation with the tape recorders struck him as the most infantile bit of all. The room at Los Hermanos had to be kept dark, and at times there was an endless whispering, scarcely loud enough to hear unless he remained in there purposely to listen; then the repeated phrases seemed to grow in volume and fill every corner.)

That period had been a strain; Thorny and Dirk worked in four-hour shifts. The schedule had to be observed with absolute precision. Each day Grove made three round trips up to the capital; on arriving back at Los Hermanos he was often short-tempered.

"Anyway," Thorny said, the morning they drove to the station and he helped Grove carry the old man onto the train for San Felipe, "whatever happens now, we've done everything we could." He knew better than to say, I've done everything. But Grove turned on him with irritation.

"What is this always about things happening?" he demanded. "Things don't happen. It depends on who comes along."

"You're right," he agreed, and he recalled the remark shortly afterward at the ranch. Grove had telephoned him the following day, saying he needed him; when he arrived he was waiting for him in the little library off his own bedroom. He got up and shut the door.

"You'll eat in here," he told him. "Your job is to tune in on all conversations, whatever room we're in, and tape everything. She's not being honest with me."

"I thought you said she was responsive," said Thorny, trying not to grin.

"That doesn't mean she's being honest now."

Thorny listened before, during, and after mealtimes, and was impressed. There was no doubt that neither of them remembered anything at all about Puerto Farol; they were convinced that they had first met Grove down there at the dock.

"There's something she's holding back," Grove complained, after he had studied the recordings.

"Get her mad if you can. Catch her off guard," Thorny advised.

"She's going to give me trouble yet."

With that in his mind, Grove could be counted on to react badly to the news about the bonfire; with misgivings Thorny went in to tell him. Earlier in the day Grove had handed him a pile of papers to burn, most of them typewritten notes of the sort he was always making. He would not have bothered to call it to Grove's attention had he not seen the girl wandering around out there in the garden, near the spot where he had burned them. When she had gone in, he left his hammock in the bamboo brake and walked over to check. One of the servants, before going off to the fiesta, must have spilled water on the fire, he decided, for the papers had not burned completely. He picked up those that remained and carried them into the kitchen, pinching off the charred edges on the way. At the sink he washed his hands, and while he dried them he glanced over the top fragment.

fer
as scaffolding f
(Note: for therap
rd day—tape of beach at La Lib
h "Dawn will be breaking soon."
nto RED notebook a

It went on in this way; there was not even another complete sentence—only bits of phrases and truncated words. However, there was nothing to do but take the stuff in and report what had happened.

"What?" Grove sprang up out of his chair, grabbed the papers.

Thorny was silent. He heard the steady spray of a sprinkler in the courtyard rattling as it hit the big banana leaves. After a lapse, Grove said, looking fixedly at him, "This makes it bad."

"For Christ's sake! She just walked past!"

Grove still glared at him. He raised his voice, "Believe me when I say it's bad."

"I believe you." Thorny moved toward the door.

"Stay here," said Grove sharply, beginning to walk around the center of the room. Then for nearly ten minutes he talked without stopping. Finally he threw himself onto the divan and stretched out at full length. "It's as though I'd known all along it was going to be this way. Unbelievable how things can dovetail."

Thorny looked at the floor. "It depends on who comes along. Isn't that what you said?"

Grove's glance was cold. "I'm as much against it as you are. It's just where the whole thing is now. You can see that."

"You know what you're doing."

It was not much later when Thorny went out into the courtyard and saw the girl standing on the rocks down below; quickly Grove brought an immersion heater and made the doctor his tea.

A good while after dark, while Grove and the girl were in the kitchen, Thorny went down and got Pablo, who had stayed on at the generator. ("There's a señor who's sick, and I have to take him to San Felipe.") Together they carried the old man from the bed to the truck. Thorny got in and shut

the door. Then he drove off alone in the dark, down the trail
that ultimately led to Barrancas, until he got to the dangerous
stretch edging the cliff. If there was even a mule coming
along here, you had to stop the car. In the daytime, far below,
you could see the round tops of the big trees down there. He
had to do the rest alone, but even so, it did not take more
than two minutes. Then he went on down a mile or so until
he came to a place where he could turn the car.

No one ever went down into that part of the country; it
was empty land. Scrub mimosa and cactus at the foot of the
cliff, and then terrible formless thickets of thorned bramble,
like rolls of barbed wire. And still lower, the tufted forest of
high green trees. And nothing lasted long down there, in any
case, he thought, glancing out over the vast moonlit lands below: the buzzards, flopping and tugging, and the ants hurrying in endless lines, night and day.

"Why don't you go to bed?" Grove asked him when he got
back.

"Yeah," he said, and went down to see Pablo at the generator. Earlier they had made some grifas together. Now they
sat smoking in the moonlight, listening to the radio. Before
he relaxed completely, for he had no idea how long he might
stay down there with Pablo, he made himself stand up and go
over to the truck: he had left the keys in the ignition. He was
almost down to the generator again when Pablo called out,
and it was a shock to find the girl standing there; he had
imagined she would be with Grove. The only thing possible
was to go up to the house for a consultation.

Grove's face grew nasty when Thorny told him. "Oh, she
wants it to be at San Felipe, does she? O.K., take her. It's perfect!" Then he explained, and told Thorny exactly what to do.

"You're out of your bloody mind!" said Thorny, in spite of
himself.

Grove smiled broadly. "I'll give you ten minutes' start."

Bravado, thought Thorny, tramping back down to the generator. It was dangerous enough anyway, without the acro-
batics. He stopped for a moment beside a high cactus and
finished off a partly smoked grifa from his pocket.

He was very high driving up to San Felipe, and the girl had
decided to be hostile. The confusion of the alameda, the fire-

works and the yelling, made him even more nervous. When he had spotted Grove and knew Grove had seen him and the girl, he pushed into the crowd, looking straight ahead, and fought his way through to the open. Quickly he passed between the rows of silent seated Indians, and into the dark street where he had parked.

Five

31

THE OLD woman's face lost its contented look; turning her head away from the birdcage, she frowned, and then shuffled across to the door. And there he was in a white sweater, suave and gleaming. Day watched him take the old woman's measure and alter his personality to fit the need. He assumed a courteous, almost deferential air, and said a few gentle phrases to her; then he stepped past her into the patio. Grinning at Day across the birdcage, he began to talk very fast.

"'I admit I was crazy about the dame,' the suspect told police after the six-hour grilling. 'I followed her everywhere. I wanted to know what made her tick. But that don't make me the killer.'"

If only he really were mad, she thought, his behavior would be less frightening. As she did not reply, but merely stood staring at him, he went on. "In the next edition they print the full confession. What are you doing here?" The insolent tone of his final words reawakened her anger.

"I'm sleeping here," she said without expression. The night was growing colder.

The old woman still stood holding the door ajar, watching Grove with an admiration only faintly tempered by mistrust. He was so clearly a young lover; it was so natural of him to come and try to persuade the girl to go out into the fiesta. She called over to her: "*Andale, guapa! Salga un poco con su novio.*" It was ridiculous enough, but Day could not laugh.

Grove stepped around the cage to her and touched her arm. "It was just what I thought. He felt like going outside for some air. He took a walk."

She wanted passionately to believe him; it was difficult, and she may have allowed her doubt to show. "All right," he said, giving her an ugly smile. "He's been kidnaped and probably murdered. Is that better?"

Ignoring the irony, agreeing to accept the story, she went on. "Does he seem like himself?"

"More like himself than anybody else, anyway," he said with impatience. "Why don't we go up the street for a drink? Then you come back and sleep here, and in the morning I'll get Solera and bring him around and pick you up. That's what you want, isn't it? Isn't that why you came to San Felipe?"

She considered him a moment. He still thinks he can manipulate me, she thought scornfully—as if anything could change the way she felt about him. He expects me to put up resistance. An unexpected compliance could throw him off balance, and she might seize the initiative in the battle. The fact that she was unable to conceive of their relationship in any other terms rather frightened her, but above all she was infuriated by being forced to engage in such a struggle.

The sputter of firecrackers and the barking of dogs never had subsided for an instant. The old woman still stood there, her hand on the door, watching them, perfectly certain that at a given moment the girl would capitulate. And sure enough, presently she moved listlessly around the birdcage, dragging the back of her hand across the meshes of chicken wire to make a rasping noise, and came walking over toward the door. The young man followed quickly, smiled at the old woman, and gently pushed the girl outside. She nodded as he passed in front of her. "*Claro. Una noche de fiesta . . .*" She shut the door.

The stars burned in the cold sky. They walked briskly through the deserted streets, with the noise of the fiesta behind them. On the outskirts of the town there was a rocky eminence, high above the wasteland. Tall trees stood near the edge. The squat adobe building in front of them looked very small. Music came through the open door.

"It'll be good tonight," he said.

The crimson and orange glow of a jukebox was the only light in the main room. Tables were grouped around the instrument; a dozen mestizos sat in a state of torpor.

Behind the café was an open garden planted with high pines. The bamboo pavilions among the trees were scarcely lit. People sat everywhere, and bands of children raced through the gloom tossing firecrackers that exploded among the cactuses. Only when Grove had taken her all the way

across the garden did she understand why a café had been
built in this particular spot. The place was at the very end of
the town; the back of its garden skirted the promontory.
Along the curve of the parapet were more of the bamboo
huts, with slivers of pale light spilling through the slits in their
walls. Down to the lower end of the garden he led her, and
they went into a booth. There was only one small bench; they
sat side by side looking out across the lightless landscape beyond the railing. An Indian waiter wearing felt bedroom slippers appeared in the doorway. Grove ordered *habanero*; there
was only beer.

She wished the night were over. Ironically she was reminded of the sentence from her dream. If only dawn *were*
going to be breaking soon, and there were not the bare little
room and the hours in the hard bed to look forward to before meeting Dr. Solera. The dry soughing of the wind when
it passed now and then through the pines made the minutes
seem much longer.

After a while the Indian came back, bringing a pail of ice
with two bottles of beer in it. He left an opener on the table
and went away.

The moon had moved in the sky; down there she could
detect certain remote shadowy canyons that had not been
visible a while ago. As she sat letting her eyes follow their faint
contours, she thought of the terrible expression she had
caught on Grove's face in the kitchen, and it seemed to her
that all the forces which had made this present scene inevitable had come into being at that time, and that nothing
had changed since then.

He sat first in one position and then in another, although
the bench was not noticeably uncomfortable. Twice he rose
and stood with his glass in his hand, looking silently over the
railing into the dark.

A family group filed across the garden and out with a great
noise of laughter and chatter. Then in a nearby booth a powerful salute was detonated. There were screams, and the
women cried, "*Ay, Dios!*"

Finally she said, "I've got to go back. I'm half dead with
the cold." Her voice sounded to her as though it were coming over an amplifier—an unreal, husky, intimate whisper.

Somewhere back in the garden another large firecracker exploded. Several strings of small ones were tossed over the cliff, crackling and flaming.

Without getting up, he leaned over the railing and looked downward. There was only the darkness there, and she knew it as well as he, yet she too found herself staring out at the same part of the invisible countryside. For an instant there was enough silence in the garden behind her for her to hear the tiny, far-off sound of a baying dog.

Presently he said, "Look, Day." She waited for him to go on, and since he did not, she turned her head toward him. His hand, resting on his thigh, held a large black revolver.

Six

32

STEERING the truck through the gate, Thorny wondered whether Pablo would still be awake. It occurred to him that there was no one at all in the house. No servants, no guests, no hosts—only the wind in the courtyard, rustling the leaves.

The light over the generator was on, and Pablo sat on the ground listening to the radio. He dropped down beside him and squinted, so that Pablo got to his feet and snapped off the light. Squatting again, now in the precise moonlight, the boy tossed Thorny a grifa.

"*Pobrecita!* She wanted to see her husband in the hospital?"

"Yes. Shut the motor off. There's nobody in the house."

They had smoked until shortly after daybreak. When Thorny wandered up to bed, the courtyard looked haggard in the pale new light; the air in his room was hot. There was a cricket singing somewhere behind the curtains. After he had bolted the heavy door he walked across and let the blinds fall with a crash. From his pillow he listened to the cricket repeat its one small glassy note, again and again.

At two o'clock there was a banging on the door. He groaned, "Oh, Christ!" got up, and opened it.

Grove stood there with a thermos of coffee, the bright sunlight shining on the leaves behind him. "Let's get going," he said. "You're driving."

On the way up to the capital they did not talk. The long reaches of the desperate outer slums were pink in the sunset as the convertible rolled down into the city. "Luchita took off for Paris this morning," Grove said suddenly. "She phoned from the airport."

Thorny made a noise in his throat.

They stood on the terrace of Grove's apartment, drinking very cold beer, looking at the decaying light in the western sky. "When can we expect a change?" Thorny asked, without having known, an instant before, that he was going to say anything.

"It'll be coming through. Your credit's good until then. Up to a point."

"Up to a hundred thousand." Thorny's voice had absolutely no inflection.

Grove turned on him. "Go on home, will you?" he snapped, his face savage and ready for tears, like a small boy's.

"Christ almighty!" Thorny set his glass down on the table with a bang and went into the *sala*. Grove's voice was shouting after him. He stood still, waiting for it to suggest that his work had not been essential, did not deserve to be paid for.

"I said up to a certain point!" Grove appeared in the doorway, black and faceless against the dying sky. "Make sense. How can you have it until I get it?"

But an unfamiliar accent of confusion in his voice had struck Thorny's ears; he watched Grove come into the room toward him, and it seemed the right moment to move for the establishment of a new status. Not to have to pay for meals, to come home and lie down in a really comfortable bed; that was all he had in his mind at the time. He turned and went out into the foyer, stood looking into the blue bedroom where he had slept the night they had come back from Puerto Farol. "My room," he thought, and he walked in, took off his jacket and shoes, and threw himself down on the bed. His hands cupped behind his head, he lay a while staring dreamily at the ceiling, waiting to see; Grove knew he was still there.

A little later he heard Grove go out. He got up, stretching, went and turned on the hot water in the bathtub. While he waited for it to fill, he wandered out into the kitchen and told Manuel and Paloma to serve his dinner at half past eight. Walking slowly back to the bedroom along the terrace, he stopped a moment to examine the pools and fountains on the way; it was the first time he had ever really looked at them.

In the bathroom he turned off the roaring water, seized a big turkish towel, and wiped the steam from the enormous mirror on the wall; it had a wide beveled edge that played tricks with the image. He ducked his head back and forth a few times, watching his face change. Then he moistened a grifa, lit it, and partially undressed. Taking a pair of curved scissors from the cabinet, he began to cut his fingernails.

Chronology

1910   Born Paul Frederic Bowles on December 30 in Jamaica, Queens, New York City, the only child of Rena Winnewisser and Claude Dietz Bowles. (Bowles family immigrated to New England in the 17th century; Paul's grandfather, Frederick Bowles, fought for the Union in the Civil War and settled in Elmira, New York. Rena Winnewisser's grandfather was a German freethinker and political radical who came to the United States in 1848; her father owned a department store in Bellows Falls, Vermont, before moving family to a 165-acre farm near Springfield, Massachusetts.) Father is a dentist. The family lives at 108 Hardenbrook Avenue in Jamaica, the building where his father has his office and laboratory.

1911–15   Bowles learns to read by age four and keeps notebooks with drawings and stories, a habit that will continue throughout his childhood. His activities are strictly regimented by father. He spends summers with paternal grandparents in Glenora, New York, or the Winnewissers.

1916–18   Family moves to 207 De Grauw Avenue in Jamaica in summer 1916. Bowles begins attending Model School in Jamaica the following year, entering at the second grade level. Mother reads him stories by Hawthorne and Poe. Beginning in 1918, Bowles goes to Manhattan twice a week for orthodontic treatment, which will continue for ten years; makes monthly visits to New York Public Library on 42nd Street, where Anne Carroll Moore, a family friend, is head of the children's department. Receives books from Moore and visits her Greenwich Village apartment. Father confiscates notebooks in a fit of rage. (Bowles would write in his autobiography: "This was the only time my father beat me. It began a new stage in the development of hostilities between us.")

1919   Bowles and parents catch influenza but survive worldwide epidemic. Father buys phonograph, collects classical recordings, and forbids his son from bringing jazz records into the house. Bowles continues to buy "dance" records.

After family buys piano, Bowles studies theory, sight-singing, and piano technique. Writes "Le Carré: An Opera in Nine Chapters" about two men who exchange wives.

1920–21   Keeps diary filled with imaginary events and made-up characters. Writes daily "newspaper." Is promoted from fourth to sixth grade.

1922   Family moves to 34 Terrace Avenue in Jamaica. Bowles gives readings of his poems and stories after school. Buys first book of poetry, Arthur Waley's *A Hundred and Seventy Chinese Poems*.

1924   Graduates from Model School and attends public high school in Flushing, New York. Appointed humor editor of *The Oracle*, the school magazine.

1925–26   Writes crime stories with the recurring character "the Snake-Woman" and reads them at the summer home of Anna, Jane, and Sue Hoagland, friends of the family in Glenora. Meets the Hoaglands' friend Mary Crouch (later Oliver). Transfers to Jamaica High School. Reads English writer Arthur Machen. Is deeply impressed by a performance of Stravinsky's *The Firebird* at Carnegie Hall. Shows talent in painting.

1927   Performs with the Phylo Players, an amateur theatrical group. Reads André Gide. Buys an issue of the Paris-based literary magazine *transition*, which has a major impact on him. Is promoted to poetry editor of *The Oracle*.

1928   Graduates from Jamaica High School in January. The Hoagland sisters help him sell his paintings; when father refuses to support his artistic aspirations, mother pays for classes at the School of Design and Liberal Arts in New York. Bowles publishes poem "Spire Song" and prose poem "Entity" in *transition*. Spends summer working in the transit department of the Bank of Manhattan. Enters University of Virginia in the fall. Reads *The Waste Land*; discovers Prokofiev, Gregorian chant, Duke Ellington, and the blues. Experiments with inhaling ether. While home on winter break, attends one of the Aaron Copland–Roger Sessions Concerts of Contemporary Music, featuring music by Henry Cowell and George Antheil.

1929   Returns to University of Virginia in January and is hospitalized with conjunctivitis. Decides to move to Paris and obtains passport with the help of Sue Hoagland and Mary Oliver; tells virtually no one else of his plans. Arrives in Paris in April and works as a switchboard operator at the *Herald Tribune*. Mother refuses request to send money to Bowles made by a friend of Oliver's. Bowles receives 2,500 francs from Oliver and quits job; takes a short trip to Switzerland and Nice. Publishes poems in English and French in the Paris-based magazines *Tambour*, *This Quarter*, and *Anthologie du Groupe Moderne d'Art*. Visits northeastern France and Germany. Loses virginity on a camping trip with a Hungarian woman he had met the day before at the Café du Dôme; has sexual experience with Billy Hubert, a family friend. Accompanies Hubert to St.-Moritz and St.-Malo. Decides to return home and sails for New York on July 24. Works at Dutton's Bookshop and rents a room at 122 Bank Street. Begins writing "Without Stopping," fictional account of his travels in Europe.

1930   Meets Henry Cowell, who calls Bowles' musical compositions "frivolous" but writes a note of introduction to Aaron Copland. Moves to parents' home in order to use piano after Copland offers lessons in composition. Returns to University of Virginia in March. Hitchhikes to Philadelphia to attend Martha Graham's ballet *Le Sacre du Printemps* on April 11; meets Harry Dunham, who will become a close friend. Decides to leave college after finishing out the term in June. Spends September and October with Copland at the Yaddo Arts Colony in Saratoga Springs, New York. Asked by college friend Bruce Morrissette to edit an issue of University of Virginia magazine *The Messenger*, solicits submissions from William Carlos Williams, Gertrude Stein, and Edouard Roditi, who becomes a lifelong friend and correspondent. Quarrels violently with parents in December.

1931   Sails for Europe on March 25. Shortly after arriving in Paris, looks up Gertrude Stein, with whom a friendship develops. Meets Jean Cocteau, Virgil Thomson, Ezra Pound, and Pavel Tchelitchew. Goes to Berlin with Copland at the end of April. Meets Jean Rhys, Stephen Spender, and Christopher Isherwood, who will give

Bowles' surname to the heroine of his *Goodbye to Berlin*. Continues composition studies with Copland but dislikes Germany. Visits Kurt Schwitters in Hannover and is impressed with his studio; Bowles will soon incorporate one of Schwitters' abstract poems into his *Sonata for Oboe and Clarinet*. Writes to friend Daniel Burns that he feels his poems are "worth a large zero" and stops writing poetry for more than two years. Spends part of July with Stein and Alice B. Toklas in Bilignan, France, where they are joined by Copland; at Stein's suggestion, the two men visit Morocco, which enchants Bowles and frustrates Copland. They live in Tangier until early October. Bowles meets Claude McKay and the surrealist painter Kristians Tonny. After visiting Fez, Bowles writes to Morrissette, "Fez I shall make my home some day!" Bowles travels in Morocco with Harry Dunham after Copland leaves; returns to Paris via Spain. Attends final Copland-Sessions concert on December 16 in London, where his *Sonata for Oboe and Clarinet* is performed.

1932   Taken ill during a ski trip in the Italian Alps. Travels with literary agent John Trounstine to Spain and Morocco. Returns in May to Paris, where he is hospitalized with typhoid. Bowles' songs are performed at Yaddo. After leaving hospital in July, travels in France, seeing Gertrude Stein for the last time and meeting mother and Daniel Burns at Morrissette's house near Grenoble. Completes *Sonata No. 1 for Flute and Piano*. Goes to Spain with mother and Burns; after their departure, stays with Virgil Thomson and the painter Maurice Grosser. Visits Monte Carlo, where he becomes friendly with George Antheil. In December, finishes *Scènes d'Anabase*, based on the poem by Saint-John Perse. Leaves for Ghardaïa, a town in the northern Sahara recommended by Antheil.

1933   Arrives in Ghardaïa and settles in nearby Laghouat, where he uses the harmonium in the town's church to compose a cantata, using his own French text. Travels around the Sahara and North Africa with George Turner, an American. Goes to Tangier, where he shares house with Charles Henri Ford, surrealist poet and editor of *View* with whom he has been friendly since 1930, and Djuna Barnes. Returns to United States after a three-week visit to Puerto Rico en route to New York City. *Sonatina for Piano* performed on WEVD in New York on June 18. Bowles has difficulty adjusting to life in America; on June 24, writes Thomson, "Certainly nobody hates New York more than I do." Writes short story "A Proposition." Writes song cycle *Danger de Mort* and *Suite for Small Orchestra* and score for Dunham's film *Bride of Samoa*. Publishes "Watervariation" and "Message" in pamphlet *Two Poems*, his first separate publication. Sublets apartment from Copland at 52 West 58th Street. Founds music publishing company Editions de la Vipère and publishes *Scenes from the Door*, songs based on passages from Stein's *Useful Knowledge*. *Sonatina for Piano* performed in December at the League of Composers' Concert, where Bowles meets John Latouche, who becomes a close friend.

1934   Bowles meets George Balanchine and Lincoln Kirstein, who are interested in commissioning a score for American Ballet Caravan. Hired as a secretary by Charles Williams, director of the American Fondouk, a foundation in Morocco working for the prevention of cruelty to animals. Pays for Atlantic passage by working as a guide for a stockbroker vacationing in Spain. Buys records of North African music. His duties end in October and, after a brief stopover in Spain, he travels to Colombia; smokes marijuana for the first time while at sea. Falls ill from unpurified water and recuperates on a coffee plantation in the Colombian mountains. Returns to the United States, visiting Los Angeles and San Francisco, where he sees Henry Cowell; Cowell offers to publish Bowles' compositions in quarterly *New Music*.

1935   Accepts job as live-in companion to a wealthy Austrian invalid in Baltimore. Collaborates with painter Eugene Berman on an aborted ballet project. Quits job and returns to New York City. Receives commission to write score for Balanchine's *Yankee Clipper*. Allows his records of North African music to be reproduced for Béla Bartók. Writes music for Dunham's film *Venus and Adonis*, which is premiered at a screening and concert featuring several other works by Bowles. Scores two short films by Rudy Burkhardt and writes incidental music for *Who Fights the Battle?*, a play by Joseph Losey. Works as copyist for the Broadway composer Vernon Duke.

1936   With the help of Virgil Thomson, receives commission to
            write music for *Horse Eats Hat*, Edwin Denby's adapta-
            tion of a Eugène Labiche farce directed by John House-
            man and Orson Welles and supported by the Federal
            Theater Project. Helps to found the anti-Franco Com-
            mittee on Republican Spain. Article by Copland com-
            mends Bowles' music in *Modern Music* as "full of charm
            and melodic invention, surprisingly well-made in an in-
            stinctive and non-academic fashion." Bowles learns or-
            chestration and works on score for production of
            Marlowe's *Doctor Faustus* directed by Welles.

1937   *Doctor Faustus* opens in January; Thomson praises the
            score in *Modern Music* as "Mr. Bowles' definite entry into
            musical big-time." In February, Bowles is introduced to
            Jane Auer (b. February 22, 1917) by John Latouche. Sees
            Auer the following week at E. E. Cummings' apartment;
            when Bowles and Kristians Tonny propose a trip to Mex-
            ico, Auer asks to join them, and Bowles goes to meet her
            parents the same evening. Orders 15,000 anti-Trotsky
            stickers to distribute in Mexico. Travels to Mexico by bus
            with Auer, Tonny, and Tonny's wife, Marie-Claire Ivanoff.
            Auer falls ill with dysentery a week after arriving in Mexico
            and returns home without telling her companions. Bowles
            meets the composer Silvestre Revueltas, who leads an im-
            promptu performance of his *Homenaje a García Lorca* for
            him. Works on pieces influenced by Mexican folk music.
            Travels to Tehuantepec and helps prepare for the town's
            May Day Festival, then visits Guatemala. At Kirstein's re-
            quest, returns to New York to orchestrate Balanchine's
            Yankee Clipper. Auer invites him to spend a weekend with
            her in Deal Beach, New Jersey, after which they see each
            other regularly. *Yankee Clipper* premieres in Philadelphia.
            Bowles begins writing music for opera *Denmark Vesey*
            (now lost), with libretto by Charles Henri Ford. The first
            act of *Denmark Vesey* is performed at a benefit for *New
            Masses*.

1938   Bowles marries Auer on February 21. The couple honey-
            moon in Central America, then travel to Paris. Jane
            Bowles works on novel *Two Serious Ladies*. The Bowles
            meet Max Ernst and the painter and writer Brion Gysin,
            who will become a friend. Marriage is strained as Jane

spends much of her time apart from Bowles. Couple separates briefly when Bowles goes to the south of France; Jane joins him after Bowles urges her by wire to do so. The Bowles rent a house for the summer in Eze-Village near Cannes. Returning to New York in the fall, they move into the Chelsea Hotel. Bowles is commissioned to write music for Houseman and Welles' production of William Gillette's *Too Much Johnson*; finishes score but when the production is canceled, transforms his music into the piece *Music for a Farce*. Nearly broke, moves with Jane to a cheaper apartment.

1939   Receives relief payments from the Federal Music Project. Joins the American Communist Party. Writes score for the Group Theatre's production of William Saroyan's *My Heart's in the Highlands* and uses the money to rent a farmhouse on Staten Island, where he works on *Denmark Vesey* while Jane resumes writing *Two Serious Ladies*. Writes short story "Tea on the Mountain." Mary Oliver moves in and becomes Jane's friend and drinking companion, causing Bowles to move out. Bowles rents a room in Brooklyn and invites Jane to live with him. Jane refuses and moves with Oliver to Greenwich Village apartment; the Bowles continue to attend parties and social events together.

1940   Bowles and Jane move to the Chelsea Hotel in March. Bowles completes music for Saroyan's *Love's Old Sweet Song*, which begins trial run in Princeton on April 6. After being hired by the Department of Agriculture to write music for *Roots in the Soil*, a film about soil conservation in New Mexico, travels to Albuquerque with Jane and Jane's friend Bob Faulkner. Finishes score in June and goes to Mexico with Jane and Faulkner. Meets Tennessee Williams in Acapulco. Reluctantly moves to Taxco when Jane rents a house there without consulting him; Jane invites Faulkner to the house and begins a romantic relationship with Helvetia Perkins, an American woman working on a novel. Bowles returns to New York alone in September to compose music for the Theatre Guild's production of *Twelfth Night*, which opens on November 19. Bowles' score is a critical success; he receives a second Theatre Guild commission for Philip Barry's *Liberty Jones*, directed by Houseman. Jane arrives in New York on Christmas Day and rents a separate room at the Chelsea, where she is joined a few weeks later by Perkins.

1941   *Liberty Jones* opens on Broadway on February 5; the play and score receive negative reviews. Bowles writes music for Lillian Hellman's *Watch on the Rhine*. Attempts to quit Communist Party and is told that expulsion is the only means of leaving the organization. Writes *Pastorela*, an opera-ballet based on Mexican themes, for American Ballet Caravan. Lives with Jane at "artist's residence" on Middagh Street in Brooklyn Heights (other residents at the time include W. H. Auden and Benjamin Britten). Publishes obituary for Revueltas and essay "On Mexico's Popular Music" in *Modern Music*. Receives Guggenheim grant in March to compose an opera and travels to Taxco with Jane and Perkins. At the request of Katharine Hepburn, writes music for the play *Love Like Wildfire*, written by Hepburn's brother Richard. Meets Ned Rorem, who will become a friend and lifelong correspondent. *Pastorela* tours South America. Bowles meets Mexican painter Antonio Álvarez, who becomes close friend. Hospitalized with dysentery in September; recovers but falls ill with jaundice and recuperates at a sanitarium in Cuernavaca. Reads manuscript of Jane's *Two Serious Ladies* and suggests revisions.

1942   Works on light opera *The Wind Remains*, based very loosely on García Lorca's *Así que pasen cinco años*, in Mexico after Jane returns to New York to look for a publisher for *Two Serious Ladies*. Jane attempts suicide by slashing wrists but does not tell Bowles for many years. Bowles returns to United States with Álvarez, who is now partially paralyzed from a suicide attempt. Moves to apartment on 14th Street and Seventh Avenue and becomes acquainted with Marcel Duchamp, its previous occupant. Sees Jane often while maintaining separate household and finances. Debuts as music critic for the New York *Herald Tribune* on November 20; will contribute reviews regularly until 1946. Drafted for military service but dismissed after psychological examination.

1943   *The Wind Remains*, conducted by Leonard Bernstein with choreography by Merce Cunningham, premieres at the Museum of Modern Art on March 30. Jane Bowles' *Two Serious Ladies* is published on April 19 to mostly negative reviews. Composes incidental music for productions of John Ford's *'Tis Pity She's a Whore* and a stage adaptation of James Michener's *Tales of the South Pacific*. "Bluey: Pages from an Imaginary Diary," a section of his childhood notebooks, is published in *View*. Bowles meets Peggy Guggenheim, who organizes a recording of five of his pieces. Meets Samuel Barber, Gian-Carlo Menotti, and John Cage. Visits Canada with Jane.

1944   Writes music for Theatre Guild production of Franz Werfel's *Jacobowsky and the Colonel* (adapted by S. N. Behrman) and for *Congo*, a film directed by André Cauvin with script by John Latouche; receives recordings of Congolese music from Cauvin that influence the score. Composes music for ballet *Colloque Sentimental*, produced by the Ballet Russe de Monte Carlo with sets by Salvador Dali, and incidental music for Williams' *The Glass Menagerie*.

1945   Moves to an apartment on West 10th Street; Jane and Perkins rent apartment in the same building. Edits special issue of *View* on Central and South America and the Caribbean, translating several articles and contributing an anonymous story supposedly taken from a Mexican magazine; story will be revised four years later as "Doña Faustina." Writes "The Scorpion," inspired by his reading of indigenous Mexican myths, later writing that "the objectives and behavior of the protagonists remained the same as in the beast legends. It was through this unexpected little gate that I crept back into the land of fiction writing." Travels to Central America with set designer and distant cousin Oliver Smith during summer. Publishes "The Scorpion" and writes "A Distant Episode." Translates Borges' story "The Circular Ruins." Develops close friendship with Australian composer Peggy Glanville-Hicks, who will set Bowles' texts to music and become a frequent correspondent.

1946   Writes music for *Blue Mountain Ballads*, with lyrics by Tennessee Williams. Works on translation of Sartre's play *Huit-clos*. Publishes "By the Water" in *View* and "The Echo" in *Harper's Bazaar*. Completes *Sonata for Two*

Pianos and several theater scores. *No Exit*, Bowles' translation of *Huit-clos* directed by John Huston, opens on
November 29 and is awarded Drama Critics' Award for
the year's best foreign play.

1947   *Partisan Review* publishes "A Distant Episode." At a
meeting with Dial Press about a possible collection of stories, Bowles is introduced to Helen Strauss, who agrees to
be his agent. Hears from Strauss that Doubleday has offered an advance for a novel; Bowles signs contract and
leaves for Morocco soon after. Writes "Pages from Cold
Point" while at sea. Works on *The Sheltering Sky*, spending the fall in Tangier. Although he will travel frequently
to Europe, Asia, and the United States, Tangier will be
Bowles' home for the rest of his life. Contacts Oliver
Smith in New York and they agree to buy a house in the
Casbah of Tangier together, which upsets Jane. Meets
Moroccan artist Ahmed Yacoubi, who will become a close
companion during the 1950s. Begins taking *majoun*, a jam
made from cannabis; tries kif, which he will begin smoking regularly and in large quantities from the 1950s
through the 1980s, when health problems force him to reduce his consumption to one cigarette a day. Goes to Fez
in December.

1948   Crosses into Algeria and travels around the Sahara. Jane
arrives in Tangier with her new lover. Edwin Denby arrives and the four visit Fez. Jane has averse reaction to
majoun, hallucinating and experiencing severe paranoia.
Bowles finishes *The Sheltering Sky* in May; travels through
Anti-Atlas Mountains with singer Libby Holman. Returns
to New York alone in July. Doubleday rejects *The Sheltering Sky* and demands return of the advance. Several
months later, English publisher John Lehmann reads
The Sheltering Sky while visiting New York and agrees to
publish it; James Laughlin of New Directions promises
to bring out the American edition. Writes music for
Williams' *Summer and Smoke*. *Concerto for Two Pianos,
Winds, and Percussion* premieres in New York. Bowles becomes friends with Gore Vidal and Truman Capote. Jane
develops an intense emotional attachment to a Moroccan
woman named Cherifa that will last for many years.
Bowles returns to Morocco, writing "The Delicate Prey"
while at sea in December.

1949   Hosts Tennessee Williams and Williams' lover Frank Merlo. Travels in Sahara with Jane, who is impressed by the desert and writes her last completed story, "A Stick of Green Candy," in Taghit. Visits Paris for a performance of his *Concerto for Two Pianos and Orchestra*. John Lehmann publishes *The Sheltering Sky*. Bowles works on novel "Almost All the Apples Are Gone," never completed. In October, travels to England, where he is feted and introduced to Elizabeth Bowen, Cyril Connolly, and other British writers. New Directions publishes *The Sheltering Sky* in a small first printing on October 14, planning a second of 45,000 for the following year. Sails for Ceylon and begins writing a new novel, *Let It Come Down*.

1950   *The Sheltering Sky* enters the *New York Times* best-seller list on January 1; reviewing it for the *Times*, Tennessee Williams praises its "true maturity and sophistication." Bowles spends several months in Ceylon and southern India, working on *Yerma*, an opera for singer Libby Holman based on the García Lorca play. Joins Jane in Paris, where she is working on her play *In the Summer House*; Jane goes to New York, hoping to see the play staged, and Bowles returns to Morocco and receives visit from Brion Gysin. John Lehmann publishes *A Little Stone*, omitting "The Delicate Prey" and "Pages from Cold Point" because of censorship concerns. American version, *The Delicate Prey and Other Stories*, includes the two stories and is published by Random House in November.

1951   Bowles buys Jaguar and hires Mohammed Temsamany as chauffeur; travels with Gysin through Morocco and Algeria. Works on *Let It Come Down* during summer in the mountain village of Xauen; returns to Tangier in the fall and finishes the novel. Translation of R. Frison-Roche's *The Lost Trail of the Sahara* is published in August. Bowles leaves with Yacoubi for India in December.

1952   *Let It Come Down* published in February by Random House and by John Lehmann in England. Accused of spying by the Ceylonese government, Yacoubi and Bowles are detained for two days before being permitted to travel to Ceylon. Bowles makes offer to buy the island of Taprobane off the coast of Ceylon. Leaves with Yacoubi for Italy, where he plays a role in Hans Richter's film *8 x 8*. Agreement to buy Taprobane is sealed.

1953   Jane Bowles completes *In the Summer House*; having
            agreed to write music for the play, Bowles sails to New
            York with Yacoubi in March. Visits Jane at Libby Hol-
            man's house in Connecticut. Holman, infatuated with
            Yacoubi, convinces him to live with her, and Bowles re-
            turns to Tangier without completing score for *In the
            Summer House*. Writes *A Picnic Cantata*, with text by
            James Schuyler. Yacoubi returns to Tangier after quarrel-
            ing with Holman. Bowles and Yacoubi go to Italy, where
            Bowles collaborates with Tennessee Williams on English
            adaptation of Visconti's film *Senso*. Bowles goes to Istan-
            bul with Yacoubi to write travel essay for *Holiday*. They
            return to Italy in October and see Williams and Truman
            Capote before returning to Tangier amid rioting against
            the French. Bowles sails alone to United States, and com-
            pletes music (now lost) for *In the Summer House* in time
            for its December 14 performance in Washington and its
            six-week Broadway run.

1954   Returns to Tangier, where he is soon joined by Jane. Falls
            ill with typhoid and sees Williams and Frank Merlo while
            convalescing. Receives brief visit from William Burroughs,
            who will live in Tangier for several years. Bowles begins
            writing *The Spider's House*, inspired by political upheaval
            in Morocco; moves for the summer with Yacoubi to a
            rented house overlooking the ocean and maintains strict
            schedule of writing. Transcribes Moghrebi tales told to
            him by Yacoubi. Moves to Casbah in fall. Bowles and
            Jane refuse to visit each other because of Bowles' suspi-
            cion of Cherifa and Jane's distrust of Yacoubi. Hoping to
            ease tensions by leaving Tangier, Bowles sails for Ceylon
            with Jane and Yacoubi in December.

1955   Works on *The Spider's House* at house on Taprobane; Jane
            dislikes the island, is unable to write, and returns to Tan-
            gier in March. Bowles finishes *The Spider's House* on
            March 16. Travels with Yacoubi in East Asia before re-
            turning to Tangier in June. Works on *Yerma*. Writes text
            for *Yallah*, a book of Saharan photographs taken by Peter
            Haeberlin. Writes to Thomson in September that "the
            possibility of being attacked is uppermost in every non-
            Moslem's mind . . . I have taken an apartment until the
            first of October next year, but whether I'll be able to stick
            it out that long remains to be seen." Develops friendship

with Francis Bacon. At Jane's request, agrees to give Casbah house to Cherifa. *The Spider's House* is published by Random House on November 14.

1956   In Lisbon, Bowles writes anonymous article on Portuguese elections for *The Nation*. Morocco gains independence on March 2, with Tangier remaining under international control; Bowles writes in *The Nation* that "in fact, if not officially, the integration of Tangier with the rest of Morocco has already taken place" and that Europeans "know better than to wander down into the part of town where they are not wanted." Bowles' parents visit during the summer. German edition of *Yallah* published in October by Manesse Verlag in Switzerland. Bowles travels to Ceylon with Yacoubi, arriving in late December.

1957   Needing money, attempts to sell Taprobane. English edition of *The Spider's House* brought out by Macdonald & Co. Bowles travels to Kenya to cover the Mau Mau uprising for *The Nation*. Upon return to Morocco in May, discovers that Jane has suffered a stroke; rumors circulate of a violent reaction to *majoun* or poisoning by Cherifa. Receives visits from poets Allen Ginsberg, Peter Orlovsky, and Alan Ansen, who are drawn to Tangier in part because Bowles and Burroughs live there. Bowles posts bail after Yacoubi is arrested for alleged indecent behavior with an adolescent German boy. Takes Jane to London for treatment in August. Returning briefly to Morocco, Jane continues to have seizures and her psychological state deteriorates; she goes back to England and is admitted to a psychiatric clinic. Bowles and Yacoubi visit Jane in September. Bowles is hospitalized with Asiatic flu and writes "Tapiama" while suffering severe fever. Contracts pneumonia and pleurisy and is bedridden for three weeks; convalesces at the house of Sonia Orwell. Jane receives electric shock treatments. American edition of *Yallah* published by McDowell, Obolensky in October. Bowles convinces English publisher William Heinemann to bring out a story collection. Returns to Tangier with Jane and Yacoubi in November; Yacoubi is arrested and charged with "assault with intent to kill" the German boy.

1958   Police interrogate Bowles about Yacoubi and begin investigating Jane's relationship with Cherifa; the Bowles leave

Tangier and Temsamany is repeatedly questioned about them. Taprobane is sold but Bowles is unable to take any of the proceeds of the sale out of Ceylon. The Bowles travel to Madeira, where Jane's condition improves. Yacoubi is acquitted in a trial lasting five minutes. Jane flies alone to New York in April. En route to the United States in June, Bowles finishes score for *Yerma*, which premieres at the University of Colorado on July 29. Jane enters psychiatric clinic in White Plains, New York, in October. Bowles goes to Los Angeles and quickly writes score for Milton Geiger's play *Edwin Booth*, directed by José Ferrer. Returns to New York; with Ned Rorem and John Goodwin, tries mescaline for the first time. Seeks financial support to record Moroccan folk music. Jane is released from the hospital and leaves the United States with Bowles in December, arriving in Tangier by the end of the year.

1959   Bowles travels to New York after he is asked to write the score for Williams' *Sweet Bird of Youth*, which opens on Broadway March 10. Sees Ginsberg frequently. Awarded Rockefeller Grant to record North African music and returns to Morocco. Heinemann publishes the story collection *The Hours After Noon* in May. Accompanied by Canadian painter and journalist Christopher Wanklyn and driver Mohammed Larbi, Bowles makes four trips to record in remote areas and takes extensive notes that form the basis of essay "The Rif, to Music." Near the end of the project, the Moroccan government forbids further recording, calling the endeavor "ill-timed."

1960   The Bowles move into separate apartments in the same building, the Inmeuble Itesa in Tangier. Bowles refuses offer of a year-long professorship from the English Department at Los Angeles State College. Writes articles for *Life* and *Holiday* about Marrakesh and Fez.

1961   Tape-records and translates tales by Yacoubi, publishing "The Game" in *Contact* in May and "The Night Before Thinking" in *Evergreen Review* in September. Ginsberg returns to Tangier and encourages Bowles to write to Lawrence Ferlinghetti, publisher of City Lights Books, with a proposal for a collection of stories about kif-smoking that were written with the aid of kif; Ferlinghetti accepts enthusiastically.

1962 Bowles continues to record and translate stories told to him by Moroccans, a pursuit that will figure prominently in his later career. Meets Larbi Layachi, who tells Bowles autobiographical tales; under the pseudonym Driss ben Hamed Charhadi, Layachi's "The Orphan;" transcribed and translated by Bowles, is published in *Evergreen Review*. Grove Press offers to publish Layachi's autobiography. When English publisher Peter Owen solicits a manuscript, Bowles collects essays and magazine pieces that will be published the following year as *Their Heads Are Green* (American edition is entitled *Their Heads Are Green and Their Hands Are Blue*); Peter Owen will be Bowles' primary English publisher for the rest of his career. *One Hundred Camels in the Courtyard* published by City Lights in September. Bowles returns with Jane to New York to write music for Williams' *The Milk Train Doesn't Stop Here Anymore*; visits parents in Florida and attends tryouts of *Milk Train* before returning to Tangier.

1963 Completes translation of Charhadi's *A Life Full of Holes*. Rents beach house at Asilah, a town south of Tangier, and spends several months there with Jane. Begins writing *Up Above the World*.

1964 *A Life Full of Holes* published by Grove Press in May. Working steadily, Bowles completes *Up Above the World* late in the year. Burroughs, Gysin, and Layachi leave Tangier for New York.

1965 Bowles and Jane visit the United States to visit his father, who has suffered a cerebral hemorrhage, and they consider buying a house in Santa Fe. Random House rejects *Up Above the World*. With Jane, Bowles returns to Tangier, where he learns that Simon & Schuster has accepted *Up Above the World*. Agrees to write book about Bangkok for Little, Brown. Begins to record and translate the spoken stories of Mohammed Mrabet, who becomes a close friend and regular visitor to Bowles' home.

1966 Film rights to not-yet-published *Up Above the World* are sold to Universal Studios for $25,000 in February; the novel is published by Simon & Schuster on March 15 to mixed reviews. Bowles receives word in June that parents have died within a week of each other. Travels with Jane to New York, then sails alone for Southeast Asia in July. Arrives in Bangkok in the fall and immediately dislikes the city. ("Most of Bangkok looked like the back streets of the nethermost Bronx relocated in a Florida swamp.") Goes to Chiengmai; records indigenous Thai music. Begins stage adaptation of story "The Garden."

1967 *Jilala*, an album featuring recordings of the Jilala religious brotherhood made by Bowles and Brion Gysin, is released in January. Bowles returns to Tangier in March after being informed that Jane's condition has worsened, her depression so severe that she can barely sleep or eat. Takes Jane to a clinic in Málaga, where she is treated until August. "The Garden" is performed in April at the American School in Tangier. Bowles abandons Bangkok book and returns advance. Translation of Mrabet's *Love With a Few Hairs* is published by Peter Owen in London; book is adapted for the BBC and shown on September 22 (American edition is brought out by George Brazillier in 1968).

1968 Peter Owen publishes story collection *Pages from Cold Point* in April. Jane returns to Málaga clinic for treatment. Bowles accepts teaching appointment in the English Department of San Fernando Valley State College in California, where he teaches a seminar on existentialism and the novel.

1969 Returns to Tangier, bringing Jane; Jane loses weight excessively and returns to the hospital in Málaga. Signs contract to write autobiography for G. P. Putnam. Publication of Mrabet's *The Lemon* by Peter Owen (American edition, City Lights, 1972) and *M'Hashish* by City Lights, both translated by Bowles.

1970 Poet Daniel Halpern, whom Bowles had met while teaching in California, starts the magazine *Antaeus*; Bowles is named founding editor. In May, Jane suffers stroke and her condition deteriorates, causing her to lose her vision. Premiere of Gary Conklin's film *Paul Bowles in the Land of the Jumblies* (retitled *Paul Bowles in Morocco* for English release and airing on CBS the following year) on December 10 in New York.

1971–72   Bowles begins translating the work of Mohamed Choukri, Moroccan writer, working from Choukri's Arabic texts. *Music of Morocco*, two-disc set taken from Bowles' recordings in the archives of the Library of Congress, is released. Black Sparrow Press brings out *The Thicket of Spring: Poems 1926–1969*. Autobiography, *Without Stopping*, is published by G. P. Putnam's Sons on March 15, 1972. Bowles discovers the stories of Swiss expatriate writer Isabelle Eberhardt (1877–1904) and begins to translate them.

1973   Jane Bowles dies in Málaga clinic on May 4 with Bowles at her side. In the years following Jane's death, Bowles will travel outside of Morocco infrequently and will be increasingly confined to the Inmeuble Itesa (in part because of health problems); receives many visitors and, choosing not to install a telephone at his home, maintains extensive correspondence.

1974   Bowles publishes three translations: Choukri's *For Bread Alone* and *Jean Genet in Tangier*, and Mrabet's *The Boy Who Set the Fire*. Resumes writing his own short stories after a hiatus of several years.

1975   Publishes translations of Mrabet's *Hadidan Aharam* and Eberhardt's *The Oblivion Seekers* in November. Stories "Afternoon with Antaeus," "The Fqih," and "Mejdoub" are collected in *Three Tales*, published by Frank Hallman in the fall.

1976–78   Black Sparrow Press publishes translations of Mrabet's *Look & Move On* and *Harmless Poisons, Blameless Sins* in 1976 and *The Big Mirror* in 1977; Bowles' story collection *Things Gone and Things Still Here* published in July 1977. Meets Millicent Dillon, who is working on a biography of Jane Bowles (*A Little Original Sin*, 1981).

1979   *Collected Stories 1939–1976* is published by Black Sparrow with an introduction by Gore Vidal. Publication of translations *Tennessee Williams in Tangier* by Choukri and *Five Eyes*, collection of stories by Abdeslam Boulaich, Mrabet, Choukri, Layachi, and Yacoubi.

1980   Translation of Mrabet's *The Beach Café & The Voice* is published. Bowles begins working on *Points in Time*, long essay about Morocco in a genre that he calls "lyrical history."

1981–82   Premiere of Sara Driver's film *You Are Not I*, based on Bowles' story, on May 12, 1981, in New York. Story collection *Midnight Mass* is brought out by Black Sparrow Press in June 1981. *Next to Nothing*, collected poems, is published by Black Sparrow the same month. Bowles completes *Points in Time*, published August in 1982 England by Peter Owen (American edition, The Ecco Press, 1984). Teaches summer writing seminars in Tangier program of the School of Visual Arts in New York. One of his colleagues in the program is Regina Weinreich, who will make a documentary about him. Bowles discovers the work of Guatemalan writer Rodrigo Rey Rosa, one of his students, whose stories he begins to translate. Translation of Rey Rosa's *The Path Doubles Back* is published in November 1982.

1983–85   Bowles publishes unpunctuated "Monologue" stories in *The Threepenny Review* and *Conjunctions*. Translation of Mrabet's *The Chest* is published. Bowles travels to Bern, Switzerland, for medical treatment in summer 1984. Publication of *The Beggar's Knife*, stories by Rey Rosa translated by Bowles, and *She Woke Me Up So I Killed Her*, collection of translations from several authors.

1986–90   Translation of Mrabet's *Marriage with Papers* is published in 1986. Bowles suffers aneurysm in the knee and undergoes surgery in Rabat in September 1986. Meets the following year with director Bernardo Bertolucci, who is interested in adapting *The Sheltering Sky*. Begins keeping a diary (which will be published as *Days: Tangier Journal 1987–1989* in 1991). Concert of Bowles' chamber music is performed in Nice. Story collection *Unwelcome Words* is published by Tombuctou Books. Shooting of *The Sheltering Sky* on location in Morocco begins in 1989. Bowles plays role of narrator, which includes on-screen appearance; becomes frustrated with Bertolucci's refusal to listen to his objections to the adaptation. Peter Owen brings out story collection *Call at Corazón* and Bowles' translation of Rey Rosa's *Dust on Her Tongue*. Bowles meets Virginia Spencer Carr, who will become his biographer. Travels to Paris for premiere of *The Sheltering Sky*, calls the film "awful." Exhibition "Paul Bowles at 80" mounted at the University of Delaware. *The Invisible Spectator*, biography by Christopher Sawyer-Lauçanno, is published by Grove Press; Bowles objects to the book and writes in *Antaeus*, "I wonder if he knows how deeply I resent his flouting my wishes." Robert Briatte's biography, *Paul Bowles: 2117 Tanger Socco*, is published in France.

1991–94   Translations of Mrabet's *Chocolate Creams and Dollars* and Rey Rosa's *Dust on Her Tongue* are published in the United States in 1992. Limited edition of essay *Morocco*, with photographs by Barry Brukoff, appears the following year. Bowles' vision is impaired due to glaucoma. Scores written for synthesizer are performed at productions of Oscar Wilde's *Salome* (1992) and Euripides' *Hippolytus* (1993) at the American School in Tangier. In April 1994, Bowles attends concert of his music at the Théâtre du Rond-Point in Paris, which is recorded and released as *An American in Paris*. Spends a month in Atlanta for medical treatment at Emory University. Show of Bowles' photographs exhibited at the Boijmans van Beuningen museum in Rotterdam; *Paul Bowles Photographs: "How Could I Send a Picture into the Desert?"* is published. Canadian filmmaker Jennifer Baichwal visits Bowles and begins filming a documentary. *In Touch*, an edition of Bowles' letters edited by Jeffrey Miller, is published. Premiere of *Paul Bowles: The Complete Outsider*, documentary film by Catherine Warnow and Regina Weinrich.

1995   Premiere of *Halbmond*, adaptation of Bowles' stories "Merkala Beach" (alternate title of "The Story of Lahcen and Idir"), "Call at Corazón," and "Allal" by German filmmakers Frieder Schlaich and Irene van Alberti, with Bowles introducing the film in an on-screen appearance. For the first time in decades, Bowles visits New York City for three days of concerts devoted to his music and a symposium at the New School for Social Research, September 19–21. Receives standing ovation at concert at Lincoln Center. Reunion with Burroughs and Ginsberg at Mayfair Hotel is filmed by Baichwal. *Paul Bowles: Music*, a collection of essays relating to his career as a composer, is published by Eos Music Press.

1996–98   Contributes essay to monograph on Tangier-based artist
          Claudio Bravo published in 1996. Makes final visit to the
          United States for medical treatment in 1996. *The Music of
          Paul Bowles*, performed by the Eos Orchestra under the
          direction of Jonathan Sheffer, is released by BMG/Cata-
          lyst. *Paul Bowles: Migrations*, performed by members of
          the Frankfurt-based Ensemble Moderne, is released by
          Largo. Mohamed Choukri's *Paul Bowles wa 'uzla Tanja*,
          a book hostile to Bowles, is published in Arabic in Mo-
          rocco in 1996 and in French translation (*Paul Bowles, le
          reclus de Tanger*) the following year; in a 1997 interview in
          the Tangier weekly *Les Nouvelles du Nord*, Bowles says
          "there's no logic" to Choukri's accusatory assessment.
          Premiere of Baichwal's *Let It Come Down: The Life of
          Paul Bowles* at the 1998 Toronto International Film Festi-
          val. Millicent Dillon's *You Are Not I: A Portrait of Paul
          Bowles* is published in 1998. Edgardo Cozarinsky's *Fan-
          tômes de Tanger*, fictional film about post-war Tangier in
          which Bowles appears as himself, is released in France.

1999   Bowles transfers the majority of his literary papers to an
          archive at the University of Delaware. Owsley Browne's
          documentary *Night Waltz: The Music of Paul Bowles* is re-
          leased. Bowles is admitted to the Italian Hospital in
          Tangier for cardiac problems on November 7. Suffers
          heart attack in hospital and dies on November 18. Bowles'
          ashes are interred near those of his parents and grandpar-
          ents at Lakemont Cemetery in Glenora, New York.

Note on the Texts

This volume contains the 52 short stories by Paul Bowles that appeared in the collections *The Delicate Prey and Other Stories* (1950), *A Hundred Camels in the Courtyard* (1962), *The Time of Friendship* (1967), *Things Gone and Things Still Here* (1987), and *Midnight Mass* (1981; expanded edition 1983); six stories published between 1983 and 1990; the travel essays collected in *Their Heads Are Green and Their Hands Are Blue* (1963); and the novel *Up Above the World* (1966). The texts of these works are generally taken from their first book publications, because Bowles did not significantly revise these works after they appeared in book form; for *The Delicate Prey and Other Stories* and *Their Heads Are Green and Their Hands Are Blue*, the first American editions have been preferred over English editions published a few months earlier because these English editions incorporate changes based on British conventions. The English version of *The Delicate Prey and Other Stories*, entitled *A Little Stone*, also omitted material because of censorship concerns.

The Delicate Prey and Other Stories comprises 17 stories written between 1939 and 1949. Bowles wrote "Tea on the Mountain" in 1939, during a period of his career when he was otherwise composing music; the remaining stories were written between 1945 and 1949. He recalled in an interview that reading and suggesting revisions to Jane Bowles' *Two Serious Ladies* in 1941 "excited" him and made him want to write his own fiction; but according to his autobiography, *Without Stopping* (1972), it was not until 1945, after reading "some ethnographic books with texts from the Arapesh or from the Tarahumara," that he "crept back into the land of fiction writing." Bowles goes on to say: "Little by little the desire came to me to invent my own myths, adopting the point of view of the primitive mind. The only way I could devise for simulating that state was the old Surrealist method of abandoning conscious control and writing whatever words came from the pen. First, animal legends resulted from the experiments and then tales of animals disguised as 'basic human' beings. One rainy Sunday I awoke late, put a thermos of coffee by my bedside, and began to write another of these myths. No one disturbed me, and I wrote on until I had finished it. I read it over, called it 'The Scorpion,' and decided that it could be shown to others. When *View* published it, I received compliments and went on inventing myths. The subject matter of the myths soon turned from 'primitive' to contemporary, but the objectives and behavior of the protagonists remained the same as in the beast legends."

Bowles began publishing stories in magazines in 1945, and by 1947 he was looking for a publisher to bring out a collection. Early in 1947, he met with editors at Dial Press, who told him that most firms would be reluctant to publish a story collection by someone who had not yet written a novel. After Doubleday offered him a contract and advance, Bowles began writing *The Sheltering Sky*, his first novel, while living and traveling in North Africa. Rejected by Doubleday, *The Sheltering Sky* was published by New Directions in October 1949 and quickly became a best-seller and a critical success; by this time Bowles had once again turned his attention to publishing a story collection. Through his agent, Helen Strauss, he offered the collection to Random House early in 1950. Despite threats of legal action by New Directions, who had already agreed to publish the book, Bowles began preparing *The Delicate Prey and Other Stories* for Random House, with publication scheduled for fall 1950. Of the 17 stories, "Tea on the Mountain," "The Circular Valley," "The Fourth Day Out from Santa Cruz," and "A Thousand Days for Mokhtar" were first published in *The Delicate Prey and Other Stories*. The remaining stories had appeared in periodicals: "At Paso Rojo" (*Mademoiselle*, September 1948), "Pastor Dowe at Tacaté" (*Mademoiselle*, February 1949), "Call at Corazón" (*Harper's Bazaar*, October 1947), "Under the Sky" (*Horizon*, June 1947), "Señor Ong and Señor Ha" (*Mademoiselle*, July 1950), "The Echo" (*Harper's Bazaar*, September 1946), "The Scorpion" (*View*, December 1945; *Life and Letters*, July 1948), "Pages from Cold Point" (*Wake*, Autumn 1949; *New Directions in Prose and Poetry #11*, December 1949), "You Are Not I" (*Mademoiselle*, January 1948), "How Many Midnights" (*World Review*, April 1950), "By the Water" (*View*, October 1946), "The Delicate Prey" (*Zero*, Summer 1949), "A Distant Episode" (*Partisan Review*, January–February 1947; *New Directions in Prose and Poetry #10*, December 1948). An English version of the collection, entitled *A Little Stone*, was published by John Lehmann in August 1950; "The Delicate Prey" and "Pages from Cold Point" were omitted to avoid possible distribution or censorship difficulties. Three months later, in November, Random House published *The Delicate Prey and Other Stories*, which contained the text printed here.

In December 1961, at the instigation of the poet Allen Ginsberg, Bowles proposed a collection of "three short stories about kif in Morocco" to Lawrence Ferlinghetti, publisher of City Lights Books. These stories had already appeared in periodicals: "A Friend of the

World" (*Encounter*, March 1961), "He of the Assembly" (*Big Table*, 1960), "The Story of Lahcen and Idir" (*The London Magazine*, October 1960, as "Merkala Beach"). In the same letter Bowles promised "to furnish an extra story to add to my three, if you felt that said three were insufficient to constitute a tome." After Ferlinghetti accepted the proposal, Bowles lightly revised the already written stories and worked on "The Wind at Beni Midar" to add to the collection. In a letter to Ferlinghetti dated January 12, 1962, Bowles wrote, "The title business has kept me thinking, but not with any great degree of productivity. The difficulty with finding a word that has some reference, even oblique, to kif, is that the word will necessarily be a Moghrebi word, and thus will have no reference at all save to the few who know the region." He proposed the title *A Hundred Camels in the Courtyard*, taken from the proverb that serves as the book's epigraph; it would, he added, "more or less capsulize the meaning, since the theme of all the stories is specifically the power of kif, rather than the subjective effects of it." *A Hundred Camels in the Courtyard* was published on September 1, 1962, by City Lights Books in an edition of 3,000 copies; the stories were incorporated into Bowles' next story collection published in America, *The Time of Friendship* (1967), as well as the English collection *Pages from Cold Point* (1968). There was no separate English publication, but 500 copies of the City Lights edition were offered for sale in the United Kingdom. The present volume prints the text of the 1962 City Lights edition of *A Hundred Camels in the Courtyard*.

Bowles gathered the four stories from *A Hundred Camels in the Courtyard* with nine others in the collection *The Time of Friendship*, published in 1967. Most were written in the 1950s and early 1960s. "Doña Faustina," the earliest of the stories, originated in an anonymous tale published in an issue of *View* that Bowles edited in 1945. The following stories from *The Time of Friendship* first appeared in periodicals: "The Successor" (*Esquire*, March 1951, as "A Gift for Kinza"), "The Hours After Noon" (*Zero Anthology* #8, 1956), "The Hyena" (*Transatlantic Review*, Winter 1962), "The Garden" (*Art and Literature*, Autumn–Winter 1964), "Doña Faustina" (*New Directions in Prose and Poetry* #12, December 1950), "Tapiama" (*The London Magazine*, May 1958), "The Frozen Fields" (*Harper's Bazaar*, July 1957). "The Time of Friendship" and "If I Should Open My Mouth" first appeared in *The Time of Friendship*, which was published by Holt, Rinehart and Winston in 1967. There was no English edition, but the collection *Pages from Cold Point*, published by Peter Owen in 1968, includes "The Time of Friendship," "The Hyena," and "The Garden," along with the stories from *A Hundred*

Camels in the Courtyard. The present volume prints the text of the 1967 Holt, Rinehart and Winston *The Time of Friendship*.

Bowles resumed writing fiction regularly in 1974, after a hiatus of several years spent working on an autobiography, essays, poems, and various translations. Apart from "Afternoon with Antaeus," published in *Antaeus* in the summer of 1970, and "You Have Left Your Lotus Pads on the Bus," written in 1971, the stories in *Things Gone and Things Still Here* were written between 1974 and 1976. In addition to "Afternoon with Antaeus," six other stories had appeared in periodicals: "Allal" (*Rolling Stone*, January 27, 1977), "The Fqih" (*Bastard Angel*, Fall 1974), "Mejdoub" (*Antaeus*, Spring/Summer 1974), "Istikhara, Anaya, Medagan and the Medaganat" (*Antaeus*, Spring/Summer 1976), "Reminders of Bouselham" (*Transatlantic Review*, June 1977), "Things Gone and Things Still Here" (*Rolling Stone*, January 15, 1976). "You Have Left Your Lotus Pods on the Bus" and "The Waters of Izli" appeared for the first time in *Things Gone and Things Still Here*, published by Black Sparrow Press on July 5, 1977. There was no English edition. This volume prints the text of the 1977 Black Sparrow Press *Things Gone and Things Still Here*.

The stories in *Midnight Mass* were written in the late 1970s or early 1980s, following the publication of Bowles' *Collected Stories 1939–1976* in 1979. All but one story, "The Empty Amulet," had appeared in periodicals: "Midnight Mass" (*Antaeus*, Winter 1979), "The Little House" (*Antaeus*, Spring 1981), "The Dismissal" (*Antaeus*, Winter 1979), "Here to Learn" (*Antaeus*, Summer 1979), "Madame and Ahmed" (*Antaeus*, Summer 1980), "Kitty" (*Antaeus*, Summer 1980), "The Husband" (*Michigan Quarterly Review*, Winter 1980), "At the Krungthep Plaza" (*Ontario Review*, Fall–Winter 1980–1981), "Bouayad and the Money" (*Ins and Outs*, July 1980), "Rumor and a Ladder" (*The Threepenny Review*, Spring 1981), "The Eye" (*The Missouri Review*, Fall 1978; *Ellery Queen's Mystery Magazine*, January 1, 1981). The first edition of *Midnight Mass* was published in 1981; an expanded edition, adding "In the Red Room" (which appeared in *Antaeus* in Autumn 1983) but otherwise duplicating the 1981 edition, was published in 1983. There was no English edition. This volume prints the text of the 1981 edition of *Midnight Mass*; "In the Red Room" is taken from the 1983 edition.

The stories included in the "Selected Later Stories" section of this volume were written in the 1980s. The texts of "Monologue, Tangier 1975," "Monologue, Massachusetts 1932," "Monologue, New York 1965," and "In Absentia" are taken from *Call at Corazón and Other Stories* (London: Peter Owen, 1988), their first book publication. "Unwelcome Words" first appeared in book form in *Unwelcome Words* (Bolinas, CA: Tombouctou Press, 1988), which provides the text printed here. The text of "Too Far from Home" is taken from *Too Far from Home: The Selected Writings of Paul Bowles* (New York: Ecco Press, 1993), its first American book publication; the story was published separately the same year in a limited edition by the Swiss publisher Editions Bischofberger.

Their Heads Are Green and Their Hands Are Blue originated in an offer from the English publisher Peter Owen, who solicited material from Bowles for a book in 1962. After turning down the request, claiming he had nothing to give Owen, Bowles changed his mind about the project and decided to collect some of his travel essays. Several of these essays had appeared in periodicals: "Fish Traps and Private Business" (*Zero*, Spring 1956, as "From Notes Taken in Ceylon"); "Africa Minor" (*Holiday*, April 1959, as "The Moslems"); "Mustapha and His Friends" (*Holiday*, August 1956, as "The Incredible Arab"); "A Man Must Not Be Very Moslem" (*Holiday*, May 1955, as "Europe's Most Exotic City"); "Baptism of Solitude" (*Holiday*, January 1953, as "Secret Sahara"); "All Parrots Speak" (*Holiday*, November 1956, as "Parrots I Have Known"); "The Route to Tassemsit" (*Holiday*, February 1963, as "Journey Through Morocco"). In November 1962 Bowles wrote to his wife, Jane, that he was "touching up" his manuscript; although the changes are not extensive, he revised some of the essays for the collection. The book was published in England by Peter Owen under the title *Their Heads Are Green*, on June 21, 1963. The first American edition, entitled *Their Heads Are Green and Their Hands Are Blue*, was published by Random House on August 26, 1963. A 1984 paperback edition published by The Ecco Press in 1984 did not include "Mustapha and His Friends" and presented the essays in a different order. This volume prints the text of the 1963 Random House edition.

Bowles began writing *Up Above the World* late in 1963 and worked steadily on the novel throughout the following year. In a letter to Richard Peabody dated February 6, 1983, he recalled, "I simply wanted to see if I could write a 'suspense' novel that would be unlike others of its genre," adding: "I wasn't so ingenuous as to imagine that it would be a commercial success, nor was it one, by any means. But I was happy to have published it, knowing that it was the best written" of his novels. Bowles finished *Up Above the World* in the fall of 1964. Upon receiving the manuscript Random House, his publisher, rejected it because (according to one of Bowles' letters) it was too "nihilistic" in outlook. It was accepted a few months later by Simon and Schuster, which published *Up Above the World* on March

15, 1966. The English edition was brought out by Peter Owen the following year. This volume prints the text of the 1966 Simon and Schuster edition of *Up Above the World.*

This volume presents the texts of the original printings chosen for inclusion here, but it does not attempt to reproduce nontextual features of their typographic design. The texts are presented without change, except for the correction of typographical errors. Spelling, punctuation, and capitalization are often expressive features and are not altered, even when inconsistent or irregular. The following is a list of typographical errors corrected, cited by page and line number: 10.36, Gongora; 11.16, the height; 12.19, came; 27.29, *Cómo* . . . much!; 82.8, lookd; 93.32, seem; 132.40, bragadoccio; 179.4, Cadi; 211.28, tea,; 229.20, kitchen; 237.12, Ramen; 250.6, thought: the; 264.29, now'.; 264.30, Yes',; 264.36, impossible',; 269.24, hindiya; 270.1, on, I; 270.8, truth. He; 270.13, it, he; 272.14, 'Yoo; 288.2, Freiluftschüle; 299.23, heard; 300.2, cholocate; 301.27, you?; 303.26, sighed; 308.12, "Madame."; 309.13, than; 328.4, was a; 329.31, while; 332.35, if; 335.10, gasped "not; 340.3, climp; 344.14, three; 348.1, Yes; 352.15, stock; 359.20, quiet; 361.1, when; 370.2, and,; 372.33, of of; 381.15, chrous; 387.5, *Guajira"*; 387.20 *todos!"*; 390.1 have; 395.26, while; 400.24, certainly; 409.5, go back; 409.37–38, everybody, he; 492.32, yes,; 514.10, opend; 536.22, satisfatction; 557.27, The she; 582.1, about.; 584.22, friend.; 584.34, me.; 590.9, nightwatchman; 612.35, that; 645.7, subscribe; 648.27, thay; 655.28, what it; 663.10, can't; 745.3, men; 771.5, you in; 803.22, Your; 813.28, and have; 826.15, monologous, 840.32, Cairo of; 867.20, credit."; 871.26, face,; 885.21, nightmare and; 910.21, he sighed; 974.1, much."

Glossary

The Moghrebi Arabic words and phrases listed below take the form of Bowles' transliterations as they appear in the text. The Moghrebi terms appearing in the glossary to *Their Heads Are Green and Their Hands Are Blue* are duplicated below.

Ach haddou laillaha ill'Allah.] Muslim profession of faith: "There is no God but God."

Adoul] Plural of *adel*, notary.

Agi!] Come!

Ahouache] In the Grand Atlas and in territories to the south of it, a formal festival involving groups of dancers, singers, and percussionists.

Aïd el Kebir] Muslim festival commemorating Abraham's willingness to sacrifice Isaac in which a sheep is slaughtered after morning prayers and eaten throughout the day. *Aïd*: feast.

Aissaoua] Sufi religious brotherhood from Meknes.

Allah imsik bekhir.] Good night.

Annah!] Me!

Aoudad] Wild sheep native to northern Africa.

Aoulidi] My son.

Bakhour] Incense.

Bakhshish] A gratuity.

B'd drah] By force.

Baraka] Blessedness; those with *baraka* are believed to enjoy divine protection. The word can also refer, as at 574.21, to an object possessing this power.

Bendir] A large disc-shaped drum with one membrane. Also *benadir*.

Berrani] Stranger.

Bled] The countryside.

Caïd] The chieftain of a tribe (or fraction of a tribe).

Caique] A rowboat or sailing boat.

Chaamba] Bedouin people of the northern Sahara.

Chechia]   Straw hat.

Chehade]   The spoken sentence affirming the Islamic faith.

Chikh]   The leader, in this case, of a group of folk musicians.

Chleuh]   Used as a synonym for "Berber"; more specifically, it refers to the Soussi people who come from the Anti-Atlas Mountains and the Sous river valley.

Chkoun?]   Who?

Chouwal]   Or Shawwal, the month after Ramadan in the Islamic calendar.

Chqaf]   Lit contents of a sebsi, i.e., kif. Plural *chqofa*.

Chta]   Rain.

Cir f'hallak!]   Go away!

Darbouka]   Large ceramic hand drum.

Djaoui]   Resin for burning, especially with benzoin in it.

Djellaba]   A hooded overgarment with sleeves. Formerly a man's garment, but now worn by both sexes.

Djenoun]   Evil spirits (plural of *djinn*).

Djilala]   Or Jilala. Islamic confraternity named after the saint Abdel Qader Jilani (1077–1166), whose itinerant musicians perform sacred music in small ensembles. Jilala music often aims to call forth spiritual healing or to induce a state of holy trance. Bowles recorded the music of the Jilala brotherhood on several occasions.

Erg]   Saharan area consisting of "sand seas," extensive accumulations of shifting sand.

Fasoukh]   Incense used to ward off evil spirits.

Fellahin]   Peasants.

Filala]   Tribe from southern Morocco, to which the Alawite rulers belong.

Fraja]   Mass dancing.

Fjer]   Morning prayer.

Fondouk]   Hotel or inn.

Fqih]   Holy man.

Gandoura]   Long dress worn by both sexes.

Gannega]   A small disc-shaped drum with a single fine membrane.

Guennaoua (singular Guennaoui)]   A religious brotherhood, most of whose members are of Sudanese extraction, descendants of slaves.

Their choreographed ritual is useful in the curing of madness, seizures, and scorpion stings. They also rid houses of undesirable spirits.

Haik] Woman's traditional outer covering, generally of fine white wool.

Hamatcha] Religious brotherhood from Meknes.

Hammada] Flat rocky desert area blown free of sand by the wind.

Hammam] Bathhouse.

Hanoute] Grocery store.

Hindiyats] Prickly pears.

Imam] Leader of prayer in the mosque.

Imdyazen] In certain Berber-speaking regions of Morocco, professional itinerant musicians.

Imochagh] Tamachek term for Touareg.

Inch'Allah] God willing.

Jduq jmel] A hallucinogenic plant.

Jilala] See *djilala*.

Joteya] Flea market.

Katib] Secretary.

Khalifa] A deputy official.

Khamstache] Fifteen.

Khlass!] Stop it!

Khoya] Brother.

Kif] The fine leaves at the base of the flowers of the common hemp plant, chopped and mixed (ideally in a ratio of seven to four) with tobacco grown in the same earth.

Kissaria] In a Muslim town, the quarter of the souk devoted to the sale of textiles, clothing, and luxury items.

Kouffa] Basket.

Ksar] Palace.

Litham] The cloth worn over the lower half of a woman's face.

Majoun] Literally, jam. In its special sense it refers to any sweet preparation eaten with the purpose of inducing hallucinations; its active ingredient is the hemp plant.

Mçid] Religious primary school.

Mechoui]   A roast, usually of lamb.

Medina]   City. In North Africa it indicates in particular that part of any
    city that was built by the Muslims and was already in evidence at the
    time of the arrival of the Europeans.

Mehari]   Camel. *Meharistes*: Saharan military cavalrymen mounted on
    trained camels.

Mejdoub]   Deranged person believed to be possessed by spirits.

Mektoub]   Destiny.

Mellah]   Jewish quarter.

Mijmah]   Brazier.

Moqqadem]   A local official, not as high in the hierarchy as a *caïd*; local
    leader of a religious brotherhood.

Mottoui]   Leather pouch for carrying kif on one's person.

Mouloud]   The holiday commemorating the birthday of the Prophet
    Mohammed; also the month in which it occurs.

Moussem]   Seasonal festival held at the tomb of a saint.

Mruq]   Sauce.

M'tarrba]   The high narrow mattresses that line the walls of the rooms in a
    Muslim home.

Msalkheir]   Good afternoon.

Mska]   A clear yellow gum resin.

Naboula]   Bladder. Specifically a lamb's bladder, dried and softened, in
    which to store kif hermetically.

Naqous]   A percussive instrument, a heavy block played by metal rods.

Nargileh]   A water-pipe consisting of a jar and a hose with a mouthpiece.

Nchaioui]   Inveterate kif smoker.

O chnou brhitsi?]   What do you want?

Ouled Naïl]   Tribe from the Aurès Mountains of Algeria known for the
    dancing of its women.

Qachla]   Garrison.

Qadi]   A Muslim judge who rules on the basis of *Shari'ah*, Islamic law.

Qaouaji]   Waiter; tea-maker. Also *qahaouaji*.

Qsbah] Large reed transverse flute with a low register.

Rhaita] An oboe-like reed instrument. Bowles called it "the perfect out-door instrument, an oboe of stridency that permits it to be heard miles away, yet capable of executing the subtlest melodic features." ("North African Music I," New York *Herald Tribune*, December 27, 1942.)

Rhmara] The Ghomara, region in northern Morocco west of the Rif.

Ronda] Card game suggestive of gin rummy.

Safsaf] Eucalyptus tree.

Sbalkheir] Good morning.

Sebsi] Long thin pipe for smoking kif.

Seguia, Allah istir!] God save us!

Serouelles] Wide trousers worn under traditional clothing.

Sidi] Sir; Lord.

S'l'm aleikoum!] Salutation; literally "Peace be upon you."

Souk (properly *souq*)] The word is used throughout North Africa to mean a market. In the larger cities it has a second, more specific use in desig-nating a street or quarter devoted to the buying and selling (and often the manufacture) of one given commodity.

Spanioline] Plural of Spanioli, a Spaniard.

Tachelhait] A dialect of Berber spoken by the Chleuhs.

Tafilalet] Region in southern Morocco, home to the Filala.

Tarboosh] High-crowned skullcap, a fez.

Tbola] Plural of *tbel*, North African side-drum, played with the sticks.

Timma] Or *temma:* There.

Tob] Mixture of straw and earth (and often manure) for masonry.

Tolba] Men who chant the Koran and hymns of divine praise.

Toubib] Doctor.

Touareg] A Berber people, an ancient offshoot of the Kabyle Berbers of Algeria, who live in the Sahara.

Tseuheur] The theory and practice of black magic.

Yehoudía] Jewish woman.

Yemkin] Maybe.

Zamar]   Riffian double-reed musical instrument.

Zaouia]   The seat of a religious brotherhood, generally comprising a
mosque, a school, and the tomb of the sect's founder.

Zigdoun]   A woman's dress used in weddings.

Notes

In the notes below, the reference numbers denote page and line of this volume (the line count includes chapter headings). No note is made for material included in standard desk-reference books such as Webster's *Collegiate*, *Biographical*, and *Geographical* dictionaries. Foreign words and phrases are translated only if meaning is not evident in context. For Arabic terms, see Glossary, page 1047, and the glossary that is part of the text of *Their Heads Are Green and Their Hands Are Blue* (pp. 860–62). For more biographical information than is contained in the Chronology, see Robert Briatte, *Paul Bowles: 2117 Tanger Socco* (Paris: Plon, 1989); Gena Dagel Caponi (ed.), *Conversations with Paul Bowles* (Jackson: University of Mississippi Press, 1993); Millicent Dillon, *You Are Not I: A Portrait of Paul Bowles* (Berkeley: University of California Press, 1998); Michelle Green, *The Dream at the End of the World: Paul Bowles and the Literary Renegades in Tangier* (New York: HarperCollins, 1991); Christopher Sawyer-Lauçanno, *The Invisible Spectator: A Biography of Paul Bowles* (New York: Grove Press, 1989).

THE DELICATE PREY AND OTHER STORIES

6.32   *Aveces la noche*]   Sometimes the night.

12.23   *garrapatas*]   Ticks.

13.31   "*Qué calor*,"]   What heat.

32.7–8   BARCELONA . . . DOSCIENTOS AVIONES]   Barcelona Bombed by 200 Airplanes.

43.34   "*Adelante.*"]   Come on.

58.2   "*Equipajes!*"]   Luggage!

68.27   *Lástima*,]   It's a shame.

69.24   "*Callate!*"]   Shut up!

72.9–10   "*Una hija del sol!*"]   A daughter of the sun!

75.28   ABARROTES FINOS.]   Delicatessen.

77.18   "*Hay que tener mucho cuidado*,"]   You must be very careful.

84.28   "*No importa adonde.*"]   It doesn't matter where.

90.1 *The Circular Valley*] In a 1980 letter to his Spanish translator José Joaquín Blanco, Bowles noted that he published a translation of Borges' "The Circular Ruins" in 1945 and wrote that "three years later, in Fez, when I wrote a story for a little magazine in Paris (*View*), I paid tribute to Borges by giving it the title 'The Circular Valley.' (It was not a very direct form to express admiration, I admit.)"

113.26 "*Ya se va la senorita?*"] There goes the lady?

126.11 "*Qué fuerza!*"] How strong!

184.39 *orgeat*] Cocktail made with a bitter almond-flavored syrup.

187.3–4 "*Es pa' . . . quiero . . .*"] Most beautiful to me is the woman I love the most.

201.23 the war of the Sarrho] In a letter to José Joaquín Blanco, Bowles noted, "The Sarrho is a mountainous region in the south of Morocco, its inhabitants the last to surrender their arms to the French in 1936."

209.16–17 Sidi Ahmed Ben Moussa] Grand vizier to Moroccan sultan Moulay Hassan I and regent, from 1894 until his death in 1901, during the reign of Hassan's son and successor, Moulay Abd-el-Aziz.

215.5 "*Ti . . . droit.*"] All you have to do is go down.

A HUNDRED CAMELS IN THE COURTYARD

241.35 the Djemaa el Fna] Central market square in Marrakesh.

245.24–25 Aïcha Qandicha] In Moroccan legend, a bewitching evil spirit who drives her victims mad.

246.2–3 fasoukh . . . bakhour] Forms of incense.

249.34 the Agdal] Large public gardens in Marrakesh.

259.3 the Hafa,] A cliff in Tangier.

264.27 Sidi Ali el Mandri] Leader of a group of Moorish refugees from Spain who rebuilt and settled Tétouan in the late 15th and early 16th centuries.

THE TIME OF FRIENDSHIP

288.28–29 *Seien . . . Maria.*] Heartfelt greetings from your Maria.

305.8 *gosse*] Kid.

315.31 *ne t'en fais pas!*] Don't worry.

316.9 "*C'est une fille.*] It's a girl.

318.3   "*Allez . . . débine!*"]   Come, enough. Let's scram!

319.2–6   "*If . . . affected.*"]   From Baudelaire's *Les Paradis artificiels* (1860).

320.22   "*Déjalo,*]   Leave it.

322.33   *Sauve qui peut,*]   Every man for himself.

326.17   "*Le temps . . . mais—*"]   The time that passes here no longer has hours, but—

326.25   "*mais . . . loisir—*"]   But, so much leisure—

326.40   "*Dame una gorda,*"]   Give me a fat one.

327.11–12   *Porqué me molestas así?*]   Why do you bother me like this?

328.5   "*Pauvre vieux,*"]   Poor old man.

331.7   *Trae otra silla!*"]   Bring another chair!

347.3   *camioneta,*]   Little truck.

347.35   "*Pregúnteles,*"]   Ask them.

350.37–38   *mais . . . parfaite——*"]   So much idleness of someone is perfect.

362.4   *finca,*]   Ranch.

362.20   *zapotes.*]   Sapodilla plums (naseberries).

364.4   *llovizna*]   Drizzle.

364.13   "*Ya veremos,*"]   We'll see.

366.19   "*Brujerías!*"]   Sorceries!

369.5   "*Caimán!*"]   Crocodile!

379.2   "*Entonces*]   Then.

379.35–36   "*Muy triste,*"]   Very sad.

380.15   "*Hay alguien?*"]   Anybody there?

381.3   "*Qué . . . Pendejo!*"]   What a brute, you! Coward!

383.30–31   *Qué . . . perros?*"]   What's with the dogs?

386.4   "*Sí quieres . . . Qué tomas?*"]   If you want. . . . What are you having?

386.29   *bigotes*]   Mustache.

386.34   *tarde tras tarde*]   Afternoon after afternoon.

386.38   *Me hizo algo; no sé.* . . .]   He did something to me; I don't know. . . .

387.20   "*Os mato a todos!*]   I'll kill you all!

390.26   "*Las doce*,"]   Noon.

394.40–395.1   Villiers . . . Psichari,]   Phillippe-Auguste Villiers de l'Isle-Adam (1838–1889), French novelist and playwright whose works include *Contes cruels* ("Cruel Tales," 1883) and the play *Axël* (pub. 1890); George Borrow (1803–1881), English travel writer and novelist, author of *The Zincali, or the Gypsies in Spain* (1841) and *Romany Rye* (1857); the French soldier and writer Ernest Psichari (1883–1914), who set his novels *L'appel des armes* ("The Call of Arms," 1913) and *Le voyage du centurion* ("The Voyage of the Centurion," 1915) in North Africa.

THINGS GONE AND THINGS STILL HERE

440.19   Moulay Abdelqader!]   A Muslim saint.

444.33   bhikkus]   Buddhist monks.

463.1   *Antaeus*]   In Greek legend, the giant Antaeus, king of Libya, renewed his strength whenever he touched the ground. He challenged strangers to wrestling matches, then killed them when they became weak and exhausted. He was slain by Hercules.

MIDNIGHT MASS

494.3   the Minzah.]   El Minzah, Tangier's most luxurious hotel.

494.26–27   *le . . . affreuse!*"]   The naughty one! He's going to have a frightful hangover!

521.39   *A mí . . . son.*]   It doesn't matter to me how they are.

530.19–20   *Me . . . contigo.*]   I want to stay with you, Tex, with you.

587.32   *ton père qui t'aime*]   Your father who loves you.

591.18   *papier timbré*]   Stamped paper.

602.34   Coromandel screens]   Decorative Chinese lacquered screens.

605.23   Temple of the Tooth,]   The Dalada Maligawa, temple in Kandy, Sri Lanka (formerly Ceylon), housing a tooth of the Buddha as a relic; the Perahara, an elaborate annual festival celebrating the relic in the lunar month of Esala (beginning in July or August) takes place over a period of ten days.

SELECTED LATER STORIES

610.21   DEFENSE ... FLEURS]   Forbidden to touch the flowers.

634.28–29   *Pareces ... Dios!*]   Looks like the Son of God!

636.35–36   *Mais . . . l'étrangler!*]   But the poor dog! You're going to strangle him!

638.31   *La Nausée*]   *Nausea*, 1938 novel by Jean-Paul Sartre.

638.34   "Ma vie est posthume."]   My life is posthumous.

639.30   *Hasta el otro mundo,*]   Until the next world.

641.30   *archicomplet.*]   Filled up.

642.27   *Tant pis et à bientôt*]   So much the worse and see you later.

653.31   *grace à Dieu.*]   Thank God.

658.20   *blessé*]   Wounded.

664.2   ausgeschlossen]   Impossible.

664.15   Halazone]   Water purification tablets.

690.33   "*Invraisemblable.*"]   Incredible.

694.33–34   *La plaie s'est fermee.*]   The wound has healed.

THEIR HEADS ARE GREEN AND THEIR HANDS ARE BLUE

699.1–2   THEIR ... BLUE]   Most of the non-English terms appear in the Glossary included in the 1963 Random House edition of *Their Heads Are Green and Their Hands Are Blue*; see pages 860–62 in this volume.

714.16   Perahera]   See note 605.23.

715.25–26   *tessitura*]   Range of tones.

720.34   from the court of Moulay Ismail]   Morocco's second Alawite ruler, Moulay Ishmail, reigned from 1672 to 1727; he established Meknes as the capital of his kingdom.

731.37   "*Toi pas . . . Toi Allemand,*"]   You not French. You German.

749.9   Haroun el Rashid.]   Caliph of Baghdad (786–809).

781.9   Kassem]   Abdul Karim Kassem [or Quassim] (1914–1963), Iraqi general who overthrew the monarchy in 1958 and ruled the country until he was killed in a coup in 1963.

786.37   kümmel] A liqueur made with caraway seed.

788.39   Abd el Krim] The Berber warlord Abd-el-Krim (1882?–1963) defeated Spanish troops at Anual in 1921 and established an autonomous region
in the Rif; his forces continued to advance into territory controlled by the
Spanish and French until the uprising was suppressed in 1926.

805.36   "*Vous . . . panne?*"] Are you broken down?

833.15–16   "*No sée . . . corazón,*"] I don't know what strange cold has
gotten into my heart.

833.20   "*Cállate!*"] Shut up!

840.36   neutralist powers] Nonaligned countries during the Cold War
(among them India, Indonesia, and Yugoslavia).

848.14   *Mais vous allez voir.*] But you'll see.

UP ABOVE THE WORLD

863.1   UP . . . WORLD] In February 1966, in a letter to Webster
Schott, who had reviewed the book for a Kansas City newspaper, Bowles
noted, "A sentence from Borges should have been included in the front of
the book, 'Each moment as it is being lived exists, but not the imaginary
total.'"

866.20   "*Hay mantequilla?*"] Is there any butter?

872.9   "*Sabe . . . pesadillas?*"] Do you know what they are, nightmares?

903.5   *cotorra*] Talkative.

905.3   *putas*] Whores.

907.22   *Apaga la luz,*] Turn off the light.

918.25   *mejorana*] Central American dance music named for a five-
stringed guitar.

927.29–30   *Ferien . . . Überlebenden.*] 1955 book ("Holiday at Waldsee:
Memories of a Survivor") by Carl Laszlo.

927.30   *L'Enfer Organisé*] Eugen Kogon's *L'Enfer Organisé: le système
des camps de concentration* ("Organized Hell: The System of the Concentration Camps"), published in French translation from the German in 1947.

927.30   *Netchaiev.*] René Cannac's *Netchaiev du nihilism au terrorism*
("Netchaiev from Nihilism to Terrorism"), 1962 study of the 19th-century
Russian anarchist Sergei Netchaiev.

927.31   *L'Univers Concentrationnaire*] Book by David Rousset ("The

Concentration-Camp Universe"), published in France in 1946 and in English translation the following year as *The Other Kingdom*.

927.31–32   *Auschwitz, Zeugnisse und Berichte.*]   Collection of personal narratives ("Auschwitz, Testimony and Reports") by H. G. Adler, Hermann Langbein, and Ella Lingens-Reiner published in Germany in 1962.

928.10–11   *Ametralladora, modelo bolsillo,*]   Machine gun, pocket model.

998.23   REVINDICACÍON . . . REVOLUCIÓN]   Claiming, redemption, revolution.

999.33   "*A sus órdenes,*"]   At your service.

1000.6   "*No se puede,*"]   You can't.

1012.27–28   "*Andale, guapa! . . . novio.*"]   Come on, good looking! Go out a little with her fiancé.

Index of Titles

Library of Congress Cataloging-in-Publication Data

Bowles, Paul, 1910–1999
  [Stories. Selections]
  Collected stories & later writings / Paul Bowles.
    p. cm—(The Library of America series ; 135)
  Includes bibliographical references.
  Contents: The delicate prey and other stories — A hundred
camels in the courtyard — The time of friendship — Things
gone and things still here — Midnight mass — Selected later
stories—Their heads are green and their hands are blue — Up
above the world.
  ISBN 1–931082–20–0 (alk. paper)
  1. Morocco — Social life and customs — Fiction. 2. Morocco —
Social life and customs. I. Title: Collected stories and later writings.
II. Title. III. Library of America ; 135.

PS3552.O874   A6   2002b
813'.54—dc21

                                        2002019452

THE LIBRARY OF AMERICA SERIES

The Library of America fosters appreciation and pride in America's literary heritage by publishing, and keeping permanently in print, authoritative editions of America's best and most significant writing. An independent nonprofit organization, it was founded in 1979 with seed money from the National Endowment for the Humanities and the Ford Foundation.

This book is set in 10 point Linotron Galliard,
a face designed for photocomposition by Matthew Carter
and based on the sixteenth-century face Granjon. The paper
is acid-free Domtar Literary Opaque and meets the requirements
for permanence of the American National Standards Institute. The
binding material is Brillianta, a woven rayon cloth made by
Van Heek-Scholco Textielfabrieken, Holland. The compo-
sition is by The Clarinda Company. Printing and
binding by R.R.Donnelley & Sons Company.
Designed by Bruce Campbell.

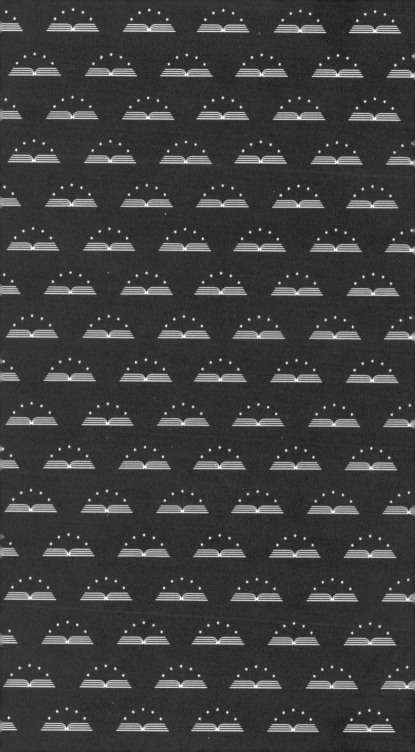